The MAGE WINDS

A VALDEMAR OMNIBUS

Also by Mercedes Lackey and available from Titan Books

THE COLLEGIUM CHRONICLES
Foundation
Intrigues
Changes
Redoubt
Bastion

HERALD SPY
Closer to Home
Closer to the Heart (October 2015)
Closer to the Chest (October 2016)

VALDEMAR OMNIBUSES
The Heralds of Valdemar
The Mage Storms (September 2015)

THE ELEMENTAL MASTERS
The Serpent's Shadow
The Gates of Sleep
Phoenix and Ashes
The Wizard of London
Reserved for the Cat
Unnatural Issue
Home from the Sea
Steadfast
Blood Red

The MAGE WINDS

A VALDEMAR OMNIBUS

MERCEDES LACKEY

TITAN BOOKS

The Mage Winds Omnibus
Print edition ISBN: 9781783293803
E-book edition ISBN: 9781783296538

Published by Titan Books
A division of Titan Publishing Group Ltd
144 Southwark Street, London
SE1 0UP

First edition: March 2015
2 4 6 8 10 9 7 5 3 1

A CIP catalogue record for this title is available from the British Library.

Printed and bound by CPI Group (UK) Ltd, Croydon, CR0 4YY

The MAGE WINDS

A VALDEMAR OMNIBUS

WINDS of FATE

A VALDEMAR OMNIBUS

BOOK ONE of
The MAGE WINDS

Dedicated to the memory of Donald A. Wollheim
A gentleman and a scholar

PROLOGUE

THE LEGEND

Long ago, in the days of the first King, for whom the Kingdom of Valdemar is named, it came to the King that he was growing old. Now Valdemar had led his people out of the hands of a tyrannical monarch and had no wish to see them fall again into the hands of tyranny. He knew that his son and Heir was a worthy, honest man—but what of his son's sons, and theirs?

He longed for a way to determine who would be a worthy successor to the throne, so that Valdemar the kingdom need never become less free than it was at that moment.

So he went into the fields and gardens beside the Palace, alone, and wrought what was half a prayer and half a spell, begging all benign Powers for their aid in this desire of his.

And as the last rays of the sun died from the sky, there was a mighty wind, and a shaking of the ground, and out of the grove of trees before him came a being like unto a white horse. And it spoke into his mind—

Then came a second, and a third, and before Valdemar could think to question why these came, his own son and his chief herald came to the place as if they had been called. And these two beings spoke into their minds also, saying, "I Choose you." So did the king know then that these Companions would choose only worthy folk to bear them company, for all their lives—and that these folk would be the instrument of justice and honor for all of the Kingdom from this moment. So did he name those Chosen by Companions to be Heralds, for only one could be a Monarch, and only one could be the Heir, but all could aspire to be a Herald. And he had made for them clothing of white, like the coats of their Companions, so that all might know them at a distance, or in a crowd; and he decreed then that only a Herald could be the Heir or the Monarch. And he decreed that there should be one Herald always to advise and serve and befriend the Monarch, so that his decisions be tempered with another view, and that Herald was to be called the Monarch's Own.

So it was. And so Valdemar has prospered. The Heralds increased, and the Monarch's justice spread.

THE CHRONICLES

In the first year of Herald Talia's investiture as full Queen's Own, Prince Ancar of Hardorn slew his father and all his father's men in a bloody and successful attempt to take the throne. He slew also Herald Kris who was there as ambassador on behalf of Queen Selenay, and imprisoned and tortured Herald Talia who was with him. She was rescued, out of all expectations, by the power of Herald Dirk, the young Heir Elspeth, and all the Companions together. Such a thing had never been known before, that the Companions would all add their strength to the Heralds to accomplish a task.

Ancar then made a trial of the strength of Valdemar, using both magic and his private army, but he was thrown back.

Some two years later, he made trial of the borders again. This time he was beaten back by the combined forces of the mercenary Company the Skybolts, under Captain Kerowyn; the armies of Valdemar; and the army of Rethwellan under Lord-Martial Prince Daren, who had come in answer to a promise of aid long forgotten. In the heat of the battle, the Prince and the Captain lost their horses and were both Chosen—and the Prince and Queen were taken with a lifebonding, a circumstance that both pleased and disturbed many.

Our ancient enemy, Karse, remains quiet, for Karse is beset with internal troubles. Ancar makes incursions on the Border from time to time; nothing but feints, however. So it has been to this day, some seven years from the last battle, when the events occurred that I now relate...

Herald-Chronicler Myste

1

ELSPETH

"**But**—" Elspeth protested weakly. The empty salle echoed back her words faintly. She stared at Herald Kerowyn and tried to make some sense of what she'd just been ordered to do. *Repair armor? Why should I repair armor? I don't even know the first thing about repairing armor! And what does that have to do with anything?* She sat down, her arms sagging beneath the weight of a set of worn-out leather practice armor, a set long past its useful lifespan, and smelling faintly of sweat, leather-oil, and dust. "But I—"

"You know leatherwork, don't you?" Kerowyn asked, her generous mouth twitching as if she were trying not to laugh. Elspeth squirmed uncomfortably on the wooden bench, feeling very much like a tiny brown mouse facing a bored cat.

"Yes, but—"

"You've seen me and Alberich repair armor before, haven't you?" the mercenary-captain-turned-Herald continued with patient logic, arms folded across her chest. Elspeth looked from Kerowyn's weather-tanned face to the dust motes dancing in the sunlight to the whitewashed walls of the salle in hope of finding an answer.

She was unable to come up with one. She'd been put directly under Kerowyn's command this week, in lieu of the "usual" duties of a Herald. Those "usual" duties—riding circuit on a Sector, acting as lawbringer, occasional judge, paramilitary advisor, and general troubleshooter—brought a Herald into areas of significant risk—risk the Council was not willing to take with the Heir to the Throne.

So her assigned duty at the moment consisted of doing whatever Herald Kerowyn told her to do. She'd assumed her tasks would be things like acting as an assistant trainer, perhaps. Learning command tactics. Perhaps even acting as liaison between Kerowyn's mercenary Company and the Council.

Especially since the Council members still weren't certain what to do with a mercenary Captain who was also a Herald.

These were all things she knew how to do—or at least make a start on. After all, those were the kinds of things Heralds were supposed to do. They were *not* supposed to be repairing armor.

"Yes, but—" she repeated weakly, not knowing what else to say.

"You don't happen to think you're *too good* to repair armor..." Kerowyn's tone held a certain silky menace that told Elspeth that *someone* had given Herald Kerowyn chapter and verse on the ill-tempered Royal Brat. Of course, the Brat was a phase she had long ago outgrown, but some people couldn't seem to forget that stage of her life.

"No!" she said hastily. "But—"

"But *why* do I want you to repair armor—especially when it's someone else's job?" Kerowyn unbent enough to smile and shifted her weight to her right foot. "Let's play 'just suppose' for a moment. Let's suppose you are—for some reason—out in the back of beyond. Not even alone. We could have a situation like the one that brought me up here in the first place—where you're with a fighting force, maybe even in command, but there *aren't any* armorers around." She gestured at the pile of leather in Elspeth's arms. "Your gear gets damaged, and there's nobody free to fix it. What are you going to do, wear something with a weak spot and hope nobody notices? Hope you can find somebody to fix it before the next engagement?"

"Did *you* ever have to fix your own gear?" Elspeth countered. She had *so* been looking forward to a free afternoon.

"I assume you mean after I made Captain?" The Herald laughed out loud, displaying a fine set of strong, white teeth. "My dear child, the Skybolts were so badly off that first year that I helped *make* armor. And arrows and lances and even some horse-gear. No, dear, you aren't going to wiggle out of this one. Leather armor isn't that hard to repair; merely time-consuming. So I suggest you get to it. As for how, you take apart everything that doesn't look solid and replace it." The former—and current—Captain of "Kerowyn's Skybolts" nodded her blonde head emphatically and turned away toward the heap of practice armor that had been tossed into the "needs repair" pile.

Resigned to the situation, Elspeth watched Kero toss her blonde braid over her shoulder, thought of her own dull brown hair, and sighed a little enviously. *If I weren't the Heir, nobody would ever pay any attention to my looks. Mother is gorgeous, the twins are adorable, my stepfather is the handsomest man at Court—and I'm the little brown sparrow. Why couldn't I have been born looking like her?*

Kerowyn was certainly an amazing person. Lithe, strong, and with a face even her critics had to call "striking," she would have had dozens of suitors if it hadn't been for the fact that she and Herald Eldan discouraged even the most persistent with their devotion to one another. The Captain had been blessed with a head of hair as bright as new-minted gold and thick as a horse's tail. And despite the fact that she was literally old enough to be Elspeth's mother, it showed no sign of graying. Whatever Kerowyn's past life had been like, it had left no outward marks on her. And from the stories Kero had told over the past few years, she'd been through enough to gray the hair of four women.

For that matter, her present was just as hectic, and it hadn't left that much of a mark on her. She juggled two dedications, Herald and mercenary Captain, either one of which would have been a full-time career for anyone else.

And there are plenty of folk who think she should stick to one or the other... Elspeth smiled to herself. Those were the same folk who were mightily annoyed that the Herald Captain wouldn't wear Whites unless it was ordered by the Queen herself. She compromised—if one could call it that—by wearing the same kind of dark gray leathers the Weaponsmaster favored. And the Queen smiled and held her peace. Like Alberich, Kerowyn was a law unto herself.

"Besides, you have all the resources of the armory at your disposal," Kerowyn said over her shoulder, as she hefted another corselet in need of repair—this one of metal scale, a mending task Elspeth didn't even want to *think* about. "You wouldn't have that in the field. Be grateful I don't demand that you fix it with what folks carry in their field kits."

Elspeth bit back a retort and spread the shirt out over the bench she was sitting on, giving the armor the kind of careful scrutiny she imagined Kero must have.

Well, it isn't as bad as I thought, she decided, after a second examination proved that some of the worst places had already been repaired. Evidently the Captain had taken *that* much pity on her...

She bent to her task, determined to make as good a job of it as Kerowyn would.

Her determination did not last more than a few moments.

Someone distracted her as soon as she turned her attention to a tricky bit of stitchery that had to be picked out without ruining the leather. A whisper of air was all that warned her of the attacker's rush—but that was all the warning she needed. What Weaponsmaster Alberich had not pounded into her, the Herald Captain was making certain she learned, and in quick-time, too. And Kerowyn was a past master of the unconventional.

:Gwena!: she screamed mentally, as she acted on what had become reflex. She tumbled off her bench, hit the hard wooden floor with her shoulder, and rolled. She came up on the balls of her feet, poised and ready, the tiny knife she'd been using to cut the stitches still in her hand. Her heart pounded, but from battle-readiness, not fear.

She found herself facing someone who had recovered just as rapidly as she had; he stood in a near-identical pose on the opposite side of the bench, and she sized him up quickly. Taller and heavier than she, an anonymous male, in nondescript clothing, his face wrapped in a scarf and head covered with a tight hood, so that all she could see were his wary eyes.

A thousand fleeting thoughts passed through her mind in that moment of analysis. Uppermost was a second mental scream for help to her Companion Gwena. Hard on the heels of that was the sudden question: *Why doesn't Kero do anything?* She glanced out of the corner of her eye. The Captain stood with arms crossed, watching both of them, no discernible expression on her handsome face.

The obvious answer was implied by the question. *Because she was expecting this.*

And because Kerowyn was a Herald and her Companion Sayvil would never permit her to betray another, and further, because Elspeth's own Companion Gwena was not beating down the doors of the salle to get in and help her stand off this attacker, it followed that the "assassin" was nothing of the sort.

Her heart slowed a little, and she dared a mental touch. Nothing: her assailant was shielded. Which meant he knew how to guard his thoughts, which only another Mindspeaker could do.

And a closer look at the bright brown eyes, and the additional clue of a curl of black hair showing outside the assailant's hood gave her all the information she needed to identify him.

"Skif," she said flatly, relaxing a little.

:Good girl,: came the voice in her mind. *:I told Sayvil you'd figure this out before it got anywhere, but she didn't believe me.:*

She shifted her gaze over to Kerowyn, though without taking Skif out of her line of sight. "This was a setup, wasn't it?" she asked the older woman. "You never really intended for me to fix that armor."

Kero shrugged, not at all discomfited. "Hell, yes, I did. And tomorrow, you *will*. But I also intended for you to figure out that you *could,*" she temporized as Skif relaxed minutely. "That's a good thing for you to know if you're ever in the situation I described. If you don't know you *can* do something, it doesn't occur to you as an option. But don't relax," her voice sharpened as Skif started to come out of his crouch and Elspeth followed suit. "Just because you've identified him, that doesn't mean that the rest of the exercise is canceled. Take it up where you left off."

"With this?" Elspeth looked doubtfully at the tiny knife in her hand.

"With that—and anything else you can get your hands on. There're hundreds of things you can use in here, including that bench." Kerowyn frowned slightly. "Anything can be a weapon, child. It's time you learned to improvise."

Kerowyn did not have to outline the reasons for that statement; even if the current interkingdom situation had been full of light and harmony, there would always be the risk of someone with a grudge or grievance—or even a simple lunatic—who would be willing to risk his life to assassinate the next in line to the throne of Valdemar.

And with at least two enemies on the borders, Hardorn and Karse, the political situation was far from harmonious.

Still—*Anything can be a weapon? What on earth is she talking about?*

But she didn't have time to question the statement in detail. Elspeth went back on guard just in time to dodge Skif's rush for her.

She sidestepped him and reversed the knife, not wanting to really hurt him, and feinted for his eyes with the wooden hilt. He recognized the feint for what it was and ignored it, coming in to grapple with her. So far he hadn't produced any weapons of his own.

So his "orders" must be to capture rather than to kill. That makes my job easier and his harder…

Relatively easier. Skif had learned his hand-to-hand skills in the rough world of Haven's slums. Even the capital of Valdemar was prone to the twin problems of crime and poverty, and young Skif had been the godchild of both. Orphaned early, he had apprenticed himself to a thieving uncle, and when *that* worthy was caught, set up shop on his own. Probably only being Chosen had saved him from hanging like his uncle—or death at the hands of a competitor, like his mother.

His "style" was a mixture of disciplines—a kind of catch-all, "anything that works," devious, dirty, and deadly. The Queen's Own Herald, Talia, had learned quite a bit from him, but no one had ever thought to have him teach Elspeth as well. At least—not that. He *had* taught her knife-throwing, which had saved her life and Talia's, but even Queen Selenay had been horrified a few short years ago at the notion of her Heir learning street-fighting. Elspeth had begged but to no avail.

Many things had changed in those few years. Among them, the arrival of Kerowyn, who had sent one of her commandos to prove to Selenay that she and her daughter needed the kind of protection only instruction in the lowest forms of fighting could provide. Alberich undertook the Queen's instruction; Kero and Skif got Elspeth's. The lessons were frequently painful.

Dirk's taught me a thing or two since the last lesson—she told herself as she circled him warily, testing her footing as she watched his eyes—*and I bet neither of them knows that.*

She sensed the pile of armor behind her, and tried to remember what was topmost. Was it something she could throw over his head to temporarily blind him?

"Pick up the pace, boy," Kerowyn said. "Take some chances. You only have a few more moments before she either calls for help herself with Mindspeech, or her Companion brings the cavalry."

Skif lunged just as she made a grab for the nearest piece of junk, a leather gambeson. He waited until she moved, then struck like a coiled snake. He caught her in the act of bending over sideways and tackled her, both of them flying over the pile and landing in a heap on the other side of it. Her knife went skidding across the floor as her cheek hit the gritty floor, all the breath knocked out of her.

She writhed in his grip and grabbed the edge of his hood and tried to pull it down over his eyes, but it was too tightly wrapped. She struggled to get her knee up into his stomach, clawed at the wrappings around his head with no effect, and kicked ineffectually at the back of his legs. He simply pinned her with his greater weight, and slapped the side of her head at the same time, calling out "Disable!"

Damn. She obediently went limp. He scrambled to his feet, heaved her up like a sack of grain, slung her over his shoulder and started for the door. She watched the floor and his boots, and wondered what her Companion was supposed to be doing while the "assassin" was carrying her off.

:Not that way: Gwena said calmly in her mind, right on cue. *:I've got the front door blocked, and Sayvil has the rear. The only way out is by way of the roof:*

"No good, Skif," Elspeth said to his belt. "The Companions have you boxed in."

"Well, then I'll have to abort and follow my secondary orders," he replied. "Sorry, little kitten, you're dead."

He put her down on her feet, and she dusted herself off. "Crap," she said sourly. "I could do better than that. I wish I'd had my knives." She couldn't resist a resentful glance at Kero, who had made her take them off when she entered the salle.

"Well," Kero told her. "You didn't do as badly as I had expected. But I told you to get rid of those little toys of yours for a reason. They aren't a secret anymore; *everybody* knows you carry them in arm-sheaths. And you've begun to depend on them; you passed up at least a half dozen potential weapons."

Elspeth's heart sank as Skif nodded to confirm Kerowyn's assessment. "Like what?" she demanded. She didn't—quite—growl. It was ironic that a room devoted to weaponswork should be so barren of weaponry. There was *nothing* in the room; at least, nothing that could be used against an enemy. The salle's sanded wooden floor stood empty of everything but the bench she sat on and the pile of discarded armor. There were a few implements for mending the armor that she'd brought in from the back room. There were no windows that she could reach; they were all set in the walls near the edge of the ceiling. Even the walls were bare of practice weapons, just the empty racks along one wall and the expensive—but necessary—mirrors on the other.

"The bench," Skif said promptly. "You were within range to kick it into my path."

"You should have grabbed that leather corselet when you went off the bench," Kero added.

"Any of the mirrors—break one and you've got a pile of razor shards."

"The sunlight—maneuver him so that it's in his eyes."

"The mirrors again; distract me with my own reflection."

"The leather-needles—"

"The pot of leather-oil—"

"Your belt—"

"All right!" Elspeth cried, plopping down heavily on the bench, defeated by their logic. "What's the point?"

"Something that you can learn, but I can't teach in simple lessons," Kerowyn told her soberly. "An attitude. A state of awareness, one where you size everyone up as a potential enemy, and everything as a potential weapon. And I mean *everyone* and *everything.* From the stranger walking toward you, to your mother—from the halberd on the wall to your underwear."

"I can't live like that," she protested. "Nobody can." But at Kero's raised eyebrow, she added doubtfully, "Can they?"

Kero shrugged. "Personally, I think no royalty can afford to live *without* an outlook like that. And I've managed, for most of my life."

"So have I," Skif seconded. "It doesn't have to poison you or your life, just make you more aware of things going on around you."

"That's why we've started the program here," Kerowyn finished. "A salle is a pretty empty room even with repair stuff scattered all over it; that makes your job easier. Now," she fixed Elspeth with a stern blue-green eye, "before you leave, you're going to figure out one way everything in here could be used against an assailant."

Elspeth sighed, bade farewell to her free afternoon, and began pummeling her brain for answers.

Eventually Kero left for other tasks, putting Skif in charge of the lesson. Elspeth breathed a little easier when she was gone; Skif was nowhere near the taskmaster that Kerowyn could be when the mood was on her. Heraldic trainees at the Collegium used to complain of Alberich's lessons; now they moaned about Kerowyn's as well, and it was an open question as to which of the two was considered the worst. Elspeth had once heard a young girl complain that it was bad enough that the Weaponsmaster refused to grow old and retire, but now he'd cursed them with a female double and it wasn't *fair!*

But then again, she had thought at the time, *what is?*

Skif grilled her for a little longer, then took pity on her, and turned the lesson from one on "attitude" to simply a rough-and-tumble knife-fighting lesson. Elspeth found the latter much easier on the nerves, if not on the body. Skif might be inclined to go easy on her when it came to the abstract "lessons," but when it came to the physical he could be as remorseless as any of the instructors when he chose.

Finally, when both were tired enough that they were missing elementary moves, he called a halt.

In fact, she thought wearily, as he waved her off guard and stepped off the salle floor, *I doubt I could be a match for a novice right now.*

"That's... enough," he panted, throwing himself down on the floor beside the bench, as she slumped down on the seat and then sprawled along the length of it, shoving the forgotten leather armor to the floor. The angle of the sunlight coming in through the high clerestory windows had changed; there was no longer a broad patch of sunlight on the floor. It was starting to climb up the whitewashed wall. Not yet dinnertime, but certainly late afternoon.

"I have to get back to drilling the little ones in a bit," he continued. "Besides, if I spend too much more time in your unchaperoned company, the rumors are going to start again, and I don't feel like dealing with them."

Elspeth grimaced and wiped sweat from her forehead with the back of her hand. The last time rumors had started about a romance between her and Skif, she'd had to placate half the Council, and endure the knowing looks of half the Heralds. She wasn't sure which group was worse.

Now I know how Mother and Stepfather felt when they were my age. Every time someone gets interested—or interesting—most of the time they're frightened off by the matchmakers. You'd think people would have more important things to worry about.

But it was too bad poor Skif had to pay the price of *her* rank. There ought to be something she could do about that, but right now her weary mind was not supplying the answer.

"I'll see you later, then," she said instead. "I've got a few things of my own I'd like to do before dinner—if you're satisfied with my progress, that is."

"You're getting there," he told her, getting up with an effort, his sweat-damp hair curled even tighter. "I was making more mistakes than you were, toward the end. What's the closest weapon to your right hand?"

"The bench I'm on," she replied without thinking. "I roll off it and kick it in your direction."

"I was thinking of the shears on the floor there, but that'll do," he said with a tired chuckle. "See you at dinner?"

"Not tonight. There's some delegation from Rethwellan here to see Father. That means all meals with the Court until they're gone." She levered herself up on her elbows and smiled apologetically. "I guess they won't believe I'm not plotting against the rest of the family unless they see us all together."

Skif was too polite to say anything, but they both knew why that suspicion of treason might occur to a delegation from Rethwellan. Elspeth's blood-father, a prince of Rethwellan, *had* plotted to overthrow his own wife and consort, Queen Selenay—and in the end, had attempted to assassinate her himself.

Not the best way to handle foreign relations…

As it happened, though, no one in Rethwellan had any idea he might attempt such a thing—certainly there was no one in the royal family who had backed him. In fact, there had been no love lost between him and his two brothers, and there had been no repercussions from Rethwellan at the news that he had not survived that assassination attempt. The Queen quietly accepted King Faramentha's horrified apologies and disclaimers, and there the matter had rested for many years.

But then war and the redemption of a promise made to Selenay's grandfather had brought one of those brothers, Prince Daren, to the aid of the Queen of Valdemar, and the unexpected result of that first meeting had been not only love, but a lifebonding. Rethwellan lost its Lord-Martial, and Valdemar gained a co-ruler, for Daren, like Kerowyn, had been Chosen, literally on the battlefield.

Whether the bedding had followed or preceded the wedding was moot; the result had been twins, nine months to the day after the ceremony. Which left the titular Heir, Elspeth, with two unexpected rivals for her position. Elspeth, whose father had tried to murder the Queen and steal her throne… And there were the inevitable whispers of "bad blood."

King Faram, the current king of Rethwellan and brother to both her father and stepfather, held no such doubts about her, but occasionally some of his advisors required a reminder that treason was not a heritable trait. Elspeth slipped out of her musings and stretched protesting muscles.

"I wish—!" she began, and stopped.

"You wish what, kitten?" Skif prompted.

"Never mind," she said, dragging herself to her feet. "It doesn't matter. I'll catch up with you tomorrow, after Council. Assuming Kerowyn doesn't have me mucking out the stables or something equally virtuous and valuable."

He chuckled and left the salle, leaving her alone with her thoughts.

She cleaned up the scattered equipment from their lesson while the sweat of her exertion cooled and dried, and took herself out before her erstwhile mentor could return and find her "idle."

A warm summer wind whipped her hair out of its knot at the back of her neck, and dried her sweat-soaked shirt as she left the salle door. She made a hasty check for possible watchers, trotted around the side of the salle, and didn't slow until she reached the edge of the formal gardens and the relative shelter of the tall hedges. The path she took, from the formal garden and the maze to the herb and kitchen gardens of the Palace, was one normally used only by the Palace's husbandmen. It ran along the back of a row of hedges that concealed a line of storage buildings and potting sheds. She wasn't surprised that there was no one on it, since there was nothing to recommend it but its relative isolation, a commodity in short supply at the Palace/Collegium complex. Not the sort of route that anyone would expect to find her taking. Nor was her destination what anyone who didn't know her well would expect. It was a simple potting shed, a nondescript little building distinguished from its fellows only by the stovepipe, a stone kiln, and the small, glazed window high up on one side. And even then, there was no reason to assume it was special; the kiln had been there for years, and had been used to fire terracotta pots for seedlings and winter herbs.

Which made it all the more valuable to Elspeth.

She opened the door and closed it behind her with a feeling of having dropped a tremendous weight from her shoulders. This unprepossessing kingdom was hers, and hers alone, by unspoken agreement. So long as she did not neglect her duties, no one would bother her here, not unless the situation were direst emergency.

A tiny enough kingdom; one bench in the middle with a stool beside it, one sink and hand pump, one potter's wheel, boxes of clay ready for working, shelves, and a stove to heat the place in the winter and double as a small bisque-firing kiln in the rear. But not one implement here reminded her of the Heir or the Heir's duties. This was the one place where Elspeth could be just Elspeth, and nothing more. A proper kingdom as far as she was concerned; she'd been having second thoughts about ruling anything larger for some time now.

Up on the highest shelf were the finished products—which was to say the ones, to her critical eye, worth keeping—of her own two hands. They began with her first perfectly thrown pots and bowls, ranged through more complicated projects, and ended with some of the results of her current efforts—poured-slip pieces cast from molds that had in turn been made from her own work.

The twins were going through a competitive stage at the moment—and any time one of them got something, the other had to have something just like it. But different. If Kris got a toy horse, *Lyra* had to have a toy horse—same size, shape, length of tail, and equipage. But if Kris' horse was chestnut, hers had to be bay, dapple-gray, or roan. If he got a toy fort, *she* had to have a toy village; same size, number of buildings, number of toy inhabitants as his fort. And so on. The only thing they agreed on was toy Companions; they had to be twins, like the twins themselves.

Not that they need "toy" Companions, Elspeth thought with amusement. *They have the real thing following them around by the nose every time Mother takes them with her into the Field. No doubts there about whether or not they'll be Chosen!*

In fact, Gwena had remarked more than once that the only question involved would be *which* Companion did the Choosing. There were apparently a number in the running. :*Mark my words,*: she'd said with amusement. :*There are going to be fights over this in a couple of years.*:

But that made gift giving both harder and easier. Trying to find—or make—absolutely identical presents in differing colors had been driving Elspeth (and everyone else) to distraction. They were able to pick out the most amazing discrepancies and turn them into points of contention over whose present was "better." Finally, though, she'd hit on the notion of making a mold and copying a successful piece. Her first effort had been a pair of dragon-lamps, or rather, night-lights; comical, roly-poly fellows who gently burned lamp-oil at a wick in their open mouths. Those had been such a hit that Elspeth had decided to try dolls, specifically, dolls that looked as much like the twins themselves as she—who was not exactly a portrait sculptor—could manage.

It's a good thing that they're in that vague sort of "child-shaped" stage, she thought wryly, as she surveyed the row of greenware heads waiting to be cleaned of mold-marks and sorted for discards. *I doubt if I could produce anything more detailed than that.*

Well, dressing the completed dolls in miniatures of the twins' favorite outfits would take care of the rest. And providing the appropriate accessories, of course. She would have to appeal for help on that. To Talia for the outfits, since she could probably bribe the Queen's Own with an offer of another doll for Talia's son Jemmie; her plain-sewing was as good as many of the seamstresses attached to the Palace staff, though her embroidery was still "enough to make a cat laugh," as she put it. To Keren for the rest. Lyra was in a horse-crazy phase at the moment, a bit young for that, perhaps, but the twins—and Jemmie—were precocious in most areas. Kris had gone mad for the Guard; half the time, when asked, he would assert that he wanted to be a Guard-Captain when he grew up (which usually made any nearby Companions snort). Tiny swords and miniature riding boots were a little out of Elspeth's line, but perhaps Keren or Sherrill, Keren's lifemate, could arrive at a solution.

The first three heads weren't worth bothering with; bubbles in the slip had flawed the castings badly enough to crack when they were fired. The fourth was perfect; the fifth, possible, and the sixth—

The arrangement of the window and door in the shed made it a regrettable necessity that she sit with her back to the door. That being the case, she had left the hinges unoiled. It simply was not possible to open the door, however carefully, without at least some noise, however slight.

She froze as she heard the faintest of telltale squeaks from behind her, then continued examining the head as if she had heard nothing. A lightning-quick mental probe behind her revealed that it was Skif— again—at the door. This time his thoughts were unguarded. He assumed that she had already put this afternoon's lessons out of her mind, a little tired and careless, here in the heart of the Palace grounds.

Not a chance, friend, she thought. And as he slipped through the door, she shifted her weight off the stool she had been using, and hooked one foot around one of the legs.

At a moment when he was poised and unbalanced, she pulled the stool over, whirled, and kicked it under his feet, all with a single motion.

He was hardly expecting opposition, much less that he would be on the defensive. He lost his balance as his feet got tangled up with the stool and couldn't recover. He fell over backward with a crash of splintering wood as her stool went with him, landing ingloriously on his rear. She stood over him, shaking her head, as he blinked up at her and grinned feebly.

"Uh—"

"Ever heard of knocking?" she asked. She picked up her stool without offering him a hand and made a face. He'd broken two of the bottom rungs and loosened all four of the legs, and it had not been that sturdy to begin with.

"You owe me a new chair," she said, annoyed all out of proportion to the value of the stool. "That wasn't just a dirty trick, Skif, that was dangerous. You could have broken some of my best pieces, too."

"Almost broke some of mine," he grumbled. "You aren't going to get an apology, if that's what you're looking for. You knew very well we'd be springing these surprise attacks on you."

But not in the one place I can relax, she thought, seething with resentment. *Not in the only place I can get away from everything and everyone.*

"You still owe me, lout," she said stubbornly, righting the stool and rocking it to check how wobbly it was going to be. She sat on it and folded her arms, making no attempt to disguise how put out she was. "You still could have broken something. I don't ask for much, Skif, and I give up a lot. I think it's only fair to be off-limits when I'm out here."

He didn't say, *Will an attacker go along with that?* and he didn't give her a lecture, which mollified her a little. Instead, he grinned ingenuously and pulled himself up from the floor, dusting off his white uniform once he reached his feet. "I really have to congratulate you," he said. "You did a lot better than I expected. I deliberately came after you when I knew you were tired and likely to be careless."

"I know," she said crisply, and watched his bushy eyebrows rise as he realized what that meant. First, that she'd detected him soon enough to make a mental test of him, and second that she'd gone ahead and read his thoughts when she knew who it was. The second was a trifle unethical; Heralds were not supposed to read other's thoughts without them being aware of the fact. But if he was going to violate her precious bit of privacy, she was going to pay him back for it. *Let him wonder how much else I read while I was peeking and sweat about it a little.*

"Oh." He certainly knew better than to chide her for that breach of privacy at this point. "I'll see you later, I guess."

"You'd better have a new stool with you," she said, as he backed hastily out the door, only now aware that she was still clutching the much-abused doll's head. She looked at it as soon as he was out of sight. Whatever shape it had been in before this, it was ruined now. She disgustedly tossed it into the discard bucket beside her bench.

It wasn't until she had a half dozen usable heads lined up on the bench in front of her, and had smashed the rejects, that she felt as if her temper was any cooler. Cleaning them was a dull but exacting task, precisely what she wanted at the moment. She didn't want to see or talk to anyone until her foul mood was gone.

So when she felt the stirring of air behind her that meant the door had cracked open again, she was not at all amused.

I'm going to kill him.

She readied a mental bolt, designed to hit him as if she had shouted in his ear—when her preliminary Mindtouch told her something completely unexpected. This was not Skif—or Kerowyn, or anyone else she knew.

And she ducked instinctively as something shot past, overhead, and landed with a solid *thunk* point-first in the wall above the bench.

A hunting knife, ordinary and untraceable. It quivered as she stared up at it, momentarily stunned. Then her training took over before the other could react to the fact that he had missed.

She kicked the stool at him as she rolled under the bench and came up on the other side. He kicked it out of the way, slammed the door shut behind him, and dropped the bar; a few heartbeats later, the door shuddered as Gwena hit it with her hooves.

Now I wish this place wasn't quite so sturdy—

The stranger turned with another knife in his hands. Gwena shrieked and renewed her attack on the door. He ignored the pounding and came straight for Elspeth. With her lesson so fresh in her mind, she flung the first thing that came to hand at him—the half-cleaned doll's head. It didn't do any damage, but it made a hollow popping sound which distracted him enough so that she could get clear of the bench, get to where he'd kicked the stool, and snatch it up. Using it as a combination of shield and lance, she rushed him, trying to pin him against the abused door with the legs.

But the battering the stool had taken had weakened the legs too much to hold; his single blow broke the legs from the seat and left her holding a useless piece of flat board. Or almost useless; she threw it at his head, forcing him to duck, and giving her a chance to grab something else as Gwena's hooves hit the door again.

That "something else" proved to be one of her better pots, a lovely, graceful, two-handled vase. But she sacrificed it without a second thought, snatching it off the shelf and smashing it against the wall of the shed, leaving her with a razor-sharp shard. A knife-edge, with a handle to control it.

She took the initiative, as he started at the crash of shattering crockery, and threw herself at *him*.

He wasn't expecting that either, and she caught him completely off guard. He tried to grapple with her, and she let him, sacrificing her own mobility for one chance to get in with that bit of pottery in her right hand.

He grabbed her, but it was too late to stop her. Before he realized what she meant to do with that bit of crockery, she slashed it across his throat, cutting it from ear to ear, as Gwena's hooves hit the door and it shattered inward.

* * *

"Are you going to be all right?" Kerowyn asked, as she wiped Elspeth's forehead with a cold, damp cloth. Elspeth finally finished retching and licked her lips, tasting salt and bile, before she nodded shakily.

"I think so," she replied, closing her eyes and leaning back against the outer wall of the shed. The others had arrived to find her on her hands and knees in the grass, covered in blood—not her own—with Gwena standing over her protectively as she emptied her stomach into the bushes.

Her stomach still felt queasy, as if she might have another bout at any moment. No matter that she had seen death before—had even killed her share of the enemy in the last war with Hardorn—she'd taken down Lord Orthallen with her own two hands and one of Skif's throwing knives.

That wasn't close, not this close. I was dropping arrows into people from a distance. I threw a knife from across the room. Not like this, where he bled all over me and looked up at me and—

Her stomach heaved again, and she quelled the thoughts. "Who was he?" she asked, wiping her mouth with the back of her hand, trying to get her mind on something else. "How did he find out where I was? And how did he get past the guards?"

"I don't know the answers to your second and third questions," Kero replied, as Elspeth closed her eyes and concentrated on the coolness against her forehead. "But I can tell you the answer to the first. There's a spiderweb brand on his palm. He's one of the followers of the Cold God. They hire themselves out as assassins, and they're very expensive because they don't care if they get caught. He was either providing a legacy for a family, or doing penance for some terrible sin. If you hadn't killed him, he'd have killed himself." Kero dropped the cloth and sat back on her heels, and Elspeth opened her eyes and gaped at the older Herald, her nausea forgotten.

"I've never heard of anything like that!" she exclaimed.

Kero nodded. "Not too many people have; the Cold One's advocates come from farther south than anyone I know has been except Geyr. He's the one who told me about them, after the last try at your mother, and told me what to look for. Said that if Ancar really got desperate and knew how to contact them, he might try hiring one of the Cold Blades." She frowned. "I didn't take the threat seriously, and I should have—and believe me, it won't happen again. Frankly, you were lucky—they usually aren't that careless. And there is nothing, *nothing*, more dangerous than a suicidal fanatic."

"But—how did he get in here, in the gardens?" she asked, bewildered. "How could he? We have guards everywhere!"

Kero frowned even harder, "If Geyr's to be believed, by m-m-m-m-magic," she said, forcing the word out around the compulsion that seemed to overtake all Heralds when discussing anything but the mental Gifts and the Truth-Spell. "There're m-mages among the Cold Ones that give them a kind of invisibility. My grandmother could do it—make people think that when they looked at her, they were actually seeing someone they knew and trusted and expected to be there. Works with the mind, like Mindspeech, but it's set up with a spell. Dangerous stuff—and now the guards are going to have to double-check everyone they think they know. There're going to be some unhappy folks, unless I miss my guess…"

He either underestimated me, or he was inexperienced, she thought soberly, as Kero left her to talk quietly with some of the Guard who were dealing with the body. *And—I don't think we're ever going to find out how Ancar found him because I have the funny feeling that he used magic.*

She shivered and stood up, her knees shaking. Her Whites were ruined—not that she'd ever want to wear *this* set again. Magic again. Whatever had protected Valdemar in the past, it was not proof against Ancar anymore.

2

DARKWIND

Darkwind k'Sheyna balanced his bondbird Vree on his shoulder, and peered out across the sea of grass below him with a touch of—regret? Envy? A little of both, perhaps. From where he stood, the earth dropped in a steep cliff more than a hundred man-lengths to the floor of the Dhorisha Plains—a formidable barrier to those who meant the Shin'a'in and their land any ill. It took knowledge *and* skill to find the paths down into the Plains, and from there, intruders were visible above the waist-high grass for furlongs.

His bondbird lifted narrow, pointed wings a little in the warm, grass-scented updraft that followed the cliff. *:Prey.:* Vree's thought answered his own, framed in the simple terms of the bondbird's understanding. Not so much a thought as a flood of images; tree-hares, mice, quail, rabbits, all of them from the viewpoint of the forestgyre as they would appear just before the talons struck.

Prey, indeed. Any would-be hunter attempting to penetrate the Plains without magic aid would find himself quickly turned hunted. The land itself would fight him; he would be visible to even a child, he would never guess the locations of seeps and springs, and without landmarks that *he* would understand, that intruder would become disoriented in the expanse of grass and gently rolling hills. The guardians of the Plains, and the scouts that patrolled the border, had half their work done for them by the Plains themselves.

Darkwind sighed and turned away, back to his own cool, silent forest. No such help for him—other than the fact that the eastern edge of k'Sheyna territory bordered the Plains. But to the south and west lay forest, league upon league of it, and all of it dangerous.

:Sick,: complained Vree. Darkwind agreed with him. Magic contaminated those lands, a place Outlanders called the "Pelagir Hills" with no notion of just how much territory fell under that description. Magic flowed wild and twisted through the earth, a magic that warped and shaped everything that grew there—sometimes for the better, but more often for the worse.

Darkwind took Vree onto his wrist, the finger-long talons biting into the leather of his gauntlet as Vree steadied himself, and launched him into the trees to scout ahead. The forestgyre took to the air gladly; unlike his bondmate, Vree enjoyed the scouting forays. Hunting was no challenge to a bondbird, and there was only so much for Vree to do within the confines of k'Sheyna Vale's safe territory. Scouting and guarding were what Vree had been bred for, and he was never happier than when flying ahead of Darkwind on patrol.

Darkwind didn't mind the scouting so much, even if the k'Sheyna scouts *were* spread frighteningly thin—after all, he *was* a *vayshe'druvon*. Guard, scout, protector, he was all of those.

It's the magic, he told himself—not for the first time. *If it wasn't for the magic*—

Every time he encountered some threat to k'Sheyna that used magic or was born of it, and had to find some way *other* than magic to counter that threat, it scorched him to the soul. And worse was his father's attitude when he returned—scorn for the mage who would abandon his power, and a stubborn refusal to understand why Darkwind had done so...

If I could go back in time and kill those fools that set this loose in the world, I would do so, and murder them all with my bare hands, he thought savagely. His anger at those long-dead ancestors remained, as he chose a tree to climb, looking for one he had not used before.

A massive goldenoak was his choice this time; he slipped hand-spikes out of his belt without conscious thought, and pulled the fingerless, backless leather gloves on over his palms. The tiny spikes set into the leather wouldn't penetrate the bark of the tree enough to leave places for fungus or insects to lodge, but it would give him a little more traction on the trunk. As would the *shakras*-hide soles of his thin leather boots.

In moments he was up in the branches. The game-trail along the edge of the territory lay below him. When two-legged intruders penetrated k'Sheyna, most of the time they sought trails like this one.

When scouts patrolled, it was often up here, where the trails could be seen, but where the scouts themselves were invisible.

He shaded his eyes and chose a route through the next three forest giants by means of intersecting limbs, stowing his climbing-spikes and removing his double-ended climbing tool from the sheath on his back. Then he picked his way through the foliage, walking as surefootedly on the broad, swaying branch as if he were on the ground, pulling another branch closer with the hook end of his tool and hopping from his goldenoak to the limb of a massive candle-pine just as the branch began to bow beneath his weight. He followed the new branch in to the trunk, then back out again to another conifer, this time stowing the tool long enough to leap for the branch above him and swing himself up onto it.

As he chose his next route, his thoughts turned back to that wild magic, as they always did. *What it has done to the land, to us, is unforgivable. What it could do is worse.*

Never mind that the Tayledras tamed that magic, cleansed the places it had turned awry, made them safe for people and animals alike to live there. Not that there weren't both there now—but they often found their offspring changed into something they did not recognize.

But that isn't our real task. Our real task is more dangerous. And my father has forgotten it ever existed, in his obsessions with power and Power.

Darkwind looked back at the treeless sky where the Plains began. The Shin'a'in had no such problems. But then, the Shin'a'in had little to do with magic. *Odd to think we were one, once.*

Very odd, for all that there was no mistaking the fact that Tayledras features and Shin'a'in were mirrors of each other. The *Kaled'a'in,* they had been the most trusted allies of a mage whose name had been lost over the ages. The Tayledras remembered him only as "The Mage of Silence," and if the Shin'a'in had recorded his true name in their knotted tapestries, they had never bothered to tell anyone in the Tayledras Clans.

Father forgets that the real duty of the Hawkbrothers is to heal the land of the scars caused by that war of magics, even as the Goddess has healed the Plains.

He often felt more kinship with his Shin'a'in "cousins" these days than he did with his real kin. *The Lady gave them the more dangerous task, truth to tell,* he admitted grudgingly. He looked back again, but this time he shuddered. The Hawkbrothers cleansed—but the Shin'a'in guarded. And what they guarded—

Somewhere out there, buried beneath grass and soil, are the weapons that caused all this. And not all of them require an Adept to use them.

Only the Shin'a'in stood guardian between those hidden weapons and the rest of the world.

I don't envy them that duty.

:Men,: Vree sounded the alert, and followed it with a vocal alarm-call. Darkwind froze against the tree trunk for a moment, and touched Vree's mind long enough to see through the bondbird's eyes.

He clutched the trunk, fingernails digging into the bark. Direct contact with the forestgyre's mind was always disorienting. His perspective was skewed—first at seeing the strangers from above, as they peered up through the branches in automatic response to Vree's scream, the faces curiously flat and alien. Then came the dizzying spiral of Vree's flight that made the faces below seem to spin. As always, the strangeness was what kept him aware that it was the forestgyre's eyes he was using and not his own—the heightened sharpness of everything red, and the colors Vree saw that human eyes could not.

He was a passive traveler in Vree's mind, not an active controller. It was a measure of the bond and Vree's trust that the forestgyre would let him take control on occasion, but Darkwind took care never to abuse that trust. In general it was better just to observe—as he found yet again. Vree spotted one of the strangers raising what was probably a weapon, and kited up into the thick branches before Darkwind had registered more than the bare movement of an arm.

Darkwind released his link with Vree, and his hold on the trunk at the same time, running along the flat branch and using his tool as a balance-aid, and leaping to the next tree limb a heartbeat later. In his first days with Vree it had taken him a long time to recover from a link—

—and some never did, especially the first time. Caught up in the intoxication of the flight and the kill, they never detached themselves. And unless someone else discovered them, they could be lost forever that way—their bodies lying in a kind of coma, while their minds slowly merged with that of the bird, diminishing as they merged, until there was nothing left of what they were.

That had never happened in Darkwind's lifetime by accident, although there had been one scout, when he was a child, who had a lightning-struck tree crush him beneath its trunk. He had been far from a Healer, and had deliberately merged himself with his bird, never to return to the crippled and dying wreck of his body. He remained with k'Sheyna within his bird's mind, slowly fading, until at last the bird vanished one day, never to return.

Slower death, but death all the same, Darkwind thought pragmatically, climbing a pine trunk by hooking the stub of a broken branch above him to ascend to a crossover branch. He preferred to avoid such a nonchoice altogether.

He slowed as he neared the strangers, and dropped to all fours, stalking like a slim tree-cat along the branch and taking care not to rustle the leaves. Not that it would have mattered to the intruders, who called to each other and laughed as if they had no idea that they were being observed, or that they were in forbidden territory. His jaw tightened. *They are about to find out differently. And they're damned lucky that it's me who found them. There are plenty of others—including Father—who would feather them with arrows or make ashes of them without waiting to find out if they're ignorant, stupid, or true hostiles. Not that they'll ever know enough to appreciate the difference, since I'm going to throw them out.*

There were seven of them, however, and only one of him, and he had not survived this long as a scout by being incautious. First he called to Vree, for his Mindspeech was not strong enough to reach to the two nearest scouts.

:*Call alert,*: he said shortly. Vree knew what that meant. He'd contact the birds of the two scouts nearest, and they, in turn, would summon their bondmates. If Darkwind didn't need their help, he would let them know through Vree, and they would turn back. But if he *did* need them, they were already on the way.

He followed the intruders for several furlongs as they blundered along the game trail, their clumsiness frightening all the creatures within a league of them into frozen silence, leaving behind them a visible trail in the scuffed vegetation, and an invisible one in the resinous tang of crushed pine needles and their own human scent. Two of the men bore no visible weapons; the rest were armed and armored.

Vree's scorn, as sour and acidic as an unripe berry, tempted him to laughter. :*Cubs,*: the bird sent, unprompted, images of bumbling young bears and tangle-footed wolf pups.

Well, this was getting him nowhere. Nothing that the intruders had said or done gave him any idea of their intent. With a sigh, he decided that there was no choice in the matter. He was going to have to confront them.

Decision made, he worked his way up ahead of them, climbed down out of the branches, restored his climbing-tool to his back, limbered his bow, and waited for them to catch up to him.

They practically blundered into him; the one in the lead saw him first; an ordinary enough fellow, his brown leather armor marking him as a fighter rather than a forester. He shouted in surprise and quite literally jumped, even though Darkwind had not moved. Of course, Darkwind's own intricately dyed scouting gear and hair dyed a mottled brown made a near-perfect camouflage, but he wasn't *that* invisible. *Citymen,* Darkwind groaned to himself. *I ought to just let the ice-drakes do my job for me…*

Except that there were no ice-drakes in k'Sheyna territory, nor anything else large and deadly enough to eliminate them. Except the gryphons or the firebirds—but that might well be what brought them here in the first place. Darkwind did not intend to have either his friends or his charges wind up as some fool hunter's trophies.

Instinctively, they closed ranks against him. He spoke before the strangers recovered from their startlement, using the trade-tongue that the Shin'a'in favored in their dealings with Outlanders. "You are trespassing on k'Sheyna lands," he said, curtly. *A bluff, but I doubt they'll know how thin we're spread. And let them wonder if they'd have been taken by Tayledras, or something else.* "You must leave the way you came. Now."

They certainly couldn't miss the bow in his hands, his hooked climbing-staff on his back, or the steely menace in his voice. One of them started to object; the man next to him hushed him quickly. The fellow in the lead narrowed his eyes and frowned, looking him up and down as if measuring him.

"There's only one," the objector whispered, obviously unaware of how keen Tayledras hearing was; his silencer cut him off with, "Only one we can *see*, you fool. Let me handle this."

The man stepped forward, moving up beside Leather Armor. "Your pardon, my lord," he said, with false geniality. "We didn't know, how could we? There are no signposts, no border guards—"

"Tayledras have no need of signs," Darkwind interrupted coldly. "And I am a guard. I am telling you to leave. Your lives will be at hazard, else."

Did that sound as stupid as I think it did? Or did I convince them that they don't dare chance that I may not be as formidable as I'm pretending to be?

"I shall not permit you to pass," he warned, as they continued to hesitate.

The Objector plucked at Speaker's sleeve; Leather Armor frowned and turned his head to listen to the others' whispered conference without taking his eyes off Darkwind. This time they spoke too softly even for him to hear, and when they turned back to face him, Speaker wore a broad, bright—and empty—smile.

Damn. They've seen through me. I look like a lad, and I didn't feather one of them before I stopped them. My mistake.

"Of course we'll leave, my lord," he said with hollow good humor. "And we're very sorry to have trespassed."

Darkwind said nothing. Speaker waited for a response, got none, and shrugged.

"Very well, then, gentlemen," he said and gestured back down the path. "Shall we?"

They turned, as if to go—

I've seen this before. They somehow know—or guess—there's only one of me right now. They think they're going to catch me off-guard. Idiots. He alerted Vree with a touch, dropped, and rolled into the brush at the side of the trail. They were making so much noise they didn't even hear him move.

They turned back, weapons in hand, and were very surprised to see that he wasn't where they expected him to be. Before they managed to locate him, he had popped up out of the brush, and the one Darkwind had mentally tagged as "Speaker" was down with an arrow in his throat.

He dropped back into the cover of the bushes as Vree dove at the unprotected head of one of the men in the rear of the party, the one who had been making all the objections. The man shrieked with feminine shrillness and clapped both hands to his scalp as Vree rose into the branches with bloody talons.

That's one down and one hit. I think that takes out anyone who might be a mage.

It didn't look as if the rest of this was going to be that easy, though. Leather Armor was barking orders in a language Darkwind didn't recognize, but as the rest of the men of the party took to cover and began flanking him, Darkwind had a fairly good idea what those orders were.

Do they want a live Hawkbrother, or a dead border guard? The question had very real significance. If the former, he could probably take them all himself; they would have to be careful, and he wouldn't. But if the latter, he was going to have his hands full.

His answer came a few moments later, as an arrow whistled past his ear, and no rebuke from Leather Armor followed. *A dead border guard, then. Damn. My luck is simply not in today…*

There were at least two men with bows that he recalled, and he was not about to send Vree flying into an arrow. He told the forestgyre to stay up in the branches and worked himself farther back into the bushes.

That proved to be a definite tactical error. Within moments, he discovered that he had been flanked.

Just my luck to get a party with an experienced commander. Now he had the choice of trying to get to thicker cover, or taking on one of the men nearest him.

Thicker cover won't stop an arrow. That decided him. He put aside his bow, and slid his climbing-staff out of the sheath at his back.

He rose from cover with a bloodcurdling shriek not unlike Vree's, the staff a blur of motion in his hands. The man nearest him fell back with an oath, but it was too late. He had misjudged the length of the staff, and the wicked climbing-hook at the end of it, designed to catch and hold on tree bark, caved in half his face and lodged in his eye socket.

Darkwind jerked the hook free and dropped, as another man belatedly aimed an arrow at him. It went wild, and Darkwind took to cover again.

That leaves four.

:*Brothers come,*: Vree said. And, hopefully, added, :*Vree hunt?*:

:*No, dammit, featherhead, stay up there!*:

:*?*: Vree replied.

Darkwind swore at himself. *Got too complicated for him again.* He thought emphatically, :*Arrows!*:

:*!*: replied Vree, just as rustling in the dry leaves told Darkwind that he was being stalked.

He Mindtouched cautiously, ready to pull back in an instant if it proved that the stalker had any mind-powers.

Ordinary, ungifted—but this one was Leather Armor. Darkwind knew he wasn't going to take *him* by surprise with a yell and a hooked stick.

He worked his way backward, wondering where the other two guards that Vree had called for him were. His Mindspeech wasn't strong enough to hear them unless they were very near, but Vree and the other bondbirds of the scouts patrolling nearby were in constant contact. Vree was trained to serve as a relay point—if there was anything to relay.

The rustling stopped, and Darkwind froze so that he did not give himself away. They remained where they were, he and Leather Armor, for what seemed like hours. Finally, just when Darkwind's leg had started to cramp, Leather Armor moved again.

Meanwhile, Darkwind had an idea. *:Vree, play wounded bird. Find a man with no arrows, and take him to the brothers.:* It was an old trick in the wild, but it just might work against citybred folk. After a moment, Darkwind heard Vree's distress call, faint with distance, and growing fainter. The rustling stopped for a moment; someone cursed softly, then the rustling began again.

That's four.

Darkwind moved again, but the cramp in his leg made him just a little clumsy, and he overbalanced. He caught himself before he fell, but his outstretched hands brushed by a thick branch and it bent, shaking enough to rustle the leaves, and betraying his location.

Damn!

No hope for it now, he half-rose and sprinted for the shelter of a rock pile, pounding feet and crackling brush not far behind him. The woods were too thick here to afford a good shot; it was going to be hand-to-hand if Leather Armor overtook him.

Ill luck struck again; just as he reached the rocks, something shot at ankle-height out of the shadows. He leapt but couldn't quite avoid the tangle-cord. It caught one foot, and he tumbled forward. He tucked and rolled as he went down, but when he came back up, he found himself staring at the point of a sword.

Behind the sword stood Leather Armor, frowning furiously. A few moments later, panting up behind him, came the man with the bloody, furrowed scalp.

"No spindly runt is going to tell us where we can go," sneered Leather Armor. "One little brat to play guardman, hmm? So much for your big bad Hawkbrothers, milor—"

Two screams from out in the woods interrupted him, and both their heads turned for a fraction of a heartbeat. Just long enough for Darkwind to reach the kill-blade he had hidden in his boot—and Vree to begin his stoop.

"What made you think I was alone?" he said, mildly. Leather Armor's head snapped back around, giving Darkwind a clear shot at his eye. A quick flick of the wrist, and the knife left his hand and went straight to the mark, just as Vree struck the second man from behind, his talons aimed for the neck and shoulders, knocking the mage to the ground with the force of the blow. As Darkwind's victim toppled over, Vree's talons pierced the back of his target's neck, and he bit through the spine, the powerful beak able to separate even a deer's backbone at need. It was over in moments.

Vree flapped his wings and screamed in triumph, and Darkwind licked the blood away from his lip; he had bitten it when he fell. The taste was flat and sweet, gritty with forest loam.

He rose slowly and brushed himself off, waiting for Vree to calm down a little before trying to deal with him. Like all raptors, the bondbirds were most dangerous just after a kill, when their blood still coursed hot with excitement, and they had forgotten everything but the chase and strike.

When Darkwind's own heart had settled, he turned, and called Vree back to the glove. The bondbird mantled and screamed objection at him, still hot with his hunting-rage, but when Darkwind Mindtouched him—carefully, for at this stage it was easy to be pulled into the raptor's mind—he calmed. Darkwind held out his arm and slapped the glove again, and this time Vree returned to his bondmate, launching himself from the body with a powerful shove of his legs, and landing heavily on Darkwind's gauntlet. The wicked talons that had so easily pierced a man's neck closed gently on the scout's leather-covered wrist.

Darkwind pointedly ignored the second body, Vree's victim, and stooped over the first corpse to retrieve his knife, Vree flapping his wings a little to keep his balance. Admittedly, it was no uglier a death than the one *he* had just delivered, but it was easy to forget that the Tayledras-bred forestgyres, largest of all the bondbirds other than the eagles, were easily a match for many wild tiercel eagles in size, and fully capable of killing men.

And when Vree did just that—sometimes the realization of just what kind of a born killer he carried around on his wrist and shoulder every day came as a little shock.

At least he doesn't try to eat them, Darkwind thought with a grimace. In fact, Vree was even now fastidiously cleaning his talons, his thoughts full of distaste for the flavor of the blood on them.

The bird looked up, suddenly. Darkwind tensed for a moment, but *:Brothers come,:* the bird said and went back to cleaning his talons.

Even to Darkwind's experienced eyes it seemed as if a man-shaped piece of the forest had detached itself and was walking toward him when Firestorm first came into view. The sight gave him a renewed appreciation for the effectiveness of the scouts' camouflage.

He'd heard somewhere that one of the Outlanders' superstitions about the Tayledras was that they were really all mirror-copies of the same person.

I suppose it might look that way to strangers...

The scouts all dressed so identically in the field that they might well have been wearing uniforms; close-fitting tunic and trews of a supple weave and of a mottled, layer-dyed green, gray, and brown. There were individual differences in the patterns, as distinct as individual fingerprints to the knowledgeable, but to an Outlander the outfits probably looked identical. And their hair *was* identical, except for length. Hair color among the Hawkbrothers was a uniform white; living in the Vales, surrounded by magic, hair bleached to white and eyes to silver-blue by the time a Tayledras was in his early twenties—sooner, if he was a mage. The scouts dyed their hair a mottled brown to match their surroundings—the rest of the Clan left theirs white.

I suppose Outlanders have reason to think us identical.

Firestorm's bondbird was nowhere in sight, but as the younger scout came into the clearing, Kreel dove down out of the treetops to land on Firestorm's casually outstretched arm. Kreel was a different breed from Vree; smaller, and with the broad wings of a hawk, rather than the rakish, pointed wings of the falcon. Neither bird had bleached out yet; since Darkwind no longer used his magic powers, and Firestorm never had been a mage, it would be years before either bird became a *ti'aeva'leshy'a,* a "forest spirit," one of the snow-white "ghost birds," with markings in faint blue-gray.

Too bad, in a way. The white ones frighten the life out of Outlanders who see them. We could use that edge, Vree and I. If this lot had seen him *first, they might not have chanced taking me on.*

Vree's natural coloration was *partially* white already. His white breast sported brown barring; the same pattern as the underside of his wings.

His back and the upper face of his wings were still brown, with a faint black barring. Kreel was half Vree's size, with a solid blue-gray back and a reddish-brown, barred breast. Kreel's red eyes had begun to fade to pink; Vree's eyes had already faded to light gray from his adolescent color of ice-blue.

"I got one of the bastards, Skydance got one, and Skydance's Raan got the third," Firestorm said, ruffling the breast-feathers of his cooperihawk. He shook his head in admiration at the gyre on Darkwind's wrist, as Vree fastidiously preened the blood from his breast-feathers. "Makes me wish I'd bonded to a gyre, sometimes. This little one is faster than anyone would believe, but she can't take down a man."

"A bird doesn't have to be able to take a man down to take one out," Darkwind reminded him. "Kreel does all right. *You're* too damned bloodthirsty."

Firestorm just chuckled, reached into his game-pouch, and fed Kreel a tidbit. Vree clucked and shifted his weight from one foot to the other, in an anxious reminder that *he* was owed a reward as well.

Darkwind scratched the top of Vree's head, then reached into his own game-pouch for a rabbit quarter. Vree tore into the offering happily. "Funny, isn't it," Firestorm observed, "We can shape them all we like, make them as intelligent as we can and still have flight-worthy birds, but we can't change their essential nature. They're still predators to the core. Who were those fools?"

"I don't know." Darkwind frowned. "I listened to them for a while, but I didn't learn anything. I think there were two mages and the rest were fighters to guard them, but that's only a guess. I don't know what they wanted, other than the usual." Flies were beginning to gather around the fallen bodies, and he moved out of the way a little. "Dive in, steal the treasures of the mysterious Hawkbrothers, and try to get out intact. Greedy bastards."

"They never learn, do they?" Firestorm grimaced.

"No," Darkwind agreed soberly. "They never do."

Something about the tone of his voice made Firestorm look at him sharply. "Are you all right?" he said. "If you got hurt but you're trying to go all noble on me, forget it. If you're not in shape for it, we can take over your share for the rest of the day, or I can send back for some help."

Darkwind shook his head, and tossed his hair out of his eyes. "I'm all right; I'm just tired of the whole situation we're in. We shouldn't *be* out here alone; we should be patrolling in threes, at least, on every section.

K'Sheyna is in trouble, and anyone with any sense knows it. Most of our mages won't leave the Vale, and the best of our fighters are out of reach. I don't know why the Council won't ask the other Clans for help, or even the Shin'a'in—"

Firestorm shrugged indifferently. "We haven't had anything hit the border that we couldn't handle, even shorthanded," he replied. "After all, we *had* cleaned this area out, that's why the children and minor mages and half the fighters were gone when—"

He broke off, flushing. "I'm sorry—I forgot you were there when—"

"When the Heartstone fractured," Darkwind finished for him, his voice flat and utterly without expression. *I'm not surprised he doesn't remember.* Darkwind had been "Songwind" then, a proud young mage with snow-white hair and a peacock wardrobe—

Not Darkwind, who refused to use any magic but shielding, who never wore anything but scout gear and wouldn't use the formidable powers of magic he still could control—if he chose—not even to save himself.

He was—*had been*—Adept-rank, in fact—and strong enough at nineteen to be one of the Heartstone anchors...

Not that it mattered. He watched Vree tear off strips of rabbit and gulp them down, fur and all. "I don't know if you ever knew this," he said conversationally, not wanting Firestorm to think he was upset about the reminder of his past. "I watched the building of the Gate to send them all off."

Firestorm tilted his head to one side. "Why *did* they send everyone off? I wasn't paying any attention—it was my first Vale-move."

"We always do that," Darkwind said, as Vree got down to the bones and began cleaning every scrap of flesh from them he could find. "It's part of the safety measures, sending those not directly involved in moving the power or guarding those who are to the new Vale-site, where they'd be safe in case something happened."

"Which it did." Firestorm sighed. "I guess it's a good thing. The gods only know where they are now. Somewhere west."

Somewhere west. Too far to travel, when over half of them were children.

"And not an Adept able to build a Gate back to us in the lot of them." Darkwind scowled. "Now that *was* a mistake. And it was bad tactics. Half of the Adepts should have been with them, and I don't know why the Council ordered them all to stay until the Heartstone was drained and the power moved."

Firestorm relaxed marginally, and scratched Kreel with his free hand. "Nobody ever tells us about these things. Darkwind, why haven't we built a new Gate and brought them back?"

A damned good question. Darkwind's lips compressed. "Father says that what's left of the Heartstone is too unstable to leave, too dangerous to build a Gate near, and much too dangerous to have children exposed to."

Firestorm raised an eloquent eyebrow. "You don't believe him?"

"I don't know what to believe." Darkwind stared off into the distance, over Firestorm's shoulder, into the shadows beneath the trees. "I probably shouldn't be telling you this, even. That kind of information is only supposed to be discussed by the Council or among mages. There's another thing; Father was acting oddly even before the disaster—he hasn't been quite himself since he was caught in that forest fire. Or that's the way it seems to me, but nobody else seems to have noticed anything wrong."

"Well, I haven't, at least not any more than with the rest of the Council." Firestorm laughed, sarcastically. "Old men, too damned proud to ask for help from outside, and too feeble to fix things themselves. Which is probably why *I'm* not on the Council; I've said that in public a few too many times."

The scout tossed his hawk up into the air and turned to go. Kreel darted up into the trees ahead, and all the birds went silent as he took to the air. Everything that flew knew the shape of a cooperihawk; nothing on wings was safe from a hungry one. And no bird would ever take a chance on a cooperi being sated. "If you're all right to finish, I'll get back to my section. Do we bother to clean up, or leave it for the scavengers?"

"Leave it," Darkwind told him. "Maybe a few bones lying around will discourage others."

"Maybe." The younger man laughed. "Or maybe we should start leaving heads on stakes at the borders."

With that macabre suggestion, the scout followed his bird into the forest, moving in silence, blending into the foliage within moments. Vree had finished his rabbit, dropping the polished bones, and Darkwind launched him into the air as well, so that they could resume their interrupted patrol.

He'd meant what he told Firestorm, every bitter word of it. *I hardly know Father anymore. He used to be creative, flexible; he used to have no trouble admitting when he was wrong. Now he's the worst of the lot. Every time another Clan sends someone to see if we need help, he sends them away. How can we not need help?*

We've got an unstable Heartstone, we don't have enough scouts to patrol a border that we had to pull back in the first place. Our children are gone and we can't get them back—and we don't dare leave. And he's *pretending we can handle it.*

That was part of the reason he spent so little time in the Vale anymore; the place was too silent, too empty. Tayledras children were seldom as noisy as Outlander children, but they made their presence—and their absence—felt.

The once-lively Vale seemed dead without them. And another part of the reason he avoided the Vale was his father. The fewer opportunities there were for confrontations with the old man, the better Darkwind liked it.

He would have to go in at the end of his patrol, though, and he wrinkled his nose in distaste at what he would have to endure. This invasion would have to be reported. And as always, the Council would want to know why he hadn't handled things differently, why he hadn't blasted the intruders or shot them all when he first saw them. And because he was an Elder, the questions would be more pointed.

I didn't kill them because they could have been perfectly innocent, dammit!

And Starblade would want to know why he hadn't used magic.

And as always, Darkwind would be unable to give him an answer that would satisfy him.

"Because I don't want to" isn't good enough. He wants to know why *I don't want to.*

Darkwind pulled his climbing-staff out of the sheath, and hooked a limb, hauling himself up into the tree and trying not to wince as he discovered new bruises.

He wants to know why. He says. But he won't accept my reasons because Adept Starblade couldn't possibly have a son who gave up magic for the life of a scout.

Even when the magic killed his mother in front of his eyes. Even when the magic ruined his life. Even when he's seen, over and over, that magic isn't *an answer, it's a tool, and any tool can be done without.*

He looked out over the forest floor and briefly touched Vree's mind. All was quiet. Even the birds, frightened into silence by the noise of the fight and the appearance of the cooperihawk, were singing again.

Well, he'd better start learning to change again, Darkwind decided, *because I've had enough. I'm taking this incident to the Council as usual, but this time I'm going to make an issue of it. And I don't care if he doesn't like what he's going to hear; we can't keep on like this indefinitely.*

And if he wants a fight, he's going to get one.

3

ELSPETH

Elspeth bit her lip until it bled to keep herself from losing her temper. Queen Selenay, normally serene in the face of any crisis, had reacted to the attack on her eldest child with atypical hysteria.

Well, I'd call it hysteria, anyway.

Elspeth had barely gotten clean and changed when the summons arrived from her mother—accompanied by a bodyguard of two. As a harbinger of what was to come, that bodyguard put Elspeth's hackles up immediately. The sight of Selenay, standing beside the old wooden desk in her private apartments, white to the lips and with jaws and hands clenched, did nothing to make her daughter feel any better.

And so far, Selenay's impassioned tirade had not reassured her Heir either. It seemed that the Queen's answer to the problem was to restrict Elspeth's movements to the Palace complex, and to assign her a day-and-night guard of not less than two at all times.

And that, as far as Elspeth was concerned, was totally unacceptable. But she couldn't get a word in until her mother stopped pacing up and down the breadth of her private office and finally calmed down enough to sit and listen instead of talking. It helped that Talia, though she was privy to this not-quite-argument Elspeth was having with Selenay, was staying discreetly in the background, and so far hadn't said a word, one way or the other.

I think if she sided with Mother, I'd have hysterics. "I can't believe you're taking this so—so—casually!" Selenay finally concluded tightly, her hands shaking visibly even though she held them clenched together on the desktop, white as a marble carving.

"I'm not taking it 'casually,' Mother," Elspeth replied, hoping the anger she thought she had under control did not show. "I'm certainly not regarding this incident as some kind of a bad joke. But I am *not* going to let fear rule my life." She paused for a moment, waiting for another tirade to begin. When Selenay didn't say anything, she continued, trying to sound as firm and adult as possible. "No bodyguards, Mother. No one following me everywhere. And I am *not* going to live behind the Palace walls like some kind of cloistered novitiate."

"You're almost *killed,* and you say *that?* I—"

"*Mother,*" Elspeth interrupted. "Every other ruler lives with that same threat constantly. We've been spoiled in Valdemar—mages have never been able to get past our borders, and the Heraldic Gifts—especially the Queen's Own's Gifts—have always made sure that we knew who the assassins were before they had a chance to strike. So—now that isn't necessarily true anymore. *I* am not going to restrict my movements with a night-and-day guard just because of a single incident. And, frankly, I'm not going to lose any sleep over it."

Selenay paled and seemed at a loss for words.

"That doesn't mean I'm going to be careless," she added, "I'm going to take every precaution Kerowyn advises. I'm not foolhardy or stupid— but I am not going to live in fear, either."

Finally Talia spoke up. "There really isn't that much more danger than there always was," she said mildly. "We've just been a lot more careless than the monarchs were in—say—Vanyel's day. We *have* been spoiled; we thought we were immune to danger, that magic had somehow gone away. The fact is, we didn't learn from the last two wars. We have to do more—much more—than we have in finding ways to counter this threat. Or should I say, in rediscovering them—"

Now that's odd. No one seems to have any trouble discussing magic when it's in the past—the stories of Vanyel's time, for instance. It's only when we're talking about it happening now—and here, inside Valdemar—that the restriction seems to hold.

But before she pursued that train of thought, she had to come up with some convincing arguments first. "Mother, I'm a Herald first, and your Heir second. The fact is, I can't do *my* job with somebody hovering over me all the time." When Selenay looked blank, Elspeth sighed. "I'm still on duty to the city courts, remember? And on detached duty with Kerowyn. What if she wants me to go work with the Skybolts for a while? What would your allies say if I went over there with a set of bodyguards at my back? They'd say you don't even trust your own people, that's what."

Not to mention what a pair of hulking brutes at my back is going to do to my love-life, she thought unhappily. *There wasn't a lot there to begin with, but I can't even imagine trying to have a romantic encounter with half the Guard breathing down my neck.*

:You could always try confining your pursuits to your bodyguards,: Gwena suggested teasingly.

:Oh, thanks. That's a wonderful idea. I'll take it under advisement,: she replied, trying to keep her level of sarcasm down to something acceptable.

"To suddenly start trailing bodyguards around isn't going to do much for my accessibility, Mother," she continued, thinking quickly. "People come to the Heir when they are afraid, for one reason or another, to come to the Monarch—and you *know* that's been true for hundreds of years. If there's something you want done, but don't want the open authority of the Crown behind it, you give it to me. Talia is your double in authority—*she* can't do that. I'm your unfettered hand, and now you want to shackle me. It just won't work, anyone could tell you that. It not only cuts down *my* effectiveness, it cuts down on yours."

:Good girl; that's the way to win your argument. I agree with you, by the way. Bodyguards are not a solution. Not unless those bodyguards were also Heralds, and we have no Heralds to spare.:

Elspeth felt a little more relaxed and confident with Gwena's support. *:Thanks. At least I'm not just being boneheaded and stubborn about this.:*

:Oh, you are being boneheaded and stubborn,: her Companion replied cheerfully. *:But it's for the right reasons, and there's nothing wrong with a little stubbornness for the correct cause.:*

Elspeth could hear the gentle good humor in Gwena's mind-voice and couldn't take offense, though for a moment she was sorely tempted.

Selenay did not look convinced by the argument, however.

"I can't see that it's worth the risk—" she began. Talia interrupted her.

"Elspeth's right, I'm afraid," she said, in her quiet, clear voice. "It *is* worth the risk. When Elspeth goes out, off the Palace grounds, you could assign her a discreet guard, but other than that I think that extra care on everyone's part will serve the same purpose. If Kero is right, simply having the guards question anyone they see who doesn't seem to be acting normally will prevent another incident like the last one."

Selenay's jaw tightened in a way Elspeth knew only too well. "You think I'm overreacting, don't you?"

Yes, Elspeth replied—mentally. And kept a very tight shield over the thought.

"No," Talia said, and smiled. "You're just acting the way any mother would. I know if it were Jemmie—let's just say I'd have him hidden away with some family—say, a retired Guardsman-turned-farmer—so far out in the country that no one could counterfeit a native and *any* stranger would cause a stir."

"Maybe—" Selenay's expression turned speculative, and Elspeth started to interrupt the thought she *knew* was going through her mother's mind.

Talia did it for her. "That won't work for Elspeth, I'm afraid. She's too old to hide that way, even if she would put up with being sent off like an exile. However—her uncle's court is very well protected..."

Not too bad an idea, Elspeth had to admit, *even if it doesn't feel right.*

"That's a thought," Selenay acknowledged. "I don't know; I'll have to think about it."

"So long as you aren't planning on putting me under armed guard, like the Crown Jewels," Elspeth said, in a little better humor.

"Not at the moment," her mother admitted.

"All right, then." She ran a hand over her hair and smiled a little. "I can put up with one guard in the city; we probably should have had one anyway. If I'm not safe on the Palace grounds, after Kero gives the Guards one of her famous lectures, I won't be safe anywhere. I should know, I got one myself today. Two, in fact. As soon as she figured I was all right, she gave me a point-by-point critique on my performance."

Talia chuckled, and Selenay relaxed a little. "I can just see Kero doing that, too," Talia said. "She doesn't ever let up. She's like Alberich. The more tired you are, the more she seems to push you."

"I know, believe me. Uh—on that subject, sort of—would there be any problem if I had a tray in my room?" she asked, drooping just a little—not enough to resurrect Selenay's hysteria, but enough to look convincingly tired. "I don't think I can handle Uncle's delegation right now..."

"After this afternoon, I doubt anyone would expect you to," the Queen replied, sympathetically. "I'll make your apologies, and hopefully, after this afternoon, the current batch of rumors will be put to rest for a while."

"And I'll see that someone sends a tray up," Talia offered. "With honeycakes," she added, giving Elspeth a quick wink.

Elspeth managed to keep from giving herself away, and stayed in character. "Thanks," she sighed, throwing both of them grateful looks. "If anyone wants me, I'll be in the bathing room, under hot water. And frankly, right now all you need to worry about is whether or not I drown in the bathtub. All I want is a hot bath and a book, dinner, and bed."

She made a hasty exit before she betrayed herself. After all, it was partially the truth. She really *was* tired; her afternoon's double-workout had seen to that even before the attack. She really *did* want a hot bath and a tray in her room. But she had no intention of going to bed early. There was too much to think about.

* * *

A candlemark later, wrapped in a warm robe and nibbling on a honeycake as she gazed out into the dusk-filled gardens, she still hadn't come to any conclusions of her own.

Things just felt wrong; she was restless and unhappy, and she wasn't certain why. The restrictions Selenay had wanted to place on her movements had merely heightened those feelings, which had been there all along.

It's almost as if there was something I should be doing, she decided, as the blue dusk deepened and shrouded the paths below in shadows. *As if somewhere I have the key to all this, if I can just find it.*

One thing she was certain of: this would not be the last time Ancar attempted an assassination, or something of the sort. He wanted Valdemar, and he was not going to give up trying to annex it. There was no way he could expand eastward; the Aurinalean Empire was old and strong enough to flatten him if he attacked any of its kingdoms. North was Iftel—strange, isolationist Iftel—guarded by a deity. He could not move against them; not unless he wanted a smoking hole where his army had been. South was Karse, and if rumor was true, he was already making moves in that direction. But Karse had been at war with Valdemar. And Rethwellan for generations, and they were quite prepared to take him on as well. Taking Valdemar would give him protection on the north, a western border he would not need to guard, and another place from which to attack Karse. Besides doubling his acquisitions.

He probably assumed that if the rightful rulers and their Heirs died, it would leave the country in a state of chaos and an easy target for takeover.

He might not be ready for another war now—but he would be, given time and the chance to rebuild his forces.

So no matter what, there's going to be another war, she thought, shoving the rest of her dinner aside, uneaten. *I know it, Kero knows it, Stepfather knows it—Mother knows it, and won't admit it.*

She turned away from the window and rested her back against the sill. She'd had a fair number of discussions with Kero and Prince-Consort Daren on this very subject. Her *stepfather* didn't treat her like a child.

Then again, her stepfather hadn't ever seen her until she was adult and in her full Whites. It was an old proverb that a person was *always* a child to his parents... but it was war she should really be worrying about, not how to make her mother realize that she was an adult and capable of living her own life. The two problems were entwined, but not related. And the personal problems could wait.

The next try Ancar makes is going to involve magic, I know it is—combative magic, war-magic, the kind they use south of Rethwellan. The kind the Skybolts are used to seeing. Kero says so, and I think she's right. She can talk about real magic, and I can... and that might be a clue to what I need to be doing right there.

For Valdemar was not ready to cope with magic, especially not within its borders. For all the efforts to prepare the populace, for all the research that was *supposed* to have been done in the archives, very little had actually been accomplished. Yes, the ballads of Vanyel's time and earlier had been revived, but there was very much a feeling of "but it can't happen now" in the people Elspeth had talked to. And she wasn't the only one to have come to that conclusion. Kero had said much the same thing. The Captain was worried.

Elspeth licked her bitten lip, and thought hard. *Kero's told me a lot of stories she hasn't even told Mother. Some of the things the Skybolts had to deal with— and those were just minor magics.*

"Most of the time the major magics don't get used," she'd said more than once. That was because the major mages tended to cancel one another out. Adept-class mages tended to be in teaching, or in some otherwise less-hazardous aspect of their profession.

Most mages, Adept-class or not, were unwilling to risk themselves in all-out mage-duels for the sake of a mere employer. Most employers were reluctant to antagonize them. But when the ruler himself was a mage, or backed by one—a powerful mage, at that—the rules changed. Mages could be coerced, like anyone else; or blackmailed, or bribed, if the offer was high enough. There was already evidence of coercion, magical and otherwise; outright control, like the men of his armies. And where there was a power broker, there were always those who wanted power above all else and were willing to pay any price to get it.

So Valdemar wasn't protected anymore because there was someone willing to pay the price of breaking the protections.

Or bending them...

All right; when the Border-protection has failed, what's been the common denominator? She rubbed her temple, as she tried to think of what those failures had in common.

It didn't keep Hulda out—but she didn't work any magic while she was here. It didn't keep some of Ancar's spells out, but they were cast across *the Border. It didn't keep that assassin out—but the spell must surely have been cast on him when he was with Ancar. And it didn't keep Need out, but Need hasn't done a blessed thing— openly—since Kero got here.*

So, as long as there wasn't any *active* magic-casting within the borders, the protections they had relied on weren't working anymore.

Or else there were now mages who were stronger than the protections, so long as they worked from outside.

And, without a doubt, Ancar had figured that out, too.

Furthermore, no matter how powerful the protections were, unless they were caused by some deity or other—which Elspeth very much doubted— they could be broken altogether, instead of merely circumvented.

And when—not if, but *when*—Ancar accomplished that, they were going to be as helpless as a mouse beneath the talons of a predator.

As if to underscore that, Elspeth heard the call of an owl, somewhere out in the gardens.

Someone was going to have to find a mage—preferably a very powerful mage, one who wouldn't suffer from whatever had kept the Skybolts' mages out—and bring him to Valdemar.

That was going to take a lot of money, persuasion, or both. The first they had—or could get. The second just required the right person. Someone who was experienced in diplomacy and negotiation. Or, failing being able to bring someone in, a Herald was going to have to learn magic herself.

That's it, she decided. *That's what I need to do—find a mage and bring him in. I'm the perfect instrument for the job. Or learn magic; Kero says there are some things—according to her grandmother—that just need a trained will. I've certainly got that.*

And as for where to find a mage—I think I know just the place to start.

This time Elspeth called the meeting, at breakfast, in her mother's suite. She hoped to catch her in a malleable mood—which she often was in the early morning. Not that Elspeth enjoyed being up that early; on the whole, she preferred never to have to view the sunrise.

But for a good cause, she'd sacrifice a bit of sleep.

She stated her case as clearly and logically as possible, before Selenay had finished her muffins, but after she'd had her first two cups of tea. She'd thought about her presentation very carefully; why someone had to go chasing mages, and why that someone had to be her. Then she sat back and waited for her answer.

She has to agree. There's no other choice for us.

"No," Selenay stated flatly. "It's not possible."

For a moment she was taken aback, but she rallied her defenses, thought quickly and plowed gamely onward. "Mother, I don't see where there's any choice," Elspeth replied, just as firmly as her mother. "I've told you the facts. Kero backs up my guesses about what's likely to happen, and she's the best tactician we have. And Alberich backs *her* up. The three of us have talked this over a lot."

"I don't—" Selenay fell strangely silent, looking troubled and very doubtful. Elspeth followed up her advantage. *I can't give her a chance to say anything. Look at her hands, she's clutching things again. It's conflict between being a mother and the ruler. I think I can convince the Council, but I have to convince her before I convince the Council.*

"We can't do this on our own anymore; we have to have help. We *have* to have a mage—'Adept-class,' is what Kero says. Someone who can work around whatever it is that keeps active mages out. We have to find someone like that who is willing not only to help us but to teach Heralds if he can."

"I don't see why—" Selenay began. "We've managed all right until now. Why can't the Gifts provide an adequate defense? They've worked so far."

"Mother, believe me, there hasn't been a real trial of them," Elspeth countered. "I've listened to Kero's stories, and frankly they won't hold against a real effort by *several* mages. I'll tell you what, I suspect that *we* have people capable of becoming mages. The Chronicles all talk about a 'Mage-Gift' just as if it were something like—oh, Firestarting; rare, but not unusual. *I* don't think it's been lost. I think that we've just forgotten how to tell what it is, and how to train it. But to do that, we need a mage. A good one. And Kero says that all the good teachers are Adept-class."

"Even if all that is true," Selenay said, after a long silence, her hands clenched around her mug. "Why should you be the one to go?"

"Well, for one thing, I've got Crown powers. When I find a mage we can trust, I can offer him anything reasonable—and I know what's reasonable; Kero's briefed me on hiring mages. For another—I'm not indispensable. You have two more heirs, and if you want to know the truth, I'm not certain I *should* wear the crown." She smiled ruefully. "I take shortcuts a little too often to make the Council comfortable."

Selenay returned the smile reluctantly, but it faded just as quickly as it came.

Elspeth shrugged. "The truth of the matter is that the twins are probably going to be better rulers than I would. The Council can't object to letting me go, with two more candidates for the throne still here. I'm a full Herald, I know what we need, Kero can probably give me contacts, and I have Crown authority. I'm the best—absolutely best—person for the job."

Selenay started to say something—Elspeth waited for the rebuke— but it never came. It was almost as if something had interrupted her before she could say anything.

Odd.

But she followed up on her advantage.

"Let me give you another reason. You wanted me safe, right? You can put forty layers of guards on the twins and they won't mind, but you know very well that *I* won't put up with it. On the other hand, if you send me to Uncle Faram, Ancar won't know where to find me at first—and when he finds out, he won't risk a try for me in Rethwellan. Uncle has a larger army, *he* has mages, and I don't think even Ancar would risk all-out war with him." She firmed her jaw and raised her head stubbornly. "Besides, I won't be there for long, I'll be looking for Kero's old mage Quenten. He has a school, she says, and if anybody can find us mages, I should think he would. When I'm there, I'll be surrounded by mages. I couldn't *possibly* be safer than that."

Selenay finally sighed and unclenched her hands. "There must be something wrong with that logic, but I can't figure out what it is," she said, her brow furrowed with an unhappy frown.

Elspeth turned a look of appeal on Talia, who bit her lip and looked very uncomfortable. *As if part of her wants to side with me, and part of her doesn't.*

"I just don't like it," Selenay said, finally. "You're far too vulnerable. Even traveling through Valdemar, I wouldn't feel comfortable unless you had a full company of troops with you. Traveling across the Comb is nearly as dangerous in summer as winter—there are thunderstorms, wild beasts— and the only decent pass is too close to Karse for *my* comfort." She shook her head. "No, I can't allow it. Bringing in a mage—that's not a bad idea. I think you're right about that much. But the person I send won't be you."

Selenay's chin came up and her voice took on a steely quality that Elspeth knew only too well. There was no arguing with her mother in *this* mood.

She *could* appeal to her stepfather and Alberich. Kero was already on her side.

But not now.

And it might take weeks, even months, to get Selenay to change her mind. By then it would be fall or winter, and she would have another excuse to keep Elspeth at home—the weather. And perhaps by then it would be too late.

She closed her eyes for a moment. The odd pressure inside her, now that she had a goal in mind and a task that really needed to be done, was already uncomfortable. Any delay would make it intolerable.

She had to go—*had* to. And she couldn't. She wanted to scream, argue, cry, anything.

But just a single word at this point would ensure that she would *never* win Selenay's permission. And without that permission, there was no point in going to the Council; they would never override the Queen on this.

If I just ran off and did it—

No, that wouldn't work, either.

She had to have Crown and Council authority to make this mission a success, and running off on her own was not going to win her either.

So instead of bursting out, as she really wanted to, she simply clamped her mouth shut.

She got up, leaving her breakfast untasted, bowed stiffly, and took herself out of the room altogether.

She managed to keep her temper as far as her rooms—where she slammed the door shut behind her, and yanked open the closet so hard she nearly took the door off the hinges. The handle *did* come loose in her hand, and she flung it across the room without a single word, grabbing a set of old clothes from the back of the closet, pulling off her uniform and throwing it in a heap on the floor, and pulling on the new clothing with no care whatsoever.

She heard several stitches pop as she pulled the shirt over her head and ignored them.

:*Kitten?*: Gwena said, tentatively. :*Dearest, don't be too discouraged. Things can change, sometimes in a heartbeat. There are events occurring out on the borders that none of us know about yet—one of those may force your mother to change her mind.*:

:*Don't patronize me,*: Elspeth snarled. :*I'm past the age when you can tell me that everything will be all right. We have trouble, and no one wants to admit it or let me do my part in meeting it. So leave me alone, all right? Let me cool down my own way.*:

:*Oh—*: Gwena replied, very much taken aback by the barely

suppressed rage in Elspeth's mind-voice. Then she remained silent though Elspeth sensed her watchful presence in the back of her mind.

She ignored it, leaving her rooms with another slamming of doors and heading defiantly out to the gardens and her pottery shed.

No one even tried to stop her. Several people looked curiously at her as she stormed past, but no one spoke.

Most of the evidence of the assassination attempt was gone, along with the remains of those pieces that were smashed in the struggle. The floor had been swept clean—much, much cleaner than Elspeth ever kept it.

No, it was more than that. There was a new stool beside the bench where the old one had stood, there was a new door in place of the shattered one. Her old stove had been replaced with a new kiln and a new stove, her shelves had been replaced with stronger ones, the walls had been scoured, the floor scrubbed, and the place had been tidied up with meticulous precision.

Elspeth stared around with a sense of affront.

Bad enough that she'd been attacked here—but someone had taken it upon himself to "improve" the place.

Her sanctuary had been violated. With good intent, but violated, just the same. It wasn't hers anymore...

But it was all she had.

Resolutely, she squared her shoulders, went to one of the waiting boxes of raw clay, and cut herself a generous chunk—quite enough to make another two-handled vase.

Better than the last one.

And she set about grimly wedging the helpless hunk of clay into submission.

Stubborn, unreasoning woman, she fumed, punching the defenseless clay as hard as she could, flattening it to a finger-wide sheet on the smooth slate top of the bench.

A lot like her daughter, whispered her conscience.

So what? she answered it. *I can see sense when I have to, whatever it costs me. She won't even consider what this could mean if I succeed—or what it* will *mean if I'm not allowed to try. I don't even know if she'll send someone else—she might decide not to. She might even forget.*

Her conscience persisted as she rolled the sheet of clay up into a cylinder and flattened the cylinder into a sphere. *You've never been a mother, so how can you know what letting you go would cost her? You heard Talia—if it were her son that was in jeopardy, she'd be just as irrational, and she is the most sensible person you know. And besides, you aren't the only one who could take this mission on and make a success out of it.*

Oh, no? she snarled at her conscience, picking the ball of clay up, and throwing it down on the slate, over and over again. *Who else is there?*

Kerowyn, for one, her conscience replied too promptly. *After all, her uncle—if he's still alive—is a White Winds Adept. And Quenten used to be one of the Skybolts' mages. She has the same contacts she would be giving you. Surely one of them could be persuaded to help.*

And if not? she challenged.

If not—there're King Faram's court mages. They aren't exactly apprentices, and they've already proved they'll work for hire by being in his employ. And Kero is Daren and Faram's very good friend. She could probably even persuade Faram to part with one or more of his mages, if they are willing to come up here.

But I'm their relative, she countered. *That should be twice as effective.*

Her conscience had no counter to that, but she had no answer for it, either. So she *wasn't* the only person who could go—so what? She was still the best choice, if not the only one, if only Selenay would admit it.

The clay was ready—but she wasn't. She continued to pound her temper out on it as she sought reasons why Kerowyn could not be spared to go in her place.

She's the Captain of the Skybolts—

Who are in Valdemar's employ. And she has perfectly adequate stand-ins.

She doesn't have Crown authority, in case she has to negotiate with someone besides the people she knows.

Well, there's always a writ.

She's too old.

That sounded like a stupid excuse even to Elspeth. *Too old, sure. She can beat me nineteen falls out of twenty. Not even close, girl.*

She doesn't know what we need.

Now that might be a good reason. The needs of a mercenary Captain and the needs of a country like Valdemar were vastly different. A Company might be able to use someone who didn't necessarily fit their profile. Valdemar was going to need someone very special.

For one thing, he's going to need a pretty good set of ethics. He'll have to be able to get along with people. He'll have to know when not to use his power. And most especially, he'll have to be someone who would never, ever, abuse either his power or position.

In other words, he would, for all intents and purposes, be as much like a Herald as possible.

And ideally, really, he would be Chosen as soon as Elspeth returned to Valdemar with him. That would be perfect.

But that would make him the first Herald-Mage since Vanyel...

She shook off the haze of speculation. What mattered was that Kero—*if* she went—was all too likely to bring back someone who was picked with a Captain's eye, rather than a Herald's. And that could be a major mistake.

She might well take the best of a dubious lot, without looking any further. She could get someone who had managed to conceal his motives. She could even get someone in alliance with Ancar, who had not only managed to conceal his motives, but his intentions.

Kero was smart, but she hadn't been a Herald for very long. She still took some folks aback by her attitudes. That was amusing inside Valdemar, but in a situation where Valdemar's well-being depended on her attitudes—a difference of opinion could be dangerous.

And there was always the possibility that she would pick someone who was not strong enough to pass the borders. Then what?

Would she simply conclude that this mage-hunting was a waste of time, and return?

Elspeth wouldn't—but she wasn't sure that the same would be true of Kero.

This may be one case where my stubborn streak is an advantage. I won't give in until I have someone. Kero might. And if she winds up having to go outside of Rethwellan—I think her reputation as a mercenary might be held against her. There might be mages with active morals who would feel that working with a mercenary, former or no, wasn't ethical, no matter how worthy the cause.

Kero had worked all of her life to keep her emotions out of her negotiations. That lack of obvious passion might work against her in a case like this.

But Elspeth might be convincing enough...

I have all the reasons and counters I need, she thought, grimly kneading her clay. *Now if only someone would be willing to listen to them.*

4

DARKWIND

"So, you have encountered another situation," Starblade k'Sheyna said coldly as he regarded his son without blinking. The *ekele* was too low on the tree trunk to sway, but the branches surrounding it moved in a gentle wind. Darkwind tried not to shift position in any way that might be interpreted as showing his discomfort. It was difficult to remain cool beneath that measuring, inscrutable gaze. Starblade's bondbird, a huge, hawk-sized crow, gazed at him with the same impassive expression as its bondmate. It might have been a stone bird, or a shadow made into flesh and feathers.

What ever happened to the Father I knew? He's gone as thoroughly as Songwind.

"Let me see if I understand this correctly. You were on patrol along the border. Your bondbird located invaders. There were some seven intruders, two of whom *may* have been mages, the rest of whom *may* simply have been in their employ." Sun poured through the leaves, beyond the open windows, engulfing them in a dappled silence.

"Yes, Elder," Darkwind replied, just as impersonally. *Perhaps if I give him a little taste of his own attitude...*

Starblade inclined his head a little, in mocking acknowledgment of the imitation, and the tiny multicolored crystals braided into his waist-length, snow-white hair sang softly as he moved, echoing the wind chimes strung in each window. "But you are not *sure.*"

"No, Elder." Darkwind knew very well what Starblade was up to and did not rise to the bait. *He wants me to get angry, and I won't. That would be an acknowledgment of weakness and lack of control.*

"Why not?" Starblade persisted, narrowing his ice-blue eyes to mere slits. "What was it that you did to try and determine what they were?"

As if he didn't know what would be the proper procedure. "I followed them for some distance, before I judged they had ventured too far into k'Sheyna territory. Nothing in their conversation gave me any clues as to their identity, Elder," Darkwind replied, holding his temper in check.

There was no real reason for this interview. They had already been over this several times; once before the entire Council, once with the other three Elders, in detail, and now, for the second time, with his father alone. The Council had heard his story without allowing him to confront them over the situation of being so shorthanded on the border. *That,* they had assigned to Starblade, as the most senior Adept, and presumably the one who could make a decision about the situation. *Perhaps he is supposed to conjure up something,* Darkwind thought bitterly.

Which meant he had to go over this as many times as Starblade wanted in order to get his point made. "I listened carefully to the conversation, what there was of it. The armed men treated the unarmed men with a certain amount of deference, but there was no outward sign that they were not—say—adventurous traders. I thought they might be mages because they were unarmed, so I moved to neutralize them first."

"You did not spellcast to determine if any of them were using magic of any kind?" Starblade settled back in his green-cushioned chair. In contrast to his son's camouflage outfit, his own elaborate clothing made him look like an exotic, silver-crested, blue-plumaged bird perched in the shrubbery.

"No, sir," Darkwind replied, allowing a hint of effrontery to carry into his voice. "I did not."

"And why not?" Starblade asked softly. "You have the power, after all."

"Because I do not choose to use that power, Father," Darkwind said, holding in his temper with an effort. "You know that. As you know my reasons."

"As I know your excuses," Starblade snapped. "They are not *reasons*. You put k'Sheyna in jeopardy because you refuse to use your abilities."

"I did no such thing. I *kept* k'Sheyna from jeopardy because I destroyed the interlopers when they would not turn back," Darkwind interrupted. "I did so *without* the foolish use of magic, which might have attracted more trouble, that close to the border. Despite being short-handed, I did so with the limited resources at my disposal."

"Without magic."

"Without magic," Darkwind repeated. *"Because* it was not needed, and *because* other things might have been attracted that it would not have been possible to combat, with *only three* guards and their birds within range to stand against the threat." He glared at his father. "If you are so insistent on having mages on the border, Father, perhaps you would care to join us for some of our patrols."

And we can lead you about by the hand.

They could not have been more of a contrast, he and Starblade. The mage wore his waist-length silver hair braided with crystals, feathers, and rainbow beads. His costume, of peacock-blue spider-silk, cut and decorated elaborately, was impressive and impractical in the extreme. Darkwind, when he was not in his scout clothing, tended to wear brown or gray, cut closely to his body, high-collared and mostly without ornament; his hair was barely shoulder-length.

Most of the mages dressed the way Starblade did, though some made concessions to camouflage by wearing white in the winter and leaf-colors in the rest of the year, garments that could blend in with the woods after a fashion. Not that long ago, he had looked like the rest of them.

This is growing tedious.

"Father, we have been over this any number of times. I did my duty; I rid k'Sheyna of the interlopers. The *point* is not that I did or did not get rid of them using magic. *The point* is that we are chronically shorthanded. We shouldn't be here at all, Father. More than half of k'Sheyna is—elsewhere. What's wrong with us? Why haven't we *done* something about this situation?"

"That is none of your concern," Starblade began coldly, drawing himself up and staring at his son in astonishment.

"It *is* my concern," Darkwind interrupted. "I'm on the Council, too. I *am* the representative of the scouts. I'm one of the Clan Elders now, which you seem to have forgotten. And as the scouts' representative, I would like to know exactly what we are doing to drain the Heartstone, or stabilize it, and rejoin the rest of our Clan." He drew himself up to match his father's pose, and looked challengingly into Starblade's eyes.

Starblade met the challenging gaze impassively. "That is the business of the mages. If you wish to have a say in the matter—" he smiled, "— you may take up your powers again. *Then* you may join the mages and have your words heeded."

Darkwind felt himself flushing with anger, despite his earlier resolutions. "What I choose to do with my powers has nothing to do with the matter. Those of us who are not mages have a right to determine k'Sheyna's future as well." He paused a moment, and added, "*That* is the tradition, after all—that every voice in a Clan has some say in the running of the Clan."

Starblade looked past his son's shoulder for a moment and took a long, slow breath. "What you choose to do with your powers is precisely at issue here." He lowered his eyes to meet Darkwind's again, and there was an anger to match his son's in his gaze. "You are risking the lives of your scouts by your refusal to use your magic. Your abilities are *required* on our boundaries, and yet you will not use them. And I *do not* accept why you refuse."

Darkwind closed his eyes, but he could not block the memories.

The Heartstone, a great crystal-laced boulder taller than he, pulsing with all the life and power of the Vale. Its surface glowed with intricate warm red and golden tracings, as the inner circle of Adepts continued to drain the excess mage-energy from the land about them, to empty the nodes and the power-lines so that there was nothing left that could be used to harm.

That was how the Tayledras left a place; concentrating all the realigned power of the area in their Heartstone; then draining the Heartstone and channeling most of its awesome energy into a new one, at the site of their new Vale.

Power crackled and seethed, pouring into the stone, as Darkwind held to his position, anchoring the West—outside the circle of Adepts that contained his mother and father. The shunting off of the great stone's energy was a dangerous task and required many protectors and guides from outside the main circle; he was an important part of the linkage. Songwind k'Sheyna was the youngest Adept of his Clan ever to take such a task and quite conscious of the responsibilities involved.

There was no warning, no unsettling current of unclean energy. Just—a brightening of the stone, more intense than the last, and a disorienting sensation like lightning striking—

Hell opened in front of him. A blaze of incandescent white, power that scorched him to the soul. Silhouetted against the hellfires, his mother—

"I don't trust my so-called 'abilities,' Father," he said slowly, shaking off the too-vivid memories. "No one knows why the Heartstone fractured, and the power broke loose."

Was it his imagination, or did his father start a little?

"I was the youngest Adept there," he persisted. "I was the only one who had never participated in moving a Heartstone's power before. What if it was something I did, and everything I do magically is forever flawed that way? I will not take that chance, Father, not when what is *left* of our Clan is at stake."

Starblade would not look into his son's eyes, but his voice was implacable. He gazed down at his hand as if he had never seen it before, examining the long fingers as he spoke. "I have told you, many times, it was nothing you did or did not do. It… it had *nothing* to do with you."

"Can you be certain of that?" He shook his head and started to stand up. "Father, I know exactly what my abilities are with my hands, my senses. I can't count on my magic—"

Starblade looked up, and his expression had changed to one of scorn. "…If you have no confidence in yourself," the Elder finished. "Your magic is flawed only if you choose to believe it is so. Songwind was not that fearful. I remember and loved Songwind. He saw his power as a source of pride, and our Clan was proud of him for it. Our children and old ones are gone from us now, and you have refused those powers to defend what is left of us here. I have little respect for you for that, Darkwind."

The heat of Darkwind's anger cooled to ice, as he felt the blood draining from his face. The golden sunlight drifting through the windows and making patterns upon the white wooden floor suddenly lost all its warmth. "The Starblade who is my Elder is not the father I remember either," he replied. "Perhaps a change of name is in order for you, as well. Iceblade, perhaps—or Brokenblade, for you seem to have lost both your courage and your compassion." He stood, while Starblade gaped at him in startled surprise. "You are unwilling to face the fact that circumstances have changed. I think that you are terrified to face that change. I don't know—I only know that you seem to think that we who work without magic are not worth aiding. If you see no reason to help the scouts, Father, then we must take what help we can get even to calling on the *hertasi*, the *dyheli*, and the others of the Hills whose well-being you scorn in your arrogance."

He started to turn, and had taken one step toward the door, when Starblade's voice stopped him.

"Arrogance?" the Elder said, as coolly as if Darkwind had not said anything at all. "An interesting choice of words from you. Songwind was the youngest Adept in the Clan—but it has occurred to me of late that perhaps that distinction was not enough for you."

Darkwind turned back to his father reluctantly. "What is that supposed to mean?" he asked, the words forced from him unwillingly.

"Songwind was only an Adept. Darkwind is on the Council—is, in fact, an Elder." Starblade shrugged. "That was an opportunity that would not have been given to Songwind for some time—but with the scouts so short-handed, and poor, newly bereft Darkwind so eager to join them—and so—charismatic—"

"If you are suggesting that I have left magic solely for the sake of another kind of power—" Darkwind could feel himself going red, then white, with anger. He struggled to control his temper; an outburst now would win him nothing.

"I am suggesting nothing," Starblade replied smoothly. "I am only saying that the appearance is there."

A hundred retorts went through Darkwind's mind, but he made none of them. Instead, he strove for and regained at least an appearance of calm.

"If that were, indeed, the case, Elder," he said quietly, but with just a hint of the rage that he held tightly bottled within, "it seems to me that I would already have been acting on those ambitions. I should have been moving to consolidate that power, and to manipulate both the nonmages and the weaker mages. As you are well aware, I have been doing no such thing. I have simply been doing the work assigned to me—like any other scout. Like any *responsible* leader. I never sought the position of leader or Elder, it was pressed upon me; I would never have used personal attraction to get them."

Starblade smiled, tightly. "I merely suggest, Darkwind, that if you returned to magic you would be forced to give up that position. In fact, in light of the fact that you are out of practice, you might be asked to return to the position of student rather than Adept. And that perhaps—unconsciously—you are reluctant to return to the position of commanded, having been commander."

"You have hinted that before, Elder," Darkwind answered him grimly. "And the suggestion was just as repellent the first time as it is now. I think I know myself very well now, and there is no such reluctance on my part for *that* ridiculous reason. If there were anyone else within the scouts who wanted the position, I would give it to him—or her—and gladly."

And if we were a less civilized people, those words would be cause for a challenge.

"I have said that I do not know this thing you have become, Darkwind—" Starblade began.

Darkwind cut him off abruptly with an angry gesture. "Indeed, Elder," he replied, turning on his heel and tossing his last words over his shoulder as he left the outer room of Starblade's *ekele*. "You do not know me at all, if you think that little of me."

It was not—quite—the kind of exit he would have liked. There was no door to slam, only a *hertasi*-made curtain of strung seeds—and it was difficult, if not impossible, to effectively stamp his feet the few steps it took to reach the ladder, without sounding like a child in a temper.

Which is how he wants me to feel, after all.

And if he rushed angrily down the ladder, even so short a distance as he needed with his father's tree-dwelling, he risked taking some stupid injury like a sprain or a broken limb. Starblade's *ekele* was hardly more than a few man-heights from the floor of the Vale, and had several rooms, like a bracelet of beads around the trunk of the huge tree it was built onto. The access leading to it was more like a steep staircase than a ladder.

So it was quite impossible to descend in any way that would underscore his mood without playing to his father's gloating.

He settled for vaulting off of the last few feet of it, as if he could not bear to endure Starblade's "hospitality" a moment more. He landed as lightly and silently as only a woods-scout could, and walked away from the *ekele* without looking back, his purposeful steps taking him on a path that would lead him out of the Vale altogether.

He knew that he was by no means as calm as he looked, but he was succeeding in this much at least. He was working off some of his anger as he pushed his way through the exotic, semitropical undergrowth that shadowed and sometimes hid the path. The plants themselves were typical of any Tayledras Vale, but the state of rank overgrowth was not.

The Hawkbrothers always chose some kind of valley for their Clansites, something that could be "roofed over" magically, and shielded from above and on all sides, so that the climate within could be controlled, and undesirable creatures warded off. Then, if there were no hot springs there already, the mages would *create* them—and force-grow broad trees to make them large enough to hold several *ekele*.

The result was always junglelike, and the careful placement of paths to allow for the maximum amount of cover and privacy for all the inhabitants gave a Vale the feeling of being uninhabited even when crowded with a full Clan and all the *hertasi* that served them.

It appeared uninhabited to the outsider. To a Tayledras, there was always the undercurrent of little sounds and life-feelings that told him where everyone was, a comforting life-song that bound the Clan together.

But there was no such song here, in k'Sheyna Vale. Instead of a rich harmony, with under-melodies and counterpoint, the music halted, limped, within a broken consort. *Hertasi* made up most of the life-sparks about Darkwind, as the little lizard-folk went about their business and that of the Clan, cleaning and mending and preparing food. And that was not right.

Further, there were no child-feelings anywhere about. Only adults, and a mere handful of those, compared to the number a full Clan should muster.

Any Tayledras would know there is something wrong, something out of balance, just by entering the Vale.

Silence; Tayledras that were not mages undertook all the skilled jobs that *hertasi* could not manage—besides the scouts, there should have been artisans, musicians, crafters. All those activities made *their* own little undercurrent of noises, and that, too, was absent. The rustle of leaves, the dripping of water, the whisper of the passing of the shy *hertasi*, sounds that he would never have noticed seemed too loud in the empty Vale.

Then there were the little signs of neglect; *ekele* empty and untenanted, going to pieces, so that *hertasi* were constantly removing debris, and trying to get rid of things before they fell. Springs were littered with fallen leaves. Vegetation grew unchecked, untrimmed, or dying out as rare plants that had required careful nurturing went untended.

It all contributed to the general feeling of desolation—but there was an underlying sense of pain, as well. And that was because not all of the *ekele* stood empty by choice.

Half the Clan had moved to the new Vale, it was true, and were now out of reach until a new Gate could be built to them. There were no mages strong enough in the far-away, exiled half of the Clan to build that Gate, and not even the most desperate would choose to take children and frail elders on a trek across the dangerous territory that lay between them. But k'Sheyna-that-remained was at a quarter of its strength, not a half. And most of those were not Adepts. The circle of Adepts that had been charged with draining and moving the Heartstone had been the strongest the Clan could muster; they had taken the full force of the disaster.

Fully half of those that had remained behind—most of the Adepts— had died in the catastrophe that claimed Darkwind's mother. Many of those that were left were still in something of a state of shock, and, like Darkwind himself, trying to cope with the unprecedented loss of so many mates, friends, and children. The silence left by their absence gnawed at the subconscious of mage and scout alike.

Only a few went to Darkwind's extreme, and changed their use-name, but he was not completely alone in his reaction. To change a use-name meant that, for all intents and purposes, the "person" described by that name was "dead."

That was why "Songwind" became "Darkwind." When he had recovered from his burns and lacerations, he repudiated magic altogether. Then, when that move brought him into conflict with his father, he moved out of the family *ekele,* and took up life on his own, with the scouts and craftsmen who were left.

Another mage, Starfire, became Nightfire, and became obsessed with the remains of the Heartstone, studying it every waking moment, trying to determine the cause of the disaster.

And the most traumatized mage of all, Moonwing, became Silence.

I could have been like Silence, he thought, beating a branch aside with unnecessary force. *I could have retreated into myself, and become a hermit. I could have stopped speaking except mind-to-mind. I could be broadcasting my pain to anyone who dared touch my thoughts. I didn't do that; I'm doing something useful.*

But that, evidently, was not enough for Starblade.

He'll have me as a mage, or not at all. Darkwind scowled at the trail before him, frightening a passing *hertasi* into taking another route. *He should look to the Clan; there are more important problems than the fact that I will not use magic.*

The physical wounds had mended, but the emotional and mental injuries were still with k'Sheyna, and they were not healing well.

But then, those that could have taken care of such deep-seated problems had all perished themselves.

There was no one skilled enough, for instance, to enter Silence's mind and Heal her—

Heal Silence? There's no one even skilled enough to Heal me...

There should have been help coming from other Clans—

There can only be one reason why there isn't, he thought, and not for the first time. *The Elders' pride. They will not admit that we failed so badly, or that we need help at all.*

Fools. Fools and blind.

In the first few weeks after the disaster, there had been messengers from other Clans. That much he knew for a fact; the rest was a guess, for he had been delirious from brain-fever and the pain of his burns. He had been in no position to make any pleas, but the visitors did not stay long, in any case. He had no doubt that they had been rebuffed. Now no visitors—or offers of help—came at all.

Darkwind reached the edge of the Vale, where the shield met the outside world. The boundary line was quite clear; within the Vale grew a riot of flowers and plants with enormous tropical leaves, all of it surrounding individual trees that reached higher than the cliffs beside them, trees with trunks as large as houses. Flowers bloomed and plants flourished no matter the season. Outside the Vale—one scant finger-length from the shield—it was pine forest, with the usual sparse undergrowth. And if Darkwind looked closely enough, he could see a kind of shimmer where the one ended and the other began.

Of course, if he cared to use Mage-Sight on that barrier—which he did not—that shimmer was a curtain of pure energy, tuned only to allow wildlife, the Hawk brothers, their allies, and select individuals across.

He paused before crossing that invisible border, and looked reluctantly at a stand of enormous bandar-plants. Behind those plants lay a hot spring, one of many that supplied the heat and moisture the plants required... and provided places of refreshment as well.

Gods above, I could use a soak… it's been a long day, and there is still more ahead of me.

Well, perhaps a short pause would not hurt anything.

He slipped between two of the plants and shed his clothing quickly, leaving it in a pile on the smooth stones bordering the spring.

This was not one of the larger springs, nor one of the more popular. It was too close to the edge of the Vale and the shield, and the reminder of the Real World outside their little sheltered Vale made many of the remaining mages too uneasy to use it.

While the scouts, who were more than a little uneasy *within* the heart of the Vale, in close proximity to the shattered, but still empowered and dangerous Heartstone, did not much care to use the larger, carefully sculptured springs there, with their pools for washing as well as pools for soaking away aches—or disporting.

Hertasi did their best to keep all the little pockets of hot, bubbling water free of fallen leaves and other debris, but they had too many other duties to attend to. This particular spring had not been attended to in some time and ran sluggishly, the surface covered with fallen vegetation. Darkwind tossed a half dozen huge leaves out to the side, and scooped out quite a bit of debris at the bottom before the spring bubbled up freely again.

Then he relaxed back into the smooth stone of the seats built into the sides, created by magically sculpting the rock before the water had been called here.

As the warm water soaked away his aches and bruises and relaxed too-taut muscles, he closed his eyes and, for once, tried to remember back to those dark and chaotic days immediately following the catastrophe.

Did we know then how bad the area was outside our own borders? He didn't think so; it seemed to him that no one had paid any attention to the lands outside the purview of the Clan, and to be fair, they had their hands full with the territory they had undertaken to cleanse.

We definitely had enough to do—and whatever was out there tended to leave us alone while we were strong. There was no reason to think that it was any worse than our own lands.

It was only after they had cleaned up their own areas, and were preparing to move, that they realized that the blight they faced on their southern border was at least as pervasive as the one they had just dealt with. And was, perhaps, more dangerous than the area to the west that they had chosen as the new Vale-site.

Why hadn't they seen the blight? Well, it might have been because there had been a clear zone between the two, a zone that disguised the true nature of what lay beyond. It was only after the disaster, when creatures from across that clear zone swarmed over the wreckage of the Vale, that anyone realized just how tainted that area was.

Now, of course, they could not deal with it, could not clean it out, and could not eliminate it.

There's at least one Adept in there, Darkwind thought, clenching his jaw involuntarily. *It was his constant "attentions" after the accident that forced us to pull back our borders in the first place.*

And now that there were no more offers of help from the other Clans, they could not ask for one of the others to lend aid. They could not even push the unseen enemies back, not without help.

I'd try to contact the other Clans myself, but I would have to do so by magic means. I don't know where the other territories are, and Father isn't about to give me a map.

And using magic would only have attracted more unwelcome attentions. He had seen all too often how blatant use of magics brought a wave of attackers from the Outside. The one mage who had been willing to work with the scouts had fallen victim, he suspected, to just that.

He was certainly overwhelmed before we could reach him. And I know there were not that many Misborn there before.

He suspected that the Adept watched for magic-use, and turned his creatures loose when he saw it. So long as k'Sheyna confined themselves and their magic to their Vale, he seemed content to pursue his own plans, only pressing them occasionally, rather than sending an army against them.

There may be more than one Adept out there, but somehow I don't think so. Dark Adepts don't share power willingly.

So far, they had been able to beat all attempts to penetrate the new boundaries. So far, they had not lost more than a handful of scouts, and a mage or two.

And right now, we seem to be operating under an uneasy truce, as if he had decided we were too weak to threaten him, but too strong to be worth moving against. At least nothing major has come out of there for about a year. And there haven't been any attacks from Outlanders that I can prove originated from there.

Nothing had made any attempt at the creatures k'Sheyna protected, either. So far the *hertasi* enclaves remained untouched, the *dyheli* herds had not been preyed upon. The firebirds had fled the area though—and that bothered him.

And there were no human villages within k'Sheyna territory anymore. Crops had failed, wells dried up, traders ceased to come; only a handful of hunters and a religious hermit or two stayed behind.

No overt attacks for a year. But who knows what that means, he thought pessimistically. *We have a weak and unstable Clan facing a nebulous enemy, and our options grow fewer with every passing day.*

Starblade's answer to their troubles was simple: more magic. More mages. Everyone who had a spark of Mage-Gift should train it, and use it in their defense, while the handful of *real* mages worked to find an answer to their unstable Heartstone. Magic was the answer to every problem.

But how many times have I seen that using magic attracts *problems? Hundreds. And what happens when we attract something we can't handle?*

No, more magic was *not* the answer. Not to Darkwind's way of thinking.

What we should *do is appeal for help to one of the other Clans; we need Adepts who can drain the old Heartstone or stabilize it and take over this Vale for us. Then we can build a Gate and rejoin the rest. So what if they can't Gate in to us? That doesn't matter; and while we wait for the Heartstone to be made safe, we can defend ourselves with stealth, with cleverness.*

He had to force his shoulder muscles to relax again, and sank a little deeper into the hot water. *In fact, that's what we should be doing about this Adept. We should find some way of luring him out into the open, maybe by "playing dead." Then we should neutralize him—but the one thing he wouldn't be expecting is a physical assault.*

He nodded to himself, the pieces finally falling together for him. *That Adept wants something—the power in the Heartstone, probably. He has to be watching constantly for magic power in use, and sending things against us only when he sees it. He really hasn't made an all-out assault against us because he's clever. He knows it would cost him less to take us by attrition than by full force.*

And right now, he's hoping to lull us into forgetting that he's out there.

He tightened his jaw, thinking about how Starblade kept dismissing the importance of the scouts, and the threats on the borders. *Right. He just might, too.*

That brought up another thought. *I wonder if he sent those intruders to test us? It could be. And not using magic told him—what?*

That we don't have mages to spare, probably. He should have a pretty good idea of how weak we really are at this point.

But what if I can use that against him? What if I can lure him out into the open, and find out who and what he is?

What if I could destroy him—or at least convince him that we're too strong, still, to be worth the trial?

He shook his head at his own ambitions. *Certainly. And what if I could grow wings and fly out of here for help? The one is as likely as the other.*

Best to stick to what he *knew* he could accomplish.

He looked up through the leafy canopy above him; not long until sunset, and that meant he had better get back to his own *ekele*. The day-scouts would be waiting to report, the night-scouts to be briefed. And Vree would be waiting for his dinner, for that bit of rabbit earlier was hardly enough to satisfy him.

Reluctantly, he pulled himself out of the spring, dried himself with his shirt, and pulled on the rest of his clothing.

If I can see what needs taking care of, then it's my job to take care of it. My duties won't wait—whether or not Father approves.

5

ELSPETH

Elspeth stood on guard, trembling with exhaustion, with the last of the dulled practice swords in her hands. The Captain went off-guard and nodded. "Right," Kerowyn said, just a hint of satisfaction in her voice. "Let's go through it again."

Did I hear satisfaction? Approval? Gods, maybe all the bruises are *worth it after all.*

Elspeth shook sweat out of her eyes, picked up the scattered practice blades with hands that still tingled from Kero's disarms, and distributed them randomly around the perimeter of the circle. It was kind of funny, really. This was the one and only time she had ever been *ordered* to just drop weapons carelessly, leaving them exactly where they fell.

This had been another one of Kero's little exercises in "attitude." Today had been entirely defensive; she had not been permitted to strike a single blow.

And she'd had one of the most strenuous workouts she'd ever had in her life.

The exercise was simple; Kero disarmed her, and she would try to get to another weapon—by whatever means possible—before Kero could corner her. Hence the rough circle of weaponry scattered around the salle.

Her setup—such as it was—completed, she stood in the middle of the circle, sword in hand, and waited for Kero to disarm her.

Kero went into "ready" stance, and Elspeth matched her.

Here it comes— Her heart beat a little faster, and her mouth dried. No matter that it was "just" a practice. With Kerowyn or Alberich, nothing was ever "just" a practice. When they delivered killing blows, they left bruises, as a reminder of what could have happened.

The Captain came in slowly this time; Kero feinted and fenced with her for a few moments, forcing her to move away from her original position. Then, when Elspeth was not expecting it, the Captain bound her blade and sent it flying out of her hand.

She didn't waste a moment; the instant she lost the blade, she dove to one side, rolled, and came up with another in her hand; a shortsword, this time. Without thinking, she shifted her grip until the balance was right.

This time Kero rushed her before she had a chance to settle herself, catching her off-guard while she was still finding the balance for the blade.

Crap!

She back-pedaled but not fast enough; Kero got to her and literally swatted the blade out of her hand.

She did the unexpected—as Kero had been *trying* to get her to do. She rushed the Captain, barehanded, shouldering past her and springing for the next sword on the floor.

This time, she didn't even get a chance to get her hands on it. Kero beat her to the spot and kicked it away before she reached it.

She dove after another, sliding belly-down across the wooden floor; she got it and started to roll over—but Kero was on top of her, and swatted that one out of her hands, too.

This one fell short, and Elspeth made a short dive and grabbed it again; her hand tingled, and she had trouble feeling her fingers, but she got it all the same, just as Kero reached her and cut down.

This time she didn't lose it. This time she managed to hold onto the hilt long enough to counter Kero's first three attempts at disarming her—even though her grip was an entirely unorthodox, two-handed one, and she never managed to return a blow.

"That's enough," Kero said, stepping back and wiping the sweat from her forehead with the back of her hand. Elspeth simply collapsed where she lay for a moment, spread-eagled on the floor. She blinked several times to clear her eyes, and rolled over onto her side. And when

Kero offered her a hand to help her up, she took it without shame.

"Not bad," the Captain said, as she started to pick up the scattered swords. "Not bad at all." Elspeth cast her a startled glance. "Oh, I mean it," the Captain grinned. "You were exhausted, your hands were numb—and you still *always* managed to get a weapon in your hands before I could close with you. Good job, kitten."

And this is the person Alberich *says is better than he is.* For a moment Elspeth truly did not know what to say in reply. Finally, she managed to think of something that wouldn't get her into trouble. "Do you think I could have kept myself alive for a little while longer?" she asked.

"At least until help came—and if Gwena couldn't get to you in time to help, you'd be in deeper compost than *anyone* could be expected to get out of," Kero told her, as she got the remainder of the practice blades and took them over to the wall to rack them. "And that is all anyone can ask for."

Someone cleared his throat conspicuously, and Skif emerged from the shadowed entry of the door leading to the outside of the salle. "Excuse me, Captain," he said meekly, "but if you're through with Elspeth, the Circle and Council want to talk to her."

"Now?" Kero asked, her eyebrows arching.

Dear gods, now what? Elspeth wondered. Skif looked very odd, and unusually subdued.

"Well, yes, sort of," he replied, uncomfortably. "I mean, they're meeting now, with the Queen, and they really wanted to talk with her now."

"Well, they can just give her a moment to sluice herself off," Kero replied firmly. "There's no sense in making her show up looking like a shambles."

:Kitten,: she Mindspoke, in private-mode, *:there's a set of my Whites and a kind of wash area in my office; you'll fit my uniform closely enough. I know from experience that it's easier facing an official situation if you feel as if you look presentable.:*

:Thanks,: Elspeth replied gratefully, surprised a little at the Mindspeech. Kero seldom used it, except with Eldan and her Companion, having had to conceal the fact that she had the Gift for most of her life. She was almost as flattered by Kero's use of it with her as by the Captain's earlier compliments.

Elspeth darted into the Weaponsmaster's office before Skif had a chance to stop her; there was, indeed, a pump and a deep basin in a little room in the back behind a screen, and a stack of thick towels beside it. The basin was deep enough for her to duck her head under water, and she did so. The water, fresh from the pump, was cold enough to make her yip, but it revived her considerably. She was toweling off her hair when the promised set of Whites appeared over the screen.

She scrambled into them, and discovered, as Kero had promised, they were a close fit.

I didn't think Kero had a set of Whites—I thought she'd convinced everybody she was never going to wear them. Well, there are times when she plays the uniform game with everyone else. Not often, but I've seen her do it. I suppose if she absolutely has to show up as a formal Herald, this is as good a place to keep her Whites as any.

They were a little loose across the shoulders and tight in the chest, but no one was likely to notice. And she realized, as she wound her wet hair into a knot at the back of her neck, that she *did* feel a little more confident.

Skif was still waiting for her when she trotted out of the office, and he didn't look *too* impatient. "Let's go," she said; he just nodded, and fell into step beside her. The two left the building side-by-side, setting a brisk pace toward the Palace.

She glanced at him in open inquiry, but he avoided her eyes. *Dear gods. What is it I'm supposed to have done?* she wondered. *Is this over that argument I had with Mother about recruiting mages?* She tightened her jaw stubbornly. *If it is—I'm not backing down. I'm right, I know I'm right.*

Why would they take her to task about that, though? What was the problem? It wasn't as if she was espousing open revolt against the Crown...

On the other hand, she'd been pressuring Selenay to allow *her* to do the mage-hunting. That might well be the problem. Some of the Councilors considered her to be impetuous, and sometimes hotheaded. *Maybe they figure I intend to go riding out of here anyway, with or without permission.*

Now *that* was a stupid idea, if that's what they were thinking. *Not that I hadn't considered it... if I could get Gwena to go along with it.*

But I didn't think about it for more than a couple of heartbeats. Really, it was a stupid idea. The only way I could get a decent mage to go along with this, would be if I had official blessing—and how would I have gotten that by running off on my own?

But while she had been thinking about that, would anyone have "eavesdropped" on her? She didn't think so.

But if they had—

She stifled a slow wave of hot anger. No use in getting angry over something that might not have happened.

But if it has—someone is going to pay.

* * *

They kept her cooling her heels for some time before finally letting her into the Council Chamber. Skif left her at the door and disappeared, leaving her no one to question, and being kept there did not help her smoldering temper any.

But after she had waited, impatiently, for what seemed like hours, she heard footsteps coming down the hall leading to the Council Chamber. She turned to see the rest of the Council approaching—and at that point the door to the Council Chamber opened, and they *all* filed in to take their places. Elspeth no longer felt quite so annoyed at being dragged off to see the Circle, then left in the hall.

Though it would have been nice if someone had bothered to tell her they were waiting for the other Council members to arrive.

She took her seat with the rest, casting covert glances at the faces of those Councilors who were also in the Heraldic Circle: Teren, who had taken Elcarth's place as Dean of the Collegium; the Seneschal's Herald, Kyril; the Lord Marshal's Herald, Griffon; the Queen's Own Herald, Talia; Selenay; and Prince Daren. Their expressions didn't tell her much; their faces were tightly controlled. That, in itself, was something; it meant they were worried. And since there was a White-clad Herald with the silver-arrow insignia of the Special Messenger sitting on the extra chair reserved for guests and petitioners, chances were slim that the Circle and Council were going to take Elspeth to task for her notions.

She relaxed and sat back a little into the familiar bulk of her Council seat. *So this is just Council business after all.* If the others hadn't looked so serious, she'd have chuckled at herself. *See, Elspeth, the world* doesn't *revolve around you!*

Selenay rose when the others had settled themselves. "This messenger arrived from the Eastern Border earlier this afternoon, from Shallan, one of Herald-Captain Kerowyn's lieutenants. She had ordered this messenger to come to me first, before reporting to his Captain."

Elspeth stifled a smile. *There's one in the eye for anyone who still wonders where Kero's loyalties lie. Or the Skybolts', for that matter.*

"Since the Circle was in session, and since I understood that his message was fairly urgent, I had him brought here. After hearing what his message was, I decided to call an emergency Council meeting." She nodded at the messenger as she sat down. "Herald Selwin, the floor is yours."

The messenger cleared his throat—though not self-consciously, Elspeth noted—and stood. "I think most of you know that the Eastern Border is considered a sensitive enough area for messengers to be posted at garrisons full time. My current post is the town garrisoned by Kerowyn's Skybolts. Now, what you probably don't know is that the Skybolts have—with the Queen's knowledge and permission—been engaging in some—ah—covert activities."

He flushed a little, and Elspeth raised a surprised eyebrow. Some of the other Councilors muttered a little, and one of them stood up: Lady Kester, speaker for the West. "Just what do you mean by 'covert' activities?" she asked sharply, looking a great deal like a horse who is about to refuse a jump.

"Well—" Herald Selwin glanced at the Queen, who shook her head imperceptibly. "Some of them—I can't talk about. I'm sure you'll understand—the Queen and the Consort both know every move, but it's very much a situation where the fewer who know, the better."

"I trust the situation that brought you here is something you *can* talk about," the woman said dryly.

"Uh—yes, of course." Selwin quickly regained his aplomb. "We've been smuggling people and information out of Hardorn, and—uh—supplies in. One of the people we just smuggled out was not just one of Ancar's farmers who has been pressed too far; this was an escaping prisoner."

We? Huh, that means Selwin's involved, too. He's not just a messenger. Elspeth glanced around the table; from the looks of speculation, she suspected that this had not come entirely as a surprise.

"This wasn't an ordinary prisoner, either," Selwin continued. "He had been one of the under-secretaries in Ancar's officer corps." This time murmurs of surprise met the statement. "He held the same position under Ancar's father, and the reason he was never replaced, like so many *were*, is that he is so ordinary as to be invisible. He says—and we've Truth-Spelled him, so we believe him—that he didn't know what was going on until recently."

Elspeth was very skeptical of *that* statement, until Selwin finished describing the former prisoner. Then she could believe it. Lieutenant Rojer Klinseinem was exactly the kind of focused, obsessive individual their own Seneschal and Lord Marshal prayed to see come into their secretarial corps. His life was in his accounting books; he never left his office except to eat and sleep, and he truly never thought about what those figures he totted up daily meant.

Until Ancar's excesses among his people began to affect even him. He found officers and court officials he had known all his life vanishing without a trace. He discovered friends, neighbors, even children in the street avoiding him when he wore his uniform. Then he noted some odd discrepancies in his accounts. One of his duties was to take care of the prison accounts. The number of prisoners in the cells had gone up, substantially, but the amount of money allotted for their maintenance had *not* increased in the corresponding amounts. Furthermore, the names of those imprisoned changed, sometimes weekly. For all his shortsightedness, he was an ethical man, and all these things worried him, so he decided to investigate them himself, an investigation that led him eventually to the prisons and the barracks rooms, then the king's own dungeons.

What he discovered horrified him. Then one of the king's sorcerers caught him.

He'd had the sense to keep his mouth shut about most of what he'd learned, and because he was so completely ordinary, with no record of ever thinking for himself, he was actually put under house arrest until he could be questioned by someone they called the "Truth-finder General." He didn't wait to discover who or what that was; he got out a back window, stole a horse, and fled toward Valdemar.

He remembered the old days, the days of friendship with Valdemar and its Queen, and he was no longer inclined to believe the official stories about the cause of the hostilities between Valdemar and Hardorn. He fled toward a hoped-for sanctuary with the hounds on his heels.

"I won't go into all the details," Selwin said. "You can question him yourself when we bring him here. Right now he's not up to much traveling."

Elspeth nodded, grimly. Nothing Rojer said would surprise her, not after some of Kero's stories—and not after what had happened to Talia.

"What's important at the moment is that he learned where the prisoners were vanishing to. They're being used as sacrifices in blood-rites—and there are more of them dying every week. Ancar is bringing in mages, *lots* of mages, and those he is not buying outright or coercing, he's making alliances with. Rojer says that Ancar's long-range plans include another major war with Valdemar, and this one is going to include those mages as a major part, rather than in a support capacity. The one that caught him boasts that not even a god would be able to hold defenses against all the mages Ancar is gathering."

Now the muttering around the Council table grew louder, and there were distinct undertones of alarm.

"That's not all," Selwin said, over the voices. The Councilors quieted, and some looked at him with real fear in their eyes. "Right after we got

Rojer out, there was an attack on the Skybolts' garrison town. A magical attack, and *it* got across the Border. Past the protections."

"Why?" asked the Lord Patriarch—Father Ricard, who had replaced elderly Father Aldon. At the same time, the Lord Marshal asked "How?"

"Why should be fairly obvious," Prince Daren said, the first time he'd spoken since the meeting began. "They knew we had Rojer, and they felt what he had to tell us was important enough to try to silence him."

Selwin nodded. "Precisely, Your Highness," he replied. "As for 'how,' I presume the mage managed to overcome the Border-protections somehow. I saw the attack. At first, I thought it was some kind of mist, and I didn't think it looked all that dangerous. But Lieutenant Shallan said the Skybolts had seen this sort of thing before, and got us all evacuated; she said they had something to take care of it, but it would only work at a distance. The 'mist' turned out to be a swarm of tiny insects, no bigger than gnats, but poisonous enough to drop a man. And they were guided, there's no doubt of that. They came out of a kind of hole in the sky." He shook his head. "I really can't properly describe it. But the hole appeared near the outskirts of town, *inside* the Valdemar Border."

"These insects," the Seneschal asked, "are they gone now?"

"Not gone, my lord," Selwin replied. "Dead. The Skybolts, as I said, have seen this kind of weapon before. They evacuated the town, then used small catapults to lob pots of burning herbs into the streets. The insects were killed so completely that there were none to follow us, and few to return when the hole in the sky reopened."

He sat down again when no one else had any more questions. Prince Daren stood up in his place. "This is not going to be the last attempt, my lords and ladies," he said grimly. "I think we can count ourselves fortunate that it *was* the Skybolts who encountered this first. If it had not been—if it had been a regular garrison—they would have died to a man, and we would never have known what it was that killed them."

Prince Daren sat down and took his wife's hand; Selenay looked very pale.

"I must admit," she said, "that I doubted when Kerowyn and my daughter swore that Ancar would find a way to penetrate our Border with magic. I was wrong."

Selenay looked over at Elspeth, and bit her lip. "My daughter also proposed a solution that I rejected out of hand; she suggested that Valdemar seek out magical allies as well, and find some mage who was strong enough to pass our borders to help us from within, and perhaps even teach new mages. She suggested that, since the Chronicles all speak of a 'Mage-Gift,' that there may still be Heralds carrying that Gift. She thinks that Gift has simply gone unrecognized and untaught because there was no one to teach it. She also suggested that *she* be the one to leave Valdemar, find such a mage, and bring him—or her— back to us."

Silence met her words as the Councilors turned looks of doubt toward Elspeth's end of the table. She did her best to look as mature and competent—and confident—as any of them could have wished. She was very glad now that Kero had insisted she wash and change before the meeting. She doubted she would have been able to convince any of them looking like a disheveled hoyden.

"May I speak?" she asked. At Selenay's nod, she stood up.

"Always speak to the Council from a standing position, kitten." Kero had tutored her a few weeks ago, after watching one of the sessions from the visitor's seat. The Council had wanted a report on what the Skybolts had been assigned to—and now Elspeth knew why Kero had been fairly reticent.

But what the Council didn't realize was that Kero had learned more about them than they had from her. The Captain had made careful assessments of the Council and their reactions to Elspeth, and had some fairly shrewd observations to make afterward.

"Always speak to them from a standing position. That will put your head higher than theirs, and give you an emotional advantage. Put your hands on the table, and lean forward a little. Showing your hands tells their guts that you have nothing to hide, leaning says that you are comfortable with your power, and leaning forward tells them that you are earnest. Never raise your voice; in fact, if you can, speak a little lower than usual. That tells their guts that you're not just an emotional female. But if you feel passionately about something, choose your words carefully, and put some punch behind them."

Talia and Selenay did all these things, but they did them without thinking, without knowing the reasons why they worked. Talia analyzed the audience through her Gift of Empathy, and adjusted herself accordingly, all without ever thinking about it. Selenay had been trained by her father—who may have known why his advice worked, but didn't bother to explain it to his daughter. Kerowyn, on the other hand, had to fight her way up to the top in a predominantly male profession—and she was a superb tactician in any arena. She knew how to deal with authority figures, and *why* the tactics she used worked.

Elspeth tried to keep all her advice in mind as she began.

"Herald-Captain Kerowyn and I have had several conversations about this eventuality," she said, quietly. "That in itself is unusual, because until now, it seems as if it has been very difficult even to *speak* about magic within the bounds of our realm, especially for Heralds. Please think back, think about what has happened every time in the past that you've spoken about magic in this Council Room—you've gone outside these walls, and gradually forgotten all about it, haven't you?"

She looked around, and got slow nods from most of the Councilors. "Somehow, as urgent as the threat seemed to be, it became less urgent once the immediate danger was over, didn't it? It did for me, too, until I met Kerowyn. I suspect that 'forgetting' may be a symptom of whatever it is that has protected us until now. But now—if you'll notice, we're speaking about magic, all of us, and I don't think we're going to forget about it outside the room. And I am terribly afraid that this is a symptom of something else—a symptom of the fact that this protection is weakening."

A swift intake of breath was the only sound that broke the silence following her words, but she couldn't tell who it was that had gasped. She glanced around the horseshoe-shaped table. Several of the Councilors were nodding, though not happily. She continued.

"I don't think we have a choice; I believe we *must* find a mage or mages to help us. I have several reasons why I think that the person who goes to look for one should be me." She paused again, waiting for opposition, but she didn't see anyone leaping to his—or her—feet to object. "A Herald *must* be the person we send to find us a mage—or mages. That is because only a Herald is likely to be able to weigh the motives of those we consider, and find a person of sufficient ethics to do us any good. As to my qualifications, first of all, my rank is such that I'm not likely to encounter anyone who doubts my ability to negotiate. Now, Talia *is* the Queen's Own, but she also has a small child. I think it would be unreasonable to ask her to leave him for an indefinite length of time. And there is a very sinister reason for her to avoid taking him with her; if someone captured her child, Jemmie could be held to be used against her."

Emphatic nods around the table gave her confidence to continue. "As you know, Ancar has made an assassination attempt on me. I think he will find it harder—as Kero would say—to hit a moving target. There may be other Heralds who have sufficient rank to be able to negotiate, but of all of them, only Kero and I seem to be able to even *speak* of magic clearly, much less assess the capabilities of a mage. And Kero was a mercenary—frankly, the kind of mage we are looking for may hold that against her." She spread her hands and shrugged. "The answer seems obvious to me. And if I may be so blunt as to say so, I *am* expendable. Mother has the twins, either of whom can easily succeed me as Heir."

She sat down carefully, and then the uproar began.

Elspeth had a pounding headache before it was over, and the arguments went on long past dinnertime and well into the night. Servants were sent out for cold meat, cheese, and other provisions, then called in again to light the lamps. Because of the nature of the arguments, young Heraldic trainees in their final year were brought in to serve at the table, and keep a steady supply of tea and other non-intoxicating drinks on hand. This was not the longest Council session on record, but it was certainly right up with the record holders.

And Elspeth was right in the middle of it all. Half the time, the Councilors went at her like a horde of interrogators, shouting questions, each one trying to make himself heard over the rest. The rest of the time, they acted as if she weren't even there, arguing about her and her competence at the tops of their lungs. Talia spared her a sympathetic glance or two, but she had her own hands full.

And besides, this was Elspeth's fight. It was up to her to win it; no one else was as convinced of her mission as she was. And her mother was still dead set against it.

So she fought by herself, grimly determined that she *would* win, no matter how long it took.

She did notice something odd, however. Every time it looked as though one of the Heralds would say something against her decision—he or she would freeze for a moment, sometimes in mid-sentence, and then fall silent.

Heralds often did that when their Companions were speaking to them, but Elspeth had never seen it happen so many times—or so abruptly. It was almost as if the Companions were arguing on her behalf, against their Chosens' better judgment. Elspeth even caught her mother in that momentary "listening" pose.

Shortly before midnight, the Council was finally in reluctant agreement. Elspeth could go; in fact, *must* go. She had succeeded, she and Selwin, in persuading everyone of the urgency of the situation. She had persuaded even her mother that she was the only person with the right combination of talents and credentials to successfully carry it off.

However, her route and ultimate destination would be watched over, at least inside Valdemar, and she would not go alone.

"You can't possibly go without an escort," the Lord Marshal said firmly. "I would say—twenty armed at the least."

"Thirty," said the Seneschal, over her squawk of outrage. "No less than that."

"Absolutely," Lady Cathan of the Guilds seconded. "Anything less would be inappropriate."

I'm trying to track down mages, she thought in exasperation. *I'm trying to find people who are notoriously shy, and they want me to bring an entire army with me?*

But she didn't say that; instead, she waited while the Councilors argued about the size of her escort, building it up until it *did* resemble a small army, then entered into the affray again when she thought she had a chance of being heard over the din.

"Impossible," she said, clearly. All heads turned in her direction. "Absolutely impossible," she repeated, just as firmly. "You're asking me to haul an entire armed force along with me. I'm trying to make speed—and I doubt if you could find fifty fighters with beasts able to keep up with a Companion even among the Skybolts. I may have to leave Rethwellan, and the presence of a troop like that could greatly offend the rulers of other countries that I might find myself in. But most importantly of all, insofar as my movements remaining a secret from Ancar, you might just as well post him a message every day telling him where I'm going, because that's how visible I'd be with that many armed fighters around me."

That brought all the arguments to a dead silence. The Lord Marshal actually looked sheepish.

"Now," she continued reasonably, "if you really *want* to make a big, fat target out of me, I wish you'd tell me. There are easier ways to get rid of me."

"Oh, come now," replied Lord Palinor, the Seneschal, wearing a superior expression that made her want to bite something. "Surely that's an exaggeration."

"Is it?" she asked raising one eyebrow, but otherwise keeping her expression sweetly innocent. "You just heard a description of something that could have destroyed an entire garrison—a weapon Ancar deployed inside our borders, and without having to come within sight of Valdemar. *Protected* Valdemar. What's likely to happen if he knows my every movement outside our borders?" She chuckled dryly. "Kind of negates the benefit of being a moving target, I'd say."

Silence for a moment, while they thought that one over. "Well," said Prince Daren. "What do *you* want to do?"

"My preference is to go alone," she admitted. "Basically, I'm safest if no one else knows where I am."

But the Prince shook his handsome head. "No," he said, with a touch of regret. "If it were anyone else, that wouldn't be a problem—but not you. You may think you're expendable, but you're still the Heir right now. You can't go running off the face of the earth all alone. And there is one argument that applies to Talia that also applies to you. If *you* were taken, you could be used as a hostage as well."

Elspeth sighed, but nodded in agreement. "That's true, Stepfather. I admit that I hadn't thought too much of that—but frankly, between Gwena and myself, I don't think we could be taken by anything but a small army."

"There's always treachery," Daren said firmly. "You'll have to take at least one other person with you. And personally, I would suggest a Herald."

"Someone responsible, capable—" said Father Ricard.

"Crafty and clever," said Talia.

"Fine," she agreed—and then, before they could engage in a till-dawn debate on exactly who she could take with her, said, "But it's going to be Skif, or no one. There is no one in the entire Heraldic Circle who is better suited to watching my back."

She expected an explosion of argument; after all, given the fuss there had been over the rumors started simply by being in Skif's company, the Councilors should, one and all, roundly denounce such a notion.

And after they argued themselves into exhaustion, she just might be able to talk the Council into letting her have her own way and going out alone.

"Fine," Selenay said, instantly. "Skif is perfect. He's everything we could ask; responsible, capable, clever, crafty—"

Lord Palinor laughed. "Aye, and tricky, the young devil. Ancar wouldn't catch *him* napping, I'd wager."

And while Elspeth gawked, caught entirely flat-footed with surprise, every single one of the Councilors agreed to the choice she would have bet money they thought unsuitable. Before she quite realized what was happening, they approved her authority as negotiator for the Crown, approved her escort, and closed the session.

And began filing out, heading straight for their beds, while she stared at them, dumbfounded. Talia even patted her on the shoulder as she left, whispering, "Good choice, kitten. I think it was the only thing that could have convinced them."

Finally she was alone in the Council Chamber, sitting back in her seat, staring at the guttering candles, still wondering what on earth had happened.

And wondering just who, exactly, had been outmaneuvered.

6

DARKWIND

Council meetings. Endless dithering about nothing, while we guardians dance with death out there on the border. And no help for us, either. If I could get anyone else to do this, I'd give up the Council seat in a heartbeat.

Darkwind pushed aside a tangle of vines covered with blue, trumpet-shaped flowers and restrained himself from pulling the whole curtain of vegetation down in a fit of anger. It had been days—weeks—since his confrontations with his father and the Council, demanding that they *do* something about the situation of the Clan, of the scouts, and what had they done?

Nothing. Or rather, they had "taken it under advisement." They would "weigh all the possible options." They were "studying the problem."

They're sitting on their backsides, afraid to do anything, *that's what's really going on. Father won't let them act because* he's *afraid of what it will do to the Heartstone. And they still won't go outside k'Sheyna for help.*

Not that he had really expected anything else after the way Starblade had treated him. Really, when it came to anything important, especially where magic was concerned, the entire Council spoke with Starblade's words.

I'll have to start considering those other plans of Dawnfire's, using the hertasi *and some of the others. They've left us no choice; if we're going to guard them effectively, we'll have to use whatever allies we have.* And he didn't particularly care if pulling the *hertasi* away from their other duties left some of those jobs undone. So what if the Vale got a little more overgrown? It didn't look to him as if it would make much difference. And maybe if some of the Elders had to suffer a little, if their *ekele* went unrepaired and their gardens untended because the *hertasi* were out helping keep their Vale safer—well, maybe then they'd notice that there was something wrong with their little world. And maybe they'd decide that it might be a good idea to try and fix what was wrong.

I hope. But I'm not going to count on anything like sense out of them.

He took the shortest possible route to the pass out of the Vale, cutting down long-neglected paths until he reached the boundary and the shield-wall. As he burst through a stand of wildly overgrown, flowering bushes, he saw Vree waiting for him in a tree growing just outside the mage-barrier. The gyre preferred not to enter the Vale itself if he could help it; many of the other bondbirds demonstrated Vree's distaste for the Vale proper, and tried to stay outside of the shield. Darkwind wasn't sure if it was because they shared their bondmates' dislike of magic, or sensed the problems with the Heartstone. One thing was certain, he *knew* that aversion dated back to the disaster, and not before.

He just wished *he* could avoid the Vale as well.

The place made him uneasy, for all its luxury. Here, near the edge, it wasn't so bad. The flora were tropical and wildly luxuriant, but it was nothing that couldn't be found in a glassed-over hothouse. But the closer he came to the damaged Heartstone, the stranger the plants became— and the odder he felt; slightly disoriented, off-balance, lethargic. As if something was sapping his energy, clouding his thoughts.

And it's not my imagination, either, he thought stubbornly. *If Vree and the other birds don't like the Vale, that should tell us all something. No matter what Father claims. What would he know, anyway? His bondbird is that damned crow— hardly bred out of the wild line, and it might as well be a metal simulacrum for all the intelligence it shows. It does what he tells it to, it doesn't talk to the other birds at all, and most of the time it sits on its perch in the corner of the* ekele, *like some kind of art object.*

He passed through the barrier—a brief tingling on the surface of his skin—and emerged into the real world again. Already he felt lighter, freer, and it seemed to him as he walked out on the path taking deep breaths of the pine-scented air, that even his footfalls were more confident. No cloying flower-scents, no heavy humidity—just an honest summer breeze. No one to answer to out here. No one questioning his judgment unless it really needed to be called into question.

:Vree!: He Mindcalled the gyre, suddenly anxious to feel the bird's familiar weight on his shoulder. Vree obliged him by sweeping down out of the top of the nearest pine, landing on his leather-covered wrist with a thunder of pinions, and stepping happily from there to his favorite perch, on the padded shoulder of Darkwind's jacket.

:Don't like Vale,: the falcon complained. *:Too hot, too empty, feels bad. Don't like crow, stupid crow. Don't go back.:*

He Sent agreement tinged with regret. *:I have to, featherhead. But you don't have to go in if you don't want to. And I don't have to go back for a while.:*

The bird crooned a little, and preened a beakful of Darkwind's hair, as the scout laughed softly. Feeling considerably more cheerful now that he was outside the Vale and wouldn't have to face another Council meeting for days, Darkwind returned the bird's affectionate caress, scratching the breast and working his fingers up to the headfeathers. Vree made a happy chuckling sound, and bent to have his head scratched a little more.

"Sybarite," Darkwind said, laughing.

:Feels good,: the bird agreed. *:Scratch.:*

:Report, featherhead,: he told the gyre. *:Or no more scratches.:*

Vree actually heaved a sigh, and reluctantly complied. The bondbirds had some limited abilities at relaying and reporting messages; while Darkwind was in the Vale, he depended on Vree to keep in contact with the rest of the scouts under his command. Vree had messages from most of the scouts; all those who had not reported in person before Darkwind went to the Council meeting this afternoon.

Most of the messages were simple enough, even by Vree's standards: "Nothing to report," "All quiet," "All is well." A normal enough day; he'd been half expecting that something disastrous would happen while he was out of touch, but it seemed that all the scouts had things well in hand.

All except for the handful of scouts who shared the southern boundary with him.

Those sent back messages that there were problems. Three of them said that they had turned their watch over to the night-scouts and would meet him at his *ekele,* to make their reports in person. Vree could not imitate the emotional overtones of those Mind-sent messages, relayed through their birds to Vree, but the terse quality did not augur well.

He swore silently to himself; the last time he'd had to take reports in person, he and the rest of the scouts had faced a week-long incursion of magically twisted creatures that ultimately cost them two scouts and the only mage who had deigned to work with them.

That had been shortly after he'd joined the scouts, and before they made him their spokesperson. He could only hope that if this was the situation they faced again, they were sufficiently aware of the problems *now* to deal with it without more losses.

:Home?: Vree asked hopefully when he'd finished listening to the last of those messages.

:Yes,: he confirmed, to the bird's delight. *:Meet me there.:* He let Vree hop back down to his wrist and tossed the heavy gyre into the air; Vree pushed off and flapped upward, driving himself up through the branches with thunderous wing-claps. Darkwind waited until he had disappeared, then started off through the forest at a trot—*not* on one of the usual paths, but on a game-trail—heading for his *ekele*.

He never took the same route twice; he never approached his *ekele* the same way. While he ran, as silently as only a Tayledras scout could, he kept his mind as well as his other senses open, constantly on the alert for traces of thought that were out of the ordinary, for the scent of something odd, for a color or texture where it didn't belong, or movement, or the sound of a footfall in the forest beyond him.

Other scouts had not been that cautious. Rainwind hadn't; he'd been ambushed halfway between the Vale and his *ekele* after a long soak in one of the springs. He'd been lucky; his bondbird had spotted one of the ambushers first, so he had only had to deal with one enemy. The creatures had not sported the kind of poisoned fangs and claws so many others had and he'd escaped with only a permanent limp from a lacerated thigh.

Others had not been so fortunate; they had been just as careless, and had paid for it with limbs or lives.

That was the cost of living outside the Vale. No single Tayledras could hope to shield more than his *ekele*, even if he were an Adept-class mage. Since most of the scouts *weren't*, they paid the price of freedom in personal safety.

But anyone who lived out here felt it was worth that cost.

There were too many other things that were bad about living in the Vale these days; it was good to have a little distance from the Heartstone, and space between themselves and the mages.

The run stirred up his blood, and made him feel a little readier to face whatever trouble was coming. He Felt the presence of the other scouts long before they knew he was there. Out of courtesy, they had not climbed to his *ekele* while he was not in it; instead, they waited below, patiently, while Vree perched above, impatiently.

:Hungry,: Vree complained, as soon as his keen eyes spotted Darkwind approaching. The three scouts waiting caught the edge of the Mind-sent plaint, and he Felt their attention turning toward him, little brushes of thought, as they each tested for him and found him with their individual Gifts.

They waited until he came into view, though, before tendering some very subdued greetings. And not the usual *"zhai'helleva,"* either; Winterlight and Stormcloud only raised their hands in a kind of sketchy salute, and Dawnfire tendered him a feather-light mental caress, a promise of things to come, but also carrying overtones of deep concern.

This did not indicate good news at all. He signaled to Vree, who swooped down and landed on one of the lower branches. Although he could not see the bird, hidden as he was by growth, he knew what Vree was up to. The gyre sidled along the branch to the trunk, and pulled a strap on the hook holding his rope ladder out of reach. The ladder dropped down to the ground with a clattering of wooden rungs; Darkwind motioned the others to precede him, and followed after with the strap that was attached to the end of the ladder tucked into his belt.

The others were far above him on the ladder; he had to go slowly, as he was bringing the end of it up with him. They were already hidden in the branches when he was only halfway up. His *ekele*, like those of the other scouts, was actually more elaborate than any of those inside the Vale. It had to be; it had to withstand winter winds and summer downpours, snow and hail, and the occasional "visit" from some of the distinctly hostile creatures from the Outlands.

At last, after penetrating the growth of the first boughs, he reached the place where the ladder-release was fastened to the bark of the trunk. He hooked the end of the ladder back in place, and followed his guests up through the trapdoor in the floor of the first chamber of the *ekele*.

The tree holding his home was an amazing forest giant, but it was nothing like the trees that supported a half-dozen *ekele* apiece, back in the Vale. Like them, though, it was a huge conifer, with a girth more than ten men could span with outstretched arms, and an arrow-straight trunk that towered without a single branching up for several man-heights above the forest floor. The first branches concealed his ladder; his *ekele* began, well sheltered, another man-height above that.

He pulled himself up onto the floor, closed and locked the trapdoor, then went to the glazed window of the first chamber, unlocked the latch at the side, and held it open for Vree. The forestgyre dove through it in a rush, landing on his outstretched arm, then hopped to his shoulder. Darkwind shut the window and relatched it, then turned to climb the stairs to join his guests.

The entire *ekele* was built of light, strong wood, stained on the outside to resemble the bark of the tree, but polished to a warm gold within. The first chamber was nothing more than a single, barren room, meant to buffer the effects of the wind coming up from below; there were all-weather coats hung on pegs on the wall, some climbing-tools and weapons, but that was all. The other scouts had already gone ahead of him, following a staircase built into the side of the trunk, a stair that spiraled up to the next chamber.

Each chamber was built upon the one below it, in a snailshell-like spiral pattern, using the huge branches as supports for the floor. The next chamber was one commonly used for the gathering of friends; it was considerably larger than the entrance chamber, and covered an arc fully one-third of the circumference of the trunk. Heated in winter by a clever ceramic stove that he also used for cooking, it supplied warm air to the two chambers above it. One of those was a sleeping room, the other, a storeroom and study. To bathe, he had to descend to the ground. As soon as his head and shoulders had cleared the doorsill—if one could rightly call an entrance that was placed in the floor a "door"—Vree hopped off his shoulder and bounced sideways toward his perch, in the ungainly sidling motion of any raptor on the ground. The floor and wall-mounted perch was a permanent fixture of the room, placed in the corner, where it could be braced against two of the walls, and near one of the windows. Vree leapt up onto it, roused his feathers, and yawned, waiting for his dinner.

Aside from the perch and the stove, the only other permanent features of the room were the low platforms affixed to the floor. Those platforms, upholstered in flat cushions, now hosted the three scouts: Winterlight, Stormcloud, and Dawnfire.

Three of the best. If they have problems, it's not from incompetence.

Winterlight was the oldest of all of them; he had held the position of Council-speaker and Elder but had given it to Darkwind with grateful relief when the others suggested him.

Now I know why he gave it up. I'd gladly give it back.

He seldom dyed his hair; longer than his waist, he generally kept the snow-white fall in a single braid as thick as his own wrist. Winterlight was actually Starblade's elder by several years but was of such a solitary nature that he had lived outside the Vale for most of his life. He was also unusual in that he flew two bondbirds; a snow-eagle, Lyer, by day; a tuft-eared owl, Huur, by night. Both birds had mated, and although the mates had not bonded to the scout, they provided extra security for Winterlight's *ekele*, nesting near each other in a rare show of interspecies tolerance, for given the chance, owls and eagles would readily hunt and even kill one another. Huur and Lyer's offspring had been in high demand as bondbirds.

Had been—but the reduced population and the absolute dearth of children meant that this year's crop of nestlings would probably go unbonded, and fly off to some other Clan to seek mates. Unless one of the scouts chose to bond to a second bird, or lost his bird before the eyases fledged and became passagers. Darkwind had briefly toyed with the notion of bonding to an owlet, but Vree had displayed a great deal of jealousy at the idea, and he had discarded it, albeit regretfully.

Stormcloud might have been a mage, but as a child his Gift was not deemed "enough" by Starblade and the other Adepts, and now he refused to enter training at all. His argument, using their own words against them in a direct quote, was, "It's better to have a first-quality scout than a second-class mage."

And I don't blame you, old friend. No matter what Father says about "ingratitude and insolence." I'd have said and done the same as you.

He was Darkwind's oldest and best friend, their friendship dating back to when they were both barely able to walk. His features differed from the aquiline Tayledras norm considerably, with a round chin and a snubbed nose. He alone among k'Sheyna cut his hair short, with a stiff, jaylike crest. He flew a white raven, Krawn, that was as loquacious as Starblade's crow was silent. Krawn was easily the brightest of all the corbies flown in k'Sheyna, and very fond of practical jokes, as was Stormcloud. It was a measure of how serious the situation among the scouts was that neither Krawn nor his bondmate had played any of their famous jokes for months.

Dawnfire flew a red-shouldered hawk, Kyrr, a bird as graceful—and as sought-after for mating—as her bondmate. Dawnfire cast Darkwind a look full of promise as he entered the room, and he marveled that he, of all the scouts, had captured her fancy. She typified the opposite end of the extreme from Stormcloud; in her the aquiline Tayledras features had been refined to the point that she resembled the elfin *tervardi*, the lovely flightless bird-people she often worked with. That was her strongest Gift; she Mindspoke the nonhuman races with an ease the others could only envy, and communicated equally well with animals of all sorts. Her hair, now bound tightly into three braids, was as long as Winterlight's when she let it down. An errant beam of light reflected from the snow-goose lanterns touched her head, giving her an air of the unearthly as Darkwind watched her.

That light was provided during the day by four windows, all of which could be opened, that were glazed with a flexible substance as clear as the finest glass, but nearly impossible to break. Tayledras artisans created it; how, Darkwind had no idea, but it was as impervious to wind and weather as it was to breakage. By night, the light came from Darkwind's single concession to magic; mage-lights captured in the lanterns, that began glowing as dusk fell, and increased their pure light as the external sunlight faded.

Darkwind dug into his game-pouch as soon as his feet touched the floor of the room; Vree had waited long enough. He came up with a half rabbit; a light meal by Vree's standards, but enough to hold him until the discussion was over. Vree looked up at him with an expression of inquiry when presented with the rabbit. *:?:* the bird said, reminding Darkwind of his hunger.

:More, later,: he promised the bird. *:I have a duck waiting for you.:*

Vree chirped a happy acknowledgment, and began tearing the meat from the bones, gulping it down as fast as he could. One thing the bondbirds were not, and that was dainty eaters.

"So," he said, leaving Vree to his snack, and sitting cross-legged on one of the couches. "What's the problem?"

"The barrier-zone," said Winterlight succinctly, his hands resting palm-down on his knees, a deceptively tranquil pose. "We've got some real problems on the south. Things moving in, things and people, and we don't like the look of either. They're coming in from that bad patch of Outland, and it looks like they're settling. They're making dens, lairs, and fortified homes. I don't like it, Darkwind; it's got a bad feel to it; these creatures aren't overtly evil, but they make the back of my neck crawl. They're *inside* the old k'Sheyna boundaries now, and not just in the old 'barren' zone. You know how one bird will 'crowd' another, getting closer and closer until the other one either has to peck back or be forced off a perch? That's what it feels like they're doing to us."

"I've got the same," Stormcloud told him, wearing a slight frown. "And I've got enough Mage-Gift to read some other things as well. There's a new node that's being established just off my area, and a lot of ley-lines have been diverted to feed it. There's a new line going off that node, too—and it's feeding straight into Outland territory, into one of the places we *know* that Adept has made his own. It's bad, Darkwind, it's feeding him a lot of power, and anyone that can divert lines is damned good. He's pulled some of the lines away from us completely. And I've caught him trying to read the Vale for power, too. I think he might be planning to use one of the lines to tap into the Vale itself."

Darkwind frowned. "This is a new tactic for him, isn't it? He's never stolen power before that I can recall."

"Exactly," Stormcloud said, and bit his lip. "I don't like it, Darkwind. And I like it even less that our own mages haven't sensed him doing anything. Unless that was what this meeting you had to attend was all about—?"

Darkwind shook his head. "No. At least, that wasn't on the agenda. So unless they're keeping it from me—and they could be, I'll admit—they haven't noticed either the new node or the diversion of the ley-lines."

Winterlight snorted his contempt. "You could probably start a mage-war out here and they'd never notice inside the Vale. They're lost in their own little dream of what-was-once. Even if they were alert, the Heartstone just blanks out everything that's not in there with them."

Darkwind's frown deepened a trifle; that was *not* the way it was supposed to be. The Heartstone was supposed to sensitize the mages to what was going on with energies outside the Vale, not destroy or bury their sensitivity. But he realized that Winterlight was right; that was another of the side effects he disliked about being inside the Vale. When he was within the shield-area, it was as if he had been cut off from the energy-flows outside.

No one had said anything about that, not even right after the Heartstone shattered—which meant either that the effect was new, another developing side effect of living next to the broken stone—

—or it's been that way since the disaster, and nobody noticed. Which is just as bad.

Dawnfire had been silent up until now; he turned toward her and raised an eyebrow.

"Well," she said, with a frown that matched his own, "Stormcloud is the one who knows energies, and Winterlight's Huur is absolutely the best at spying. So I'll just say that I think the same things have been happening in my area, but I'd like someone to check to be sure. What I have that they don't is a network of allied species acting as my informants—*hertasi, dyheli, tervardi,* and a few humans who aren't fond of civilization. Most of the humans are a little crazy, but they're sharp enough when it comes to noticing what's going on around them."

Darkwind nodded; Dawnfire was the one who had suggested taking volunteers among the nonhumans in the first place, and she had proved the idea was viable by establishing a network outside the k'Sheyna boundaries.

"Well, some of my informants are missing," she said, some of her distress coming through despite her best efforts to control it. "And when I sent someone to try and find them, there was nothing. They haven't just disappeared, they've gone without a trace. That wouldn't be too hard to do with *dyheli,* but *hertasi* have real homes—they actually build furnishings for their caves and hollow trees—and *tervardi* build *ekele,* and even those are gone. It's as if they never existed at all."

"Gone?" Darkwind repeated. "How could anyone make a tree vanish?"

Dawnfire shook her head. "I don't know—though the trees themselves don't vanish, just the hollows and *ekele.* But the caves *do* vanish; there's solid earth and rock where the cave used to be. At least, that's what my bird tells me."

Winterlight frowned. "Could that be illusion?"

"It could," she acknowledged with a nod. "Kyrr can't tell illusion from the real thing, and she's not particularly sensitive to magic. I wasn't about to ask her to test it. But my *tervardi* and *hertasi* aren't mages, either, so they wouldn't have used illusion to conceal their homes. Something took them, then covered its tracks by making it look as if there had never been anything living there."

"Who, why, and how?" Stormcloud asked succinctly. "There *is* an Adept out there—"

"But again, this isn't like anything he's ever done before," said Winterlight.

"That we know of," Darkwind added. "He might have decided to change his tactics. And it might not be him—or her—at all. It might be another Adept entirely. 'Why' is another good question; why take them at all, and why try to make it look as if they never existed?"

"To confuse us?" Stormcloud asked facetiously. "And make us think we're crazy?"

"Why not?" was Dawnfire's unexpected reply as she sat straight up, with a look of keen speculation on her face. "He has to know how badly the Heartstone has been affecting us. If we were only in sporadic contact with those particular creatures, erasing their very existence *might* make us uneasy about our own sanity."

Winterlight nodded, slowly, as if what she had said had struck a note with him, too. "A good point. But the question is, what are we going to do about it?"

"About losing neutral territory—there's not much we *can* do," Darkwind sighed. "We could make things uncomfortable for the things moving in, I suppose; uncomfortable enough that they might move back without our having to force a confrontation we haven't the manpower to meet."

"Like some really nasty practical jokes?" For the first time in the meeting, Stormcloud's eyes lit up. "Krawn and I could take care of that. Now that it's summer, there are a *lot* of things we can do to make them miserable, as long as we have your permission." He grinned evilly. "I know where there are some *lovely* fire-wasp nests. And Krawn can bring in absolute swarms of other corbies. They aren't going to be able to leave anything outside without having it stolen or fouled."

"Do it," Darkwind told him. "And don't stretch yourself too thin, but if you can extend your reach into Dawnfire's and Winterlight's areas, do so."

"I can," Stormcloud replied, with barely concealed glee. "The thing about tricks is that they're more effective if they're sporadic and unpredictable. Krawn is going to love this."

"What about the power-theft?" asked Winterlight anxiously. "We can't do anything about that—just as well try to bail water with a basket—but surely someone should."

"I'll tell the mages," Darkwind said, "but I can't promise anything. They might seal off the leaks, they might not. There's no predicting them these days."

"And my missing creatures?" Dawnfire was giving him that look of pleading he found so hard to resist, but there wasn't anything he could do that would satisfy her.

"They'll have to stay missing," he said, and held up his hand to forestall a protest. "I know, I know, it's not right, but we haven't enough guardians to spare to send even one into the neutral territory to find out what happened to them and protect the rest."

"If your gryphon friends were the ones missing," she said, her eyes sparking with momentary anger, "would you still be saying that?"

"Yes, I would," he replied, "*If* they had nested outside our boundaries. And even then, well, anything Treyvan and Hydona couldn't take care of themselves, I rather doubt *we* could handle. But I promise this much; if you and Kyrr can catch our predator in the act, we'll see what can be done to save whoever he's after. And if we can catch him in the act, we may have a chance at figuring out a defense for the rest of your friends."

Dawnfire obviously didn't like the answer, but she knew as well as he did that it was the only one he could give her.

"Anything else?" he asked, stifling a yawn, and casting a look at the windows. The sky beyond the branches was a glorious scarlet; they had spoken until sunset, and if the others were to get back to their *ekele* before dark, they'd have to leave soon. "I'm going to have to get out on patrol before dawn to make up for stealing a couple of hours of Amberwing's time so I could go to the blamed meeting. So I've got a short night ahead of me."

"I think we've covered everything," Winterlight said, after a moment of silence. "I'll catch up with the others, and let them know what we've decided."

He got up from the couch, and started down the stairs. Stormcloud followed him, then paused at the top of the stairs just long enough for a slow wink.

Dawnfire glanced at the windows, at the heavy branches standing out blackly against the fire of the sunset. "Are you really that tired?" she asked. She didn't get up from the couch.

"Not if you're going to stay a while," he replied, with a slow smile.

"You haven't taken back your feather," she said, somehow gliding into his arms before he was aware she had moved. "And I certainly don't want mine back. Of course I'll stay a while."

The scent of her, overlaid with the musky trace of her bird, was as intoxicating as *tran*-dust, and the soft lips she offered to him made his blood heat to near-boiling. He lost himself in her, their two minds meeting and melding, adding to the sensuality of the embrace. Her hands caressed the small of his back and slid down over his hips; his right was buried in her hair at the nape of her neck, his left crushed her to him.

He had just enough wit to remember he still had to pull up his ladder.

So did she, fortunately. "Go secure the door. The sunset, if I recall correctly, is incredible from upstairs."

She pushed him away; he moved down the stairs in a dream. The trapdoor was still unlatched; he brought the ladder up, rung by rung, and rehung it, latched down the trapdoor, and keyed the mage-light to a dim blue.

Then he ran up the two flights of stairs to the sleeping room.

She was waiting, clothed only in her loosened hair, curled like a white vixen on the dark furs of his bedspread, her hair flowing free and trailing behind her like a frozen waterfall.

She turned a little at his footfall, and smiled at him, holding out her hand—and they didn't see a great deal of the sunset.

:Brother comes, fast,: said Vree. Then, with an overtone of surprise, *:Very fast.:*

Vree's alert interrupted what had been an otherwise completely dull and uneventful patrol along the dry streambed that formed part of the k'Sheyna border. It hadn't always been dry—in fact, a week ago, there had been a stream here. Evidently not only ley-lines were being diverted.

Darkwind had not been overly worried when he discovered the condition of the stream; the diversion could easily have had perfectly natural causes. It could have gone dry for a dozen reasons, including the "helpful" work of beavers. But it was one more thing to investigate...

That was when Vree's call alerted him. Before Darkwind had a chance to wonder just what that "fast" meant, he heard the pounding of hooves from up-trail. A moment later, a *dyheli* stag plunged over the embankment above him, coming to a halt in a clatter of cleft hooves, and a shower of sand and gravel. The graceful, antelope-like creature was panting, his flanks covered with sweat, his mane sodden with it. As Dawnfire slid from his back, he tossed his golden head with its three spiraling horns and Mindspoke Darkwind directly.

:Cannot run more—help my brothers—:

Then he plunged back into the brush, staggering a little from exhaustion, as Darkwind turned toward his rider.

"What—"

"There's a *dyheli* bachelor herd just outside the boundaries," she said, her words tumbling over each other with her urgency. "They're trapped in a pocket valley, one they can't climb out of. I don't know what chased them in there, or even if they just went in there last night figuring it was a good place to defend in the dark—but they've been trapped, and they're going mad with fear—"

"Whoa." He stopped the torrent of speech by placing his hand over her lips for a moment. "Take it slowly. What's holding them there?"

"It's—it's like a fog bank, and it fills the outer end of the valley," she replied, her voice strained. "Only it's bluish, and anything that goes into it doesn't come out alive. Darkwind, we have to get them out of there!"

"You say they're outside the borders?" he persisted.

She nodded, her enormous, pale-silver eyes fixed on his.

"I—" he hesitated, presented with the pleading in her expression. *I shouldn't. It's outside, it could be a diversion to get several of us out there—it could be an attempt to ambush us—*

But her eyes persuaded him against his better judgment. "I—all right, *ashke.* I'll come look at the situation. But I can't promise anything."

It took them a while to reach the spot, even with the assistance of two more *dyheli* from a breeding herd inside k'Sheyna borders. By the time they reached the valley, the situation had worsened. The fog had crowded all the young *dyheli* bucks into the back of the valley, and they milled around the tiny space in a state of complete, unthinking panic. Trampling everything beneath their churning hooves, with horns tossing, their squeals of desperation reached to Darkwind's perch on the hill above them.

He studied the situation, his heart sinking. The sides of the valley—it was really a steep cup among the hills, with a spring at the bottom—were rocky, and far too steep to bring the *dyheli* up, even if they'd been calm. In their current state of panic, it was impossible.

The fog was mage-born, that much he could tell, easily. But the mage himself was not here. There was no one to attack, and no way to counter such a nebulous menace. Even calling up a wind—if he could have done so—would not have dispersed the evil cloud.

It roiled beneath him, a leprous blue-white, thick and oily, too murky to see into. Twice now, he'd seen young bucks overcome with fear and madness try to break through into the clear air beyond. They had never come out on the other side.

"We have to do something!" Dawnfire pleaded. He hesitated a moment, then gave her the bad news.

"There isn't anything we can do," he said, closing his mental shields against the tide of fear and despair from below. The *dyheli* were so panicked now that they weren't even capable of thinking. "Maybe the rain tonight will disperse it in time to save them."

"No!" she shouted, careless of what might overhear her. "No, we can't

leave them! I'm a guardian, they're my responsibility, I *won't* leave them!"

"Dawnfire—" he took her shoulders and shook them. "There isn't anything we can do, don't you understand that? They're too panicked to get harnesses on and haul them up—even if we had enough people here to try! And I *won't* call in all the scouts from their patrols. It's bad enough that I left mine! Don't you see, this could easily be a diversion, to clear the way for something else to come in over the border while it's unguarded!"

She stared at him, aghast, for a long moment. Then, "You *coward!*" she spat. "You won't even try! You don't care if they die, you don't care what happens to anyone or anything, all you care about is yourself! You won't even use your magic to save them!"

As the envenomed words flew, Darkwind kept a tenuous grip on his temper by reminding himself of how young Dawnfire was. *She's only seventeen,* he told himself. *She lives and breathes being a guardian, and she doesn't understand how to lose. She was barely assigned her duties when the Heartstone blew. She doesn't mean what she's saying...*

But as her words grew more and more hurtful and heated in response to his cool silence, he finally had enough. His temper snapped like a dry twig, and he stopped the torrent of abuse with a mental "slap."

And as she stood, silent and stunned, he folded his arms across his chest and stared at her until she dropped her eyes.

"You say you are a guardian. Well, you pledged an oath to obey *me,* your commander, and abide by my decisions. Have you suddenly turned into a little child, regressed to the age of ten, when sworn oaths mean only 'until I'm tired of playing'? No?" He studied her a moment more, as she went from red to white and back again. "In that case, I suggest you calm yourself and return to your assigned patrol. *If* you comport yourself well and *if* you can keep yourself under control, I will consider leaving you there, rather than reassigning you elsewhere. Is that understood?"

"Yes, Elder," she replied, in a voice that sounded stifled.

"Very well," he said. "Go, then."

7

ELSPETH

"Elspeth?"

Despite the anxious tone of Skif's voice, Elspeth didn't look up from her book. "What?" she said, absently, more to respond and let Skif know she'd heard him than a real reply. She was deep in what was apparently a firsthand description of the moments before Vanyel's final battle.

It was then that we saw how the valley walls had been cut away, to widen the passage, and the floor of the vale had been smoothed into a roadway broad enough for a column of four. And all this, said Vanyel, was done by magic. I knew not what to think at that moment.

"Elspeth, don't you think we should be getting out of here?" Skif persisted. "On the road, I mean." She looked up from her page, and into Skif's anxious brown eyes. There was no one else to overhear them; they were the only ones in the library archives, where the oldest Chronicles were stored.

Sunlight damaged books, so the archive chamber was a windowless room in the center of the library. Smoke and soot damaged them as well, so all lighting was provided by smokeless lanterns burning the finest of lamp oil, constructed to extinguish immediately if they tipped over. No other form of lighting was permitted—certainly not candles. Elspeth realized, as she looked into Skif's anxiety-shadowed face, that she didn't know what time it was. If any of the Collegium bells had rung, she hadn't noticed them.

Her stomach growled in answer to the half-formed question, telling her that it was past lunchtime, if nothing else.

She rubbed her eyes; she'd been so absorbed in her reading that she hadn't noticed the passage of time. "Why?" she asked, simply. "What's your hurry?"

He grimaced, then shrugged. "I don't like the idea of riding off south with just the two of us, but since you seem so set on it—I keep thinking your getting the Council to agree was too easy. They didn't *argue* enough."

"Not argue enough?" she replied, making a sour face. "I beg to differ. *You* weren't there. They argued plenty, believe me. I thought they'd never stop till they all fell over from old age."

"But not enough," he persisted. "It should have taken weeks to get them to agree to your plan. Instead—it took less than a day. That doesn't make any sense, at least, not to me. I keep thinking they're going to change their minds at any minute. So I want to know why we aren't getting out of here before they get a chance to."

"They won't change their minds," she said, briefly, wishing he'd let her get back to her researches. "Gwena says so."

"What does a Companion have to do with the Council changing its mind?" he demanded.

That's what I would like to know, she thought. *Gwena's playing coy every time I ask.* "I don't know, but ask yours. I bet she says the same thing."

"Huh." His eyes unfocused for a moment as he Mindspoke his little mare; then, "I'll be damned," he replied. "You're right. But I still don't see why we aren't getting on the road; everything we need is packed except for your personal gear; I should think you'd be so impatient to get out of here that I would be the one holding us back."

She shrugged. "Let's just say that I'm getting ready. What I'm doing in here is as important as the packing you've been doing."

"Oh?" He shaded the word in a way that kept it from sounding insulting, which it could easily have done.

"It's no secret," she said, gesturing at the piles of books around her. "I'm researching magic in the old Chronicles; magic, and Herald-Mages, what they could do, and so forth. So I know what to look for and what we need."

If he noticed that some of those Chronicles were of a later day than Vanyel's time, he didn't mention it. "I suppose that makes sense," he acknowledged. "Just remember, the Council could change their decision any time, no matter what Gwena says."

"I'll keep that in mind," she replied, turning her attention back to her page. After a moment, Skif took the hint; she heard him slip out of his chair, and leave the room.

But her mind wasn't on the words in front of her. Instead, she gave thought to how much Skif's observations mirrored her own.

This *was* too easy. There was no reason why the Queen should have agreed to this, much less the Circle and Council. The excuse of the magical attack on Bolton, the Skybolts' deeded border town, was just that; an excuse. She had checked back through the Chronicles of the past several years, and she had uncovered at least five other instances of magical attacks on Border villages, all of which looked to her as if they showed a weakening of the Border-protections. The records indicated no such panic reaction as she'd seen in the Council Chamber; rather, that there was a fairly standard way of responding. A team of Heralds and Healers would be sent to the site, the people would be aided and removed to somewhere safer, if that was their choice, then the incident was filed and forgotten. Farther back than that had been, Talia's encounter with Ancar, that had signaled the beginning of the conflicts with Hardorn. There had been long discussions about what to do, how to handle the attacks of mages; Elspeth remembered that perfectly well. And there *had* been some progress; the Collegium made a concerted effort, checking the Chronicles following Vanyel's time, to determine how Heralds without the Mage-Gift could counter magical attacks. Some solutions had been found, the appropriate people were briefed and trained—

And that was all. The knowledge was part of the schooling in Gifts now, but there was no particular emphasis placed on it. Not the way there should have been, especially following Ancar's second attempt at conquest.

File and forget.

For that matter, there was even some evidence that Karse had been using magic, under the guise of "priestly powers." No one had *ever* followed up on that, not even when Kero had made a point of reminding the Council of it.

There had to be another reason for letting her go on this "quest." Especially since there were overtones in the Council meetings she attended of "the Brat is getting her way." It would have been obvious to anyone with half a mind and one ear that now that the initial excitement was over, they regretted giving her their permission to leave, even to as safe a destination as Bolthaven, deep in the heart of her uncle's peaceful kingdom.

Even the Heralds on the Council gave her the unmistakable feeling that they were *not* happy about this little excursion, and they'd gladly use any excuse to take their permission back.

But they didn't. Gwena had said repeatedly that they wouldn't. There was something going on that they weren't talking about. And it didn't take a genius to figure out that, whatever it was, the Companions, *en masse*, were hock-deep in it.

And did it have something to do with her growing resistance to this compulsion to forget magic, to avoid even thinking about it?

Once her suspicions were aroused, Elspeth had decided that, before she ran off into unknown territory, she was going to do a little research on the Herald-Mages. Not just to find out their strengths and weaknesses, nor to discover just what the limits and gradations of the "Mage-Gift" were, but to see just how extensive the apparent prohibition against magic was; how deeply rooted, and how long it had been going on.

And what she had learned was quite, quite fascinating. It dated from Vanyel's time, all right—but not exactly.

To be precise, it dated from the time that Bard Stefen, then an old and solitary man, vanished without a trace.

In the Forest of Sorrows.

At least, that was Elspeth's guess. He was supposed to be in the company of some other young, unspecified Herald, on a kind of pilgrimage to the place where Vanyel died. He never arrived at his destination, yet no one reported his death. Granted, he had not yet achieved the kind of legendary status he had in Elspeth's time, but still, he was a prominent Bard, the author of hundreds of songs, epic rhymed tales and ballads, and the hero of a few of them himself. He was Vanyel's lifebonded lover, the last one to see him alive, and Vanyel *did* have the status of legend. *Someone* would have said something if he had died—at the very least, there should have been an impressive Bardic funeral.

No mention, no funeral. He simply dropped out of sight.

Nor was that all; even if he had vanished, someone *should* have noticed that he disappeared; surely searches should have been made for him. But no one did notice, nor did anyone look for him.

He simply vanished without a trace, and no one paid any notice. And that—possibly even that precise moment—was when it became impossible to talk about magic, except in the historical sense. That was when the Chronicles stopped mentioning it; when songs stopped being written about it.

When encounters with it outside the borders of Valdemar—or, occasionally, just inside those borders—were forgotten within weeks.

Fortunately those encounters were usually benign, as when ambassadors from Valdemar would see the mages in the Court of Rethwellan performing feats to amuse, or ambassadors from outside of Valdemar would mention magic, and some of the things their kingdoms' mages could do. The Chronicler of the time would dutifully note it down—then promptly forget about it. So would the members of the Council—and the Heralds.

Did they attribute all of that to boasting and travelers' tales? Now I wonder if, when other people read the Chronicles over, do their eyes just skip across the relevant words as if they weren't even there?

It wouldn't surprise her. Elspeth herself had noticed whole pages seeming to blur in front of her eyes, so that she had to make a concerted effort to read every word. She had initially ascribed the effect to fatigue and the labor of reading the archaic script and faded inks, but now she wasn't so sure. It had gotten easier, the more she had read, but she wondered what would happen if she stopped reading for a while, then came back to it.

She had even found a report from Selenay's grandfather, back when he was plain old "Herald Roald," and the Heir, about his encounter with Kero's grandmother Kethry and *her* partner.

Tarma shena Tale'sedrin, a Shin'a'in Kal'enedral, sworn to the service of her Goddess, was plainly some kind of a priest. In fact, much to Roald's surprise, she had achieved a physical manifestation of her Goddess right before his eyes. Never having seen a Goddess, he was rather impressed.

So would I be!

He'd described the manifestation; the impossibly lovely young Shin'a'in woman, clothed as one of her own Swordsworn—but with strange eyes with neither pupil nor white; just the impression of an endless field of stars.

Brrr. I would probably have passed out.

He and Tarma had become quite firm friends after that; Roald's Companion approved of both the priest and her Goddess, which Roald had found vastly amusing. But if Tarma was a powerful priest, Kethry was just as clearly a talented and powerful mage. Roald had quite a bit to say about her; it was evident that he was quite smitten with her, and if it hadn't been for the fact that she was obviously just as smitten with the Rethwellan archivist they had rescued, he hinted that he might well have considered a try in that direction.

A superb tactician, however, he knew a hopeless situation when he saw one and wisely did not pursue his interest any further.

It was Roald's account of Kethry's magical abilities that interested Elspeth. It was in this account that she got a clearer idea of the differences between Journeyman class and Master, of Master and Adept. That alone was useful, since it proved to her that what Valdemar needed was indeed an Adept, more than one, if at all possible. Certainly a teacher.

There was no reason why the Mage-Gift should have vanished from the population of Valdemar, when it was clearly present elsewhere.

Roald did not have a great deal to say about Kethry's magical sword, "Need," other than the fact that it was magical, with unspecified powers, and would only help women. So at that point in time, the song "Threes" had not migrated up to Valdemar, or Roald would have made certain to mention it.

Interesting about songs…

As evidence of just how strong that magic-prohibition had been, Elspeth had come across another fascinating bit of information in the Bardic Chronicles, which were also stored here. The song "Kerowyn's Ride" had preceded the arrival of the real Kerowyn by several years—ascribed to "anonymous." Which it wasn't; several times visiting Bards had attempted to set the Valdemaran record straight. Each time the attribution was duly noted, then the very next time the song was listed in a Court performance, it was ascribed to "anonymous."

It was the habit of Master Bards, particularly the teachers, to write short dissertations on the meaning and derivation of popular songs to be used as teaching materials. Out of curiosity, Elspeth had made a point of looking up the file on "Kerowyn's Ride."

At that point, it would have strained the credulity of even a dunce to believe that there was nothing working to suppress the knowledge of magic—for even *after* the arrival of the real Kerowyn, Master Bards were writing essays that claimed it was an allegorical piece wherein the Goddess-as-Crone passed her power to the Goddess-as-Maiden at Spring Solstice. She found several other papers stating that it described an actual event that had taken place hundreds of years ago, as evidenced by this or that style.

That was quite enough to get Elspeth digging into more of the Bardic Chronicles, and that was when she discovered corroborating evidence for her theory that something was suppressing the very idea of magic.

Despite the fact that there had been a concerted effort to get the songs about Herald-Mages and magical conflicts back into the common repertory, despite the fact that this was Bardic Collegium's top priority—and despite the fact that perfectly awful, maudlin songs like the unkillable "My Lady's Eyes" stayed popular—the "magic" songs could not be kept in repertory. Audiences grew bored, or wandered away; Bards forgot the lyrics, or found themselves singing lyrics to another song entirely. When given a list of possible songs for various occasions, a Seneschal or

Master of the Revels would inexplicably choose any song but the ones describing magic.

Only those songs that did not specifically mention magic, or those where the powers described could as easily be ascribed to a traditional Gift, stayed in popular repertory. Songs like the "Sun and Shadow" ballads, or the "Windrider" cycle, songs that were hundreds of years older than the Vanyel songs and written in archaic language, were well known—was it because not once was there a reference to a specific spell, only vague terms like "power" and "curses?"

Furthermore, Elspeth herself had heard the "problem" songs being sung, not once, but fairly often, and with a great deal of acclaim and success. So it wasn't that there was anything wrong with the songs themselves. It *had* to be because of their content. And was it possible that the reason the songs had been successful was that they were sung in the presence of many Heralds? For that seemed to be the common factor. It was when they had been sung with no Heralds present at all that the worst failures occurred.

She had learned several other things from the Chronicles of Vanyel's time—things which had no direct bearing on her present mission, but which explained a great deal.

For instance: there had been something called "The Web," which demanded the energy and attention of four Herald-Mages. Those four apparently had been somehow tied to one-quarter of Valdemar each, and were alerted to anything threatening the Kingdom by the reaction of the spell. The problem was, by the end of Queen Elspeth the Second's reign, there were not enough Herald-Mages to cover the four quarters... not and deal with enemies, too.

That was when Vanyel altered the spell, tying *all* Heralds into this "Web," so that when danger threatened, *everyone* would know. Before that, it was only chance that a ForeSeer would bend his will to a particular time and place to see that something would be a problem. After, it was *guaranteed*; ForeSeers would see the danger, and would know exactly what Gifts or actions were required to counter it. Heralds with those Gifts would find themselves in the saddle and heading for the spot whether or not they had been summoned. The Chronicles were not clear about how he had done this, only that it definitely worked, and there was a great deal of relief knowing that the Kingdom no longer depended on having four powerful Herald-Mages to act as guardians.

Vanyel had done something else at that time, though whether or not it was part of the alterations to this "Web" or not, the Chronicles were unclear. He had summoned—something. Or rather, he had summoned *things*. Having called them, he did something to them or with them, somehow gave them the job of watching for mages and alerting Herald-Mages to their presence in Valdemar.

What happened when there weren't any more Herald-Mages? she wondered. *Did they just keep watching, or what? Have they been trying to alert Heralds, or not?*

At least this accounted for something Kero had said, about why Quenten and the rest of the Skybolts' mages couldn't stay inside Valdemar. "He said it felt like there was someone watching him all the time," she'd told Elspeth. "Like there was someone just behind his shoulder, staring at him. Waking or sleeping. Said it just about drove him crazy."

That certainly made a good enough reason for Elspeth; she didn't think *she* would want to stick around anywhere that she felt eyes on her all the time.

Unless, of course, she was a truly powerful mage, one able to shield herself against just about anything. One that knew she was so much the superior of other mages that she felt totally confident in her ability to hide from the enemy.

Like Hulda, maybe? We still don't know everything she can do. We've been assuming she was just Ancar's teacher and attributing all his success to Ancar himself... But what if it's really Hulda, letting him think he's in control, while she is really the power and the mind behind his actions?

Again, that would explain a great deal, particularly Ancar's obsession with eliminating Talia, Selenay, and Elspeth.

It could be he simply hated suffering defeat at the hands of women.

But it also could be Hulda, egging him on. If he felt somehow shamed at being defeated by females, she could be playing on that shame, making him obsessive about it. After all, *she* had very little to lose. If Ancar was goaded into defeating Valdemar, she won. And if he lost, or was killed during the conflict—she would be there to inherit his kingdom and pick up the pieces. And Hulda would never repeat his mistakes...

It all made hideous sense, a good explanation of otherwise inexplicable behavior. And Elspeth didn't like the explanation one bit. Ancar as an enemy was bad enough. But the idea of an enemy like Hulda who had been plotting for decades—

It was enough to send a chill down the toughest of spines. It was more than enough to give Elspeth nightmares for three nights running.

* * *

Elspeth closed the book she'd been reading, fighting down a queasy sensation in her stomach.

She had just finished reading the passages in the Chronicles about Tylendel, Vanyel's first lover; his repudiation and his suicide. It didn't make for easy reading; it had been written, not by the Chronicler of the time, but by a non-Herald, a Healer, who had been a friend of Tylendel's mentor. Evidently the Heralds had all been affected so strongly by this incident that they were unable to write about it.

But that was not why she was fighting uneasy feelings.

Tylendel—at seventeen—had evidently been able to construct something called a "Gate" or a "Gate Spell," which enabled him to literally span distances it would take a Companion days or even weeks to cross.

Her blood ran cold at the idea, and even though the author had hinted that the mage who used this spell had to know precisely where he was going, that fact was no comfort. Hulda had been to Valdemar—and it would not be very difficult to insert other agents into Valdemar simply to learn appropriate destinations.

What if Ancar were to control this spell? What if he were able to get it past the protections? There would be no stopping him; he would be able to place agents anywhere he chose.

In fact—Hulda had been in the Palace. For years. There was probably very little she *didn't* know about the Palace.

She could place an agent in the Queen's very bedroom, if she chose, and all the guards in the world would make no difference.

That might even be how that assassin got onto the Palace grounds. She shuddered. *I think I'm going to have nightmares again...*

This had not been an easy day for reading. Elspeth was just as disturbed by the Chronicle she had completed before this one, the one describing Vanyel's last battle.

The Herald-Mage had commanded tremendous power; so tremendous that the author had made an offhand comment to the effect that he could have leveled Haven if he so chose. Granted, Haven was a smaller city then than it was now, but—the power to level a city?

It simply didn't seem possible; destruction on that kind of scale seemed absurd on the face of it. Yet for the writer, such power seemed to be taken for granted.

At first reading, she had been skeptical of such claims; Chroniclers had been known to indulge in hyperbole before this. She had assumed that the descriptions were the embroideries of a "frustrated Bard," a Chronicler's version of poetic license. But on the second reading she had discovered the signature at the end, modestly tucked away in small, neat handwriting that matched the rest of the Chronicle, but not anything else in the book.

Bard Stefen, for Herald-Chronicler Kyndri.

Now there was no reason for Stefen to have invented outrageous powers for his lifebonded. There was *every* reason for him to have been absolutely factual in his account. He was not a would-be Bard, like many of the Chroniclers; he *was* a Bard, with all the opportunity to play with words that he wanted, outside of the Chronicles. And everything else in those Chronicles had been simple, direct, without exaggeration.

So it followed that Herald Vanyel *had* that power, that ability. The ability to level a city.

And if Vanyel had commanded that kind of power, there was no reason to suppose that Ancar could not ally himself to a mage with that same power, sooner or later. There probably weren't many with that kind of ability, but if there was one with the same kind of lust for conquest that drove Ancar, the King of Hardorn would eventually find him.

Elspeth sat for a moment with her head in her hands, overwhelmed by a feeling of helplessness. How could Valdemar possibly stand against the power of a mage like that?

By finding another like him, she finally decided. *If there is one, there have to be more. And surely not all of them will find Ancar's offers attractive. And that's exactly what I'm going to have to do.*

She shook back her hair, and pushed her chair away from the book-laden table. She was a little surprised by the bulk of her scattered notes; she'd been so engrossed she hadn't noticed just how much she'd been writing down.

All right, she decided. *I've learned all I can from books. Now it's time to get out there and see how much of it applies to current reality.*

She collected her notes into a neat stack, and shoved them into a notebook. Then she rose, stretched, and picked up the books, restoring them to their proper places on the shelves. Finally, though, she had to admit to herself that she wasn't being considerate of the librarians, she was putting off the moment of departure.

She squared her shoulders, lifted her head, and walked out of the archives with a firm step—showing a confidence she did not feel.

Not that it really mattered. This was her plan, and she was, by the gods, going to see it through. And the first step on that road was to go find Skif and tell him it was time to leave; that she had everything she needed.

If nothing else, she told herself wryly, *Skif will be ready. Even if I'm not sure I am.*

Skif *was* ready; he had wisely refrained from repeating just how ready he was, but he was so visibly impatient that she decided to get on the road immediately, instead of waiting for morning. She headed back to her room at a trot, to throw her personal things into packs, while he had the Companions saddled and loaded with saddlebags. It was, after all, only a little after noon. They could conceivably make quite a bit of progress before they had to stop for the night.

From the look on his face, that was exactly what Skif intended.

She intercepted a young page and sent him around with farewell messages for everyone except her mother and Talia; those farewells she would make in person.

Mother would never forgive me if I just sent a note, she thought ruefully, as she stuffed clothing into a pack. *Not that I wouldn't mind just slipping out of here. She's bound to raise a fuss...*

Selenay still was not resigned to the situation; Elspeth was as sure of that as she was of her own name. She had been so involved in her researches that she hadn't spent much time in her mother's company, but the few times she had, she'd been treated to long, reproachful looks. Selenay hadn't said anything, but Elspeth would have been perfectly happy to avoid any chance of another motherly confrontation.

She fully intended to plead the need for a hasty departure, putting the blame on Skif and his impatience if she had to. *If I can just get this over quickly—*

Just as she thought that, someone tapped on her door. She started, her heart pounding for a moment, then winced as she forced herself to relax. She hadn't realized just how keyed up she was.

A second tap sounded a little impatient. *Don't tell me; Mother's already found out that I'm leaving!*

"Come in," she called, with a certain resignation. But to her surprise, it wasn't Selenay who answered the invitation, it was Kero.

A second surprise: the Herald-Captain was carrying a sword; Need to be precise. Not *wearing* it, but carrying it; the blade was sheathed in a brand new scabbard, with an equally new sword-belt, both of blue-gray leather. And before she had a chance to say anything, Kero thrust the sword—sheath, belt, and all—into her hands.

"Here," she said gruffly, her voice just a little hoarse, as if she was keeping back emotions of some kind. "You're going to need this. No pun intended."

Her hands left the sheath reluctantly, and it seemed to Elspeth as if she was wistful—unwillingly so—at parting with the blade.

For her part, Elspeth was so dumbfounded she felt like the village idiot, unable to think at all coherently. *I'm going to what—she's giving me— that's* Need, *it's magic, she can't mean me to have it! Why—what—*

"But—" was all she could say; anything else came out as a sputter. "But—why?"

"Why?" Kero shrugged with an indifference that was obviously feigned. "Right after you and I met, Need spoke for you. I couldn't do without her, not right then, and she hasn't said anything since, but there's never been any doubt in *my* mind that you're the one she was supposed to go to."

"Go to?" Elspeth repeated, dazedly. Now that the blade was in her hands, she felt—something. An odd feeling. A slight disorientation, as if there was someone trying such a delicate mental probe on her that it was at the very edge of her ability to sense it. It was a little like when she'd been Chosen, only not nearly as strong.

"It's something like being Chosen, I suppose," Kero said, echoing her thought. "She picks the one she wants to be passed to. Better that than just getting picked up at random, or so I'd guess, though women are the only ones that can use her. Grandmother got her from an old female merc when she left her mage-school; she gave Need to me, and now I'm giving her to you. You'd have gotten her from me in any case eventually, but since you're going out past the borders, I think it would be a good idea if you take her with you."

Suddenly, the blade seemed doubly heavy.

"You mean the sword talks to you?" Elspeth replied vaguely, trying to sort out surprise, the odd touches at the back of her mind, and just a touch of apprehension.

"Not exactly talks, no," Kero chuckled. "Though let me warn you now, she is going to try and exert a lot of pressure on you to do what *she* wants—which is to rescue women in trouble. Don't give in to her more than you have to. She'll try two things—she'll either try to take over your body, *or* she'll give you a headache like you've never had in your life. You can block it and her out; I learned to eventually, and I

106

should think with all the training you've had in the Gifts you should be able to manage just fine. After all, when I faced her down, I was only half-trained at best. Whatever you do, don't give in to her, or you'll set a bad precedent, as bad as giving a troublesome falcon its own way. She manipulated my grandmother, but I never let her manipulate me if I could help it."

Elspeth regarded the gift dubiously. "If she's that much trouble—"

"Oh, she's worth it," Kero said, with a rueful chuckle. "Especially for somebody like you or me, somebody who doesn't know beans about magic. For one thing, she'll Heal you of practically any injury, even on the battlefield in the middle of a fight. That alone is worth every bit of bother she ever gave me. But for the rest of her abilities, if you're a swordswinger, she'll protect you against magic—and I mean real protection, as good as any Adept I've ever seen. I had some encounters with some mages of Ancar's that I haven't talked about—there wasn't anything any of them threw at me that she couldn't deflect." Kero chuckled. "Gave them quite a surprise, too."

"But your grandmother was a mage," Elspeth said.

"Right. If you're a mage, she protects you, too—but she doesn't do anything for you magically."

"She takes over your body and makes you a good fighter?" Elspeth supplied.

"Right! But she doesn't do anything for a fighter in the way of fighting ability."

"I think I remember something about your grandmother being a fighter in some of the songs, only I knew you said she was a mage," Elspeth said, looking down at the blade in her hands with a touch of awe. "I never could figure out how the confusion happened. From everything I've read, becoming a mage takes up so much of your time you couldn't possibly learn to fight well."

Kero shrugged. "Yes and no. It really depends on how much you want to curtail your social life. If you want to be a celibate, you could learn to be both."

Huh. Like Vanyel...

"Anyway, Need makes you a swordmaster if you're a mage, protects you from magic if you're a fighter. And if you aren't either—"

"Like in 'Kerowyn's Ride'?" Elspeth asked, with a sly smile.

Kero groaned. "Yes, gods help me, like in that damned song. If you aren't either, she takes over and makes you both. *Her* way, though, which tends to make you almost as big a target as one of your 'Here I am, shoot me' uniforms."

Elspeth chuckled; Kero was, as usual, *not* wearing Whites. Then she sobered. "But you said I can fight the compulsion, right?"

Kero nodded. "I did it. It takes a little determination, if you don't know what you're doing, but it can be done. I had to threaten to drop the damned thing down the nearest well. And I've already told it that you'll do the same if it gives you too much trouble."

Seeing Elspeth's hesitation, she added, "If you don't want it, don't draw it—it can't force you to take it, you know. If you don't draw it, it won't have any kind of hold on you."

Elspeth wasn't entirely sure of that—not after the tentative touches in the back of her mind, but she was certain that the hold the blade had on her could be fought. If she chose to. If Kero could, so could she.

Carefully, she weighed all the factors in her mind. This was not going to be a decision to make lightly.

She'll have a hold on me—but she'll protect me from things I not only don't understand, but might not detect until it's too late. And the Healing—that's damned important. If I'm hurt, I may not be able to get to a Healer, but I won't have to if I have her.

Not such a bad trade, really. And since Elspeth had already been Chosen, perhaps the hold would be that much less. Gwena would surely help fight it; she could be very possessive when she wanted to be.

Another good reason to take the blade suddenly occurred to her. One that Kero might not have thought of. *If I* don't *find a mage—I'm a woman, and Mother's a woman. How well would this magic sword work against Ancar, I wonder?*

Given that scenario, how could she *not*, in good conscience, accept the blade?

Without hesitation, she pulled Need from her sheath.

For a moment, nothing at all happened.

Then—

Time stopped; a humming, somehow joyful, gleeful, filled the back of her head. *It* is *just like being Chosen*, she thought absently, as the blade glowed for a moment, the fire coalescing into script, runes that writhed, then settled into something she could actually read.

Woman's Need calls me, as Woman's Need made me, she read, as her eyes watered from the fiery light. *Her Need will I answer, as my Maker bade me.*

The runes writhed again—then faded, the moment she had the sense of them. The hum in the back of her mind stilled, and Time hiccupped, then resumed its stately progress.

"What the hell was that supposed to mean?" she demanded, as soon as she could speak again.

Kero shrugged. "Damned if I know," she admitted. "Only the gods know her history now. Grandmother said that's what happens when she gets into the hands she wants. But that, my dear, is the first time she's roused since I brought her inside the borders of Valdemar."

Elspeth slid the blade gingerly into her sheath.

Her. I doubt I'll ever call her "it" again…

"What happens when I take her outside Valdemar?" she asked with trepidation. There had been such a feeling of power when Need had responded to her—a feeling of controlled strength, held back, the way a mastiff would handle a newborn chick.

And I'm not sure I like feeling like a newborn chick!

"I don't know," Kero admitted. "She hasn't been outside Valdemar for a long time. Whatever happens, you're going to require her, of that much I'm certain."

"But what about you?" Elspeth was forced by her own conscience to ask. "Where does that leave you?"

Kero laughed. "The same as before; I haven't *ever* depended on her to bail me out of a tough spot. And to tell you the truth, I don't think I'm going to be seeing anything worth being protected against."

"And I am." Elspeth made that a statement.

"I'd bet on it." Kero nodded, soberly. "I'll tell you this much; while she's given me trouble in the past, she's always been worth the having. I may not have depended on her, but she's bailed me out of things I could never have gotten myself out of alone. I feel a lot better knowing you have her."

"I—" Elspeth stopped, at a loss for words. "Kero, 'thanks' just doesn't seem adequate…"

"Oh, don't thank me, thank her," Kero grinned. "She picked you, after all."

"I'm thanking you anyway." Elspeth hugged her, sword and all, then bade her a reluctant farewell. It was hard saying good-bye; a lot harder than she thought it would be. She stood with the sheathed sword in her hands for a long time after Kero was gone.

Finally Elspeth buckled the swordbelt over her tunic, and wriggled a little to settle Need's weight. Once in place, the sword felt right; most swords took some getting used to, they all weighed differently, their balance on the hip or in the hand was different.

But most swords aren't magic.

The thought was unsettling; this was the stuff of which ballads and stories were made, and although Elspeth had daydreamed herself into a heroine when she was a child, she'd given up those daydreams once she achieved her Whites.

I thought I had, anyway.

That made for another unsettling thought, though; stories all had endings—and she was beginning to feel as if the ending to this one was already written.

As if she had no choice in where she was going, or how she was going to get there; as if everyone knew what her goal was except her.

"Destiny" was one word she had always hated—and now it looked as if it was the one word that applied to her.

And she didn't like the feeling one bit.

8

DARKWIND

: *Stupid,:* said Vree, with profound disapproval.

Darkwind's stomach lurched as Vree made another swooping dive—not *quite* a stoop—skimming through the pocket valley that held the trapped *dyheli* bucks.

There were times when the gyre's viewpoint was a little—unsettling.

The gyre wheeled above the *dyheli* herd, just above the highest level of the mist, giving Darkwind the loan of his keener eyes and the advantage of wings and height. :*Stupid, stupid. We should go.:*

Not that Darkwind needed a bird, even a bondbird, to tell him that. The gentle *dyheli* huddled together in an exhausted, witless knot, too spent by panic to do anything sensible.

Through the gyre's eyes he looked for anything that might pass as a track out of the valley—and found nothing. The spring dropped from a height five times that of the *dyheli* to the valley floor, down a sheer rock face. The other two sides of the valley were just as sheer, and sandstone to boot.

Nothing short of a miracle was going to get them out of there.

Vree's right. We should go. I can't risk all of k'Sheyna for the sake of a dozen dyheli. *I made pledges, I have greater responsibilities.*

So why was he here, lying under the cover of a bush, just above the mist-choked passage out of the dead-end valley, searching through his bondbird's eyes for a way out for the tiny herd? Why was he wasting his time, leaving his section of the border unpatrolled, tearing up his insides with his own helplessness?

Because I'm stupid.

One of the bucks raised a sweat-streaked head to utter a heartbreaking cry of despair. His gut twisted a little more.

And because I can't stand to see them suffering like that. They're fellow creatures, as intelligent as we are. They looked to Dawnfire for protection and help, even if they did range outside our boundaries. They acted as her eyes and ears out here. I can't just abandon them now.

Which was, no doubt, exactly the way Dawnfire felt. There was no difference in what he was doing now, and what she wanted to do.

Except that I'm a little older, a little more experienced. But just as headstrong and stupid.

The mist—whatever it was—rose and fell with an uneasy, wavelike motion, and wherever it lapped up on the rock wall, it left brown and withered vegetation when it receded. And it took quite a bit to kill those tough little rock-plants. So the mist was deadly to the touch as well as deadly to breathe. There was no point in trying to calm the *dyheli* enough to get them to hold their breath and make a dash for freedom... they'd never survive being in the mist for as long as it would take them to blunder through.

As if to underscore that observation, the mist lapped a little higher just below his hiding place. A wisp of it eddied up, and he got a faint whiff of something that burned his mouth and throat and made his eyes water. He coughed it out as the mist ebbed again.

Poisonous and caustic. First, burns to madden them further, then the poison. They're horribly susceptible to poisons; they'd probably get fatal doses just through skin contact, through the area of the burn.

No, no hope there.

He rubbed his eyes to clear them, and sent Vree to perch in the tree over his head. Another of the *dyheli* called mournfully, and the cry cut into his heart. He knuckled his eyes again, blinking through burning eyes, but still could see no way out of the trap.

Even the spring-fed waterfall was not big enough to do more than provide a little water spray and a musical trickle down the rocks. There was no shelter for even one of the *dyheli* behind it.

I can't bear this, he decided, finally. *All I could do is shoot them and give them a painless death, or leave them, and hope that whatever this poison is, it disperses on its own—or maybe won't be able to get past the mist that the waterfall is throwing.*

Two choices, both bad, the second promising a worse death than the first. His heart smoldered with frustration and anger, and he swore and pounded his fist white on the rock-hard dirt, then wiped the blood off his skinned knuckles. *No! Dammit, it's not fair, they* depended *on Tayledras to protect them! There has to be someth—*

He looked back into the valley, at the tugging of an invisible current, a stirring in the fabrics of power, the rest of his thought forgotten.

A sudden shrilling along his nerves, an etching of ice down his backbone, that was what warned him of magic—magic that he knew, intimately, though he no longer danced to its piping—the movements of energies nearby, and working swiftly.

His fingers moved, silently, in unconscious response. He swung his head a little, trying to pinpoint the source.

There—

The mist below him stirred.

The hair on the back of his neck and arms stood on end, and he found himself on his feet on the floor of the valley before the wall of mist, with no memory of standing, much less climbing down. It didn't matter; magic coiled and sprang from a point somewhere before him, purposeful, and guided.

Striking against the mage-born wall of poison.

The mist writhed as it was attacked, stubbornly resisting. Magic, a single spell, fought the mist, trying to force it to disperse. The mist fought back with magic and protections of its own. It curdled, thickened, compacted against the sides and floor of the valley, flowing a little farther toward the *dyheli*.

The spell changed; power speared through the mist, cutting it, lancelike. A clear spot appeared, a kind of tunnel in the cloud. The mist fought again, but not as successfully this time.

Darkwind *felt* it all, felt the conflicting energies in his nerves and bones. He didn't have to watch the silent battle, he followed it accurately within himself—the spell-wielder forcing the mist away, the mist curling back into the emptying corridor, being forced away, and oozing back in again. He reached out a hand, involuntarily, to wield power that he had forsaken—

Then pulled his hand back, the conflict within him as silent and devastating as the conflict below him.

But before he could resolve his own battle, the balance of power below him shifted. The magic-wielder won; the mist parted, held firmly away from a clear tunnel down the middle of the valley, with only the thinnest of wisps seeping in.

But he could feel the strain, the pressure of the mist on the walls of that tunnel, threatening to collapse it at any moment.

It can't hold for long!

But again, before he could move, the balance shifted. The ground trembled under his feet, and for a moment he thought it was another effect of the battle of mist and magic being fought in front of his very eyes. But no—something dark loomed through the enshrouding mist, something that tossed and made the ground shake.

The *dyheli!*

Now he dared a thought, a Mindspoken call.

It didn't matter that someone or something might overhear; they had been started, or spooked, but without direction they might hesitate, fatally. :*Brothers—hooved brothers! Come, quickly, before the escape-way closes!*:

There was no answer except the shaking of the ground. But the darkness within the mist began to resolve into tossing heads and churning legs—and a moment later, the *dyheli* bucks pounded into sight, a foam of sweat dripping from their flanks, coughing as the fumes hit their lungs. And behind them—something else.

Something that ran on two legs, not four.

It collapsed, just barely within the reach of the mist. And as it collapsed, so did the tunnel of clear air.

He did not even stop to think; he simply acted.

He took a lungful of clean air and plunged into the edge of the roiling, angry mist. His eyes burned and watered, his skin was afire. He could hardly see through the tears, only enough to reach that prone figure, seize one arm, and help it to its feet.

He half-dragged, half-carried it out, aware of it only as lighter than he, and shorter, and still alive, for it tried feebly to help him. There was no telling if it was human or not; here in the borderland between k'Sheyna and the Pelagirs, that was not something to take for granted. But it had saved the *dyheli,* and that was enough to earn it, in turn, aid.

The mist reached greedily for them; he reached clear air at the edge of it; sucked in a lungful, felt his burden do the same. Both of them shuddered with racking coughs as a wisp of mist reached their throats.

He stumbled into safety at the same moment that the other collapsed completely, nearly carrying Darkwind to the ground with him.

Him?

At that moment, Darkwind realized that this was no male. And as he half-suspected, not human either.

:*Run!*: Vree screamed from overhead, with mind and voice, and Darkwind glanced behind to see the mist licking forward again, reaching for them, turning darker as if with anger.

From somewhere he found the strength to pick her up, heave her over his shoulder, and stumble away at a clumsy run.

He ran until exhaustion forced him to stop before he dropped the girl, fell on his face, or both. Vree scouted for him, as he slowed to a weary walk, muscles burning, side aching. He figured he must have run, all out, for furlongs at least; he was well out of sensing range of the evil mist, if that still existed and had not been dissipated. That was all that mattered. By the time he came to a halt, in the lee of a fallen tree, he was sweating as heavily as the *dyheli* bucks.

He knelt and eased his burden down into the grass beside the bark-stripped trunk of the tree, and didn't bother to get up. He sat right down beside her, his legs without any strength at all, propping himself against the tree with his back against the trunk.

For a long time he just sat there, his forehead against his bent knees, wrists crossed over his ankles, every muscle weak from the long run, relying on Vree to alert him if anything dangerous came along. Sweat cooled and dried, his back and scalp itched, but he was too tired to scratch them. He was only aware of his burning muscles, his aching lungs, the pain in his side.

After a while, other things began to penetrate to his consciousness as his legs stopped trembling and the pain in his side and lungs ebbed. Birds called and chattered all around; a good sign, since they would have been silent if there had been anything about to disturb them.

He began to think again, slowly. His mind, dull with fatigue, was nevertheless alert enough to encompass this much: as a nonhuman *and* an Outlander, she was not going to be welcome in k'Sheyna. She was not, as he recalled from the brief glimpse he'd had before he had to pick up and run with her, a member of any of the non-human races k'Sheyna had contact with. And unknown meant "suspect" in the danger-ridden lands beyond the borders of the Vale.

Now what am I going to do with her? he wondered, exhaustion warring with the need to make a quick decision. *I'd better take a closer look at her. We aren't inside the Vale yet. If she isn't badly hurt, maybe I can just leave her here, keep an eye on her until she comes around, then make sure she takes herself off, away from the Vale.*

He raised his head and turned his attention to his silent companion—still unconscious, he saw. As he turned her over to examine her, everything about her set off ripples of aversion.

Not only was she nonhuman, she was only-too-obviously one of the so-called "Changechildren" from the Pelagirs, creatures modified from either human or animal bases—at their own whims, frequently, if the base was human; or that of their creators if they were modified from animals. It was what the Tayledras had done with the bondbirds, and what they had done to horses on behalf of the Shin'a'in, taken to an extreme. An extreme that many Tayledras found bordering on the obscene—perhaps because of the kinds of modifications that had been done at the time of the Mage Wars. It was one thing to modify; it was quite another to force extreme changes for no good reason, be the base human or animal.

His experienced eye told him which it was; there was only so much that could be done with an animal base. You couldn't grant equal intelligence with humans to an animal, except over the course of many generations. It had taken the *hertasi* many generations to attain enough intelligence for a rare mage to appear among their ranks, and that event itself had been centuries ago. *Human base, modified to cat...*

Even unconscious, she oozed sexual attraction, which made him both doubly uneasy and pitying. That attraction—it was a common modification, based on smell and the stimulation of deep, instinctual drives in the onlooker. Whether he decided ultimately on pity or revulsion would depend on whether she'd had it done to her, or done it herself. If herself—

Already he felt a deep, smoldering anger at the idea. *I may pitch her back into the damned mist.*

Those who modified themselves for sexual attractiveness were generally doing so with intent to use themselves and their bodies as a weapon. And not an honest one, either.

On the other hand, if she'd had it done *to* her—it was likely with the intent of her master to use her as a kind of sexual pet. That was as revolting to Darkwind as the first, but it was not a revulsion centered on the girl.

For the rest, the overall impression was of a cat, or something catlike. Her hair was a dark, deep sable, and rather short, with a subtle dappled effect in the direct sunlight, like his own dyed hair-camouflage. Her face was triangular, with very little chin; her ears, pointed, with furlike tufts on the ends. Her eyebrows swept upward, her eyes were slanted upward, and when he pulled an eyelid open to see if she really *was* conscious, he was unsurprised to see that her golden-yellow eyes had slit pupils. Which were dilated in shock; her stunned condition was real.

She wore the absolute minimum for modesty; a scanty tunic of cream-colored leather, and skin-tight breeches that laced up the side, showing a long line of dark golden-brown flesh beneath. Not practical garb for woods running.

Even unconscious, she lay with a boneless grace that echoed the cat theme, and her retractile fingernails were filed to sharp points, like a cat's claws.

Whatever she had been, she was not even as human now as the Tayledras. The changes had been made to her from birth; possibly even before. In fact, in view of the extensiveness of the changes, it was increasingly unlikely that she'd done them to herself. *Unless she was born in one of the contaminated areas, the poison twisted her in this direction, and she decided to continue the shift.*

She was barefoot, but the tough soles of her feet convinced him that she had spent most of her life without wearing foot coverings. Again, not practical for woods running, which argued that she had run away from something or someone.

Then he saw the patterns of old and new bruises over much of her body, as if someone had been beating her on a regular basis. Nothing to mar the pert perfection of her face—but everywhere else, she was marked with the signs of frequent blows. The darkness of her skin had hidden it from him at first, but she was covered with the greenish-yellow of old, healing bruises, and the purple-black of fresh ones. Some of them, on her arms, were as big as the palm of his hand. He could only wonder, sickened, about the parts of her hidden under her clothing. The evidence was mounting in her favor.

She was thin—*too* thin, with bones showing starkly, as if she never had quite enough to eat.

Darkwind sat back on his heels, no longer certain what to think. The Changechild was a bundle of contradictions. If she was, as she seemed, the escaped chattel of an Adept-level mage, how was it she had commanded the power to free the *dyheli* herd? No mage would have permitted a "pet" to carry the Mage-Gift, much less learn how to use it.

But if she was an enemy, why did she bear the marks of beatings and semistarvation? And why had she freed the herd in the first place?

She represented a puzzle he did not have enough information to solve.

I have to give her the benefit of the doubt, he decided, after pondering the question for a moment. *She did save the* dyheli. *Whatever else she is, or is not, will have to wait. But I can't make a decision until I know what she is.* He thought a moment more. *I have to see that she stays safe until she wakes. I do owe her that much, at the very least—and I owe her the protection of a place to recover afterward.*

At a guess, she hadn't breathed enough of the poison to have put a healthy creature into the unconscious stupor she lingered in. But she had not been healthy, and she had depleted her resources considerably in fighting that evil mist. She was *not* Adept-level; that much was obvious. She was not even a Master; no Master would have exhausted herself in fighting the mist directly. A Master would have transmuted the mist into something else; an Adept would have broken the spell creating it and holding it there. Both would have involved very powerful and difficult spells and would have alerted every mage within two days' ride that there was another mage plying his powers. That was what Darkwind would have done—before he swore that nothing would ever induce him to wield magic energies again. Before it became too dangerous for him to draw the attentions of other Adepts to the depleted and disrupted Clan of k'Sheyna.

She had not—probably could not—either break or change the spell. She could only fight it. That meant she was Journeyman at best, and that the energy to create the tunnel of safety had come directly from her. It was what made Journeymen so hard to track; since the only disturbances in the energy-flows of mage-energies were those within themselves, they couldn't be detected unless one was very nearby. And, thank the fourfold Goddess, that was what had kept her magics from attracting anything else. Probably he had been the only creature close enough to detect her meddling.

But that was also what limited a Journeyman's abilities to affect other magic, and limited his magical "arsenal" as well. When the energy was gone, the mage was exhausted, sometimes to the point of catatonia depending on how far he wanted to push himself, and there was no more until he was rested.

That was what brought the Changechild to this pass; depleting herself, on top of her poor physical condition, then taking one whiff too many of the poison mist. She might be a long time in recovering.

But Darkwind could not, in all conscience, leave her where she was. It wasn't safe, and he could not spare anyone to protect her. And even if it was safe, she might not recover without help; he didn't know enough of Healing to tell.

He rested his chin on his knee and thought.

I need someplace and someone willing to watch her and keep her out of mischief. But I can't take her into the Vale; Father would slit her throat just for looking the way she does. I need a neutral safe-haven, temporarily—and then I need a lot of good advice.

He knew where to find the second; it was coming up with the first that was difficult.

Finally with a tentative plan in mind, he hefted her over his shoulder again—with a stern admonition to his body to *behave* in her proximity, as her sexual attraction redoubled once he was close to her.

His body was not interested in listening.

Finally, in desperation, he shielded—everything. And thought of the least arousing things he could manage—scrubbing the mews, boiling hides, and finally, cleaning his privy. That monthly ordeal of privy-scrubbing was the only thing that ever made him regret his decision to move out of the Vale…

The last worked, and with a sigh of relief, he headed off to the nearest source of aid he could think of.

:Vree!: he called.

The bondbird dove out of the branches of a nearby tree; he felt the gyre's interest at his burden, but it was purely curiosity. The Changechild—thank the stars—was of the wrong species to affect Vree.

If she'd been tervardi, *though—she'd have gotten to both of us. And I don't think Vree's as good at self-control as I am. I would truly have had a situation at that point.*

:Where?: the bondbird replied, with the inflection that meant "Where are we going?"

:The hertasi, *Vree,:* he Mindspoke back. *:The ones on the edge of k'Sheyna. This one hurt-sleeps.:*

:Good.: Vree's mind-voice was full of satisfaction; the *hertasi* liked bondbirds and always had tidbits to share with them. He could care less about Darkwind's burden; only that she was a burden, and Darkwind was hindered in his movements. *:I guard.:*

Which meant that he would stay within warning distance just ahead of Darkwind, alert at all times, instead of giving in to momentary distractions.

Unlike his bondmate…

Latrines, he thought firmly. *Cleaning out latrines.*

Nera looked up at Darkwind—it was hard for the diminutive *hertasi* to do anything other than "look up" at a human—his expressive eyes full of questions.

:*And what if she wakes?:* the lizard Mindspoke. He turned his head slightly, and the scales of the subtle diamond pattern on his forehead shifted from metallic brown to a dark gold like old bronze. Nera was the Elder of the *hertasi* enclave and an old friend; Darkwind had brought his burden—and problem—straight to Nera's doorstep. Let the mages discount the *hertasi* if they chose, or ignore them, thinking them no more than children in their understanding and suited only to servants' work. Darkwind knew better.

:*I don't think she will,:* Darkwind told him honestly. :*At least not until I'm back. I risked a probe, and she is very deeply exhausted. I expect her to sleep for a day or more.:*

Nera considered that, his eyes straying to the paddies below, where his people worked their fields of rice. The *hertasi* settlement itself was in the hillside above a marsh; carefully hollowed out "holes" shored with timbers, with walls, floors and ceilings finished with water-smoothed stone set into cement, and furnished well, if simply. The swamp was their own domain, one in which their size was not a handicap. They grew rice and bred frogs, hunted and fished there. They knew the swamp better than any of the Tayledras.

That had made it easy for Darkwind to persuade the others to include them within the bounds of the k'Sheyna territory. The marsh itself was a formidable defense, and the *hertasi* seldom required any aid. A border section guarded by a treacherous swamp full of clever *hertasi* was something even the most stubborn mage would find a practical resource.

Though they knew how to use their half-size bows and arrows perfectly well, and even the youngest were trained with their wicked little sickle-shaped daggers and fish-spears, the *hertasi* preferred, when given the choice, to let their home do their fighting for them. Enemies, for the most part, would start out chasing a helpless-looking old lizard-man, only to find themselves suddenly chest-deep and sinking in quicksand or mire.

The *hertasi* were fond of referring to these unwelcome intruders as "fertilizer."

Nera was still giving him that inquisitive look. Darkwind groaned, inwardly. There were some definite drawbacks to a friendship dating back to childhood. Old Nera could read him better than his own father.

Thank the gods for that.

The Changechild's attraction didn't work on Nera, any more than it did on Vree—but Darkwind had the feeling that the *hertasi* knew very well the effect it was having on the scout. And he was undoubtedly giving Darkwind that *look* because he assumed the attraction was affecting his thinking as well as—other things.

Darkwind sighed. *:All right,:* he said, finally. *:If she wakes and gives you trouble, she's fair game for fertilizer. Does that suit you?:*

Nera nodded, and his flexible mouth turned up at the corners in an approximation of a human smile. *:Good. I just wanted to be certain that your mind was still working as well as the rest of you.:*

Darkwind winced. Nera was so small it was easy to forget that the *hertasi* was actually older than his father, and was just as inclined to remind him of his relative youth. And *hertasi*, who only came into season once a year, enjoyed teasing their human friends about their susceptibility to their own passions.

It didn't help that this time Nera's arrow hit awfully near the mark.

:I'm still chief scout,: he reminded the lizard. *:Anything that comes out of the Pelagirs is suspect—and if it's helpless and attractive, it's that much more suspect.:*

:Excellent.: Nera bobbed his muzzle in a quick nod. *:Then give my best to the Winged Ones. Follow the blue-flag flowers; we changed the safe path since last you were here.:*

With that tacit approval, Darkwind again shifted his burden to the ground, this time laying her on a stuffed grass-mat just inside Nera's doorway. When he turned, the *hertasi* Elder had already rejoined his fellows, and was knee-deep in muddy water, weeding the rice. He might be old, but he had not lost any of his speed. That was how the *hertasi*, normally shy, managed to stay out of sight so much of the time in the Vale; they still retained the darting speed of that long-ago reptilian ancestor.

Darkwind pushed aside the bead curtain that served as a door during the day, shaded his eyes, and looked beyond the paddies for the first of the blue-flag flowers. The *hertasi* periodically changed the safe ways through the swamp, marking them with whatever flowering plants were blooming at the time, or with evergreen plants in the winter. After a moment he spotted what he was looking for, and made his way, dry-shod, along the raised paths separating the rice paddies.

Dry-shod only for the moment. When he reached the end of the cultivated fields, he pulled off his boots, meant mostly for protection against the stones and brambles of the dryland, fastened them to his belt, and substituted a pair of woven rush sandals he kept with Nera.

Rolling up the cuffs of his breeches well above his knees, he waded into the muddy water, trying not to think of what might be lurking under it. The *hertasi* assured him that the plants they rooted along the paths kept away leeches, special fish they released along the safe paths would eat any that weren't repelled by the plants, and that he himself would frighten away any poisonous water snakes, if he splashed loudly enough, but he could never quite bring himself to believe that. It was very hard to read *hertasi* even when someone knew them well, and it was all too like their sense of humor to have told him these things to try and lull him into complacency.

He could have gone around, of course, but this was the shortest way to get to the other side of the swamp, where the marsh drained off down the side of the crater-wall into the Dhorisha Plains. The swamp, barely within k'Sheyna lands, ended at the ruins he sought—and when he had apportioned out the borders, he had made sure that both were within his patrolling area.

One advantage of being in charge: I could assign myself whatever piece I wanted. Dawnfire gets the part facing on the hills that hold her friends, and I get the area that holds mine. Seems fair enough to me...

Normally he didn't have to get there by wading through the swamp. This was *not* the route he chose if he had a choice.

The water was warm, unpleasantly so, for so was the heavy, humid air. A thousand scents came to his nostrils, most of them foul; rotting plants, stale water, the odor of fish. He looked back after a while, but the *hertasi* settlement had completely vanished in waving swamp-plants that stood higher than his head. He thought he felt something slither past his leg, and shuddered, pausing a moment for whatever it was to go by.

Or bite me. Whichever comes first.

But it didn't bite him, and if there had been something there, it didn't touch him again. He waded on, watching for the telltale, pale blue of the tiny, odorless flowers on their long stems, poking up among the reeds. As long as he kept them in sight, he would be on the path the *hertasi* had built of stone and sand amid the mud of the swamp. There were always two plants, one marking each side of the path. The idea was to stop between each pair and look for the next; while the path itself twisted among the reeds and muck, it was a straight line from one pair of plants to the next. And there were false trails laid; it wasn't a good idea to break away from the set path and take what looked like a more direct route, or a drier one; the direct route generally ended in a bog, and the "dry" one *always* ended in a patch of quicksand or a sinkhole.

Once again he was sweating like a panicked *dyheli*, and that attracted other denizens of the swamp. Below the water all might be peaceful, but the *hertasi* could do nothing about the insects above. Darkwind had rubbed himself with pungent weeds to enhance his race's natural resistance to insects, but blackflies still buzzed about his eyes, and several nameless, nearly invisible fliers had already feasted on his arms by the time he reached dry land again.

There was no warning; the ruins simply began, and the marsh ended. Darkwind suspected that the marsh had once been a large lake, possibly artificial, and the ruins marked a small settlement or trading village, or even a guard post, built on its shore. If whatever cataclysm had created the Plains had *not* altered the flow of watercourses hereabouts, he would have been very surprised—and after that, it would have been logical for the lake to silt up and become a swamp. He climbed up on the stones at the edge of the swamp, slapping at persistent insects, vowing silently to take the long way around on his return.

He looked up to make sure of Vree, and found the bondbird soaring overhead, effortlessly, in the cloud-dotted sky.

Not for the first time, he wished for wings of his own.

:*And what would you do with them, little one?*: asked a humor-filled mind-voice. :*How would you hide and creep, and come unseen upon your enemies, hmm?*:

:*The same way you do, you old myth,*: he replied. :*From above.*:

:*Good answer,*: replied Treyvan, and the gryphon dove down out of the sun, to land gracefully on a toppled menhir in a thunderous flurry of backwinging, driving up the dust around him and forcing Darkwind to protect his eyes with his hand until the gryphon had alighted.

"Sssso, what brings you to our humble abode?" Treyvan asked genially, somehow managing to do what the *tervardi* could not, and force human speech from his massive beak.

"I need advice, and maybe help," Darkwind told him, feeling as small as the *hertasi* as he looked up at the perching gryphon. Those hand-claws, for instance, were half again as wide and long as his own strong hands, and their tips were sheathed in talons as sharp and black as obsidian. Treyvan jumped down from the stone, and his claws clenched and released reflexively as the gryphon changed its position before him, absentmindedly digging inch-deep furrows into the packed earth.

"Advissse we will alwayss have forrr you, featherlessss sson. Advissse you will take? That iss up to you," Treyvan smiled, gold-tinged crest raising a little in mirth. "Help we will alwaysss give if we can, wanted orrr not." Darkwind smiled, and stepped forward to grasp the leading edge of the great gryphon's folded wing, and leaned in to run a hand through the spicy-scented neck feathers, seemingly unending in their depth. "Thank you. Where is Hydona?"

"Sssearrrching for nessst-lining, I would guess." Treyvan let a trace of his pride show through, fluffing his chest feathers and raising his tailtip.

"So soon? When... when will you make the flight?"

"Sssoon, sssoon. You will be able to telllll..." Treyvan chuckled at Darkwind's blush, then half-closed his eyes, and Darkwind felt the wing-muscles under his hand relax.

It was easy—very easy—to fall under the hypnotic aura of the gryphon, a state of dreamy relaxation brought on by the feel of the soft, silky feathers, the faintly sweet scent, the deep-rumble of Treyvan's faint purr. It was the gryphon himself who broke the spell.

"You have need of usss, Darrrkwind," he reminded the scout. The muscles in the wing retensed, and he stood, wings tucked to his side under panels of feathers. "Let usss go to Hydonaaa."

He turned and paced regally on a path winding deeper into the ruins. Darkwind had to hurry to keep up with his companion's ground-eating strides.

The gryphons had arrived here, in these ruins, literally out of the sky one day, when Darkwind was seven or eight. He'd claimed these ruins—then, well within the safe boundaries of k'Sheyna territory—as his own solitary playground. There *was* magic here, a half-dozen leylines and a node, but the mages had decreed it safe; tame and unlikely to cause any problems. It was a good place to play, and imagine mysteries to be solved, monsters to conquer, magics to learn.

Watching Treyvan's switching tail, he recalled that day vividly.

He had rounded a corner, the Great Mage investigating possibly dangerous territory and about to encounter a Fearsome Monster, when he encountered a *real* one.

He had literally walked into Treyvan, who had been watching his antics with some amusement, he later learned. All *he* knew at the time was that he had turned a corner to find himself face-to-face with—

Legs. Very large legs, ending in very, very large claws. His stunned gaze had traveled upward; up the furry legs, to the transition between fur and feathers, to the feather-covered neck, to the beak.

The very, very, *very* large, sharp, and wickedly hooked beak.

The beak had opened; it seemed as large as a cave.

"Grrr," Treyvan had said.

Darkwind had turned into a small whirlwind of rapidly pumping arms and legs, heading for the safe-haven of the Vale, and certain, with the surety of a terrified eight-year-old, that he was not going to make it.

Somehow he had; somehow he escaped being pounced on and eaten whole. He had burst into the *ekele*, babbling of monsters, hundreds, thousands of them, in the ruins. Since he had never been known to lie, his mother and father had set up the alarm, and a small army of fighters and mages had descended on a very surprised—and slightly contrite—pair of gryphons.

Fortunately for all concerned, gryphons were on the list of "friendly, though we have never seen one" creatures all Tayledras learned of some time in their teens. Treyvan apologized, and explained that he and Hydona were an advance party, intending to discover if these lands were safe to live and breed in. They offered their help in guarding k'Sheyna in return for the use of the ruins as a nesting ground. The Elders had readily agreed; help as large and formidable as the gryphons was never to be disdained. A bargain was struck, and the party returned home.

But all Darkwind knew was that he was huddling in his parent's *ekele*, his knife clutched in his hand, waiting to find out if the monsters were descending on his home.

Until his parents returned: unbattered, unbloody, perfectly calm.

And when he'd demanded to know what had happened, his father had ruffled his hair, chuckled, and said, "I think you have a new friend—and he wants to apologize for frightening you."

Treyvan *had* apologized, and that had begun the happiest period of his life; when everything was magical and wondrous, and he had a pair of gryphons to play with.

He hadn't realized it at the time, but it hadn't entirely been play. Treyvan and Hydona had taught him a great deal of what he knew about scouting and fighting, playing "monster" for him as they later would for their fledglings, teaching him all about dangers he had not yet seen and how to meet them.

Now he knew, though he had not then, that they had chosen the ruins deliberately, for the magic-sources that lay below them. Magic energies were beneficial for gryphon nestlings, giving them an early source of power, for gryphons were mages, too. A different kind of mage than the Tayledras, or other humans; they were instinctive mages, "earth-mages," Hydona said; using the powers about them deftly and subtly for defense and in their mating flights, for without a specific spell, a mating would not be fertile.

That was what Treyvan had meant by "you will know;" when he and Hydona flew to mate for their second clutch, any mage nearby would know very well that a spell with sexual potency was being woven.

The last time they'd risen, he'd been fourteen, and just discovering the wonders of girls. Fortunately he had been alone, and there had been no girls within reach…

The offspring of that mating were six or seven years old now, fledged, but not flying yet, and still sub-adult.

Pretty little things, he thought to himself, with a chuckle, though the term "little" was relative. They were bigger and stronger than he was. At fourteen he'd already acquired Vree, and the appearance of the gryphlets hadn't appalled him the way it might have. Vree had looked *much* scrawnier and—well—awful, right out of the egg. Lytha and Jerven were born alive, and with a reasonable set of fluff-feathers and fur—and Treyvan hadn't let him see them until their second or third day, when their eyes were open and they didn't look quite so unfinished.

The gryphons' nest was very like an *ekele*, but on the ground, presumably to keep the flightless gryphlets from breaking their necks. The pair had created quite an impressive shelter from stone blocks, cleverly woven vegetation, and carefully fitted logs.

As Darkwind neared it, he realized that it was bigger than it had been; it wasn't until he got close enough to measure it by eye that the difference was apparent. From without it looked almost like a tent made of stone and thatch, with a roof quite thick enough to keep out any kind of weather; it looked very much as if the gryphons had dismantled and rebuilt it, keeping the same shape with an increase in size.

He glanced in the door as Treyvan turned, a look of proprietary pride on his expressive face. Obviously he was waiting for a compliment.

Inside, there were three chambers now, instead of the two Darkwind remembered; the fledglings', the adults', and a barren one, which would probably be the new nursery. The other two were basically large nests, piled deep with fragrant grasses that the pair had gathered down on the Plain, and changed periodically.

Treyvan's neck curved gracefully, and he faced his human friend eye to golden eye. "Well?" he demanded. "Whaaat do you think?"

"I think it's magnificent," Darkwind replied warmly—which was all he had time for, as the gryphlets heard and recognized his voice, and came tumbling out of their chamber in a ball of squealing fur-and-feathers. Darkwind was their favorite playmate—or play*thing*, sometimes he wasn't entirely certain which. But he'd used Treyvan and his mate the same way as a child, so turnabout only seemed fair.

Mostly they tried to be careful, but they didn't always know their own strength—and they *were* very young. Sometimes they forgot just how long and sharp their claws and beaks were.

They hit him together, Lytha high, Jerven low, and brought him down, both shrieking in the high-pitched whistles that served the gryphons for howls of laughter.

Darkwind tried not to wince, but those whistles were enough to pierce his eardrums. *I'll be glad when their voices deepen. Human children are shrill enough as it is…*

Lytha grabbed the front of his tunic in her beak and "worried" it; Jerven "gnawed" his ankle. He struggled; at least they were big enough now that *he* didn't have to watch what he did; he could fight against them in earnest and not hurt them, provided he didn't indulge in any real, killing blows. They seemed to have improved in their "playing" since the last time; he'd needed a new tunic when Jerven got through with him. Treyvan watched them maul him indulgently for a moment, then waded in, gently separating his offspring from his friend, batting at them so that they rolled into the far corners of the chamber, shrieking happily.

Darkwind *did* wince.

Treyvan whistled something at them; they bounced to their feet and bounded out the door. Darkwind still wasn't fluent in Gryphon; it was a very tonal language, and hard to master, but he thought it was probably the equivalent of "Go play, Darkwind needs to talk to Mother and Father about things that will bore you to sleep."

Treyvan shook his head, then turned, and settled himself into a graceful reclining curve, with his serrated, meat-rending bill even with Darkwind's chin, bare inches away, gazing into the human's face. "Your indulgenssss, old friend. They aaare veeeery young."

"I know," he replied, picking himself up off the floor, and dusting himself off. "I distinctly remember doing the same thing to you."

Treyvan's beak opened in a silent laugh. "Aaaah, but I wassss ssstill *thissss* ssssize, and you were much ssssmaller, yesss? The damagesss were much lessss."

"I think I'll survive them," Darkwind responded. "And I owe you both for more than just being gracious about playing 'monster' for me."

Treyvan shook his head. "Weee do not think of ssssuch," he said immediately. "Thissss issss what friendssss do."

Darkwind remained stubbornly silent for a moment. "Whether or not you think of it, I do," he said. "You two helped me cope with Mother's death; you've been a mother and father to me since. It's not something I can forget."

The memory was still painful, but he thought it was healing. It certainly wouldn't have without their help.

"Sssstill," Treyvan objected. "You are uncle to the little onesss. At consssiderable perssonal damage."

He shrugged. "To quote your own words," he replied wryly, "'that's what friends do.' I think they're well worth indulging. So, you've obviously enlarged the nest—and it's wonderful; the new chamber doesn't look tacked-on, it looks like it was built with the original. What else are you planning to do?"

"We thought, perhapsssss, a chamber for the younglingssss to play in foul weather—"

They discussed further improvements for a moment until a shadow passed over Darkwind, and he looked up at the sound of his name whistled in Gryphon.

Then once again, he had to protect his eyes, as Hydona, Treyvan's mate, landed in the clearing before the nest, driving up a stronger wind with her wings than Treyvan had.

Darkwind rose to his feet to greet her. She was larger than Treyvan, and her dusty-brown coloration was a muted copy of his golden-brown feathers. There was more gray in her markings, and less black. Her eyes were the same warm, lovely gold as Treyvan's, though, and she was just as pleased to see him as her mate had been.

She nuzzled him and gripped a shoulder gently, purring loud enough to vibrate his very bones. He buried his hands in her neck-feathers and scratched the place at the back of her neck she could never reach herself; the most intimate caress possible to a gryphon, short of mating behavior. She and Treyvan had been extraordinarily open with him, especially after the death of his mother, allowing him glimpses of their personal life that most humans were never allowed to see. They were, all in all, quite private creatures; of all the Tayledras, only Darkwind was considered an intimate friend. They had not even allowed Dawnfire, who was possibly the best of all the k'Sheyna at dealing with nonhumans, to come that close to them.

"Sssssso," Hydona sighed, after a long and luxurious scratch. "Thisss is your patrol time—it musst be busssinesss that bringsss you. And bussinesss isss ssseriousss. How can we help?"

Darkwind looked into her brilliant, deep eyes. "I want to ask advice, and maybe some favors," he said. "I seem to have acquired a problem."

Hydona's ear-tufts perked up. "*Acquired* a problem? Interesssting word choicssse. Ssssay on."

He chose a comfortable rock, as she curled up beside her mate. "Well," he began. "It happened this way…"

9

ELSPETH

Master Quenten reread the message from his old employer, Captain Kerowyn. *Herald* Captain Kerowyn, he was going to have to remember that. Not that the new title seemed to have changed her much.

"Quenten, I have a job for you, and a sizable retainer enclosed to make you go along with it. Important Personage coming your way; keep said Personage from notice if possible; official and sensitive business. Will have one escort along, but is capable of taking care of self in a fight. Personage needs either a mage-for-hire, a damn good one, or training. Or both. Use your own judgment, pass Personage on to Uncle if you have to. Thank you for your help. Write if you find a real job. Kerowyn."

He smiled at the joke; no, Kerowyn hadn't changed, even since becoming one of the white-clad targets for the Queen of Valdemar— although Quenten also had no doubts that she refused to wear the white uniform without a royal decree. Quenten thanked the courier for the message, and offered him the hospitality of the Post for his recovery-stay. It was graciously accepted, and the young man—one of King Faram's squires—offered to share gossip of the Rethwellan Court with him in return come dinner. *And people wonder how we get our information.*

The squire was an affable youngster, fresh from the hill district, with the back-country burr still strong in his speech. He made Quenten quite nostalgic for the old days with the Skybolts; a good half of them came out of the hill district facing Karse, with their tough little ponies and all their worldly goods in a saddle-pack up behind them. What they lacked in possessions, they tended to make up for in marksmanship, tracking, and a tough-minded approach to life; something Kero had called "Attitude."

He had all of that, with a veneer of gentility that told Quenten he was from one of the noble families that hung on there, after fighting their way to the local high seat and holding it by craft, guile, and sheer, stubborn resilience. His eyes went round at Quenten's pair of mage-lights over the table, though he never said a word about them. He knew how to use the eating utensils though, which was more than Kero's hill lasses and lads generally did. He'd gotten that much out of civilization.

But because he was so new to Court, he couldn't tell Quenten what the mage really wanted to know—just who and what this Personage was.

"There's two of 'em, about a day behind me, I'd reckon," the young man said around a mouthful of Quenten's favorite egg-and-cheese pie. "One man, one girl, done up all in white, with white horses. Fast, they are, the horses I mean. I say about a day 'cause I started out a week ahead, but I reckon they've made it up by now, that's how fast them horses are."

Well, "done up all in white" in connection with the note from Kero meant they were Heralds out of Valdemar, but what Heralds could possibly want with a mage was beyond him. He recalled quite vividly his encounter with Valdemar's Border-protections. He didn't think they'd be able to pay *any* mage enough to put up with that.

Still, that wasn't for him to say; maybe there was a way around it. He'd have to wait and see.

But who were these Heralds? They'd have to be important for Kero to exert herself on their behalf—and equally important for King Faram to have sent one of his own squires on ahead with Kero's message to warn him that they were coming.

He put that question to the youngster over dessert, when the squire had sipped just enough of Quenten's potent, sweet wine to be a little indiscreet.

Ehrris-wine does it every time.

The young man rolled his wide blue eyes. "Well as to that," he replied, "no one's said for sure. But the young lady, I think she must be related. I overheard her call His Majesty 'Uncle,' when the King gave me the packet and instructions just before I left. I reckon she's Daren's get, though I'd never heard of her before."

Daren's child? Quenten snorted to himself with amusement. *And a Herald of Valdemar? Not unless the twins are aging a year for every month since they've been born. But Selenay's oldest child, now that's a possibility, though I wouldn't have thought they'd let her out of the city, much less the Kingdom. Interesting. Something must be going on in that war with Hardorn that I don't know about. I'd thought it was back to staring at each other across the Border.*

He sat back in his chair while the young man rattled on, and sipped his own wine. Suddenly the stakes were not just Kero asking a favor; not with a princess riding through Rethwellan incognito, looking for mages to hire. This had all the flavor of an intrigue with the backing of the Valdemaran Crown, and it promised both danger and the possibility of rapid and high advancement. Quenten had a good many pupils that would find those prospects attractive enough to chance the protections keeping mages out. *Maybe they even found a way to cancel them. That might be why they're finally coming down here now.*

In fact—now that Quenten was Master-Class, and could be a low-level Adept if he ever bothered to take the test—it was possible that it was attractive enough to interest *him.* It might be worth trying to find a way around those "watchers," whatever they were, if they hadn't been countered already.

Court Mage of Valdemar… For a moment visions of fame and fortune danced in his head. Then he recalled *why* he wasn't a Court Mage now—the competition, the rivalry, and above all, the restrictions on what he could and could not do or say. He'd been offered the position and more than once. So had Jendar, as far as that went. Both of them had preferred to help friends to the post—friends who would tell them what was going on—and keep up casual ties with the rulers of the time. Sometimes a King preferred to go outside his Court for advice… to a mage, say, with no other (obvious) axes to grind.

He laughed at himself, then, and bent his attention to the amusing stories the young squire brought from Court. And remembered what he had once told Kero.

If I have to choose between freedom to do what's right, and a comfortable High Court position, I'll take the freedom.

She had shrugged, but her smile told him that she tacitly agreed with him. Which was probably why she was making a target of herself in Valdemar right now.

We're both fools, he thought, and chuckled. The squire, who thought the mage was chuckling at one of his jokes, glowed appreciatively.

Quenten used the same office and suite of rooms that the Captain had, back when Bolthaven was the Skybolts' winter quarters, and not a mage-school. Placed high up in a multistory tower that overlooked most of the town as well as the former fortress, he had a clear view of the main gate and the road leading to it, the exercise yard, and most of the buildings. Kero might not recognize the place at first sight anymore; the exercise yard had been planted and sodded, and turned into a garden, he'd had trees and bushes brought in and scattered about to provide shade, and most of the buildings had been refaced with brick. The barracks were a dormitory now, and looked it, with clothing drying on the sills, food or drink placed there to cool, kites flying from the rooftop, and youngsters sitting or hanging out of most of the windows. The main stable was a workshop, where anything that was likely to blow the place up could be practiced in relative safety. Only the smaller visitors' stable remained to house the few horses Bolthaven needed. While he kept the stockade, as a means of defining boundaries beyond which the students were not permitted without permission, the place didn't look like a fortress anymore, it looked like what it was: a school. And not just any school; the largest White Winds school in Rethwellan. The only one that was larger was the school Kethry had attended, in Jkatha. Her son Jendar, Quenten's teacher, had founded a school near Petras, the capital of Rethwellan, in a little town called Great Harsey, but it had never been this large.

Then again, mage-schools can be dangerous for the innocent townsfolk. Sometimes things get a little out of hand. Townsfolk can get downright touchy over the occasional earth-elemental in the scullery. Can't imagine why…

That hadn't been a problem for Quenten. The town of Bolthaven had been built around the garrison, the folk here depended on it for their custom. They'd been relieved to learn that there would still *be* custom here, and most of them had been able to turn their trades to suit young mages instead of young mercs. And, all told, an earth-elemental in the scullery did less damage—and was less of a hazard to the problematical virtue of the help—than any drunken merc bent on celebration.

The worst that ever came up from Bolthaven now was an urgent call for one of the teachers, followed by a polite bill for damages.

Quenten's desk was right beside the window; a necessity, since he spent very little time in doing paperwork—that's what he had clerks for—and a great deal of time in overseeing the pupils and classes. Some of that "overseeing" was conducted from his desk—an advantage mages had over mercenary captains. He could "look in" on virtually anything he chose, at any time, simply by exercising a little of the power that came with the rank of Master mage.

Just now he was keeping an eye on the road, in between considering the proposed theses of four would-be Journeymen. The messenger had departed early this morning; since then, he'd been waiting for the Personage. Not with impatience—a mage soon learned the futility of impatience—but with growing curiosity.

He wasn't certain what to expect, really. On rereading the note, he saw that Kero had said that he should give this girl training, something he hadn't taken a great deal of notice of the first time around. Now that was interesting—Kero herself was not a mage, but she had somehow managed to spot potential mages in the past and send them to either him or her uncle. Had she seen something in this girl?

Or was it simply something the girl herself wanted? Had she absorbed tales of what Kero's mages had done until she had convinced herself that she, too, could become a mage?

Well, that was possible, but not without the Talent for it. Unless you could See *and* manipulate the energies mages used, she could fret herself blue without getting anywhere.

Even those who followed the blood-paths had at least a little of the Talent. There were varying degrees in what mages could do, too. Not only did the strength of the Talent vary—thus dictating how much energy a mage could handle—but the kind of Talent varied—thus dictating the kind of energy he could handle. Some never became more than earth-mages and hedge-wizards, using their own life-energies to sense what was going on in the world around them, augmenting the natural attributes of plants and animals to serve them, and Healing. Not that there was anything wrong with that; Quenten himself had seen some very impressive merc work done by hedge-wizards with a firm grasp of their abilities and a determination to make the most of them.

The tiniest change at the right moment can down a king… or an army.

But he rather doubted that being told she would never be anything other than a hedge-wizard would satisfy a headstrong princess. Nor would being told she could not be any kind of a mage at all.

He was prepared for just about anything, or so he told himself; from a spoiled brat who thought a white uniform and a coronet entitled her to anything she wanted, to a naive child with no Mage-Talent whatsoever, but many dreams, to someone very like some of his older pupils—

That would be the best scenario in many ways, to have her turn out to *be* teachable; with Mage-Talent present, but unused, so that he *could* give her what she wanted, but would not have to force her to unlearn bad habits. Theoretically, the discipline required by the Heralds' mind-magic would carry over, and give her a head start over Talented youngsters who had yet to learn the value of discipline.

A flash of white on the road just below the gate alerted him, and he paused for a moment to key in his Mage-Sight. That, in particular, had improved out of all recognition since joining the Skybolts and his elevation to Master-class. If this child had any ability at all, he would be able to See it, even from the tower. *Then* he would know what to tell her if she asked for training. And he'd have some time to think about just how he was going to phrase it, be it good news, or bad.

Two dazzlingly white-clad riders on pure white horses entered the main gate and paused for a moment in the yard beyond before dismounting.

And that was when Quenten got one of the greatest shocks of his life.

Whatever he had been expecting—it wasn't what he Saw.

The ordinary young woman with the graceful white horse was—not ordinary at all. She *was* the bearer of an untrained but major Mage-Gift; one so powerful it sheathed her in a closely wrapped, sparkling aura in his Mage-Sight, that briefly touched everyone around her with exploratory fingers she was apparently unaware of. Quenten was astonished, and surprised she hadn't caused problems with it before this. *Surely* she must have Seen power-flows, energy-levels, even the nodes that he could See, but could not use. Surely she had wondered what they were, and how could she not have been tempted to try and manipulate them? Then he recalled something; these Heralds, one and all, had mind-magic and were trained in it. If they didn't know what Mage-Talent was, it could, possibly, be mistaken for something like Sight. And if she was told that this was just another way of viewing things, that she could not actually affect them, she might not have caused any trouble.

They have no idea how close they came. If she had ever been tempted to touch something...

That was not the end of the surprises. She was carrying at her side something that radiated such power that it almost eclipsed her—and only long familiarity with Kero's sword enabled him to recognize it as Need. The sword had changed, had awakened somehow, and it was totally transformed from the relatively simple blade he had dealt with. Now there was no doubt whatsoever that it was a major magical artifact—and it radiated controlled power that rivaled the Adepts he knew.

It's a good thing I never tried mucking around with it when it was like this. It probably would have swatted me like a fly.

He wondered how he could have missed it when they were riding in; it must have been like a beacon. And how the mages at Faram's Court could have missed it—

He had his answer, as it simply—stopped what it was doing. It went back to being the simple sword he had known; magical, yes, if you looked at it closely enough, but you had to look very closely and know what you were looking for.

Did it put on that show for my benefit? he wondered. Somehow that idea was a little chilling. No one he knew could detect Mage-Sight in action; it was a passive spell, not an active one.

No one *he* knew. That didn't mean it couldn't be done. That notion was even more awe-inspiring than the display of power had been. Need was old; perhaps the ancient ways of magic it was made with harbored spells he couldn't even dream of.

The creature she was riding—not a horse at all, even if it chose to appear as one—rivaled both the young woman and the sword, but in a way few would have recognized. The aura enveloping it was congruent with the creature's skin, as if controlled power was actually shining *through* the skin. Which was very much the case... Although few mages would have known it for what it was, Quenten recognized it as a Guardian Spirit of the highest order. And from the colors of its aura, it was superior even to the Ethereal Spirits he had once, very briefly, had conversation with when some of the Shin'a'in relatives came to Bolthaven for the annual horse-fair—the ones Kero's other uncle called "spirit-Kal'enedral," that served the Shin'a'in Goddess. The "veiled ones," shaman Kra'heera had called them; the unspoken implication being that only the spirit-Kal'enedral went veiled. They were to this "horse" what an eating knife is to a perfectly balanced rapier.

One blow after another, all within a heartbeat. He practically swallowed his tongue with shock and dropped his arms numbly to his sides.

For a moment, he felt like an apprentice again, faced with *his* Master, and the vision of what that Master had become after years and years of work in developing his Talent to its highest pinnacle placed before him. All that power—all that potential—and he hadn't the slightest idea what to do with it.

His mind completely froze for a moment as he stared at her. *I can't take her on!* his thoughts babbled in panic. *One slip—and she wouldn't just blow up the workshop, she could—she could—and that Guardian—and the sword—and—and—*

Only years of self-discipline, combined with more years of learning to think on his feet with the Skybolts, enabled him to get his mind working again so that he could stop reacting and start acting like a mage and a competent Master, instead of a dumbfounded apprentice.

And the first thing he did was to turn away from the window. With *her* out of his sight and Sight, he was able to take a deep breath, run his hand through his sweat-damp hair, and *think*. Quickly. He had to come up with an answer and a solution.

One thing was certain; it wasn't a question of whether she could be trained or not; she *had* to be trained. One day, she might be tempted to try to manipulate some of the energies she could sense all around her, and then—

No telling what would happen. Depends on what she touched, and how hard she pulled.

It could be even worse if she were in a desperate situation and she simply reacted instinctively, trying to save herself or others. With the thrust of fear driving her—

Gods. And the very first thing we are taught is never, ever, act in fear or anger.

She would be easy prey for anyone who saw her, and wanted to use her. There were blood-path Masters and even Adepts out there who wouldn't hesitate to lure her into their territory with promises of training, and then exploit her ruthlessly, willing or not. Anyone could be broken, and no mage had gotten to the Master level without learning the patience it took to break someone and subvert them, even if it took a year or more.

No, she had to be trained. Now the question was, by whom?

Kero said if I couldn't handle her to send her on to old Jendar, her uncle. He's an Adept; hellfires, he taught me, he ought to be able to handle anyone. He can deal with her. I don't have to.

That burden off his hands, he sighed and relaxed. Gradually the sweat of panic dried, his heart went back to its sedate pace, his muscles unknotted. The problem was solved, but he wasn't going to have to be the one to solve it. He was glad now that he'd delegated one of the teachers—a very discreet young lady, who was, bless the gods, an Herbalist-Healer earth-witch with *no* Mage-Sight worth speaking of—to greet them when they arrived, just in case he suddenly found himself with his hands full.

God only knows what I'd have been like if I'd met them at the gate. Babbling, probably. Hardly one to inspire confidence. By the time word reached him that they had arrived, he was back to being the calm, unruffled image of a school-master, completely in control of everything around him.

"Yes?" he said; the child poked his head inside, cautiously. All the apprentices were cautious when the Master was in his office. Quenten had been known to have odd things loose in the room on occasion, just to keep people from interrupting him. The legend of the constable's scorched backside was told in the dormitory even yet, and that had happened the first year the school had been founded.

"Sir, the people you expected are here. The lady's name's Elspeth, the gen'man is Skif, Elrodie says. If you're able, sir, you should come down, Elrodie says." The child looked the way he must have a few moments ago; it wasn't often an apprentice got to see the inside of the Master's office. Usually he met the youngsters on their own ground, and when he wasn't actually in the office, he kept it mage-locked, for his office also served as his secondary workroom. There were things in here no apprentice should ever get his hands on.

"I'll be right there," he said. The child vanished. He waited a few moments more to be certain his stomach had settled, then turned, and started down the stairs.

By the time he reached the ground he felt close to normal, and was able to absorb the shock of his visitors' appearance without turning a hair. Outwardly, anyway. The sword was "quiet"—but the girl and her so-called horse weren't.

So long as they don't do anything…

He turned first to greet the young lady, as her companion held back a little, diffidently, confirming his guess that she was much higher-ranked than he was. And given her strong family resemblance to King Faram, she was undoubtedly the "Elspeth" that was Heir to the Valdemar throne. She took after the dark side of the family, rather than the blond, but the resemblance was there beyond a doubt.

To all outward appearances, she was no different than any other young, well-born woman of his acquaintance. Wavy brown hair was confined in a braid that trailed down her back, though bits of it escaped to form little tendrils at her ears. Her square face was not beautiful or even conventionally pretty and doll-like—it *was* a face that was so full of character and personality that beauty would have been superfluous and mere "prettiness" eclipsed. Like Kero, she was handsome and vividly alive. Her brown eyes sparkled when she talked; her generous mouth smiled often. If he hadn't had Mage-Sight, he would have guessed that she had Mage-Talent in abundance; she had that kind of energy about her.

She'd studied her Rethwellan; that was evident from her lack of accent. "I am very glad to meet you at last," she said, when she'd been introduced. "I'm Kero's problem child, Master Quenten. She's told me a lot about *you,* and since she's a pretty rotten correspondent, I guess you're rather in the dark about me." Her smile widened. "I know what her letters are like. The last time she was with the Skybolts, there was a flood that got half the town, and all she wrote was, 'It's a little wet here, be back when I can.'"

He chuckled. "Well, she neglected to supply me with your name and she kept calling you a Personage. I expect that was for reasons of security? You *are* the Elspeth I think you are—the one with a mother named Selenay?"

Elspeth nodded, and made a face. "I'm afraid so. That was part of what I meant by being a problem child. Sorry; can't help who my parents are. Born into it. Oh, this is Skif; he's also assigned to this job."

"By which she's tactfully saying that my chief duty is to play bodyguard," Skif said, holding out his hand. Quenten released his Mage-Sight just a little, and breathed a silent sigh of relief. This young man was perfectly ordinary. No Magical Artifacts, no Adept-potential.

Except that he was also riding a Guardian Spirit. Not as exalted a Spirit as the girl's, but—

The mare turned, looked him straight in the eye, and gave him a broad and unmistakable wink.

He stifled a gasp, felt the blood drain from his face, then plastered a pleasant smile on his lips, and managed not to stammer. "Since there is only one Elspeth with a mother by *that* name that I know of—that Kero would have been so secretive about—I can understand why you are in that role," he said. "It's necessary."

"I know it is," they both said, and laughed. Quenten noted that they both had hearty, unforced laughs, the laughter of people who did not fear a joke.

Elspeth made a face, and Skif shrugged. "We know it's necessary," Skif replied for both of them. "But that doesn't mean Elspeth much likes it."

Quenten had not missed the sword calluses on her hands, and the easy way she wore her blade. She had the muscles of a practiced fighter, too, though she didn't have the toughened, hard-eyed look the female mercs had after their first year in the ranks.

He coughed politely. "Kero did, at least, tell me what brings you here, and I have to be honest with you. I wish I could help you, but I can't. None of my teachers are interested in anything *but* teaching, and none of the youngsters ready to go out as Journeymen are up to trying to cross your borders and dealing with the magical guards of that border. I assume you know about that; I couldn't pass it when Kero first took the Skybolts north, and I don't know that I could now that I'm a more practiced Master with years in the rank."

Elspeth's face fell; Skif simply looked resigned.

"What about you teaching us?" she asked—almost wistfully. "I mean, I don't suppose either of us are teachable, are we?"

Do I tell her right now? He thought about that quickly; well, it couldn't do any harm to tell her a little about her abilities right off. It might make her a little more cautious. "I'm afraid Skif isn't—but, young lady—you are potentially a *very* good mage. Your potential is so high, in fact, that I simply don't feel up to teaching you myself. And you have to be taught, there is absolutely no doubt about that."

Her face was a study in contradictory emotions; surprise warred with disappointment, elation with—was it fear? He hoped so; she would do well to fear that kind of power.

"I don't have the time," he said truthfully. "You're coming to the teaching late in your life, and as strong as you could be—well, it will require very personal teaching. One to one, in fact, with someone who will be able to deal with your mistakes. And I can't do it; it would take time away from the students I've already promised to teach. That wouldn't be fair to them. And I gather that you're under some time considerations?"

Both of them nodded, and Elspeth's "horse" snorted, as if in agreement.

Dearest gods, it's looking at me the way old Jendar used to when I wasn't up to doing a particular task and said so. Like it's telling me, "at least you know when not to be stupid."

"It wouldn't be fair to you to give you less attention than you need, especially given that."

Her shoulders sagged, and her expression turned bleak. "So I've come on a fool's errand, then?"

"Not at all," he hastened to assure her. "What I *can* and will do is send you on to my old master, Kero's uncle, Adept Jendar. He's no longer teaching in his school—he will, on occasion take on a very talented pupil like yourself. But without my directions, introduction, and safe conduct, you'd never find him. He's very reclusive."

"I don't suppose we could get him to come back with us, could we?" Skif asked hopefully. "That would solve all our problems."

Quenten shrugged. "I don't know; he's very old, but on the other hand, magic tends to preserve mages. I haven't seen him in years and he may still be just as active as he always was. He's certainly my superior in ability and knowledge, he's just as canny and hard to predict as Kero, and I won't even attempt to second-guess him. The best I can offer is, ask him yourself."

Skif looked a great deal more cheerful. "Thanks, Master Quenten, we will."

Quenten felt as if a tremendous burden had just been lifted from his shoulders. *There's nothing quite like being able to* legitimately *pass the responsibility,* he thought wryly. And, feeling a good deal more cheerful himself, he told both of them, "Even if I can't offer you the dubious benefits of my teaching, I can still offer the hospitality of the school. You *will* stay for at least the night, won't you? I'd love to hear what Kero's been up to lately. You're right, by the way," he concluded, turning with a smile for Elspeth. "She's a terrible correspondent. Her letter about you was less than half a page; the letter I'm going to give you for Jendar is going to be at least five pages long, and I don't even know you that well!"

The young woman chuckled, and gave him a wink that was the mirror image of the one Skif's spirit-horse had given him. He racked his brain for the right name for them—Comrades? No, Companions, that was it.

"I can even offer something in the way of suitable housing for your—ah—friends," he said, bowing a little in their direction. "Your 'Companions,' I believe you call them. I don't know what kind of treatment they're accustomed to at home, but I can at least arrange something civilized."

Elspeth looked surprised at that, but the Companions themselves looked gratified. Like queens in exile, who had discovered that someone, at last, was going to give them their proper due.

"We have two loose-boxes, with their own little paddock, and you can fix the latch-string on the inside, so that they can open and shut it themselves," he said, hastily, trying to look as if he had visits from Guardian Spirits all the time. "Kero always had Shin'a'in warsteeds, you know, and they needed that kind of treatment; they aren't Companions, of course, but they're a great deal more intelligent than horses."

"That's lovely," Elspeth said as he fell silent, her gratitude quite genuine. "That really is. I can't tell you how hard it is even in Valdemar to find someone who doesn't think they're just horses."

"Oh, no, my lady," he replied fervently, convinced by the lurking humor in both sets of blue eyes that the Companions found him and his reactions to them very amusing. "Oh, no—I promise you—I know only too well that they aren't horses."

:And you don't know the half of it, friend,: whispered a voice in his mind.

For a moment he wasn't certain he'd actually heard that—then the light of amusement in the nearest one's eyes convinced him that he had.

I think I should ignore that. If they wanted me to treat them like heavenly visitors, they wouldn't look like horses, would they? Or would they? Do the Heralds know what they are? If they don't—no, I don't think I'd better tell them. If the Companions want them to know, they'll know. If not—no, it would not be a good idea to go against the wishes of a Guardian Spirit, in fact, it would be a very stupid idea—

He realized that he was babbling to *himself* now, and decided to delegate the tour of the stables and school to someone else. He was going to need a chance to relax before he dealt with these two again.

Dinner, held without being under those disturbing blue eyes, was far easier. They exclaimed over his mage-lights, and over the tame little fire-elemental that kept the ham and bread warm, and melted their cheese for them if they chose. They marveled at a few of his other little luxuries, like the stoves instead of fireplaces, which kept his quarters much warmer in winter, even without the aid of more fire-elementals. He exchanged stories with them of what he knew of Kero, and Faram and Daren, from the old days with the Skybolts, and what Kero was up to now, at least, as a Herald. He actually got quite a bit of useful Court gossip from her; she knew what to look and listen for.

But he got even more from Skif, who evidently didn't miss anything.

That young man bore watching; he reminded Quenten of another one of the Shin'a'in, one he knew was trained as an assassin, who'd been one of the Skybolts' specialist instructors for a while—an instructor in techniques he *knew*, without being told, that he didn't want to know anything about.

There was a great deal more to Skif than met the eye. Quenten had the feeling that he was not only very resourceful, he could probably be quite dangerous. He also had the feeling that Skif's presence had a great deal to do with the reason why Elspeth hadn't been bothered by mages eager to use her before this.

Elspeth was, he discovered, an extremely well-spoken young lady, but in many ways she was still a girl.

She knew how she was treated inside Valdemar, and how her rank worked within that Kingdom, but had very little notion of how knowledge of her rank would affect people, for good or ill, outside it—or how they could and would exploit her, given the chance.

"You see," Skif said, after he'd explained some of the ways in which she would have to be careful around local nobility. "I told you it was complicated down here."

She made a face, and the mage-light picked up golden glints in her eyes as she turned toward her partner. "You told me a lot of things, and some of them *I* was right about."

Quenten intervened. "It's not her fault, Skif; she's always dealt with very highly ranked nobles. It's the local lordlings you have to be really careful with around here. I'd say that half of them were never born to their titles—or at least, weren't the first sons. They didn't get where they are now by being nice, and most of them want to climb a lot higher before they die. You can't even count on blood relations to be honest with you. Well, take Kero's brother, for instance. *He's* all right, but the Lady Dierna is pretty much an information-siphon for her relatives. And there are a couple of *them* that none of us trust, not even the King. Go to Lordan and within half a day every one of Dierna's relatives will know that something brought Heralds down out of Valdemar. Let Lordan know who and what you are, and I personally wouldn't vouch for your safety once you got off his lands. Ransom is too tempting a prospect."

"Huh," was Skif's only comment. He reached for another piece of smoked ham, thoughtfully. There were odd markings on his hands; old scars that looked like they might have been left by knife fights.

Interesting, Quenten thought. *A strange sort of partner for a princess.* For

Skif *was* a partner and not "just a bodyguard;" the body-language of both of them said that. *More than a partner, a lover, maybe?* That seemed likely at first—

Then again, maybe not. They were both Heralds, and the little he'd managed to pry out of Kero on the subject indicated that Heralds had an even closer brotherhood than the tightest merc company. Emotionally, sexually, whether the two were lovers didn't bear any thought after that; they were Heralds, and that was a good enough answer for Quenten.

"Even if you were left alone, they'd find a way to use your presence," he continued. "Believe me, the more you act like common folk, the better off you are." He waited for understanding to dawn, then said, patiently but forcefully, *"Get out of the white outfits."*

Skif snickered; Elspeth simply looked bewildered.

"Look, *common people* don't ride around in immaculate white outfits. The horses are bad enough, add the uniforms, and you might as well hire barkers to announce you in every little village. I'll get you some clothes before you leave; save the white stuff for when you need to impress someone. Your simple presence as someone's guest could lend weight to some quarrel they have that you know nothing about."

And I wish there was a way to dye the Companions, too, but I'm afraid the amount of magic energy they have simply by being on this plane is going to bleach them again before they get half a day down the road. That's assuming dye would take, which I wouldn't bet on.

Elspeth sighed, and finally nodded a reluctant agreement. "Damn. Being able to pull rank on someone who was being stupid would have been awfully useful. All right. You know more about the way things are around here than we do."

"That's why he's got Bolthaven as a freehold of the King," Skif put in unexpectedly. "As long as it's a freehold, none of the locals can try and bully each other by claiming he's with them." He turned to Quenten, gesturing with a piece of cheese. "Am I right?"

"Exactly," he replied, pleased with Skif's understanding. "Not that anyone who knew anything about magic would ever suspect a White Winds school of being on anyone's side. We don't do things that way."

Skif grinned crookedly. "I kind of got the impression from Kero that you folks were the closest thing there was to Heralds down here."

"Oh," he replied lightly, trying to keep away from that subject. The brotherhood of the White Winds mages wasn't something he wanted to confide to an outsider. There were things about White Winds people that weren't shared by any other mage-school, and they wanted to keep it that way. "We aren't that close."

:*I'll second that,*: whispered that voice in his mind. He started involuntarily.

"So what exactly are these 'mage-schools,' anyway?" Skif persisted, showing no notice of his momentary startlement. "I mean, some of you are real schools, and some of you seem to be philosophies, if you catch my meaning."

"We're—both," he replied, wondering who, or what, had spoken. Surely not the Companions? Surely he would have detected them "listening in" on the conversation. Wouldn't he?

"Each method of teaching *is* a philosophy," he continued, mind alert for other intrusions. "We differ in how we use our magic and how we are willing to obtain power."

How much should he tell them, and how much should he leave in Jendar's hands?

Better stick to the basics. "White Winds takes nothing without permission, and we try to do the least amount of harm we can. We also think that since Mage-Talent is an accident of birth, we have the obligation to use it for the sake of those who were never born with it." Then he grinned. "But there's no reason why a mage can't make a living at the same time, so long as he doesn't knowingly use his powers to abet repression or aid others who abuse their powers. But that's why you don't find many White Winds mages working with mercenary companies. When you're a merc, you can't guarantee that you're going to be working for the right side."

"At least we don't have to worry about that," Elspeth said. Skif simply raised an eyebrow—and Quenten had the distinct feeling that Skif was debating how much to tell *him*.

"I assume you've heard of blood-path mages?" he asked, and was surprised when Skif shook his head. "Oh. Hellfire, I guess *I* had better tell you, then. They're mages who take their power from others." He waited expectantly for them to make the connection, then added, a little impatiently, "By *killing* them. Usually painfully. And by breaking and using them, if they have the time to spare."

Elspeth's eyes widened. "That's what Ancar is doing—or at least, that's what some of the people who've escaped from Hardorn say he and his mages are doing. I didn't know there was a name for them."

Skif scowled. "So, which school teaches people to do *that?*" he asked, growling a little.

Quenten shrugged. "There are schools, but the moment anyone

finds out about them, they're destroyed. If the mages haven't scattered first, which is what usually happens. No sane ruler wants that on his soil. But to tell you the truth, that kind of magic usually isn't taught in a school, it's usually one-to-one. A blood-path mage who decides to take an apprentice just goes looking for one. They try to find people who have potential but are untrained."

"And can't tell one mage from another?" Skif asked, with a hard look at him. Quenten nodded; Skif had already seen what he was driving at.

"Sometimes; sometimes they look for someone who is impatient, who is power-hungry and ruthless. That's the kind that usually rebels eventually; has a confrontation with his master, and either dies, wins, or has a draw that both walk away from. And that is how they reproduce themselves, basically." Quenten did *not* mention what happened in the first example; he decided, all things considered, it was better to wait until Elspeth was gone.

"Now, there's one thing I have to warn you about, and it's back to the same old story of 'you aren't in Valdemar anymore.' For every rule there's an exception—and this is the one to blood-magic. There are perfectly *good* people that practice a couple of forms of magic that require a blood-sacrifice. The Shin'a'in shamans, for one. Sometimes they spill their *own* blood, just a little, because any spillage of blood releases a lot of power. And in times of a very dire problem, a shaman or Swordsworn may actually volunteer as a sacrifice, as a kind of messenger to their Goddess that things are very bad, they need help, and they are willing to give up a lot to get it."

Elspeth's eyes got very wide at that. "You're joking—"

Quenten shook his head. "I am not joking. It's very serious for them. It hasn't happened in the last three or four generations—and the last time it did, the Plains were in the middle of a drought that had dried even the springs. People and herds were dying. One of the shamans threw himself off the top of the cliffs that ring the Plains. Right down onto an altar he'd set up down there."

"And?" Skif asked.

"And the drought ended. They say that he roams the skies of the Plains as a spirit-bird now. Some even say he transformed as he fell, that he never actually hit the ground." It was Quenten's turn to shrug. "I'm not their Goddess, it's not my place to make decisions. What's better; answer every little yelp for help, or make people prove they need it?"

"I don't know," Skif admitted. Elspeth just bit her lip and looked distressed. "But I can see what you mean; we really aren't home, are we?"

"There's a lot of gray out here, and precious little black and white," Quenten replied with a hint of a smile. "The Shin'a'in aren't the only odd ones, either. There're the Hawkbrothers, what the Shin'a'in call *Tale'edras*. Nobody except the Shin'a'in shamans knows anything about them, mostly because they tend to kill anybody that ventures into their territories."

Skif scrutinized him closely for a moment. "If you're waiting for a gasp of horror, Master Quenten, you aren't going to get one. There's a reason you told us this, and it has to do with the situation not being black and white. So? Why do they kill people who walk across their little boundary lines?"

Quenten chuckled. "Caught me, didn't you? All right, there's a reason that I think is a perfectly good one—and to be honest, they will *try* and turn you back; it's only if you persist that they'll kill you. The Shin'a'in say that they are the guardians of very destructive magics, that they 'purify' a place of these magics, then move on. And that they kill persistent intruders so that those intruders can't get their hands on that magic. Seems like a good reason to me."

Skif nodded. "Any evidence to support this?"

Quenten raised an eyebrow. "Well, their territories *are* all in the Pelagirs, and there are more weird, twisted, and just plain evil things in there than you could ever imagine. And they *do* periodically vanish from a place and never come back, and once they're gone, anybody that moves in never has trouble from the oddling things again. So? Your guess is just as valid as mine. I'd believe the Shin'a'in, personally."

Skif's eyes were thoughtful, but he didn't say anything. Elspeth stifled a yawn at that moment, and looked apologetic.

"It isn't the stories, or the company, Master Quenten," she said ruefully. "It's the long ride and the wonderful meal. We started before dawn, and we got here just before sunset. That's a long day in the saddle; Skif's used to it, but I'm a lot softer, I'm afraid."

"Well, I can't blame you for that," Quenten chuckled. "The truth is, I'm not up to a day in the saddle myself, anymore. Why don't you find that bed I showed you? I was thinking of calling it a night, myself."

"Thanks," she said, and finished the last of the wine in her glass, then pushed herself away from the table. She gave Skif an opaque look but didn't say anything.

"Good night, then," Quenten supplied. "I'll see you off in the morning, unless you want to stay longer."

"No, we're going to have to cover a lot of ground and we're short on time," she replied absently, then smiled. "But thank you for the offer. Good night."

Skif looked after her for a moment after the door had closed, then turned to Quenten. "There's something else you didn't want her to hear," he said. "About those blood-path mages. What is it?"

A little startled by Skif's directness, Quenten came straight to the point. "It's about the ones who are looking for an 'apprentice'—or at least they call it that—who is untrained but powerful. The ones looking for someone who is totally naive about magic. Like your young friend there."

Skif nodded, his eyes hardening. "Go on."

"What they're looking for is the exact opposite of someone like themselves. They have two ways of operating, and both involve subversion." He paused to gather his thoughts. "The first is to corrupt the innocent."

"Not possible," Skif interjected. "Trust me on that one. If you've ever heard that Heralds are incorruptible, believe it."

Well, anyone who rides around on a Guardian Spirit probably is, no matter what people say about everyone having a price. I suppose Heralds do, too, but it's not the kind of price a blood-path mage could meet. "Well, the other is destruction. Luring the innocent into a place of power, then breaking him. Or her." Quenten gave Skif a sharp look. "And don't tell me that you can't be broken. *Anyone* can be broken. And a blood-path mage has all the knowledge, patience, and means to do so. Their places of power are usually so well guarded that it would take a small army to get in, usually at a terrible cost, and by the time they do, it's usually too late. That's if you can *find* the place because besides being protected, it will also be well-hidden."

Skif had the grace to blanch a little. "Nice little kingdom you have here."

"Oh, there aren't ever a lot of that kind, but they do exist," Quenten replied. "And that's why I'm warning you. *You* don't have the ability to see the kind of potential she carries—but I do, and so will anyone else of my rank who happens to see her. That's Master and above. And there are not only blood-path Masters, there are Adepts, trust me on that. One of *those* would be able to persuade you that he was your long-lost best friend if you weren't completely on the alert for someone like that. In fact, the truth is that unless you've got introductions like I'm going to give you, I would be *very* wary of anyone who seems friendly. The friendlier they are, the warier I'd be. There isn't a mage out here who has to go looking for pupils—they come to him. It's a matter of the way things work; power calls to power. So if someone is out looking, it usually isn't for anyone's purposes but his own. The only people as a group that you can trust without hesitation are the Shin'a'in and whoever they vouch for. Anyone else is suspect."

Skif's eyes narrowed. "And you say she looks attractive?"

Quenten nodded soberly. "I hate to send you to bed with a thought guaranteed to create nightmares, but—yes. More than attractive. To put it bluntly, my friend, you are riding out into wolf territory with a young and tender lamb at your side. And the wolves can look convincingly like sheep."

Skif licked his lips, and the look in his eyes convinced Quenten that he hadn't been wrong. This man *was* very dangerous, if he chose to be. And he had just chosen to be.

Quenten could only hope the man was dangerous enough.

1 0

DARKWIND

Vree dove down out of the sky with no warning whatsoever, coming straight out of the sun so that Darkwind didn't spot him until the last possible second, seeing only the flash of shadow crossing the ground.

"Treyvan! Look out!" he shouted, interrupting whatever it was Hydona was about to say.

Treyvan ducked and flattened his crest, and Vree skimmed right over his head, his outstretched claws just missing the quill he'd been aiming for.

Then, without faltering in the slightest, he altered his course with a single wingbeat, and shot back up toward the clouds, vanishing to the apparent size of a sparrow in a heartbeat.

That was the single bad habit Darkwind had *never* been able to break him of. The gyre was endlessly fascinated by Treyvan's crest feathers, and kept trying to snatch them whenever the gryphon wasn't careful about watching for him.

"Sorry," Darkwind said, apologetically. "I don't know what gets into him, I really don't…"

Hydona smothered a smirk. Treyvan looked up at the bird—who was now just a dot in the sky, innocently riding a thermal, as if he had never even *thought* about snatching Treyvan's feathers—and growled.

"Darrrrkwind, I do love you, but ssssome day I aaam going to *ssssswat* that birrd of yourrrsss." Hydona made an odd whistling sound, half-choked; Treyvan transferred his glare to his mate.

"Sorry," Darkwind repeated, feebly. "Ah, Hydona, you were saying?"

"Oh, that therrre ssseems no rrreassson for the Changechild to haave sssaved the *dyheli.*" Hydona's eyes still held a spark of mirth as Treyvan flattened his crest as closely to his skull as he could. "Unlessss she trrruly meant to be altrrruissstic. And I sssuppose you could not judge how powerrrful a mage ssssshee iss?"

He shook his head. "Not on the basis of a single spell. If I were an Adept trying to worm my way into a Clan, I'd probably try and make myself look as harmless as possible, actually."

"Shhheee isss Otherrr," Treyvan said, unexpectedly. Both Darkwind and his mate looked at him in surprise. "It iss the clawsss. Thossse cannot be changed from human bassse, only brrred in. Which meansss that she isss Otherrr, for the clawsss come frrrom the unhuman, and only the Othersss brrreed with them. Ssso ssshe is Otherrr, at least in parrt."

Hydona nodded, slowly. "That iss trrue. I had forrgotten that."

Darkwind bit back a curse. That would make her even harder to slip past his father if he had to. A Changechild he might accept, with difficulty—but one who was even in part of the Others, the blood-path mages of the Outlands? Not a chance.

"But if she's Other, what was she doing that close to k'Sheyna?" he asked.

Treyvan ruffled his feathers in the gryphon equivalent of a shrug. "It ssseemsss obviousss that sshe could haave many motivessss."

True. Darkwind could think of several. She could be a spy; she could still have been trying to escape a cruel master. She could even be an Adept herself, and have inflicted all those hurts on herself with the intent of lulling their suspicions. "We could," Hydona offered unexpectedly, "quesstion her for you. We arrre asss effective asss the *vrondi* at sssensssing falsssehood. It isss insstinct."

They are? That was news to him—though welcome news. Somehow the gryphons kept pulling these little surprises out of nowhere, keeping

148

him in a perpetual state of astonishment.

"That would be—damned useful," he replied honestly. "The Truth-Spell is still a *spell,* and I don't want to use it. Not this close to the border. I can't chance attracting things to the *hertasi* settlement, or to k'Sheyna, either."

"It isss insstinct with usss," Treyvan repeated, to reassure him. "Not a ssspell. Perhapsss, though, you ought to be therrre alsso. Ssshe will probably be verrry afrraid of usss."

He smiled. "Considering that you're large enough to *really* bite her head off if you wanted to, you're probably right," he said. "And that might not be a bad thing, either. If we keep her frightened, we have a better chance of catching her in a lie, don't we?"

"Yessss," Treyvan agreed. "It doesss not affect the trrruth asss we sssensse it, fearr."

"Good; I'll be with you, so that she doesn't try to run, but you two *loom* a little bit. Be the big, bad monsters, and I'll be her protector." But another thought occurred to him, then. He'd been planning on what to do to find out more about her; he still had no idea what to do *with* her.

"What do I do with her if she seems all right?" he asked. "I can't possibly take her into the Vale."

"Worrry about that when—and if—the time comesss," Treyvan said quietly. "It isss eassy to make a decission about a frrriend. I would worrrry more about how to disssposss of herrr. If ssshe isss falssse, leave herrr to usss. If you like. We can disssspatch her."

"No," he said, quickly. "No, that's my job." It made him sick to think of killing in cold blood, but it *was* his job, and he would not put the burden on someone else. *Not them, especially. There's such an—innocence—about them. I won't see it stained with a cold-blooded murder, no matter how casually they think of doing it. It would matter to me, even if it doesn't seem to matter to them.*

Treyvan shrugged. "Very well, then," he said. "Ssshall we meet you therrre?"

"Fine," he replied. And couldn't help but grin. "Even if it *does* mean another trek through the marsh. The things I do for duty!"

Treyvan just laughed, and spread his wings. "Jussst keep that birrrd frrom my crrrest. He beginsss to look tasssty!"

And as Darkwind turned to head back, he was mortally certain that the gryphon was thinking of all those quill-snatching attempts by Vree, and chuckling at the notion of dining on the poor gyre. The gryphons were very catholic in what they considered edible; just as Vree would happily dine on a kestrel, a fellow raptor, the gryphons would probably be just as willing to make a morsel of Vree.

Except that Vree was Darkwind's. That alone was saving him from becoming Treyvan's lunch—in reality, if not in thought.

:Featherhead,: he Mindspoke up to the dot in the blue. *:You have no notion how close to the cliff you've been flying.:*

:Cliff?: responded Vree, puzzled. *:What cliff? Where cliff?:*

I can't tell if he's playing coy, or he really doesn't understand me.

Darkwind sighed, and waded into the murky water. *:Never mind. Just stop teasing the gryphons. Leave Treyvan's feathers alone, you hear me?:*

:Yes,: said Vree slyly. "Yes," that he'd heard Darkwind, not that he'd obey.

Darkwind groaned. *No wonder Father doesn't listen to me. I can't even get respect from a bird.*

Nera met him at the edge of the swamp, popping up out of nowhere right into his path and scaring a year out of him. He yelped, one foot slipped off the path and into who-knew-how-deep, smelly water, and he teetered precariously for a moment before regaining his balance.

He glared at the *hertasi*, snarling silently. Nera blithely ignored the glare. *:The winged ones are here,:* he Mindspoke. *:The creature you brought is also awake.:*

And with that, he vanished again, melting back into the reeds.

Darkwind closed his eyes for a moment and tried to think charitable thoughts. *He let me leave the girl here, and he's worried because of her, the threat she represents. He was startled to see the gryphons. He's preoccupied with other things. He forgets that I'm a lot clumsier in the swamp than he is.*

He grimaced. *Sure he does. And I'm the Shin'a'in Goddess.*

Not that it mattered; nothing was going to change Nera; the *hertasi* was far too fond of playing his little games of "eccentric old creature," and insisting that if Darkwind really *tried*, he could move as well as the *hertasi* could in the swamp. He *enjoyed* watching Darkwind come out of the reeds covered in muck.

Vree, Nera, Dawnfire, the gryphons... With friends like these, why do I need to look on the border for trouble? All I need to do is sit and wait. They'll bring trouble to me.

But he did hurry his steps a little, as much as he dared without losing his footing. Nera would not have come looking for him if the *hertasi* weren't at least a little worried—truly worried—about the Changechild.

And rightly; it *was* possible the girl was an Adept; she seemed a little young for the rank, but Darkwind had just attained Adept-class when the Heartstone fractured, and he had been younger.

And it didn't follow that she was as youthful as she looked. One of the commonest changes for a blood-path Adept to make in himself was to remove years. Most of them kept their bodies looking as if they were in their mid-twenties, but some even chose to look like children.

Those were the really nasty ones for Tayledras to cope with; given the Hawkbrothers' strong reaction to children, it was easy to play on their emotions until the enemy Adept had them in exactly the position he wanted them. K'Vala had been decimated by an Adept using that ploy several hundred years ago, back when their territory was on the eastern shore of the Great Crater Sea, the one the Outlanders called "Lake Evendim" now. Their lesson was one no Tayledras could afford to ignore.

He found himself thinking of his options if she *was* an Adept, and how he might be able to trick her into revealing her abilities.

She'll have to pull power from the nearest node just to Heal herself, he thought, as he felt his way along the submerged path. *Treyvan should be able to sense that if she does; from what he told me, he's tied his magic into that node. If she's a Master, she'll draw from the ley-lines. That's going to be subtler, and harder to catch. Hmm.* If he had someone "trap" the lines, so that any interference would be noted, *she* might note it as well. What he needed was a Sensitive, someone who was so attuned to the local energy-flows that he would notice any deviation from the norm.

Wait a moment; didn't Treyvan tell me that the gryphlets are Sensitive to the power-flows in their birth area? That might work—assuming he can convince them to keep their minds on it.

He tried to think of something that would have convinced *him* to keep a constant watch for something when he was that young, and failed to come up with anything. Children were children, and generally as featherheaded as Vree.

Well, I'll mention it to the adults, and see what they say.

He emerged from the reeds to the walkways rimming the rice paddies and stopped long enough to dry his feet and put his boots back on. A quick look around showed him nothing amiss, which meant there had been no real need to hurry, only Nera's impatience.

Old coot. Just likes to see me lose my balance. And he's not happy unless he's the one in charge of everything.

He knew Nera was watching him, and he deliberately took his time.

On the hill above Nera's tunnel, two pairs of huge, waving wings told him that Treyvan and Hydona were waiting, too, but with more patience than the little *hertasi*. He picked his way across the paddies, taking time to be courteous to the farmers who bent so earnestly over their plants. One of them even stopped him to ask a few questions about one of his kin who lived in the Vale—and he could sense Nera's impatient glare even from the distant tunnel mouth.

He looked up, and sure enough, there was a shadow, just within the round entrance to the tunnel. He smiled sweetly at it and bent to answer the *hertasi's* questions, in detail and with extreme politeness. After all, he was the only Tayledras any of them saw regularly, and he *did* make a point to keep track of those Vale *hertasi* with relatives out here. They were so shy that they seldom asked him about their Vale kin, and it was only fair to give them a full answer when they did inquire.

And if Nera says anything, that's exactly what I'll tell him.

When he reached the hill and set foot on the carefully gravelled trail leading up the side, he debated on going first to Nera's tunnel, but Treyvan's Mindspoken hail decided him in favor of the gryphons instead. It seemed that his charge was not only awake, but moving.

:Featherless son, your prize waits up here. She can walk, slowly, and there is more room for us up here. She did not ask what we were and does not seem particularly frightened.:

Well, that was a little disappointing. *:She must have known about you—or else she's seen gryphons before. So much for you playing monster. I'm on my way up.:*

When he reached the top of the sun-gilded bluff, he found his charge reclining on another of the stuffed grass-mats, neatly bracketed between the two gryphons. They were also reclining in the cool, short grass, wings half-open to catch the breeze coming over the top of the hill.

His eyes went back to the Changechild as if pulled there. She seemed even more attractive awake, with sense in those slit-pupiled eyes and life in the supple muscles. He was only *too* aware of how fascinating she was; her very differences from humankind were somehow more alluring than if she'd been wholly human.

She nodded a greeting to him, then shifted her position a little, so that she could watch him and the gryphons at the same time. He noticed that she moved stiffly, as if more than her muscles were hurt.

"Sssso, your charrge iss awake," Treyvan said genially. "We have been having interesssssting conversation. Nyarrra, thisss iss Darrkwind."

She fixed him with an odd, unblinking gaze. "I remember you. You saved me," she said, finally, in a low, husky voice that had many of the qualities of a purr. "From the mist. You helped me get out when I fell."

"After you saved the *dyheli* herd," he pointed out. "It seemed appropriate—though I could not imagine why you aided them." He lifted an eyebrow. "I assume you had a reason."

"I was fleeing my own troubles when I saw them." She shrugged, gracefully. "I am what I am," she replied. "A Changechild, and not welcome among the Birdkin. When I saw the *dyheli* trapped, it came to me that it would be good to free them, and also that your folk value them. If I freed them, perhaps the door might be open for one such as I. And also," she added, looking thoughtful, "I have no love for he who trapped them."

"And who might that be?" Darkwind asked, without inflection. He could see what Treyvan had set up, even without a Mindspoken prompting; since the girl was not afraid of the gryphons, their planned positions would be reversed. *They* would be friendly, and *he* would be menacing.

A little harder to pull off, with her lounging on the ground like an adolescent male dream come to languid life, but certainly a good plan. It seemed that she was perfectly willing to believe that he would be hostile to her, even with her sexual allure turned up to full force.

"My master," she said, pouting a little at his coldness. "Mornelithe Falconsbane."

"Not a frrrriendly name," Hydona said, with a little growl.

"Not a friendly man," replied Nyara, with a toss of her head and a wince. "Not a *man* at all, anymore, for all that he is male—or at least, very little human. He has worked more changes upon his own flesh than he has upon mine."

"An Adept, then," Treyvan said with cheerful interest. "And one you did not carrre for, I take it? From yourrr hurtss, I would sssay he wasss even less kind than he wasss frriendly."

Nyara nodded, her supple lips tightened into a bitter line. "Oh, yes. I was the creature upon which he attempted his changes, and if they proved to his liking, he used them also. And he made his mistakes upon me, and often did not bother to correct them. Other things he did, too— beatings, and—"

Her eyes filled with tears and she averted her head. "I—he hurt me, once too often. That is all I would say."

"So, you ran away from him, is that it?" Darkwind interrupted the attempt to play for sympathy rudely. "How did you get away from someone as powerful as that? I don't imagine he let you simply walk away. And when you saw the *dyheli,* then what did you do?"

She blinked away the tears, and rubbed her cheeks with the back of her hand, without raising her head. "I have stolen little bits of magic-learning from time to time. I have a small power, you see. When Mornelithe was careless, I watched, I learned. I learned enough to bend the spells of lock and ward and slip free of his hold. Then I went north, where I have heard from Mornelithe's servants that there were Birdkin, that he hated." She watched him out of the corner of her eyes. "Do you think less of me, that I thought to use you? You are many, I am one. You have been the cause of some of my hurts, when *he* was angered with you and could not reach you. I thought with Birdkin between me and him, he would ignore my flight and harry the Birdkin. He might even think I was with the Birdkin, and turn his anger on them. Then I saw the horned ones, and felt his magic upon them, and thought to buy myself sanctuary, or at least safe passage, with their freedom." Her head came up, and she looked defiantly into his eyes. "You owe me safe passage, at least, Birdkin. Even though I thought to trick Mornelithe and set him on you. *You* have defeated him many times. I am but a small thing, and could not even defy him, and escaped him only with guile."

He looked sideways at Treyvan, who nodded ever so slightly. Everything she'd said was the truth, then. It was probably safe enough to give her what she asked for.

"We do owe you that and a place to rest until you can journey again," he admitted, softening his icy expression a little. He caught the glint of scales out of the corner of his eye, and Mindspoke Nera, watching her closely to see if she detected the thoughts. *:Nera, this Changechild seems friendly, and she's going to need your help; shelter for a week or two at least, maybe more. Have you got any tunnels no one is using?:*

The hertasi forgot whatever it was that had brought him, now that Darkwind had invoked his authority again. *:Hmm. Yes. The old one at the waterline that belonged to Rellan and Lorn, that flooded this spring. Again. They finally listened to me and moved out. Unless we have three or four weeks of rain, it should stay dry.:*

And it was right on the edge of the bluff, with the swamp on one side, a hillside too steep for someone in her condition to climb above, and all the *hertasi* between herself and freedom. That should do.

:Perfect,: he said.

And Nyara showed no signs of having heard the conversation.

:We will make it ready,: Nera told him, full of self-importance, and content now that he was a major part of whatever was going on. *:The creature can walk, but slowly—my Healer says that there are half-healed bones and torn muscles. Send her in a few moments and there will be a bed and food waiting.:*

"We can give you a place to stay for as long as you need it," he told her. "And I will see about getting you safe passage, once you're fit to journey again. I—don't think you can hope for sanctuary. The Elders of this Clan hate Changechildren too much."

"But you do not," she replied, her voice a caress.

"I—don't hate anyone," he said, flushing, and averting his eyes, much to Treyvan's open amusement. "But I don't determine what the Elders will say or do. At any rate, Nera and the others are moving some basic things in now, and as soon as you are ready, one of them will come show you where it is."

"I am grateful, Darkwind," she said, bowing her head a little and looking up at him from under long, thick lashes. "I am very grateful."

He felt his blood heating from that half-veiled glance, and wondered if she knew what she was promising him with it. Then he decided that she must know; sex was as much a part of her weaponry as her claws.

"Don't worry about being grateful," he said gruffly, while Treyvan hid his amusement. "Just get yourself healed up, so we can get you out of this Mornelithe's reach. The sooner you're gone, the safer we'll all be."

They removed themselves to a place farther along the bluff, well out of earshot of the *hertasi* village, before any of them said anything.

It was a golden afternoon, near enough to nightfall for things to have cooled down, sunlight as thick and sweet as honey pouring over the gold-dusted grass of the bluff, with just enough breeze to keep it from being too warm. The gryphons fanned their wings out to either side of themselves, basking, their eyes half-lidded, and beaks parted slightly. Treyvan's crest was raised as high as it could go, and his chest feathers were puffed out.

They looked extraordinarily stupid. Darkwind had to fight off gales of laughter every time he looked at them.

Vree, on his good behaviour now that both Darkwind and Treyvan were ready for his tricks, joined them on the grass. He had just taken a bath, and looked even sillier than the gryphons. Even though he was behaving, he kept eyeing the quills of Treyvan's crest with undisguised longing.

"Will the little ones be all right with you gone so long?" Darkwind asked with concern.

Hydona nodded, slowly and lazily. "The ruinsss are sssafe, temporrrarrrily. We caught the *wyrrrsssa*. They were wild, masssterless."

"What about that serpent you thought moved into the ruins this spring?" he asked. "The one I found the sign of. It's certainly large enough to make a meal of one of you, let alone Lytha or Jerven."

"It made the missstake of bassssking on the sssame ssstone alwaysss," Treyvan replied, his voice full of satisfaction. "It wasss delicioussss."

"The little onesss will be fine," Hydona assured him. "Their Mindsssspeech isss quite sssstrong now, and if they are threatened, they will call. We can be there verrrry quickly."

Having seen the gryphons flying at full speed once, he could believe that. They were even faster than Vree, and that was saying something, for Vree was faster than any wild bird he had ever seen.

"So, was she lying about anything?" Darkwind asked, as he pulled the hair away from the back of his neck to let the sun bake into his neck and shoulder muscles. "Nyara, I mean."

"No," Hydona said. "Orrr—mossstly no."

"Mostly?" Darkwind said sharply. "Just how much was she lying about?"

"The one ssshe claimed wasss her massster," Treyvan said, slowly.

"Mornelithe Falconsbane," Darkwind supplied. "Sounds to me as if he really does hate Tayledras, if he's taken a use-name like that." Most Adepts assumed use-names; the Tayledras did it simply to have a name that was more descriptive of what they were, but the blood-path Adepts did so out of fear. Names were power, though not in the sense that the foolish thought, that knowing someone's "true name" would permit you to command him. No, by knowing the real name, the birth-name, of someone, you could discover everything there was to know about him, if you were thorough and patient enough—you could even see every moment of his past life, if you knew the spell to see into the past. And by knowing that about him, you knew his strengths and weaknesses. And most importantly, you could learn the fears that were the strongest because they were rooted in childhood. It was characteristic of blood-path Adepts that they had many, many weaknesses, for they generally had never faced what they were and conquered those old fears. There had been cases of mere Journeymen besting Adepts, sometimes even by illusions, simply by knowing what those fears were, and playing to them.

But blood-path mage or any other kind, the use-name told the world something about what the mage was *now*. A name like "Mornelithe

Falconsbane" did not call up easy feelings within a Tayledras.

"I do not like that name, Darrrkwind," Hydona said uneasily. "It does not sssit well in my mind."

"Nor mine, either," Darkwind admitted. "I don't imagine he cares much for anything with wings and feathers. *Mornelithe*, now, that's Old Tayledras; it's actually Kaled'a'in, the language we and the Shin'a'in had when we were the same people—"

"Yesss," Treyvan said, interrupting him. "We ssspeak Kaled'a'in. Fluently."

"You do?" he replied, surprised again. *That's something to go into with them later. In detail. Where on earth did they ever learn Kaled'a'in? I thought it was a dead language.* "Well, I knew what it was, but what's it mean?"

"Hatrrred-that-returnsss," Treyvan said solemnly. "A name that sspeaksss of return over the agesss, not once, but many timesss. It isss not rebirrth, it isss actual returrn, and return looking for rrrevenge. It isss an evil word, Darrrkwind. Asss evil as you find 'Falconsssbane' to be."

The words hung heavy and ill-omened between them, silencing all three of them for a moment, and bringing a chill to the air.

"Typical blood-path intimidation," Darkwind said in disgust, attempting to make light of it and dispel the gloom. "Trying to frighten people with a portentous name and a fancy costume. Frankly, *I'd* like to know where they're finding people willing to make clothing like that, those ridiculous cloaks and headdresses. They look as if they were designed by an apprentice to traveling players with delusions of grandeur. Half the time they can't even walk or see properly in those outfits."

Treyvan laughed. "Oh? And who isss it hasss an entire collection of Ravenwing'sss feather masssksss on hisss wallsss?"

"That's different," he replied, defending himself. "That's art. Back to the subject; what was it Nyara lied about in connection with her master? Wasn't he her master after all?"

"Oh he wasss her massster, yesss. But he wasss more. Sssomething more—intimate." Treyvan shook his head and looked over at his mate, who nodded.

"Yesss," said Hydona. "But not intimate, asss in loversss. There isss no love there. It wasss something elsssse."

Darkwind tried to puzzle that one out, then gave it up. "I'll think about that for a while; maybe the connection will come to me. She *did* escape, though, right?"

"Oh, yesss," Hydona replied emphatically. "Yesss, sshe did esscape, and wass purssued. I would ssay that her sstory isss trrrue—all of it that ssshe told usss, that isss."

"I wish I'd been able to ask her more questions," he said, chewing at his lower lip as he thought. "I wish I'd been able to *think* of more questions."

"It ssseemss clear enough," Treyvan said lazily, stretching his forelegs out into the sun a little more. "Ssshe isss exactly what sshe ssseemsss."

"A Changechild, used to try out the changes her master wanted to perform on his own body—used as a sex toy when he wished."

"Yesss," Hydona nodded. "And usssed alssso to rrraissse and hold powerrr for him. You did not ssssee that upon herrr?"

He looked up at the sky in exasperation. "Of course! I missed that aspect completely! I could not imagine why Falconsbane would allow her to keep her Mage-Gift intact, when an Adept should be able to block it or render it useless by burning the channels. But if she didn't have enough to challenge him—but *did* have enough to carry power—"

"Ssshe would make the perrrfect vesssel," Treyvan concluded.

"Exactly," Hydona replied. "He could ussse herrr to carrrry powerrr from hisss sacrificesss; he could generrrate powerrr *frrrom* herrr by hurrrting herrr."

"And best of all," Darkwind concluded grimly, "he could exhaust *her* power without touching his own. That made it possible for him to work spells that don't disturb the energy-flows around here at all, because it's all internal power. *That* is how he's been doing things without my sensing them!"

"Sssensing them?" Treyvan opened one eye. "I thought you had given up yourrr mage-sssskillsss."

"I have," he replied firmly. "But I can still sense the power flows and the disturbances when someone tampers with them. As long as I'm not inside the Vale, that is."

"That Heartsssstone isss a problem, Darrrkwind," Treyvan said, unexpectedly. "It isss distorting everrrything in the area of the Vale, asss if it were a thick, warped pane of glasss. And when thingsss come into thiss area, like the ssserpent, it isss attracting them. I am ssssurprisssed that no one in therre hasss noticed the problemsss."

Darkwind shook his head, compressing his lips tightly.

"If I say what I'd like to—well, that's Vale business, and the Elders' business, and you—"

"Are Outsssssidersss," Treyvan replied, rolling his eye in exasperation. "And if your father dissscovered you had been ssspeaking of Vale busssinesss to Outsssiderssss, what then? Would he cast you out? It might be worth it, Darrkwind. Thisss isss involving more than jussst k'Sssheyna. The broken Heartsssstone beginsss to affect the area outssside the Vale."

"No." He shook his head emphatically. "I have a duty to my Clan, and to what the Tayledras are supposed to be. I guess—" he thought for a moment, "I suppose I'm just waiting for the moment that they all bury themselves, and I can find out where k'Vala or k'Treyva are now, and I can go get some help."

"May that be ssssoon," Hydona sighed.

"Too true." He eyed the sun and stood up, then hesitated a moment. "You know my personal reasons for giving up magic—and—well, I wouldn't admit it to anyone but you, but—I'm beginning to think that may have been, well, a little short-sighted."

Treyvan tilted his head. "I will not ssay that I told you the ssame."

"I know you did. But now," he frowned, "if the Heartstone is attracting uncanny things, it is probably a good idea not to rescind that vow. Look what happened to the one mage who *tried* casting spells outside the Vale."

"A good point," Treyvan acknowledged. "But you ssstill show Adept-potential, do you not? Would that not attract creaturesss asss well ass sspellcasssting?" He tilted his head the other way. "A dissstinct liability to a ssscout, I would sssay."

He flushed. "Treyvan, I'm not stupid. I thought of that. I swore I wouldn't spellcast. I *never* swore I wouldn't keep my shields."

Treyvan laughed aloud. "Good. You are asss canny as I could wish, flightless ssson."

He had to laugh, himself. "Well, Nera has things well in hand for now, you have youngsters to get back to, and I—I guess I'd better finish out my patrol, tell Dawnfire the good news if she doesn't know already, and figure out how best to phrase Nyara's request to the Elders."

Treyvan chuckled. "Ssshe won't be moving far or fasst for a few dayss, if I'm any judge of human ssshapesss. You'll have ssome time to think."

Darkwind sighed. "I hope so," he replied. "It isn't going to be easy. Starblade is *not* going to like this."

11

ELSPETH

Skif peered through the foggy gloom of near-dawn, wishing he had eyes like a cat. He watched for possible trouble, as Elspeth stood—literally—on her saddle, trying to read the signpost in the middle of the crossroads. Gwena stood like a stone statue; a distinct improvement over a horse in a similar situation.

Before they had left Bolthaven, Elspeth had taken Quenten's advice quite literally—and very much to heart. For one thing, she'd consulted with him about disguises, in lieu of being able to ask Kerowyn. Now they wore something more in the line of what a pair of prosperous mercenaries would wear. "Mercs would be best," Quenten had decided, after a long discussion, and taking into consideration the fact that no amount of dye would stain the Companion's coats. "Tell people who ask you've been bodyguards for a rich merchant's daughter, and that's where you got the matched horses. If you say you're mercs, no one will bother you, and you can wear your armor and weapons openly. Just put a coat of paint on those shields, or get a cover for them."

They'd given him carte blanche, and a heavy pouch of coin. He'd grinned when Skif lifted an eyebrow over the selection of silks and fine leathers Quenten's agent brought back from the Bolthaven market, clothing that was loose and comfortable, and so did not need to be tailored to them to look elegant.

"We want you two to look prosperous," he'd said. "First of all, only a prosperous merc would be able to afford horses like yours, even if you did get them in the line of duty. And secondly, a prosperous merc is a *good* fighter. No bandit is ever going to want to bother a mercenary who looks as well-off as you will. The *last* place a merc puts his money is in his wardrobe. If you can afford this, *you're* not worrying about needing cash for other things."

"But the jewelry," Skif had protested. "You've turned most of our ready cash into jewelry!"

"A free-lance merc wears his fortune," Quenten told him. "If you need to buy something, and you don't want to spend any of those outland gold coins because it might draw attention to you, break off a couple of links of those necklaces, take a plate from the belt, hand over a ring or a bracelet. That's the way a merc operates, and no one is going to turn a hair. Very few mercs bother with keeping money with a money-changing house, because it won't be readily accessible. In fact, only about half of even bonded mercs have a running account with the Mercenary's Guild, for the same reason. Where you're going, every merchant and most good inns have scales to weigh the gold and silver, and they'll give you a fair exchange for it."

Skif thought about what he said, then sent Quenten's agent back to the bazaar to exchange the rest of their Valdemaren and Rethwellan gold and silver for jewelry. He had to admit that the ornaments he got in exchange, a mixture of brand new and worn with use, were a great deal less traceable than the Valdemaren coin. He felt like a walking target—his old thief instincts acting up again—but he knew very well that when *he* was a thief, he'd never, ever have tackled *two* wealthy fighters, especially when they walked with their hands on their hilts and never drank more than one flagon of wine at a sitting. Quenten had been right; a wealthy, cautious fighter was someone that tended not to attract trouble. Still, he'd complained to Elspeth their first night on the road that he felt like a cheap tavern dancer, with his necklaces making more noise than his chain-mail.

Elspeth had giggled, saying *she* felt like a North-province bride, with all her dowry around her neck, but she had no objections to following Quenten's advice.

He still resented that, a little. He'd made a similar suggestion—though he had suggested they dress as a pair of landed hill-folk rather than mercs—and she had dismissed the notion out of hand. But when *Quenten* told them to disguise themselves, she had agreed immediately.

Maybe it was simply that he'd suggested plain, unglamorous hill-folk, and Quenten had suggested the opposite. Skif had the feeling she was beginning to enjoy this; she was picking up the kind of swaggering walk the other well-off mercs they met had adopted, and she had taken to binding up her hair with bright bands of silk, and some of the strands of garnet and amethyst beads Quenten had bought. There were eye-catching silk scarves trailing from the hilt of Need, and binding the helm at her saddlebow. She looked like a barbarian. And he got the distinct impression she *liked* looking that way. Her eyes sparkled the moment they crossed into a town and found a tavern, and she began grinning when other mercs sought them out to exchange stories and news. One night she'd even taken up with another prosperous female free-lance, Selina Ironthroat, and had made the rounds of every tavern in town.

:The gods only know what they did. I don't even want to think about it. At least she came back sober, even if she was giggling like a maniac. If half the stories those other mercs told me about Selina are true, her mother would never forgive me.

Not only that, she took the inevitable attempts at assignations with a cheerful good humor that amazed him.

He'd expected her to explode with anger the first time it happened. She had been the center of a gossiping clutch of Guild mercs, but as the evening wore on, one by one, they'd drifted off, leaving her alone for a moment. That was when a merc with almost as much gold around his neck as she wore had tried to get her to go off with him—and presumably into his bed. He readied himself for a brawl. Then she'd shocked the blazes out of him. She'd *laughed*, but not in a way that would make the man feel she was laughing *at* him, and said, in a good approximation of Rethwellan hill-country dialect, "Oh, now that is a truly tempting offer, 'tis in very deed, but I misdoubt ye want to make me partner there feel I've left 'im alone."

She'd nodded at Skif, who simply gave the merc The Look. *Don't mess with my partner.* And turned back to his beer, with one cautious eye on the proceedings.

"He gets right testy when he thinks he's gonna be alone, truly he does," she continued, a friendly grin on her face, her eyes shining as she got into her part. "Ye see, his last partner left 'im all by 'imself one night, and some sorry son of a sow snuck up on 'im when he wasn't payin' attention, an' hit 'im with a bottle." Her face went thoughtful for a moment. "'Twas sad, that. 'E not only took it out on 'is partner, gods grant th' puir man heals up quick, 'e took it out on th' lads as took the puir fellow off. He hates havin' no one to watch 'is back, he truly do."

The other merc looked at Skif, who glowered back; gulped, and allowed as how he, too, hated having no one to guard his back.

"Then let's buy you a drink, lad!" she'd exclaimed, slapping him so hard on the back that he'd staggered. "When times be prosperous, 'tis only right t' share 'em. No hard feelin's among mercs, eh? Now, where are ye bound for?"

Oh, yes, indeed, she *looked*, and acted, the part; a far cry from the competent but quiet princess of Valdemar, who never had seen the inside of a common tavern in her life.

As he waited for her to decipher the sign, he wondered, as he had wondered several times before this, if she wasn't enjoying it a bit too much.

She dropped down into her saddle by the simple expedient of *doing* just that, her feet slipping down along the sides as she fell straight down—and he winced. That was one of Kero's favorite tricks, and it *always* made men wince.

"We're on the right road if we go straight ahead," she said. "That's 'Dark Wing Road,' and we don't want it; it's going into the Pelagiris Forest in a couple of leagues, and it doesn't come out until it hits the edge of the Dhorisha Plains. No towns, no inns, no nothing. We want this one; it's still the Pelagiris Road, and in a while it'll meet the High Spur Road, and *that* takes us to Lythecare."

On the map, this "Dark Wing Road" had looked to be a very minor track, but it was just as well-maintained in reality as the High Spur Road they expected to take. Of course, now that she'd pointed out what it was, it was obvious that it went in the wrong direction, but with all this dark mist confusing his senses—"I'm all turned around in this fog," he complained.

"That's what you get for being a city boy," she replied, ridiculously cheerful for such an unholy hour. "Get you off of the streets, and you can't find your way around." She sent Gwena to join him, then took the lead. His Companion followed after with no prompting on his part, the fog muffling the sounds of hooves and the jingle of harness.

His nose was cold, and the fog had an odd, metallic taste and smell to it. He hated getting up this early at the best of times; the fog made it that much worse.

"You're just as much city-bred as me," he countered, resentfully, a harder edge to his voice than he had intended. "Since when did you get to be such an expert on wilderness travel?"

She swiveled quickly and peered back at him, hardly more than a dark shape in the enshrouding fog. "What's wrong with you?" she asked, astonishment and a certain amount of edge in her voice as well.

"Nothing," he said quickly—then, with more truth—"Well, not much. I hate mornings; I hate fog. And there's something that's been bothering me—you're different. It's as if you're turning into Kero."

Or even Selina Ironthroat.

"So what if I am?" she countered. "Who would you rather have next to you in trouble—Kero, or mousy little princess Elspeth, who would have let *you* try and figure out where we were going and what we were doing? What's wrong with turning into Kero? That's assuming that I *am;* I happen to think you're wrong about that."

Now it was his turn to be surprised. He'd never heard her refer to herself as a "mousy little princess" before. And while she had sometimes railed *about* things to him, she'd never turned on him before. "Uh—" he replied, cleverly.

"Or is it just that I won't let you take care of me? Is that the problem?" He heard the annoyance in her voice that meant she was scowling. "You've been sulking since we left Bolthaven, and I'm getting damned tired of it. As long as I let *you* make all the decisions, everything was fine—but this is *my* trip, and I'm the one with the authority, and you know it. I pull my own weight, Skif. I was perfectly capable of doing this trip by myself, in fact, I was ready to. I admit I didn't think about disguises—and you *were* right about that idea. But the fact is, if I'd been able to go on my own, I was intending to travel by night and hide by day. And if anyone saw me, I was going to pretend I was a ghost-rider and scare the blazes out of him."

"It's not that you're making the decisions. It's just the changes in you. You're so—hearty," he said feebly. "You're kind of loud, actually. Everybody notices us, wherever we go. I thought the point was to keep from drawing attention to ourselves."

She snorted, and it wasn't ladylike. "You think these costumes *aren't* going to draw attention to us? Come on, Skif, we're walking advertisements for the life of the merc! Sure, I'm loud. That's what a woman like Berta *would* be. Like Selina Ironthroat. I spent that night studying her, I'll have you know. I'm competing for men's money in a man's world, and I'm doing damn well at it, and the more I advertise that fact, the more jobs I'll be offered. In fact, I've *been* offered jobs, quite a few of them; I turned them down, saying we were going off to take another job with a caravan we were picking up at Kata'shin'a'in."

"Oh," he replied, feeling overwhelmed. Admittedly, he hadn't thought much about the part he was supposedly playing. Certainly not the way she had. She had everything; motives, background, character— even an imaginary job that would give them an excuse to turn down any other offers.

"Don't *cosset* me, Skif," she said, her voice roughened with anger. "I'm sick to death of being cosseted. Kero wouldn't, and you know it. This is exactly the kind of job she'd love. She'd be right beside me, slapping those drunks on the back—and if she had to, I bet she'd be hauling them off to bed with her, too."

"*Elspeth!*" he yelped, before he thought.

"There!" she said triumphantly. "You see? What's the matter, don't you think I know about the simple facts of a man and a woman? An *ordinary* man and woman, not Heralds, the kind of people who are driven by the needs of the moment? Just what, exactly, are you trying to protect me from? The idea that drunk strangers grab each other and hop into strange beds and proceed to form—"

He tried, but he couldn't help himself. He emitted an inarticulate moan.

"—each other's tails off?" she finished, right over the top of him. "And I deliberately didn't use any of the ten or so rude words I know for the act, just to avoid bruising your delicate sensibilities. I can swear with the worst of the mercs if I have to, and I know hundreds of filthy jokes, and furthermore, I know exactly what they mean! I've spent lots of time with Kero's Skybolts, and they treated me just like one of them. Skif, I *grew up.* I'm not the little sister that you used to leave candy for. *And I don't need you to shelter me from what I already know!*" A pause, during which he tried to think of something to say. "Stop treating me like a child, Skif. I'm not a little girl anymore. I haven't been for a long time."

And that's the problem, he thought, unhappily. She *wasn't* a little girl anymore, and he wasn't sure how to act around her. It wasn't that competence in women bothered him—he loved Talia dearly, and he looked up to Kero as to his very own Captain, for she was one of the few at Court to whom his background meant nothing in particular. It was seeing that confidence in *Elspeth* that bothered him. He couldn't help but think that it wasn't confidence, it was a foolish overconfidence, the headiness of freedom.

The warnings Quenten had given him had made him wary to the point of paranoia. Every time someone approached her, he kept examining them for some sign that they weren't what they seemed, that they were really blood-path mages stalking her, like a cat stalking a baby rabbit.

:She just doesn't understand,: he confided to his Companion, thinking that she, at least, would sympathize. *:There're all those mages out there Quenten warned us about. She doesn't even think about them, she doesn't watch for them, and she's not trying to hide from them.:*

:But you warned her about everything Quenten said,: Cymry said, answering his thought. *:You told her everything you knew. She may be right about hiding in plain sight, you know. Why would a mage look for someone like her to have Mage-Gift? Everyone knows mages can't be fighters. Besides, don't you think she's as capable as you are of telling if someone is stalking her?:*

:Yes, but—:

:In fact,: she continued, thoughtfully, *:it's entirely possible that she would know sooner than you. She does have mage abilities, even if they aren't trained. Quenten said that power calls to power, and she's keeping a watch on the thoughts*

of everyone around her. Don't you think she'd know another mage if one came that close to her?:

:Yes, but——: He lapsed into silence. Because that wasn't all, or even most, of what was bothering him.

She'd grown up, all right. She was no longer anything he could think of as a "girl." And whether it was the new attitude, or the new clothing, or both—he couldn't help noticing just how much she had grown up. Certainly the new clothing, far more flamboyant than anything she wore at home, enhanced that perception. It seemed almost as if she had taken on a new life with the new persona.

Maybe it was also, at least in part, the fact that no one was *watching* them together. There was no one to start rumors, no one to warn him that she was not exactly an appropriate partner for an ex-thief; no one to wink and nod whenever he walked by with her, no one to ask, with arch significance, how she was doing lately. The friends had been as annoying as the opponents.

But now both were gone, far out of distance of any gossip. And he was free to look at her as "Elspeth" instead of The Heir To The Throne.

And he was discovering how much he liked what he saw. She was handsome in the same vibrant way Kero was—*and, admit it,* he thought to himself, *you're more than half in love with Kero.* Clever, witty, with a ready laugh that more than made up for her whiplash temper. Oh, she was a handful, but a handful he wouldn't mind having by his side...

Dear gods. A sudden realization made him blush so hotly he was very glad that the fog was still thick enough to hide it. It wasn't outraged sensibilities that made him yelp at the idea of her entertaining one of those mercs in bed—it was jealousy. The very last emotion he'd ever have anticipated entertaining, especially over Elspeth.

He didn't *want* her running off with someone else, he wanted her to run off with *him.*

He must have been giving an ample demonstration of his jealousy over the past few days; surely she had guessed long before he had.

But now that he thought about it, she didn't seem to notice anything except his increasing protectiveness—"mother-henning," she called it. This wasn't the first time she'd complained about it.

But it was the first time she had done so at the top of her lungs. She might not have noticed his attraction, but she had certainly noticed the side effects.

I guess she's really mad, he thought guiltily. And cleared his throat, hoping to restart the conversation, and get it turned back onto friendlier ground.

She didn't say anything, but she didn't turn around and snap at him, either. The growing light of dawn filtered through the fog, enveloping them both in a glowing, pearly haze—and it was a good thing they *were* both wearing their barbaric merc outfits; the Companions just faded into the general glow, and if they'd been wearing Whites, they'd have lost each other in a heartbeat. This kind of mist fuddled directions and the apparent location of sound, too. He peered at her fog-enshrouded shape up ahead of him; it looked uncannily as if she was bestriding a wisp of fog itself.

Try something noncommittal. Ask something harmless. "Did Quenten say why Adept Jendar is living in Lythecare, when the school he founded is all the way back up near Petras in Rethwellan?" he asked, trying to sound humble.

"Don't try to sound humble, Skif," she replied waspishly. "It doesn't suit you." Then she relented and unbent a little; he thought perhaps she turned again to make certain he was still following, and hadn't halted his Companion in a fit of pique. "Sorry. That wasn't called for. Ah—he did tell me some. Jendar wants to be down here in Jkatha so he's somewhere nearer his Shin'a'in relatives, but he doesn't want to be in Kata'shin'a'in, because it's really just a trade-city, and it practically dries up and blows away in the fall and winter."

"What did he mean by that?" Skif asked, puzzled. "I should think a trade-city would have anything he'd want."

She paused. "Let me see if I can do a good imitation of Quenten imitating Jendar."

Her voice shifted to that of a powerful old man's, with none of the querulousness Skif expected.

"'I want fabulous food! Carpets! Hot bathhouses and decent shops! Beautiful women to make a fool of me in my old age! Servants to pamper me outrageously, and merchants to suck up to me when I'm in the mood to buy something!'"

Skif chuckled; Elspeth did an excellent imitation when she was in a good mood—and from the sound of it, she had shaken her foul humor. *I have the feeling I'm going to like Kero's uncle as much as I do her.*

"I think I'm going to like the old man," she said, echoing his thought. "Quenten also said that there were two reasons Jendar didn't retire in Great Harsey, even though the school and the village begged him to. The first was that Great Harsey is a real backwater, too far for a man his age to travel to get to Petras, even if it is less than a day's ride away. The other is that he said that if he stayed, the new head would never *be* a head, he'd always be 'consulting' with Jendar and never making any decisions for himself. He thought that would be a pretty stupid arrangement." Her voice shifted again. "'Let the youngster make his own mistakes, the way I did. *You* certainly haven't been hanging on my coattails, Quenten, and you're doing just fine.'"

She paused again, and said, significantly, "Jendar obviously believes in letting people *grow up.*"

"I get the point," Skif muttered. "I get the point."

It wasn't far now to the turnoff, but Elspeth was beginning to wonder if she'd make it that far. And she wondered also what happened to a Herald who murdered his Companion... Once in a while, she wished there was such a thing as repudiation by the *Herald,* and this was one of those times. The summer heat was bad down here; it was worse, without trees to give some shade. The Pelagiris Forest lay somewhere to their right, but there wasn't a sign of it along this road way, except for the occasional faint, fugitive hint of pine.

:Well, you're certainly smug today,: Elspeth finally said to Gwena, when, for the fourth time, a sensation as of someone *humming* invaded the back of her mind. She pushed her hat up on her forehead and wiped away the sweat that kept trickling into her eyes.

:What?: Gwena replied, her ears flicking backwards. *:What on earth do you mean?:*

:You were humming to yourself,: Elspeth told her crossly. *:If you were human, you'd have been whistling. Tunelessly, might I add. It's damned annoying when someone is humming in* your *head; it's not something a person can just ignore, you know.:*

:I'm just feeling very good,: Gwena replied defensively, picking up her pace a little, to the surprise of Cymry, who hurried to match her, hooves kicking up little clouds of dust. *:Is there anything wrong with that? It's a lovely summer day.:*

Oh, really? *:A candlemark ago you were complaining about the heat.:*

:Well, maybe I'm getting used to it.: Gwena tossed her head, her mane lashing Elspeth's wrist, and added, *:Maybe it's you. Maybe you're just being testy.:* Her mind-voice took on a conciliating tone. *:Is it the wrong moon-time, dear?:*

:No it's not, as you very well know. Besides, that has nothing to do with it!: Elspeth snapped, without thinking. *:Skif is being a pain in the tail.:*

168

:Skif is falling in love with you,: Gwena replied, dropping the conciliating tone. *:You could do worse.:*

:I know he is, and I couldn't *do worse,:* she said, conscious only of her annoyance. *:I'm not talking about differences in rank or background, either. And don't you start playing matchmaker. He's a very nice young man, and I'm not the least bit interested in him, all right?:*

:All right, all right,: Gwena said, sounding surprised at her vehemence. *:Forget I said anything.:* Gwena closed her mind to her Chosen, and Elspeth sighed. It wasn't just Skif and his problem that was bothering her—or even primarily Skif. It was something else entirely.

It was a feeling. One that had been increasing, every step she rode toward Lythecare. The feeling that she was being *herded* toward something, some destiny, like a complacent cow to the altar of sacrifice.

As if she were doing what she "should" be doing.

And she didn't like it, not one tiny bit.

Everything had fallen into place so very neatly; she could almost tally up the events on her fingers. First, Kero showed up, with a magic sword. Then, Elspeth, having seen real magic at work, firsthand, just *happened* to get the idea that Valdemar needed mages. Then, Kero just *happened* to back that up, having had to deal with mages herself in her career.

All that could have been mere coincidence. But not the rest. Why was it that within a month, *she* was attacked by an assassin who may have been infiltrated into Haven magically, there was a magic attack on a major Border post—manned by Kero's people, so an accurate report got back, *and* the Council, for some totally unknown reason, seemed to be forced into letting her go look for mages?

And lo, as if in a book, Kero just *happened* to have kept up contact with her old mage, who *happened* to have kept up contact with his old teacher, who *happened* to be Kero's uncle and doubly likely to cooperate. No one had stopped them on this trek, no one had even recognized them as far as Elspeth knew. Everyone was so helpful and friendly it was sickening. Even the mercs seemed to take her stories at face value. There was no sign of Ancar or his meddling. Everything was ticking along quietly, just like it was *supposed* to occur.

They were barely a candlemark away from the turnoff for Lythecare. And the Companions were so smug about something she could taste it.

Gwena was humming again.

And suddenly she decided that she had had enough.

That is it.

She yanked so hard on her reins that Gwena tripped, went to her knees, and scrambled back up again with a mental yelp—and Cymry very nearly ran into her from behind.

She turned to look at Skif; he stared stupidly back at her, as if wondering if she had gone mad.

"That's it," she said. "That is *it*. I am *not* playing this game anymore."

"What?" Now Skif looked at her as if *certain* she had gone mad.

"I am being herded to something, and I don't like it," she snapped, as much for Gwena's ears as his. "I did want to do this, and Valdemar certainly needs mages, but I am *not* going to be guided by an invisible hand, as if I were a character in a badly written book! This is *not* a foreordained Quest, I am *not* in a Prophecy, and I am *not* playing this game anymore."

With that, she dismounted and stalked off the side of the road to a rough clearing. Like seemingly all wayside clearings in this part of Jkatha, it was a bit of grass, surrounded by fenced fields of grain, with a couple of dusty, tall bushes, and a very small well. She sat down beside the well defiantly and crossed her arms.

Skif dismounted, his expression not the puzzled one she had expected but something she couldn't read. He walked slowly over to her, the Companions following with their reins trailing on the ground.

"Well?" she said, staring up at him.

He shrugged, but the conflicting emotions on his face convinced her that he knew something she didn't.

"I am not moving," she said, firmly, suppressing the urge to cough as road dust went down her throat. "I am not moving, until you tell me what you know about what's going on."

He looked helplessly from side to side; then his Companion whickered, and looked him in the eyes, nodding, as if to say, "You might as well tell her."

I thought so. She glared at Gwena, who flattened her ears. :*You should have told me in the first place.*:

"It—was the Companions," Skif said, faintly. "They, well, they sort of—ganged up on their Heralds, when you first wanted to go looking for mages. The Heralds that didn't want to let you go, like your mother— well, they kind of got bullied."

"They *what?*" she exclaimed, and turned to Gwena, surprise warring with other emotions she couldn't even name.

:*It had to be done,*: Gwena replied firmly. :*You had to go. It was important.*:

"That's not all," Skif said, looking particularly hangdog. "For one thing, they absolutely forbid you to be told what they were doing. For another, they're the ones that suggested Quenten in the first place. They said he was the only way to an important mage that they could trust."

"I *knew* it!" she said, fiercely. "I knew it, I *knew* it! I knew they were hock-deep in whatever was going on! I *knew* I was being herded like some stupid sheep!"

She turned to Skif, ignoring the Companions. "Did they say anything about the Shin'a'in?" she demanded. "If I'm going to do this, I am by *damn* going to do it my way."

"Well," he said, slowly, "No. Not that I know of."

:We don't know anything about the Shin'a'in Goddess,: Gwena said, alarm evident in her mind-voice. *:She's not something Valdemar has ever dealt with. We're not sure we trust Her.:*

"You can't manipulate Her, you mean," she replied flatly.

:No. She could be like Iftel's God; She could care only for the welfare of Her own people. That's all. We know some of what She is and does—but it's not something we want to stake the future of Valdemar on.: Gwena's mind-voice rose with anxiety. Elspeth cut her off.

"What do *you* have to say about this?" she asked Skif. "You, I mean. Not the Companions."

"I—uh—" he flushed, and looked horribly uncomfortable. "I—don't know really what the Companions think of it."

He's lying. His Companion is giving him an earful.

"But I—uh, from everything Kero's said, the Shin'a'in probably could give you the teaching, and if *they* couldn't, they would know someone who could." He gulped, and wiped sweat from his forehead with his sleeve. "Kero trusts them—not just her relatives, I mean—and so does *her* Companion, I know that much."

Gwena snorted. *:Of course Sayvil says she trusts them. Contrary old beast, she'd say that just to be contrary.:*

Elspeth ignored the waspish comment. "Fine." She turned to stare into Gwena's blue eyes. "I am going to Kata'shin'a'in, and I am going to see if the Shin'a'in know someone to train me." She turned the stare into a glare. "That *is* where I am going, and you are not going to stop me. I'll *walk* if I have to. I'll buy a plowhorse in the next village. But I am *not* going to Lythecare. And that is my final word on the subject." She raised her chin and stared defiantly at all of them. "Now, are you with me, or do I go on alone?"

Less than a candlemark later, they passed the turnoff to Lythecare, heading straight south, to Kata'shin'a'in.

And Gwena was giving her the most uncomfortable ride of her life, in revenge.

But every bruise was a badge of victory—

And I hope I'll still believe that in the morning when I can't move...

1 2

DARKWIND

This patrol—like all the others lately—had been completely uneventful. *This is almost too easy,* Darkwind thought, making frequent checks of the underbrush beside the path for signs of disturbance. *A week now, that Nyara's been hiding with us, and there's nothing from the other side. Nothing hunting her, except that couple of* wyrsa *I caught on her trail, no magic probes, nothing.*

The very quietude set all his nerves on edge. *Of course, her shielding is really outstanding. Falconsbane might not know she's here, or even that she headed this way when she ran. He could be hunting for her in another direction altogether.*

That was what Treyvan said; Hydona was of the opinion that Falconsbane knew very well she'd come this way but assumed she was in the Vale. She pointed out that in all the time Falconsbane had been on their border—and everything Nyara said indicated that he had been there for a very long time—he'd never directly challenged k'Sheyna. He was only one Adept, after all, and there were at least five Adepts and ten times that many Masters in k'Sheyna. And even though none of them were operating at full strength, the mages of k'Sheyna could still be more than he cared to meet in conflict. Especially when the conflict was over the relatively minor matter of the loss of a single Changechild.

"He can alwaysss make anotherrr," Hydona had said, callously. "It isss unusssual for one like himsssself to keep a pet forrr longerrr than a few yearsss."

And oddly enough, Nyara agreed with Hydona's analysis.

"If he was angered at all, his anger would have been for a loss; not for the loss of *me,*" she'd said, more than a little piqued at having to admit that she was worth so little to her former master. "As an individual, I mean very little to him. He has threatened many times to create another, to then see how I fared among his lesser servants as their plaything. All that would goad him into action was that he had lost a possession. If something distracted him from that anger, he would have made only a token attempt to find me, more to appease his pride than to get me back."

So it seemed, for other than the pair of *wyrsa,* there had been nothing in the way of activity—not along Darkwind's section, nor Dawnfire's—not, for that matter, anyone else's. Except for Moonmist; *she* ran into a basilisk who'd decided her little patrol area was a good one to nest in. Prying *that* thing out had taken five scouts and three days. They didn't want to kill it if they didn't have to; basilisks were stupid, incredibly dangerous, and ravenous carnivores who would eat anything that couldn't run away from them—but they weren't evil. They had their place in the scheme of things; they dined with equal indifference on their own kills or carrion, and there were few things other than a basilisk that would scavenge the carcasses of cold-drakes or *wyrsa.*

But no one wanted a basilisk for a near neighbor, not even the most ardent animal lover. Not even Earthsong, who had once unsuccessfully tried to breed a vulture for a bondbird.

But that was the only excitement there had been for days, and there was no way that incident could have been related. No one could herd a basilisk. The best you could do was to make things so unpleasant for it that it chose to move elsewhere. No one, in all the history of the Tayledras, had ever been able to even *touch* what passed for one's mind, much less control it. The histories said they were a failed and abandoned experiment, like so many other creatures of the twisted lands; a construction of one of the blood-path mages at the time of the Mage Wars. But perversely, once abandoned, the basilisk continued to persist on its own.

It's just a good thing they only lay two or three fertile eggs in a lifetime, he thought wryly, *or we'd be up to our necks in them.*

A broken swath of vegetation caught his attention, and he looked closer, only to discover the spoor of a running deer and the tracks of its pursuer, an ordinary enough wolf pair. From the small hooves, it was probably a weanling, separated from its mother; it wouldn't have broken down the bushes if it had been an adult.

This is ridiculous, he thought. *I might as well be a forester in the cleansed lands. There hasn't been anything worth talking about out here for the past week.*

That was the way the area around a Vale was *supposed* to look, just before a Clan moved to a new spot. No magic-warped creatures like the giant serpent, no mage-made things like the basilisk; just normal animals, relatively normal plant life.

Maybe Father's been right about sitting and waiting for the Heartstone to settle…

Up ahead, the forest thinned a little, the sunlight actually reaching the ground in thick shafts. These golden lances penetrated the emerald leaf canopy, bringing life to the forest floor, for the undergrowth was thicker here, and there was even thin grass among the wild plum bushes. He looked up at the hot blue eye of the sky as he reached a patch of clearing; framed by tree branches, Vree soared overhead, calmly. *He* hadn't seen anything either; in fact, he'd been so bored he'd taken a rock-dove and eaten it while waiting for Darkwind to catch up. It had been a long time since he'd been able to hunt and eat while out on scout.

Starblade's answer to the fracture of the Heartstone had been to wait and see what would happen. He'd insisted that the great well of power would drain itself, slowly—Heal itself, in fact—until it was safe to tap into it, drain the last of its energies, construct a Gate, and leave.

Darkwind had disagreed with his father on that, as he had seemingly on everything else. And up until the past week, it certainly hadn't looked as if the Heartstone was following his father's predictions. In fact, if anything, the opposite was true. There had been *more* uncanny creatures; more Misborn attracted, more actually trying to penetrate the borders. And recently, there had been the other developments; the fact that the mages within the Vale had been unable to sense the changes in energy flows outside it, the fact that now most of the scouts' bondbirds refused to enter the Vale itself, the perturbations that Treyvan sensed.

But maybe that was all kind of the last gasp—maybe things have settled down. Maybe Father's right.

But when he considered that possibility, all his instincts revolted.

Yes, but what if I just feel that way because if Father is right, it means that I am wrong? What if I am wrong, what does it matter? Other than if I'm wrong, Father will never let me forget it…

He stopped for a moment, hearing a thudding sound—then realized it was only a hare drumming alarm, hind foot beating against the ground to alert the rest of his warren—probably at the sight of Vree.

Is it just that I can't admit that sometimes he might *be right?*

On the other hand, there was a feeling deep inside, connected, he now realized, with the mage-senses he seldom used, that Starblade was wrong, dead wrong. A Heartstone that badly damaged could not Heal itself, it could only get worse. And this calm they were experiencing was just a pause before things degenerated to another level.

I guess I'll enjoy it while it lasts, and stay out of the Vale as much as possible.

He sent another inquiring thought at Vree, but the gyre had no more to report than the last time.

It was very tempting to cut everything short and go to see how Nyara was doing. So tempting, that he fought against the impulse stubbornly, determined to see his patrol properly done. It might make up for the other days he had neglected it.

Not really neglected it—there were the dyheli, *and then Nyara.*

His efforts at appeasing his conscience came to nothing. *It still wasn't done. And if I hadn't been very lucky, things could easily have slipped in.*

He no longer worried that these temptations were caused by anything other than his own selfish desire to spend more time with the Changechild. Nyara was good company, in a peculiar way. She was interested in what he had to say and just as interesting to listen to.

At least I can appease my conscience with the fact that I'm learning something about our enemy.

She was also as incredibly attractive as she had been the first time he'd seen her. If he had been a less honorable man, her problematic virtue wouldn't have stood a chance. Which led him to revise his earlier assumptions; to think that she *wasn't* in control of that part of herself. She might even be completely unaware of it.

That would fit the profile of her master.

Mornelithe Falconsbane would not have wanted her in control of anything having to do with sexual attraction; *he* would have wanted to pull the strings there. Which was one reason why Darkwind had continued to resist letting her lure him to her bed. He had no prejudice against her, but he was not sure what would happen, what little traps had been set up in her makeup that a sexual encounter would trigger.

That would fit Falconsbane's profile, too. Make her a kind of walking, breathing trap that only he could disarm. So anyone meddling with the master's toy would find himself punished by the thing he thought to enjoy.

With a set of claws—and sharp, pointed teeth—like she had, he didn't think he was in any hurry to find out if his speculations were true, either. Darkwind was not about to risk laceration or worse in a passionate embrace with her.

He was so lost in his own thoughts that he almost missed the boundary marker, the blaze that marked the end of his patrol range and the beginning of Dawnfire's. He glanced at the sun, piercing through the trees, but near the horizon; it was time for Thundersnow to take over for him. And if he hurried, he *would* have a chance to chat with Nyara before he went to the council meeting.

He was already on the path to the *hertasi* village before the thought was half finished.

"I think this is the best chance I'm going to have; things have been so quiet, they can't blame disturbances on your presence. So I'm going to tell the Council about you, and put your request to them," he told her as they both soaked up the last of the afternoon's heat on the top of the bluff.

She didn't answer at first; just turned on her back and stretched, lithe and sensuous—and seemed just as innocent of the effect it had on him as a kitten. She wasn't even watching him, she was watching a butterfly a few feet away from them.

That didn't stop his loins from tightening, or keep a surge of pure, unmixed lust from washing over him, making it difficult to think clearly for a moment.

He sought relief in analyzing the effect. *That sexual impact she has can't be under conscious control. She couldn't fake the kind of nonchalance she's got right now.*

"When?" she asked, yawning delicately. "Is it tonight, this meeting?"

He nodded; he'd explained to her the need to wait until a regular meeting so that her appearance would seem a little more routine. She'd agreed—both to his reasons and to the need to wait.

But in fact, his real reasons were just a little different. He'd put off explaining what had happened in its entirety until he wouldn't have to face his father alone. Starblade in the presence of the rest of the Elders was a little easier to deal with than Starblade in the privacy of his own *ekele*, where he could rant and shout and ignore anything Darkwind said— and he tended not to take quite so much of his son's hide in public, where there were witnesses both to his behavior and to what Darkwind told him.

"It is well," Nyara purred, satisfaction brimming in her tone. She blinked sleepily at Darkwind, her eyes heavy-lidded, the pupils the merest slits. "Though I still cannot travel, should they grant me leave. You *will* say that, yes?"

"Don't worry," he replied, "I'm going to make that very clear."

In fact, that was one of the points he figured he had in his favor; Nyara obviously could not move far or fast, and he wanted to have a reason for why he had left her with the *hertasi*, instead of putting her under a different guardian. "More competent," Starblade would undoubtedly say. "Less sympathetic," was what he would mean.

And if worse came to worst, he wanted to have a reason for continuing to leave her here, instead of putting her with a watcher of Starblade's choice.

"You still seem fairly weak to me," he continued, "and Nera's Healer seems to think it's a very good idea for you to stay with us until those cracked bones of yours have a chance to heal a bit more. And that reminds me; have you had any problems with the *hertasi?*"

"Have they complained of me?" she snapped sharply, twisting her head around, to cast him a look full of suspicion.

He was taken a little aback. "Why, no—it's just that I wanted to make certain you were getting along all right. If there was any friction, I could move you—maybe to the ruins where the gryphons are. It's pretty quiet there—"

"No, no!" she interrupted, her voice rising, as if she were alarmed. Then, before he could react, she smiled. "Your pardon, I did not mean that the way it may have sounded. Treyvan and Hydona are wonderful, and I like them a great deal—as I expected to like anything Mornelithe hated. I learned early that whatever thwarted him he hated—and that what he hated, I should be prepared to find good."

"He knows about Treyvan and Hydona—"

"No, no, *no*," she interrupted again, hastily. "I am saying things badly today. No, it is only gryphons in general that he hates. As he hates Birdkin, so I was prepared to like you. He never told me why." She shrugged indifferently, and by now Darkwind knew he'd get nothing more out of her on the subject. She had all the ability of a ferret to squirm her way out of anything she didn't want to talk about.

But if she likes them, why wouldn't she want to stay near them?

"It is the little ones," she sighed, pensively, as if answering his unspoken suspicion. "I am very sorry, for I am going to say something that will revolt you, Birdkin, but I cannot *bear* little ones. No matter the species." She shuddered. "Giggling in voices to pierce the ears, running about like mad things, shrieking enough to startle the dead—I cannot *bear* little ones." She looked him squarely in the eyes. "I have," she announced, *"no* motherly instinct. I do not *want* motherly instinct. I do not want to see little ones for more than a short time, at *long* intervals."

He laughed at her long face. "I can see your point," he replied. "They are a handful—"

"And soon there will be two *more*, this time the *very* little ones, who cry and cry all night, and will not be comforted; who become ill for mysterious reasons and make messes at both ends. No," she finished, firmly. "I care much for Treyvan and Hydona, but I will not abide living with the little ones."

"You've been getting along all right with the *hertasi*, though?" he asked anxiously. If he had to leave her here for any length of time, it would be a good idea to make sure both parties were willing. Nera had indicated that *he* had seen no trouble with her, but Darkwind wanted to be sure of that. Sometimes the *hertasi* were a little too polite.

"As well as one gets along with one's shadow." She shrugged. "They are quiet, they bring me food and drink, they are polite when I speak to them, but mostly they are not there—to speak to, that is." A wry smile touched the corners of her mouth, and the tips of her sharp little canine teeth showed briefly. "I am well aware that they watch me, but in their place, *I* would watch me, so all is well. I pretend to ignore the watchers, the watchers pretend they are most busy counting grass stems, we both know it is pretense, and politeness is preserved."

Darkwind laughed; she smiled broadly. *Now I know why Nera called her "a very polite young creature."*

"As long as you're doing all right here—" he glanced at the setting sun. "I have to get back for that meeting. I expect to have some trouble with it."

Nyara's smile faded to a wistful ghost. "I wish I could tell you it would be otherwise, but I doubt it will be so. I only hope you do not come to regret being my champion."

He sighed, and got to his feet. "I hope so, too."

The windows of the *ekele* shook as his father pounded the table with his fist. "By all the gods of our fathers," Starblade stormed, "I *never* thought my own son would be so much of a fool!"

Darkwind stared at a patch of the exposed bark of the parent-tree, just past his father's shoulder, and kept his face completely expressionless. At least it sounded like most of the tirade was over. This was mild compared to the insults Starblade had hurled at him at the beginning of the session.

Then again, it might simply be that Starblade had run out of insults.

Starblade shook his fist in the air, not actually threatening Darkwind but the implication was there. "If I didn't know better, I'd swear I couldn't be your father! I've never—"

"That's enough, Starblade," interrupted old Rainlance tiredly. "That is quite enough."

The quiet words were so unexpected, especially coming from Rainlance, that both Starblade and his son turned to stare in surprise at the oldest of the four Elders. Rainlance never interrupted anyone or raised his voice. Except that he had just done both.

"By now we all know that you think your s—hmm, Darkwind—is the greatest fool ever born. We also know precisely why you think that." Rainlance leveled a penetrating stare at Starblade that froze him where he sat. "The fact is, I've known you a great deal longer than Darkwind, and I think there are times when you allow some of your opinions to unbalance your judgment. This is one of them. It just so happens I've never shared your peculiar prejudice against the Changechildren. I won't go into why, right now, but I have several good reasons, strong ones, to disagree with you on that. And I *also* do not share your view of Darkwind's incompetence." He coughed, and shook his head. "In point of fact, I think Elder Darkwind has done a fine job up until now, a *very* fine job. His peers trust him, he has never let *his* private opinions interfere with his judgment, and I don't see any reason to make a snap decision about this Other of his. I don't see any reason, in fact, why we *shouldn't* continue to help her."

Rainlance looked pointedly at the other Elder, Iceshadow, who shrugged, the crystals braided into his hair tinkling like tiny wind chimes. "She's not a danger where she is," Iceshadow said. "She hasn't caused any trouble—"

"That we know of," snapped Starblade.

Iceshadow gave Starblade a look of disapproval, and Darkwind knew he'd scored at least one point. Iceshadow hated to be interrupted. "Very well. If you insist on that phrasing. That we know of. Frankly, I see no harm in letting her stay where she is until she's healthy, and considering her request for safe passage then."

Rainlance nodded. Starblade frowned angrily, then pounced. "Under *strict watch.* Darkwind may be a gullible boy being led by a pair of come-hither eyes and a sweet voice, but I'm not so sure this Other may not be playing a deeper game. I say she stays under *strict* watch, with careful observers."

"You can't get more careful than *hertasi*," Iceshadow remarked to the ceiling of his *ekele.* "And if she's leading Darkwind around by his urges, that ploy won't work on *hertasi*. Even stubborn, pigheaded old—ah—mages will admit to that."

It was Iceshadow's turn to receive a glare, but the Elder ignored it, winking broadly at Darkwind when Starblade turned away in disgust.

"I think the *hertasi* will do as watchers," Rainlance said smoothly, soothingly, as he sought to heal the split in the Council. "They are certainly quite competent. But I do agree she should be kept as far from the Vale itself as possible. And if she causes any trouble—"

"If she even *looks* like she's causing any trouble," Starblade growled.

Rainlance raised his voice a little, and annoyance crept into it. "— she'll have to be dealt with."

"She'll find herself bound and staked, and you can tell her so!" Starblade shouted.

"*Are* you quite finished?" Rainlance shouted back, his temper frayed to the snapping point. "I'd like to get on with this if I may!"

Starblade sank back into his seat with an inarticulate mumble, confining himself to angry glares at anyone who happened to glance at him. Rainlance closed his eyes for a moment and visibly forced himself to calm down. Darkwind had no sympathy to spare for him; he'd been on the receiving end of his father's tempers too often to feel sorry for anyone else.

"Really, Darkwind," Rainlance continued, opening his eyes, his voice oozing reason and conciliation. "You must see this in the perspective of the Vale and Clan as a whole. We really can't take her into the Vale. We can't take the chance, however slim, that she might be some kind of infiltrator."

"I'm not asking for her to be brought into the Vale," Darkwind replied, echoing Rainlance's tone as much as he was able. "I'm just asking that she be allowed nearer. Right now she's in jeopardy; she's hurt, and she can't run the way the *hertasi* can. I doubt she'd be able to get away if something comes over the border, especially if it's something that's come hunting especially for her. She can't run, she can't hide, and Mage-Gifted or not, she probably can't protect herself from any kind of trained mage."

Iceshadow shook his head regretfully; Darkwind got the feeling that if this hadn't been so serious an issue, he was so annoyed with Starblade right now that he would have been glad to agree with Darkwind just for a chance to spite his father. "No. It's just not possible. And I'm sure she realizes that, even if you don't. After all, look at what she is and what we are—we're enemies. Or at least, she's been on the enemy side. And yet she came to us, supposedly for help. She *admitted* she was going to use us as a kind of stalking horse. No, she stays where she is, and that's the end of it."

"Well," said Starblade, his voice penetrating the silence that followed

Iceshadow's speech like a set of sharp talons, his eyes narrowed, and a tight little smile on his lips. "Since you seem so worried about her, since you brought her into our boundaries in the first place—and since she *is* in your territory—I think it's only fair that you be the one to undertake her protection. Even if it means you have to fall back on magery." He looked around at the other Elders. "Isn't that fair?"

"I don't know——" Rainlance began.

"*I'd* say it is," Iceshadow said firmly. "I've never been happy that when Songwind left us, his magic did as well, Darkwind. I understand your feelings, but I've never been happy about it. You could be quite a mage if you'd give it another try."

Rainlance shrugged. Starblade cast his son a look of triumph. "It seems there's a consensus," he said smugly.

Darkwind managed not to jump up and hit him, scream at the top of his lungs, or do anything else equally stupid and adolescent. In fact, his reaction, so completely under control, seemed to disappoint his father. He thought quickly, and realized that, unwittingly, his father had not only left him an out, he'd given the scout a chance to do something he'd been campaigning for all along. He'd have to phrase this very carefully.

"Very well, Elders," he replied, nodding to each of them in turn. "I am overruled. Nyara may stay, under the eyes of the *hertasi*. I will undertake to keep the Changechild protected—using all the resources at my disposal. Is that your will?"

Rainlance nodded. "That's fine," Iceshadow said. Starblade looked suspicious, but finally gave his consent.

"Done," said Rainlance. "You have the Council's permission, as stated."

"Good," Darkwind said. "Then if that is the consensus, I will have the other scouts keep an eye out for her and stand by for trouble, I will recruit whatever *dyheli* I can find to stand guard, and I have no doubt there will be plenty of volunteers, since she helped save one of their herds—I will ask Dawnfire to look for help among the *tervardi*, and I will see if the gryphons are willing to work some of their protective magics."

He managed *not* to grin at Starblade's expression. For once, he'd managed to outmaneuver his father.

But there was no feeling of triumph as he left the meeting; the fight had been too hard for that. Instead, he was weary and emotionally bruised.

Like someone's been beating me with wild plum branches.

He climbed down out of the *ekele* before anyone else. It would have been a courtesy to wait for the eldest to descend first, but he wasn't feeling particularly courteous right now—and he really didn't want to chance his father ambushing him for a little more emotional abuse. It was dark enough around here that he should be able to escape, provided he did the unexpected. And he was getting rather good at doing that...

So he hurried off into the cover of the thick undergrowth, taking exactly the *wrong* path—one leading to the waterfall at the head of the Vale, instead of the exit. It passed the Heartstone, though not near enough to see the damaged pillar of stone, its cracked and crazed exterior only hinting at the damage echoed across the five planes, and visible to anyone with even a hint of Mage-sight.

He felt it, though, as he passed; an ache like a bruised bone, a sense of impending illness, a disharmony. If he'd had any doubts about it Healing itself earlier, they were dispelled now. It hadn't Healed itself, it had only gotten worse. Now it left a kind of bitter, lingering aftertaste in the back of his mind; if it had been a berry he'd tasted, he would have labeled it "poisonous" without hesitation.

So he did something he had never thought he would do in his lifetime. He shielded himself against it.

The air immediately seemed cleaner, and the sour sense of sickness left him. There was only the hint of incenselike smoke from the memorial brazier at its foot, the flame that commemorated the lives lost when the Heartstone fractured. Now all he had to contend with was the bad taste the meeting had left in his mouth.

He started to look for a way to double back to the path he wanted to take, when he remembered that there was another hot spring at the foot of the waterfall. It wasn't a big waterfall, but it was a very attractive one; it had been sculpted by Iceshadow himself, back when the Vale had first been constructed, and the cool water of a tiny stream fell into a series of shallow rock basins to end in the hot pool of the spring below. Each of the basins had been tuned, although Darkwind had no idea how something like that was done. The music of the falls was incredibly soothing.

Just what I need right now.

That decided him; instead of retracing his steps, he took the path all the way to the end. And as if to confirm that he had made the right decision, as he entered the clearing containing the pool, the moon rose above the tree level, touching the waterfall, and turning it into a shower of flowing silver and diamond droplets. *If you didn't know better, you'd swear there was nothing wrong here in the Vale, it's that peaceful.*

And no one, absolutely no one, was there.

Of course, that might have been because this particular pool had once been a popular trysting spot, and there was not a great deal of romance going on in the Vale anymore. Most of the young Tayledras were scouts, and they seldom came this far in now. As for the rest—Darkwind suspected the mages were suffering, perhaps without realizing it, from the same, sickened feeling the Heartstone induced in him. That was not the sort of sensation likely to make anyone think of lovemaking...

He wondered how many of them had thought to cut themselves off from the Stone. *Not many*, he decided, shedding his clothes and leaving them in a heap beside the pool. *It's their power, their lifeblood. They'd rather feel ill than lose their connection to it. They wouldn't be able to draw on it if they shielded themselves against it.*

Idiots.

Then he left all thought of them behind, as he plunged in a long, flat dive into the hot water of the pool.

He came to the surface, and floated on his back, letting it soothe the aches in his muscles as it forced him into a state of relaxation. Only then did he realize how tightly he had been holding himself, and how many of those aches were due to tension.

He drifted for a while, losing himself deliberately in the sound of the falling water, the changing patterns of the sparkling droplets, the silence.

"Turning merman?" said a shadow at the entrance.

He swam lazily to the edge, rested his arms on the sculpted rim, and looked up into Dawnfire's amused eyes. She looked down on him, a faint smile playing on her lips, her hair loose, her boots in her hand. "Not that I'm aware of," he said lightly. "Unless you saw something I didn't know about."

"Probably not." She knelt down beside him, put her boots down beside her, then unexpectedly seized his head in both her hands, leaned down to water-level, and presented him with the most enthusiastic— and expert—kiss he'd ever had from her. His mouth opened under her questing tongue, and he clutched the rim with both hands, convulsively.

What—she never *gets aggressive—* He became aware that not all the heat coursing through his veins was due to the temperature of the water. He closed his eyes, went passive, and let her lips and tongue play with his, until he was breathless. Her hair fell around him, enveloping him in her own silken waterfall.

She released him, and he nearly slid under.

"*That* was for going back and saving my *dyheli*," she said, sitting back on her heels, balancing there as if she had no weight at all.

"I didn't—exactly—" He regretted having to confess that he had very little to do with it, if *that* was what she had in mind for a reward.

She dismissed everything he was going to say with a wave of her hand. "I know, there's that Changechild involved in it, and it did the magic—but *you* stayed with them, and *you* Mindcalled them. They'd never have found their way out without that."

"It" did the magic. She doesn't know Nyara is female... His attention was captured and held, as she began removing her clothing in the most provocative way, slowly, teasingly. He found himself watching her with parted lips. First the tunic—lacings loosened, then pulling the garment slowly over her head. Then the breeches, inching them down over her hips, sliding them a little at a time down her long, lithe legs—all the while maneuvering so that the shirt covered all the strategically important parts of her. Then the shirt followed the tunic at the same tantalizingly slow speed.

At that moment she seemed just as exotic as Nyara, and just as desirable.

Nyara— *If she doesn't know Nyara's a female, there's no harm in not telling her*—

She was down to a short chemise now, and she winked, once, then vanished into the shadows, reappearing before he had time to think why she had left.

"I put the 'in use' marker at the entrance," she said. "Not that there's anyone likely to be here tonight. I knew you were at the meeting, and I waited to catch you to thank you properly. But you didn't go the way I thought you would. I had to chase you, loverhawk."

She stood in an unconscious pose at the rim, moonlight softening the hard muscles, and turning her into something as soft and quicksilver as a Changechild.

"I wanted to avoid Father," he said, filling his eyes with her.

"I thought so," she said, and laughed. "I figured, knowing you, that as long as you were here you'd probably decide to soak him out of your thoughts. I've been checking every pool between here and Rainlance's *ekele.*"

"I'm glad you found me," he said softly.

She sat on the rim, slid out of the chemise, and into his arms. "So am I," she whispered, and buried her hands in his damp hair, her lips and tongue devouring him, teasing him, doing things no woman had ever done to him before.

His hands slid down her back, to cup her buttocks and hold her against him. She strained into the embrace, as if she wanted to reach past his skin, to merge with him. Her kiss took on a fiercer quality, and she worked her mouth around to his neck, biting him softly just beneath his ear, while he ran his hands over every inch of her, re-exploring what had become new again, and making her shiver despite the heat of the pool. He gasped as she nuzzled the soft skin behind his ear, then worked her way back to the hollow of his throat, and gasped again when she untangled her fingers from his hair, and slid them down *his* chest, slowly—teasingly.

"Not in here—" he managed to whisper, as he grew a little light-headed from the combined heat of the water and his blood.

She laughed, low and throatily. "All right." She began to back up, one tiny step at a time, rewarding him for following her with her clever fingers, which were now hard at work well below the waterline and threatening to make his knees go to jelly at any moment.

They reached the edge of the pool, right beside the waterfall, where some kind soul had left a pile of waterproof cushions and mats. She turned away from him to hoist herself up on the rim. He caught her by the waist, lifted her up, and held her there, nibbling his way up the inside of her thighs until it was her turn to gasp. She buried her hands in his wet hair and her fingers flexed in time with her breathing.

Then she clutched two fistfuls of hair, pulled him away, and swore at him, half laughing. "Get up here, you oaf!" she hissed, "Or I'll get back in the water and do the same to you! You *just* might drown!"

"We can't have that," he chuckled, and joined her; tumbling her into the cushions, nibbling and touching, making her squeal with laughter and surprise.

He only had the upper hand for a moment. Then she somehow squirmed out from beneath him, and pulled a wrestler's trick on him. Then she had him on *his* back, bestriding him, a wicked smile on her face as she lowered herself down, a teasing hair's breadth at a time.

He arched to meet her, his hands full of her breasts, catching her unawares. She cried out and arched her back, driving herself down onto him.

Their minds met as their bodies met, and the shared pleasures enhanced their own, as she felt his passion and he experienced every touch of his fingers on her flesh.

She roused him almost to the climax, again and again, building the passion higher and higher, until he thought he would not be able to bear another heartbeat—

Then she loosed the jesses, and they soared together.

"Dear—gods," he whispered, as they lay together in a trembling symmetry of arms and legs.

She giggled. "The reward of virtue."

"I think I shall strive to be virtuous," he mumbled, then exhaustion took him down into sleep before he could hear her reply. If she even made one. Verbally.

When he woke, she had moved away from him to lie in a careless sprawl an arm's length away. He'd expected as much; he'd learned over the past few months that she was a restless sleeper—after more than once finding himself crowded onto a tiny sliver of sleeping pad. The moon was just retreating behind the rock of the waterfall. He slipped into the pool for a moment, to rinse himself off after his exertions, warm up his muscles, and to cross to the other side without rustling the undergrowth. *That* would surely wake her, as the sound of someone swimming would not. On the other side of the pool, he used his shirt to dry himself and pulled on the rest of his clothing. He hated to leave her like that.

But she is as curious as two cats, and I am not certain I want to answer all the questions she is likely to have when she wakes.

She *would* ask about the rescue, and she would also want to know about the Changechild. And when she found out that Nyara was female—

I am not ready to fend off fits of jealousy, he thought, wearily. *Father's accusations are bad enough. Hers would be worse. And there is no reason for them.*

Yet. Not that he hadn't entertained a fantasy or two.

But they are only fantasies and will remain so, he told his conscience firmly. *Still, they are things I would rather she did not know about. She is not old enough to accept them calmly, for the simple daydreams that they are. However satisfying. Or accept that sometimes the fantasy can be as fulfilling as the reality.*

He moved quickly and quietly along the paths of the Vale, pausing now and then to take his bearings. Once outside, he went on alert. Although this *was* where the scouts had their *ekeles,* they did not equip them with retractable ladders for nothing.

But the night lay over the forest as quietly as a blanket on a sleeping babe. Only twice did he pause at an unusual sight or sound. The first time, it was a pair of bondbirds, huge, snow-winged owls, chasing each other playfully. He recognized them as K'Tathi and Corwith, and relaxed a little. If they were up, it meant the trail was under watch. The second time he stopped was to hail his older half brother, Wintermoon, the bondmate of those owls, who knelt beside the trail, dressing out a young buck deer. Wintermoon, one of two children of Starblade's contracted liaison with a mage of k'Treva, had none of either parent's Mage-Talents, and only enough of Mind-magic to enable him to speak with his bondbird. The other child, a girl, had apparently inherited it all, but *she* was with k'Treva and out of Starblade's reach. The Adept had never forgiven his eldest son for his lack of magery, and Wintermoon had responded by putting as much distance between himself and his father as Clan and Vale would permit. He had no wish to leave k'Sheyna; he had an amazing number of friends and lovers for so taciturn and elusive an individual—it was simply that he also had no wish to deal with a father who had nothing but scorn for him.

"Good hunting," Darkwind said with admiration, eyeing the size of the buck's rack. "Wish I could do that well in the daylight!" He had no fear that Wintermoon had taken anything other than a bachelor; his brother was too wise in the stewardship of the forest to make a stupid mistake in his choice of prey.

Wintermoon laughed; part of his attempt to put distance between himself and Starblade had been to bond exclusively to owls. He had become completely nocturnal, and was one of the night-hunters and night-scouts, and encountered his father perhaps twice in a moon, if that often. "It becomes easier as time goes on. And K'Tathi there lends me his eyes; that's most of it."

"How does—" Darkwind began, puzzled.

Wintermoon followed the thought with quicksilver logic. "He perches above my head. I simply have to adjust my aim to match. Practice enough against trees, and it's not so bad. So, little brother, do you want any of this?"

Darkwind shook his head. "No, I'm fine for the next few days. Dawnfire could use some, though. She was telling me her larder was a little bare."

That should make up for my leaving her like that.

"I'll see she gets it. All's clear the way back to your place. Fair skies—"

That was a clear dismissal—and really, about as social as Wintermoon ever got outside of the walls of his *ekele*. "Wind to thy wings," Darkwind responded, and continued up the trail. He didn't entirely release his hold on caution, but he did relax it a little. Wintermoon was completely reliable; if he said it was clear, he didn't mean just the trail, he meant for furlongs on either side.

Once at his *ekele*, he woke Vree up to let down the ladder-strap for him. There was still enough moon for the gyre to see, though he complained every heartbeat, and went back to sleep immediately, without waiting for Darkwind to climb up. Even though he was relaxed and utterly weary, he couldn't help thinking about Nyara, as he drifted off to sleep. He found himself thinking of her suspiciously, the way his father would.

Or Wintermoon, for that matter. He's more like Father than he knows. Or will admit.

He wished he'd been able to persuade the Elders to allow her closer. And not just for her protection. No, it would have been much easier to keep a watchful eye on her, if she'd been, say, in one of the dead scouts' abandoned *ekeles.*

Of course, Starblade would have opposed that out of its sheer symbolism.

Still, she was within reach. The *hertasi* were clever and conscientious. There were the gryphons, three or four *tervardi,* several *dyheli* herds, and Dawnfire between here and the Vale, and her only other escape routes lay across the border, into the Outlands.

I can't see her going back that way, he yawned, finally giving in to sleep. *She was running away. Why in the name of the gods would she ever run back?*

1 3

INTERLUDE

Nyara huddled before her father, abject terror warring with another emotion entirely.

Pure, wanton desire.

She hated it, that need, that fire that drove her to want him—and even as she hated him, she hated herself for feeling it.

Even though she could not control that need, even though she knew it was built into her; as he had sculpted her flesh to suit him, he had also sculpted her mind and her deepest instincts.

It didn't matter; none of it mattered. Half the time she suspected he had inserted that same self-hatred into her, purely for amusement.

And when he had called her this night, she had obeyed the call. *That* was built into her, too, for all that she had run away from him, for all that she had deluded herself, telling herself that she could, would resist him. She could not, and had not, and now she groveled here at his feet, longing for his touch, hating and fearing it. Despising herself for thinking that she could escape him so easily.

It had been no trouble to deceive the little *hertasi* who guarded her; they were not creatures of the night, and a simple illusion of her slumbering form in the darkness of the little cave they had given her was enough to satisfy them.

She had not lied. Until tonight, she *had* thought she could escape his reach. She had not purposefully misled the *hertasi* Healer, either—her weakness and pain were not feigned, nor were her injuries. But what the Healer did not know, was the extent to which she could ignore pain and fight past weakness when she had to.

That was how she had found the strength to counter her father's magic and free the *dyheli* herd. That was how he had forced her to come to him when he called, overriding the pain with his own commands.

And, as usual, he said nothing at first; merely smiled and waited until she had abased herself sufficiently to drive home how helpless she was, how much of her life lay within his power.

If she resembled a cat, Mornelithe Falconsbane *was* a feline; one that stood upon two legs, and walked, and talked, but there his connection with humanity ended. Long silky hair poured uncut down his back, the color a tawny gold that he maintained magically, else he would have been as bleached-silver as any Tayledras Adept. Long, silky hair grew on most of his face, carefully groomed and tended by a maidservant whose only role was to brush her master whenever he called. His slit-pupiled eyes were a golden-green, like watery beryls; his canines sharper and more pronounced than hers. His pointed ears were tufted at the tips, and the silky hair continued down his spine in a luxurious crest, ending at the clefts of the buttocks. For the rest, he was as perfectly formed and conditioned as a human could be, with a body any sculptor would have wept to see.

As Nyara knew, intimately.

Since he had emerged from his stronghold to call her to the border of k'Sheyna and the beginnings of his domain, he had chosen to dress for the occasion in soft, buckskin leather that perfectly matched his hair. Darkwind's disparaging comments to the contrary, Mornelithe seldom wore elaborate costumes; in fact, within his own quarters, he went nude as often as not.

Which Nyara *also* knew, intimately. She knelt before him until her legs ached from the stones and bits of branch beneath them—which he would not permit her to clear away. He lounged on a blanket of fur spread over a fallen tree trunk by a servant, making him an impromptu throne. The golden mage-light above his head glistened on his hair, the tips of the fur, and on the bat-wings of his two giant guardian-beasts, half wolf, half something she could not even name, creatures whose heads loomed even with his when he stood.

Some of her scars had come from the teeth of those beasts, lessonings in her proper place in the scheme of things, and the proper demeanor to display. Thus she had learned not to move until told, or speak until spoken to.

"Well," he said at last, his voice deep, calm, smooth and soothing. There was a wealth of warm amusement in his voice, which meant he was pleased. She soon discovered why.

"You took my invitation to flee to the Birdfools as if you had thought of it yourself, dear daughter," he chuckled. "I am proud of you."

She burned with humiliation. So it had all been *his* idea, from the inattentive guards, to the captive *dyheli* herd. Without a doubt, he had planned everything, knowing how she would react to anything he presented in her path. She should have known...

"You followed my plan to the letter, my child," he said with approval. "I am very pleased with you. I assume that they invoked a Truth-Spell upon you?"

"Of a kind," she whispered, shivering with shamed pleasure as his approval warmed and excited her. "The Birdkin do not trust me, yet. They keep me in a dwelling of sorts at the border, with *hertasi* and one Birdkin scout to watch."

"One scout only?" Mornelithe threw back his head and laughed, and the guardian-beasts hung out their tongues in frightening parodies of a canine grin. "They trust you more than you think, little daughter, if they set only one to watch you. Are there no other watchers on you?"

She could not help herself; she was compelled to answer truthfully. But she *could* make him force it out of her a word at a time, and perhaps he would grow tired before he learned all the truth. Let him think it was fear that tied her tongue. "Two," she whispered.

"*Hertasi?*"

She shook her head. He frowned, and she trembled. "*Tervardi,* then?"

She shook her head again, hope growing thin that he would lose interest.

"Surely not *dyheli*? No?" His frown deepened, and she lost any hope of hiding her friends' identities. "What are they? Speak!"

He reached out a tendril of power to curl about her. A hand of pain tightened around her mind, though not so much that she could not speak. Her body convulsed. "Gryphons," she whimpered, through tears of agony and anger. "Gryphons."

The pain ceased, and she slumped over her knees, head hanging, hands clasped together tightly. She fought to control her tears, so that he would not know how she had come to like the pair, and so have yet another weapon to hold over her.

"Gryphons." His voice deepened, and the guardian-beasts growled. "Gryphons, *here*. This requires—thought. I will have more of these gryphons out of you, my child. But later."

She looked up, cheeks still wet with tears. He was looking past her, into the dark forest, his mind elsewhere than on her. Then he took visible hold of himself, and gazed down on her, smiling when he saw her tears. He leaned down, and lifted a single drop on a long, talon-tipped finger, and licked it off, slowly, with sensuous enjoyment, his eyes narrowed as he watched her closely.

She shook with a desire she could not control, and that only he could command. He smiled with satisfaction.

"This Birdfool," he said, leaning back into his fur. "His name."

"Darkwind," she told him.

His eyes lit up from within, and again he laughed, long and heartily, and this time the beasts laughed with him in gravelly growls. "Darkwind! The son of my *dear* friend Starblade! What a delicious irony. Has Starblade seen you, my dearest?"

She shook her head, baffled by his words.

"What a pity; he'd have been certain to recognize you, as you would recognize him if you saw him." He laughed again, and she dared a question.

"I have seen him, this Starblade?"

"Of course you have, my precious pet. He was my guest here for many days." Mornelithe's smile deepened, and he licked his lips. "Many, many days. You dined upon his pet bird, do you not recall? And I gave him the crow to replace it, once he learned his place beneath me."

Nyara's eyes widened, as she remembered the Tayledras Mornelithe had captured and broken; how she had been so jealous of the new captive, who had taken *her* place, however briefly, in Mornelithe's attentions. How she had so amused Mornelithe with her jealousy that he had chained her in the corner of his bedroom, like a pet dog, so that she was forced to watch him break the new captive to his will.

And he, the former captive, without a doubt would remember her.

"My little love, if you can contrive a way for Starblade to see you, I should very much be pleased," Mornelithe said caressingly. "It would enlarge my vengeance so well, to know that *he* knew that I had an agent in place on his ground, subverting his beloved son. It would be delicious to know how his mind must burn, and yet he could do and say nothing about it."

"I do not think I can manage that," she told him timidly. "He never leaves the Vale, and I may not go within it."

"Ah, well," Mornelithe said, waving the idea aside. "If you can, it would be well. But if not, I am not going to contrive it at the moment."

His expression grew abstracted for a moment.

She ventured another question. "Is there something that I should know, my lord?"

He looked down at her, and smiled, shaking his head. "It is no matter. There are other matters requiring my attention just now, a bit weightier than this. My vengeance has waited long, and it can wait a little longer."

She sighed with relief, thinking that he was finished with her, that he had forgotten about Treyvan and Hydona—

Only to have her hopes crushed.

"The gryphons," he said, suddenly looking down at her again, and piercing her with his eyes. "Tell me about the gryphons. *Everything.*"

Compelled by his will, she found herself reciting all that she knew about them, in a lifeless, expressionless voice. Their names, the names of their two fledglings; what they looked like, where they nested. *Why* they had chosen to nest there.

And that there was going to be another mating flight shortly.

He sat straight up at that—and she huddled in on herself, shivering, her teeth chattering, free from his compulsion and sick inside with her own treachery.

She looked up at him, from under her lashes. His eyes were blank, his thoughts turned entirely within. Even his guardian-beasts were quiet, holding their breath, not wanting to chance disturbing him.

Then—he stared down at her, and pointed his finger at her, demandingly, the talon fully extended. "More!" he barked, his words and will lashing her like barbed whips. "Tell me more!"

But she had nothing more to tell him, and so he punished her, lashing her with his mind, inflicting pain that would leave no outward signs, nor anything that a Healer could read, but whose effects would linger for days.

And the more he hurt her, the more she yearned for him, burned for him, until the pain and desire mingled and became one obscene whole. She groveled and wept, and did not know whether she wept because of her shame or because of her need.

Finally he released her, and she lay where he left her, panting and spent, but still afire with longing for him.

"Enough," he said, mildly, softly. "You will learn more. I will call you again, when my other business has been attended to, and you will tell me what you have learned. You will try to ensnare Darkwind, if you can, but you *will* learn more of the gryphons."

"Yes," she whispered.

"You will return here to me when I call you."

"Yes," she sobbed.

"You will remember that my reach is long. I can punish you even in the heart of the k'Sheyna Vale if I choose. Starblade has put *my* stamp on their Heartstone, and I can reach within at my will." His eyes glittered, and he licked his lips, slowly, deliberately.

"Yes."

"Do not think to truly escape me. I created you, flesh of my flesh, my dearest daughter, and I can destroy you as easily as I created you." He reached down and ran a talon along her chin, lifting her eyes to meet his, and in spite of herself, she thrilled to his touch.

She said nothing; she only looked helplessly into his eyes, his glittering, cold, cruel eyes.

"Should you try to hide, should you reach k'Sheyna Vale I will call you even from there. And when you come to me, you will find that what you have enjoyed at my hands will be paradise, compared to what I deal you then." He held her in the ice of his gaze. "You do understand, don't you, my dear daughter?"

She wept, silent tears running down her cheeks, and making the mage-light above his head waver and dance—but she answered him. Oh, yes, she answered him.

"Yes, Father."

"And what else?" he asked, as he always asked. "What does my daughter have to tell her doting father?"

And she answered, as she always answered.

"I l-l-l-love you, Father. I love you, Father. I love and serve only you." And her tears poured down her cheeks as she repeated it until he was satisfied.

1 4

ELSPETH

Kata'shin'a'in was a city of tents.

At least that was the way it looked to Elspeth as she and Skif approached it. They had watched it grow in the distance, and she had wondered at first what it was that was so very odd about it; it looked *wrong* somehow, as if something about it was so wildly different from any other city she had ever seen, that her mind would not accept it.

Then she realized what it was that bothered her: the colors. The city was nothing but a mass of tiny, brightly colored dots. She could not imagine what could be causing that effect—was every roof in the city painted a different color? And why would anyone do something as odd as that? Why *paint* roofs at all? What was the point?

As they neared, the dots resolved themselves into flat conical shapes— which again seemed very strange. Brightly colored, conical roofs? What kind of odd building would have a conical roof?

Then she realized: they weren't buildings at all, those were *tents* she was looking at. Hundreds, perhaps thousands, of tents.

Now she understood why Quenten had said that Kata'shin'a'in "dried up and blew away" in the winter.

Somewhere amidst all that colored canvas there must be a core city, with solid buildings, and presumably inns and caravansaries. But most of the city was made up of the tents of merchants, and when trading season was over, the merchants departed, leaving behind nothing at all.

She glanced over at Skif, who was eyeing the city with a frown.

"What's the matter?" she asked.

"Just how are we ever going to find the Tale'sedrin in there?" he grumbled. "Look at that! There's no kind of organization at all—"

"That *we* can see," she interrupted. "Believe me, there's organization in there, and once we find an inn, we'll find someone to explain it to us. If there *wasn't* any way of organizing things, no one would ever get any business done, they'd be spending all their time running around trying to find each other. And when in your entire life have you ever known a successful disorganized trader?"

His frown faded. "You have a point," he admitted.

:I don't like this,: complained Gwena.

:I am perfectly well aware that you don't like this,: Elspeth replied crisply.

:I think this is a mistake. A major mistake. It's still not too late to turn back.:

Elspeth did not reply, prompting Gwena to continue. *:If you turned around now, we could be in Lythecare in—:*

Elspeth's patience finally snapped, and so did the temper she had been holding carefully in check. *:Dammit, I told you I* won't *be herded into doing something, like I was the gods' own sheep! I don't believe in Fate or Destiny, and I'm not going to let you lot move me around your own private chessboard! I* will *do this my way, or I won't do it at all, and you and everyone else can just find yourself another Questing Hero! Do you understand me?:*

Her only answer was a deep, throaty chuckle, and that was absolutely the final insult. She was perfectly ready to jump out of the saddle and *walk* to Kata'shin'a'in at that point.

:And. Don't. Laugh. At. Me!: she snarled, biting off each mental word and framing them as single words, instead of an entire thought, so that her anger and her meaning couldn't possibly be misunderstood.

Absolute mental silence; then Gwena replied—timidly, as Elspeth had *never* heard her speak in her life with her Companion, *:But I wasn't laughing.:*

Her temper cooled immediately. She blinked.

It hadn't really *sounded* like Gwena. And she'd never known a Companion to lie. So if it wasn't Gwena—

:Who was it?: she asked. *:If it wasn't you, who was it?:*

:I—: Gwena replied hesitatingly, lagging back a little as Skif rode on ahead, blithely oblivious to what was going on behind him. *:I—don't know.:*

A chill crept down Elspeth's spine; she and Gwena immediately snapped up their defensive shields, and from behind their protection, she Searched all around her for someone who could have been eavesdropping on them. It *wasn't* Skif; that much she knew for certain. The mind-voice had a feminine quality to it that could not have been counterfeited. And it wasn't Cymry, Skif's Companion; other Companions had only spoken to her *once*, the night of Talia's rescue. She could not believe that if any of them did so again that it would be for something so petty as to laugh at her. *That* was as unlikely as a Companion lying.

And besides, if it *had* been Cymry, Gwena would have recognized her mind-voice and said something.

Kata'shin'a'in stood on relatively treeless ground, in the midst of rolling plains. While there were others within Mindhearing distance—there were caravans both in front of and behind them—there was no one near. Certainly not near enough to have provoked the feeling of intimacy that chuckle had.

In fact, it was incredibly quiet, except for the little buzz of ordinary folk's thoughts, like the drone of insects in a field.

The chill spread from her spine to the pit of her stomach, and she involuntarily clutched her hand on the hilt of her sword.

:You—: said a slow, sleepy mind-voice gravelly and dusty with disuse as she and Gwena froze in their places. *:Child. You are… very like… my little student Yllyana. Long ago… so very, very long ago.:*

And as the last word died in her mind, Elspeth gulped; her mind churned with a chaotic mix of disbelief, astonishment, awe, and a little fear.

It had been the *sword* that had spoken.

Skif looked back over his shoulder. "Hey!" he shouted, "Aren't you coming? You're the one who wanted to go here in the first place."

But something about their pose or their expressions caught his attention, and Cymry trotted back toward them. As he neared them, his eyebrows rose in alarm.

"What's wrong?" he asked urgently. Then, when Elspeth didn't immediately reply, he brought Cymry in knee-to-knee with her and reaching out, took her shoulders to shake her. "Come on, snap out of it! What's wrong? Elspeth!"

She shook her head, and pushed him away. "Gods," she gulped, her thoughts coming slowly, as if she was thinking through mud. "Dear gods. Skif—the sword—"

"Kero's sword?" he said, looking into her eyes as if he expected to find signs that she had been Mindblasted. "What about it?"

"It talked to me. Us, I mean. Gwena heard it, too."

He stopped peering at her and simply *looked* at her, mouth agape. "No," he managed.

"Yes. Gwena heard it, too."

Her Companion snorted and nodded so hard her hackamore jangled.

"A sword?" He laughed, but it was nervous, very nervous. "Swords don't talk—except in tales—"

:But… I am *a sword… from a tale. Boy.:* The mind-voice still had the

quality of humor, a rich, but dry and mordant sense of humor. :*And horses don't talk... except in tales, either.*:

Skif sat in his saddle like a bag of potatoes, his mouth still gaping, his eyes big and round. If Elspeth hadn't felt the same way, she'd have laughed at his expression. He looked as if someone had hit him in the back of the head with a board.

His mouth worked furiously without anything coming out of it. Finally, "It talks!" he yelped.

:*Of course I talk.*: It was getting better at Mindspeech by the moment, presumably improving with practice. :*I'm as human as you are. Or I was. Once.*:

"You were?" Elspeth whispered. "When? How did you end up like *that?* And why—"

:*A long story.*: the sword replied. :*And one that can wait a little longer. Get your priorities, child. Get in there, get shelter. Get a place to sit for a while. Then we'll talk, and not before.*:

And not one more word could any of them get from it, although the Companions coaxed and cajoled along with the two Heralds. And so, with all of them wondering if they'd gone quite, quite mad, they entered the trade-city of Kata'shin'a'in.

The inn was an old one; deep paths had been worn into the stone floors and the courtyard paving, and the walls had been coated so many times with whitewash that it was no longer possible to tell whether they had been plaster, brick or stone. The innkeeper was a weary, incurious little old man, who looked old enough to have been the same age as his inn. The stone floors and the bathhouse indicated that the place had once catered to prosperous merchants, but that was no longer the case. Now it played host to a variety of mercenaries, and the more modest traders, who would form caravans together, or take their chances with themselves, their own steel, and a couple of pack animals.

Their room was of a piece with the inn; worn floor, faded hangings at the window, simple pallet on a wooden frame for a bed, a table—and no other amenities. The room itself gave ample evidence by its narrowness of having been partitioned off of a much larger chamber.

At least it was clean.

Elspeth took Need from her sheath, laid the sword reverently on the bed, and sat down beside it—carefully—at the foot. Skif took a similar seat at the head. The Companions, though currently ensconced in the inn's stable, were present in the back of their minds.

So now is the time to find out if I'm having a crazy-weed nightmare.

"All right," she said, feeling a little foolish to be addressing an apparently inanimate object, "We've gotten a room at the inn. The door's locked. Are you still in there?"

:Of course I'm in here,: replied the sword acerbically. Both she and Skif jumped. *:Where else would I be?:*

Elspeth recovered first, and produced a wary smile. "A good question, I guess. Well, are you going to talk to us?"

:I'm talking, aren't I? What do you want to know?: Her mind was a blank, and she cast an imploring look at Skif. "What your name is, for one," Skif said. "I mean, we can't keep calling you 'sword.' And 'Hey, you' seems kind of disrespectful."

:My holiest stars, a respectful young man!: the sword chuckled, though there was a sense of slight annoyance that it had been the male of the two who addressed her. *:What a wonder! Perhaps I have lived to see the End of All Things!:*

"I don't think so," Skif replied hesitantly. "But you still haven't told us your name."

:Trust a man to want that. It's—: There was a long pause, during which they looked at each other and wondered if something was wrong. *:Do you know, I've forgotten it? How odd. How very odd. I didn't think that would happen.:* Another pause, this time a patently embarrassed one. *:Well, if that doesn't sound like senility, forgetting your own name! I suppose you'd just better keep calling me 'Need.' It's been my name longer than the one I was born with anyway.:*

Skif looked at Elspeth, who shrugged. "All right—uh—Need. If that doesn't bother you."

:When you get to be my age, very little bothers you.: Another dry mental chuckle. *:When you're practically indestructible, even less bothers you. There are advantages to being incarnated in a sword.:*

Elspeth saw the opportunity, and pounced on it. "How *did* you get in there, anyway? You said you used to be human."

:It's easier to show you than tell you,: the blade replied. *:That's why I wanted you locked away from trouble, and sitting down.:*

Abruptly, they were no longer in a shabby old room in an inn that was long past being first quality. They were somewhere else entirely.

A forge; Elspeth knew enough to recognize one for what it was. Brick-walled, dirt-floored. She seemed to be inside someone else's head, a passive passenger, unable to do more than observe.

She rubbed the sword with an oiled piece of goatskin, and slid it into the wood-and-leather sheath with a feeling of pleasure. Then she laid it with the other eleven blades in the leather pack. Three swords for each season, each with the appropriate spells beaten and forged into them.

A good year's work, and one that would bring profit to the Sisterhood. Tomorrow she would take them to the Autumn Harvest Fair and return with beasts and provisions.

Her swords always brought high prices at the Fair, though not as high as they would be sold for elsewhere. Merchants would buy them and carry them to select purchasers, in duchys and baronies and provinces that had nothing like the Sisterhood of Spell and Sword. But before they were sold again, they would be ornamented by jewelers, with fine scabbards fitted to them and belts and baldrics tooled of the rarest leathers.

She found this amusing. What brought the high price was what she had created; swords that would not rust, would not break, would not lose their edges. Swords with the set-spell for each season; for Spring, the spell of Calm, for Summer, the spell of Warding, for Fall, the spell of Healing, and for Winter, the spell that attracted Luck. Valuable spells, all of them. Daughter to a fighter, and once a fighter herself, though she was now a mage-smith, she knew the value of being able to keep a cool head under the worst of circumstances. Spring swords generally went to young fighters, given to them by their parents. The value of the spell of Warding went without saying; to be able to withstand even some magic was invaluable to—say—a bodyguard. With one of her Summer swords, no guard would ever be caught by a spell of deception or of sleep. Wealthy mercenaries generally bought her Fall swords—or the noble-born, who did not always trust their Healers. And the younger sons of the noble-born invariably chose Winter blades, trusting Luck to extract them from anything. The ornamentation meant nothing; anyone could buy a worthless Court-sword with a mild-steel blade that bore more ornament than one of hers. But her contact had assured her, over and over again, that no one would believe her blades held power unless they held a trollop's dower in jewels on their hilts. It seemed fairly silly to her; but then, so did the fact that most mages wore outfits that would make a cat laugh. Her forge-leathers were good enough for her, and a nice divided wool skirt and linen shirt when she wasn't in the forge.

Once every four years, she made eleven swords instead of twelve, and forged all four of the spells into a single blade. Those she never sold; keeping them until one of the Sisterhood attracted her eye, proved herself as not only a superb fighter, but an intelligent and moral fighter. Those received the year-swords, given in secret, before they departed into the world to earn a living. Never did she tell them what they had received. She simply permitted them to think that it was one of her remarkable, nearly unbreakable, nonrusting blades, with a simple Healing charm built in.

After all, why allow them to depend on the sword?

If any of them ever guessed, she had yet to hear about it.

There was one of those blades waiting beneath the floor of the forge now. She had yet to find someone worthy of it. She would not make another until this one found a home.

:That's what I was,: whispered the sword in the back of Elspeth's mind.

The scene changed abruptly. A huge building complex, built entirely of wood, looking much like Quenten's mage-school. There were only two differences that Elspeth noticed; no town, and no stockade around the complex. Only a forest, on all four sides, with trees towering all about the cleared area containing the buildings. Those buildings looked very old—and there was another difference that she suddenly noticed. Flat roofs: they all had flat roofs and square doorways, with a square-knot pattern of some kind carved above them.

She was tired; she tired often now, in her old age. A lifetime at the forge had not prevented joints from swelling or bones from beginning to ache—nor could the Healers do much to reverse her condition, not while she continued to work. So she tottered out for a rest, now and then, compromising a little. She didn't work as much anymore, and the Healers did their best. While she rested, she watched the youngsters at their practice with a critical eye.

There wasn't a single one she would have been willing to give a sword to. Not one.

In fact, the only girl she felt worthy of the blade wasn't a fighter at all, but was an apprentice mage—now working out with the rest of the young mages in the same warm-up exercises the would-be fighters used. All mages in the Sisterhood worked out on a regular basis; it kept them from getting flabby and soft—as mages were all too prone to do—or becoming thin as a reed from using their own internal energies too often. She watched that particular girl with a measuring eye, wondering if she was simply seeing what she wanted to see.

After all, she had started out a fighter, not a mage. Why shouldn't there be someone else able to master both disciplines? Someone like her own apprentice, Vena, to be precise.

Vena certainly was the only one who seemed worthy to carry the year-blade. This was something that had never occurred in all the years she'd been forging the swords. She wasn't quite certain what to do about it. She watched the girls stretching and bending in their brown linen trews and tunics, hair all neatly bound in knots and braids, and pondered the problem.

The Sisterhood was a peculiar group; part temple, part militia, part mage-school. Any female was welcome here, provided she was prepared to work and learn some useful life-task at the same time. Worship was given to the Twins; two sets of gods and goddesses, Kerenal and Dina, Karanel and Dara; Healer, Crafter, Fighter, and Hunter. Shirkers were summarily shown the door—and women who had achieved self-sufficiency were encouraged to make their way in the outside world, although they could, of course, remain with the Sisterhood and contribute some or all of their income or skills to the upkeep of the enclave.

All this information flashed into Elspeth's mind in an eyeblink, as if she had always known it.

Those girls with Mage-Talent were taught the use of it; those who wished to follow the way of the blade learned all the skills to make them crack mercenaries. Those who learned neither supported the group by learning and practicing a craft or in Healing—either herb and knife Healing, or Healing with their Gifts—or, very rarely, taking their place among the few true Priests of the Twins at the temple within the Sisterhood complex.

The creations of the crafters in that third group—and those mages who chose to remain with the enclave—supported it, through sales and hire-outs. The Sisters were a diverse group, and that diversity had been allowed for. Only one requirement was absolute. While she was with the Sisterhood, a woman must remain celibate.

That had never been a problem for the woman whose soul now resided in the blade called "Need."

Interesting, though—in all her studies, Elspeth had never come across anything about the "Twins" or the "Sisterhood of Sword and Spell." Not that she had covered the lore of every land in the world, but the library in Haven was a good one—there had been information there on many obscure cults.

On the other hand, there had been nothing in any of those books about the Cold Ones, and Elspeth had pretty direct experience of *their* existence.

She'd never found any man whose attractions outweighed the fascination of combining mage-craft with smithery. Of course, she thought humorously, the kind of man attracted to a woman with a face like a horse and biceps rivaling his own was generally not the sort she wanted to waste any time on.

She sighed and returned to her forge.

The scene changed again, this time to a roadway running through thick forest, from a horseback vantage point. The trees were enormous, much larger than any Elspeth had ever seen before; so large that five or six men could scarcely have circled the trunks with their arms. Of course, she had never seen the Pelagiris Forest; stories picked up from mercs along the way, assuming *those* weren't exaggerated, had hinted of something like this.

The Fair was no longer exciting, merely tiring. She was glad to be going home.

But suddenly, amid the ever-present pine scent, a whiff of acrid smoke drifted to her nose—causing instant alarm.

There shouldn't have been any fires burning with enough smoke to be scented out here. Campfires were not permitted, and none of the fires of the Sisterhood produced much smoke.

A cold fear filled her. She spurred her old horse which shuffled into a startled canter, rolling its eyes when it scented the smoke. The closer she went, the thicker the smoke became.

She rode into the clearing holding the Sisterhood to face a scene of carnage.

Elspeth was all too familiar with scenes of carnage, but this was the equal of anything she'd seen during the conflicts with Hardorn. Bodies, systematically looted bodies, lay everywhere, not all of them female, none of them alive. The buildings were smoking ruins, burned to blackened skeletons.

Shock made her numb; disbelief froze her in her saddle. Under it all, the single question—why? The Sisterhood wasn't wealthy, everyone knew that—and while no one lives without making a few rivals or enemies, there were none that she knew of that would have wanted to destroy them so completely. They held no secrets, not even the making of the mage-blades was a secret. Anyone could do it who was both smith and mage, and willing to spend one month per spell on a single sword.

Why had this happened? And as importantly, who had done it?

That was when Vena came running, weeping, out of the forest; face smudged with ash and smoke, tear-streaked, clothing and hair full of pine needles and bark.

Again the scene changed, to the forge she had seen before, but this time there was little in the way of walls or ceiling left. And again, knowledge flooded her.

Vena had been out in the forest when the attack occurred. She had managed to scale one of the smaller trees and hide among the branches to observe. Now they both knew the answer to her questions.

"Who" was the Wizard Heshain, a mage-lord who had never before shown any notice of the Sisterhood. Vena had described the badges on shields and livery of the large, well-armed force that had invaded the peaceful enclave, and she had recognized Heshain's device.

"Why—"

His men had systematically sought out and killed every fighter, every craftswoman, every fighter apprentice. There had been mages with them who had eliminated every adult mage.

Then they had surrounded and captured every apprentice mage

except Vena. They fired the buildings to drive anyone hiding into the open and had eliminated any that were not young and Mage-Talented.

The entire proceedings had taken place in an atmosphere of cold efficiency. There were no excesses, other than slaughter, not even rape—and that had struck Vena as eerily like the dispassionate extermination of vermin.

Afterward, though, the bodies of both sides had been stripped of everything useful and anything that might identify them. There had still been no rapine, no physical abuse of the apprentices; they had been tied at the wrists and hobbled at the ankles, herded into carts, and taken away. Vena had stayed in the tree for a full night, waiting for the attackers to return, then she had climbed down to wander dazedly through the ruins.

Vena had no idea why the wizard had done this—but the kidnapping of the apprentices told her all she needed to know.

He had taken them to use, to augment his own powers. To seduce, subvert, or otherwise bend the girls to his will.

They had to be rescued. Not only for their own sakes and that of the Sisterhood, but because if he succeeded, his power would be magnified. Considerably. Quite enough to make him a major factor in the world.

A man who sought to increase his power in such a fashion must not be permitted to succeed in his attempt.

He had to be stopped.

Right. He had to be stopped.

By an old, crippled woman, and a half-trained girl.

This was a task that would require a fighter of the highest skills, and a mage the equal of Heshain. A healthy *mage, one who could ride and climb and run away, if she had to.*

But there was a way. If Vena, a young and healthy girl, could be endowed with all her *skills, she might well be able to pull off that rescue. One person could frequently achieve things an army could not. One person, with all the abilities of both a mage of some strength—perhaps even the superior of Heshain—and a fighter trained by the very best, would have advantages no group could boast.*

That was their only hope. So she had sent Vena out, ostensibly to hunt for herbs she needed. In actuality, it was to get her out of the way. She was about to attempt something she had only seen done once. And that *had not been with one of her bespelled swords.*

She took the hidden sword, the one with the spells of all four seasons sealed to it, out of its hiding place under the floor of the forge. She heated the forge, placed it in the fire while she wrought one last spell—half magic, and half a desperate prayer to the Twins.

Then, when the blade was white-hot with fire and magic, she wedged it into a clamp on the side of the forge, point outward—

And ran her body onto it.

Pain seared her with a white-hot agony so great it quickly stopped being "pain" and became something else.

Then it stopped being even that, and what Elspeth felt in memory was worse than pain, though totally unfamiliar. It was not a sensation like anything Elspeth had ever experienced. It was a sense of wrenching dislocation, disorientation—

Then, nothing at all. Literally. No sight, sound, sense of any kind. If she hadn't had some feeling that this was all just a memory she was reexperiencing, she'd have panicked. And still, if she had any choice at all, she never, ever wanted to encounter anything like this again. It was the most truly, profoundly horrifying experience she had ever had.

A touch. Connection. Feelings, sensations flooded back, all of them so sharp-edged and clear they seemed half-raw. Grief. Someone was weeping. Vena. It was Vena's *senses she was sharing. The spell had worked!* She *was now one with the sword, with all of her abilities as mage and as fighter, and everything she had ever learned, intact.*

Experimentally, she exerted a bit of control, moving Vena's hand as if it had been her own. The girl plucked at her tunic, and it felt to her as if it was her own hand she was controlling. Good; not only was her knowledge intact, but her ability to use it. She need only have the girl release control of her body, and an untrained girl would be *a master swordswoman.*

Vena sobbed helplessly, uncontrollably. After the first rush of elation, it occurred to her that she had probably better tell the child she wasn't dead. Or not exactly, anyway.

The sword released its hold on them, and Elspeth sat and shook for a long time.

It was a small comfort that she recovered from the experience before Skif did. She had never been so intimately *one* with someone's thoughts before. Especially not someone who had shared an experience like Need's death and rebirth.

She had never encountered anyone whose thoughts and memories were quite so—unhuman. As intense as those memories were, they had *felt* old, sounded odd, as if she was listening to someone with a voice roughened by years of breathing forge smoke, and they contained a feeling of difference and distance, as if the emotions Need had felt were so distant—or so foreign—that Elspeth couldn't quite grasp them.

Perhaps that made a certain amount of sense. There was no way of knowing quite how old Need was. She had gotten the distinct impression that Need herself did not know. She had spent many, many lifetimes in the heart of the sword, imprisoned, though it was by her own will. That was bound to leave its mark on someone.

To make her, in time, something other than human? It was possible.

Nevertheless, it was a long time before she was willing to open her mind to the blade again, and to do so required more courage than she had ever mustered up before.

:I wish you wouldn't do that,: the sword said, peevishly, the moment she reestablished contact.

"What?" she replied, startled.

:Close me out like that. I thought I made it clear; I can only see through your eyes, hear through your ears. When you close me out, I'm deaf and blind.:

"Oh." She shivered with the recollection of that shared moment of pain, disorientation—and then, nothing. What would it be like for Need, in those times when she was not in contact with her wielder?

Best not to think about it. "Can you always do that?" she asked instead. "As long as you aren't closed out, I mean."

Skif showed some signs of coming out of his stunned state. He shook his head, and looked at her, with a bit more sense in his expression, as if he had begun to follow the conversation.

:Once I soul-bond, the way I did with Vena, and most of my other wielders, yes. Unless you deliberately close me out, the way you *just did. I had forgotten that there were disadvantages to bonding to someone with Mindspeech.:* Need seemed a little disgruntled. *:You know how to shield yourselves, and unless you choose to keep me within those shields with you, that closes me out.:*

Given some of what Kero had told her about her own struggles with the sword, Elspeth was a little less inclined to be sympathetic than she might ordinarily have been. Need had tried, not once, but repeatedly, to get the upper hand and command the Captain's movements when she was young. And she *had* taken over Kero's grandmother's life from time to time, forcing her into situations that had often threatened not only her life, but the lives of those around her. Granted, it had always been in a good cause, but—

But Kero—and Kethry—had occasionally found themselves fighting *against* women, women or things in a woman's shape. Creatures who were frequently the equal in evil of any man. And when that happened, Need had not only not aided her wielder—she had often fought her wielder.

More than once, both women had found themselves in acute danger, with Need actually helping the enemy.

Given that, well… it was harder to be in complete sympathy with the sword.

Poor Kero, Elspeth thought. *I'm beginning to understand what it was she found herself up against here…*

And that made something occur to her. "Wait a minute—Kero had Mindspeech! Why didn't you talk to her before this?"

:I was asleep.: the sword admitted sheepishly. *:There was a time when all I could bond to were fighters, with no special abilities whatsoever. During that rather dry spell, there was a long period between partners. I am not certain what happened; I didn't get a chance to bond properly, because she didn't use me for long. Perhaps my wielder put me away, perhaps she sold me—or she might even have lost me. I don't know. But my bond faded and weakened, and I slept, and my wielders came to me only as dreams.:*

"What woke you?" Skif asked. He sounded back to his old curious self.

:I think, perhaps, it was the one before you. Kerowyn, you said? She began to speak to me, if crudely. But because I had been asleep for so very long, I was long in waking. Then, as I gradually began to realize what was going on and came to full wakefulness, she brought me to your home.:

Need fell silent, and all of them—Elspeth Felt Gwena back with her again—waited for her to speak. Gwena finally got tired of waiting.

:Well?: she snapped. *:What then?:*

Elspeth clearly felt the sword react with surprise.

:What then? I stayed quiet, of course! The protections about your land are formidable, horse. Someone has changed the nature of the vrondi *there. They—:*

"The what?" Elspeth asked, puzzled by the strange reference.

:The vrondi, *child,:* Need responded, impatiently. *:You know what they are! Even though you have no mages within your border, you use the* vrondi *constantly, to detect the truth!:*

Unbidden, the memories of first learning the Truth-Spell sprang into her mind.

"Think of a cloud with eyes," said Herald Teren. *"Think of the spell and concentrate on a cloud with eyes."*

She must have spoken it aloud, for the sword responded. *:Exactly.:* Need replied with impatience. *:Clouds with eyes. Those are* vrondi. *Did you think they were only creatures of imagination?:*

Since that was precisely what she had thought, she prudently kept that answer to herself.

:Someone, somehow, has changed the nature of the vrondi, *and they are not the same in your land,:* the blade said peevishly. *:They look now, they look for mage-energies. When they see them, they gather about the mage, and watch, and* watch, *and they do not stop watching unless they see that the mage is also a Herald, and has one of your talking horses with him.:* If a sword could have produced a snort, this one would have. *:So I kept silent. What else was I to do? I did not wish to call attention to myself. That was when I drifted back to sleep again.:*

:Not as deeply, I trust,: Gwena responded, dryly.

:Well, no. And I waited, not only to be able to leave your land, but to be passed to the one I had sensed—you. Not only a fighter, but one with Mage-Talent as well, and Mindspeech.:

"Then I took you out—"

:And I woke. Just as well, I think. If you will forgive me, child—you need me.:

Elspeth groaned inwardly, though not at the pun. The last thing she had any use for was yet another creature with an idea of what she "should" be doing.

Oh, gods, she thought. *Just what I wanted. Another guardian. Someone else with a Quest.*

That was not the end of her troubles, as she soon learned.

Both she and Skif were exhausted, but Skif seemed a little more dazed than she. Possibly it was simply a matter of sex; Need had shown herself to be a little less than friendly to males, and Elspeth had no doubt that the sword had not made mental contact easy on him.

Skif lay down on the bed, his face a little dazed. Elspeth, though she was tired, also felt as if she needed to get on with her plans quickly, before Need could complicate matters.

It was possible, of course, that *Need* could prove to be the magic-teacher she so eagerly sought. Possible—but a last resort, to be considered only when she had exhausted all others. Including seeking the Adept in Lythecare. She wasn't certain of Need's powers, and she wasn't certain if the blade was entirely to be trusted. If she would run roughshod over Skif, what would she do to handicap other Valdemaran males? Would she actually sabotage *their* training? Elspeth couldn't be sure, so she wasn't going to take the chance.

When the sword had been put in her sheath, with a promise that Elspeth would not again block Need out of her mind without ample warning and cause, she went out for a breath of air, and to begin to explore the tent city. As she had been expecting, there *was* a logical pattern to the "streets" of

Kata'shin'a'in. The farthest tents, those all the way downwind, belonged to the beast sellers. Near to them were those who sold the things one would need for a beast, everything from simple leads and halters for sheep and collars for dogs, to the elaborate tack for parade horses.

Then came leather workers in general, then the makers of glass, metal and stonework.

Then textile merchants, and finally, nearest the core city, sellers of food and other consumables.

The core city itself contained very few shops. It consisted mostly of the dwellings of those few who remained here all year and the inns.

There were dozens of those inns, ranging in quality from a mud-walled, dirt-floored, one-room ale house, to a marble palace of three stories, whose supposed amenities ranged from silk sheets through mage-crafted delicacies to the very personal and intimate attendance of the servant of one's choice.

The innkeeper had not gotten any more explicit than that, but Elspeth reckoned wryly that a whore by any other name still plied his or her trade—presumably, with expertise.

It might be nice to experience service like that, one day—*though without,* she thought with a little embarrassment, *anything more personal than a good massage.*

But for now, she had a great deal more on her mind than that. For one thing, she had to find Shin'a'in. This *was* Kata'shin'a'in, "City of the Shin'a'in," after all. Once she found Shin'a'in, she had to get them to talk to her. Then she had to find someone willing and able to put her in touch with Tale'sedrin, Kero's Clan.

And she reckoned that the best place to find the Shin'a'in would be in the beast market. They not only bred horses, after all, they also had herds of sheep and goats; presumably they bought and sold both.

Failing that, she would try the textile merchants. The Shin'a'in were great weavers and among those who treasured such pieces of art, their carpets, blankets, and other textiles and embroideries were famed all the way up into Valdemar.

So she went out to scout the beast market first.

She had hoped to slip away without disturbing Skif, who had fallen asleep on the bed, exhausted by the strain of the strange day.

But no matter what Need claimed about her own powers, evidently "attracting Luck" was no longer one of them. She had no sooner gotten outside the door of the inn when Skif came panting up behind her.

She sighed and kept from snapping at him. It was fairly obvious that he was not going to let her go out alone. And it wasn't simply more of his mother-henning. The peculiar look in his eyes told her all she needed to know.

He was infatuated with her.

And I ought to recognize infatuation when I see it, since I've suffered under it myself. He undoubtedly had convinced himself that he was in love with her.

Wonderful, she thought to herself, as she headed determinedly toward her goal, despite having him trailing along behind her. *Just wonderful. My partner thinks he's in love with me, my Companion wants me to become some kind of Foretold Hero, my sword has a mind of its own, and I'm going to have to find someone from an elusive tribe of an elusive people all on my own, in a city where I don't even speak the language.*

No, somehow I don't think that attracting Luck is on the list of active spells…

1 5

DARKWIND

Treyvan roused his feathers, fluffing his crest and shaking his head, his claws digging long furrows into the thick weedy turf. He held his head high, his muscles stiff with impatience. Darkwind glanced sideways at him and smiled a little.

A shadow passed over the scout, and he looked up automatically, but it was only a cloud passing across the sun. Vree was waiting for him back in the forest, away from the temptation of Treyvan's crest feathers. "How long have you and Hydona been mated?" he asked, with pretended innocence.

"Twelve yearsss," the gryphon replied, rousing his feathers again, and casting his own glance upward. "What'sss that got to do with anything?"

"And you've made quite a few mating flights, haven't you?" the scout continued, his smile broadening. Treyvan was so preoccupied he didn't even realize that Darkwind was teasing him.

"Well," Treyvan said, with a sidelong glance at Hydona. Hydona only roused her own feathers, watching him coyly. "Yesss."

"If you've got so much experience at it," he laughed, reaching up to scratch behind Treyvan's ear-tufts, "don't you think you ought to be able to take your time about this one?"

Treyvan closed his eyes, wearing an expression of long-suffering patience. "You, a human, *always* in ssseason, with matesss ambusshing you even when you are bathing—you tell *me* that? You crrreaturess neverrr *ssstop.*"

Hydona made a choking sound; her mate pointedly looked away from her. Darkwind knew that faint gargling from past exchanges with the pair; she was trying not to chuckle. He raised his eyebrows at her, then gave her a broad wink. She hid her head by turning it to the side, but her shaking shoulders told him she was stifling outright laughter.

"Anyway," Treyvan continued, in an aggrieved tone, "you know very well that I casst the initial ssspell thiss morrrning. *And* you know verrry well that until we complete it with the sssecond ssspell, it'sss going to make me itchierrr than a plague of sssand-fleasss. I explained it to you often enough." He shook his head and made a grinding sound with his beak. "I feel asss if my ssskin isss too tight," he complained.

Darkwind bit his tongue to keep from making a retort to that particular complaint. "In that case," he said, soothingly, "I had probably better leave you two alone."

"Oh, he'll live," Hydona countered, controlling herself and her humor admirably. "Trrruly he will. You're rrready for what we'll do thisss time, I hope? Not like the lassst time?"

He flushed at the memory of the "last time," when he had been much younger. He had been close enough to them, and unshielded, so that he had gotten caught up in the extremely potent magic of their mating spell. The first spell that Treyvan had mentioned was what actually made the mating fertile; otherwise their sexual activity was purely for enjoyment. The second would ensure conception. And despite Treyvan's acerbic comment about "humans always being in season," the fact was that the gryphons were at least as active in that area as any humans Darkwind knew.

"I'll be fine," he told her. "I'm not fourteen anymore."

Hydona laughed. "I'd notisssed," she teased.

"Essspecially around Dawnfirrre. When will *you* be picking a mate?"

"Uh—" the question took him by surprise, so he settled for a gallant answer. "When I find a mate as magical as you are."

"Flattererrr," she replied, dryly. "Well, when you do, perhapsss we'll all be rrready to ssssettle a new place together, ssso that we can keep eyesss on each other'sss sssmall onesss." She looked over his head a moment, off into the distance. "That isss the ultimate goal of ourr being herrre, you know," she said thoughtfully. "We'rrre pioneerssss, of a sssort. Our kind came from sssomewhere about herrre, you know, very, very long ago, and Trrreyvan and I are here now to sssee if it isss the time to rrreturn."

"So you told me," he said, "A long time ago."

She nodded as Treyvan sighed and lay down in the long grass with a long-suffering look.

"Oh, yesss," she said, ignoring her mate, with a mischievous twinkle in her eyes. "We arrre herrre to sssee if we can raissse little ones, brrring them into the magic of the land, and prossssper. If we do well, more will come. You know, ourrr people and yoursss arrre ancient parrrtnersss, from the daysss of the Kaled'a'in. The *hertasi*, too, and othersss you may not have everrr ssseen beforrre. It would be good if we could be partnersss again."

Another surprise; this time, a much greater surprise. He'd been astonished to learn that the gryphons were fluent in the ancient tongue of Kaled'a'in, a language so old that very few of either the Tayledras or the Shin'a'in could be considered "fluent," despite the fact that both their current languages were derived from that parent. But this revelation was a total surprise, for there was nothing in the Tayledras histories to indicate that the two species had been so close.

While he pondered the implications of that, Hydona reached over and gently bit Treyvan's neck. The male gryphon's eyes glazed and closed, and the cere above his beak flushed a brilliant orange-gold. Obviously, her mind was no longer on the far past, but on the immediate future. And from the look on Treyvan's face, his mind had been there for some time.

Darkwind coughed. "Uh—Hydona?"

"Hmm?" the gryphon replied dreamily, her own eyes bright, but unfocused, her thoughts obviously joined to Treyvan's.

"Who's watching the little ones?" he asked. "I can't; I've got to be out on patrol. I don't trust this quiet."

"They'll be fine," Hydona replied, releasing her mate long enough to reply. "They've been told not to leave the nessst, and if they called, nothing could get to them beforrre we'd be on top of it."

"Are you sure?" he persisted, but Hydona was nuzzling Treyvan's neck again and he knew there was no way he was going to get any sense out of her at the moment.

"They'll be fine," she mumbled, all her attention centered once more on her mate.

Despite being under shielding, the sexual euphoria began penetrating even his careful defenses. This was obviously the time to leave.

As he picked his way through the ruins, a feeling of light-headedness overcame him for a moment. He looked back over his shoulder to see the two of them surging up into the cloudy sky, Hydona a little ahead of Treyvan. Even as he watched, they began an elaborate aerial display, tumbling and spiraling around each other, in a dance that was half-planned and half-improvisation. This "dance" itself was part of the spell; the rest—Treyvan's extravagant maneuvers—were designed to inflame himself and his mate.

And judging by the faint excitement *he* was feeling, even through his shields, it was having the desired effect.

As he turned his eyes back toward the ground, another moving speck caught his eye. Though it was very high, long experience enabled him to identify it as a red-shouldered hawk, one of the many breeds often used as bondbirds by the Tayledras.

That made him think reflexively of Dawnfire, whose bird *was* a red-shouldered. And that—given all that he'd been exposed to in the past few moments—made his thoughts turn in an entirely different direction than they *had* been tending.

Dawnfire rode the thoughts of her bondbird with the same ease that the bird commanded the currents of the sky. Theirs was a long partnership, of seven years' standing, for she had bonded to Kyrr at the tender age of ten. Darkwind's Vree had been with him only four or five years; the bird he had bonded to before that had been a shorter-lived shriek-owl, gift of his older brother.

A shriek-owl was not a practical bird for a scout, but the tiny creatures were perfect for a mage, which was what Darkwind had been in that long-ago, peaceful time. Shriek-owls in the wild seldom lived beyond three years—the bondbird breed in general tripled that lifespan. That was nothing near like the expected lifespan of the scouts' birds—twenty-five to fifty years for the falcons, larger owls, and hawks, and up to seventy-five years for the rarer eagles. And shriek-owls were tiny; scarcely bigger than a clenched fist. They ate mostly insects, flew slowly, and generally flitted from tree to tree inside a very small territory. They could hardly be counted on to be an effective aid either on a scouting foray or to aid in an attack. But the owls were charming little birds, by nature friendly and social—in the wild they nested several to a tree—and the perfect bird for a mage who only needed a bird to be occasional eyes and ears and to pass messages. A mage did not necessarily need to bond to his bird with the kind of emotional closeness that a scout did, nor did he need a bird with that kind of long expected lifespan. All of the mages that Dawnfire knew that she liked, personally, *did* bond closely with intelligent birds, but it was not as necessary for them as it was for scouts.

Scouts had to develop a good working, partner-like relationship with their birds, and that required something with a long anticipated lifespan. Scouts spent as much as a year simply training their birds, then it took as much as four or five more years to get the partnership to a smooth working relationship. Like the scouts, the lives of the bondbirds were fraught with danger. There had already been casualties among the birds, and Darkwind had warned his corps to expect more. Their enemies knew the importance of the birds, as well as the impact a bird's violent death had on his bondmate, and often made the birds their primary targets. Dawnfire tried not to think about losing Kyrr, but the fact was that it could happen.

Darkwind's father Starblade had lost *his* bird in circumstances so traumatic that the mage had returned to the Vale in a state of shock, and actually could not recall what had occurred. Since he had been investigating a forest fire ignited by firebirds, and since the birds themselves seldom reacted so violently that they set their homes aflame, the other Tayledras assumed that whatever had frightened the firebirds had probably caught and killed Starblade's perlin falcon. That had been a set of very strange circumstances, actually; Dawnfire remembered it quite vividly because her mother had been one of the scouts who had found the mage and had talked it over one long night with friends in her daughter's presence.

There had been a sortie that had drawn most of the fighters off when word of the fire had reached the Vale. Starblade had gone out to take care of it.

He had then vanished for many days. He was found wandering, dazed, within the burned area, near nightfall on the third day. His bondbird was gone, and he himself could not remember anything after leaving the Vale. Injured, burned, dehydrated, no one was surprised at that—but when days and weeks went by and he still could not remember, and when he chose to bond again with a crow, from a nest outside of the Vale—some people, like Dawnfire's mother, wondered...

Darkwind had once said something after another of his angry

confrontations with his father—something about his feeling that Starblade had changed, and was no longer the father he had known. *He* blamed the change on the disaster, Dawnfire wasn't so sure.

Starblade had not been that close, emotionally, to Darkwind's mother, though Darkwind had never accepted that. Dawnfire was not at all certain that Starblade would have been so badly affected by her death that his personality had changed. She blamed the change on the death of Starblade's bird. It seemed to *her* and her own mother that Starblade had become silent and very odd afterward. And that crow he'd bonded to was just as odd.

She pulled her thoughts away from the past and returned them to the present. She was off-duty today and had decided to indulge her curiosity in something.

Darkwind's gryphons.

She had been terribly curious about them for a very long time, and had even gone to visit them a time or two. But the gryphons, while still being cordial and polite, had made one thing very clear to her: the only visitor they truly welcomed was Darkwind.

That—had hurt. It had hurt a very great deal, and not even Darkwind knew how much it hurt. She brooded on that, as Kyrr neared the ruins, coming in high over the forest.

I've never had anyone rebuff me like that, she thought resentfully. *Every other nonhuman I've ever met seems to think I'm a good person to deal with and to have as a friend. Tervardi, kyree, dyheli, hertasi—even firebirds, teyll-deer, wolves, the nonsentients... Why don't the gryphons want me around?*

She'd asked that question any number of times. Darkwind wouldn't tell her a great deal, citing the gryphons' desire for privacy. That had only inflamed her curiosity—at the same time, she felt she had to respect that need. But why wouldn't they be willing to meet with her, once in a while, away from their nest? Why was it that only Darkwind was worthy of their attention?

Over the months and years, the unfulfilled questions ate at her, and she had slipped over to the ruins more than once to watch the gryphons and their offspring from a distance. Darkwind had never forbidden her that; in fact, he said once that she had eased one of his worries, helping to keep an eye on the young ones while the adults were off hunting.

They had to spend a great deal of time in hunting; they were very large, flighted carnivores, like the birds of prey they resembled, and they needed a lot of meat. They ranged very far in order to keep from overhunting any area, and they often spent an entire morning or afternoon away from the nest. Dawnfire had taken this tacit approval as permission to watch them whenever she wasn't otherwise occupied, so long as she did it from afar, feeling that she might be able to earn the acceptance of the adults with her unofficial guardianship of their offspring.

But then, a week or so ago, Darkwind had specifically forbidden her to go anywhere near the ruins today, without giving any explanation. And that had driven her curious nature wild, as well as rousing resentment in her that he had simply ordered her as if it was his right.

He probably shouldn't have told me, she admitted to herself, as her bird soared just at the border of the gryphons' territory. *If he hadn't told me, I probably wouldn't be doing this—*

But then anger at him and his authoritative attitude burned away that thought—an anger nearly a week old, born of resentment, and nurtured on his continued silence. How *dare* he forbid her to go where she wanted to go on her own time? He had no authority over her, over her freedom! He hadn't *asked* her, simply and politely, he'd *demanded* that she promise, then and there, refusing to answer any questions, either before she reluctantly promised, or after. He refused to explain himself, or even talk about it. Her anger smoldered, hot, and grew hotter with every day that passed.

Following anger had come suspicion, slowly growing over the course of several days; a feeling that he was hiding something, and nothing had alleviated it since.

Her suspicions centered around the Changechild. He was always with the gryphons—he was with them, and with that Changechild. He wouldn't talk about either. It was not unreasonable to suppose that the two were connected—and that there was something about the Change-child that Darkwind didn't want her to know.

He'd never hidden anything from her before. There was no reason why he should want to start now.

Or so she had thought. Until this morning, when an overheard comment told her something very important that Darkwind had somehow left out of his few stories about the Changechild.

"Has Darkwind said anything more about the Changechild?" Ice-shadow asked someone. "Is she ready to leave, yet?"

She? This Changechild, neuter in her mind, suddenly took on a different face. "It" was a *she.*

Suddenly the senseless questions had sensible answers. And there were plenty of reasons why Darkwind would want her kept in the dark about this female. Especially if she was attractive.

And Dawnfire's imagination painted her as very attractive. Most Changechildren were. And there were the attractions of the exotic, of course...

Not that I care if he's enamored with the girl, she told herself, as Kyrr soared a little closer to the gryphons' nest. *It's not as if we're lifebonded or something. We haven't even traded bondbird primary feathers. I would if he offered, but we haven't, just coverts. I don't exactly have a hold on him...*

Excuses, excuses, and none of them meant anything, not really.

Damn him, anyway.

She had given a promise, and she never broke one—no matter what.

Even if the person she had given the promise to turned out to be a worthless sneak.

So she had spent most of the morning trying to think of a way around that promise, so that she could see what Darkwind was really up to when he slipped off to his gryphon friends. She wasn't entirely certain why she was tormenting herself, it was as if she kept biting at a sore tooth. It hurt, but she just couldn't seem to stop doing it.

Then the answer to her dilemma had occurred to her; she had promised that *she* wouldn't go near the gryphons, but she hadn't promised that Kyrr would stay away. And what Kyrr saw, she could see. Kyrr could be her way to see just what Darkwind was really up to.

The only problem was that to do that, she would have to hole up in her *ekele* and go into a full trance. That was something she was secretly ashamed of; that she could not make full contact with Kyrr's mind unless she performed a full bonding. She didn't know why; scouts generally had no trouble using their bird's senses. There *were* one or two others who had the same trouble, but no more than that. Darkwind had speculated that she found the experience of having her consciousness split to be too traumatic to deal with unless she was in a full trance—since in a full trance, her consciousness wasn't really split.

Normally this wasn't a handicap; her communication with Kyrr was otherwise excellent. The big hawk was one of the most intelligent of all the scouts' bondbirds, and had no trouble with simply *telling* her what she needed to know. Kyrr could "speak" in full sentences, she had a sense of humor, and had no trouble in cooperating with her bondmate. There had never been any rebellion or any real disagreements with Kyrr.

But Kyrr could not read facial expressions; she could not pick up the nuances of behavior that Dawnfire needed to know. She wanted to *know* how he really felt about this Changechild. Kyrr only understood things as they related to raptor feelings and instincts. And she didn't want Kyrr to misinterpret things that she saw in light of those instincts. After all, it was entirely possible that Darkwind had other reasons for keeping her away, legitimate reasons.

It's entirely possible that pigs will fly, too, she thought sourly.

Darkwind wasn't at the gryphons' nest, and neither were the gryphons. Surprised, she sent Kyrr ranging out to find them. After a bit of searching, she spotted them, near the edge of the ruins, where the forest began; she must have passed them at a distance when Kyrr flew in. Darkwind's figure blended into the landscape of tumbled stones and overgrown hillocks, rendering him very difficult to see, but the gryphons stood out against the ruins very clearly. More clearly than she remembered, in fact; their feathers shone with color, gold and red-brown, and they seemed to capture and hold the sunlight, shining in all the colors that Kyrr could see and she couldn't. For a moment, their striking beauty drove all other thoughts from her mind.

Then she wrenched her attention away, to look for anything that might be the Changechild. But there were only the gryphons and Darkwind, with no sign of anyone else, nor any of the signs that several days of occupancy would put around a hiding place in the ruins. Unless they were trying to conceal it—and they had no reason to—there would be distinctive signs of habitation.

Her anger faded and died, giving way to embarrassment.

Was I wrong? she wondered, as the gryphons fanned their wings in the sun, and she and Kyrr circled nearer. She had never felt so stupid in her life. She was just glad that she hadn't made this blunder in public. *Was I just a suspicious, jealous bitch? Was I overreacting to something that hadn't even happened?*

It certainly looked like it. As Darkwind bade farewell to his two friends and slipped into the shadows of the forest, she very nearly sent Kyrr home. But sheer curiosity kept her aloft, circling above the two gryphons, and something about their colors nagged at the back of her mind, reminding her of a memory she couldn't quite put her finger on.

Then it came to her, as the larger of the two gryphons bit the neck of the smaller one in an unmistakable act of sexual aggression.

Gods and ancestors—they're going to mate. That's why he didn't want me around them.

For a moment, that was even more embarrassing. She felt as if she'd been caught watching the *dyheli* stallions and their mares for the sheer, erotic amusement of it…

But they'd had mating-flights before, lots of them, and Darkwind had never forbidden her to go near. What was it that was so different this time?

Curiosity overcame embarrassment. Whatever it was, she was going to find out.

As first one, then the other of the gryphons launched themselves into the air, she circled the sky around them, keeping them in sight at all times.

The male—Treyvan—wheeled and stooped and circled his mate, who hovered as he circled, followed him in his dives, and climbed beside him as he dove upward again. This was not simply "flight"—this was an aerobatic dance, breathtaking and beautiful, and as impressive as anything she had ever witnessed.

The gryphons moved higher with every turn of the dance, gaining altitude as the dives grew shallower, the climbs steeper, and the circles more fluid and sensuous. They came even with Kyrr, then climbed above her, continuing to climb higher as she tried to follow. Finally they climbed into regions where she couldn't follow, leaving her gazing in wonder from below…

Then there was just one single dot in the blue. And it was growing larger.

Dear gods—they mate on the wing, like eagles—

For two minutes they fell together, claws locked in ecstasy—plummeting toward the earth so fast that the wind whistled in their feathers, eyes closed—

—they aren't going to—

At the last possible moment they broke apart, spreading their wings with a *crack* as they caught the air and shot upward again, side by side, beauty so incredible that she couldn't breathe—

When the beauty of the moment was shattered by the *thunk* of a heavy crossbow firing, and a bolt streaking toward Hydona.

Dawnfire was watching the female at the moment that the broad-bladed bolt ripped through the air, changing its arc to meet the wing and shred it.

The female screamed as the wing collapsed; the uninjured wing flailed wildly as she fell in a barely controlled spiral towards the ground.

The male's scream of rage echoed his mate's scream of pain; he did

218

a wing-over and turned his climb into a killing dive, claws extended, as he followed his mate down.

The female crashed into the trees at the edge of the forest and was lost to sight; the male followed an eyeblink behind her.

Then a sudden flare of light from beneath the trees enveloped him in a tongue of white flame; he screamed again, but this time in pain, not in rage. The light held him suspended for a moment, as he went limp. Then he simply dropped, unconscious, through the leafy roof of the forest.

All that saved him from a broken neck was the fact that it was a relatively short drop.

Anger filled her, white-hot anger, and the urge to kill.

Without stopping to think, Dawnfire sent Kyrr in a near-vertical stoop down after them; Kyrr's instinct was to shriek with rage, but Dawnfire clenched the hawk's beak shut. No point in warning whoever it was that had perpetrated this—outrage.

As she dove through the branches, snaking through the obstacle course with desperate adjustments of her wings, Kyrr's blood boiled with rage. It was all that Dawnfire could do to keep her under control and quiet. The bondbird wanted blood, she wanted it *now*, and she wasn't going to accept less.

:*Kill!*: she shrilled in Dawnfire's mind. :*Kill them all!*:

Dawnfire gritted mental teeth, and held to her tenuous control as they penetrated the last of the branches and broke out into the clear air beneath the forest canopy. *If I lose her now, I lose her for all time. I'll never be able to control her in a rage again—*

There were two men with the unconscious gryphons; she saw that in a moment. One, the one with the crossbow, was standing guard over the unconscious male who lay in a pathetic and boneless heap at his feet.

The other was beside the female, who was, at least, semiconscious. He was unarmed, dressed in close-fitting leather—and he was without a doubt a mage, one of the Others, who had manipulated himself into a form that was scarcely more than half human.

And he was doing something to the female gryphon.

Dawnfire barely had time to take that all in; at that moment, the female gryphon sent up a shriek of heartrending agony. The scream goaded Kyrr into a rage that tore her loose from Dawnfire's control.

Not that it mattered, because Dawnfire herself was so angered that she released control to Kyrr, to give her all the edge she needed.

Screaming outrage, they dove together in a full-scale attack, claws extended and aimed for the mage's eyes.

He looked up—

And his eyes were all Dawnfire could see—just before something slammed into her, and darkness swallowed her. His eyes—his slitted eyes...

And his hate-filled, sharp-toothed smile...

1 6

ELSPETH

Elspeth swore silently as she caught a familiar profile out of the corner of her eye. Skif was following her again.

The turbaned merchant implored her to examine the clever workmanship of the leather pouch she was holding, conveying grief that his profit margin had already been slashed to nothing. Elspeth lingered over her purchase, haggling a few more coppers off the price of the belt-pouch, as she watched Skif ghosting around the edge of the crowd, keeping an eye on her. He was very good; it was unlikely that anyone around her realized that he was shadowing her. In a bazaar full of foreigners of all shapes, sizes and costumes, neither of them stood out from the crowd. Trade season was at its height, and the crowds of small traders, mercs, and the occasional pleasure traveler filled the aisles between the tent-booths. It was not the easiest thing to spot Skif as he skillfully used the crowds to cover his movements, but *he* had trained *her,* and she knew his moves better than anyone else could.

It was just a good thing that she was conscientious enough to keep her own watch out for other followers. He could easily be distracting her enough to put her at hazard.

The scent of fine leather rose from the pouch in her hands as she pretended to examine it further. The merchant swore she was impoverishing him.

This was getting annoying. No, it had gotten annoying already. She had begun to lose her patience with him.

Twice now, she had gotten close to someone who had hinted he might know a Shin'a'in or two—and twice, it had come to nothing. The Clansmen were proving incredibly elusive.

"Alas, you should have been here in the spring," said the folk in the fabric bazaar. "They are only here in the spring. But I have some fine Shin'a'in rugs, and you couldn't get a better bargain on them from a Clansman herself..."

"Oh, you should wait until the fall," said the horse traders. "They never come here except in the fall. Now, I have some outstanding Shin'a'in saddle mares..."

"Well, they were just here," said the shepherds, in a dialect so thick she could scarcely make out what they were saying. "Tale'sedrin, you say? That's the blonds, no? Ah, you just missed them; here last week, they were, buying up them new long-haired goats."

Here last week, here last season, not here yet—the herders were the closest she had gotten; at least they knew that Kero's Clan had a number of blond members, legacy of Kero's grandmother Kethry.

But the Shin'a'in were proving horribly hard to find. It seemed that no matter where she went, they had either been and gone, or they had not yet appeared.

"Cakes yesterday, cakes tomorrow, but never cakes today," she muttered to herself, keeping one eye on Skif as she paid for the leather pouch and attached it to her belt. Clever pouch; well worth having, with a catch designed to foil pickpockets, and a belt loop with woven wire glued between two layers of leather, to outwit cut-purses.

Well, she wasn't going to get anywhere today. The leather market was as empty of contacts as any other. It was time to try something else.

But before she did that, she was going to have to deal with Skif. Before he drove her to give him a bloody nose.

The crowds hadn't thinned any; sometimes she wondered what they were all doing here—they couldn't all be selling to each other, or there wouldn't be anyone in the booths. But there were smaller merchants who had no booths, picking up bargains for the luxury trade; there were plenty of people who seemed to be here just to shop and enjoy themselves. Kata'shin'a'in seemed to provide a kind of ongoing Fair that lasted for months. The security provided by the discreet bazaar guards encouraged folk to wear their finery and indulge themselves. She headed back to the inn with her other purchases, fruit and cheese and fresh bread, in a string bag at her side. She moved through the crowd briskly, at a fast walk, taking Skif by surprise so that she managed to lose him around a corner.

Well, while *he* had been busy following her, she had been paying attention to the layout of the bazaar. She took a shortcut through the saddlers, coming out in the midst of the rug sellers; from there it was a another skip across to the food vendors. She stopped just long enough to buy a parchment bag full of sugared fried cakes; her nose caught the scent and she discovered she couldn't resist the rich, sweet odor. Then she cut down the aisle of the scent sellers and from there, she strolled directly into the inn.

She unlocked the door of their room, and as she had expected, she had beaten him back. Since he was *supposed* to have been taking a nap—

:I wish you'd take me with you,: Need said querulously, from beneath the bed. *It may be just a bazaar, but you know very well there are people who are out there looking for you.:*

Wonderful. Another mother hen. "I can't take you with me," she said, trying to keep her patience intact. "It's bazaar rules; no long weapons in the bazaar, nothing longer than a knife, unless it's a purchase, and then it has to be wrapped up."

:You could carry me wrapped,: the blade suggested hopefully. *:There wouldn't be any problem then.:*

"Then you'd do me about as much good as a stick," she snorted. "Less; you're not much good as a stick, you're too awkward and not long enough."

Before the sword could retort, there was a sound of a key in the door, and it opened as soon as the lock disengaged.

"Welcome back," she said dryly.

"Uh. Hello," Skif said, first startled, then sheepish.

"I suppose you couldn't sleep, hmm?" She put her purchases on the rickety little table that was supplied with the room. "You know, there's a little story I've been meaning to tell you—I wonder if you've ever heard it? It's about Herald Rana and her old suitor from home."

He shook his head, baffled.

:You're a cruel child,: said Gwena.

:I'm getting tired of this,: she replied.

"Herald Rana went back home for a visit last year, and a young man who wouldn't give her a second glance back when she was the cheesemaker's daughter decided that she was the most wonderful woman he'd ever seen." She shrugged. "It might have been the Whites, it might have been that she'd matured quite a bit since the last time he saw her. It really doesn't matter. He followed her back to Haven and then out on her circuit. He got to be such a nuisance that she decided to do something about him. So the next time he came up behind her in a market and put his arms around her, she put him to the ground." She raised one eyebrow at him. "That wasn't enough for him, apparently, because he kept following her, but at a distance. So she waited until he followed her out into the forest when she went to hunt a little fresh meat."

She paused, significantly.

"Well?" Skif finally responded.

"She ambushed him and planted an arrow right between his legs. I'm given to understand that she came close enough to his assets to shave them."

Skif gulped.

"I trust you take my point." She turned away from him, drew her knife, and lopped off the tip of the cheese roll with an obvious enthusiasm that made him wince. She stabbed the piece and offered it to him. He declined.

:You are a very cruel child.: Gwena sounded more amused than accusatory.

:Very practical,: Need retorted, with a chuckle.

:Very weary,: she replied to both of them. And took the cheese herself. *:Let's hope he gets the point—before I have to give it to him.:*

The sword and Gwena joined in laughter. *:Oh, I think he did,:* Gwena chuckled. *:I'll have a talk with Cymry and see if she can't have a word with him.:*

:She'd better do something,: Elspeth replied grimly. *:Or I will. And this time, Herald or not, I'll be more direct.:*

Priests and other religious travelers had their own special camping ground reserved for them away from the bazaar, on top of a rise. Shaman Kra'heera shena Tale'sedrin looked out over the crowded tents of the bazaar from his vantage point above it and smiled a little. Somewhere down there was a young woman, accompanied by a tall young man, who was looking for them.

Not them, specifically. Just the Tale'sedrin. Since he and Tre'valen had arrived late this afternoon, no less than four traders had come strolling up to their tent with the casually proffered information that someone was looking for Tale'sedrin.

To each of those four, Kra'heera had said nothing. He had simply gone about his business of raising their tent. His apprentice, Tre'valen, had thanked them politely, but when he had shown no further interest in the subject, the four had strolled onward, ostensibly to visit some other tent dweller farther on. But Kra'heera read the set of their shoulders, and knew that they went away disappointed because he had not been interested in buying the rest of their information. There was as much traffic in information in the bazaars of Kata'shin'a'in as there was in material goods.

He had not bought their intelligence because he did not need to. And he let them know by his manner, since they were no fools, that he had his own ways of information. Reinforcing the shamans' reputation for uncanny, timely knowledge never hurt.

As sunset touched the tops of the tents with a sanguine glow, another visitor reached the encampment of the Shin'a'in, but this visitor had no interest in selling her information. Not to folk of the People of the Plains; not when her own son rode with them, adopted into the Clan of Tale'sedrin by marriage.

This scarlet-clad visitor was welcomed within the newly pitched tent with jokes and news; the brazier was fired for her, and cakes and sweet tea were offered and accepted. And when all the civilized amenities were completed, and *only* then, did rug seller Dira Crimson say what she came to say.

She, Kra'heera, and Tre'valen sat comfortably on overstuffed cushions, placed on a carpet any of the rug traders would have offered their firstborn offspring for. "There is a girl," the woman said, her plump, weathered face crinkling with a smile as she arranged the folds of her scarlet skirt about her feet. "She is a stranger, and speaks with an accent that I would not know, had I not journeyed once into Valdemar with the Clan—where we had much profit, the gods be praised."

Kra'heera's lips curled up in his own smile, and he filled her cup with more tea. "I think that the gods had less to do with that than your own wit and fine goods, trade-sister."

She waved the suggestion aside. "Na, na, one does one's best, and the gods decree the rest. So. There is a girl. There is a young man with her. *She* looks for Tale'sedrin. *He* watches her with the eyes of a young dog with his first bitch."

Kra'heera laughed at the old woman's simile. There was no repressing Dira; she told things as she saw them, and if anyone objected, why, she felt they need not listen.

"Young men are ever thus. What of this girl of Valdemar, who seeks the Children of the Hawk?" he asked.

"Well, it is said that she comes from Kerowyn, on whom be peace and profit, if such a thing is possible for one whose livelihood is by the sword. It is said that she bears the mage-sword given her from the hand of Kerowyn as a token of this." The old woman's black eyes peered at him sharply, from within a nest of wrinkles. "This is the sword of Clan-Mother Kethryveris, the blade called 'Need.'"

"It is said?" Kra'heera pondered the information. "You have seen this?"

Dira shook her head. "No, not with my own eyes. Nor have I heard her claim this with my own ears. I have spoken with her but briefly, a few words at most. She seems honest. That is all I can say."

Kra'heera nodded, and Dira smiled her satisfaction. No Shin'a'in ever moved on purely hearsay evidence. No Shin'a'in dared move on hearsay. But Dira had reported what she knew, and Kra'heera would not be caught by surprise.

The last of the light faded, and Tre'valen lit the scarlet lamps that marked the tent as priestly and not to be disturbed. They exchanged a few more pleasantries, and Dira took herself back to her own tent, somewhere in the labyrinthine recesses of the rug seller's bazaar.

Kra'heera nodded to his apprentice to take her place beside the brazier. The elder shaman sat in thought while his apprentice seated himself. "Will you do nothing about this Outlander?" Tre'valen wondered aloud. "Will you seek her out?"

"Perhaps." Kra'heera studied the bottom of his paper-thin porcelain teacup. "Perhaps. She may be of some use to us, whether she speaks the truth or no. But we have a more urgent appointment, you and I."

"We do?" Tre'valen asked, surprised, his black brows arching upwards in surprise. Tre'valen was one of the pure-blood Shin'a'in—by no means the majority among the mixed-blood Clan of Tale'sedrin. His ice-blue eyes were startling to an outsider, set beneath his raven-black hair, in an angular, golden-skinned face.

"Surely you did not think that we came riding over the Plains in the heat of summer for the pleasure of it?" Kra'heera responded wryly. "If that is so, you have an odd notion of pleasure."

Tre'valen flushed a little but held his tongue. Kra'heera's wit sometimes tended to the acidic, but his apprentices had to grow used to it. That was part of becoming a shaman; to be able to face any temperament with calm.

"We go out now," Kra'heera announced, standing up from his cross-legged position with an ease many younger men would envy. *That* took Tre'valen by surprise; the apprentice scrambled to his feet awkwardly, just in time to follow his superior out into the night. To Kra'heera's veiled amusement, Tre'valen first turned toward the bazaar, and only altered his steps when he realized that the shaman was heading into the Old City.

And not just the Old City, but the oldest part of the city. The city swallowed them, wrapping them in a blanket of sound and lights. Kata'shin'a'in did not sleep in trade season; business went on as usual after nightfall, although the emphasis shifted from the general to the personal, from the mundane to the exotic. In the bazaar the perfume sellers, the jewelers, the traders in mage-goods would be doing brisk business. In the Old City, within the inn walls, food, drink, and personal services were being sold: Kra'heera wondered if his apprentice felt as odd as he did, moving silently between walls, with the sight of the land and much of the sky blocked out by masonry. The wind could not move freely here, and the earth beneath their feet had been pounded dead and lifeless by the countless hooves of passing beasts.

Yet the Shin'a'in had once known cities—or rather a city, one that had once stood in the precise middle of the Dhorisha Plains. Once, and very long ago, that had been the home of the Kaled'a'in.

Kra'heera led the way confidently between the walls of alien stone, through the scents and sounds that were just as alien, the evidences of Outlanders conducting further business—or pleasure. He moved without worry, for all the fact that he wore a sword at his back, for the rule of the bazaar did not apply to Shin'a'in; not here, in their own city, where they only visited, but never lived.

The deeper they went into the core city, the darker and quieter it became—and the stranger grew the scents and the sounds. Voices babbling in chaos became voices chanting quietly in unison; raucous song became the sweet harmony of a pair of boy sopranos. The mingled scents of perfume, wine, and cookery gave way to the smoke of incense and the fragrance of flowers. This was the quarter of the temples, and the doors spilling forth yellow light yielded to those with lanterns on either side, held invitingly open for the would-be worshiper.

Yet these were all Outlander places of worship, not places that belonged to the Shin'a'in. Kra'heera continued past them as Tre'valen gazed about in interest. The lanterns at the temple doors became fewer; the doors, closed and darkened, until there was no light at all except what came from the torches kept burning at intervals along the street. Sound faded; now they heard the dull scuff of their own boot soles along the hard-packed dirt of the street.

Finally they reached their goal, near where the street ended in a blank wall; a single closed door, with a lantern burning low beside it. Kra'heera knocked in a pattern long familiar to his apprentice, as the beginning of one of the drum chants.

The door opened, and Kra'heera again hid his amusement to see Tre'valen's shock. She who opened the door for them was Kal'enedral, Swordsworn—and at first glance, she looked to be garbed in black, the color of blood-feud.

A closer look as she closed the door behind them, however, showed Tre'valen what Kra'heera already knew; the color of her costume was not black, nor brown, but deep midnight blue.

Which was *not* a color that Swordsworn ever wore.

"What—" said Tre'valen.

"She is special," Kra'heera said, anticipating his question. "She is Sworn, not only to the Warrior, but the Crone as well. She bears her blade—but she uses it to guard wisdom. There are a dozen more like her here, and this is the only place where you will find them."

The Kal'enedral led them down the corridor, into a single square room, with a roof made of tiny square panes of glass set in a latticework of lead. The full moon had just begun to peer through the farther edge of the window-roof. Tre'valen stared at it in fascination; glass windows were a wonder to a Shin'a'in, and a glass roof a marvel past expectation. He almost stumbled onto the weaving carpeting the floor of the room; Kra'heera caught him before his foot touched the fragile threads, and steadied him as he looked down in confusion.

"It is too old to hang," he explained. "And besides, as you know, there are things that need the moon to unlock."

The Kal'enedral slipped out of the room unnoticed; Kra'heera took a seat on one of the many cushions placed around the woven tapestry at the periphery of the room. After a moment's hesitation, Tre'valen joined him.

"You know the story of our people," Kra'heera said softly, as he waited for the moon to sail above the walls, shine down through the window, and touch the threads of the weaving. "Let me remind you again, to set your mind upon the proper paths."

Out of the corner of his eye he saw Tre'valen nod, and waited for a moment, absorbing the silence—and the dust of centuries rising from the weaving.

"In the long-ago time, we and the Hawkbrothers were one people, the Kaled'a'in. We served and loved an overlord, one of the Great

Mages, and when he became drawn into a war, so, too, did we. The end of that war brought great destruction, so great that it destroyed our homeland. The mage himself had great care for his people, and he gave the warning and the means for us to escape before the destruction itself was wrought. It took us many years to return from whence we had escaped; when we came here, to this very spot—"

The moon crept through the roof-window; it had been edging down toward the weaving. He had paced his words to coincide with it reaching the first threads of the border, as he reached with the power She gave her shamans, and invoked the magic of the weaving.

"—this is what we saw."

Shaman Ravenwing passed her hand over her eyes, wishing she could change the reality as she blotted out the sight.

The debris that they had encountered on their way here, the flattened trees, complete absence of animal and bird life, the closer they came to the site, had given them some warning. The ridge of earth they had approached had told them more. But nothing prepared them for the reality.

There was no homeland. Only a vast crater, as far as the eye could see, dug many, many man-heights into the ravaged earth. So intense had been the heat of the blast that had caused it, that the earth at the bottom had been fused into a lumpy sheet of glassy rock.

Ravenwing took her hand from her eyes and looked again. It was no better at second viewing, and Ravenwing reached out blindly for the two Clansfolk standing beside her. She stood with her arms about their shoulders, theirs about hers; and her eyes streamed tears as she forced herself to face the death of all she had ever known.

She sat inside the hastily pitched Clan Council tent, erected to provide shade—and to block the sight of the destruction. With her sat the shamans, the Clan Elders, every leader of every Clan of the Kaled'a'in. They were here to make decisions—and possibly, to settle a rift that was threatening to split the People in twain.

The dispute centered about magic. Five of the Clans used it, four did not. Traditionally, the four who tended and bred the horse herds were the Clans which avoided the use of magery; Hawk, Wolf, Grasscat, and Deer. The five Clans which—among other things—actually manipulated the breeding of the horses, as well as other creatures, did so by means of magic. These five had fielded many mages and Healers to their overlord, Mage Urtho. Falcon, Owl, and Raven Clans were protesting that they were not going to give up their powers, as the previous four were insisting. Two more Clans, Eagle and Fox, were ambivalent, but were disturbed by the idea of sacrificing something so integral to their lives.

Ravenwing's own Clan, Taylesederin, was foremost in demanding that magic be eliminated from their lives.

"Our warsteeds are everything anyone could wish; there have been no changes made to them for generations. The bondbirds are not entirely all one could wish, but is it worth holding such a dangerous, double-edged power simply to improve them a little more?"

That was Ravenwing's Clan Chief, Silverhorse, the foremost opponent of magic in all its shapes and colors.

Firemare Valavyska, Elder for the Owls, widened her eyes with contempt. "What, you think that is all magic does? Precisely what do you intend to do about those who do not share your scruples, our enemies who would use any weapon they have against us? Who will protect you from the attacks of mages if you banish magic from our lives?"

"Who protected us this time?" Silverhorse shouted, gesturing wildly at the desolation beyond the tent flap. "Is it worth a repetition of that simply to have a little more power?"

"Magic protected you this time by giving you the means to escape, little brother," rumbled Suncat Trevavyska, of Falcons. "Magic has saved you before, and it will again. Besides, how do you propose to cleanse this land if not by magic? Only magic can undo what magic has done."

It was but the opening blow of a dispute that was to continue for days...

The last member of the Five Clans vanished into the north, and Ravenwing dried her eyes on her sleeve, swallowing the last of her tears. In the end, the dispute could not be healed, not by the softest words of the most reasonable and coolest heads in the Clans nor by any appeals to brotherhood and solidarity.

The Five Clans—now calling themselves "Taylesederas," or "Brothers of the Hawks," for their association with the corvine and raptor bondbirds they had been developing—had determined to split from the Four Clans who wished to banish magic from their lives for all time. The Four Clans had no name for themselves at the moment—and no home, no purpose. Their only plan had been to do away with magery. Now that was done, and they had no idea of what to do next.

But Ravenwing and her fellow shamans—from all of the Nine Clans—had been in separate consultations after they had determined that there would be no compromise. And Ravenwing had been chosen to present their thoughts to the Elder of Hawks.

Silverhorse stared after the departing ones long past when the last of the dust had settled. His face was blank, as if he had not truly expected that the People could be sundered. It seemed as good a time as any to approach him.

"Well?" she asked, jarring him from his enhancement. "You have succeeded in this

much; there is no longer magic among the People, other than that She and He give the shamans. Now what is your plan? Where do we go? What do we do? Will we find a homeland? Do we seek a new overlord?"

He turned eyes upon her that were bleak and sad. "I do not know," he confessed. "This land is torn and poisoned by magic turned awry; there is nowhere for us to go that we may claim without displacing someone else. Yet we cannot remain here—"

"We could," she offered. He answered with a short bark of a laugh.

"What? And eat rock? Drink our own tears? Watch our little ones warped and changed by the magic gone wild and twisted in this place?" He laughed again, but the pain in his laughter tore at her heart. "Is that all you can offer me, shaman of the Hawk?" He continued to laugh, but it was becoming wild and hysterical.

She silenced him with a single, open-handed slap. He stared at her—for in all her life, she had never once raised her hand to anyone, Clansman or not. She had been known as one of the softest and gentlest women in all the Clans—certainly among the shamans.

But the past days had hardened and toughened her; and the days to come would only mean more of the same. This she knew, though she was no Seer.

"You told me when you urged that we forsake magic, that we must trust in the Powers for our protection. Are you telling me now that you no longer believe that?" She let the acid of her words drip into the raw wound of his soul without mercy. "If that is true, then perhaps I should take my beasts and ride out after my Sundered brothers!"

"I—" his mouth worked for a moment, before he could produce any words. "I believe that... but..."

"But what?" Ravenwing looked down her long nose at him, from beneath half-closed lids. "But you do not believe They would answer if we called on them? Or is it that you are not willing to pay the price They might put on our aiding?"

"Would They answer?" he asked, hope springing into his eyes. "Have you done a Seeking, shaman of the Hawk?"

She nodded, slowly. "I have done a Seeking and a Calling, and I have been answered. But the price of Their aid will be in blood."

He took a deep breath. "Whose?"

"The Elders of each Clan that is left," she replied with authority. "Yours, and the other three."

She watched his face change as her words struck him. It was not an easy decision that he was being asked to make. He was a relatively young man; as yet unmated, with all of his life before him. And that was part—and no small part—of the sacrifice. Yet when he had taken the Oath of the Elder, he had pledged just this thing; to lay down his life for his people at need. But he had, no doubt, thought if it came to that, it would be in the heat of battle—not the cold loneliness of self-sacrifice.

His eyes widened in a glazed shock, turned inward, then focused on hers again. She nodded as she saw his attention return to her.

"It is not an easy question," she said quietly. "Your three brother and sister Elders are being posed the same question even now. We do not expect you to answer at once—but it must be soon. The People, as you pointed out, cannot remain here long."

"And if I decline this—honor?" he asked, with a touch of painful irony.

"Then I spill my blood in place of yours," she replied steadily, having faced this possibility herself, and made her own decision. "It must be one or the other of us."

"Leaving Hawk without a shaman."

She shrugged. "It must be one or the other of us. That is the Price the Calling named. We four chief shaman have spoken, and agreed. All of the apprentices have promise, but none is fit or trained to function on his own. If any of the chiefs must go, that Clan must live without a shaman until an apprentice is ready." She stepped away from him, and turned to go. "I will leave you to think on this. Come to me by moonrise with your decision."

He touched her shoulder as she turned away, stopping her.

"I do not need until moonrise," he said, in a tone that made her heart sore. "It is not all that difficult a choice to make, after all."

He smiled, a smile sweet and without fear, and she held back her tears.

"When will you require me?" he asked.

It had taken a full moon for the Clans to position themselves about the glassy crater that had been their homeland, one to each prime direction. It had been hardest for Cat Clan; they had to make the half-circle around the rim to position themselves in the West.

At sunset—in whatever manner they chose—the four Elders gave themselves for their people. Silverhorse had simply stepped off the top of the ridge, vanishing into the darkness of the crater without even a sigh. Now Ravenwing stood above the place he had fallen, her arms spread to the sky, calling on the Powers with every fiber. Behind her in a rough half-circle stood the rest of the Clan, from the infants in arms to the oldest grandsire, adding their prayers to hers.

And with the moon, She came. Her face changed, moment to moment, from Maid to Crone, from stern Warrior to nurturing Mother, and back again. She filled the sky, and yet She stood before Ravenwing and stared deeply and directly into the shaman's eyes.

She spoke, and Her voice filled Ravenwing's ears and mind so completely that there was room for nothing but the experience.

"I have heard your prayers," She said, gravely, "as I have heard the prayers of your Sundered brothers. There was a price to be paid for what they asked, and there is a price to be paid for what you ask."

"In blood?" asked a quiet voice, which Ravenwing recognized as that of Azurestar,

231

shaman of Cat Clan. A tiny bit of her was left to wonder that she could hear the voice as clearly as if Azurestar stood beside her.

She shook Her head. "Not in blood—in your lives, all of you. I shall give you back your homeland, but the price is vigilance."

She held out Her hand, and cupped within it was the crater. In the center of the crater, and scattered about it, beneath the slag and fused stone, were shapeless things that glowed an evil green.

"Three things destroyed the homeland," She said gravely. "The destructive spell of an enemy, the self-destruction of the Gate that you fled through, and the Final Strike of your master Urtho's death by his Champion, meant to remove his enemy as he himself died. Yet despite all this, there are many weapons of Urtho's making that still remain and could be used, buried beneath the slag and rubble. There are weapons there that are too dangerous even for those with good intentions to hold. But you have forsworn magic for all time—they will be no temptation to you."

Ravenwing nodded, and felt the agreement of the rest.

"Here, then, is the price. You must guard your new land, which you shall call the Dhorisha Shin'a—the Plains of Sacrifice, and yourselves the Shin'a'in—the People of the Plains. You must keep strangers out at all cost, unless they pledge themselves into the Clans, or are allies that you, the shamans, must call on Me to judge. Those will be marked in ways that you will recognize. You will never swear to any overlord again, but will remain always sworn only to each other and to the Powers. You have forsworn magic, and you must keep that vow. Any of your children that are born with Mage-Gift, you must either send to your Sundered brothers, bring into the craft of the shaman, or permit the shaman to block the Gift for all time."

It was a sacrifice indeed; of freedom, and to a small extent, of free will—and not just for them, but for all generations. They would swear to an endless service, an endless guardianship.

But the gain was their home.

She felt the assent of her people, and added her own to it.

The Goddess smiled. "It is well," She said, and spread out Her hands, stepped down into the crater, and began to walk.

Where Her feet touched, a carpet of flowers, grass, and trees sprang up, and spread, flowing over the ruined earth like a green flood, as She walked westward...

Kra'heera blinked, and smiled faintly. He had forgotten how powerful the memories knotted into this weaving were. Ravenwing had been a formidable, strong-minded woman, and had managed to weave in not only the memories, but the emotions she had felt at the time.

That, of course, was the secret of the shamanic weavings; they held the memory of every shaman who worked upon them. This weaving held not only Ravenwing, but the half dozen who had followed her in those eventful days. Other weavings held the memories of more shamans than that; often in the Plains these days, there was little to record for years or even decades.

The most significant weavings were kept here, where all the Clans could have free access to them. There were more than four Clans now, and it was part of the training of a shaman that he come here, to experience the beginning of the Shin'a'in, the People of the Plains, for himself.

Ravenwing was responsible for making a great deal of the early training of shaman a part of the education of every Shin'a'in, so that every Shin'a'in could invoke the Powers at need. In the event of a Clan losing their shaman, it would be less of a problem to wait on the training of another than it had been in the old days.

She had also been responsible for insisting that whenever possible, more than one shaman and apprentice be resident with each Clan. And she had been the shaman who created the first of the Kal'enedral, those warriors who served not any one Clan, but all of the Clans together.

Altogether a remarkable woman, indeed.

Kra'heera turned slowly toward his own apprentice, and waited for the memories the shaman had invoked to release the younger man. Finally Tre'valen blinked, and shook his head slightly.

"All that is left is for you to learn the unlocking of these memories, and the weaving of them yourself," Kra'heera told the apprentice. "But that was not why I brought you here now. Have you guessed why?"

Tre'valen, who had already recovered from the effect of the alien memories on his own mind, nodded. "It is because of the rumors, I think," he said. "There are rumors that the Plains have been disturbed. You wanted me to see for myself why it is the People guard them."

Kra'heera considered moving—but the memory-trance relaxed one rather than leaving one tense, and there was nowhere more secure from listeners than this place.

"The rumors are true," he said. "There have been intruders on the Plains, intruders that only the shaman have been able to detect. The border guards cannot stop them, indeed, they have only recently caught sight of them at a distance. They are some kind of magic-made creatures from past the Tale'edras lands, and they have entered from the northern side of the Plains, where the Plains meet the territory of the Tale'edras Clan k'Sheyna."

"The Falcons?" Tre'valen said, curiously. "I do not know them."

"I know a little, but not a great deal," Kra'heera admitted. "I know this much of the enemy: the things that have been looking about have an incredible ability to vanish and have never been seen clearly. They have been sniffing out magic, I think, and when they find it, I think they will call that which created them."

"They could find many things," Tre'valen said grimly.

"And worst case, they could find the remains of the stronghold of Mage Urtho." Kra'heera nodded agreement. "I do not know if it would be possible for an attack to be mounted against the center of the Plains—but I do not know that it would *not* be possible."

"What of k'Sheyna?" Tre'valen asked anxiously. "Are the Hawkbrothers not pledged to help us when dangers come from out of *their* lands?"

"Yes, but k'Sheyna, from the little I know, is a Clan with troubles of its own," Kra'heera responded, after a moment to gather his thoughts. "I do not think they are capable of repulsing a single Adept just now, and if these creatures are the servants of not one, but an alliance of Adepts—well, I do not think there is much hope of aid from them."

Tre'valen grimaced. "So. What is it we need do?"

Kra'heera mentally congratulated his apprentice; the youngster had cut to the heart of the matter, without wasting time on things that might or might not be.

"We need to bring together the shamans of two Clans, at least. Then, we must invoke the Kal'enedral—the *leshya'e*-Kal'enedral, as well as what physical Swordsworn we can muster."

"The spirits?" Tre'valen said in surprise. "We can invoke the spirit Swordsworn?"

"If needs must, yes, we can," Kra'heera told him. "It must be done through the living Swordsworn, but it is not done lightly. I think, however, we have little choice at this moment. The spirits bring with them some of Her power, Her magic, and with these, I think we can withstand these intruders. But to accomplish all this, there is one thing more we must have."

"Time," Tre'valen responded promptly.

"Time," Kra'heera agreed. "And to gain time, we need a distraction for these things."

"Hmm." Tre'valen's face grew thoughtful, and Kra'heera felt a lifting of his heart. He had not been mistaken in this young man. Tre'valen did not simply wait to do what he was told—he looked for answers.

"The young woman that Dira spoke of—" Tre'valen said, slowly. "Just what is she? Why would she seek us?"

Kra'heera wondered for a moment why Tre'valen's mind had turned to the strangers, but the younger man was Gifted with the ability to sift through bits of information and extract unusual solutions. So here, in this safest of all places, the elder let his own mind range for a moment, asking for a vision that would sum up what these strangers were.

In a moment, he had that vision; the young woman and her friend— with white uniforms, and *leshya'e* horses.

They were Heralds of Valdemar. He had no trouble recognizing the uniform; his cousin Kerowyn had one—though she seldom wore it willingly.

Only one Herald had ever entered the Plains—the great and good friend of Tarma shena Tale'sedrin, long before Kra'heera had ever been born. Herald Roald was something of a minor legend among Tale'sedrin, with his spirit-horse, and his undeniable charm. Other Clans' children envied Tale'sedrin, who had hosted the *ver'Kal'enedral*, the "White Swordsworn," who brought them presents and took them for rides on his beautiful spirit-horse. Kra'heera's father had been one of those so honored, and for years thereafter he had told the children and grandchildren his tales of the wind-swift horse that had the understanding of a man.

"They are Heralds, from the Queen in Valdemar," he told his apprentice. "I do not know what brings them, but since our cousin Kerowyn is also one of them, I think that everything Dira told us could be true."

"Hmm." Tre'valen nodded thoughtfully. "That must be tested, of course. As they must be tested."

"But not by us," Kra'heera reminded him. "She must test and mark them. But—what were you thinking?"

"That they might prove worthy allies, perhaps enough to help us with these intruders." Tre'valen blinked, owlishly, in the moonlight. "Did you have any other thoughts?"

"Yes," Kra'heera responded, smiling slowly. "I have in mind that they might become our distraction. They have to be tested in any case; why not make their testing a matter of seeing how they respond to these intruders?"

Tre'valen frowned, which surprised his teacher. "Is this fair?" he demanded. "They do not know what it is they will encounter, nor do they know the Plains. *We* know the girl carries a magic thing, the spirit-sword. If these hunters are seeking out magic, will they not sniff *it* out? And what then?"

"Then they must defend themselves if the hunters come for them," Kra'heera said with a shrug. "They are outsiders, are they not? They must prove their worth, must they not? If She finds them worthy, perhaps She will aid them."

"But what of us?" Tre'valen asked. "Should we not aid them?"

"Why?" Kra'heera responded. "I see no reason to aid them. If they survive, very well. If they survive and grant us the time we need, we will aid them. If they do not?" He shrugged. "The Plains are *ours* to guard. *She* never told us that we were to take in random strangers who come looking for help from us. In fact, by allowing them to cross the Plains, we are granting them more than any other in all of our history. It is only because they are Heralds, and because they come from our cousin, that I allow this at all."

Reluctantly, Tre'valen nodded. "It is in the interest of the Clans," he admitted. "But I cannot like it."

"That which does not overcome us, strengthens us," Kra'heera replied callously. "This will be good for them. And here is what we shall do…"

Elspeth knew by a sudden change in the air that she was no longer alone in her little room.

Tonight she had demanded another room, separate from Skif's. She was not going to share a room, much less a bed, with him anymore. She had hoped that would make it clear to him that she was not going to put up with his nonsense any more.

Skif had protested, but she had overruled him. Now she was sorry she had.

There was an intruder in her room, and if she was very lucky, it would only prove to be a thief.

She risked a quick mental probe, and met a block as solid as a wall of seamless marble.

Crap. It's not a thief—

She started to reach for the knife under her pillows, and started to call for Gwena—only started; no more. She was frozen in place by a sudden flare of light.

It was the candle at her bedside, lighting itself. And at the foot of her bed was a sinister shadow, arms folded.

Clad in black from head to toe, veiled—there was no mistaking that costume. Kero had described and sketched it in detail, and no one here in Kata'shin'a'in would dare counterfeit it. Not here, not on the edge of the Plains.

Her intruder was Kal'enedral—one of the Swordsworn. She relaxed marginally. If this one had wanted her dead, she would *be* dead, and there would have been none of this drama with the magically lighted candle.

The Swordsworn flicked his (her?) hand, tossing something at the bed. It glinted as it spun, coppery and metallic on one side, enameled on the other. It landed enamel side up; it bore the image of a gold-feathered hawk.

Tale'sedrin. Children of the Hawk! She recognized it instantly; she had one identical to it in her belt-pouch, given to her by Kero as a way of identifying herself when she finally found the Tale'sedrin.

It seemed that *they* had found *her.*

"What—" she whispered—or started to. But the Swordsworn shook her (his?) head, and threw something else onto the bed. This time it was a piece of rolled vellum. Her eyes, caught by the movement, followed it for just a moment—hardly more than an eyeblink. But that was long enough. When she looked up again, the black-clad stranger was gone. There was no movement at either door or window to say which way he had taken—if, indeed, he had taken either.

:What happened?: Gwena demanded. *:Are you all right?:*

:Yes. Yes, I'm fine.: She told Gwena absently about her visitor as she picked up the vellum gingerly and unrolled it. Her heart, which had all but stopped, leapt and hammered with excitement.

It was a map of the Plains, the first such that she had ever seen. Or rather, the first such that she trusted. There had been plenty of folk who had offered her maps, but their reliability ranged from laughable to pathetic. This, from the hand of a Kal'enedral of Kero's own Clan, was something she thought she could put her trust in. One thing stood out, on a map crowded with detail and closely written markers; an enigmatic little drawing, perched on the northern rim of the Plains, circled in bright red, very fresh ink.

The Clans migrated with the season; could that be Tale'sedrin's current location?

Well, what else could it be? They know I'm looking for them; this is their answer. I have to come to them, they won't be coming to me.

She said as much to her Companion.

:I don't like it,: Gwena said, unhappily. *:I don't like it at all. You aren't planning on going out there, are you? Well? Are you?:*

Elspeth ignored her, letting her silence declare her intent. She was not about to argue with her Companion on this, and Gwena should have been able to anticipate just that reaction.

:I'd go for it, girl,: Need chuckled. *:Hell of an opportunity. Probably testing you to see if you've got the guts to go into their stronghold.:*

:You would *go for it,:* Gwena complained resentfully. *:The worst that could happen to you is that you'd have to find yourself another bearer. Don't listen to her, Elspeth.:*

:You just want her to do what you planned for her,: the sword jeered.

:Both of you, shut up, *dammit,:* she "shouted"—and was rewarded by blessed silence.

She was going of course; there was nothing that was going to stop her. Not Gwena's disapproval, or Skif's; not the possible risk, or the distance involved. She was finally charting her *own* course and following a path that no one had planned for her.

And that, in itself, was reason enough.

1 7

DARKWIND

As he passed beneath the trees and away from open sky, Darkwind redoubled his shielding. When he had been fourteen and had been caught up in his friends' mating-spell, it had been an accident, and one that brought all of them a great deal of chagrined amusement. But if he were to "eavesdrop" now, it would be deliberate—and since he had not been invited, he was not going to intrude on this most private of moments for them.

Or at least, he had not intended to intrude—

But he was given no choice, after all.

Everything seemed quiet up by the swamp, and he didn't think there was any particular reason to double back and check the area beside the ruins; the gryphons themselves had made an aerial patrol of the forest before the flight. He doubted that anything large would have gotten in under cover of the trees.

On the other hand, it wouldn't hurt to check the trails for signs of intruders. It wouldn't take all that long.

He had just called to Vree, and was halfway through this particular patch of forest. He was heading in the direction of the path to the swamp and the *hertasi*, when a scream of agony cut the sky. A second scream answered the first. A heartbeat later, the world came apart for an instant.

At least that was what it felt like. He *knew* what it was as he slammed down another kind of shield and fought his senses clear; the resonating effect of a magic-blast, powerful, crude, and close at hand. And the tortured scream that had accompanied it, that echoed across the sky and pierced all his mental shields, had come from Treyvan!

Vree was already shooting up through the treetops, streaking off in the direction of the shriek of rage and pain, screaming a battle cry of his own. Running all out, Darkwind followed on the ground as best he could.

This was wild land, hard to cross at any speed. He ran through it without any of his usual care—breaking branches, leaving behind tracks an infant could read, crashing through the undergrowth like a clumsy young deer in a panic. But still the terrain itself held him back; bushes clutched at him, roots tripped him up, thickets too thick to be forced blocked his way. Heedless of his own risk, he opened his mind to the gryphons, but heard—nothing.

And that was even worse than the cries had been.

Rage and fear blinded him to pain; rage and fear drove him through plum thickets, across a tumble of razor-sharp stone fragments, and loaned him wind and strength. His heart pounded too loudly for him to have heard danger coming up behind him; his soul was torn with claws of agony for what that silence might mean.

:Ahead!: called Vree, shooting under the tree branches like a winged arrow, turning faster than the eye could follow, and shooting away again. :Here!:

The bird was too excited and angry to manage anything more coherent than that. Darkwind plunged after him, his lungs burning, his side pierced with a lance of pure pain. Just when he thought that he could not possibly run any farther, he literally stumbled into a tangle of broken branches, then over a fur-covered leg, and fell into a mass of broken brush before he could regain his balance.

The leg belonged to Hydona, who was sprawled in an unconscious tangle, bleeding from one torn and wounded wing.

* * *

"Come on, Treyvan," Darkwind crooned, cradling the gryphon's head in his hands, and slapping his beak lightly. "Come on, old boy. Wake up. Come on, Hydona needs your help; I can't move her without you." Treyvan lay in the middle of a half-crushed bush. It had obviously saved him worse injury when he hit the ground, but Darkwind couldn't free him from the snarl of broken branches unless he could revive the male gryphon and get some help from him.

The eyelids fluttered, the beak opened a fraction, and closed again. The head stirred in Darkwind's hands and Treyvan protested his treatment wordlessly. "Arrwk—rrrr—Daaa—Daaarrrwk—"

"That's right, it's Darkwind. Come on." Darkwind slapped the beak a little harder, pulled at Treyvan's crest-feathers. "Come on. Say something with some sense in it. Wake up, old friend."

"Rrrrrr." The eyelids fluttered and stayed open this time; the weight of the gryphon's head left Darkwind's hands as Treyvan raised it a trifle. "Hydona—" the gryphon croaked, whining wordlessly with pain, as he tried to turn his head. "Hydona—"

"She's hurt," Darkwind told him, "but I think she'll be all right. Her wing's hurt; I don't think she's broken anything, and she's kind of half-conscious, but I can't get her out. I need to get you out of this tangle, so you can help me get her out of hers."

"Can't—move—" the gryphon said, starting to thrash weakly in alarm. It was obvious then to Darkwind that Treyvan wasn't really hearing him—that, in fact, he was only half-conscious.

He opened his shields to the gryphon, and touched him directly, mind to mind. *:Don't move till I tell you. You're caught. Hydona is all right, but she's hurt and tangled up in some brush, and I'm going to need your help to move her.:*

He glanced back over his shoulder to the right, where the female gryphon lay, eyes half-closed, one wing folded awkwardly beneath her, the other oozing blood from a wound. Vree sat right beside her head, *his* eyes closed in concentration. He was in complete mental contact with her, helping to keep her calm and unmoving. He'd done this before, with wounded bondbirds, and he was remarkably good at it—in fact, if there were such a thing as a Healer among the bondbirds, Vree might well qualify. He might not have been able to hold Hydona if she had been completely awake and aware enough to fight him, or if she'd been delirious and raving, but like Treyvan, she had been—at best—half-conscious when the two of them arrived.

The mental contact seemed to steady Treyvan; he stopped thrashing, and held still. Satisfied that the gryphon wasn't going to lose control, panic, and disembowel his rescuer (a very real possibility with a predator as large and strong as a gryphon), Darkwind moved over to his side.

:All right, old friend. I'm going to start with your left wing. Lift it just a little— that's it—:

It took them much longer than Darkwind wanted to get Treyvan free; by the time they finished, Hydona had slipped a little farther away from consciousness. It took all three of them, Vree included, to rouse her—and all three of them to get her on her feet.

"What happened?" Darkwind asked, glancing sideways at what appeared to be fresh human remains—shredded—as they finally got Hydona, swaying, into a standing position.

"I—don't rrrremember," Treyvan said unhappily. "We completed the flight—yesss—and—"

"Aahhh," said Hydona. She shook her head, and gave a faint cry of pain. "There wasss—a man. Below. Usss. With a weapon. A crosssbow."

"Yesss, a man—" Treyvan nodded, as he put his shoulder to Hydona's to support her. "He sssshot Hydona—that isss all I rrrrremember—"

"Can you hold her up a moment by yourself?" Darkwind asked. "I think I see something, and I didn't get a chance to look over there."

Treyvan nodded and winced as if his head hurt. That gave Darkwind another little piece of information, confirming one of his suspicions. The male gryphon had been the one receiving the blast of magic that Darkwind had felt smash into his own shields, as if it had been nonspecific, and unfocused. Magic was a poor way to render someone unconscious—rather like taking a boulder to smash a fly. The amount of sheer power required to overwhelm was ridiculous—in fact, it was far easier to shape a bit of energy into a dart and shoot them with it. Better far to use a true mind-blast, if one had the Gift, or a physical weapon like the crossbow. A magic blast to the mind had certain side effects— and a headache was only one. It was not the weapon of choice, even against a flighted target.

That meant that the gryphons' attacker had no mental abilities of his own. And might not have had any magical ones, either.

Darkwind made certain that Hydona was balanced well, before leaving her side and walking over to what was left of the human who had attacked them.

He bent over the remains and poked at them with the tip of his dagger where he saw a glint of metal. Sure enough, there was a tarnished amulet of some sort about the neck, and the remains were as much blackened and burned as they were clawed.

He checked back over his shoulder; Hydona seemed to be doing better by the moment, so he spent some time investigating the state of the corpse. When he stood up and returned to the gryphons, Hydona was standing on her own, and Vree had taken a perch in the tree above them, showing not the slightest interest in Treyvan's crest-feathers.

"Well, it looks like I can piece together what happened," Darkwind said, as he reached out for the leading edge of Hydona's injured wing. "At least I think I can."

"I wisssssh I could," Treyvan fretted. "I do not like thisss, not rrrememberrring."

"Treyvan... you may never get the memory back," Darkwind told him, fighting off his own guilty feelings. *I should have stayed nearby. I should have guarded them. It wouldn't have taken that long, just to wait around until they were through and on the ground again.* "Here's what I think happened. This fellow was watching you, and when Hydona got within range, he shot, wounding her. Treyvan, when you dove at him, he hadn't yet had time to reload the crossbow—I think he was counting on you to be very slow, since you're very large. I think your speed took him by surprise. He has an amulet around his neck, the kind that can be used to store very basic magic. When you dove at him, he blasted you with it as kind of a reflex action."

"But—we have defensssessss," Treyvan said in surprise. "Magic defenssessss."

"True—but they were partially down because of your mating. I remember noticing that as you took off, then thinking it wouldn't matter." *Now I wish I'd said something.*

Treyvan hissed. "Trrrue. It isss neccesssary. I had forgotten that. Not fully down, but—reduced."

He nodded. "Anyway, they were down enough that the blast knocked you unconscious, but *up* enough that you reflected part of it back to him. Since he didn't have any defenses at all, you got him with the back-blast. I don't know if you killed him, but in the end it didn't matter. If he wasn't, Hydona, you definitely killed him when he fell and was within your reach. See?" He pointed to her foreclaws. "There's blood on your talons, and he's fairly well shredded."

"But why don't *I* remember?" she asked unhappily.

"Because you weren't more than half-conscious at the time," he told her. "It was mostly reflex on your part."

"Ah." She accepted that, carefully putting one foot before the other, while Darkwind walked beside her, holding up the drooping wing so that it wouldn't drag on the ground.

"I... will have an aching head for a while, then," Treyvan said ruefully. "And I did not even rescue my mate—"

"Oh, you did, it was just rather indirect," Darkwind soothed him. "I wouldn't worry about the headache; I'm going to get the *hertasi* to send over their Healer as soon as I leave you. She'll put you both right."

He was making light of the incident—because he was afraid it might mean more than a simple trophy-hunter, trying to shoot down the gryphons.

How had he found out about them, whoever he was? How had he traced them here? Where had he gotten a protective amulet powerful enough to have knocked Treyvan out of the sky? Why did he use the crossbow instead of magic, if he'd had access to magic that formidable?

And why had he gone after them in the first place?

There were more questions. What were those faint traces Darkwind had seen, before he had gotten the two gryphons to their feet—traces of a second person who had been moving about the two of them?

He'd been forced to destroy those traces, much against his will; there was no way to get to the gryphons without doing so. Getting in to disentangle their limbs and move brush away was the only way to help Treyvan and Hydona up and get them moving. He hadn't seen the scuffs and prints anywhere else, not even entering the area—and they had been quite clear around *Treyvan's* body, which meant, whoever it had been, the print-maker had *not* been the same person as the archer. The archer had been stone cold by the time the unknown had meddled with Treyvan's unconscious body.

If I had gotten here sooner, I could have caught him— Yet another lance of guilt, none of which was going to be assuaged until Treyvan and Hydona were safely back at their nest, and both of them were healed enough to take to the skies again.

The gryphlets boiled out of their nest as the quartet approached, hysterical with fear, so completely incoherent that not even their parents could get any sense out of them. They simply crowded under the adults' wings, pressing as closely to their bodies as they could, whimpering and trying to hide.

This, of course, did not help at all, but the little ones were too terrified to be reasoned with.

Darkwind couldn't tell if something had frightened them directly, or if they had linked in with their parents and experienced what had happened to the adult gryphons indirectly.

Whatever had happened, it rendered them completely irrational, and also turned them into complete nuisances.

He wanted to comfort them—and Hydona was nearly frantic with maternal worry—but they were in the way, underfoot, and demanding the total attention and protection of their parents, neither of whom were in any shape to give it.

Finally, in desperation, he tried the only one of them who wasn't already fully occupied. *:Vree!:* he called, hoping the bird might be able to at least chase the little ones out of the way.

The gyre came down from his protective circle above them in a steep dive, braking to a claws-out landing on the top of one of the stones. He looked sharply at the shivering, meeping gryphlets, and opened his beak to give a peculiar, piercing call.

The little ones looked straight at him, suddenly silent. Then they resumed their cries, but ran away from their parents and straight for Vree.

Vree, for his part, hopped down to a rock that stood just shoulder-height to the youngsters; he spread his wings and the little ones huddled up to the rock, one on either side, trying to cower under his wings, the tone of their cries changing from frantic to merely distressed. Vree replied to them with reassuring chirps of his own, "protecting" them with his wings.

It would have been funny, if the little ones hadn't been in such distress.

Whatever the cause of their fear, it could be dealt with later, once Treyvan and Hydona were settled into their nest, and the *hertasi* Healer brought to help them.

He left Treyvan leaning up against the stones with Vree and the little ones, while he helped Hydona into the nest area to clean her wing wound. The bolt had passed completely through the wing, leaving a ragged, round hole. It needed a Healer; there was no way for him to bandage it properly, and it continued to ooze blood, despite the primitive pressure-bandage he put on it. She clamped her beak shut and obviously tried not to complain, but moaned softly despite her best efforts as he bound the cloth in place. Darkwind found himself sweating and apologized clumsily for her pain. He returned to help Treyvan into the nest, keeping the little ones back until the still-unsteady gryphon had settled himself.

"I'm going to get the Healer," he said. "Do you want me to leave Vree with you?"

"Yesss," Treyvan sighed, as the forestgyre herded the youngsters in with all the skill of an expert nursemaid. "If it would not leave you in danger. He issss much help. And after thisss," he concluded, with a hint of his old sense of humor, "I may even *give* him my cresssst featherssss."

One thing at a time, he told himself. *First the gryphons, then the little ones— and then I find out who and why—and what this attack on them really means.*

One thing is certain. The quiet we've been enjoying was just a momentary lull. We're in for more and worse trouble; I can feel it.

He had felt trouble ahead, like the ache before a storm in once-broken bones. Like a storm, that trouble would strike—and with no warning where or when. He little thought that this time the fury would strike straight at his heart.

He gave Nera and the rest of the *hertasi* a brief explanation of what had happened, while Nyara listened unobtrusively in the background. The Healer, Gesta, left halfway through without waiting for permission—so like the Healers of the Tayledras that Darkwind had to smile. No one gave *them* orders either, and they were not much inclined to wait for permission when they thought their services were needed. Vree came winging in over the swamp just after he answered the last of the lizard people's questions—mostly concerned with their own safety, and what, if anything, they could do to safeguard it.

With Vree back, there was no reason to postpone his regular patrol—and every reason to complete it. There might be traces of those invaders—they might even still be within Tayledras territory, though Darkwind doubted it. In the past, those who had invaded to strike at the Hawkbrothers generally moved in, made whatever action they had come to take, and moved out again.

And there was still no telling if this was a danger to the Tayledras, or simply the foolishness of a trophy-hunter.

But when in doubt—assume the worst. The Hawkbrothers stayed alive by that rule, and it had always been the precept Darkwind operated on. He went over his ground with eyes sharpened by anxiety, looking for traces of the interlopers.

He found only vague tracks, places where something had passed through, but the ground was too dry to hold marks, and it was impossible to tell what had made those traces. It could have been the marksman and his (presumed) companion; a thread caught on a thorn showed it was not simply an animal, despite the trace of lynx hair below it.

At sunset he completed the last of his circuits, being replaced by Starsong, Wintermoon's current lover. He thought she looked at him strangely when she passed him—a pitying glance as she vanished into the underbrush. He puzzled over that odd expression as he headed back toward his *ekele*, thinking only of changing, getting food for himself and Vree, and going back to the gryphons.

But as he hurried up the path, Vree suddenly swooped down in front of him, crying a warning. He froze, one hand on his dagger, as a man-shaped shadow separated itself from the rest of the shadows beneath the trees.

Then Vree swerved away, his cry changing from warning to welcome, as a huge, cloud-white owl rose on silent wings to meet him. Darkwind's hand fell from the hilt of his dagger, as he recognized Wintermoon's bird K'Tathi.

"Brother—" he called softly. "What brings you out here? I thought you were on hunt-duty for a while."

Wintermoon said nothing; only came forward, slowly, worriedly searching Darkwind's face with his eyes. "Then—you have not heard?"

Darkwind shook his head, alarmed by his brother's expression, and his words. "Heard? No—nothing from the Vale, anyway. Why? What—"

Wintermoon clasped Darkwind in his arms, in a rare display of emotion and affection. "Little brother—oh, little brother, I wish it were not so... I grieve for you, *sheyna*. Dawnfire... is dead."

He searched his brother's face... and saw only regret. Darkwind was prepared for almost anything but that. He stood within the protection of his older brother's arms, and tried to make sense of what he had just heard.

"Dawnfire? But—this was her rest day! She wasn't even going to leave her *ekele*, she told me so! Surely you must be mistaken."

"No," Wintermoon said, his voice soft with seldom-heard compassion. "No, there is no mistake. She was found in her *ekele*—"

Then it hit him, with all the force of a blow to the gut.

"No!" he shouted, pulling away and staring at Wintermoon wildly. "*No!* It can't be! I don't believe you!"

But Wintermoon's pitying expression—exactly like Starsong's—told him the truth that he did not want to hear.

He was too well-trained and disciplined to break down—and too overcome with shock to move. His knees trembled, and threatened to give way beneath him. Wintermoon took his shoulders and gently steered him over to a fallen tree at the side of the trail. He urged Darkwind to sit as Vree dove in under the tree branches and landed, making soft whistling noises in the back of his throat.

Darkwind felt blindly behind his back and got himself down on the log before his legs collapsed. "What—happened?" he asked hoarsely, his throat choked, his eyes burning. He blinked, and two silent tears scorched down his cheeks.

"No one knows," Wintermoon replied quietly. "Thundersnow came to see if she wanted to go hunting for game birds, and found her this afternoon. She was—" he hesitated. "Little brother, did she full-bond with her bird often?"

"Sometimes," Darkwind croaked, leaning on his left side. He stared out at nothing, more tears following the first. "She—could not full-bond without trance, but Kyrr was so bright, she didn't need full trance often."

How can she be dead? Who could have touched her in her own home?

His fists knotted, and his stomach. More tears welled up and flowed unnoticed down his face.

"Little brother, it appeared that she was in full trance; that at least is how Thundersnow found her. There were no signs of violence or sickness upon her." Wintermoon paused again. "I would say… she must have undergone full-bond with her bird, and that some ill befell the two of them." He paused. "She was not known for caution. It may be that she sent Kyrr into the Outlands, and met something she could not escape from." He rested his hand on Darkwind's shoulder. "I am very sorry, little brother. I—am not known for words. But if I can help you—"

Darkwind seized the comfort he had thrust away earlier, and clasped Wintermoon to him, sobbing silently into his older brother's shoulder. Wintermoon simply held him, in an embrace of comfort and protection, while Vree whistled mourning beside them.

Nyara twisted on the sleeping mat in her little cave, a ball of misery and confusion. When Darkwind came to the *hertasi* with his story of attack on the gryphons, she had been as confused and alarmed as any of them. But now she'd had some time to think about what he had said—and to think back to that last confrontation with her father.

Mornelithe Falconsbane had always hated gryphons, just as a general rule, although *she* was not aware that he had ever had contact with the species. Not directly, at least. But he had been very interested in Treyvan and Hydona, to the extent of pulling every detail she knew about them out of her. She had the horrible feeling, fast growing into certainty, that *he* and no other was behind this attack.

And yet a direct attack was so unlike him. Mornelithe *never* did anything directly; he always layered everything he did in secrecy, weaving plots and counterplots into a net not even a spider could untangle. Why *would* he send someone to shoot at them? And why would he send someone armed with the crudest of amulets, a protection that was bound to fail? It made no sense at all...

The *hertasi* Healer passed the mouth of her cave. Gesta paused a moment, peering shortsightedly into the doorway. "Nyara?" she said, softly. "Are you there? Are you awake?"

Nyara blinked in surprise. "Yes," she responded. "Yes... I could not get to sleep. Is there something you need from me?"

Gesta coughed politely. "A favor, perhaps. The winged ones are better, but they need a full night's sleep. Yet they are fearful to sleep, fearing another hunter, this time in the dark. You, I think, can see well in the dark, no?"

"Yes, I can," Nyara responded, and in spite of her worries, a pleased little smile curled the corners of her mouth. *They trust me—or Gesta does, anyway—and they're willing to give me something to do.* "I think I see where you're tending. You want me to guard them, do you not? So that the winged ones may have some sleep."

"Yes," Gesta breathed, in what sounded like relief. "You need not defend them; you need only stand watch and pledge to rouse them if danger comes. You can do that, I think, without harm to yourself. And they asked after you, saying you were a friend. *We* would, but—"

The thin little figure silhouetted against the twilight sky shrugged, and leaned against its walking stick.

"But you do not see or move well by darkness, I know," Nyara responded. "I should be happy to attend them." She uncoiled from her mat and glided silently out to the *hertasi*, who blinked at her sudden appearance.

"Do you go across the swamp?" Gesta asked, taking an involuntary step backward and looking up at her. Nyara realized then that this was the first time the *hertasi* Healer had seen her on her feet. Her slight build might have deceived the little lizard into thinking she was shorter than she actually was. In reality, she was perhaps a thumb-length shorter than Darkwind, but certainly no more than that.

"No," she replied, wrinkling her nose in distaste at the thought of slogging through all that mud and water—and in the dark, no less. "No—if I go around about the edge, I shall find the ruins, no?"

"It will be longer that way," Gesta warned.

"But swifter if I need not feel my way through water in the dark," Nyara chuckled. "I go, good Healer. Thank you for giving me the task."

She slipped down to the path that led to the edge of the marsh before the *hertasi* could reply. And once out of sight of the *hertasi* village, she slipped into the easy run she had been bred and altered for, a ground-devouring lope that would have surprised anyone except those who were familiar with the Plains grass-cats on which she had been modeled.

While she ran, she had a chance to think; it was odd, but running always freed her thoughts, as if putting her body to work could make her mind work as well.

She thought mostly upon the notion that her father might have been involved in this attack upon the gryphons. If he was, what was she to do about it?

Treyvan and Hydona are my friends, she thought, unhappily. *They are, perhaps, the only true friends I have ever had. And Darkwind—oh, I wish that Father had not ordered me to seduce him! He makes my blood hot, my skin tingle. Never have I desired anyone as I desire him—not even Father. Father I hate and need—Darkwind I only need—*

The very thought of Darkwind, of his strong, gentle hands, of his melancholy eyes, of his graceful body, made her both want to melt into his arms, and to pounce on him and wrestle him to the ground, preparatory to another kind of wrestling altogether.

But Mornelithe has ordered me to take him—and therefore—I will not. She set her chin stubbornly, tucked her head down, and picked up her pace a bit.

But what if Mornelithe were behind this; what then?

I think it may depend upon if he sends more creatures against them tonight. Or if he has left a taint of himself that I can read. If I find nothing, I shall be silent. But if I find traces—then if I can—I must speak.

The decision seemed easy until she realized that she had actually made it. The realization took her by surprise.

I—why have I thought that? What are they to me, besides creatures who have been friendly—kindly—

No one had ever been friendly or kindly to her, not since Mornelithe had eviscerated her nurses, and given her sibs and playmates, failures by his reckoning, to his underlings to use as they would.

As he would give me to his underlings, if he judged me a failure. As he would kill me, if he knew of my rebellion.

Therefore he must not learn of it…

She reached the border of the ruins before she expected; she slowed to a walk, and sharpened her eyes to catch the glow of body heat. She knew in general where the gryphons' nest was, but not precisely. She also freed her ears from her hair, and extended them to catch any stray sound.

It didn't take her long to determine where the nest was; she heard the murmur of voices echoing among the stones of the ruins, and traced them back to their source. She froze just behind the shelter of a broken-down wall, hearing not only the gryphons, but Darkwind as well.

"There was a red-shouldered hawk circling around you when I left," he was saying. His voice sounded odd, thick with emotion, and hoarse. "Dawnfire's Kyrr was a red-shouldered—you know, I made her promise me that she *wouldn't* come around here today—"

"Which may have been a missstake," Treyvan interrupted wearily. Nyara peeked around the end of the wall. "Sssshe wasss curiousss. Very curiousss. It isss entirely posssible ssshe did full-bond with her birrrd. And whoeverrr it wasss that attacked usss, may have attacked and killed herrr asss well. If the birrrd diesss, the bondmate diesss, no?"

"Yes," Darkwind replied, but he sounded uncertain. "If they are in full-bond at the time. But I didn't see any dead—" he faltered, "—birds—"

"You might not," Hydona said, emerging slowly from the entrance of the nest, the little ones trailing after her. "It might not have ssstruck the grround. Perrrhapsss it wasss caught in a tree…"

She went on to say more, but Nyara didn't hear her. All of her attention had been caught by the female gryphon and the nestlings.

They bore the unmistakable stamp of her father's taint.

Hydona wore the contamination only lightly, a glaring red tracery like burst veins… and it was fading, as if Mornelithe had attempted something against her, and had failed. But the gryphlets— She moaned silently, to herself, as she had learned only too well to do.

Now she knew that it *had* been her father who had masterminded the attack on the gryphons. And how, and why.

The physical attack had never been intended to succeed. It had been intended to bring the gryphons down out of action, and only incidentally into his reach. He had attempted to subvert Hydona, to insert his own will and mind into hers. He surely found her too tough for him to take, at least, given the short amount of time he had to work in. She knew he had never really meant to do more than make a cursory attempt to take them, on the off chance that he would succeed by sheer accident. Because what he had really wanted was the opportunity to get at the little ones and work with them, undisturbed. She knew from bitter experience that it would not take him long at all, with a young thing, to subvert it to his will. The gryphlets would not be as useful as quickly as the adults—but they were more malleable, and far less able to defend themselves against him.

And they had one thing the adults did not; a direct tie into the power-node beneath their birthplace.

Mornelithe wanted that; he could pull power away from nodes, by diverting some of the power-flows into them, but he had no direct access to any nodes. The only nodes anywhere near this area were the one beneath k'Treva, and the one beneath the gryphons' nest. Both were within k'Treva territory, and out of Mornelithe's reach.

The power-node here was very deep, but very strong, and its ley-lines ran into k'Treva Vale. Through the young, tainted gryphons, Mornelithe would have direct access to the node, the line, and very possibly, could drain the node beneath k'Treva.

Or move it to his own stronghold.

It was entirely possible he would also have access to lines and nodes in the Plains; she had no idea if the node here was connected there or not.

And these ruins themselves could conceal artifacts from the ancient Mage Wars. Mornelithe had been trying to collect those for as long as she had been aware of his activities; he had only been marginally successful in his quests, gathering in creatures and devices either flawed, broken, or only marginally useful. His ambition was to acquire something of great power; one of the legendary permanent Master Gates, for instance. One of those would give him access to the old Citadels of the Lord Adepts; and *those*, however ruined, wherever they were hidden, would undoubtedly contain things he would find useful.

But having access to this node is going to be bad enough! She shuddered at the idea of Mornelithe with that much power in his hands. This nexus was far more important, far more powerful than the Birdkin guessed. If they had known, they would have either drained it or built their Vale here. Nyara closed her eyes and saw her father's face, slit eyes gleaming down at her, gloating with power beyond her weak imagination as she trembled.

With that much power, she would never be free of him. She straightened and walked into the circle of stones before the nest. Her foot stirred a tiny stone as she moved, and the human and gryphons sprang up, gryphons with talons bared, Darkwind with his dagger drawn. They relaxed when they saw her, Treyvan sitting back down with a sigh.

"Gesssta sssaid that ssshe would assk Nyarrra to come ssstand watch thisss night for usss," Treyvan told Darkwind. "Ssshe sssseesss well by night, and we trusssst herrrr—"

"You shouldn't," Nyara replied, stifling a sob. "Oh, you should not have trusted me."

Darkwind seized her by the arm, and pulled her into the stone circle. "Just what do you mean by *that*?" he snarled.

And slowly, holding back tears, she told them.

1 8

ELSPETH

This was, possibly, the strangest land Elspeth had ever crossed. There were no roads and no obvious landmarks; just furlong after furlong of undulating grass plains. There were clumps of brush, and even tree-lines following watercourses, but grassland was the rule down on the Dhorisha Plains. It was truly a "trackless wilderness," and one without many ways of figuring out where you were once you were in the middle of it.

Right now, the Plains were in the middle of high summer; not the best time to travel across them. Nights were short, days were scorching and long; the grass was bleached to a pale gold, insects sang night and day, down near the roots. Otherwise there wasn't much sign of life; no animals running through the grass, no birds in the air. Or rather, there was nothing *they* could spot; the Plains might well teem with life, as hidden in the grass as the insects, but silent. Here, where the tall, waving weeds made excellent cover, there was no reason for an animal to break and run, and every reason for it to stay quietly hidden where it was.

A constant hot breeze blew from the south every day, dying down at sunset and dawn, and picking up again at night. And not just hot, but dry, parchingly dry. Thirst was always with them; it seemed that no sooner had they drunk from their water skins than they were thirsty again. Elspeth was very glad of the map; since they had descended into the Plains near a spring, she'd puzzled out the Shin'a'in glyph for "water"—the water that was very precious out here in the summer. This was *not* a desert, but there wasn't a trace of humidity, day or night, and there would be no relief until the rains came in the fall. The mouth and nose dehydrated, skin was flaking and tight, and eyes were sore and gritty, most of the time. Many of the water sources shown on the map were not springs or streams, which would have been visible by the belt of green vegetation along their banks, but were wells. There was no outward sign of these wells anywhere; in fact, they were frequently hidden from casual searching and could only be found by triangulating on objects like rocks, a mark on the cliff wall, a clump of ancient thorn-bushes. There were detailed, incredibly tiny drawings of the pertinent markers beside each water-glyph. Elspeth marveled again and again at the ingenuity of the Shin'a'in and their mapmakers. And she was very glad that she did not have to travel the Plains by winter. A bitter winter wind, howling unchecked across those vast expanses of flat land, would chill an unprotected horse and rider to the bone in no time. And there was little fuel out here, except the dried droppings of animals and the ever-present grass. Would it be somehow possible to compact the grass into logs? There were no natural shelters from the winter winds either, at least that she had seen. Small wonder the Shin'a'in were a hardy breed.

Since their goal was the northern rim of the Plains, they had chosen to follow the edge, keeping it always on their right as they rode. But Elspeth wondered aloud on their third day out just how the Shin'a'in managed to find their way across the vast Plains, once they were out of sight of the cliffs. And soon or late, they must be out of sight of those natural walls. How could they tell where they were?

Skif shrugged when she voiced her question. "Homing instinct, like birds?" he hazarded. "Landmarks we can't see?" He didn't seem particularly interested in the puzzle.

The sword snorted—mentally, of course. *:They use the stars, of course. Like seafarers. With the stars and a compass, you can judge pretty accurately where you are. I expect some of those little scribbles on your map are notes, readings, based on the compass and the stars. And I know the lines they have cross-hatching it are some way of reckoning locations they have that you don't.:*

Elspeth nodded; she'd heard of such a thing, but no one in landlocked Valdemar had ever seen the sea, much less met those who plied it.

They both had compasses, bought in Kata'shin'a'in, though Skif had complained that he couldn't see what difference knowing where north was would make if they got lost. She'd bought them anyway, mostly because she saw them in places where the Shin'a'in often bought made-goods. She reckoned that if the Clansmen needed and used them, she should have one, too. She bit her tongue when he complained, and somehow kept herself from pointing out that on a featureless plain, if he knew which way north was, he would at least be able to prevent himself from wandering around in a circle.

The cliff wall loomed over their heads, so high above them that the enormous trees on the top seemed little more than twigs, and one couldn't hope to see a human without the aid of a distance-viewer. Elspeth had one of *those*, too, purchased, again, in Kata'shin'a'in. Skif hadn't complained about that, but he had coughed when he'd learned the price. It was expensive, yes, but not more than the same instrument would have been in Valdemar—if you could find one that the Guard hadn't commandeered. Here they were common, and every caravan leader had one. The lenses came from farther south, carried between layers of bright silk, and were installed in their tubes by jewelsmiths in Kata'shin'a'in. The workmanship was the equal of or superior to anything she had seen in Valdemar.

Elspeth ignored Skif's silent protest over the purchase of the distance-viewer, as she'd ignored the vocal one over the compasses. She had saved a goodly amount of their money on the road by augmenting their rations with hunting; she also had a certain amount of discretionary money, and some real profit she had made by shrewd gem-selling. She had a notion that Quenten had known these gemstones, amber and turquoise, change-stone and amethyst, were rarer here, and therefore in high demand, for he had invested quite a bit of their Valdemaren gold in them. She was very glad the mage had. It enabled her to make those purchases without feeling guilty about the expense.

She'd done very well with her first attempt at jewel trading, so she didn't feel that Skif had any room to complain about how she spent some of that money. There was a curious slant to his complaints—a feeling that it wasn't so much that she had spent the money, but that she hadn't first consulted him. She also had a sneaking suspicion that if she had spent that same money on silks and perfumes, he would not have been making any complaint. And that, plainly and simply, angered her.

Not that she hadn't wanted silks and perfumes, but this was neither the time nor the place for fripperies. Instead of buying those silks and perfumes, she had bought other things altogether; the compasses and distance-viewer, some special hot-weather gear, and a full kit of medicines new to her, but which the Healers here seemed to depend on. If she could get them home intact, she would let Healer's Collegium see what they could do with these new remedies. She had bought two sets of throwing knives, in case she had to use and leave the set she now wore. She had purchased an enveloping cloak, and had gotten one for Skif as well—because as they left Kata'shin'a'in at the break of dawn, they had been wearing their Whites again, and she had wanted to disguise the fact until they were well down onto the Plains.

Wearing their Whites again was not something she'd insisted on just for the sake of being contrary, though Skif seemed to think so. It had seemed to her that since the Shin'a'in already knew what Heralds were, it would be a good thing to travel the Plains in the uniform of their calling.

Skif argued that they'd been in disguise to avoid spies. She pointed out that it would make no difference one way or another insofar as possible spies were concerned. If Ancar could *get* spies near enough the Plains for them to be seen, he was more powerful than any of them had ever dreamed, and whether or not they wore their Whites would make no difference.

But if he were not that powerful, then wearing their uniforms could provide them with a modicum of protection from the Shin'a'in. The Plainsfolk had a reputation for shooting first, and questioning the wounded. Being able to identify themselves as "nonhostile" at a distance was no bad idea.

Except that even with all the best reasons in the world, Skif didn't like *that* idea, either.

She was just about ready to kill him in his saddle. Now that he had her "alone," he seemed determined to prove how devoted he was to her safety. But he was going about it by looking black every time she did something that was "unfeminine" (or rather, something that asserted her authority), by disagreeing with her decisions, and by repeating, whenever possible, his assertion that this was a mistake, and they should go back to the original plan. If that was devotion, she was beginning to wish for detestation.

Tonight they camped beside a spring; easy enough to spot from leagues away as a patch of green against the golden-brown of the waving sea of grass. Because of that, she had decided to bypass the well they encountered earlier in the afternoon and journey on into darkness to reach the spring. After all, they were supposed to be making as much time as possible, right? They couldn't possibly bypass the place; it was the *only* spot ahead of them with trees. They couldn't even miss in the dark; they'd *smell* the difference when they reached water and the vegetation that wasn't scorched brown. And even if, against all odds, they did miss it, the Companions would not.

Skif, predictably, had not cared for that either. He only voiced one complaint, that he didn't think it was a good idea to push themselves that hard in unknown territory. But he did brood—she was tempted to think "sulked" but did not give in to the temptation—right up until the moment they made camp. She couldn't think why he should have any objections, not when they'd already agreed to make as much time as possible. All she could think was that it was more of the same—he didn't want her to make the decisions.

Once there, they had chores, mutually agreed on. She avoided him with a fair amount of success. While he set up camp, she collected water and fuel. Not too much of the latter; they didn't need much more than to brew a little tea. Elspeth was nervous about grass fires; one spark could set the entire area ablaze, as dry as this vegetation was. In her view, Skif was simply not careful enough. When she returned with her double handful of twigs and fallen branches, she discovered he had etched a shallow little pocket in the turf, just big enough to hold the fire she intended to build. Plainly that was not good enough; but Skif was a child of cities, and likely had never seen a grass fire. It was hard for someone like Skif to imagine the fury or the danger of a grass fire. A *city* fire, now, that was something they could comprehend—but grass? Grass was tinder, it wasn't serious, it burned up in the blink of an eye and was gone with no damage.

Right.

Elspeth knew better. It *was* tinder; it caught fire that easily and burned with incredible heat. But there was a lot of it out here—acres and acres—and that was what Skif couldn't comprehend. She had never, ever forgotten the description Kero had given her of a patrol caught in the path of a grass fire during her days as merc Captain of the Skybolts. Kero had described it so vividly it still lived in her memory.

"It was a wall of flame, as tall as a man, driving everything before it. Herds of wild cattle were followed by a stampede of sheep. That was followed by a sea of rabbits, frightened so witless they'd charge straight up to a man and run into his legs.

That was followed by the little birds that lived in the grass, and a river of mice—and then the wall was on top of you. You could hear it roaring a league away, and nearby it was deafening. It moved as fast as a man can run, and it sent up a great black pall of smoke, a regular curtain that went straight up into the sky. The burning area was farther than I could jump—at the leading edge the ends of the grasses were afire, in the middle, all of this year's growth—but on the trailing edge, all the previous years' growth that was packed down was burning as fiercely as wood, and hotter—"

Kero paused and passed her hand over her eyes. "Everyone let go their beasts; you couldn't hold 'em, not even Shin'a'in-breds. A couple of the youngsters, I'm told, tried to run across the fire. It was unbelievably hot; their clothing, anything that was cloth and not leather or metal, caught fire. Not that it mattered. The hot air stole the breath from them; they fell down in the middle of the flames, trying to scream, and with no breath to do it, burning alive. The rest, the ones that survived, wet their shields and cloaks down with their water skins, put their shields over their backs and their wet cloaks over that, and hunkered down under both. 'Like turtles under tablecloths' is what one lad told me. They stuck their faces right down into the dirt, and did their best to breathe as little as possible. That was how they made it. And even some of those got scorched lungs from the burning air." She shook her head. "Don't ever let anyone tell you a grass fire is 'nothing,' girl. I lost half that patrol to one, and the rest spent days with the Healers, for burns inside and out. It's not 'nothing,' it's hell on earth. My cousins fear fire the way they fear no living thing."

No, a grass fire was nothing to take lightly. On the other hand, there was no purpose to be served in giving Skif a lecture, especially not the way she felt right now. Anything she told him would come out shrewish; anything she said would be discounted. Not that it wouldn't anyway.

Rather than risk sounding like a fishwife, she simply took out her knife and cut a larger circle in the turf, removing blocks of it and setting them aside to replace when they were finished. She made a clear space about half as wide as she was tall. Skif sat and seethed when he saw her kindling a tiny fire in the middle of this comparatively vast expanse of clear earth, but he didn't comment. Then again, he didn't have to; she didn't even have to see his face, his posture said it all.

Even without her saying a word, he took what she did as criticism. Was it? She couldn't help it. Better to do without a little tea than risk a fire. She decided that he was going to seethe no matter what she did, whether or not she said anything.

And when the tea was boiled and their trail rations had been toasted over the fire, she put the fire out and replaced the blocks of turf— enjoying, in a masochistic kind of way, the filthy mess she was making of her hands—again to the accompaniment of odd looks from Skif.

:He thinks you're doing this just to avoid him,: the sword observed cheerfully.

:I don't particularly care what he thinks,: she retorted. *:I do care about making sure any watchers know that we're being careful with their land. It seems to me that since we're here on their sufferance, we'd better think first about how they're judging us. And I know they're out there.:*

:Watchers?: the sword responded.

:They're there,: she replied.

:There're at least four,: Need said, after a moment. *:I didn't know you could See through shields. You must be much better than I thought.:*

She came very close to laughing out loud. *:I can't. I simply guessed. The Shin'a'in are notorious for not allowing strangers on their land; and that they not only allowed us, they gave us a map, says that they are bending rules they prefer to leave intact. That didn't mean that they were going to leave us on our own, they don't trust us that much; if we didn't actually see anyone watching us, it followed that they were hiding. They aren't going to stop us, but I'll bet that if we did something wrong, we'd be dis-invited, and if we strayed from the path, we'd be herded back.:* She thought about it for a moment; it was the first thing that had offered her any amusement all day. *:Might be fun to do it and see how they'd get us back on track. I bet it wouldn't be as straightforward as riding up and helping us back to the "right" way. I bet they'd start a stampede or something.:*

The sword was silent for a moment. *:Convoluted reasoning, that; 'if we can't see them, they must be there.':*

:Merc reasoning,: Elspeth replied, and let it go at that. When she finished replacing the turfs, she looked up to see Skif still sitting there, watching her. There was no moon tonight, only starlight, but his Whites stood out easily enough against the high grass and the night sky, and seemed to shimmer a little with a light of their own. He looked like something out of a tale.

Or a maiden's dream, she thought scornfully. *A hero, a stalwart man to depend on for everything. Perfect, strong, handsome—and ready to take the entire burden of responsibility on* his *shoulders.*

She stood up; so did he. She moved off a little, experimentally. He followed.

More than followed; he came closer and put his arms around her, and she stiffened. She couldn't help herself; it just happened automatically, without thinking. She didn't want him to touch her—not like that. Not with the touch of a lover.

"Don't!" he said, sharply.

"Don't what?" she asked, just as sharply, trying to pull away without being obvious about it.

"Don't be like that, don't be so cold, Elspeth," he replied, softening his tone a little. "You never used to be like this around me."

"You never used to follow me like a lovesick puppy," she retorted, getting free of him, walking away a little to get some distance, and turning to face him. "You used to be my 'big brother' until all this started."

"That was before I paid any attention to—how much you'd grown up," he responded. "All right, so I was a fool before, I wasn't paying any attention to what was in front of my nose, but I've—"

Oh, gods, it's a bad romantic play! She didn't know whether to laugh or cry. Both would have been so full of anger that they would have made her incoherent.

"You've been paying too much attention to idiot balladeers," she interrupted, rudely. "All of which say that the young hero is supposed to finally notice the beauty of the young princess, fall madly in love, rescue her and carry her off to some ivy-wreathed tower to spend the rest of her days in sheltered worship." She took a deep breath, but the anger didn't fade. "I've heard all of that horse manure before, I didn't believe in it then, and I don't now. You're not a hero and neither am I. I'm not a beauty, I just happen to be the only woman who's a Herald around here. I don't need rescuing, and I *don't* want to be sheltered!"

"But—" he said weakly, taking a step back, overwhelmed with her vehemence.

"Stop it, Skif!" she snapped. "I've been nice, I've hinted, I've tolerated this, and I am not going to take any more! *Leave me alone!* If you can't treat me as your partner, *go home.* Nothing is going to happen to me in the middle of the Dhorisha Plains, for Haven's sake!" She waved her arm out at the expanse of trackless grass to the south of them. "There're half a dozen Shin'a'in out there right now, and I doubt any of them is going to let something get past them."

"That's not the point, Elspeth," he said, pleadingly. "The point is that I—"

"Don't you *dare* say it," she snarled. "Don't you *dare* say that you love me! You don't love *me,* you love what you *think* I am. If you loved me, you wouldn't keep trying to prove you were better than me, that I should follow your lead, let you take over, permit you to make all the decisions."

"But I'm not—"

"But you are," she retorted. "Every decision I make, you find a reason not to like. Every job I try to do, you try to do better. Every idea I have, you oppose, *except* in those times when I'm acting, thinking, like a good little girl, who shouldn't bother her pretty head about warfare, and should go where she's been told and learn the pretty little magics she's been told to learn."

"I'm not like that!" he bristled. "Some of my best friends are female!"

She very nearly strangled him.

"So—any female you're not interested in can be a human being, is that it?" she said, her voice dripping scorn. "But any female you *want* had better keep her proper place? Or is it just that every female who outranks you can have her position and be whatever she needs to be, and anyone who's your peer had better let *you* be the leader? Oh that's noble, that truly is. How nice for you, how terribly broad-minded."

"Just who do you think you are?" he shouted.

"*Myself,* that's who!" she shouted back. "Not your inferior, not your underling, not your child to take care of! Not your doll, not your toy, not your princess, and not your property!"

And with that, she turned and stalked off into the grass, knowing she could lose him in a scant heartbeat—and knowing that Gwena could find her immediately if Elspeth needed her.

She ducked around a hillock, and dropped down into the dusty-smelling grass. She held her breath, and listened for his footsteps, waited for him to blunder by in pursuit of her, but there was nothing.

:Gwena?: she Mindcalled, tentatively.

:He's just sitting here on his bedroll,: she said, and the disapproval in her mind-voice was thick enough to cut. *:That was cruel.:*

Elspeth slammed her shields shut before Gwena could reproach her any further. She didn't want to hear any more from that quarter. Gwena was on Skif's side in this, like some kind of matchmaking mama. She'd escaped her real mother's reach, and she wasn't about to let someone else take over the position.

She lay back into the fragrant grass; it was surprisingly comfortable, actually—and looked up at the night sky. The night was absolutely clear, and the stars seemed larger than they were at home.

Her back and neck ached with tension; her hands had knotted themselves into tight fists. Her stomach was in an uproar, and her throat tight.

This was no way to handle a problem.

She tried to empty her mind, just empty it of all the anger and frustration, the need that was driving her out into the unknown, and the heavy burden of responsibility she was bearing. Gradually the tension drained out of her. Her stomach calmed, her hands relaxed. She concentrated on the muscles in her back and neck until they unknotted. She stopped thinking altogether. She simply—was. Watching the stars, letting the warm, ever-present breeze blow over her, inhaling the dry, dusty scent of the grasses she lay in, feeling the earth press up against her back.

This place felt very much alive, as if the warm earth itself was a living being. It calmed her; she found her tension all drained out of her, down into the earth, which accepted it into a tranquility that her unhappiness could not disturb.

Gwena's right. I was cruel. She felt her ears flushing hotly, and yet if she had the chance to do it over, there was nothing she would not have repeated. *What happened to us? There was a time I would have gladly heard him say he loved me. There was even a time when I might have been able to fall in love with him. Gwena was right; I could do so much worse.*

Tears filled her eyes; they stung and burned. Not from what she had done to Skif—he was resilient, he'd survive. But from what she was going to face in the years ahead. *If we all survive this, I probably* will *do worse. I'll probably have to marry some awful old man, or a scrawny little boy, just to cement an alliance. We'll need all the help we can get, and that may be the only way to buy it. If I took Skif, I'd at least have someone who loves me for a little while...*

But that wasn't fair to him; it was wrong, absolutely wrong. She'd be using him and the affection he was offering, and giving him nothing in return. She *didn't* love him, and there was no use pretending she did. Furthermore, he was a Mindspeaker; he'd know.

Besides, when she married that awful old man, whoever he was, she'd have to break with Skif anyway, so what was the point?

What was the point of all of this, at all? When it all came down to it, she was just another commodity to be traded away for Valdemar's safety. And intellectually, she could accept that. But emotionally—

Why? she asked the stars fiercely as tears ran down into her hair. *Why do I have to give up everything? Why can't I have a little* something *for myself? That's not being selfish, that's just being human! Talia has Dirk, Kero has Eldan, even Mother has Daren... Why isn't there anyone for me?*

There was no answer; she held back fierce sobs until her chest ached. Maybe she wasn't as sophisticated as she had thought, after all. Maybe all her life she *had* believed in the Bardic ballads, where, after long struggle, the Great True Love comes riding out of the shadows.

All right, maybe it's childish and stupid, but I've seen it happen—

Happen for other people. The fact was, the notion was childish and stupid—and worse, if she spent all her time waiting for that One True Love, she'd never get anything done for herself.

But, oh, it hurt to renounce the dream...

1 9

INTERLUDE

Dawnfire woke all at once, her heart racing with fear, but her body held in a strange kind of paralysis. She couldn't see anything. All she could feel was that she was so hungry she was almost sick, and that she was standing; her position seemed to be oddly hunched over, but—

No, it wasn't hunched over, it was a perfectly normal position—for *Kyrr's* body. She was still in the body of her bondbird. Only—Kyrr was gone. She was alone.

She opened her beak to cry out, and couldn't—and then the paralysis lifted, and a hazy golden light came up about her, gradually, so that her eyes weren't dazzled.

She was on a perch.

As she teetered on the perch, clutching it desperately, trying to find her balance without Kyrr to help her, she saw that there were bracelets on her legs, and jesses attached to them, and that the jesses were fastened to a ring on the perch.

The light came up further; she moved her head cautiously at the sound of a deep-throated chuckle to discover that now she could see the entire room. An empty, windowless room—except for a bit of furniture, one couch, and its occupant.

She couldn't help herself; panic made her bate, and she flapped uncontrolled right off the perch. She couldn't fly even if she hadn't been jessed; she hadn't Kyrr's control—and she hung at the end of the leather straps, upside-down, swinging and twisting as she beat at the air and the perch with her wings.

I can't get back up!

That sent her into a further panic, and she flailed wildly in every direction but the right one, with no result whatsoever. She twisted and turned, tangled herself up, and banged her beak against the perch support, and never once got a claw on the perch itself.

Finally she exhausted herself; she hung in her jesses with her heart beating so hard she could scarcely breathe, listening to it thunder in her ears, growing sicker and weaker with every moment she stayed inverted. She had gone, as any raptor would, from a state of uncontrolled panic to a state of benumbed shock.

She was hanging facing the wall, not the room beyond, and its bizarre occupant; she didn't even hear the footsteps coming toward her because of the sound of her own heart.

Suddenly there was a hand behind her back, and another under her feet. She clutched convulsively as she was lifted back up onto the perch. She released the hand as soon as she was erect, transferring her grip to the sturdy wood, as the Changechild took his gloved hand away, and smiled enigmatically down on her.

"Having trouble, dear child?" he purred, stepping back a pace or two to observe her. The glove was the only article of clothing he was wearing, and now he pulled it off, and tossed it on a shelf next to her perch. He really didn't need much in the way of clothing—long, silky, tawny-gold hair covered him from head to toe—except for certain strategic areas.

If she could have blushed, she would have. It wasn't as if she hadn't seen nude males before, certainly there was no nudity taboo among the Tayledras, but he seemed to flaunt his sexuality like some kind of weapon. It was somehow obscene, even though he wasn't doing anything overtly to make it so. It was all in posture, unspoken body-language.

He seemed to sense her embarrassment and take amusement from it—and that made it even more obscene.

He looked like a cat—a lynx—and he moved like a cat as he padded back to his couch. That was where she had seen him when the light came up; reclining with indolent grace on a wide couch piled high with silken pillows, in black and golden tones that matched his hair. He resumed his position with studied care, and a fluidity not even a real cat could have matched, then rested his head on one hand to watch her with unwinking, slitted eyes.

Her feet twitched a little and she teetered on the perch.

That was when she realized just how helpless she truly was. He didn't *need* the jesses, except to keep her from falling to the floor every time she bated. Without Kyrr, she was as helpless in this body as a newborn chick. She could do simple things that were largely a matter of reflex—like perching—but anything more complicated than that was out of the question. She could no more fly now than she could in her own body.

She stared at him in despair; he smiled, and slowly, sensuously, licked his lips.

"I," he said, in a deep, echoing voice, "am Mornelithe Falconsbane. You made the fundamental mistake of attacking me. And I am afraid that you, dear child, are my prisoner. To do with as I will."

Fear chilled her, and made all her feathers slick tight to her body, as he said that. *Mornelithe Falconsbane*—this must be the Adept that Darkwind's Changechild had fled from; the Adept that had trapped and tormented her *dyheli* herd—his name did not invoke a feeling of comfort in a Tayledras.

"It's a pity that you managed to have yourself trapped in that bird's body," he continued. "The ways that I may derive pleasure from it are so limited, but I'm sure you can be flexible."

He mock-sighed and lowered his lids over his slitted, green-golden eyes, looking at her through thick lashes. She clutched the perch nervously, swaying back and forth, her mouth dry with fear as she waited for him to do something. He raised a single finger. The door beside his couch opened, and a human in golden-brown leather that clung to his body as if it had been sewn around him entered the room, carrying a deep pannier. He went straight to her perch, as she flapped in alarm, and put the basket down underneath it. Then he untied her jesses from the ring, tied a leather leash to it instead, and attached the leash to her jesses.

Then he turned his back on her and left her, all without saying so much as a single word.

She looked down into the basket. Cowering in fear, and looking up at her, were three live mice.

Now her stomach growled with hunger, even while her mind rolled with nausea. She stared down at the mice, ravenous, and feeling just as trapped as they were.

She was starving—this was food. And she didn't have the slightest idea of how to kill and eat it.

Kyrr would, but Kyrr was gone.

Then it hit her. Kyrr was *gone*. Not waiting patiently in the back of the bird's mind, but gone completely. Dead. Part of her soul, her heart, her life—gone without a trace. She was completely alone, in a way she had not been since she was ten.

The grief that descended over her was so total that she forgot everything, including her hunger.

Oh, Kyrr—

Her beak gaped, but nothing happened. Not even a single sob.

She couldn't cry, she wasn't even human anymore. How could she mourn as a hawk? She didn't know, and the inability to cry out her pain and loss redoubled it. They were both lost, she and Kyrr—and they would never come home again.

She closed her eyes and rocked from foot to foot, trapped in a sea of black grief, drowning in it.

A satisfied chuckle made her snap her head up and open her eyes wide. Mornelithe was watching her with amusement.

Her grief turned to rage in the blink of an eye; she mantled and screamed at him, her cry piercing the silence and shattering it—though she was careful to keep a tight grip on the rough wood of her perch as she shrieked her defiance at him.

He found that even more amusing; his smile broadened, and his chuckle turned into a hearty laugh.

"Perhaps you won't be a disappointment after all, clever bird-child." He caressed her with his eyes, and her rage spilled away, leaving her weak and frightened again.

He returned his gaze to something in his lap, and as he shifted a little, she could see that it was a dark crystal scrying-stone. He stared at it, his gaze suddenly going from casual to penetrating—and what he saw in it made him frown.

2 0

DARKWIND

Starblade turned away from the little knot of Tayledras Adepts and Healers surrounding Dawnfire's *ekele* in despair, and sought the sanctuary of his own *ekele*. The fools were trying to thrash out what could have killed Dawnfire, and why—when it was obvious, as obvious a taint on the girl's body as the taint on his own soul, and the contamination that had cracked the Heartstone.

He knew it the moment he saw it. And he could not say a single word.

He felt old, old—burdened with secrets too terrible to hide that he *could not* confess to anyone, weary with the weight of them, sick to his bones of what he had done. As he had so many times, he climbed the stairs to his *ekele*, then sought the chamber at the top, and stood looking down on the Vale, wondering if *this* time he could find the strength to open the window and hurl himself to the ground.

But the crow on his shoulder flapped to its perch as soon as he entered the room, and sat there watching him with cold, derisive eyes. And he knew, even as he fought the compulsion to turn away from the window and suicide, that Mornelithe Falconsbane still had his soul in a fist of steel, and there was nothing he had that he could call his own. Not his thoughts, not his will, not his mind.

He flung himself down on the sleeping pad, hoping to lose himself in that dark oblivion—but sleep eluded him, and Falconsbane evidently decided to remind him of what he was.

The memory-spell seized him—

Smoke wreathed through the trees as he paused in an area he had thought safe, and the acrid fumes made him cough. The fire was spreading, far faster than it should have. For a moment, Starblade wondered if perhaps he should go back for help. But other emergencies had emptied the Vale of all but apprentices and children, and he had a reputation to maintain. He was an Adept, after all, and a simple thing like a forest fire shouldn't prove too hard to handle. He sought shelter from the smoke down in a little hollow, a cup among some hills, and closed his eyes to concentrate on his first task.

No, you fool, Starblade cried at his younger self. *Go back! Get help! Nothing trivial would frighten that many firebirds!*

But this was a vision of the past, and his younger self did not heed the silent screaming in his own mind.

He reached out with his mind, seeking the panic-stricken firebirds first of all. Until he could get them calmed and sent away, he would never be able to put the flames out. One by one he touched their minds; turned their helpless panic into a need for escape instead of defense, and sent them winging back to the Vale. One of the beast-tenders, the Tayledras who spoke easily to the minds of animals, would take care of them. He had a fire to quench.

There were more firebirds than he had expected, and they were in a complete state of mindlessness. It took time to calm them.

But while he had stood there like a fool, the fire had jumped the tiny pocket of greenery where he worked, and ringed him. He opened his eyes, weary with the effort of controlling the birds, to find himself surrounded by a wall of flame and heat. The leaves were withering even as he watched, the vegetation wilting beneath the heat of the hungry flames. Fear chilled him, even as the heat made him break into a sweat. That was when he realized, when he reached for the power to quench it, that he had exhausted himself in calming the birds—

—and that he was cut off from the node and the nearest ley-lines. Something had sprung up while he worked; something had arisen to fence him away from the power he needed, not only to quell the fire, but even to save himself. He was enveloped in a wall of shielding as dangerous as the wall of flame.

Smoke poured into the hollow; something brushed against his leg, and he glanced down to see that a rabbit, blind with panic, had taken shelter behind his ankle. The heat increased with every passing moment; it wouldn't be long before this little valley was afire, like the rest of the forest here. He was not clothed for a fire; he had run out in his ordinary gear, a light vest and breeches. He had nothing to protect him from the flames, nothing to breathe through. There was only one thing he could do—wrap the remains of his power about him in as strong a shield as he could muster, and run—

As the nearest flames licked toward him, he sent his bird up into the safety of the skies, and sprinted for what he hoped was the easiest way out. Straight into hell.

On the sleeping pad, his body writhed in remembered agony, his mouth shaping screams of pain he was not permitted to voice.

Flames licked his body, hungry tongues reaching out from burning scrub, a tree trunk. There was no pain at first—just a kind of warm pressure, a caress as he ran past. Then came the pain, after the flame had touched—red heat that blossomed into agony. Sparks fell on him as he dashed under a falling, blazing branch. He wrapped his hair around his mouth, and still the air he breathed scorched his lungs. Within moments, there was nothing but pain—and the fear of a horrible death that drove his legs.

Then—cool, smokeless air. He burst out past the fireline, into the unburned forest. Freedom.

But not from pain. He fell into a stream, moaning, extinguishing his smoldering leather clothing and hair. The stream cooled him but did nothing for the pain, for the horrible burns where the skin was blackened and crisped on his arms. How long he lay there, he did not know. Smoke wreathed over him, but the flames did not grow nearer. He could not tell if it was the smoke that darkened his sight—or his pain. Only that after a dark, breathless time of agony, salvation loomed out of the smoke, a spirit of mercy—vague and ghostlike.

NO! he screamed. NO! Don't believe him! Kill yourself, draw your knife, kill yourself while you have the chance!

He reached out toward the mist-wreathed shape, who seemed to be someone he *knew, yet could not identify. Hazy with an intimation of power, the stranger's white hair was a beacon that drew his eyes. White hair—a Tayledras Adept, surely. Yes, he knew this one; he must. Rainwing? Frostfire? Both were recluses. No matter—he managed a croak, and the other started and turned his steps in Starblade's direction.*

No—he moaned. No—

"I thought I heard someone Call," said the other, stooping over him in concern. "I see I was right."

His lips shaped words he could not speak for lack of breath. "Help me—"

Silver hair wove a web of light that dazzled his eyes. The Adept's own eyes, gilded-silver, held his. "I will have to take you to my home," *the other said worriedly.* "The fire has cut us off from Tayledras Vale. But I can tend you there, never fear. Will that be all right?"

Starblade nodded, giving consent, and as a consequence of that consent, relaxed all of his defenses. And as the other bent closer over him, to lift him in amazingly strong arms, he thought he saw a peculiar gleam in the other's eyes...

He awoke again, resting on something soft, his arms thrown over his head, with a tawny silken coverlet swathing him from chest to feet. He still hurt, but he was no longer covered with angry, blackened burns, and he took a deep, experimental breath to find his lungs clear again.

Then he tried to move his arms—and couldn't.

He tried harder, struggling against silk rope that bound him hand and foot—with no better success. A deep chuckle answered his efforts.

He twisted his head to face the source of the sound.

"So eager to take leave of my hospitality?" *said the tall, catlike Changechild, smiling as he paced toward the couch on which Starblade lay tethered. The creature had modeled himself on a lynx; was clothed mostly in his own tawny-silk hair, but wearing a supple, elaborately tooled and beaded leather loincloth.* "How—uncivilized of you."

It—he—smiled, with sensuously parted lips. Starblade wrestled furiously against his bonds. "My Clan will know where I am," *he warned.* "Even if you kill me, they will know where I am, and they will—"

"They will do nothing," *the Changechild yawned, examining the flex of his own fingers for a moment, admiring his needle-sharp talons.* "You accepted my offer of help, consented to come away with me. You will leave no trail of distress for them to follow—and you are behind my walls and shields now. Call all you like, they will not hear you."

Starblade snarled his defiance. "You forget, Misborn—I am Tayledras. My bird will bring them here!"

He sought for Karry's mind with his own, even as the Changechild moved slightly aside and gestured. "If you mean that—it tried foolishly to attack me."

Starblade followed the gesture to a shadow-shrouded corner, where something thin and almost-human looked up with wild, unfocused eyes, its hands and mouth full of feathers.

Perlin falcon feathers.

Karry's feathers.

Silent tears ran into his hair; silent sobs shook his body. None of it brought Karry back.

The crow cawed; it sounded like scornful laughter.

The Changechild sat on the edge of the couch, and flicked away the covering, leaving him naked and unprotected, even by a thin layer of silk. He shrank away, involuntarily. "I am called Mornelithe, rash birdman," the creature said, idly gliding a talon along Starblade's side. "I think I shall take another name, now. Falconsbane." He glanced sharply at Starblade, who continued to fight his bonds, though his eyes blurred with the tears for Karry he would not—yet—shed. "And believe me, my captive. In a shorter time than you dream possible, you will have another name for me." He paused, and a slow, lascivious smile curled the corners of his mouth. "Master," he said, savoring the word.

Then he bent over his captive and transfixed him with a pair of green, slit-pupiled eyes, that grew and grew until they filled Starblade's entire field of vision.

"I think we shall begin the lessoning now."

Mercifully, he could no longer remember that lessoning, not even under the goad of Mornelithe's spell. It involved pain; it also involved pleasure. Both hovered at the edge of endurance. Mornelithe was a past master at the manipulation of either, of combining the two. When it was over, Mornelithe had the keys to his soul.

He knelt before the Changechild, abasing himself as fully as he could; worshiping his Master, and detesting himself for doing so. All that was in his line of sight at the moment was the golden marble of the floor, and Mornelithe's clawed feet. Thankfully, he had not yet been required to kiss them this time.

"Ah, birdman," Mornelithe chuckled. "You grovel so charmingly, so gracefully. It is almost a pity to let you up."

Starblade felt himself flush with shame, then chill with fear. Too many times in the past, such seemingly casual words had led to another "lesson."

"You have learned your place in the scheme of things quite thoroughly, I think," Mornelithe continued. "It is time to let you return to your lovely home."

Instead of elation, the words brought a rush of sickness. Bad enough, what he had become—but to return to the Vale, bringing this contamination with him—

He wanted to refuse. He wanted to rise, take the dagger at his belt, and slay his tormentor. He wanted to take that same dagger and slay himself.

He tried to assert his will; he closed his eyes and concentrated on placing his hand on the hilt of that dagger. He was *an Adept—he had training, experience, his own personal powers. His will had been honed to an instrument like the Starblade of his use-name. Surely he could reclaim himself again. Yes... yes, he could. He could feel his will stirring, and opened his mouth to denounce his captor.*

"Yes, Master," he heard himself say softly. "If it is your will."

He felt his lips stretching in an adoring smile; his head lifted to meet Mornelithe's unwinking eyes. His hand did not move from the floor.

There were two Starblades inside his mind. One worshiped Mornelithe and looked to his Master for all direction. That was the one that was in control, and there was no unseating it. But buried deep inside, away from all control, bound and gagged and able only to feel, was the real Starblade.

Mornelithe could have destroyed even this remnant; he had not, only because it amused him to see his victim continue to suffer, long after the contest of wills had ended.

"I do not entirely trust you, dear friend," Mornelithe said, softly, as he reached down and touched Starblade's cheek. "You were a stubborn creature, and I do not entirely trust you away from my sight. So, I shall send you a watcher, also—one that the rest will take for your new bondbird. Here—"

He snapped his fingers, and held out his hand—and a huge crow, identical in every way to those the Tayledras bonded with, flapped out of the shadows beside Mornelithe's chair to land on the outstretched arm. The Changechild gestured with a lifted finger that Starblade should rise from his crouch to a simple kneeling position; the Tayledras' body obeyed instantly, even while his helpless mind screamed a protest.

The crow lifted silently from Mornelithe's wrist, and dropped down onto his shoulder.

And what little remained of Starblade's will was frozen with paralysis.

"There," Mornelithe said with satisfaction. "That should take care of any little problems we may have, hmm?"

The crow cawed mockingly, joining Mornelithe's laughter...

The memory-spell released him, leaving him limp and shaking, with the echo of that laughter in his ears.

From the moment he had left Mornelithe's stronghold—which leavetaking he did not remember—he had been completely under the Adept's control. And Mornelithe was an Adept; there was no doubt of that. All that he lacked to make him a major power was control of a node.

The only two for any distance around lay in the hands of the Tayledras.

Mornelithe intended to change that. And at the time of his release, that was all that Starblade had known; he had no idea what Mornelithe planned.

Nor, when he was found wandering in the heart of the burned area, did he even remember that he had been taken.

Instead, he had false memories of being overcome with smoke, of losing Karry somewhere in the heart of the fire—of taking a blow to the head from a falling tree. Then vague and confused recollections of crawling off and hiding in a wolverine's hole until the fire passed, of smoke-sickness that pinned him in the area for several days, of bonding to a huge crow who brought him fruit to feed him and supply his fevered body with liquids, and his final desperate attempt to get back to the Vale.

And the false memories passed muster. The crow was unremarked-upon. He had only an unusually touchy temper that caused his friends and son to give him some distance until he should regain his normal calm. Any changes in him, they—and he—ascribed to the trauma he had endured, and they all felt that those changes would pass in time.

All else seemed well, until the ritual to move the Heartstone.

Only then, *after* the disaster, did his true memories return. And it was then that the rest of his hidden memories emerged—

Memories of going to the Heartstone every night, and creating a flaw in it, leeching the power away from a place deep inside, and creating an instability that would not be revealed until the entire power of the Vale had been loaded into it, preparatory to bridging the distance between the old Heartstone and the new.

That was the first night he had tried to fling himself from the top of his *ekele*.

Once again, Mornelithe exerted his power over him, through the compulsions planted as deeply within him as he had planted the flaw in the stone. The crow was the intermediary of those compulsions, and since it never left his side, Mornelithe's hand was always upon him.

And when he tried to confess his pollution, he found his tongue uttering simple pleasantries. When he tried to open his mind to let others see the traitor within their ranks, he found himself completely unable to lower his own shields. As he had been in Mornelithe's stronghold, he was bound, gagged, and paralyzed, a prisoner within his own mind, still toyed with and controlled for Falconsbane's pleasures and purposes. At least half of the time, that tiny portion of himself that was still free was buried so deeply that it was not even aware of what passed, what Mornelithe made him do, and say.

All he could do, in the moments he was free to speak and act, however circumspectly, was to alienate his son, in the barren hope that, once made into an enemy, anything Starblade supported, Darkwind would work against. It looked as if the ploy was working.

At least, it had until the death—no, murder—of Dawnfire. Once again the hand of Mornelithe Falconsbane had reached out to take what he wanted, and again Starblade had been helpless to prevent it.

There was only one further hope. Darkwind had withdrawn from the company of mages after the disaster. Darkwind lived outside the influence of the flawed and shattered Heartstone. So Darkwind's powers *should* be uncontaminated by Mornelithe's covert influence. If he could just get Darkwind to take up his powers again—Darkwind would call for help from the nearest Clan. The deceptions that had held for so long would shatter under close examination, and Mornelithe would find himself locked out, once again.

But how to get Darkwind to resume his powers, after all that Starblade had done to keep him from doing just that?

Starblade groaned, and threw his arm over his eyes. There seemed no way out; not for him, nor for anyone else.

K'Sheyna was doomed, and his was the hand that had doomed it. The only way out was death, and even that had been denied him.

Damn you, Falconsbane! he shrieked inside his own mind. And it seemed to him that he caught a far-off echo of derisive laughter.

Darkwind felt torn in a hundred pieces, divided within himself by conflicting emotions, responsibilities, and loyalties. Treyvan had kindled a mage-light; a dim orange glow in the center of the ceiling of the lair. Yet another surprise to Darkwind; he hadn't known the gryphon could do *that*, either.

He slumped in one corner of the gryphons' lair with his head buried in his hands and his mind going in circles. Hydona curled protectively around her youngsters, trying to minimize whatever harm Falconsbane had already done them. *Her* shields were up at full strength, with Treyvan's augmenting them. Darkwind's shields augmented *both* of theirs; he had never renounced that part of his magecraft, and he squandered his own energies recklessly to stave off any more disaster that might befall his friends.

Nyara sat curled into a ball in the opposite corner of the lair, with as much distance between herself and the rest of them as she could manage.

After his initial outburst of rage—during which he had come very close to breaking her neck with his bare hands—Darkwind's anger toward the Changechild faded. After all, none of this was of Nyara's plotting. He should have known better than to leave her with the *hertasi*, who were mostly creatures of daylight, to keep her watched at a distance by *tervardi* and *dyheli* who also moved mostly by day.

I should have found a night-scout willing to watch her, he thought distractedly. *Hindsight is always perfect.*

"All right," he said, breaking the silence, and making everyone jump. He turned to Nyara, who shrank farther back into her corner, her eyes wide and frightened. "Stop that," he snapped, his tightly strung nerves making him lash out at her as the only available target. "I'm not going to kill you."

"Yet," Treyvan rumbled. He had taken Nyara's news much worse than Hydona. His mate tended to ignore the past as beyond change, and was interested only in what she could do to fix what had been done to her younglings. Treyvan felt doubly guilty; because he had failed to protect Hydona, and because he had failed to protect his offspring.

Darkwind knew exactly how he felt.

Nyara tried to melt into the rock behind her, her eyes now wide and focused on Treyvan.

Darkwind recaptured her attention. "I want to know everything that *you* know about us, and what *he* knows that you're sure of. I mean not only what you've told your f—Falconsbane, but what he knew before this."

Nyara shivered but looked as if she didn't quite understand his question.

He stood up, walked over to her, and towered over her. "What does he know about the Vale?" he asked, speaking every word carefully. "Begin from the very first thing you knew."

Nyara began, stuttering, to tell them fairly simple bits of intelligence that anyone could have figured out for himself. That the only nodes Falconsbane could possibly access were in Tayledras hands. That he had made several attempts to get at one or the other of the nodes. She identified each attempt that she knew of, going back to long before the arrival of the gryphons. Most of these trials had been low-key, tentative feints. And as she spoke, she gained confidence, until she was no longer stuttering with fear, and no longer speaking in short, choppy sentences.

Most of the feints she described, Darkwind had already been aware of. But then she took him by surprise.

"Then F-father decided to take the Vale from within, I think," she said, her hands crooking into claws, as her eyes glazed a little. "This was when he was angry with me, and he was—he was—he was angry with me." Her expressive face was as still as stone, and Darkwind sensed that this had been one of those periods when Falconsbane had "trained" her, using methods it made him ill even to contemplate.

But this was important. She had said that Falconsbane meant to "take the Vale from within." He had to know what that meant, and what had happened.

"What did he mean by that?" he prompted. She gave him a frightened, startled look, as if she had forgotten he was there.

"He set a trap," she replied tightly. "He set a very clever trap. He sent many of his servants to create diversions—emptying the Vale of all but one of the Adepts."

This was beginning to sound chillingly familiar—but she was continuing.

"When that one was alone—he knew that there was but one Adept still present by the level of power within the Vale—he created a disturbance that required an Adept." She licked her lips nervously and gave him a pleading glance. "I truly do not know what that was," she said, "I was not in favor. He did not grant me information."

"I understand that," he said quickly. "Go on."

"When the Adept came to deal with the disturbance, Mornelithe sprung the trap and closed him off from the Vale. He was hurt—and that was when Mornelithe cast illusions to make him appear to be of the Birdkin, so that the Adept would accept him as rescuer. The bird, Father slew. It was not deceived, and attacked him. But by then the Adept's hurts were such that he was unconscious, and did not know. Father took him to the stronghold and imprisoned him to break him to Father's will."

"And you know who this Adept is?" Darkwind felt himself trembling on the brink of a chasm. If it *was* his father—it would explain so much. And yet he dreaded the truth—

She looked directly up at Darkwind, and said, clearly and forcefully, "I did not know until Father called me on the night of moon-dark who that man was. It was your father, Darkwind. It was he that is called Starblade." She licked her lips, and raised one hand in a pleading gesture. "He wanted you, as well, the son as well as the father—he wanted me to—entice you. I told him 'yes,' but I told myself 'no,' and I kept myself from working his will, as he worked it upon your father."

There it was, the blow had fallen. He surprised himself with his steady, cold calm. "So Falconsbane succeeded?"

She nodded, dropping her eyes, her voice full of quiet misery. "When he sets out to break one to his will, he does not fail. I was—present—for much of it. It was part of my t-t-training. That this could be happening to me. Both the pleasuring, and the punishment. I can tell you some of what he did, what he ordered Starblade to do when he returned to the Vale. You do not want to know... what was done to control him."

Darkwind tried to speak and could not. Treyvan spoke for him, in a booming, angry rumble. "Continue! All that you know."

"He was, firstly, to forget what had happened to him. Mornelithe gave him false memories to replace what had truly occurred—until Mornelithe chose otherwise. Then he was to creep in secret to the heart of the Vale." She gave Darkwind a look of entreaty. "I have not the words—"

"The Heartstone," Darkwind supplied, at her prompting, feeling sick.

"The Heartstone," she said. "Yes. He was to go to it in secret, and change it—he was one who created it, so he would know best its secrets. Father did not *know* that his trap would ensnare someone of that quality, but he was so pleased that he had, he forgot, often, to mete out punishment to me."

"Return to the subject, Changechild," Treyvan growled. She wilted, losing some of the confidence she had regained.

"What was it Starblade was supposed to do to the Heartstone?" Darkwind prompted her, with a bit more gentleness. She turned gratefully to him.

"He was to make a flaw in it, a weakness, one that would not appear until the Birdkin prepared to move. *Then* he called back all his creatures, to make it appear that all was made safe here. He even sent *his* creatures to guard beyond *your* borders, so that you would be prepared to shift your power elsewhere."

Darkwind held up his hand. "How much does he know—how can he continue to control Starblade, and does he know our strength?"

She shrugged. "I do not know what he knows, but he has long patience and is willing to move slowly, so that each move he makes is sure. But as to how he controls Starblade, it is with a crow."

"His bondbird." Somehow that was simply the crowning obscenity. To take the closest tie possible to a Tayledras other than a lifebond, and pervert it into an instrument of manipulation—

"He cannot speak, move, or let his thoughts be known. All that is under Father's control, from compulsions planted when he was broken, and held in place by the crow." She hesitated a moment. "There is little, I think, that he can learn unless Starblade goes to him, and that, he has not done. The barriers still in place about the Vale prevent that. But there is much that he can do with the compulsions already in place."

"Not for long," Darkwind said, with grim certainty, heading for the door of the lair. "Hydona, forgive me—I can't do anything about the younglings yet. But I *can* do something about this."

"Go," she replied. "Frrree thisss placsse of the viperrr, then perrrhapsss we can frrree the little onesss asss well."

"*I* will guard the Changechild," Treyvan said, before Darkwind even thought of it.

And before Darkwind could think to ask "how?" the gryphon turned to face Nyara, his eyes flashing. She looked surprised—

And then she slumped over, unconscious.

Darkwind returned to Nyara's side. She was asleep, deeply asleep, but otherwise unharmed.

Treyvan sighed. "I have not hurrrt herrr, Darrrkwind. But it isss better to have the enemy underrr yourrr eye."

"She isn't exactly the enemy," Darkwind said, uncertainly.

"She isss not exactly a frrriend," Treyvan replied. "Ssshe isss at bessst, a weaknesss. I will watch herrr, for my magic isss ssstronger than herrsss. Go."

Darkwind did not have to be told twice. He was out the door of the lair and running for the Vale before the last sibilant "s" had left Treyvan's beak. Dawn's first light flushed the eastern horizon, and Vree shot into the sky from his perch on a stone beside the lair crying greeting to his bondmate, projecting an inquiry. While running, Darkwind tried, as best he could, to give Vree an idea of what He had learned, in simple terms the bird could understand.

He conveyed enough of it that Vree screamed defiance as he swooped among the forest branches, preceding Darkwind and making sure the way ahead was clear of hazard. The bird was angered, but he had not lost his head or his sense of responsibility.

:Where?: Vree demanded, his thoughts hot with rage.

:The Vale,: Darkwind replied, as he leapt a bush, and took to the game trail that led most directly to the k'Sheyna stronghold.

:I go,: the bird said. *:I go* in, *with you.:*

Once again, Darkwind was surprised, but this time pleasantly. *:I go,:* Vree repeated firmly.

That took one worry off his mind. It would be a great deal easier to handle that thrice-damned crow with Vree around.

Now he concentrated on running; as hard and as fast as he could, keeping his attention fixed on the ground ahead and leaving his safety in Vree's capable talons.

Where would Starblade be at this moment? He was an early riser, as a rule. By the time the sun was but a sliver above the horizon, he was generally in conference with one or more of the Adepts. There was a kind of informal ceremony there, as the memorial fire at the foot of the Heartstone was fed with fragrant hardwoods and resinous cedar. Those Adepts remaining—even the most reclusive—generally attended at least one of these meetings; they remembered those who had been lost, and monitored the Heartstone very carefully, looking for changes in it morning and night.

With Father carefully making sure they accomplish nothing, he thought with nausea. *Now I know why he never misses a meeting.*

Now he was on safer ground; he passed his own *ekele,* and that of his brother; passed night-scouts coming in and day-scouts going out, both of whom stared at him in equal surprise. He ignored the ache of his lungs and his legs, dredged up extra reserves of energy and ran on, long hair streaming out behind him. He caught sight of other bondbirds flying beside him, peering down at him curiously, and guessed that their bondmates were somewhere behind. He ignored them; he would take no chances that a carelessly shielded thought would warn Starblade—or more importantly, the thing that controlled him in the guise of a black bird.

Up hills, and down again; he took the easiest way, not the scouts' way—using game trails when he could find them. Finally he came out onto a real path, one that led to the border with the Dhorisha Plains, and had, in better days, been used by visitors from both peoples. It terminated at the entrance to the Vale, and Darkwind took deeper breaths, forcing air into his sobbing lungs. It would not be long now...

The shimmer marking the shields that guarded the entrance flickered between the hills. This was where Vree usually left him.

A cry from above alerted him, and Vree swept in from behind in a stoop that ended with the forestgyre hitting him hard enough to stagger him, and sinking his talons into the padded shoulder of Darkwind's jerkin. A fraction of a heartbeat later, he was through the shields, a tingle of pure power passing through him as the shields recognized him and let him by.

He was inside the Vale, but this was no time to slow down. He flung himself down a side path, bursting through the overgrown vegetation, and leaving broken branches and a flurry of torn leaves in his wake.

He was nearing the Heartstone; he heard voices ahead, and he felt its broken rhythms and discordant song shrilling nauseatingly along his nerves. Vree tightened his talons in protest but voiced no other complaint.

He staggered, winded, into the clearing holding the Heartstone, taking the occupants by complete surprise.

Vree did not wait for orders; he had an agenda of his own. Before Darkwind could say a word, the forestgyre launched himself from Darkwind's shoulder, straight at the crow that sat like an evil black shadow on his father's shoulder, as if it was whispering into Starblade's ear.

The crow squawked in panic and surprise, and leapt into the air— heading for the shelter of the undergrowth, no doubt counting on the fact that falcons never followed their prey into cover. But the evil creature did not know Vree; his speed, or his spirit. The gyre hit the crow just as he penetrated the cover of the lower branches; hit him with an impact audible all over the clearing. Rather than taking a chance that his stunned victim might escape, instead of letting it fall, Vree bound on with both sets of talons, and screamed his victory as he brought his prey to the ground. And Starblade collapsed.

The action of Darkwind's bird stunned the Adepts, all but Stormcloud, who shouted something unintelligible, and flung out his hand in Darkwind's direction. The scout found himself unable to move *or* speak, and fell hard on his side—

Vree bent and bit through the thrashing crow's spine, ending its struggles.

Darkwind fought against his invisible bonds as the outraged Adepts converged on him—but as they started to move, an entirely unexpected sound made them freeze where they stood.

"Free—" Starblade moaned, the relief so plain in his voice that it cut to the heart. "Oh, gods, at last, at last—"

The Adepts turned to stare at their leader, and Darkwind took the momentary distraction to snap his invisible bonds.

He stumbled to his father's side and reached for his hands. Starblade took them; his mouth trembled, but he was unable to say anything. It seemed as if he was struggling himself, fighting against a horrible control that even now held him in thrall.

"He's been under compulsion! Put a damn *shield* on him!" Darkwind shouted, throwing his own around his father, and startling the others so much they followed suit. And just in time; Darkwind felt a furious blow shuddering against his protections as the others added their strength to his. Another followed—then another. A half dozen in all, before the enemy outside gave up, at least for the time being.

And now I know your name and face, Darkwind thought with grim satisfaction. *I know who you are. Now it's just a matter of hunting you down.*

Starblade groaned, still fighting the binding that kept him silent. "I know, Father," Darkwind said, urgently, as the other Adepts gathered around them. "I know at least some of it. That's why Vree killed that damn crow. We'll help you, Father. I swear it, we'll help you."

Starblade nodded slightly, and closed his eyes, silent, painful tears forming slowly at the corner of his eyes and trickling down his ghost-pale cheeks as Darkwind explained what he had learned from Nyara as succinctly as possible. The others wasted no time in argument; Starblade's own reactions told the truth of Darkwind's words.

"Let me tend to him," Iceshadow said, when Darkwind had finished. The scout moved over enough for the older Adept to take a place cradling Starblade's head in both his hands. Iceshadow stared intently into Starblade's eyes, but spoke to the son, not the father. "Tell me in detail everything you know."

Darkwind obeyed, detailing Nyara's explanations of how Falconsbane had caught Starblade, and how he had broken the Adept and set the compulsions. Iceshadow nodded through all of it.

"I think I have enough," he said, then looked down into Starblade's eyes. "But first, old friend, I must bring down your shields. *He* has trained you to respond only to pleasure, or pain. And since I do not have time for pleasure—forgive me, but it must be pain."

As Starblade nodded understanding, Iceshadow caught Darkwind's attention. "Take his left hand," the Adept said. "Spread it flat upon the ground."

As Darkwind obeyed, mystified, Starblade closed his eyes and visibly braced himself.

"Take your dagger and pierce his hand," Iceshadow ordered. And when Darkwind stared at him, aghast, the older Tayledras frowned fiercely. "Do it *now*, young one," he snarled. "That evil beast has tied his obedience to pain, and I cannot *break* his shields to free his mind without driving him insane. Now do what I tell you if you wish to help him!"

Darkwind did not even allow himself to think; he simply obeyed.

Starblade's scream of agony sent him lurching to his feet and away, tears of his own burning his eyes and blurring his sight.

When he could see again, he found Vree standing an angry and silent guardian over *his* victim, the crow that Mornelithe Falconsbane had used to control Starblade and shatter the lives of everyone in k'Sheyna. Showing a sophistication that Darkwind had not expected of him, Vree had neither eaten his victim, nor abandoned it. The first might have left him open to Falconsbane's contamination—the second might have given Falconsbane a chance to recover his servant, perhaps even to revive it. Almost anything was possible to an Adept of Falconsbane's power. It only depended on whether or not he was willing to expend that power.

Even if they buried the crow, it was possible that Falconsbane could work through it, to a limited extent. There was only one way to end such a linkage.

Destroy it completely.

There was always a fire burning beside the Heartstone; that memorial flame to the lives of those who had died in its explosion. Darkwind picked up the bird carefully by one wing, and took it to the stone basin containing the fire of cedar and other fragrant woods long considered sacred by both the Shin'a'in and the Tayledras.

He raised his eyes to the shattered Heartstone, truly facing it for the first time since the disaster.

The surface of the great pillar of stone was cracked and crazed, reflecting the damage beneath. The invisible damage was much, much worse.

And none of it—*none*—was his fault. The personal burden he had carried for so long, the ghost of guilt that had haunted his days, was gone.

Darkwind bent over the basin's edge and closed his eyes in a prayer to the spirits of the woods and an apology to the spirits of the Tayledras that had died when the Heartstone sundered.

Mornelithe Falconsbane, you have a great deal to answer for.

He drew back and hurled the body of the crow into the fire pit—so hard that something shattered with a splintering *crunch* as it hit—perhaps the bird's bones, perhaps the branches of the fire…

The Adepts were so intent on Starblade that they didn't even look up, but a sudden heavy weight on his shoulder, and the soft trill in his ear, told him that Vree approved.

The feathers caught fire quickly; the rest took longer to burn—but the flames from the resin-laden branches were hot, and eventually the flesh crisped and blackened, then burst into flame. He watched until the last vestige of the bird was ash and glowing coals, and only then turned back to the rest.

Iceshadow still cradled Starblade's head in both his hands. A pool of blood had seeped out around Starblade's hand, with Darkwind's knife laid to the side. The expression on Iceshadow's face was just as intent, but Starblade's expression had changed entirely.

Darkwind wondered now how he could ever have mistaken the changes in his father for anything other than a terrible alteration in his personality. *Here* was the father he had loved as a child—despite the pain, the grief, and the suffering etched into his face.

Starblade opened his eyes for a moment and saw him; he smiled, and tried to speak.

And couldn't. Once again, he came up against a terrible compulsion. His face twisted as he strove to shape words that would not come.

"Keep trying," Iceshadow urged, in a low, compelling voice. "Keep trying, I'm tracking it down."

Iceshadow was seeking the root of the compulsion, and reversing it; since Falconsbane had changed his father's will rather than placing a simpler block, it was not a matter of removing a wall. Instead, Starblade's mind had to be altered, set back to normal bit by bit as each compulsion was found and changed, so he could regain the use of all of his mind.

The internal struggle, mirrored in Starblade's face, ceased as Iceshadow found the series of problems, and corrected them one by one.

Darkwind dropped to his knees beside his father, and took the poor, wounded hand in his own. Blood leaked through an improvised bandage, but Starblade managed a faint ghost of a smile, fleeting, and full of pain.

"I made you my enemy," he whispered. "I made you hate me, so that anything I told you to do, you would do the opposite. Then, when M-M—" his face twisted with effort.

"Mornelithe," Darkwind supplied.

Starblade sighed. "When *he* twisted my thoughts, so that they were no longer my own, I knew that *he* would want you to take up magic again.

If you did, eventually *he* would find a way to take you, too, through me. And blood of my blood, you would have been vulnerable."

"He almost had what he wanted," Darkwind replied grimly, thinking of all Nyara had told him.

Starblade nodded. "The only way I could think of to protect you was to drive you away from me. So that the more I tried, beneath his compulsion, to bring you back to magic, the more you would fight it. Then... when my mind was not my own... you were safe." He looked up tearfully, entreatingly, at his son. "Can you... ever forgive me?"

Darkwind blinked away tears. "Of course I can forgive you," he said quickly, and took a deep breath to calm himself. He looked up at Iceshadow. "How clear is he?" he asked.

Iceshadow shook his head. "I've only begun," the Adept replied, exhaustion blurring his words a little. "It's going to be a long process. The bastard set the compulsions in a few days, but they've had all this time to work and develop. We'll have to keep him under shield the whole time."

"Put him in the work area," Darkwind suggested. "It has strong shields, and there aren't any apprentices who need it right now. Those shields are the best we have."

"Which is why I was not—permitted—to go there," Starblade whispered. "The bird would not let me."

"Then that is a good indicator that the shields will hold, don't you think?" Darkwind responded. He started to let go of Starblade's hand, but his father clutched it despite the pain that must have caused.

"Wait," he coughed. "Dawnfire—"

Darkwind froze. Iceshadow asked the question he could not manage to get out.

"What about Dawnfire?" the Adept asked. "She's dead."

"No," Starblade said urgently. "The bird was never found, but M-M—*his* sign was on her body. I think he has her—trapped in her bird. Still alive, but helpless. A—another toy." Starblade's face was twisted, but this time with what he remembered. "It would—please him—very much."

2 1

ELSPETH

The sky burned blue, but eight hooves pounded their own frantic thunder on the earth of the Plains; grass stems lashed their legs and the barrels of the Companions as they fled. Elspeth risked a look back, her hair whipping into her face and making her eyes water. The pack of fluid brown shapes streaming through the grasses behind them seemed a little closer. It was hard to tell for certain; they were visible only as a flowing darkness in the grasses, and the movement of the vegetation as they disturbed it. Then the lead beast leapt up, showing its head, and she was sure of it.

"They're gaining on us!" she shouted at Skif. He looked back, then bent farther down over Cymry's neck like a jockey. She did the same, trying to cut her wind resistance.

The Companions were running as fast as they could—which was very fast, indeed. The ground flowed beneath their hooves at such a rate that after one look that made her dizzy, she kept her eyes fixed ahead. She could not imagine how any creature could be capable of keeping up with them. It seemed impossible that *they* could be moving this fast.

:What are these things?: she asked Gwena, who flattened her ears a little more and rolled her eyes back at her rider.

:I don't know,: the Companion replied, bewildered. *:I've never heard of anything like them.:* Sweat streamed down her outstretched neck, and the ends of her mane lashed Elspeth's face and got into her mouth.

:I have,: the sword cut in gruffly. *:Damn things are magical constructs; beasts put together by an Adept. Probably all they're good for is running.:*

Elspeth looked back again, nervously. The pack leader gave another of those jumps; that took it briefly above the level of the grass stalks, this time showing its head clearly. Its mouth was open, its tongue out like a dog's. All she really *saw* were the jaws, a mouth full of thumb-length fangs.

:Well—running and killing,: Need amended. *:Whatever, they're not of a type I've seen before. That makes them twice as dangerous; I can't tell you what they're capable of.:*

"Thanks," Elspeth muttered under her breath. She peered ahead, wishing there was any way she could use her distance-viewer. Somewhere on the cliff ahead of them—hopefully somewhere near—was a path like the one they had descended. This trail was next to a waterfall, and she strained her eyes for a glimpse of water streaming down the side of the cliff into the Plains. If they could reach that path, they could probably hold the things off. They might be able to climb it faster than the beasts could; certainly they would be able to hold the narrow trail against their pursuers if they turned to stand at bay.

At the top of that path lay the place circled on the map. Whether or not there was any help for them there—

The Companions were getting tired. How long could they keep this pace up?

Her nose caught the scent of water as they topped a rise, just as she saw the line of green, a line of verdant trees and bushes, at the edge of a long slope, down below them. There was a glint of reflected light from the cliff; she assumed that was the promised waterfall.

She closed her eyes for a moment, and set loose her FarSight, looking for a place to make a stand. There wasn't much else she could do at the moment, other than make certain she was in no danger of being tossed off if Gwena had to make a sudden move.

Nothing at the bottom of the cliff; no, that was definitely no place to make a stand. The waterfall splashed down onto rocks right beside the beginning of the trail; the rocks were wet and slippery, marginal for booted feet, treacherous for hooves. In fact, the entire path was like that, winding beneath the waterfall at times, skirting the edge of it at others. This was not a straight fall; the water dropped through a series of basins and down many tumbles of rocks, keeping spray to a minimum. It might almost have been sculpted that way, and the path appeared to be an afterthought, cut into the stone around the fall as best as could be.

The path was narrow, too narrow to allow more than one rider at a time. She scanned the entire length of it, and found no place wide enough for the four of them to hold off their followers. If they made a stand, it would have to be at the top.

So she turned her FarSight to the top—and there, at last, was the shelter she had been searching for.

There were ruins up there; tumbles of massive rocks, identifiable only as ruins because of the regular size and shape of the stones, and the general shapes of what might once have been walls. Right where the path reached the top, there was a good place to hole up.

:There's magic there,: Need said suddenly, looking through Elspeth's

"eyes." *:Do you see that kind of shimmer? That's magic energy. With luck I can use it to help with defense.:*

:I don't intend to get close enough to those things to have to use a blade,: Elspeth retorted.

:Dunce. I didn't mean for you to fight. *I mean to channel my magic through you. I was a fairly good mage. You may even learn something.:*

Elspeth felt stunned. *:I thought you only protected—:*

:That was when I asleep,: the sword said shortly. *:Why don't you see what you can do about picking off some of those beasts? Maybe if you kill one, the others will stop to eat it.:*

Well, it was worth trying. The long slope gave the Companions some relief; though tiring, they were running with a bit less strain. Gwena's coat was still sweat-foamed, but her breathing beneath Elspeth's legs was easier.

Elspeth pulled her bow from the saddle sheath; freed an arrow from the quiver at her knee. She clamped her legs tight around Gwena's barrel, and turned, sitting up a little higher in her saddle as she did so.

The leader of the pack had a peculiar bounding rhythm to his chase; it was, she discovered, rather like sighting on a leaping hare. And she had done that so many times she had lost count; hunting had been one of the few ways she could escape the Palace and her rank and position.

Although I wish I had a hawk right now to set on them. A big hawk. With long, long talons...

The leader's bound carried him below the grass; she nocked and loosed—and he leapt right into the arrow's path.

Soundless they were on the chase, soundlessly he fell, and he fell right under the feet of his pack. Whether or not they would—as Need had so gruesomely suggested—stop to eat him, it didn't matter. At least not at the moment, not while at least half the pack tumbled over the body of the leader, and the rest stopped their headlong chase to mill aimlessly around the dead and the fallen.

She nocked and loosed another arrow, and a third, both finding targets, before Gwena carried her out of range. Never once did any of those she hit utter a single sound.

:Good work,: the Companion said, without slowing. *:That should buy us some time.:*

:Assuming something else doesn't take their place, or join them,: the sword pointed out grimly. *:I hate to say this, but I do sense things stirring; energies being*

disturbed, and some kind of communication going on that I can't read. I'm afraid we're going to have something else on our trail before long.:

She didn't say what she was thinking; it wasn't as if Need had willfully called these things up. *:Will we have a chance to get up on that path first?:*

:I think we'll make it up to the top. But there's more trouble up there. It's at the border of a bad area, and it has its own energies that are reacting to the changes elsewhere. I think you should know that disturbance brings predators and scavengers alike.:

Well, that was no more than the law of nature. She sheathed the bow again and looked back down their trail. There was nothing immediately in sight.

But there *was* a dark golden clot of something on the horizon, something tall enough to be visible above the grass, and it was coming closer. She rather doubted it was a herd of Shin'a'in goats.

The scent of water was stronger; she turned to face forward. The belt of greenery was near enough now to make out individual trees and bushes, and the waterfall dashed down the side of the cliff with a careless gaiety she wished *she* shared.

She knew what awaited them and held Gwena back a little to let Skif shoot ahead of her. Cymry's headlong pace slowed as she met the slippery rocks of the trail. Gwena's shoulders bunched beneath Elspeth's knees as she prepared to make the climb.

The scramble up the trail was purest nightmare. If it had not been that the Companions were far more surefooted than the Heralds were, and far, far faster even on footing this treacherous, she would have stopped to dismount. As it was, she clung to the saddle with legs and both hands, drenched with water spray and her own sweat of fear. If she dared, she would have closed her eyes. Gwena skidded and slipped on the spray-slick rocks; she went to her knees at least once for every switchback, and there seemed to be hundreds of those. Every time Gwena lurched sideways, Elspeth lurched with her—further unbalancing the Companion and hindering her recovery. The only good thing was that the slower pace enabled Gwena to catch her breath again.

Ahead, Cymry and Skif were in no better shape. That presented a second danger, that they might lose their balance and careen into Gwena and Elspeth, sending all four of them to their deaths.

Gwena might have read her mind; the Companion stopped for a moment, sides heaving, to let Cymry put a little more distance between them. She stood with her head hanging, breathing deeply, extracting everything she could from the brief rest.

Elspeth used the respite to peer through the spray, down to the foot of the trail.

The entire trail was visible from this vantage point, and there was nothing on it except them. Yet. But peering up at her—at least, she presumed they were peering up at her—were several creatures of a dark-gold color that would have blended imperceptibly into the grasslands. They stood out now, only because of the brilliant green of the vegetation below the waterfall. Milling around them were some dark-brown slender beasts, whose fluid movements told her that the pack that had pursued them had recovered from the loss of its leader. In fact, there seemed to be more of them.

I think I know what that blot on the horizon was now. I wonder where the other "hounds" came from, though...

And mingling with those creatures was something else; black, small animals that hopped rather than walked.

She guessed from their behavior that there was some kind of consultation going on. The black creatures seemed to be the ones in charge, or conveying some kind of orders. As she watched, the thin creatures arrayed themselves below the cliff, providing a kind of rear guard. The golden-brown forms lined up in an orderly fashion, and started up the path with a sinister purposefulness. And the black dots sprouted wings and rose into the air.

Crows—she realized. Then, as they drew nearer— *Dearest gods—they're so big!*

They were heading straight for the Heralds. And they could do a great deal of damage with those long, sharp bills, those fierce claws.

Without being prompted by the sword, she pulled her bow again, hoping that dampness hadn't gotten to the string. She nocked and sighted, and released; and repeated the action, filling the air below her with half a dozen arrows.

Only three reached their mark, and one of those was by accident, as a crow flew into the path of one of the arrows while trying to avoid another. Of those three, one was only a wound; it passed through the nearest crow's wing, and the bird spiraled down to the earth, cawing its pain, and keeping itself aloft with frantic flaps of its good wing.

Poor as the marksmanship had been, it was enough to deter the rest of the birds. They kited off sideways, out of her arrow range, caught a thermal, and rowed through the air as fast as their wings could flap to vanish over the top of the cliff.

Gwena lurched back into motion, and Elspeth was forced to put her bow away and resume her two-handed clutch on the saddle pommel. They were barely a third of the way to the top of the cliff and the shelter of the ruins.

She hoped they would see that shelter—and that what awaited them at the top was not a further nest of foes.

Wherever the crows had gone, they had not managed to herd another clutch of magically constructed creatures to the ruins to meet them. And they didn't return to harass the Heralds themselves.

Elspeth heaved a sigh of relief that was echoed by Gwena as they approached the edge of the cliff without seeing any further opposition to their progress. They reached the end of the path without meeting any other dangers than the treacherous path itself—though the last third, so high above the floor of the Plains, had put Elspeth's heart in her throat for the entire journey. She tried to use her FarSight to spy out the land ahead, but either her fear or something outside of herself interfered with her ability to See. She *thought* the way was clear, but she drew her bow—again—just in case it wasn't.

They scrambled up the final switchback, with Elspeth praying that there wasn't anything lying in ambush, and found themselves on a smooth apron of masonry, uneven and weathered, with weeds growing through the cracks.

But there was no time to marvel. A new threat climbed the trail behind them—a threat that was surefooted enough to have closed the gap between them. Elspeth had not had any chance to shoot at these new followers, but they were much bigger than the first creatures that had pursued them across the Plain as well as being armored with horny plates, and she was not terribly confident that their arrows would make much of an impression on these beasts. And they were barely two switchbacks behind the Heralds.

She and Gwena pushed past Skif and scrambled for the shelter of that ruined towerlike edifice she had Seen. He followed right on Gwena's crupper; the Companions' hooves rang on the stone in perfect rhythm, sounding like one single horse.

They reached the shelter of the stones just barely ahead of their pursuers; the first of the creatures came over the edge of the cliff as they whisked into a narrow cleft between two standing walls, a cleft just wide enough for the two of them, or one of them and a Companion, but deep enough for several to work unhindered behind whoever held the front.

Skif and Cymry reached the cleft last, which put them in the position of initial defenders. As Elspeth threw herself from the saddle, she reached for bow-case and quiver. As she fumbled with the straps that held both in place on the saddle-skirt, the sword at her side uncoiled its power, and struck.

At her.

Her hand closed on the hilt of the blade before she was quite aware of what was happening. But as Need moved to take over the rest of her body, she fought back.

It was a brief, sharp struggle; it ended in the blade's surprised capitulation.

:What in hell is wrong with you, girl?: Need shrilled in her mental "ear." *:I thought you were going to let me work magic against those things!:*

:Through me, not using me,: she snarled back. *:That's my body you're trying to take over. You didn't ask, you just tried to take.:*

Need seemed very much taken aback. While the blade pondered, Elspeth retrieved her bow and quiver, and counted out her shots. There were depressingly few arrows left; what she had, she would have to use carefully.

:You've got a mothering-strong Mage-Gift,: the blade said, as Elspeth positioned herself behind Skif, with one arrow nocked to her bowstring. *:I think if I guide you through it, we ought to be able to fend these things off long enough to give us a breathing space. Relax a little, will you?:*

Elspeth let down her guard, reluctantly. *:That's all I need,:* Need said. *:This will be like learning how to shoot. My hands on yours, guiding. That's all. Now look, with your FarSight, below us.:*

Elspeth obeyed, wondering if this was a waste of time. But to her amazement, there *was* something down there.

A kind of web of light, with a bright glow where the lines all met.

:Those are ley-lines; the thing in the middle is a node. Reach out and touch it. I'll help you.:

There *was* an odd sensation that was similar to that of having hands on hers; she followed the guidance of those invisible "hands," reaching out to touch—just barely touch—that bright glow.

Although her physical hands merely pointed off into the heart of the ruins, those other "hands" penetrated deeply beneath the ground—deeper, she sensed, than the Plains below them. It was *not* effortless. She was sweating and trembling by the time she made contact; weak-kneed with the effort, as if she had run up a second cliff trail as long as the one they had just traversed.

Then she touched this "node"—and was hit with a blast of power, as if she stood in the path of an onrushing torrent. If she could have cried out, she would have. She had never felt so entirely helpless in her life.

:Dammit—: Those invisible hands caught her, steadied her. She saw how they were holding her against the power, and altered her "stance," opening to it instead of resisting it. Opening what, she didn't know; in point of fact it "felt" like opening a door that she hadn't been aware existed.

Now instead of being swept away by the flood of power, she had become a conduit for it. It filled her, rather than overwhelming her.

:Good,: the sword said, with grudging admiration. :I wasn't that quick even when I was your age. And I never could handle nodes, only local energy, shallow lines, and power-pools. I think I'm jealous.:

Elspeth opened her eyes to discover that the creatures that had followed them were only now lining up in front of their shelter. Amazingly, hardly any time at all had passed.

:Well, child,: Need said, with grim satisfaction. :Let's show these beasts that the mice they thought they trapped have fangs.:

Elspeth followed the blade's direction, raising her hands above her head and clasping them together for a moment while the power built within her, flooding channels she discovered as they were being filled, then letting it loose with a gesture of throwing.

:You won't need to do that forever,: Need told her, as a lance of energy, like a lightning bolt, leapt from her hand to impact squarely in the chest of one of the creatures. :Eventually, you'll be able to send power without making those stupid gestures. And you'll be able to use it less—crudely. But this will do for now.:

Even as the blade spoke, she guided Elspeth through another three such displays. Skif and the Companions had been taken entirely by surprise; they stood looking at Elspeth as if she had suddenly grown an extra head, staring despite the danger outside the cleft, as if they did not recognize her.

For that matter, she wasn't entirely sure she recognized herself. Here she was, flinging *lightning bolts* about as if they were children's balls— Elspeth, protected Heir, who had never been outside of Valdemar. Elspeth, otherwise very ordinary Herald, who had never been thought to have a particularly strong Gift, much less something like this. The power sang through her mind, light coalescing at her fingers and striking out in showers of sparks.

Unfortunately, when the dazzle cleared from her eyes, it was apparent that her fiery attacks had not impressed the hunters that much.

:Damn,: the sword swore. *:They've been given some protection against magic attack. I didn't know that could be done with constructs.:* And, as if to herself, *:I wonder what else has changed…*

As the exhilaration of power and the impetus of fear both faded, Elspeth leaned against the rock wall and blinked to clear her eyes. For the first time Elspeth got a good look at their foes, as they huddled at a respectful distance from the opening of the cleft, their heads together as if they were discussing something. Perhaps they were…

They were shaped rather like cattle, with horny plates instead of hair, and all of that uniform golden-brown that resembled the color of the parched grasslands of the Plains. They were not as clumsy, however, and were as tall at the shoulder as any of the Ashkevron warhorses. Nor were their heads or legs at all bovine; they bore resemblance to no animal that Elspeth recognized. From sharp, backswept horns, to wide, slitted eyes, to fanged mouths, their heads were alien and as purposeful as the pack of beasts that had chased the Heralds across the Plains. And there were odd feet on those legs, a kind of claw-hoof; the front legs more like a dog's than a cow's.

The consultation ended, and half of the beasts trotted out of sight. Elspeth had no fear that they would come in from behind; those hooves were never made for climbing rock, and the tumble of stones behind them was beyond the capability of anything lacking humanlike hands and feet. What they were undoubtedly doing was making sure that the *Heralds* did not escape by climbing the rocks and slipping away.

The remainder of the creatures settled down, as if perfectly prepared for a long wait.

:I hate to tell you this,: Need said gloomily, *:but if these things have defenses to magical attacks, they have probably been constructed very well. They might not need to eat, drink, or even sleep.:*

She sighed, and pulled her damp hair behind her ears. "Well, that was just what I needed to hear," she muttered.

"What was?" Skif asked, and she realized that the blade had left him out of the conversation again. Probably deliberately.

Elspeth explained, as she and Cymry traded places.

"Oh, hell," he groaned. "We're safe for now, I guess, but how are we going to get out of here? Poison the damn things?"

"They *have* to have a weakness somewhere," she replied absently, studying the beasts with narrowed eyes. "If they're protected in one area, that probably means they've given up protection somewhere else."

Suddenly, one of the beasts, which had been utterly silent up until then, let out a bloodcurdling shriek. The one nearest the opening reared up to its full height, pawing at something in its throat, its head and neck extended as far as they could reach while it shrieked again. As it reared, they saw what had hit it.

An arrow, buried to the fletchings in its throat.

The underbody was covered with soft skin, unlike the horny hide-plates. The area of weakness Elspeth had been hoping for. Her heart surged with elation, and her energy returned redoubled.

A second arrow whirred past and thudded into the creature's chest as it teetered on its hind legs. It bellowed again, then collapsed, and did not move.

While its fellows began to look about confusedly, Skif darted out of cover before Elspeth could stop him. As a third arrow skimmed past him, just beyond his shoulder, and bounced off the hide of the nearest beast, distracting it, he flung one of his throwing knives at the beast's eye. It hit squarely; the tiny knives were razor-sharp and heavy for their tiny size. The second beast threw up its head and collapsed like its brother.

Skif darted back into cover.

Before he had done more than reach the shelter of the cleft, a huge shadow passed overhead.

They both looked up, as a second shadow followed the first, and a cry, like that of an eagle, but a hundred times louder, rang out.

Dear gods—

Elspeth gasped, and for one moment she could not even think.

:What—the hell—are those?: the sword asked.

Elspeth shook with nerves and fear, as the huge gryphons stooped on their pursuers. She had known, intellectually, that gryphons existed; Heralds had seen them in the sky north of Valdemar, but no one she knew had ever seen one this close.

Or at least, if they had, they'd not lived to report the fact.

For one panicked moment, she thought they had come to join the other beasts against them—and *these* creatures would not have the limitations of the hooved ones in prying the Heralds out of their shelter.

But they attacked the strange creatures with talons and beaks, knocking one of them entirely off the cliff, and killing another before Elspeth could react, shrieking defiance as they shredded flesh and flew off again.

Well, whatever they are, even if they aren't on our *side, they aren't on* their *side either.*

The rest of the beasts turned to defend themselves, forming a heads-out circle, and it was clear that there would be no more easy kills.

It was also clear that the gryphons were not going to give up. Nor, from the carefully placed arrows, was their still-unseen ally.

And damn if I'm going to let them do this alone. Maybe they've heard the old saying about how "the enemy of my enemy is my friend."

She ran out, nocking another arrow to her bow, before Skif could grab her and haul her back to safety.

"Come on!" she shouted back at him, allowing a hint of mockery to enter her voice. "What are you waiting for? Winter?"

Elspeth rested her back against a rock, and slid down it. Skif slumped nearby, with his head hanging, his forearms propped on his bent knees, and his hands dangling limply. There was a long shallow gash in her leg that she didn't remember getting, and another wound (a bite) on her arm that she only recalled vaguely. It was a good thing she had more clothing with her; all Whites, though, the merc outfits were filthy. She'd taken both hits after she'd run out of arrows and knives, and the damned sword had insisted on getting in close to fight hand-to—tooth, horn, whatever.

Neither wound was bleeding, and neither one hurt…

:I told you. That's my doing.: That was Need, still unsheathed and in her hand. It was covered in dark, sticky blood, and she had not yet regained the energy to clean it. She had the feeling that the sword wouldn't care—but if she ever put any blade in its sheath without cleaning it, she knew in her soul that Kero *and* Alberich would walk on air to beat her black and blue. The smug satisfaction in the sword's tone would have been annoying if she hadn't been so tired. *:I let 'em bleed enough to clean 'em out, then I took care of 'em.:*

:Well, you were the one that was responsible for my getting hurt in the first place,: she retorted, watching the gash and bitemarks Heal before her eyes. *:I should think you'd take care of them!:*

The sword muttered something about ingratitude; Elspeth ignored it. The gryphons—and presumably the archer—had gone in pursuit of the enemy creatures once their combined attack had broken the beasts' circle and forced them into flight. Neither the Heralds nor their Companions had been in any shape to join the chase.

Gwena plodded over to Elspeth's side and nosed her arm. *:At least that piece of tin is useful as a Healer,:* the Companion observed. *:Are we going to find somewhere safe to rest, do you think? Someplace secure? I'd really like to go sleep for a week or so.:*

"Unless those gryphons saved us just to eat us themselves, I think we are," Elspeth responded, unable to muster much concern over the prospect of becoming gryphon-fodder. She had just learned the truth of something Quenten had warned her about. It took energy to use energy—and hers was spent, and overspent. Right now she was just about ready to pass out, safe or not.

But the sound of a falcon's cry made her look up; there was an enormous raptor skimming along, barely clearing the tops of the stones, winging his way out of the forest. An omen? That would be all they needed now; something more to wonder about.

For a moment, she thought it was her weary, blurring eyes that made the vegetation behind him seem to move, as if part of the forest had separated and was walking toward her. But then, the "vegetation" stepped a little farther out into the open and became a man.

Her hiss of warning brought Skif's head up, and they both struggled to their feet to meet the stranger standing, their Companions moving a little into the shadows out of immediate sight as they rose. She stood so that Need was not so obviously still in her hand; no point in looking belligerent.

He was a somber-looking young man, tall, taller than Skif, and slender. And handsome, strikingly handsome, with a sculptured face and tough, graceful body. He'd already slung his bow across his back; a longbow, much more finely crafted than anything Elspeth had ever seen in use before. His green, gray, and brown clothing blended so well with the forest that he faded into the background every time he paused. His long hair was an odd, mottled brown that helped with the camouflage-effect considerably. As he neared, Elspeth saw that he had the same piercing, ice-blue eyes and bone structure of the Shin'a'in she had seen, though his complexion was a paler gold than theirs. As the man drew nearer, the falcon wheeled and returned. Without looking, the stranger held out his gauntleted wrist, and the falcon—*much* larger, she realized, than any bird she had ever seen, other than, say, an eagle—dropped down gracefully to his fist, and settled itself with a flip of its wings.

That was when she finally made the connection. *Dear gods—he must be one of the Hawkbrothers.* She felt as if she really *had* stepped into the pages of a legend; first she was visited by a Shin'a'in Kal'enedral, then chased by monsters, then rescued by gryphons—and now here was a Hawkbrother, a creature out of legends so remote that she had only found references to them in Vanyel's chronicles. *Moondance and Starwind, Vanyel's friends—Mages, Adepts in fact, from the Clan of k'Treva.*

The man paused at a polite distance from the Heralds, and frowned, as if he wasn't certain how to address them, or which of them to speak to first. She wondered if she should solve his quandary.

But before she could speak, he made up his mind. "Who are you?" he demanded arrogantly in trade-tongue. "What are you doing in Tayledras lands? Why are you here?"

And who are you to ask? I didn't see any boundary markers! She drew herself up, answering his arrogance with pride of her own. "Herald Elspeth and Herald Skif, out of Valdemar. And we were chased here by monsters, as you likely noticed," she replied stiffly, in the same language. "We didn't exactly plan on it, and we didn't stop to ask directions. Any more questions?"

To her surprise, he actually started to smile, at least a little. But that was when Gwena poked her nose from behind her Chosen, and looked at him with a combination of inquiry and tentative approval. His eyes widened and, to Elspeth's amazement, he paled.

She took an involuntary step backward, and that brought Need into view. He glanced down, took a second, very surprised look, and went a little whiter.

He mumbled something under his breath that sounded like Shin'a'in, but was different enough that she couldn't make out what he was saying. It seemed to have something to do with bodily functions.

Well, as long as he'd seen the damned sword and hadn't interpreted it as hostility, she might as well put it away properly. She turned a little, fished a cleaning rag out of Gwena's saddlebag as he watched her warily, and began wiping the blade clean.

It practically cleaned itself. Then again, maybe that wasn't surprising, all things considered. The Hawkbrother mumbled something again, and she looked up as she sheathed her sword properly, and wiped off her filthy hand. "What did you say?" she asked politely, but with a touch of the same arrogance he had been showing them.

He shook his head, but he did seem to be unbending just a little.

"Never mind," he said, "It matters not. It would seem that I am to add you to the colony of Outlanders I am collecting."

"And what if we don't want to go?" she retorted, taken aback by his assumption that she would obey him without a second thought. "There are four of us and only one of you."

"This is our land you trespass on. There are four of us," he corrected mildly, as the gryphons swooped in from behind her to land at his side, the wind created by their wings as they landed making a tiny tempest that blew dust into her face and made her squint. "And I think two of us are bigger than all of you."

She tightened her jaw, refusing to be intimidated. "Is that a threat?" she snapped. "I think we might surprise you, if it is."

He sighed. "No, it is not a threat; if you wish to descend to the Plains, you are free to do so. But I must tell you, there *are* four of us that stand guard here, I will not permit you to pass through Tayledras lands, and your escort still awaits you below the cliff. Our Shin'a'in brethren have not chosen to disperse them, and we above do not trespass upon the Plains without invitation."

"Oh," she said, deflated. *:What do you know about these people?:* she asked the sword.

:Not a damn thing,: Need replied. *:Never heard of them, and I don't recognize the language. They're either something I never ran into, or they sprang up after my time.:*

The young man cleared his throat, delicately, recalling her attention. "I feel as if I must point out that you would not be safe from *anything* with *that* at your side."

He pointed to the sword with his chin.

She raised an eyebrow and looked back at Skif. He shrugged. "I don't think we have much choice," he said quietly.

"Your friend speaks wisely," the Hawkbrother put in. "It may be your escort was attracted by you, or by the weapon you carry. It is magic, and such things are drawn by magic. I think that you would be safer in the company of two mages."

"*Two* mages?" boomed out a new voice. Elspeth's heart leapt right out of her body, and only Gwena's shoulder behind her kept her on her feet as her knees dissolved from a combination of startlement and fear.

"*Two* mages?" repeated the smaller of the gryphons. "Darrrkwind, do my earrsssss decssseive me?"

It talks, Elspeth thought, faintly.

The Hawkbrother—Darkwind, if the gryphon had called him by

his correct name—shrugged again. "This is neither the time nor place to speak of my decisions," he replied, and turned to the Heralds. "I phrased myself poorly. I think that you have no real choice. I think you must accept my hospitality, for your own safety and the safekeeping of that which you carry. Though what the Council will say of this," he added, looking at the gryphon who had spoken, and shaking his head ruefully, "I do not care to contemplate."

The arrogance was back, an imperious quality more suited to a prince of some exotic realm than this—whatever he was. She wanted to angrily deny the fact that they needed protection of any kind, much less *his*. But much as she hated to admit it, she *didn't* want to have to face any more bizarre monsters. Not right away, anyway.

:I think we'd better go along with him, Elspeth,: Skif Mindspoke tentatively, as if he expected her to turn on him and lash him with her anger for such a suggestion. *:I don't know about you, but we can't face any more without some rest. And I really would like to know a little more about what's going on around here before we go charging off on our own.:*

He's some kind of Border Guard, she thought, though not without some resentment. *It* is *his land. I could do with a little less of an attitude, though…* She would have preferred to tell him exactly what he could do with his so-called "protection"—to tell him that she would be perfectly fine—to inform him in no uncertain terms, that whatever he *thought,* she had been sent here, to this very place, by those "Shin'a'in brethren" of his, and that she intended to wait here for them.

On the other hand, she had no idea *why* the Shin'a'in had sent her here, nor if they themselves intended to meet her. Maybe all they had meant was to put her in the hands of these Hawkbrothers…

:What do you think?: she asked Gwena.

:That he is right, we have no choice,: came the Companion's prompt reply. *:It is not necessarily a bad thing; you were in search of mages. He is a mage, so is the gryphon. And according to the chronicles, many of the Hawkbrothers are mages. They taught Vanyel, did they not, when the Herald-Mages could not?:*

:Let's see if someone's willing to come with us, or teach me, first,: she replied sourly. So, it was fairly well unanimous.

"He's right," she told Skif shortly, in their tongue, much to the older Herald's relief. "And so are you. We're all tired, and as long as this isn't an imprisonment—"

"I don't think it is," Skif replied. "I think he'd let us go if we really wanted to. I've got the feeling that we're kind of an annoyance to him, not something he'd keep around if he had the choice."

That didn't make her feel any better. "All right," she told the Hawkbrother, trying to conceal her annoyance. "Where is it you want us to go?"

Instead of replying, he gestured curtly for them to follow; she seethed a little at the implied discourtesy. As the gryphons lofted themselves into the air, she stood aside for Skif and Cymry to get by her. She did not want to follow him too closely just now; she was afraid she would lose what was left of her temper.

She had gotten used to being the one making the decisions. Now she was again following someone else's orders. That galled her as much as this Darkwind fellow's arrogance.

In fact, she decided somewhat guiltily as she led Gwena in Cymry's wake, it probably galled her more...

2 2

Darkwind led the way for this strange parade of Outlanders, winding through the piles of stone on the weed-grown path that led from this end of the ruins to the gryphons' lair. It was a good thing that they had enlarged it; between two Outlanders, their spirit-horses, and Nyara, it would have been crowded otherwise. He wished strongly for something to ease his aching head, or to make him able to forget everything that had happened for the past several days. Or both.

Well, perhaps not everything.

I have my father back again. That was no small gain, even when weighed against all the grief and pain.

He concentrated on staying on his feet, glad beyond telling that this incursion would likely mean there would be nothing more today. If only he were in his *ekele*—he had begun this day wearied and emptied of all strength, or so he thought. He had not found anyone able to take his patrol for him, so he had taken to the border, resigned to another stretch without rest. It had been two days without sleep, now.

But it had been quiet, amazingly so—until, when (of course) he was at the very opposite end of his patrol, he sensed magic, powerful magic, being used somewhere near the gryphons' lair.

He'd thought it might have been Treyvan, doing something to free the gryphlets from Falconsbane's control. But any hope he'd had of that had been shattered by Treyvan's Mindcall.

There was a massing of Misborn beasts, Falconsbane's creatures, in pursuit of two humans—and one of those humans was using magic to try and drive them off. Without success, as it happened. The gryphons were going to their aid. It was his territory; so must he.

He, and they, had arrived on the spot simultaneously, to play rescuer to Outlanders. That had irritated him beyond reason; he was tired, and he saw no reason to save ignorant fools from the consequences of their own folly. He had intended to send them back where they came from, whether they were still in danger or not—until he actually *saw* who, or rather, *what,* he had rescued.

He glanced back over his shoulder at them, trying not to look as if he was doing so. "Unsettled" was the mildest term for the way he felt right now. "Shaken" probably came closer; profoundly shaken.

Well, it is not every day that a pair of Guardian Spirits and a pre-Mage-War Artifact fold wings on your doorstep...

And when one added the fact that the person bearing the Artifact—and in the charge of the more potent of the Guardian Spirits—was a completely untutored mage of Adept potential—

If this is a trial of my abilities—the gods have no sense of proportion.

He was exhausted, bewildered, and one step short of collapsing. All he could think of was to take these Outlanders to the gryphons' lair, where they had left Nyara. Treyvan agreed; and concurred with his judgment that they did not dare let these two—four—*five*—wander about with things as unsettled as they were. If Falconsbane got his hands on them, as he was so obviously trying to do, Darkwind was not willing to think about what uses he might make of them.

With any luck, the Elders were so concerned with Starblade that they would not find out about these "visitors" until they were long gone.

And meanwhile, perhaps he could find somewhere safe to send them. To the Shin'a'in? No, they had forsworn magic...

Could these two have *stolen* that sword from the soil of the Plains? That horrifying thought nearly stopped him in his tracks, until he remembered that the blade did *not* have the air of disuse about it that something of that nature would—and that it *did* have the air of something that was alien to the kind of magics that lay buried in the Plains. *Woman's magic;* that was it. No, this was nothing that had been created by the thoroughly masculine Mage of Silence—and it did not have the look or feel of anything forged by the Shin'a'in. Weapons made for the servants of the Star-Eyed were as sexless as the Kal'enedral; this artifact was as female in its way as—as Nyara.

He staggered a little as he neared the lair; recovered himself before the Outlanders noticed. Above all, he *had* to present a strong front to them. There was no telling what kind of unwitting havoc they could cause if they thought he was less than vigilant, ineffectual—he was certain now that they meant no harm, not with Guardian Spirits hanging about them, but they could cause a great deal of trouble if they chose to meddle without knowing what they were about.

I could wish they were Shin'a'in; then we would have two more useful allies at this moment...

Hydona was already in the lair when they reached it; Treyvan waited outside. "In there," he said, shortly, wishing he dared shake his head to clear his eyes. "If you have gear, Hydona will tell you the chamber you may use."

When the young man looked from him to the spirit-horse doubtfully, he added, "The white ones, too. We will find them food if you do not have it." He bowed a little to the mare. *"Zhai'helleva,* lady. You honor k'Sheyna with your presence."

The spirit-mare looked flattered and surprised—so did the young man.

:You do not look well,: Treyvan noted.

:I do not feel well, but I shall survive,: he replied. He gave Vree a toss to send him to a perch above the lair "doorway" and stood, leaning (he hoped) casually, against the doorpost. The young man entered with his spirit-horse. The young woman's spirit-horse started to follow, and he averted his eyes with discomfort—

Then he found himself sliding dizzily toward the ground, clinging not-so-casually to the rock as his knees buckled.

Quickly, the young woman knelt beside him and unsheathed her sword.

:Peace, brother, she means no harm,: Treyvan said calmly.

Darkwind wasn't so sure. He tried to get up a hand to fend her off—but instead, she put the hilt of the thing *in* his hand.

And he heard a strange, gravelly voice in his mind—

:She says if I don't Heal you she's going to drop me down the nearest well,: the sword told him, annoyance warring with amusement in the overtones of its—her—mind-voice. *:I think she must have been taking lessons in rudeness from her predecessor. And knowing Her Highness, she probably would.:*

He nearly dropped the thing in shock, and only long training—never, never, *never* drop a blade—kept his numb fingers clutched to the hilt.

:Huh. Nothing too bad—overwork, under-rest. And—: He Felt the thing

probing him and his memory, then suddenly pulling back. *:Oh, youngling,:* the sword said, dropping all cynicism. *:You've had more heartbreak than anyone should ever face in a lifetime, and that much I can't Heal. But I'll do my best for you. Open your shields to me.:*

She sounded so much like one of his teachers, an old, old Adept who had ordered him about as if she had been his mother, that he obeyed without thinking twice. She took instant action; in the next moment a gentle warmth stole over him, making him relax still further. He closed his eyes gratefully and let it in. Healers had worked on him before, but that had been for a major injury, not for general exhaustion.

First came the warmth and relaxation; then came new energy, new strength. It rose in him like a tide, rather than a flood; a rising tide of warmth and golden-green light that touched him within and without, folding him in great wings of brilliance, sheltering him as he had not been protected since he was a child. But the blade not only filled him with renewed physical energy, she also reopened his long-unused mage-channels, replenishing him with magical power as well.

He was vaguely offended at first, but then practicality took hold. He *had* said he was a mage. Any reasons for renouncing powers were gone. There was, in fact, every reason why he *should* take up magecraft again.

:Thank you,: he told the blade.

:Thank the girl,: Need responded. *:Oh, I was an Adept, but never with the ability she has. She and her teacher were the first in I don't know how long that fought me and won. And all this power—it's coming through her. So save your thanks for her. I'll be done soon.:*

The blade was as good as its word; the dizziness and weakness were gone, and shortly after that, he felt as refreshed as if he had never endured the stresses of the past five days.

He stood up and gingerly passed the sword back to its bearer. "That was kindly done," he said, with all the courtesy he could muster, embarrassed by the awareness that his dealings with her had been woefully short of courtesy up until this moment. "Thanks is not adequate, but it is all I can offer."

She seemed first surprised, then pleased, then blushed, averting her eyes. "That's all right," she said, "I mean, you looked like you needed help. *She* doesn't like men much, but I figured I could convince her to do something for you."

He looked to the young lady and spirit-mare, nodding gravely. "There have been troubles here," he told her. "There still *are* troubles—

evil ones—and you have tumbled unwitting into the midst of them. My time is short, my powers are strained, and my patience, alas, never was particularly good. Please, even if I offend you, never hesitate to follow my orders or Treyvan's. It may well mean not only your life but ours."

She looked back up at him, resentment warring with respect in her eyes. Respect won.

"I will," she said, a little grudgingly, and he sensed that she was not often minded to follow anyone's orders, much less a stranger's. "You're right, I suppose. We're not from around here; we can't possibly know what's going on."

Imperious, he noted thoughtfully. *Used to giving the orders, not taking them. The sword called her "Highness." That may well be truth, rather than sarcasm.*

"I am Darkwind k'Sheyna," he told her. "This ruin is nominally part of k'Sheyna territory; Treyvan and Hydona are the actual guardians here. There are few who would care to dispute boundaries with them."

He meant that as a subtle warning, but she cocked her head to one side, looked from him to Treyvan and back again, and said accusingly, "There is something very wrong here. You said we've walked into a situation we don't understand—but everything, absolutely everything I've seen tells me that it's worse than that. You people are in trouble."

He narrowed his eyes speculatively. "Why do you say this?" he asked before he thought.

"Well, I'm thinking of you, for one thing," she said. "Need says you were exhausted, that you'd gone days without rest. You don't do that unless you're in some kind of trouble. Everything around here seems— well, it feels like being on the edge of a battlefield, on the eve of a war. And if that's what we've walked into, I'd like to know." She gulped. "I think, on the whole, I'd just as soon take my chances with those things you chased off. I'd rather not get caught in another all-out war. Especially not a war involving magic."

Again, he spoke before he thought, with a little more scorn than he had intended to show. "And what do *you* know of warfare?"

She scowled. "I've fought in a few battles," she snapped. "Have you? And you still haven't answered my question."

"Why should I?" he retorted. He raised his head proudly, planting his fists on his hips. "I know nothing of you, other than that you came across the Plains—and *that* you likely did without the knowledge of the Shin'a'in—"

"What, you want my credentials?" she scoffed, now obviously very angry, but keeping a firm grip on herself. She turned quickly to her saddlebag and turned round again with a roll of vellum and something else. "All right, I'll give you what you'll recognize. My teacher's teacher was Tarma shena Tale'sedrin. My teacher is Captain Kerowyn of the Skybolts, cousin to most of the Tale'sedrin. She no longer rides a warsteed, but when she did, it was *always* called Hellsbane. I came to Kata'shin'a'in looking for Tale'sedrin. One found me; a Kal'enedral. He, she, or it gave me these."

She thrust the roll and an enameled copper disk at him. The latter, he recognized. It was one of the Clan tokens customarily used to identify Clansfolk passing through Tayledras lands. And it was, indeed, a genuine Tale'sedrin token. He even recognized the maker's glyph on the back. That they had given this Outlander one meant that they expected her to be passing through both the Plains and Tayledras territory, and had granted her as much safe passage as they could.

But the other thing, the roll of vellum, proved to be as great a shock as the spirit-horse.

It was a map of the Plains. Darkwind had heard of such things, but the normally secretive Shin'a'in had never before let one out of their hands, to his knowledge, not even to their cousin, Captain Kerowyn. And it *was* a genuine map, not a fake. It showed every well and spring in the Plains, used the correct reckonings, and showed the correct landmarks—at least as far as he could verify. For that much it was priceless. It showed more than that; it showed, if you knew what to look for, the locations of common camp-sites of the four seed-Clans and the offshoot Clans. Anyone who had that information would know who held which territories, and where to find them…

And it also showed the ruins here on the rim, circled in red ink, fresher than anything else on the map.

"That was where I was supposed to go, at least that's what I guessed," she said assertively, stabbing her finger at the red mark. "I don't know what it was I was intended to find, but it certainly looks to *me* as if I was to come here. If you know better, I'd be pleased to hear where I'm supposed to be."

"No," he replied vaguely, still staring at the solid evidence of Shin'a'in cooperation in his hands. "No, I would say that you are correct."

This incident was rapidly turning into something he was not ready to deal with. It had looked like a simple case of Outlanders wandering where they didn't belong.

Then it became a case of keeping these people out of Falconsbane's hands. But now it looked as if the *Shin'a'in* had sent these Outlanders here. And what that could mean, he did not know.

"Please," he said, rolling up the map and handing it back to her. "Please, if you would only rejoin your friend, the young man, I need to speak with Treyvan."

She set her chin stubbornly, but he could be just as stubborn. He crossed his arms over his chest and stood between her and the pathway out, silent, and unmoving except for his hair blowing in the breeze. Finally she stuffed the map back in her belt with an audible sniff and turned to enter the lair.

She went inside—but the white spirit-horse did not. The mare stared at Darkwind for so long he began to feel very uncomfortable. It was very much as if she was measuring him against some arcane standard only she knew. In fact, she probably was, given the little he knew about manifesting spirits; Starblade had once seen a *leshya'e* Kal'enedral, but he never had, and he had been perfectly content to have it remain that way.

Evidently the gods had other ideas.

:A word with you,: the spirit-mare said. Then she looked up at Treyvan and included him in the conversation. *:Both of you,:* she amended.

Treyvan looked down at the little mare from his resting place atop the lair, and rumbled deep in his throat. *:We have many problems and little leisure, my lady,:* he replied in Mindspeech. *:I do not mean to belittle your troubles, but we have no time for yours.:*

She tossed her head and stamped one hoof with an imperiousness that matched her rider's. *:That is exactly what I wish to speak with you about,* your *troubles! You are being very foolish to dismiss us so lightly. I tell you, you* need *us, and I swear to you that you may trust us!:*

With every word, she glowed a little brighter to his Mage-Sight, until he finally had to shield against her.

:Lady, I know you think I can trust you,: he replied, stubbornly, *:but you and she are not of my people; your ways are not ours, and what you think important may mean nothing to us.:*

:And please to dim yourself.: Treyvan added. *:You do not need to set the forest afire to prove what you are.:*

Her glow faded, and she pondered for a moment. *:It is true that we are not of the same peoples, but I will tell you what brings us here. The child needs tutoring in magecraft. That is the most important of our tasks. Other than that, we have no agenda to pursue. And we are four more to stand at your side in your troubles.:*

She snorted delicately. *:We have departed from the road that had been planned for her. At this point, I do not see how further deviation from that plan can matter.:*

The road that had been planned for her? Interesting words, and ones that explained a great deal about the girl's temperament. *I doubt I would much care for being blown about by the winds of fate. In fact—I just might become as belligerent as she has.* He began to feel a bit more in sympathy with the girl. And quite a bit more inclined to trust her.

:Lady, we may not agree on what is to be done here,: he warned. *:This is Tayledras land; we follow the task given to us by our Lady, and nothing is permitted to interfere with that.:*

She shook her mane impatiently. *:Does it matter in whose name good is done? Evil done in the name of a Power of good is still evil. And good done in the name of a Power of evil is still good. It is the actions which matter, not the Name it is done for. You stand against evil here; we will help if you will have us. And then—perhaps—you may help us.:*

Well, that seemed reasonable enough. He raised an eyebrow at Treyvan; the gryphon, adroit at reading human faces, cocked his head to one side. *:She seems sincere. She is—something that cannot speak falsely. And—Darkwind, we and k'Sheyna are not strong enough that we can afford to neglect any form of aid. Especially if we are to free Dawnfire and my children.:*

He nodded. *:If that's the way you feel, then I agree.:* He turned to the mare. *:Lady, we accept your offer with thanks.:*

The spirit nodded emphatically. *:Good. Shall we confer on what needs to be done?:*

Things to be done—the rescue of Dawnfire, for one thing. After Starblade's revelations, he was certain that she *was* in Falconsbane's hands. He *could* not leave her there—he told himself it was for k'Sheyna's sake, that the Clan could not afford another like Starblade—but it was as much for his sake as the Clan's. Over and over the thought had plagued him, intruding into everything, that if he had only been more vigilant, if he had only taken the time to explain why he had wanted her to stay clear of the gryphons that day, none of this would have happened to her. He knew now that he was not to blame for the shattering of the Heartstone—but this he *was* guilty of. He had allowed Falconsbane to lure him into relaxing his guard. And this was the result.

:Bring your people out,: he told the spirit. *:As soon as they are ready to talk. And I will see if I can explain this before night falls. And explain,:* he added grimly, *:just what it is that we mean to do.:*

* * *

To his surprise—although he should not have *been* surprised—the Outlanders had a very good grasp of the situation once he sketched it. As the young man said, "It's not much different from our position at home. Except that the scale is a lot smaller."

The girl sat with her chin resting on both her hands as she listened, then offered a question. "Why is it that this Falconsbane hasn't made a frontal assault on k'Sheyna? He has to know that you're in trouble, and this would be the perfect time to take you."

This Elspeth seemed much easier and more relaxed, now that her blade was out of its sheath and away from her. The spirit penned within the sword—"Need" was its name—had stated that there was very little it could contribute. It had never been a tactician or a leader and did not care to begin learning the craft now. Furthermore, there *was* a great deal she could do to shield the gryphlets from further tampering; so that was what she had been left to do.

Elspeth *had* been a leader and a tactician—at least in small skirmishes—and she had studied her craft under one of the legendary mercenary Captains of the modern times. Word of the Shin'a'in "cousin" had penetrated even into Tayledras lands, via the few Bards that had congress with Tayledras and Shin'a'in. And her pupil's question had merit.

"I do not know," he replied frankly. "I am fairly certain that he has the power to pursue a frontal assault. It may be that he has not simply because he does not think in those terms; because he prefers to weaken from within, and gnaw away from without, until little by little he has wrought such damage that he can overcome his target with little effort or losses."

"That only works if you don't know what he's doing," she pointed out. "Once his victim knows—"

"It may be too late," Treyvan rumbled. "I sssussspect hisss tacticsss have done verrry well in the passst."

"He probably *enjoys* working that way," the young man—Skif, a very odd sort of name, to Darkwind's mind—put in. "I mean, it's obvious from what the cat-lady said that he positively revels in making people suffer. Seems to me he wouldn't get half the pleasure out of being straightforward."

Elspeth bit off an exclamation. "That's it!" she exulted. "That's his weakness! That's what makes him vulnerable! He's so busy with his convoluted plans that if he sees us trying one thing, he might not expect a second attack that was perfectly straightforward. Look, Darkwind, if I were you, that's what I'd do; I'd pretend to try to negotiate with him, and while he thought he was tying me in knots, I'd make a straight assault to get Dawnfire free. I'd also try and do as much damage as I could on the way out," she added thoughtfully, "but then, I'm well known to be a vindictive bitch."

She glanced sideways at Skif as she said that, and the young man looked sour. Evidently she was using words he had thrown at her at some point, and he was not enjoying hearing them now, tossed back in his face.

For his part, Darkwind was a little surprised by this interchange. He had been under the impression that these two were lovers, but evidently this was not so. He tucked the information into the back of his mind for later use in dealing with them. There were niceties needed with a pair of lovers that could be disposed of when working with a pair of friends or colleagues.

Such as splitting them up, for instance, sending one on one mission, and the second on another.

"It is a good notion," he told the girl. "Except that we are not supposed to know that Falconsbane even exists, much less that he holds Dawnfire."

"Damn," she said, with a frown. "I'd forgotten that. Well, what about that daughter of his, Nyara? Can she be useful?"

Now that was a thought. Treyvan rose, anticipating his next words.

"I sssshall wake herrr," the gryphon said, folding his wings to fit more easily through the door of the lair. "We ssshall sssee if ssshe isss rrready to be morrre frrriend than enemy, asss ssshe claimsss."

Darkwind nodded, grimly. Now was the time for Nyara to show her true allegiances. There was a great deal about her father and her father's stronghold and abilities that she could tell them, if she chose. And—just perhaps—some of his weaknesses.

And if she did not choose to help them—well, she would see the Vale after all, as she had often wished. From inside, as he turned her over to the Adepts to be judged. He wondered what they would think of the creature that had eaten Starblade's bondbird before his eyes. No matter how extenuating the circumstances, he did not think they would be inclined to kindness.

Dawnfire stood on her squeaking mouse, killed it messily, and leaned down to pick it up head-first. She started swallowing it whole, trying her best not to think about what she was doing.

At least I'm not like a poor, stupid eyas that doesn't know which end to start on, she thought unhappily. *At least I know enough to kill the things before I try to eat them. And I knew how to kill them in theory, if not in practice.*

In fact, she had learned a lot more than she was displaying. She blessed the many times she'd spent in full-bond with Kyrr, and blessed Kyrr's memory for the way the hawk had shared every experience with her. No, she was *not* a bird—but she had the memories of what it had been like to be a raptor, and once she had overcome her initial despair, those memories had helped her learn the ways of her new body.

They did not help her overcome her fear.

Fear of Falconsbane was only part of it. There was another fear, a constant fear that never left her, waking or sleeping. She knew what would happen as she remained in Kyrr's body—the longer she remained, the more of herself she would lose, until there was nothing left but the hawk. The fact that she had adapted to the body so quickly was both bad as well as good. The more comfortable she felt, the easier it would be to lose herself.

She tried to hold onto herself, with utter desperation. She tried to remember everything about the scouts, the Vale, Darkwind—and she panicked when she found herself in the midst of a memory and could not remember a face, a name, a setting. Was it just that these things had slipped her mind—or was it that her mind was slipping? There was no way to know.

And what had happened to her body, back in the Vale? What if Falconsbane had killed that along with Kyrr's soul? What would she do then?

The past two days had felt like two months. Time stretched out unbearably—and there was nothing to distract her from fear and brooding.

When those thoughts drove her into a state of frenzy, there was only one way to break the cycle. She plotted her escape. She had been taken outside enough times on a creance to know all the places where escape might be possible. If she could get away—no, *when* she got away, she would *not* think "if"—she would head straight up, as high as a red-shouldered could go. From there, she would have an unparalleled view of the countryside; her scouting experience would tell her where she was. If she didn't recognize anything, she would circle until she did see a landmark she knew. And Falconsbane shouldn't be able to touch her.

Planning kept her sane; planning and practice.

When Falconsbane was not in the room, she practiced, as she had

seen the fledglings practice; flapping until she lifted herself just above
the perch; hopping down the length of her jesses and flying back to her
perch. When she had to kill her food, she did so with a clumsiness that
was feigned more and more often. She took out her anger on the hapless
mice, ripping them with talons and beak after she had killed them.

Though it was still all she could do to force herself to eat the mice
afterward.

Falconsbane was not paying a great deal of attention to her, but she
continued the charade, lurching clumsily up to the perch and taking
a long time to get settled. She watched him carefully as she cleaned
her talons and beak. He'd been very preoccupied today; and he had
evidently forgotten, if he had ever known, just how wide a field of vision
a raptor had. She could watch him easily without ever seeming to pay
attention to him.

He had been staring at the scrying stone; no longer relaxed, and no
longer so infernally pleased with himself. She had finally decided that
the scrying stone wouldn't work anywhere except this room; certainly
he never took it with him, and there was nothing else here but her
perch, his couch, the cabinets he kept his toys of pain and pleasure in,
and the stone. For the past two days he had spent more and more time
here; watching the stone, and getting very intent about something. She
overheard him muttering to himself; evidently he had also forgotten how
sharp a raptor's hearing was.

There was something about "heralds," though what that would
have to do with anything, she had no notion. There was more about
"Valdemar" and a "queen;" "Hardorn," and "Ancar." He seemed very
preoccupied with two quite different sets of people. One set seemed to
be traveling, and they had something he wanted.

"Wanted?" That was like saying that she "wanted" her freedom. He
lusted over this object, whatever it was, with an intensity she had never
seen him display before.

The other people were connected with this "Ancar," who seemed
to be the enemy of the first group of people. From the pacing and
muttering that went on after he had watched this person, she gathered
that he was toying with the notion of contracting with this "Ancar" and
proposing an alliance.

That was something new for him, or so she gathered. He wanted
to—and yet he did not want to chance losing the slightest bit of his
own power.

Then, this afternoon, something had changed. The people he had been watching escaped what he had thought was a perfect trap. And they had taken the thing that he wanted with them.

Falconsbane flew into a rage and flung the stone against the opposite wall with such force that he splintered the rock of the wall and reduced the stone to fragments, and she shrank back onto her perch, doing her best not to attract him to her by moving or making a sound. He paid no attention to her whatsoever; he roared for one of his servants to come and clean up the mess, and stood over the trembling boy, looking murderously at him as the terrified child carefully gathered the sharp shards in his shaking, bare hands.

Dawnfire trembled herself, expecting at any moment that he would take out his temper on the boy as he had on the stone. There would be true murder then—

With a sick feeling, she watched him reach down, slowly, clawed hands spread wide—

But before he touched the boy, the door flew open, and two men in some kind of ornate uniform flung themselves into the room to abase themselves at his feet, babbling of "failure" and "mercy." Falconsbane started, then grabbed the child to cover his surprise. He pulled the boy up to his feet by his hair, and threw him bodily toward the door, showering the shards around him. This time the boy did not try to pick them up; he simply made good the chance to flee. The guards blanched and immediately went back to groveling with more heartfelt sincerity than before.

He listened to them a while, then cut them short with a single gesture. "Enough!" he growled, the fingers of his right hand crooked into claws, with the talons fully extended.

The two men fell absolutely silent.

"You failed to capture the artifact," he said, his voice rumbling dangerously. "You failed to corner the quarry, you failed to keep them from finding aid, and you failed to acquire the artifact when you had the opportunity. I should take your lives; I should—remake you."

The men whitened to the color of fresh snow.

"There is nothing you can say that will redeem your complete stupidity," Falconsbane continued. "You will report to Drakan for your punishment. I have not the time to waste upon you."

The two men started to get up; a single snarl from Falconsbane sent them back to their faces.

"I *do* have time to retrieve from your worthless bodies a modicum of the power you *wasted* in this effort." He stretched out his right hand and spread it over the two prone men.

Dawnfire was not certain what exactly he did—but she saw the result clearly. The two men sat back on their heels suddenly, jerked erect like a pair of puppets. Their white faces were frozen in masks of pain, and their limbs trembled and jerked uncontrollably. Their mouths were open, but they uttered not so much as a single sound.

What was truly horrible about the entire tableau was the expression on Falconsbane's face.

He looked like a creature in the throes of sexual ecstasy. He had tossed his long, flowing hair back over his shoulders, and he stared off into nothingness with his eyes half-closed in pure pleasure. His fingers flexed; every time they did, the two men's bodies jerked, and their faces took on new lines of agony. Falconsbane's eyes closed completely, and he lifted his face to the light in obscene bliss.

Finally, he knotted his hand into a fist; the men shuddered, then collapsed.

He opened his eyes, slowly, and gazed down on his victims with a slow, sated smile. "You may go," he purred. *"Now."*

Limbs stirred feebly, heads raised, and the two men began to move. Too weak to do anything else, they crawled toward the door, slowly and painfully.

And that wasn't even their "punishment." That was just Falconsbane's way of reminding them that he was their master in all things.

The first man reached the door and crawled out. All of Dawnfire's feathers slicked down flat to her body in fright. She couldn't have moved now if she had wanted to.

"Greden," Falconsbane said, as the second man started out the door.

The guard stopped, frozen; in a macabre way, he looked funny, like someone caught pretending to be a dog.

"Greden, send Daelon to me on your way out." Falconsbane turned, ignoring the man's whispered acknowledgment, and began pacing beside his couch.

In a few moments, another man entered; an older man, lean and fit, with elaborate, flowing garments and dark gray hair and beard. "My lord?" he said, waiting prudently out of reach. Falconsbane ignored him for a moment, his face creased with a frown of concentration. The man waited patiently; patience was a necessity with Mornelithe

Falconsbane, it seemed. Patience, and extreme care.

Finally Falconsbane stopped pacing and flung himself down on the couch. "Daelon, I am going to propose an alliance, to King Ancar of Hardorn."

"Very good, my lord," Daelon responded, bowing deeply. "Alliances are always preferable to conflict."

Falconsbane smiled, as if he found the man's opinions amusing. "I've been in contact with him for some time, as you know; with him, and some other rulers of the East. He agreed to meet with me in person, but he would not set a time." Falconsbane's smile faded. "When he would not specify a date, I insisted that he must come here, and that it was to be within three months of the initial agreement."

"I assume that he has set a date, my lord?" Daelon asked smoothly.

"Finally." Falconsbane scowled. "He told me just before that disaster Greden was in charge of that he will be arriving in three days' time."

"Very good, my lord. By Gate, my lord?" Daelon asked, with one eyebrow raised.

Falconsbane snorted with contempt. "No. The fool calls himself a mage, yet he cannot even master a Gate. That, it seems, was the reason he would not set a date. He had to travel overland, if you will, and he did not wish anyone to know that he was en route."

Daelon produced a superior, smug smile. "Then you wish me to ready the guest quarters, my lord?"

"Exactly," Falconsbane nodded. "I expect I will be able to persuade him to accept my hospitality after several weeks of primitive inns and the like."

Daelon raised one eyebrow. "Do I take it he will not be coming directly here?"

Once again, Falconsbane snorted. "He prefers, he says, to remain in 'neutral' lands. I directed him to the valley I flooded with death-smoke a while ago. It is secure enough, the horned vermin will not be using it again soon, and if he proves unreliable, well—" the Adept shrugged, rippling his hair and mane. "I flooded it once and can do so again."

"Very good, my lord," Daelon bowed, and smiled. "Better to eliminate a menace than deal with a conflict."

Falconsbane chuckled; the deep, rumbling laugh that Dawnfire knew only too well. She crouched a little smaller on her perch. "Ah, Daelon, your philosophy is so—unique."

Daelon bowed again, smiled, but said nothing. Falconsbane waved negligently at him. "Go," he said. Then as Daelon started for the door, he changed his mind. "Wait," he called, and scooped something up from beside his couch. As Daelon turned, he tossed something at him; and as the servant caught it, Dawnfire saw it was the falconer's glove.

"Take that bird with you," he yawned. "I am fatigued, and she no longer amuses me. Take her to the mews; it is time for her to learn her place in life."

"Very good, my lord," Daelon repeated. When the servant approached Dawnfire, she tensed, expecting trouble, but evidently he was so unfamiliar with falconry that he did not even attempt to hood her. He merely took the ends of her jesses, clumsily, in his free hand, and stuck his gloved hand in her general direction.

If he didn't know enough about falconry to hold her jesses properly, he might not know enough to hold them tightly.

She hopped onto his hand as obediently as a tamed cage-bird, and remained quiet and well-behaved. And as he carried her out of the room, and away from Falconsbane's sight, she saw with elation that he was barely holding the tips of her jesses. Of course, she had fouled them; she couldn't have helped that. He evidently found that very distasteful, and he was avoiding as much contact with the chalked leather as possible.

And he was holding the arm she rested on stiffly, far away from his body, lest (she supposed) she also drop on his fine robes. And if that particular function had been within her control, she would have considered doing just that.

He could not find a servant anywhere as they passed through silent stone corridors on the way to the outside door; that elated her even further, even as it visibly annoyed him. He was going to have to take her outside himself...

He dropped the jesses, leaving them loose, as he wrestled with the massive brass-bound wooden door, trusting in her apparent docility. She rewarded that trust as he got the door open; a real hawk would have bolted the moment a scrap of sky showed, but she was not sure enough of her flying ability to try for an escape. The man was so fussy she was hoping he would take the time to make sure the door was closed before reaching for her jesses again.

Please, Lady of Stars, please don't let him see a servant out here...

He looked about him, squinting in the light, as he emerged from behind the bulky door into the flagstoned courtyard, frowning when he found the courtyard as empty as the corridors. He held her with his arm completely extended, away from his body, as he started to shove the door closed.

YES!

She crouched and launched herself into the air, wings beating with all her might, just as she had practiced. With a cry of despair, Daelon made a grab for her dangling jesses—

But it was too late. She flung herself into the freedom of the blue sky, putting every bit of her strength into each wingbeat, exaltation giving her an extra burst of power, as Daelon dwindled beneath her, waving in wild despair.

2 3

S kif sat very quietly in his corner of the gryphons' lair and made up his bedroll with meticulous care. Elspeth had complained a few days ago that she felt as if she were being written into a tale of some kind. Now he knew how she felt. Strange enough to see gryphons this close—but to be rescued by them, hear them talk—

No one at home is ever going to believe this.

The fighting had been real enough, and he'd seen plenty of misshapen things in the ranks of Ancar's forces. Too many to be surprised by the creatures that had been sent against them. But talking gryphons, Hawkbrothers—

No, they're going to think we made this up.

He tried not to show his fear of the gryphons, but one of his friends was an enthusiastic falconer, and he *knew* what a beak that size, and talons that long, could do.

The bigger of the two gryphons was already inside the roofed-over ruin when he entered it. The place was ten times larger than his room at Haven, but it seemed terribly crowded with the gryphon in it.

"Excuse me, my lady," he'd said humbly, hoping his voice wouldn't break, "but where would you like me?"

"Hydona," said the gryphon.

He coughed, to cover his nervousness. "Excuse me?"

"My name isss Hydona, youngling," the gryphon said, and there was real amusement in its voice. "It means 'kindnessss.' You may put yourrr thingsss in that chamberrr. The Changechild will ssshow you."

That was when he noticed a girl in the next chamber over, peering around the edge of the opening; obediently he had hauled his saddlebags and bedroll across the threshold, wondering what on earth a "Changechild" was.

Then the girl moved out of his way, and fully into the light from the outer door, and his eyes nearly popped out of his head.

She didn't have fur, and she didn't walk on four legs—but she had sharply feline features, slit-pupiled eyes, and the same boneless, liquid grace of any pampered house-cat he'd ever seen.

He managed to stammer out a question about where he was to put his things. She answered by helping him; and that was when he noticed that once the initial shock of her strangeness wore off, she was very attractive. Quite pretty, really.

He smoothed his bedroll and watched her out of the corner of his eye as she brought armfuls of nest-material to put between it and the hard rock. She was more than pretty, she was beautiful, especially when she smiled.

"Thank you," he said, just to see her smile again. Which she did, a smile that reached and warmed those big golden eyes. There hadn't been a lot of smiles out of Elspeth lately... it was nice to see one.

"Let me aid you," she said softly, and knelt beside him to help him arrange a more comfortable bed without waiting to hear his answer.

There hasn't been a lot of help out of Elspeth either, lately, he thought sourly. In fact, this girl was Elspeth's utter opposite in a lot of ways. Quiet, soft-spoken, where Elspeth was more inclined to snap at the most innocent of questions.

"What's your name?" he asked her, as they took the opposite ends of the bedroll, and laid it over the bedding prepared for it.

"Nyara," she said and looked shyly away.

That was when Elspeth came in and put her own gear away, efficiently and without a fuss, but it broke the tentative conversation between himself and Nyara, and the girl retreated to her corner.

She's so—mechanical. She's like a well-oiled, perfectly running clockwork mechanism. She's just not human anymore.

In fact, for all of her exotic strangeness, Nyara seemed more human than Elspeth did.

He stripped off his tunic and changed his filthy, sweat-sodden shirt for a new one, with sidelong glances at Elspeth.

She changed torn shirt and breeches, both cut and stained with blood, although there was no sign of a wound on her. She took no more notice of him and Nyara than if they had been stones.

No heart, no feelings, no emotion. No patience with anyone who isn't perfect. As cold as… Nyara is warm.

A sound at the door made him start, as he laced the cuffs of his shirt. The man who had rescued them—Darkwind—stood shadowing the door. Skif had not heard him until he had deliberately made that sound. *He* spoke with gryphons, moved like a thought, hid in the shadows—he was far more alien than Nyara, and colder than Elspeth.

He looked slowly and deliberately into Skif's eyes, then Elspeth's, then Nyara's. "Come," he said, "it is time to talk."

"Why does it seem as if a whole week has passed since this morning, and a year since we first entered the Plains?" Elspeth asked, her dark brown eyes fixed on the horizon as the last rays of the sun turned the western clouds to gold and red streaks against an incredibly blue sky. The young man called "Skif" was contemplating Nyara, as he had been since she had been awakened.

Darkwind was watching Elspeth and her friend—though mostly Elspeth—rather than the sunset. She had washed and changed into another of those blindingly white uniforms, and he found himself wondering, idly, how she would look in one of the elaborate robes Tayledras Adepts favored. In better days, he'd had time to design clothing for his friends; Tayledras art had to be portable because they moved so often, and clothing was as much art as it was covering. His designs had been very popular back then; not as popular as Ravenwing's feather masks, but she had been practicing her art for longer than he'd been alive.

In fact, he had been proud, terribly proud, that his father had worn some of his designs. One of the things that had hurt him had been finding those outfits discarded soon after he had joined the scouts, in the pile of material available to be remade into scout-camouflage. Now he knew why his father had done that; discarded the clothing where he would be certain to find it. He'd meant to drive Darkwind farther away, to save him. The knowledge turned what had been a bitter memory into something more palatable.

As he contemplated Elspeth, he imagined what he would design for her. Something hugging the body to the hips, perhaps, showing that magnificently muscled torso, then with a flaring skirt, slit to properly display those long, athletic legs—definitely in a brilliant emerald green. Or maybe something that would enable her to move and fight with complete

316

freedom; tight wine-red leather trews laced up the side, an intricately cut black tunic, a soft red silk shirt with an embroidered collar and sleeves…

What in hell am I doing? How can I be thinking of clothing right now?

Maybe it was that she cried out for proper display. White was not her color. The stark uniform only made her look severe, like a purposeful, unornamented blade. After talking with her at length, there was no doubt in his mind that she was a completely competent fighter—that this was an important part of her life. But there was more to her than that; much more. Her outer self should mirror her complicated inner self.

She needed that kind of setting, with her spare, hard-edged beauty. Unlike Nyara, who would never look anything other than lush and exotic, sleek and sensuous, no matter what she wore.

Nyara sat on the opposite side of Skif, glancing sideways at him; Skif couldn't take his eyes off her. She had proved, once revived, not only cooperative but grateful that all Treyvan had done was put her to sleep. Her reaction—completely genuine, so far as Darkwind was able to determine—had shamed him a little for behaving with such suspicion and cold calculation toward her.

On the other hand, she herself had confirmed what Darkwind and Treyvan had suspected; that she was a danger. She confessed that she could be summoned by her father at any point, and if unfettered, she would probably go to him, awake or asleep. She did not know if he could read her thoughts at a distance, but was not willing to say that he couldn't.

"If you have any doubt, you must send me to sleep again, and tie me," she had said humbly. "Do not waste shields upon me that you may give to the little gryphons."

That last had won Treyvan; Darkwind was still not so sure, but his own misgivings were fading. She had given them an amazing amount of information about Mornelithe's stronghold; the problem was, the place was a miracle of defensive capability. Nyara bitterly attributed her easy escape now to the fact that her father had wanted her to get away. Extracting Dawnfire from that warren was looking more and more difficult. Active discussion had died before the sun sank into the west.

But Elspeth was still thinking about the problem and not simply admiring the sunset. "Darkwind, she's a bird, right? What about getting in, turning her loose, and making some other bird look like her?" Elspeth turned toward Darkwind as the last sliver of sun vanished. "One person, maybe two, could get away with that."

:Now that is the kind of sortie I know how to run,: the sword put in.

Darkwind looked pointedly at Nyara.

She coughed politely. "This would be a good time for me to absent myself. Could I take a walk, perhaps?" she asked. "Could someone go with me?" And she glanced significantly at Skif, who flushed but did not look as if he would turn down the invitation.

Darkwind found himself torn by conflicting emotions. He knew very well what was likely to happen as soon as those two found themselves alone, and while on the one hand he was relieved that Nyara had found herself a safer outlet for her needs than himself, he also was unreasoningly jealous.

He didn't trust himself with her. He didn't trust *her;* she had already told them that Falconsbane had ordered her to seduce and subvert him. Doing anything except exchanging pleasantries with her was the worst possible idea at the moment.

That didn't stop his loins from tightening every time she looked at him.

And it didn't stop him from being envious of anyone else she cast those golden eyes upon.

"I've done my share of breaking into buildings in my misspent youth," Skif said hesitantly, with one eye on Nyara. "But I have the feeling you're thinking of using magic, and that's where you lose me. I suppose we could go take that walk, out of earshot. If only one person goes in, I guess it wouldn't be one of us Heralds—so what I know is pretty superfluous."

Darkwind glanced at Elspeth; he thought he saw a little smile playing at the corners of her mouth, but the light was fading, and he couldn't be sure. He wondered if she would be so amused if she knew what *he* knew about Nyara.

But there didn't seem to be any reason to object. "Stay within the ruins," he said, curtly. "Skif, I hold you responsible for this woman. Remember what she's told us; she can't even trust herself."

Skif nodded, but he also rose to his feet and courteously offered Nyara his hand to help her rise as well. Nyara took it, though she didn't need it any more than Darkwind would have. And she held it a moment longer than she needed to.

I don't think he has any idea of what he's in for. She just may eat him alive.

He stopped himself before he could say anything. *She isn't my property. She's too dangerous right now for me to touch. It doesn't matter what I want. Acting on what you want is something only children think is an adult prerogative.*

So he held his tongue and watched the two of them walk slowly into the shadows of the ruins, side-by-side, but carefully not touching.

The sexual tension between them was so obvious that they might just as well have been bound together by ropes.

"I know I'm being incredibly obnoxious to ask this," Elspeth said behind him. "But were you two lovers?"

"No, lady," he said absently, as he struggled to get his jealousy under control. "No, we weren't. She has that much control of herself; her father ordered her to seduce me, therefore she would not. Otherwise——" he paused, then continued, sensing that this particular young woman would not misinterpret what he was saying. And sensing that he could somehow reveal anything to her, without fear of coming under judgment. "Otherwise we might well have been. She was created for pleasure, I think you know that, or have guessed. It drives her before hunger or pain. She is probably quite——adept at it. She has had most of her life to learn it, and practice."

Elspeth considered his words for a moment, as he turned back to face her. "You aren't angry at Skif, I hope."

He uttered a short, humorless laugh. "Angry, no. She cannot help what she is. Envious—yes. Much as I hate to admit it. Envy is not a pretty trait. And you?"

Her soft laugh was genuine. "I am so relieved that he has finally found someone to—well——"

"Drag off into the ruins?" Darkwind suggested delicately.

"Exactly. I can't tell you how relieved I am. He has been a very good friend for many years," she said, tilting her head to one side as she sat silhouetted against the indigo sky. "And he has been under a great deal of strain lately."

"And were *you* lovers?" Darkwind asked sharply, in a tone that surprised even him. *Why should I care?* he wondered. *They're Outlanders. They'll get what they need and leave, like the breath of wind on a still pond. The only impression they can make is a fleeting one.*

She didn't seem to notice. "I haven't been entirely candid with you, Darkwind—though mostly it was because I didn't think rank was going to impress you any, and might have made you reject us out of hand."

Ah, so my surmise was right.

She took a deep breath. "I'm next in line for the throne. Not that I particularly want it," she added, and there was a kind of chagrined surprise in her voice, "Which is odd, because when I was little, I thought that being made Heir was the highest possible pinnacle of success. But there it is; now I have it, and I rather wish I didn't. Skif has always been a kind of big brother to me, and there were always rumors about the two of us."

"But were they true?" he persisted. He shifted a little; not because he was uncomfortable outside, but because he was acutely uncomfortable inside. Jealousy again, and this time for *no* damned reason!

It must be overflow from Nyara, he decided. *Gods of my fathers, this is embarrassing... have I no self-control?*

"No," she said calmly, relieving his jealousy by her answer. "No, he always thought of me as a little sister. Until we went out on this trip together. *Then* he suddenly decided that he was in love with me." She sounded annoyed, to his great satisfaction. "I cannot for the life of me imagine why, but that's what he decided, and I've been trying to discourage him. Maybe once I would have been happy for that, but—it's not possible, Darkwind. I have duties as the Heir, if I ever get back in one piece. If I were to make any kind of alliance, I have to consider my duties first. And anything permanent would be weighed against them. Love—even if genuine—could only be secondary. Mother married for what she *thought* was love the first time, and it was a total disaster. Skif is so blinded by his own feelings that he won't even consider anything else."

"Ah," he replied, "I take it that you are far from convinced that what your friend feels is love."

She snorted. "Infatuation, more like it. I've been trying to emulate my teacher—Kerowyn—since we left Valdemar, and he worships her. That may have been the problem."

So she feels no tie beyond friendship for this Skif, he thought, with a feeling of satisfaction. *Well, if she is going to learn magic, that's just as well. She'll have a great deal to learn, coming to it this late, and she'll have no time for anything but study.* "That may have been the situation," he responded, sensing she was waiting for some kind of a reply. "But—you sounded very annoyed just now with him. May I ask why? If there is friction other than what you have told me, I need to know."

"Nothing other than that once he became infatuated, he wanted to wrap me in silk and stick me in a jewel box," she replied, the annoyance back in her voice. "I think I have him cured of that, but in case I haven't, the problem may come up again."

He nodded, forgetting that it was dark enough that she wouldn't see the nod, then coughed politely. "Thank you, Elspeth. That could cause some problems. I hope I have not caused you distress by asking you these questions."

"No, not at all," she replied, surprise in her voice. "You are a very easy person to confide in, Darkwind. Thank you for giving me the chance to unburden myself. My Companion thinks Skif is perfect for me, and Need thinks he's an utter loss, so any time I say anything to either of them, all I get is lectures."

Companion? Oh, that must be the spirit-mare. But she said it as if it were a name...

"Companion?" he asked, as the first breath of the evening wind flowed through the stones and breathed the hair away from his face.

"My not-horse," she replied, and there was a smile there that he felt across the darkness between them. "The one you have very graciously been treating not like a horse. We call them 'Companions'; every Herald in Valdemar has one—they Choose us to be Heralds."

"They—" he hesitated in confusion. "Could you please explain?"

"Certainly, if you don't mind my coming closer," she replied. He peered through the darkness at her to see if she was being flirtatious—but she appeared to be swatting at her legs. "There seem to be some kind of nocturnal insects on this rock, and they like the taste of Herald."

"By all means, come sit beside me," he replied, grateful to the night-ants. "There are no night-ant nests here."

She rose, brushing off her legs, as he moved over on his rock to give her room.

"Now," he continued, "about these 'Companions' of yours—"

"Shouldn't we be discussing how to get Dawnfire free?" she replied as she seated herself, her tone one of concern. "It's easy to get distracted."

"We are discussing Dawnfire," he told her, a little grimly. "You and this 'Companion' of yours may be better suited to the task than I. I need to know as much as possible about you."

"But Skif—"

"Won't be back for some time," he assured her. "And I have but two concerns regarding him. The first—that her father not attempt to contact or call her while he is with her."

"And the second?" she asked.

He sighed, and leaned back on his hands. "That she leave enough left of him to be useful."

She chuckled, and he felt the corners of his mouth turning up in a smile. "Now," he continued. "About this 'Companion'..."

* * *

Nyara could have shouted her joy aloud, as Darkwind gave them tacit permission to go off alone. Skif could have been ugly, foul-breathed, pot-bellied, bow-legged, bald and obnoxious, and she would not at this moment have cared. He was *safe*, that was what mattered. Mornelithe had not ordered her to seduce him; did not even know that he existed, so far as she knew. She could ease the urges that had been driving her to distraction since her body began to heal, and do so without the guilt of knowing she would be corrupting him—do so only to pleasure herself and him, and not with any other motive of any sort.

That he was cleanly handsome, well-spoken, well-mannered—that turned the expedition from a simple need to a real desire.

She wanted him, in the same way she wanted Darkwind, but without the guilt. Likewise, he wanted her. She guessed, however, that he was shy, else he would have proposed dalliance when they were first alone, in the gryphons' lair. So, it would be up to her.

She had a cat's hearing, to be able to discern a mouse squeak in the high grass a furlong away; and a cat's eyes, so that this light of a near-full moon was as useful to her as the sun at full day.

So when he had just begun to turn to her, to tentatively reach for her hand, she already knew that they were well out of earshot, and that there was a little corner amidst the pile of rocks to their left that would suit his sense of modesty very well. No ears but those equal to hers would hear them; and no eyes but an owl's would spy them out.

Thank the gods—not Mornelithe—that she had learned trade-tongue, and that these strangers spoke it well.

"Nyara," Skif said shyly (oh, she had been right!), taking heart when she did not pull her hand away, "I'm sure this sounds pretty stupid, but I've never met anyone like you."

"You have no Changechildren in your lands?" she asked, stopping, turning to his voice, and standing calculatedly near him. Near enough that her breast brushed his arm.

He did not (oh, joy!) step away. "No," he replied, his voice rising just a little. "No Ch-changechildren, no magic."

"Ah," she purred. And swayed closer. "You know what my father made me for? Darkwind has told you?"

A slight increase in the heat of his body told her he blushed. "Y-yes," he stammered.

"Good," she replied, and fastened her mouth on his.

He only struggled for a moment, mostly out of surprise, and the anticipation that this was part of a ruse, that she meant to escape. Since that was the last thing on her mind, she told him so, with every fiber of her body.

He stopped struggling, believing her unspoken message. She molded herself to him, each and every separate nerve alive and athrill. Then, as he finally began responding instead of reacting, she led him back into the little alcove, step by slow, careful step.

She was on fire with need, and so was he; she felt it, and, for the first time in her life, Felt it as well, a flood of emotion and urgency that washed over her and mingled with her own.

That was such a surprise that she came near to forgetting her own desire. She melted in his need, pulling him down into the shadows, marveling at this precious gift from out of nowhere. To Feel his pleasure, his desire—it heightened her own beyond any past experience.

I am an Empath? I had never dreamed—my own hatred and fear must have shielded me.

But that didn't matter at the moment. All that was truly important was getting him out of his clothing. Or part of it, anyway.

He pulled away, and she clutched him, ripping his shirt with her talons. Why was he trying to evade her? She could Feel his overwhelming need so clearly.

"—rocks!" he gasped, as she tried to fasten her mouth on his again. "You'll hurt your—"

She proceeded to prove to him that the setting didn't matter, and neither did the rocks. Soon they were writhing together, joined in body and mind, and she bit her hand to keep from screaming her pleasure aloud. Mornelithe knew her body as no one else; he knew every way possible to elicit reactions of all sorts from her. But *this* was pleasure unmixed with anger, hate, self-hatred. She had never been so happy in all of her short life.

He reached the pinnacle; she followed, and they fell together.

They lay entwined, panting, sweat-soaked and exhausted. He stroked her hair, with a gentle hand, murmuring wonderful things that she only half heard. How amazing she was; astonishing, a dream come to life. These things were never to be believed if a would-be lover whispered them before the bedding—but after?

She probed his feelings delicately, taking care with this new sense. And there was some truth there, a little something more than mere infatuation. Yes, he was infatuated, but he thought her brave for even trying to resist her father, he thought her admirable for giving them the aid that she had.

And he thought her lovely, desirable, beyond any dream. Nor did he despise her for using her body as she had, or even (and she held her breath in wonder) for being used by her own father.

But there was a bitterness to the joy; he imagined her to have been forced into submitting.

He could never understand the forces that had been bred and formed in her; that her father would call, and she would come, willingly, abjectly, desiring him as fervently as she desired anyone...

She resolved not to think about it. The chances were, she would never see him again after the next few days. If they freed Dawnfire, she would use the Tayledras' gratitude to enable her to put as much distance between herself and her father as her feet would permit.

If they did not—

She would not think of it. Not now. And there was a most excellent distraction near at hand.

She reached for Skif again; he pulled her closer, pillowing her head on his shoulder, thinking she only wished comfort.

She was going to give him such a lovely surprise...

In speaking to Elspeth, Darkwind found himself baffled and dazzled by turns. By the time Skif and Nyara returned, disheveled and sated, smelling of sweat and sex, Darkwind had begun to realize that there was even more to this complicated princess than he had thought.

She had her flaws, certainly. An over-hasty tongue; not in saying what she should not, but in doing so too sharply, too scathingly. A habit of speech, of speaking the truth too clearly and too often that could earn her enemies—and probably had. A hot temper, which, when kindled, was slow to cool. The tendency to hold a grudge—

Hold a grudge? Dear gods, she treasures a grudge, long past when it should have been dead and buried.

She would, without doubt, pursue an enemy into his grave, then make a dancing-floor of it. Then return from time to time for a jig, just to keep the triumph alive.

She flung herself into the midst of disagreements before she entirely understood them, basing her response on what had just happened, rather than seeing what had led to the situation. She was impatient with fools and scornful of those who were ruled by emotions rather than logic. And she took no care to hide either the scorn or the impatience; without a doubt, that had earned her enemies as well.

But to balance all that, she was loyal, faithful, and truly cared for people; so blindingly intelligent that it amazed him, and not afraid of her intellect as so many were. She tried, to the best of her ability, to consider others as often as she considered herself. Her sense of responsibility frightened him, it was so like his own. So, too, her sense of justice.

Dawnfire had been—was, he told himself, fiercely—a paragon of simplicity compared to her. Of course, Dawnfire was ten years her junior, or thereabouts, but he wondered if Elspeth had ever been uncomplicated, even as a child.

Probably not; not with all the considerations the child of a royal couple had to grow up with. Every friend must be weighed against what he might be wanting; every smile must be assumed to be a mask, hiding other motives. Such upbringing had made for bitter, friendless rulers in the Outlands.

It was a very good thing that these people had their Heralds; a very good thing that the monarch was a Herald, and could know with certainty that she would always have a few trustworthy friends.

He didn't entirely understand what the Heralds did, but he certainly understood what they were about. They embodied much the same spirit as the Kal'enedral of the Shin'a'in; like them, it appeared that they were god-chosen, for if the Companions were not the embodiment of the hand of the gods, then he would never recognize such a thing in his lifetime. Like them, they were guided, but subtly—for the most part, left free to exercise their free will, and only gently reminded from time to time if they were about to err. It seemed that the unsubtle attempt to steer Elspeth down a particular course was the exception, and not the rule—and it appeared to him to have failed quite dismally. And as a result, Elspeth's Companion Gwena was now, grudgingly, going to admit her defeat and permit Elspeth to chart her own way from this moment on.

The Heralds were very like the Kal'enedral in another way; for as each had his Companion, so each Kal'enedral had his *leshya'e* Kal'enedral, the spirit-teacher that drilled him in weaponry and guided his steps on the Star-Eyed's road.

And the Heralds themselves were blissfully unaware of the fact.

If they didn't know—and the Companions chose not to tell them— he was not inclined to let the secret slip. *"It is not wise to dispute the decisions of the Powers,"* he thought, wryly quoting a Shin'a'in proverb. *"They have more ways of enforcement than you have of escape."* The decision to set Elspeth on a predetermined path was probably less a "decision" than a "plan." Another Shin'a'in proverb: *"Plans are always subject to change."*

He found himself making a decision of his own: when all this was settled, he would teach her himself. He would find a teaching-Adept, perhaps in another Clan, like k'Treva, and as he relearned, he would teach her. He had the feeling that she respected what he had done, and she would continue to respect him for going back to pick up where he had left off.

Besides, as Tayledras had learned in the past, those who were in the process of learning often discovered new ways and skills, just by being unaware that it "couldn't be done." Perhaps they would discover something together.

But that was for the future; now there was a rescue to be staged.

"We have decided," he said, as Skif reclaimed his boulder, and Nyara seated herself near it. Not quite at his feet, but very close. Darkwind suppressed a last fading twinge of jealousy. "We think we have a plan that will work."

"It's going to need a lot of coordination, though," Elspeth added. "It's going to involve more than just us. Skif, can you get Cymry listening in on this? I just called Gwena."

"Cymry?" he responded, sounding confused. "Uh—sure—"

"They don't need to be with us to be in on conferences," Elspeth said in an undertone to Darkwind. "The Herald-Companion link is even closer than a lifebond in many ways; no matter how weak your Gift of Mindspeech is, your Companion can always hear you, and, if you choose, listen to what you hear."

"And right now they need very badly to be eating," he supplied. "Indeed, the *dyheli* are so, after a long, hard run."

He felt her smile, though he could not see it. "Why don't you start, Darkwind, since this was your idea."

"What of me?" Nyara asked in a small voice. "Should I—"

"You are going to be *inside* the Vale by midmorning," Darkwind told her. "I am going to tell Iceshadow something of your past, and put you in his custody, asking him to keep you always within the shields of the apprentice's working place, where my father is. If your father can break the Vale shields *and* the working-shields, he is merely toying with us, and anything we do is trivial against him. I am going to ask you to answer all of Iceshadow's questions about my father's captivity, no matter how painful they are to you."

"Why?" she asked, huddling a little smaller.

"Because you will be helping Iceshadow determine what was done to him, and so break the bonds Falconsbane placed upon him," Darkwind told her, letting the tone of his voice inform her that he would grant her no more mercy than he granted himself. "That much, at the least, you owe him."

Skif made a little movement, as if he wanted to leap up and challenge Darkwind, but wisely kept himself under control.

"I will then summon the nonhumans that Dawnfire worked with," he continued. "They will help be our diversion; *tervardi* and *dyheli,* they will concentrate on a place where you, Heralds, will be. In the neutral area, as if you had passed across Tayledras lands and were going westward. It will look to Falconsbane as if you have summoned them, and he will assume it is through your sword, Elspeth."

Elspeth took up the explanation where he paused. "All he can tell is that it's magic, Skif. That's probably why those things were chasing us across the Plains. He wants it, and he hasn't got a clue that he can't use it."

:Oh, he could try, I suppose,: the sword said dryly. *:But he doesn't know I'm in here. It's quite likely that it would be impossible for him to make any real use of me without destroying me.:*

"I suspect he will decide that it is one of the ancient devices used to control the nonhumans in warfare." Darkwind rubbed the bridge of his nose. "I can tell you that if he thinks *that,* he will be mad to have it. And he will be equally determined after his last failure that he will not leave the task in the hands of others."

"So he'll come in person," Skif stated, and he was plainly not pleased with the idea. "Where does that leave us?"

"Standing inside the Vale," Darkwind chuckled, wishing he could see Skif's face. "It will be your images and your auras in the neutral area, and no more. It is a spell that is not often cast, for it is broken as soon as one moves more than five paces in any direction. Need reminded us of it. In fact, Need intends to be the mage casting it." He made a little bow in Elspeth's direction.

:Thank you for the confidence, but save your applause for if it works. And it'll be Elspeth casting it; I'll just be showing her how.:

"That leaves me outside," he continued, "and I shall be the one making the attempt to free Dawnfire. If I have the time, I shall place the illusion of the proper hawk on some other bird in his mews, and blank the beast's mind. He will assume that Dawnfire's personality has at last faded. Or so I hope."

He hated to subject an innocent bird to that, but with luck, it would be one of Falconsbane's own evil creations.

"If I do not have the time," he continued, "I shall simply free her and attempt to escape. I do not think he will return before I am away again."

Skif whistled softly. "That's going to take some good timing," he observed. "And you're the one taking the packleader's share of the risks."

"But it could not be done without all of you," he responded. "I cannot ask you to take the kinds of risks that I will—but I cannot make this succeed without you."

"And afterward?" Elspeth asked softly. "When you have Dawnfire free, but still trapped in a hawk's body, her true self fading with every day—what then? You didn't speak of that."

He remained silent because he didn't know—and he didn't want to contemplate it, having to watch her struggle against the inevitable, and lose.

A long, unhappy silence descended, which the sword finally broke.

:Oh, worry about it when she's free,: the blade replied irritably. *:For one thing, I know a bit about transfer spells. Maybe I can get her into something with a big enough brain that she can stay herself. Or maybe I can get her into something like a sword.:*

"Would that not be just as bad?" Nyara asked doubtfully, voicing exactly what Darkwind was thinking. He suppressed a groan.

:At least she'd stay herself, girl,: the sword retorted with annoyance. *:There're worse fates than being hard to break, heart included.:*

Darkwind decided to end the discussion right there. "Enough; we have a great deal ahead of us—"

"And not much time," Elspeth said firmly. "And best to work on it in the morning."

They returned to the lair, and gave Treyvan and Hydona the basics of what they had decided. Treyvan did not ask about the fate of his own young, but Darkwind could tell that he was gravely worried and weary; evidently Falconsbane had tried something while they were talking and had been beaten back, but at a cost. They were all too tired for anything more, and put off further discussion. Nyara bedded down in the same chamber as Skif and Elspeth, with Darkwind across the door and Treyvan blocking the entrance for added security.

But Darkwind could not fall asleep as easily as the rest. He lay staring at the silhouette of the sleeping gryphon, watching the shadow climb up the wall as the moon set. And over and over, the question repeated in his mind.

What do I do once she is free?

She would never again wear the body of the girl he had traded feathers and favors with. At worst case, he would watch her fade, slowly, into the hawk. If Falconsbane had slain the spirit of her bird with Dawnfire's body, she might well hold on longer, but the end would be the same. And whether she stayed in the hawk, or Need managed to find a way to put her in another form, the result was the same. She would never again be "Dawnfire," she would be something else, something he could no longer touch.

What, in the gods' names, do I do when she is free?

2 4

The alarm cry of a falcon woke him at dawn—and the answering, deeper scream of a hawk.

He started awake, all at once, and knew he was not at home. The rock floor, the lack of movement, and the darkness told him that much before he even opened his eyes. His hand was on his knife-hilt as he blinked the haze of sleep away, running rapidly through all the possibilities of where he was and what had become of his *ekele—*

Treyvan's lair— That was all he had a chance to remember as the falcon cried alarm again. He cast about for the door, still disoriented by the strange surroundings.

That's Vree—but whose was the hawk?

:Out!: Vree demanded, his mental cry as shrill and penetrating as his physical scream. *:Out now! Hurry! Help!:*

That wasn't the "Help me" version, it was "I need your help." He scrambled over Treyvan's prone body as the gryphon struggled up out of sleep. "Grrrruh?" Treyvan responded, as Darkwind slid down his haunches and into the sunlight. "Wrrrrhat?"

There were two birds up above, one flapping as clumsily as a just-fledged crow, the other unmistakably Vree. The gyre circled in guard-fashion above the first, protecting it as it tried to come in to land. It was a red-shouldered hawk. It was—*Dawnfire!*

:Help me,: came the faint and faltering mental cry. *:Help me—:*

She doesn't know how to land—he realized, just as Treyvan shouldered him aside, leapt into the sky, rose to meet her, and scooped her from the air with his outstretched talons. He wheeled and dropped, cradling her safely in his foreclaws, coming to rest delicately on his hind feet only, in a thunder of wing-claps, before Darkwind realized what he was doing.

Treyvan balanced precariously as he alighted, keeping himself from falling with his outstretched wings. The bird lay exhausted in Treyvan's claws, every last bit of energy long since spent. Darkwind took her from the gryphon, and held her in his arms, like an injured, shocked fledgling. She lay panting, eyes closed, as he folded her wings over her back, and stroked her head.

Another hand joined his; a hard, but feminine hand. It was Elspeth, wearing only a thin undershift and hose, but carrying her blade unsheathed in her other hand. Her eyes were closed; a slight frown was her only expression—but the moment her fingers touched Dawnfire's back, the bird began to revive.

Her head lifted, and she craned it around to stare up at him. *:Darkwind?:* she Mindspoke, softly. *:Is this real, or some illusion* he *created to torment me? Am I truly free? And home?:*

"You're free, *ke'chara,*" he replied, anger and grief combined rising to choke off his words. It was one thing to know intellectually that she might have been trapped in her bird's body; it was another to see it, Sense it.

:I saw Vree, or he saw me, I forget,: she said, closing her eyes again, and bending her head, as if she did not want to see him through the hawk's eyes. *:He brought me here, but I was so tired—:*

"The sword will work better through direct contact," Elspeth said quietly. "If you can put her down on my bed, and I can lay Need next to her—"

No sooner spoken than done; and with the blade touching her, Dawnfire gained strength quickly, asking for water and food. The latter Darkwind fed her as he would an eyas: little morsels cut from a fresh rabbit that Vree brought back within moments of her asking for something to eat. She took each tidbit daintily, and it was plain from her condition that she had not been feeding well in Mornelithe's hands.

Outwardly he was calm. Inwardly he was in turmoil. How to tell her that her body was dead—that she was still as trapped now as she was in Falconsbane's hands? There was no hint of Kyrr in her thoughts—so the blade's guess, that Mornelithe had killed the bird's spirit with her body, was probably right. That gave them a little more time than if she'd had to share Kyrr's mind—but it would only postpone the end a little longer.

Joy at her recovery, anguish at her condition, rage at the one who had brought her to this—guilt because he was partly to blame. Warring emotions kept him silent as he fed her, wondering what to say and how to say it.

"Dawn—" he began, hesitantly.

:Darkwind, you're in danger,: she interrupted urgently. She twisted her head to look at the strangers. :You're all in danger, terrible danger!:

Quickly she told them of all she had heard; and most importantly, of Falconsbane's new plan, his decision to make Outland alliances.

Alliances? Oh, blessed gods— He forgot his other worries in the face of this new threat, for Falconsbane alone was bad enough. Falconsbane with allies was a prospect too awful to contemplate. Allies with mage-powers, allies with armies—either would spell disaster for the precarious hold k'Sheyna maintained on power here, but this Ancar evidently had mages and armies, according to Elspeth. K'Sheyna would be obliterated, and every other Vale faced with a formidable threat.

If he gets help like that, there won't be anything beyond him—

The Heralds—and their Companions—questioned Dawnfire closely as he closed his eyes and tried to think of all the possibilities. Their reaction was identical to his—not too surprising, given that he thought this "Ancar" that Dawnfire said Falconsbane was meeting was undoubtedly the same man who had been doing his best to level their land. It was not a common name; it was beyond likely that there were two of them.

And although it seemed a terribly long way to travel just for a meeting with a possible ally, Mornelithe was a powerful Adept, and a desirable acquisition, so far as Ancar's position was concerned. The King of Hardorn needed mages; he'd been actively recruiting them. He might not yet have any Adept-class; it might be well worth it to him to come this far.

And a similar search had already brought Elspeth and Skif just as far.

:He said he was meeting the man in three days,: Dawnfire was saying when he opened his eyes again to pay attention to what was going on around him. Now there were seven sets of eyes fixed on the exhausted hawk; the two Heralds, the two gryphons, the pair of Companions, and Nyara, who seemed as upset as any of them.

331

He thought he knew the reason why. *Perhaps she sees herself in Dawnfire's entrapment...*

:That was two days ago,: Dawnfire continued. *:I escaped that afternoon, and I've been flying in circles ever since, trying to find my way home. So today, or the day after, they will meet.:*

"Ancar wouldn't have come all this way just to turn around," Elspeth said grimly. "He wants this alliance, wants it badly. He's got no other reason to leave his own realm, and I don't care how much Hulda taught him, he wouldn't leave the place even in *her* hands if there was any other way out. Gods—with Falconsbane's power and Ancar's armies—and his recklessness—we won't have a chance. We've got to stop this before it happens."

"We have an opportunity to put paid to both our enemies," Darkwind growled, his hands clenched into fists. "Not only to stop this alliance, but take both our enemies at one stroke. I must talk to the Elders."

He started to get up; Skif caught his elbow and his attention. "You'd better include Elspeth in your plans, no matter what else you do," he whispered, "or she's likely to march right in there on her own."

She, who holds a grudge like an eyas binds to a kill. He nodded curtly, annoyed, but knowing Skif was right.

The gryphons had a grudge of their own to settle. They probably wouldn't try to stop her.

:Settle down, you lot!: Need growled suddenly, startling all of them. *:I don't know what's set the burr under your tails so you aren't thinking, children, but I stopped falling for tricks like this one a millennium ago and I'm not going to let you cart me into a trap now. I said he likely wouldn't be able to use me; I'd prefer not to put that to the test, if you don't mind.:*

They stared at each other in shock, Dawnfire included.

"What?" Darkwind asked.

:Let me spell it out for you. Dawnfire was allowed to escape, so that she could bring you this trumped-up story. So that you lot would go charging off straight into his loving arms.:

Nyara was the first to recover. "Oh, no," she whispered. "It is too, too like my own escape—an escape that was not. This sword is right!"

Elspeth set her chin stubbornly, her eyes flashing for a moment, then sighed, and threw up her hands. "Bright Havens, I *want* to believe it, I really do, because it's such a good chance to get the bastard now, while he's away from his support and his army—but you're right, you're both right. It's too damned pat, too coincidental. Mother's intelligence web had Ancar safe in his own palace when we left. We made much better time than he could have because we're riding Companions. The only way he could possibly have matched our time would be to ride in relays, and how would he manage that off his own lands? He has farther to come than we did on top of all that. So how could he *possibly* be arriving here just at the same moment we did?"

"And why sssshould he perrrmit Dawnfirrre to overhearrrr hisss plansss?" Treyvan rumbled. "Mossst essspecially, why ssshould he have given herrr to one who wasss not competent with hawksss to take to the mewsss? He wanted herrr to fly to usss with thisss."

"And then wanted us to—what?" Elspeth asked. "Falconsbane never does anything for just one reason. He wants us not only to try and break up this nonexistent meeting, he wants us moved. Why? What's so special about this neutral area where the supposed 'meeting' is? Is it a particularly good place to stage a double ambush?"

"There's nothing special about it that I know of," Darkwind replied, frowning with concentration.

:He can't have meant to catch you as he caught the dyheli, *can he?:* Dawnfire asked, drooping a little, as she, too, acknowledged the fact that her escape had been too easy. *:He deliberately reminded me of what he had done to them there—:*

"Which probably means he wanted us to concentrate on that as well," Skif mused aloud. "We know he wants the sword. From what Quenten told me, he probably wants Elspeth as well."

"Oh, yes," Nyara agreed, nodding her head vigorously. "Yes, an untrained mage? He uses such as tools. He would be pleased to have you in his hands, lady."

"So, is there anything else he wants? Something we'd leave unprotected—something even the whole Clan might leave unprotected, if we went to them and got more help for this?" Skif continued.

Elspeth glanced sideways at Darkwind. "The Vale itself?" she hazarded. "Or your father?"

He shook his head. "No, the static protections are too much for him to crack easily. We could return and entrap him before he had even begun to break the outermost shields."

"The Heartsssstone?" asked Treyvan, then answered himself. "No, it isss the sssame as for the Vale—"

The squall of a hungry young gryphon cut across their speculations, and sent all eyes in the direction of the inner lair.

"No," Treyvan whispered, his eyes widening.

"Yes!" Nyara cried, in mingled pain and triumph. "Yes—that is what he wants—as much as sword and mage, and Starblade and Starblade's son! Revenge, and the souls of your younglings!"

"And I…" Treyvan whispered, his eyes wide with horror, "nearrrly gave it all away to him… again."

It had taken Darkwind no time at all to create a scale-model of the area around the lair, using rocks, twigs, and the flat expanse of sand near the entrance. It was the only place big enough for all of them. Elspeth shook off the many memories of time spent bending over a sand-table with Kero, and paid close attention to Darkwind. She wondered now how she could have mistaken simple stress for arrogance.

Not thinking clearly lately, are we? she asked herself. *Not observing at all well. When this is over, it might be a good idea to take a few days to rest and think. About a lot of things.*

"You'll be here," Darkwind said to Skif, placing a pinecone on the bits of rock representing the ruins to the left of the lair.

"And I'll be moving around if I can't get a good knife or bow-shot from there," Skif added.

The Hawkbrother nodded. "Exactly so. You are best as mobile as possible. Now, the little ones, Dawnfire, and the sword will be *here*, in front of the lair." He placed a cluster of weed-stripped seed-heads and a sliver of wood before the large stone representing the lair, and gave Elspeth a penetrating glance. "You are certain you are willing to give up the use of the blade? It seems unfair."

Elspeth shrugged. "It was Need's choice, remember," she pointed out. "We've got to protect the bait somehow, and two of the three of them are female."

:Crap, I'll take care of the little male, too,: the blade said gruffly. *:What do you think I am, some kind of baby-killer? Besides, the bastard would twist him up as badly as he has Nyara, if he got his claws on the lad.:*

"You are not such poor bait yourself, blade-lady," Darkwind replied. "He wants you as well, as I recall."

:Just make sure he doesn't get me.:

"No help coming frrrom the Vale?" asked Hydona, leaning over Skif's shoulder to look at the setup.

Darkwind shook his head. "Not since the message I sent them by bondbird-relay. They are rightly fearful that this may be a double ruse—a feint at the little ones, a pretense that draws us into ambush, and a real strike at the Vale. They have been badly shaken by what they have seen done to my father and do not share my confidence in their own shields. They have called in all the scouts but myself, and are bracing for attack."

"Firrrssst ssssmarrrt thing they've decided in agesss," Treyvan growled, "Even if it doesss leave usss to bearrr the burrrden of ourrrr own defensssessss. I take it we are herrre, and herrrre?"

The gryphon pointed a talon at two feathers stuck in the sand on the opposite side of the lair from Skif's initial position, behind a line of rocks representing the wall the lair had been built into.

"Precisely," Darkwind agreed, "And here are Elspeth and myself." He dropped two rough quartz-crystals opposite the gryphons and nearer to the lair than Skif. "Then the Companions, watching for his creatures coming at us from behind." Two large white flowers, one beside Skif's pinecone, one beside Elspeth's crystal. "Treyvan, we will try to bracket him with magic; once that occurs I do not think he will be looking for a physical attack. That is where you come in—" he nodded at Skif. "And you, because of that, are the pivotal point of the defense. You look for your opening and take it. The man is as mortal as any to a well-placed knife or arrow. You are our hidden token, our wild piece."

"What about me?" Nyara asked, in a small voice. "Is there nothing I can do?"

Elspeth bit her lip to keep from saying what she was thinking; that there was no way they could trust the Changechild enough to give her a part to play. They certainly couldn't make her part of the bait; neither the gryphons nor Darkwind wanted her near enough to be in range for an attack on *them* if her father regained control of her.

"Falconsbane does not know you are still with us," Darkwind said, after an uncomfortable silence. "The longer this remains so, the better."

"Stick with me," Skif suggested. "I'm staying out of sight."

:Is this wise?: Darkwind asked Elspeth worriedly. She shook her head just enough to make her hair stir imperceptibly.

:He's assassin-trained,: she replied, wishing there were somewhere safe they could leave Nyara until this was all over. :And Cymry will be with him, watching his back, the way Gwena will be watching ours. She won't be able to catch him with an unexpected attack. I just hope he doesn't find himself in the position of being forced to let Cymry kill her.:

:Or killing her himself,: Darkwind added.

Anything more he might have intended to say was lost, for at that moment, Vree sounded the alert from overhead.

:He comes!: the bird shrieked, with mind and voice. *:He comes now!:*

They scattered for their posts.

Falconsbane prowled the woods that the Birdmen thought were theirs with an ease they would have found appalling, noting the increased levels of shielding about the Vale with a mixture of contempt and anger. There was no doubt of it; they had poured more power into their old shields, added new, and every Adept within the Vale was undoubtedly on alert. The tentative plan he'd formed to extract Starblade from his protectors and retrain him for further use was obviously out of the question now.

He paused in the shelter of a wild tangle of briars and searched for a weak point. There was nothing of the sort. Since there was no one to see him, he permitted himself a savage snarl. All that work, all the patience, the careful planning, the investment of power in Starblade's transformation to puppet, and in the construct that controlled him— all wasted!

He wished he had been able to see through the simulacrum's eyes, but the protections about the Vale had made that impossible. He still had no real idea what had happened when he'd lost his contact with the simulacrum. Starblade had been near the Heartstone; he knew that much. Since it had been near dawn, Falconsbane assumed that he must have been conducting his usual nonproductive assessment of the state of the Heartstone. Then, out of nowhere, a flash of panic from the crow—

And then, the backlash of power as the bird was destroyed. Why, or by whom, he'd had no clue.

He had immediately diverted the wild, uncontrolled power, killing one of his servants—the toady of a secretary, Daelon, who had the misfortune to be nearest.

That wasn't too much of a loss; Daelon had been useless as a mage, and only moderately useful as a secretary. But any loss at all angered him. He had lashed back immediately, flinging spells intended to resnare Starblade before anyone could protect him. It might have been an accident; it might have been the foolish simulacrum venturing into someone's protected area, or even bumbling into something—doing something as stupid as frightening a pet firebird. Any of those things could have killed it.

But as his spells battered against a new and powerful set of shields, it became obvious that it had not been accident that killed the simulacrum. It had been deliberate; his plots had been discovered.

And later tries against Starblade had proven just as fruitless. The Birdman had been well protected within shields that predated Falconsbane's interference with the Heartstone; strong, unflawed shields that he could find no way past.

Now he passed within easy striking distance of the Vale—"striking" distance, only if he'd had that alliance with Ancar of Hardorn that he had feigned, if he'd had a dedicated corps of mages, Masters and Adepts—and as he saw the shimmer of power above the Vale he could only curse at his own impotence. Somehow, some way, someone within k'Sheyna had learned what he had done to Starblade, had surmised how he controlled the handsome fool. Perhaps it had been one of the Adept's former lovers; in retrospect it had been a mistake to force Starblade to retreat into hermitlike isolation. But he had been afraid that the new persona he had laid over the old would not withstand the scrutiny of close examination.

I should have let him keep his lovers; should have had him employ some of the pleasuring techniques he learned at my hands. That would have kept them quiet enough. Nothing stops questionings like unbridled lust and the exhaustion afterward.

It was too late now; he'd not only lost Starblade, he'd lost the Vale. The Birdmen were alert now; there would be no subterfuge clever enough to bypass their protections, and though weakened, they were too formidable for him to take alone.

With luck, the two Outlanders and Starblade's son were on their way to the trap he'd laid for them. Camped within the valley even now were a host of human servants, garbed in the livery of Ancar of Hardorn, led by one who was like enough to that monarch to be his twin. And no illusion had been involved; the conscript was already similar in height, build, and coloring—the same spells that sculpted changes into Falconsbane's flesh had been used at a subtler level to reform this human's face. There would be lingering traces of magic, but that was what the Outlanders would expect. Ancar was a mage, after all.

Once the Outlanders were in place, watching, the rest of his army would take them from behind.

If I cannot have Starblade, I will have Starblade's son. If I cannot take my vengeance upon the Vale, I can take it upon his sweet, young flesh.

There would be that other young man—malleable, possibly of some use as well. Certainly an entertaining bit of amusement. Likely to be a bargaining chip in some way.

And then there was the girl. Her potential as a mage was high. She was curiously naive in some areas; and that left her a wide range of vulnerable points for Falconsbane to exploit. It had been a very long time since he'd broken a female Adept to his will. He was going to take his time with this one; there would be no mistakes that way—and it would, not incidentally, prolong the pleasure as well.

He slid from shadow to shadow beneath the trees, as surefooted and quiet as the lynx he had modeled himself on. As keen of ear, swift of eye, and cunning—

Not even the Birdmen, the scouts and their so-clever birds had ever caught him. He had been wandering freely amid their woodlands since k'Sheyna first settled here. And they never once guessed at his silent presence.

My fighters will take Starblade and the Outlanders, and kill or catch the gryphons. I hope they can catch them. I want the satisfaction of killing them myself.

The deep hatred that always rose in him at the thought of *gryphons* choked his throat and made him grind his teeth in frustration. No matter how remote the memories of his other lives were, *that* one was clear, balefully clear.

Gryphons. They had foiled his bid for supremacy in the Mage-Wars, they had defied his power, ruined his plans, destroyed his kingdom—

Gryphons. Wretched beasts, they were no more than jumped-up constructs. How *dared* they think of themselves as sentients, equal to human, independent and proud of their independence? How dared they use magic, as if they had a right to do so? How dared they *breed* at all?

Animals they were, and one day he would reduce them to the position of brute animals again. And in so doing, he would achieve the sweetest revenge of all, for he would undo everything that the wretched beast who had brought him down had lived and worked for. Only then would he be able to face the memory of Skandranon, the Black Gryphon, with satisfaction.

I will have the parents, he thought, snarling, as he slipped through the underbrush without leaving so much as a footprint behind. *But most importantly, I will have the children. And through them I will not only control the node, but have the downfall of the entire race in my hands. Through them I can spread a plague and a poison that will destroy the minds of any gryphon they meet, and turn them into mere carnivorous cattle. My cattle. To use as I wish. And it is time and more than time that I have that pleasure.*

He entered the area of the ruins, skirting the edge just within the cover of the forest. The lair lay beneath the shadows of the trees in the morning, though it enjoyed full sunlight in the afternoon. This was the nearest he had been, save for that one quick foray to place his hand and seal on the youngsters, binding them to himself.

They can't have left the young ones alone, without some form of protection. There may be shields, or some of the beast-guardians. He paused for a moment, one deeper shadow within the shadows, his spotted pelt blending with the dappled sunlight on the dead leaves beneath the trees, with the mottled bark of the trunk beside him. He wore scouting leathers very similar to what the Birdmen wore; that was one subterfuge that had stood him in good stead in the past. If he *was* seen, he had only to create a fleeting illusion of Birdman features, and other scouts would assume he was one of their number.

A quick glance upward showed him nothing was aloft—nothing but what he expected. Two tiny specks, hardly large enough to be seen, circling overhead. Waiting. That would do.

He set out a questing finger of Mage-Sight, looking for what might have been left behind with the gryphon young.

A shimmering aura flickered about the lair in a delicate rainbow of protection. But beneath the shimmer—a brighter glow of power. *The shields I knew of—yes—and something more—*

He paused; Looked, and Looked again, hardly able to believe his luck.

They had left the artifact behind to guard the young ones! Its protections were unmistakable, and just the touch of them awoke avarice in his heart. *The age—the power—woman's power, but there is little I cannot overcome and turn to my own use—I must have this thing. I must! And they have left it for my taking!*

Elation faded, replaced by cold caution. Perhaps the Outlanders would be that foolish, and even the gryphons—but would Darkwind? The boy was a canny player; surely he had left more protections behind than that, for all that he had renounced magic.

Falconsbane Looked farther, deeper into the ruins than he had ever bothered before; looking for traps, for any hint of magic, even old, or apparently inactive magic. It was always possible that some ancient ward or guardian still existed here that Darkwind had left armed against him.

But there were no signs of any such protections.

He Looked farther still. He had assumed that they knew by now what he had done to the young ones. Was it possible, barely possible, that they did not *know* of his hand on the gryphlets? Had he overestimated their intelligence, their caution? Was it possible after all that they had been so caught up in what he had done to Starblade and Dawnfire that they had missed his sign and seal on their own young? Or could it be that the advent of the Outlanders had distracted them?

No. No, that is why they left the artifact, I am sure of it. To protect the young against me. The shields are too obviously set against my power; even the shields of the artifact itself.

Then, just when he thought perhaps he was searching in vain for further traps, he caught a hint of magic-energy, a tremor of power. Old magic.

Very old magic.

It was not active, but the presence of magic that ancient attracted his curiosity anyway. He had time to spare; such potentials were worth investigating. It was probably nothing; perhaps some long-abandoned shrine, or an ancient talisman, buried beneath a mound of rubble. It might be worth retrieving at some point, if only as a curiosity.

He moved in for a closer Look, half-closing his eyes, his talons digging into the bark of the tree beside him as he concentrated.

And he tore an entire section of bark from the tree trunk as his hand closed convulsively.

A Gate!

No. Yes. It couldn't be. Not the site of a temporary Gate, but one of the rare, powerful, *permanent* Gates—

No more than a handful of Adepts at the time of the Mage-Wars had ever constructed permanent Master Gates; they required endless patience, vast expenditures of energy that could have gone into constructing armies and weapons. Those few who had done so had made a network of such Gates, all tied into one another, crisscrossing their little kingdoms. Urtho had been one of those; that was how the Kaled'a'in had survived the downfall of his kingdom to become the Shin'a'in and Tayledras—they had fled through the Gate at the heart of his citadel to one on the edge of the area. Possibly even this one. Falconsbane had never built one—not in any of his lifetimes. He'd known of the network Urtho had built, of course, but he had never once entertained the idea that even part of that network could still exist.

A Gate, even a Master Gate, couldn't have survived the Wars, or the years, could it? It simply wasn't possible—

Falconsbane could not ignore the proof of his own senses. It was possible. And the Gate had survived.

The touch of it drove him wild with the desire to have it under his control. The node, the gryphons, the artifact, and now this—

He had to have it. He *would* have it. Then he would excavate it, study it, learn how to set it—and *use* it, use it to penetrate to the remains of Urtho's stronghold at the heart of the Plains. With a Gate like this one, he could bypass all the protections of the damned horse-lovers, get in, get what he wanted, and get out with no interference. He could go anywhere there was another permanent Gate, whether or not he knew the territory. He could construct temporary Gates no matter where he was and link into this one at any distance, once he keyed it into himself. Working that way would drain only a fraction of the energy of an ordinary Gate-spell from him. That was the deadly burden of Gating; the energy for the Gate came from the mage.

Or from someone tied to the mage with the kind of bond as deep as a lifebond. Not many knew that a mage tied by a lifebond to another mage could feed his beloved with the energies needed to fuel the Gate-spell.

Fewer knew what Falconsbane knew, that there was another bond as deep as a lifebond; the bond he built between himself and his victim when he made that victim an extension of himself.

As deep as a lifebond; it had to be, to survive the endless struggle of his victims to be free. Built out of both pleasure and pain at the most primitive, instinctive levels, it made his servants need him more than they needed food, drink, sleep—

That opened all their resources to him; to the point, if needed, that he could drain them to their death. He could use those resources to open the Gate and make it his in a way that no other Adept ever had.

But first—he had to make the area his. And that meant retrieving and subverting the young gryphons, to open up the node to his use. Right now there didn't appear to be anything in the way of that.

He released the trunk of the tree, dropping bits of wood and bark as he shook his tingling hand, and stepped cautiously out into the sunlight.

He kept to the shadows, still. There was no point in walking about in the open and alerting a perfectly ordinary guard. It was entirely possible that one or more of those tiresome scouts had been posted here, and Falconsbane had no intention of walking into one of them.

Still, there seemed to be nothing at all blocking his way as he approached the site of the nest. Finally he straightened, and moved into the open, taking a deliberate pace or two forward before the young ones noticed him.

They looked at him curiously, with their heads cocked to one side, as if they had never seen him before. He smiled with satisfaction.

Good. The spell I cast before I left them, to cloud their memories, worked. They do not fear me, so they will not call for help until it is too late.

"Hello, little ones," he purred, and moved into the open. But then something fluttering on the ground caught his eye, and he stopped, suddenly wary.

Flowers. Feathers. Rocks laid in deliberate patterns that teased his memory; he paused for a moment, frowning, as he tried to match pattern with memory.

Then he recognized it for what it was.

So that's the plan, is it? He noted the position of the lone brown pinecone. *I think not.*

He stood very still, listening for movement behind him. There—the scrape of leather on stone; the whisper of wood on wood, sliding.

Oh, I think not, young fool.

He whirled, both hands spread before him, and caught the white-clad young man full in the chest with the bolt of magic, before the Outlander could loose the arrow he had nocked to his bowstring.

A second power-blast left Falconsbane's hands before the first reached its target; this one aimed, not at the man, but at the horse behind him. The "horse" that radiated the same kind of power as some of those damned nomad shamans.

The bow snapped, the arrow shattered, and the young man was blasted off his feet to land in an unconscious heap some distance away.

The "horse" toppled like a fallen tree.

Mornelithe smiled with great satisfaction. He had deliberately held back his strength when he recognized the Outlander clothing. He wanted to—discuss a few things with this young man.

But a feline shriek of pure rage tore through the air, startling him, and he turned again as Nyara—*Nyara?*—leapt upon him, teeth and talons bared, prepared to rip his throat out.

He had no time for other than a purely instinctive reaction; he backhanded her with all his strength, catching her in mid-leap, and sending her flying across the clearing and into the two young gryphons. There was a squeal of outrage from the largest as Nyara landed atop it, and a squawk of fear from the smallest.

But there was another attack coming—

He drew his arms up in a defensive gesture, his powers massing around him in his shields as bolts of mage-energies blasted him from either side.

"What's he doing?" Elspeth whispered to Darkwind, as the Adept calling himself "Mornelithe Falconsbane" paused just outside the ambush zone. He was certainly everything that Darkwind and Nyara's stories had painted him.

Her very first sight of him had terrified her, despite having seen his daughter Nyara and fought his monsters, the things Darkwind called "Misborn," and she had no idea why. Perhaps it was the fact that Falconsbane was so obviously once human, but had given up that humanity. Perhaps it was the cold and focused quality of his gaze. Perhaps it was simply what she knew of him. Darkwind had confided to her—and her only, perhaps because he trusted her, perhaps he thought these were things she in particular needed to hear—some of the horrors that Iceshadow had extracted from Starblade. Nyara wore a haunted look that made her certain—horrible as the idea was—that Falconsbane had visited some of those same torments on his own daughter.

Yet what she knew of him was no worse than some of what she had learned concerning Ancar. Neither made for easy dreams... but Falconsbane was nearer right now than Ancar.

I might feel the same way about Ancar, if I ever see him.

Falconsbane was surely the stuff of which nightmares were made; there was very little of the human left after all the changes he had wrought upon himself, but the effect he had created was of something warped, and not for the better. If one took a lynx, sculpted a perfect human body with a half-human face, then granted it an aura of power that was nothing like anything she had ever experienced before—it still would not be Mornelithe Falconsbane. He was sinister and beautiful, all at the same time, and Elspeth found herself shivering at the mere sight of him.

He had simply appeared, some time after Vree's cry of warning. She had not seen him approach; he was simply *there*, standing amid the rocks, looking down at the earth. "What is he looking at?" she repeated, as Darkwind frowned.

"I don't—*shaeka!*" he spat.

She had no chance to ask him what was wrong; even as he rose to

343

a half-crouch, Falconsbane whirled and dropped to one knee, arms outstretched, hands palm out. Elspeth's stomach knotted with fear.

Darkwind uttered a strangled cry and rose to his feet, flinging one hand protectively toward Skif.

Too late. Elspeth choked on a cry of horror as Falconsbane's bolt of magic struck Skif and threw him into the stones of a ruined wall.

And too late for Cymry, as well; a second bolt struck her, dropping her where she stood like a stricken deer.

Elspeth's horrified *"No!"* was lost in the scream of pure hatred that tore the air like a jagged blade as Skif's limp body dropped to the stones beyond Cymry's.

It was Nyara, leaping in defense of Skif, who attacked her father with the only weapons at her disposal; her claws and teeth, her face a snarling animal-mask of pain, anguish, and hatred.

He intercepted her in mid-leap, and with a single blow of his powerful arm, flung her across the open space to land stunned atop the largest of the young gryphons.

There was no time to wonder if Skif and Cymry survived; no time even to think. She bottled her fear, her anger, though they made her want to run to her old friend's side—or run and hide. The Hawkbrother had joined in combat with the Changechild Adept, and there was no turning back now. Elspeth joined her power to Darkwind's, feeding him with the raw energy she drew up from the node. He knew how to use it; she could only watch and learn—for when he tired, it would be her turn to strike. From the other side, lances of fire rained down on Falconsbane, power pouring from the outstretched claws of Treyvan, with his mate backing him as she backed Darkwind.

For a moment, it was impossible to see the Adept beneath the double attack—and during that moment she dared to hope.

But then, a shadow appeared amid the glare of power—then more than a shadow—then—

Pain.

She thought she cried out; she certainly fell back a pace or two and covered her eyes with her upraised arm, as Darkwind's blast of power reflected back into their faces.

When she blinked her tearing eyes clear, Falconsbane stood untouched, within a circle of scorched earth.

Darkwind had taken the brunt of the blast on their side, as had Treyvan on the gryphons'. Treyvan crouched with head hanging, panting; Darkwind was on his knees beside her, shaking his own head, dazed and unable to speak.

Falconsbane ignored the rest and concentrated his cold gaze on her. Her stomach turned into a cold ball of ice. He smiled, and she stepped back another pace, her hand reaching for a sword she no longer wore, palms sweating, feeling the blood drain from her face.

"Well," he said, his voice full of amusement. "So you have some fight still. I will enjoy breaking you, Outlander." His eyes narrowed, and his voice lowered to a seductive purr. "I will enjoy taking both your mind and your body—"

"*Not this day,*" called a high voice, in pure Shin'a'in, from the ruins behind Falconsbane.

Falconsbane's head snapped around; Elspeth gathered her primitive, clumsy power just in case this was nothing more than a ruse.

But there were people behind the Adept; perched atop rocks, peering from behind walls, an entire line of people. Black-clad, one and all, some veiled, some not, but all with the same cold, implacable purpose in their ice-blue eyes. And one and all with drawn bows pointed at Falconsbane's heart.

"Not this day, nor any other," Darkwind coughed, struggling to his feet. Elspeth gave him a hand, and stood beside him, helping him balance. He did not look to be in any shape to enforce those brave words; he swayed as he stood, even with Elspeth's unobtrusive support, and his face was drawn with pain.

But there were all those arrows pointed at Falconsbane; surely they had him now—didn't they?

Or did they?

After the first flash of surprise, Falconsbane straightened again and laughed, sending a chill down Elspeth's back. "Do you think me so poor a player, then, to show all my counters before the game is over?"

Elspeth did not even have a chance to wonder what he meant.

She had *no* idea of where the thing came from, but suddenly it was dropping down out of the clouds—a huge, black, bat-winged creature that seemed big enough to swallow her whole and have room for Gwena afterward. It buffeted her with its wings, knocking her off her feet with a single blow, then slammed her into a rock—all the breath was driven out of her by the impact; her head snapped back against the stone, and she slid down it, seeing stars.

She blacked out for a moment, but fought back from the dark abyss that threatened to swallow her consciousness. As she struggled back, shaking her head and swallowing the bile of nausea, Falconsbane laughed again.

Her eyes cleared. That was when she saw that there were two of the things. One of them had Hydona trapped beneath it, its talons on her throat, ready to rip it out if she struggled. She looked out helplessly as the creature drew blood and looked expectantly at its master. Then Elspeth could only stare in horror—

The other had Gwena in the same position.

Darkwind lay in a heap just beyond her; eyes closed, unmoving. Treyvan faced the beast that had his mate with every feather and hair standing on end, kill-lust making him tremble. Muscles rippled as he restrained himself from attacking, and the stone beneath his talons flaked away in little chips from the pressure of his claws.

:Gwena—: she Sent.

:Don't!: the Companion shot back. *:Don't move, don't anger it!:* Her mind-voice died to a whisper as the beast tightened its grip on her, and little beads of blood stained her white coat under its talons. *:Don't do anything. Please.:*

"Stalemate, I think?" Falconsbane said genially. The arrows of the Shin'a'in did not waver, but neither did the archers loose them.

"Well, then. In that case, I think I shall fetch what I came for."

Hydona uttered a wail that was choked off by the brutal grip of the beast prisoning her. Treyvan seethed with rage, eyes burning with fury.

"It is not yours, Changechild," said one of the Shin'a'in, in a hollow voice that sounded as if it came up from the depths of a well. *"It was not made by you, it does not obey you; it is not yours."*

Falconsbane lifted an eyebrow. And half-turned to lash out with yet another bolt of power; this one aimed at the young gryphons, a flood of poisonous red.

"NO!"

The cry was torn from Elspeth's throat—but from others as well. One of those others was free to act.

Nyara leapt to her feet, her hands full of Need's hilt, holding it between herself and her father. The bolt of power struck the blade instead of the young gryphons, and built with an ear-shattering wail as Need collected the blast—

And changed it; from sickly red to burnished gold. Elspeth's heart stopped as she watched, not fully understanding what was happening but fearing the worst. She heard Darkwind mutter something about "transmuting," and then he trailed off into a stream of what she guessed to be incredulous Tayledras curses.

Need split the sphere of power in two, one half enveloping each young gryphon, filling them with light. Falconsbane's scream of rage drowned Elspeth's gasp of joy, but it could not stop what was happening. The golden light burned away at a kind of shadow within the two youngsters—the shadows melted even as she watched, melted and evaporated, leaving them clean of its taint.

Distracted by the light and their master's cry of outrage, Mornelithe's dark beasts loosed their grip a little.

Darkwind moved.

Faster than a striking viper, he whipped the climbing-stick that never left him from the sheath on his back, and hooked it into the beast's throat. He never gave the creature a chance to realize what had happened; he yanked the hook toward himself, giving Gwena the opening to kick and buck herself free of it as the creature tried to both right itself and disengage the hook that was tearing its flesh from inside. The Companion scrambled out of the way, sides heaving, legs trembling, blood pouring from a dozen puncture wounds, to collapse at Elspeth's feet.

The creature paid her no heed; all of its attention was taken up with Darkwind.

Elspeth hovered protectively over Gwena; the Companion was shaking like an aspen leaf in the wind, but her wounds were already closing. She leapt up to stand between Gwena and the beast, but there was no need for her protection. She had wondered about Darkwind's peculiar weapontool; now she saw how an expert used it.

Darkwind's face was contorted into a snarl of rage as he attacked the creature, forcing it to go on the defensive; the spiked end of the tool drove into an eye, blinding the beast, as Darkwind backed it into a rock and it staggered. He slashed in a broad flat stroke, laying the beast's belly open, and it fell forward to protect itself. It screamed, and Darkwind reversed the stick, hooking the beast's mouth and tearing at the tongue and lips. It tried to buffet him with its wings, screaming as its eye and mouth dripped thick, brownish blood; he simply hooked the membrane of the wings and tore them, while he ducked under claw-strikes, or fended them off with the spike. Every time there was an opening, he darted in and stabbed again with the spike; he wasn't yet doing the beast lethal damage, but he had to be causing it a lot of pain. It bled from a dozen wounds now, and Darkwind showed no signs of tiring.

Screams of bestial pain from across the court made her dare a glance in that direction. Hydona, bleeding, but still full of fight, stood defiantly between Falconsbane and her children. Her wings were at full spread, mantling over her young, every feather on end. Treyvan clung to the back of the other beast, trying to sever its spine, each strike succeeding in removing a foot-long strip of meat from its neck. The creature screamed and tried in vain to throw him off, leathery wings flailing. No matter the gryphon was half this beast's size; he was going to win. Treyvan was astride the beast's back even if it tried to roll, his claws gouging deep and holding fast with its every swift move, then moving upward as if he was walking up the thing's back like it was a rock, driving deep holes in with every step, and taking a clump of meat with him at every opportunity. Elspeth swallowed in surprise; she had imagined what the gryphons' fearsome natural weaponry could do, but actually seeing it was another matter.

Falconsbane seemed to be ignoring both the beasts, his attention fixed on the Shin'a'in. A moment later she knew why, as a flight of arrows sang toward him, only to be incinerated a few arm's lengths away.

Another scream in her ear reminded her that there was equal danger, nearer at hand. Darkwind's beast was holding its own against him now, and even regaining a little ground, its one good eye mad with rage and fixed on its target. Even if Treyvan won his contest, he could still lose if this beast killed Darkwind.

She had to help him, somehow—

One good eye—

She acted with the thought; dropped one of her knives into her hand from its arm-sheath, aimed, and threw, as one of the beast's lunges brought that good eye into range.

It missed, bouncing off the eye-ridge. The creature didn't even notice.

She swore, and dropped her second knife, as Darkwind slipped on blood-slick rock and fell.

Crap!

The beast lunged with snapping jaws, managing to catch his leg in its teeth. He screamed and beat at the beast's head with his stick, trying to pry the jaws apart, stabbing at the eye.

Suddenly calm, Elspeth waited dispassionately for her target to hold still a moment—and threw.

The creature let Darkwind go, throwing its head up and howling in agony—and instead of scrambling out of the way as Elspeth expected, Darkwind lunged upward with the pointed end of his staff, plunging it into newly revealed soft skin at the base of the thing's throat, and leaning on it as hard as he could.

The creature clawed at the stick, at him, falling over sideways and emitting gurgling cries as he continued to lean into the point, thrashing and trying to dislodge it from its throat, all with no success. Darkwind's eyes streamed tears of pain, and he sobbed under his breath, but he continued to drive the point deeper and deeper.

It died, breathing out bubbles of blood, still trying to free itself.

Across the stretch of scorched earth, Treyvan had clawed his way up his enemy's back to the join of neck and spine. As Elspeth looked briefly away from Darkwind's beast, Treyvan buried his beak in his foe's neck, and jerked his head once. The beast collapsed beneath him.

Treyvan's battle shriek of triumph was drowned in Falconsbane's roar of rage.

Before anyone could move, the Adept howled again, his eyes black with hate, his hands rending the air as he clawed at it. Elspeth did not realize he was making a magical gesture until an oily green-brown smoke billowed up from the ground at his feet, filling the space between the ruined walls in an instant, completely obscuring everything that it rolled over.

Poison! That was her first, panic-stricken thought, as the cloud washed over her before she could scramble out of its path. There was a hum of dozens of bowstrings as the Shin'a'in loosed their arrows.

But though the thick, fetid smoke made her cough uncontrollably and brought tears to her eyes, it didn't seem to be hurting her any. She reached out a tentative Mindtouch for Gwena.

:I'll be all right,: came the weak reply. *:Don't move; the nomads are still shooting:*

And indeed, she heard bowstrings sing and the hiss of arrows nearby. But not a great deal else.

"Darkwind?" she called. "Are you all right?"

"As well as may be, lady," he replied promptly, pain filling his voice. He coughed. "Stand fast, I am going to disperse this. I have enough power for that, at least."

A moment later, a fresh wind cut through the fog, thinning it in heartbeats, blowing it away altogether as Elspeth took in deep, grateful breaths of clean air and knuckled her eyes until they stopped tearing.

She looked first for Falconsbane; he was no longer there, but where he had stood were dozens of arrows stuck point-first into the earth—and leading away from the place was a trail of blood.

That was all she had time to recognize; in the next moment, a surge of powerful energy somewhere nearby disoriented her for a moment. She might have written it off as a spasm of dizziness, had she not seen Darkwind's face.

He stared off into the ruins, his mouth set in a grim line.

"He used the last of his energies to set a Gate-spell back to his stronghold," the Hawkbrother said, bitterly. "*Shaeka.* He has escaped us."

2 5

This isn't finished yet.

Tension still in the air knotted her guts like tangled yarn. And it wasn't just Falconsbane, either. Something was going to happen. There was unfinished business here—but whose it was—she couldn't tell.

The trail of blood ended in a little pool of sticky scarlet, directly in front of an archway in a ruined wall, or so said the Shin'a'in who had followed it to its end. There wasn't any reason for them to lie, and although they did seem a bit too calm and detached for Elspeth's liking, she assumed she could trust them. Darkwind apparently did. He made no effort to see for himself, but simply allowed the Vale Healer to continue working on him, although his lips moved with what Elspeth suspected were curses.

Elspeth swore under her breath herself as she tested Cymry's legs for any more damage than simple bruises and sprains. Skif's Companion was suffering mostly from shock; somehow between them, the Companion and Darkwind had managed to shield Skif and herself from the worst of Falconsbane's blows. That was nothing short of a miracle.

Gwena's talon-punctures had been treated, and would soon heal completely on their own. She was in pain, but it wasn't as bad as it could be, and she said so.

Skif was in the hands of one of the Shin'a'in, the one who had introduced himself as the Tale'sedrin shaman, Kra'heera, and who had seemed oddly familiar to Elspeth. Skif had evidently suffered no worse than a cracked skull that would keep him abed until dizziness passed, and several broken ribs that would keep him out of the saddle for a while. He was unconscious, but not dangerously so. Nyara had satisfied herself on that score even before Elspeth and had taken a place by his side with Need in her hands. Since the blade's Healing power was working on the cat-woman's hurts, and might well aid Kra'heera's efforts with Skif if Nyara managed to persuade the blade, Elspeth saw no reason to take it away from her.

She herself had gotten off lightly, with scratches and cuts; but Darkwind and Treyvan looked like badly butchered meat. When Hydona had flown limpingly into the Vale to fetch help, the Vale's own Healer had timidly come out of protection to treat them and bandage them, then had scuttled back to safety like a frightened mouse. Elspeth didn't think much of him; oh, his skills were quite excellent—but she didn't think highly of any Healer who wouldn't stay with his patients until he knew they were well. Darkwind saw her thinly veiled scorn, though, and he'd promised an explanation.

It better be a good one.

The Shin'a'in were still searching the ruins for Falconsbane, though Darkwind was certain that he was long gone out of reach, and Elspeth agreed with him.

Of them all, only the gryphons were happy, despite wounds and pain. Somehow Need had transmuted the power of Falconsbane's magic into something that burned the little ones clean of his taint. Need might not think much of her own abilities, compared with Elspeth's potential, but Darkwind was impressed. Transmuting was evidently a very rare ability. The adults had taken the young ones to the lair and curled up in there, refusing to budge unless it were direst emergency.

Beside her, Darkwind leaned back against the rock supporting him, and stared at the red-shouldered hawk perched above the door of the lair, her head up and into the wind, her wings slightly mantled. He looked haunted, somehow. As she studied his face, Elspeth thought she read pain and anxiety there, though it was hard to tell what the Hawkbrother was truly feeling.

But when he looked at Dawnfire, *that* was when the feeling of tension solidified.

It's her. That's what isn't finished. She can't stay the way she is—

She wrapped Cymry's foreleg to add support, and looked over at the bird herself.

Dawnfire—what were they going to do about *her?* She was still trapped in the body of a bird.

Even the Shin'a'in seem to feel sorry for her—or something.

The Shin'a'in were returning from their hunt by ones and twos, all of them gathering as if by prearrangement on the area below Dawnfire's perch, all of them silent. They seemed in no hurry to leave, and Elspeth mostly ignored them in favor of the task at hand despite the growing tension in the air. Even if something was about to happen, there wasn't much she could do about it.

Then Cymry's nervous snort made her look up.

As far as she could tell, all of the Shin'a'in had returned and now they were standing in a rough circle below Dawnfire. All but the shaman, that is; he had left Skif and now knelt beside Darkwind, with an odd expression as if he were waiting...

This is it. This is what I've been feeling—this is the cause of all the tension and pressure—

Were they glowing slightly, or was that only her imagination? There seemed to be a hazy dome of light covering them all.

One of the Shin'a'in, a woman by the build, finally moved.

Kra'heera grabbed Darkwind's shoulders and physically restrained him from standing up, as the woman put up a hand to Dawnfire. The bird stared measuringly at her for a moment, then stepped down from her perch onto the proffered hand, and the woman turned to face the rest.

Like all the others, this one was clad entirely in black, from her long black hair to her black armor, to her tall black boots. But there was something wrong with her eyes... something odd.

Darkwind struggled in earnest against the shaman, but he was too weak to squirm out of Kra'heera's hands. "Be silent, boy!" the shaman hissed at him as he continued to fight. "Have *you* any life to offer her? Would you watch her fade before your eyes until there is nothing left of her?"

Elspeth paid scant attention to them, concentrating instead on the black-clad woman who had taken Dawnfire. There was something very unusual about her—a feeling of contained power. Elspeth felt the stirring of a kind of deeply running energy she had never experienced before, and found herself holding her breath.

The woman raised Dawnfire high above her head and held her there, a position that must have been a torment after a few moments, and as she did so, the entire group started to hum.

Softly, then increasing slowly in volume, until the ruins rang with the harmonics—and Dawnfire began to glow.

At first Elspeth thought it was just a trick of the setting sun, touching the bird's feathers and making them seem to give off their own light.

But then, the light grew brighter instead of darker, and Dawnfire straightened and spread her wings—and began to grow larger as well as brighter.

Within heartbeats, Elspeth couldn't even look at her directly. In a few moments more, she was averting her face, though Darkwind continued to stare, squinting, into the light, a look of desperation on his face. The light from the bird's outstretched wings was bright enough to cast shadows, the black-clad Shin'a'in seeming to be shadows themselves, until the bird appeared to be ruling over a host of shades.

The Shin'a'in shaman caught her staring at him. He met her eyes, then returned to gaze fearlessly into the light, and seemed to sense her questions. "Dawnfire has been chosen by the Warrior," he said, as if that explained everything.

Oh, thanks. Now of course I understand. I understand why a hawk is flaming brighter than any firebird; I understand why Darkwind looks as if he's at an execution. What in Havens is going on?

Gwena looked at her as if the Companion had read those thoughts. :*It's business,*: she said shortly, :*And not ours.*:

And I suppose that's going to tell me everything.

Darkwind's eyes streamed tears, and she longed to comfort him, but she sensed she dared not; not at this moment, anyway.

The light was dying now, along with the humming, as she looked back toward the circle of Shin'a'in.

The bird on the female fighter's fist was no longer a red-shouldered hawk; it was a vorcel-hawk, the emblem of the Shin'a'in Clan Tale'sedrin, and the largest such bird Elspeth had ever seen. The light had dimmed in the bird's feathers, but it had not entirely died, and there was an otherworldly quality about the hawk's eyes that made her start with surprise.

Then she recognized it; the same look as the female fighter's. There were neither whites nor pupils to the woman's eyes, nor to the bird's—only a darkness, sprinkled with sparks of light, as if, rather than eyes, Elspeth looked upon fields of stars.

That was when she remembered where she had heard of such a thing. The Chronicles—Roald's description of the Shin'a'in Goddess.

Her mouth dried in an instant, and her heart pounded. If she was right—this was a Goddess—

And Dawnfire was now Her chosen avatar.

And at that moment, she found she couldn't move. She was frozen in place, as a string of bridleless black horses filed into the clear area, led by no one, each going to a Shin'a'in and waiting.

The Shin'a'in mounted up, quite literally as one, and rode out in single file; the woman and the hawk last, heading for the path that wound around the ruins and led down into the Plains. Those two paused for just a moment, black silhouettes against the red-gold sky, sunlight streaming around them, as they looked back.

Darkwind uttered an inarticulate moan. It might have been Dawnfire's name; it might not.

Then they were gone.

Sunset did not bring darkness; Darkwind and Treyvan used their magecraft to kindle a couple of mage-lights apiece, and they all crowded into the lair. Right now, no one wanted to face the night shadows.

Darkwind looks as if he's lost. Not that I blame him. He and Dawnfire were... were close. Whatever happened to her, I have the feeling she's pretty well gone from his life.

"Where's Nyara?" Skif said, struggling to sit up, the bandage around his head obscuring one eye.

"Right there." Elspeth glanced at the niche among the stones by the door that Nyara had been occupying since the fight, Need on her lap, only to find her gone. And she didn't recall seeing the girl move.

Darkwind glanced up at the same time, on hearing Skif's voice; their eyes met across Nyara's now-empty resting place.

"I didn't see her leave," Darkwind began.

"Nor did I," Elspeth replied grimly. "And she's got my sword."

:What do you mean, your sword?: Need's mind-voice asked testily, the quality hollow and thin, as if crossing a bit of distance. Elspeth had started to get to her feet; she froze at the touch of the mind-voice, and a glance at Darkwind showed he had heard it, too.

:I'm not your sword, Elspeth, I'm not anybody's sword. I go to whom I choose. And frankly, child, you don't require my services anymore. You're a fine fighter; a natural, in fact. You're going to be a better mage than I am. And you are ridiculously healthy in mind and body. Nyara, on the other hand...: A feeling of pity crept into the sword's tone. *:Let's just say she's a challenge to any Healer. And if she's not going to fall back into her father's hands, I figured I'd better take an interest in her. She needs me more than you ever would.:*

The mind-voice began to fade. *:Fare well, child. We'll see you again, I think.:*
Then it was gone.

Elspeth stared at Darkwind with a mingled feeling of relief and annoyance. At least this meant there was one less thing to fight, but she'd gotten used to having the blade around to depend on.

I'd gotten used to it—well, maybe she was right. If what she told us was the truth, she never let anyone depend *on her powers.*

"Do you think the artifact will be strong enough to keep Nyara out of *his* hands?" Darkwind asked, worriedly.

Elspeth shrugged. "I don't know. She was strong enough to turn Falconsbane's spell against him."

Darkwind nodded, slowly; his face was in shadow so that Elspeth could not read it, but she had the feeling he was somehow at war within himself. As if he was both relieved that Nyara was gone, and regretting the fact.

Then he moved a little, and the cold light showed a look of such naked loss and loneliness that Elspeth looked away, unable to bear it.

She turned to Skif instead, who was still trying to sit up. "Nyara," he said fretfully, squinting at her. He was doubtless experiencing double vision, and a headache bad enough to wish he were dead. "Where's Nyara? Is she all right?"

"Need's taking care of her," Elspeth told him, giving him the bare truth. "She's fine."

Satisfied, he stopped trying to fight his way into a sitting position, and permitted her to feed him one of the herbal painkillers she had picked up in Kata'shin'a'in. Shortly after that, he was snoring; and she looked up to find Darkwind gone as well, taking his thoughts and his pain into the night.

She hugged her knees to her chest and waited for a while, but he did not return. Finally she went to bed, where she lay for a long time, listening to Skif's drug-induced snores and the young gryphlets making baby noises in the next room.

It was a long night.

Darkwind returned to the gryphon's lair late the next morning; it had been a long night for him, as well, and it had ended with a morning session of the Council of Elders.

He had found himself in the odd position of Council Leader; he was not certain he liked it. Virtually anything he thought to be a good idea would be adopted at this point, when his credit was so high with the rest of the Elders, but how was he to know whether what he wanted was going to be good for the rest of the Vale?

Especially where these Outlanders were concerned.

But he wanted them to stay. Although he was tired, heartsore, and uncertain of many things, of that much he was sure.

He found the young woman outside the lair, taking advantage of a cool breeze and a chance, at last, to rest in the open without fear of attack. She rose on seeing him, and he made idle talk for a moment before finally coming to the subject.

"Falconsbane is gone; perhaps for good. Your sword is no longer with you. I can and will direct you to a teacher among the Vales, and k'Sheyna is not likely to be a comfortable place to live for a while. So what is it you would do now?" he asked, refusing to meet Elspeth's eyes. "There is no need for you to stay."

She set her chin stubbornly. "You promised to teach me magic; are you going back on that promise?"

"No," he replied slowly. *Is this wise? Perhaps not—but I am weary of being wise.* "But—"

"Does the Council want us to leave?" She looked very unhappy at that idea; he rubbed his hand across his tired eyes. Was it only because she thought there would be opposition that she would have to fight without an advocate if she went to another Vale?

"No, not at all," he said wearily. "No—it is—I thought perhaps you and Skif—"

"Skif isn't going to leave here unless you force him to," she told him bluntly. "It's that simple. He can't travel any time soon, and after that—" She shrugged. "He may go home, he may decide to stay, that's up to him. Nyara's out there somewhere; he may decide to try to find her, and personally, I think he will. But I plan on staying, if you're still willing to teach me."

"I am," he replied soberly, "But I must warn you that I have never taught before. And you are a dangerous kind of pupil; you come late to this, and you wield a great deal of power, very clumsily."

She bristled a little. "I haven't exactly had a chance to practice," she retorted. "I don't think you'll find me unwilling to work, or too inflexible to learn."

"I, too, will be a kind of pupil," he reminded her. "I have not used my powers in a long time; I shall have to relearn them before I can teach you."

But it is easier for two than one. And my friends are few enough. Elspeth has become one.

She shrugged. "If you don't care, I don't. What I do care about is that you can teach me as quickly as I can learn. I don't have a lot of time to spend here."

Dark thoughts shadowed her face; he guessed they were thoughts of home, and all that could be taking place there. He softened a little, understanding those worries only too well. "If you will give me your best, I will give you mine," he replied.

She met his eyes at last. "I never give less than my best," she said.

He glanced at the slumbering Skif out of the corner of his eye. "Not even to him?" he asked, a little cruelly, but unable to help himself. *You must know yourself, strengths and weaknesses, before you dare magic.*

"I gave Skif my best," she replied instantly, without a wince. "It just wasn't what he thought he wanted. He's still my friend."

He nodded, satisfied, and rose, holding out his hand to her. "In that case, lady, gather your things again."

This time she did wince. "Why? Did you change your mind just now about throwing us out?" She sounded a little desperate.

"No." He stared at the forest for a moment, wondering again if he was doing the right thing.

But he was doing something, and his heart told him it was right. And that was infinitely better than doing nothing.

"No... no, Elspeth," he replied after a moment, tasting the flavor of the strange name, and finding he liked it. "I have not changed my mind. As soon as you are ready, I will have Skif brought to the Vale, and conduct you there myself." He turned toward her and found himself smiling at the look of complete surprise she wore. "You have succeeded in winning a place where no Outlander has been for generations."

He clasped her forearm in his hand, searching in her eyes for a moment... then speaking to her softly.

"As Council Leader of Vale k'Sheyna, I offer you the sanctuary and peace of the Vale; I offer you the honor and responsibility of the Clan. If you will take it, I give you the name Elspeth k'Sheyna k'Valdemar..."

Somewhere overhead, a forestgyre called his approval as he rode the winds, watching over the forest; for Vree's bondmate had begun his healing at last.

AUTHOR'S NOTE

Just as the Companions are *not* horses as we know them, so the Tayledras bondbirds are *not* hawks and falcons. They have been genetically altered to make them larger, more intelligent, telepathic, and *far* more social than any terrestrial bird of prey. The "real thing" bears the same resemblance to a bondbird as a German Shepherd does to a jackal.

The ancient art of falconry can be thrilling and enjoyable, but the falconer must be prepared to devote as much or more time to it as he would his job. The birds must be fed, trained, and exercised every day without fail, and frequently will not permit anyone but their handler to feed them. For the most part, the falconer must make all his own equipment. And in order to obtain the licenses for his sport, he must pass a lengthy Federal examination, and the facilities for his bird must pass a Federal inspection. The licenses themselves must be obtained from both the Federal and State governments. All native birds are protected species, and possession without a permit is subject to a Federal fine as well as confiscation of the bird. The Apprentice falconer is only permitted to train and fly the red-tailed hawk or the kestrel (North American sparrowhawk), and must do so under the auspices of a Master. This is not a hobby to be taken on lightly, nor is it one that can be put in a closet on a rainy day, or if the falconer doesn't feel well that day. For the most part, birds of prey are not capable of "affection" for their handler, and the best one can expect is tolerance and acceptance. Falconers speak of "serving" their bird, and that is very much the case, for this is a partnership in which the bird has the upper hand, and can choose at any moment to dissolve the relationship and fly away. And frequently, she does just that.

Falconers are single-handedly responsible for keeping the population of North American peregrine falcons alive. They were the first to notice the declining numbers, the first to make the connection between DDT and too-fragile eggshells, and the first to begin captive breeding programs to save the breed from extinction. They are intensely involved in conservation at all levels, and are vitally interested in preserving the wilderness for all future generations.

WINDS of CHANGE

A VALDEMAR OMNIBUS

BOOK TWO of
The MAGE WINDS

Dedicated to the Tayledras and Heralds of our world: police, firefighters, and rescue workers everywhere, whose accomplishments in everyday life outdo anything in fiction.

PROLOGUE

For long years, the rich northern kingdom of Valdemar, ruled by Queen Selenay and her consort Daren, had been under siege by the forces of Hardorn (*Arrows of the Queen, Arrow's Flight, Arrow's Fall, By The Sword*). Ancar, its ruthless and cunning leader, had first tried treachery against the rival country's court; that had been foiled by the Heralds of Valdemar, the judges, lawgivers, and law-enforcers of their people. He could not corrupt them, for it was not in the nature of the Heralds, Chosen for their duties by the horselike creatures called "Companions," to be corrupted. He then tried direct attack—that was foiled by the forces of neighboring Rethwellan to the south, brought by an old promise of aid, long forgotten in Valdemar. Those forces included the mercenary company of the Skybolts, commanded by Captain Kerowyn, grand-daughter of the mage Kethry (whose own story is related in *The Oathbound* and *Oathbreakers*). Kerowyn brought more with her than just arms and fighters; she brought with her an ancient and powerful enchanted weapon, the sword her grandmother had borne; Need, who for reasons then unknown could be commanded only by a woman. With her she brought the King of Rethwellan's own brother, Prince Daren, the Lord Martial of his country, also the younger brother of Selenay's former treacherous husband. The result was the successful defeat of Ancar's forces—and the Choosing of both Daren (for he was nothing like his brother) and Kerowyn by Companions, much to the consternation of some of Selenay's nobles.

And Daren and Selenay had loved each other at first sight.

Five years later, they had produced both progeny and an uneasy peace, although Ancar continued to make attempts across the border, and insinuated spies inside Valdemar. But the one thing of which all felt sure, was that they were safe from magic.

In fact, few people in Valdemar even believed in "real" magic, although the mind-magic of the Heralds was commonplace. An ancient barrier, attributed to the work of the legendary Herald-Mage Vanyel, seemed to hold the *working* of real magic at bay inside Valdemar's borders, if not its effects. Further, it seemed as if there was some prohibition about even *thinking* of real magic; those who discussed it soon forgot the discussions; those who witnessed it soon attributed their memories to dreams. Even old chronicles that spoke of it were forgotten, and those who tried to read them found their interest lagging and put them away without a memory of why they had sought them out in the first place.

But one day, it became plain that this barrier was no longer as effective as everyone believed and hoped. The Queen's Heir, her daughter by her first marriage, made the decision that the time had come for Valdemar to have the same manner of magic its enemies wielded (*Winds of Fate*), and perhaps new magics as well.

She fought for the right to seek out the mages of other lands herself—more successfully, after a magically enhanced assassin sent by Ancar nearly killed her—and set off with the sword Need and one other Herald, Skif, to find mages for Valdemar.

She had not gone far beyond Rethwellan when she deduced that she had not done this alone—that the Companions had acted on her behalf, and were, in fact, forcing her toward a goal only they knew. Angered by this, and swearing that she would follow her own path in this venture, Elspeth turned off the road she had been intended to take, and headed instead for Kata'shin'a'in and the nomads of the Dhorisha Plains— who, she hoped, would lead her to the mysterious Hawkbrothers of the Pelagirs. The last of the Herald-Mages, Herald Vanyel, had been reputedly taught by them (*Magic's Pawn, Magic's Promise, Magic's Price*) and she hoped that she could find either allies or teachers there.

The Shin'a'in had their own set of plans for her, once they learned of her destination. They intended to test her, watch her, and allow her to face some of their enemies as she crossed their land.

Meanwhile, the sword she carried, that she had thought was "only" a magic weapon, proved to be more than that. In her hands it awakened— and proved to be a once-human mage of times so long past that there was no record of her previous life, or anything Need referenced, in the Chronicles of Valdemar.

Together the Heralds, their Companions, and the newly awakened blade crossed the Dhorisha Plains, only to find themselves going from old dangers into new—for the Tayledras territory they headed for, following a map that the Shin'a'in shaman Kra'heera and Tre'valen gave to Elspeth, was as much under siege as the kingdom of Valdemar.

Among the Hawkbrothers, a former mage, Darkwind k'Sheyna, had been fighting his own battle against enemies within and without. Without, were the forces led by the evil Adept and Changemaster, Mornelithe Falconsbane—not the least of which was his half-human daughter, the Changechild Nyara. Within, the Clan was split— physically, for more than half their number, including all of the children and lesser mages, were stranded in the intended site of a new Vale when their Heartstone cracked. And split in leadership, for Darkwind was the leader of a faction that wanted to bring in help from outside to heal their Heartstone and bring back the rest of the Clan—while his father, who led the mages, swore this could not be done.

But Darkwind's father had been subverted by Falconsbane, and even in the heart of the Vale was still under his control. It was Darkwind's father, the Adept Starblade k'Sheyna, who had actually *caused* the fracturing of the stone.

Darkwind was aided by a pair of gryphons and their young, who had served as surrogate parents to him when his own mother died and his father turned strange and alien. Treyvan and Hydona did their best to support him, but despite being powerful mages in their own right, there were few in the Vale who would listen to their advice.

Falconsbane elected to close his hand tighter around k'Sheyna Vale, and sent his daughter—under the ruse that she was escaping his power—to seduce young Darkwind. Nyara herself, sick of her father's mistreatment, was not aware of Falconsbane's larger plan. Loyalty to his lover Dawnfire kept Darkwind from succumbing to his attraction to Nyara, but by Falconsbane's reckoning, it was only a matter of time before he had both father and son in his grasp.

Elspeth, bearing an enormously valuable artifact, and a powerful, if untrained mage herself, aroused Falconsbane's avarice as soon as she came within his reckoning. He turned some of his creatures that had been searching the Plain for the artifacts guarded by the Shin'a'in to pursue Elspeth. And meanwhile, in pursuit himself of an old hatred for gryphons, he launched an attack on Treyvan and Hydona and their young. And in the wake of the attack, he managed to trap Dawnfire's spirit in the body of her bondbird, and slay her human body along with the spirit of the bird.

On discovering that the young gryphlets had been contaminated by

Falconsbane's power, Nyara confessed her hand in the matter, and was confined in a corner of the gryphon's lair.

Elspeth, Skif, and the rest arrived at the borders of the k'Sheyna territory, pursued by Falconsbane's creatures. Darkwind and the gryphons came to their rescue, and recognized both the sword and the Companions for what they were. Unsure of what to do with them, Darkwind led them back to the lair. There, Skif met Nyara and fell in love with her—and the fascination was mutual.

Things that Nyara knew and confessed proved to Darkwind that his father was in thrall to the evil Adept. He succeeded in breaking Falconsbane's hold on his father and in destroying the creature through which the control had come, but that alerted Falconsbane to the fact that they now knew who and what he was and, presumably, what he had planned. He permitted Dawnfire to overhear that he was planning to meet with Ancar of Hardorn to discuss an alliance—then allowed her "accidental" escape.

The name meant nothing to Dawnfire, but a great deal to the Heralds. This was their worst fear realized; that Ancar should unite with a truly powerful Adept—

But Need, who had centuries of experience recognizing trickery, pointed out that Dawnfire's "escape" was a little too easy—and that they would be leaving both the gryphlets and possibly even herself unguarded to disrupt a spurious "meeting."

So the allies planned a reverse ambush, lying in wait for Falconsbane when he came to take the young ones.

Falconsbane was cannier than they thought; he detected the ambush at the last moment, and mounted an effective counterattack. He attempted to take control of the gryphlets, but Need deflected the magic, and turned it against him, using it to purge the unsuspecting young ones of his taint. He attacked Skif, but before he could kill the Herald, he was attacked by his daughter Nyara, in the first open act of defiance in her life. Nevertheless, Falconsbane's powerful magics and allies succeeded in taking down both Companions and trapping Hydona.

All would have been lost but for the tenacity of Darkwind and the gryphons—and the intervention of the Shin'a'in Swordsworn, the black-clad servants of the Shin'a'in and Tayledras Goddess, who had been secret players in events all along. They surrounded the combatants and forced Falconsbane to a stalemate.

Snarling in rage, the Adept escaped—barely—leaving behind a trail of blood and the survivors' hope that a Shin'a'in arrow had been fatal.

But the intervention of the Shin'a'in was not complete. The Swordsworn and the two shaman took up Dawnfire—who, trapped in a bird's body, was fated to fade and "die," leaving nothing of her human self behind. Before the eyes of the Heralds and the rest, the Goddess herself intervened on Dawnfire's behalf, transforming her into a shining Avatar in the shape of a vorcel hawk, the symbol of the shamans' clan, Tale'sedrin.

And in the awed confusion afterward, Nyara vanished, taking Need with her—at the blade's parting insistence that Nyara required her more than Elspeth did.

But the Clan was united once more, and Darkwind agreed to take up his long-denied powers again, to teach Elspeth the ways of magic, that she might return home an Adept.

So dawns the new day...

1

Elspeth rubbed her feather-adorned temples, hoping that her fears and tensions would mercifully go, and leave her mind in peace for just once today.

This isn't what I expected. I wish this were over.

Herald Elspeth, Heir to the Crown of Valdemar, survivor of a thousand and one ceremonies in her twenty-six years, brushed nervously at a nonexistent spot on her tunic and wished she were anywhere but here. "Here" was the southern edge of the lands held by the Tayledras, whom Valdemarans spoke of as the fabled Hawkbrothers. "Here" was a rough-walled cave, presumably hewn by magic, just outside the entrance to k'Sheyna Vale. "Here" was where Elspeth the Heir was stewing in her own juices from anxiety.

Elspeth was still getting used to these people and their magic. As far as she could tell the cave hadn't been there before yesterday.

Then again—the walls didn't have that raw, new look of freshly cut stone, and the sandy, uneven floor seemed ordinary. Even the entrance, a jagged break in the hillside, appeared to be perfectly natural, and healthy plants lined the edges. Greenery grew anywhere roots could find a pocket of soil to hold onto. And the smell was as damp and musty as any cave she'd ever seen during her Herald's training.

Maybe she was wrong. The cave might always have been there, but its entrance may just have been well-hidden.

Now that she thought about it, that would be a lot more like the style of the only Hawkbrother she knew, Darkwind k'Sheyna. He wasn't inclined to waste time or energy on anything—much less waste magical power. He took a dim view of profligate use of magery, something he'd made very clear to Elspeth in the first days of their acquaintance. If something could be done without using magic, that was the way he'd do it—hoarding his powers and doling them out in miserly driblets.

That was something she didn't understand at all. When you had magic, shouldn't you use it?

Darkwind didn't seem to think so.

Neither did the Chronicles she had read, of Herald-Mage Vanyel's time and before. Incredible things were possible to an Adept—and that, of course, was *why* she was here. If she'd dared, she'd have used her powers now, to shape a more comfortable seat than the rock she perched on, just inside the cave's entrance.

That at least would have given her something to *do*, instead of working herself up into a fine froth of nerves over the coming ceremony.

She glanced resentfully at Skif; *he* looked perfectly calm, if preoccupied. His dark eyes were focused somewhere inward, and if he was at all nervous, none of it showed on his square-jawed face. In fact, the only sign that he wasn't a statue was that he would run a hand through his curly brown hair once in a while.

Elspeth sighed. It figured. He was probably so busy thinking about Nyara that none of this mattered to him. The only thing that being made a Tayledras Wingbrother meant to him was that he'd be able to stay in Hawkbrother territory for as long as it took to find her.

Assuming the sword Need *let* him find Nyara. The blade not only used magic well, it—she—was a person, a woman who'd long ago traded her aging fleshly body for the steel form of an ensorceled sword. It wasn't a trade Elspeth would have made. Need could only hear, see, and feel through the senses of her bearer—and in times when her bearer wasn't particularly MindGifted or when she had no bearer at all, she had drifted off into "sleep."

She'd been asleep for a long time before Elspeth's teacher, Herald Captain Kerowyn, had passed her on to her pupil. But something—very probably something Elspeth herself had done—had finally roused her from that centuries-long sleep. Once she was awake, Need was a hundred times more formidable than she had been asleep.

She had quite a mind of her own, too. She had decided, once Elspeth was safely in the hands of the Hawkbrothers and the immediate troubles were over, that the Changechild Nyara required her far more than Elspeth did. So when Nyara chose to vanish into the wild lands surrounding the Tayledras Vale, Need evidently persuaded the catlike woman to take the sword with her.

That left Elspeth on her own, to follow her original plan; find a teacher for Valdemarans with mage-talent, and get training herself.

Among the few hundred-odd things she hadn't planned on was being made a member of a Tayledras Clan. *How did I get myself into this?* she asked herself.

:Willingly and with open eyes,: her Companion Gwena replied, the sarcastic acidity of her Mindspeech not at all diluted by the fact that it was a mere whisper. *:You could have gone looking for Kero's great-uncle, the way you were supposed to. He's an Adept and a teacher. You could have followed Quenten's very clear directions, and he would have taken you as a pupil. If necessary, I would have made certain he took you as a student. But no, you had to follow your own path, you—:*

Elspeth considered slamming mental barriers closed against her Companion and decided against it. If she did, Gwena would win the argument by default.

:I told you I wasn't going to be herded to some predestined fate like a complacent ewe,: she snapped back, just as acidly, taking Gwena entirely by surprise. The Companion tossed her mane as her head jerked up with the force of the mental reply, her bright blue eyes going blank with surprise.

:I also told you,: Elspeth continued with a little less force and just a touch of satisfaction, *:that I wasn't going to play Questing Hero just to suit you and the rest of your horsey friends. I will do my best by Valdemar, but I'm doing it my own way. Besides, how do you know Kero's uncle would have been the right teacher for me? How do you know that I haven't done something better than what you planned by coming here and making contact with the Shin'a'in and the Hawkbrothers? Vanyel was certainly a well-trained Adept, and the Chronicles say that the Hawkbrothers trained him.:*

Gwena snorted scornfully, and pawed the ground with a silver hoof. *:I don't know whether you've done better or worse,:* she replied, *:but you were asking how you got yourself into this—this—brotherhood ceremony. And I told you.:*

Elspeth stiffened. Gwena had been eavesdropping again. *:That was a purely rhetorical question,:* she said coldly. *:Meant for myself. I wasn't broadcasting it to all and sundry. And I'd appreciate it if you'd let me keep a few thoughts private once in a while.:*

Gwena narrowed her eyes and shook her head. *:My,:* was all she said in reply. *:We're certainly touchy today, aren't we?:*

Elspeth did not dignify the comment with an answer. If anything, Gwena was twice as touchy as *she* was, and both of them knew why. The only way for Elspeth—or Skif—to be able to remain in the lands guarded by the Tayledras was to be made Wingbrothers to the Clan of k'Sheyna. But that required swearing to certain oaths—which none of their informants had yet divulged, saying only that they'd learn what those pledges were when they actually stepped into the circle to *make* them.

Elspeth had been trained in diplomacy and statecraft from childhood, and undisclosed oaths made her very nervous indeed. It wasn't so bad for Skif—*he* wasn't the Heir. But for her, well, the things she pledged herself to here could have serious consequences for Valdemar if she wasn't very careful. She carried with her the Crown's authority. The fact that a *forgotten* oath had made a crucial difference to Valdemar in the recent past only pointed up the necessity of being careful what she swore to here and now.

"Nervous?" Skif asked in a low voice, startling her out of her brooding thoughts.

She grimaced. "Of course I'm nervous. How could I not be? I'm hundreds of leagues away from home, sitting in a cave with you, you thief—"

"*Former* thief," he grinned.

"Excuse me. *Former* thief and a bloodthirsty barbarian shaman from the Dhorisha Plains—"

Tre'valen cleared his throat delicately. "Pardon," he interrupted, in the Tayledras tongue, "But while I am both shaman and bloodthirsty, I am not, I think, a barbarian. We Shin'a'in have *recorded* history that predates the Mage Wars. Can you say as much, newcomer?"

For a moment, Elspeth was afraid she had offended him, then she saw the twinkle in his eye, and the barely perceptible quirk of one corner of his mouth. Tre'valen had proved to have a healthy sense of humor over the past few days, as they waited out the response of the k'Sheyna Council of Elders to their petition to remain. She had heard him refer to himself as bloodthirsty *and* a barbarian more than once. In point of fact, the shaman seemed to enjoy teasing and challenging her...

"I stand rebuked, oh Elder of Elders," she replied formally, bowing as deeply as she could. She was rewarded with his broad grin, which grew broader as she continued, "Of course, the fact that you don't *do* anything with all that recorded history has no bearing at *all* on whether or not you're barbarians."

"Of course not," he replied blandly, evidently well-satisfied with her return volley. "Dwelling overmuch upon the past is the mark of the *decadent*. We aren't that, either."

"Point taken." She conceded defeat, and turned back to Skif. "So I'm here in a cave waiting for some authority to come along and demand that I swear something unspecified, which may or may not bind me to something I'd really rather not have anything to do with—why should I be nervous?"

Skif chuckled, and she restrained herself from snarling. "Now think a bit," he told her, fondly, but as if she were thirteen again. "You've read the Chronicles. Both Vanyel and his aunt swore the Wingbrother Oaths. They *had* to, or they couldn't have gone in and out of the Vales the way they did. If there was nothing in the oaths to bother them, why should you be worried?"

"They do not differ," Tre'valen said serenely, "and they have not changed in all of our *recorded* history. Many shaman of the Shin'a'in swear to Wingsib; and believe me, the oaths our Goddess requires of us bind us to far more than your own oaths to your Crown and country. And *She* can move her hand to chastise us at her will. I think you need not be concerned."

Well, that was some comfort, anyway. Elspeth had seen for herself how the Shin'a'in Goddess—who was, so Darkwind said, also the Goddess of *his* people—could and did manifest herself in very tangible fashion. And she had a sure and certain taste of how seriously the Shin'a'in took their oaths to protect their land from interlopers. Well, if Tre'valen knew all about the oaths and felt comfortable with them, she probably didn't have to worry.

Much.

This would be the first time she and Skif had been permitted inside the Vale of k'Sheyna itself. The Hawkbrother mage—or was it scout?—Darkwind had dismissed it with a shrug as "not what it once was" with no indication of what it could be like; and Tre'valen, if he knew what the Vale was like in its prime, was not telling. Descriptions in the Chronicles of Vanyel's time had been sketchy, hinting at wonders without ever revealing what the wonders were.

:Probably because they didn't know,: Gwena said, most of the sarcasm gone from her mind-voice. *:Vanyel and Sayv—Savil had too much on their minds to give descriptions of where they'd been. Besides, why describe somewhere no one else would be allowed to visit? It might tempt them to try, and that would be fatal. The Tayledras tend to perforate first and apologize after.:*

:Are you snooping in my head again?: Elspeth replied, with a bit less venom than before.

:No, you're echoing at me,: Gwena told her candidly. *:I can't help it if your surface thoughts echo down our link unless you block them. And I can't help it if you forget to block because you're nervy.:*

:All right, all right. I stand rebuked. I apologize.: Elspeth carefully put up her lightest shields, and went back to her brooding.

There was a fourth party sharing the title of Wingbrother with them, but shaman Kethra had sworn her vows a long time ago. She was considerably older than Tre'valen, though not as old as his superior, Kra'heera, and she had been a wingsib for at least a dozen years. She was a Healer as well as a shaman, and she was tending to Darkwind's father, Adept Starblade. Darkwind seemed reluctant to discuss what Mornelithe Falconsbane had done to his father, and Elspeth wasn't about to press him for answers. She did want to know, however, and badly; not because of morbid curiosity, but because one day she might need to know just how one Adept could so completely subvert another. One of Weaponsmaster Alberich's precepts was that "anyone can be broken." If it was possible she might find herself on the receiving end of an attempt to break her, she'd like to know what she could expect…

Elspeth had been a bit surprised that Tre'valen was staying on, though. He had said only that his own master had asked him to remain with k'Sheyna "because it is important." Whatever it was, it couldn't have anything to do with what Falconsbane had done to the Clan—Darkwind and Kethra were tending to that.

Could it be because of what had happened to Dawnfire?

The memory was so vividly etched in her mind, she had only to think of the hawk Dawnfire to relive what she'd seen.

The Shin'a'in stood in a rough circle below Dawnfire's perch. The red-shouldered hawk had taken a position just above the door of the gryphons' lair, her head up and into the wind, her wings slightly mantled. Then one of the Shin'a'in, a woman, put her hand up to the hawk.

Dawnfire stared measuringly at her for a moment, then stepped down from her perch onto the proffered wrist. The woman turned to face the rest.

Like all the other Shin'a'in who had come to their rescue, this one was clad entirely in black, from her long black hair to her black armor, to her tall black boots. But there was something wrong with her eyes. Something odd.

Elspeth had sensed a kind of contained power about her; the stirrings of a kind of deeply running energy she had never felt before.

The woman raised Dawnfire high above her head and held her there, a position that should have been a torment after only a few moments, no matter how strong she was. Tayledras hawks were the size and weight of small eagles, and Dawnfire was by no means the smallest of the kind. But as the woman continued to hold Dawnfire aloft, the entire group began to hum—softly at first, then as the volume increased, and as the ruins rang with harmonics, Dawnfire started glowing.

At first Elspeth had thought it was just a trick of the setting sun, but the light about the bird grew brighter instead of fading. Then Dawnfire spread her wings and grew larger as well as brighter.

Before long, Elspeth couldn't even look at her directly; she had averted her eyes, for the light from the hawk was bright enough to cast shadows.

Kra'heera had looked at her and said, "Dawnfire has been chosen by the Warrior." She hadn't known what that meant then. She did now.

When the light and sound had faded, and she was able to look at the bird again, she saw that it was no longer a red-shouldered hawk. It was a vorcel-hawk, the emblem of Kra'heera's Clan, and the largest such bird she had ever seen. Although the light had dimmed, it had not died, and there was an otherworldly look in the hawk's eyes that had made her start with surprise.

It was the same look as in the eyes of the female warrior who held her—their eyes held neither whites, irises, or pupils—only a darkness, sprinkled with sparks of light that were visible even where Elspeth stood. As if instead of eyes, they had fields of stars.

That was when she had remembered the description of the Shin'a'in Goddess—and had realized exactly what she was looking at. Small wonder the memory was as vivid as it was; it wasn't every day an ordinary mortal saw a living Goddess and her Avatar.

She eyed Tre'valen with speculation. No matter how casually the elder shaman had treated the event afterward, she wondered if he hadn't been just as surprised as everyone else by the appearance of his Goddess. From what little she understood, change came to the Plains seldom and slowly. When Kerowyn had regaled them with tales of her Shin'a'in cousins, had she ever said *anything* about their Goddess creating Avatars? Elspeth didn't remember anything like that...

So maybe this was something new for them. Maybe that was why Tre'valen was here; to watch for Dawnfire, and to try and figure out the reasons behind his Goddess' actions.

Well, if that was the case, he must have told the Hawkbrothers, or at least their leaders. On the surface none of this seemed to have anything to do with her—but Elspeth didn't take anything for granted anymore. After all, why should the Shin'a'in have shown up at all then? Who could have predicted she'd get involved with the Tayledras, and wind up adding their enemies to her own rather formidable list? *I ought to ask him later if I'm right about all that. Maybe we can help each other out.*

Gwena walked to the entrance of the cave and looked out—

impatiently, Elspeth thought. Her Mindspoken words to her Chosen confirmed that. *:I wish I knew what it was they were spending so much time doing in there,:* she said. *:They've certainly been keeping us cooling our heels long enough. At this rate, that ceremony of theirs won't be over until dark.:*

Elspeth wondered why *she* was so impatient—the Companions weren't the ones being sworn in, even though they wouldn't be permitted in the Vale until the Heralds were. Evidently, by common consensus, the Tayledras regarded the Companions as creatures that simply didn't require oaths to hold them.

Hmm. That requires thought. Do they think Gwena is some kind of Avatar herself? The idea was kind of funny. *If they ever listened to her moaning and griping they'd soon lose that particular illusion! I rather doubt Gwena's hiding that kind of secret.*

Not that she hadn't been hiding other kinds of secrets. This "plan" for Elspeth's future that the Companions had been plotting, for one. And there were others...

Shortly after Nyara had vanished, taking Need with her, Elspeth noticed that Gwena was missing. Worried about her—since Gwena had been injured in the fight with Falconsbane's mage-beasts—she had tried to find her Companion, and when she failed, tried to Mindtouch her. When *that* failed, she had been alarmed and had gone looking for her.

Gwena had been perfectly all right—but she'd been locked in a self-induced trance, shielded even against the prying of Elspeth's thoughts. And when she'd come out of it, she'd been very unhappy to find her Chosen standing there, tapping her foot impatiently, waiting for an answer.

Under pressure from both Elspeth and Skif, she reluctantly admitted that she had been in contact with another Companion in Valdemar all during this journey. Elspeth had expected that Companion to be her mother's—and had been both surprised and relieved to find that it was actually Rolan, the Companion of the Queen's Own Herald, Talia.

Then she had been annoyed, though she hadn't made much of an issue about it. She hadn't known that Companions could relay messages that far—and so far as she was aware, *no one* knew that little fact. Was it just Gwena and Rolan, or could others do it, too? One way or the other, it was one more thing that the Companions had been hiding. So how much more could they do that they hadn't revealed?

Gwena had said crossly that Elspeth should have expected that "arrangements would be made." And Elspeth had been forced to agree.

After all, she was the Heir, and she'd been allowed to go haring off into the unknown with only one Herald to guard her back. For all that she'd managed to get complete agreement from the Council and Heraldic Circle, it was still rather irresponsible. If Queen Selenay had *not* had a way to get news about her errant offspring, she'd likely have had strong hysterics before a month was out. Especially after Elspeth departed from the agreed-upon itinerary, and "vanished" into the Dhorisha Plains.

Still, she hadn't much liked the idea that little reports on her progress were being sent back home, as if she was some kind of child on her first outing without Mama.

On the other hand, Gwena had told them, when Elspeth pressed her for *exactly* what she'd been telling Rolan, that the "reports" she'd been sending Rolan were edited. "Heavily edited," in fact, was what the Companion had said, rather glumly. Which was just as well. If Selenay had the smallest inkling just how much danger Elspeth and Skif had gotten themselves into—

She'd have found a way to haul me back, that's what she'd have done, and plunked me down in nice safe embroidery classes for the rest of my natural life.

How could she possibly explain to her mother that ever since she'd started on this trip—even before she'd started—she'd had the feeling that the Crown wasn't something she was ever going to wear? Even if she had tried to tell her, Selenay would have taken it the wrong way; she'd have been sure that Elspeth had some premonition of doom, and there she'd be in embroidery class again, away from all possibility of danger.

What an awful idea.

And it wasn't a premonition of "doom," or anything like one. It was just the feeling that she was never going to rule. That one of the twins was going to have the throne, and the other—

The other would be King's Own. Not a bad arrangement, since they aren't at all alike. Wouldn't be the first time that sibs were Monarch and Monarch's Own.

Her fate was something else entirely—though what, she hadn't the faintest notion. Even though her conscience bothered her now that she was so far away from home, she'd been doing some useful work, assigned to Kerowyn and the Skybolts. And, though she would never have believed it when she left Haven, she was homesick.

She kept telling herself that there wasn't much she had been doing that couldn't be done by Talia and Daren… and that though she wasn't a ForeSeer, she'd never been wrong when she got really strong feelings about something. There was something she had to do, and it was tied up with learning magic.

She'd said as much to Gwena, who'd agreed with her. "Even though you *aren't* following the course we'd planned for you," she'd added.

Too bad. So I'm a stubborn bitch. I do things my way, or not at all, and if Mother, Gwena, and Rolan don't like it, I'm not at all sorry. So there. Nyah, nyah. She grinned to herself at her own childish thought. Really, it was a very good thing that the messages were going through Rolan to Talia and only *then* to Selenay. Rolan had more of a sense of humor than Gwena—and a little more tolerance. And Talia knew her former charge very well indeed. Further, Talia had told Elspeth privately that she thought the Queen was reacting like most mothers to the evidences of her daughter growing up and developing a mind of her own.

Badly.

Oh, not as badly as she could have, but all things considered, it was much better for Elspeth to be off beyond Mama's reach for a while. By the time she returned, it might be possible for Queen Selenay to admit that her daughter wasn't a foolish, headstrong, *stupid* child anymore.

I've managed to acquire a little sense, anyway...

:Gather yourself, my dear,: Gwena Mindspoke, interrupting her thoughts. *:They're coming for you. Finally.:*

Elspeth glanced out of the corner of her eye at Skif and Tre'valen. Skif looked as if he were concentrating on every word that the Hawkbrother called Iceshadow spoke. Actually, he probably was; his command of the Tayledras tongue wasn't anywhere near as good as hers. Odd; she'd slipped right into the language as if she had known it most of her life.

Oh, that's probably because it's like Shin'a'in, and Kero taught me some of that.

Tre'valen wore that inscrutable face that Kero always put on when she was determined not to let anyone know what she was thinking. "Gambling-face," she called it.

The more she thought about it, the better she liked the idea of approaching Tre'valen later to see if they could do anything for each other. She felt a lot more comfortable around him—around any of the Shin'a'in, really—than she did around the Tayledras. That was probably because she *could* read him, a little. He and Kethra reminded her of Kero; well, that shouldn't surprise her. Kero had trained *her*, and Kero had, in turn, been trained by a Shin'a'in Swordsworn, so there was a lot of Shin'a'in attitude and thinking patterns in the way Kero looked at things. A good bit of that had rubbed off on her pupil, without a doubt. The Tayledras, however, were very exotic, and Darkwind had been so hard to read that Elspeth had given up even trying.

I wonder if they seem that way to Tre'valen?

They hadn't had much of a chance to see the Vale; as Gwena had predicted, it was sunset when the Hawkbrothers came for them, and most of the Vale was shrouded in shadows as they passed through it. Elspeth had gotten some impressions that had taken her breath away, however—of luxuriant growth that made any forest she'd ever seen look sparse by comparison, and trees so enormous her mind refused to accept their size. The Companions had trailed along behind as they followed a well-worn path past curtaining vines covered with cascading flowers the size of her hand, and bushes with leaves bigger than a saddle. Elspeth couldn't wait to see the place in the daytime.

Darkwind himself had come to fetch them, as their sponsor into the Clan; Kethra was Tre'valen's. With him had come at least a dozen more Tayledras—and Elspeth had done her best not to stare, but it had been very difficult. She had thought that Darkwind was a typical Hawkbrother, and she had been just a little disappointed, given the hints in the Chronicles of how strange the Hawkbrothers were, at his shoulder-length, mottled-brown hair and his drab clothing. The Chronicles had talked about Moondance and Starwind being as "brightly plumaged as firebirds" and she'd cherished images of brilliant colors and weird clothing, maybe things that didn't look like clothing at all.

She wasn't disappointed any longer. The dozen Tayledras with Darkwind had been garbed as wildly and beautifully as she could have wished. Every one of them had hair that was waist-length or longer, white as ice, and twined with feathers, crystals, bells, slender chains, or strands of silk matching their—costumes. That was the only word she could arrive at. "Clothing" certainly wasn't adequate—not for robes with layered sleeves that trailed on the ground, hugged the arm like silken skin, were scalloped, bejeweled, embroidered, and tapestried. "Garb" didn't describe tunics and gowns that mimicked feathers, leaves, flower petals, frozen waterfalls. Every one of the dozen was unique; every one was incredible and complex. And yet, the costumes weren't any less functional than, say, Valdemaran Court gear; although she wouldn't have known how to move in those outfits without tripping over something.

She felt for the first time as if she had truly left the world she knew and had stepped into the pages of a tale.

Even Darkwind—drab, disappointing Darkwind—had been transformed. Although his hair was still shoulder-length, he had somehow managed to get *patterns* dyed into it. She assumed it was dye; it might not have been. How would she know? It might have been magic. Birds flickered whitely against a dark gold background every time he moved his head, as if his hair was a forest in autumn with doves flying through it. And his costume was as fanciful as the rest—although a little more practical. He had eschewed trailing sleeves and hemlines for embroidery and something that stayed fairly close to his body. But he was just as eye-dazzling in his way as the others were in theirs.

He smiled shyly when he saw the surprise and approval in her expression, but said nothing, simply gesturing for her and Skif to follow him into the depths of the Vale. Kethra led Tre'valen in a similar fashion; the rest of the Tayledras came behind, with mage-lights bobbing above their heads, and the Companions bringing up the rear. Above the walls of the valley and the tops of the towering trees, the sky still glowed blue, with the west a warm gold—in the shelter of the massive branches, dense blue shadows obscured all but the trail they walked.

They had emerged in a clearing, ringed and paved with stone. In the very center of the circular area stood a cracked and half-broken stone with a brazier at its foot, all of it lit by more mage-lights. This strange monolith, she assumed, was the Heartstone—damaged, its wild energies barely restrained by multiple layers of shielding. Darkwind had warned her to keep tight personal shields about her when she was near it; she saw no reason to argue with him. Even through her protections she felt something vaguely *wrong* with the stone, a kind of sickness about it. It wasn't something she could put a finger on, or point to, but the uneasy feeling was definitely there.

Iceshadow—wearing an elaborate costume that made him look as if he was half a man and half a delicate, frozen fountain—took his place before the stone. In the transparent, unwavering illumination of the mage-lights, he could have been a dream, an illusion—an ice sculpture brought to life. Then he moved, gracefully, holding up his hands—and with no more preparation than that, Elspeth found herself surrounded by a blue glow that was quite familiar.

Truth Spell? Bright Havens, did we get it from them, or did they get it from Vanyel?

The other question that occurred to her, with a touch of envy, was how Iceshadow had managed to call the spell up with no preparation and in no more than a heartbeat. It took her a good bit of time to call up a Truth Spell, and she was one of the best in her class at that particular exercise. Iceshadow hadn't even needed to *think* about it, so far as she had been able to tell. He just gestured, and there it was. That was as impressive as all the lightnings and thunders she'd seen—and cast— fighting Falconsbane and his creatures. Iceshadow had not only cast the spell as easily as breathing, he had made it *look* effortless.

Iceshadow lowered his arms, and a white horn-tufted owl drifted down out of the trees to land on his shoulder. He watched the three of them serenely for a moment, and then folded his hands in his sleeves. "Do you bring any ill-intent into this Vale?" he asked, conversationally.

Was this the beginning of the oathtaking? It must be. She shook her head, and Skif mouthed the word "No."

Iceshadow smiled slightly, and continued; still calm, still casual. "Is it your wish to be made a brother of this Clan?"

They both answered with nods.

Now Iceshadow sobered; the owl settled itself and turned unblinking eyes upon them, as if it, too, was weighing the truth of their intent. Elspeth was suddenly hyperaware of everything about her; the faint, cool breeze on her back, the way it stirred Iceshadow's clothing, Skif's hair, the fringe on Tre'valen's sash. The way the blue light from the spell reflected in the onlookers' eyes. The call of a bird, somewhere out in the Vale. Iceshadow took a deep breath, and spoke, in a soft voice that still carried incredible intensity. "Hear, then, the privileges of brotherhood: to come and go freely within all lands held by Tayledras k'Sheyna; to call upon your brothers in times of need; to ask of us teaching; to make your home among us. Hear also the responsibilities of brotherhood: to keep the secrets of the Clan; to neither bring nor lead strangers among us; to keep our lands and guard them as we do; to answer to our need if no other oath prevents; to teach when it is asked of you, aid when it is asked of you, give shelter and succor to your brothers of the Clan, of Tayledras, and of Shin'a'in. Can you be bound to these conditions?"

"Yes," Elspeth breathed. It would not have been unreasonable to swear them to absolute secrecy, or to require that they pledge a formal and complicated alliance to the Clan. Skif seemed just as surprised as he answered in the affirmative.

The breeze gusted past again, and the owl roused its feathers, shaking himself vigorously before settling down to resume his stare at them. Iceshadow watched them as unblinkingly as his owl. "Then there is another vow you must make," Iceshadow continued. "But it is one that you must not make in ignorance. So listen—watch—and heed—"

He gestured again, and as Elspeth caught her breath in startlement, a globe of glowing white mist rose up from the pavement between them, obscuring everything on the other side of the circle. As Elspeth turned her attention from the Hawkbrother to the globe of starlight, she saw that there was a picture forming in it. She bit her lip when the picture cleared, this time with a feeling of incredulity and horror; she had seen her own land ravaged by warfare, but this was beyond anything she had ever dreamed in her worst nightmares. Encased in the glowing globe was the image of a devastated land; the viewpoint was from the edge of a blasted crater so wide she literally could not see the other side. She blinked and swallowed, finding it hard to comprehend destruction on so vast a scale, and nauseated by the very idea that such a thing could have happened. To see a place that must once have been green, been full of people, animals, trees and plants—to see it not only ravaged, but utterly *annihilated*—the shock of it drove any real thoughts from her head for a moment. Beside her, Tre'valen started in surprise, as if this was something *he* knew about but had not expected to see here.

"This was the homeland, long and long ago." Iceshadow's voice drifted across the silence, a voice filled with such sadness and loss that it seemed as if what Elspeth saw might have happened a day ago, rather than centuries ago. "This was the homeplace of the people called Kaled'a'in. This was all that remained, at the end of the First and Last conflict, the Mage Wars."

The scene shifted, to a group of armed, subdued people, all with the long black hair and golden skin of the Shin'a'in, gathered on the edge of the crater. There was some confusion as they and their animals—horses, huge dogs, hunting cats, and birds of prey—milled about, and then it was apparent that about half of them were packing up and moving off, away from the crater, while the rest stayed.

"We fled from the destruction, and returned when we could. This was what we found, and there was mourning and confusion. Then came anger, at what had happened, at what had caused it. There was dissent over what the people should do. Some wished to renounce all magic; some, to make *further* use of magic to keep the Clans alive in this new and alien world. There was no compromise possible between those positions—dissent became argument, and argument became hate. That was when, rather than turn dissent to feud, the two sides agreed to divide, and with this decision came the Sundering of the Clans. Those who renounced magic became the Shin'a'in, while those who sought magery removed themselves from the rest, calling themselves *Tayledras*, after the birds that they had helped to bring into being. These, our Fathers and Mothers, went north."

Again the scene shifted, to something that had probably been a forest. Once.

Now it was another kind of nightmare; instead of lifelessness, twisted and contorted wildlife ran riot. The vegetation grew so thick it formed a solid green wall on either side of the road, except that it was hard to tell some of the flora from some of the fauna. There were plants that groped after the passing Clansfolk, and animals that were rooted to the spot like plants, some watching them with indifferent eyes, others that screamed unendingly. There were creatures she half-glimpsed through the veils of vines hanging from every branch that made Elspeth shudder. As she tried to make sense of confusion of color and motion, the group shown was attacked by things that were horribly worse than the creatures Falconsbane had sent against them—things that seemed to be nothing but teeth and claws, with armored plates covering everything but their joints.

Iceshadow's voice made her jump. "The five Clans that were now Tayledras found that the lands beyond the homeland were ravaged by the forces of twisted and tainted magic. No human or bird could survive there for long. Either they must starve, for they could not spare a moment from defense to grow or hunt their food, or they must give up defense and perish at the hands of the monsters that inhabited these lands. They despaired, for there was nowhere else for them to go."

The scene fogged for a moment, and re-formed. The band of Tayledras had made a camp on the top of a hill, the earth scorched bare by fire, with a temporary palisade of thorny branches about the camp— but it was obvious it could not last for long against any kind of attack.

"They knew they could go no farther," Iceshadow concluded. "So, as their kindred that would become the Shin'a'in would do, they prayed to their Goddess. And She answered. Here is her answer to their plea."

Nothing Elspeth had watched prepared her for what happened as the mist clouded again.

Suddenly there was no ball of glowing mist with pictures in it before her; suddenly there was no clearing, no Hawkbrothers, no Skif—

—no light, no sound, no *world.*

Only herself, a sky full of stars stretching in every direction—

—including *down*—

And out of this starry nothingness arose a white-hot flame that was somehow also a woman. Too bright to see clearly, She changed from moment to moment, and the raw Power emanating from Her made Elspeth tremble. She'd have fallen to her knees—if she could have figured out how to do so in the midst of all this starry space.

I have heard your prayers, She said, in a voice that filled Elspeth's mind, leaving no room for anything, not even fear. *There is a price to be paid for what you ask, and that price is in your lives, and your freedom.*

She gestured, and in the palm of Her hand was cupped the weirdly twisted landscape of the forest the Clansfolk had entered. *Terrible magics have warped this land, and only magic can heal it again. Therefore I offer this, that you have asked of me. I shall grant you safety here, long enough to establish each of you a Clan holding. I shall teach you the means of creating a place in the midst of the holding wherein you shall dwell in protection. I shall grant you the knowledge of Adepts, to use and concentrate the magic—and a knowledge even Adepts have not—to create a center of such power that the greatest of the mages who caused these changes would look upon you with envy.*

To this you shall swear, in return. You will cleanse these lands—restore them to what they were before the Wars. You shall destroy the creatures of evil intent, cherish and succor the innocent victims of this catastrophe, and find shelter for those that are merely animals, meaning neither good nor ill. You shall destroy those old weapons you may find, that they may not be misused again. You shall cleanse the land you hold—and then you shall move on, to another place, to begin again. All of your children that are Mage-Gifted shall follow this path. All who are not shall guard and aid the ones who are. You shall be the Healers and Protectors—and you shall never permit the magics you manipulate here to be used for ill, nor shall you permit strangers within your ranks, unless they be sworn to the Clans. This you must do, at whatever cost to yourselves.

Abruptly, the vision was gone. Elspeth shook her head, blinking and still trembling with reaction, more than a little disoriented. There was nothing now in the clearing but what had been there when they entered; even the glowing mist was gone.

She tried to shake off the effect of the vision—if that was what it had been. She had *been there* for a moment; she didn't at all doubt that she had experienced exactly the same thing as those long-ago Hawkbrothers had. What she couldn't understand was why Skif didn't seem particularly affected, but Tre'valen looked just as dazed and bedazzled as she felt. Long ago, when she was younger, she had first heard the story of King Valdemar and the first appearance of the Companions, and had thought it a very pretty tale. *Now* she had the glimmering of what King Valdemar just *might* have experienced when his prayers were answered. It shook her to the soul. It made her understand why some people became ardent, abject devotees of deities.

Iceshadow was silent for a long moment, while she and Tre'valen gathered their scattered wits. Elspeth thought that he watched her particularly closely, although she couldn't be sure of that. Finally, he spoke again.

"This is the last oath you must swear—that you will aid your brothers of the Clan in their duty, as your own oaths permit—and that never will you use what is taught you here for the sake of your own power, pride, and status."

He held his hand up, to forestall their immediate answers. "I shall not ask you to swear never to use it to harm—for one day you may find yourself facing an enemy who would destroy far more than you if he is given the opportunity to do so. But you must *never* use your learning for selfish purposes, to increase your own importance, to make your life one of pointless leisure, to merely indulge your fancies. Can you swear to that?"

Elspeth heaved a sigh of relief; that was enough like the oaths a Herald took before the Circle that the wording made very little difference. She gave her assent with a much lighter heart, grateful that all of the vows she'd been asked to make seemed to take into account the fact that those outside the Clan had other duties and oaths of their own that might take precedence.

Now as long as both sets of promises never come into conflict, I should be all right.

Throughout the entire oathtaking, the blue glow of the Truth Spell remained steady around all three of them. Now Iceshadow banished the spell with another gesture, just as the deepening blue of the sky above them took on the golden-red streaks of the last moments of sunset. Elspeth looked up for a moment, as some movement against the luminous blue above caught her eye, and discovered that what had attracted her attention was the steady circling of a bird over their clearing. A bird of prey, by the shape.

Nothing unusual, not here in the heart of a Tayledras Clan territory, but something about the bird made her take a second, closer look.

It was big; much bigger than she had thought, at first. In fact, it was easily the size of the largest eagle she had ever seen. But it had the distinctive tail-striping of a vorcel-hawk; that was *one* bird she would never again mistake for anything else.

A vorcel-hawk the size of an eagle, or larger—and unless it was a trick of the light, it was glowing.

Dawnfire? The thought was inevitable. She glanced back down at Tre'valen, only to see that he was watching the hawk as well, though no one else seemed to notice that it was there. The expression on his face was a most peculiar one; he looked both excited and obscurely disturbed, at one and the same time.

The hawk made a final circle above, then spiraled upward, to be lost in the scarlet-and-golden glory of the sunset. Tre'valen licked his lips and looked down again; reluctantly, it seemed to her. He caught her watching him before she could look away, and something in his eyes made her nod, once, slowly; admitting, without actually saying anything, that she had seen the bird as well.

His lips formed the merest ghost of a smile, and he turned his attention back toward Iceshadow.

Less time had passed than she had thought. The Tayledras Adept was only now finishing *his* words of acceptance, admitting them into the Clan as Wingsiblings, and welcoming them as allies and friends.

She shook her head again, feeling another shiver of disorientation. Time was doing strange things around her, today. And Skif didn't seem to be affected by any of it. Was it because she was a mage, or was it something else entirely?

Or was it just nerves?

Not that it really mattered at the moment. The ceremony wasn't *quite* over yet, although the formal pledging of vows was. Darkwind had explained this afternoon as he brought them to the cave to wait, that Iceshadow wanted to talk to her, Skif, and their Companions before he unleashed the rest of the Clan on them.

"He wants to give you a clearer idea of what you're getting involved with," he had said; she had wondered at the time if he was joking a little or being completely serious.

But Iceshadow was, indeed, walking across the paving toward them with another strange Hawkbrother at his side, and Darkwind and the Companions following behind. The other Tayledras drifted off, seeming to melt into the luxuriant foliage.

"So, I meet the Heralds at last," the Adept said, as he got within easy conversational distance of them. "The last of your kind to be within a Clan was—what?" He looked to the other Tayledras for an answer.

"Near seven hundred years ago," the stranger supplied. Elspeth noticed, now that he was near enough for her to note details, that he was very pale, very tired-looking; there were lines of pain around his eyes and mouth. He made a little grimace. "That was k'Treva, though. They always were—hmm—unconventional."

"I would say innovative, Starblade," Iceshadow chided gently. "The experience certainly did them no harm and much good, from all I have heard out of the tales."

At his naming the stranger, Elspeth took a moment for a second, closer, but covert examination of him. So this was Darkwind's father? They didn't look all that much alike, but that could be illness and the differences in their hair as much as anything. Starblade was wearing a more—conservative costume than the rest of his fellows; in fact, there was something about it that seemed very similar to the one Darkwind was wearing; something that invoked birds and their wings, without actually imitating feathers. As if they had been designed by the same mind. Interesting.

"The k'Treva Tayledras that welcomed the Heralds back then—that would have been Moondance and Starwind k'Treva, wouldn't it?" she replied, obviously startling all three of the Hawkbrothers, and earning a covert grin of approval from Tre'valen. "That was in the Chronicles of Herald Vanyel's time; I read them, and that was why I came here, to try and find more Tayledras, if I could. The Heralds were Vanyel Ashkevron and his aunt, Savil—Vanyel was the last of the Herald-Mages. The Chronicles said that he spent quite a lot of time there, in k'Treva Vale, especially when he was young, and that Starwind taught him most of what he knew about magic."

"That is quite true, young one," Starblade replied, his voice warming a little with what sounded to her like approval. "Or at least, that is what *our* records told me. Iceshadow, my friend, would it be possible for us to move to somewhere a little less formal for the rest of this?" He gestured apologetically to her, and to Skif and Tre'valen, "I am sorry, but I fear I must beg your indulgence and find a place to sit."

"What about the fishpond over there?" Darkwind asked, pointing with his chin somewhere behind Iceshadow's shoulder. "It's quiet enough, and there shouldn't be anyone there after the sun sets."

"Good enough," his father replied—gratefully, Elspeth thought. "There should be room for your large friends, and seating enough for all of us."

Iceshadow gestured to the younger Hawkbrother to lead the way; Elspeth followed him, and the rest trailed behind her. By now it was becoming quite dark, and she was grateful for the mage-lights Iceshadow and Starblade produced. She found that distances were deceptive in the Vale; the ornamental fishpond Darkwind spoke of was actually hardly more than a stone's throw away from the Heartstone circle, and yet it might easily have been halfway across the Vale. Once they had arranged themselves around it, there was no way of telling that the Heartstone was anywhere nearby.

"Well," Starblade said, once he had settled himself in a comfortable "chair" formed of the roots of a tree with moss cupped where a cushion would be. Elspeth took a second, similar seat, and found it incredibly comfortable. "Iceshadow has asked me to explain to you just what sort of a—ah—situation you have unwittingly involved yourselves in. And since I am the partial cause of that situation, I think it only fair that I make the attempt."

Elspeth met his eyes and recognized what she saw there. Pain, mental and physical. This conversation was going to cost him something—but she had seen some of that same pain in Darkwind's eyes whenever he had spoken of his father, and she knew that Starblade had put that pain there. The man was right. It *was* only fair.

She settled herself and nodded to him, decisively. "Go ahead," she said. "I don't think anything you say is going to make us change our minds, but I was trained as a tactician; I like to know what I can expect." She smiled, slightly. "Good or bad."

Starblade nodded gravely, and leaned forward. He cradled his right hand around his bandaged left hand—surely there must be a story behind that as well. This was either going to be very short, or very long. Whichever it was, it was going to be interesting.

She had told the truth about not changing her mind; she only hoped what she learned wasn't going to make her regret her own decisions. It was a little too late for regret now.

It was not, however, too early for strategy. It was *never* too early, or too late, for that.

2

"Iknow you are an Outlander... but I know not how much my son has told you of our troubles here," Starblade began, with a sober glance at Darkwind, "so I shall tell my tale from the outset, and beg your patience if I repeat what you know." He glanced down at the pond, with its patient, colorful carp skimming just below the surface of the water. "I shall be as brief as I can."

He paused for a moment, clearly organizing his thoughts. "Mornelithe Falconsbane," he said at last. "It all comes down to him."

Darkwind nodded grimly, but said nothing.

"The Heartstone—" Starblade closed his eyes, but not before Elspeth had seen another shadow of pain pass across them. "Its shattering is his doing, but by my hand. I was foolish and vain; I thought myself clever, and I found out differently. He caught me through my foolishness, and my pride. He broke me, and he used me."

Terse speech, but obviously each word cost him dearly. "Through me, he set his darkness upon the Heartstone, disrupted our magics, broke it from the inside, and in so doing, caused the deaths of many of our mages. Because of me, three-fourths of the Clan are lost somewhere in the wilderness."

"How?" Elspeth asked, puzzled. "I mean, how could you lose that many people?"

Starblade toyed with a glass-beaded feather braided into his hair. "When a Clan moves, it is our way to establish the children, the lesser mages, the weak and the old, with the bulk of our scouts and warriors to protect them, at a new site. We send them by means of a Gate, we drain the Stone of its power and send it to the new Stone, then we follow. But when we filled the Stone with all the Clan's power in preparation for diverting the power to the new site, the Heartstone shattered, and the Adept holding the Gate open died with the shattering. We had no one among us who could use the Heartstone, damaged as it was, to go to them by Gate. We barely know the true location of the rest of the Clan, for the scouts who had found the new place were with them."

"And they couldn't reach you without sending badly needed fighters," Elspeth supplied. "I take it none of the lesser mages were able to build these Gate things?"

"Only an Adept can master the Gate Spell," Iceshadow replied. "And we fear that even if they had one who could cast it, the Stone is too unstable and there may be no way of bringing a Gate near to it."

"All the scouts that knew the overland way to the new Vale are at that Vale," Darkwind repeated. "Our number would be decimated trying to get to them by foot—leagues traveled are hard-won going North—and they cannot come to us, burdened with the old, the young, the sick."

His father nodded. "Indeed. So—to make the bad much the worse, Falconsbane continued to work through me, keeping the Clan from reaching for help, keeping the Adepts still remaining from stabilizing the Stone, and keeping those who knew me well at a distance." Starblade averted his eyes from Darkwind, but the reference was plain enough. "He hoped, I think, to wear us down until he could penetrate our defenses at his leisure and usurp the Stone and the power it still held. But he had not reckoned on our clever allies, the gryphons—and he had not reckoned on the courage and good sense of my son."

"He couldn't have guessed Nyara would turn against him, either," Skif put in, with a hint of pride.

"No—nor the appearance of you and all that you represented," Tre'valen told him, his eyes showing a hint of sardonic humor. "To tell you true, there was an unexpected marshaling of powers from all sides. Falconsbane certainly did not plan on that, nor the involvement of the Shin'a'in. That was his downfall."

"If he lives still, he cannot be prospering," Iceshadow put in. "Shin'a'in arrows found a mark in him; that much we know. And he has lost much in the way of power and creatures."

"I wonder at that; Shin'a'in do not often miss in such attacks, their Goddess oft assists the arrow to the mark. But, despite that, I doubt that he lives," Starblade sighed. "I think that the arrows of the Shin'a'in found their mark; that he fled only to die. There has been no sign of him or his creatures, and his escape was by blood-magic... with his own blood. That is an act of finality among mages."

Elspeth shrugged. "I don't know one way or the other about him, but the point, it seems to me, is that he has left the Vale in one snarled mess."

Starblade nodded, and smoothed his braided hair back behind his ears. "My son has said he will teach you in the use of your Mage-Gift; that is a good thing, I think—but he will need to relearn much as he teaches you. It would be hazardous for you to do much practice of that learning within the Vale itself; though you would be protected from threats that are outside the Vale, the Stone is yet dangerous."

Gwena stamped a hoof and snorted agreement, bobbing her head vigorously. Elspeth nodded; she felt the same. Starblade bore many years' experience, and knew the magics involved as only a Tayledras Adept could. Better to err on the side of safety.

"I think," Darkwind said slowly, "that we may practice outside the Vale for some time in relative safety. It will only be as we approach the greater Adept-magics that we will need the shieldings of the Vale."

"By then, the Council and I should have come to some decision on the Stone," Iceshadow told them. "Either we shall have begun to heal it ourselves, or we shall have found a way to deal with it."

He glanced at Elspeth, with a certain amount of expectation in the look. She sighed, knowing what that look meant. "If you're wondering if you can count on my help with this Heartstone of yours, I *do* remember those oaths I just took," she said, with a little shake of her head. "I can't say I *like* the idea of mucking about with that much power gone wrong, but what I can do, I will."

Both Iceshadow and Starblade gave her nods of approval, but she wasn't quite done. "What I need to know, here, is this—how much more trouble from outside can we expect while we're doing all this? Starblade, I hope you'll forgive my asking this, but you were a point of weakness before. Just how vulnerable are you to more meddling?"

Starblade wet his lips with the tip of his tongue before replying. "To meddling—I would say not at all. Even if Falconsbane still lives, and as I said, I do not think that he does, Iceshadow and Kethra have changed all the paths that made me open to him. To have me so his slave again, he would have to have me in his hand. He would break me faster—for I am that much more fragile than I was—but he would have to have me to break me."

"And?" Elspeth raised an eyebrow.

"And I shall not leave this Vale until I walk through the Gate to a new one," he told her. "I have been broken and am mending, but I am still weak to be broken again, and will not chance it, for the sake of all of us."

Elspeth nodded, satisfied, but Skif frowned. "What about attack?" he asked. "Are you weaker to attack than—say Iceshadow?"

Starblade looked mildly surprised by the question. "I—think not," he said immediately. "The weaknesses I have still require someone who *knows* me to exploit, and to have me, if not within physical touching, certainly within sight."

Skif glanced over at Tre'valen, who shrugged. "The only magics I know intimately are those of the Goddess," he said. "I am of no help nor hindrance in these things. These are good things to know, Starblade. I thank you for telling them."

"I can't think of any more questions," Skif admitted. "I'm no mage, and I'm no help to you. Frankly, I'll be a lot more help in finding Nyara and that damned sword she carries."

"Now *that* I need to know something of," Starblade said immediately. And Elspeth found herself the focus of every eye in the little clearing.

She fidgeted a little, uncomfortably. "I don't know as much about Need as I'd like," she replied, reluctantly. "She predates the Mage Wars, I think. At least, I didn't recognize anything she showed us when she let us into her memories. So she's either very old, or from awfully far away."

"I would say, very old," Darkwind opined, toying with a feather in a gesture uncannily—and probably unconsciously—like his father. "I would say, she is as old as the oldest artifact I have ever seen. She gave me the impression of great age, as great as any of the things I have stumbled upon in the ruins."

Elspeth tilted her head back and took a deep breath of the cool, flower-scented air, using the moment to think. "What I do know is she was a member of some kind of quasi-religious order, with gods I never heard of—male and female twins."

She gave the Hawkbrothers a glance of inquiry; all three of them shrugged as if the reference meant nothing to them either. "Well, even though at one time she'd been a warrior, she called herself a Mage-Smith." Elspeth closed her eyes for a moment, to call up the memories that Need had shared with her and Skif. "As to how she became a sword in the first place—someone attacked the Order while she was gone—wiped out the older members, enslaved the young girls, stole everything they could carry. The only ones left were Need, who was too old to fight, and a young apprentice. So Need took a special sword that she'd forged spells into, spells of healing and luck—and forged *herself* into it as well."

"How?" Iceshadow asked, genuinely interested.

Elspeth shook her head. "It wasn't something I'd have done. She did some kind of preparation, then she killed her human body with the blade so that she could move her spirit into the sword. Then as long as the girl carried her, Need could give her both the skills of a fighter and of a Mage-Smith."

All three of the Adepts looked startled at that. "How could that be?" Starblade asked.

"Well, she could operate on her own as a mage, or through her bearer," Elspeth told him. "Or she could direct her bearer, if the bearer was Mage-Gifted—that was how she worked with me, after I refused to let her take me over. But for fighting skills, you had to let her completely take control of your body." She grimaced. "I'm afraid I wouldn't let her, artifact, mage, or no. She didn't much care for my attitude."

A hint of smile appeared around Starblade's mouth; Darkwind grinned openly. "Why am I not surprised by that?" the younger mage said, to no one in particular.

Elspeth was glad that the darkness hid her flush; Darkwind seemed to have an uncanny ability to poke pins into her pride. Maybe it was just ill-luck, or bad timing.

She licked her lips and kept her temper. "I think that she wasn't used to being thwarted," she said carefully. "Captain Kerowyn, who had her before I did, told me that I would have to be prepared to counter her, that she'd have me haring off to rescue whatever female nearby was in trouble, whether or not it was a good idea to poke my nose into her problems. That, though, was while she was still—" Elspeth thought a moment. "As I remember, she called it 'being asleep.' I gathered that the personality was dormant, unconscious for a long time. Need never told me why."

"The blade may not have wanted you to know why," Tre'valen said smoothly. "Certainly, if you contradicted her will, she would not be so free with revealing secrets."

"That's true," she acknowledged. "Anyway, she didn't start to wake up again until I was at Kata'shin'a'in. So I don't know as much as I'd like to about her. I think she *is* likely to take over Nyara; I think that after years of her father molding her to his whim and will, Nyara is inclined to be manipulated like that."

Skif bristled, and started to say something. Darkwind's thoughtful statement forestalled him.

"That would not be entirely ill for her," the Hawkbrother said quietly. "Especially since—it seems, at least to me—Need has no intention of doing anything detrimental. I think she seeks to make her bearer a stronger woman. It is just that she does not like to have *her* will thwarted."

Elspeth smiled ruefully. "I can testify to that," she said.

"It seems to me this might be a good thing for the Changechild," Starblade added thoughtfully. "Despite what has happened, I—I can feel pity for Nyara. She and I—" he faltered "—we have much, much in common. What Falconsbane did to her—it is very like what he did

393

to me. It may be that this sword, if it has healing magics like those of Kethra and Iceshadow, can reverse some of the things that were done to the girl, even as Kethra is aiding me. I hope that is so. For her sake, and for ours."

There didn't seem to be anything else to say; Elspeth sat there awkwardly for a moment, until Iceshadow cleared his throat conspicuously. "If there is naught else that we can tell you—" he said.

Elspeth shook her head; so did Skif. "Not that I can think of," she replied. "Although I probably will come up with a dozen questions I should have asked just before I drop off to sleep tonight."

Iceshadow chuckled; Starblade nodded knowingly. "If you can recall them when you wake, feel free to ask them," Iceshadow said, rising. "In the meantime—we hold celebration, to welcome you to the Clan and Vale. Your fellow k'Sheyna are anxious to see you; they are as curious about you as you are about them."

In a way, that statement was something of a relief. It meant that the secretive Hawkbrothers were human enough to be curious. For all the time she had spent in Darkwind's presence, there was more that was a mystery about him and his people than there was that was familiar.

"In that case," she replied, rising from her own seat, "let's not keep them waiting any longer."

Elspeth followed Darkwind's direction, as Iceshadow escorted Starblade in another direction—presumably, to rest. "We have had little enough to celebrate, of late," Darkwind told the two Heralds and their Companions in a quiet voice, as he shepherded them down yet another path bordered by wild growth. "The stalemate with the Stone, the constant harassment on our borders, the separation—it has been difficult for everyone here. Add to that my father's attempt to foster dissension between the scouts and the mages, and there was more tension than many could bear."

"That particular dust-up was all because of Falconsbane, wasn't it?" Skif asked. "I hope that's been settled. I'd just as soon not find myself in the middle of a private quarrel."

"You won't," Darkwind actually chuckled, as Elspeth hid a sigh of relief. "It's been settled. I can pledge you, everyone is ready for a good celebration. The fact that you are the cause of it—*and* are strange Outlanders into the bargain—will make you very popular."

That gave Elspeth a bit of a qualm; not because she was ill at ease at the idea of being the focus of so many strangers, but because of what Darkwind had called her.

Outlander.

She was a stranger here. There was nothing in this place that would remind her of home. If Darkwind seemed alien to her, his words were a reminder that she must be just as alien to him, and by extension, to his people. *She* wasn't used to being the stranger; it made her feel disconnected and unbalanced.

And now, for the first time since she had arrived, she felt completely alone, completely without roots. And felt a wave of terrible homesickness wash over her.

At that moment, she was within a breath of weeping. Her throat closed, and she couldn't speak. Her eyes clouded, and she stumbled—

But when she looked up, she found herself on the edge of another clearing, but this one was full of light—people.

Her training took over; there were people waiting to meet her out there. She was the Heir to the Throne, she was a Herald. Her homesickness could wait. She must put on a good face for them, impress them, so that they would see that Valdemar was worth aiding.

She blinked once or twice, clearing her eyes. The Companions, Skif, and Darkwind got a pace or two ahead of her, giving her the chance to compose herself further. She took a deep breath, another, then followed them out into the radiant clearing.

She had expected mage-lights, and mage-lights there were in plenty, but the chief illumination came from the moon. The soft, silvery light blurred and softened details; and as she looked around her, she suddenly realized that not all of the exotic occupants of the clearing were human.

Hertasi, the shy lizardlike creatures that were roughly half the height of a very tall man, she had seen once or twice before, in colored beads and satins—and the gryphons of course.

Their presence was a welcome surprise, and she waved at Treyvan when she knew he had seen her. She hadn't known that the gryphons were coming, and Treyvan's wide-beaked grin from across the clearing chased away the last of her homesickness. She couldn't help herself; the gryphon grin was so contagious it left no room for such trivialities. Hydona saw that Treyvan was staring in their direction and turned to see what he was looking at. When she saw them, she nodded; her smile matched her mate's and welcomed the newcomers with a warmth that surpassed species boundaries.

The gryphons occupied one entire nook of the clearing all by themselves, but beside them were three graceful, horned creatures that Elspeth guessed must be *dyheli*. And scattered among the Hawkbrothers were a handful of two-legged creatures whose feathers were real, and growing from their heads, not braided into their hair.

Tervardi! Elspeth's years of protocol schooling kept her from staring, even though she would dearly have loved to. Along with the gryphons and the *hertasi*, these creatures were the stuff of legend in Valdemar. Legend said the *tervardi* were shapechangers, that they sprouted wings and turned into real birds when they chose. One of them turned, and Elspeth caught sight of a still, serene face with a mouth rimmed by something that was either a small, flexible beak, or hard, stiff lips. The creature gestured before she turned back to her conversation group, and Elspeth saw the stunted, colorful feathers, the last vestige of her wings, covering her arm.

As she moved hesitantly into the clearing, she realized that the previous occupants were—not ignoring her, but permitting her politely to fit into their group. That was certainly more comfortable than being mobbed and was exactly what a similar gathering of Heralds would have done.

She looked around; there were birds everywhere, some sleeping on perches, some awake and perched on shoulders or poles. The Companions both had joined a small group of mixed humans and nonhumans, along with Tre'valen; somehow, Darkwind and Skif had vanished, she had no idea how, but it left her on her own. With all those people carefully, politely, *not* looking at her, she felt more conspicuous than she would if they had been staring at her.

She hurried across the rest of the grassy space between her and the gryphons. Odd that of all of that gathering, they were the strangest physically, and the most familiar in every other way...

"Sssso!" Treyvan greeted her, extending a taloned foreclaw in a token of welcome. "You are now Tayledrasss, Clansssssib! Do you feel any different?"

"Well, yes and no," she replied. "No—I mean, I'm still a Herald, and I'm still everything I was before."

"But yesss?" Hydona spoke gently. "I think perhapsss it isss homesssicknesss?"

She blinked, surprised, and in an odd way, grateful. "How did you guess?"

The female gryphon nodded at the rest of the gathering. "We arrre the only two of *our* kind herrre asss well, except for the little onesss. We know how ssstrange you musst feel."

She flushed, embarrassed that she could have missed something so very obvious. "Of course. It's just that you and Darkwind are such friends, it never occurred to me—"

Treyvan laughed. "If it neverrr occurred to you, then I would sssay that iss a compliment on how well we have come to fit in herrre!" he exclaimed. "And trrruly, the humansss of the Valesss arrre not that unlike the humansss of our own landsss."

"Ah," she replied vaguely, not knowing what else to say. "Oh, where *are* the little ones?"

"Therrre." Hydona indicated another corner of the clearing with an outstretched talon; there, in the shadows, the two young gryphlets were sprawled on the grass, listening sleepily to what appeared to be—

A *very* large wolf?

—except that it wasn't speaking, so how could they be listening?

"That isss a *kyree;* they arrre not often in thisss Vale," Hydona said, as if she had heard Elspeth's unspoken questions. "It isss a neuter. It hasss taken a liking to the little onesss and hass been kind enough to tell them taless sssince we arrived. I believe it iss called—" She turned to her mate for help.

"Torrl," Treyvan supplied promptly. "It wass a great friend of Dawnfire, and iss sstill a great friend of Darrrkwind. *Kyree* neuterss are often verry fond of little oness of any speciessss; it iss a good thing the children arrre both sstrong Mindspeakersss."

And that, of course, was how the *kyree* was "telling tales" to the young gryphlets; directly mind-to-mind, as the *kyree* who helped Vanyel at the last had spoken to Stefen. Elspeth's mouth had gone very dry; this was like being inside of a tale herself, the experience being made even more dreamlike under the delicate illumination of mage-lights and moonlight.

She managed not to jump, as something tugged at the hem of her tunic. She looked down quickly; it was one of the *hertasi*, carrying a tray laden with fruits and vegetables that had been carved into artful representations of flowers. It offered the tray to her, and she took one; she hadn't the faintest notion of what she'd taken, but she didn't want to offend the little creature by refusing.

It slipped into the crowd, and she bit cautiously into her "prize." Crisp and cool, it had a faint peppery taste, and a crunchy texture;

encouraged by her success, when the next *hertasi* came by, this one with a tray of drinks, she took a glass with more enthusiasm.

This proved to be a light wine; she sipped it and continued to chat with the gryphons, deliberately keeping the subject light, asking innocuous questions about the *kyree* and the other nonhumans, until other Tayledras drifted up to join the conversation. Gradually she began to relax, and to enjoy herself.

When a touch on her elbow made her turn, she found that Darkwind had found his way back to her. He handed her a slice of something breadlike, with something like a tiny, decorative flower arrangement atop it, and slid into the group beside her.

"Your friend Skif and my brother seem to have discovered that they have much in common," he said by way of joining the conversation, "and they have gone off to discuss weaponry. Knives, I think."

She shook her head. "That figures. Offer to talk about knives, and you'll have Skif's undivided attention for as long as you like. Do I eat this, or wear it?"

He chuckled. "You eat it. I think you will like it; it is smoked fish."

She nibbled the edge of it, tentatively. The smoked fish *she* was used to generally had the consistency and texture of a slab of wood, and tasted like a block of salt dipped in fish oil. She was pleasantly amazed at the indescribable blend of delicate flavors. As Darkwind chuckled again at her expression, she devoured it to the last shred.

"I have been asked," he continued, both to her and to the gryphons, "to request the presence of my good friends Treyvan and Hydona at the waterfall, and my wingsib Elspeth at a gathering of the scouts."

"Ssso?" Treyvan replied. "What isss at the waterrfall? And whom?"

"Kethra, Iceshadow, and my father, among others," Darkwind told him. "And, I am told, a very large selection of fresh fish and uncooked meat and fowl. Some of our more sensitive guests, like the *dyheli* and *tervardi*, might be distressed by refreshments of that nature, so we took them out of the way."

"Wissse," Hydona acknowledged. "But the little onessss——"

"Torrl assures me that they are not too far from falling asleep," Darkwind answered, "And when they do drift off, the *hertasi* have promised to keep an eye on them."

"I am *famisshed,*" Treyvan said, with a look of entreaty at his mate.

Across the clearing, Elspeth noticed the *kyree* raising its head from its paws, and looking directly at them.

:Every parent deserves some time without the young,: she heard, just as clearly as if the *kyree* was her own Companion. *:They are too tired to get into mischief that I cannot distract, and anything that wishes to harm them will have to come at them through not only me, but all the defenses of the Vale. And, I suspect, the large white hooved ones.:*

Hydona gave in; Elspeth readily understood her reluctance to have the gryphlets out of her sight, considering all that had happened to them, but the *kyree* was right. If the little ones weren't safe *here,* none of them were. They rose to their feet, folded their wings tightly against their sides to avoid knocking anything or anyone over, and took their leave.

Darkwind led the way up and down yet another path; this one ended beneath one of the enormous trees she had only glimpsed through curtains of bushes and vines. There were quite a few Tayledras gathered beneath it, but for the first few moments, all her attention was taken up by the tree itself.

Simply put, it was so large that an entire house could have been built within the circumference of its trunk. A curving staircase had been built around it, leading up to a kind of balcony three stories above the clearing. Soft lights hung from the bottom of the balcony, preventing her from seeing anything above that level, but she had the feeling that the staircase continued upward. When she shaded her eyes and peered upward, she caught sight of other, fainter lights near the trunk, half-obscured by the enormous branches. The Chronicles had once referred to the Hawkbrothers as the "tree-dwelling Tayledras," and she knew that Darkwind lived in a kind of elaborate platformed treehouse. So it looked as if that was the norm for the Hawkbrothers, rather than a concession to danger.

At least now she knew *why* they made a point of cultivating those enormous trees. Such marvels could support not one, but several dwellings.

When she turned her attention back to the gathering, she discovered that most of the Tayledras here were dressed very like Darkwind; in relatively "plain" clothing, and with hair either cut or bound up to be no longer than just below the shoulders, dyed in patterns of mottled brown and gold. They looked more like the Shin'a'in than the mages did, and it wasn't just that their hair wasn't white...

It's because they're scouts, fighters, she realized, after a moment. Like Darkwind, they couldn't wear clothing that interfered in any way with fighting movements, nor could they afford to indulge themselves with elaborate hairstyles. Like Darkwind, they had a certain economy of movement; nothing dramatic, nothing theatrical—nothing done just for the effect. There were strong, well-trained muscles under those silken tunics, hard bodies that saw furlongs of patrolling every day.

She felt herself relaxing further in their presence, even before Darkwind began introducing them to her. These were people who, although they were familiar with magic, had very little to do with it; they were somehow more down-to-earth than the mages in their sculptural robes. And they were more like Heralds than anyone she had met yet.

She took careful note of the names as they were introduced to her, the habit of someone born into politics. Winterlight and Stormcloud, Brightmoon and Daystar, Earthsong, Thundersnow and Firedance— she matched names with faces, with smiles shy or bold, with personality quirks. Darkwind had explained the Tayledras habit of taking use-names, names that described something of what the person was like. She had to admit that it wasn't a bad system; it was much easier to match a name with a face when Winterlight (one of the few scouts to grow long hair) had a thick mane that, when he was persuaded to unbraid and unbind it, looked like moonlight pouring down on snow—when Daystar was as sunny of disposition as the twins—and when Firedance was always in motion, never quite still, mercurial in temper and bright with wit. She wondered if she ought to take a use-name as well, though it shouldn't be hard for *them* to remember Elspeth, Skif, Gwena, and Cymry. Four names were easier to remember than an entire Clanful.

"These are the k'Sheyna scouts," Darkwind said, when he'd finished the introductions, confirming her guess that there wasn't a mage among them. "Not all of them, of course; we still have a full patrol out tonight. But enough for now, I think; any more of us, and you would be overwhelmed with names and faces."

She smiled, but said nothing. This wasn't the time to point out that she'd coped with four times their number at ordinary state dinners. True, she had Talia's and Kyril's help, and the nobles and dignitaries didn't look quite so alike...

"You are lucky, Elspeth," the young fellow called Stormcloud told her. "Truly. We are in festival gear now. If you were to see us tomorrow, you might find it hard to tell one from the other."

Earthsong nodded vigorously. "There is a tale among Outlanders that we are all mage-born copies of a single Tayledras."

"I can see how they would think that," she replied after a moment of consideration, imagining them all garbed in Darkwind's drab scouting clothing, with their hair bound up against snags. If the women—already slender and athletic—bound their breasts, it would even be difficult to tell male from female. "Of course, I'm sure you don't do *a thing* to encourage that now, do you?"

She was pleased when they laughed at her sally; sometimes the most difficult thing about dealing with a new people was finding out what they considered funny. And as she had discovered on her own, knowing what made someone laugh was the surest shortcut to making him your friend.

"Oh, no, of course not!" Firedance exclaimed, eyes wide and round with mock innocence. "Why would we ever do anything like that?"

The others laughed again at his disclaimer, then settled themselves back where they'd been before Darkwind brought her into the clearing. "We were just having some music and a little dancing," Earthsong said, as he picked up a flat drum. "We thought you might like to see and hear some of it, so we asked Darkwind if he'd go pry you away from the gryphons."

"Not that we're great artists," Winterlight spoke up quietly, "But we do enjoy ourselves, and I think music is better than any amount of words at telling people about each other. A language that needs fewer words."

"That's what our Bards say," she replied, looking for an inconspicuous spot to put herself, and finally giving up and taking a seat on one of the tree's enormous roots.

Winterlight gestured in agreement, and picked up something that she didn't recognize; a trapezoidal box strung like a harp. He set it on his lap and pulled a couple of hammers from under the strings, then glanced at Earthsong. The young scout evidently took that for a signal; he began to produce an elaborate rhythm on his flat drum with a single, double-ended stick; Winterlight listened for a moment, then joined him, not by plucking the strings as Elspeth had expected, but by striking them deftly with the hammers. Within a few moments, others had joined in, either on instruments of their own or simply by clapping. Some of their instruments were things that Elspeth recognized; most weren't, with sounds that were not—quite—like anything she knew.

The music was far from unpleasant. There were unexpected bellsounds in the rhythm, a wailing wind instrument that added an unearthly element like a singing hawk's scream, and the occasional whistling improvisation by one of the scouts. It was quite infectious, and she found herself clapping along with it.

It wasn't much longer before the Tayledras got up to dance. Here was another difference between the Hawkbrothers and her own people. At home, folks danced in groups—ring dances or set pieces, with a definite sequence to the steps. The Tayledras danced singly, or in couples, or trios at most, and there was no set pattern to the dance steps. The nearest she had ever seen to this kind of exuberant chaos had been at a Herald celebration when a number of the younger Heralds just in from the field had gotten involved in a kind of dancing contest, demonstrating the wilder steps from their various home villages.

Two or three songs later, she noticed that some of the original contingent had vanished somewhere, and there were a few additions, wearing costumes more like those of mages than of scouts.

She started watching the onlookers as well as the dancers, and figured out from overheard bits of conversation that there were dozens of these little gatherings, scattered all around the Vale, although this was probably the most lively. Several scouts turned up in the next few moments with wet hair, attracted by the sounds of the music from the pools in which they had been swimming. That, it seemed, was the essence of a Tayledras celebration; to roam. People came and went; sampling little bits of this and that, food, music, conversation...

She decided to do as the natives were doing, taking the opportunity to explore the Vale a little, and slipped off by herself, wandering down a randomly chosen path until she heard the sounds of a softer melody than the dancing music.

She discovered a single singer, a woman in silvery-gray, slender as a birch tree, playing a huge diamond-shaped wire-strung harp. There were a half dozen of the mages listening to her, sitting on benches arranged in a half-circle around her, and Elspeth stayed through three songs before moving on.

She found her way back to the original clearing. By now the gryphlets were sound asleep, oblivious to all the light and movement and the sounds of conversation around them. Both Companions were still there, with that relaxed attitude and cheerful, ears-up, tail-switching pose that told her they were enjoying themselves. Their conversational partners were Torrl, the *kyree*, two of the mages, one of the scouts, and an old *hertasi*. Seeing them, she relaxed as well, since they were enjoying themselves. As she wandered off again, it occurred to her that this was the one thing that was often missing from parties that the Heralds held—Dirk and Talia's wedding had included the Companions, but all too often, they were left out of things. As she watched Gwena and Cymry, she made a mental note; when she got home again, that was one thing that would change. She'd find a way to make certain they weren't left out again. They were as responsible for the success of the Heralds as the Heralds themselves. Surely they deserved that much consideration.

Gwena turned around at that moment and gave her an unmistakable wink before returning to her conversation.

Even if they do snoop in our heads.

But she was smiling as she chose another path, not looking for anything in particular, but thinking that a swim might be nice.

She heard water trickling off to one side, and someone giggling; she didn't really stop to think, she just started to make her way down the little path.

Suddenly Darkwind slipped in front of her, stopping her before she could part the branches that shielded the end of the path. "Pardon," he said apologetically. "The marker beside the path—it was turned to face red. It means that—"

The giggling changed to an unmistakable gasp of pleasure. Elspeth found herself blushing. "Never mind," she whispered, backing up hastily. "I think I have a good idea what it means."

She turned, and started back toward the clearing; Darkwind intercepted her again. "Oh, no," he said earnestly. "No, if they had not wanted to be disturbed, the marker would have been blue. No, the red marker means that they would welcome—ah—all other—" he coughed "—participants—"

She blushed even deeper, her ears and cheeks aflame. She'd always been told that the Heralds were uninhibited. It seemed that the Hawkbrothers had even fewer inhibitions.

"I thought perhaps no one had warned you," he continued. "If, perhaps, you might want to enjoy one of the hot springs, I can take you to one where there is nothing more active than hot water."

What else could she do but accept gracefully, and hope that by the time they reached this spring, her blushes would have cooled?

A curtain of steam announced the location of the spring, but when Darkwind pulled aside the branches at the entrance and waved her into the area around the pool, she found herself flushing all over again. There were about ten of the Hawkbrothers she remembered seeing at the dancing, all soaking muscles that must certainly be complaining, but they weren't wearing much except hair.

"Darkwind!" one of them hailed. "Fifteen split-jumps! Beat that, if you can!"

"Oh, yes," the young woman next to him said mockingly. "Fifteen split-jumps indeed—and now you see him soaking here, because he could scarce walk when he completed the fifteenth!"

"Sunfeather!" the young man exclaimed indignantly. "You weren't supposed to tell him that!"

Darkwind peeled off his tunic, as Elspeth averted her eyes and slowly took off her boots. "Perhaps you should think less about split-jumps, and more about what Sunfeather's expectations for the evening were *before* you tried to displace your hipjoints," he suggested mildly. "Then you might have the answer as to why she revealed your secret."

As the rest of the Tayledras teased the discomfited dancer, Darkwind removed the rest of his clothing and slid into the water beside Sunfeather. The spring-fed pool was quite a large one; the dozen Tayledras were scattered about the edge of it, each one of them lounging at full length, and they were hardly taking up more room than a dozen peas in one of the Collegium kitchen's biggest pots.

The analogy to a pot was a lot more apt than she had thought; when she finally got up enough courage to shed the rest of her clothing, she slid into an unoccupied niche. The hot spring was a good deal hotter than she had thought; not *quite* painful, but not far from it.

Steam rose about her face and turned her hair limp, but after a moment she stopped thinking she was about to have her hide boiled off, and began to enjoy the heat.

She slipped out again, after a relatively short time; she was *not* used to turning herself into a scalded turnip. Much to her surprise, someone— perhaps one of the ubiquitous and near-invisible *hertasi*—had left a towel and robe beside her clothing.

For the rest of the evening, she alternated between the larger clearing and the one the scouts had taken for their dancing. One of the mages treated the group to a guided flight of befriended firebirds—like the fireworks displays at home, except that these fireworks didn't fade or die. Gwena loved every moment of it, although Elspeth would have liked to have seen the firebirds come closer. The demonstration was very impressive, especially when they flew among the branches of the huge, shadow-shrouded tree. *That* wouldn't have been possible with real fireworks.

She lost track of time, wandering around the Vale, as fatigue caught up with her and her nerves relaxed. Finally she found herself back beneath the tree; most of the lights hanging from the balcony had been extinguished, but there were more people, human and not.

They were all "people" to her now, after an evening of trading jokes with *hertasi*, commiserating with *tervardi* on the likelihood of a bad winter, and telling the *dyheli* exactly what had happened to Nyara. So far as the *dyheli* were concerned, Nyara was still their heroine. *She* hadn't known that their entrapment had been a setup by her father, to ensure that the k'Sheyna would look on her favorably. She had acted in the belief that she was saving them. They knew that, and honored her for it.

So the facts of her disappearance were of great interest to them; they promised Elspeth that they would watch for signs of the Changechild, and report anything they learned back to the Tayledras scouts.

All but the most die-hard of dancers had given up by now; Elspeth found herself a seat in the shadows. Tre'valen was the center of a cluster of the scouts, who were trying to persuade him to dance. Finally he shook his head, shrugged, and gestured to the musicians. "Hawk Dance?" Iceshadow called back.

Tre'valen laughed. "Indeed!" he said, taking a stand in the middle of the illuminated area. "What else would I do for you? But only on condition that Darkwind follow with a Wind Dance."

Elspeth hadn't seen Darkwind before Tre'valen called out his name, but when he waved agreement from across the clearing, she saw that he had stripped off the fancier over-tunic, and now looked more like the Darkwind she knew, in a deep-cut sleeveless jerkin and tight breeches, his only ornaments the feathers in his hair.

Tre'valen had changed after the ceremony into his Shin'a'in finery of scarlet, black, and gold; embroidered vest with fringe to his knees, fringed and belled armbands. Loose breeches with fringed kneeboots, all of it topped with a horsehair and feather headdress like some strange bird's crest—he was a striking sight.

The drummer began first; Tre'valen marked the time with one foot, the fringe shivering with each beat. When the instruments came in, Tre'valen leapt into action.

Elspeth soon saw why it was called the "Hawk Dance." Tre'valen was aloft more often than he was on the ground; whirling, flying, leaping. He never paused, never rested; no sooner did his foot touch the ground than he was in the air again. His arms curved like wings cupping the air. Elspeth's heart kept time with the beat, her eyes unable to leave him. He didn't seem much like a human at the moment—more like a creature akin to the *tervardi* or the firebirds. But then, perhaps that was the essence of being a shaman.

The dance came to an end on a triple beat and one of the highest leaps of the dance that left Tre'valen standing still as stone, exactly in the same place where he had begun the dance. Elspeth had no idea how he had known the music was about to end; she had heard nothing to signal the end of the piece. It left her staring, dumb with astonishment and delight.

Tre'valen sat down on a root amid the shouts and applause of the others. Darkwind took the shaman's place in the center of the circle, composed himself, and nodded to the musicians.

This time the music began slowly, with a glissando on the odd hammered instrument, followed by another on the harp, a softer echo of the first. Then Darkwind began to dance.

The Tayledras and Shin'a'in music were related; that much was obvious from a root similarity of melody, but dancing and music had changed from the time the two races were one. Either the Shin'a'in had gotten wilder, or the Tayledras had become more lyrical, or both.

Darkwind didn't leap, he floated; he didn't whirl, he flowed. He moved as if he had no bones, flew like his own bird, glided and spun and hovered. There was nothing feminine in the dance, for all of that; it was completely, supremely masculine. Besides his supple grace, what Elspeth noticed most of all were his hands—they had to be the most graceful pair of hands she had ever seen.

Darkwind finished the dance like a bird alighting for the night, coming to rest with a final run from the harp. There was a faint sheen of sweat over his body and face, shining in the moonlight. As he held his final pose, he was so completely still that he could have been a silver statue of a forest spirit, looking up in wonder at the stars.

That was the image that Elspeth took with her, as she slipped out of the clearing and found one of the *hertasi*. She asked the little creature to show her the quarters Darkwind had promised were waiting for her here.

The little lizard grinned at her, and led her down so many twisting dark paths that she was soon lost. Not that it mattered at the moment. Darkwind had also pledged that he would send someone to lead her about until she knew her own way.

She recognized the area, once they got near it; they were very close to the entrance to the Vale, the farthest they could be from the Heartstone and still be inside the Vale shields. The *hertasi* showed her a staircase winding up the side of a tree. For a moment she was afraid that she would have to climb up several stories, and she wasn't sure she had the head for it.

But the *hertasi* scrambled up ahead of her, and her waiting quarters proved to be a mere single story above the floor of the Vale, a set of two rooms built just off the stairs, lighted and waiting for her.

She fell into the bed as soon as the *hertasi* left her—but for a surprisingly long time she lay looking at the moon, as sleep deserted her.

She felt a little less like a stranger, but no less lonely. Skif had Nyara— or at least, he had the dream of Nyara, wherever he was now. She still had no one.

Only her duty, her omnipresent duty. To learn everything she could about magic; learn it quickly, and bring it home to Valdemar.

That was cold comfort—and no company—on a silvered, moonfilled night...

3

Darkwind accepted the applause of his fellow scouts along with a damp cloth and a healthy gulp of cold water. It had been a long time since he had performed the Wind Dance in full, although dance was a part of his daily workout. He enjoyed it, and enjoyed the applause almost as much. It was good to know his skill could still conjure approval from his brethren.

The Outlander, Elspeth, had been watching the dancers when Tre'valen began his display. He knew she had enjoyed the Hawk Dance; from the look on her face, she had probably never seen anything quite like it before. He thought she'd enjoyed *his* dancing as well—and he meant to talk to her afterward. He was disappointed, after he'd caught his breath, to find she had gone.

He settled for a moment to let his muscles recover; he felt them quivering with fatigue as he sat down. He had pushed himself in this Wind Dance, to far closer to his limits than he usually tried to reach. The steps, which appeared deceptively easy, required perfect balance and control and required fully as much effort to sustain as Tre'valen's more energetic Hawk Dance.

He listened to some of the others discussing dances and dancers past, nodding when someone said something he particularly agreed with. No one else wanted to follow his performance, and some of the players took that as a signal to put their instruments away and rest their weary fingers. As Darkwind settled his back against the tree and slowly sipped his water, he considered the Outlanders—Elspeth in particular. They were less of an enigma than he had feared they would be, although he still wished he knew a great deal more about their culture.

Elspeth was more of a problem than her friend Skif, simply because of her position as his student. She was sometimes fascinating, sometimes infuriating, often both.

She compounded his own problems as he resumed his position as an Adept. As his father had pointed out, he had a great deal to re-learn; how much, Darkwind was only now figuring out. What Starblade didn't know was that his son was already giving Elspeth lessons, even while he was retraining his own powers.

Elspeth posed a peculiar hazard, that of half-knowledge. She had full training in the Gifts of mind-magic, though no true training in her mage-powers—but some of the mind-magic disciplines were similar enough to give her a grasp on magery, but without controls. Her sword had at one time provided some guidance and tutelage, but Elspeth had a great deal to learn about even rudimentary magics. Without the blade Need about to keep her in hand, he had not felt safe about having Elspeth walking around loose without beginning those early lessons in basic control.

What he had not reckoned on—although, given her quick temper, he should have anticipated the difficulty—was her impatience with him.

She wanted answers, and she wanted them immediately. And when he was already impatient with himself, he didn't feel like explaining himself to an Outlander who had barely even seen magic in action before she came south.

Her insistence on forcing years' worth of learning into a few weeks was enough to drive the most patient of savants to distraction, much less her current teacher. *She can be so irritating...*

He leaned his head back and stared up into the pattern of faint light and deep darkness created by moonlight, mage-lights, and tree branches. There was randomness, no discernible pattern, just as there was no discernible pattern to his life. A season ago, he would never have been able to imagine the events of the past several weeks. A year ago, he never would have believed his life would change in any meaningful way, except for the worse.

He sighed, and ran his hand through his hair, fluffing it to cool and dry it. Elspeth was a disruption to an already confusing situation. The problem was, she had the infuriating habit of being *right* now and again in matters of magic—matters in which she had no experience and little knowledge.

He'd dismissed all of her suggestions initially. Then, when she'd been proven right a time or two, he'd thought at first that it was pure luck. No one could *always* be right or wrong after all, but a day or so ago, he'd finally seen the logic to her ideas' successes. In general, when she saw something that she thought could be done magically, but that *he* had never learned, her theories turned out to be, in principle, correct.

One case in point that still annoyed Darkwind was treating the lesser lines of power as if they were a web, and the mage was a spider in the midst of that web. She'd reasoned that anyone working magic within the area a mage defined as his "web" would create a disturbance in the lines of power, which the mage at the center would feel, in the same way a spider felt an insect in its web. The advantage of this was that it was a passive detection system; there was nothing to alert the intruding mage that he'd been detected.

It was nothing he'd been taught. He'd been certain it wouldn't work—until she sketched a diagram, extended a few tendrils of energy, and proved to him that it would. It had been something of a shock to his already-bruised pride, and he followed along numbly as she refined the idea.

As if it weren't enough that she was attractive, in her unadorned way. She had to be innovative, too.

The mage-lights dimmed, sending the boughs above vanishing into shadows; and he looked back down from his perusal of the branches to find that everyone had left the clearing but him. The celebration was winding down, as couples and groups sought *ekeles* or hot springs, and the rest, not ready to seek beds, gathered in the meeting-circle or beside the waterfall.

He stretched his legs, carefully, to make certain they hadn't stiffened up on him. They weren't cramping as he'd feared; he was in better shape than he'd thought, apparently. But he didn't feel much like rejoining the rest who were still celebrating; he rose slowly, and began pacing, making a point of walking as silently as he could. It was a lot easier to do that here, on the clear paths, than out in the forest. There was no point in losing his hard-won scouting skills just because he was resuming his position as an Adept. There was a Tayledras saying: "No arrow shot at a target is ever wasted, no matter how many break." It meant that no practice or lesson, however trivial it might seem, was a loss.

Now, reclaiming his magery, he was discovering the downside of that saying.

I didn't realize how much I'd forgotten until I started trying to teach her, he admitted to himself. *If she'd just be a little more patient with me...*

When something went wrong, Elspeth wasn't particularly inclined to sit and wait quietly until he got it right again. Magic wasn't simple; spells had to be laid out methodically, and when something got muddled, a responsible mage couldn't just erase things and start over. Spells gone awry had to be unmade. Generally Darkwind had to retrace his steps carefully, in order to find out exactly where he'd made those mistakes. Only then could he undo what he'd done, go back to the beginning, and start again, constructing correct paths.

Whenever he was forced to do that, Elspeth would invariably ask questions at the worst possible time, when interruptions would be the most irritating. She never seemed to know when to keep quiet and let him work. Why was she in such a hurry to master every aspect of magic? Mastery took time and practice; surely she was bright enough to realize that.

Even now, he realized, she was irritating him. *How can she do that?* he asked himself, pausing in his pacing for a moment to examine his reaction. *How can she annoy me when she isn't even here? It has to be me, not her—*

As he folded his arms and pondered the question, he recalled something that seemed to have nothing to do with Elspeth. It was the reason why he had given in so quickly to the demand that he perform the Wind Dance. And it had nothing to do with Tre'valen's request, either; he'd have found some excuse to perform that dance before the evening was over, no matter what.

The reason? Stormcloud's boast of fifteen consecutive split-jumps.

Challenge. He couldn't resist it. And Elspeth annoyed him because she challenged him in a way no one else ever had—or at least, no female ever had. He wasn't facing the challenge of a teacher toward a student's potential, nor, precisely, was he facing the risks of an explorer. There was, though, that annoying realization that he didn't have the safety of being able to lord skill over her; he was as uneducated in *his* way as she. It didn't sit well with him, but that was the truth of the matter. Therein lay the challenge: she was a virtual equal.

Now that he had identified the source of his irritation, he realized that he wasn't going to be able to do anything about it. Perversely, he enjoyed the frustration, just as he enjoyed Elspeth's company though she grated on his nerves.

She was too impatient, but that was not damning. There was no reason why she shouldn't intrigue him, just as what he was teaching should be a challenge to her. She was, after all, a bright student. Alert and eager.

Hmm. That's not the only challenge she represents. He enjoyed her company quite a bit more than he was fully willing to admit. Of all the possible partnerings he could have made tonight, he had only considered one. She attracted him quite as much as she irritated him, although he was certain that he was not ready emotionally for anything as deep as he had shared with Dawnfire. And there had only been one consideration that held him back from offering Elspeth a feather tonight.

Sadly, that consideration was a major one; one that was going to require any association with her—other than pure friendship—to be choreographed as carefully as any major spell. She was an Outlander; he had no idea of the ways of her people. It might be that the folk of Valdemar took sexual liaisons very seriously; they might even reserve sexual activity for formal bondmates only. Until he knew more about her and her people, he was not going to take the risk of offending her or her country by propositioning her. Even if she would accept an apology, the offense would continue to taint everything he did or said to her.

Lust is easy to come by, after all. I couldn't enjoy it with too much worry, anyway. There is simply too much at stake to permit a night of pleasure to complicate matters.

Not to mention the possible repercussions of bedding the designated heir to a foreign monarchy. Who knew where that would lead? He doubted anyone would declare war over it, but what if a liaison with Elspeth would make her subject to problems when she returned home? She was too important a personage.

Ah, now there's another thing that irritates me!

He began walking again, turning his steps out of the clearing and down the path that led to the waterfall at the end of the Vale. Now that he'd figured out what it was that was bothering him, it might help to have a talk with someone about it. He could do his best to try to watch his own reactions, but there wasn't a great deal that he could do about Elspeth's attitude.

It's this Heir To The Throne business. She never actually says anything about it, but she radiates it. As if—she doesn't wear a crown, but she carries herself as if she did. As if she is always *thinking that she's being watched and admired, that she is an important person, and expects everyone else to be aware of that.*

Never mind that the only Tayledras around who knew of her land were Starblade and Iceshadow, who had studied the old histories. Never

411

mind that even those two had no interest whatsoever in her country and the Heralds who populated it, except as a curiosity and as it had impact in the past on Tayledras concerns.

Treyvan and Hydona might have some ideas about his concerns; they were ambassadors, of sorts—Hydona was female. That could help. In either case they might have some idea how to deal with another Outlander. Particularly an impatient, high-ranking, annoyingly impressive female Outlander.

At the waterfall, all the mage-lights had been extinguished. The moon was still high overhead, though, providing plenty of illumination, pouring down over this end of the Vale and touching the mist rising from the falls with silver. The two he sought were still there, lazing beside the pool like a pair of creatures from legend; both gryphons looked up at his footfall, but to his disappointment he saw that they were not alone. The shaman Tre'valen was with them, and he felt a certain reluctance to discuss one Outlander in front of another. For that matter, he wasn't certain he wanted to discuss Elspeth with anyone except the gryphons. He trusted them unfailingly.

Nevertheless, since they had seen him and nodded greetings, it would have been impolite to ignore them and walk on. It would be even worse to return the way he came. *It isn't going to do any harm to make some idle chat. And Her Highness Elspeth isn't a problem I can't cope with on my own, if I just think carefully before I say or do anything.*

So he approached the little group—which, he saw as he grew nearer, included the gryphlets. The little ones were tucked under their mother's wing, quietly sleeping, curled together into softly huffing balls of wings and limbs.

"Tre'valen brought the younglingsss when they began to fret and did not want to sssleep without usss near. And have you had enough of cccelebration?" Treyvan said softly as he neared. The shaman lounged beside Hydona, along the edge of the pool, his hair wet and rebraided.

Looks as if Tre'valen has been swimming. I didn't know that the Shin'a'in knew how to swim. I didn't think there were any bodies of water on the Plains deep enough for them to learn.

"Quite enough, I think," he replied, and nodded to the shaman. "Your Hawk Dance is very good, Wingbrother. In fact, I don't know that I've ever seen better. I should like to see you dance one day in full home regalia, with a proper set of Shin'a'in musicians and singers."

"If you enjoyed my dance, you should see my brother; I learned it from him." Tre'valen stretched, and turned to look him straight in the eyes. "I have been greatly curious, Wingbrother, and I think you will be willing to answer an impertinent question. Was it my imagination, or was there an air of desperation about all of this? As if folk were doggedly determined to enjoy themselves?"

Darkwind had been wondering if he was the only one to notice that. "It was not your imagination," he replied quietly.

"I thought not." Tre'valen nodded. "Your people escaped the hand of Falconsbane by a very narrow margin. Whether it was the hand of the Goddess or of chance, or both together, there was little they could have done of themselves to free this Clan from his influence. I wondered if they knew how narrow their escape was. Your father, for instance—"

"They know," Darkwind replied, carefully steering the conversation away from his father. That was another whole situation he was not quite ready to deal with yet. "They simply don't dwell on it. And they know that our troubles are not yet over, which accounts for that desperate enjoyment you noted."

"But the urgency iss lesss," Hydona said. "All that hass occurrred, hass bought k'Sheyna time. Thisss celebration—it wass a good thing. It iss a relief from the tenssion. Bessidesss… other changess arre coming."

Darkwind decided to leave that typically gryphonish—meaning cryptic—remark alone.

"You could be reading Iceshadow's mind," he smiled. "After all the troubles, the fear—"

—and the other things no one wants to talk about, like discovering what had been done to my father—

"It was just a good idea to give everyone something pleasurable to think about for a little while. A relief." He scratched Hydona's neckruff absently, and she half-closed her eyes with pleasure. One of the gryphlets rolled over, chirring contentment in its sleep. "A day or two of rest isn't going to alter the Heartstone question, but it might make all the difference in letting us gain a fresh outlook."

Tre'valen raised an eyebrow, but said only, "Some look as if they need a rest more than a fresh outlook. Starblade, for instance."

Don't ask too many impertinent questions, shaman. I might answer them, and you might not care for the answers. I am not altogether certain that the Shin'a'in are ready to embrace the problems of their cousins, no matter how many Wingsib Oaths are sworn. What you do not officially know, you need not act upon.

Treyvan raised his head from his foreclaws. "*You* look rrready for a

413

frresh outlook, Darrkwind," he said, as Darkwind tried unsuccessfully to suppress a yawn. "The outlook you may have frrom yourrrr bed."

"I think you're right," he admitted, glad of the excuse to escape from a conversation that was becoming increasingly uncomfortable. *He* didn't particularly want to discuss the problems of k'Sheyna, at least not now, when his tired mind and tongue might let things slip he would rather were not revealed.

The way he felt about Starblade, for instance. His heart was still sore and shaking from the revelation that the cold, critical "father" of the past several years had *not* been the father who had taught him his first lessons in magic—and who had worn the costumes his son had designed for him with such open pride.

The fact that Starblade had worn one of those costumes tonight, which was not only the Wingsib Oathing, but the first time he had taken part in the social life of k'Sheyna since Darkwind had freed him, had left him on very uncertain emotional ground. In a very real sense, he had a new father—but Darkwind was years older, and there was deep-set pain between them. It was going to take some time before his feelings were reconciled.

He imagined it was much the same for Starblade. The only difference between what he and his father had to cope with was that Starblade had known the truth but had not been able to act upon it, while Darkwind had been able to act but had not known the truth. Equally painful situations.

He yawned again, and this time did not take the trouble to hide it. "I think I must be getting old," he said. "My ability to celebrate until sunrise is not what it once was. And I did promise young Elspeth that her lessons would continue when we both arose from sleep—" He ignored Tre'valen's suggestive smirk, "—so rather than finding her waiting at the foot of my *ekele*, I think I will seek my own bed and see if I might wake before she does."

"A good plan," chuckled Tre'valen. *"Zhai'helleva."*

"And to you, all," he replied, and rose from the soft turf beside the pool, brushing off his seat. He retraced his steps, this time heading for the path that ultimately led out of the Vale. Even though he was reconciled with Starblade the fluctuating power of the Heartstone made him uncomfortable, and he disliked having to sleep near it. Starblade and the rest understood, and his "eccentricity" of maintaining a dwelling outside the safe haven of the Vale was no longer a subject of contention.

His path tonight, however, was not a direct one. Three times he had to interrupt his path with detours to avoid trysts-in-progress. He should have expected it, really; the end result of a celebration was generally trysting all over the Vale, of whatever tastes and partners.

So why am I going back to my ekele *alone?*

He'd never lacked for bedmates before. Actually, if he hadn't been so choosy—or was it preoccupied—he wouldn't have lacked for bedmates tonight.

He could say that he mourned for Dawnfire, and that would have been partially true. He missed her every time he thought of her, with an ache that he wondered if he would ever lose. She had been the one that he'd thought would actually work out as more than a bedmate; their interests and pleasures had matched so well. The fact that she hadn't *died* made the situation worse, in some ways. She had become something he could see, but could not touch. Now at least, after much thought, the first, sharp sorrow had passed, the sorrow that had been like an arrow piercing his flesh. Now what he felt was the pain of an emotional bolt lodged in place, poisoning his blood with regret.

He also knew that Dawnfire would have been the first to tell him to get on with his life. If she had been with him, if he had lost another lover, she would whisper to him to take a bedmate, and some pleasure, to ease the pain. That was just her way, another thing he had loved her for.

So why hadn't he taken one or more of those offers for companionship tonight?

Because he didn't *want* any of them. They simply didn't fit his real, if vaguely defined, desires.

And to tell the truth, he wasn't sure what he wanted. Elspeth was the only person tonight who had attracted him. But along with every other way she made him react, he was afraid—afraid that she might draw him into a deeper relationship than he intended.

She would leave the Vales and return to her Valdemar; and his people were here. There could be nothing lasting between them emotionally, save wistfulness over what might have been. But they would be spending most of their time together, now that she was a Wingsister; it was his duty to teach her, and hers to help defend the Vale for as long as she dwelled here. The Council had made it clear that *he* was responsible for her. If it turned out that Elspeth was equally attracted to him—that her ways were similar to his people in the matter of loveplay and they became more than casually involved—perhaps they could pursue some of the techniques in which sexual magic could be tuned and sublimated, and in so doing—

No. I couldn't do it. I just lost Dawnfire, I can't lose another lover. I'm not made of such stern stuff.

He finally reached the path to his *ekele* without incident—without encountering anything more hazardous than a flight of moths. That in itself was a pleasant change. The sharp bite to the air and the faint aroma of leaves in their turning reminded him that there were other changes on the wind that were not so pleasant. Autumn was at hand; winter would follow, and although the Vale would remain green and lush, outside it the leaves would fall, and snow and ice-storms would come. Winter would bring a new set of dangers from outside; predators would grow hungry, and the fear that kept them away from the Vale in the summer might not be enough to overcome their hunger's insistence. Winter would make it difficult for infatuated young Skif to track the Changechild. And it would be much harder for the remains of k'Sheyna to trek across the country in search of the rest of the Clan, if that was ultimately what they had to do to reunite.

Despite the fact that k'Sheyna territory was now much safer than it had been before the confrontation with Mornelithe Falconsbane, Darkwind had reverted to his old habits the moment he passed the barrier at the mouth of the Vale. It only took one slip at the wrong time to make someone a casualty. Tayledras had been killed even in tamed territories, simply by thinking they were secure. He kept to the deepest shadows, walked silently, and kept all senses alert for anything out of the norm. The moon was down beneath the level of the trees by the time he reached his *ekele;* he kindled a tiny mage-light in the palm of his hand and—with some misgiving—loosed the ladder from its support above and lowered it by means of another exercise of magic. With a tiny spell, he tripped the catch that held the rope-ladder in place.

If this had been in daylight, he'd never have used magic, he'd have had Vree drop the trigger-line to him. He still felt uneasy about using anything except mage-shields outside of the Vale. True, Falconsbane was no longer out there, watching for the telltale stirrings of magic-use and waiting to set his creatures attacking anything outside the protection of the Vale. But caution was a hard habit to break, especially when he wasn't certain he truly wanted to break it.

Still, the presence of the mage-light made climbing the ladder a lot easier, and the use of the spell eliminated the need to scale the trunk in the dark to release the ladder. It was worth the risk, at least tonight.

Perhaps, now, there were many things that were worth the risk of attempting them...

Skif could hardly believe what he'd just heard. He rubbed his tired eyes, and stared across the tiny firepit at his new friend. The conversation had begun with knives in general, proceeded to other things, such as forging, tempering, balance and point structure, throwing styles—but it had just taken a most unexpected turn. "Forgive me, but I'm not—ah—as good in speaking Tayledras as Elspeth. Did you say what I think you said?"

Wintermoon chuckled, and passed him a cup of a spicy—but, he'd been assured, nonalcoholic—drink, poured from a bottle he'd asked one of the *hertasi* to bring. "I will speak in more plain words," the scout told him, slowly, reaching for one of the sausages warming on the grill above the coals of their fire. "I wish to help you to find the Changechild Nyara. If you tell me 'aye,' I shall come with you. You say you have no true learning in woods-tracking; I am not a poor scout. I think I would be of real help."

:He's one of the best scouts and trackers in k'Sheyna, Chosen,: Cymry told him. Her ears were perked up, showing her excitement and interest. *:He's being very modest. The* dyheli *told me he's one of the few that can even hunt and track by night, maybe even the best.:*

He wanted Wintermoon's help—wanted it badly. He *needed* it. Without it, all he'd do would be to crisscross k'Sheyna territory, virtually randomly, hoping to come across some sign of Nyara. With Wintermoon's skillful help, he would be able to mount a systematic search. But was this a test of his oaths and his loyalties?

"I—uh—I don't know what to say," he stammered, watching the tall Tayledras with his strange hair and pale eyes. "Wintermoon, I want your help more than I can say, but you're a scout, a hunter, a good one. What about the Clan? Don't they need you? I mean, I'm a Wingbrother, but doesn't that mean I need to think of the good of the Clan first?"

Wintermoon blinked slowly, and turned away toward the trees. He held up a gauntleted wrist. That was the only warning Skif had that something was happening; a heartbeat later, a huge white shape hurtled by his ear, soundlessly. As he winced away, the shape hit Wintermoon's wrist and folded its wings. It resolved itself into a great white owl, which swiveled its head and stared unblinkingly at him before turning back to Wintermoon, reaching down with its fierce hook of a beak and nibbling the fingers of his free hand gently.

"This is K'Tathi," Wintermoon said, stroking the owl's head gently. "Corwith is in the tree above. There are not many Tayledras who bond to the greater owls."

"You didn't answer my question," Skif said pointedly.

"Ah, but I did." Wintermoon transferred the owl from his wrist to his shoulder, where it proceeded to preen his hair. He sighed, and gave Skif a look full of long-suffering patience.

"There are not many Tayledras who bond to the greater owls. While my bondbirds can hunt by day, they prefer not to. They are also a different species from the hawks and falcons, and there is instinctive dislike between them and the birds of other scouts. It can be overcome, but it requires great patience." He shrugged, as the fire flared up for a moment from the cooking. The flare flushed the owl with ruddy light. "More patience than I care to give. Thus, I hunt by night, and mostly alone. That makes me something that can be done without when times are not so chancy."

"In other words, your absence won't cause any problems?" Skif persisted, clutching the cup.

The owl found Wintermoon's ear, and began nibbling it. Wintermoon sighed, and gave it his finger instead. "The new plan is for mages to help the scouts," he explained. "There will be more watchers. Your friend, Elspeth—she is clever, and will make up for my absence. So, I am free to aid you."

:There is a hole in this, somewhere,: Cymry said.

Skif agreed; he could sense it. "What is it that you aren't telling me?" he demanded. "Is it something about Nyara?"

The owl let go of Wintermoon's finger, roused its feathers, and settled, staring at Cymry as if it found her fascinating. Wintermoon nodded. "I thought perhaps you might think that, and yes, it concerns the Changechild. But you must pledge not to take offense."

:Offense?: he asked Cymry. *:Why would I—oh. Of course. They still don't trust Nyara, they want her under control, and they probably feel the same way about that damn sword.:*

:Can you blame them?: she asked reasonably.

:About the sword, no,: he replied. Then, to Wintermoon, "You Tayledras

don't trust Nyara or the blade, do you? The rest of the Clan wants you to go along and make sure she isn't out there trying to set up some more trouble for you."

Wintermoon nodded. "Quite. I beg pardon, but that is only the truth of the matter. But, Skif—I do wish to help you, for yourself. You are not schooled in tracking, you have said as much yourself. Think of it this way," he grinned. "I have no wish for your friend Elspeth to be sending me out in an ice-storm to *find* you!"

"Oh, I'm not that bad," he replied with a rueful smile. "I've had *some* field training. But it was all in Valdemar—there were Herald way-stations all over."

"And you cannot track or trail," Wintermoon repeated. He turned to Cymry. "Lady, you cannot track or trail, either. Nor can you see as well at night as my Corwith and K'Tathi can. Nor do you know our territory."

Cymry bowed her head in agreement.

"And, Skif, I would like to help you, for I know that you feel very much for the Changechild." His face sobered. "I do not know if the Changechild is near as dangerous as the Council think she might be. I think she deserves to have someone looking for her that will give her that benefit. I think it is a good thing for her to have someone besides yourself that will do that. You are a Wingbrother—but an Outlander as well. I am k'Sheyna."

Skif was well aware of what the Tayledras meant; just as his own word would hold more weight in Valdemar than Wintermoon's, no matter how many oaths the latter swore, so Wintermoon's held more weight here. If there were any doubt as to Nyara's allegiances, Wintermoon's opinion might well be the deciding factor.

And it would be a very good thing to have company out there in the wilderness...

:Take his offer,: Cymry urged. *:He's a good man; he could become a good friend.:*

"All right, Wintermoon," Skif said decisively. "I would be very, very glad to have you help me. Cymry wants you along, and I never argue with her."

:Never?: she snorted.

:Well—I never argue with you when you're right.:

"Good." Wintermoon rose to his feet, then held up his wrist again. For the second time, a white shape dove past Skif's ear; this time the owl came in from the side, then swooped up and alighted on Wintermoon's gauntlet with grace and silence. "This is Corwith," he said, transferring the owl to his other shoulder. "We three will be most happy to give you our help. Then I shall see you in the morning?"

"Make that when we wake up," Skif amended. "It's already morning."

Wintermoon squinted at the west, where the moon was going down. "So it is. Well, the night is my chosen time of departure, when I am given a choice. That will be good. There will be fewer eyes that will see us leave. *Zhai'helleva,* Wingbrother. May your dreams bring you peace and good omens."

"And yours—friend." On impulse, Skif offered his hand; Wintermoon took it after a moment, clasping first his hand, then his wrist.

As Wintermoon vanished into the darkness under the trees, and Skif turned to climb up into the *ekele* that had been given him, Cymry reached over and nuzzled his shoulder. *:That was well done,:* she said warmly. *:I like him. I think we might have accomplished more than we realized.:*

:I think you're right,: he answered, yawning. *:I've got a good feeling about this.:*

So good a feeling, that for the first time since Nyara disappeared, he fell asleep immediately, instead of lying awake and staring at the darkness. And for the first time, it was a calm sleep, untroubled by dreams of silken skin and crying, cat-pupiled eyes.

4

Skif tied the final knots on his packs, expecting at any moment to have a *hertasi* pop its head over the edge of the treehouse with a summons from Wintermoon. It was difficult to tell time here, where the position of the sun was obscured by the towering trees and where the temperature seldom varied by much, but he thought he'd awakened about noon. There had been cheese, fruit, and fresh bread waiting in the outer room of his little treehouse along with all of his belongings and Cymry's tack, brought from the gryphon's lair. By *hertasi* or one of the scouts, he presumed; they were the only ones who knew where his possessions were, besides, of course, the gryphons. He and Elspeth had stayed with the gryphons since they had first arrived here in k'Sheyna territory; they were kindhearted creatures, but certainly not pack animals; he'd assumed he would have to go fetch all of the gear himself. This was yet another instance of Tayledras thoughtfulness; or at least, of *hertasi* thoughtfulness. He was even more surprised and delighted to discover that every bit of his clothing had been cleaned and neatly folded before being put in the pack, and all but one of his hidden knives and garrottes from said clothing laid out neatly by the pack.

Old habits die hard.

He descended long enough to clean himself up at a hot spring set up as a kind of bathhouse—and to thank the first *hertasi* he saw for having his things brought. He found the lizard first. He was a little ashamed that he couldn't tell the difference between individual lizard-creatures; surely there was a way, and it seemed doltish not to know it. He covered it as best he could by asking the diminutive creature to pass on his thanks to the others. The *hertasi* didn't seem to mind. In fact, it thanked *him,* and showed him where to go to bathe and find provisions for his journey.

Back in the treehouse, he launched into packing feverishly. The strange provisions he'd gotten from a hidden kitchen area—learning only then where all the food for the celebration had come from—weighed much less than the dried fruit and beef and travelers' bread that the Valdemaran forces, Heralds and Guards alike, carried into the field.

Just so that they were marginally edible. Marginal was all he asked for. *They can't taste any worse than the clay tablets they expect Karsite troops to eat. Starch for shirts or old glue would taste better.* That much he was certain of; some folks would rather eat their saddles than the Karsite field rations.

"I trust you are ready?" Wintermoon called up from below, startling him. He went to the balcony, and looked over the edge.

Beneath him were the scout—now with his hair bound up in a tail and wearing clothing identical to the kind Darkwind had worn—and a pair of handsome *dyheli* stags. One carried a light pack, the other did not even have a cloth on its back. Beside them was Cymry, looking up at him with merry blue eyes, as if she was amused by his startlement.

"I'm ready," he replied to all of them. "I'm pretty much packed. Look out, I'm going to toss the stuff down."

Wintermoon and the rest backed up a little, giving him room for the drop. He dropped the saddle and the pack containing his clothing and nonbreakables over the edge of the balcony; he brought the rest down the staircase, slung over his back.

By the time he reached the ground, Wintermoon had already saddled Cymry for him, and was waiting for the rest of the gear. "You should try the Shin'a'in saddles," the Tayledras scout observed, as Skif pushed aside an enormous leaf that overhung the trail to join them. "I think you both would find them more comfortable."

"Maybe," Skif replied, dropping his pack on the ground, and holding up the hackamore for Cymry so that she could slip her nose into it. "But the Shin'a'in don't have to contend with anything other than the plains. We've got a lot of different terrain to cross, a lot of jobs to do, and sometimes we have to be able to sleep in the saddle or strap ourselves on because of wounds." He faltered for a moment, as an ugly memory intruded; he resolutely ignored it, and continued. "I'll try their saddles some time, but we've put a lot of time and work into that design, and I'm not sure there's any way to improve it."

Cymry nodded, which apparently surprised Wintermoon. Skif was going to ask where his birds were, when one of them dropped down out of the tree to land on the laden *dyheli's* pack, and the other followed to land on the unladen one's horns. The stags were both evidently used to this; the second *dyheli* held his head steady until the owl hopped from the horns to Wintermoon's shoulder. "Mobile tree branches," the Tayledras grinned.

"So I see. I told Elspeth that I was going out to hunt for Need," Skif told the scout, "I told her that I didn't think we could afford to have a major power like that out loose and not know where it was or what it was doing. She agreed, but I don't think she believed that was the only reason."

"I doubt you could fool your friend on matters of the heart," Wintermoon replied. "At least, not for long. Except, perhaps, for her own; I have noted that few people are good judges of their own hearts."

Skif flushed, and decided not to answer that statement. "Have you got any ideas about where we should start looking?" he asked instead. "I mean, I know you haven't had much chance to think about this since last night, but—"

"Actually, I have," Wintermoon interrupted, surprisingly. "I spent some time last night reviewing what I would do if I were in her place. So I know where she might be, I think—or rather, I know where we need not look. Here—"

He pulled out a map from a pouch at his belt and spread it on the ground. Skif pulled the last buckle on Cymry's packs tight and crouched down on his heels beside the scout. Cymry craned her neck around to look over his shoulder.

"—here, is the Vale." Wintermoon pointed at an oval valley on the rim of the crater-wall that marked the rim of the Dhorisha Plains. "Nyara will not have run to the west, neither south nor north; to the west and south were her father's lands. To the west and north, *that* is untamed, unhealed, tainted land, full of creatures that are as bad or worse than anything that her father commanded."

"And she knows this?" Skif asked.

Wintermoon snorted. "She cannot have avoided knowing. No matter how closely he kept her mewed, if she had any contact with the world outside his walls, she would have known. We had intended to bracket the area between this Vale and the new one—well, that is of no matter now. She will not have gone west unless she is an utter fool. Nor will she have gone south."

"Because that's the Dhorisha Plains," Skif said, absently, studying the map.

"Yes. So, that leaves east and north. She may have gone east—she *can* go east—but here—" he indicated a shaded area on the map. "This pattern means that the lands here *are* healed. If she goes there, she will encounter farms and settlements. If she goes further, she must meet towns, villages, and people who are unused to seeing creatures that are not wholly human. She will surely encounter trade-roads, traders, caravans. No, I do not think she would go very far to the east."

"And if she went due north?" Skif asked.

"Ah—again, she will encounter a border, this time the territory guarded by another Clan. They may not be as kindly disposed toward her as we. Certainly, since they will not know her, they will regard her with suspicion and even hostility." Wintermoon sat back on his heels. "So you see, she must be within *this* area." His forefinger described a rough oblong on the map. "Those are the lands we once claimed but we have let run wild, as we pulled back our borders. *That* is where I think we shall find her."

Skif nodded, and considered the map. "None of it is very far from where the scouts patrol," he observed. "In fact, we *could* go out there and start our search, and come back to the Vale every few days to see how matters are progressing here—and whether or not we're going to be needed after all."

"My thought exactly," the scout said, picking up the map and folding it. He stood up, stowing the folded parchment in his pouch again. "In this way we fulfill our own wishes and our duty to the Clan as well." He gave Skif an odd sideways grin that Skif returned.

"Why do I have the feeling that you're as good at that as I am?" he asked slyly. "Getting your own way by threading through rules and obligations, I mean."

"What, I?" Wintermoon replied, widening his eyes innocently. Then he laughed. "Come, we are birds of the same flock, you and I. We know each other. Yes?" He turned and mounted the second stag bareback, saving Skiff from having to answer that question.

Skif took his time mounting, settling himself into the saddle with a sigh. Not that he didn't enjoy partnering with Cymry, but it had been a long journey and he'd been glad it looked as if they were staying in one place for a while. Well, it *had* looked that way, until he'd realized that Nyara was gone and wasn't coming back. Now they were on the trail again...

:Oh, you won't be in the saddle as much as you think,: Cymry told him affectionately. *:Don't forget, Wintermoon is going to have to look over the ground out there very closely for clues. Actually, if I were you, I'd let him teach me about tracking in the wild; I think you could learn a lot from him. I know I'll be paying attention.:*

Skif was a little surprised at her matter-of-fact acceptance of this excursion. He had more than half expected her to object to leaving Elspeth on her own—after all, he was supposed to be looking after her, wasn't he? He was supposed to be her bodyguard, *and* he was supposed to keep her from getting into too much trouble.

:Elspeth's quite capable of taking care of herself, Chosen, as she has reminded you more than once.: This time the tone was teasing, lighthearted. But she quickly sobered. *:There is no way that Ancar can get to her here—even if he could learn where she was. She's got to go her own way now, you know that. You know she's going to have to deal with things you can't even guess at. Whatever trouble she's likely to get into, I don't think it's going to be anything a couple of arrows or knives would fix.:*

Skif ducked out of the way of a branch stretching over the path, and sighed. That, no matter how his pride felt about it, was only the truth. She was a mage now, under the protection and tutelage of mages. He would be as out of his element as if he tried to teach a candlemaking class.

:And I don't have any of this Mage-Gift, whatever it is,: he added. *:Probably I'd only be in the way. Probably I'd get myself in trouble without ever helping Elspeth.:*

:Probably,: Cymry agreed. *:Nyara, now—that's something you can do something about. I think you should. If nothing else, when you find her, you'll discover for yourself if there can be—or ever was—anything between you two. And you'll finally stop worrying about her.:*

While her words were practical, the tone of her mind-voice was unexpectedly sympathetic.

She was his best friend, barring no one else. She knew all of his secrets, even the ugly ones. He stared at the trail ahead and at Wintermoon's back for a while, thinking about that, thinking about how close they were. *:Cymry, were you ever in love?:* he asked abruptly.

:Bright Havens, what a question!: she exclaimed. *:Me? In love? Why do you want to know?:*

After all these years, he'd managed to surprise her. *:Because—I don't know if I'm in love or not—or if I was ever in love with anyone.:* Silence fell between them for a heartbeat. *:I thought if you were ever in love, you'd be able to tell if I was. Am. Whatever.:*

They reached the barrier-shield at the end of the Vale at that moment; the tingling of energies as they crossed it distracted Skif from his question.

When they emerged into slightly cooler air on the other side, Cymry shook her head, and shivered her skin as if she was shaking off flies. *:Skif, yes, I do know something of emotional involvement. That doesn't simplify matters any. You weren't in love with Elspeth, I can tell you that much,:* she said, slowly. *:That was a combination of a lot of things, including, my dear Chosen, the fact that you finally saw her as a very attractive woman for the first time and had a predictable reaction.:*

He choked; turned it into a cough when Wintermoon looked back at him in inquiry. Cymry wasn't usually so frank with him.

Or blunt. *:You made matters worse, I'm afraid, by acting far too strongly upon those feelings.:*

:I'd kind of figured that part out,: he replied wryly. *:But now, this time?:*

She shook her head. *:I honestly don't know. You have some very strong feelings, but I can't sort them out any better than you can.:*

Well, at least the Companions didn't know everything. Sometimes he wondered about that. They certainly didn't go out of their way to dispel the idea that they did.

Skif turned his attention to the woods surrounding the trail, trying to get used to these new forests, so that he could learn to identify what was a sign of danger and what wasn't. He did the only thing he could do; he assumed that this area was safe, and studied it. Anything that differed from this might be dangerous.

Most of his experience outside of towns consisted of the single circuit he'd made with Dirk when he first got his Whites, and his occasional duty as courier and messenger. At neither time had he really had to deal with *wilderness;* with places where people simply did not live. He had traveled roads, not game-trails; spent nights in way-stations, not in a tent, or a blanket roll under the open sky. Even on the journey here, the first time he had encountered true wilderness was when they descended into the Dhorisha Plains.

There, on that trackless expanse of grassland, there had been no real sign of the hand of man. Perhaps that was why the Plains intimidated him so much. Never had he felt so completely out of his element.

Maybe that had been why he had persisted in clinging to Elspeth...

Well, here was wilderness again; once outside the Vale, there were no tracks of any kind, for the Tayledras went to great lengths to avoid making them. The only creatures making trails of any sort were wild ones: deer, bear, boar. Even the *dyheli* did their best to avoid making trails, for trails meant places they could be ambushed. Skif couldn't help wondering if the only reason Wintermoon rode the *dyheli* stag now was to keep from leaving human footprints.

The signs of fall were everywhere; in the dying, drying grasses, in the leaves of the bushes which were just starting to turn, in the peculiar scent to the air that only frost-touched leaves made. This wasn't a comfortable time of the year to be traipsing about in wild country.

On the other hand, it would be harder for anything hostile to hide, once the leaves started falling in earnest. If there was anything noisier for a skulker than a carpet of crisp, freshly fallen dry leaves, Skif had yet to run into it; even in his days as a thief and a street brat, he'd known that, and stayed clear of rich folks' gardens in the fall. And he was not looking forward to camping out in the cold, riding through chill autumn rains...

On the other hand, it probably wouldn't get horribly cold this far south, at least, not for a while yet. Game would be plentiful at this time of year, a lot of it birds and animals in their first year—inexperienced, or just plain stupid, which to a hunter translated as "easy to catch." Darkwind had quoted a Shin'a'in saying about that, one day when Vree brought back a rabbit that couldn't have been more than two months old: "If it gets caught, it deserves to be eaten." On the whole, Skif agreed. With fresh meals volunteering their lives to their owls, arrows, and snares, they might not even need to resort to their traveling rations much. Maybe this wasn't going to be so bad after all.

Cymry's ears flicked, the way they did when she was Mindspeaking, and he caught the barest edges of something in the back of his mind. But he couldn't make anything out, just a mental "sound." It was as if he was several rooms away from two people having a conversation; no matter how hard he strained, all he could hear was a kind of murmur in the distance.

:Who are you talking to?: he asked her, puzzled. He hadn't thought Cymry could Mindspeak with anyone except himself and another Companion.

:Elivan,: she replied, shortly.

Elivan? Who—

Then the *dyheli* that Wintermoon was riding turned its head on its long, graceful neck and gave him a look and a nod.

The *dyheli?* She was Mindspeaking the *dyheli?* Frustrated, he tried to make sense out of the far-off murmuring, unable to make out a single "word." Even more frustrating, he caught Wintermoon in a kind of "listening" attitude, and heard a third "voice" join the other two in what sounded like a brief remark.

Whatever they were saying, Wintermoon seemed vastly amused; Skif got a look at his expression as he ducked to avoid a low-hanging vine, and he looked like someone who has just been let in on a private joke.

Skif felt a surge of resentment at being left out. Just how much mind-magic did the Hawkbrother have? Why couldn't he hear the *dyheli,* if Wintermoon and Cymry could? And was it only Wintermoon who had that particular Gift, or did all the Tayledras share it?

They'd been free enough with information about real magic; why keep this a secret?

Except that they weren't exactly keeping it a secret—not from Skif, anyway.

Unless they couldn't block what they were doing. But in that case, why did Cymry tell him matter-of-factly that she was talking to the stag?

The murmur of far-off voices stopped; finally Wintermoon signaled a halt at the edge of a tiny, crystalline stream. The Tayledras dismounted, and the two *dyheli* moved up side-by-side to dip their slender muzzles into the water. Another sign of the stags' intelligence— the pack-laden stag was not being led, and Wintermoon made no move to limit their drinking.

:I could use a drink too, dear,: Cymry prompted him. Skif slid out of his saddle to let Cymry join them. Wintermoon strolled over, stretching to relieve the inevitable stiffness of riding any distance at all.

"We are at the edge of the territory k'Sheyna still patrols," he said. "After this point, the hazards begin. It may be dangerous to break silence; if I note anything, I shall warn your lady mind-to-mind."

"Why not warn me?" Skif asked, doing his best not to sound sullen, but afraid that some of his resentment showed through anyway.

Wintermoon only looked mildly surprised. "Because I cannot," he replied. "The mind-to-mind speech of the scouts is only between scouts and those who are not human." His brow furrowed as he thought for a moment. "Perhaps you caught the edge of my conversation with Elivan. I apologize if this seemed rude to you, but your Cymry told me that you did not share the Gift of Mindspeech with one other than her—or perhaps another Herald. I thought, then, that you did not hear us." He shrugged, apologetically. "I am sorry if you thought we had left you out a-purpose. Many Tayledras have this Gift, but I am one of the strongest speakers, as was Dawnfire. Sometimes it only extends to bondbirds. I am fortunate that I share my brother's ability to speak with other creatures as well, although I do not share his gift of speaking with other humans."

Skif flushed. That was one possibility that simply hadn't occurred to him—that Wintermoon might not know that he was aware of the conversation without knowing what was being said. *Well, now I feel like a real idiot...*

"Is that what makes the nonmages scouts, and not something else?" he asked, trying to cover his misstep.

Wintermoon shook his head, and smiled. "All Tayledras have mind-to-mind speech, usually only with their bondbirds," he replied. "It is a part of us; one of the many things that the Goddess granted to us to help us survive here, but although those who can speak with other creatures make the best scouts, if they are also mage-born, then mage-craft is oft the course of their life."

Skif looked beyond him for a moment, across the stream. It didn't seem any wilder or more threatening there than it did on this side. Frost had laced the trees on both sides of the stream, perhaps because they were more sensitive to it; the leaves were a yellow-brown, and some had already fallen, carpeting the ground and occasionally drifting off on the current of the brook. Jays called somewhere out there—or at least, something with the same raucous scream as a scarlet jay. A hint of movement on the other side of the water caught his eye, and he turned his head slightly just in time to catch the tail of a squirrel whisking over to the opposite side of the trunk—presumably, with a squirrel attached to it, although if what he'd been told was true, that didn't necessarily follow.

"Just what's so bad out there?" he asked, curiosity overcoming pride. "It doesn't look any different to me, but I wouldn't know what to look for."

"There—not much," Wintermoon replied, scanning the trees and the ground beneath them with eyes that missed nothing. "Farther out—

I've heard there are *wyrsa*, though at this season they do not run in packs. Bears, of course, and Changebears. Treelions and Changelions, wild boars and Changeboars. Perhaps *bukto*, and—"

"Wait a moment," Skif interrupted. Those names—that was something he'd been wanting to ask about, and hadn't had an opening. "Changebears, Changelions, Changeboars—what are you talking about? Darkwind called Nyara a 'Changechild,' does this have anything to do with her?"

"Yes and no," Wintermoon replied maddeningly. Skif stifled his impatience as Wintermoon paused, as if searching for the proper words. "Do you not recall what you were shown by Iceshadow? How magic, uncontrolled and twisted, warped all that it touched here?"

"Yes, but wasn't that a long time ago?" he said, thinking back to those images, strange and only half understood. The part where that bright light had appeared to the Hawkbrothers—he'd understood what the Goddess had asked of them, but he hadn't seen more than that light. Elspeth and the Shin'a'in had plainly experienced more than that.

"Not long enough," the scout replied, looking soberly out at the innocent-looking land beyond the stream. "There was a time when magic in all its 'colors' and 'sounds' worked together. The time we call the Mage Wars shattered that order. The structure of magic—and its energies—were stressed to their limits. In the great disaster that ended the Final War, those bonds were broken. Their crystalline patterns, like branches of light to a mage, became as distorted as pine needles dropped to the ground. And every place they touched, on a scale vaster than we can see, they made the land dangerous, and caused creatures that should never have lived to appear."

Skif shook his head, unable or unwilling to comprehend it. Wintermoon continued.

"When we first came here and established this Vale, the land hereabouts was as fearful as anything you saw before the Lady appeared. We have tamed it somewhat, and it is a fortunate thing that few of the magic-twisted creatures breed true. That also is due in part to Tayledras magery."

"But some do?" Skif asked.

Wintermoon nodded. "Those we call 'Changebeasts.' They plainly have parentage of normal creatures, but they have new attributes, generally dangerous. Changelions, for instance—oft they have huge canine teeth, extending far beyond their jaws, and have a way of being able to work a kind of primitive magic that can keep them invisible even when one looks directly at them, so long as the Changelion does not move. That is... a common Change. Some are unpredictable or unrecognizable." He hesitated, gathering his thoughts. "When the parentage was human, we call the result a 'Changechild.' And—in general—true humans do not—mate with them."

He glanced sideways at Skif, gauging the effect of his words. Skif didn't take offense, but he wasn't going to accept that particular judgment without a fight, either. "Why not?" he asked, bringing his chin up aggressively. "I mean, what's the difference? Who would care?"

Wintermoon sighed. "Because it is said that to mate with a Changechild is the same as mating with a beast, because the Changechildren are one with the beasts." He held up a hand to stop the angry words Skif started to speak. "I only say what is commonly thought, not what I think. But you must know that it *is* the common thought, and there is no escaping it."

Skif frowned. "So most Tayledras would think—if Nyara and I made a pair of it—that I was some kind of deviant?"

The Hawkbrother sighed. "Perhaps fewer in this Clan than in others, but some would. And outside the Clans altogether, among Outlanders who live in Tayledras lands and hold loyalty to us, or among those who trade with us—there would be no escaping it. They would all feel that way to some degree."

So I'll deal with it when—if—it happens. He nodded his understanding, but not his agreement.

Wintermoon continued. "There is another problem as well; there are either no offspring of such a mating, or as often as not, they truly *are* monsters that are less able to reason than beasts. This, I know, for I have seen it. The few children of such a union that *are* relatively whole are like unto the Changechild parent. And that is only one in four."

Not good odds...

Wintermoon flexed his hands. "The likeliest to happen is that there are no children of the union. I would say that is just as well."

"So Nyara is a Changechild," Skif said, thinking out loud. "Just what makes her that, and not some—oh—victim of an experiment by her father on a real human child?"

"That there are things the human form cannot be made to mimic," Wintermoon replied too promptly. "Her eyes, slitted like a cat. Fur-tufts on her ears."

"Oh?" This time Skif expressed real skepticism. "That's not what Darkwind told me. He said that it *was* possible that she'd been modified from a full human. He said that it would take a lot of magic to do it, but that if Falconsbane was using her as a kind of model for what he wanted to do to himself, he might be willing to burn the magic."

"He did?" Skif's assertion caught Wintermoon by surprise. "That— would make things easier." The Hawkbrother chewed his lip for a moment. "That would make her entirely a victim, among other things. That would bring her sympathy."

"I've got another question." Cymry returned from the stream and came to stand beside him; he patted her neck absently. "What if she wasn't a Changechild—but she wasn't a human either?"

Wintermoon shook his head in perplexity. "How could she not be either?"

"If she was someone from a real race of her own—" He chewed his lip, and tried to come up with an example. "Look, you don't call the *tervardi* Changechildren, or the *hertasi*. What makes them different from Nyara?"

"There are many of them," Wintermoon replied promptly. "They breed true; they have colonies of their own kind, settlements."

"So how do you know that there *aren't* settlements of Nyara's kind somewhere?" he interrupted. "You didn't know there were gryphons before Treyvan and Hydona arrived!" He smiled triumphantly.

"Gryphons were upon a list handed down from the time of the Mage Wars," Wintermoon said immediately, dashing his hopes. "As were the others. Every Tayledras memorizes it, lest he not recognize a friend—or foe. There is nothing on that list that matches Nyara."

Well, so much for that idea. At least she isn't on the "foe" list; I suppose I'd better consider us fortunate.

Nevertheless, he couldn't help wondering if there *could* be creatures that were like the *hertasi* that simply hadn't made the all-important list. Or if there were creatures that had developed since the Mage Wars that couldn't have made the list because they hadn't been in existence then...

Oh, this is ridiculous. It doesn't matter what she is. What matters is what she does. Every Herald he'd met had told him that as he grew up in the Collegium. They had been right then; that should hold true now.

"It will be dark, soon," Wintermoon said, glancing at the sky. While they had been talking, the quality of the light had changed, to the thick gold of the moments before actual sunset. Filtered through the golden-brown leaves, the effect was even more pronounced, as if the very air had turned golden and sweet as honey.

"Are we going to camp here, or go on?" Skif asked. The question was pertinent; if this had been an expedition with two Heralds, they would camp now, while there was still light. But it wasn't; Wintermoon had abilities and a resource in his bondbirds that no Herald had.

"We go on," Wintermoon replied promptly. "Although we will feign to make camp. If there is anyone watching us, they will be deceived. Then once true night falls, we shall move on."

It didn't take them long to unload the packs and Cymry's saddle and make a sketchy sort of camp; Wintermoon unstrung and tied out a hammock, and padded it with a bedroll, then produced a second one and guided Skif in setting it up. That done, they cleared a patch of forest floor and built a tiny fire.

As they sat beside the fire, one of the owls lumbered into their clearing, laden with a young rabbit. It dropped its burden at Wintermoon's feet, and before it had taken its perch on his shoulder, the second followed with a squirrel in its talons.

"Well," Wintermoon chuckled, as the second owl dropped its burden beside the first and flew to a perch in the tree above Wintermoon's head, "it seems that my friends have determined that we shall have a meal, at least."

"That's fine by me," Skif said, and grinned. "I was about to dig out those trail rations."

"I thought I heard something growling—I thought it might be a beast in the bushes. 'Twas only your stomach," Wintermoon teased as he began gutting and skinning the rabbit. Both owls hopped down from their perches to stand on the ground beside him, waiting for tidbits.

They took the proffered entrails quite daintily; seeing that, Skif had no hesitation about picking up the squirrel and following the scout's example. When the darker of the two owls saw what he was doing, it joined him, abandoning Wintermoon.

Skif got two surprises; the first, that this little "squirrel" was built more like a rabbit than the scrawny creatures he was used to—and the second, that the owl took so much care in taking its treats from him that its beak never touched his fingers. "Which one have I got?" he asked Wintermoon. "How hungry is he likely to be?"

"K'Tathi," the scout replied without looking up. "The scraps will suffice for now; they will hunt again after we make our second camp, this time for themselves. Give him what you wish to spare from your meal."

Head, entrails, and the limbs from the first joint out seemed appropriate. K'Tathi took everything that was offered with grace, never getting so much as a spot of blood on his gray-white feathers. Skif offered the skin as well, but the owl ignored it, so Skif quickly tossed it into the bushes as he saw Wintermoon do. That would have been foolhardy if they had been planning to stay, for the bloody skins might well attract something quite large and dangerous. But since they weren't—well, there was sure to be something that would find the skin worth eating, and if there *was* someone watching them, possibly following them—

Well, if they try to go for the camp and there's something big, with teeth, still here, they're going to get a rude surprise.

When he finished his task, he once again followed Wintermoon's example and spitted it on a sturdy branch to hold over the fire. Meanwhile, the sun continued to set, the sky above the trees turning first orange, then scarlet, then deepening to vermilion-streaked blue. By the time the meat was done, the sky was thick with stars.

He was halfway through his dinner when Wintermoon said abruptly, "I envy you, did you know that?"

He looked up, a little startled, into the ice-blue eyes of the man across the fire. There was no sign of Wintermoon's dinner, other than the pile of small, neatly stacked bones at his feet, each of them gnawed clean.

What did he do, inhale the thing?

On the other hand—it was in the interest of the scout's survival to learn to eat quickly. No telling when a meal might be interrupted by an uninvited, unwelcome dinner-guest.

"Why?" he asked, puzzled by the question. "What is there about me to envy? I'm nothing special, especially around Heralds."

"My—liaisons—tend to be brief, and informal," the scout replied. "One reason I wished to guide you was because Starspring returned my feathers, and I am at loose ends."

Skif wondered if he should tender sympathy, surmising from the content that "returned his feathers" meant his lover had dissolved the relationship. But Wintermoon evidently saw something of his uncertainty in his expression and shook his head, smiling.

"No, this was not painful. I have no wish to *avoid* the Vale, or her. But I simply have no partner now, and there is no one else I care to partner with at the moment. So I am at loose ends, and would just as soon have other things to think on." He wiped his fingers clean on a swatch of dry grass, and tossed it into the fire. "That is what I envy you, do you see," he said, watching the grass writhe and catch. "Strong feelings. I have never experienced them."

Skif coughed, a little embarrassed. "I don't know that this is anything other than infatuation or attraction to the exotic."

"Still, it is strong," Wintermoon persisted. "I have never felt anything strongly. Sometimes I doubt I have the ability for it."

The statement was offered like a gift; Skif was wise enough to know that when he saw it. He searched his mind for an appropriate response.

:The birds,: Cymry prompted.

"You feel strongly about Corwith and K'Tathi, don't you?" he countered.

Wintermoon nodded slowly as if that simply hadn't occurred to him in such a context.

"Well then," Skif said and gestured, palm upward. "Then I wouldn't worry. You're capable. The way I see it, we all feel strongly about things, we just might not know we do. Valdemar is like that for Heralds; we lay our lives down willingly for our country and Monarch when we must, but most of the time, we just don't think about it. If you encounter someone you *can* feel strongly about, you will. You haven't exactly been given much of a choice of potential mates what with three-fourths of the Clan gone, and your tendency to, well, stay to yourself."

"True." The scout sat back a little, and only then did Skif realize, as he relaxed, that he had been tensed. "My father thinks that being born without the Gift for magery shows a serious lack in me. Sometimes I wonder if I have other, less visible lacks."

Before Skif could change the subject, Wintermoon changed it for him—to one just as uncomfortable. "What do you intend when we find Nyara?" the scout asked, bluntly. "We shall, I promise you. I am not indulging in vanity to say that I am one of the finest trackers of k'Sheyna."

"I—uh—I don't know," Skif replied. "Right now, to tell you the truth, all I'm thinking about is finding her. Once we do that—" He shook his head. "It just gets too complicated. I'm going to worry about it when it happens. What she says and does when we find her will give me my direction."

"Ah," the scout replied, and fell silent.

After all, I spent less than a week in her company, he thought. *I could have been misreading everything about her.*

Except that she had saved his life at the risk of her own. She'd attacked her *own father,* a creature that had held absolute control over her all of her life, and for Skif's sake.

She'd gone after Falconsbane with nothing; nothing but her bare hands—

—or rather, claws—

And thoughts like that made him realize all over again just how alien she was, yet that realization didn't change how he felt in the least. Whatever it was, it was very strong and very real.

What's going to make a difference is what's happened to her—and what happens to us. If she's handling the things her father did to her. And if we can find someplace where people will accept her—and maybe even us.

That place might not be Valdemar; that was something he was going to have to admit. They might not be able to deal with someone who had tufted, pointed ears, catlike eyes, and a satiny-smooth pelt of very, very short fur. It wasn't obvious, but a close examination would show it. The Heralds were open-minded, but were they open-minded enough for *that?* To accept someone who looked half animal?

And he was going to have to go home eventually…

That question kept him thinking until Wintermoon shook his shoulder. After that, he was too busy breaking camp and following the scout through the darkness to worry about anything else. And when they finally made camp again, he was too *tired* to think at all.

5

The two hunters began using a different pattern than a follower might expect; they were on the move from about mid-afternoon to after midnight. With the owls helping him, Wintermoon was completely happy doing most of his scouting after darkness fell, and even Skif's night-vision gradually improved with practice. He would never be Wintermoon's equal, but he grew comfortable with searching the forest in the darkness. There were advantages to this ploy that outweighed the disadvantages; the strongest advantage being that with K'Tathi and Corwith scouting for them, there was nothing that was going to surprise them—and nothing that would be able to follow them easily. Few creatures hunted the night by preference, and those few, though formidable, could be watched for. So for several days, they hunted and camped, and remained unmolested even by insects. But Skif knew that the situation could not last. Sooner or later, they were going to run into one of the kinds of creatures that had driven the Tayledras borders back in the first place. Sooner or later, something was going to come hunting them.

That, in fact, was what he was thinking when they paused along a deer trail, and Wintermoon sent the owls up to quarter the immediate vicinity, looking for disturbed areas or other signs of someone who was not especially woodswise. Cymry began acting a little nervous, casting occasional glances back over her shoulder. But Wintermoon, who was sitting quietly on Elivan, didn't seem to sense anything out of order.

His first real warning that something really was wrong and that Cymry just wasn't being fidgety was when Wintermoon suddenly tensed and flung up his hand, and Corwith came winging in as fast as a slung shot, landing on his outstretched arm, and hissing with fear and anger. Skif held out his hand as Wintermoon had asked him to do if one of the owls ever came in fast and showing distress. K'Tathi arrived a moment later, and K'Tathi hit his gauntleted wrist as if striking prey. It was the first time that the owl had landed on Skif, and nothing in his limited experience in hawking with merlins and kestrels prepared him for the power and the weight of the bird as it caught his wrist and landed. Those thumb-length talons closing—even with restraint—on his wrist could easily have pierced the heavy leather of the gauntlet. They did not, although the claws exerted such powerful pressure that Skif could not possibly have rid himself of the bird short of killing it. K'Tathi hissed angrily, and swiveled his head away from Skif, pointing back the way he had come.

Before Skif could ask what was wrong, Wintermoon cursed under his breath and the *dyheli* stag he rode tossed its antlers and reared, its eyes shining in the moonlight, wide with fear. Wintermoon kept his seat easily, but Corwith flapped his wings wildly to keep his balance.

Tilredan, the second stag, the one laden with their provisions and extra gear, bolted; it was Skif's turn to swear, and not under his breath. But he had reacted too soon; in the next breath, Wintermoon's mount followed the other stag, and Skif only had Cymry's warning Mindcall of *:Hold on!:* before she was hot on his heels.

Hold on? With an owl on one arm?

He dropped the reins—useless in a situation like this one—and grabbed for the pommel of the saddle with his free hand, deeply grateful that he had *not* given in to Wintermoon and exchanged Cymry's old saddle for a Shin'a'in model. Shin'a'in saddles had no pommel to speak of...

K'Tathi continued to cling to his wrist, mercifully refraining from using his wings to keep his balance. One strong buffet to the head from those powerful wings would lay Skif out over Cymry's rump before he knew what had hit him.

Instead, the owl hunched down on the wrist, making himself as small as possible, leaning into the wind of their passing. Skif tried to bring him in close to his body, but he wasn't sure how much K'Tathi would tolerate.

:What in——: Skif began.

:A pack of something, that scented us and is hunting up our backtrail,: Cymry answered shortly. *:Not something we've seen before, but something Wintermoon and the others know. Worse than wolves, worse than Changewolves. And smart—we're running for a place where we can defend ourselves. K'Tathi found it just before Corwith sighted the pack.:*

He could only hope that an owl's idea of what was defensible and theirs was the same; sheer cliffs were fine if you could scale them, and a hole in a tree would be all right if the tree was the size of a house, but otherwise they'd be better off making a back-to-back stand.

And he hoped his idea of "nearby" and the owl's was the same, too.

For behind him, he heard an uncanny keening sound; not baying, not howling, not wailing—something like all three together. The noise gave him chills and made the hair on the back of his neck stand up, and it sounded as if it was coming from at least eight or nine throats. He glanced back over his shoulder and saw nothing, but his imagination populated the darkness. If he heard eight, how many were really in the pack? Twelve? Twenty? *Fifty?*

K'Tathi clutched his wrist a little harder, and the deadly talons pricked him through the leather. This was not a good way to carry the bird, but there was no way to turn K'Tathi loose to fly. The *dyheli* were nearly a match for a Companion in speed, and they were going flat-out; neither owl could have hoped to keep up with them by flying through the canopy, which was why both birds were clinging desperately to their perches on his wrist and Wintermoon's. But K'Tathi, at least, was having a lot of trouble holding on. If the owl exerted a little more pressure—

:Cymry! Can you talk to K'Tathi?: he asked Cymry, frantically.

Her mind-voice was colored with surprise and annoyance at what probably seemed like a supremely inappropriate question. *:Yes, but this is no time—:*

He interrupted her. *:Tell him not to move, I'm going to try something with him, before he goes through my wrist.:*

He pulled his arm to his chest, and brought the bird in close to his body, sheltered against his body. This left the owl unbalanced, with its face shoved against his tunic, but K'Tathi displayed his agility and intelligence; somehow he managed to get himself reversed, so that his head faced forward and his tail and wings were tucked down between Skif's wrist and his chest. Now the bird wasn't having to fight the wind by himself, he was braced against Skif. The painful pressure on Skif's wrist relaxed.

That takes care of one problem.

Cymry's muscles bunched and flexed under his legs, the sound of hooves drowning out anything else except the chilling cries behind them. The wailing behind them seemed closer. Skif didn't ask Cymry if it was; it wouldn't make any difference. They'd either reach safety in time, or not.

He just wished he knew how far it was to that promise of "safety." If he knew, he might be able to guess whether they had any chance of making it, or whether it might be better to turn and make a stand.

And he wished that he had Wintermoon's night-sight, far superior to his own. To him, the moon-filled night was full of shadows his eyes couldn't penetrate. There could be nothing in those patches of darkness, or an enemy, or a hiding place. Though the moon was bright, there were still enough leaves on the trees to keep most of the light from reaching the ground.

The pack behind them cried again; this time there was no doubt in his mind about the peril of their situation. They were closer; if he looked back, he might be able to see them. The brush obscuring the path behind them didn't seem to be slowing the pack at all. In fact, they were probably breaking a trail for the pursuers to follow along. He'd learned long ago that being the pursued in a chase was more difficult than being the pursuer.

He crouched a little lower over Cymry's neck; as low as he could without flattening the owl. K'Tathi seemed to realize what he was doing, and didn't object or struggle, only giving him a warning stab with his talons when he crouched too low for the owl's comfort. Soft feathers pressed against his chin, and K'Tathi hunched down on his wrist so that the bird's chest-feathers warmed his hand.

He glanced up; saw the gray bulk of a rock formation looming ahead of them through the trees. In this light, it looked very like the one in which he and Elspeth had sheltered when they first arrived in Tayledras territory. A moment later, he saw that this one was bisected by a good-sized crack. Just like the one he and Elspeth had used.

He seemed to spend a lot of time hiding in rock crevices lately. Whatever had happened to hiding in rooms, behind drapes, or under furniture?

He had a moment to think—*Oh, no, not again*—and then Cymry braced all four legs for a sudden stop, skidding to a halt beside the *dyheli*. At least the owls did seem to have some idea of what constituted a good shelter for the rest of the party. The crevice would be a little crowded for three plus the two humans, but it was better than facing what howled on their backtrail with nothing to protect their backs!

All three of them crowded into the narrow crevice between two halves of a huge boulder; the rock was easily two stories tall, and the crevice ended in the stone face of a second stone that was even taller. There was barely enough room for Cymry to turn around, but that was fine; less room for them meant less room for those things out there to try to get past them.

A strangled hoot and the booting of K'Tathi's head against his chest reminded him to turn the poor owl loose. He raised his arm and launched it clumsily into the air, thrown off by the confined quarters and the fact that the owl was considerably heavier than a merlin. It wasn't much of a launch, or much help to the owl in gaining the air; K'Tathi hit him in the side of the head with a wing, recovered, and got free of the crevice, just as the pack reached them.

Skif looked up when a note of triumph entered the wailing. A strange, yellowish flood burst through the bushes and into the area around the rocks. *Dear gods*—

He needn't wish for night-sight after all. The damned things glowed. Now that he saw them, he wished, perversely, he didn't have quite such a good view.

They looked—superficially—like dogs; they had the lean, long-legged bodies of greyhounds, the close-cropped ears, the long, snaky tails and pointed muzzles. But their faintly glowing, pale yellow hides were covered with scales, each scale outlined by a darker yellow. Their heads, shaped like an unholy cross between dog and viper, held eyes that burned a sulfurous yellow much brighter than the bodies, and rows of sharply pointed fangs.

They flowed, they didn't run; they drifted to a halt outside the entrance to the crevice and wound around each other in a vicious, impatient, ever-moving tangle. A snarl of ropes, with teeth at one end. A ball of vipers. They confused the eye and baffled the senses with their hypnotic restlessness. Wintermoon slid off the back of his mount; Skif followed his example a moment later.

They couldn't get in; the sharp hooves of Cymry and the *dyheli* bucks awaited them if they tried, not to mention the bows that Skif and Wintermoon unlimbered from the sheaths at each saddle. But those who had taken refuge here couldn't get out, either.

Stalemate.

Skif strung his bow and nocked an arrow to the string, Wintermoon shadowing every movement. *All right, here we are. Now what?*

"What are those things?" Skif asked quietly, as the creatures continued to mill about in front of the crevice. He blinked his vision clear as they blurred for a moment. Was that just his tired eyes acting up, or were they doing it?

"Wyrsa," Wintermoon replied, frowning as he sighted along his arrow. He loosed it in the next moment, but the *wyrsa* that was his target writhed aside literally as the point touched its hide, evading the deadly metal hunting point in a way that Skif would have said was impossible if he hadn't seen it himself. He'd never seen anything move so fast in his entire life.

Wintermoon muttered under his breath; Tayledras words Skif didn't know, but recognized for intention if not content.

The Tayledras nocked another arrow, and sighted, but did not fire. "They have no magic weapons, but they do not tire easily, and their fangs are envenomed," Wintermoon continued, watching as the beasts flowed about each other. "Once set on a quarry, they do not give up. They know how to weave patterns that confuse the eye, and as you see, they are swift, agile. Alone, we do not consider them a great problem, but together in a pack, they are formidable."

"Great," Skif replied, after a moment. "So what do we do about them?"

"We kill them," the Hawkbrother said calmly, and loosed his arrow. This time, although the beast he aimed at evaded the shaft, the one that was behind it could not get out of the way, and took the arrow straight in the chest.

In any other beast, the wound might not have been fatal. There was no blood, and Skif honestly thought the creature was going to shake the strike off, even though it had looked like a heart-shot. But it stood stock still for a moment, jaws opening soundlessly, then toppled over onto its side. The light died from its eyes, and a moment later, the light faded from its hide, until it was a dull gray shape lying on the darker ground, revealed only by the moonlight.

The entire pack surged to one side, leaving the dead one alone. For a moment they froze in place, unmoving and silent.

He thought for a moment that they might prove Wintermoon wrong, that after the death of one of the pack, they might give up and leave their quarry to go its own way.

But then they all turned burning, hate-filled eyes on Wintermoon, then pointed their noses to the sky and howled again.

The sound was much worse at close range; it not only raised the hair on Skif's head, it rang in his ears in a way that made him dizzy and nauseous. The pack of *wyrsa* wavered before his blurring eyes, and he loosed the arrow he had nocked without even aiming it.

Luck, however, was with him. Two of the *wyrsa* dodged aside, accidentally shoving a third into the arrow's path. A second *wyrsa* dropped to the ground, fading as the first had done the moment it dropped. The pack stopped their howling, and tumbled, hastily, out of the way.

They stood near the bushes at the head of the path, this time staring at the cornered quarry. Skif got the feeling that there were cunning minds behind those glowing eyes; minds that were even now assessing all five of them. *Two down—how many to go? I can't make out how many there are of them, they keep blurring together.*

They advanced again, as a body, but with a little more separation between each of the beasts, so that they could dodge out of the way without sending another into the line of fire. He and Wintermoon loosed another five or six arrows each without hitting any more of the beasts. At least they had stopped their howling; Skif didn't think he could have handled much more of that. After the last fruitless volley, Wintermoon nocked his arrow but did not bother to draw it. Instead, he looked out of the corner of his eye at Skif and said, "And have you any notions?"

Skif had been trying to think of something, anything that could be done about the beasts; shook his head, wordlessly. Wintermoon grimaced.

One of the *wyrsa* separated from the pack when they held their fire, and slunk, belly-down to the ground, to stand just in front of the crevice, as if testing them. When they didn't fire on it, another joined it, and another, until all of them had gathered directly before the entrance to their shelter. While they were moving one at a time, Skif got a chance to count them. There were eight in all, not counting the two dead.

He'd gone against worse numeric odds, but never against anything with reactions like these creatures had. *We're rather outnumbered.*

"If this were a tale," he offered, "our rescue would come out of the woods at this point. A herd of *dyheli*, perhaps, something that would come charging up and flatten everything in sight. Or a mage that could kill them with lightning."

"Would that it were a tale," Wintermoon muttered, his eyes following every move the beasts made. "The things move too swiftly to shoot."

If we had a way to distract them, it might be possible to get at some of them before they figured out what we were doing. "Are K'Tathi and Corwith fast enough to avoid those things?" he asked. "Could they—oh, fly down and make strikes at their heads and eyes, keep them busy while we tried shooting?"

Wintermoon shook his head, emphatically.

"No," he replied. "Owls are agile flyers, and silent, not swift. If they were to dive at the *wyrsa*, the beasts would have them. I will not ask them to do that."

Well, so much for that idea. Unless—well, they don't have to dive at them to distract them.

"All right, what about this," he said, thinking aloud. "Can they fly just out of reach, and hiss at them, get them worked up into forgetting about keeping an eye on us, maybe tease them into trying to make strikes even though they're out of reach?"

"Not for long." Wintermoon frowned. "Not long enough for us to pick off all the *wyrsa* with arrows."

"But what if we used the last of the arrows, waited, got the owls to tease them again, then charged them, all of us? Cymry and the *dyheli*, too?" Skif had a good idea that the hooved ones might account for as many as one *wyrsa* apiece—that would leave less for him and Wintermoon. "We can always retreat back here if we have to."

"It is worth a try." Wintermoon left his arrow nocked, but did not sight it. Even as Skif did the same, two ghostly white shapes swooped down out of the dark treetops, hissing and hooting. The *wyrsa* looked up, startled, as the owls made another swoop. At the third pass, even though they were plainly out of reach, the nearness of the owls, and the taunting sounds they made, broke through their control. They turned their attention from their trapped quarry and began lunging upward at the birds.

Wintermoon gave the *wyrsa* a few moments more to fix their attention on the "new" targets—then pulled up his bow and fired his last three arrows, just as fast as he could get them off. Skif did the same.

The *wyrsa* quickly turned their attention away from the owls, but it was already too late. Each arrow had found a mark; two more *wyrsa* lay dead, and four were wounded. It seemed that only a heart-shot was effective in killing them; the wounded *wyrsa* limped, but did not bleed, and in fact took a moment to gnaw off the shafts of the arrows piercing front and hind-quarters.

Now they were even more angry; Skif felt the heat of their gaze as a palpable sensation on his skin, and the hatred in their eyes was easy to read. As he put up his now-useless bow and drew his sword, he thought he read satisfaction in those eyes as well.

Wintermoon drew his sword as well, and K'Tathi and Corwith swooped down again, harrying the *wyrsa* from above, carefully gauging their flights to keep them just barely out of range. Skif would have thought that the ploy wouldn't work the second time, but either the *wyrsa* had not made the connection between the owls and the attack, or now that the last of the arrows was spent, they had reasoned as a human would that the quarry would not be able to use the owls as the cover for an attack.

They grew frustrated by their inability to do anything about the flying pests, and, sooner than Skif would have thought, turned their full attention back to the owls. That was when Wintermoon gave the signal to charge.

Cymry, larger and heavier than the *dyheli*, charged straight up the middle of the pack, striking with forehooves and kicking with hind, before whirling and retreating to the safety of the crevice. The *dyheli* came in on either side, just behind her, and trampled the *wyrsa* that dodged out of the way. They too retreated, as Skif and Wintermoon followed as a second wave, swords out and swinging.

Skif's world narrowed to his enemies and himself; nothing more. As always, fear temporarily evaporated, replaced by a cool detachment that would last only as long as the battle. Talia had told him that he was really temporarily insane when this came over him—as emotionally dead and uncaring as an assassin. He hadn't always been this way, but like so many in Valdemar, the war with Ancar had changed him.

He ducked away from snapping jaws, and decapitated one *wyrsa*. Two more came for him, poisoned fangs gleaming in the moonlight, but one of the *dyheli* got in a kick that distracted the first, and he fatally disemboweled the second when it couldn't limp out of the way fast enough.

Cymry screamed a warning, and he ducked the one that the *dyheli* had kicked; hit it with the flat of the blade, and knocked it into Cymry's path. She trampled it; bones crunched and popped, and a hoof crushed its skull as it snapped at her.

He saw movement out of the corner of his eye, and struck at a third as it jumped for Wintermoon's back. His strike wasn't clean; he only sliced at its foreleg, but that disabled it. Wintermoon finished that one off, and Skif looked around for more of the beasts.

There weren't any more.

"We did it." Skif could hardly believe it. It had happened so quickly—he leaned on his sword, panting, his heart still in his mouth over the near-misses he'd had with the creatures' poisoned fangs. Very near misses; the cloth of his breeches was torn in one place, and his tunic damaged by claws.

"We were lucky," Wintermoon said flatly. "Very, very lucky. Either these were very stupid *wyrsa*, or your tactic took them by surprise. One touch of a fang begins to dissolve flesh far worse than any poisonous serpent. And *wyrsa* often travel in packs twice the size of this one. We would not have defeated a larger pack this easily."

Skif nodded, and the battle fever that had sustained him drained out of him in a rush, leaving him weak-kneed and panting. He cleaned his sword on a handful of dry grass, and sagged against the stones that had sheltered them. "Havens. No, if there had only been one more of those things, I don't think we could have done this. I've never seen anything move as fast as they did." He closed his eyes as a rush of exhaustion hit him.

"I think," Wintermoon said, in a voice as drained-sounding as Skif felt, "that we should camp now."

Wintermoon decreed a fire, after they cleared the carcasses of the *wyrsa* out of the way, pitching them into the forest, upwind of the camp, for scavengers to squabble over. Not the easiest task in the dark; they were heavier than they looked, and their fangs were still deadly and had to be avoided. Then they collected arrows and arrowheads, all that could be found. There were more arrows in their packs, but every arrow was precious, and every broken-off head might be needed. By the time they had the fire going in front of their crevice, there was *something* out there, fighting over the remains with other *somethings*, all of them squalling and barking. Skif wondered how they would dare to sleep; he kept glancing at the forest where the noises were coming from, even though he knew the chances that he'd actually see anything were remote. Hopefully, they hadn't attracted anything *too* large...

"We stay awake until they carry away the remains," Wintermoon said, as if answering his thought. Skif was only startled by it for a moment; he was probably pretty transparent, and Wintermoon had read his expression. "Once the carcasses are gone, the scavengers will go. The fire will keep them away until then. The night-scavengers are cowards, and fear fire. We had best not move away from it."

The Hawkbrother settled down on his blanket roll, got one of his packs and took out a small, fire-blackened pair of pots, and filled both with water from one of their bottles. He looked up to see Skif watching him with puzzlement.

"So long as we are confined to the fire we might as well make use of it," he said. "The owls will only be able to hunt enough to fill *their* bellies; they are too weary to hunt for us tonight. I prefer not to resort to unembellished trail rations if I have any choice at all."

With that, he reached into his pack for a slab of dried venison and a few other things. He broke off bits of meat and dropped them into the first pot, which was already simmering, following that with the multicolored contents of a gray paper packet, and a sprinkling of what looked to be herbs. Into the second pot went more herbs, dried fruit, and several small, round objects that Skif didn't recognize.

"Can I help?" Skif asked. "I should warn you, I tend to ruin anything I cook on my own, but if you keep an eye on me, I should do all right."

The scout chuckled, and handed him a wooden spoon. Skif pulled the edges of his cloak a little closer around his body, and stirred the meat pot as he'd been directed. He was very glad of the fire; now that they weren't moving or fighting, the air, though windless, was very chilly. He expected to see thick frost on the ground in the morning.

"I have needed this myself," Wintermoon said, breaking the silence. "I am often out alone, and the *hertasi* do not care to be outside the Vale or their settlements. My lovers have always been casual, so there has never been anyone to share such—domestic chores with."

"Forgive me if I am stepping beyond the bounds," Skif said, "but I can't imagine why. You seemed popular."

Wintermoon coughed politely. "Well, none of the scouts have felt easy about having long-term affairs with one who hunts the dangerous hours of night by choice, and no woman of the Clans would ever consider a long liaison with a man who has no magic."

"But you have magic," Skif felt moved to protest. "Better than mine, in fact."

Wintermoon shrugged. "It is not magic by Starblade's definition," he said, too casually. "I do not know how these things are reckoned in other Clans, but it is that way in k'Sheyna."

Skif stirred the pot vigorously, and tried to think of a tactful way to approach the subject of Starblade. Darkwind had been so relieved at the release of his father that he was likely to look no further, but Skif did not trust Starblade's ability to assess his own strengths and weaknesses. Tact had never been his strong suit; he finally gave up searching, and tried bluntness instead.

"What do you think of Starblade?" he asked. "Now, I mean—now that he isn't being manipulated. Do you trust him?"

"Much the same as I have always thought of him," came the surprising answer. "Not often, and not a great deal. This revelation has changed very little between Starblade and myself, whatever it has done for Darkwind."

"But—" Skif began. Wintermoon looked up from his task, briefly, and the firelight flickering over his face obscured whatever faint expression it might have held.

"Starblade disassociated himself from me when testing proved me to have no real magic," he said carefully. "Do you really wish to hear this? It is not particularly interesting."

"Why don't you let me judge that?" Skif replied, just as carefully. "It will help me to know k'Sheyna through you."

Wintermoon raised an eyebrow at that, but made no other comment. "So, then," he began. "My mother was a k'Treva mage, who came to k'Sheyna to look for a father for outClan children. She bargained with Starblade for twins, male and female, the male to leave, the female to take back with her. I do not know if my sister had mage-powers, but *I* did not, and I am told I was a great disappointment to my father. *I* did not know that, and I only knew he was my father because I was told, for I scarcely saw him."

"At least you know who yours is," Skif replied, with a bitterness that took him by surprise. "I don't. If I have any sibs, I don't know that, either. Mother never got around to telling me anything; she was too busy teaching me to pick pockets. Then someone decided to get rid of her—a rival thief—and I was on my own."

He snapped his mouth shut, appalled at the way he had simply blurted that out to a near-stranger; things he hadn't told anyone except his dear friend Talia.

"You were a thief? In a city?" Wintermoon seemed more intrigued than anything else. "I should like to hear of this one day. I have never seen a city."

"You haven't missed much," he replied. "Cities aren't all that impressive. And I'd give a lot to have a brother."

Once again, the Tayledras dropped his eyes. All of Wintermoon's apparent attention was again on his half of dinner. "At least I do have Darkwind, that is true. I am actually glad that I am so much older than he; if I had been younger, I would have hated him for stealing Starblade's love and care. But I was old enough to know that what occurred was no one's fault, that without magic, I would never represent anything but failure to Starblade, and that Darkwind was no more to be blamed for that than the magic itself, which declined to manifest in me. Still, I stay away a great deal. It is very easy to find myself envying him, and envy oft turns darker."

He sighed, as Skif nodded. He stared into the fire for a moment and continued. "I think I will never have other than mixed feelings for Darkwind. I do love him. When he was very young, it was easy to love him, for his disposition was sunny, and his mother treated us both as if we were sons of her body. Even as he came into his power, he was not prideful—he rather delighted in the learning, in finding what could be done—in showing it to me, like any young man with a new accomplishment. Magic was like a huge and complex puzzle to him. But at the same time, there was always the envy…"

"I don't see how you could have gotten away from it," Skif put in quietly, hoping he wasn't going to break Wintermoon's mood by speaking. This was instructive; it gave him an idea of how some of the more complex situations in the Clan had evolved.

"Ah, but I am also jealous," Wintermoon said with a lightness that did not in the least deceive Skif. "Darkwind has so many things come easily to his hand, from his bondbird to his magic. Things that I must struggle to achieve, and often have not even a hope of having. Women, for instance. If you have gotten the impression that he could have any partner in the Vale that he chose, you are substantially correct. That is not the least because he was—or is—a powerful mage."

They sat in silence for a while as their dinner cooked, and ate in silence. Finally Wintermoon broke it. "I think, perhaps," he told Skif, slowly, "that I have said too much. You must think badly of me. I do not ordinarily speak of such things even to friends; I cannot think why I did so now."

"Maybe because we're more alike than either of us guessed," Skif replied. "And, if you don't mind, I think I'd like to talk. There's been something bothering me for a long time, and I can't really talk about it to anyone—at home. They wouldn't understand." He looked straight into Wintermoon's eyes. "I think you might."

Maybe it was that Wintermoon was *so* strange—and yet so very like him. Maybe it had something to do with everything the entire Clan had just endured. Maybe it was just time. Skif didn't know, but when Wintermoon nodded, he drew a deep breath and began choosing the simple, painful words to tell the story of his failure.

"You know we are at war with a country to the east of us, right?"

Wintermoon nodded.

"And I told you that I was a thief, once. Well, for a little while, I was working across the Border, because I'm used to doing things that are— outside a Herald's usual skills." He paused for a moment, then continued, keeping his voice as expressionless as he could. "I was supposed to be helping people escape across the Border, and I was working with a series of families that were providing places for escapees to hide as they fled across the country. I lived with one of those families. Hunters, the husband and wife both—he hunted game, she hunted herbs that won't grow in gardens. They had two children, an older boy and a little girl. They were—kind of the family I never had."

Wintermoon nodded knowingly. "As Darkwind's mother played mother to me."

"Exactly." His stomach churned, and a cold lump formed in his throat. "I never thought I'd like living out in the middle of nowhere— and I used to tease them about being backwards—but I kind of got to enjoy it. Then we got a message saying there was someone waiting at the next house in, waiting for me to guide him to the place on the Border. I went and fetched him—and damn if he wasn't *just* like me. Same background, used to be a thief before he joined Ancar's army, all that."

I trusted him. I should have known better, I should have, but I liked him, I trusted him...

"He had to stay a couple of days before it was safe to make the crossing. We talked a lot."

He acted and reacted just like me, teased the kids, helped with the chores—but I should have known, I should have—

"Anyway, it was finally clear, and he went off. I *thought* he made the crossing. I left him, though, because I had to check back with the people he'd stayed with before, bring them some news and money. That was when I found out—"

"That they were no longer there," Wintermoon interrupted. "That the plausible fellow you had trusted was a traitor."

"How did you know?" Skif's jaw dropped, and Wintermoon grimaced.

"Because I am older than you, by more than you know," the Hawkbrother said, gently. "I have seen a great deal. Remember who was the unwitting traitor in *our* midst. To be effective, one who would betray others must be likable and plausible—while all the time actually being something else entirely. He must be a supreme actor, projecting warmth and humanity, while having a cold, uncaring heart. Someone who was a criminal is likely to be all of these." He looked up at Skif, thoughtfully. "I do not think he was likely to have been a thief, though he may well have associated enough with them to have collected the tales he traded with you. He is likelier to have been something darker. I would say, one who kills in cold blood for pay."

Skif blinked, and tried to collect his thoughts. All he could think of to say, was, "How old are you?"

Wintermoon did not seem surprised at the non-sequitur. "You are Darkwind's age, I would guess. I am sixteen summers his senior." He half-smiled, wryly. "It is difficult to determine the age of a Tayledras, even if you are of the Clans yourself."

"Oh." Skif gathered his scattered and perambulatory wits, and continued his story, but this was the most difficult part to face.

"I—I went back, as fast as I could—but—" He swallowed the knot of grief in his throat. He didn't close his eyes; if he had, he'd see them, hanging from the crossbeam of their own barn. See what had been done to them by Ancar's toadies before they were hanged. He still saw them, at night. "The only one left was the little girl; the family had managed to get her out before the troops caught them, and she was hiding in the woods." *Thank the gods, she never saw any of it, never knew what had been done to them.* "I got her across the Border; left her with friends. Then—then I went back. Against orders. The bastard shouldn't have told so many stories; he gave me more clues than he knew, and I *know* cities. I tracked him down."

And I did to him what had been done to them before I killed him.

Wintermoon nodded, and waited.

Skif hesitated, then continued. "Nobody ever said or did anything, even though they must have known what I did. And I'd do it again, I swear I would—"

"But part of you is sickened," Wintermoon said softly. "Because what you did may have been just, in the way of rough justice, but it may have been—excessive." He stared up at the sky for a moment. "It is better to kill cleanly," he said, finally. "If you did not, you are at fault. A creature like the one you described is not sane, any more than Mornelithe Falconsbane is—was—sane. But you do not torment something that is so crazed it cannot be saved; you kill it, so that its madness does not infect you."

Skif was astonished. "After all he did to your people—if you had Falconsbane in front of you now—"

"I would kill him cleanly, with a single stroke," Wintermoon said firmly. "I learned this lesson when I was a little older than you, now—when I visited similar retribution on a very stupid bandit that had been tormenting *hertasi* and killing them for their hides. It does no good to visit torments upon a creature of that nature. It teaches him nothing, and makes your nature closer to his. And that is why you are troubled, Wingbrother. You knew this all along, did you not?"

Skif hung his head, and closed his eyes. "Yes," he admitted, finally. "I did."

Wintermoon sat in silence a moment longer. "For what it is worth," he said finally, "what was done, was done in the heat of anger, and in the heat of anger, one loses perspective—and sanity. *Now* you are sane—and sickened. Do not forget the lesson, Wingbrother—but do not let it eat at you like a disease. Let it go, and learn from it."

Skif felt muscles relaxing that he hadn't known were tensed, and a feeling of profound relief. There. It was out in the open; Wintermoon had guessed most of it without Skif having to go into detail. And the result: he had just discovered he wasn't alone in depravity after all.

"*I visited similar retribution upon a stupid bandit, who had been tormenting* hertasi *and killing them for their hides.*"

He would never have guessed from Wintermoon's serene exterior.

"Others will forgive you this, Wingbrother," the Tayledras said softly, "but only you can forgive yourself. You must never, never forget."

"I won't," Skif promised, as much to himself as to Wintermoon. "I won't..." He shook his head, in part, to clear it. "I—after that, though—I got myself assigned back at the capital. I just lost my taste for adventure."

Wintermoon chuckled. "In that case, Wingbrother, why are you here?"

"I also couldn't resist Elspeth. It's strange how, even if you know inside that there isn't a chance, you'll pursue something anyway because the thought of it is so attractive. I've known it for a long time, but I wouldn't admit it to myself. Elspeth has her own plan for her life, and my role in it is not as her lover. Still, there it is. The only way they were going to let her make this journey was if I came along." He smiled, and shrugged. "But, when this is all over, if I'm given a choice, I'd like to have a place like that family had. For me… or maybe for their memory." Skif pursed his lips, then looked back up at Wintermoon. "Oh, I'd probably be awful at country living—I'd probably have everyone in the county laughing at me, but it would be good trying. I know I'd like to have a home. A family." He smiled, a little wistfully. "Nobody at Haven would believe that of me."

"You have seen enough blood, enough death," Wintermoon surmised. "You fought in battles, as a soldier?"

"Yes." Once again he was amazed at Wintermoon's insight. Or was it something more? "Are you talking with Cymry?"

The other man nodded, and poked at the fire.

:I told him only a few things.: Cymry didn't sound at all apologetic. :When you started talking to him and it looked like you were going to talk about That—I prompted him a little.:

:Why?: He wasn't angry, not really; Cymry was in and out of his thoughts so much she was part and parcel of him. She was his best and dearest friend; he loved her so deeply that he would sooner cut off his arm than lose her. And if he knew nothing else, he knew that she would never, ever do anything to harm him in any way. She had been a part of the revenge scheme, although she had not known his plan until he'd ambushed the bastard and begun. And even then, she kept silent after her initial protests. He didn't think she'd even betrayed his secret shame to other Companions. So why reveal it now?

:Because I thought it sounded and felt like you were ready to speak, and he was ready to hear,: she replied, matter-of-factly. :And as much as being ready to speak, you were ready to listen. Was I wrong?:

He shook his head. :No. No, you were right. Thank you, love.:

Wintermoon sat quietly through the silent exchange, and watched Skif and Cymry alternately. When the Companion nodded, he sighed, and smiled thinly. "I hope you are not angered with us," he said, in half apology. "You see, I had a similar discussion after *my* ill-conceived vengeance, with Iceshadow. He is not a Mind-Healer, but he is closer to being one than he thinks. He has the insights, at least."

The Hawkbrother fixed him with a penetrating stare. "I will tell you this, out of my own experience. Although you feel relief now, this is likely to be the source of many sleepless nights for you. You will lie awake, look upon your heart, and find it unlovely. You will be certain that, regardless of what I have said, you are the greatest of monsters. This is a good thing; although you may forgive yourself, you must never come to think that your actions were in any way justifiable. But—" He chuckled, ironically. "As Iceshadow told *me*, being a sane, honorable human is not always *comfortable.*"

:He should go set up shop on a mountaintop somewhere,: Cymry said. *:He'd make a prime Wise Old Teacher. He's already got the part about tormenting the students down perfectly.:*

Wintermoon drew himself up and stared at her in mock affrontery. "I heard that," he protested.

:I meant you to.:

Skif grinned, and the grin turned into a yawn. Wintermoon caught it, and pointed an admonishing finger at him.

"We still have work ahead of us, and that work requires rest. As you *both* know." He spread out his bedroll by way of making an example, and climbed into it. "Stars light your path, Wingsibs," he said pointedly, and made a show of turning on his side and closing his eyes. *"Wyrsa* have no respect for crisis of conscience."

Well, that about sums the evening up, he thought as he rolled out his own bedroll and crawled into its warmth. And then he thought nothing more, for sleep crept up and ambushed him.

6

Nyara slicked back her sweat-soaked hair, hardly feeling the cold as the chill breeze dried her scalp. She licked salt from her lips and crouched in the shelter of the bushes for a moment, surveying the open expanse of cracked and crazed pavement that kept the forest from encroaching on the foot of her tower. Though the stones were fragmented, even melted in places, they must have been incredibly thick, for nothing but grass grew in the cracks. It looked similar in construction to the ruins around the gryphons' home, though the tower's age and makers were unknown to her.

There was no sign of anything waiting for her, but she had learned to leave subtle telltales, things easily disturbed by interlopers. The "random" lines of gravel, for instance; not so random, and placed so that one or more of them would be scuffed by anyone crossing the paving. The faint threads of shields that would vanish if breached—or, just as importantly, if even touched by a mage's probing. With her feeble command of magic, she could scarcely hope to build a shield that would hide her presence from a greater mage, so she didn't even try. Instead, she concentrated on things that would let her know if she had been discovered, so that she had the time to run and hide somewhere else.

But once again, her refuge seemed secure; the threads were still in place, the pavement clear. Nevertheless, she stayed in the shelter of the evergreen bushes, and sent a careful probe up into the heart of her shelter.

:Well?: That was all she Mindsent. Anything more could reveal her location to lurkers. There were creatures—some of them her father's—that were nothing more than compasses for the thoughts of those who could Mindspeak. Normally only the one Spoken to could Hear, but these creatures could Hear everything, and could follow the thoughts of a Mindspeaker from leagues away.

:All's clear,: came the gravelly reply. *:Come on up, kitten. I trust you had good hunting.:*

Now she relaxed; nothing got past her teacher. *:Quite good,:* she replied shortly. *:No visitors?:*

:None,: came the answer. *:Unless you count our daily cleanup committee.:*

She would have worried if *they* hadn't shown up. Anything bad enough to frighten off a vulture was a serious threat indeed. *:I'm coming up,:* she Sent, and only then arose from her shelter, pushing through the bushes and trotting out into the open—as always, with a thrill of fear at leaving her back exposed to the forest, where someone *else* could be lurking.

She padded quickly across the paving, taking care to avoid her own traps. The less she had to redo in the morning, the sooner she would be able to get out to hunt. The sooner she got out to hunt, the more practice she would have. She was under no illusions about her hunting successes; the colder the weather grew, the scarcer the game would become, and the harder it would be for her to catch it. She had never truly hunted for her meals before this, and was no expert. She was lucky; lucky that game was so abundant here, and lucky that she was getting practice now, while it *was* abundant, and a miss was not nearly so serious as it would be later in the winter.

The wall of her tower loomed up before her, the mellowed gray of weathered granite. The tower had that look about it of something intended to defend against all comers. She took the neck of the pheasant she had caught in her teeth, and set her finger- and toe-claws into the stone, and began climbing. The scent of the fresh-killed bird just under her nose made her mouth water. Just as well there had been no blood, or she would have been in a frenzy of hunger.

As she climbed, it occurred to her that it was not going to be pleasant, if indeed *possible*, to make the climb in winter. Ice, snow, or sleet would make the rock slippery; cold would numb her hands and feet. The prospect daunted her.

Well, no point in worrying about it now; truly dismal weather was still a few weeks off, and anyway, there was nothing she could do about it at the moment. Not while she was clinging to sheer stone, three stories above the pavement, with another to go.

Perhaps a ladder, like the Tayledras outside the Vale use for their treehouses. True, she did not have a bird to let the ladder down for her, or to hide the line that pulled it up, but she had magic. Not much, but she was learning to use every bit of what she had, and use it cleverly. A bit of magic could take the end of such a ladder up, and drop it down again when she returned.

So many trips up and down that stone had taught her where all the holds were, and now she didn't even need to think about where she was putting her hands and feet. This was the most vulnerable moment in her day—this, and the opposite trip in the morning. There was a staircase up the inside of the tower, but although it looked sound, appearance was very deceptive. It was, in fact, one more of her traps and defenses, and anyone chancing it would find himself taking a two- or three-story drop to the ground, depending on how far he got before the weakened stone gave way beneath him.

But then, she privately thought that anyone trusting his weight to an unproven stair—in a ruined tower, no less—probably deserved what he found.

Her mind wandered off on its own, planning lightweight ladders and imagining what she might use to make them, discarding idea after idea. She came to the conclusion that she might be trying to make things a little *too* elaborate; after all, by virtue of her breeding she was a much better climber than the best of the Tayledras. A simple, knotted rope might serve her better.

At that point, her hand encountered the open space of her window, and she grasped the sill with both hands, and hauled herself up and over the stone slab. She swung her legs inside and dropped down to the floor, crouching there for a moment. She took the pheasant out of her mouth and grinned, as her teacher and weapon growled in her mind *:I hate it when you do that. You look like a cat that's just caught someone's pet bird.:*

"But it is not a pet bird, Need," she replied pertly. "It is my dinner."

:So is the pet bird for the cat,: the sword said, *:But nobody ever asks the bird how it feels about the situation.:*

She sat down cross-legged on the bare stone of the floor, and began industriously plucking her catch. "If it gets caught, it deserves to get eaten," she told the sword.

:You stole that from the Hawkbrothers.: Need accused.

She shrugged. "So? That does not make it less true. And like all Hawkbrother sayings, it is double-edged. If it gets caught, it *deserves* to be eaten—to be appreciated, used entirely and with respect, and not robbed of something stupid, like a tail-feather, and discarded as useless. I honor my kill, and I am grateful that I caught it. If it has a soul, I hope that soul finds a welcome reward."

Need had nothing to say in reply to that. Nyara smiled, knowing that "no comment" was usually a compliment of sorts.

She put the best of the feathers aside; the large, well-formed ones she would use to fletch arrows, the rest would go to stuff her carefully-tanned rabbit hides. Need had been teaching her a great deal; she had come to this tower with nothing but a knife she had filched from Skif and the sword. Now she had clothing made from the hides of animals she had caught; a bed of furs from the same source, with pillows of fur stuffed with feathers on a thick pallet of cured grasses. And that was not all; over in the corner were the bow and arrows Need had taught her to make and was teaching her to use. Need had already taught her the skills of the sling she had used to take this pheasant.

The sword had also unbent enough to conjure—or steal by magic—a few other things for her, things she couldn't make herself. Not many, but they were important possessions; a firestarter, four pots, three waterskins and a bucket, one spoon, a second knife, and a coil of rope. The latter was precious and irreplaceable; she had used it only to haul heavy game and her water up the side of her tower.

:Are you going to eat that raw?: Need demanded. She licked her lips thoughtfully; she was very hungry and had been considering doing just that. But the way the question had been phrased—and the fact that her teacher had asked the question at all—made her pause.

"Why?" she asked. "Is there something wrong with that?"

If the sword could have moved, it would have shrugged. *:Not intrinsically,:* Need replied. *:But it gives the impression that you are more beast than human. That is* not *the impression we are trying to give.:*

Nyara did not trouble to ask just who would be there to observe her. True, there was no one except herself and her mentor at the moment, but she sensed that Need did not intend either of them to be hidden away in the wilderness forever.

She doesn't want me to seem more beast than human. Need had been trying to reverse the physical changes Nyara's father had made to her; now she had an inkling of why. Need wanted to make her look…

Less like an animal. Perhaps she should have been offended when that thought occurred to her, and she was, in a way, but rather than making her angry with Need, it made her angry at her father. *He* was the one who had made so many changes to her body and mind that Need had been incoherent with rage for days upon discovering them. *He* was the "father" that had made her into a warped slave, completely in thrall to him, often unable even to act in her own defense.

Need had done her best to reverse those changes; some she had, but they were all internal. There was no mistaking her origin; the slitted eyes alone shouted "Changechild."

If the world saw a beast—the world would kill the beast. It was not fair, but very little in Nyara's life had ever been fair. At least this was understandable. Predictable.

Mornelithe Falconsbane had never been that, ever.

No one was here to see her now except Need, but when she finished plucking the pheasant, instead of tearing off a limb and devouring it raw as her stomach demanded, she gutted and cleaned it as neatly as any Tayledras hunter or *hertasi* cook, and set it aside.

She tried not to think about how loud her stomach was complaining as she uncovered the coals in her firepit and fed them twigs until she had a real flame. Once she had a fire, she spitted her catch, and made a token effort to sear it.

Once the outer skin had been crisped, she lost all patience; she seized the spit and the bird, and began gnawing.

Need made an odd little mental sound, and Nyara had the impression that she had winced, but the sword said nothing, and Nyara ignored her in favor of satisfying her hunger.

But when she had finished, sucking each bone clean and neatly licking her fingers dry, the blade sighed. *:Tell me how the hunt went,:* she said. *:And show me.:*

"I saw the cock-pheasant break cover beside the stream," she said, picturing it clearly, as she had been taught. "I knew that the flock would be somewhere behind him…"

The stalk had taken some time, but the end of the hunt came as swiftly as even Need could have wanted. She had lost only one of her carefully rounded shot, which splintered on a rock, and took one of the juvenile males with the second. She felt rather proud of herself, actually, for Need was no longer guiding her movements in hunting, or even offering advice. Although the blade could still follow her mentally if she chose, it was no longer necessary for her to be in physical contact with her bearer to remain in mental contact.

When Nyara had fled from the Tayledras as well as her father, she had no clear notion of where she was going or what she would do. She had only known that too many things were happening at once, and too many people wanted her. Their reasons ran from well-intentioned to darkly sinister, and *she* had no real way of telling which from which. So she ran, and only after she had slipped out of Darkwind's ken had she discovered herself in possession of Elspeth's sword. She honestly had no memory of taking it; the blade later confessed to having influenced her to bear it off, making her forget she had done so.

At first she had been angry and afraid, expecting pursuit; the blade was valuable enough that her father had wanted it very badly. But pursuit never came, and she realized that Elspeth was actually going to relinquish the blade to her. Such unexpected generosity left her puzzled. It would not be the last time that she was to be confused over matters in which Need was involved.

Nyara had found the tower after a great deal of searching for a defensible lair. Need had rebuilt the upper story with her magic, strengthening it and making it habitable. It still looked deserted, and both of them had been very careful to leave no signs of occupancy. Any refuse was taken up to the flat roof and left there; vultures carried off bones and anything else edible, and the rest was bleached by the sun and weathered by wind and rain. Eventually the wind would carry it away, and it would be scattered below with the dead leaves.

:You're doing well,: the sword said, finally. *:Even if you do eat like a barbarian. I don't suppose table deportment is going to matter anytime soon, though.:*

Nyara was silent for a moment; now that her stomach was full and the little chamber warmed by the fire, she had leisure to consider the blade's remarks, and feel a bit of resentment. Nyara appreciated all that Need had done for her, attempting to counter the effects of twenty years of twisting and abuse, teaching her what she needed to survive. Still, sometimes the sword's thoughtless comments hurt.

"I'm not a barbarian," she said aloud, a little resentfully. "I've seen Darkwind bolt his meals just like I did."

:Darkwind is fully human. You are not. You are clever, intelligent, resourceful, but you are not human. Therefore you must appear to be better than humans.:

Once again, Nyara was struck by the injustice of the situation, but this time she voiced her protest. "That's not *fair*," she complained. "There's no reason why I should have to act like some kind of—of trained beast to prove that I'm just as human as anyone else!"

:You were *a trained animal, Nyara,:* Need replied evenly. *:You aren't any longer. And we both know why.:*

Nyara shuddered, but did not reply. Instead, she cleaned up the remains of her meal, saving a few scraps to use as fishing bait on the morrow, and took everything up to the roof. As Need had mentioned, the vultures had been there already; there was little sign of yesterday's meal.

Although the wind was cold, Nyara lingered to watch the sunset, huddled inside her crude fur tunic with her feet tucked under her. Need was right. She *had* been little more than a trained animal. Her father had controlled her completely, by such clever use of mingled mind-magic, pain and pleasure that a hint of punishment would throw her into uncontrollable, mindless lust, a state in which she was incapable of thinking.

Need had freed her from that; Need had worked on her for hours, days, spending her magic recklessly in that single area, to heal her and release her from that pain-pleasure bondage. Need had watched the nomad Healer working on the Tayledras Starblade from afar, studying all that the woman did and applying the knowledge to Nyara.

In this much, she was free; she would no longer be subject to animal rut. Although Need had not been able to "cure" her tufted ears, pointed canines, or slit-pupiled eyes, the blade had put *her* in control of her emotional and physical responses.

Must I really be more than they are to be accepted as an equal? Nothing less would do, according to Need, and as she watched the stars emerge, she came to the reluctant conclusion that the blade was right. She *had* to be accepted as at least an equal to claim alliance with the Hawkbrothers. She needed them, and knew it, although they did not yet know how much they needed her. She had information that would be very useful to them, even if some of it was information they might have to get at using Need's mind-probing tactics. She would gladly submit to that, to have their protection.

But to earn that, did she have to give up what she was, to take on some kind of mask of what *they* considered civilized? That simply wasn't fair, not after everything she had already been through! What Falconsbane had done—she didn't want to think about. And under Need's tutelage, she had not only undergone the pain that preceded Healing, but nightly—and sometimes daily—vision-quests. She had to admit there was one positive result of that; her real dreams were no longer haunted, and her nightmares had vanished completely. The sword was as hard a teacher as she could have imagined, driving her without allowance for weakness. Not only did she take Nyara through trials in her dreams, and teach her the skills that helped her survive on her own, but she launched Nyara like an arrow against whatever target she deemed suitable, giving her lessons in real combat as well as practice. Nyara had already defeated a wandering bandit and a half-mad hedge-wizard. Both had been left for the vultures when they had seen only a female alone, and attempted to take her. In both cases, Need had ultimately taken command of her body, as soon as she reckoned that Nyara had gone to the very edge of her abilities, and moved her with a skill she did not, herself, possess. There would, doubtless, be more such in the future. So why must she prove that she was something other than she was to be accepted?

No, she decided as she watched the moon rise above the horizon. It was *not* fair. Need wanted too much of her.

She descended to her tower-top chamber only to find the fire burning down to coals and the sword silent. She watched it for a moment, then shrugged philosophically and heated just enough water for a sketchy sort of bath. One advantage of her breeding, besides her owl-keen nightsight, was that the pelt of very short, very fine fur that covered her body made bathing less of a chore than it was for full humans. And one had to be very, very close to her to learn that it was fur, and not just smooth skin. She wasn't entirely certain that either Skif or Darkwind had figured it out. Well—perhaps Skif had. He hadn't seemed to mind.

Morning would arrive far too early. Although she intended to fish and not hunt, it would still be better to do so in the early morning when the fish were hungry. So as soon as she had cleaned herself, she banked the fire, and crawled into her bed of furs.

Only then did Need speak, just as she was falling asleep.

:Let's explore that business of "fair,": the sword said, with deceptive mildness. *:Shall we?:*

Nyara was no longer Nyara; no longer a Changechild. In fact, she was no longer in the world or the body she knew.

Except that she *was* Nyara; she was herself and someone else, too. She relaxed; this was something she had experienced in Need's dream-quests many times, although this was someone she'd never been before. Then she realized that this was different; strange, in a way she could not quite describe. This life—was ancient, heavy with years, and faded. She felt the experience as if through a series of muffling veils, each of which was a century.

Her name was Vena; she was once a novice of the Sisterhood of Spell and Sword. Now she was alone, except for the sword that had once been her teacher, the Mage-Smith Sister Lashan—and ahead of her was an impossible task.

A mage that Lashan identified as Wizard Heshain had come to the enclave of the Sisterhood with an army of men and lesser mages, capturing the Sisterhood's mage-novices and slaughtering everyone else. Vena had escaped mostly by luck, and by hiding in the forest surrounding the enclave until they all left. She had thought she was completely alone until Sister Lashan had come riding up, returning from her yearly trip to the trade-markets where she sold her bespelled blades to weapons' brokers to profit the Sisterhood.

When she saw her teacher, she'd had no thought but to escape with her to somewhere safe. But Lashan had other ideas.

She had questioned Vena very carefully, probing past the girl's hysteria to extract every possible detail from her. Then she had sat in silence for a long, long time.

Her decision had not been the one that Vena had expected; to make their way to some other temple of the Twins, and seek shelter there, since it was plainly impossible for anyone to rescue the captured novices from such a powerful mage-lord. Sister Lashan had told her stunned apprentice that they—the two of them—were going to rescue their captive Sisters. She admitted that she did not know what he planned to do with the novices exactly—mostly because there were so many things he *could* do with a collection of variously mage-talented, untrained, mostly virginal young women. But all of the fates she outlined to her apprentice were horrible. Eventually, even Vena had to agree. They could not leave their Sisters in Heshain's hands.

Rescue *was* possible. Especially if rescue could come before the caravan reached Heshain's stronghold. But there was no time to gather another small army to rescue them, assuming that anyone could be found willing to commit themselves and their troops against a mage like Heshain.

That had left only Vena and Sister Lashan, who had decided, unbeknownst to her bewildered apprentice, that her old, worn-out human body was just not going to be up to the task. So instead, she had chosen a new one; a body of tempered steel. A sword, to be precise; a bespelled blade, the kind she had been teaching Vena to make.

Vena was still not certain how Sister Lashan, who had ordered her to forget that name and call her "Need" now, had ensorceled herself into the blade. She wasn't certain that she *wanted* to know. It had certainly involved the death of the mage herself, for she had found the Sister spitted on her own sword. She had thought that despair had overcome her mentor, and had been overwhelmed with grief—when the sword spoke into her mind.

Now she was on the trail of Heshain and his minions, armed with a blade she scarcely knew how to use, ill-provisioned, and without the faintest idea of what she was doing. And winter was coming on. In fact, since the trail led northward, she would be walking straight into the very teeth of winter.

But if she did not try to do something, no one would. She had no choice. No choice at all.

All this, she knew in an instant, as if she had always known it. And then, she was no longer aware of Nyara—only of Vena. Only of a moment that was dim and distant, and yet, now.

Vena crouched above the road, belly-down in the snow, and tried to think of nothing. There was no sign that Heshain had any Thought-seekers among his men—but no sign that he didn't, either. Despite her wool and fur-lined clothing, she was aching with

461

cold. It had been a very long time since she'd last dared to light a fire, and she couldn't remember when she'd last been warm.

She was hungry, too. The handful of nuts and dried berries she'd eaten had only sharpened her appetite. And down below her was everything she craved. Shelter, a roaring fire, hot food—

Trouble was, it was all in the hands of the enemy.

And the enemy wasn't likely to share.

She Felt Sister Lashan—or rather, Need—studying the situation through her eyes. She wasn't certain how Need felt about it, but it looked pretty hopeless from here. The group that had captured the novices seemed to have divided up. This was the hindmost bunch, and the girls they guarded seemed to be the ones in the worst shape. Most were in deep shock; some were comatose, and carried on wagons. The rest hardly seemed aware of their surroundings. None of them were going to be of any help at all—at least, not until Vena could physically get Need into their hands, for contact-Healing was one of Need's abilities. But that could only happen after they were rescued, and not before.

So just how was one half-trained Mage-Smith apprentice going to successfully take on twenty or more well-trained fighters?

:Cleverly, of course,: *Need's voice grated in her mind.*

:There are twenty or more tired, bored, careless males down there. What do you think would distract them the most?:

"Women?" she whispered tentatively, thinking of conjuring an illusion of scantily clad girls, and getting into the camp under the cover of the excitement. But then what? The illusion wouldn't hold past the first attempt to touch one of the girls, unless Need could somehow make it more than mere illusion—

Her teacher made a mental sound of contempt. :And a troupe of dancing girls rides up out of nowhere. I don't think so, dear. These are also seasoned fighters; they're suspicious of anything and everything. Try to think like one of them. Look at their camp; what are they doing?:

As if she hadn't been doing just that, ever since they cleared a space for the first tent, and freezing her rear off too. "They're eating," she offered tentatively.

:Closer. What are they eating?:

Vena's mouth watered as she stared down at the fire. "Looks like winter-rations. Beans and bread, I think." Oh, she would gladly have killed for some of those hot spiced beans and a piece of bread.... "I don't see—"

:Meat, Vena. They don't have any. They're on winter-rations, and they haven't been allowed time to hunt, so they don't have any meat. And these are fighters; they're used to having it. They don't seem to have any wine, either, but I can't think of a way to get that to them without making them suspicious of their good fortune. Back down the ridge, slowly. I'm going to try calling in an elk. I used to be good at this.:

In the end, it was a deer Need managed to attract, and not an elk, but in all other ways it was precisely what she wanted. Old, with broken antlers, already looking thin this early in the winter, the aged animal would not have outlasted the snows. Vena followed her directions carefully, as they poisoned the poor beast by means of counter-Healing, hamstrung one leg, as if it had just escaped from a wolf, and drove it over the ridge and down into the enemy camp.

The men there fell on the weakened beast, seeing only their good luck, and never thinking that there might be something wrong with it other than exhaustion and injury. The toxin Need had infused into the deer's blood and flesh was only slightly weakened by cooking. A clever poison, there was little or no warning to the victims of their fate; most ate, fell asleep, and never woke. By daybreak, all twenty men were dead or dying—and Vena came down into the camp to dispatch the dying, and found herself in charge of eleven of her fellow novices.

Not one of whom could be trusted even to look after the others, much less find her own way back to safety.

Confidently, she turned to Need for advice.

:Damned if I know what to do with them,: *the blade replied.* :I can Heal their injuries, but the rest is up to you. Demonsbane, girl, I only made blades before I made myself *into* one! You're the one with the hands and feet, and they know *you*, they probably never even met me! I'm fresh out of clever ideas. Time for you to come up with one or two.:

So it was up to Vena to deal with the girls; to try to rouse some of them from their apathy, and to figure out what to do with the rest. And to drag the bodies of the poisoned fighters out of the camp, to get her eleven charges fed and sheltered, to make sure the horses were tended to.

It was nothing less than hard labor, although she gave herself a selfish moment to build the fire back up, and warm herself by that fire until her bones no longer ached. Then she took a little more time to stuff herself on the bread and oat porridge (not beans, after all) that was cooking over the fire—avoiding the charred venison and the pot of venison stew.

She freed the novices from their cages in the four prison wagons, but most of them didn't recognize her, and the ones that did reacted to her as if they'd seen a ghost— terrified and huddling speechless in the corners. She tried not to look too closely at them after the first encounter; the girl wasn't one she had known, but her eyes were so wild, and yet so terrified, that she hardly seemed human anymore.

She led the girl, coaxingly, away from there, across the snow, and into the only wagon without bars and chains; the one that held the provisions. When she offered the girl a blanket, taken as an afterthought from one of the bedrolls beside the fire, the poor child snatched it from her, and went to hide in the darkest corner of the wagon.

She repeated the process until she got them all herded into the wagon, where they huddled together like terrified rabbits, their eyes glinting round and panic-stricken from the darkness of the back.

During the long process of getting her former fellow students into the provision wagon, she'd tossed out everything else that had been in there. Now, in the last of the daylight, she sat on a sack of beans and went through everything she had thrown on the ground, and all the personal belongings that were still in the camp. She felt very strange, rifling through other peoples' possessions, at least at first. But soon sheer exhaustion caught up with her and she no longer saw them as anything other than objects to be kept or discarded in the snow. Blankets went straight into the wagon behind her; hopefully, the girls still had enough wit left to take them. The best blankets she kept for herself, as well as enough food for the girls for a few days more, and in a separate pack, provisions for herself.

Finally, the unpleasant job she had been avoiding could be put off no longer. She tethered all the horses next to the wagon, then harnessed up one, the gentlest, the one she had marked for her own. Trying not to look at the bodies of her former enemies, she threw a hitch of rope around their stiffening feet, and towed them one by one to a point far beyond the camp, leaving them scattered around a tiny cup of a valley like dolls left by a careless child.

Then she returned to the shelter of the wagon, and the non-company of her charges. All of that work had taken another precious day. She got the girls fed and bundled up in blankets as best she could, spending a sleepless night listening to the screams of scavengers when they found the bodies, and making sure none of the eleven wandered off somewhere on her own. It was, possibly, worse even than the nights she had spent waiting for the raiders to return.

In the end, it was the horses that gave her the idea of how to move them, and what to do afterward. Vena was a country girl; where she came from, a horse was a decent dowry for any girl. A pair of horses apiece ought to be enough to pay for their care until someone could come get them, later.

She roused six of the girls to enough self-awareness and energy that they could cling to the saddle-bow of a horse—even if half the time they stared in apathy, and the other half, wept without ceasing. The other five she put in one wagon, with the rest of the horses following behind, tethered in a long string. Then she coaxed Need into using her magic to find the nearest farm. It proved to be a sheep-farmer's holding rather than a true farm; hidden away in a tiny pocket-valley, she would never have found it if not for Need.

To the landowner she told the truth—but cautioned him to tell any other inquirers a tale she and Need concocted, about a plague that caused death and feeble-mindedness, killing all the men of a village where she had relatives, and leaving only the healthiest of the girls alive. She offered him the entire herd of horses (save only the one she had chosen for herself) to tend to the novices. Her only other condition was that as soon as possible he was to send a message to the nearest temple of the Twins, telling what had happened and asking for their aid for the girls.

As she had expected, the offer was more than he could possibly refuse, and when Need read his thoughts to be certain he would keep the bargain, she found no dishonesty. Winter was an idle time for farmers and herders; he had a houseful of daughters and servants to help tend the girls. And sons to find wives for… it would be no bad thing to have a mage-talented girl for a bride for one of his boys. Such things tended to breed true even if shock made the girl lose her own talent, and a man could do much worse than have a wife who could work bits of magic to help protect herself and her home, and to enrich the family, if she was able to keep practicing. Hedge-wizardry and kitchen-witchery was easy to learn; it was having the power to make it work that was granted to only a few.

She agreed on their behalf that if any of them chose to stay with him and his boys, there would be no demands for reparations from the Sisterhood. Then she saddled and mounted her horse, and turned back to the hunt.

They were now weeks, not days, behind the enemy, but he was burdened with wagons and hysterical girls, and Vena was alone, and now a-horse. As she turned her mare's head back along the trail, Need finally spoke.

:Demonsbane, girl! Why didn't you put that fatuous sheep-brain in his place? Brides for his sons—what did he think you were, some kind of marriage-broker? And where did he ever get the idea any of them would want to live out their lives making hero-charms and tending brats and lambs?: *The sword grumbled on, for a while, and Vena let her. The novice had plenty of other things to think about; most notably, finding the now-cold trail of the rest of the captives. It wasn't easy, not with two weeks' worth of wind and weather eating at the signs.*

But she had the right gear for the job, at last. Sheepskin boots and coat, woolen leggings, sweater and cotton undertunic. And all the provisions and equipment she needed.

Or at least, all that she needed until the next encounter.

But she told herself she wasn't going to think about that until it happened.

Finally she found the track, half-melted prints of hooves and wagon-wheels in the snow, and Need finally finished venting her spleen.

Vena waited for a moment, both to be sure she had the trail and to be certain Need was talked out. "Look," *she pointed out,* "after everything those girls have been *through, one or more of them are bound to change their minds about a life dedicated to High Magery and the Sisterhood. That farmer was trustworthy and kindhearted; not a bad thing in a father-in-law. And the boys were a little rough around the edges, but no worse than the lads in my home village. You and I can never give back what those girls—our Sisters—have lost, but we can at least give them options."*

Need stayed silent for a moment. :You could be right,: *she finally said, grudgingly.* :I don't like it, but you could be right.:

Vena decided not to tell her that she was having second thoughts, herself… she doubted she'd survive long enough to consider being a farmer's wife. Right now, despite this early success, she wasn't going to give herself odds on that.

Nyara woke with the sun in her eyes, and for a moment, her arms and legs still ached with that long-ago cold; her hands expected to encounter those heavy blankets instead of furs, and she was exhausted with a phantom weariness that vanished as soon as she realized who she was, and where.

Phantom weariness was replaced by real weariness. She lay where she was for a moment, despite her resolution of the night before to get up early to fish. Dream-quests did not, as a rule, leave her tired. Nor did they leave her feeling a weight of years…

:*That's because I never took you back so far before,*: Need said, and it seemed as if the sword was just as tired as her student. :*I've granted you what I seldom grant my bearers; now you know the name I had forgotten, my name as a human.*:

But that wasn't what mattered to Nyara; suddenly she sat bolt upright and stared at the sword leaning against the wall with a feeling of anger and betrayal. "You didn't help her!" she accused. "You didn't help her at all!"

:*I did what I could,*: the blade replied, calmly. :*I was new to my form and my limitations. I had as much to learn as she did, but I didn't dare let her know that, or her confidence would have been badly undermined. I've had a long, long time to learn more of magic, Nyara. I didn't know a fraction then of what I know now.*:

Nyara stared at the sword propped in the corner, aghast. "You mean—you did not know what you were doing?"

:*Oh, I knew what I was doing. I was herding us both into trouble. But what else was I going to do? There were all those youngsters in danger, and if Vena and I didn't do something about it, nobody would.*:

Nyara blinked, and started to say, "But that's not f—"

:*Fair? No, it wasn't. Not to Vena, not to me, and certainly not to the novices.*: The blade's matter-of-fact attitude took Nyara aback.

She climbed out of her bed of furs as her thoughts circled around something she could not yet grasp. Need was not cruel—not on purpose, at any rate. She *was* driven by expediency, and by a dedication to the longer view. But she wasn't cruel…

So what was she trying to say?

She had sacrificed herself for the bare chance of saving the novices through Vena. The girl herself had done the same. And it was all so unf—

It was unfair. But so was what Father did to me, what he did to the Hawkbrothers, what happened to the gryphons…

Life was unfair. She *knew* that, and so did Need. But she'd been complaining about that unfairness a great deal lately.

:Very good, kitten,: Need said in her mind. *:You've figured that part out. I find it a wonder that you can even grasp "unfairness," knowing so little else in your life besides it. I am still working on that; it seems inconsistent with what your thrice-damned father taught you. Know this, though: oftentimes the concept of fairness can be a wall to accomplishing what must be done. Worrying over fairness can sometimes impede justice, and that in itself is not fair.:*

Nyara nodded, as more awareness of Need's teaching came to her.

:Now let me show you what real *unfairness is…:*

Vena clung with her fingers and toes to the side of the cliff, and prayed that Heshain's Thought-seekers would not find her…

7

Darkwind had been struggling for several days now to maintain his dignity, his composure, and above all, the signature Tayledras detachment, and failing dismally. The cause, ever and always, was Elspeth. He wondered if all teachers felt like this, or if he was particularly blessed—or cursed—with a student so intelligent and quick that she threatened to run right over her hapless instructor.

"I can't keep ahead of her, and sometimes it's all I can do to fly apace with her," he confessed to Treyvan, as he helped the gryphon affix a set of shelves onto a wall of an interior room, a bit of work that only small, nimble, human hands could manage. Treyvan and his mate had expanded the original lair quite a bit since things calmed down, reconstructing the original walls of the building that had stood here, then creating several rooms where there had once been only two. Why the gryphon would want shelves, he had no idea—but then, there were a great many things he still didn't know about the gryphons. For all he knew, they collected *hertasi* carvings and wanted to display them.

Darkwind hammered on a stake and tied support cords from it. Finished flat boards such as the gryphons had discovered were hard to come by, and he wasn't going to waste them on wall mounts; he was using a variation on the Tayledras' *ekele* construction, that of anchored, co-supporting lines.

"Ssso what iss the trouble?" the gryphon asked genially. "You have had much more tutelage than she, and access to more knowledge." He lounged in the corner and watched Darkwind with half-lidded golden eyes, not out of laziness, but because he had just eaten, and the gryphons, like the raptors Darkwind knew so well, rested after filling their crops.

"I can't do everything," Darkwind admitted, with a touch of annoyance. He shook his hair out of his way, and aligned the support he was working on with the others. "I haven't actively worked magic in years, and my memory of what to do is a little foggy. My magical skills are—well—as stiff as muscles get if not exercised regularly. And, the Mage-Gift fades if not used."

"Asss any other attribute," the gryphon agreed. "Asss in hunting, sswordsskill, or musssic."

"Well, mine's creaky with disuse," Darkwind sighed, "And I can't re-learn everything I'd forgotten *and* teach Elspeth, too. It was all right when she didn't know anything about mage-craft, because I could set her to work on something basic, while I practiced something else. But now—that won't work anymore."

The gryphon stopped in the middle of a lazy stretch, and blinked at him, claws still extended, back arched. "Ssshe isss that quick?"

"She's that quick," Darkwind told him, setting the last support firmly into the wall. "The problem is that her people have made quite a science of mind-magic, and she's very good at it. Although she says she isn't particularly outstanding." He snorted. "Either it's the one and only time I've caught her being modest, or her people are frightening mind-mages. Good enough to stand equal with an Adept."

"And in mind-magic there isss enough sssameness to give her a basssisss in true magic," Treyvan supplied. "Isss there alsso enough sssameness to causse her trouble?"

Darkwind wedged the heavy shelf into the support loops and eyed it critically, ignoring the question for the moment. "How level do these have to be?" he asked. "What are they for?"

"Booksss," Treyvan replied, completing his stretch. "Jussst booksss, many of them. Ssso long asss they do not fall, it iss level enough."

Books? Where is he getting books? He sighted along the shelf again. It slanted just a bit, but not enough for most people to notice. Or it just might be the uneven stone floor that gave the illusion that it slanted; it was hard to tell. It would certainly do for books—wherever the gryphons had gotten them. And whatever they planned to do with them. He couldn't imagine them reading, either—

"Yes," he admitted, finally. "There is just enough that mind-magic has in common with true magic to make her ask me some really difficult questions and to occasionally get her in trouble. And that's the problem—if she's asking me questions, I'm distracted from polishing my own skills. And when she gets into trouble, it's sometimes difficult to get her out again, because I am, well, rusty. I've forgotten most of the specifics. It's more annoying than anything else at the moment, but it's going to be dangerous when facing an enemy."

And how would I explain that to her countrymen? "I'm sorry, but I seem to have let your princess get killed. I hope you have a spare?"

"Can you not asssk anotherrr Adept to train herrr?" the gryphon asked, his crest-feathers erect with interest.

He sighed, put his back to the wall, and slid down it to sit braced against the cool stone. "That's just the difficulty, you see. I sponsored her as Wingsib; unless I *really* get into trouble, she's my problem and my responsibility. We don't have that many Adepts in the first place, and, frankly, none to spare to teach Elspeth."

Besides, I can just imagine what would happen if she were to pull one of her impertinent little questions on, say, Iceshadow. And how would I explain that? "I'm sorry, but your princess seems to have gotten a bit singed. Don't worry, truly, I'm sure everything will grow back as good as new."

Treyvan scratched meditatively for a moment, then said, "Well, what of me?"

Darkwind frowned, not understanding the gryphon's question. "What about you?" he asked.

The gryphon coughed, and cocked his head to one side. "It ssseemsss to me that I could train herrr. I am Masssterrr, and my ssskillsss, while not Adept-classs, arrre quite finely honed and in usssse. I am sssurely good enough to answswer herrr quessstionsss, get her out of tanglesss, and drill you both. Anything I cannot deal with, you can sssurely answswer, sso long as the child isss not breathing firrre down yourr neck." His beak gaped in that familiar gryphon grin. "Besssidess, I doubt ssshe will give me asss much backtalk asss sssshe givess you!"

This was the answer to all his problems. He'd known the gryphon was *some* kind of mage. He'd seen it proven, and levels were largely a matter of power rather than skill, once one reached anywhere near to Master.

"Would you?" he said eagerly. "Would you really do that?"

The gryphon made a chirring sound, something between a snort and a chuckle. "I ssssaid that I would, did I not? Of courssse I will. It will be amusssing to teach a human again." He eyed Darkwind speculatively. "What isss more, featherrrless sson, I sshall drrrill you asss well. I sshall assk Hydona to help me."

Darkwind suddenly had the feeling a sparrow must have when caught out in a storm. He could bluff Elspeth when he didn't know an answer or concoct a spur-of-the-moment fake that would hold until he recalled the real answer. He wouldn't be able to do that with Treyvan.

And what was more, by the glint in Treyvan's eye, the gryphon knew he'd been doing exactly that.

On the other hand, he needed the drill badly, and Treyvan was the only one likely to offer. He didn't like to go to the other mages and beg for their help; many of them were working themselves into the ground, first shielding, then trying to Heal the Heartstone. The rest, now that the rift between mages and non-mages had been dealt with, were often working the borders with the scouts. Thanks to them there were proper patrols and reasonable work shifts, and the scouts were no longer spread so thin that if one of them were ill or injured, it meant a gaping hole in their border coverage. Those holes were how Falconsbane had gotten in and out of their territory at his leisure.

But that meant there was no one Darkwind really wanted to ask to help him re-train. Except Starblade—but there were too many things between Starblade and he that had yet to be resolved. Besides, Starblade had task enough in simply being healed.

"There isss ssomething more about Elssspeth, iss there not?" Treyvan asked. The gryphons' perceptiveness was a constant source of annoyance for Darkwind. It was impossible to be self-indulgent around them. "You have feelingsss beyond the ssstrictly necesssarrry. Sssomething—hmm—perrrsssonal?"

He flushed. "Not really," he replied, more stiffly than he would have liked. "I'm attracted to her, of course. But that would happen with any beautiful young woman that became my pupil. It's a natural occurrence in the student-teacher relationship, when both student and teacher are young, and their ages are close." He winced at saying that; he'd sounded pompous, and he'd come perilously close to babbling. But better that than have Treyvan think there was more between them.

"Of coursse," Treyvan said blandly. Too blandly. He could hardly take exception to that. He could suspect that Treyvan was teasing him, but he could prove nothing—which was, of course, exactly what Treyvan wanted. So long as Darkwind couldn't prove a real insult, the gryphon could tease all he wanted.

Crazy gryphon. Treyvan and his sense of humor, he thought sourly. *He'd laugh at his own funeral.*

"Anyway," he continued, as if Treyvan had said nothing at all, "with you drilling her, that won't come up. I will be too busy with my learning, as will she, and I sincerely doubt she will have any interest in you as a... uhm... I wouldn't worry about it, if I were you."

"Oh," Treyvan replied, a definite twinkle in his eyes, "I won't."

Darkwind gritted his teeth; Treyvan was trying to annoy him, and there was no point in letting the gryphon know he was succeeding. That would only encourage him.

And after all, Treyvan had put up with plenty of harassment from Darkwind's bondbird, Vree. The forestgyre had a fascination for Treyvan's crest-feathers, and attempted to snatch them any time he had the chance, no matter how often or forcefully Darkwind warned him off. Sometimes, much to Treyvan's discomfort, he succeeded in getting a claw on them, too. Once when Treyvan was in molt, he'd even managed to steal one.

I suppose I can put up with a little teasing. Unlike Vree, Treyvan is at least not snatching at body parts in his joking.

But he would rather that Treyvan had chosen another subject for the teasing besides his feelings toward Elspeth...

Hydona hissed and clacked her beak to get Elspeth's attention; Darkwind ignored her, for he had learned that Treyvan would use any moment of distraction to send lances of carefully tempered power at the Hawkbrother's shields. And Treyvan was watching him very carefully without seeming to; the advantage of the placement of the eyes on gryphon heads. They had excellent peripheral vision; a full three-quarters of a circle, and sharper than Darkwind could believe.

Despite Treyvan's comment about asking his mate, Darkwind had not expected that both gryphons would show up to tutor them. But when he and Elspeth traveled across the pass-through to the Practice Ground, four wings, not two, lifted to greet them.

"Hydona hass more patience than I," Treyvan had said jovially. "And ssshe hasss taught morrre than I. Ssshe thought ssshe might be a better teacherr for Elssspeth." His eyes glinted. "That leavesss me morrre time to tutorr you."

Hydona trilled. "Tutorr orr torturrre?"

"What about the young ones?" Darkwind had asked, worriedly, trying to ignore Hydona's remark. "The Heartstone still isn't safe for little ones to be near, even with all the shielding we've put on it."

"They are at the lair," Treyvan had replied. "The evening of the celebrrration had an unexpected outcome. The *kyree*, Torrl, hasss decided to ssstay with usss to aid yourr folk in ssscouting, and hisss young cousin, Rris, arrrrived yesssterday to join him. Rris watches the younglingsss. He ssays he isss glad to do ssso." Treyvan grinned hugely. "It ssseemss that we are sssuch thingss of legend that it isss worrth it to him to be the brrrunt of the younglingsss' gamesss to be nearrr usss."

Darkwind could only shake his head. The *kyree* were large, yes, but by no means the size of a half-grown gryphlet. Lytha and Jerven could bowl *him* over without even thinking about it; they would certainly give that poor *kyree* plenty of reasons to regret his offer.

I can just imagine the games they'll get up to. Pounce and Chase, Scream and Leap, Who-Can-Send-Rris-Rump-Over-Tail...

Unless, of course, Rris was very agile—or very clever. If the former, he could probably dodge the worst of their rough-and-tumble games, and if the latter, he could think of ways to keep them out of mischief without getting flattened.

"I hope this Rris has a great deal of patience, my friend," was all he had said. "Your offspring are likely to think he's some kind of living tumble-toy."

Treyvan had only laughed. "Think on Torrl," he had replied. "Young Rrisss isss asss clever asss hisss cousin, and verrry good, I am told, with younglingsss. All will be well."

Then Darkwind had no more time to worry about the well-being of the brave young *kyree* who had taken on the task of tending Jerven and Lytha, for their father launched him straight into a course of practice aimed at bringing him up to full and functional Adept status in the shortest possible period of time. It was aggressive, and Treyvan proved to be a merciless teacher.

Interestingly enough, he proceeded very differently from the way that Darkwind had initially been taught. In his years of learning before, he had mastered the basics of manipulating energies and shielding, then learned the offensive magics, *then* the defensive. But the first thing that Treyvan drilled him in were the Master-level *defensive* skills.

As now; he was constructing a structure of shields, onionlike in their layering, while Treyvan watched for any sign of weakness in them and attacked at that point. The object was to produce as many different kinds of shields as possible, so that an enemy who might not know every kind of shield a Tayledras could produce would be defeated by one, perhaps the third, fourth, or fifth.

The outermost was not so much shield as misdirection; it bent the mental eye away from the wearer and refracted the distinct magical image of the mage into resembling his surroundings, as if there was no one there. Beneath that was a shield that deflected energy, and beneath that, one that countered it. Yet deeper was one that absorbed energy and transmuted it, passing it to the shield beneath *it*, which simply resisted, like a wall of stone, and reflected the incoming energy back out through the previous layer. It was the transmutational shield that was giving Darkwind trouble. It would absorb Treyvan's attacks, right enough, but it wasn't transmuting the energy-lances into anything he could use.

"Hold," Treyvan said, finally, as Hydona lectured Elspeth on the need to establish a shield and a grounding point *first*, before reaching for node-energy. He had been trying to get that through her head for the past two days; finally, with someone else telling her exactly the same thing, it looked as if she was going to believe that he was right.

No, she's going to believe the information was right, he chided himself. *That's what's important, not the source of the information. If hearing it from Hydona is what it takes, then fine, so long as she learns it now and not the hard way—*

No one in k'Sheyna had ever learned that lesson "the hard way," not within living memory, but there were tales of a mage of k'Vala who had seized a node without first establishing a grounding point, and discovered that the node was rogue. Nodes could go feral, flaring and dying unpredictably, without the stabilizing focus of a Heartstone. The node he seized had done just that; it flared, and with no ground point to hold him and shunt the excess away and no shield to shelter him, he had burned up on the spot, becoming a human torch that burned for days—or so the tales said.

In fact, it had probably happened so fast that the mage had no notion of what had gone wrong. But whether the tales were true or not, it was still a horrible way to die.

Maybe all she needed was for it to be a female that taught her, he thought, watching as her grave eyes darkened and lightened according to her mood. *Her weapons teacher, the Tale'sedrin-kin that she worships so, is a female; and so is her oldest friend. And her Companion is female. Maybe she just responds better to female teachers.*

A reasonable thought—

Thwap!

A mental slap across the side of his head woke him to the fact that he was supposed to be working, not woolgathering. Once again, Treyvan had taken advantage of the fact that his attention had wandered to deliver a stinging reminder of what he was supposed to be doing.

Damn you, gryphon. That hurt.

With his "ears" still ringing, he turned his attention back to his teacher, whose twitching tail betrayed his impatience.

"If you do not pay heed, I ssshall do more than ssswat you, Darrrkwind," Treyvan warned him. "That isss the third time today your thoughtsss have gone drrrifting."

He grunted an assent, without mentioning that each time Elspeth had been the cause of his wit-wandering. He needn't have bothered. Treyvan brought it up on his own.

"Can you not worrrk about a young female without having yourrr mind drrrift?" he asked acidly. "Humanss! Alwaysss in sseasson!"

Darkwind felt his neck and ears heat up as he flushed. "That's not it," he protested. Treyvan cut his protests short.

"It mattersss not," the gryphon growled. "Now *watch* thiss time. *Thisss* is how the transssssmutation ssshould look to you. Crreate the texturrre *sso,* pussh it frrrom you asss if rrreleasssing a brreath. Halt it *herrre* frrom yourr body."

Darkwind blotted everything out of his mind except the sense of the power-flows, and the magic that the gryphon manipulated. As Treyvan built the proper shield, step by slow, tiny step, Darkwind finally saw what he had forgotten.

Treyvan had woven a complex texture into the shield, in one area directing power only *in,* and in another place filtering it *out,* giving him *two* power flows—one from himself, the other ready to take in energy directed at him by an enemy, and transmute it. That was the problem; he'd only allowed for the single power-flow from himself. The energy coming in from outside took over the field that was supposed to channel power from himself into the first shield. Back-pressure, as in a wellspring, with only the inevitable leaks to relieve that pressure. Once there, since it wasn't shield-energy, it eddied or stood idle—or worse, waited to react with another "color" of magic—in all cases, more than frustrating. Potentially deadly, in fact. It never reached the transmutational part of the working, so it never channeled to the last shield.

Mentally cursing himself, he rebuilt his shields; this time the transmutational shield worked correctly, giving him two shields for the personal-energy cost of one. At least for as long as the enemy chose to sling spellweapons at him.

"Now, you know how thisss ssshield can be countered, yess?" Treyvan asked, when the shields had been tested and met with his approval.

"Two ways—well, three, if you count just blasting away with more energy than the shunt can handle," Darkwind replied. "The first is to find the shunt—where he's grounded—and use it to drain energy out of the shield—hooking into it yourself, and taking the energy back. If that happens, the shield starts draining the mage that's holding it. If you do that fast enough, all his shields will collapse before he can react."

Treyvan's crest-feathers rose with approval. "And?"

"Attack where the mage isn't expecting it," he said. "That can be one of two things—attacking through the shunt, which is structurally the weakest part of the shield, or attacking with something else entirely." He thought for a moment. "At this point, if I were the attacker, I'd go for something completely unexpected. Like… a physical attack. Send Vree in to harass him. Toss an illusion at him. Demonsbane—throw a *rock* at him to make him lose his concentration!"

Treyvan laughed. "Good. Now—could you have done what the sssword Need did? Could you now transssmute the energy of an attack and sssplit it?"

He thought about that for a moment; thought about exactly what the sword had done. "Yes," he said finally. "But only by doing what she did—holding no shields at all between the attack and the transmutation-layer. That might work for a thing made of metal and magic, but it would be pretty foolhardy for a flesh-and-blood creature."

Treyvan nodded. "Neverrrthelesss," he said, pointing a talon at Darkwind, "it did worrk. And ssso long asss Falconsssbane kept launching magical attackss against herr, it continued to worrrk. Only if he had ssseen what ssshe wass doing and launched a physical attack, or ssome otherr type of magic, would he have failed. He ssufferrred frrrom sshort sssight."

Darkwind countered that statement with one of his own. "We were lucky," he said flatly. "Falconsbane was overconfident, and we were *damned* lucky. I have the feeling that if he'd had the time to plan and come in force, he could have taken us, all the Shin'a'in, and maybe even their Goddess on, and won."

Treyvan hissed softly. "Your thoughtsss marrch with mine, featherlesss ssson," he said, after a pause. "And it isss in my mind that we ssshall not alwayss be ssso lucky."

"In mine, too." Darkwind nodded toward Elspeth, and tried to lighten the mood. "For one thing, that woman seems to *attract* trouble."

The gryphon's beak snapped shut, and he nodded. "Yesss, sshe doess. Sshe hass attracted you, forr one. Ssso, let usss sssee if you can conssstruct thossse ssshields corrrectly a ssecond time—and thisss time, hold them againssst me."

Elspeth paid careful attention to every hissed word Hydona spoke, finding it unexpectedly easy to ignore the fact that her teacher was a creature larger than the biggest horse she had ever seen, with a beak powerful enough to snap her arm off at a single bite. Even with a motivation to pay attention such as that, the gryphon already made more sense than Darkwind did. Neither she nor the gryphons were native speakers of the Tayledras tongue; Hydona was being very careful about phrasing things in unambiguous terms that Darkwind likely thought were intuitively obvious.

Another case for being careful about what you assume in translation. Interesting. That is a consideration I would expect of a Court-trained person, not a creature like Hydona.

Hydona related everything she taught Elspeth to the mind-magic Elspeth already knew. *That* made a lot more sense than Darkwind's convoluted explanations of power-flows and energy-fluxes. They seemed clear to him, apparently, and seemed to make sense, except when he tried to fake; she had seen bluffs in enough Court functions to recognize the signs.

Hydona clearly detailed making an anchor point and shielding, for instance; that was a lot like grounding and centering, and was done for many of the same reasons. When put that way, Elspeth stopped subconsciously resisting the idea of having to effectively double-shield, once against mental intrusions and once against magical attacks. The other thing that made sense was that Hydona had pointed out the sword Need had done all that *for* her; the sword was in itself a permanent anchor point, radiating a seemingly ungraspable power into the earth, forever acting as a ground for the bearer it was bonded to. Need had shields on it that Hydona doubted were under conscious control anymore—if they ever had been. She seemed to think that they hadn't been; that they were some part of the sword itself, before the spirit came to reside in it.

So that was how Elspeth had managed to work magic without all the preparations the Hawkbrothers and their large friends deemed necessary. The precautions *had* been taken, they simply hadn't been taken by her.

And now that Need was no longer in Elspeth's possession, Elspeth was going to have to learn how to do everything Need had done so that she could manage for herself. With an ironic smile, she thought how easily Need could have become less a sword and more a crutch.

Oh, Need would have forced her to learn it all anyway. The only reason Need had aided her for as long as she had was because they had been in something of an emergency situation. In all probability, Need would have insisted on her learning to fend for herself as soon as there had been some breathing room.

Obediently, she "watched" as Hydona led her through the steps of anchoring and shielding, then practiced until they came easily. First, feeling the stable point in the power-flows about her and setting mental "hooks" into it, then erecting a shield against mage-energies that was remarkably similar to mental shields. Hydona drilled her over and over, and after a while the exercises stopped being something foreign and started feeling like second-nature. Best of all, they took about the same effort it took to stay on a galloping horse. She was a little surprised by how quickly it all came to her, but Hydona said nothing of it. She seemed to think it was only natural.

"Now," the gryphon said, after she'd repeated the patterns until she was weary of them, and thought she could do them in her sleep. "Here isss when you rrreach for powerrr; when you arrre ssafe in yourrr protectionsss, and anchored against fluxesss. Now, there isss a ley-line to the eassst of you; a young one, eassily tamed—but you do not know that. Ssso. Asssssume you know nothing. Searrrch for it. When you find it, rrreach forr it, asss Need ssshowed you, and ssample it. Sssee if you can usse it, orrr if it isss too ssstrong forr you."

She closed her eyes, found the line Hydona spoke of, and *reached* for it, dipping the fingers of an invisible hand into it, as if it were a kind of stream, and she wanted to drink of it.

She "tasted" it; tested the textures, the strength of the flow and the complexity. It was very tame, and bland. Not terribly strong. Kind of boring, in fact, compared with the rush of power she had gotten when she'd tapped into the node under the gryphons' ruins for the first time.

I can't do much with this, she thought, and began to trace it out to whatever node it was linked into, without thinking twice about doing so.

She felt her skull resound with a hard mental *thwap!* Her eyes snapped open, and she rocked back on her heels for a moment, staring at the female gryphon, aghast.

"What did you do that for?" she cried, angrily, "I was just—"

"You were jussst about to find yourrr way to the Hearrtssstone," Hydona interrupted. "And *that,* little child, would have eaten you whole, and ssspit out the piecessss. A trrrained and warry Adept can stand againssst it, but not you."

She licked her lips and blinked. "I thought the Heartstone was shielded. I thought nobody but Adepts *could* reach it now. Isn't that what all the mages have been working on since we got rid of Falconsbane?"

"And ssso it isss," Hydona nodded, "But you arrre within the prrotectionsss of the Practice Ground. The ssshieldsss do not extend herrre, so that those who arrre trrrying to Heal the Ssstone can rrreach it without dissrrupting thossse sssame ssshieldsss."

"So the Adepts healing the Stone come *here* to work?" she asked. Hydona nodded. Her voice rose with alarm; if the shields didn't extend here— "Isn't it dangerous for us to be here, then? I mean, what if we interfere with what's going on?"

"Therrre isss no one herrre at the moment," Hydona said calmly. "Arrre you afrrraid?"

Reluctantly, she nodded. After all she'd heard about the Heartstone and how dangerous it was in its current, shattered state, she wasn't very happy being somewhere that had no protections against it. The idea made her skin crawl a little with uneasiness.

"Good," Hydona said, with satisfaction. "You ssshould be afrrraid. Verrry afrrraid. It isss nothing to disssregarrd, thisss Ssstone. It isss lightning harrnesssed, but barrrely, in itsss perfect sstate." She refolded her wings, and settled her tail about her forelegs. "Now, *why* werrre you wanderrring off like that?"

She shuffled her feet, uncomfortable beneath the gryphon's dark, penetrating gaze. "I—there wasn't much power there," she stammered. "I wanted more than that. I mean, there was hardly enough there to do anything with."

"Morrre than you think," Hydona scolded gently. "Tcha. You are a child who hasss alwaysss had a forrtune at herrr beck, and hasss never learrrned how to make do with less." The gryphon shook her massive head, and the scent of cinnamon and musk wafted over Elspeth. "You musst learrrn to budget yourrrssself." She cocked her head sideways and watched Elspeth with a knowing eye. "The mossst effective mage I know neverr rossse above Journeyman-classss. He wasss effective becaussse he knew *exactly* what hisss limitsss werrre, and he did everrrything possible inssside thossse limitssss. *He* neverrr perrrmitted lack of powerrr to thwart him; he sssimply found wayss for lesss powerrr to accomplisssh the tasssk."

That was the harshest speech she'd ever gotten from Hydona, the closest the gryphon had ever come to giving her a scolding.

Although the *thwap* a few moments ago was a great deal like one of Kero's "love-taps."

She rubbed her temple, and considered the similarities between the two teachers. *"Delivered for your own good," Kero used to say. Well, this is another kind of weaponswork I suppose. And what was it Kero always says? "On the practice ground, the weaponsmaster is the one true God." And this is the same as the practice ground, I guess.* She nodded meekly, and Hydona seemed satisfied, at least for the moment.

"Ssso, do asss I told you in the firrrsst place. Find the line, tesst it, and link with it." Hydona sat back on her haunches and gave her a steady, narrowed-eyed look that Elspeth interpreted as meaning she would not permit the slightest deviation from her orders.

So, with a purely mental sigh, she found the tame, boring line of power again, and tapped into it. The amount of energy possible to get from a source so slight was hardly more than a trickle, compared to the sunlike fury that was the Heartstone. This time, she made the connection without even closing her eyes. The relationship between the inner world of power, unseen by physical eyes, and the outer world no longer confused her. Part of that was simply all the work she'd done with FarSight over the years; another instance of how working with mind-magic made work with *real* magic much easier.

Ah, but as Hydona pointed out, less power does not mean less effective power. Mind-magic is still strong. If there are more Heralds with the MageGift, after this I should be able to teach them in a reasonable length of time—not in the six or eight years it takes Quenten's students to become Journeymen. I could just work from their own mind-magic Gifts outward.

When she finished her assigned task, sealing the connections with a bit of a flourish, Hydona nodded with satisfaction. "Good. Now, channel the powerrr to me." Her beak opened in a hint of amusement at Elspeth's dropped jaw. "What, you did not know sssuch a thing wasss posssible? Becaussse it isss not posssible in mind-magic? Ah, but it *isss* possible in Healing, isss it not? Asss there are ssssimilaritiesss, there are differencesss asss well, and those differencesss might kill you. Trrrussst yourrr intuition, but neverrr asssume any thing."

What Hydona did not say—because she didn't need to—was that Elspeth needn't think she knew everything just because she was well-versed in the magic of her own people.

All right, so I'm a bonehead. She reached a tentative "hand" to Hydona, and was relieved to find the gryphon's shields down, and Hydona waiting for her "touch." She had no idea how to proceed with someone who was uncooperative, or worse, unable to cooperate. It took several false starts before she was able to create a channel to Hydona without losing the first one to the ley-line, but once she had it set up, she was able to redirect the power without too much difficulty.

She was tempted to set up a channel from Hydona to the line, directly, but she had a notion that Hydona would be able to tell the difference, and that the gryphon would not be amused.

Hydona broke the contact, and Elspeth maintained the channel without drawing any more energy from it while she waited for the gryphon's next instructions.

"Ssso, you can ssseek, sssample, channel, and sssend. Now we sssshall practice all of thossse," Hydona said genially. "We sssshall prrractice, and prractice, until you can ssseek, sssample, channel and sssend underrr any circumssstancesss."

Elspeth smothered a groan, and broke her contact with the ley-line neatly, letting its newly freed power wisp away harmlessly. This was starting to get frustrating. Hydona sounded more and more like Kero with every passing moment. *If she starts being any more like Kero, the next thing she's going to do is quote a Shin'a'in proverb at me.*

"It isss sssaid that 'Whatever isss prreparred forr neverrr occurrrssss,'" Hydona quoted. "That isss an ancient Kaled'a'in sssaying. Ssso, let usss prrepare you for finding yourrrssself alone, sssick, wounded, exhaussted, ssssurrounded by enemiessss and needing powerrr, and it will neverrr occurrr. Yesss?" Elspeth could only sigh.

Later, after the gryphons were gone, Darkwind rubbed eyes that ached and burned with the strain of DoubleSight, and was mildly surprised to find Elspeth still there. She sat quietly on a stone bench, leaning against the curved marble wall of their corner of the Practice Ground with her eyes closed. He wondered if she was waiting for him to show her the way out—or just waiting for him.

He walked up to her, and she stared up at him with eyes as tired as his own. "We should leave, Elspeth," he said carefully, uncertain of her temper, as weary as she looked. "The others will be here soon to work on the Heartstone, and we shall be in the way."

"We'll be more than in the way, if what Hydona said is any indication," she replied, getting slowly to her feet. "We'd be in danger—and a danger to them. Well, I would be, anyway. Like having a toddling baby underfoot on a tourney field. Nobody would ever hit it on purpose, but... well."

He nodded, relieved. "There you have it, truly. Would you care to come with me, to find something to eat?"

She hesitated a moment, then shrugged. "I'm not hungry, though."

"All the more reason that you should eat," he told her warningly. "Until you are used to it, the manipulating of mage-energies dulls the appetite. You must take care that you do not starve yourself."

She looked at him in surprise, and must have seen by his expression that he wasn't joking. "Well, that's not such a bad thing if you're on the plump side, but—"

"Hmm. There are no fat mages," he pointed out as he walked, "except those who habitually and grossly overindulge themselves; those for whom overeating is either a self-indulged vice or a disease. Manipulating mage-energies also costs one in terms of one's own energies, which means that you have just done *work*, Wingsib. Very hard, physical work, that deceives your own body."

He led her to the peculiar Gatelike construction called a "pass-through" that led to the Practice Ground. It was yet another way to ensure that the unwary and unready did not intrude on students at practice, or the Adepts at their work.

Because of the wall about it, the grounds could not be seen from outside, nor the Vale from within. They were a place and a time unto themselves. And in fact, he sometimes wondered if time moved a bit differently there.

She shook her head as she recovered from the jolt of disorientation that accompanied the transition across the pass-through. "How do you ever get used to that?" she asked. "That kind of dizzy feeling, I mean."

He raised an eyebrow at her. "We never do," he said simply. "There is a great deal that we never get used to. We simply cease to show our discomfort."

She said nothing, but he caught her giving him a speculative look out of the corner of his eye. For his part, he was more concerned with finding one of the *hertasi*-run "kitchens" before his temper deteriorated. Hunger did that to him, and he couldn't always predict what would set him off when his temper wore thin.

He didn't want to alienate her; the opposite was more like it, but he often felt as if he was dancing on eggs around her. He wondered if she felt the same around him. There was no cultural ground that they could both meet on, and yet they had a great deal in common.

The "kitchen" was not a kitchen as such; just a common area, a room in one of the few ground-level structures, that the *hertasi* kept stocked with fresh fruits, bread, smoked meat, and other things that did not spoil readily. Those Hawkbrothers who either did not have the skill or the inclination to prepare their own meals came here to put together what they pleased. The fare was not terribly varied, but it was good. And at the moment, Darkwind had no inclination to make the trek to his own *ekele* for food. Not while his stomach was throttling his backbone and complaining bitterly.

He indicated to Elspeth that she should help herself, and chose some fruit and bread, a bit of smoked meat, and a handful of *dosent* roots that had a cheesy taste and texture when raw. They found a comfortable spot to sit, in an out-of-the-way clearing, and fell to without exchanging much more than nods.

"So, what was it that Hydona tutored you in?" he asked, when the edge was off his hunger.

"Baby-steps." She made a face. "This is childish of me, I know, but she had me tapping into a very low-power ley-line, over and over, until she was certain that I could handle it in my sleep. But I was working the node under the lair with Need, and she *knows* that!"

"So you wonder why is she insisting that you work with minimal energy?" he replied, trying very hard to see things through her eyes.

Elspeth nodded, and nibbled a *chasern* fruit tentatively.

He licked the juice of another *chasern* from his fingers, and tried to answer as he thought Hydona would. "Firstly, there are some sources of power that are much too dangerous even for a single Adept to handle. Yes, even here, in our own territory. I mean besides the Heartstone." He nodded at her look of surprise. "There are pools of tainted magic, like thin-roofed caves, left by the Mage Wars. Difficult to see from the surface, and deadly to fall into. That is what a Healing Adept must deal with, and at the moment, we have none. There are even perfectly natural sources too strong for one Adept to handle by himself—any node with more than seven ley-lines leading into it, for instance, or rogue lines, which fluctuate in power levels unpredictably. Add in the tendency of lines to move, and you find the only way to use these sources is with a group of Adepts, each one supporting the others, each doing a relatively small amount of work so they have a reserve to deal with emergencies."

"I can see why she doesn't want me to just tap into whatever powerful source I See," Elspeth replied impatiently, "but *why* is she insisting that I only work with a bare trickle of power when energy is everywhere?"

"Ah, but it *isn't*," he replied, happy to at last discover the misconception that was the source of her impatience. "There is a limit on all Gifts, no matter how powerful. There is a limit on how far you, personally, can FarSee, yes?"

She nodded, slowly, and focused on him intently, paying very close attention to his words.

"And when you Mindspeak, you can only do so within a given distance, true?" he continued. "Well, power is *not* everywhere—or rather, great power is not everywhere. There are places where there are not even weak ley-lines for a day's ride in any direction. There are places where even the nodes are weaker than the line you worked with today. We are *Tayledras*, Elspeth, and we are enjoined by the Goddess to cleanse these lands of magic. To that end, we concentrate it here. The energy level is unnaturally high in and around a Vale, even one as damaged as this one, and unnaturally high in and about the lands you call the Pelagir Hills, which we call the Uncleansed Lands."

She swallowed the bite she had begun with a bit of difficulty. "So you're saying that when I get home, I might find that there's no magic energy to work with?" She looked horrified, and he hastened to assure her.

"No. I am saying that when you return, you may find you have lower levels of energy available than you have here. Or the power may be there, but buried deeply." He ate the last of his fruit. "That is why there are schools of mages, who build up reservoirs of power that are available to the Masters and Adepts of those schools. And that is why blood-mages build power for themselves by exploiting the pain and death of others. So, you must know how to work subtly. You must learn that raining down blows with pure power is not always the correct response. It was not with some of Falconsbane's creatures; that you witnessed."

She shook her head; whether stubbornly or for some other reason, he couldn't tell. "Listen," he said, "Hydona believes you are doing well. Once you have mastered the fainter sources of power, and in using the energy you yourself have stored within you, she and Treyvan wish us all to take our places on the border."

She perked up at that, and he smiled to see her interest. "Really?" she exclaimed. "I've felt so useless. I know you have to learn theory before you practice anything, but—"

"But you came here to become a weapon against the enemy of your land, I know," he replied. "Now please—I know that you are impatient, but believe me. It is better to use little power rather than too much. Using a poleaxe to kill small game destroys the game thoroughly, rendering it useless. So it is with magic. Too much can attract things you do not wish to have to deal with, as a dead creature can attract things more dangerous than it was to scavenge upon it. Master the subtlety Hydona tries to teach you. There will be time and more than time for the greater magics."

He watched her face; she seemed thoughtful, and he hoped she believed him, because whether she knew it or not, her life depended on believing him—and sooner than she might think.

For Hydona had not meant that suggestion in jest, that both of them take up a scout's position on the border of k'Sheyna. When they did that, there were no longer any shields, any protections, or any rules. It would be only themselves and the gryphons, and it might well be that there were things out there that were more powerful and deadly than Mornelithe Falconsbane.

8

So now I'm a scout on the border of the Tayledras territories. In the Pelagirs. Me, who never even rode circuit. Mother would have a cat. Elspeth's heart raced every time a bird called an alarm or a stray twig broke, even though she knew very well that potential danger was likely to be upon them long before there were any such warnings. Gwena was jumpy too, and that didn't help her nerves any. She had all her shields down toward Gwena, and whatever her Companion felt, she felt, and vice versa.

Or was it that Gwena was jumpy after all? The Companion was ill at ease, but it didn't quite have the feeling of nerves.

:All right,: she said, suddenly suspicious. *:What are you hiding this time?:*

:I wasn't hiding it—at least, not from you,: the Companion temporized. *:I've been keeping something from the others. Well, maybe I have and maybe I haven't—I mean, I don't know how much they've guessed about Cymry and me. So I wasn't really hiding it from you, but—:*

Elspeth choked and coughed to cover it. *:Gwena, dear, you can stop babbling, all right? I'd say the Tayledras know plenty about you two, from the way Darkwind dances around you, and they aren't telling me about what they know, either. So you might as well let this great secret out, whatever it is, because even if I don't know about it, they probably do.:*

She couldn't hide her resentment at that, and didn't try. It was obvious—would have been plain even to a child—that the Hawkbrothers considered the Companions something quite special, according them more reverence than they even got at home in Valdemar. But the Tayledras wouldn't discuss the Companions at *all* without one of them being present, as if they were determined not to offend the Companions or reveal something they shouldn't.

And even if there was nothing to this dancing about the bushes, it drove Elspeth to distraction.

:Well,: Gwena said slowly, *:I would have to tell you soon, anyway. It's not really all that complicated. Now that you know how to channel mage-energies, and you know how to feed someone else and be fed in turn—well—I can feed you.:*

Elspeth was past being surprised. She simply nodded. *:And of course it would have been no use telling me this before I had the skill, I know.:* She closed her eyes and counted to ten, very, very carefully. *:You aren't keeping anything else back, are you?:*

:No,: Gwena replied in a subdued voice. *:No, not really. I can feed you if you need it, but I'm subject to the same limitations you are. Except—:*

Elspeth counted to ten a second time. *:Except?:*

Gwena waited a long time, and Elspeth sensed that she was choosing her words very carefully. *:Except that you and I are a special pairing; so special that distance doesn't matter between us. That's all. I'm—different that way. It's like a lifebonded pair working together. Ask Darkwind about that some time, if you like; there are things a pair can do that even two Adepts working together can't do.:*

A vague memory fluttered at the back of her mind; something about a dark, windy night, the night when Gwena had Chosen her.

But the memory escaped before she could grasp it and she gave up trying to get it back after a fruitless moment of concentrating. *:I won't say I'm unhappy to hear that,:* she told Gwena sincerely. *:If things ever go badly for us, you and I might need that edge. I—don't suppose this means you're a mage, too—does it?:*

:Oh, no!: Gwena replied, her mind-voice bright with relief. *:No, not at all! I can just tap into nodes, energy-lines, and fields. All Companions can, just most of them can't use it for more than—oh, the usual. Healing themselves quickly, extended endurance, and running faster than a horse can. And they certainly can't feed their Chosen. That's why we're white, you know—ask Darkwind about node-energy and bleaching.:*

She sat up straighter, and looked up in the tree above her at Darkwind, who was "taking the tree-road." Except that right now he was just sitting, letting Vree do his scouting for him before they all moved on to another spot on their patrol. "Darkwind?" she whispered.

He looked down at her, but did not give her the hand signal that indicated she should be quiet.

"Gwena says I should ask you about node-energy and bleaching. She says that's why Companions are so white, because they use node-power to increase speed and endurance." She shook her head, still trying to figure it out.

But Darkwind seemed to get the point immediately; his eyes lit up, and he grabbed the branch beneath him. He swung down off his branch perch like a rope dancer, to land lightly beside her. "So! That is the piece of the puzzle that I have missed!" he said cheerfully. "I think you need not fear lack of nodes and power in your land, if all your Companions are able to tap them to enhance their physical abilities. That must mean that there is no scarcity of mage-energy."

Well, that was a great weight off her mind. "About bleaching?" she prompted.

He tugged at his own hair, and she noticed that white roots were starting to show and that the color had faded to a dull tan. "Use of node-energy gradually bleaches a mage; the color-making dyes in skin, hair, and eyes, and the color that is already there is leeched away. I do not lie when I say that magery changes a person. So—your Companions use node-energy, and thus are blue-eyed, silver-coated, gray-hooved."

:*Silver-hooved,*: Gwena said with dignity. He chuckled softly, and tapped her nose.

"If you insist, my lady." He turned back to Elspeth. "My hair is not white, because as a scout I dye it. Tayledras all *live* with node-energy, whether we are mages or no, so nonmages bleach as well. Mages are silver-haired usually in their fifth year of practice; any other member of the Clan will have made the change at, oh, thirty summers, or thereabouts. Even with dye, I must renew the color every few days now that I am a mage again."

Elspeth could only cast her eyes upward. "It's like continuous sun on them, then? No wonder dye won't take on them," she said. "The gods know we've tried often enough—you know, it's damned *hard* to disguise a big white horse!"

:*Sorry,*: Gwena put in. :*Can't help it.*:

"In a trade-off between endurance and the rest of it, and being unable to disguise them, I think I'll take the endurance," Elspeth said, as much for Gwena's ears as Darkwind's. And for Gwena's ears only, :*I'll take you just the way you are, oh great sneak,*: and felt Gwena's rush of pleasure, much like a pleasantly embarrassed flush.

He shrugged. "It is the choice I would make. Besides, now that you are a mage, you may make her seem any color you choose, by illusion."

Before she could answer that, he was back up in the tree again, swarming up the trunk like a squirrel, and hooking the branches above him with the peculiar weapon-tool he kept in a sheath on his back. She still didn't see how he could possibly climb that quickly, even with the spike-palmed climbing gloves he wore; humans shouldn't be able to climb like that.

She was about to ask him what was going on, when he gave her the hand signal indicating that she should remain quiet. She and Gwena froze, statue still, trusting to the bushes they sheltered in to keep them from sight.

She didn't dare let down her shields to probe about her. Darkwind had warned her of the danger of that, and after hearing more about Mornelithe Falconsbane and the creatures he had commanded, she was inclined to listen to him and believe. But she was free enough to use every other sense, and she did. At first she couldn't tell that there was anything at all out of the ordinary, but then she realized that the forest was a little too quiet. No birdcalls, no wind stirring the branches, nothing but the little *ticks* the red and golden leaves made as they fell.

:Elspeth?: came the tentative mental touch, as soft as the caress of a feather. *:Vree has found someone. I sense only a void, which means that there is someone inside a shield where Vree sees a two-legged creature.:*

Darkwind had told her that he would use Mindspeech only if he had determined that an enemy could not hear it, and had explained that he would test with a quick mental probe of his own, too swift to fix on. She had wanted to object, but it *was* his land and he was used to scouting it; she had to assume he knew what he was doing. And evidently he did…

:We're going to have to work out what I should do if someone ever does *catch a probe and lock horns with you,:* she interjected, sending a mental picture of stags in full battle.

A rush of chagrin accompanied his reply. *:You are right. But—not now.:*

:No,: she agreed. *:Not now. What do you want me to do? Should I try a probe? Are the gryphons going to get in on this?:*

:Not unless there is no other choice,: he replied firmly. *:We need to keep their existence as quiet as possible; there are surely others besides Falconsbane who might covet them or the small ones. And you may try a mind-magic probe, but I think you will encounter the same shields as I have. No, you and I will confront and warn him. If he does not heed the warning, we will deal with him—:*

He broke off his link with her so suddenly that she was afraid that something *had* locked him in mental battle after all. But then, a heartbeat later, his mind-voice returned. *:There is an additional complication,:* he said dryly; she looked up to find him looking down at her with a face full of irony. *:It seems our intruder is a Changechild.:*

Her first thought had been: it must be Nyara. Her second thought had been that it couldn't be Nyara, but that it must be another of her father's creatures, running wild with Falconsbane gone. She tried a mental probe and discovered that just as Darkwind had said, the creature had very strong shields, well beyond her ability to counter. So the only way to learn anything about it was to confront it.

As she and Darkwind watched the intruder from their respective hiding places, she knew all of her guesses about it had been wrong.

She didn't know whether to be relieved that this interloper was not their Nyara, or not. If it *had* been Falconsbane's daughter, the situation between herself and Darkwind would have been complicated enormously. Her own instincts warred with her on the subject; she trusted Nyara to a limited extent, and she certainly felt that the Changechild had been greatly wronged and abused, but—

But Nyara was incredibly, potently, sexually attractive. She couldn't help herself. Elspeth would have to have been blind not to see that Darkwind had wanted her as much as Skif had and that if anything had kept them from becoming intimate, it wasn't lack of attraction. She suspected that his own innate suspicion, lack of opportunity, and perhaps something on Nyara's part had kept him from playing the role of lover. As it was, that night before Dawnfire had returned to them, trapped in the body of her bondbird, it had been Skif, not Darkwind, who had taken that role. And, perhaps, guilt had kept Darkwind at arm's length. Guilt, that kept him from taking a new lover when his former love was a captive, confined to a bird's body by the temptress' father.

But Falconsbane was dead, or the next thing to it, and Dawnfire was out of reach of any of them. That left him free. And if he encountered Nyara before Skif did, would he be able to stand against temptation a second time? Especially if Nyara were to make overtures?

Knowing men, she didn't think so.

But at the same time, discovering that this stranger was *not* Nyara was a disappointment. However brief their acquaintance had been, Elspeth *liked* Nyara, and felt a great deal of sympathy for her. And she sometimes spared a moment to worry about her, put there in the wild lands that k'Sheyna no longer held, with a mage-sword who might not even *like* her. She had few or no provisions, no shelter against the coming winter unless she had somehow found or made one…

Well, this wasn't the time to worry about their errant Changechild. Not with another standing on k'Sheyna lands, within k'Sheyna borders—and by the blood on its hands and the circle about its feet, one who was up to no good.

Elspeth had done enough hunting in her time not to be sickened by the blood of a butchered deer. What made her ill were the fact that it was a *dyheli* that had been slain, and the signs that the butchery had taken place *before* it was dead, not after.

Blood-magic. Wasn't that what Darkwind and Quenten both mentioned, but wouldn't talk about?

Well, here it was—a "blood-mage"—and now that she knew what to

Look for, she Sensed the power that the mage had drawn into himself as a result of his work. It wasn't power *she* could have used under any circumstances; in fact, it made her a little nauseous to brush against it just long enough to figure out what it was. But it *was* power, and she had a notion that the death of a thinking, reasoning creature like a *dyheli* would have given this mage four times the strength that a deer would have. Perhaps more, depending on how long it had suffered.

Easy power, easily obtained, from a source you can find anywhere. And if you're sadistic by nature, a source that gives pleasure when exploited. No wonder Ancar is attracted to it.

If Nyara was feline in nature, this creature was serpentine. As he moved about, disposing of his victim, he glided rather than walked, and many of his motions had a bonelessness to them that made her shiver in an atavistic reaction to the evocation of "snake."

Odd. The hertasi don't do that to me, and they aren't half as human. I wonder why this thing does?

What exposed skin she saw—mostly hands and a glimpse of cheek—gleamed in the late afternoon light, with a kind of matte reflectivity that hinted at hard, shiny scales.

He dressed for deep cold, rather than the autumnal chill of the season; heavy leather boots, thick hose, a fur-lined tunic and cloak, and a heavy velvet shirt beneath the tunic. The colors were curious; a strange, dappled golden brown shading into deep orange—colors that blended surprisingly well into the foliage. Whatever else he was, this Changechild was canny. If he lay unmoving in the heart of a thicket, no one would ever see him.

The Changechild looked up at the first rustle of leaves, and froze in a combat-ready crouch. Darkwind dropped out of the branches like a great hawk coming to land, his knees flexed, and his hands in front of him, wary and ready to launch into an attack or defense as the need arose. The creature faced her fully now, and she saw that beneath the hood of his cloak, his face was curiously flat, with a thin, lipless mouth, and unblinking eyes as round as marbles. He straightened, but did not relax his wary pose.

Neither did Darkwind.

"You trespass," the Hawkbrother said clearly and slowly, in the most common of the trade-tongues used hereabouts. "You trespass upon the lands of the Tayledras k'Sheyna, and you pollute those lands with blood needlessly spilled."

That thin mouth stretched in what might have passed for a smile in any other creature. He straightened with arrogant self-assurance. "Not needlessly," he said, "and who or what are you to tell me what I may or may not do?"

"Tayledras k'Sheyna," Darkwind replied flatly. "These are our lands. We do not permit this. You will depart, taking your filth with you."

The mouth stretched a little more, and the creature's hands flexed a little. "What? Run from a single foe? I think not."

He made no gesture, but the circle he had drawn about his feet in blood flamed with sullen power—

—and, horribly, the disemboweled *dyheli* on the ground beside him heaved itself to its feet. It stood swaying a little, a gaping hole where its belly should have been, its eyes red with that same sullen power, and a dull glow about its hooves and horns.

"You are only one," the Changechild said softly. "One single Hawkbrother is hardly a threat. This weak creature was not enough. I think you will do to serve me."

Elspeth did not need Darkwind's signal to step from concealment, with Gwena at her side. She took up her position near enough to the Hawkbrother that they could not easily be separated, but distant enough that they would not interfere with each other.

"We are Tayledras k'Sheyna," Darkwind said, firmly, but with no hint of anger. "And you will leave now."

This time Hydona was not around to keep her from using the strongest source of power she could Sense, and there was a three-line node not more than a furlong from where they stood. She tapped into it, quickly; to her Othersight it glowed with healthy green fire, and touching it was a pleasant jolt, as if she took a deep draught of cold spring water on a hot day. She established her link and channeled power to herself and her shields before the stranger had a chance to respond to Darkwind's challenge. She kept the level of her outermost shield the same so as not to warn him; at minimal strength, the kind of mage-shield a beginner would build. But, like a paper screen hiding a stone barrier, beneath the disguising energies of the first shield was a second, and it was linked to the node-power.

It was just as well that she did, because the Changechild's reply was to attack.

He was no Falconsbane, but he was no Apprentice, either. He chose his target cleverly, launching his initial onslaught against Elspeth rather than Darkwind. Perhaps he was deceived by the rudimentary outer shield, or perhaps he was under the impression that a female would be less prepared and less aggressive than a male.

If that was the case, he judged wrongly.

She Saw his attack as he launched it; a flight of white-hot energy-daggers that he flung at her with both hands. She anticipated the direction of his attack by his eyes—and was ready in time to reflect them straight back at him, holding up mirror-shielded hands that doubled the flame-bright weapons back on themselves and sent them back on their original path. *That* must have been something of a shock to him, for he did not even deflect them properly, much less reabsorb them. They impacted on his shields, splintering silently into a thousand shard-sparks, and he flinched away.

Before he had a chance to recover from that shock, Darkwind had launched an attack of his own, but not one he likely would have expected. He attacked the mage's shields with a needle-lance of force, not the mage himself, boring through the protections at their weakest point, where some of the energy daggers had impacted. The blue-white lance split the air between them, and Darkwind held it straight on target, despite the Changechild's best efforts to shake it off. Elspeth readied a second attack, arrows of lightning, but did not launch it, holding it in reserve.

The Changechild sent his unliving creature to attack them; the shambling, bloody thing charged with a speed quite out of keeping with the condition it was in. It was halfway to them before Elspeth realized that it *was* an attack, but Gwena intercepted it, like a trained war-horse, as if she had dealt with such things all her life. She sidestepped the wicked horns neatly, and twisted sideways to launch a cruel double-hooved kick with her hind legs as the thing passed, that sundered its hips with a meaty *thunk* and a wet *crack*.

The dead thing staggered and went down again, and tried to heave itself erect. But it could not struggle upright again, for its hip and one of its hind legs were broken and would no longer bear its weight.

At that same instant, Darkwind penetrated the Changechild's shields, and Elspeth launched the lightning-arrows she had been readying, targeting them at the hole Darkwind had bored and was even now spreading open. The first one missed slightly, impacting just to one side of the hole, splintering as had the mage's own energy-daggers.

The second did not miss, nor did Darkwind's fireball that followed in the arrow's wake.

Within the enemy's shields and contained by them, a storm of utterly silent fireworks erupted. The Changechild stood frozen for a moment, a dark silhouette against a background of coruscating energies—

Then he collapsed to the ground as his shields collapsed around him, and, like the *dyheli* that had been his victim, did not move again.

They patrolled the border until nightfall and the arrival of Summersky, the scout that was to relieve them, but there wasn't so much as a leaf out of place. As they headed homeward toward the Vale, Elspeth found herself very glad that she was riding. Although Hydona had warned her that a mage-duel would take *far* more out of her than she would ever believe, she hadn't really understood what the gryphon meant. Now though—now she knew Hydona was not only right, she had understated the case. Mostly all that she wanted right now was a soak in one of the hot springs, a meal, and her bed.

But besides being weary, she was very confused; a poor combination, all things considered. She was dissatisfied with her first foray on k'Sheyna's border. Certainly there were questions that had not been answered adequately.

And as she followed in Darkwind's wake, watching him stride tirelessly along with one hand on Treyvan's shoulder and folded wing, and Vree perched on a padded perch on his shoulder, she tried to reconcile her mixed emotions. It didn't help matters any that from this angle she had such a good view of his tight, muscular...

Hydona trilled to herself, apparently amused by a private joke. The female gryphon walked beside her as her mate strode beside Darkwind, all of them following a dry stream bed back to the Vale. Hydona's head was easily level with Elspeth's, which was a little unsettling, since it underscored how very large the gryphon was. It was easy to forget that, when one often saw them lounging about like overgrown house cats.

"And what arrre you thinking?" Hydona asked, as if she were following Elspeth's thoughts.

"I'm not sure," she said, frowning, trying to put her emotional reactions into words. "This isn't the first time I've been in combat—it isn't even the first time I've been in magical combat. I think we did all right—"

"You did," Hydona confirmed. "Verrry well, essspecially forr a beginnerrr. But asss you pointed out, you have had combat experrrience, and I expected nothing lesss than competence." She cocked her head at Elspeth. "How do you feel you will manage againssst that enemy of yourrrsss?"

She thought for a moment, weighing what she could do now with what she knew Ancar could produce. "Well, providing Ancar hasn't acquired an army of mages, I should be able to do something about him, if I can keep progressing at this rate. I mean, it isn't easy, but so far I haven't lost any body parts. Provided I don't reach an upper limit to my powers in the near future, and Ancar hasn't learned to tap nodes. I know he should be a Master-class mage by now at the very least."

"One should neverrr trrusst an enemy to be placssid. What about yourrr perrrforrrmance?" Hydona asked shrewdly. "How would you rrrate yoursssself?"

"Darkwind and I worked together as a team *quite* well, I think. At least we did once he got around to *doing* something." There it was; that was what she had been trying to pinpoint as the root of her discontent. "But that was the problem; he gave that damned thing a warning even after we knew it had worked blood-magic!"

She couldn't keep indignation from creeping into her voice, and didn't try. Kero would have cut the interloper down where he stood; filled him full of so many arrows that he would have looked like a hedgehog.

"The oddssss werrre two to one," Hydona responded. "Thrree to one, if we count Gwena. Don't you think that the crrreaturrre dessserrved a fairr warrrning with oddsss like that?"

Elspeth shook her head, stubbornly. "No," she said flatly, and her voice shook a little with intensity. "I don't. We knew he was a blood-mage; there's no point in giving something like that a chance to get away or hurt you. I *sure* as Havens don't intend to give Ancar a shred of warning. In fact, if I get the chance, I'll ambush him!"

As always, the mere thought of Ancar and what he had done made her blood boil. The tortures he had inflicted on Talia—the rape of his own country—the hundreds, thousands of lives he had thrown away— but most of all, the careless *glee* he had taken in it all—

No, when she thought of Ancar, all she could think of was the chance of getting him in her power and shredding him. She hated him, she hated everything he'd ever done, and she wanted him *dead*, safely *dead*, so that he couldn't hurt anyone any more.

Ever.

In fact, if there was a way to destroy his very soul, she'd do it, so that there wouldn't even be a chance he'd be reborn and start over again, as some mages could.

"You arrre angrrry," Hydona observed. "This enemy of yourrrsss angersss you."

"I'm always angry when I think about Ancar," she replied fiercely. "I can't help it; the man's another Falconsbane, just as evil and as corrupt, and I want him dead as much as any Tayledras could ever have wanted Falconsbane dead." She raised her chin defiantly. "More than that, I want Ancar's liver on a plate, so I can feed it to something vile. I not only want to kill him, I want to *hurt* him so that he knows some of what his victims felt. I hate him, I'm afraid of him, and if there were any way to put *him* through what he has put others through, I'd take it."

Hydona shook her head with open admonition. "You arrre *too* angrrry," she said. "It isss not underrr control, thisss angerrr. Hate will not serrve you herrrre. And ssssuch hate, sssuch angerrr will weaken you. You musst learrrn to contrrrol them, orr they will contrrol you. Thisss I know."

Elspeth grimaced, but kept her lips clamped tight on what she wanted to say. This wasn't the first time she'd heard this particular lecture; the first time, it had come from Darkwind. And it just made her angrier.

How could she *not* hate the bastard, after everything he'd done to her friends and her land? How could she not hate him after seeing what he had done to his own people? How could she not feel enraged at everything he had done?

And how in Havens could an emotion that strong possibly be a weakness? It was a contradiction in terms.

But there was absolutely no point in getting into an argument over it, so she elected to keep her thoughts to herself, and her tongue on a very short leash, until they reached the sanctuary of the Vale.

Hydona said nothing more.

The gryphons left them once they were well within the "safe" area that was kept under close watch by the mages, and full of alarms that would be tripped by strangers. By the time they arrived at the shielded entrance to the Vale it was already dark, and her temper had cooled considerably. Not that she had changed her mind about anything she'd said, but she wasn't quite so ready to bite off someone's head over it.

One thing had calmed her down a bit; she discovered that Gwena felt the same as she did—at least about Ancar. The Companion was of two minds about Darkwind warning the Changechild, admitting that there were good reasons for either decision, whether to warn or not—but on the subject of Ancar of Hardorn, Gwena was in full accord with her Chosen.

:*The man is a mad dog,:* she told Elspeth flatly. :*You don't give a mad dog a chance to bite you, and you don't try and cure it. You get rid of it, before it destroys something you love.:*

That backing of her own thoughts on the matter made her feel a bit more secure about her own judgment, and that Gwena shared her anger eased her own somewhat. That helped her temper to cool a lot faster.

She was quite ready to see the Vale long before they actually reached it. She discovered, somewhat to her surprise, that it was no real effort to keep her Mage-Sight invoked—and since Mage-Sight gave her an enhanced, owl-like view of her surroundings, she left it in force. It occurred to her, as she noted how every living creature and some things that were not alive each bore a faint outline of energy, that this must be what Companions used for night-sight. After all, in order to tap into and manipulate mage-power, you had to be able to See it, and since this kind of Sight worked equally well by day or night, why not use it to give you a nighttime advantage? Yet another Companion power she could explain away, which gave her a perverse feeling of satisfaction.

Once they approached the shields surrounding the Vale, she had to drop the Sight; the energies there were so powerful they threatened to "blind" her.

Well, that's one reason not to count on it for night-sight. And if powerful energies can "blind" you—well, that's something to be wary of. Hmm. And something to keep in mind as a weapon.

The faint tingle of her skin as they passed the entrance to the Vale, as if lightning were about to strike her, told her that they had crossed the shields and protections standing patient guard over the only way in and out. But even if she had not felt that little tingle, she would have known they were inside k'Sheyna Vale, for in the space of half a heartbeat they went from deep autumn to high summer. Suddenly her clothing was much too warm.

Gwena stopped as Darkwind went on ahead, pushing through the foliage draped over the path and vanishing into the shadowy gloom. Elspeth dismounted, unfastened her cloak, and draped it over the saddle. Even then she was a little too warm; she rolled up the sleeves of her shirt and opened the collar to the balmy night air, heavy with the scent of night-blooming flowers she could not even put a name to.

This place was the closest thing on earth that she had ever seen to the Havens of scripture and sermon. *Too bad I can't bring a little bit of this back with me,* she thought wistfully. *Fresh fruit and flowers in the dead of winter, hot springs and cool pools to bathe in—trysting nooks, and I can think of plenty of people who'd enjoy those! Near-invisible servants. Balmy breezes. No wonder Vanyel visited k'Treva whenever he was exhausted.*

Darkwind had said more than once that this Vale wasn't even a real showplace of what the Hawkbrothers could do. K'Sheyna, he'd wistfully related, was the smallest of the Clans even when they were at full strength, and the Vale was neglected and run down. Half tended at the very best, with no water-sculptures, no wind-harps—more than half the *ekeles* untenanted and falling to ruins—no one making vine-tapestries or flower-falls. No concerts except on the rarest of occasions, no artists except Ravenwing and the *hertasi*. Still, Elspeth found it beautiful beyond her wildest dreams.

She could only wonder what the rest of the Vales must be like. And— could the Heralds create something like this, if only in miniature?

But—should they?

She brushed aside a rainbow-threaded dangling vine and wondered about that.

This Vale was a very seductive, hedonistic place, and many people already thought that the Heralds were a bit too randy as it was. It was also a place that could encourage sloth; she found it very easy to justify sleeping a little later, lingering in the hot spring, or sitting and watching a waterfall and thinking about nothing at all.

Her footsteps made no sound on the soft sand of the pathway, sand that cradled her feet luxuriously. Everything about this Vale hinted at luxury—a luxury that few outside the Vales enjoyed. In fact, not even the Tayledras "cousins," the Shin'a'in, got to enjoy this sort of life. For that matter, could the Heralds really justify making themselves a private paradise when there were so many other things that needed doing?

A pair of long-tailed birds sang sweetly nearby, scarcely an arm's length from Gwena, reminding her by their presence that outside the Vale the songbirds had long since gone south. Even if Heralds could justify building a place like this, there was no way that they could justify lounging about in it the way the Tayledras did. Frolicking in flower-bedecked bowers and lounging in hot pools didn't get circuits ridden. Too much living like this, and she'd find herself wasting time designing feather-masks and festival-garb instead of getting her work done.

A feeling of moral superiority crept into her thoughts, and she let it. She led Gwena up the path to her loaned *ekele* and the tiny, sculpted hot pool beneath it, and felt a bit smug.

The stone path wound across another just ahead of her, and the murmur of voices to her right warned her that several folk were going to cross ahead of her. She paused—

And her sense of moral superiority vanished as soon as the Hawkbrothers came in view.

"Elspeth," called the first of the group as he caught sight of her, "We should like the use of your pool. The *hertasi* are cleaning several of the others, and yours is the nearest that is prepared. May we?"

The mage-light that danced over his head revealed the little group of five pitilessly. The one in the lead, a mage named Autumnwing, was the best off, physically—and he was worn right down to the bone. Overextended, to say the least; his eyes were sunken, his skin pale, and he trembled with weariness. Behind him were two of Darkwind's scouts, both bruised and bloody, and supporting them were two more mages who looked in no better shape than Autumnwing. Even as she watched, one was redressing a wound that gleamed dark and wet, while her partner held the arm steady.

"What in Havens happened to you?" she exclaimed, before she could stop herself.

Autumnwing shrugged. "I have been with the rest on the Heartstone; it fluxed again today. Be glad you were not within the Vale, or we would have conscripted you with or without training. But I am not so bad— these four met with a pack of Changewolves that had cornered one of k'Sheyna's *dyheli* herds, and if it had not been for them, there might have been a score of Changewolves hounding the Vale itself tonight." As Elspeth's eyes widened, he added, "They are very valiant. Had I been in their place, I fear I would have fled."

The arm-wounded woman grunted and said, "Forty-arrow fight." Then she shrugged.

"P—please," Elspeth stammered, "feel free to use the spring. I was going to find some food; shall I bring you back some, or send a *hertasi* with it?"

"Either," replied one of the scouts wearily. "I could happily eat one of our fallen enemies at this moment, raw, and without salt."

:I'll take care of it, if you'll pull off the tack,: Gwena told her. *:I can probably find a* hertasi *before you can.:*

In answer, Elspeth bent to loose the saddle-girth, and saddle and blanket slid to the ground as she unbuckled the hackamore and hauled it over Gwena's ears. The Companion vanished into the undergrowth.

"She's gone to recruit you some food," Elspeth told the others, as she bent to retrieve the fallen saddle.

"Our thanks," Autumnwing told her gravely; she waited for them to make their way past her, then gave them a head start, before following in their wake.

Hot pools and life in an eternal summer don't compensate for that, she thought, balancing the saddle on her shoulder. *And given the Goddess' edicts, I suppose that even in Vales where the Heartstone is whole the mages aren't sitting around discussing water-sculpture.*

So much for moral superiority.

The Vales must seem like paradise itself when they're out in the Pelagir wilds— but one that wouldn't be there to return to if they weren't out in those wilds to defend it. Is Valdemar any different to a Herald?

Willfully faulty memory caught up with reality. This wasn't the first time she'd seen Hawkbrothers in such poor condition. The mages, half-Healed Starblade among them, worked themselves to a thread every day, shielding the Vale from attack, and trying to do something about their Heartstone. She had her own experience today to show her the hazards of being a scout on the bonier of the k'Sheyna territory, where every league held new and deadly honors.

For that matter, she'd been an inadvertent witness to the worst— save only death—that could befall a Hawkbrother. She'd seen what had happened to Dawnfire, and she'd been asked to feed power to Kethra one day, when the mage that usually augmented the Healer-shaman was too exhausted to continue. Kethra put Starblade through purest agony that day, explaining only that this was a necessary part of Healing what had been done to him. Elspeth still felt uncomfortable with the memory. Although she repeated to herself again and again that it was for the better, she still felt like a torturer's apprentice for it.

We're pampered, we Heralds, she realized, stopping long enough to shift the weight of the saddle to her other shoulder, and shake some of the aches out of the arm that had balanced it. *We have everything we need taken care of for us. We live in prepared quarters, we have servants picking up after us. The Hawkbrothers have Vales; we have our rooms at the Collegium. They have hertasi, we have human servants. They have their food and clothing made for them; so do we. Neither of us have physical pleasures that are adequate compensation for what we do.*

She reached the foot of the tree that held her *ekele;* muted voices and faint splashing told her that the pool was occupied. She hung her saddle and hackamore over the railing at the bottom of the stair, and took herself up the staircase.

Darkwind had pointed out something about the Vales; that anyone with sufficient magic power could create one. They were really just very large hothouses, with a mage-barrier serving in place of glass. Nothing terribly exotic about a hothouse. She pulled aside the door to her *ekele*, and looked down over the edge of the staircase for a moment. Kerowyn's grueling lessons in strategy and tactics caused her to realize something else as well.

The *ekeles* were not simply exotic love nests. They were based directly on the quite defensible treetop homes of the *tervardi*. How defensible they were could be demonstrated by the *ekeles* built outside the Vale; once the ladder to the ground had been pulled up, there was virtually no way to reach them. They were warded against fire, even, by set-spells and a transparent resin painted around the tree trunks well past two man-heights.

Even the *ekele* here could be made quite defensible simply by destroying the rope-and-truss suspended staircases, making them an excellent place to retreat if the Vale defenses were ever breached.

Gwena must have found her *hertasi* right away, for there was a tray of food waiting for her, and the herb tea in the pot was still hot and steeping. She helped herself to bread and meat, and collapsed onto her pillow-strewn pallet.

My people build walls. The Tayledras put themselves up in the trees. Differences in philosophy, really. More like the Heralds than like the ordinary folk of Valdemar. They think in terms of evasion, the way we do, rather than the stand-and-fight of the Guard.

She finished as much of her meal as she wanted at the moment, and stripped off her filthy, blood-speckled clothing. *Dyheli* blood, of course, and not of herself or Darkwind, but it was still going to be a major task to get it out. She could bleach it with magic of course, and she probably would, but that was a waste of mage-power.

Maybe she'd just shift over to scout clothing. It was more practical for all this woods-running, anyway.

She wrapped a huge towel around herself and descended the staircase, heading for the spring. Occupied or no, she was going to use it. After all, she deserved a good soak as much as her visitors did; she'd just spent *her* day doing the same things they had done. She had earned a little luxury.

They all had.

9

Vree stayed calm on Darkwind's shoulder after they passed the protections at the entrance to the Vale, even though until recently the bondbird had not wanted to enter the Vale itself. The rogue energies of the Heartstone had disturbed Vree badly, and the bondbirds of every other scout as well, but the additional shielding on the Stone seemed to be having some beneficial effect.

:Are you all right?: he asked Vree, just to be sure. *:We can turn around and leave if you want; I can hold the scouts' meeting at the* ekele *just as well as here. The mages will just have to climb a rope ladder instead of a staircase, and they'll all have to squeeze into my rooms. I* think *it would bear their weight.:*

Vree ducked his head a little, and yawned. *:Fine. Happy,:* he replied sleepily. Then, anxiously, *:Food soon?:*

:Soon,: he assured the bird. *:Quite soon. As soon as we get to the meeting.:* The other scouts would have hungry birds as well; the *hertasi* would have provided a selection of whole game birds and small mammals for the raptors, along with some kind of meal for the birds' bondmates.

For the first time in a very long time, this would be a meeting of day-watch scouts and scout-mages. Stormcloud would hold a similar meeting for those on night-watch. Yesterday Darkwind had asked them to gather because there was something important to be addressed. He hadn't specified what that was.

He had been the scouts' representative to the k'Sheyna Council during the most divisive period in their history—the period when Starblade, as directed by Mornelithe Falconsbane, was creating rifts between mages and nonmages, to weaken the Clan and make it easier for Falconsbane to destroy them. Darkwind had been willing to serve then, knowing that no one else had the edge he did, having his own father as chief of the Council. It was a bitter truth that his advantage then was not in currying favor, but knowing the other's weaknesses. He had sometimes been able to manipulate his father. Equally painful to recall was the fact that Starblade had done the same to him.

But now that he was devoting more time to mage-craft, he had less time to spend elsewhere. The scouts were his friends and charges, and with his attentions divided so, they could conceivably suffer for it.

It was time for a change. Now the question was whether or not he could get the others to agree with him. In general the kind of person who became a successful scout was *not* the kind who enjoyed being in a position of authority, or who relished dealing with those who were.

The best place for the gathering was the central clearing that had been used for the celebration, but that was closer to the Heartstone than Darkwind liked, shielding or no shielding. So he had asked them all to gather in the smaller clearing beneath the tallest tree in the Vale; the one that the scouts had used for dancing.

When he arrived, he found a near replication of the celebration, except that there was no music or dancing, the clothing was more subdued, and the conversation level was considerably quieter. Birds stood on portable perches, the exposed roots of trees, or in the branches, most of them with talons firmly in their dinner, the rest eyeing the mound of fur and feathers with a view to selecting something choice. Brighter mage-lights than those conjured for the celebration hung up in the branches, illuminating everything below with a clear yellow light, sunlike but for its intensity. Tayledras sprawled all over the clearing, eating, talking, or both. Darkwind did a quick mental tally and came up a few names short, as Vree yearned toward the heap of "dinner," making little plaintive chirping noises in the back of his throat.

:Hungry!: he urged his bondmate, as Darkwind tried not to laugh at the ridiculous sounds he made. The uninitiated were often very surprised at the calls of raptorial birds; most of them, other than the defiant screams of battle and challenge, were very unimpressive chirps, clucks, and squeals. One species, the Harshawk, even croaked, sounding very like a duck with a throat condition. And owls hissed; not the kinds of things one expected to hear from the fierce hunters of the sky.

But silly sounds notwithstanding, Vree's hunger was very real and quite intense, and the bondbird had more than earned his dinner. Darkwind took him on the gauntlet and tossed him into the air, to give him a little height. Vree gave two great beats of his wings, reaching the lowest of the branches, then dove straight down at the pile, shouldering aside lesser and less-famished birds to get at a fat, choice duck. One of the Harshawks quacked indignantly as the tasty morsel was snatched right from under his talons, and two of the owls hissed angrily at being shouldered aside, but Vree ignored them all. The gyre heaved himself and his prize up into the air, and lumbered off to a nearby branch, where he mantled both wings over it and tore into it with his sharp, fiercely hooked beak.

"Here—" Shadowstar shoved sliced meat and bread at Darkwind, and snatched back her fingers, laughing, when he grabbed for it as if he were a hungry forestgyre himself. "Heyla! Sharp-set, are we? In yarak?"

"Something like," he admitted. "It's been a long day, with a mage-duel at the end of it." He took a healthy bite of the food, and bolted it, suddenly realizing just how hungry *he* was. "Where are Summerstar and Lightwing? And—ah—" it took him a moment to remember the names of the mages that had been assigned to help the two scouts.

Shadowstar beat him to it. "Songlight and Winddance. Gone to get injuries tended again; they ran into Changewolves. Nothing serious."

A tentative Mindtouch from an unfamiliar source reassured him. *:Songlight here. We are mostly soaking bruises, Darkwind. I will stay in Mindtouch and relay to the others, if you like.:*

:Please,: he replied, taking a seat where he could see the others. *:This shouldn't take long.:*

He took out his dagger and rapped the hilt of it on the side of the tree; it rang hollowly, and got him instant attention and instant silence.

"I hope that most of you have guessed why I asked for these meetings—" he began.

Shadowstar stood up, interrupting him. "We pretty much figured it out," she said dryly, as the others nodded. "We were talking it all over before you got here. And we're all agreed that while we *don't* want to lose you as our leader, you deserve a rest, and you aren't going to get one at the rate you're going."

Nods all around confirmed her words, and Darkwind felt an irrational surge of relief—both that the scouts still wanted him as leader, and that they were willing to let him go.

"Have any of you got a candidate in mind?" he asked. Surprisingly, it was one of the mages who answered him.

"Winterlight," the young man said promptly. "He did it before you had the position, and now that we aren't at each others' throats, he says he would be willing to take it again."

Darkwind turned to his old friend, one of the oldest scouts in the Clan, raising an eyebrow inquisitively. Winterlight coughed and half-smiled. "I know the job," he answered, confirming the mage's words. "And since it's no longer the trial that it was—"

Darkwind grinned openly. "Then as far as I am concerned, the position is yours, my friend—if the rest agree, that is."

He was going to open the meeting up to discussions, but the others forestalled him with their unanimous assent. Even the bondbirds seemed pleased with the choice. It was a good one; although he was not a mage, Winterlight seldom dyed his hair, and wore it long, as a mage did. So he looked like a mage, and he was a contemporary of Starblade and Iceshadow, which made him doubly acceptable to the Elders of the Council.

"As long as the night-watch agrees, then, it's yours," he told Winterlight happily. "And if they come up with a different candidate, you'll have to deal with that yourself."

"If they come up with a different candidate, we'll split the duties," Winterlight replied immediately. "I've had my fill of dissension."

Darkwind shrugged. "That's fine with me," he responded.

Winterlight smiled. "It wasn't just a rest that the youngsters decided you need," he said, in a confidential whisper. "I overheard one of them saying that you've been living like a sworn celibate and you needed to take that pretty Outlander off to a bower and—"

The rest of Winterlight's whispered suggestion made Darkwind flush so hard he was afraid he was glowing.

The rest of the scouts howled with laughter.

Winterlight just smiled enigmatically and asked if Darkwind needed to borrow any feathers. Darkwind deliberately turned his attention first to Vree to make sure the gyre was all right, then to his food, both to cover his confusion. When he looked beside him again, Winterlight was gone—

—but the Shin'a'in shaman Kethra had taken his place.

Oh, my. I wonder what I owe this pleasure to.

He brushed invisible crumbs from his tunic, self-consciously. Kethra was another source of confusion entirely for him, and not just because she was his father's lover.

Although that was a part of it—

"Is Father well?" he asked her, quickly.

She nodded, her bright green eyes as cool and unreadable as a falcon's, and smoothed her long black hair behind her ears. She wore a birdfetish necklace that sparkled in the magelight, and a braided length of cord adorned with feathers hung from her left temple.

"He is relatively well," she told him, as the assembled scouts collected their birds as if at an unspoken signal, and drifted not-too-casually off, back to their respective *ekeles*. There wasn't any people-food left, and the few carcasses that remained were taken by those who lived outside the Vale.

Kethra, however, was not leaving. "There are some things I need to discuss with you before I proceed to the next steps with him. They concern you, and your relationship to him."

"What about it?" he asked, more brusquely than he intended. Suddenly it seemed as if everyone in k'Sheyna was interested in his private life! *Am I to be allowed no thoughts to myself?* He glanced around the clearing, hoping for a distraction, but all of the scouts who had thronged the area had evaporated like snow in the summer sun, as if there was some kind of conspiracy between them and the Shin'a'in. She only pursed her lips and shook her head at him, allowing him no evasions.

"I need to know what you think of him now—and what you think of me." She fixed him with an unflinching gaze. "You know I am Starblade's lover."

He flushed, painfully embarrassed. "Yes," he said shortly. "And Iceshadow told me why—why it was necessary."

"What did he tell you?" she asked. "Humor me."

He averted his eyes for a moment, but she recaptured them. "Because so many of the things that were done to Father, and the magics that were cast to control him, were linked with sex, it has required sexually oriented Healing to undo them. That meant Father's Healer should be a lover as well."

Kethra nodded, and leaned back, her slender hands clasped around one knee. "That is quite true," she said quietly, "And in case you had wondered, I knew that was the case when I came here at Kra'heera's request. But had you also deciphered that I am your father's love as well as his lover, and he has become mine as well?"

Darkwind tried to look away in confusion, and found that he could not. "I—it had occurred to me," he admitted. "I am not blind, and your attitude toward one another shows."

She set her jaw with the perpetual half-smile that shamans always seemed to have. "And what do you think of that?" she asked bluntly, a question he had not expected. "What do you think of me, when you picture me in that role?"

Gods of my fathers. She would ask that. "I am confused," he said, as honestly as he could. "I do not know what to think. I admire you for yourself, shaman. You are a very strong, talented, and clever woman. You force my father to be strong again, as well. I think that he must need this, or you would not do it. I see you encourage him to go to his limits; you permit him to do for himself what he can. Yet you do not let him fall when you can steady him, and you match your talents with his when he cannot do something alone."

"You are describing a partner," Kethra said calmly. "An equal.

Someone who is likely to go on being one for the foreseeable future."

He nodded, reluctantly, aware that his uneasiness was making him sweat.

"And this makes you ill at ease." She stated it as an observation rather than a question. "Uncomfortable in my presence whether or not I am with your father."

He sighed. "Yes, lady. It is not just because you are a shaman, though there is something to that."

Kethra chuckled. "Shamans make you nervous?"

Darkwind took a deep breath and chose his words carefully. "Shamans as a rule can make one uncomfortable by seeing more than one would like. That is not the whole of it, though. I do not know what to say to you, or how to treat you. You are the first of my father's lovers who has been a full partner since my mother's death. And when I am looking objectively at my memories, it seems to me that you have more patience and compassion than my mother had. And yet—"

"And yet, what of your loyalty to your true mother, now that I have come to replace her? Surely I seem an interloper. I suffer by comparison with your memory of her."

"It is easy to regard someone who is dead as without peer," he told her candidly. "I have lost enough friends and loved ones to be aware of that." He cocked his head to one side, and nibbled his lower lip. This was, possibly, one of the oddest conversations he had ever taken part in. "Say this. I know that I can call you friend. I think if you will give me time, I can even come to call you more than that. Will this serve?"

Her smile widened, and she reached out a hand to clasp his, warmly. "It will serve," she told him. "Friend alone would have served; I am pleased you think of me that well. I was not sure, Darkwind. You are adept at hiding your true feelings—you have had need to, I know. That is not unique to Tayledras, Shin'a'in, or any other people. Trust me, we shamans need to hide our feelings ourselves sometimes, to struggle through pain."

He shrugged. "We all have needed to hide true feelings here, to one extent or another. Events have made it necessary."

She nodded. "Well, at least you and I have looked beneath the masks, and not run from what we have found."

He smiled, impressed by her steadfast sense of humor. "Now the unpleasant news. Your father is still far from recovered. It will not take weeks or even months to cure him; it will be a matter of years."

He took a deep breath and ran his hand through his hair. He felt his shoulders slumping, and remembered that it made a poor impression of strength, but he knew Kethra would see through any attempts to hide his emotions, either by words or body language. He closed his eyes. "I had thought so, but I had not liked to believe it. Father has always been so—strong. He has always recovered quickly from things. Are you quite certain of this?"

A deep, somewhat strained male voice spoke from behind them.

"You must believe it, my son," said Starblade. Darkwind jerked his head up and turned to face him. Starblade wore a thin, loose-cut resting-gown that Songwind... Darkwind had designed for him a decade ago. The Adept walked slowly into the clearing, and now that he knew the truth, Darkwind saw the traces of severe damage done to him, physically as well as mentally.

Starblade found a space beside Kethra and joined her. "You must. I am but a shadow of what I was. In fact," he chuckled as if he found the idea humorous, "I have considered changing my use-name to Starshadow. Except that we already have a Shadowstar, and that would be confusing for everyone."

Darkwind clenched his hands. It wasn't easy hearing Starblade confess to weakness; it was harder hearing him admit to such profound weakness that he'd thought of altering his use-name. That implied a lasting condition, as when Songwind had become Darkwind, and sometimes an irreparable condition.

Starblade sat carefully down beside the shaman, and took her hand in his. His left hand—the one that Darkwind had pierced with his dagger as part of his father's freeing from Mornelithe Falconsbane. It showed a glossy, whitened scar a half-thumblength long now that the bandages had been removed. "I hope that you and I have reconciled our differences, my son," he said, as Darkwind tried not to squirm, "because I must tell you that I do not trust my decision-making ability any more than I can rely on my faded powers."

Darkwind started to blurt out a protest; his father stopped him. "Oh, not for the small decisions, the everyday matters. But for the decisions that affect us all deeply—and the ones I made in the past—I do not feel that I can continue without another view to temper mine. In our Healings, I see my actions laid on bare earth, without order. As I am rebuilt, Kethra helps me to understand the motivations behind those actions, and reject those that Falconsbane engineered. It is a slow process, Darkwind. I do not *know* which of the decisions I have made were done out of pride, out of good judgment, or out of the direction of our enemies. I need you, my son; I need your vision, and I need your newly regained powers. More so: k'Sheyna needs them."

Now Darkwind was numb. At the moment, all he could do was to nod. But this—this was frightening, inconceivable. Even at his worst, when Starblade had been trying to thwart him at every turn, he had been in control, he had been powerful. He had been someone who at least could be relied upon to know what he was doing, a bastion of strength. Full of certainty.

This was like hearing that the rock beneath the Vale was sand, and that the next storm could wash it away.

Kethra and Starblade both were waiting for some kind of response, so he got himself under some semblance of control, and gave them one. "What is it you want me to do?" he asked.

"I want your opinions, your thoughts," Starblade told him, his lined and weary face showing every day of his age. "I need them. The most pressing concern is the Heartstone; what do *you* think we should do about it? You know enough to make some educated guesses about it. We cannot stabilize it, not without help. I do not think that we can drain it, either. When we try, it fluxes unpredictably. And after you have given me your opinion, I want your help in doing whatever it is that we must to end this trouble—I want you to take *my* place as the key of the Adepts' circle."

He shook his head at that, violently. "Father, I can't. I haven't even begun to relearn all I've forgotten and—"

"The strength of your will and youth will counter that lack of practice," Kethra said, interrupting him. "The key need not be the most experienced Adept, but he must be the strongest, and you are that."

Starblade coughed, then settled himself, fixing Darkwind with a sincere look. "I will explain it to you in this light, then. Your mother and I raised you to be a strong and responsible person, Scout or Mage. Now, the strength that I taught you has been taken from me. You are at least in part the vessel of my old personality. I would appreciate relearning what I was from you, and learning your strength."

Given a choice, he would have told them it was impossible; turned and fled from the Vale, back to his *ekele*. But he had no choice, and all three of them knew that. He bowed to their will. "If that is truly what you want," he said unhappily. "If it is, then I shall."

"Thank you," Starblade said, simply. As Kethra stood up, he rose to his feet to place one hand on his son's shoulder. "This—confession has cost me a great deal, but I think it has gained me more. I have given over wanting you to be a copy of me, and I wish that Wintermoon and I had not drifted so far apart that I cannot say those same words to him and be believed. Perhaps in time, he will not be lost to me. I do not wish you to be anything but yourself, Darkwind. Whatever comes of this, it will have happened because you went to the limit of your abilities, and not the sum of my expectations. In all that happens, I shall try to be your friend as well as your father."

With those words, which surprised him more than anything else that had happened tonight, Starblade turned and walked slowly back into the shadows, with Kethra at his side.

Vree swooped down off his perch, and backwinged to a new one beside his bondmate. He swiveled his head, turning it upside down to stare at Darkwind from a new angle, as only a raptor would do. Hard to manage, with his crop bulging as if the bird had swallowed a child's ball. And possibly the silliest pose any bird could take.

:*Sleepy,*: he announced. :*Sleep now?*:

Darkwind held out his gauntlet automatically, and Vree swiveled his head back and hopped onto his bondmate's wrist. :*I think so,*: he replied, absently, all the while wondering if, after all this, he still *could* get to sleep.

He flailed up out of slumber, arms windmilling wildly, with sparkling afterimages of confused dream-scenes still in his mind and the impression of someone shaking him.

Someone *was* shaking him. "What?" he gasped. "Who?" The hammock-bed beneath him felt strange, the proportions of the room all wrong.

Light flared, and he blinked, dazzled; the shaker was Sathen, the *hertasi* who usually tended Starblade's *ekele* for him. The little lizard was holding a lit lantern in one claw, with the other on Darkwind's shoulder. And the proportions of the room were wrong because he was not in his own *ekele*, he was in Starblade's, in the guest quarters. Vree dozed on, oblivious, on a block-perch set into the wall, one foot pulled up under his breast-feathers and his head hunched down so far there was nothing visible in the soft puff of white and off-white but a bit of beak.

I need to find Father a new bondbird, came the inconsequential thought, as Sathen waited patiently for him to gather his wits and say something sensible.

"What?" he obliged, finally. "What's wrong?"

"Trouble," the little *hertasi* whispered. "Trouble-call it is, from Snowstar.

Needing mage. Needing *mages,*" he corrected. "More than one."

Marvelous. Well, I'm probably the least weary. "What for?" he asked. It couldn't be for combat; by the time he reached Snowstar's patrol area, any combat would have been long since resolved. He reached for his clothing and pulled on his breeches. *Well, at least this means that someone else will have to take our patrol in the morning. And* I *don't have to be the one to decide who it is.*

"Basilisk," Sathen said, his nostrils closing to slits as he said it. The lizard-folk did not like basilisks—not that anyone did, but basilisks seemed to prefer *hertasi* territories over any others.

Darkwind groaned, and pulled his tunic over his head, thinking as quickly as his sleep-fogged mind would permit. "Go leave a message for Winterlight that—ah—Wingsister Elspeth and I went out to deal with the basilisk, and he'll have to get someone else on day-watch to cover for us. Then go wake up the Outlander and tell her I'll be coming for her in a moment."

Fortunately Elspeth's *ekele* was not that far from Starblade's. She wasn't going to like being awakened out of a sound sleep—but then, who did? *She took the oath,* he told himself a little smugly as he pulled on his boots. He splashed water from the basin Sathen had left onto his face to wake himself up. *She might as well find out what it means.*

Besides, being shaken awake in the middle of the night might also shake up that attitude problem of hers. And once she saw a basilisk for herself, he had a shrewd notion that she might start paying better attention to him when he told her something. Particularly about the dangers that lurked out in the Uncleansed Lands, and how you couldn't always deal with them combatively.

This would be a good exercise in patience for her, as well; now that he thought about it, he realized he couldn't have *planned* this encounter more effectively.

Other than staging it by daylight instead of darkness.

For a basilisk could not be moved by magic power—it grounded attacks out on itself, sent the power out into the earth, and ignored the attackers. And it could not be moved by force.

It could *only* be dealt with by persuasion. And a great deal of patience, as Elspeth would likely discover the hard way.

He took the gracefully curved stairs down to the ground, jumping them two at a time, suppressing the urge to whistle.

This promised to be very, very entertaining.

* * *

It was not just any basilisk. It was a basilisk with a belly full of eggs.

Snowstar held his torch steady, no doubt trusting in the cold to keep the creature torpid. It blinked at them from the hollow it had carved for itself in the rocky bank of the stream, but remained where it was. Torchlight flickering over the thing's head and parts of its body did nothing to conceal how hideous the poor creature was.

"Havens, that thing is ugly," Elspeth said in a fascinated whisper. Basilisks came in many colors—all the colors of mud, from the dull red-brown of Plains-mud, to the dull brown-black of forest-loam mud, and every muddy variation in between. This one was the muddy gray-green of clay. With the face of a toad, no neck to speak of, the body of an enormous lizard, a dull ash-gray frill running down the head and the length of the spine and tail, a mouth full of poisonous half-rotted teeth, and a slack jaw that continuously leaked greenish drool, it was definitely not going to appeal to anything outside of its own kind. And when you added to that the sanitary habits of a maggot, and breath that would make an enraged bull keel over a hundred paces away, you did not have anything that could be considered a good neighbor.

And that was when it was torpid. As soon as the sun arose, and warmed the thing's sluggish blood, it would go looking for food. It wasn't fussy. Anything would do, living or dead, so long as it was meat.

But as soon as the blood warmed up, the brain would warm up, too—and when that happened, nothing nearby would be safe. Not that the basilisk was clever; it wasn't—it wasn't fast either, or a crafty hunter. It didn't have to be. It simply had to feel hunger and look around for food, and everything within line-of-sight would freeze, held in place by the peculiar mental compulsion it emitted.

Then it could simply stroll up to its chosen dinner, and eat it.

As Snowstar explained this to Elspeth, Darkwind created a heatless mage-light and sent it into the basilisk's shelter, so he could get a better idea of how big it was. Elspeth shuddered in revulsion as the light revealed just how phenomenally hideous the creature was.

"Are we going to kill it now?" she asked; Darkwind had the feeling that she wanted to get this over with quickly. Well, he didn't blame her. Being downwind of a basilisk was a lot like being downwind of a charnel pit.

Snowstar answered for him. "Gods of our fathers, no!" he exclaimed. "If you think it stinks *now*, you don't want to be within two days' ride of a dead one! That's assuming we *could* kill it. It has three hearts, that warty skin is tougher than twenty layers of boiled hide, and it can live for a long time with what we'd consider a fatal wound. It can live without two legs, both eyes, and half its face. Altogether. Assuming you could get near enough to it to take out an eye. Personally, I'd rather not try."

Elspeth shook her head, not in disbelief, but in amazement. "What about magic?"

"Magic doesn't work on them," Darkwind told her, as he reckoned up the length of the beast and judged it to be about the size of three horses, not counting the tail. "It just passes around them and goes straight into the ground. *We* should have shields like that! An amazing animal."

"You sound like you admire it," Elspeth replied in surprise.

He shrugged, and walked around a little, to see if the basilisk noticed him, or if it had gone completely torpid. "In a way I do," he said, noting with satisfaction that the creature's eyes tracked on him. "It is said that they were created by one of the Great Mages, not as a weapon, but as a way of disposing of the carcasses of those creatures that *were* weapons, that even dead were too dangerous to touch and too deadly to leave about. Nothing else will eat a dead cold-drake, for instance." His brief survey complete, he returned to Elspeth's side. "They weren't supposed to be able to breed, but neither were a lot of other creatures. Most of their eggs are infertile, but there are one or two that are viable now and again."

He turned to Snowstar. The scout wiped the back of his hand across his watering eyes, and stood a little straighter. Snowstar was one of the youngest of the scouts; Darkwind was grateful that he had known enough to send for help and not attempted to move the basilisk himself. It *could* be done without magic, but the odds of success, especially in the uncertain weather of fall or spring, were not good. "Have you found any place for us to put her?" he asked.

"Yes, but it's not as secure as I'd like," the scout replied, wiping his eyes again. The wind had turned, and the fumes were—potent. Darkwind's eyes had started to burn a few moments ago, and Snowstar had been here for some time. Small wonder he had watering eyes. "I've got a rock-bottomed gully along this stream; the sides are too steep to climb and there's always lots of things falling into it to die. The only problem is that the mouth of the valley is open to the stream, and I couldn't see a way to close it off."

"Isn't there a swamp somewhere off that way?" Darkwind asked, waving vaguely in the direction where he thought he sensed water.

"Can you get the thing that far?" Snowstar asked, incredulously. "If you can, that would be perfect. There's plenty for it to eat, no *hertasi* like it because it's full of sulfur springs, and the sulfur's enough to make sure any eggs it lays won't hatch."

"If we can get it moving, we can get it that far," Darkwind told him. "The problem is going to be getting it moving without getting it worked up enough to think about being angry or frightened. If it's either, it'll start trying to fascinate everything within line of sight."

"Right." Snowstar spread his hands. "I'll leave that up to you. Get it moving and I'll guide you to the nearest finger of the swamp and make sure nothing interferes with you on the way."

"That will do." Darkwind studied the hideous beast, trying to determine whether it was better to lure it out of its rudimentary den, or force it out.

Force it out, he decided at last. He didn't think that the beast was going to take any kind of bait at the moment.

"Here's what we're going to do," he said, turning to Elspeth, who still watched the basilisk with a kind of repulsed fascination. "It's comfortable and it feels secure in that den. You and I are going to have to make it feel uncomfortable and insecure, and make it come out. Once it's out, it will try to go back in again; we'll have to prevent that. Then we'll have to herd it in the direction we want it to go."

Elspeth licked her lips and nodded, slowly. "We use magic, I presume?"

"That, or mind-magic, or a combination of the two," he told her. He yawned as he finished the sentence, and hoped he wasn't going to be too fuddled from lack of sleep to carry this off. Elspeth looked as if she felt about the same. "Got any ideas about what might drive it out?"

She leaned back against a tree trunk and frowned at the beast. "Well, what would drive you or me out of bed? Noise?"

Interesting idea. "That's one nobody I know of has tried." He thought for a moment. "If it were warmer, we could lure her out with an illusion of food, but she isn't hungry in the semi-hibernation she's in right now. Heat and cold in her cave—no, too hot and she'll just wake up more, and we don't want that. Too cold and she'll go torpid."

"How about rocks in her bed?" Elspeth hazarded. "Sharp, pointy ones. Maybe combine it with noise."

"Good. Good, I like that plan. It should irritate her without making her angry, and if we make her uncomfortable she won't want to go back in there." He scratched his head. "Now, which do you want? Rocks or noise?"

"Rocks," she said, surprising him. "I've got an idea."

Since he already had a notion about the noises that might irritate the basilisk, that suited him very well. He had been afraid that Elspeth wouldn't think herself capable of manifesting good-sized stones, but evidently she already had a solution in mind.

"Do it, then," he said, shortly, and concentrated all his attention on a point just behind the basilisk's body. The one thing he *didn't* want to do was frighten her—just make her leave her lair. If he frightened her, she might be aroused enough to set all her abilities working, and that would do them no good at all.

Fine thing if I met my end as a late-night snack for a foul-breathed, incredibly stupid monster.

He already knew how some pure, high-pitched sounds irritated wolves and birds; he reasoned the same might well be true of this beast. It just had to be loud enough and annoying enough.

Dissonance, he thought suddenly. That might work even better; two pure tones out of tune with each other.

He'd done this before as a kind of game, when he was just learning very fine control. He'd gotten good enough that he had been able to produce recognizable voices out of the air. Producing pure tones wasn't all that hard, it just took a lot of energy.

He started near the top of the human-audible scale, figuring to go up if he had to. It took him a moment to recall the trick of it, but when he got it, Snowstar jumped as a nerve-shattering squeal rang out from the basilisk's lair. The young scout clapped both hands over his ears, his expression pained. Darkwind wished he had that luxury. *He* had to listen to his creation in order to control it.

When he glanced out of the corner of his eye at Elspeth, he saw she had blocked both her ears with her fingers, and her brow was creased with concentration.

His sounds didn't seem to be having any effect, although already he noticed the basilisk shifting her weight, as if she found her position uncomfortable. He raised the notes another half step and waited to see the effect.

Another increment followed that, until he had gone up a full octave, and still he was not getting the reaction he wanted, although the monster turned occasionally to snap at the empty air, as if trying to rid her lair of its noisy visitor.

Finally, he took the sounds up past the range where even *he* could hear it, and he had one of the longest ranges in the Clan. Elspeth had taken her fingers out of her ears two steps earlier, and Snowstar had taken his hands down before that, with an expression of deep gratitude. This was the range that animals other than man could hear; he wasn't about to give up this plan until he'd passed the sounds that bats used. And from the look on Elspeth's face, *she* wasn't going to give in until she had produced rocks the size of small ponies.

Neither of them had to go that far, although whether it was Darkwind's dissonant howls or Elspeth's stones that finally tipped the balance, he couldn't tell. The basilisk had been snapping and shifting uncomfortably for some time when he changed the tone again, and the basilisk came pouring out of her lair, burbling with anger and frustration.

She stood there for a moment, wavering between the discomfort of the lair, and the exposure of the outdoors. If she dove back in again, they might never get her out.

Before Darkwind could say anything, Elspeth solved the problem for him. He sensed her grabbing the underlying web of earth-energies at the mouth of the half-dug lair and yanking.

The lair collapsed in on itself, leaving the basilisk nowhere to go.

The monster rumbled deep in her chest, and turned, heading downstream and away from them, into the darkness. "That will do for a few furlongs, but then we're going to have to turn her out of this stream when it forks," Snowstar said, as the basilisk plodded out of the range of his torch and Darkwind's mage-light.

"Don't worry, I think we can deal with it," he said, breaking into a trot along the graveled streamside, sending his mage-light winging on ahead until it illuminated the unlovely rump of the basilisk. She was moving at a pretty fair pace; he'd had no idea they could move that fast. In fact—was he going to be able to keep up with her?

Elspeth supplied his answer, as she and the Companion trotted up alongside and she offered him a hand up. "Gwena can carry two for a while," she said. He took her at her word and got himself up behind her. "Are you going to use that sound of yours to drive that thing?" she asked once he was settled and Gwena was bounding after the tail of the monster.

"Yes," he said—shortly, as it was difficult to speak when bouncing along on the rump of a trotting mount. "That—was—the—idea—"

:I have another idea,: Elspeth said by Mindspeech. *:It's a reptile, which means it can probably sense heat very well. Let's create a ball of warmth about her size, and lure her along with it. Keep it a couple of lengths ahead of her until she's where we want her, then dissipate it. What do you think?:*

He switched to Mindspeech as well. *:That is an excellent idea. This is going to be great news when we get back to the Vale,:* he told her, and smiled at the glow of well-earned self-congratulation that met his words. *:You've helped uncover something entirely new, and very useful to us. The other forms of driving these monsters have all been much riskier. You are going to make your Clansibs quite happy with this news.:*

For that matter, she was making *him* quite happy. The basilisk responded to guidance by noise and the heat lure beautifully. They were going to be returning to the Vale much sooner than he had thought.

Much sooner, and flushed with success. Not a bad combination.

Not a bad combination at all.

Everyone wanted to hear about the basilisk drive. This was the first time that a basilisk had been moved with fewer than a dozen people and with no injuries. Small wonder that the Vale had been astir when they returned, and that the mages had all wanted to hear the story in detail. It seemed that if he and Elspeth hadn't used unorthodox tactics because there had only been two of them, they would never have budged the thing. And if Snowstar hadn't been so inexperienced in the ways of basilisks, he'd never have called for just a pair of mages.

"You weren't lucky," Iceshadow finally said. "Snowstar was relatively lucky because he got you. But you two—you were quite clever. Or am I being overly optimistic?"

Darkwind laughed tiredly, and drank another full beaker of cold water—the aftereffect of all that basilisk stench was incredible dehydration. He and Elspeth together had drained a small lake, it seemed, and they were still thirsty.

"No, we were bright enough that if we hadn't been able to budge the old girl with methods that wouldn't enrage her, we would have called for help," he assured the Adept. "I pledge you that. I don't trust anything that can entrance you to the point that you let yourself be swallowed whole."

When the others finally left them in peace, Darkwind realized that he was much too keyed up to sleep, at least not without a long soak in hot water to relax him.

He stood up abruptly, catching Elspeth by surprise; she jumped when he moved and looked up at him with round eyes.

"I need a bath and a soak," he said, "and the pool under your *ekele* is the nearest two-layered one I know of. Would it disturb you if I used it?"

"Would it disturb you if I joined you?" she asked.

At first, he thought she was making some kind of an overture, but a moment of reflection told him that she couldn't possibly be doing anything of the sort. She was just as tired as he was—even if she wasn't bruised from riding for furlongs on the sharp and protruding hipbones of her Companion. Even if the two of them had been ready to tear one another's clothes off in a fit of unbridled lust, neither of them would have had the energy to do so. No, she was just being polite.

But at least she wasn't as shy as she had been. And she was still an attractive woman. There might be some hope after all.

"It surely won't disturb me," he told her, and offered her a polite hand to help her rise. "In fact, I doubt very much if it would disturb me to share a pool with—"

He stopped himself before he said "with that basilisk;" realizing at the last moment that the comment could be construed as saying that he did not find her attractive. Which was not the case, at all.

"—half the Clan," he concluded. "All I want is to get this stink off and soak my muscles until I can sleep."

"Good plan," she said, and smiled. "I'll make you a bargain. If you find some of that fruit drink, I'll get soap, robes and towels from my treehouse."

"I'll take that," he said instantly. Elspeth disappeared into the greenery while he sought one of the storage areas, and dug out a tiny keg of a peculiar, mineral-rich drink Elspeth had gotten very fond of. Normally he didn't care much for the stuff, but when he was as parched and exhausted as he was now, he downed it with the same enthusiasm as she did.

Keg under one arm and a pair of turned wooden mugs in the other hand, he retraced his path and followed in Elspeth's wake. When he arrived at the pool, he found that she had been as good at keeping her word as he. There was strongly herb-scented soap beside the lower of the two heated pools, and towels and robes hanging nearby on a couple of branches, with one small mage-light over each pool providing just enough light to see by.

Elspeth was already in the upper soaking pool. He left the keg and mugs beside it as she waved at him indolently from the steam, then he stripped and plunged straight into the lower pool.

It took three full soapings before the last of the stench was gone and he felt clean again. By then he was more than ready for a mug and a long, soothing soak.

"I think I took all my skin off," Elspeth complained languidly from her end of the pool as he slipped across the barrier between the pools and into the hotter water of the second. "I scrubbed and scrubbed—every time I thought I was clean, I could still smell that thing."

"Worse than skunk or polecat," he agreed. She seemed very relaxed for the first time since he had met her. "Did you see how much Iceshadow liked that idea of yours, moving the basilisk with noise?"

"But it was your idea to use pure-tones in dissonance," she said immediately. "I had just thought of using volume, or maybe make it sound like the cave was falling in."

He allowed himself to feel pleased about that part of it. "Well, I guess that I'm going to have to admit that you *are* right about trying new things even in magic. Just because they aren't the way we've always done something, that doesn't mean new ideas aren't going to work. Change comes to the Vales; quite a concept."

She laughed heartily. "I thought I'd never hear you say that! But I have to make a confession to you, though. I *have* been pushing you, just because you were being such a—mud-turtle about things. Not wanting to try *anything* new. But—well, now I know that there's good reasons why some things aren't done in the Vales and in this one in particular. Hydona's been explaining things to me…"

Her voice trailed off, and he thought she was finished, until she spoke up again. "You know, Hydona reminds me a great deal of Talia."

That old friend of hers. The one that's some kind of aide to her mother, and not the one that's the weapons teacher.

"In what way?" he asked.

She waved steam away from her face. "She made me give her a promise back when I was a child—that I would never simply dismiss anything she told me just because I didn't want to hear it, or that I was angry at her or anything else. That I would always go away and think about it for a day. Then if I couldn't agree with *any* of it, I had the right to be angry, but if I could see that she was right in at least some of what she'd said, I would have to come back to her and we'd talk about it as calmly as we could."

Well, if that isn't an opening chance to talk about her attitude—

"I know we don't know one another as well as you and Talia do," he said tentatively, "but could you grant me that same promise as a Wingsib?"

"Oh, dear," she said, her voice full of ironic chagrin. "Been a bitch, have I?"

He wanted to laugh, and decided against it. Still, he smiled. "Not exactly a bitch. But your attitude hasn't been helping me teach you. That was one reason why, when the gryphons volunteered to help, I agreed."

"Attitude?" she asked; her voice was carefully controlled to the point of being expressionless. Not a good sign.

"Attitude," he repeated, getting ready for an outburst. "You're very self-important, Elspeth. Very aware of your own importance, and making sure everyone else is aware of it, too. Take what you just said, about being a bitch. You laughed about it; deep down, you thought it was funny. You think you are so important it doesn't matter if you're offending those around you. You just make some perfunctory apology, smile and laugh, and that's that. But nothing has really changed."

She was quite silent over there in the steam, but he wondered if he'd just felt the temperature of the water rise by a bit. That silence was not a good sign, either.

"The truth is, Elspeth, right now you're an enormously talented liability." She wasn't going to like *that*, one bit. "I never heard of your land, outside of something vague from the old histories. You could be a bondslave from Valdemar, and we would be treating you the same as we are now. Your title doesn't matter, your country doesn't matter, and your people don't matter. Not to us."

Little waves lapped against him as she shifted, but she remained silent.

"What does matter is that you did help us; for that, we made you a Wingsib. Because we made you a Wingsister, you became entitled to training. *Not* because of a crown, and not because of a title. Not even because you asked us. Because you are part of the Clan. And what's more, the only ones willing to train you were myself and the gryphons. Everyone else has more important matters to attend to."

That wasn't precisely the truth, but it was close enough that it might shake her up a bit.

"So." No doubt about it, she was angry. "I don't matter, is that it?"

"No, that's not it. You matter; your title doesn't." He hoped she could see the difference. "So you might as well stop walking around as if there was a crown on your head. Kings don't mean much, out here. Anyone can call himself a king. Having the power to *enforce* authority—that's something else again. Until you have that, you'd best pay a little closer attention to the way you treat those around you because we are not impressed."

"Oh, really?" He sensed an angry retort building.

But then, she said nothing. Nothing at all. He tensed, waiting for an outburst that never came. He wondered what she was thinking.

Finally she yawned and stretched, water dribbling from her arms.

"I'm tired," she said, yawning again. "Too tired to think or react sensibly. I'll sleep on what you just said."

"Please do, and carefully, Elspeth. More could depend on it than amiable learning conditions." He looked down and sighed. "I do like you, and would prefer not to spend my time with you deciphering what you really mean under the royal posturing."

She rose, surprising him, and hoisted herself out of the pool, wrapping a towel around her wet hair, then bundling one of the thick, heavy robes around herself. She turned and looked down at him.

"You've said quite a bit," she told him quietly. "And I'm not sure what to think. Except that I'm certain you weren't being malicious. So—good night, Darkwind. If there's anything to say, I'll say it tomorrow."

She gathered her dignity about her like the robe, and walked off into the darkness, leaving him alone.

10

Twice Darkwind tried to wake up; twice he turned over to climb out of bed. Twice he closed his eyes again, and fell right back to sleep. And since no one came to fetch him, and there was hardly ever any noise around Starblade's *ekele*, he slept until well past midmorning unaware of how long he'd been dreaming.

When he finally awakened and *stayed* awake, he lay quietly for a moment, feeling confused and a bit disoriented. The light shouldn't have been coming in at that angle...

Then it finally occurred to him why it was doing so.

I haven't overslept like this in I can't think how long.

Feeling very much as if he'd done something overly self-indulgent, he snatched his newly cleaned clothing from a shelf and hastily donned it. There was no one in the *ekele* except Vree, who was still dozing. He vaulted the stairs to the ground and hurried down to Elspeth's *ekele* only to find her gone.

He was both embarrassed and annoyed. Annoyed that she had left without him; embarrassed because she'd needed to. She had at least left a note.

It looked like gibberish, until he realized that she had apparently spelled things the way they sounded to her.

Takt tu Starblaad n Winrlit sins we r not owt. Taa sed tu werk on bordr majik wit grifons. We r al waading fer u wen u waak up.

It took him a moment to puzzle out that she had checked with Starblade and Winterlight about what she and he should do since they weren't on patrol. He surmised that they had both asked her to work on border protections under the gryphons' tutelage. All three of them were expecting Darkwind whenever he got there. She hadn't even told him *where* they were working. They could be anywhere.

Once again, as with everything Elspeth did, he had mixed feelings. Pleased that she had taken it upon herself to find something useful to do; miffed that she hadn't consulted him.

He snatched a quick meal, and wondered if he should try to find Winterlight. Presumably the scout leader would know where they were.

Then it occurred to him that he hadn't bothered to ask the most obvious "person." Vree. The forestgyre was still back at Starblade's *ekele.* Undoubtedly, recovering from the way he'd stuffed himself yesterday.

He sent out a mental call, and was rewarded within a few moments by a flash of white through the high branches. He held out his arm, and Vree winged in, diving down to the ground and pulling up with spread wings in a head-high stall. He dropped delicately down onto Darkwind's wrist.

The gyre chirped at him, and inclined his head for a scratch. *:Messages?:* he asked.

:From Horse,: Vree replied. Horse—with the mental emphasis of importance—could only mean the Companion.

Vree's intelligence was limited; he had to get messages in pieces. *:Who is the message from Horse about?:*

:Female and Big Ones.: Vree leaned into the scratch, his eyes half-closed in pleasure.

:What is the message?: He had long ago given up being impatient with this slow method of finding things out. It was simply the way Vree and every other bondbird worked.

:At magic-place,: Vree replied.

Well, he *wouldn't* have to ask Vree to track them down. Good thing, too, since Vree was still drowsy from a long night of digestion. He'd be so fat Darkwind wouldn't be able to find his keelbone if he was fed that way all the time. Interesting, though, that the Companion could talk to Darkwind's bird. He wasn't surprised, but it wasn't something that Gwena had shown she could do—or wanted to do—before this.

And he wasn't going to have to leave the Vale, which was a bit of a relief. His backside was still a little sore and stiff from the ride yesterday.

:Do you need to leave the Vale?: he asked Vree. After all, the poor bird had been in here for more than a day. The gyre turned his head upside down as he considered the question and his bondmate.

:No,: Vree decided. *:Head not itch.:* That was how he had described the way that rogue powers of the Heartstone had affected him; that his head had itched. It had taken Darkwind a while before he had figured out that the bird meant *inside* his head, not outside.

:Go back to Starblade's, then,: Darkwind told him. *:Or hunt, if you want— just don't go too far from the Vale. I'm going to the magic-place and I don't want you in there. Your head would* really *itch.:*

:Yes,: Vree agreed, and half-spread his wings, waiting for Darkwind to launch him. The scout gave him a toss, and the gyre gained height rapidly, disappearing into the branches above.

No need to guess what the "magic-place" was: the Practice Ground. It was entirely possible to direct the border defenses from in there, although it would require great patience and careful shielding to keep the Heartstone from affecting whatever the three of them did in there.

Maybe that was the idea.

It'll certainly test the integrity of my shielding. And if I can shield against the Stone and work at the same time—I just might be ready to help handle the Stone myself. The gods only know that there'll be no peace for k'Sheyna until I do.

Well, if they were waiting for him, they were probably wondering if he'd fallen down a well or something. He'd better go prove he was still alive.

He had heard a mutter of conversation before he crossed the pass-through in the barrier that divided the rest of the Vale from the Practice Ground. The sudden silence that descended as he appeared told him that *he* had been the topic of discussion between Elspeth and the gryphons. He suppressed a surge of irritation at being talked *about*.

"Sorry I slept so late," he said, trying not to let his irritation show. "What are we doing?"

"Conssstructing ward-off ssspellsss," Hydona said mildly, as if she hadn't snapped her beak shut in mid-syllable the moment he came into view. "Elssspeth had one of the *hertasssi* look in on you, but you were sssleeping ssso deeply we decsssided you mussst need the ressst."

His irritation faded a little. At least they had checked on him before doing anything on their own. This particular task was not something he would have expected for the four of them. Ward-offs were simple things, but they had to be constructed and set carefully, another task of patience. Intended to discourage rather than hurt, ward-offs were the first line of defense on the border; the more intelligent the creature that encountered one, the more likely it was to be affected by it. A basilisk, for instance, would not be deterred by one, but a Changewolf probably would, unless it happened to be very hungry. Humans certainly would be; especially wanderers, peddlers, and the like—people who had crossed into Tayledras lands by accident.

Treyvan roused his golden-edged crest and refolded his wings with the characteristic rasp of feathers sliding across feathers. "You and I arrre not to make ward-offsss. Ssstarblade hasss a tasssk forrr usss; to move ley-linessss," he said. "We work while Elsspeth watchesss. We are to diverrrt them to the node beneath the lairrr, sssevering them from the Heartsssstone."

Darkwind frowned. That came under the heading of "tedious and necessary," as well. But anything to do with the Heartstone had its own share of danger involved. Certainly this was *not* beneath his abilities. It was along the lines of doing his share to work with the imbalanced Stone.

"Do you have any idea why we're doing this?" he asked.

"Thessse are minorrr linesss," Treyvan told him. "Ssstarrrblade wantsss all the minorrr linesss rrremoved, to sssee if they can be, and to sssee if thisss weakensss the Ssstone."

"Hmm. It could well be that once the minors are removed, the majors could be split into minors, and diverted in the same manner to other nodes, perhaps other Heartstones if there were any near."

Treyvan gave him one of those enigmatic, purely-gryphonish expressions of his, the one that always looked to Darkwind like "I know something you would dearly like to know." He spoke slowly. "It isss not imposssible."

Darkwind nodded, watching Elspeth with his Othersight; taking note of how she built the ward-off layer by layer, with the deft and delicate touch of a jeweler.

Showing no signs of impatience. And no signs of attitude, either.

And that irritated him all over again. Why couldn't she just have been reasonable in the first place?

Because no one put things to her in a way she understood, he reminded himself. *She's as much an alien here as the gryphons, no matter how comfortable she looks or how well she seems to fit in.*

And she did look as if she fit in, wearing the clothing he'd had made for her instead of those glaring white uniforms or the barbarian getup she'd had in her packs. She didn't quite look Tayledras, not with that hair—but until she spoke, no one would know she was not one of the Tayledras allies.

Get your mind on the task, Darkwind, and off the female.

"Hasn't anyone tried this line-diverting with the Stone before?" He couldn't believe that they hadn't. It seemed like the logical sort of thing to do.

"Yesss," the gryphon said, switching his tail restlessly. "But it did not worrk. And not asss we will be worrrking. Parrrtially the Sstone ressissted having the linesss taken; and parrrtially it rrreclaimed them within a day. We will give the linesss a new anchorrr, fixing them in place, rrrather than letting them find theirrr own anchorrr. Beforrre, they werrre allowed to drrrift, and the Sstone rrreclaimed them."

Elspeth put the final lock on the ward-off, and sent it away to settle into its place on the border. In his mind's eye it drifted away like a gossamer scarf blown by a purposeful wind—or a drift of fog with a mind of its own.

"I'm done," she announced, dusting off her hands. "Your turn." She took a seat nearby, her face alight with interest. "I thought these lines were like rivers or something. I didn't know you could change where they went."

"Generally only the little ones," Darkwind told her as he stretched. "At least, the major lines take all the mages of a Clan to reroute. That's something we do when we start a Vale; we find a node or make one, then relocate all the nearest big lines to it, so that we can drain the wild magic of an area into the Heartstone."

"It isss much like crrreating a riverrrbed before therrre isss a rrriver," Hydona said. "When the waterrr comess, it will follow the courssse laid forrr it. Ssso isss the wild magic to the grrreaterrr linesss. The grrreaterrr linesss have theirrr bankssss widened. The unsssettled magicsss join theirrr flow."

"I can see how that would make sense. And when you leave, you drain the magic from the Stone—along a new-made set of 'riverbeds,' I assume," Elspeth said, with a measure of surety in her voice.

"That, or a series of reservoirs are made temporarily."

"Then what?" she asked Darkwind.

"Then we sever the lines and let them drift back into natural patterns, and physically remove the Stone," he told her as he concentrated more of his attention on the complex of shields and probes he would need to handle his task. Shields against the Heartstone, some set to deflect energy away, some to resist, sensory probes to know what it was doing. Heartstones were not precisely *aware*, they certainly weren't thinking creatures, yet they were alive in a sense and normally tractable. But this one was no longer normal.

"But didn't you redirect the greater ley-lines in the first place to get rid of wild magic?" she asked, puzzled. "Or am I missing something?"

At least this time she didn't phrase it in a way that made me sound like I didn't know what I was talking about.

"We did—" This juggling of preparations and explanations was going to get him into trouble if he wasn't very careful, which, again, was probably Treyvan's intention. In a job like this, "trouble" had the potential of being very serious indeed. The gryphons were merciless in their testing. "We do. And by the time we leave, it's gone, changed into a stable form. The magic we're draining… isn't in its natural state." *Set the shield just—so—got to be able to sense through it without getting blinded if the Stone surges—*

"It doesn't belong here, and certainly not in a random state. Once we finish, the only thing left is the natural magic flow."

"Ah, so you take down the Stone and leave, and everything goes back to the way it was before the Mage Wars." Both he and Hydona had already explained the natural flow of magic energy to her; how it was created by living things, how it collected in ley-lines and reservoirs in the same way that water collected in streams and lakes.

"Probably not exactly, but at least a human can live here without fear that his children will have claws or two heads. And there won't be any other Changecreatures there either, unless they manage to get past our lands somehow." *I'll need a secondary shield to slap between the end of the severed line and the Stone…* "And when we leave, we take the innocent or harmless mage-created creatures with us, so *they* don't have to fear the full-humans who inevitably arrive."

Her face changed subtly at that, as if it was something that hadn't occurred to her until that moment. He would have liked to know what she was thinking.

Well, time enough for that later.

"I would like you behind as many shields as you can put up," he told her. "I do not know what is likely to happen; there has been so much work with the Stone that it may have changed the way it is likely to react. Can you watch through my 'eyes,' or Treyvan's?"

She nodded and extended a tentative "hand" to him, waiting for him to take it.

Well, that's promising. She didn't just fling a link at me without asking. He took her up, making certain that everything including surface thoughts was well-shielded against casual probes. He didn't *think* she would intrude, but there were always accidents. Some of his personal thoughts were less than flattering to her; most he would rather not share with anyone.

Treyvan indicated his readiness to act with a nod and a "hand" of his own. He settled into partnership with the gryphon with the same ease that one half of an acrobatic team has with the other.

But Treyvan waited for *him* to initiate the action. The gryphon's intention was clear; he meant to observe the act as a backup in case of trouble but to otherwise let Darkwind take the lead. The Heartstone glowered before them, sullen red, pulsing irregularly, with odd cracklings of random energy discharge flowing over and through it. The lines were anchored firmly in its base, concentrated amidst the major lines like roots from a crystalline tree of lightning, their rainbow-patterned raw power transformed by the stone itself.

Was he ready?

He would have to find out sooner or later. Might as well get it over with.

:All right, old friend,: he Mindsent. *:Let's make this one clean and quick.:*

Clean it was; quick, it was not.

The Stone resisted their attempts to sever the lines, as Treyvan predicted; he was not prepared for the uncanny way in which it reacted when he severed the first of them, though.

He formed his own power into a thin, sharp-edged "blade," sliding it into the join of Stone and line, intending to excise the line as if cleaning a rabbit hide. To his surprise, though, it Felt precisely like trying to cut the leg from an old, tough, and overcooked gamebird; he encountered a flexible resistance that was at once yielding and entangling.

He changed his tactic; changed from trying to cut his way through the join, to burning his way through. It resisted that as well, so he changed to a mental image of wielding bitter cold at the join, to make it brittle, then breaking it away. That worked, but it was a good thing he had secondary shields ready to protect the raw "ends," because the moment he got the line loose and held in one of his "hands," he Sensed movement from the Stone.

He passed the line to Treyvan, protected the end with an expanding shield. Just in time. The Stone itself created tiny tentacles of seeking power, probing after the line it had lost. Thin, waving strands of sullen red energy groped toward him, lengthening as they searched. The hair on the back of his neck rose as they came to him, then ignored him, and sought after the line. For one frightening moment, he thought they were coming after him, that the Stone *knew* he had taken the line and wanted retribution. They reminded him of the filaments of energy cast out in the creation of a Gate, the filaments that sought for and found the terminus at the other end and drew the two "together." They found the line—and slid along the surface of the shield protecting the severed end. Before they could seek further, perhaps touch past the sides of the shield, Treyvan hauled the line out of reach.

He shivered, watching the red fingers weaving and groping after the line. There was something very *wrong* about this. In all of his training, in all of the tales he had ever heard, there had been nothing like this behavior noted in a Heartstone.

Fortunately, these tentacles were neither as powerful nor as persistent as the Gate-energies; they receded into the seething chaos of the Stone moments after they pulled the line out of reach. But he certainly remained aware of them—and aware that the Stone might have more surprises.

He did not like the feeling that it knew exactly what he had done, and was angry with him.

With one "eye" on the Stone, he and Treyvan put their strength into relocating the line and, to some extent, the pathway it would take in the future. Moving the line was a great deal like pulling one end of a very heavy, very long rope—a rope that was, perhaps, as thick as his waist. The line resisted being moved from its accustomed course, just by pure inertia. By the time he got the severed end within easy distance of the new node, he felt as if he had run a long uphill race.

Treyvan's mind was focused on his and Hydona's home. He manipulated the node beneath the lair; that was appropriate, since he was the most familiar with it. He created a kind of "sticky," or "rough-surfaced" place on it; at least that was the analogy Darkwind used for himself. Whatever he did, it made the raw end of the line seek it as soon as Darkwind removed the shield; they joined, jumping together as a thread will jump to a silk-rubbed amber bead, or a bit of iron to a magnet. Then he ran magical pressure along the line, to straighten and broaden it slightly, so it would seat in place easier.

Darkwind studied the join for a moment, and mentally shook his head. :*I don't want to take any chances, this time,*: he said to Treyvan, feeling Elspeth in the back of his mind, watching with interest. :*I didn't like what the Stone did back there, and I don't want it to recapture these lines. Let's armor and shield the joining.*:

:*A good plan,*: Treyvan agreed.

It was probably not necessary. They were probably doing far more work than they needed to. But Darkwind could not get those seeking tentacles of power out of his mind—

—*and the more I weaken the Stone, the less chance it has of turning the tables on us when we finally drain it. Or whatever we do when we finally take it down.*

He was aware that he was thinking of the Stone as if it were a living, sentient creature. A discomforting fact of magic, also, was that often *thinking* about something made it happen, especially with skilled Adepts. Magery was not a matter of spell components and rituals at Adept level, it involved a high measure of subconscious skill and influencing of the physical world.

He had no doubt that there were others among the Hawkbrothers who thought of the Stone as having a mind—a half-mad, malicious one, to be sure. Personifying a problem was also not unheard of among people of all ages and races, much less mages. It *might*, by now, have a kind of mind. That might even be the root cause of its behavior back there. If it did, the last thing he wanted to do was underestimate it.

So he and Treyvan spent some time in ensuring that the Stone would *not* be able to get that particular ley-line back. And the next. And the next.

Four lines later, and he was quite ready to call an end to the exercise. So, he surmised, was Treyvan. When he disengaged his attention from Othersight and glanced over at the gryphon, poor Treyvan's crest drooped, and his neck-ruff had a decidedly wilted look about it.

:*That's enough,*: he said. :*We know this will hold. And even weakened, my father could do this alone. In fact, if I can do this, any pair of the Adepts should be able to. I think I'll advise that they work in pairs, though. I don't think anyone should ever turn an unguarded back on that Stone from now on.*:

Treyvan acknowledged his decision with a weary nod, and broke the link. As Darkwind brought all of his attention and concentration back to his physical body, the gryphon slumped over his foreclaws and sighed.

"That Sstone isss *mossst* ssstubborn, Darrkwind," the gryphon complained, his crest-feathers slowly rising. "I have neverrr ssseen anything like it."

"Let's get out of here," Darkwind urged. "I'm too tired to really trust my shields."

"I agrreee," Hydona rumbled, and turned to lead the way across the pass-through. On the other side of the barrier, Treyvan resumed his interrupted observation.

"I have neverrr ssseen anything like the way the Ssstone behaved," he repeated, his voice troubled, and his crest rising and falling a little with his agitation.

"You mean the way it tried to reach after the line once we severed it?" Darkwind asked. "By the way," he added in an aside to Elspeth, "Treyvan is right in that what you Saw wasn't normal behavior for a Heartstone. It's not supposed to reach out after things like that on its own."

The gryphon shuddered. "It acted asss if it werre alive and thinking. It issss jussst a *node.* Nodesss arrre not sssupposssed to be alive!"

"Yes and no," Darkwind replied. "Although this is sheer speculation on my part, I must remind you. But I have seen another kind of magic-imbued object act like that; when you build a Gate, the energy integrated into the portal does the same thing."

"Yesss, but *not* on itsss own," Treyvan corrected. "You make it do sssso!"

"Initially, perhaps," Darkwind argued, "but eventually, a mage can work parts of the spell without consciously thinking on it. After a while the process proceeds without direction—"

A flash of white in the branches up above should have warned him, but he was too tired to think of more than one thing at a time, and his mind was already occupied with the problem of the Heartstone. So it wasn't until Vree had made three-fourths of his dive at Treyvan's crest that he realized what was about to happen. And by then it was too late.

"NO!"

This time, Treyvan was tired, irritable—

Vree reached out claws to snatch and encountered something he had not expected.

Treyvan had suffered the bondbird's behavior enough.

Vree found himself flying straight for Treyvan's enormous beak; easily large enough to engulf the bird.

Darkwind reached out his hand in a useless gesture. He didn't even have time to *think*. It was all happening too fast. Vree frantically tried to pull up out of the dive.

Too late.

Crack.

The sound of Treyvan's beak snapping shut echoed across the Vale like nothing that had ever been heard there before. Like the sound of an enormous branch snapping in two, perhaps, or the jaws of a huge steel trap closing.

Or the hands of a giant slapping together. Clouds of songbirds took wing in alarm.

Vree screamed in pain and dove for the safety of Darkwind's wrist. Treyvan spat out the single tail-feather he'd bitten off with an air of aggrieved triumph.

Darkwind heaved a sigh of relief. Treyvan was a carnivore, as much a raptor as Vree was; something *he* never forgot. Vree was lucky; incredibly lucky—

Because Treyvan hadn't missed. He'd snapped off exactly what he intended to. The gryphons' reflexes were as swift and sure as the fastest goshawk, and if Treyvan had chosen, it would have been Vree's neck that was broken, not a tail-feather.

:I warned you,: Darkwind said, as Elspeth hovered between sympathy for the badly frightened bird and the laughter she was obviously trying to repress. *:I warned you, and you wouldn't listen!:*

Treyvan fixed the trembling, terrified bondbird with a single glaring eye. "You arrre jussst forrrtunate that I wasss not hungerrred," he hissed, and Darkwind "heard" him echoing his words in simple thought-images the bondbird would have no difficulty understanding. "You may not farrrre so well a sssecond time."

Vree cowered against Darkwind's chest, making tiny sounds of acute distress and pain.

:Now you're going to be minus that feather until you molt, unless I can imp it back in.:

:Hurts,: Vree wailed. *:Scared!:*

:I know it hurts. You should be glad he didn't pull it out, or bite your tail off.: Darkwind caressed the gyre until he stopped trembling, as Elspeth bent to pick up the feather and offered it to him.

He took the gesture at face value, and not for the one implied by Hawkbrother custom. *:Tell Treyvan you're sorry,:* he told Vree sternly, holding the bondbird out to the gryphon's face, within easy reach of that enormous beak.

Maybe this will impress him enough that he won't try the game again. He sighed. *I certainly hope so.*

The gyre looked up into the huge amber eyes as Darkwind held him up to the gryphon's face. *:S-s-s-sorry,:* the bird stuttered—no mean feat, mentally. *:S-s-s-sorry!:*

He certainly sounded sincere.

:Promise you won't do it again,: Darkwind ordered.

Vree shook, and slicked down all his feathers with unhappiness. *:Not snatch again,:* he agreed. *:Not ever. Never, never, never, never.:*

Darkwind transferred the bird from his wrist to the padded shoulder of his jerkin, where Vree huddled against his hair, actually pushing himself into the hair so that it partially covered him, hiding. Darkwind examined the feather carefully, hoping that it hadn't been too badly damaged. Vree depended on his tail for steering; the loss of one feather might not seem like a great deal, but it would make a difference in his maneuverability.

"You did a good job," he remarked to Treyvan, whose crest was rising slowly again. "It's a nice clean cut, only cracked the shaft a little. I won't need to use one of last year's set. I should be able to imp this one back in with no problems."

The gryphon chuckled. "It isss in part Vree'sss doing. If he had not turrned, I ssshould not have been able to catch the tail-featherssss. If he did not turrrn, I wasss going to catch him and hold him, then let him go."

"He'd have been frightened to death. Well, I think you've finally made an impression on him," Darkwind replied—*not* chuckling, though he wanted to, for fear of hurting the bird's feelings. "He finally sees you as a bigger, hungrier, meaner version of a bondbird, and not something like a glorified firebird. To tell you the truth, I think he's just fascinated by beautiful feathers, like your crest and the firebirds' tails. He snatches *their* feathers all the time."

Treyvan's crest rose completely, with mock indignation. "I ssshould hope we arrre not *glorrrified firrrebirds*," he snorted. "I am a vain birrrd, and I appreciate that he findsss my cressst ssso attrrractive, but we arrre not anything like firrrrebirrrdssss."

"What are you, though?" Elspeth asked, suddenly. "I mean, you don't really look like anything I know of—other than vaguely like hawk-eagles and falcons."

"Oh, well, we arrre not anything you know," Hydona replied, vaguely. "Not hawk, not falcon. It isss not asss if sssomeone took bitsss and piecesss of birrrd and cat and patched usss togetherrr, afterrr all!"

"Yes, but there *are* supposed to be gryphons north and west of Valdemar," Elspeth persisted. "But there aren't any in any of the inhabited lands I know—so where do you two come from?"

"Wessst." Hydona shrugged. "You would not know the place. Even the Hawkbrotherrsss had not hearrrd of it."

Elspeth wasn't giving up that easily. "Well, is that where your kind comes from? Is that why there aren't any gryphons in Valdemar?"

Treyvan gave her a droll look out of the corner of his eye. "If you arrrre asssking if we arrre a kind of Changechild orrrr Pelagirrr monsssterrr," he replied, "I can tell you that we arrre not, and thanksss be to Sssskandrrranon forrr that. We werrrre crreated by one of the Grreat Magessss, the Mage of Ssssilence, whom we knew asss Urrrtho. That wasss a long time ago, beforrre the Mage Warrrs. He crrrreated the *herrrtasssi* asss well, and othersss. That wasss hisss grrreat powerrr and joy, to crrreate new crrreaturessss. Ssso they sssay."

Before Elspeth could leap in with another question, Hydona yawned hugely and looked up at the sky. "It isss late," she said abruptly, "and I am hungerrred, even if Trrreyvan isss not."

"Not hungerrred enough forrr falcon," Treyvan chuckled. "But a nicsse clawful of geesssse, now—orrr a young deerr…"

Hydona parted her beak in a gryphonic smile. "I think we will leave you now, Darrrkwind."

"Until tomorrow, then," he said, smoothing Vree's feathers with one hand. "Sleep well, and pass my affections on to Lytha and Jerven."

"Mine, too," Elspeth piped up, to Darkwind's surprise.

"Tomorrrrow," Treyvan agreed. The two gryphons moved off down a side path that would take them to the entrance of the Vale; they couldn't possibly take off from within it, for the interlacing branches of the great trees would make it too difficult for them to fly without damage to themselves or the trees.

Elspeth looked after them for a moment, then made a little shrug and turned back to Darkwind. From her expression, there was a lot going on behind her eyes.

"Is there something bothering you?" he asked, thinking she might have questions about the lesson just past.

But her observations had nothing to do with magic. "They are certainly very good at avoiding questions they don't care to answer," she pointed out dryly. "This isn't the first time I've tried to pin them down about where they come from and what they are, and their answers have always been pretty evasive."

"You can trust them," he felt moved to protest.

"Oh, I have no doubt of that; after all, Need trusted them, and she's about the most suspicious thing in the universe. But they seem to have as many secrets as a Companion!" This, with a glance at Gwena, who shook her head and mane and snorted. "I had the feeling that they hadn't told the Tayledras much more than they've told me."

He nodded slowly. She was absolutely right about that, anyway. He hadn't quite realized how little he knew about them, really. The fact that they had been his friends for so long had obscured the fact that what he knew about them was only what they had chosen to reveal.

There had been any number of surprises from them, lately. The fact that they were fluent in the ancient Kaled'a'in tongue, for instance, and just how much of a mage Treyvan really was. That they spoke of Urtho as if *they* knew the lost history of the Mage Wars in much greater detail than any Tayledras did.

As if that history hadn't been lost to their people, whoever and wherever those people were.

Interesting. Very interesting. But it was so *frustrating!* They didn't even work at being mysterious, the way Elspeth's friend Skif did. They just *were.*

It gave him enough food for thought that he remained silent all the way back to Elspeth's *ekele*, and from the expression on her face, she found plenty of room for speculation there herself.

11

Skif packed the new supplies he had gotten from the *hertasi* carefully; Cymry needed to be able to move with the same agility she had without packs once they got back on the trail. Lumpy and unbalanced packs would not make either of them very happy.

"You look like a Hawkbrother," Elspeth observed from the rock beside him; like everything in the Vale, it had been made to look natural, while being placed in the perfect position to be used as a seat, and had been carefully sculpted to serve that very purpose. She sat cross-legged with a patch of sun just touching her hair. There were already a few white threads in it; he wondered how long it would be before she was completely silver. Wintermoon had confided that Elspeth was handling more of the powerful energies of node-magic in her first few months than most Tayledras Adepts touched in a year or more. And she spent a great deal of time in the unshielded presence of the Heartstone. While Wintermoon was quite certain that none of this would harm her, he did warn Skif that her training and the discipline needed to handle such powers might cause some changes in his friend, and not just physical ones.

Indeed, there were some changes since he had left the Vale. Elspeth seemed a little calmer, and considerably more in control of her temper. She no longer reminded him of Kero, or her mother... she was only, purely, Elspeth. His very dear friend—but no more. He could not imagine anyone having a romantic attachment to this cool, contemplative person; it would be like having a fixation on a statue.

He glanced up at her and smiled. "So do you," he said. "It suits you."

She really did look like a Hawkbrother; she was growing her hair longer, and although it wasn't yet the stark white of a mage, or the mottled camouflage colors of a scout, she had somehow learned the Tayledras tricks of braiding it so that it stayed out of the way without looking severe. And the tunic and trews she wore—flowing silk in deep burgundy, cut so that the tunic fastened up the side with little antler-tips—well, it suited her much better than anything she'd ever worn at home.

"What happened to your Whites?" he asked.

She laughed. "They disappeared, and I have the feeling I won't see them again until we're ready to leave. I have the feeling that the *hertasi* disapprove of uniforms on principle. Whenever I ask about them, the *hertasi* give me this *look*, and say 'they're being cleaned.' It's been weeks now, and they're still being cleaned."

"Mine are probably with yours," Skif said. "Wintermoon wouldn't let me bring them; he said they weren't even suited to winter work. He made me get scouts' gear."

She chuckled a little. "I'm beginning to agree with Kerowyn about Whites," she told him. "At least, about the way they're made. You get tired of them. They can't have changed in hundreds of years—you know, we really could stand to have a style choice, at least."

He shrugged. "Probably nobody ever thought much about it." He lifted the pack experimentally. It was about as heavy as he wanted Cymry to carry, and after all, it wasn't as if they were cut off from k'Sheyna and more provisions. "That's going to do it, I think."

Elspeth measured the pack with her eyes. "What's that—two weeks' rations at the most?"

"About. We'll be back in by then." He fastened both packs to Cymry's saddle, and turned back to Elspeth. "I'm sorry I didn't have any news for you."

She shrugged. "I'll tell you the truth, big brother—I really don't think it's all that important for me to get Need back, even assuming she'd be willing to return to me, which I doubt. I think it *is* important for you to find Nyara, for both your sakes."

He flushed but didn't reply to that directly. Another change; she was either much improved at reading body language or she had picked up an uncanny ability to intuit things. "I don't know how much you're aware of the weather in here, but we're just about on to winter out there," he said. "We won't be able to cover as much ground once it starts snowing."

She didn't seem concerned. "Take as much time as you need. Our orders haven't changed; no one needs us back home, and I need training as complete as I can get. Gwena says that things haven't deteriorated with Ancar and Hardorn any more than they had the last time we got word. It might simply be the weather. They're already into winter up there."

"And no one, sane or insane, attacks in winter." He nodded. "With luck, you'll be ready by spring."

He had other, unspoken thoughts. *And with more luck, your Darkwind will be willing to come along when we leave.* He smiled, but only to himself. Elspeth wasn't the only one good at reading body language.

Elspeth shifted her position a little. "Well, we've also got the possibility of some new allies. According to Gwena, there's some indication that Talia, Dirk, and Alberich are getting somewhere in negotiating with the Karsites."

"The—what?" He felt his eyebrows flying up into his hairline with astonishment. Last thing *he* had heard, people were simply grateful that the Karsites were too embroiled with Ancar and their own internal politics to harass the Border they shared with Valdemar. "When did all this start?"

"Early fall—about when we reached here," she said. "Sorry; I forgot that I didn't hear about it until after you left." She looked up and frowned a little. "Let me see if I can tell you this all straight; I've been getting it in bits and pieces. Alberich got some tentative contacts with someone supposedly official in the Karsite army through a really roundabout path. It was supposed to be someone he knew and tentatively trusted."

"From Karse?" He could hardly believe it. "How did anything get out of Karse?"

"Convolutedly, of course; Gwena said the pathway involved traders and the renegade faction of the Sunlord that keeps allegiance with Valdemar." She raised an eyebrow. "Not the most secure line of communication, and the message was pretty vague. Sort of—'we might be willing to talk to you people if you happened to show up at this place and time'; he wasn't sure he trusted it at all, but it was the first positive gesture we've had from those people in hundreds of years, so he didn't want to dismiss it out of hand."

"He wouldn't, and he'd be right," Skif agreed. "But it could have been a trap, counting on the idea that he might be homesick."

She snickered. "Surely. Anybody who'd think that doesn't know Alberich. Anyway, that was about a month ago; he and Eldan and Kero checked the stories out, and they seemed to be genuine. Two weeks ago, they were actually approached officially. Then a week ago Mother arranged for Talia and Dirk to go down to the Border, the Holderkin lands, and meet an envoy from the Karsite government."

"Which means the Sun-priests." He tried the thought out in his mind. "Any idea what started all this?"

Elspeth started to chuckle. He gave her a quizzical glance.

"If Gwena is relaying what Rolan told her correctly—it's as convoluted as the Karsites are. The infighting settled this fall—and the Priest-King suddenly seems to be a Queen now. The envoys are half women, and Talia had picked up a kind of grim 'we're all women together' kind of feeling from them, though whether that's their feeling about her, or the Priest-Queen's feeling about Selenay, I don't know."

"Interesting," Skif said absently. In either case, the chances of coming to an agreement were much better.

"That's only the first factor. Ancar has been harassing them much more than he has us, probably because they don't have that anti-magic defense we do. That, it seems, was bad enough, but now he's stealing the Sun-priests' pet demons, and that was absolutely the last straw." She grinned like a horse trader who's just sold an ill-tempered Plains-pony as a Shin'a'in stud. "That must have doubly stuck in their throats—not only to have to come to *us*, the unholy users of magic, but to have to admit that *they* were using magic themselves!"

"Ah, if I know Talia, she was very careful about not rubbing their noses in the fact." He shook his head and chuckled. "That's something I would have had a hard time doing."

"You and me both," she admitted. "Anyway, that's where things stand at home. With luck, we can at least get them to promise not to harry our borders until Ancar is dealt with once and for all."

Skif rubbed the back of his neck, and stared off into the distance. North and east. "I'd like to be there," he said, more than half to himself. "I really would. Peace with our old enemy… Havens, wouldn't that be something!"

"I'll believe it when it happens," she replied. "For now, it's enough to know we aren't the only ones that Ancar's been hurting. That at least opens up the possibility of uniting against a common enemy."

He shook off his reverie. "Amazing. But I have my own job to take care of. Standing here and biting my nails over something happening hundreds of leagues away is not going to accomplish much of anything."

"I have patrol with Darkwind," she told him. "We're taking an evening shift, with one of the scouts that flies an owl. He's got some beasties hanging about at night that he wants a mage to have a look at."

"Gryphons, too?" he asked with interest. He liked Treyvan and Hydona a great deal, and his sole regret in going out with Wintermoon was that he was unable to learn more about them.

"No, they're going to stay with the little ones; we monopolize enough of their time as it is." She started to chuckle.

"What's so funny?" Skif wanted to know. "Oh, just their *kyree*-friend, Rris. The *kyree* are usually so dignified; Torrl is, anyway. But Rris is like—like a big puppy. All bounce and friendliness. But what's funniest is that he's just *full* of stories about 'my famous cousin, Warrl.'"

That sounded familiar, somehow. "Warrl. That—that can't be the same *kyree* that was Kero's teacher's bondmate, is it?"

She nodded vigorously. "The same. And hearing the same stories Kero used to tell us told from the *kyree* point of view is an absolute stitch!"

He sighed. Another thing he was missing. Well, he couldn't be here and out there at the same time, and on the whole, he was doing better and more productive work out there. There had been an encounter with another pack of *wyrsa*—this time on their terms, and he and

537

Wintermoon had destroyed them. There'd been more of those *gandels* that they'd had to lure into a pit-trap—and some smaller, but still nasty, encounters.

All of which meant hazards no k'Sheyna scout would have to face, something that Winterlight, the new scout-leader, had been quick to point out to the Council. Permission to return to the search had been readily given.

Though several of Wintermoon's friends told him he was crazy, staying out in the winter-bound forest when he could be warm and comfortable in the Vale; in his off-duty hours, anyway.

Skif still wasn't quite certain of Wintermoon's motivation, but the scout had told him repeatedly that even if he had been running patrols, he would have continued to live in his *ekele* outside the Vale. That to him, winter camping was no great hardship.

If that was the way he felt, Skif would take his words at face value.

"We'd better get going, then," he said. "Wintermoon should have gotten the cold-weather gear together by now." Already he wanted to be back on the hunt...

"Darkwind and Gwena are probably waiting for me. I'd better go get my scout gear on." She bounced to her feet and planted a kiss on his cheek. "See you in about two weeks?"

"Right." He patted her on the head as if she were a very small child; she mock-snarled at him. "Don't get into too much trouble, all right?"

"Hah! Me?" With a wave, she was gone.

The first snow of the season was going to be a substantial one. "Does winter always start so—enthusiastically?" Skif asked his guide, as they arranged things in the shelter they had rigged beneath the overhanging limbs of a huge pine. It was a very small shelter, compared to the way-stations the Heralds used, but it was big enough for two if no one moved much. Skif couldn't begin to guess what it was made of; some kind of waterproof silk, perhaps. Wintermoon had taken it from a pouch scarcely bigger than a rolled-up shirt. Light for now came from a tiny lantern holding a single candle suspended from the roof; not much, and not very bright.

Wintermoon shrugged. "Sometimes yes, sometimes no," he replied. "Often it depends upon what the mages have done. Great fluxes in the energy-flow of magic can change the weather significantly, usually to make it worse."

"Now he tells me," Skif said to the roof of the tent. "Havens, if I'd known that, I'd have kept everyone out of that to-do with Falconsbane!"

"Oh, that was not significant," the Hawkbrother replied carelessly. "Not enough to make any real difference. Building a Gate, now—one has to make certain that the weather is going to hold clear for several days, if one has a choice, or any storm will worsen. If they manage to drain the Heartstone—that would be significant, very much so. That is why we try always to work the greater magics in stable times of the year."

"For a nonmage you certainly know a lot," Skif observed. Wintermoon only laughed.

"One must, if one is Tayledras. As one must know horses, even if one is a musician or weaver, if one is also Shin'a'in. Magic is so much a part of what we do that we *all* of us are affected by it, if only in the bleaching of hair and eyes." He completed rigging his own sleeping place, and eyed Skif's pad of pine boughs dubiously. "Are you certain that you wish to sleep upon that? It looks very cold and stiff, and I brought a second hammock."

"I'm used to it," Skif replied. "I'm not used to being suspended like a bat."

"Well, it is warmer so." Wintermoon looked out of the flap of the tent, and resecured it. "This will be a heavy storm. I think we will be here until well past midmorning at the least. Nothing is like to be moving this night, not even a cold-drake."

"Comforting. At least nothing can wrap us up in our tent and carry us away." The two owls, Corwith and K'Tathi, had perches in one corner of the shelter; packs took up the remaining space, including beneath Wintermoon's hammock, making the area very crowded. Cymry and the *dyheli* had a lean-to rigged against the side of the shelter, and were huddled together under blankets.

:Are you all right?: he asked his Companion. *:If you're too cold, we'll find some other way—:*

:No worse than if I'd been up north,: she told him. *:Better, in fact. The snow may be heavy, but it isn't that cold, really. And the* dyheli *are warm, and good company.:*

Well, if she wasn't going to complain, he wasn't going to worry.

Hawkbrother winter gear was a lot better than his own; lighter, for one thing. Instead of relying on layers of wool, fur and leather for their bedrolls and heavy-weather coats, they had something light and fluffy sandwiched between layers of what he knew to be waterproof spider silk, because the *hertasi* had told him so. No cloaks for them, either. Cloaks were all very well if you were spending most of your time on horseback, but not if you were trying to make your way through a pathless forest. Cloaks caught on every outstretched twig; the slick-finished coats did not.

"Would we were mages," Wintermoon observed wistfully. "We could make lights, heat—I have a brazier, but it needs a smoke hole, and that lets in as much cold as the brazier supplies heat in any kind of wind."

"According to Elspeth, an Adept doesn't need to make heat; he can ignore the cold." Skif shook his head. "I don't know about that."

"Oh, that is possible, but there is a price in weariness," Wintermoon told him. "Keeping warm requires some kind of power, whether it be the power of the fire, or the power of magic. If she has not learned that yet, she will."

"Ah." He felt a bit better. "I thought that sounded a bit too much like—well—magic."

"Tayledras magic is no more than work with tools other than hands," Wintermoon laughed. "Or so I keep telling my mage-friends. My brother said that. I think of all the mages I know, he is the most sensible, for he never relies on his power when his hands will do."

It occurred to Skif that, given that philosophy, Darkwind was probably the best teacher Elspeth could have. She tended to fall prey to enthusiasm about anything new, and look to it as the solution for every problem. Darkwind should keep her from falling prey to that fault. "Are you changing our tactics now that we've had heavy snow?" he asked.

"Actually, it will be easier." Wintermoon slid into his hammock with a sigh; bundled up to the neck as he was, he looked like a human-headed cocoon. "The trees are leafless, snow covers the ground. Nyara will be hard put to hide the signs of her passing, of her living. The owls will most probably find her. *We,* though—we will be facing more of the hunters, and performing our secondary task for the Clan. The season of stupid young is over, the season of dying old not yet on us. This is the season of hunger for the hunters. This is when we truly prove our worth to k'Sheyna."

Skif climbed into his own bedroll, and shivered as he waited for it to warm around his body. The hot springs and summerlike atmosphere of the Vale seemed a world away. "The Clan means a lot to you, doesn't it? Even though—"

"Though my father rejected me, the Clan saw to it I was not left parentless," Wintermoon said firmly. "It is more than simple loyalty. K'Sheyna is my family in every way that matters. Can you understand that, who had no real family? I sometimes wonder."

"Maybe if I hadn't been Chosen…" Skif listened to the soft ticking of snow falling on the fabric of the shelter, listened to the creaking of boughs in the forest beyond. "I do have a family, you know. More fathers and mothers, brothers and sisters than I can count. The Heralds gave me that, and they are *my* family in every way that counts."

"So—the Heralds are a kind of Clan?" Wintermoon asked curiously. "A Clan that is not related by blood, but by—purpose."

"I guess we are." It was an intriguing thought, one that had its own logic. Interesting. "I want my own family, though. Eventually. Well, I told you all about that."

"Where?" Wintermoon wanted to know. "Have you a place that has won your heart?"

His first thought was that farmhouse, so long ago. That was something he had to think about. "Back at Haven, I suppose, though it could be anywhere. Come to that, there's a lot of peace here. More than there is at home." Now that he thought about it, if there was any one place he'd seen in all of his travels that he felt called to him, it was here. "The Vale seems serene, tranquil. I don't really understand why you don't spend more time there."

"Appearances can be deceiving," Wintermoon replied dryly. "If you were at all sensitive to the currents of magic, you would find it less than peaceful, even if the Stone were intact. And every Vale is under a constant state of siege. When it isn't, it is time to move on to a new one. But you—how could *you* bear to leave the city? I should think you would miss the people and all the doings. There must be much to keep you busy there."

"Not that much." He considered the question. "It's just as easy to be lonely in a city as out in the wilderness. Easier, really. It's harder to get to know someone when you meet in a crowded place. People can freely ignore you in the city; they can assume they don't have any responsibility for you. When there are fewer people, I think they begin assuming some kind of responsibility, simply because you naturally do the same."

"Perhaps. But let me show you how a Vale appears to me, before you assume that it is a kind of wonderland." There was silence for a moment. "Take the Vale itself; there is the constant undercurrent of magic, even in a Vale with an intact Heartstone, because magic is how the place is maintained. It is as if there were always bees droning somewhere nearby, or something humming in a note so low it is felt more than heard. Then there are ever the *hertasi* underfoot." Wintermoon sighed. "They mean well, but they are so social they are nearly hive-minded. They cannot understand that one might wish to be without company."

"I'd noticed that," Skif chuckled. "If I'm not asleep, there always seemed to be a *hertasi* around wanting to know if I needed anything."

"And if you are asleep, they are there still. It can get tiresome," Wintermoon said with resignation. "They also do not see that some of us can live without certain luxuries. For instance—did they steal your clothing?"

Skif blinked with surprise. "Why—yes—"

"They do not approve of it," Wintermoon told him. "I am certain of that. It is too plain, too severe. You will not see it again until you are ready to leave. And even then, I fear they will have made alterations to it."

Skif choked on a laugh.

"Oh, no doubt this is amusing, but what if one *prefers* simpler clothing? What if one *prefers* to make one's own food? What if one would rather his quarters were left undisturbed? Then there is the matter of my Clansfolk."

"What about them?" Skif asked.

"Several matters. The one which concerns both of us is the attitude that those with little magic are less important." Wintermoon's voice conveyed faint bitterness. "It matters not that someone must do the hunting, must keep the borders secure, must meet with the Shin'a'in and arrange for those few things we cannot make. There are a hundred things each day that must be done that need no magic. Yet those of us whose magic is only in the realm of thought and not of power are, at least in this Clan, often discounted."

"That might only be because of Starblade," Skif pointed out. "It could change."

"Indeed. It may, and I hope it will. But if it does not—you, Wingsib, will, soon or late, find yourself accounted of less worth than your friend Elspeth."

The bedroll warmed, and Skif relaxed into it. "That wouldn't be anything new," he replied drowsily. "Back home, after all, she's the Queen's daughter, and I'm nobody important."

"Ah." The tiny candle dimmed and died, leaving them in the darkness. On the other side of the tent wall, one of the *dyheli* snored gently, a purring sound like a sleepy cat. "They also do not much care for Changecreatures."

"You mean Nyara." Skif forced himself to think of her dispassionately. "Well, we'll worry about that when we find her. No point in getting worked up over something that hasn't happened yet."

"They have other prejudices," Wintermoon warned. "Outsiders in general tend to be met with arrows and killing-bolts. And that is not the k'Sheyna way only; that holds for all Clans. Only your acceptance by the Shin'a'in and the presence of your Companions kept you from gaining a similar welcome."

Skif yawned. "I'm sorry, Wintermoon, but I'm drifting off. I wish I could concentrate on what you're saying, but I can't."

The Tayledras sighed. "I suppose it is just as well," he admitted. "I am losing track of my thoughts."

Skif gave up trying to fight off sleep. "We can take this up in the morning, maybe," he muttered after a while. And he never heard Wintermoon's answer.

There was too much light coming in the tower window.

Nyara unwrapped herself from her furs and winced as cold air struck her. She wrapped a single wolfskin about her shoulders, and moved cautiously to the narrow slit in the eastern wall. She looked out of her tower window on a world transformed, and panicked.

Snow. The forest is covered in snow!

It was at least knee-deep; deeper in some places. The wall below her glittered with patches of ice—predictably, wherever there were hand-and foot-holds.

What am I going to do ?

She wasn't ready for this. She still hadn't worked out a way of getting up and down her wall in snow and ice, and he wasn't nearly good enough a hunter yet.

All the game must have gone into hiding, or worse, into hibernation; it will see me coming long before I'm in range, and I can't run or leap as fast; it'll be like trying to run in soft sand, but so cold.

Her mind ran around in little circles, like a frightened mouse—and it was that image that enabled her to get hold of herself.

Stop that, she told herself sternly. She forced herself to sit and *think,* as Need had taught her; to use all that energy that was going into panic for coming up with answers.

The first, and most immediate problem, was how she was going to get down out of the tower to hunt in the first place.

And she had already come up with one possibility; she just hadn't done anything about it yet. Well, now she was going to have to.

We have plenty of rope, and no one is going to cross all that snow without leaving tracks a baby rabbit could see, so there's no harm in using a rope to get up and down with. No one will get in here to use it without my knowing. I can just secure one end of the rope up here and climb down that way. That isn't perfect, but then, what is?

And as for game, well, whatever hampered her would also hamper the game. In fact, as cold as it was, she could even think about creating a hoard for emergencies; if she hung the carcasses just inside the tower, they'd stay frozen. If she put them high enough, they'd be out of reach of what scavengers were brave enough to venture inside with her scent all over everything. She could even take deer, now, and not worry about spoilage.

And since she hadn't bothered the deer yet, they did not yet regard her as a predator. Snow would be at least as hard on them as it was on her.

I can pull the carcasses easier through the snow, too; I won't have to try to cut them up to carry them back...

With a plan in mind, at least for getting into and out of her shelter, and the possibility of new game to augment the old, she looked down on the forest with curiosity rather than fear.

She had never seen snow before, not like this. Falconsbane had copied the Tayledras, whether he admitted it or not, keeping the grounds of his stronghold free of ice and snow, and warmed to summer heat. He had hated winter; hated snow and ice, and spent most of the wintry days locked up inside his domain, whiling away the hours in magery or pleasure. The only time she had ever seen snow was when she had ventured to the gates, and had looked out on a thin slice of winter woods and trampled roadway from the tiny and heavily barred windows. She was not permitted on the tower tops, lest she attempt to climb down and escape, and the windows in wintertime were kept shuttered and locked against the season.

She had always dreaded the coming of winter, for during the winter months her father often became bored. It was difficult for his creatures to move through the snow; even more difficult for them to slip into the Hawkbrothers' lands unseen. And of course, Falconsbane would not venture outside unless it was an absolute emergency, so his own activities were greatly curtailed. Humans tended to keep to their dwellings in winter, and the intelligent creatures to band together, so the opportunities for acquiring victims were also reduced. He dared not be too spendthrift with the lives of his servants, for there were only so many of them, and fewer opportunities to get more. They were trapped within the walls, too, and if he pushed them too far, they might become desperate enough to revolt. Even he knew that. So Falconsbane's entertainments had to be of his own devising.

When he grew bored, he often designed changes he wished to make in his own appearance, and worked them out on her, an activity that, often as not, ranged from mildly to horribly painful. And when that palled, there were other amusements in which she became his plaything; the old games she now hated, but had then both loathed and desired.

No, until now, winter had not been her favorite season. Spring and fall had been best—spring, because her father was out of the stronghold as often as possible, eager to escape the too-familiar walls, and fall, because he was seizing his last opportunities to get away before winter fell.

But this year, the coming of winter had not induced the fear that it had in the past.

Odd. I wonder why?

Then she realized that all the signs of winter that she had learned to fear were things Falconsbane had created; the increasing number of mage-lights to compensate for the shortening days, the rising temperature in the stronghold, and the shuttering of the windows against the gray sky.

Any mage might do those things—there were other signs in Falconsbane's stronghold that marked the season of fear.

Forced-growth of strange plants brought in to flower in odd corners, creating tiny, often dangerous, mage-lit gardens. Many of those plants were poisonous; some had envenomed thorns, or deadly perfumes. It was one of her father's pleasures to see who would be foolish enough to be entrapped by them.

More slaves in the quarters reserved for those Falconsbane intended to use up, slaves usually young and attractive, but not terribly bright. Her father tended to save the intelligent, warping their minds to suit his purposes, keeping them for two or even three years before pique or a fit of temper brought their twisted lives to a close.

Strained expressions on the faces of those who hoped to survive the winter and feared they might not. Sometimes, usually in the darkest hours of the winter, her father's temper exceeded even his formidable control—though most of the victims were those former "favorite" slaves...

There had been none of that this year. The shortening of the days had not signaled anything to her, and she had simply reacted to the long nights by sleeping more. There had been no blazing of lights in every corner to wake old memories, merely the flickering of her own friendly fire. There was no tropic heat to awaken painful unease, only the need to move everything closer to the firepit, and to build up a good supply of wood.

This place that she lived in could be called squalid, compared to the lush extravagancies of an Adept's lair, but it was *hers*. She had made it so with pride, the first place she could truly call her own, unfettered by her father's will. The wood and rope and furs were placed by her desires alone, with the advice and help of Need, who had become a trusted friend. Taken as a sum of goods, it was insignificant; taken in its context, it was delightful.

The view from her window surprised her with unexpected beauty; the ugliest tangles of brush and tumbled rock had been softened by the thick blanket of snow.

It was astonishing; it took her breath away. She simply admired it for many long moments before turning her thoughts back to the reality that it represented.

It could also be deadly to one who had no real experience in dealing with it.

For a moment, a feeling of helplessness threatened to overwhelm her with panic again.

She quelled it. *No point in getting upset—I have Need. She can always help me solve any problems that come up. If we have to, she can deal with them with magic.*

She turned her mind to her sword—

And met only blankness.

She never quite remembered the first few hours; hours when she had huddled in her furs, alternately weeping and howling. It was a good thing nothing dangerous had come upon her then; she would have been easy prey.

When she exhausted herself completely, she fell asleep, doing so despite her fears, despite her despair, she had drained herself that badly.

When she woke again, in the mid-afternoon, the sheer, unthinking panic was gone, although the fear remained. Somehow she managed; that day, and the next, and the next.

She found game, building a blind beside the pond where the ducks and geese came to feed, and covering it with snow. She caught a goose that very night, and not content with that, hung it in her improvised larder to freeze and scoured the forest for rabbits. She didn't catch any of those, but she discovered a way to fish in the ice-covered ponds, using a bit of metal found in the tower, scuffed until shiny, as bait.

She hauled wood up to her shelter, and kept it reasonably warm and dry; made plans for a blind up in one of the trees above a deer-trail, so that she could lie in ambush for one.

Somehow she kept panic from overwhelming her at the thought that the sword was no longer protecting her from detection.

For if something had happened to Need, she would have to protect herself. She had no choice, not if she wanted to live. Sooner or later, something would come seeking her.

She spent hours crouched beside the fire, bringing up everything Need had ever told her about shielding, about her own magic. Then she spent more hours constructing layer after layer of shields, tapping into the sluggish power of the sleeping forest and into her own energies. But to tap into her own power, she needed a great deal of rest and food—which brought her right back to the problem of provisions. She decided that she *must* start hunting deer; that there was no choice, that it was the only way to buy her the necessary days of rest and recovery when she built up her shielding. The rest of the time—the hours of darkness before sleep finally came—she spent bent over the sword, begging, pleading with it to come back to life. Prodding and prying at it, to try and discover what had gone wrong. Something must have; there was no reason for the blade to simply fall silent like that, not without warning.

And all with no result. The blade was a sword now; no more, no less. A weapon that she could not even use properly, for without Need's skill guiding her, she was as clumsy as a child in wielding it.

Finally, after trying so hard on the evening of the third day that she worked herself into a reaction-headache, she gave up, falling into an exhausted sleep, a sleep so deep that not even her despair penetrated it. A dreamless sleep, so far as she knew.

When she woke again, quite late on the morning of the fourth day, the clouds had vanished overnight, and sun blazed down through the windows of her tower with cold, clear beams. When she looked out of her window, she had to pull back with her eyes watering. It was *too* bright out there; too bright to see. The sun reflected from every surface, and although there were shadows under the trees, they were not dark enough to give her eyes any rest.

Now she knew what her father's men had meant when they spoke of "snow blindness."

There was no way she was going to be able to see out there without getting a headache, unless she found some way to shade her eyes.

Shading her eyes probably wouldn't do that much good; there would still be all the light reflecting up from the snow.

Wait, though, she could *change* her eyes. After all of Need's lessons, she had a little control over her body; she might be able to make her eyes a little less sensitive, temporarily… perhaps darken them to let less light through…

:It's about time you started looking inside yourself for answers,: came the raspy, familiar mind-voice.

She whirled, turning away from the light, peering through shadows that were near-black in contrast with the intense sunlight. "You're back!" she cried, staring at the vague shape of the sword leaning against the firepit where she had left it the night before.

:I never left,: Need said smugly. *:I just decided to let you see you could manage completely on your own for a while.:*

Anger flared; she took a deep breath and fought it down. Anger served no purpose unless it was channeled. Anger only weakened her and could be used as a weapon against her. She reminded herself that Need never did anything without a good reason.

Anger faded enough so that she was in control, not the emotion. She tried not to think of the fear, the first hours of desperation—of all the endless hours when she had been certain that she would not live through this season. That would only make her angry again.

"Why?" she asked bluntly. "Why did you *do* that to me? I didn't do anything to warrant being punished, did I?"

The sword didn't answer directly. *:Look around you. What do you see? The game stocked away, the firewood, all the defenses you constructed.:*

She didn't have to look, she knew what was there. "Get to the point," she snapped. "Why did you leave me alone like that? Why did you leave me defenseless?"

:Did I do any of that, any of the things you've accomplished in the last few days? Did I hunt the game, catch the fish, rig that hidden ladder to the top?: There was a certain quality in Need's words that overrode Nyara's anger completely.

"No," Nyara admitted slowly. She had done quite a bit, now that she thought about it. Without any help at all.

:Did I rig all these shields?: the sword persisted. *:Did I figure out the way to*

548

make them cascade, so that the only one under power is the first one unless something contacts it?:

"No," Nyara replied, this time with a bit of pride. "I did that." Given that her magic was pathetically weak compared to Need's, or even the least of the mages that her father controlled, she really hadn't done too badly.

:If I really was destroyed tomorrow, would you be able to get away, to hide, to keep yourself alive?: The sword waited patiently for an answer, and the answer Nyara had for her was a very different one than the one she would have had a few days ago.

"I think so," she said, nodding to herself. "Yes, I think so. Was that the point?"

:It was. Four days ago if I had asked that question, you would have said you couldn't do without me. Now you know that you can.: Need's mind-voice conveyed a hint of pride. Nyara smiled a little, despite the remains of her anger.

Need chuckled at her smile. *:It wouldn't be easy for you to do without me, and any number of creatures could take you in a heartbeat, but I would give you even odds of being able to hide and stay hidden if you chose that route over fighting. You were coming to depend on me too much, and I am not invincible, dear. I can be hurt, or even destroyed. Your father could have done it, if he'd known how. Any of the Tayledras Adepts could. You needed to know you could survive if I was not here.:*

Nyara considered that for a moment and let her anger cool. Another of Need's ongoing lessons—anger used to make her incoherent; now, once it was under control, it made her think with a little more focus. That *could* be a problem, too; being too focused meant that you could miss something, but it was better than being paralyzed and unable to think at all.

"What about what you've been doing to fix what Father did to me?" she asked. "I can't do *that*. And it isn't finished—"

:It may never be finished,: Need told her frankly. *:It could take a Healing Adept—which I am not—years to change all the things that were done to you. But you are doing some of that for yourself. If you didn't recognize the problems and want the changes, if you weren't consciously helping me, there wouldn't be any changes. I can't work against resistance, my dear.:*

"Oh." Nyara couldn't think of anything else to say.

:There's something else I want you to consider.:

A breath of chill breeze came in the window. Nyara shivered and moved away from it, returning to the warmth of her furs. She wrapped up in them, cuddling down into their warmth, and let her eyes readjust to the darkness of her tower room. "What?" she asked, expecting something more along the same theme—perhaps something about using her own magic more effectively.

:What do you want?: asked the voice in her mind.

The question took her completely by surprise. "Wh-what do you mean by that?" she stammered.

:It's a question no one has ever asked you before—and one that you were never in a position to decide, anyway,: Need said patiently. *:But you are out here in the wilderness. No one knows where you are yet. You are in a position to decide* exactly *what is going to happen to your life because there's no one here to affect you, to do things you don't expect and haven't planned for. So what do you want? Assume all the power in the world—because, my dear, you have many powerful people who consider you a friend worthy of helping, and they might just do that if you came to them and asked it of them.:* The sword's voice warmed. *:You are quite worthy of being helped, child, though I don't want you to come to depend on it.:*

What *did* she want? To be left alone was the first thing that sprang to her mind—

To be left alone… there were no complications out here. Nothing to get in the way of simply living. No emotional pain—that is, when Need wasn't deserting her! This was the first time in her life that she had been in a position of control over her own actions and reactions. There was something very attractive about that.

But—no. It was lonely out here. She was often too busy to think about the isolation, but in the dark of the night, sometimes, she felt lonely enough that she had to fight back tears. At first, she had been too busy to think about it, and then Need had been enough company, but now she wished there was someone else to talk to, now and again. Someone who wasn't a teacher, who was just a friend.

Or… maybe a little more than a friend? The frequent urges of her body had not gone away, they had simply become less compulsory, and more under her own control.

But if she didn't want to be left alone, that meant rejoining some portion of the outside world. North meant other Birdkin Clans, and she had been warned they were far less tolerant of Changechildren. South was Dhorisha. There were only two real directions for her, east to the *real* "outside" world, or west, back to the k'Sheyna Vale.

There were problems with both directions. Should she leave the area entirely, and try to find someplace in the east where she could go?

But then what could she do? She would have to find some way to support herself. She had to eat—there was little or no hunting in lands that were farmed. She would have to have clothing, and a place to live, and in civilized lands, one couldn't wear rough-tanned furs or live in a cave. Even assuming there were caves about to live in.

"I could go to the lands where the Outsiders came from. When I am there, I can track and hunt," she said aloud. "I could hire out as a hunter or a guide... or maybe as some kind of protector."

Need indicated tentative agreement. *:True, but what are the drawbacks of running off like that, into places you know nothing about and where you have no friends? Remember, out there, no one has ever seen anything quite like you. They might not treat you well, they might greet you with fear or hatred, and you would be one against many if it came to hostility.:*

There was another option—one in which her alien appearance might be of some use. "I could... hire out as a bed-partner." There. She didn't like the idea, but it was a viable one. It was one thing she was well-trained in. Skif had certainly been pleased.

Again, Need indicated tentative agreement, but with reservations. *:You could do that, and you would probably do very well. But is that what you want? I thought that was the point of this discussion.:*

She sighed. "No, it isn't what I want. It would be a choice, but not a good one. I suppose—if I had to, it would be better than starving. But I don't have to east, do I?" If she didn't go east—

Then she went west. Back to k'Sheyna. Back to where the Outland strangers were...

No point in avoiding it. The one person in the whole world that she thought of with longing was that stranger. The young man called Skif—who was with k'Sheyna. And the only Hawkbrothers in the world who *might* look upon her with a certain amount of kindness were the k'Sheyna. She had helped them, after all—fought against her father's controls. *She* was the reason they had known that one of their own was Falconsbane's slave. In a sense, they did owe her a debt...

In more than a sense, so did Skif. She had saved his life at the risk of her own.

And they had shared so much in such a relatively short period of time, enough that the intensity of her feelings had frightened her. That was more than half the reason why she had run away from him. She did not want him near her while her father's directives still ruled her so closely.

Not while she wanted him so very badly...

:I rather thought so,: Need said, following her thoughts, with a feeling of wry humor. *:I rather thought that your Skif would be in the equation somewhere.:*

"Is there anything wrong with that?" she asked defensively, a little apprehensive that Need would not approve. After all, when she had been a woman, she had been celibate. And now that she was a sword, did she still understand feelings?

:No, child, there is absolutely nothing wrong with that. I think your emotions are quite healthy. I think it's just as well that you feel this way, especially since he's out here looking for you.:

She held quite still, rigid with surprise. *What?*

Nyara had never experienced such mixed emotions in her life, all of them painfully intense. Elation and fear. Joy and dismay. She hugged her furs to herself and trembled.

:I rather imagined you'd react this way.: The sword all but sighed, but there was an undercurrent of satisfied humor. *:I suppose I have seen true love often enough to recognize it when it smacks me between the quillions. From at least a dozen of my bearers. And lately—first that sorceress who went into repopulating the Plains all by herself, then that Kerowyn child, and now you. I am beginning to feel like a matchmaker. Perhaps I should give up my current calling and set up as a marriage broker. Very well.:*

Nyara fought all of her emotions down enough to get some kind of answer out. "Very well, what?" she asked.

:We know what you want. So. Now we get you ready for it. That young man needs and wants a partner, *youngster—not a little girl, not just a bedmate, not someone he has to drag about like an anchor and rescue at regular intervals. So, we'd better start building you in that direction. If,:* the sword finished, with a hint of dry sarcasm, *:that suits you.:*

She sat up straighter. A partner. Someone who could stand alone, but chose to stay with another. Someone who just might come rescue *him* once in a while.

"Yes," she said, quietly, calmly, with her chin up. "That suits me very well."

1 2

Trevalen closed his eyes and narrowed his consciousness, pulling his concentration within himself until he was aware of nothing but himself. A moment only, he paused, finding his balance and center, and from deep within—he stepped out. Onto the Moonpaths, into the spirit realms.

By virtue of their close bond with the StarEyed, any Shin'a'in could walk the Moonpaths; provided that it was at night, under the full moon, and he sought the place with unselfish intent and enough concentration. Any Swordsworn could walk the Moonpaths on any night, and call and be answered by the *leshy'a Kal'enedral*, the spirit-warriors sworn to the martial aspect of the Goddess.

A shaman could walk the Moonpaths into the spirit world at any time he chose, and call and be answered by any spirit that lingered there, if the spirit he sought was willing...

That knowledge brought no comfort, only doubt and trepidation. *And that is the question, indeed. Is Dawnfire willing?*

Dawnfire. Of Tale'edras, but called by the Shin'a'in Aspect of the Goddess, to serve in a form a Shin'a'in would recognize—the emblem of one of the four First Clans. He had called and spoken with her on several occasions now, but each time he called, it was with questioning and fear deep in his heart. Fear that this time she would not answer.

Questioning his own motives.

Kra'heera had ordered him to remain at k'Sheyna Vale to learn the Star-Eyed's motive and purpose in creating a Shin'a'in Avatar out of one of the Hawkbrothers. Never had She created an Avatar before, much less one from a child of the Sundered Kin, the magic-users. If Kra'heera had speculations, he kept them to himself. Tre'valen had no guesses at all.

He had learned nothing of Her motivation in all the time he had dwelt here. He had, however, learned far too much of his own heart, a heart that ached with loss, and yearned for one that he could not touch. Ironic that he should discover the love of his life and his soulmate only after she was—technically at least—dead. But was that not like the Goddess, to create such ironies for Her shamans?

Keep to the journey, traveler. The Moonpaths are peril enough without your wandering off them. He walked the Moonpaths, dream-hunting in the spirit world; keeping safely on the trails meant for the living, and sending his call out into the golden mist beyond where lingering spirits lived. Golden mist, for he hunted by daylight; at night, the mist would be silver. This was not wearisome for a shaman, though one who was not so trained returned to his body weary and drained if he dared to venture here. And as a shaman, he knew that time meant very little in this realm, so he walked onward with patience, waiting for the sign that would tell him that Dawnfire was coming—or not.

One moment he was alone; then she was there, before him, in her hawk-form, hovering above the pathway on sun-bright wings. A great vorcel-hawk, glowing with a fierce inner light, so full of energy that the mist about her crackled.

But this time, instead of coming to rest upon the path as she always had before, she spoke one word into his mind.

:Follow.:

Then she was gone, diving out of the spirit realm with speed he could not match—but leaving behind a glowing trail that he followed back, back, back to his body, to the material world. He sank into himself; feeling crept back to arms and legs, he put on the shell of himself as a comfortable garment.

He took a deep breath, then opened his eyes to find the hawk that was Dawnfire poised before him. She watched him; before he could blink his eyes twice, the hawk shimmered, a trembling like a heat haze passing over her, intensifying the glow of her inner fire. Soon she glowed like a tiny sun, as she had when she first transformed.

He looked away for a moment, his eyes watering with the brightness. When he looked back, the hawk no longer perched there.

In its place was the transparent and radiant form of the woman. He had never seen her this way in the real world, only in the spirit realm. *A woman made of glowing, liquid glass…*

He took a deep breath of surprise, as she examined her hands and a smile crossed her lips. He rose from his cross-legged pose, and approached her; not certain that he should, but unable to keep at a distance. "I was not certain that I could do this, though my teachers assured me it is no great accomplishment for me now," she said, a little shyly. "I was never a mage; I am not really certain how I accomplish the half of what I do."

This was true speech, and not the stumbling, mind-to-mind talk he had gotten from her aforetimes. He willed his hands to still their trembling and nodded. "I think I can understand how you feel," he replied. "We are not mages, either, we Shin'a'in. That, we leave to Her."

She dropped her eyes from his hungry gaze. "I wanted—I wished to be with you, in as real a way as I could," she said, slowly. Then she looked up, and there was no mistaking the expression she wore, even though her "face" was little more than air and power. It showed a hunger and a desperation as great as his own. "I am *not* dead. I'm just different, and I wanted to be like I was, for a while."

He had never wanted anything more in his life than to take her hand; he reached for her, shaking a little, stretching one hand across more than a gulf of physical distance—

And she reached toward him.

Their hands met—one of solid flesh, one of ephemeral energy. He felt a gentle pressure, warmth—and it was enough, almost. So, they could touch, for just a moment, letting touch and eyes say what words could not.

He withdrew first; she brought her own hand back and set her face in a mask of calm, although longing still stood nakedly in her eyes.

He did not know what to say to her. "I am not only here with you for my own sake," she said after a moment of strained silence. "I am here— my teachers tell me that I must speak with you, telling you what I have learned because I can see things anew, being what I am now. Things they did not know, and could not see. Maybe that is *why* I became what I am—not quite in the spirit world and not quite in the material world."

He nodded and set his own feelings aside; this was the first time she had said anything like this, the first time that she had given any hint of what Kra'heera wanted to know. Not that he had not asked her questions, for he had. Until now she had shown great distress when he had asked her those questions about her current state, so he had stopped asking them. He feared she might stop coming to him; he was afraid he might have frightened her with all his queries.

Apparently not. But then, she was a brave woman, and I do not think that she has ever run from what frightened her.

"When you started asking me questions—I didn't want to think about them, but I had to anyway," she told him slowly. "Like this, there is no sleep, no dreams to run to. Once I started thinking, I started asking questions myself…"

She stared off somewhere above his head for a moment, and he held his breath, as much to try and still the pain in his heart as in anticipation of what she might say next. She could say she had to go, leave him forever, for the Goddess willed it so.

This was far from easy for him. He had dreamed of this woman for years, ever since becoming a man. Since he had been initiated as a shaman, the dreams had more power. He had known in the way of the shaman even then that this woman was his soul-partner, and yet he had never seen her. When Kra'heera had asked him to stay and learn of her, he had thought no more of it than any task the Elder Shaman had set him.

Until she had first come to him on the Moonpaths, this Dawnfire, this transformed Tale'edras. Until he had seen *her* face, and not the hawk-mask of the Avatar.

Now he knew who and what she was, and after the initial joy of discovery, the knowledge was a burden and an agony to his soul, for she was untouchable—out of reach—not truly dead, but assuredly not "alive" in the conventional sense. There was no way in which she could become the partner his dreams had painted her as. How could his dreams, the dreams of a shaman, which were supposed to be accurate to within a hair, have been so very wrong?

"There are threats and changes on the winds," she said, finally, bringing his attention back to something besides his own pain. "Terrible changes, some of them—or they have the potential to bring terror, if they are not met and mastered. One is a lost man of your own people, whom we have faced once already. No Shin'a'in, no Tayledras, no Outlander has the answer to these changes, only pieces of the answers."

He groped after the answers that her words implied. "Are you saying that the time for isolation to end is at hand?" That in itself was a frightening thought, and a change few Shin'a'in would care for.

"In part." She did not breathe, so she could not sigh, but he had the impression that she did. "It is easy for me to see, but hard to describe. All peoples face a grave threat from the same source, but three stand to lose the most; the Shin'a'in—"

"For what we guard," he completed. *That* was a truism, and always had been.

She nodded emphatically. "Yes. The Tayledras, also, for what we know—and the Outlanders of Valdemar, for what they *are*. And somehow those threats are as woven together as the lives of the Outlanders and the Sundered Kin have become in these last few days." She shook her head in frustration. "I cannot *show* you, and I do not have the words that I need; that is the closest that I can come."

But Tre'valen understood; what she said only crystalized things he had half-felt for some time now. "This is no accident, no coincidence, that things have fallen out as they have," he said firmly.

"It is less even than you guess," she responded immediately. And that confirmed another half-formed guess—that it had been the careful hands of the gods that had worked to bring them all here together. Him—and the Outlanders. "This path that we are all on was begun farther back than even our enemies know. I can see it stretching back to the time of the Mage Wars. There were cataclysms then that are only now echoing back to us."

A cold hand of fear gripped his throat at that, driving out other thoughts. "What do you mean?" he asked, carefully.

She searched visibly for words, her gaze unfocused as though she were watching something that she meant to describe for him, like a sighted woman describing the stars to a blind man. "Neither Urtho nor his enemy were truly aware of what they unleashed upon the world. It is as if what they did has created a *real* echo, except that this echo, rather than being fainter than the original catastrophe, has lost none of its strength as it moved across time and the face of the world. And now—it returns, it sweeps across our world back to its origin."

"But what has this to do with us?" Tre'valen cried. "Those were mages of awesome power—what has this to do with us and what we can do? Surely *we* cannot counter their magics! It is all we can do to hold them away from those who would use them!"

She shook her head dumbly, at a complete loss for an answer. "I can only tell you what I see," she replied, slowly, unhappily. "You asked me of the past and present, and this is what I see. The future is closed to me."

He was at as much of a loss as she, and slowly lowered himself to a stone within arm's reach of her translucent form.

They sat together for a long and painful moment, as he tried to think of words to give her; something with a bit of meaning to it.

"This, I think, must be what Kra'heera sensed when he charged me with remaining here," he said, finally. "He is my senior in much. Perhaps he can give us an answer; perhaps Kethra can, or one of your own people. I shall speak with Kethra and my teachers; I shall relay this to the Kal'enedral…"

"When you do this, speak of the need to speak to one another, Hawkbrothers, Shin'a'in, and Outlanders all," she said, interrupting him. "That much I do see. There has been overmuch of sundering, of the keeping of secrets. It is time for some of this to end."

"Secrets…" He looked up at her, and he knew that longing and pain were plain upon his face, plain enough that any child would see and know them and the cause.

"I must go," she said abruptly; she did not "stand up" so much as gather her energies about her and rise. Her form began to fluctuate and waver, and he held back frustration that she was so near, and yet untouchable except for a moment or two. Despite all that she had told him, his heart cried out for her—his own pain eclipsing the importance of her words.

She turned toward him; held out her hand. "I—" she said falteringly. He had not expected to hear her speak again, and the sound of her voice made him start in surprise.

She was in a kind of intermediate form; womanly, with her human face, but a suggestion of great wings. Again, the power in her made her difficult to look at as she wore the glory of the noon sun on her like a garment, but he would not look away, though his eyes streamed tears.

"I have seen your true heart, and I see your pain, Tre'valen," she said. "I—I share it. Beloved."

Then she was gone, leaving him with a heart torn in pieces, and a mind and soul gone numb.

Darkwind waited for his brother at the edge of the Vale, packs in his hand, and shivered as he looked out on the snow. He was not hardened to this weather, not as he would have been at this time last winter. Then he had sheltered outside the protection of the Vale, and most time not spent in sleeping had been spent in the snow.

He had not gone back to his old *ekele* except to gather his things and bring them back to the Vale with the help of several friends. He had been one of the first to do so, but now that the Vale no longer troubled the bondbirds, most of the scouts had followed his example and returned to the shelter and safety of the rocky walls and enclosing shields. Probably even Wintermoon would join them when his search was over. Darkwind's brother was stubborn but not foolish.

Shelter and safety the Vales held indeed—and comfort, which was something only someone who had never been without comfort scorned. This was going to be a hard winter; it had begun that way, and all signs pointed to the weather worsening before spring. The Vale was warm, with *hertasi* to take care of everyday tasks... difficult to resist such comforts, when the winter winds howled around one's windows and drafts seeped in at every seam. Especially when the *ekeles* of those within the Vale needed no protections from the cold; when hot springs waited to soak away aches and bruises, when windows could stand open to the breeze—

Well, they could if one lived on a lower level, at any rate. The *ekeles* near the tops of the trees tended to find themselves whipped by wilder winds than those near the ground. He smiled through his shivers at recalling when Nightsky had left her windows ajar—and came back after a lesson to find belongings strewn about the room. She had learned quickly that it was as well to leave the windows closed.

Few lived in those upper levels, in k'Sheyna. With the population so reduced, there was little competition for dwellings nearer the Vale floor. One or two still preferred heights, but never scouts. After returning from a long day on patrol the very last thing anyone cared to do was to climb a ladder for several stories just to get home to rest.

Darkwind was no different in that respect from any of the rest of the scouts, once the general consensus was reached that a move back to the Vale would be a good thing for all. He had stayed with his father for a brief while, in part to help Kethra at night, then moved into an *ekele* in the lowest branches. His tree stood near the waterfall end of the Vale, so that both the cool water of the waterfall pools and a nearby hot spring were available. He ran his patrols with Elspeth and her Companion as he had since the coming of autumn, but now he returned with gratitude to the warmth and the comfort of the Vale. And he pitied Wintermoon for his self-chosen exile to the winter-bound forest.

On the other hand, we can't seem to track down Nyara from within the Vale. I've tried looking for her, but she—or that sword—have shielded themselves too well to spot. I am glad it isn't me out there.

K'Tathi had flown in just before he and Elspeth went out on patrol, carrying a message; a written one, since it was fairly complicated. Wintermoon and Skif had given a good portion of food to a *tervardi* temporarily disabled by an encounter with Changelions. Rather than lose any great amount of time, Wintermoon was leaving Skif with the bird-man, and coming in to fetch replacements and enough food over to keep the *tervardi* fed while he healed. So would Darkwind be so good as to put together thus-and-so, and meet him and his *dyheli* friends at the mouth of the Vale at sunset?

Darkwind not only *would*, he was glad to. It often seemed to him that there was never a great deal he could do for Wintermoon; he and his brother had very little in common, and Wintermoon's position as elder often led to him being the one to lend aid to the younger brother. Wintermoon seldom asked favors of anyone; he was as much a bachelor falcon as Darkwind, if not more so.

With that in mind, Darkwind went out of his way to root through some of the old storehouses and uncover the last few cold-lights, mage-cloaks, and a fireless stove left from the days when mages in k'Sheyna could lend their powers to making aids to the scouts. It had been a very long time since scouts of k'Sheyna made overnight patrols—and a very long time since any of them had been willing to use mage-made things, for fear that the creatures of the Uncleansed Lands might sense them. He thought that Skif and Wintermoon might well be willing to chance that, since they were between k'Sheyna and the Cleansed Outland. The cloaks kept the wearer warm and dry; there were five, enough for both humans and the Companion and *dyheli* to sleep beneath. The stove should be good for several weeks of use, or so his testing had confirmed—and should heat the tiny tent his brother and the Outlander shared quite cozily.

When he asked for permission to take the things, Iceshadow had queried with a lifted eyebrow whether they needed it—or were keeping warm some other way. He had answered the same way that the notion was wildly unlikely. He still was not certain about Outlander prejudices in that regard, but he knew his brother well enough to be certain that young Skif was *not* likely to become Wintermoon's bedmate unless they encountered some wild magic on the borders that wrought a complete change of sex in either of them.

The last gray light of afternoon faded and died away, creeping from the forest by imperceptible degrees, and deepening the shadows beneath the trees. He shivered in a breath of cold air that crept across the Veil and hoped that Wintermoon would arrive soon. It had been a very long day, and he was bone weary. He and Elspeth had tracked and driven off a pair of Changelions—perhaps even the same ones that injured that *tervardi*, in fact—and it had not been an easy task in knee-deep snow. Even Elspeth's Companion had been of little help, not with the snow so deep and soft. The cats, with their snowshoelike paws, had a definite advantage in weather like this.

It had been snow with ice beneath; they had slipped and slid so often that he reckoned they were both black and blue in a fair number of places. He wanted to get back to his *ekele*, to the hot pool beneath it. He thought, briefly, about seeking one of the other scouts for company, then dismissed the idea. There were several women of k'Sheyna who were friends, willing and attractive, but none of them were Elspeth…

Stupid. Don't be an idiot. Don't complicate matters. She's your friend, sometimes your student; be wise enough to leave it at that. You aren't living a romance-tale, you have work enough and more to do.

Still—she was a competent partner now as well; *he* felt more confident in his magic, and so did she. As a team, they were efficient and effective. Working with the gryphons had been a stroke of genius.

A white shape flickered through the branches ahead, ghosting just under the branches in silence; a breath of snow-fog, with a twin coming in right behind it.

Vree cried a greeting; not the challenge scream, but the whistling call no outsider ever heard. A long, deep *Hooo, hoo-hooo,* answered him, and one of the two owls swooped up across the Veil and onto a branch just above Darkwind's head.

The second followed his brother, and as he flew up to land above, Darkwind made out the distant figure of someone riding through the barren bushes and charcoal-gray tree trunks of the unprotected forest.

The *dyheli* waded through the soft snow easily, his thin legs having no trouble with drifts a man would be caught in, his sharp, cleft hooves cutting footholds in the ice beneath. Astride him was Wintermoon. Behind the first *dyheli* came the second, unladen, his breath puffing frostily out of his nostrils.

Wintermoon waved as soon as he saw Darkwind, grinning broadly. Since he was not normally given to such things as broad grins, Darkwind was a bit surprised.

Being with that Outlander has done him some good, then. Loosened him up.

It occurred to him that Wintermoon might have found himself a real friend—rarer still, a close friend—in the Outlander Herald. Could it be mutual? Perhaps they had learned that they had a lot in common; Skif had struck him as rather a loner himself. A close friend was something, so far as Darkwind knew, his brother had never had before.

About time, too.

Wintermoon and the *dyheli* crossed the Veil and the scout slid from the *dyheli's* back to land beside his brother. "Darkwind!" he said, obviously pleased. "Thank you for doing this yourself, and thank you for fetching the supplies for me at all. What's all this?" Wintermoon briefly embraced his brother and indicated "this" with a toe to one of the extra bundles. "I did not ask you for nearly so much."

"And it doesn't look like provisions, I know." Briefly, Darkwind told his brother what he had put together for the little expedition.

Wintermoon frowned at that. "I don't know. I hesitate to use anything magic made out there."

"I've shielded it as best I can," Darkwind pointed out. "We have been using magic without attracting trouble for many weeks now. And if I were the one doing the scouting, I would weight the benefits of warmth and light very heavily in any decisions I made. Winter is only just upon us, and already it has the Vale locked around with ice and snow. It will be worse out there."

"It already is worse." Wintermoon eyed the bundle dubiously, but then heaved it onto his mount's back. "You were the first of us to object to using magic on the border; if you say it is probably worth the risk, I will believe you. I have very little to return you for your gift, I am afraid."

"No sign of Nyara?" Darkwind asked, expecting a negative.

"Very little sign, and old," Wintermoon replied, as he helped his brother tie the bundles securely to the *dyheli* backs. "But there are things that tell me she passed the way we are going. I have some hope that we will find her, though I have not told this to Skif, for I do not wish to raise his hopes with nothing more substantial than old sign. It is a difficult secret to keep, though."

"That is probably wise," Darkwind said carefully, balancing the first *dyheli's* load.

His brother looked up at him from the other side of the stag's back. "He is a man who has had many disappointments," the scout said suddenly. "I would not add to them, if I can avoid it. He is Wingsib; more than that, he does not deserve it."

"We seldom deserve disappointment," Darkwind observed dryly. "But I do agree with you."

He fastened the last of the bundles to the second *dyheli*, and straightened from tightening the cinch. "If you are worried about losing time and need someone to meet you with supplies, send K'Tathi again," he said. "It's no trouble, and perhaps I can find you something else useful, rummaging around in the old stores."

"You might indeed, and thank you." Wintermoon peered out into the growing darkness beyond the Veil. "I had best get on the trail; it will take some time getting back with all these supplies."

Darkwind nodded, and Wintermoon mounted the second stag, so that the work of bearing him could be shared between the two. With a wave of farewell, Wintermoon urged his mount and its brother out of the Vale and into the night, vanishing into the darkness beneath the trees, followed by two silver shadows, ghosting out and above.

Darkwind turned his own face back toward the Vale, figuring to find some dinner, soak himself in hot water, and go to bed. A headache was coming on, and he assumed it was from fatigue. It had been a very long day. Bed, even one with no one in it but himself, had never seemed so welcome.

So when he passed his father's *ekele* and saw the Council of Elders, even old Rainlance, huddled in conference with most of the mages of k'Sheyna, including Elspeth, he was tempted to retrace his steps before anyone saw him. Such a gathering could only mean trouble. Surely he had done enough for one day. Surely he deserved a rest.

But—

Damn. This looks important. I can do without food and sleep a little longer. I've done it before.

The mage-lights above them were few and dim, and if he had gone another way, they would never have known he was there, now that the shadows of night had descended. Elspeth was the first to spot him, but as soon as the rest realized she was looking at someone and not staring off into the darkness, they glanced his way. Their glances sharpened as soon as their eyes fell on him, and with a resigned sigh, he joined them.

I guess I was right. It is important.

The very first thing he noticed, once he joined their circle, was that they were all, barring the few scouts among them, drained and demoralized. They slumped in postures of exhaustion, faces pale and lined with pain, white hair lying lank against their shoulders.

All? There was only one thing that would affect them all.

"The Heartstone," he said flatly. Iceshadow nodded, and licked dry lips.

"The Heartstone," the Elder replied in agreement. He passed his hand over his eyes for a moment. "Precisely. We have failed in our attempt to stabilize it. And there will be no more such attempts."

"The spell not only did not drain the Stone," one of the others whispered wearily, "it enabled the Stone to drain *us*. We will be days, perhaps even a week, in recovering."

So that's why Iceshadow said there would be no more tries... if it could do that once, it will do so again. Thank the gods that the mages worked within shields, or we would likely all be in the same condition.

"K'Sheyna will not be defenseless, thanks to good planning," Iceshadow sighed. "The mages that are also scouts were not involved in the spellcasting, nor you and Wingsister Elspeth. But it is only thanks to that caution that we still have magical defenders."

There was one face missing from the group, one who *should* have been there. "My father?" he asked sharply.

Iceshadow winced. "A side effect we had not reckoned on," he replied, averting his eyes from Darkwind's. "Starblade's life is bound to the Stone in some way that we do not understand and did not sense until too late. When our spell backlashed, it struck him as well."

Darkwind tensed. "What happened to him?"

Iceshadow said nothing. Rainlance spoke softly. "It nearly killed him, despite the shaman Kethra throwing herself into the link to protect him."

"He lives, and he will recover," someone else said hastily, as he felt blood drain from his face. "But he and the Healer are weak and in shock. The shaman, Tre'valen, is tending them."

They are in the best hands in the Vale. If I have regained him only to lose him— "Is this a Council meeting, then?" he asked, keeping back all the bitter things he wanted to say. They were of no use, anyway. How could anyone have known the deep plans that had been laid against them, all the things that had been done to Starblade? They severed his links to Mornelithe Falconsbane, but there had been no reason to look for any others. *Even gone, Falconsbane's influence lies heavily upon us. Even gone, he left behind his poison in our veins.*

"A meeting of the Council and of all the mages," Iceshadow replied. "We have determined that we have tried every means to neutralize the Heartstone at our disposal, and all have failed. There is no other way. We must look outside, to other Clans, for help."

The faces in the dim light showed how they felt about it; that it was an admission of dependence, of guilt, of failure. Darkwind had urged them all for years to seek help from outside, and swallow that pride. Bitter and sweet; victory at last was his, but it had nearly cost the life of his father. Caught between two conflicting sets of emotions, he could only stare at the leader of the Council.

"You must send the call," Iceshadow said, finally. "You, the Wingsister, and the gryphons. Elspeth has already agreed, as have Treyvan and Hydona. You are the only ones that we can turn to now, you and Elspeth. You remember the way of constructing a seeking-spell strong enough to reach who and what we need."

He nodded numbly, still caught in a web of surprise and dismay.

"You look ready to drop," Elspeth said firmly into the silence. "You're tired—I'm tired—we aren't going to get anything done tonight." She stood up and nodded to Iceshadow. "With respect, Elder, we have had a long day, and we need to rest. We'll see what we can do tomorrow."

"It has waited until now, it can certainly wait another night," Iceshadow agreed wearily. "And there is no sense in exhausting you two as well. Tomorrow, then."

"Tomorrow," she agreed, and signaled Darkwind to follow her down the path.

"I had the *hertasi* bring food and that mineral drink to the pool near your treehouse," she said as soon as they were out of sight and sound of the circle of exhausted mages. "I thought you would probably need both. And a good soak."

"You were right." He rubbed his temple, as a headache began to throb behind his eyes. "When did all this happen?"

"Just at sunset," she told him. "That was when they had timed the drainage to begin, and that was when the spell backlashed. I didn't feel it, and neither did anyone else outside of the Working area except Starblade; I first knew something was wrong when two of them staggered out the pass-through looking for help, and I happened to be nearby. Some of them had to be carried out."

"Gods." He shook his head. "So there are only four of us to work this seeking-spell."

:Five,: corrected a voice in his head.

He had not noticed Gwena's presence until that moment; she moved so quietly behind them that she might have been just another shadow. "Five?" he repeated. "But, lady, I did not know you were Mage-Gifted."

Elspeth's glare could have peeled bark from the trees.

"Neither did I," she said flatly, her voice so devoid of expression that the lack alone was a sign of her anger. She stopped; so did he and the Companion.

Before Gwena could jerk her head away, Elspeth had her by the bottom of the hackamore. "Look," she said tightly, "you *know* how important strategy is. That, and tactics. Especially here and now."

Gwena tried to look away; Elspeth wouldn't let her. *:Yes,:* she agreed faintly.

"You have been withholding information," Elspeth continued, her voice still dangerously flat and calm. "Information that I—*we* need to have to plan intelligently. What would you do to someone who had deliberately withheld information that vital?"

Gwena shook her head slightly, as much as Elspeth's hold on her hackamore would permit.

"I. Have. Had. Enough." Elspeth punctuated each word with a little shake of the halter. "If you haven't worked *that* into your 'great plan,' you'd better start thinking about it. No more holding back. Do you understand?"

Gwena rolled her eyes and started to pull away. Elspeth wouldn't let her, and Gwena was obviously not going to exert her considerable strength in something that might harm her Herald. But from the look of shock in her bright blue eyes, she had not expected this reaction from Elspeth.

"I said, *do you understand me?*" Elspeth pulled her head down and stared directly into her eyes.

Darkwind stood with his arms crossed, jaw set in a stern expression. He was trying his best to give the impression he supported Elspeth's actions completely. In fact, he did.

:*Yes,*: Gwena managed.

"Are you going to *stop* holding back information?"

Gwena pawed the ground unhappily, but clearly Elspeth was not going to let her go until she got an answer she liked.

:*Yes,*: she said, meekly, obviously unable to see any other way out of the confrontation.

"Good." Elspeth let go of the halter. She straightened, put her hands on her hips, and gave Gwena a look that Darkwind could not read. "Remember. You just gave your word."

Darkwind did not think that Gwena was going to forget.

1 3

A gray sky gave no clue as to the time, but Darkwind thought it was not long after dawn. He had spent a restless night, haunted by the exhausted faces of the k'Sheyna mages. He had not been expecting anyone so early and the first words out of Darkwind's mouth when Elspeth appeared at his *ekele* were, "We cannot do it here."

He had been thinking hard about what they were to do; all during his meal, the long soak before bed (in the midst of which he had fallen asleep until a *hertasi* woke him), and into the night before sleep took him. And he had decided on certain provisions as he dressed. *What* they were to do was no problem; thanks to Elspeth and Treyvan he was accustomed now to improvising on existing spells. This would be a variation on the seeking-spell. But *where*—that was different. It could not be done within the confines of the Vale, even outside the shielded Practice ground. He knew that with deep certainty that had only hardened during sleep. Every instinct revolted when he even considered the idea.

Something was happening to the Heartstone, or possibly within it.

He had no notion of what was going on, but now he did not want to do anything that affected it while within its reach. It was not just that the Stone had drained k'Sheyna mages, it was the way it had happened. It had waited, or seemed to, until they were certain of success and off their guard.

Perhaps that had been an accident, but what if it was not? He did not know. It didn't seem likely, but less likely things had been happening with dismaying regularity. These were strange times indeed.

He realized as soon as he said the words that Elspeth would have no idea what had been going through his mind since the meeting. He felt like a fool as soon as he closed his mouth.

She's going to think I've gone crazy, that I'm babbling.

But instead of confusion, Elspeth met the statement with a nod of understanding. "Absolutely," she replied, as if she had been talking to him about the problems all along. "Too much interference from shields and set-spells, plus the Heartstone's proximity itself. I've been thinking about that since last night. That Heartstone of yours is acting altogether too clever for *my* comfort. I don't want to do something it might not like when I'm anywhere around it. It might decide that since I'm an Outlander, it'll do more than just drain me."

"It is not a thinking being," he protested, but without conviction.

"Maybe not, but it acts like it is." She glanced back over her shoulder, in the direction of the Stone. "Maybe it's all coincidence, or maybe it's something that Falconsbane set up a long time ago. But when it acts like it can think, I'm I going to assume that it *is* thinking and act accordingly." She grinned crookedly. "As my Shin'a'in-trained teacher would say, 'Just because you feel certain an enemy is lurking behind every bush, it doesn't follow that you are wrong.'"

Shin'a'in proverbs from an Outlander. God help me. But he couldn't help but smile ruefully in reply. "The trouble with proverbs is that they're truisms," he agreed. "You make me think that you are reading my thoughts, though."

It was a half-serious accusation, although he made it with a smile. It was no secret that these Heralds had mind-magic—but did they use it without warning?

She laughed. "Not a chance. I don't eavesdrop, I promise. No Herald would. It was just a case of parallel worries. So, where are we going to go to work?"

No Herald would. Perhaps the Companion might… but I suspect she knows that.

He wasn't worried about her Companion reading his thoughts. It was not likely that there was anything he would think that a Guardian Spirit had not seen before.

"Have you eaten yet?" he asked instead. When she shook her head, he went back into his *ekele* and rummaged about in his belongings and what the *hertasi* had left him. He brought out two coats draped over his arm, and fruit and bread, handing her a share of the food. She took it with a nod of thanks. "I thought," he said after she had settled beside him on the steps, "that we might work from the ruins."

"The gryphons' lair?" She tipped her head to one side. "There *is* a node underneath it. And we're likely to need one. But what about—well—attracting things when we do the magic?"

"We won't have the shields of the Vale, and that's a problem," he admitted, biting into a ripe *pomera*. "I don't know how to get around that."

She considered that for a moment, then shrugged. "We'll deal with it, I suppose," she replied. "Gwena can't think of any way around it either, but she's in agreement with both of us on not working near the Heartstone." She finished the last of her bread and stood up, dusting her hands off. "So, what, exactly, are we doing?"

He licked juice from his fingers and followed her example, handed her a coat, then led the way down the stairs to the path below. "Well, we can't do a wide open Mindcall," he began.

"Obviously," she said dryly. "Since we don't want every nasty thing in the area to know that k'Sheyna is in trouble. I wouldn't imagine we'd want to do a focused Mindcall either; something still might pick it up, even though we meant it only for Tayledras. There might even be something *watching* for a Mindcall like that, for all we know."

"And what's the point in wasting all the energy needed for a focused Mindcall to all the Clans when there may not be more than one or two Adepts that can help us?" he concluded. "No, what I'd thought that we should do is to send a specific message-spell; that is a complicated message that can be carried by a single bird." He smiled to himself; she wouldn't believe what kind of bird would carry the incorporeal message, but it was the most logical.

"To whom?" she asked in surprise, as Gwena joined them, following a polite ten paces behind. "I thought—" she stopped in confusion.

"I don't know *who* to send it to, but I know *what*," he explained, brushing aside a branch that overhung the path. "Somewhere in the Clans is a Healing Adept of a high enough level that he either knows or can figure out what we need to do. Now I know that no one here can, so I send out a message to the nearest Clan, aimed at any Adept that's of our ability or higher. In this case, the nearest Clan is k'Treva. And I'm pretty sure they have someone better equipped to deal with this than we are. They offered their help a while back, and Father refused it."

"And if no one there can help us after all?" she asked, darkly.

He shrugged. "Then I ask them to pass on the word to the others. *They* don't have a flawed Heartstone in their midst. *They* can send out to any Clan Council. To tell you the truth, our biggest problem with getting the Stone taken care of has been isolation. Solve that, and we can solve the rest."

The Vale was unusually silent, with all the mages abed and recovering. Their steps were the only sounds besides the faint stirring of leaves in the breeze and the bird songs that always circulated through the Vale. She was quiet all the way to the entrance and the Veil that guarded it. Beyond the protections, another winter snowstorm dropped fat flakes through the bare branches of the trees.

They shared a look of resignation, wrapped themselves in their coats and crossed the invisible barrier between summer and winter. The first sound outside was of their boots splashing into the puddles of water made by snow melted from the ambient heat of the Vale's entrance.

There was no wind, and snow buried their feet to the calf with every step they took. Flakes drifted down slowly through air that felt humid on Darkwind's face, and not as cold as he had expected. Above the gray branches, a white sky stretched featurelessly from horizon to horizon; Darkwind got the oddest impression, as if the snowflakes were bits of the sky, chipped off and slowly falling. Beneath the branches, the gray columns of the tree trunks loomed through the curtaining snow, and more snow carpeted the forest floor and mounded in the twigs of every bush. There were no evergreens in this part of the woods, so there was nothing to break the landscape of gray and white.

Snow creaked under their feet, and the cold crept into his boots. Their feet would be half frozen by the time they reached the ruins.

Darkwind didn't mind the lack of color. After the riot of colors and verdant greens within the Vale, the subdued grays and gray-browns were restful, refreshing. He wished, though, that he had time and the proper surroundings to enjoy them.

This is a good day for bundling up beside a fire, watching the snowfall and not thinking of anything in particular.

"This is the kind of day when I used to curl up in a blanket in a window and read," Elspeth said quietly, barely breaking the silence. "When I'd just sit, listen to the fire, watch the snow pile up on the window ledge, and think about how nice it was to be warm and inside."

He chuckled, and she glanced at him. Gwena moved around them to walk in front, breaking the trail for them.

"I was just thinking the same thing," he explained. "If we only had the time. I used to do much the same."

"Ah." She nodded. "I'd forgotten you used to live outside that glorified greenhouse. I like it, the Vale, I mean—but sometimes I miss weather when I'm in there. It's hard to tell what time of day it is, much less what season."

"Well, I imagine Wintermoon and Skif would be willing to trade places with us right now," he replied thoughtfully. "This is good weather to be inside—but not for camping. Snow this damp is heavy when it collects on a tent. Oh, if you're wondering, I sent Vree on ahead with a message about what we want to do; I expect Treyvan and Hydona will be waiting for us."

"I was wondering." She glanced at him again, but this time she half-smiled as she tucked her hair more securely inside the hood of her coat. "Not that I expected them to object, but it is considered good manners to let people know that you are planning on setting off fireworks from the roof of their house—and you plan to have their help in doing it."

He laughed; this was a very pleasant change from the Elspeth of several weeks ago. Reasonable, communicative. And showing a good sense of humor. "Yes it is," he agreed. "My message to them was that if they objected to the idea, to let me know immediately. That was when I first woke; since Vree didn't come back, I assume they don't mind."

"Either that, or he forgot his promise and made a snatch at a crest-feather again," she said with mock solemnity. "In that case, you'll have to find yourself another bondbird."

Elspeth enjoyed the walk, for with Gwena breaking the trail for them, the trip to the lair was something like a pleasant morning's hike. They had to keep a watch for unexpected trouble, of course, but nothing more threatening appeared than a crow scolding them for being in his part of the forest.

This is the most relaxed I've been since I got here, she thought. Perhaps it was because the waiting was finally over. She'd had the feeling all along that the mages of k'Sheyna would never be able to solve the problem by themselves. Darkwind felt the same, she knew, but he never discussed it. He was relieved, too—but too conscientious to feel pleased with the failure of his Clan's mages, even though it proved that he was right. He wasn't a shallow man.

The ruins were cloaked in snow, which gave some portions an air of utter desolation, and others an uncanny resemblance to complete buildings. Passage of the gryphons in and around their territory kept the pathways they used relatively free of snow. It was easier to move here, but with the last of the trees out of sight, the place felt like a desert.

Vree was on his best behavior, it seemed, for when they approached the gryphons' lair, they found him up on the "rafters" of the nest, pulling bits from a fresh-killed quail with great gusto.

He didn't have time to do more than call a greeting to Darkwind, though. The gryphlets tumbled out of the nest and overran all three of them, knocking Darkwind off his feet and rolling him in the snow, wrestling with him as if they were kittens and he was a kind of superior cat-toy.

Elspeth laughed until her sides hurt; every time he started to get up, one of the youngsters knocked him over again. He was matted with snow; he looked like an animated snowman, and was laughing so hard she wondered how he caught his breath.

Gwena watched the melee wistfully, obviously wishing she could join in.

Elspeth decided that Darkwind could use a rescue. She waded in and started pulling tails, which turned the gryphlets on *her.* Within a heartbeat, she found herself going ramp-over-tail into a snowdrift, with a squealing Jerven on top of her, flailing with his short, stubby wings and kicking up clouds of the soft snow in all directions.

That was when Gwena joined the fun; making short charges and shouldering the youngsters aside so that she tumbled them into the snow the way they had knocked Darkwind and Elspeth over. The gryphlets loved that; Gwena was big enough to hold her own with them, and provided they kept their foreclaws fisted, they didn't have to hold back with her in a rough-and-tumble.

In a few moments, their parents appeared, and rather than calling a halt to the game, they joined it. Now the odds were clearly against the gryphlets, and first Darkwind, then Elspeth switched sides, coming to the youngsters' defense while Gwena sided with the parents. In moments, snow flew everywhere. It looked like a blizzard from the ground up.

The best strategy seemed to be seizing the tail of an adult, hampering movement, while the young one batted away at the front end with blows of their wings and with their claws held tightly into a fist to avoid injury.

That wouldn't work for long, however.

Just as Elspeth was getting winded, Hydona turned the tables on them. The gryphon whirled, dragging Elspeth along with her and bringing her into the range of the huge wings. Suddenly she went tumbling, buffeted into another snowbank by a carefully controlled sweep of a wing; landing right beside Jerven who had gotten the same treatment. Before either of them could scramble to their feet, Hydona was upon them, pinning each of them down with a foreclaw.

"Trrruce?" the gryphon asked, her head cocked to one side, her beak slightly open as she panted. Steam rose in puffs from her half-open beak. Elspeth sensed the controlled power in the claw pinning her carefully into the drift, and marveled at it, even as she signaled her defeat laughingly. Hydona let both of them up, extending the claw again to help Elspeth to her feet.

"Thanks," she said, looking for Gwena, and finding that Darkwind and Lytha had taken Gwena hostage, holding her against Treyvan's continued good behavior. The Companion's blue eyes sparkled like sapphires, and her ears were up and tail flagged—

In short, they only *thought* they had her.

Elspeth kept her mouth shut, waiting for Gwena to make her move.

Treyvan feinted, and Darkwind turned just a little too far to block him. For one moment, he took his eyes off the Companion.

That was when Gwena grabbed his collar in her teeth, and, whipping her head around on her long, graceful neck, jerked him off his feet and flung him sideways into Lytha.

Darkwind *whuffed* with surprise; Lytha squealed. They both went down in a tangle of legs and wings.

Elspeth giggled uncontrollably, then took a huge double handful of snow, packed it tight, and lobbed it at Gwena. It impacted against Gwena's rump, and she whirled to glare at her Chosen indignantly. Darkwind howled with laughter, and the gryphlets joined in.

"I was afraid you were going to break the game up," Elspeth told the female gryphon, as Darkwind and his partner surrendered to her mate.

Hydona shook her head to rid it of snow. "No," she replied. "The little onesss werrre resstlesssss. Now they will sssettle, and let usss worrk in peace."

Elspeth stretched and began beating the snow out of her cloak, feeling vertebrae pop as her muscles loosened. "I feel like I've worked off a bit of nerves, too," she began, when another creature popped its head out of the gryphon's lair, ears pricked forward and eyes wide with interest.

:Is the battle over?: the *kyree* asked. *:Or is this a temporary truce?:*

"I think we've been defeated too soundly to make another attempt," Darkwind said cheerfully. "Despite Gwena's indignation. Am I right, my shieldbrother?" he asked, turning to Lytha.

The gryphlet nodded vigorously, and sneezed a clump of melting snow from her cere and crown. "Wet," she complained. "Got sssnow in my featherssss."

"If you fight in sssnow, you mussst expect sssome in your feathersss," Hydona told her, with a twinkle.

:My famous cousin Warrl used to say, "You cannot have a battle without getting your fur in a mess.": The *kyree* scratched meditatively at one ear. *:He used to say, "You know how fierce the fighting was by how long after it takes to clean up." If you two want to come inside, I can start a mage-fire for you to lie beside, and tell you a story.:* The *kyree's* head vanished into the lair again.

Jerven beat Lytha inside by less than half a length.

"I take it that was Rris?" Elspeth said, trying not to laugh.

"Yesss," sighed Hydona. She looked at Treyvan, and the two of them said, in chorus, "That wasss Rrisss Let-me-tell-you-of-my-famousss-cousssin-Warrl of Hyrrrull Pack."

"The childrrren love him," Treyvan added. "I think I can bear with hisss famousss cousssin sstorriess sssince he doesss not repeat them."

"Only the proverbsss and advice." Hydona shrugged. "It isss no worssse than living with a Ssshin'a'in."

"Surely, but what could be?" Darkwind agreed, and squinted at the sky. "We have all of the afternoon and some of the morning left. Do you want to start now?"

"I thought it might be wisssse," Treyvan replied. "The lair isss not dirrrectly above the node. When I found the place that wasss, I built it into a ssshelter asss well. Would you follow?"

Darkwind waved him ahead; he and Hydona took up the lead, with the two humans following, Gwena between them. Elspeth laid a hand on her shoulder.

:Did you enjoy yourself?: she asked. *:You looked like you were having a wonderful time.:*

:Very much,: Gwena replied, her breath steaming from her nostrils, her

573

eyes still bright and merry. *:That was fun! I'd nearly forgotten how much fun it is to be a child. Or to be with a child. No matter how serious things are, they can always play.:*

:A good thing, too,: Elspeth chuckled, patting her on the neck. *:They can remind us grownups that there's a time to forget how serious things are. I miss the twins.:*

:So do I: Gwena sighed gustily. *:I miss a lot of things.:*

Elspeth realized Gwena must feel rather alone. *She* at least had other humans around, however alien they were.

With Skif out on the hunt for Nyara, Gwena didn't even have Cymry to talk to.

Gwena must have guessed the direction her thoughts were taking. *:Oh, don't feel too sorry for me,:* she said, poking Elspeth in the shoulder with her nose. *:I can do that well enough on my own!:*

Elspeth made a face at her, relieved. *:I'm sure you can,:* she teased. *:And I wouldn't even have to encourage you.:*

:Too true.: Gwena's ears pricked forward and she brought her head up. *:I do believe we have arrived.:*

Before them loomed another rough building-shape, much like the lair, but cruder. Where the lair was clearly a dwelling, this was no more than a simple shelter; the most basic of walls and a roof. But it was fully large enough for the gryphons and their guests, with room to spare.

It was clear that Treyvan and his mate had constructed this place before the first snow fell. Elspeth wondered why they had built it. Had they always intended to work magic here in their ruins? Or had they some other purpose in mind?

They entered, to find that Treyvan had already started a mage-fire inside; the glowing ball gave them both heat and light. The interior of the crude building was appreciably warmer than the outside, although an occasional draft whipped by at ankle height. Elspeth decided to leave her coat on; it wasn't *that* warm inside.

"What, exactly, arrre we doing?" Treyvan asked, settling down on his haunches. "I know of one kind of messssage-ssspell, but I do not know that it isss like the one you ussse."

"Ours requires a carrier," Darkwind explained carefully. He looked around and found a block of stone to sit on. "We generally use a bird of some kind. There are a lot of advantages to that. The spell itself weighs nothing, and it can't be detected unless a mage is quite close to the bird. The bird doesn't need to remember anything, so it doesn't have to be a bondbird. The spell is in two parts; one is the message, and the other will identify the target. That part will tell the bird when it has found either the specific person that the message is for, or in our case, the *kind* of person the spell is for."

"Interessssting." Hydona nodded. "Better than oursss; lesss inclined to be detected. What bird arrre you usssing?"

"This one." He pointed to the hood of his coat; a tiny head peeked out from beneath his hair. Very tiny; mostly bright black eyes, and a long, sharp beak. Elspeth blinked, and looked again.

"A *hummingbird?*" she said incredulously. "Where did that come from?"

"The Vale," Darkwind grinned. "He was in my cloak hood until just before the children ran at us. He went up to shelter with Vree while we played; Vree knows better than to molest a hummingbird, since we use them for message-spells all the time. He ducked back inside my hood when I told him it was safe, and that was how I brought him here."

"But a hummingbird?" She frowned; it was not the choice she would have made. The tiny birds were pretty enough, and certainly they did very well in the artificial world of the Vale, but it seemed to be a poor choice for carrying a message for what might well be hundreds of leagues. "Isn't he going to freeze to death in this weather? What's he going to eat? And how is he going to defend himself?"

Darkwind held his hand up to his hood; the bird flew out and hovered for a moment before settling on his finger. It was no larger than the first joint of his thumb. "As long as he keeps moving, he'll be fine; he won't have any trouble with the cold. He won't have to stop to eat, because I will have given him a tiny store of mage-energy that will carry him as far as k'Treva. And look at him."

Elspeth kept her reservations to herself and took the time to examine the tiny bird closely. It was not one of the little flying jewels she was used to seeing; the bird was black, with only a hint of dull purple at his throat.

"This little fellow doesn't need to defend himself because very few creatures or birds will be able to see him," Darkwind continued. "The fact that you didn't see him fly out of my hood or back in is proof of that. His speed is his defense; that and his size. He's so small that even if something sees him, it isn't likely to catch him. And if something is foolish enough to try to catch him, it is going to discover that it's nearly impossible to try and catch a hummingbird in full flight."

"Hmm." Treyvan bent his head to examine the bird at short range. It looked right back at him, completely without fear, despite the fact that the gryphon could have inhaled the tiny creature and never noticed he had done so. "Ssso you will create a pocket of mage-enerrgy to feed the birrd? That ssshould make no morrre ssstirr than the ssspell itssself."

"Exactly." Darkwind looked very pleased. "These little fellows move so quickly that even if someone detected a spell, by the time they got to the place where they'd first detected it, the bird would be a hundred furlongs gone."

"From the maps I've seen, it's an awful long way to k'Treva," Elspeth said doubtfully.

"Wild hummingbirds migrate so far to the south in the winter that we don't even know where they go," Darkwind replied.

:He's right,: Gwena put in. *:One of Kero's men, the black fellow—I listened to him tell stories once to some of the trainees. He said that hummingbirds spent the winter in his land. And we have no notion of how far north he came.:*

Well, if hummingbirds really traveled that far—

"He can do it, don't worry," Darkwind replied firmly. "These little ones have carried messages like this one before, even in winter. And once he gets to k'Treva and finds our Adept, someone will see to it that he gets the best honey-nectar and will find a territory for him in their Vale."

Once again she was struck by the care the Tayledras had for the creatures that they shared their lives with—even a tiny hummingbird that was in no way the kind of partner that their bondbirds were.

Darkwind shook his head. "The little fellow is ready and eager to go. Let's get to this, so that he doesn't have to wait."

Elspeth couldn't imagine how he would know that, but she agreed. This was likely to take a fair amount of time.

"Indeed," Hydona said, nodding. "Rrrisss cannot keep the little onesss quiet forever."

Elspeth was very glad Gwena had come along and even happier that the Companion wasn't as tired as she was.

The walk back to the Vale, which had been so pleasant on the way out, was a daunting prospect now.

:Neither of you are heavy,: Gwena said, as the three of them followed the gryphons out into the snow. *:The Vale is not that far. I can carry both of you, or you can lean against me, if you like.:*

The sun was faintly visible through the thick clouds; there was perhaps a candlemark until sunset. "What do you think?" Elspeth asked the Hawkbrother. "Walk, or ride?"

:I can get you there by sunset,: Gwena said, coaxingly.

"Ride," Darkwind replied decisively. "If you have no objection."

"None at all." In fact, this might prove to be an intriguing opportunity…

Darkwind was possibly the single most attractive man she had ever met, and not just because he was so exotic. And once she had figured out that he wasn't being obtuse in his lessons just to aggravate her, she found him even more attractive.

Admittedly, most of the Tayledras were attractive, either physically, mentally, or both. But Darkwind drew her as no one else had. She wanted to know more about him—and she wanted him to know more about her. It was one thing to be attracted to someone. It was another thing entirely to act on that attraction.

Especially if it proved to be only one-sided.

Horrible thought. But possible.

And her pride would not permit her to go panting after him like a puppy. Skif's example of slavish infatuation was enough to decide her on that. She would never put herself in the position to be humiliated the way he had been.

She mounted first; Darkwind, less experienced, used a handy chunk of fallen rock to mount up behind her.

:I promise I'll be gentle,: Gwena teased, reminding them both of the uncomfortable jog Darkwind had taken, perched behind Elspeth over Gwena's hipbones, as they hurried to the aid of another scout. :Nothing more than a fast, smooth walk.:

"Thank you," Darkwind said fervently.

The gryphons had already made their weary farewells; as custodians of this node, they had used the most strength in linking into it and feeding the power to Darkwind, Gwena, and Elspeth. The hummingbird was on his way, shooting into the sky like a slung stone. There was nothing holding them here.

Snow continued to fall, but the light was fading, and the ruins had a haunted look to them that made Elspeth's skin crawl. Gwena responded to her uneasiness by heading out by the most direct route, one that would skirt the *hertasi* swamp but would not go in. That was no place to be in weather like this.

"What happens to the *hertasi* in the winter?" she asked, suddenly. "The ones that live out in the marsh, I mean?"

"They don't precisely hibernate, but they do not leave their caves much," Darkwind said into her left ear, while Gwena waded through the soft snow at a fairly brisk pace. His hands felt good on her hips.

"They seal themselves into their caves; sleep much, and eat little, stay close to fires. What time they spend awake, they use in making small things. Carvings, mostly. Everything they own is carved or ornamented, at least a little."

"I gathered they had a fondness for that sort of thing," Elspeth replied. "You know, they don't approve of my uniforms. Too plain, I suppose."

"Precisely." He chuckled. "That is one reason why they enjoy working with us. They have a number of traditional designs they use, but we are quicker at creating new ones than they are. Or perhaps it is simply that we are more uninhibited. That is part of the trade they have with us; when one of them wants a new design for something, he goes to one of us craftsmen, and we create it for him. That, and protection and shelter, and we earn their service."

"Us craftsmen?" she said, puzzled. "I didn't know you were a craftsman."

"I do clothing design, or I did. I am no great artist like Ravenwing," he replied, and she had the impression that he was a little uncomfortable, perhaps embarrassed. "Odd as it may seem, when they are at leisure, the *hertasi* of the Vale enjoy having elaborate clothing to wear."

She considered teasing him and decided against it. She recalled the festival clothing that he and Starblade had worn; clothing that seemed to have been created by the same hand. Now she knew it probably had been. His hand. Had that been a kind of silent signal of reconciliation? What other signals was she missing?

"You know," she said slowly, "back at home there's an entire set of codes in the flowers people wear, that they give to one another. It's even more elaborate at Court. People have carried on entire conversations, wordlessly, with the flowers they have worn during the course of a day."

"Really?" He seemed amused and relieved that she had turned the topic to something else. "Here there is only one meaning to a gift of a flower."

"And what is that?" she asked.

"The same as a gift of a feather—that one wishes intimacy." She blinked, now understanding a number of exchanges she had seen but hadn't understood.

"If the feather is from any bird, the relationship is casual," he continued. "If it is from one's bondbird, however, the meaning is that it is to be one of deeper intentions."

A sudden image flashed from memory, of the shaman Kethra, a string of feathers braided into her hair when she had never seen the Shin'a'in wear feathers before.

"Is that why Kethra——" she exclaimed, then stopped, blushing at her own rudeness.

But Darkwind didn't seem to think it was rude. "Yes," he said simply. "Those were feathers from the birds he bonded to before that raven—a gray owl, and a falcon called a perlin. When our birds molt, we save the feathers. Those we do not need to use for repair when a bird breaks a feather, we keep for special purposes, and for gifts."

"He needs another bird," she said, thinking out loud. "You know, watching you and the others with your birds—it isn't like a Herald with a Companion, but it's an important relationship. He needs a bird, and I don't think either he or Kethra realize how much, or the good it would do him to have one."

Silence then, as Gwena continued to push her way through the snow beneath the barren, gray branches of the forest, as the light slowly leached from the sky and the shapes of trees far away lost their definition, blurring into charcoal shadows. She wondered if she had broken some unspoken taboo among the Hawkbrothers. Or if, perhaps, she had sounded arrogant, as if she thought that she knew it all.

"Odd," he said, finally. "That is precisely what I have been thinking. Father lost his last bird to Falconsbane, and may hesitate to ask someone to help him find another. Kethra knows nothing of the bond of Tayledras and bird, how important it is to us. *All* of us have a bird of one sort or another, Elspeth. The mages often bond to a small owl, or to one of the corbies, but all of us have birds, and all of enhanced breeding."

"It seems to me that the birds you have are more like—well—house-cats. They have that kind of independence of thought, but willingness to *be* somewhat dependent." She shook her head, at a loss to explain what she meant. "They're not like dogs—well, mostly they aren't. But they sure as fire are *not* like the falcons and accipiters *I* know! The best you can get from them is tolerance, unless you can Mindspeak with animals."

"You are very observant. That is very true. They have that capacity for real affection that most of the true raptors lack; they are social, and they are intelligent enough to work together instead of preying on one another. Because of that capacity, the bond between us is as much of friendship as dependence. The only trouble is, this is not breeding season, and all the adult birds within the Vale are already bonded."

Perhaps the waning light had made her other senses sharper; perhaps it was just that she had become accustomed to listening for nuances in the way Darkwind spoke. "Within the Vale?" she repeated.

"Are there birds of Vale lineage outside the Vale?"

"Many. All those that are not claimed by someone as an eyas are left free to follow their own will." He was silent for a moment. "But without the bond, their wild instincts come to the fore, and aside from size, it is difficult to tell them from their wild cousins. We could trap a passage bird, perhaps. But that would be a poor way to begin a relationship that is based in trust."

"I see your point." And she did. A wild-bred bird never connected the trap with the human that took him from it. In fact, a wild-bred bird often woke to his surroundings when securely mewed, and the falconer began the careful process of manning him. But a bird as intelligent as one of bondbird stock would make the immediate connection between trap and trapper. And he would not be pleased, however good their intentions. "Have you asked Vree what he thinks we should do?"

"Actually, no." She could tell by the tone of his voice that she had surprised him, probably by saying something one of his people wouldn't have thought of. But she was used to asking Gwena's advice, and while she wouldn't have considered posing a complicated question to the bondbird, this was something he could realistically handle.

The gyre dropped down ahead of them out of the trees, circled about beneath the branches, and chirped at Darkwind before regaining the height he preferred with a few strong wingbeats.

Darkwind laughed aloud. "You pleased him, Wingsib," he said. "He was very flattered by being asked his opinion. And in his own very direct way, he has the perfect answer. He says that we must wait for one of the birds of the proper lineage to be injured. It is winter; first-year birds are injured all the time, trying for difficult kills. In the normal way of things, they will heal upon their own; sometimes other birds of Tayledras breeding, even their parents, will feed them while they heal. And in the way of things, if they do not heal properly and there is none to feed them, they die. But if the other birds of the Vale know we are looking for an injured bird, they will watch for one such, and we may play rescuer."

"Giving us a grateful bird instead of an angry one." She smiled; it was the best kind of solution. "I take it that he's going to speak to the other birds?"

"Once again, you guess correctly." Darkwind's voice was as warm as the gathering night was chill. "Elspeth, if it will not offend you, I would like to say that you are a much easier person to be around now."

She flushed. "Well... Darkwind, some of what you didn't like was something I *have* to do when I am around my own people. They expect me to lead; they expect me to act in certain ways. That 'attitude' you accused me of having is a big part of that. I'm sorry it had become a habit that I wasn't conscious of. I think some of it was associated with a kind of reflex; if the person I was with wasn't wearing a white uniform, then I acted a certain way without even considering what I was doing." Would he understand? Would he even try? "I *am* royalty, Darkwind. No matter that my land matters less to you than one of Vree's broken feathers, I still am royal, I am expected to act in a certain way, and I can't escape that. I've been bred and raised to it."

"Ah." She hoped that what she read into the tone of that single syllable was dawning understanding.

She sighed. "There's something else," she said, through painful shyness. "I'm rather the plain-plumaged bird of my family. Everyone else is so handsome it's like—like living among Hawkbrothers. So the only reason *I* can think of for a young man to be attracted to me is because of my rank. And there have been those. I try to keep them at a distance."

"I can understand that," he said after a moment, in which the sound of Gwena's breathing and the muffled sounds of her hooves in the snow filled the twilight forest and defined the borders of their little private universe. "But, Elspeth, those young men who were blinded by your rank were fools. Or else they failed to see the quiet beauty inside the showy. Or—"

She sensed, rather than saw, the grin behind her.

"Or perhaps they were dazzled by the stark white attire."

She groaned. "Don't tell me *you're* in on the conspiracy to steal my Whites!"

"Only a little." She waited for him to continue. "I will admit to advising Lursten on a choice of substitute wardrobe."

She chuckled, and they passed the rest of the journey in silence, as the twilight darkened to true night and the air chilled further. Before it became too dark for him to see to fly, Vree came winging in to land on Darkwind's wrist. He held the bird between them, keeping him warmed with the combined heat of their bodies, something *no* raptor of Elspeth's acquaintance would have tolerated, much less enjoyed.

True to her promise, Gwena brought them to within sight of the Vale just as the last of the dull light of sunset faded from the western sky.

Darkwind slid from her back as soon as they passed the entrance to the Vale, Vree balancing carefully on his wrist. "I am for sleep," he said with a smile. "Do not take this amiss, Wingsib, but take it as a compliment, please. I have wished to offer you a feather since the days of our first acquaintance, for *I* find you a very attractive woman. More so when you smile, rather than frowning on me so formidably!"

She blinked at him in shock, then tentatively smiled in return.

"Thank you," she said simply, blushing. "Ah—Darkwind, if I wasn't so tired—oh, that sounds like such a transparent excuse but—"

"But it is, sadly, true. Elspeth, even if you were not weary, I feel that I am like to fall asleep even as I walk to my *ekele*. Shall we take it as true and not an excuse?"

Something warmed deep inside her. "I think that's reasonable."

:And I think you should both go to bed. To sleep,: Gwena chided gently.

"All right, little mother," Darkwind said, amused. "We shall. Tomorrow we will be dealing with all the creatures our magics attracted, at any rate. We will need a good rest."

She couldn't be disappointed, she thought. Not after all that. But no, that would not do. It was not enough.

She dismounted and went to him, wrapping her arms around his waist. With an inner flush, she looked up into his clear eyes.

Darkwind held Vree a little further from his body, inviting her in closer. She smiled, not knowing how well it could be seen, and felt Gwena send a quiet touch of approval.

Elspeth raised a hand to Darkwind's face, caressed the hair at his temple. He licked his lips as Vree spread his wings, and bent his neck down just a little, enough for one loving kiss, framed by the rich light and warmth of the Vale behind them.

1 4

Darkwind woke to a cool, pebble-scaled hand shaking him awake. He raised his head from his pillow and blinked to clear his eyes.

It was still dark.

:Darkwind,: said the *hertasi* at his elbow. *:There is a disturbance.:*

He recognized the mind-voice as that of Suras, one of the three *hertasi* who had attached themselves to Darkwind when he moved back into the Vale. The lizard-folk did that; it was one of their many peculiarities. They simply decided who they wanted to serve and proceeded to do just that. One day, Darkwind was living in the clutter created by moving, and putting together his own meals, doing his own laundry and cleaning up after himself and Vree. Then, with no warning at all, he arrived home to find everything straightened, folded, and put away, and a meal waiting.

There were advantages and disadvantages to being back in the Vale. He'd felt a pang of displeasure at his loss of autonomy. However, with *hertasi* serving him, it was much easier for people to find him when he was needed. That, too, could be a disadvantage, especially when he was trying to sleep off the last time he'd been needed.

Suras patted his arm again. *:Disturbance, Darkwind. You are needed, please.:*

"What kind of trouble is it this time?" he asked—or rather, mumbled into his pillow—hoping it was something he could get someone else to take care of.

:Magical,: Suras said curtly. His tone told Darkwind everything he needed to know. He was not getting out of this one. *:A magical disturbance between here and the ruins.:*

No doubt about this; he, Gwena, and Elspeth were responsible for dealing with it. "I'll be right there."

Suras lit a lantern and vanished. Darkwind clenched his eyes closed, opened them reluctantly, and dragged himself out of bed. Vree roused and blinked sleepily, then yawned widely. *:Awake again? Rather sleep.:*

Darkwind yawned in response. "You and I both, beloved. I'll go on ahead, and call on you if you're needed. Fair enough?"

:You go. I sleep. Fair deal.:

Vree settled and tucked his beak under feathers again while Darkwind felt around for the clothing Suras would have laid out before waking him. *I can't say I wasn't expecting this,* he thought glumly. *But I wish it had waited until after sunrise to start. Maybe we should have just stayed with the gryphons.*

He had known that when they worked a spell requiring that much power and concentration, things would be attracted. There were too many power-hungry creatures in the Pelagirs for any educated mage to think that magical workings of any scale could go unnoticed. Odd how much had gone into so simple and tiny a package as that hummingbird messenger, though.

Well, tiny, yes. Simple, no. There had been all manner of enhancements on that little bird, for speed, for endurance, plus the pocket of energy it would use to feed. Then all the spells needed to hold the message, to deliver it, to recognize the right kind of person to unlock it…

We did what we could to shield, everything we could spare from the spells themselves, without harming the little thing itself, he told himself. *We did everything we knew how to do, but I suppose the bleedoff was noticed. There hasn't been anything really troublesome around since the basilisk. If luck is with us, these things will be small. Something we can run off, rather than killing.*

He dressed carefully, knowing that he would probably be spending the whole day out in the cold, wrapping his joints and neck in brushed-cotton and insulation. It was still dark by the time he descended the steps to the Vale floor, and he had no idea how long it would be until dawn. It was going to be a very long day indeed.

Another messenger *dyheli* came galloping closer just as they ran the younger of the *lodella* pair off with its fuzzy tail tucked down between its legs, all its dorsal spines flat, and its hairless head ducked low. The elder had already flagged its surrender with its retreating back, but the younger one had less sense and more bravado. They'd actually had to pound it a bit with hammer-spells before it gave up.

Darkwind waved to his partners, who came up beside him just as the stag neared. "Now what?" Elspeth asked, as she propped herself against her Companion's neck, then shifted toward the saddle to avoid being caught in Gwena's steaming breath.

Elspeth hadn't spent a lot of time in the saddle; the Companion had been far more effective helping as a third herder when they met with creatures that were willing to be shepherded away. It wasn't just her size; she also seemed to be able to project a "presence" that played a factor in discouraging hostilities from the less-intelligent creatures.

These "disturbances" had actually included a fair percentage of "browsers;" creatures that meant no real harm, but could not be allowed close to habitations. But the rest—

The rest of the beasts facing them would have been only too happy to work some harm, but the beasts faced the three of them, plus the two gryphons, and Falconsbane was no longer there to support his creatures with magic.

The gryphons had tackled the first real problem; the half-dozen *gandels* that tried to force their way into the ruins. But without Falconsbane's will driving them, they were inclined to fold at the first show of resistance. A few feints of Hydona's claws and a stooping dive by Treyvan convinced them elsewhere would be far safer.

That set the tone for the day; to frighten the creatures away rather than actually closing to fight with them.

Illusions proved as effective as real threats; after the *gandels*, they had sent a pack of Changewolves running with the illusion of a bigger, stronger pack downwind facing them to claim the territory. Illusions were exhausting, though; they took more magical energy from the caster than actually fighting, but certainly left the user less winded, and less likely to strike at shadows. After a full day of active casting, though, illusions could deaden even the most ardent of mages.

On the other hand, one generally doesn't get wounded casting illusions. Or bitten, gored, horned, or worse. As Vree would say, "Fair deal."

It actually had a certain entertainment value, as he and Elspeth got into an impromptu contest over which of the two of them could create the most imaginative counter to the problem at hand. He'd conceded defeat when Elspeth began dropping huge illusionary clay pots on the dumber creatures' heads, or sending blizzards of wildflowers in their faces. They'd both found themselves laughing after that.

So far, they had been incredibly lucky; the illusions hadn't failed yet to drive away their targets, though once or twice they'd needed to reinforce the illusion with a bit of magical force.

The *dyheli* stopped and pawed at the snow, a signal for attention. Was their luck about to run out?

:You are called to the ruins,: the *dyheli* said, before Darkwind could ask him why he had been sent. *:The gryphons say there is a message waiting for you there. Three of the Vale mages are following me, to take your place.:*

Darkwind slumped against a tree in relief. He had completely forgotten that the mages of k'Sheyna would recover from their draining eventually. He had been so used to depending on himself and no one else, used to the idea that there was no one to relieve him. It had literally never occurred to him that someone would be along to take their places.

"So what is it?" Elspeth asked. "Who are we going to have to rescue this time?"

"No one," he said, mentally thanking the messenger at the same time. "Believe it or not, no one. We've had a reply to our call for help. It came to the ruins, since that was where the hummingbird started from. Keyed to us, of course, so no one else can break into it."

:Would that be the kind of personally keyed message we would have sent if we'd been able?: Gwena asked, her tiredness fading as her interest was caught. *:But it hasn't been more than a day—I had no idea that little bird could fly that fast or far!:*

"I hoped he would find a good carrying wind somewhere up above the clouds," Darkwind told her. "That, and the enhancement spells we put on him would have made all the difference. Once k'Treva got the message, of course, it wouldn't take them very long to reply—they knew where to send it and who to send it to; it takes a little longer than straight Mindspeech, but not much."

"Then the bird probably reached them just as we tackled the wolves," Elspeth replied thoughtfully. "It hardly seems possible, but I suppose that if a falcon can be carried off for hundreds of leagues by a high wind, there's no reason why a hummingbird couldn't have that happen to him, too."

She straightened, and looked around. "We're going to have to walk," she told Darkwind. "Gwena is in no shape to carry us."

She bent down and scooped up a little snow, and rubbed Gwena's forehead with it. When Gwena didn't protest that she was fine, thank you, Darkwind figured that Elspeth was right. While the Companion hadn't been working any direct magic, she had been acting as an energy source for both of them, plus giving the more timid creatures a good scare when she charged them. She must be as exhausted as they were.

"That's all right," he said. "It isn't that far." He oriented himself, recognizing a clump of mingled evergreen and goldenoak, stand of willows, and a rock formation. "We've been working in circles, actually. We're hardly more than a dozen furlongs from the edge of the ruins."

"Then what are we waiting for?" Elspeth asked.

"For me to get my second wind," he told her. "I haven't your youthful resilience." She chuckled. He closed his eyes for a moment, drew up reserves of energy, then pushed away from the tree he had been leaning on. "Let's go see what the news is."

The visible component of the message was a tiny, incandescent spark that danced in the air above the exact center of the crude building in the ruins. It brightened as soon as they entered the building, and the moment they were both in place, with Darkwind to the east of the node and Elspeth beside him, the spark flared suddenly.

Then it—unfolded, was the only word Darkwind could think of. It stretched down in a line that just touched the ground, then the line opened up on either side, until it formed a soft-edged mirror that hung in the air between them.

For a moment, Darkwind saw only his own reflection. Then the mirror dimmed and darkened to blue starlight, and the face of another

Tayledras, this one a contemporary of his father at a guess, looked solemnly out at him.

It was hard to remember that this was only a message, that he could not actually speak to the one in the mirror, any more than he could hold a conversation with a piece of parchment. The illusion was so complete that it took an effort of will to keep from greeting the stranger.

:K'Treva has heard the need of k'Sheyna,: came the mind-voice of the stranger. *:While we are grieved by your situation we are relieved that you came at last to us. We feared for you but saw no way to help you without acting like tyrants or well-meaning but intrusive siblings.:*

Darkwind nodded; that made sense. No Clan interfered in the affairs of another without some kind of truly catastrophic emergency involved.

:We have the help you need,: the other continued. *:A Healing Adept, strong and well-versed in his craft, and who is one of the most creative mages this Clan has ever held.:* The other smiled, briefly. *:Such praise may seem excessive, but as the Shin'a'in saying goes, "It is no boast when it is fact." I will build him a Gate to a place I know within your territory, one that I hope will be far enough away that it will not disturb your Stone. From the Gate terminus, I believe it will be about a half day's ride to your Vale under good conditions, and certainly no more than a full day. Expect him within that time once you feel the perturbations of the Gate. If Firesong cannot help you, no one of k'Treva can. Be of good cheer, brothers.:*

With that, the entire construction sparkled and winked out. Darkwind stared across the room at Elspeth, unable to believe their good fortune.

"You look like a stunned bird," she observed.

"I feel like a stunned bird," he admitted. "It's incredible."

"I have to tell you," she said, shaking off her daze, "I was standing here waiting for the ax to fall. I never thought there'd be anyone in the first Clan we sought help from powerful enough—and willing—to handle this mess. Especially not after what it did to our mages."

"Nor did I," he admitted. "I thought that surely even if there was a Healing Adept within k'Treva that we would have to convince him to come here. And then we would have to convince his Clan to permit him to put himself at risk. They must have been convinced already that we needed their help and were just waiting for us to ask for it."

Elspeth crossed the room to stand closer to him. "Was I missing something, or did he imply that he was here after the Stone shattered and that his Clan was worried about yours?"

Darkwind winced, but felt comfortable enough with her now not to bother covering it. "You are correct. He said—or implied—exactly that."

Memories, though dimmed with time, still had the power to hurt him. *Heart and mind in agony, as well as body—the dim shapes of strangers in his sickroom. Shock holding him silent in the face of their gentle questioning. Then the voice of his father, harshly telling them to leave the boy alone...*

"Right after the Stone shattered, I was told that k'Treva sent mages to discover what had happened and to volunteer their help," he told her. "I was—still in shock, hurt, and I do not recall most of it. But they went away without doing much except to help treat some of the worst wounded. I suppose that Father must have sent them away as soon as he could."

"Evidently if he tried to cover things up, he didn't manage as well as he thought he had," she replied, dryly. "Not if they were still concerned after all this time."

"Or he managed to let them see enough that there were still doubts; kept from completely covering things up, despite Falconsbane's control." That seemed the more likely, given what else Starblade had done. *Like protecting his son by driving him away...*

Elspeth shook her head. "I wonder sometimes if you realize just how strong your father is. When you think what that kind of attempt must have cost him... I can't imagine doing half that much. It took some kind of cleverness, too, to get around Falconsbane's compulsions. Starblade's a strong man."

"It is a brittle strength," he replied, sadly. "And like a bit of metal that has been bent too often, he is apt to break if he is stressed again." He shook his head. "Ah, this is gloomy thinking and poorly suited to our good news. Who knows? It may speed Father's recovery."

"It might at that." It seemed to him when she stood up that she moved with a bit more energy; certainly he felt that way. A great burden had been taken from his shoulders. K'Sheyna would have the help it needed. The long nightmare would soon be over.

He refused to think beyond that. There would be time enough for plans later. Let the Stone be dealt with first, and worry about what followed that when the time came.

He stopped at the gryphons' lair long enough to give them the good news, then they trudged back to the Vale through the snow, though it was nowhere near the job it was yesterday. They had been this way so often they were making a trail between the ruins and the Vale. A few months ago he would have worried about that, but not now. There wasn't any real reason to worry about leaving signs of where they had been. He sighed with relieved contentment, and relaxed a bit more, feeling muscles unknot all over his back. Shortly this would all be true Tayledras land again, and things like the Changewolves would not get past the borders—

:Up! Help!:

His head snapped up to a call only he heard. Vree!

He froze where he stood and linked with the gyre, fearing the worst. Dawnfire and her red-shouldered hawk all over again. Elspeth and Gwena stared at him for a half-heartbeat, then went into defensive postures. He prepared to break the link with Vree if he had to, to save himself—

—but caught no pain, no feeling of imminent danger. Vree felt him link and welcomed him in, his mind seething with agitation but not pain. He had given a distress call, but the bondbird himself was uninjured.

:Here! Help! Look-look-look!: the bird Mindcalled again, and this time gave Darkwind a look through his eyes.

A disorienting look, for Vree circled and twisted wildly, but Darkwind was used to looking through his bird's eyes. He recognized the spot immediately; on the edge of the swamp, but he did not recognize the man that was the source of Vree's anger and distress, a man laying out what could only be a *hertasi* trap. The view dipped and swung, as Vree circled, his silent rage burning in Darkwind's mind, making the Tayledras clench his fists and long with the bird to screech out a battle-cry. Then with another turn, Darkwind saw what must have triggered that rage.

The man had three pack-mules with him, and on the third was a raptor, a big one, bound on its back and hooded. From the little he could see, it looked to be a crested hawk-eagle; from the size of it, it could only be of bondbird breeding.

He had no idea that he was running until he saw Elspeth pounding beside him, already astride her Companion, and offering him a hand up. He seized it, and scrambled behind her. Then they were off, plunging through the thick snow. This was not like the last wild ride he'd made, for Gwena could not run or trot in the heavy snow. Her progress was a series of lunges or leaps; it was harder for him to keep his balance on her back, but easier on his bones.

Their quarry knew they were coming, for they made no effort to hide the noise of their passage. But their quarry did not know two very pertinent facts.

He was nearer the *hertasi* village than he knew. And while they were sluggish in the cold, they were by no means impotent. Anger alone was enough to keep their blood warm in the snow and give them the same agility they had in the high heat of summer. They, too, could dress for the cold and preserve some body heat when action outside was needed.

And although the encroaching mage had prevented the bondbird he had caught from calling its distress, Vree was under no such handicap. Nor was Darkwind; while he was nowhere near as adept at Mindspeaking with other creatures as his brother Wintermoon, he was still one of the best in the Clan. The soundless cry went out for assistance.

While Vree was calling his fellow bondbirds, Darkwind was rousing the *hertasi* village, starting with old Nera. The attack was conceived and coordinated in a matter of moments. The three forces converged on their target at nearly the same instant.

If the mage—for mage he was; he had a lightning-flare ready for them the moment they plunged over the top of the hill and began the sliding descent toward him—had only had to face Darkwind and Elspeth, he might have won. They were tired, and he was fresh. If he had only faced the *hertasi*, with their simple fishing spears, he *would* have won. And he had already proven he was capable of felling bondbirds from the sky.

But, since only Darkwind's party was making any noise, he had no idea that the others were on the way until it was too late to do anything about them.

Darkwind flung a shield up before them to deflect the first bolt. The second went awry as Vree dove, his claws ripping through the cloth of the man's hood, narrowly missing the scalp. Behind Vree came another forestgyre, in the same stooping dive, then a gyrkin, then a trio of perlins, all of them slashing at head and face with their long, sharp talons. They struck to hurt, not to blind; the perlins in fact struck close-fisted, as if they were trying to knock a duck out of the sky. The mage screamed in pain as the talons scored deep gashes in his scalp, staggered under the blows of the perlins, any of which would have been hard enough to stun him had they hit the temple.

He tried to protect himself with his arms. Apparently, like most Pelagir-wilds mages, there were severe gaps in his education. He seemed unable to summon any physical shields.

The birds retreated to the protection of the skies, gaining altitude as one. The mage stood, one hand on his bleeding scalp. From behind him, a thicket of spears boiled up out of the half-frozen swamp.

Darkwind struck then, gesturing behind Elspeth's back with two clenching fists. Gray and green stripes of a binding spell tangled the mage's hands and his magic for a moment. That moment was all that was needed. The *hertasi* did the rest.

They swarmed about the mage, casting their fishing spears and pulling on the lines. He tried to run, then slipped and floundered in the heavy snow. He scrambled to his feet again, and fell for the last time. The *hertasi* overran him, and he writhed to avoid the wicked points of the spears.

In moments, he looked like nothing so much as a hedgehog. In heartbeats, he was dead.

Gwena skidded to a halt in the snow beside the man's string of pack animals, a trio of tired mules who gazed at them with absolute indifference. Darkwind slid down off her back and hurried to the last one, the one bearing the bird like just another bundle of forest gleanings.

This much the man had known; he had bound the talons into fists, tied them together, bound the wings to the body so that it would not injure itself, then hooded the bird so that it could not see and would not struggle. The hood was strung to the bound feet by a cord, to prevent further movement, and from the cord dangled a carved bead.

As Darkwind's hands touched the bundle, he felt—something. It was akin to the draining effect of the Heartstone, and was centered in that bead, and spread throughout the bindings.

He drew back and examined the bird with mage-sight—and swore. Small wonder he had not Heard the thoughts of this bird; it was bound by magic as well as by bands of fabric, a binding that linked its life-force to the spell that held it. And that could only have been for one purpose.

Elspeth bit her lower lip and peered at the bindings on the captured hawk-eagle. Her face looked as it did when she was hearing news she didn't like.

"He was going to use this bird as some kind of sacrifice, wasn't he?" Elspeth said, her own voice tight with anger. She put a hand toward the hawk-eagle. "That's not all, Darkwind, this bird is in pain. He hurt it when he caught it."

She had been quicker than he; though she could not sense the bird's thoughts, she had felt its pain. He was glad he hadn't touched the poor thing; he could only have hurt it worse, unknowingly.

First things first; destroy the mage-bindings so that the bird's mind could roam free and it could hear his Mindspeech. Until then, it would struggle against him, thinking he was an enemy, hurting itself further.

The man had been a Master, but no Adept; Darkwind snapped the shackles of magic with a single savage pull but left the physical bindings in place. With a carefully placed dagger cut, he removed the carved bead. Beneath the bindings, the bird was in a state near to shock, but not actually suffering from that ailment. Darkwind could still touch its mind, talk to it sensibly, and know he would be heard.

He stretched out his thoughts—carefully, gently, with a sure, but light touch.

:Friend,: he said, soothingly.

The hawk-eagle tossed up its head as far as it could and struggled fruitlessly against the bindings. *:NOT!:* it screamed.

:Friend,: Darkwind repeated firmly, showing it a mental picture of its former captor lying in the stained snow. *:The enemy is dead.:*

The bird struggled a moment more, then stopped. Its head came up again, but this time slowly, as fear ebbed and the bird's courage returned. It considered his words for a moment, and the image he had Sent; considered the sound of his mind-voice.

:See!: it demanded imperiously.

"I'm going to unhood him," Darkwind warned. The *hertasi* backed off, but both Elspeth and her Companion stayed. "I don't know what he might do. He's bondbird stock, and right now he's sensible, but he may go wild once he can see again."

Elspeth reached forward with gloved hands. "You need four hands to undo those wrappings. I'll take my chances."

"Don't say I didn't warn you." No matter how intelligent, bondbirds were raptors, and likely to do unexpected things when injured and in pain, even one like Vree, brought up from an eyas and bonded before he was hard-penned. And this bird had never bonded to anyone. Still, she was right, and the sooner they got the bird untied, the more likely it was to listen.

The bird had been hooded with an oversize falcon's hood; a little too small; uncomfortable, certainly, and it would have been impossible for the bird to eat or cast through the hood. But Darkwind doubted that this man had made any plans to feed his catch, through the hood or otherwise. He got the end of one of the ties in his teeth, and the other in his free hand, and pulled, continuing the motion with his hand to slip the hood off the magnificent hawk-eagle's head.

It blinked for a moment, as the feathers of its crest rose to their full, aggressive height, the pupils of its golden eyes dilating to pinpoints as it got used to the light. Then it swiveled its head and saw for itself what Darkwind had shown it.

It opened its beak in a hiss of anger and satisfaction, then turned those intelligent golden eyes back to Darkwind. *:Out,:* it demanded, flexing bound wings once in a way that left no room for doubt about what it meant. *:Out!:*

It seemed calm enough, if still in pain. *:Let me get your feet free first,:* he replied. *:Then you can stand while I get the rest of this mess off of you.:*

Once again, the bird gave careful consideration to what he had said, weighing his reply against what it wanted. Darkwind marveled at the bird's intelligence; even Vree seldom *thought* about what Darkwind told him.

:Good,: the hawk-eagle said shortly, and stopped any effort to free itself. It held itself completely still, and while Elspeth held the huge creature, Darkwind picked delicately at the mess of rags and string muffling the hawk-eagle's talons and tying them into fisted balls.

Finally he got them free, and Elspeth placed the bird on the saddlepack. Its talons closed convulsively on the leather, and it flexed its claws once or twice to assure itself of its balance.

The hawk-eagle stood on the saddlepack and looked Darkwind straight in the eyes. *:Good,:* it said. *:Out now!:*

It waited while they picked the wrappings from its bound wings, talons digging deeply into the leather covering of the pack. Those talons were as long as Darkwind's fingers, and the cruel, hooked bill would have had no trouble biting through the spine of a deer. Darkwind wondered at the temerity of the dead man who had caught the bird, mage though he was. Vree could kill a man, with enough precision—and had done so in the past. This bird was nearly double Vree's size, and not only could kill a man, he could do it as easily as Vree killed a rabbit.

If the hawk-eagle hadn't been of bondbird stock—and hadn't Mindspoken with such clarity and relative calm, given the situation— Darkwind would never have dared to unhood him. It would have been suicide. The bird could have seriously hurt him, even bound, with a swift stroke of that terrible hooked beak.

When the last binding had been cut, the magnificent hawk-eagle spread wide brown-banded wings to the fullest—and winced, dropping the left one immediately. The wing continued to droop a little, after he had folded the right and tucked it up over his back.

He looked at Darkwind demandingly. *:Hurts,:* he said. *:Chest hurts, wing hurts. Hurt when fell.:*

Darkwind ran careful hands over the bird's breast, and quickly found the problem. A cracked wishbone. There was only one cure for that injury; resting quietly, while the bone set and mended. It would take weeks to heal properly, for bone Healing did not work well on birds, and the great hawk-eagle might never fly with the same ease and freedom again. Winter would bring special problems; cold would make the old injury ache, and the stiffness in the wing would make it harder to catch swift prey.

A tragedy—if he continued to live wild. No special problem—if he lived in the Vale.

But a bondbird, when not bonded as a fledgling or even an eyas, was traditionally given a choice. Freedom, or the bond.

Darkwind explained it to the hawk-eagle in simple terms. If he would come and live in the Vale, his life would be thus. He would bond to Starblade, who was himself wounded and in need of healing...

It was not his imagination; the bird's interest, dulled by the pain he was in, sharpened at that.

:Show,: he demanded. Darkwind obeyed, showing him mental images of Starblade as he was now—and one of Starblade and his cherished perlin Karry.

:Yes,: the bird said, thoughtfully. *:Ye-es.:* He dropped his head for a moment, and it seemed to Darkwind that he was thinking. Then his head came up again, and he stared directly into Darkwind's eyes. *:I go— we go to that one,:* he ordered, *:To warm place, to wounded one. We belong, him, me. Need, him, me.:*

And although Darkwind dutifully offered him his continued freedom after healing, the bird refused to consider it. *:We go,:* he insisted, and Darkwind gave in gladly to him, but with no little wonder. He had never had a bondbird speak so clearly to him—nor had he ever seen one exhibit genuine abstract thought before. There was no doubt in his mind that the bird was quite certain Starblade *needed* him. And there was no doubt that the bird had responded to that need.

He had heard that the crested hawk-eagles were different, that way— that they had a greater capacity for bonds of affection than any other breed. They often hunted in family groups and shared kills in the wild, something most other raptors never did. But no one in k'Sheyna had one of their kind, so he had only hearsay to go on.

Until now, that is. And he wondered; since no one in k'Sheyna had ever flown the crested hawk-eagles, where had this one come from?

"I was following that, a little," Elspeth said as she dumped the packs from the mules, leaving them for the *hertasi* to paw over. "So he does want to come with us?"

"So it would seem," Darkwind replied, a bit amazed by how readily the bird had fallen in with their idea. Could it be a trap of some kind?

:Stupid,: Vree said contemptuously, from his perch in the tree above. *:Hyllarr goes to Vale. Gets good food, warm place, safe place, hunts only when he wants. Gets good friend. Hyllarr wants good friend, mind-friend. Hyllarr flies, he gets winter snow, summer storms, has to hunt, get hurt again, dies alone.:*

Darkwind laughed, and so did Elspeth, though she looked a little surprised that she could hear the gyre's "voice."

"Put that way, it makes all the sense in the world, doesn't it," she said, with a bright sparkle in her eyes. "Here—" she offered her leather-clad arm. "I'll take him for a moment while you get up on one of those mules. Then I'll pass him back when you're mounted."

Hyllarr looked at her arm for a moment, then directly into her face—and with a delicate care that in no way hid the fact that his talons could pierce through her arm if he chose, he stepped onto her forearm and balanced there while Darkwind hoisted himself onto a mule's back. Elspeth blanched and inhaled abruptly when Hyllarr dug in while balancing himself.

No point in doing anything with the others. He would leave them to wander or follow as they chose; if they followed his mount to the Vale, someone there could always put them to good use. If they didn't, they would survive—or not—as their fate and wits decreed.

Elspeth held the hawk-eagle—*Hyllarr,* she reminded herself—steadily, despite the fact that it was a heavy weight, there on her wrist. But once he got himself settled, and before he could reach out his own wrist to take the bird back, Hyllarr half-spread his wings and hopped from Elspeth's arm to Darkwind's shoulder.

He tensed, expecting the talons to close through his leather coat and into the flesh beneath. But Hyllarr shifted a little, getting his balance, and then closed his feet slowly, carefully.

:Hurt?: he asked Darkwind, increasing the pressure a little more.

:No—no—there.: As the claws just pricked his skin, he warned the bird, and Hyllarr eased off just that trifle needed to pull the talons back through the leather.

:Good,: the bird replied with satisfaction. *:No hurt. Good. Go to warm place now.:*

That was an order, if Darkwind had ever heard one. He turned to Elspeth, to see her own eyes alight with laughter and a little wonder. "I heard him that time!" she exclaimed. "I think—maybe—I've got the knack of talking to the bondbirds now. They're kind of—pitched higher than human mind-voices."

"Yes, exactly," he replied, as pleased by her accomplishment as she was. "That's excellent! Well, then, you heard. We've gotten our marching orders."

She eyed the long, sharp talons—the fierce beak—and grinned. "You know, given where he's perched right now, I wouldn't argue with those orders if I were you."

"I don't intend to," he assured her, and kicked the mule into a reluctant walk toward the Vale, Elspeth and Gwena following.

When Darkwind turned the mule over to the *hertasi*, he got them to find a stout branch that he could brace across his shoulder and hold with one hand. That gave Hyllarr a much more secure perch, and one that eased Darkwind's aching shoulder quite a bit. He was going to be very glad when he delivered the bird to his father. After that, Starblade could figure a way to carry him; it would no longer be Darkwind's problem.

The hawk-eagle reveled in the heat of the Vale, rousing his feathers with a careful shake and raising his crest fully. Darkwind had decided on a tentative approach to his father on the slow ride to the Vale; now it only remained to convince the bird to cooperate.

He got Hyllarr's attention with a little mental touch, the kind he used with Vree.

:?: Hyllarr replied, definite feelings of relaxation and satisfaction coming along with the reply.

:Starblade is hurt,: he said, hoping he could convey the complex idea in a way the bird would understand.

:Hurt,: Hyllarr agreed. And waited.

That was encouraging. *:Starblade is proud,:* he continued, showing the bird an image of Hyllarr himself, hurt, but refusing all aid, trying to fly and unable to.

:Proud,: the bird said, agreeing again. Then, *:Stupid. Like first year. Try too much.:*

:Exactly!: Darkwind said, astonished that the bird understood so much. He was to have an even bigger surprise.

For suddenly, Hyllarr drooped on his shoulder, dropping the injured wing even further. *:Hurts,:* the bird moaned, making little chirps of distress. *:Oh, huuuurts. Need Starblade! Need Starblade, make better!:*

Then the bird straightened again, a distinct gleam of humor in the eye nearest Darkwind. *:Good?:* he asked. *:Good for proud Starblade?:*

Darkwind wanted to laugh, both at the bird's astonishing ability to *act* and at Elspeth's expression. "I'm as surprised as you are," he grinned, then returned his attention to the bird.

:Very good!: he replied. *:Exactly right!:*

The bird roused again with satisfaction. *:Hyllarr plays hurt-wing-eyas, Starblade feels good, Hyllarr gets many good eatings, tender eatings, tasty prey, make Hyllarr better. All good.:*

"You," he said, shaking an admonitory finger at the bird, "are going to wind up too fat to fly."

Hyllarr bobbed his head to follow Darkwind's fingertip, then blinked in mock drowsiness. Darkwind felt his amusement. He turned his head to look at Elspeth, who was fairly bursting with laughter. "Don't you dare give this away," he warned. "I don't know how Hyllarr managed to grasp it, but Father really *does* need him. This is going to make all the difference in his recovery, if we don't ruin everything."

She nodded. Darkwind smiled his thanks to her.

As soon as they were within sight of Starblade's *ekele,* he gave a silent cue to the hawk-eagle, who immediately went into full droop, complete with weak, pathetic chirps.

Weak they might have been, but Starblade heard them readily enough. He appeared at the door of the *ekele,* leaning against it heavily, with Kethra supporting him from behind, his face full of concern. "Darkwind?" he said, peering down at them in the gloom of late afternoon. "What is wrong with—"

His eyes widened. "That is *not* Vree!"

Darkwind gave his father a brief version of the rescue. "Hyllarr needs quiet, and someone to care for him, Father. He's in a lot of pain. I don't have the time to coax him to eat or keep an eye on that injury— and Kethra's a Healer, I thought she might be able to help him a little."

Hyllarr chose just that moment to raise his head and look directly into the elder Hawkbrother's eyes. *:Hurts,:* he said plaintively. *:Oh, huuuuurts.:*

Darkwind suspected that he himself might have worn that stunned expression a time or two. The first time Vree spoke directly into his mind, perhaps. But it was more than he had expected to see it on Starblade's face.

It was only there for a moment; then it was replaced by concern and something else. A fierce protectiveness—and the unmistakable look of the bondmate for *his* bird. "Bring him up," Starblade ordered, turning to go back inside.

Darkwind struggled up the stairs as best he could with the weight of the bird on his shoulders, overbalancing him. He managed to make it to the door of the *ekele* without mishap, but he had a feeling that the next time Hyllarr went from ground to door, it would be under his own power. Starblade was not going to be up to carrying Hyllarr any time in the near future.

One of the *hertasi* squeezed by him as he moved inside, and Kethra met him at the door itself. He tensed himself for her disapproval, for Starblade was moving about the room, putting things aside, readying a corner of the place for the "invalid." But her eyes were twinkling as she asked, "Will he let me touch him?"

"Yes, I think so," Darkwind replied, and as Kethra placed a gentle hand on the hawk-eagle's breast-feathers, she leaned in to whisper in Darkwind's ear.

"You just gave him the best medicine he could have had," she said softly. "Something to think about beside himself. Something stronger and prouder than he was, that is hurt as badly and needs as much help. Thank you."

He flushed, and was glad that it wasn't visible in the darkness of the room.

"He has a cracked keel and wishbone, *ke'chara,*" Kethra said to Starblade, who had taken spare cushions from beneath the sand pan all Tayledras kept under their birds' perches, and in the case of Starblade's *ekele,* for guests' bondbirds. "He must be in tremendous pain. It will take a great deal of care for him to fly again."

"He'll have it, never fear," Starblade said, with some of his old strength. "You brought him to the right place, son."

His eyes met Darkwind's and once again Darkwind flushed, but this time with pleasure. Starblade actually *smiled* with no signs of pain, age, or fatigue. Darkwind's heart leapt. *That* was his father!

Before he could say anything, the *hertasi* returned, with two of his fellows. Two of them bore bags of sand for the tray; the third had an enormous block-perch, as tall as the lizard, and very nearly as heavy. The perch went into the tray, and the other two *hertasi* poured their bags of clean sand all around it, filling it and covering the base of the perch for added stability. Kethra stood aside and watched it all, a calculating but caring expression on her face, curling a length of hair between her fingers.

Darkwind took Hyllarr over to his new perch; the bird made a great show of stepping painfully onto it, but once there, settled in with a sigh; a sigh that Darkwind echoed, as the weight left him. He put a hand to his shoulder and massaged it as he headed toward the exit; Kethra nodded to him with approval.

Starblade took his place beside the perch. The look of rapt attention on his father's face was all Darkwind could have hoped for, and the look of bliss in the bird's eyes as Starblade gently stroked under his breast-feathers was very nearly its match.

1 5

His partner and her Companion had waited below while he presented Starblade with *his* new partner. "Well?" Elspeth asked as soon as he got within whispering distance, her face full of pent-up inquiry.

"It worked beautifully," Darkwind told her. He permitted himself a moment of self-congratulation and a brief embrace, then gestured for her to follow so that there would be no chance of Starblade overhearing them. "He's already up out of bed and fussing around Hyllarr—it's a definite match. I don't think either of them have any idea how well they mesh, but I've seen a hundred bondings and this is one of the best."

"Is Hyllarr going to heal up all right?" she asked, dubiously.

He shrugged. "As long as he isn't in pain, it doesn't really matter how completely he heals. Even if the bird never flies again, it won't make any real difference to Father. Starblade isn't a scout; he doesn't need a particularly mobile bondbird. Hyllarr will be able to get by quite well with the kind of short flights a permanently injured bird can manage."

Elspeth considered that. Gwena nodded. :*I see. Injuries that would doom a free bird wouldn't matter to one that is never likely to leave the Vale. It is relief of pain that matters, not mobility.*:

He chuckled his agreement. "In fact, I remember one of the mages from my childhood who had a broken-winged crow that couldn't fly at all, and *walked* all over the Vale. If it came to it, Hyllarr could do the same. And be just as pampered."

Gwena snorted delicately. :*That makes an amusing picture; Starblade with the bird following him afoot or, more likely, carried by a* hertasi. *Well, Hyllarr isn't going to get fat if he finds himself walking. I doubt that anyone as frail as your father is right now* could *carry that great hulk.:*

"*I* couldn't carry him for long," Darkwind admitted. "I have no idea how scouts bonded to hawk-eagles manage. I thought my shoulders were going to collapse."

"The important thing is Starblade," Elspeth pointed out, "and it sounds like having Hyllarr around is going to make the difference for him."

Darkwind nodded, and then the insistent demands of his stomach reminded him that they were both long overdue for a meal.

Both? No, all. Surely Gwena was just as ravenous.

Unless she and Elspeth, too, were suffering from something that often happened with young mages, where the body was so unused to carrying the energies of magic that basic needs like hunger and thirst were ignored until the mage collapsed. Just as the impetus of fear or anger made the body override hunger and thirst, so did the use of magic—at least until the mage learned to compensate and the body grew used to the energies and no longer confused them.

"If you two aren't hungry, you should be," he told them. "Elspeth, I warned you about that happening, but I don't think I told Gwena; it never occurred to me that she might be susceptible."

Gwena paused, her eyes soft and thoughtful for a moment. *:I should be starving. Hmm. I think I shall find a* hertasi, *and have a good grain ration. If you'll excuse me?:*

With a bow of her head, she trotted up the trail, leaving them alone.

"A wise lady," he observed. "Let's drop by Iceshadow's *ekele* long enough to give him the good news from k'Treva, and then take this conversation to somewhere there's food for us."

Elspeth grinned. "I think I'm used to magic enough now because my stomach is wrapping around my backbone and complaining bitterly. Let's go!"

Iceshadow was overjoyed at the good news from k'Treva and almost as pleased with the news about Starblade. They left him full of plans to inform the rest of the mages, and with unspoken agreement, reversed their course, back to the mouth of the Vale.

There were "kitchens" on the way, but somehow, that "somewhere" wound up being Darkwind's *ekele*, where his *hertasi* had left a warm meal waiting. The *hertasi* information network was amazing; word must have gotten around the moment they'd crossed into the Vale. Before them were crisp finger vegetables and small, broiled gamehens; bread and cheese, fruit, and hot *chava* with beaten cream for two for dessert. Darkwind dearly loved *chava*, a hot, sweet drink with a rich taste like nothing else in the world. Sometimes the *hertasi* could be coaxed into making a kind of thick cookie with *chava*, and the two together were enough to put any sweet-lover into spasms of ecstasy.

And while he had a moment of suspicion over the fact that the *hertasi* had left food and drink for two, he had to admit that they had done so before. And given his past, perhaps the preparation was not unwarranted. Until Elspeth had entered his life, he had certainly eaten and slept in company more often than not. This was a lovers' meal, though. And they knew very well that he had not had any lovers since they had begun serving him. Was this an expression of hope on their part? Or something else?

Well, the *chava* could be used as bait to tempt Elspeth into his bed, that was certain. He knew any number of folk who would do astonishing things for—even with—the reward of *chava*.

It was Elspeth's first encounter with *chava*, and Darkwind took great glee in her expression of bliss the moment she tasted it. Once again, another devotee was created. They took their mugs over to the pile of cushions in the corner that served as seating and lounging area.

"You look just like Hyllarr when Starblade started scratching him," he told her, chuckling. "All half-closed eyes and about to fall over with pleasure."

"No doubt," she replied, easing back against the cushions with the mug cradled carefully in her hand, so as not to spill a single drop. "Complete with raptorial beak, predator's eyes, and unruly crest."

She spoke lightly, but Darkwind sensed hurt beneath the words. That was the same hurt he had sensed when she spoke of being afraid that most men were interested only in her rank, not in her. "Why do you say that?" he asked.

She snorted, and shook her head. "Darkwind, I thought we were going to be honest with each other. I've mentioned this before, I know I have. Can you honestly say that I am *not* as plain as a board?"

He studied her carefully before he answered; the spare, sculptured face, the expressive eyes, the athletic figure, none of which were set off to advantage by unadorned, white, plain-edged clothing—or, for that matter, the drab scout gear she wore now. The thick, dark hair—which he had never seen styled into anything other than an untamed tumble or pulled back into a tail. "I think," he replied, after a moment, "that you have been doing yourself a disservice in the way you dress. With your white uniform washing out your color and no ornaments, you look very *functional,* certainly quite competent and efficient, but severe."

"What I said: plain as a board." She sipped her *chava,* hiding her face in her cup. "I like the colored things the *hertasi* have been leaving out for me, but they don't make much difference that I can see."

"No," he corrected. "Not 'plain as a board.' Improperly adorned. Scout gear is still too severe to display you properly. You should try mage-robes. Mages need not consider impediments such as strolls through bramble tangles."

Many Tayledras costumes were suited to either sex; Elspeth, with her lean figure, would not distort the lines of some of his own clothing. There were a number of costumes he had designed and made, long ago, that he had never worn, or worn only once or twice. When Songwind became Darkwind, and the mage became the scout, those outfits had been put away in storage as inappropriate to the scout's life. They were memories that could be hidden.

And, truthfully, he had not wanted to see them again. They belonged to someone else, another life, another time. Their cheerful colors had been ill-suited to his grief and his anger. He had not, in fact, even worn them now that he was a mage again and in the Vale, though he had brought them out of storage, with the vague notion that he might want them.

They were here, now, in this new *ekele,* in chests in one of the upper rooms. He studied her for a moment, considering which of those half-remembered robes would suit her best.

The ruby-firebird first, he decided. *The amber silk, the peacock-blue, the sapphire, and the emerald. Perhaps the tawny shirt and fawn breeches—no, too light, they will wash her out. Hmm. I should go and see what is there; I can't recall the half of them.*

"Wait here," he said, and before she could answer, ran up the ladderlike stair to the storage room at the top of the *ekele.*

Maybe the tawny with a black high-necked undergarment for contrast...

He returned with his arms full of clothing; robes and half-robes, shirts and flowing breeches in the Shin'a'in style, vests and wrap-shirts, all in jewel-bright colors, made of soft silks and supple leathers, and scented with the cedar of the chests. Light clothing, all of it, made for the gentle warmth of the Vale. There were other mage-robes, heavier, made to be worn outside the Vale, but none of those were as extravagant as these outfits. Tayledras mages did not advertise their powers in outrageous costumes when outside the confines of their homes, unless meeting someone they knew, or knew would be impressed.

"Here—" he said, shaking out the ruby-colored silk half-robe and matching Shin'a'in breeches, cut as full as a skirt, and bound at the ankles with ribbon ties. The half-robe had huge, winglike sleeves with scalloped edges, and an asymmetric hem. "Try this one on, while I find some hair ornaments."

She stared at him, at the clothing, and back again, as if he had gone quite mad. "But—"

He grinned at her. "Indulge me. This is my art, if you will, and it has been long since I was able to spare a moment for it. Go on, go on—if you're modest, there's a screen over there you can stand behind to dress."

He turned to his collection of feathers and beads, crystals and silver chains, all hung like the works of art they were, on the walls. By the *hertasi*, of course; when he'd lived outside the Vale he'd had no time to sort through the things and hang them up properly. They winked and gleamed in the light from his lamps and candles as he considered them. Some of them he had made, but most had been created by other Tayledras. Most of them, sadly, were either dead or with the exiles. But the delicate works of their hands remained, to remind him that not every hour need be spent in war and defense.

After a moment he heard Elspeth rise and take the clothing behind the screen; heard cloth sliding against cloth and flesh as she undressed, then the softer, hissing sounds of silk against that same flesh. He closed his eyes for a moment, reflecting on how good it felt to be doing this again—after all that had happened, that there was still a skill he could use without thought of what it meant tactically.

A moment later, she slipped from behind the screen, and he heard her bare footfalls against the boards of the *ekele* floor. "I hope I have this stuff on right," she said dubiously, as he selected three strands of hair ornaments from among those on the wall.

He turned, his hands full of beaded firebird feathers, and smiled with pleasure at the sight of her.

She made a sour face, and twisted awkwardly. "I look that silly, do I?"

"On the contrary, you look wonderful." She pursed her lips, then smiled reluctantly. He admired her for a moment; as he had thought, the variegated, rich rubies and wines of the half-robe heightened her otherwise dull coloring. With her face tanned by the wind and sun, and her dark brown hair, without the help of color reflected up from her clothing, it was no surprise that she thought herself plain. But now, she glowed, and her hair picked up auburn highlights from the ruby-red silks. And with her hair braided and ornamented instead of being simply pulled back from her face—

She is going to look magnificent when her hair turns white, he thought admiringly. *But now—no, this severe style is not going to work. Color's a bit too strong. It looks wrong now.*

Before she could move, or even protest, he had his hands buried in her hair, braiding the beaded cords of feathers into one side. Then he created a browband with another cord, pulling some of the rest of her hair with it across her forehead to join the braid on the other side. It didn't take long; her hair was ridiculously short by mage-standards, and even many of the scouts wore theirs far longer than hers. But when released from that severe tail, it had a soft, gentle wave that went well with the braids and beaded feathers.

"There," he said, turning her to face the mirror that had been left covered, as was customary, with an embroidered cloth. He whisked the cloth away, revealing her new image to her eyes. "I defy you to call yourself plain now."

Her mouth formed into a silent "Oh" of surprise as she stared at the exotic stranger in the mirror. She flushed, then paled, then flushed again, and her whole posture relaxed and softened.

"I would give a great deal to see you appear in your Court dressed this way," he said, a little smugly. He was rather proud of the way she looked in his handiwork. Better than he had imagined, in fact. "I think that you would set entirely new fashions."

She moved carefully, holding out her arms to see the fall of the sleeves, twirling to watch the material slip about her legs and hips, her eyes sparkling with unexpected pleasure. "I had no idea. The last time I wore anything like this, it was for Talia's wedding. I was a cute little girl, but, well, cuteness wears off. I never thought I could look like this." She shook her head, her eyes still riveted to the mirror. "I thought that the clothing the *hertasi* had been leaving for me was nice, but compared to this—"

"Scout's clothing, it was, really," he said, with a shrug. "Quite as practical as your Herald uniforms. Mages tend to prefer more fanciful garb, and certainly more comfortable. *These* are for delight. Showing off. Dancing. Display, as our birds do, for the sheer joy of doing so, or for—" Before she could respond to that, he had picked out a full robe in monochrome intensities of vivid blue. "Come," he said, coaxingly. "Let us try another. I wish to see you in all of these."

"Me? What about you?"

"What about me?" he repeated, puzzled. "What have I to do with this?"

"You're a mage, aren't you? And aren't these *your* costumes?" She folded her arms stubbornly across her chest. "I'd like to see what *you* look like in these things!"

Try as he would, he could not dissuade her. Before she would consent, she insisted that if *she* was going to prance about in bright feathers, he would have to do the same. So nothing would have it but that he must don a set of dancing gear before she would change her costume for another. The evening hours passed, the two of them playing among the costumes like a pair of children at dress-up, laughing and admiring together.

Some time later, he had draped her in a swath of amber-gold that brought sunlike highlights to her hair and a Tayledras-sheen to her skin. Any of the vivid colors suited her, but she glowed in the warm colors, he had decided. This particular robe, though he did not tell her so, was a lounging robe—a dalliance robe, in fact. A lover's robe. Meant for display to one person, not to many. He had made it for himself, but had not liked the color once he had tried it on—one of the few times he had misjudged color for himself.

But on her—

"You must keep that," he whispered, as she turned and twisted, plainly taking sensuous pleasure in the soft slip of the silk against her skin. "No, indeed, you must," he insisted, as she turned to protest. "It was never suited to me, but I think I must have somehow designed it with you in mind."

The words had been meant to come out teasingly, but somehow, they turned in his mouth and hung in the air between them with more meaning in them than he had intended. He reached delicately to a glass box and opened it, and before he knew what he was doing, he reached toward her, his hand holding a single brightly beaded feather.

Not one of Vree's—though at this moment, he would have offered her that, if he had thought she might take it. But he dared not. He hardly believed that he dared this.

She knew what that meant now—and as she stared at it and at him with her expression gone quiet and unreadable, he feared that he had just undone all that had been built between them.

But her hand reached for his—and gently took the feather.

And carefully, as if it, or she, might break, she braided it into her hair, then took a deep breath, her eyes wide and dark, waiting.

They both stepped forward at the same moment; he reached up with both hands and cupped her face between them, as carefully as he would grasp a downy day-old falcon. Her skin was as soft as the washed silk she wore, and very warm beneath his hands, as if she was flushed or feverish. It occurred to him then that she might—no, must—be shy, of him, and of what was to come; with a last, weary exercise of his magic, he dimmed the mage-lights.

The comparison and the contrast was inevitable; this was no Dawnfire. Elspeth, for all her courage elsewhere, all her eagerness, was trembling and half-frightened with him. It came to him in a rush how far away from her home she was—all the trials she had faced, and now this—it was up to him to take the lead. She was unsure of herself and not certain what he wanted of her, but there was desire there.

So, he would go as gently with her as he would with caring for a frightened wild bird. She was not likely a virgin, but it did not necessarily follow that she was experienced in lovemaking; he could by accident frighten her with a technique she had never experienced. With all sincerity, he hoped there would be ample times in the future to explore.

He kissed her, once, then dropped his hands, catching hers, and led her back to the bower of cushions on the floor. He slowly drew her down beside him, and there they stayed while he caressed her, letting the silk slide over her body beneath his hands. He touched her gently; shoulders, back, breasts, neck—let the silk carry the movement of his hands. She shivered again, but now it was not from half-formed fear, but from anticipation.

Her lips parted in a gentle moan of pleasure, and she lay her head back with a visible expression of delight.

After a moment, she returned his caresses, hesitantly at first, then with more boldness. Her hands wandered as freely as his, and he kept careful control over himself, lest he move too quickly with her.

But it had been a very long time since his last lover... a very long time. Controlling himself was as difficult as any magic he had ever attempted.

Now they drew closer, and her lips met his.

If he had any thoughts until that moment that she might regret having accepted his feather, they were dismissed by the eagerness with which she returned his kiss. He allowed his mind to brush hers for a moment, as his mouth opened for her. He garnered two important things from that brief contact; she was by no means as experienced a lover as he, but she was as perfectly willing to be his pupil in this as in the other subjects he had taught her. She had confidence in his skill abed.

So, take things slowly. The greater her desire, the calmer at first, the more fully she felt their bodies, the better the experience.

He slid his hands under the silk of the robe, and continued his slow, sensual caresses; continued until any thought of fear was a long-forgotten triviality. Then he joined his mind to hers, very lightly, and showed her wordlessly what would pleasure him, as he noted what pleasured her. She was soft silk in his hands, and warm honey in his mouth; feather-caress and nectar. Her scent was of sandalwood, cinnamon, and herbs. His was of musk and rich *chava*. Her skin tasted salty-sweet, and where their bodies touched, liquid fire poured between them.

When their minds were so entwined that there was no telling where one ended and the other began, only then did he join his body into hers.

A pair of hawks spiraling slowly up a thermal, talons entwined, they rose together, and soared into the sun...

Elspeth lay in silk and warmth, and thought of absolutely nothing, content to savor the warm glow that bathed every pore. Content to listen to Darkwind breathing beside her. Content, for the moment, to forget everything she was, and simply be.

Darkwind lay quietly beside her, his breathing slow and even. She listened to him, thinking that sleep could not be far off for her, either, but hoping to hold it away a little longer, and savor the moment.

"I trust I achieved your expectations."

She started; he laid a calming hand on her shoulder, and she laughed, breathlessly, willing her heart to calm. "I thought you were asleep," she said. "I mean, you sounded like you were."

"That would be unforgivably crude," Darkwind replied, with just a hint of laughter in his voice. "At least, it would be by our customs."

She thought of the few—to be honest, three—lovers she had taken to her bed, not counting the almost-lover whose tryst Talia had interrupted so long ago. Skif had never been one of them—which might have accounted for the way he had overreacted when they were alone on the road together.

They were all friends, she and her lovers, but never more than that, and they had trysted with the understanding that it would remain that way. Heralds, all of them, of course; Talia had been right about that. Only a Herald could be trusted to be completely discreet about making love with the Heir. Two of them had always fallen asleep immediately afterward, and she had slipped out of *their* rooms to return to her own.

Oh, they were always tired, she thought, in their defense. *And no sooner were they rested than they were haring off again, out on circuit. They couldn't help it. And it would have been an awful scandal for me to act openly as their lover.*

Neave never fell asleep, but then he never *ever* fell asleep with anyone else in his bed. He couldn't. Not after what he'd been through. He was healing, but sometimes she wondered if he would ever really be *healed.* Perhaps not. And her times with him had been as much comfort for him as lovemaking. Oh, he was skilled; he'd had no choice but to learn skill... poor child. How anyone could make a child into an *object* like that; to use a child, an unconsenting, terrified *child*—

She deliberately turned her thoughts away from the past. "I think I could learn to like your customs," she said, keeping her tone light. "It seems a bit more civilized than to simply roll over and forget one's partner when the moment is gone."

"Well, but it is no jest, not really," he replied, with a finger-brush along her cheek. "Wait a moment—"

He gently disentangled himself from her, and with a whisper of cloth, faded into the darkness. Her ears strained to hear what he was doing, but she could not make anything out except some vague sounds of moving about.

He returned in a moment, and took his place beside her again; felt for her hand, and pressed a cool cup into it. She sipped, and found that it was delightfully cold and sweet water. Before she knew it, she had drained the cup, and feeling for a secure place to put it, set it down on a table beside her with a sigh.

"Sometimes I suspect the *hertasi* of prescience," he said, after a moment. "A meal for two waiting, *chava* for two to inflame the senses, with cool water waiting with two cups to quench the thirst—"

She chuckled. "Maybe. Is that one of your customs? Pampering your partner?"

"Oh, the custom is simpler than that," he replied, setting his cup down somewhere with a faint *tick.* "It is that one does not simply fall asleep without expressing one's delight in one's partner." His voice was warm with approval, and she found herself blushing.

"That is a most civilized custom," she replied, after a moment. "And," she groped for something to say that would not make her blush even harder, "consider it expressed."

"Would you care to accept my feather in the future, Wingsib?" he persisted.

She couldn't help it; she flushed so hotly that she feared she must be glowing in the dark. "I—would very much like it," she stammered.

"Ah, now I embarrass you, forgive me," he said quickly. "We are a forward people, we Tayledras. The Shin'a'in claim that like kestrels, we have no shame. But I hope you will not take it amiss that I am very glad to hear your reply."

"No—no, not at all." Oh, she must sound like a schoolchild in the throes of infatuation!

"Thank you, bright lady." That gentle hand touched her cheek again, and this time, he did not withdraw. "Are you rested?" he asked, his finger tracing a line down her cheek, then further down, along the line of her throat.

"I—think so—" she stammered again. What was he about?

"Well, then—there is another custom," he chuckled, "Which is why the Shin'a'in compare us to kestrels... in more than being shameless."

Then to her astonishment, he pressed gently against her, and began all over again.

At first she was too surprised to respond, but her astonishment did not outlive the realization that he was quite serious. And quite intent.

And quite, quite splendid.

This time, she brought the water, with help from a tiny mage-light to find where the *hertasi* had left the pitcher. He accepted it with a sleepy smile, and a kiss in the palm of her hand.

She took her place beside him, quite certain that even if she had wanted to, her legs would not have carried her as far as her own *ekele*. And she didn't want to leave, not really. Her bed was cold and lonely, and Darkwind was warm and quite ready to cradle her in his arms.

Who would she outrage, anyway? Not Gwena. Not the *hertasi*. Not any of the Hawkbrothers, who partnered whomever they pleased. Even Skif could not take her to task. There were no Court gossips here. No word of this would get back to scandalize whatever potential bridegrooms there might be.

Not that there seemed to be any in the offing. *Nothing* would persuade her to wed Ancar, and it was not likely that Karse had any royal sons to wed to satisfy an alliance... her mother had satisfied any need for bonds with Rethwellan. Who would she wed? Some fur-covered hulk from the North? They didn't even *have* any government; they were a series of warring tribes.

Perhaps she *could* choose a partner to suit herself...

"And now," Darkwind whispered, "custom satisfied—I fear—I *must* sleep—" A yawn punctuated the sentence, and she found herself echoing it.

"Custom satisfied—" she yawned again "—I agree—"

"Then, good night—" he whispered. *"Zhai'helleva—"*

Sleep had her by the shoulders and was dragging her down into darkness. But had she heard what she *thought* she heard?

Had he whispered, with the sigh of one drifting into slumber, *"Zhai'helleva, ashke?"*

Wind to thy wings—beloved?

The *hertasi* brought her clothing and laid it beside breakfast for two without so much as a single eyeblink to show that they considered her spending the night anything out of the ordinary. Gwena appeared shortly afterward, to tell them that they had been relieved of the duty of chasing away what had been attracted by their profligate use of power. And even her Companion had nothing to say on her choice of sleeping places and partners.

:Iceshadow approved of your choice of nonweaponry.: she told them. *:Illusions make a less visible use of power. He has some other mages out there doing what you did—with backups, of course, in case the beasties don't frighten away. Right now he wants you to meet with him and the Elders and anyone else that is free—he's holding a Clanwide general meeting.:*

"I assume he wants us to tell them all exactly what the message said?" Darkwind replied after a moment of thought, as he braided his hair away from his face.

:Probably. He didn't tell me.: She tossed her head with feigned indignation, but Elspeth could tell that she didn't mean it. *:I told him that it was my opinion that you two needed a day of rest, anyway. He seemed inclined to agree. His exact words were "as much rest as the Clan can afford them, at any rate."*

Darkwind chuckled. "Meaning that we are still on call. Ah, well. It is better than being out in the snow!"

They ate slowly, Elspeth being very aware of Darkwind's eyes lingering on her, and being unable to resist taking a few, long, lingering glances herself.

He certainly provided a pleasant place to rest the eyes. He no longer seemed so exotic—although he did look a bit odd, with white showing at the roots of his hair; she couldn't help but think of certain "blonde" ladies whose hair often showed the opposite coloration at its roots. It no longer seemed strange to have the bondbird sitting beside them, taking bits of raw meat from Darkwind's fingers. For that matter, it no longer seemed revolting to eat her breakfast and watch the bird bolting his tidbits…

She remembered, then, that she had been able to hear the bird yesterday. Was that still true?

Well, why not test it?

:Vree?: she called, tentatively, pitching her mind-voice up high, trying to reach the same place she had Heard him.

The bird looked up, startled, and immediately turned his head upside down to look at her.

:?: he Sent. :/:

"Yes, she's speaking to you, silly bird," Darkwind said lightly, with an approving glance at her that warmed her all the way down to her toes. "It's considered polite to answer."

:Ye-es?: Vree replied, cautiously, righting his head again.

:How is Hyllarr?: she asked, figuring that was an innocent enough question, and one the bird should be able to answer easily enough.

:Hungry. Healing. Happy.: Vree roused all his feathers, evidently tickled by his own alliteration. :Very good. Is good bonding.:

:Thank you,: she told him, and he bobbed his head at her before turning his attention back to Darkwind's tidbits.

"Why can I talk to him now when I couldn't before?" she asked, hoping he knew the answer.

"I think—mostly because you know now that he Mind-speaks, so you began listening unconsciously for where he was Speaking," Darkwind hazarded. "The gryphons Speak high, but in the ranges you were listening in already—but listening to them made you ready to listen even higher. I think. I don't *think* that you are developing a new Gift."

"Good," she replied, a little relieved. "One at a time is enough."

He laughed, and fed Vree the last bit of meat. "Shall we go?" he asked, standing up and offering her his hand.

* * *

The meeting was relatively uneventful, until Starblade put in an appearance. He leaned heavily on Kethra and a walking stick, and sat down immediately, but it was already obvious that despite his physical weakness there was new life in his eyes, and new hope in his spirit.

He listened to both of them recount what they remembered of the message, and waited for the buzz of conversation to die down, before clearing his throat to speak.

He got immediate silence.

"Before any of you speculate," he said, carefully, "Yes—k'Treva *did* send mages to see if we needed help immediately after the Stone shattered. And I did turn them away, with protests that we were fully capable of dealing with the situation ourselves. You all know why I did that. I am sorry. But this may have been all to the good, in some ways. When they offered help, the healing Adept of which they speak had only just come into his power. Now he is at full strength. Had he tried to deal with the Stone as it was, it might have killed him and the rest of us as well. Certainly it would have damaged him, and our great enemy would have had a way into the power of a Healing Adept as a result. And that would have been even more of a catastrophe."

Murmurs around the circle showed that most of the Clan agreed with him. Elspeth didn't even want to *think* about Mornelithe Falconsbane having that much power. The little that she had seen of him had convinced her that he had been far too powerful as it was.

"Now—" Starblade continued, "I believe that with the help of Darkwind, Wingsib Elspeth, honored Gwena, and our gryphon allies, all will be well. But I am only one. I think that every voice should be heard in this. It is the fate of our entire Clan that we are discussing."

Elspeth followed as much as she could, but the Hawkbrothers were more than a bit agitated, and as a result, spoke a little faster than she preferred. She gathered that they were, on the whole, inclined to agree with Starblade, but they had been deceived before and were determined to do what they could to see that it did not happen again.

As the meeting went on, Starblade wilted visibly—yet seemed stubbornly determined to remain and prove that he was no longer acting against the good of the Clan. Finally Elspeth couldn't stand it any more. She stood up.

All eyes focused on her, and the babble of speech cut off, abruptly, leaving her standing in silence.

"I haven't endured what you have," she said, slowly. "And I haven't been a mage for very long. I've certainly never seen a Healing Adept, so I have no idea what they can or can't do. But we took a lot of time preparing that message; we told k'Treva everything we knew, in as much detail as we could. *Surely,* since they were already worried about us, this Adept they are sending has had time to prepare for trouble! Surely he comes not only armed but armored!"

She sat down again, wondering if she'd managed to insult all of them, or if she'd made some sense.

Evidently the latter, since she saw Iceshadow smiling, slowly, and there was very little muttering and much nodding of heads.

"Has everyone said what is needed?" Iceshadow asked, once the last of the muttering died down. He looked about, but no one seemed inclined to jump to his or her feet. "Very well, then, I—"

The bottom dropped out of Elspeth's stomach, and although she hadn't moved, it felt as if she had suddenly plummeted about five feet.

What in— She looked wildly about. Was it an attack? Had something gone wrong with the Stone?

But no one else seemed alarmed, and she calmed her pounding heart. Iceshadow actually grinned at the expression on her face, whatever it was.

It probably looks like someone hit me in the back of the head with a board.

"That, I think, makes the rest of the arguments moot," Iceshadow said. "So, if no one has any objection, I will declare the meeting closed."

Under cover of the rest standing up and moving off in twos and threes or more, Elspeth leaned over to Darkwind and asked, "And just what *was* that? Was that an earthquake? I've heard of them, but—"

"Not an earthquake, no, although I am told that the feeling is very similar, save that the earth itself does not move," Darkwind replied. "No, that was the establishing and closing of a long-ranging Gate that you just felt. Very abrupt—probably to keep from disrupting the Stone too much. Normally the flux is much more gradual and less noticeable."

"You mean—"

He took her hand and squeezed it, his smile inviting her to share in his triumph. "Yes. At last. There is very little that is likely to stop him. And there is no more chance for argument. Our help is on the way. We have won."

16

Darkwind took nothing about Elspeth for granted, but when she returned with him to his *ekele*, he thought it reasonable to assume that she was not displeased with him in the clear light of day. He had not been certain; she was so self-possessed, she rarely revealed what was in her mind. As important as her mind, he was not certain what the reaction of her Companion would be to their assignation, despite the fact that Gwena had left them alone together.

But there were inevitable awkward moments to come. The early moments of a new liaison were always full of such things… when neither knows quite what to say or do, and neither is familiar enough with the other to read body and voice. Trying not to appear too distant, yet not wanting to seem possessive, making the dance moves of courtship and trying not to stumble through them—all of this was universal.

He paused at the foot of the stairs and cleared his throat at the same time that she said, "Darkwind—"

They looked at each other and laughed self-consciously.

"I was about to suggest that we take advantage of our temporary freedom to soak away some bruises," he said, offering a neutral occupation which had the potential to become something else entirely. In this, at least, he had more experience than she. He had sky-danced through a fair number of courtships. "The *hertasi* are skilled at massage, if you like. They use carved wooden rollers instead of claws, and thick oils."

She stretched in a way that suggested that she might well be suffering from sore muscles, stiffly, and with a little wince of pain, rather than coyly or provocatively. "I would like that," she replied. Then she smiled, wryly. "Now the pertinent question—were you thinking of soaking in the same pool as me, or going off on your own? I would enjoy your company, but I won't be upset if you'd like to have some time to yourself." Her smile became a grin. "Astera knows you've seen quite enough of me and my over-sharp tongue. I wouldn't blame you if you'd like a respite!"

"Actually, I was hoping you'd join me, but in the pool near *your* tree," he said, relieved at her words, and even more so at the touch of self-deprecating humor. "Yours is the warmest pool in the Vale. I will ask my *hertasi* to bring oils, once I find them. They haven't established a summoning method yet."

"Shall I meet you there?" she suggested gracefully. "You've got things to do—and I'm still something of an appendage to the Clan."

It didn't take him too long to find the two lizard-folk; it took him even less time to make his way to the pool he now thought of as "Elspeth's." But by the time he got there, she was already chin-deep in hot water, her hair piled up on the top of her head and her eyes half-closed in pleasure.

"We must have slipped and fallen in the snow a hundred times. I have bruises in places I didn't even guess at. I have got to find some way to reproduce these pools once I get back home," she said, as he shed clothing and joined her. "A hot bath is no substitute for this."

The two lizard-folk busied themselves in setting up cushions and towels beside the pool; once they were ready, he and Elspeth could go to their skillful hands with their muscles warm and pliant. *Much* easier to take the knots out of muscles that were relaxed and warmed than those that were stiff and tense.

"Have you no hot springs in your homeland?" he asked lazily, slipping into the hot water with a sigh of pleasure. "I would find that very strange."

"You would find a lot of things about my land very strange," she said. "At least as strange as Skif and I find the Vale. And speaking of Skif—"

He felt a chill in spite of the heat of the water. Was she about to reveal that she and Skif were betrothed, or something of the sort? While he had no claims on her, nor had any right to think of such things—the idea disturbed him in a way that he did not want to examine too closely.

But she was continuing, and there was nothing in her tone to give him any kind of clue to her feelings about the other Herald. "Speaking of Skif—Darkwind, what should I do about Nyara? If—when he finds her. Should I worry? Should I even try to do anything?"

"I do not know," he said, carefully, choosing his words in the hopes that they would not turn to stones and bruise his already shaken pride. "First I must ask you this—what is Skif to you?"

"To me?" She opened her eyes and looked him full in the face, and he was relieved to see that there was nothing hiding there. No hitherto undisclosed passions. No pain. Only simple concern. "My very good friend. My blood-brother. My—Wingsib, if you will, for the Heralds are the closest thing to a Tayledras Clan that my people know. He *has* no other kin but the Heralds, and I'm one of the closest friends he has among them. I'm *worried* about him, Darkwind."

There was something she hadn't told him yet. "Why should you worry?" he asked. "He seems perfectly capable to me."

She sighed, and chewed her lower lip. "I've known him a long time, and the Skif you know isn't the Skif I first made my brother. I haven't talked to anyone about this, but something happened to him a couple of years ago, something to do with the war with Hardorn, and it changed him. He hasn't been the same since. But he never said anything to me about it, and I don't feel that I should press him on the subject. I mean, he values his privacy."

He considered her words for a moment, hoping that the relief he felt on learning that Skif was no more than a brother to her did not show too clearly. But changes in a personality—oh, he was all too familiar with that. Though this was not likely to be the kind of sinister change that had overcome Starblade.

No, more like the change of shock that had made Songwind become Darkwind.

"I think that if it was something he felt comfortable about revealing to you, he would have done so," he said carefully. "That may have been because he considered you to be too sheltered to reveal it, because he was ashamed of it, or even because you are female and he is male. Do I take it that this experience—whatever it was—damaged him in some way?"

"Not physically, but he was never as—carefree afterward," she replied thoughtfully. "Yes, I would say that it damaged him. Probably all three reasons have something to do with why he has never told me about it."

"In that case, he might well reveal it to Wintermoon," Darkwind mused aloud. "That would be a good thing. My brother is a remarkable man and has his own burdens he might be pleased to reveal. That would be a good thing as well."

She gave him a glance filled with hope and speculation. "Do you think so? He's been so—I don't know. Before, he was always eager for the next adventure. Now it seems as if adventure has soured for him, and all he's looking for is peace. And I think that Nyara just *might* be able to ease some of what is hurting him. *If* she doesn't hurt him further."

"A good point. I do not think that she would do so a-purpose," he said, raising a dripping hand from the water to rub his temple. "She has been both cause and receiver of too much harm to wish to work further such, I think." Nyara… oh, *there* was a potential to become the lash of a whip if not carefully dealt with. "But there is pain waiting for him, with that one, be she ever so well-intentioned."

Elspeth nodded. "You're thinking what I'm thinking. If he—no, when he finds her, if she is not in love with him, he's going to be hurt."

"Would it were only as simple as that. You know that if she *does* love him and ran to save him before for that reason, he is destined for even greater hurt." Darkwind raised himself a little higher in the water, rested his arms on the ledge around the pool, and propped his head on one hand. "You must know that, Elspeth. Think on it. Suppose she loves him truly. Suppose she *accepts* his love. *My* people would have trouble in accepting a Changechild as the lover of one of their kin. But yours? To them, will she not seem a monster?"

She groaned, and rubbed her eyes. "I wish I could tell you no, but I can't. Gods, Darkwind, the Shin'a'in are looked at askance when a rare one comes to Valdemar. The Hawkbrothers are legends only. They'd try to put *her* in a menagerie!" She shook her head. "No matter what we did, how we tried to disguise her, I doubt it would hold for long."

"Soon or late, any disguise is unmade, any illusion is broken," he agreed. "Nor is that the only problem with Nyara. She is utterly, totally foreign. Her ways could never be yours. Gods of my fathers, her ways are utterly alien to *my* people! Among yours, she would be like unto a plains-cat given a collar and called a pet!"

Elspeth groaned. "And that—that aura of sexuality she has—that isn't going to win her any converts, I can tell you that. Havens, she even made *me* annoyed, sometimes, and there was nothing for me to be irritated with her over!"

"Except that every male eye must ever be on her," he said ruefully. "Be he ever so faithful to his lover, he *still* must react to her like a male beast in season! Even I—well, I entertained fantasies, and I knew well the danger she implied. You say that Skif seems to seek only peace. Well, he will not find it with *that* one on his arm! Every male with no manners will be trying to have her for himself. Every female will react as you—or more strongly."

"And she can't help herself." Elspeth's mouth quirked in a half smile at his confession, but she quickly sobered. "Darkwind, what should I do?"

"Should you do anything?" he countered. "Can you do anything? Is there even any advice that you could give him that he would heed?"

She shook her head sadly. "Probably not. I guess there's only one thing I can do—to be ready for whatever decision he and she make."

"That is all that a friend can do, Elspeth," he agreed. "And I think perhaps that is all that a friend *should* do. But you know, there is another course that he might take that you do not seem to have considered. What would you and your people think if he should choose to stay here—with her?"

"If he—" She stared at him now as if the very idea were so alien that she couldn't quite grasp it. "But he's a Herald!"

"He is also a human—and a man. And he is very much in love." Darkwind had a fleeting feeling of disorientation, as if he were not talking only about the Herald Skif. "Would your people make him choose between his love and his land? Would this cause his Companion to abandon him?"

"I don't know," she said helplessly. "The subject has never come up."

"Interesting." He leaned back into the water again. "Perhaps you and Gwena should discuss this at length. I have the feeling that it may be important."

"So do I," she replied, slowly. "So do I…"

The Adept from k'Treva did not appear by nightfall, at which point Darkwind felt that he had most probably taken the wise course of finding a secure place to rest for the night. When he and Elspeth sought out Iceshadow just after dusk, the Elder said words to that same effect.

"I do not think our Clansbrother is likely to arrive on our doorstep until the morning," Iceshadow predicted, as the three of them strolled back to the Elder's *ekele*. "Were I he, I would find a *tervardi* and share his shelter for the night. I have sensed nothing amiss, and I think if he were in trouble, we would certainly *know* it."

Darkwind nodded. Very few Tayledras traveled by night by choice. Even fewer did so in unknown and possibly dangerous territory. "He knows that our borders are shrunken, and that the land within them is not certain. The heavy snows of the past few days have probably slowed him down. I doubt the one who replied took the difficulties of winter riding into account when he sent the message and told you the Adept would arrive in half a day. Even on *dyheli* I would not undertake to go anywhere in this snow in half a day."

They reached Iceshadow's home at that moment; the Elder stretched, and paused with one hand on the railing. "I would not worry, were I you. *I* am not concerned. We will see this marvel when he arrives and not before, and the matter of one or two days more is not going to make a great deal of difference to our situation. True?"

When they agreed, he chuckled, and bid them a pleasant evening, a certain twinkle in his eyes as he looked from Elspeth to Darkwind and back.

Not that Darkwind minded the delay. Once the Healing Adept arrived, he and Elspeth would start on a round of magic-use that would leave them quite exhausted at day's end. He knew *that* from experience. Sadly, heavy magic-use tended to leave one too weary for dalliance. They would have one more night together, at least—

Or so he hoped.

This time, since they were so near, she had invited him to her *ekele* for supper, while the *hertasi* turned them both into limp yarn dolls. At the time he had thought he saw Faras, the one working on her back, smile a little when she made the invitation. He said nothing, though, then or now; she knew that the lizard-folk used Mindspeech as easily as humans used their voices. Though what she might not know was the way the little folk liked to play at matchmaking...

They took a second soak in the pool, then slipped into a pair of thick robes that the *hertasi* had left there for them, leaving the pool when dusk was only a memory and full darkness shrouded the Vale. Darkwind was not certain how Elspeth felt, but *he* had not been so relaxed or content for a very long time. He followed her up to her *ekele*, pretty well certain of what he would find there.

He was not disappointed. The robe of amber silk, clean again, was waiting for her—and his favorite, of deep blue, lay beside it across the cushions. And on the table there waited another intimate supper for two. This one was a bit different, though.

He recognized it, though she would not have. This was a lovers' supper, a trysting meal. Sensual delights. Things to tease the palate and the four senses. Light foods, the kind found at festivals, arranged in single bite-sized pieces. Food made to be eaten with the fingers—

—or fed to another.

Oddly modest, she caught up the robe and carried it into the next room to change into it, although she had not seemed so shy at the pool. He would have enjoyed seeing the soft silk slip over her young, supple body. Well, that would come in time as she lost her shyness with him.

If they had the time...

He pushed the thought from his mind. He would enjoy what they had, and not seek to shape their future. He slipped into his own robe as she returned, the amber silk caressing her and enveloping her like a cloud of golden smoke. She made a circuit of the room, lighting scented candles to perfume the air; he watched her with pleasure, and wondered a little at her grace. Had she always moved like that? Or had he only now begun to notice?

He waited until she had made herself comfortable before moving toward her. She patted a place beside her and he settled next to her. His most urgent appetite was not for food, but he contented himself with nibbling on a slice of quince as she hesitantly took a piece of cheese.

"What do you think he'll be like?" she asked abruptly, proving that whatever his thoughts were, hers were elsewhere.

The question took him by surprise, and he had to drag his thoughts away from contemplating *her,* and apply them to something a bit more abstract.

"The Healing Adept, you mean?" he hazarded. That was the only "he" the question seemed apt for. "The one from k'Treva?"

She nodded, and he made a half shrug. He hadn't thought about it; he was far more interested in the Adept's skills than in anything else.

"It usually takes a Healing Adept years to come into his full power, so I suppose that he is probably about the age of my father," he said, after a moment. "Probably very serious, very deliberate. Although—" he frowned, trying to recall the message's exact words, "—they did say that he was a kind of experimenter. That is an interesting point. He might be more like Kra'heera than my father."

"What, that funny kind of trickster?" She nibbled at a piece of fruit. "But powerful."

"Oh, that, at the least," he agreed. "He would have to be, to be willing to ride alone across uncertain land. I think that he will definitely have that kind of air about him that Iceshadow has when he is truly certain of himself. Except that he will have it all the time."

"You have that air sometimes," she said suddenly.

"No—" Now that startled him. "I do?"

"Yes." She licked juice from her fingers and gave him a sidelong glance. "You did last night. Sometimes I think you don't give yourself enough credit."

He shook his head. "I think you are being flattering, but—"

"I'm not really hungry," she interrupted him. "Are you?"

He laughed, now knowing where the pathway was leading. "Not for this sort of food," he said.

Bondbirds carried the message in midmorning that the k'Treva Adept was less than a league away. Those of the Clan that were not otherwise engaged in Clan duties gathered at the entrance of the Vale to await his arrival. Although the snow was knee-deep beyond the Veil, it would not have been a proper welcome to greet him within.

Elspeth and Darkwind were among them, and she thought privately that this mysterious mage could not have contrived a more perfect backdrop for his first appearance. The clouds of the past few days had cleared away by dawn, and the sun shone down out of a flawless blue sky, filling the snow-bedecked woods outside the entrance of the Vale with pure white light. There wasn't even a breath of wind, and the woods were completely silent except for a few calls of birds off in the distance. As they waited in the snow, straining their ears for the sound of hoofbeats, Elspeth fretted a little beneath the suspense of the moment. Even Gwena seemed tense with anticipation.

Finally, the sound they had been waiting for echoed beneath the trees; the muffled thud of hooves pounding through snow. From the cadence, Elspeth knew that he had urged his mount into a gallop. Not that *dyheli* had any objection to galloping, but he could not possibly have kept up that pace all the way here. Only a Companion had the stamina to gallop for hours at a time.

Either he's impatient for the end of the trip, or he wants to make an impressive entrance, she thought with amusement.

And then the object of their anticipation came pounding in, sprays of snow flying all about him, and a magnificent, snow-white firebird skimmed just beneath the branches precisely over his head, its tail streaming behind it as the Adept's long hair streamed behind him.

The firebird was the biggest one she had ever seen—and never had she ever heard of anyone using one for a bondbird. It threw off the little false-sparks of golden light as it flew, glittering, a creature of myth or tales.

From the murmurs of surprise, she surmised that no one among the Hawkbrothers had ever seen a firebird bondbird before, either.

It was at least as large as Darkwind's forestgyre. It seemed to be larger, because of the length of its magnificent tail. The head, with its huge, ice-blue eyes, was just as large as any bondbird's head, which meant it could be as intelligent as the rest.

But the firebirds were seed and fruit eaters. Not carnivores or hunters...

Well, why not? He's a mage. He doesn't need *a combative bird to help him, the way the scouts do.*

The Adept pulled up before the entrance to the Vale in a shower of snow and a flurry of hooves, like some kind of young god of winter, or an ice-storm personified. Even his mount gave Elspeth pause for a moment, until she saw the curving horns over the two ice-blue eyes, for he rode a *dyheli* bleached to snowy white just as the bondbirds were.

He *posed* for a moment, and she realized that he was doing it deliberately. Not that she blamed him. She smiled, but kept it to herself.

Oh, what a vain creature he is! And how he basks in the admiration he's getting. Rightfully.

They had expected a venerable wise man; another Iceshadow with more presence, perhaps. What they had gotten was something else entirely.

He swept his arm out and the firebird drifted down to rest on his snow-white leather gauntlet, alighting as silently as one of its own feathers would fall. Only then was it clear that the firebird was fully as large as any of the greater hawks, and approached the size of the hawk-eagle. Its tail trailed down gracefully to within a hand's breadth of the snow, and it, too, posed, as if perfectly well aware of its unearthly beauty.

He was dressed all in white; white furs and leathers, long white hair with white feathers in a braid to one side, white coat draped over the rump of his white *dyheli*. Three sets of ice-blue eyes looked over the assembled Clansfolk dispassionately; the eyes of the *dyheli* and the firebird held only curiosity, but the eyes of the Adept held more than a touch of a self-confidence that was surely forgivable—both for his Adept status (and indeed, he could never have achieved that complete bleaching of hair and eyes and bird if he had *not* been controlling node-magic since he could toddle) and for his absolute physical perfection.

Never in all her life had Elspeth seen anyone so beautiful. That was the only word for him. He was beautiful in a way that transcended sexuality and yet was bound up with it.

So some arrogance and self-assurance could certainly be forgiven, even if he was no older than Darkwind.

Gwena was staring at him intently, much more intently than Elspeth expected.

:What's wrong?: she asked the Companion quietly. *:Is there anything wrong?:*

:Nothing wrong, exactly,: she said slowly. *:No, that's not true. There's nothing wrong at all. But it almost seems like I've seen him before, though I can't imagine how I ever could have. But there certainly is something familiar about him—:*

:Of course there is, my dear,: a deep, masculine mind-voice interrupted. And the k'Treva Adept winked at the Companion, slowly, and unmistakably.

Elspeth was left floundering in surprise—and as for Gwena, clearly, if the Companion's jaw could have dropped in shock, it would have. Gwena stepped backwards.

"Greetings, Clansibs," the Adept called to them all, as calmly as if he had not just utterly flabbergasted Gwena. "I am Firesong k'Treva, and I trust I have not made you wait for too long for my arrival."

With that, he dismounted, sliding from the back of the *dyheli* so smoothly that the firebird was not in the least disturbed. There was a pack on his back—also of white leather—which had been hidden until he dismounted. The *dyheli* paced beside him as he walked forward to the Veil and the Tayledras waiting to greet him, one hand still on the *dyheli's* shoulder, a half-smile on his handsome face. Iceshadow and the other Elders greeted him first, as was only proper, but when he had done clasping arms with them, he turned immediately to Elspeth and Darkwind.

"And here are those whose message summoned me," he said, tossing his head to send his braid over his shoulder, his lips curved in an enigmatic smile. "I see one Clansib—and two Outlanders. A fascinating combination."

"This is Wingsister Elspeth k'Sheyna k'Valdemar, and her Companion Gwena k'Valdemar," Darkwind said carefully. A little too carefully, Elspeth thought. "I am Darkwind."

"K'Valdemar, hmm?" Firesong repeated, his smile increasing by just a hair. "*And* a Companion. *Zhai'helleva*, Wingsibs. The tale of your coming here must be a fascinating one indeed."

"Elspeth is a Herald of Valdemar, if you have heard of such things." Darkwind's voice was carefully neutral. "There is another Herald out on the borders of k'Sheyna who was also made Wingsib, one Skif k'Sheyna k'Valdemar—but it is pressing business that keeps him there, and at any rate, he is no mage."

"Which you, bright falcon, most certainly are." Firesong's handclasp was warm and firm as he took Elspeth's hand in greeting. "And as it happens I have heard of Heralds before. It is something of a k'Treva legend, the visits of Heralds. But then, k'Treva has always been considered—hmm—unconventional." He glanced aside at Iceshadow, who coughed politely.

"But here I am keeping you out in the snow and cold, when we could be in the welcoming warmth of the Vale!" he exclaimed, turning swiftly in a graceful swirl of snowy hair, feathers, and clothing. "Come, Clansibs! Let us continue these greetings in comfort."

Darkwind struggled against annoyance. This Firesong—this *young* Firesong—displayed a body-language that flaunted his arrogance. And a confidence that implied a competence fully as great as the arrogance.

Well, the firebird resting on his shoulder said something of his competence. It had been generations since one of the Tayledras thought to breed up a new species of bondbird—and to do so from firebird stock was doubly amazing. Firebirds were shy, highly territorial, easily startled—none of those being traits that augured well for their potential as bondbirds. Yet here he was, this Firesong, bearing a snow-white firebird that sat upon his shoulder as calmly as ever a forestgyre sat on a scout's.

Small wonder that his Clan described him as an experimenter.

He *could* be older than he looked; it often took an Adept up to sixty years to show any signs of aging. But Darkwind doubted that. The arrogance that Firesong flaunted was that of youth, not age; Darkwind reckoned that he *might* even be a year or two younger than *he* was.

Just as annoying was Elspeth's obvious fascination with the newcomer.

He is as beautiful as a god, a traitorous whisper said in the back of his mind. *How could she not be attracted to him? How could anyone?*

He took small comfort in the fact that Firesong chose an *ekele* near the opposite end of the Vale from Elspeth's. Right beside Starblade's in fact, a little higher in the same tree. But no sooner had the Adept tossed his white pack carelessly up into the open door, sent his white firebird to a perch, and shed his heavy outer garments, than he turned and looked down at Darkwind with that annoying half-smile on his face.

"I should like to see your father Starblade, if I may," he said without preamble. "If you will excuse me."

And with that, he ran lightly down the stairs and tapped upon the doorpost of Starblade's *ekele* as if he were expected.

Perhaps he was, for Kethra beckoned him inside, leaving Darkwind *outside*. She did not beckon him in, although she clearly saw him standing there.

He felt like a fool, and only felt like less of one because there was no one there to witness his exclusion from what was obviously a private conference.

He gritted his teeth, and went off to find something marginally useful to do, before he did something decidedly the opposite.

"Ho, Darkwind!"

The unfamiliar voice hailing him could only be Firesong's. Darkwind stopped, put a pleasant expression on his face with an effort of will, and turned to face the young Adept.

Firesong had changed his costume, from the winter whites he had ridden in wearing, to something more appropriate to the warmth of the Vale. A half-robe and trousers of fine silk—and if Darkwind had not seen it, he would not have believed that it was possible to create a costume that was *more* flamboyant than that of his arrival.

Firebird gold, white, and flame-blue were the colors, and they matched the blue of his eyes, the silver of his hair, and the gold of his skin to perfection. Someone—*hertasi*, probably—had taken great pains with his hair. Darkwind felt positively plain beside him.

"Darkwind," Firesong said, cheerfully, as he strode up beside him. "I have had speech of Starblade and Kethra, of the Elders, and also of the Shin'a'in shaman Tre'valen. What they have told me has confirmed the impression your message gave to me. We can do nothing about the Heartstone for a brace of days; I must study it at close hand."

Well, at least he has that much sense.

"I trust I don't need to warn you to be careful about it," Darkwind said.

Firesong nodded, for once, seeming entirely serious. "There is no doubt in my mind that the Stone is treacherous," he stated. "It has behaved in a way that no such Stone in the history of either of our Clans has ever done before. I shall take *no* chances with it."

That much gave Darkwind a feeling of relief. However arrogant this young man was, he was at least no fool.

"There is something else, however," Firesong continued. "Something I think you have probably anticipated. There are only two among the humans of the Vale who are of a power and an ability to aid me in dealing with this Stone. Yourself, and the Outland Wingsister. But you are not yet tested and confirmed as Adepts."

Darkwind grimaced, and began walking back toward his *ekele*, the direction in which he had been going when Firesong hailed him. "That is true. Although we have Adepts among us, there were none who felt strong enough to do so."

"I have seen that, and I think it was wise of them to work within their strength," Firesong replied, keeping pace with him easily. "But that must end now. I shall complete your training, and Elspeth's, and confirm you, for I shall need you at full ability to aid me." He stared ahead, down the trail, as Darkwind glanced at him out of the corner of his eye. "I shall be accomplishing something with your father as well, but it is nothing you need to concern yourself over."

No, of course not. He's only my father. Why should I worry about what you are going to do with him?

But Darkwind kept his thoughts and his comments to himself, simply nodding shortly. "When do you want to see us, then? And do you want to work with us singly, or together?"

"Oh, together," Firesong replied, carelessly, as if it did not matter to him. "Since I shall need you to work as partners, that is best, I think. And, tomorrow. But not *too* early." He yawned, and smiled slyly. "I am weary. And the *hertasi* have pledged me a massage. It was a cold and fatiguing journey; I believe I shall go and rest from it."

And with that, he turned abruptly off on a sidepath, one that would take him back to his own *ekele*.

And Starblade's.

Of course he already has hertasi, Darkwind thought with irritation. *They flock to beauty and power, and he has both in astonishing measure. He probably had a half dozen begging to serve him within moments of his arrival. If he walked by the swamp village, they would follow him in hordes, for all that they consider that they are independent. Nera would probably lead them.*

He turned his steps toward Elspeth's dwelling to give her the news of their new tutor.

And how was *she* reacting to this arrogant youngster, he wondered. This powerful, breathtaking youngster...

And he was surprised by the stab of jealousy he felt at the memory of the open admiration he had caught in her eyes.

1 7

Nyara woke to the thunder of great wings above her tower, and the sound of something heavy landing on her roof. She slipped out of bed, hastily snatching up the cloak she had made from the skin of a winter-killed bear.

Before she had a chance to panic, or even to shake herself out of the confusion of interrupted sleep, Need spoke in her mind. *:It's the gryphons. Tell them hello for me,:* Need said casually, as she stood, blinking, and trying to shake her dreams off.

The gryphons? She wrapped the cloak around her narrow shoulders and slipped up the steep stone stairs to the rooftop.

The gryphons? But—why have they come here?

"Brrright grrreeetingsss, little one!" Treyvan called, as she poked her head cautiously over the edge of the stair opening. "How goesss the lessssoning?" He looked as cheerful—and as friendly—as she had ever seen him, his wings shining in the sunlight, his head and crest up. As if she had never betrayed his little ones, his trust. As if she had never fled his lair with a stolen sword. As if nothing had ever happened between them but friendship.

She tried not to show her surprise, and ventured the rest of the way onto the rooftop. "Well, I think," she said shyly, bobbing a greeting to Hydona, who had landed behind her mate. "Or at least Need says that I do well. She says to tell you hello. How did you find me?"

"Ssstand, and let me look at you," Hydona demanded, turning her head from one side to the other, like a huge bird surveying something that intrigued it. Nyara obeyed, instantly.

"Good," Hydona pronounced. "The taint isss gone, and you arrre looking lesss—ferrral. We knew wherrre you werrre becaussse Need told usss, of courssse."

"Of course," she said faintly.

"Sssomeone had to know," Treyvan admonished with a flick of his tail. "What if you encounterrred sssomething you could not deal with? What if crrreaturresss of yourrr fatherrr found you? Need judged usss able to defend you, and otherrrwissse likely to leave you in peace."

"Morrre ssso than the Hawkbrrotherrrsss," Hydona said. "But that isss why we arrre herrre. Becaussse of Ssskif and Winterrrmoon."

She inadvertently brought her hand to her throat. "Are they near?" She had not thought she would have to deal with Skif so soon…

"Verry," Treyvan said shortly. "The trrrail isss hot. You will not brrreak passst Winterrrmoon without him ssstriking yourrr esscape trrrail. The owlsss will find thisss place tonight or tomorrrrow night."

Hydona nipped at her mate. "And we mussst leave, if we arrre not to brring dissscovery on herrr soonerrrr." She hesitated a moment. "Nyarrra, we have all forrrgiven you. You did yourrrr bessst. We wisssh you verrry well. And Ssskif would make a fine mate. But I think you know that alrrready."

With that, she launched herself from the tower like a sea-eagle, in a dive that ended with a great *snap* as she opened her wings and turned the dive into a climb. Treyvan only nodded, then turned and did the same.

Within moments, they were far out of sight. Nyara stared after them—comforted, and yet tormented.

She descended the stairs to her living quarters slowly, still not certain what to do. Should she wait for him to find her? Should she hide somewhere, so that he found only her empty lair? Should she hide *here* and pretend that she was not here?

:Go find him, girl,: Need replied. *:You heard Hydona; now you have a second opinion. A little stronger than mine, really—but then Hydona has a mate of her own. She tends to favor matings.:*

"But—" Nyara began.

:But nothing. Don't let the opinion of someone who never had a man get in your way.: Need actually chuckled. *:Look, girl, I never, ever, put my bearers between a boulder and a rock, making them choose between me and a man. Just because I have always chosen to* defend *women, that doesn't mean I despise men. Demons take it—that would be as blind as the opposite! I am not about to go copy the behavior of some woman-hating man! Now go on out there and deal with your feelings. Meet them, instead of waiting for them to trap you.:*

"I still don't know," Nyara said, feeling as helpless as a kitten in a flood.

:You don't need to know. Get it over with one way or another. If you don't—girl, don't you know *that's something your father will use against you? Make it into a strength, and not a weakness! It worked before. Remember?:*

Yes, she remembered. Remembered attacking her father with tooth and claw, for striking at Skif. Recalled the surprise on his face before he struck her.

:The beast just does not understand the strength of true feelings, and he never will. It makes you unpredictable to him. Use that.:

Nyara sighed and moved to her window, looking out over the peaceful countryside that up until this morning had been only hers. Only white. And now seeing the shadows. They had been there all along, but she had chosen not to see them. "I suppose I should be grateful that he has been sulking and licking his wounds for so long, and has not come looking for me."

:You're waking up, girl. The gryphons were my hedge against Skif or Mornelithe finding you. Well, Skif showed up before the beast did; I suppose we should be grateful for that, too. Skif's a good one, as young men go.:

"So." She settled her cloak firmly about her shoulders. "If he is hunting with Wintermoon and the owls, he hunts by night."

:True enough.:

"He will be sleeping now," she said, thinking out loud. "I should be able to approach without Cymry rousing him, and be there when he wakes. Yes, I think that now is the time to go and meet him."

:Good girl.:

She turned to face the sword. "So," she said, feeling a kind of ironic amusement after all, "since I am sure that you know—or can find out—where is he?"

Mornelithe Falconsbane reclined on a soft couch in his darkened study, and brooded on revenge, like some half-mad, wounded beast. He had not left the room since his return, sore in body and spirit, depleted, but refusing to show any weakness. Weakness could be fatal to someone in his position. A show of weakness would give underlings... ideas. He had learned that decades ago.

His own people hardly dared approach him; they ordered slaves to bring him food and drink, silently, leaving it beside the door. The slaves obeyed out of immediate fear of the lash, fear of pain even overcoming their fear of Falconsbane, praying that he would not notice them. For sometimes, the slave in question would find those glowing golden eyes upon him, shining out of the darkness of the study-corner where he lay...

And when that happened, more slaves were summoned later, to take the remains away. The remains were not pretty. Usually, there were pieces missing. No one looked into the study to find them.

He had used his own blood to open the great Gate in the ruins; had wrenched that Gate from its set destination to a portal of *his* choosing. He had done so out of desperation, not knowing if the thing would work, not knowing if he had the strength left to make it work. Not knowing if it would take him where he willed, or somewhere unknown. He chose to risk it anyway, preferring to die fighting rather than be taken by the cursed Horse-Lovers and the Bird-Fools.

In the end, he stumbled from the mouth of a cave at the very edge of his own realm, fell to the ground, and lay in a stupor for over a day. Only the strength he had cultivated, the stamina he had spelled into himself, had saved him. A lesser being would have died there. A lesser Adept would have been stranded in the nothingness between Gates, trapped, unless and until some accident spewed him forth—perhaps dead, perhaps mad, certainly tortured and drained.

But he was not a lesser Adept, and it would take more than a day of exposure to kill him.

He woke, finally, ravenous and in pain from wounds within and without. His mage-channels had been scorched by the unrestricted torrent of energies he had used. The first thing he had needed was food.

He had caught and killed a tree-hare with his bare hands; eaten it skin and bones and all.

He had chosen his exit point well; once he had strength to move, he turned his attention to his next need, shelter. That was not a problem, for wherever he had established a possible Gate-anchor, he had always built a shelter nearby. That was a habit so ingrained he never even thought about it, centuries old, but this time it had saved his life.

He had staggered to the hunting shelter, a small building of two rooms, but well-stocked with food, wood, and healing herbs. He spent over a moon-cycle in recovering from the worst effects of wounds and spells. His own slaves and servants had not known whether he lived or not, until he had limped home. Only their fear of him had kept them at their posts. Only sure knowledge of his retribution when he recovered completely kept them there once he returned.

Fortunately, obedience was a habit with them. He was at a reasonable fraction of his strength once fear and habit weakened, and someone thought they might try for freedom.

Since he had neither the strength nor the time for finesse, he simply killed the offenders.

Fear of what he was now continued to keep them here.

He reinforced that fear, periodically, by killing one of the slaves. Reminding them what he had done; what he could do. Reminding them all that their lives rested in his hands.

It was a diversion, anyway.

There was an ache inside him that no herb and no rest could touch—a hunger for retribution. That was what drove him to killing the slaves. The deaths themselves did nothing to ease the pent-up rage that smoldered in his soul. There were only three things that would slake his thirst for blood.

Nyara.

He flexed his claws into the leather of his couch, and considered what he would do to her once he found her. She would die, of course, but not for a very long time. First he would ease his lust in her, repeatedly. He might share her; it depended on his own strength and how deeply he wished to wound her spirit. Then he would flay her mind with the whip of his power until she was nothing more than a quivering, weeping heap of nothingness—until the *person* that had dared to defy him was utterly destroyed. Then, only then, would he carefully, delicately, flay the physical skin from her body—leaving her still alive. Then he would see that what was left was placed in a cage and hung over his towers for the carrion crows to pick at. An example for those who considered treachery. His magic would see to it that she lived for a very long time.

Perhaps he would make a rug of that skin, or wear it.

K'Sheyna.

That was the second cause for his anger and hate. Only the destruction of the entire Clan would do. He had held back his power until now, enjoying the challenge, but now he would take them, one by one. First the scouts. Then the mages. Then, last of all, Starblade and his sons, plucking them from the heart of the Vale and bringing them to grovel at his feet before they died. The others he would kill however he could, but those three—those three he would deliver to the same fate as his treacherous daughter. Then, when the Vale was empty of all but the hangers-on, he would suck the power from the Heartstone and blast it back again, turning the Vale into an inferno of melting stone and boiling water.

Then the last—and greatest—cause for rage. *The gryphons.*

Oh, the gryphons. Creatures that he had thought long gone. Returning to these lands, after all these many centuries. Returning to live here once again. Returning to the home of Skandranon...

The gryphons. My hated ancient adversaries. Something very... special... for them.

He brooded in the hot darkness of his study, and never quite knew the moment when his brooding slipped over the edge into dreaming.

He watched himself through other eyes and knew that he was An'desha shena Jor'ethan, Shin'a'in of the Clan of the Bear, an offshoot of Wolf-Clan. A young almost-man, in his early teens. He stood on the edge of all that he had known, and shivered.

He was not yet a warrior, this youngling of the Plains. Only—he was Shin'a'in no more. He could no longer hold place in the Clans, for he had the power of magic, and yet he had not joined the shamans. The Goddess had declared that no one but Her shamans could work magics within the bowl of the Plains, for the task of the Shin'a'in was to keep magic from their homeland. He had felt no calling for such a life-task, and no liking for it, either.

For such a one, one with the gift of magery, yet unwilling to go to Her hands, there was only one choice. Exile, to the Kin-Cousins, the Tale'edras, the Hawkbrothers. They had magic; they were permitted—nay, encouraged—by the Goddess to use it. They would freely adopt any of their magic-bearing Kindred into their ranks, so it was said, to teach the use of such a gift.

So he had come, to the edge of Hawkbrother lands. Yet he had come without the knowledge of the rest of his kin, nor the guidance of the shaman, for no one else in his Clan knew of this secret power. He had feared to disclose it, for he was not a strong-willed young man, and he knew only too well what such a disclosure would bring to his lot.

And now, as he stood in the silent forest, he wondered. Should he have confided in Vor'kela, the shaman? Should he have confessed his fatal gift before the rest of the Clan? Should he not have claimed his rights, and been given guidance to the nearest of the Tale'edras?

Yet even as he wondered, he knew that he could not have born the weight of Vor'kela's insistence that he take up the shaman's staff and drum. No one in all of the Clan would have been willing to let him go to the Kin-Cousins without great outcry and argument. There would have been those who said that his gift was unclean, and the result of his father's liaison with the Outlands woman at Kata'shin'ain, even as he was the result of that liaison. There would have been those who would have said he should take vows of celibacy, that this gift not be passed to others of the Clan. There would not have been a single one of his Kin willing to let him pass out of their hands without long argument and contention.

And he—he would have folded beneath the weight of their words. He would have taken up a place at the shaman's side. And there he would have been utterly miserable. He trembled at the thought of all the years of sacrifice the place as shaman's apprentice would cost him. He was revolted at the idea of being forced to serve at Vor'kela's side and bear the brunt of the shaman's humor.

Better that he had done what he had done; to creep away in the dead of night, and seek out a new life among the Kin-Cousins. He had taken only what was his by right. He had violated no laws.

Because of this, he had no guide. He had never been outside the Plains. As he stood at the top of the path that led from the bottom of the great bowl of the Plains to the top of the rim, he wondered at the forest before him. Huge trees, more trees than he had ever seen in his life, towered before him, and marched endlessly to the horizon. Only there was no horizon, only trees, trees, endlessly trees.

Trees were a rarity on the Plains, and never grew to the height of these. He could not see their tops, only their interweaving branches.

Trees that bent over him, as if watching. Trees that murmured on all sides of him, as if whispering. Trees that had a secret life of their own.

With a bravery born of desperation, he shouldered his pack—for he had left his horse at the base of the path, to find her way back to the Clan—and marched into the cool shadow of the endless trees. Always he had heard how jealously the Hawkbrothers guarded their lands. Surely he would be found and challenged before long.

Before midday, he was lost. By nightfall, he was lost, cold, and terribly afraid. He had heard all too many tales of the strange beasts that lived beneath these trees—the beasts that the Tale'edras fought and penned. Strange mage-created creatures that no arrow could harm. Beasts with the cunning minds of men. He knew none of the sounds of the forest around him; he could not tell if they were the voices of harmless things, or terrible predators, or even demon-spawn.

If only he had a fire—but he had left his fire-making tools behind, for they did not belong to him only, but to all of his family. He was so cold—and all men knew that true beasts feared fire. If he had a fire, it would shine through the darkness of this forest like a beacon, drawing the Tale'edras to him. If only he had a fire...

But wait—had he not heard that a mage could call fire? Even so untutored a one such as himself? He knew where the currents of power ran; he felt them beneath his very feet. He had felt them, even stronger and wilder, on the Plains. Why could he not use them to bring a spark to waiting tinder?

No sooner thought, than he hurried about in the gathering gloom, scraping a dirt hollow in the moss, gathering twigs, dried pine-needles, bits of dry bark; laying larger branches close to hand. When he had his tinder going, he would soon have his fire built as high as he needed.

He closed his eyes, reached for the power, and thought of the springing flames—

And got what he had not expected.

YES!

He came with a roar, filling the boy's body, thundering out of his hiding place, into the body of the blood of his blood, his coming triggered by the moment of Fire-Calling. As it had always been. Once again he took and lived. From the time when Ma'ar, Mage of Dark Flames, had fought and conquered Urtho and had learned of a way to preserve himself down through the ages...

Using the power of the death of his body to hide himself in a tiny pocket of the nothingness between the Gates, he preserved his own person, sealed himself there with spell upon carefully wrought spell. And when one with a trace of the blood of great Ma'ar in his veins learned to make Fire, he came, and overwhelmed the boy's fledgling personality with his own. So he lived again. And when the time came for the death of that body, he moved again into hiding...

Hiding to live again.

So it had gone, down through the centuries, taking new bodies and taking on other names. Krawlven. Renthorn. Geslaken. Leareth. Zendak.

And now, a new rebirth, a new body, a new name. As the young spirit struggled beneath his talons with fear and hopelessness, as the spirit grew quiet, then disappeared altogether, he baptized himself in the blood and flesh of a new incarnation.

Mornelithe. I am Mornelithe! And I live again!

The sound of his laughter rang beneath the branches of the pines, and shocked the forest into sudden stillness.

Then he gathered his powers about himself and vanished into the night, to build his empire anew.

Mornelithe woke with a sudden start. He had not thought of that moment in... decades. Why now?

And why had he first felt the long-vanished spirit of the Horse-Loving halfbreed whose body he had taken?

Never mind, he told himself impatiently. *It matters not at all. Or if it matters, it was to remind myself that I have lived more lives than this, and I am surely wiser for all of that living. And stronger. Wiser by far than the Bird-Fools. It is the gryphons that should concern me. The gryphons, K'Sheyna. Nyara.*

He stretched and sat up on his couch. Discontent weighted his shoulders like a too-heavy garment. In the days that he was Ma'ar, he would merely have had to stretch out his hand to have them all—

But the power that was so rich and free in his day as Ma'ar was a poor thing now. Shattered and scattered, dust in the storm. Like his power, his empire was a small thing. He was constrained to harbor allies he would never have suffered in the old days.

For a moment, he felt a kind of shame, that he should be reduced to this meager existence. Yet what had worked in the long-ago days could work now, if only on a smaller scale.

The gryphons. The gryphons. Why is *it that they do not fade, but prosper?* In his mind's eye the male gryphon took on the black-dyed elegance of Skandranon, and his lip lifted in a snarl. There was no mistaking the beast's lineage. And that should not have been. The gryphons of Urtho's pride should not have survived him.

Nor should those too-faithful servants, the beast-breeding Kaled'a'in. They should have perished, they should all have perished in the cataclysm that destroyed his kingdom *and* Urtho's. There should have been nothing left but a pair of smoking holes. Every trace of Urtho's handiwork and Urtho's allies should have been erased for all time.

Yet, here they were. The Kaled'a'in, Urtho's faithful servants, still prancing about in the guise of the Bird-Fools and the Horse-Lovers. Sundered, yet still prospering. Half of them guarding what remained of the old magics, half of them removing the scars and taint of the destruction. Both halves working beneath the eye of that wretched Goddess who took so deep an interest in their doings.

And the gryphons—thriving! Clearly established in the west, and moving eastward!

How? How did this happen?

He flung himself off of his couch, and began to pace the room, like a restless, caged lion. He had been brooding here for too long. He needed to act! He needed to stir his blood, to exact some token of vengeance before his followers lost their fear and began to desert him.

He needed a show of strength that would convince them that he was still as all-powerful as ever. And he needed the sweet taste of revenge to completely heal him.

Nyara. She was the weakest, the most vulnerable—and the most personal target. Yet she was inexplicably out of his reach. He had sought for her ever since he returned to his stronghold, and yet it had been in vain. He searched as far as his strength was able to take him. There was no trace of her.

Or rather—something was hiding her. He would have known if she had perished, for the power he had invested in her would have come rushing back to him. There was someone, or some power, hiding her.

K'Sheyna, perhaps?

A possible, if surprising, thought. He had thought the Bird-Fools of k'Sheyna too bound up by long custom to change. *Could* the Bird-Lovers have lost their hatred of Changechildren enough to shelter her? Was it possible?

After the way she had fought at cursed Darkwind's side—after the way that she had defended the gryphons—yes. It was possible. In fact, now that he gave it consideration, it was likely.

The gryphons—

The target he longed to strike.

No, the time was not right to exact his revenge upon them. Besides, they too lay under the shelter of k'Sheyna. He might ambush them, but he had no major mages at his disposal now. The last of them had vanished during a hunt for spell-components. He would have to go in person to deal the blow. That was too risky; there was too much he did not know about them.

That left—*k'Sheyna.*

The most logical choice, if he was to impress his followers with his still-vital power.

He would have to do something to hurt the Clan, and hurt it badly. But it would have to be something swift and decisive, and something they had not guarded themselves against.

If he struck at the Clan, his followers would see that he was strong again, and fear to desert him. In striking at the Clan, he might persuade the Bird-Fools to give up the shelter of all those not of their blood. If he were clever enough, he could make it look as if the blow had come through them. K'Sheyna would never shelter them, then. That would put not only Nyara within his reach, but the Outlanders and the gryphons.

The gryphons.

Yes, then he would gather in his dearest daughter—and her winged friends...

And the Outlanders as well, the strange ones. The girl, now—she had all the potential for an Adept. When he saw her last, she had but the most rudimentary of tutelage. It was unlikely anyone in k'Sheyna could be persuaded to give her lessons, and the half-taught were the most vulnerable. He would need a plaything when Nyara was dead.

Yes, he would slay the Outland man, but keep the Outland woman. She might do well to carry his seed for the next generation, since Nyara had proved barren, and turned traitor in the bargain. He might even make the transfer without waiting for the death of his body. Yes. That was a good plan. An excellent plan. It would be good to have a young, strong body again, full of vigor and energy.

That left only one question to be answered.

If I am to hurt k'Sheyna, where must I strike?

His lips twisted in a feral smile.

Where else, but at the weakest bird in the flock, the broken-winged, broken-souled Starblade? He will no longer be mewed up away from my power. They surely think me dead. They must be getting very careless at this point.

An attack on Starblade in and of itself would not hurt the Clan as a whole. But if he used Starblade's link to the Heartstone, and completed the work that he had begun there—

Yes, if I shatter the Heartstone—it might not destroy everything in the Vale, but it will surely destroy most of what is important, and at least half of the mages will die in the backlash of power.

It went against the grain to loose all that power.

But if I cannot control it, then I shall destroy with it.

If he were truly fortunate—although his revenge would be a little less—the gryphons would be destroyed with the rest.

Or better, far better, the gryphons would be *hurt* when the Stone shattered completely. Leaving them weak, and vulnerable.

Yes, that would be the best of all.

He flung himself back down upon his couch, chewed the last pain-spiced flesh from a former servant's thighbone, and began to plan.

Firesong deemed most of the Vale too near the Heartstone to work in, and although Darkwind agreed with him, this tiny clearing at the far end was a damned awkward spot to get to. It had been made as a trysting-spot, but had gotten overgrown. To reach it, they had to wind their way through tangles of vines and bushes, only to discover when they got there that most of the clearing itself had been eaten up by encroaching vegetation. "So, clear it," Firesong said casually, and sat down on a stone to await the completion of their task. Darkwind seethed with resentment that he held closely, permitting none of it to slip. He had thought that Elspeth tested his temper; he had never thought that one of his own people would bring it so close to the snapping point.

Except, perhaps, his father.

The Adept did not even watch them; he called in his snow-white firebird and fed it flowers and bits of fruit while they worked, clearing the vegetation by hand since using magic would have been fairly stupid for so simple a task. "Good enough," Firesong said at last, when the earth of the clearing had been laid bare, and all the seats were free of vines and overhanging bushes. "Now, we return to basics. Darkwind, you will tap into the ley-line beneath us."

Back to basics? For what? Or doesn't he trust our training?

"Stop," Firesong said, with calm self-assurance, as Darkwind obeyed him; he grounded himself carefully, centered his personal power, and prepared himself to grasp for the power of the ley-lines. "What are you doing?"

"I am grounding myself," Darkwind told him, not adding, *as any fool could see,* for it was obvious that Firesong had some deeper intention in mind. Sunlight trickled through the leaves above them, making patches of brilliance in the Adept's hair. This morning Firesong wore blue, the same blue as his eyes. He looked good enough to have his will of any female in the Vale, and no few of the males.

"Why?" the Healing Adept asked, flicking his hair over his shoulder with one hand. "Why are you grounding yourself and your shields?"

"Because—because that is the way that I was taught. That—" he groped after long-forgotten lessons "—if I am not grounded when I reach for the ley-line power, it will fling me away by the force of its current." His resentment continued to seethe at being forced to dredge up those long-ago lessons. What difference did it make? It was something you *did*.

"All well and good," Firesong replied, with that same maddening calm, and a smile that said volumes. "But what if you release your ground *after* you have the power? What, then? And *why* must you always sink your ground into the earth below you? Why not elsewhere?"

Darkwind only gaped at him, unable to answer questions that ran counter to everything he had ever been taught.

"I will show you." The young Adept centered and grounded faster than Darkwind could blink; seized upon the ley-line beneath them as if he owned the deed to it. He made the energies his own, feeding them into his shields with an ease that called up raw envy in Darkwind's heart.

Then he cast loose the ground. "Now, strike me. Full force, Darkwind, trust me." The shields stayed where they were, contrary to everything Darkwind supposed would happen.

Darkwind struck—with more force than he had consciously intended, all of his pent-up frustration going into the blow. All of his fury and bruised pride combined to make the blow one that *would* have done harm if it had properly connected. It should have completely shattered Firesong's shields, the outer one, at least.

But instead of meeting the blow, the shields, no longer anchored by the ground, slid aside. Darkwind watched in complete shock as his angry blast did no more than to bow the shields slightly. The energy of his strike was neither absorbed, nor reflected; it was deflected, routed around the outside, skittering away in bright eddies of flame. Nothing touched the mage inside.

"This *is* dangerous, cousin," Firesong warned, smugly cradled within his untouched shields. "A clever mage will see at once that without the ground protecting the essential flow of magic energy from the line to myself, that tie is vulnerable. A clever mage could also force the shields toward me, then instead of striking a blow, could lance through them at the nearest, thinnest, weakest point. But until he does that, I sit untouched, allowing all his force to spend itself uselessly. I need not even fear the contamination of his magic, for it never touches me or my shields."

To Darkwind's great chagrin, Elspeth nodded, her face aglow with admiration. "A clever mage could also create a whirlwind of edged mage-bolts around you," she pointed out. "Those things can shred a shield in next to no time. And although they can't touch you physically, that would leave you open to attack."

"Ah, but that whirlwind would have no effect, Wingsib," he said, turning a dazzling smile upon her that caused a shaft of jealousy to stab his "cousin." Darkwind chewed his lip and looked away, at the tangle of vines behind one of the empty seats. "A whirlwind that would erode a grounded shield would only cause this one to spin with it. It would find purchase but spin freely. Since I am not connected to the shield, it would have no effect on me."

"I see." She prodded the shield with a bit of power, experimentally, and Darkwind saw for himself how the shield simply bent away from it. "Interesting. So if the enemy doesn't know that this is possible, you can let him wear himself out against you."

Firesong imploded the shield and collapsed it down around himself. "Aye, and a bit of acting, and he'd continue to do so, as I looked 'worried.' Now—this is the trickier task. Grounding in something other than the earth." His face sobered for a moment. "Take heed, cousin. This is something only a powerful Adept can attempt, and never with impunity. I think that you can do this, but it is very dangerous."

Once again, Firesong centered, grounded, and shielded, all within the blink of an eye. To Darkwind, he looked perfectly "normal," insofar as a mage of his power could ever look "normal." But then he took a closer look.

"Where is your ground?" he asked, perplexed.

"You'd like to know, wouldn't you?" the young mage taunted. "Find it! You already know it is not sunk into the earth at my feet. Look elsewhere! Have I somehow grounded into the air? Perhaps I have only created an illusion of being grounded."

Elspeth only shook her head, baffled. Darkwind was not prepared to give up so easily. He studied Firesong carefully, ignoring the mage's mocking smile. Finally he acted on a hunch, and moved his Mage-Sight out of the real world and onto the Planes of Power. There he saw it— and a cold sweat broke out all over him at the Adept's audacity.

He stared at Firesong and could not believe that the mage simply stood there, calm and unmoved. As if he did this sort of thing every day.

Maybe he did. If so, he was the bravest man that Darkwind had ever seen. Or the most foolhardy. Or even both, at the same time.

"You grounded it—in the place between Gates!" he managed to get out, after a moment. "I can't believe you did that! You could call a deadly storm that way—or find yourself drained to the dregs!"

Firesong shrugged, and dismissed the shield, ground and all. "I told you, no mage does that with impunity. I would not attempt it while someone else held a Gate near me, or during a thunderstorm. But that place makes an energy-sink that is second to none. If you wish to drain an enemy, ground yourself in the place, tie your shields to the ground as always, and let him pour all of his power out upon you. It will drain into the place and be swallowed up, exhausting him and costing you no more than an ordinary shield."

He held out a long, graceful hand to Darkwind. "Touch it," he ordered. Darkwind did so. The hand was as cold as ice. "Therein lies the danger there. The place is an energy-sink. It will steal your energies as well, and there is no way to keep it from doing so. You had best hope that you can outlast your enemy, if you ground there; work him into an irrational fury before trying it."

He turned to Elspeth, who was again visibly impressed. "Take nothing for granted, Wingsib. No matter what you have been told, most anything in magery *can* be done, despite the 'laws' that you have been taught. The question is only whether the result is worth it."

It galled him to see the admiration on her face. Oh, Firesong had undoubtedly earned the right to arrogance; his Clansfolk had not exaggerated when they said that they considered him a powerful experimenter. He was, without a doubt, a genius as well.

But none of that meant that Darkwind had to like it.

At the end of the day, when he was exhausted, and Firesong was still as outwardly cool and poised as he had been that morning, Darkwind was ready to call a halt to the entire thing.

But Firesong didn't give him that opportunity.

"You'll do," he said, with cool approval. "At least, you aren't hopeless. I'll have a different course of action for you two tomorrow."

And with that, he simply turned on his heel and left, he and his bird together, melting into the greenery.

18

Darkwind and Elspeth walked together to her *ekele*. They were going to hers, because it was nearer; Darkwind was so drained that he didn't think he could go any further without a rest and something to drink. He was glad that it was still mid-afternoon. If it had been dark enough that he'd had to conjure a mage-light, he'd have fallen over, he felt that tired.

"So what do you think of Firesong?" Elspeth asked as they crested the gentle curving path between six massive flowering bushes. The flicking tail of a *hertasi* ducked under a trellis, distracting him for just a moment.

He cast her a suspicious glance, gauging the import of her question, but her expression, like her voice, remained carefully neutral. "Well, he's certainly brilliant," he admitted grudgingly. "And unconventional. But I don't think I've ever met anyone so arrogant in all my life."

"He's earned the right to be," Elspeth replied, to his increased annoyance. "I mean, there are a lot of people who think Weaponsmaster Alberich is arrogant—or Kero. And they're right, but there's a point where you're so good that you've earned a certain amount of—hmm—attitude."

He didn't reply. He couldn't. Not and maintain his own calm. In a certain sense, Elspeth was completely correct. In fact, if he mentioned Firesong's arrogance to Iceshadow or his father, he would probably be told that it *wasn't* arrogance at all, it was simply self-assurance, and a pardonable pride.

Firesong was the best mage Darkwind had ever seen in his life; perhaps the best living mage that there was. Not just a Healing Adept, but an innovator; a brilliant creative genius. Not fearless—at the levels at which Firesong was working, being fearless could get him killed quite quickly—but so knowledgeable that he was able to judge risks to within a hair.

He was worlds away better than Darkwind was now, and what was more, he was better than Darkwind, or anyone known to the Vales, would ever be. And that did not come as a comfortable revelation.

Darkwind was not used to seeing himself as second-best. It stung his pride, even as Firesong's attitude made him angry. And then, on top of it all, for the cocky mage to be so cursed *handsome!*

Elspeth openly admired him. That was just as difficult to take. How short a step was it from admiration to something else more personal—more physical?

It was only then, when he caught himself seething with completely unwarranted jealousy, that he realized the trend his thoughts were taking. *All right. Stop right there. Think whatever you like, but be careful about anything you say. Right now it would be the easiest thing in the world to say something that would completely alienate her—to make accusations that you have no right to make.*

Elspeth wouldn't react well to that. And never mind that it galled that Firesong's power and beauty were enough to make anyone inclined to throw themselves at his feet. If Elspeth chose to join the crowd, Darkwind had no say in the matter.

You don't own her. She consented to share pleasure with you. That gives you no rights, remember that. She can continue to share your bed and *Firesong's and you have no right to demand that she cleave only to you. She can throw you over for Firesong if she wants. That is up to her.*

"You're thinking very hard," Elspeth said, glancing at him.

"I'm thinking that — I am likely to be very irrational about Firesong." That was all the warning he could bear to give her. But hopefully, it would be enough. "He is right when it comes to magic, anyway. I've never seen anyone as skilled or as powerful as he is, except maybe Falconsbane."

"He's going to try something different with the Stone no one even guessed could be done," she said. "We knew he was going to be doing *something* like that, but I honestly didn't think he was going to include us in it." She gave him a lopsided smile. "I guess we must be good for something after all."

Darkwind suddenly saw a way to get some of his own pride back, especially if the Adept planned on training the two of them together. Firesong wasn't the only one who could be innovative.

Gwena joined them a moment later, and Darkwind swallowed down some of the things he wanted to ask Elspeth. *Is she attracted to him? Just how attracted is she? Is she thinking of asking* him *to continue her teaching? And if he's teaching her magic, does that mean she goes to k'Treva after the Stone is dealt with?*

He shouldn't care, and he couldn't help himself. He had no holds on her. She shared his bed sometimes. He shared hers. She was not truly of the Vales; she was an Outlander. All the arguments against Skif and Nyara's success together held true for the two of them, too.

Tayledras simply didn't leave their Vales. How could he continue the work he had sworn to do, if he left the Vale? He was a Hawkbrother; a Pelagirs healer of ruined lands. He could never leave the Vale, the Pelagirs—it was impossible. She was the Heir to a throne, vital to the safety and government of her land. She couldn't stay here. *That* was impossible.

She would go, and he would stay, no matter what happened here. He began building himself a kind of emotional bulwark to save what was left of his pride and heart. He would have to watch his tongue, and not *drive* her away—she would be leaving soon enough. He would deal with that when it came. He would fight back the tears that he knew, somehow, would come when his Wingsib Elspeth left.

There was little enough in his life now. No need to act like his namesake—Darkwind, an approaching storm-cloud. It made no sense to ruin what there was, least of all by voicing his own foolishness.

"Elspeth," he said, with cheerfulness that didn't sound *too* forced, "once we recover from being run like rabbits, did you have any plans for this afternoon?"

Starblade eased himself down onto the couch beside the huge block-perch Hyllarr had taken for his own, and scratched beneath the hawkeagle's breast-feathers. Hyllarr all but purred, pulling one foot up in complete contentment.

In this alone, Hyllarr was like Karry, but in no other way. Starblade was grateful for that. There were no poses, no lifts of the head, nothing to haunt him. Hyllarr was Hyllarr, and unique. Uniquely intelligent, uniquely calm, uniquely charming. He had succeeded in charming Kethra, who had been immune to the blandishments even of Darkwind's flirt-of-a-bird, Vree. Hyllarr had her securely enchanted.

Kethra settled beside him, with an amused glance at the bird. "I have no idea how you're going to carry him around once he's well, *ashke,*" she said. "He'd be a burden even for someone like Wintermoon. I can't even begin to think how you're going to have him with you."

"I shall worry about that when the time comes," he told her serenely. He already had some notions on the subject. Perhaps a staff across the shoulders... "Is your kinsman coming?"

"He should be here at any moment," she began, when footsteps on the staircase heralded their visitor. And, as Starblade had expected, it was Tre'valen who appeared at the doorway—a Tre'valen who, to Starblade's pained but keen eyes, was a young man in serious emotional turmoil.

Starblade had been seeing the signs of trouble in Tre'valen's face for some time now, but it had never been as obvious as it was now. So, he had been right to ask the shaman here. There was something going on, and the Clan needed to know what it was.

"Sit, please, shaman," he said mildly.

Tre'valen obeyed, but with a glance at Starblade that told the Hawkbrother that this shaman was quite well aware Starblade had not asked him here to exchange pleasantries.

Good. In these times, it was no longer possible to hide behind a veil of politeness. Some of the others of the Clan had relaxed, thinking that now that the Adept was here, all their troubles would be over. They had not stopped to consider the fact that Firesong was here to solve only *one* of the Clan's problems. When he had dealt with the Stone, he would be gone. Then there would remain the rest of the puzzle-box. How to safely reunite the Clan. What to do about Dawnfire. What to do about this territory. How to deal with Falconsbane's daughter, who was a danger—and *in* danger—as long as there was any chance her father was still alive.

How to discover Falconsbane's fate. What to do about him if he still lived…

"There was a time," he began, "when I could afford to hint, to be indirect. I no longer have the strength for such diplomacy. Tre'valen, your Wingsibs of the Clan know why Kethra is here, why Kra'heera asked us to allow her to stay. She was already a Wingsister, and there was obviously a great need for her help."

Kethra's left hand found his right, and she squeezed it, but said nothing.

Starblade smiled at her, and took strength and heart from her support. "Kra'heera asked us to grant the same status to you, and the same hospitality, but with no explanations. I had not pressed you for such an explanation, but I think the time has come for one."

Tre'valen looked very uncomfortable and glanced at Kethra.

"You need not look to me for aid, Clanbrother," she replied to his unspoken question. "I am in agreement with Starblade."

Tre'valen sighed. "It is because of Dawnfire," he said, awkwardly.

Starblade nodded. "I had already surmised that," he said dryly. "I should like to hear what the reasons are."

Tre'valen was clearly uncomfortable, more so than Starblade thought the situation warranted. "Kra'heera wished me to seek her out—if I could find a way to bring her to me—and speak with her as much as I might. It seemed to him quite clear that she has become some kind of avatar of the Star-Eyed, but it is not an avatar we recognize. But it also does not seem to be anything your people had seen before, either. He wanted me to discover what the meaning of this was, if I could. This is a new thing, an entirely new thing. We have had no direction upon it. Kra'heera does not know what to think."

He paused, and rubbed the side of his nose, averting his eyes from Starblade's unflinching gaze.

"New things simply do not occur often in the Plains, *ashke*," Kethra put in. "The Star-Eyed has been a lady more inclined to foster the way things *are* rather than bring on changes."

But Starblade was watching Tre'valen very closely, and there was more, much more, that Tre'valen had not told them. For a moment he was at a loss as to what it could be.

Then the memory of the young shaman's face, gazing up at a bird that *might* have been Dawnfire, suddenly intruded. He had not seen that particular expression of desire very often, but when he had, it always meant the same thing.

"You long for her, do you not?" Starblade asked quietly, and to his own satisfaction, he watched Tre'valen start, and begin to stammer something about emotions and proper detachment.

"Enough," Kethra interrupted her younger colleague. "Starblade is right, and I should have recognized this when I saw it. You *have* become fascinated—enamored. With Dawnfire. I think perhaps you may have fallen in love with her."

"I—have—" Tre'valen looked from one to the other of them, and capitulated, all at once. "Yes," he replied, in a low, unhappy voice. "I have. I tried to tell myself that I was simply bedazzled, but it is not simple, nor it is bedazzlement. I—do not know what 'love' is, but if it means that one is concerned for the other above one's own self—I must be in love with her, with that part of her that is still human in spirit. And I know not what to do. There is no precedent."

It was one thing to suspect something like that. It was quite another to hear confirmation of it from Tre'valen's own mouth. Starblade looked to his beloved for some kind of an answer, and got only a tight-lipped shrug. *She* did not know what to make of this, either.

A nasty little tangle they had gotten into... a worse thing still to offend a deity. If indeed, they were doing so.

"Do I take it that the Star-Eyed has offered you no signs?" Starblade said delicately. "No hint as to how *Her* feelings run in this matter?"

Tre'valen shook his head. "Only that She has permitted us to continue to meet, either in this world or in the spirit realms. And she has granted Dawnfire the visions that I told you, the ones I do not understand, about ancient magic returning. And about the need for peoples to unite and change in some way."

Starblade closed his eyes for a moment, but no answers came to him, so he analyzed the few facts in the matter. Dawnfire was not dead, at least not in the accepted sense. But she was no longer anything like a human being. Mornelithe Falconsbane had destroyed her body, but left her spirit—her soul—alive and in her bondbird. Such a tragedy would have meant a slow fading until at last there was nothing of the human left, leaving a mentally crippled raptor to live as long as it could. But in this, there was a powerful being that had shown Her interest in the situation by creating some kind of different creature out of Dawnfire. Dawnfire was not like the *leshy'a* Kal'enedral, who were entirely of the spirit world, yet could, on occasion, intervene in the physical realm. And not like a mage, who could on occasion intervene in the spirit world. She seemed to dwell in both worlds at once, and yet truly touched neither.

The Shin'a'in face of the Goddess—her Warrior face, in fact— seemed to have created her, then abandoned her. It was most unwise to second-guess a deity; what appeared to have been abandoned may have, in fact, been left to mature.

"All that I can say is that I warn you to be careful," he said at last. "These are strange waters that you swim in, and I know not what lurks beneath the surface. Whatever it is, is fearsome, shaman."

"I know," Tre'valen said at last, after a long pause. "I know this. The Star-Eyed marked Dawnfire for her own, but to what purpose, She has not revealed. She might not approve of my—inclinations and intentions."

Starblade could only shrug. "I am not a shaman," he pointed out. "You are. I say only—be careful and consider first what is best for Dawnfire and those you have sworn to serve."

"I shall." Tre'valen stood, and moved toward the door. "I will keep you closely informed from this moment of what I see. And—of what I feel."

He bowed, turned, and descended the stairs quickly, but the air of trouble he had brought with him remained. Kethra held Starblade's hands wordlessly for a long time afterward.

Darkwind tossed his head, and sent his soaking-wet hair whipping over his shoulder. Sweat poured down his forehead and stung his eyes, but external vision did not matter. *Internal* vision did.

No matter that he had picked a quarrel with Elspeth not half a candlemark before they joined Firesong in the glade that he had made into their Working Place. No matter that he had left her without a reply to the hurtful words he had not truly meant, but said anyway. Once across the invisible boundary, he and Elspeth were two halves of a working whole, and there was no quarrel dividing them.

He frankly had not expected that of her. He had been faintly surprised when her power joined to his with no hesitation. But he could not be less than she, his pride would not permit it.

But he wondered, in a tiny, unoccupied section of his mind, if he had deliberately quarreled with her in hopes that she would storm off, making it impossible for them to practice with Firesong driving them?

Firesong lived up to his use-name; his power-signature crackled with illusory flames, and he used music, drumbeats, to focus it. That made it easier, rather than harder, for Darkwind to follow him; all of his training as a dancer came to the fore, guiding him where he might otherwise have stumbled blindly. So Darkwind had gone Firesong one better; now in the circle he *danced* his magic, eyes closed, moving in place.

I am going to be much leaner before this is all over... and a better dancer.

Elspeth, interestingly enough, chose to follow his dancing with a manifestation of power he had heard of, but had never seen: lightweaving. She created patterns of energy that matched his dancing and Firesong's drums, uniting them, in a way that he didn't understand, but fit well.

It seemed that Firesong didn't understand it either, for the first time Elspeth had woven her light-web he had been drilling them in the creation of a kind of containment vessel that was meant to contract down around something and hold it—

Firesong had been startled and had lost the beat—Darkwind had seen only the pattern and danced it—and the web contracted around *Firesong.*

The Adept had managed to extract himself from it before it closed convulsively and vanished with a little *pop,* but it had clearly been a near thing. They had afforded him a bit of a thrill. Ever since then he had guided them through a refinement of this technique; honing it down and making a weapon of it. Sometimes making a *real* weapon of it. Darkwind Felt something beginning to form before him. Firesong was about to create an enemy for them to face—a very real enemy, for all that it was made of mage-energy.

He changed his steps, and Felt the light above him weaving into a protection. And he sensed Firesong's surprise. He guessed that Firesong had intended Elspeth to weave a mage-blade, or even two, for them to fight with. But Elspeth had her own ideas. Perhaps the weariness of his dance steps had told her that defense would be better than offense. Whatever; he followed the pattern she sketched, and the power wove about them into an hourglass-shaped flow, a double-lobed shield, and the fire-creature Firesong had conjured hissed about the outside in frustration, unable to burn a way through. Since the walls of energy *flowed*, it could not focus its flames on any one place long enough to do any significant damage; the lances of energy dissipated and swirled, but did not burn through.

It sends out extensions of itself, as tongues of flame. Hmm. I think I can work with that.

The next time the creature attacked, Darkwind changed his steps. The protection suddenly became "sticky," if energy could be sticky.

An attractant, perhaps. Whatever the name of his defense might be, Darkwind caught the tongue of the creature's energy, and before Firesong had a chance to react, he spun the fire-shape into his shields, integrating it and making its power his.

The drumming stopped; Darkwind danced on for a moment, letting the power return into the flow of the ley-line beneath them, rather than permitting it to drain away into the air to hang like lightning threatening to strike. Then he stopped and opened his eyes, to gaze somewhat defiantly at their instructor.

"That was not at all a bad solution," Firesong said, calmly. "Not what I had in mind, but not at all bad."

"Darkwind couldn't have fought that thing off," Elspeth said flatly, with no inflection at all. "He was already exhausted from everything else you'd sent at us today."

"So you improvised a defense and solution in one; I like that." Firesong smiled at Elspeth, and Darkwind fought down a surge of irrational anger. "The Shin'a'in say—when you do not like the fight, change the rules. I have often found that to be a useful solution."

Firesong looked no more weary than if he had just taken a fast walk across the Vale. Not a hair was out of place, nor a thread of clothing, for all of his furious drumming.

I should have known. Perfect, as always.

As Darkwind had anticipated, Firesong had been very popular among the k'Sheyna, human and non. Power and beauty are both powerful attractants, and Firesong had both in abundance. He, in return, accepted the attentions as only his due—and his devotees seemed to find his very insolence appealing.

Including Elspeth.

And as for the *hertasi*—well, his borrowed *ekele* swarmed with them. He would not even have had to dress, feed, or bathe himself if he had chosen otherwise. Perhaps he hadn't.

Now, Darkwind, your claws are showing.

But how could he have gone through this past training session without a hair out of place?

Because he's a greater mage, a greater Adept, than you or anyone in your Clan has ever seen, that's how. He's likely enhanced his endurance for year upon year. Elspeth and the rest are perfectly right to admire him. And there is nothing wrong with him being proud of himself and what he can do…

"I think that you are near to ready," Firesong said, standing up, and putting the drum away in the elaborate padded chest he used as a seat. "You work remarkably well together. We can begin planning what we will be doing with your rogue Stone tomorrow, hmm?"

Darkwind nodded, but Firesong wasn't done yet. Elspeth headed straight out of the clearing, going for the hot spring and a long soak, but Firesong caught Darkwind by the elbow before he had a chance to leave.

"There is trouble between you and the Outlander," he said, making it a statement rather than a question. Darkwind couldn't meet his eyes, nor could he say anything. "There are also thorns between you and me."

Darkwind faced him, resentment smoldering. "Nothing I cannot deal with," he said—keeping himself from snarling.

Firesong gave him a most peculiar look as he retook his position on the padded chest. He crossed his legs and intertwined his slender fingers across one knee.

Then he spoke.

"Darkwind, I have been working magery since I was barely able to walk," the Adept said slowly. "My hair was white by the time I was ten. I have ever had a fearsome example to live up to, for my great-great-many-times-great-grandfather was one Herald Vanyel Ashkevron out of Valdemar. Even as Elspeth's was, though she knows it not."

"But—" Darkwind was surprised he managed to get that much out, stunned as he was, "—how?"

"A long tale, which I shall make as short as I may." The Adept held up his hand, and his firebird came winging out of the tree cover above, a streak of white and gold lightning that alighted haughtily on his wrist. "This is the tradition, as it was handed down from Brightstar's foster-parents, Moondance and Starwind. One of k'Treva wished a child and there was no one in the Clan she favored. Moondance and Starwind also longed to be parents. Vanyel was well favored by all within the Clan, and consented to be father to twins, one of whom was my forefather, Brightstar. But in Valdemar, also longing for a child, was the King's Own and lover of the Monarch, Shavri. Vanyel obliged her in part so that it would seem that Randale was able to father children, which he was not. That child, Jisa, wedded the next Monarch, Treven, a cousin of the King, and from that line of descent springs yon Outlander."

Firesong chuckled at Darkwind's expression.

I must look like a stunned ox.

"Nay, cousin, we of k'Treva are not so well-versed in Outlander doings as you think. It is simply that Brightstar knew of his half-sister and her young suitor, and that the Ashkevron blood calls to blood; we know each other, though she does not know how." Now Firesong raised one winglike eyebrow. "That may be the source of the Outlander's fascination with my humble self."

Darkwind snorted. "As if *you* could ever be humble," he said sardonically.

"It has happened a time or two, but not recently." Firesong shrugged, and transferred his firebird to his shoulder. "I thought a word to you was appropriate. I have *much* more training than you, more thorough, and more consistent. I have never abandoned my magic. Considering all you have—experienced—you do far better than I had expected. Take that for what it is worth. There is more I would say when the time is appropriate."

He hung his head for a moment, then raised it again and brushed the moon-white hair from his forehead. Then he stood, an inscrutable expression on his face, and left by the trail Elspeth had taken, white-feathered firebird on his shoulder.

I should at least apologize to her, if he is not with her, Darkwind thought, finally. *Or even if he is with her… though I doubt I could.*

So eventually he, too, followed the pathway out of the clearing to the end of the Vale where Elspeth's *ekele* stood. He waited for a moment, listening at the entrance to the hot spring near her tree. There were splashing sounds; someone was definitely in there. There was no "in use" marker at the entrance…

He hesitated a moment longer, then went in.

For a moment he thought he had made a terrible mistake, for Elspeth was lying beside the pool, wrapped in a lounging robe, head pressed against another, crowned with flowing white—

:Oh, for Haven's sake, don't be more of a young fool than you are already.: Gwena snapped. He recognized, just before he backed out of the clearing, that it wasn't Firesong she was lying against, it was her Companion.

"Do you—mind if I use the pool?" he said awkwardly. She propped herself up on one elbow and gave him a long, penetrating look.

"I mind only if you plan on being as hateful as you were this morning," she said, levelly.

"I didn't exactly plan on being hateful," he replied weakly. "It just happened."

"Hmm," was all she said, and she laid herself back down again on the cushions.

:If you don't mind, I'm going to leave you two alone,: Gwena said, getting gracefully to her feet. *:I suggest whatever in the nine hells is bothering the two of you, that you get it dealt with before it shows up in the magic. That youngster and I agree on one thing, at least—that you'd better* not *bring your emotional upheavals into the reach of the Stone.:*

And with that, she melted into the undergrowth.

Darkwind stripped hastily, and slipped into the water. Elsspeth stayed where she was, neither moving nor talking. He finally decided to break the silence before he got a headache from it.

"I'm sorry. I didn't mean to be nasty."

"I'm sure you didn't," Elspeth replied. Then she turned on her side and met his eyes. "Something occurred to Gwena, and she pointed it out to me. You're getting a dose of what your brother gets all the time, did you realize that?"

"What?" he said cleverly. "Wintermoon?"

"Certainly." Elspeth turned over onto her stomach, and pillowed her head on her arms. "Think about it. *You* were always the Adept, the one with all the power. The one who had anything he wanted, from Starblade's approval to his pick of lovers in the Clan. *He* was a lowly scout, no magic, and in a position of risk, so that even if someone had considered getting close to him, they were afraid to because he was as likely to die as return every patrol. Even when you gave up the magic and no longer were the darling of your father's eye, you still had high rank, a place in the Council, the friendship of the gryphons, and Dawnfire. Now you've taken the magic up again, and you have it all back. And there stands good old reliable Wintermoon, upstaged again."

"I never thought of it that way," he said, slowly. "It never occurred to me."

"I didn't think so. Ever wondered why he spends so much time outside the Vale—why he volunteered to go wandering about the countryside with Skif in tow?" She rubbed her forehead on her sleeve. "I did. Gwena says she thinks he does it so that he won't get jealous of you. He really loves you, just as truly as any brother—but *hellfires*, Darkwind, it must be awful to stand around and watch you, and see everything you want just fall into your hand like a ripe fruit!"

"Oh," he replied, feeling very—odd. Very taken aback.

"So, now you're confronted with Firesong, and you're feeling the same way Wintermoon has since you started showing Mage-Gift." Her bright brown eyes regarded him soberly from beneath a lock of hair. "Doesn't feel very good, I'd imagine."

"No, it doesn't," he admitted. "But—you—"

"Oh, I'm used to not being the best." Elspeth shook her hair back. "Talia was better than me at classes, Jeri was better than me at swordsmanship, Mother is much prettier than me, Kero's better at strategy, Stepfather at diplomacy, Skif at being sneaky—the only thing I was really good at was pottery, and I didn't deceive myself into thinking I was the best in the Kingdom." She spoke airily, but Darkwind sensed that old hurt under her words.

"Elspeth, I think the thing that bothers me the most is that Firesong has your admiration," he said, unhappily. "I *am* jealous of him. He is so much more my master at magic—I feel like a bare apprentice. But it is the fact that you admire him so that angers me, and I cannot help myself."

It truly cost him in pride to admit that, and she stared at him a moment longer. "You know, Kero told me something once. She said—'you'd think being able to speak mind-to-mind would put an end to all the misunderstandings between people, but it doesn't.' She was right, too."

He shook his head ruefully. "I have often found that when there were misunderstandings, both parties found reasons not to share their thoughts."

"Exactly." She widened her eyes, and he felt the delicate touch of her mind on his. :*Firesong has Power. Firesong is too beautiful to be human. Firesong is worth admiring. But from a distance. He's not called Firesong for nothing—he breathes in the admiration and everything else around him. Fire can warm you from a distance, but it burns when you get too close to it.*:

There was no doubting the truth of the feelings behind the words. He ducked under the water for a moment, then emerged and hoisted himself up onto the bank beside her. "Then you forgive me for being a beast?"

She grinned. "I think you could persuade me to."

* * *

Tre'valen soared the spirit-skies in a new form; that of a vorcel-hawk. Smaller than Dawnfire—as was only appropriate for a tiercel—and with nowhere near her power, he still hoped that in this form she would see that he was trying to meet her halfway. She had avoided him for days now, and he was not certain if the reason was anything to do with him, or if it was something outside of both of them.

Surely the Goddess knew of his feelings toward Dawnfire. Could She not approve, to let him continue to pursue Dawnfire? It would take the barest blink on Her part to slap him to the ground, away from Her Avatar—yet Tre'valen sought Dawnfire still. Surely the Goddess knew that he was still devout, that he searched always mindful of serving Her people better. No matter how his heart might cry to him of how Dawnfire needed him, and he needed her—he was still a sworn shaman, and owed his loyalty to Her and Her purposes.

Hold, though—had he truly just *assumed* Dawnfire needed him? He did not know for certain if he read her emotions or his own. Her eyes were no longer human when he saw her. Could he believe the desire for companionship he saw in them? It was all so complex, and he had so few real facts to work with. He could only do the one thing a shaman ultimately must: trust in who he was and let his long-learned morals determine his actions.

He had always been bright-eyed and adventurous; the Goddess had not been displeased by it when She took him as Her shaman. It would be senseless to deny his nature—better to act on it.

He had walked the Moonpaths to no effect—so now he tried a desperation move. He left the Paths altogether, and turned his flight into the starry night between them.

Prudent Kra'heera had never left the Paths in all of his long life as a shaman. Tre'valen had heard of some—very few—who had, and lived to do so again. They were not many, but their adventures had been in times calmer than these. There were new things happening, strange and promising and frightening at once, and risks were somehow more appropriate. The risk of leaving the Moonpaths paled before the danger of his courting the Goddess' own Avatar.

Still, if Dawnfire would not come to him, he must go to her.

He felt the lift in his "belly" as he lifted from the Paths, on wings made of glittering golden stardust and lit by his own life. A shiver as though from a cold wind, a knifelike wash through his sunlight-feathered body, and the Moonpaths dropped away below him.

Foolishness it might be—but glorious it certainly was.

He soared and wheeled above and under the Paths, able now to See the patterns upon patterns they coursed into, and the colors and layers as far as his spirit-eyes could discern.

But she was nowhere to be found.

Perhaps he was looking in the wrong place entirely? Well, there was nothing keeping him from using this form in the "real" world—and if she soared the physical skies in her hawk-form, she would *surely* see him in this guise.

He closed the eyes of the hawk, then turned within—sought the twist that brought him home—

And opened them again as warm sun flooded through him. Through, because as a spirit-hawk in the real world, he was slightly transparent. A tiercel-vorcel of golden glass...

Was it not exactly like a lovesick tiercel to court a mate with fancy flying? Leaving the Moonpaths, diving from the starry soul-sea into the physical world—was that not the equivalent of skimming a cliff face to attract a lover's eye?

He couldn't help but laugh at himself over it all, still a little giddy from the feel of the soul-sea between the Paths. Should he continue with the analogy and hope that Dawnfire would be impressed? Could they be enough alike somehow that she would fly with him? So many mysteries, but then, there were few answers to begin with in his life's work. That was, he felt, part of its appeal—in searching for Truths, he'd found few absolute ones and thousands of personal ones. He'd follow his heart, wherever it led.

Perhaps his willingness to risk was only adaptability. He felt at home in this Vale of summer nestled amidst cruel winter, as he did wherever he traveled. So many times he'd been berated for his brashness by Kra'heera; perhaps his brashness was but unrefined bravery?

He increased his physical mass, steadied in the chilly breeze above his brothers' Vale. They, too, followed their hearts as certainly as they followed the Goddess' laws. He admired them. They fought for a goal that would come many centuries from their own lifetimes as though it would be enjoyed at day's end.

They were not so different from his own people, who guarded the Plains and the deadly things under it. The Hawkbrothers actively fought; the Shin'a'in had the equally difficult tasks of unending vigilance and precise response. The Kal'enedral and the Hawkbrother Adepts were alike in some respects, were they not? Different but complimentary.

He had seen history drawn in tapestries in Kata'shin'a'in. Was it time now for a new tapestry to be woven?

Ah, if his thread and Dawnfire's could be woven together, it would be like the satisfying ending to a tale, and he would feel reborn...

He angled over the Vale, careful of the sense of wonder that he felt. He couldn't let it blind him to his goal. The point of taking flight this way was to find Dawnfire, to speak with her. Tre'valen scanned the skies, widened his view—and saw something bright hurtling toward him and the Vale.

It was without physical form, a fiery spear of crackling magical energy, larger than two men. It came roaring toward him, rushing, unrelenting, like a storm-driven grass-fire across the Plains—and struck him full in the chest. A shower of splintered mage-energy burst around him and he screamed out.

He fell half a furlong, stunned; recovered; held himself in place with unsteady wingbeats. The next blow was coming, and he warded against it as best he could.

For one moment, he thought that his fears were coming to pass, that the Star-Eyed herself had decided to punish him for his audacity. But no—

No, he was not even the object of the attack. He had been in its bound-path, and it had diverted to him—and *through* him. He had only been in the way. The second strike was approaching differently; it struck at him, hurt him, but lost little of its power, continuing to its true target. That target was below him, in the Vale.

Starblade—

He Saw the Adept taking the force of the blow and falling to his knees while his bondbird screamed in anger and frustration; Saw him recover. Even as he folded his wings and dove to add his own small—and probably futile—strength, he Saw Kethra fling herself physically over the Adept, and magically join her power to his. Then he watched in astonishment as Starblade gave up control to Kethra, letting her spread the force of the attack over both of them.

It is Falconsbane!

A third blow came, and then a fourth; the pair sagged beneath the force of the brutal attack, their shields eroding. Kethra cried out, face toward the sky, fists clenched, transmuting the attack-energies into another form. A circle of intense cold spread out from her, covering everything it touched with a thick layer of frost. Furniture split and shattered as it was overcome; drinking vessels and pitchers burst; the very structure of the *ekele* was warping and cracking as it was engulfed in bitter cold.

Falconsbane—

Hyllarr shrieked in agitation and abandoned his perch, falling to the floor and backing against the wall of the *ekele* as the lethal white circle spread. Already, Tre'valen knew the victims were in pain from the deadly cold—which told him that withstanding the effects of the attack must have been worse even than its transmutation.

Even without ForeSight, the next few moments were writ clear for anyone to see. Help would not come from the rest of the Vale in time. Falconsbane had been merely testing their strength. The next blow would rip through their defenses, and surely channel through from Starblade inside the Vale, into the Vale—

And pour into the Heartstone, shattering it, and sear the country for leagues. The devastation would kill everyone, and unleash a score of wild ley-lines to tear through the landscape.

I must stop this—

He knew he would die.

It did not matter. Too many would be hurt—

:Here!:

He looked up; Dawnfire was above him in her hawk-form, a blazing creature of glory. She had more than enough power to shield Starblade from the next attack. Whether he would survive the encounter, he could not know, but his brethren must be saved. And here, with him, was Dawnfire...

She had the power. *He* had the knowledge.

:Now! Together!: he cried, and folded his wings to plummet down. She fell beside him, both of them rushing just ahead of the blast of power that they felt hot on their necks...

Firesong took up the drum and faced the Heartstone, his fingers pattering a little anticipatory run on the taut skin. Darkwind shook out his muscles, a chill of nervousness running down his spine. This was only to be an exploratory venture, a preliminary, to see what the three of them could do with the rogue Stone.

:Haiee!:

It was not so much a call, as a mental shriek of pain. And Darkwind knew immediately whose pain it was.

:Father!: He reached for power, blindly.

But Firesong reacted first, reaching, clenching fists until his knuckles whitened, flinging the tightest shield Darkwind had ever seen around—

—the Heartstone.

What—

Darkwind had no time for anything other than a gasp of outrage. It was Starblade and Kethra who needed protection, not the damned Stone!

Firesong fell to his knees, hands spread wide, muscles straining as he built shield after shield around the Stone. The Stone flared and a dozen fire-red tendrils stabbed out toward Starblade's *ekele*, to be stopped short by Firesong's shields. They sought purchase in the inner shields, and half of them penetrated; Firesong built another layer and another, sucking in power from all around him.

The tendrils were all reaching out to Starblade.

Darkwind's Sight clearly showed him the next huge fire-bolt coming in through the Vale's shields. Streaking down before it were two sun-bright vorcel-hawks. They dove wing to wing, turned as one above Starblade and Kethra's *ekele*—

—and caught the fire-bolt together. Power flared around his father and his lover, and then all was still, except for the hoarse protests of Hyllarr and a subsiding thrum from the Heartstone. Firesong constricted the shields, his eyes closed tightly in concentration. The tendrils receded.

Darkwind reached his power to Elspeth, without conscious thought of it—and found her doing the same toward him. They wove a counterattack, lanced it up into the sky—and let it sputter off into nothing. The enemy—*Mornelithe Falconsbane*, he knew—had aborted his remaining attack and dispersed its power into a huge, flickering mantle over the Vale.

There was no path for a counterattack to follow.

Mornelithe Falconsbane had escaped again.

1 9

"That was Falconsbane!" Elspeth gasped, climbing to her feet and swaying in her tracks with shock at Darkwind's side. "That was Falconsbane—I know it was! What stopped him?"

"I don't know," Darkwind replied. "I can't tell, Elspeth." His head rang with the echoes of power, and there was no reading anything subtle this close to the Stone. He stepped across the pass-through on the warded threshold that sealed the Stone away from the rest of the Vale, and sent out a fan of questing energy.

The trace was clear and clean, though quickly fading, and it ran back to a center that was not disturbed, but oddly empty.

No—more than empty—

When he realized what he felt, he recoiled and snapped up his own shields. Elspeth crossed the threshold, and Gwena appeared at her side. Both breathed hard from sprinting.

Vree, who had been sunning in the falls area of the Vale, shot overhead, alert for new danger. He abruptly sideslipped and landed in a tree outside the threshold, and sent a mental query, followed by a wordless message of support when he sensed how distraught his bondmate was.

Darkwind waved to warn Vree away, then began running toward a particular remote corner of the Vale—a place where he had sensed, not only the remains of burned-out power, but something more. The kind of emptiness only a Final Strike left behind.

Death.

Someone had died protecting Starblade, and given that it was a power-signature he didn't recognize, he was horribly certain he knew who that someone was.

Hoofbeats gained behind him and Gwena and Elspeth drew up just ahead of him. Elspeth's hand was open to him, and he grasped it and vaulted up onto Gwena's back. Together, they rode crouched, into the far reaches of the Vale. Gwena sprinted and stooped, dodging trees, limbs, and other obstacles. The lush, relaxing decorations of the Vale were now clinging distractions; Gwena could only make speed in clearings.

They were overtaken within moments. Gwena dove off the trail in time to avoid being trampled by Firesong's white *dyheli*, who streaked past them, lightning-fast and surefooted. The stag bore Firesong clinging bareback, and behind them flew the firebird, streaming controlled false-sparks of agitation along the flowing length of its tail.

By the time Darkwind, Gwena, and Elspeth reached their goal, Firesong was lifting the body of Tre'valen in his arms as if it weighed nothing, his face utterly blank and expressionless. Firesong's complexion had turned ashen; the firebird clutched at his shoulder and cluttered angrily, then fixed its eyes on Tre'valen's lifeless face and went silent.

Firesong looked from Darkwind to Elspeth and back again, but said nothing. There was a chill in his eyes that made Darkwind reluctant to say anything. Elspeth stifled a sob behind her clenched fist; Gwena moved away, stepping backward very deliberately.

Firesong stalked carefully between them, eyes focused straight ahead. He carried his dreadful burden out of the clearing and into the depths of the Vale, without saying a single word to either of them.

Darkwind's thoughts seethed with anger. *He killed Tre'valen. He shielded the Stone and not my father, and Tre'valen died for it. And he knows it, the arrogant bastard. Why? Why did he shield the damned Stone? He saw the strike coming before I did—he knew what was going to happen!*

"Darkwind—your father," Elspeth said urgently, recalling to him the *other* casualties in this catastrophe.

"Gods—" he said, despairingly, and headed off at a run again, in the opposite direction that Firesong had taken. The *ekele* was not that far, but it seemed hundreds of leagues away as he hurtled through the foliage, taking a narrow shortcut. Branches whipped at his face, leaving places that stung until his eyes watered. His lungs ached, his legs felt as unsteady as willow twigs. But there was no time, no time—

Despite the fact that it seemed an eternity since the attack, he and Elspeth reached Starblade's home moments ahead of the rest of the mages of k'Sheyna. Hyllarr was shrieking alarm and outrage to the entire Vale. Darkwind pounded up the steps of the *ekele* and burst into the main room, and stepped back, shocked by the destruction.

Starblade was sprawled inelegantly across the floor, with Kethra lying atop him in an attitude of protection. He was awake, if dazed; she was not moving. Elspeth pushed past him and reached for Kethra, levering her off the k'Sheyna Adept so that Darkwind could get to his father. She slipped and steadied, after a floorboard shifted under her. All the wood in the room was splintered; moisture covered every part that was not patched in frost. Very little was intact within four arm spans of Starblade and Kethra; the floor and walls were warped and cracked. This *ekele* could not possibly be livable again.

Hyllarr quieted as soon as they entered the room, though he continued to shift from one foot to the other, crooning anxiously and craning his neck to watch what they were doing. He came as far as the outer edge of the ice, then waited.

Starblade blinked up at his son, and tried to rise; Darkwind decided that it would be better to help him onto the couch than try to prevent him from moving. Starblade's fingers showed signs of frostbite.

"Falconsbane," Starblade murmured, bringing a trembling hand up to his eyes. "That touch again—filthy—"

He shuddered, and Darkwind got him lying back against a heap of pillows, then ran to fetch water and cups from the far side of the *ekele*. One cup he handed to Elspeth, who had managed to get Kethra into a sitting position. The other he handed to his father, who seized it in shaking hands and drained it as if it contained the water of life itself. Darkwind daubed his fingers into the pitcher and traced wet fingers across his father's brow and eyes and blew gently, an old mage's technique to help focus concentration.

"What happened?" he asked, as Starblade closed his eyes and lay back again, the lines of pain in his face even more pronounced than ever before.

"I am not certain," Starblade faltered. "It was Falconsbane—he tried my defenses." His face mirrored his confusion and his fear, the fear that he had once again betrayed his Clan.

"It seems he could not break them," Darkwind reminded him. "The beast *could not take you,* Father. His hold over you is gone forever— do you see?"

Starblade shook his head, though not in negation. "I—he attacked. Kethra tried to protect us both." He propped himself up onto one elbow, with obvious effort, and looked around.

"She's in shock," Elspeth said calmly. "She needs a lot of rest, and she needs her energies restored. But I'm sure she's going to be all right."

By now, they had an audience, but only Iceshadow pushed through to join them. He went first to Kethra, then to Starblade, and seeing that they were only badly shaken and depleted, shook his head.

"It is strange," Iceshadow said in puzzlement. "There was no time for *any* of us to have protected them. Yet someone did."

"There were hawks," Starblade whispered. "Two shining hawks with wings of fire. They dove from the sun, and sheltered us beneath their wings. That is what protected us."

"That was Tre'valen," said a new voice, flatly. Firesong stood just inside, keeping his face in shadow.

"That was Tre'valen, in spirit-form. And likely that one of k'Sheyna who was taken by the Shin'a'in Goddess." He seemed to be waiting for the name, and Darkwind supplied it, carefully controlling his own anger at the Adept's failure to shield his father.

"Dawnfire," he said, his own voice as expressionless as Firesong's.

Firesong did not even acknowledge that he had spoken. "Dawnfire.

It was also Dawnfire. That was shamanic magic; it would have been the only thing this Falconsbane could not counter, for it is spirit-born, and he knows not how to use it, nor how to negate it." Firesong bent down for a moment, and laid his hand gently on Starblade's head, above his closed eyes. Starblade did not seem to even notice that he was there, so deep was his exhaustion. "He must have known he could not survive such a blow in spirit-form."

Darkwind kept a tight curb on his tongue, afraid to say *anything*, lest he lash out with words of challenge. But Firesong straightened, and looked into his eyes.

And the sheer agony Darkwind saw there killed whatever accusations had been forming in his mind. Firesong's ageless, smooth face, which bore only confidence scant hours ago, now showed creases of tension and grief.

"I could not shield your father and the Stone, both, Darkwind," Firesong said quietly, with unshed tears making his voice thick. "Tre'valen died because I was a fool. I did not think to look for your enemy; I did not ward the Stone against him. I had to make a choice; your father, or the Vale.

"Look," he said, and picked up a stoneware cup spiderwebbed with cracks from the cold. "Look here, how this is like the Stone. All the damage runs from this place, tied to Starblade. And a single blow *here*—channeled through Starblade—you see?" He dropped the cup, which shattered between his feet.

Indeed, Darkwind did see. That one blow, had Firesong not intervened, would have shattered the Heartstone completely, releasing all the pent-up energies at once.

It would not have created as large a crater as made the Dhorisha Plains, but it would have dug down to bedrock, and killed every living thing within the Vale, and far outside it.

"I am—sorry," Firesong said, and sighed heavily. "You will never know how sorry. I did what I had to. As did Tre'valen."

And with that, he retreated, with the rest of k'Sheyna parting before him.

It was a fair amount of time later when Darkwind left the *ekele*, having put Starblade and Kethra under the care of Iceshadow and the other mages. Iceshadow was confident that they would both be near recovery by morning; Elspeth had volunteered to stay with them, channeling energies through Gwena to renew what they had lost, helping the k'Sheyna Healers. Vree had wanted to stay with Elspeth.

Darkwind could think of no way to be of use. His own strength was not what it should have been; he had cast much of it into that fruitless counterattack on Falconsbane. And his mind was in turmoil. He did not know what to do, or to think. He would have been of no use to the Healers, muddled as he was.

So he wandered the Vale instead, coming at last to the curtain of energies that hid the entrance. Snow was falling again. The last daylight dwindled beneath the trees. He reached the cleft in the hillside, and realized that the odd outcropping of snow there was not snow at all.

Firesong turned slowly, saw him, and nodded. It felt like an invitation. Darkwind stepped across the Veil and into the snow to stand beside him.

After a moment, Firesong spoke.

"He goes home now——" the Adept said dully, "——his body does."

Darkwind saw that one of the shadows at the limit of vision was moving; was not a shadow at all, but a black-clad rider on a ghost-gray horse, with a large bundle carried across the saddlebow. Moving away; toward that path that led down to the Plains.

"And what of the spirit?" Darkwind asked, finally.

"I am not a shaman. I cannot say."

Darkwind rubbed his arms as the residual heat of the Vale wisped away from his body into the silent snowfall.

"I want you to know, you did the right thing. In protecting the Heartstone. It would have killed us all."

Firesong stiffened, and looked up; white crystal flakes settled on his forehead and brows, laced his eyelashes and crown of white hair. "Knowing it was the better of two ills changes little." His hair rippled like silk in a breeze. "It makes Tre'valen's death hurt no less."

Darkwind nodded.

Firesong shifted his loose robes and lifted a long bone pipe to his lips. Thin, breathy notes fell softly upon the ear, mingled with the silence. Darkwind knew the tune, a Shin'a'in lament.

A second voice joined the flute's, though Darkwind could not have told what it was until he saw the white firebird perched in the tree branches above the Adept, its head and neck stretched out, its graceful bill open and its throat vibrating.

The scene etched itself into Darkwind's memory. After so many years in the company of Adepts, he knew the outward signs of self-induced trance; after a while, he realized that the Adept was paying no attention to anything but his music.

Darkwind turned and walked back into the Vale, leaving Firesong and his bondbird pouring out mournful notes into the dark and silence.

As he walked away, he thought he caught sight of something wet glittering on Firesong's cheek, though the notes never faltered, and the face remained utterly remote and as lifeless as a marble statue's. Perhaps it was only a melting snowflake.

Perhaps it wasn't.

A scream rang out and was cut short.

Falconsbane slashed, all claws extended, and the hapless slave fell to the stone floor, choking on his own blood. Falconsbane watched him with anger raging unappeased through his veins, as the boy gurgled and clutched desperately at his throat. Blood poured between his fingers and splattered against the cold gray marble as the slave twitched and gasped and finally died, his eyes glazing, his body twitching, then relaxing into the limpness of death.

Not enough. Falconsbane looked for something else to destroy, cast his eyes about the study, and found nothing that he could spare or did not need. He had already shattered the few breakable ornaments; the upholstery of his couch was slashed to ribbons. The table beside the couch was overturned, and he would not touch the books; they held knowledge too precious to waste.

So he turned back to his final victim, and proceeded to reduce the body to its fundamental parts, using only his hands.

When he was done, he was still full of burning rage. He kicked the door of the study open, hoping to find someone lurking in the hall, but they knew his temper by now, and had cleared out of the corridors. Likely they were all cowering behind locked doors and praying to whatever debased gods they worshiped—besides him—that he would appease his anger with the slave they had sent him. Cowards. He was surrounded by worthless, gutless cowards.

He growled deep in his chest. *Not as gutless as the slave is now.*

He stormed out into the corridors of his fortress, and ran upward, toward the rooftops. The place stifled him with its heat and luxury. He wanted to destroy it all, but instead, he went seeking the darkness of the night and the quiet of the snow to cool his temper.

He found a spot where he would not be tempted to destroy anything more because there was nothing to destroy—the top of one of the four corner towers.

It was open to the wind and weather, and since the quiet and cold did nothing to cool his anger, Falconsbane found another outlet for his rage. He reached out to the storm about him and whipped it from a simple snowstorm to a blinding, howling blizzard, taking fierce comfort in the shrieking wind. Wishing that it was the shrieks of dying Hawkbrothers he heard instead.

Thwarted. Again! It could not have happened. He'd posted sentries to spy upon them. They had done nothing out of the ordinary. They made no efforts at all to *use* the twisted power of their Stone. Instead, they had sought to drain power from it, and it, of course, had resisted as it had been trained to do. Their mages were exhausted; they had no reserves, no Great Adepts.

The timing could not have been better. And yet he had been thwarted.

First, his attempt to retake his pawn Starblade failed. All of the channels he had so carefully established into the Bird-Fool's heart and mind were *gone*. Not blocked, but gone completely, healed by some strange application of magics with a taste he could not even begin to sort out. Strongly female and laced with an acid protectiveness that made him flinch away.

That was bad enough, having to abandon his best tool, but when he tried to turn his controlling of Starblade into an attack on the k'Sheyna Heartstone as planned, he could not springboard to the Stone. Infuriating!

Not once, but *twice;* blocked at the Stone itself, by shields he could not penetrate, and blocked again at the channel he had tied to Starblade's life-force! *Where* had those fools gotten the Adept that had shielded the Stone? There had been no one, not even the Outland girl, with so much as the potential for power like that! And *what* had they used to block his death-strike on Starblade? Not only did he not recognize it, but his mind still reeled beneath the blinding counter it had made to his strike. What had intercepted his fire-bolt? It had taken all his power and transformed it into a force he could not even remotely name.

Either of those alone would have been bad enough. Together they awoke a killing rage in him that demanded an outlet. He had stormed out of his working-place and into his study, intending mayhem.

He discovered there was more—much more.

His outriders had been waiting for him; they had come in to him, all bearing the same story. Black-clad riders on black horses, haunting the edges of his domain. Riders who *did* nothing; simply appeared, watching for a moment, as if making certain that they had been seen, and vanished again. Riders who left no mark in the snow; whose faces could not be seen behind their veilings of black cloth.

His *mages* had come to him with more news of the same ilk, hundreds of tiny changes that had occurred while he was dealing that aborted attack to k'Sheyna. Along and inside all of his borders, there were tiny pinprick-upsettings of his magic. Traps had been sprung, but had caught nothing, and there was not even a hint of what had sprung them. Ley-lines that had been diverted to his purposes had returned to their courses, but they went *to* nothing specific nor any new power-poles. Areas that he had fouled to use for breeding his creatures had been cleansed. Yet there was no pattern to it, no plan. Some lines had been left alone; traps side-by-side showed one sprung, the other still set. Areas near to the Vale had been left fouled, while others, farther away, had been cleansed.

He snarled into the howling wind. He *hated* random things! He *hated* fools who worked with no plans in mind, and changes that occurred with no warning! And most of all, he hated, despised, things that happened for no apparent reason!

Every one of those pinpricks had taken away his order, interfered with his careful plans—and left chaos behind. And all to no purpose he could see!

He shouted into the night, and let the wind carry his anger away, let the cold chill his rage until it came within the proper, controllable bounds again. How long he stood there, he was not certain, only that after a time he knew that he could descend into his stronghold again, and be in no danger of destroying anything necessary.

He dismissed the stormwinds; without his will behind them, the winds faded and died away, leaving only the snow still falling from the darkened, cloud-covered night sky.

He opened the door into the warmth and light of the staircase and found one of his outriders waiting there for him.

He snarled and clenched his fists at his side; this was more of that *news*, he knew it, and he wanted so badly to maim the bearer of it that he shook with the effort to control himself.

The man's face was white as paper; he trembled with such fear that he was incapable of speech. He held out an intricately carved black box to his master, a box hardly bigger than the palm of his hand.

Falconsbane took it and waited for the man to force the words past his fear to tell his master where this trinket of carved wood had come from. But when the man failed utterly to get anything more than an incoherent hiss past his clenched teeth, Falconsbane ruthlessly seized control of his mind with yet another spell, and tore the story from him. It only took a moment to absorb, mind-to-mind, but what he learned quelled his anger far more effectively than the wind had.

His hand clutched convulsively on the box as the tale unfolded, and he left the man collapsed upon the stairs in a trembling heap, ignoring whatever damage he had done to the outrider's mind. He took the stairs two at a time back to the safety and security of his newly cleaned study; there was no sign of where the dead slave had been except a wide wet spot. And only there, with all his protections about him, did he use a tiny spell to open the tiny box from arm's length.

If this was a rational, ordered universe, it would contain something meant to cripple or kill him.

He held his shields about him, waiting.

Nothing happened.

The box contained, cradled in black padded suede, a tiny figurine carved of shiny black onyx.

The figure of a perfectly formed black horse, rearing, and no bigger than his thumbnail.

There was no scent of magic upon it—no trace of who or what had made or sent it. Although he *knew* what had delivered it, if not who it was from.

One of the black riders.

He retreated to his newly covered couch and held the delicate little carving to the light, pondering what he had ripped from his servant's mind.

This particular outrider had seen these black-clad riders three times before this, but always they had vanished into the forest as soon as they knew they had been seen, leaving not even hoofprints behind. But this time had been different. This time he had seen the rider cleave a tree with a sword blow, and leave something atop the stump. The rider sheathed the sword and slipped into the shadows, like another shadow himself. When the outrider had reached the spot, he discovered this box.

And it weighted down one other thing. A slip of paper that had burned to ash in his hand as soon as he had read it. A slip of paper bearing the name of his Master, Mornelithe Falconsbane, in the careful curved letters of Trade-speech.

As if there had been any doubt whatsoever who this was meant for—

He turned the figurine over and over, staring at it. There was nothing here to identify it or the box, with its stylized geometric carvings, as coming from any particular land or culture. Was it a warning, or a gift? If a gift, what did it mean? If a warning—who were these riders, who had sent them, and what did they want?

Skif and Nyara talked idly about the chase; this rabbit they were dressing out had been far more trouble than it was worth, but Nyara's capture of it was as worthy of admiration as any hawk's stoop. Wintermoon was gently cleaning a deep scratch one of the *dyheli* had suffered, several feet from the two of them.

Nyara had reentered their lives by simply coming into camp and waiting to be discovered. They'd found her between the two *dyheli* when they awoke, sitting with her knees tucked up to her chest and the sword Need at her feet. She looked different now—more human, and with sharply defined muscles. She also moved with purpose rather than slinking like a cat; she had visibly undergone many changes, all of which served to fascinate Skif further.

There was no sign of any trouble, but suddenly Cymry's head shot up, and her eyes went wide and wild, with the whites showing all around them. Her body went from relaxed to tense; she stood with all four legs braced, and there was no doubt in Skif's mind what she sensed.

Danger. Terrible danger. Something was happening.

Skif stood and put one hand on her shoulder to steady her, as Nyara's face went completely blank. Nyara leapt to her feet and stared off in the same direction as Cymry, her own eyes mirroring a fear that Skif recognized only too well.

He felt nothing, but then, if it was magic that alerted them, he wouldn't. But he recognized what direction they were both staring in.

The Vale—where Elspeth was.

He tried to Mindtouch his Companion, but all of her attention was on the danger she had sensed. It was Need's mind-voice that growled in the back of his head, as he tried to break through Cymry's preoccupation.

:Leave her alone, boy. She's talking to Gwena. There's big trouble back with your bird-loving friends.:

He dared a tentative thought in Need's direction, waiting for an instant rebuff. He still had no idea what Need thought of him, beyond the few things she had condescended to say to him. *:What kind of trouble? Something involving us?:*

The sword hesitated a moment. *:Hmm. I'd say so. Your kitten's sire just tried to flatten the whole Vale. And I think—yes. No doubt. There's been a death.:*

Before Skif could panic, the sword continued. *:Not Elspeth; not Darkwind. More, I can't tell you. There's some shamanic magic mixed in with the rest, and damned if I can read it.:*

Wintermoon stared at all of them with the impatient air of a man ready to strangle someone if he didn't get an explanation soon. Skif didn't blame him, and he broke off communication with the blade to tell the Hawkbrother what little Need had been able to tell him. The name of Mornelithe Falconsbane got his immediate attention. "Falconsbane! But I thought—"

"We all thought—or, we didn't think," Skif replied, trying to make his thoughts stop spinning in circles. "We just assumed. Not a good idea where magic is concerned." *Of where Falconsbane is concerned. Next time I won't believe he's dead until I burn the body myself and sow the ashes with salt.*

"If there is trouble, we *must* return, with all speed. And it must be with Nyara or without her, for we cannot delay to argue," Wintermoon said firmly. "I had rather it were 'with' but I shall not force her."

The mention of her name seemed to wake Nyara from her trance. "Of course we go, night-hunter," she replied. Her eyes still looked a little unfocused, but her voice was firm enough. "And I go with you. I know too much about my father to remain outside and watch your people struggle to match him again. I shall not hide while he tries to destroy your Clan, hoping he will miss me as he concentrates on you."

She shook her head, then, and hesitated, looking fully into Skif's eyes. "If I had a choice, I would tell you this when we are alone, *ashke,*" she said softly. "But I think that Wintermoon must hear this so he can bear witness if need be."

Skif tensed, wondering what she was going to say to him. Things had seemed so promising a few moments ago.

"I care for you, Outlander," she said with quiet intensity. "More than I had ever realized when I saw your face this morn. I would like—many things—and most of all, to share my life with you. But you and I can do nothing until I come to terms with my father. There is much that I have not told you of him—and myself. It must be dealt with."

Skif had seen such looks as he saw in her eyes more than once, before he became a Herald—and after, among some of the refugees from Ancar's depredations. He saw it in the eyes of a woman who spoke of her father, and horrors between them.

He knew. He knew of many things that decent people would only think of as horrible nightmares, and deny that they truly happened. He knew the sordid tales that could be hidden behind those bleak eyes. She didn't even have to begin; he knew before she started. And he blamed her no more for what had been done to her than he would have blamed a tree sundered by lightning.

She was all the more beautiful for her strength.

Maybe it was just that he was too busy wanting to hold her and tell her that nothing in her past could make him want her any less. Falconsbane was dismissed from any redemption in his mind; to him he rated no more thoughts, not even hate—as his friend Wintermoon had taught him, such emotions can cloud purpose. Maybe that purpose was too important for him to have any room left for anger, now. That might change if he ever actually saw Falconsbane again, but that was the way he felt at this moment.

All things could change. If he were the same person he was only a few years ago, he'd have already been sharpening knives, plotting revenge on Falconsbane; now, simply eliminating the Adept was more important. Revenge seemed foolish somehow; it would not help Nyara at all. How strange, that after a life like his, revenge seemed hollow compared to simple justice.

Nyara deserved far more consideration than her father.

He didn't even think about the sword's propensity to eavesdrop, until she spoke to him.

:Well, bless your heart, boy—I'm beginning to think there's hope for you yet.: Need's harsh mind-voice rattled in his head as she chuckled. *:You are all right! Hellfires, I'd even be willing to nominate you as an honorary Sister!:*

He felt his ears redden, as Nyara looked at him curiously. *:Uh—thank you,:* he said simply, not wanting to offend the blade by adding *I think.*

:Tell her, boy. Don't go into detail, keep it short and simple, but tell her. She needs to know.:

"Look, Nyara—" he said haltingly, wishing he could say half of what he wanted to. "I—I love you; I guess you've figured that out, but I thought I'd better say it. There. Nothing's going to change that. I'm not the picture of virtue—or innocence—I've seen more than you might think. I've spent time on Ancar's Border. I've seen girls—women— who've had pretty bad things happen to them. Who've been—I don't know. I guess you could say they've been betrayed by the parents who should have protected them. I know what you mean. You and I can't do

669

anything about us until we get *him* out of our lives."

:*A little confused, boy, but I think she got the gist of it. I'll have a little talk with her and lay things out for her later.*: Again, that gravelly chuckle. :*I'll let her know you weren't just making pretty talk; you've seen things as rough as she's lived through. Who ever would have figured me for playing matchmaker. And at my age!*:

Nyara only stared at him in dumb surprise, clutching the sword to her chest beneath her cloak of fur. But then one hand crept off the scabbard and moved down; searched for his and found it.

She gave him the ghost of a smile then. "Either you are lying, which Need says not—you are a saint, which she also says not—or you are as great a fool as I." She shook her head, but her eyes never left his.

"Well, then—let's be fools together," he whispered, staring down into her bottomless eyes. "I'm willing to work at it if you are."

Commotion at the entrance end of the Vale caught Darkwind's attention and broke into his brooding. Darkness had fallen some time ago, but he had not bothered to call any lights. Part of him still wanted to be angry with Firesong—angry at *someone*—but the rest of him knew that the Adept was punishing himself already. Anything he said or did would be superfluous, and likely cause much harm.

The disturbance was enough to let him know that a larger party than usual had crossed the Veil, and since the second shift of scouts had already gone out, this was not something expected. Something unexpected today could only mean trouble.

He sent a tentative inquiry to Vree, and the answer he received sent him shooting down the stairs of his *ekele* like a slung stone.

He met the tiny parade just past the first hot pool, and when he saw who had met Wintermoon's little troupe, as well as who was riding with it, he thought that he was dreaming.

The Outlander Skif rode his white Companion. Beside him to his right was Wintermoon on one of the two *dyheli* stags that had gone out with them. But on the left hand of the Herald was the second stag, who also bore a rider, and that was what caused him to stare and question his sanity. Nyara sat astride the *dyheli,* as if she had always known how to ride. She was clad in a rough bearskin cloak, carrying the blade she had taken across her lap.

Walking *beside* her, holding a mage-light to show the way and engaged in easy conversation with her, was Firesong.

Wintermoon held up his hand, and they stopped long enough to dismount. The *dyheli* walked off, into the side of the Vale, where the Clan kept grazing and water for their kind. Firesong stepped back to allow Skif to aid Nyara from her mount, but then he fell in beside them, still deeply in conversation with both of them. Still more than a little stunned, Darkwind took his place beside his brother. Wintermoon thanked his mount and sent the stag on his way with a pat on the withers. Cymry walked ahead, but Darkwind had no doubt that she was following every word of Firesong's conversation.

"Who in the name of all gods is that?" Wintermoon asked, after hearty greetings between the two brothers.

"Firesong k'Treva. Healing Adept. The Council let us send for help," Darkwind replied. "He's—"

"Impressed by himself," Wintermoon completed. "But I'd guess that he must be something very special." He shook his head. "Brother, so much has happened to us since dawn this morning that I do not know where to begin."

"Then let me," Darkwind suggested. "After the last time you came in, Elspeth and I were permitted to call for aid. Firesong is what we received. He was more than we expected. And yes—he is of such power and ability that this arrogance of his is little more than pardonable pride, and almost a game to him."

Wintermoon only snorted. "Perhaps. I would like to see him in a situation where his pretty face means nothing, and he only frightens with his power. Take away the things he was born with, and I will be prepared to admire his accomplishments. But then, I am a crude man. Magic has never much impressed me."

Darkwind came so close to laughing that he choked, and gave his brother a quick embrace. "Nevertheless, he has been training me and the Outlanders."

"He has been training you, between attempting to impress the Outlander—"

"How am I to finish this tale?" Darkwind chided, then sobered. "Listen, there were ill things happened here, today. We were to attempt something small upon the Stone—when—"

"When Falconsbane raised his ugly head and attempted to foul the Vale," Wintermoon interrupted. "Do not fear to alarm me. That much we knew. Nyara felt the taint of her father, as did the Companion, and the sword knew where and that there had been a death. She said she did not think it was someone she knew. Whose death, then?"

"Tre'valen, the Shin'a'in shaman," Darkwind said, sorrow rising in him again. Wintermoon's eyes went wide with surprise. "He—the beast struck at our father, Wintermoon. Firesong shielded the Stone—no, do not interrupt me this time—had he not, none of us would be here to greet you. You would have returned to a smoking hole, and that I pledge you. I could do nothing, nor Elspeth; we were not quick enough."

"But—Father obviously lives—was it Tre'valen that shielded him, then?" Wintermoon shook his head, amazed. "Surely though he is— was—a shaman, he could not have protected Father against the beast in his wrath!"

Darkwind nodded at everything his brother said, and was no little amazed at how much Wintermoon guessed correctly. "Firesong thinks that he was not alone—that it was he and—and Dawnfire together who shielded Father." Now it was Darkwind's turn to shake his head. *"He does not know what happened to them, besides that Tre'valen is dead. I do not know what all this means. But there will be a little time to try to find meanings later. What is your tale?"*

"Simple, compared to yours." Wintermoon took off his coat and slung it over one shoulder. "I had struck signs of Nyara's presence and narrowed the search. I thought that we were within a day, perhaps two, of finding her. But instead, I woke to find her seated quite calmly in the midst of our camp."

"Oh, so?" He raised an eyebrow at that.

"The sword advised her to seek us out. Well, to seek Skif out, is closer to the truth. It was he that her eyes were upon, and it was he she wished to speak to, so I woke him. There was much sighing and exchanging of speaking looks." Wintermoon smiled, a smile tinged with sadness. "I would be laughing if there were not so many things now that would make a laugh so greatly out of place. It was quite charming. A meeting out of a silly ballad, Darkwind, I could almost hear a harp a-playing. Skif would not thank me for telling you that. Well, I think I can safely say that the two are fairly smitten, absence from each other has only made the bond stronger, and that if I were a betting man, I would bet on them pairing as eagles. A true lovebond."

Darkwind considered the two; considered what he and Elspeth had spoken of. "I would not bet against you, but there are many obstacles in their way." *Not the least of which is her father—and what he will do to her if he finds her.*

"They know that. Which makes it—well—a better pairing, for my thinking. They know what they face, and face it together." Wintermoon gazed at the backs of those in front of him and smiled again. "A good thing, to see some love in the midst of so much pain. But I should continue. Once we had gotten past the sighing and the looking and into the speaking, she would, I think, have spoken of those obstacles. But then came the attack upon the Vale." Wintermoon rubbed the back of his neck with one hand. "We decided to return. *She* determined to go with us, saying there was much she could tell us to aid against her father. I was not certain then of the wisdom of this, for she could be a breach in our defenses."

"Not with Need beside her," Darkwind said firmly. "I have spoken to Elspeth of the blade. Although she is not an Adept as we know them, she is very powerful, and has knowledge we do not."

Wintermoon nodded. "It did seem to me that Nyara was less feral and more human, but I only saw her once, and I thought I might have misremembered. Perhaps the sword is even able to change her. I knew, danger or no, that she must come here long enough to be given some kind of protection. If you have so powerful an Adept here, perhaps he can weave shieldings for her that will protect her. We cached the packs to make more speed, and returned as quickly as we could."

"When you arrived, was Firesong still at the entrance to the Vale?" Darkwind could not resist asking.

"That he was; quiet as an ice-statue, though he came to life quickly enough when he saw us." Wintermoon raised his eyebrows. "And that bird of his. It lit our way in. Is he always such a showman?"

Darkwind shrugged. "I cannot see how he could be anything less. I think it is part of his nature. But tell me, what did he make of the Changechild? I have heard that k'Treva is less forgiving of such creatures than we."

"If that is a trait of his Clan, he does not share it," Wintermoon said, a hint of speculation in his voice. "He did not even seem particularly startled, although if he viewed us from afar with the eyes of his bondbird, he would have known what she was long before we rode through the Veil."

"And now he speaks with her." Darkwind ran a hand through his hair. "It is not what I would have expected of him."

:Well, he's reserving judgment, boy,: said a harsh mind-voice. *:He isn't terribly happy about having Falconsbane's daughter in his lap, but he thinks that he has some foolproof ways of telling if she's an enemy plant.:* A snort of laughter. *:As if I would leave any of the bastard's hooks in her!:*

Darkwind belatedly recognized the voice of the sword. *:I think you fully capable, warlady:* he said carefully. *:Let me ask you this; is she ready to face her father?:*

:Alone? Hellfires, no. Not in a century. There's only so much I can do with the raw material. Only so much I can do. I'm no great Adept, just a mage-smith: The sword sounded surprisingly—humble? Darkwind found the changes in Need as interesting as the changes in Nyara. *:I'll promise you this, though; give that girl proper backing, and she'll defy her father. Though she hasn't quite figured it out yet, she's not his frightened slave anymore.:*

That was good news; the first of the day.

"Unless you have something planned—" Wintermoon began. Firesong stopped, turned, and interrupted him.

"I think," the young Adept said, pitching his voice so that they all heard him clearly, "it is time to call a Council."

2 0

It was a strange conference, held in a clearing below Firesong's borrowed *ekele*. Firesong's *hertasi* scrambled to bring food and drink for the participants, some of whom, like Firesong himself, Darkwind, and Elspeth, had not eaten for some time. Food had not seemed particularly important to Darkwind, but of course to the *hertasi*, it was a source of much disapproval that they had neglected themselves. The lizards hovered all over them, but paid particular attention to Firesong. There were, predictably, twice as many *hertasi* attending him as anyone else.

The conference was also a small one; Iceshadow, representing the Elders and mages, Darkwind, Firesong, Wintermoon for the scouts, Nyara, the blade Need. Kethra sent her regrets that she could not attend; she would not leave Starblade's bed. Elspeth had been reluctant to join in it, but at Firesong's urging, she too took her place in the circle. Skif presented himself at Nyara's side and would not be moved, and Darkwind urged the Companions to take places beside their Heralds as well.

The conference was interrupted immediately by yet another visitor, reminding them all that there was more at stake than just the Vale.

The *kyree* bounded into the group and planted himself right next to Nyara without even asking for permission. Darkwind recognized Rris immediately, by the jaunty tilt of his head and his alert eyes and ears. Firesong was somewhat taken aback by the *kyree's* brashness, and Darkwind was so amused to see his reaction that he insisted that Rris be allowed to speak.

:I am sent from Treyvan and Hydona,: the *kyree* said, holding his head up and refusing to be intimidated by Firesong's measuring glances. *:Those are the gryphons, young cub,:* he said then, with a kindly, patronizing tone in his mind-voice, turning to give Firesong a measuring glance of his own. *:They are the allies of this Vale, and they wish to know what has happened. Beyond the obvious, that is—the action of Mornelithe Falconsbane and the death of the shaman.:*

Darkwind hid his smile behind a cough. He himself had taken the time to send a message to the gryphons, but Rris had obviously been coached. And he had a shrewd idea by whom.

:They wish to know what you intend to do,: Rris continued blithely. *:They have taken steps; they have fortified their lair, which lies near to the node in the ruins. They have shielded that node, so that no one may use it but themselves. And they have found the old, buried Gate and have shielded it, so that Falconsbane may not use it to return. But they must know what their allies intend as well. And they wish the council to know that, with the sword Need, they vouch for the Changechild Nyara; that they feel she is trustworthy, for they have been aware of her movements and actions since she left their lair.:*

He lay down then, obviously very pleased with himself. Darkwind knew why; he had delivered Treyvan's message word for word with the proper tone, and no one had interrupted him. Darkwind hoped that Firesong was reading that pleasure as a taste of Rris' own self-conceit.

Young cub. I thought he was going to lose those eyebrows up into his hair.

But there was at least one surprise in all of that for him, as well; the gryphons had known where Nyara was and what she was doing. And they vouched for her.

Firesong might have lost the initial control of the council, but he regained it as soon as he stood up to speak.

"I have been lacking in forethought," he said, quietly. "I have not thought that Mornelithe Falconsbane could still be a danger, if he even lived. That was an error, and one that has cost a precious life. Perhaps two; I do not know if the one called Dawnfire also perished with Tre'valen. I think it is time that we deal with both our problems in a coordinated fashion. Our first problem is the Heartstone, for until we remove it as a threat, Falconsbane can use it against us, as he nearly did earlier. Then we must deal with Falconsbane himself."

He looked around the circle, and got nods of agreement from everyone. "To that end let each of us say what he knows, both of what happened this day, and what in the past may have been involved. Never mind that it has all been said before; there are going to be some of us that have not heard all the tale from all the participants."

He began, with his perception of the attack. The various stories took some time to complete, but in the end, even Darkwind was satisfied. Some of the pieces were beginning to make a whole.

"Now that we have built the proper picture, I see two different needs that must be addressed at the same time." Firesong shifted restlessly from foot to foot. "*I* know what must be done with the Stone, and those of you who are to help me should hear of this now, so that there is no more mystery. But what we are to do about Falconsbane, I do not know. I think that I would be of little aid there, for I am not well-versed in combative magics. I am not versed in combat, to speak of, at all, but I am not certain that direct combat, with magic or not, is the proper way to deal with him."

Darkwind must have looked a little surprised at Firesong's confession that there was something he did not know, for he caught the Adept's sardonic glance in his direction.

"So this is my suggestion. That we have two councils. I shall have Elspeth and Darkwind, the gryphons' representative—" he bowed ironically to Rris, who only bowed gravely back at him, "—and the Companion Gwena. If Iceshadow and Wintermoon would care to lead the other, I think that Nyara may know some ways of countering her father. She will certainly know more of his ways and his stronghold than any of the rest of us. And surely the sword Need knows combat by magic *and* blade far, far better than I."

:Thank you, youngster,: came Need's dry response, broadcast clearly to all. *:I do have a little experience there.:*

Firesong's eyebrows flew up into his hair again, but he did not comment. Wisely, Darkwind thought. One did not pick quarrels with edged wit or edged weapons. "When we have all reached some sort of conclusion, we will meet again as one, this time with the full k'Sheyna Council. Will that suit you all?"

"It suits me very well," Iceshadow said cautiously. Wintermoon and Skif nodded. "Well, then, let us withdraw to my *ekele*, and leave this place to the others."

Firesong made some show of finding a place to sit while the others followed Iceshadow down one of the paths. Only when they were completely out of earshot, did the young Adept sigh, and look from Darkwind to Elspeth and back.

"Here is what I intend," he said, quietly. "Attend, sir *kyree;* you must carry this back to the gryphons as soon as I have done, for this is dangerous working that I propose, and I want—no, I need—them to participate."

Rris nodded, and pricked his ears forward eagerly.

Firesong took a deep breath.

"I intend to shatter the Heartstone."

At Darkwind's instinctive move of protest, he shook his head. "No, not as Falconsbane sought to—and not releasing the energy wildly. Faceting a precious stone is not the same as striking it with a mallet. No, I intend to do this under complete control. First, I wish to *prepare* the Stone as if it were to become a Gate. Call it a proto-Gate. I shall work only with the energy tied to the Stone, but never the Stone itself. That will anchor all of the energy but not in a physical anchor."

Darkwind nodded slowly. This made sense, but it was not something he would ever have considered. Everyone knew that creating a Gate anchored energy, but no one would have ever considered making a Stone into a Gate. It would entail circling the powers about the Stone from without; he did not even want to consider what would happen to someone who actually used such a Gate.

"K'Sheyna has prepared a new Stone in the new Vale—yes?" At Darkwind's nod, he continued. "Once *this* stone is shattered, the proto-Gate will be drawn to the point of greatest attraction and to the point that is nearest in type to the old Stone. It will seek, and we shall push it gently in the proper direction. That should be the new Stone, for both were created by the same mages. It will carry the remaining ley-lines with it. We can guide its movement from here."

"That's not going to happen quickly," Darkwind put in.

"No. It will take several Adepts in relays to move it, and they will be working for several days to do so. But this should work." Firesong looked to Rris. "The shielding will be undertaken in pairs; like the shielding when a Heartstone is moved, but with double the mages. The pairs will be male-female, to enforce the balancing. I wish the gryphons to be in the West, if they would. Can you tell them that, as well as all else you have heard tonight? Can you remember?"

:Surely,: the *kyree* replied, with a lift of his head that signified slightly offended pride. *:I know every* kyree *history-song, every tale the Tayledras have*

shared with my clan, and all of the four-hundred and twenty-three tales of my famous cousin Warrl. Carrying what I have heard to Treyvan and Hydona is no great task at all.:

Darkwind felt his lips twitching.

:With your permission, I shall go to them,: Rris finished. At Firesong's nod, he was off, leaping across the circle and into the underbrush, presumably on his way back to the ruins.

Gwena chose that moment to absent herself, leaving only Firesong, Darkwind, and Elspeth. Darkwind was about to take himself off as well, when Firesong put out a restraining hand.

"There is trouble between us, Darkwind," he said levelly. "That trouble has not been purged. There is trouble between you and the Wingsister, for you have not truly dealt with it. And there is trouble between Elspeth and myself, for there are some assumptions that she has made that I have not corrected."

Darkwind's stomach knotted with sudden tension. He would have liked to make an escape, but he did not dare.

"These must be dealt with, all, before we enter the circle together," Firesong said, but instead of turning first to Darkwind, he faced Elspeth.

"You have not been honest with Darkwind," he said levelly.

"I—" She started to protest, but the protests died on her lips under his stern gaze.

"You have not told him your true feelings concerning me," the Adept continued. "He has sensed it, but you have avoided dealing with your own feelings, and with him. You have not told him the truth."

"I—suppose not. I am very attracted to Darkwind. Very. But—you—" She shrugged helplessly. "I can't help it, and it isn't just because you're so infernally beautiful. Firesong—" She blushed furiously, and hung her head. "I've never wanted anyone—physically—quite so much."

Darkwind felt his jealousy rising to eat him alive. Had she been fantasizing that her lover was Firesong every time that the two of them had...?

"Well." Firesong nodded coolly, not in the least perturbed—or impressed. "You are not the first female to attempt to fling herself at me. Let me tell you that you are a good student, Elspeth, and worthy of the praise that I have given you. But you must know this; I am not as you think." She shook her head, obviously not understanding. For that matter, Darkwind couldn't imagine what Firesong was getting at.

"I am," he said delicately, "the true descendant of your Herald

Vanyel, on both sides of my family. It is from his blood that I have my power." Then, before Elspeth could register *that* surprise, he continued. "I inherited more than his power."

She shook her head; clearly she did not understand what he was trying to tell her.

He arched an eyebrow in Darkwind's direction. "Perhaps I should be a little more explicit. Elspeth, while I am sure you are a very attractive woman to some, it is Darkwind's hair that *I* would choose to braid feathers into if I could." He licked his lips. "In point of fact, I have been wishing that since I first laid eyes upon him. Had he not put his own feelings toward you out where anyone could see them, I should already have done so." And Firesong actually *blushed.*

Elspeth had thought she had come to the end of the surprises that living with the Hawkbrothers brought, but this last series had caught her flatfooted.

First, of course—that the famous Vanyel had left *any* offspring. There was no record of that in any of the Chronicles, and no hint of it in any of the songs and ballads. Then came the revelation that Firesong was the descendant of that child—or children. There was no reason to doubt him; he had never lied before, and why lie about something so stupid, something that couldn't be proved or disproved here? Firesong already had plenty of status—and presumably fame—on his own; he surely didn't need to boast of a bloodline like some fading, failed highborn. But the last surprise—

That he's—dear gods, what do they call it here? Shay'a'chern ? Is that where we get shaych? *Why am I thinking about where a word came from when—*

When he wants Darkwind *and not me...* First came a rush of profound embarrassment. She hadn't been made a fool of. She'd made a fool of herself quite nicely on her own, with no help from Firesong, making assumptions she had no right to make. She just wanted to crawl away and hide somewhere.

But then she was overcome by a flood of jealousy. But not of Firesong's attraction to Darkwind. No, she was jealous—and afraid of—Darkwind's possible attraction to Firesong. She *knew* the Tayledras were a lot more flexible about sexual matters than the people of Valdemar, even the Heralds. What if, now that Firesong's preferences were out in the open, Darkwind preferred him to her?

She was so jealous she was literally sick. Her stomach and shoulders were in knots, her throat too tight to speak. Firesong was watching both of them, wearing an unreadable little smile, and measuring them from beneath his long white lashes. What was he thinking? Did he know how she felt? Was he amused?

Once again, she was dizzy with embarrassment, sick with the emotions warring for control of her.

She flushed, then paled, feeling herself growing hot, then cold, then hot again. Her ears burned, and the back of her neck; her hands grew cold, and she fought dizziness as she looked up with defiance into Firesong's face.

There was no doubt that the Adept had at least some idea of her internal battling; Firesong's smile increased, just a trifle. He tossed his head, sending his hair whipping back over his shoulders, and deliberately, tauntingly, lifted his chin at her. Then he grinned insolently, and turned away, walking *off* into the darkness, leaving his mage-lights behind him. She couldn't look at Darkwind. She couldn't *not* look at him. She tried to look at him out of the corner of her eye, but caught his eyes by accident and was forced either to meet his eyes or look quickly away. She chose the former.

He coughed, and she saw to her increased confusion—as if it *could* be increased any further—that he was flushed a little himself. No, more than a little; the peculiar illumination of the mage-lights tended to wash his color out. Her hands were cold, her face still flushed, but she no longer felt so sick.

"I feel like a fool," he said, just before the silence became unendurable. "I feel like a true and crowned fool."

"Well, imagine how *I* feel," she said sharply. "Especially when I realized that I didn't care a pin how he felt about me or *you*, but—"

"But?" he prompted, and she flushed again, feeling her ears, neck, and cheeks burning.

She didn't really want to answer him, but if she didn't, she'd never know what his feelings were in the matter. "It really made me very unhappy to think you—might—" She shook her head, and finally looked right at him. "All right!" she snapped, angrily. "I was *jealous*, if that's what you wanted to know! I was jealous, because you might be more interested in him than you are in me!"

He simply watched her, soberly, without so much as twitching a muscle. He didn't say a thing, and now she was sick with embarrassment again. And with humiliation.

She knew, now that Firesong had pressed the issue and humbled her by forcing her to reveal things she had kept only to herself, that her attraction to Firesong had been nothing more than simple infatuation. It had only been complicated because she had so admired his competence, his intelligence, as well as his stunning looks.

But Darkwind was competent and intelligent. And her attraction to him was something a great deal deeper. Deep enough to move her to jealousy; deep enough to make her willing to make a fool of herself, if it came to that.

"I have *been* a fool," Darkwind said quietly. "Even as you. Perhaps it was as much due to stress as anything else. We have been living a lifetime in the past few moons. We have both of us changed, sometimes profoundly. I can only take comfort in one of the Shin'a'in sayings—'No one has lived who has not been a fool at least once.' And," he summoned up a ghost of a smile, "with luck, we have had our entire lifetime's foolery from this."

"Oh I hope so," she replied fervently.

"But there is one other thing. I think *that* one," he nodded after the departed Firesong, "brings trouble with him as easily and purposefully as he brings baggage. I think that no matter where he went, he would leave unsuspecting folk in some kind of tangle. And I do think that at some level he enjoys doing so."

Elspeth found herself smiling a little; the heat eased from her ears and neck, and her stomach calmed. "No doubt about it," she said wryly, as her flush faded. "He would just revel in having the entire Vale fussing over him the way the *hertasi* do. I doubt he'd be happy if he wasn't the center of attention."

"Oh, and he would enjoy having us at odds over him as well," Darkwind replied. "Make no mistake about it. He is aptly named. I suspect he leaves lovers strewn in his wake like old, dead leaves. He would take great pleasure in being the centerpiece of a quarrel, only to turn about and mend it. But he is too much the Healing Adept to allow that to happen now in a situation this important. In a quieter time, perhaps."

"Well, he isn't going to get another chance from me," she replied firmly. "Let him go play his games with someone else." She shook her head, and realized that the muscles of her neck and shoulders were aching with tenseness. "Look, after all that, I need a soak. Come with me?"

He smiled, and reached for her hand. She met him halfway. "A good notion," he replied clasping his warm hand around her cold one.

Moments later, they were side by side in the hot pool below her *ekele*. She sighed as the heat and her own deliberate attempt to relax her muscles took effect, easing the stiffness and some of the pain.

It was very dark under the tree, and neither of them put up a mage-light to illuminate the shadows. He was a silent presence in the water beside her; not touching her, but there nevertheless. Above them the ever-present breezes of the Vale stirred the leaves of the tree; somewhere in the distance, a bird sang for a moment, then fell silent. Or perhaps it was someone playing a flute.

Darkwind lifted a hand out of the water, and the sound of drops falling from it to the pool seemed very loud. Elspeth emptied her mind and let it drift, full of nothing but the sounds around her.

"Do you think he meant that?" Darkwind said, finally.

"Do I think who meant what?" she asked, lazily.

"Firesong. Do you think he meant what he said about—" Darkwind hesitated, "—about me?"

"Why?" she asked, fiercely. "Because if you plan on taking him up on it, I'll—I'll—" She sought desperately for the most absurd thing she could say. "I'll *scratch* his big blue eyes out!"

Darkwind laughed, and she let relief wash over her again. "No, I do *not* plan on taking him up on it."

"Good," she replied. "Because in a cat-fight, I'd win."

"I believe you would," he said lazily.

"That's because I'd cheat," she continued.

"I *know* you would," he chuckled.

Then she reached toward him and found his hand catching hers, pulling her toward him. She decided not to fight and let her body drift to his.

"You would do that for me?" he asked. "Fight, cheat—"

"Well, fight, anyway. I'd only cheat if it was Firesong because he'd already be cheating." He put his arm around her, and suddenly it was good just to rest her head on his chest and listen to the night.

"He probably would." He took one or two deep breaths. "I do not think that you need to worry about Firesong, however." Another breath. "Or shall I show you that, so that you truly believe me?"

"Please," she said, surprising herself.

Then he surprised her.

* * *

Darkwind held Elspeth's hand, facing Iceshadow and Nightjewel across the circle, the Stone standing ominously in the middle, half-obscuring the other couple. To the right, Treyvan and Hydona faced the crazed surface of the Stone with no sign of trepidation; to the left, Starblade and Kethra stood, hand in hand, in a peculiar echo of Darkwind and Elspeth's own pose. In the middle of their carefully constructed circle was the Stone.

It *showed* its damage now, and not just to the inner eye. Trails of sullen red light crawled over its surface, strange little paths of lightning in miniature. Every line that could be severed from it, had been, and had been reattached to the node beneath the gryphons' lair. That had taken a full day, with a working team of the gryphons, Elspeth, and himself— and Firesong and Need.

He had been surprised when Firesong appeared with the blade in hand, but he was amazed when the Adept actually *used* Need's powers. The two couples had held a warding about the circle, as the Adept and the blade together severed all but two of the remaining ley-lines and relocated them to the node beneath the lair. Firesong was not inclined to explain how he could use magics so openly feminine, and Need held her peace when Darkwind questioned the Adept. Elspeth was just as astonished. It was Nyara herself who had provided the answer, with an odd shyness, when he asked her. "He is balanced," she had told Darkwind. "He is completely balanced between his masculine and feminine sides. So even as he can use man's magic, he can also use woman's magic, magic keyed only to females."

"Such as what Need holds?" he had asked. She had nodded. "And since she is willing to do so, she can feed her power through his feminine side. She would not be able to do that, were he not so balanced."

So although Nyara did not have the mage-strength to enter the circle and wield the blade effectively in this case, Need was there anyway, and lending her power to the isolating of the Stone.

Falconsbane, thank the gods, remained quiet during that day, and during the day that it took for Firesong—alone, completely unaided— to create the proto-Gate from the Stone's remaining power. He would permit no one else within the shielded area. It was too dangerous, he said, and something about his unusual grimness made Darkwind believe him completely. Darkwind and Elspeth took a patrol on the edge of the Vale, encountering nothing more dangerous than a lone *wyrsa*, and returned to linger outside the shielded area, waiting for Firesong to emerge.

That was when he finally realized just what it meant to be a mage as powerful as Firesong. What it meant to be a Healing Adept, in terms of personal cost.

As the sun set, Firesong staggered across the invisible pass-through at the boundary and fell into their arms. No longer the arrogant, self-assured young peacock; he was drained, shaking, drenched with sweat. His very hair hung lank and limp with exhaustion. He was hardly able to stand, much less walk.

They held him up, Darkwind's heart in his throat, until he told them in a hoarse voice that he was all right. "Just—tired," he had croaked. "Very—tired. I have—called help."

The white *dyheli* that had brought him to the Vale appeared at that moment as if conjured, and Darkwind helped the Adept up onto the stag's back at his direction. "My *hertasi* are waiting," Firesong had whispered, from under a curtain of sweat-soaked hair. "I told them what to expect, what I would require. Thank you for helping me."

"Shall I get some other help?" Darkwind had asked, uncertainly.

The curtain of hair had shaken a faint negative. "They know what to do. It is their ancient function. I shall be well enough in a day or so."

Darkwind had nodded and stepped back, letting the *dyheli* bear his burden away.

And Firesong *had* been well enough in a day, making a recovery that seemed little short of miraculous to anyone who had seen him the day before. It seemed he had recovery skills as remarkable as his other skills.

Darkwind and Elspeth had taken another turn as border guardians, with both of them expecting trouble from Falconsbane at any moment. But no trouble came, nothing more than some odd glimpses of shadow riders, who *could* have been little more than nerves and an overactive imagination. Certainly they left no traces on the fresh snow. At the end of that day, they had returned to find Firesong waiting for them, fully restored.

"Tomorrow," he had said. "It must be tomorrow. Starblade and Kethra are not as strong as I would like, but Nyara is afraid that with every passing day, it becomes more likely that her father will strike again. Need agrees, and I will not underestimate Falconsbane again if I can help it. I will go to instruct the gryphons this evening, and we shall gather on the morrow."

Darkwind still did not know exactly what passed between Firesong and the gryphons, but it must have been interesting. Hydona would surely have met his young arrogance with an arrogance of her own, and Treyvan would have deflated Firesong with a few well-chosen comments. Nevertheless, here they were, calmly prepared to do what they must.

And in the center of the circle, ready to strike when all was prepared—Firesong and Need.

The young Adept looked carefully at each one of his chosen pairs, meeting the eyes of each of them in turn. Darkwind brought his chin up and nodded in answer to that unspoken challenge, and Elspeth showed the ghost of a feral smile. What Firesong saw must have convinced him that they were ready, for he nodded.

"Let us begin," he said simply, with no elaborate speeches. There was no need for speeches, after all. They all knew what they were to do, they had drilled together as much as they could. If they were not ready now, nothing anyone could say would make any difference.

Darkwind already held Elspeth's physical hand; now he held out a mental hand, and felt her take it firmly, but without clutching. He let the power build between them for a moment, then he bent his attention (though not his eyes) to the left, where his father and Kethra stood. Elspeth turned hers to the right.

He sensed Kethra building the power between herself and Starblade; then having secured her ground, she bent her attention to him, and he held out another "hand" to her. She took it, fumbling a bit at first, then her "grip" firmed. It was the clasp of a warrior, for all that she was a Healer.

:But a Healer fights for the lives of her patients, does she not? As much a warrior as a bladesman,: Kethra said lightly; then she braced herself to make their bond as strong as possible.

On the right, he sensed Treyvan catching Elspeth's extended "hand." At that moment, the circle trembled for a heartbeat, until all the powers within it found their balance points. Male and female, human and gryphon, old and young; earth, air, fire, and water; Tayledras, Valdemaran, Shin'a'in, far-traveler...

Then the unexpected; when the balance came, it brought with it a sense of wholeness and astonished joy, a lift to his spirits like nothing he had felt since the Heartstone shattered. He saw his surprise mirrored in Kethra's eyes; felt it in the trembling of Elspeth's physical hand in his. He wanted to shout, to laugh, to sing—*this* was how magery should be! This marvelous feeling of rightness!

Movement at the center of the circle caught his attention, and he looked up for a moment at Firesong. The young Adept was smiling, his eyes alight—and somehow Darkwind knew that the wholeness, the joy, came from him.

Was *this* how Firesong felt every time he worked magic? No wonder it was effortless for him… no wonder he was willing to exhaust himself, drain himself to nothing, if this was his reward.

Somewhere in the back of his mind, Darkwind wondered if he would ever feel this way again—knew he never would—and at the same time, knew there would always be a little of this whenever he worked a spell. The touch of the Healer Adept had given that much to him.

The eight of them bound themselves ever closer, with Elspeth weaving their power around and about the circle until it was no longer a circle, but a shell of energy as precise as a porcelain egg, as strong as sword-steel.

Firesong began to tap his foot. He could not bring a drum into the circle, for he could not use it and Need at the same time—but standing just behind Starblade and well within the danger area was Nyara. She caught Firesong's rhythm, and began to drum with a skill Darkwind had not suspected of her. Darkwind picked up the rhythm within a few beats, moving his legs and loosening up; the others followed upon it. The stamping of his feet was enough like a dance that his own magic gained in strength; and where Elspeth's light-weaving gave their construct form, his dancing gave it movement, making it dance, so that there were no weak places, and no places holding still long enough to be weakened by an attack.

He closed his eyes and gave himself up to the rhythm, sensing Elspeth holding firm beside him. Sensing Firesong waiting, poised above the waiting Stone, choosing his moment—

Then, he *struck.*

Need rang as she impacted the Heartstone pointfirst, but instead of the shriek of agony that Darkwind had expected, there came a single bell-like tone.

The sound filled the air and filled his soul; carried all other sounds away, drowning them, and he sensed that they *must* contain it, or it would ring through the Vale and shatter everything in its path.

Nyara threw herself into the drumming, and though he could no longer hear it, he felt it. He threw all of his power and will into the effort of holding—holding—holding until he thought he must fall.

He felt himself faltering, felt the circle faltering. He steeled himself and poured more energy in. He sensed a change in the tone.

It was weakening, fading away.

That gave him his second wind and the strength to keep his place, to keep the power contained. As it faded, so did his strength, but always just a little behind the tone so that his ability to keep it contained was just enough to do so.

Finally it was gone, faded into an echo, then into nothing.

He opened his eyes, swaying on his feet, and looked around. Firesong leaned heavily on the blade, which was buried to the hilt in a pile of uneven, dull-gray shards. Starblade leaned on Kethra's shoulder, and even as he watched, Iceshadow and Nightjewel sank to the ground together. Even the gryphons' heads were hanging down with weariness. But when Treyvan finally raised his head with an effort, and looked into Darkwind's eyes, Darkwind saw satisfaction and triumph that mirrored his own there.

"Brothers," came the weary voice from the center of the circle. "Sisters. We have succeeded."

:Damn if we haven't,: Need said, and even the sword sounded exhausted. :Damn if we haven't.:

Firesong stood erect again, pulling himself up with an effort, and with a single gesture, banished the circle of power beyond them that had contained the rogue Stone for so long. He shared that power among them, equally, giving them all the strength to stand firmly again. Not much more than that, but at least they were no longer about to drop.

Darkwind did not need to close his eyes to sense the burning lens of power that had been the Stone and was now the proto-Gate. It hovered between this world and the world of Gates and ley-lines, affected by both—yet no longer the malignant, near-sentient thing it had been. Now it was only power. And now that the shields were down, the gryphons were able to draw safely on the clean power of their own node.

They lost their weariness, legs straightening, wings refolding with a *snap*, heads coming up.

Nyara entered the former circle quietly, and Firesong handed Need back to her with little bow of courtesy before he turned back to the gryphons. "Well," he said, his voice already stronger, as he shared the power they were drawing from the node they had made their own. "And are you ready for the first stage of the move?"

"Lead on, featherrlessss one," Treyvan said, cocking his head sideways. "And congratulationsssss. That wasss *well* done."

Firesong had that arrogant little smile back, but this time Darkwind was not going to fault him for it. This had been the most brilliant, innovative piece of magic he had ever seen—and, he suspected, was ever likely to see.

"Thank you," Firesong replied with no show of humility at all, false or otherwise. "That was the hardest part. The rest, though it will be tedious, will be much easier."

"Hmm. Yesss. Perrhapsss. It isss not wissse to count the eyassess until they arrre fledged." Hydona roused her feathers with a shake, so much like Vree that Darkwind chuckled despite his weariness. "Ssstill, sssoonesst begun isss sssoonessst done. Let usss deal with thisss prrroto-Gate of yoursss before it getsss the notion to wanderrr on itsss own."

As the rest of them gathered themselves up and headed for the Council Oak, where the *hertasi* had assembled food and drink, Darkwind sighed with relief and squeezed Elspeth's hand. The worst, indeed, was over. No matter what else happened, Falconsbane would not be able to destroy the Vale and Stone together. So for now, at least, they were safe.

Or as safe as they were likely to get, with Falconsbane still out there.

Still plotting. Still watching.

Still Falconsbane... a terrible and implacable foe.

2 1

There was a peculiar feeling to the Featherless Fools' Vale today. Falconsbane could not quite put his finger on what it was, but he sensed that they had redoubled their shielding on the Stone again. They had also reduced the number of lines on the Stone to a bare two, but those were the most powerful of all. It would not have been possible to sever either of them—no matter how good that Adept thought he was.

He smiled to himself, fingering the tiny carved horse—which was *not* onyx, nor obsidian, nor any other stone he knew. It could not be chipped nor marred in any way at all, no matter what he did to it. It should have been fragile. He had even ordered one of his artisans to strike it with a stone sledgehammer when nothing *he* had done had affected it in any way. It had chipped the hammer; obviously, it was anything but fragile.

A puzzle; like those who had sent it.

One he did not have time for, as matters stood. He needed to concentrate on his plan for k'Sheyna, a plan that required patience and vigilance, but would pay for that patience handsomely. The Bird Lovers could put all the shields they wanted to on that Stone of theirs; they still wouldn't be able to save it. And the moment they dropped the shielding, he would be waiting. He would not fail a second time.

Let them only drop the shield. He had been waiting for days now, buried in his study, gathering his strength, preparing a single lightning strike that would overwhelm Starblade, burn away his mind, and burn *through* him to the Stone.

It was a new sort of action for him—and thus, he thought, it would be unexpected and unanticipated. There would be no testing, no struggling of wills. Just one single, quick, clean blow, spending all of his power in that strike and holding none in reserve. A reckless kind of action, audacious. Starblade would flare up like a stick of dry kindling, and a moment later, his home would follow, Adept and all. It was not the end he would have chosen for Starblade or his followers, but it would at least be revenge.

Only let them drop the shield—

He watched, as patient as a cat at a mousehole, as a lion above a salt lick, knowing that to reestablish those lines they would have to drop the shield—to use the power of the node in the ruins to try to heal the Stone, they would have to drop the shield. Sooner or later, it would have to come down. There was not enough untainted power within the Vale to even begin to heal the Stone.

Assuming it could be healed. He didn't think that was possible. He had hundreds of years of mage-craft behind him, and he would not have cared to try it.

He had caught his attention wandering for a moment and had redoubled his vigilance when a trembling of the shields alerted him to changes within the Vale.

LIGHT!

He fell back onto his couch with a cry of pain, squeezing his watering eyes shut, holding his ears, in a futile reaction to the blinding wall of "light" and "sound" that assaulted his Sight and Hearing.

If he had not been watching the Vale and the emanations of the Stone within it, he might have missed the death of the Stone itself. If he had been concentrating on something in the material world, he would never have noticed what had happened, for the only effect was in the nonmaterial plane. But since he was, and looking right at it with all of his powers—

For a moment it blinded his inner eye when it exploded in light and sound. A lesser mage would have been struck unconscious and possibly come away with his Senses damaged.

It *did* send him graying-out for a moment, and fighting his way back to consciousness. That was all that was possible; to hold tightly to reality and claw his way back—he couldn't think, couldn't do anything else.

When he came back to himself, the Stone was gone.

He could only sit and blink in dumbfounded shock.

At first he simply could not believe what had happened. It made no sense, it was simply not in the Tayledras to have done such a thing. He thought for a moment that he *had* been Headblinded; that his Senses had failed him.

Then shock gave way to anger. All his plans—destroyed in a single moment! How could he have so completely misjudged them? They should have tried to *save* their Stone, not destroy it! This was something those suicidal Shin'a'in might have tried, but never the Tayledras!

He shook his head, growling in bafflement and increasing rage. His head pounded with reaction-pain; his temples throbbed, and a sharp, hot jabbing at the base of his skull warned him that he was overstressing himself. The pain only increased his anger. How could they have done something so completely unexpected, so entirely out of character? More than that, how had they accomplished it, without destroying the Vale as he had intended to do?

His inner eyes were still dazzled, his outer eyes streamed burning tears in reaction, but he strained his Sight toward the Vale anyway, hoping for a glimpse of something that might give him a clue as to how this unknown Adept had worked the impossible.

Then, as the dazzle cleared under the pressure of his will, he got more than a clue. Far more.

Hanging in the between-world where Gates and ley-lines were born, was a lenticular form of pure, shining Power. It occupied the same not-space that the Stone had taken—or rather, that the Power the Stone contained had taken. For a long, stunned moment, he simply stared at it, wondering where it had come from and what it was. It didn't resemble anything that had been in or near the Vale before. It didn't resemble anything he had ever seen before, for that matter. And how had it gotten where the Power-form of the Stone had been? How had those two ley-lines gotten attached to it? He had never seen lines running to anything but nodes or Stones before. He realized at that moment that it *was* the

Stone—or rather, it was what had taken the place of the Stone. Whatever that Adept had done to the Stone, destroying it had purified the Power and allowed him to give it a new shape. There were only the two lines leading into it, and it was no longer anything he could use or control—or even touch, directly. It had become something that answered to one hand only, and that hand was not his. Power with monofocused purpose, and linked to a particular personality.

In fact, it was very like a Gate. Except that there could not be more than a handful of Adepts great enough to create a Gate with power that was *not* their own.

He nearly rejected that identification out of hand; even the Bird-Fools would not be so foolhardy as to make a Gate within a node, much less within a Stone! And why create a Gate with so much power in the first place? You couldn't use it; anything passing through a Gate like that stood a better-than-even chance of winding up annihilated.

But this was not a Gate, exactly. It was something like a Gate; something that could become a Gate with more shaping. But it was not, in and of itself, a Gate. In fact, the more he examined it, the less like a Gate it became. There was no terminus; it was entirely self-contained. There was no structure that it was linked to; it was linked to the half-world, a kind of Gate doubled back upon itself. That, in fact, was what gave it all the stability it had.

It was more like one of the little seeking tendrils of power a Gate would spin out, trying to reach its terminus.

As he thought that, he Saw it move a little; watched it as it swung slightly to the west and north, seeking something—

Then he understood. It *was* seeking something, and that was why it had been made along the pattern of a Gate.

It was seeking the empty vessel that should have held it, the physical container that had been made by the same hands that had shaped its old vessel. The new Stone in the new Vale.

Unbelievable. Incredible. Something he would never have thought of doing, had he been in the same position.

For a moment, he could only blink at the astonishing audacity of it all. Bold, reckless—not only brilliant, but innovative.

A worthy foe. Not another Urtho, of course, but he was no longer Ma'ar. If he were going to be honest with himself—which he tried to avoid—he would have to admit that another Urtho would not find him much of a challenge these days. Or would he? They would both find themselves dealing with limited power... with magic that followed another set of laws, twisted by the end of their own warring.

Pah, I am woolgathering! No wonder the infant stole a march on me!

Infant? No—young, but no infant. Old in cunning and in skill—youthful only in years. I wonder... is he as beautiful as the rest of the Bird Lovers I have seen?

For another moment, he was overcome by a feeling of complete and overpowering *lust*. And not just for the power—but for the one who had created and conceived this plan. What would it be like to have such a one under *his* control, subject to his whims and fancies, placing his abilities at Mornelithe's call?

What would it be like to be under the control of such a one...?

He shook the thoughts away angrily. Ridiculous! These Bird Lovers were *winning!* He could not permit that! Surely there was something he could do to wrench control of the thing out of their hands.

Wait; go at it backward. What would he do if he had it? What would it mean?

It would attract lines to itself; set in a neutral place, it would soon be the center of a web of lines as complete and complex as the old Stone had owned.

If I had this power-locus, I would have control of the entire energy-web of this area. I could pull all the lines to myself without effort, like a spider whose net spins itself. It would be like my present network of traps and wards, but with such power to tap...

His thumb caressed the tiny horse as he chewed his lip, his mind running in furious thought. Then the image of the spider in the web came to him again. And with it, an idea. *So, little mage, we are going to try new magics, are we?* He smiled, and his smile turned vicious. *Two can play that game. There was a time when I anchored a permanent Gate upon myself, after all.*

That had been far, far back in the past, before the so-clever Hawkbrothers had ever stretched their wings over this area. When it had been *his*, and he had fought to possess it against what seemed to be an endless supply of upstarts. He had been younger then, and willing to try things no one thought possible, for he had already sired a dozen children on as many mothers, human and Changechild, and he was secure in the continuance of his bloodline. And so long as there was someone with direct descent and Mage-Gifts alive, *he* was immortal. Wild chances had been worth the risk.

No one had ever tried to shift the focus of a permanent Gate from a place to a *person*. His advisors said it could not be done, that the power would destroy the person.

And yet, in the end, the temporary Gates were all partially anchored in a person, for the energy to create them came from that person. He had thought it worth trying. Permanent Gates had their own little webs of ley-lines, and acted much like small nodes—that was before he had learned of the Hawkbrains and their Heartstones, and had learned to lust after *real* power. It had seemed a reasonable thing, to try to make himself the center of a web of that kind of power.

So he had researched the magics, then added himself and his own energy-stores to the permanent Gate in his stronghold. He had truly been like a spider in a web then, for whatever he wished eventually came to him, falling into his threads of power. There had been a price to pay—a small one, he thought. After that, he had been unable to travel more than a league from his home, for his fragile body was not able to bear the stress of physical separation for long. On the other hand, he had only to will himself home, and the Gate pulled him through itself, without needing another terminus to step through. His innovation had worked, and then, as now, being home-bound had been a small price to pay for control of all the mage-energy as far as he could See.

He studied the situation carefully, alert for any pitfalls. The most obvious was that the moment he touched the power-locus, his enemies would know what he was doing. The Adept was guiding it himself, with help from some other mages. How maddening to be able to See all of this and yet be unable to act on it!

So he would have to be subtle. Well, there were more ways of controlling the direction of the power-locus than by steering the thing itself. There were two lines on it still, and they could be used to bring it closer to him.

Carefully, he touched the line nearer himself, and pulled; slowly, gradually, changing the direction the power-locus was taking. No one seemed to notice.

Falconsbane's smile turned to a feral grin. The hunt was up, but the quarry did not yet know that the beast was on its trail.

Like all good hunters, he needed to rest from time to time. Falconsbane had pulled the power-locus as far out of line as he cared to for the moment. He had left his servants to themselves for a long while, perhaps too long; they needed to be reminded of his power over them. There were preparations he needed to make here, before he would be ready to make the Gate a part of himself and his stronghold. And before he undertook any of those preparations, or even interfered any more with the power-locus, he needed to rest, eat, refresh himself.

He left his study, and only then noticed that the air in his manor was thick with the heavy smell of incense and lamp oil, of rooms closed up too long and people sweating with fear. He shook his head at the dank taint of it in the back of his throat.

Before he got anything to eat or drink, he needed a breath of fresher air.

He turned around, and was on his way to the top of his tower when every blocked-up and shuttered door and window in his stronghold suddenly flew open with an ear-shattering crash.

Glass splintered and tinkled to the floor. Sunlight streamed in the windows, and a sudden shocked silence descended for a single heartbeat.

Then, with a wild howl, a violent wind tore through his fortress. It came from everywhere and nowhere, tearing curtains from their poles, sending papers flying, knocking over furniture, putting out fires in all the fireplaces, scattering ashes to the farthest corners of the rooms. It raced down the hallway toward him, whipping his hair and clothing into tangles, driving dust into his eyes so that he yelped with the unexpected pain.

Then, before he could react any further than that, it was gone, leaving only silence, chill, and the taste of snow behind.

That wild wind signaled the beginning of a series of inexplicable incidents. They invariably occurred at the least opportune moment. And they made no sense, followed no pattern.

They sometimes looked like attacks—yet did nothing substantial in the way of harm. They sometimes looked as if someone very powerful was *courting* him—yet no one appeared to follow through on the invitation.

Every time he set himself to work on pulling the power-locus nearer, one of those *incidents* would distract him.

The single window in his study was open to the sky since that wind had shattered both shutter and glass. A blood-red firebird—or something that looked like one—flew into his study window and dropped a black rose at his feet. It left the same way it had come and vanished into the sky before he could do anything about it.

694

A troop of black riders kept one of his messengers from reaching him, herding the man with no weapon but fear, running him until his horse foundered, then chasing him afoot until he was exhausted. Then they left him lying in the snow for Falconsbane's patrols to find. By then, it was too late; the man barely had a chance to gasp out what had happened to him before he died of heart failure, his message unspoken.

All of the broken glass in the windows of his stronghold was replaced somehow in a single hour—but not by clear glass, by blood-red glass, shading the entire fortress in sanguine gloom. *He* liked the effect, but his servants kept lighting lanterns to try and dispel it a little.

Every root vegetable in the storage cellar sprouted overnight, growing long, pallid roots and stems. The onions even blossomed. His cook had hysterics and collapsed, thinking Mornelithe would blame *him.*

Two hundred lengths of black velvet appeared in the forecourt, cut to cape-length.

All of the wine turned to vinegar, and all of the beer burst its kegs, leaving the liquor cellar a stinking, sodden mess. Another black rider waylaid the cook's helper sent to requisition new stores and forced him to follow. There were wagonloads of wine- and beer-barrels, of sacks of roots, all in the middle of a pristine, untouched, snow-covered clearing. With no footprints or hoofprints anywhere about, and no sign of how all those provisions had gotten there.

All of the weather vanes were replaced overnight with new ones. The old weather vanes had featured the former owner's arms; these featured black iron horses.

A huge flock of blackbirds and starlings descended on the castle for half a day, leaving everything covered with whitewash.

Something invisible got into the stable in broad daylight, opened all the stalls and paddock gates, and spooked the horses. It took three days to find them all.

When the last horse—Falconsbane's own mount, on the few occasions he chose to ride—was found, it was wearing a magnificent new hand-tooled black saddle, black barding, black tack. And in the saddlebag was a scrying crystal double the size and clarity of the one he had shattered in a fit of pique.

He paced the length of his red-lit study, trying to make some sense of the senseless. It was driving him to distraction, for even those acts that could be interpreted as "attacks" could have been part of a courting pattern. He had done similar things in the past—sent a gift, then done something that said, "see how powerful I am, I can best you in your own home." The courting of mage-to-mage was sometimes an odd thing, as full of anger as desire… as full of hate as lust.

But if it *was* courting, who was doing it? It couldn't be Shin'a'in, for *they* avoided all forms of magic. It couldn't be Tayledras; they hated him as much as he hated them.

Who was it, then? He thought he had eliminated any possible rivals— and only rivals would think to court him.

He stopped stark still, as a thought occurred to him. There had been a time when he had fostered the illusion that the mage the Outlanders were so afraid of had been seeking to ally with him. What if *he* was the one behind all this? It would make sense—black riders to send against white ones—black horses instead of the Guardian Spirits.

Now that he thought about it, the idea made more and more sense…

He called a servant, who appeared promptly, but showing less fear than usual. He had not blamed any of his servants for the bizarre events that had been occurring lately, and that had given them some relief. Besides, he had been getting tired of the smell of fear in his halls. Why, he hadn't even killed a slave in days…

"I want you to find Dhashel, Toron, Flecker, and Quorn," he told the servant. "These are their orders, simple ones. There is a land to the north and east: Hardorn. Its king is one Ancar; he is a mage. He is also the sworn enemy of the two Outlanders with the k'Sheyna, and at war with *their* land of Valdemar. This much I know. I desire to know more. Much more." He blinked, slowly, and fixed the servant with his gaze. "Do you understand all of that?"

The servant nodded, and repeated the orders word for word. Falconsbane was pleased; he would remember never to kill or maim this one.

Good service deserved reward, after all.

"Now go, and tell them to hurry," he said, turning back to the couch and his new scrying crystal. "I am eager to hear what they can learn."

Darkwind rose unsteadily to his feet as Iceshadow tapped his shoulder in the signal that meant Iceshadow was there to relieve him. He staggered out of the former Stone clearing and up the path toward the *ekele* shared by Nyara and Skif. He was tired, but this couldn't wait.

Something or someone was diverting the path of the proto-Gate.

Every moment spent in rapport with Firesong moving the proto-Gate toward the new Vale was a moment spent in constant battle to keep the Power-point on the right course.

They couldn't be sure who was doing it, of course, but for Darkwind, Falconsbane was high on the list. It *was* possible to anchor the proto-Gate temporarily, thank the gods, or they would all have been worn away to nothing, for what they had hoped would take only hours was taking days.

Firesong especially was under stress; since the proto-Gate was linked to him, personally, he had to be the one in charge of directing its path. Although the *hertasi* swarmed over him, bringing him virtually everything he needed, there was one thing they could not give him, and that was rest.

But since they had learned that the proto-Gate could be anchored, his helpers only needed to work in four-candlemark shifts, and he himself needed only to work for eight.

Darkwind had been very dubious about the wisdom of leaving the proto-Gate unguarded, but they really had no choice. Firesong would be helped into bed at the end of the day and sleep solidly until it was time to work again. So he had held his peace and had hoped that there was no way to interfere with the energy-point without Firesong knowing.

And once the proto-Gate was anchored for the night, it actually seemed that either there was something protecting it, or Falconsbane had not found a way to move it.

He paused for a moment, as that thought triggered a memory. *Protecting it...*

He shook his head, and continued on his way. Had he seen what he *thought* he'd seen this morning, when he and Firesong and Elspeth took the first shift together? Had there been two shining, bright-winged vorcel-hawks flitting away silently through the gray mist of the not-world? And had they, a moment before, been standing guard over the proto-Gate?

In the end, it didn't matter—except, perhaps, to Firesong. If the Adept knew that Tre'valen had survived in some form, he would be much comforted. Although Firesong hid most of his deeper feelings beneath a cloak of arrogance and flippancy, Darkwind was better at reading him now. The young shaman's death still grieved him.

Then again, it could have been a trick of the not-world, a place where illusions were as substantial as reality, where nothing was to be trusted until you had tested it yourself. It could even have been a specter of his own half-formed hopes.

There was no denying the fact that someone was trying to steal the proto-Gate, however, and Darkwind was going to assume that it was Falconsbane until he learned otherwise. That meant that some of the nebulous plans the "war council" had discussed before and after the destruction of the Heartstone were going to have to be put into motion.

Darkwind was not certain what Falconsbane intended to do with the proto-Gate, or where he planned to anchor it, for that matter. Presumably on something *like* a Heartstone, somewhere deep in his own stronghold. If he did that, it would give him access to something that had the potential to become a full *permanent* Gate. If he knew how to effect the rest of the spell, that is. Firesong did, or at least Darkwind suspected he did. Not too many did, except for Healing Adepts—and not many of those. No one had had the secret in k'Sheyna for as long as Darkwind had been alive.

But even if Falconsbane didn't know the trick, having the proto-Gate in his control would give him access to a great deal of power.

Nor was that all; unless Firesong freed himself first, access to the proto-Gate meant access to the Adept.

Darkwind did not want to see Firesong—or anyone else, for that matter—in Falconsbane's hands. Firesong *might* be able to defeat Mornelithe in a head-to-head battle. He *might* be able to hold Falconsbane off long enough for someone to help to free him.

Darkwind was not prepared to bet on either of those possibilities. Dealing with Falconsbane had taught him this: it was much safer to overestimate the beast.

He could take over Firesong the way he took my father, and have the power of a Healing Adept to pervert. With that—he could undo anything any Vale has accomplished.

Horrible thought.

If he had a permanent Gate, he could bypass our shields and send his creatures straight into the mouth of the Vale at no cost to himself. That was another unpleasant scenario.

So it was time to consult Nyara, who alone of all of them was an expert on her father.

Nyara had always liked Darkwind; now, with the pressures of her body and of her father reduced or gone altogether, she had discovered it was possible to simply be his friend. Over the past few days she had found him to be kind, courteous—and oddly protective, determined to keep his people from snubbing her or making her feel uncomfortable. That was not to be expected, particularly not with the pressures that were on him now.

She and Skif were actually working on sword practice; although Need had been putting her through exercises, this was the first time she had ever had an opponent to practice with. She welcomed the physical activity as a release from direct thinking. She did not want to consider what she would do when the time came that they both must leave the Vale. She wanted to go with him, but at the same time she was afraid to. It was much easier to lose herself in the hypnotic dance of steel and footwork.

Darkwind must have been standing at the edge of the practice circle for some time before she and Skif realized he was there. She spotted him first, and signaled a halt; only then did he enter the circle.

"You two look very good," he said quietly. "I hated to interrupt you, but I think we're going to have to figure out exactly where your f— Falconsbane is after all."

She wiped sweat from her forehead with her sleeve, and nodded. "Did you find those maps you were talking about?" Strange; not so long ago, even *thinking* of her father brought her to the verge of hysteria. Now—well, she was afraid, only a fool would *not* fear Falconsbane, but she could face that fear.

"They're in my *ekele,*" Darkwind replied, with a nod. "Could you two join me there?"

His treehouse was not far, even by Vale standards. Together he and she and Skif took an old set of Shin'a'in maps out of their leather cases and bent over them with something more than mere interest. They worked backward from the spot where Darkwind had first encountered her; Darkwind pointed out landmarks that *he* knew, as she puzzled her way through the strange notation.

"This would be it, I think," she said at last, pointing to an otherwise unremarkable spot to the north and west. "I have not had much training in the reading of these things," she continued apologetically, "but I think this is the likeliest place for my father's fortress to be."

Darkwind nodded, marked the place, and rolled up the thick sheets of vellum. "That's the direction the proto-Gate is being pulled, so that rather confirms that your guess is correct," he said. "And it confirms *my* guess as to who is behind this. Firesong is trying to second-guess our would-be Gate-thief, but I don't think at this point that there could be much doubt about motivation. If it's Falconsbane, then there is only one real answer. He wants what he's always wanted: power."

"The proto-Gate would be irresistible to him," Nyara agreed, then widened her eyes as something occurred to her. "You know—it is rather odd, but he becomes more predictable under stress, had you noted that? I do not know why, but it is true. I have seen this over and over again, when I was still with him.

The more he is forced to react to the surprises sprung upon him by others, the more likely he is to act as he has always acted, and think it is a clever new plan."

Darkwind nodded, as if what she had just told him confirmed something he had thought himself. "What do you think he's planning on doing with the proto-Gate when he captures it?"

"Oh, he will install it in his stronghold," she said immediately. With no effort at all, she could picture him gloating over his new-won prize as he had gloated over so many in the past. "That is predictable, too. Probably in his study; he is jealous of his things of power and often will not put them where other mages may even see them. He will want such a thing as near to him as may be."

"That would be a bad place to put a Gate," Darkwind observed. "A Gate works both ways—"

"No, I *suspect* he will try to anchor it in a stone or crystal of some kind, rather than as a Gate," she said, trying to remember if Falconsbane had ever indicated that he knew how to make the Greater Gates. "I am not sure. I believe he *knows* how to make a Gate but has not the strength. I think he would rather create something to use as a power-pole, to bring in more lines, if he can."

"What, use it to create his own kind of Heartstone?" Darkwind asked in surprise, and was even more surprised when she nodded. "Make a Heartstone like a Hawkbrother?"

"It seems amazing that he should imitate you," she told him earnestly, "but he has seen your success. He is *not* good at creating things. He is good at twisting them to his own ends, or warping them to suit his fancies, but not at creating them. He will imitate you, therefore, and tell himself that he is making something entirely new."

"So, whatever he tries is going to have a focus," Darkwind mused. "The personal link will have to be taken from Firesong, of course—but if he has to have a focus, he has to have something physical. Focus; his ideal choice would be something shaped the way the proto-Gate looks in the halfworld. And we can attack that."

"What are you thinking of?" Skif asked, sounding just a little belligerent and definitely protective.

Darkwind looked up at the tall Herald, and shook his head. "You are not going to care for my notions," he said. "No, you are not going to like them at all."

"Probably not," Skif agreed. "On the other hand, I don't like the idea of Falconsbane with all that power."

"Nor do I." Darkwind turned back to Nyara. "Before I broach any ideas, there's something I really need to know, both from you, and from your friend in the sheath." He nodded at Need. "Do you think you can hold out against your father's control now? I mean in a face-to-face confrontation; can you hold against his will?"

:Good question, boy. My vote is yes—but she won't unless she believes she can.:

Nyara looked deeply and carefully into his eyes. "I think so," she replied after a long moment of thought. "I know that I can for some time if we are not near one another. I think that I can, if we are not in physical contact. If he had me in his hands—" She shrugged, trying to hide her fear, but Darkwind saw it and sympathized with it anyway. "I would have no chance with him, if I were in his hands. But the old means by which he controlled me no longer work. He tried upon me what he perfected upon your father. Because none of this was perfected, there were places where Need and I could break what he had done to me. He would have to work magic—perhaps even cast actual spells—to get new controls on me. And just at the moment he might not realize that."

"Part of the way he reacts in a typical fashion when he feels himself under pressure?" Darkwind asked.

She nodded. "Especially if he were distracted or busy," she told him. "The more distractions he has, the more likely he is to revert to what has worked in the past."

:Absolutely.: Need agreed. *:Half the reason I was able to help her so much was because I was watching Kethra Heal your father. His problems are a superior copy of hers. We've thrown Falconsbane off-balance by destroying the Heartstone, and he's reacting predictably, by trying to steal the power it harbored. There are a dozen other things he could do with it, or about it, but instead, he's doing exactly what I would have predicted for him.:*

"I could prolong the moment that he thinks he still has me controlled by feigning it," Nyara offered, trembling a little inside from fear. "Need might be able to help with that."

Nyara watched Darkwind turn all that over in his mind—and she wondered. One plan, with a fair likelihood of success, had already occurred to her. She wondered if he was thinking the same thing that she was. She had been thinking about something like this for some time—fearing the idea, yet knowing it had logic to it. And knowing that if she were asked, she would follow through with it. Skif was most definitely not going to like it.

2 2

Falconsbane stepped back and surveyed his work, nodding with satisfaction. He had done very well, given the short notice he'd had. And it had been at minimal cost to himself. There were, after all, two ways to create power-poles. The first way was to produce the power from yourself; much in the same way that a Gate was created. That was not the ideal way to proceed, so far as he was concerned.

The other way was to induce it from the body of another—as skilled and powerful a mage as one could subdue. The drawing out of the power would kill the mage in question, of course; there was no way to avoid that. A pity, but there it was.

Then, given the plan he had created, one needed to fix the pole in place—that required another mage. Fixing the pole absolutely required the life of that mage, this time by sacrifice, although Falconsbane had managed to crush the man's heart with no outward signs and no blood spilt. It would have been a pity to stain the new carpets.

And lastly, in accordance with the plan, *he* had needed the full power of a human life *and* the full power of a mage to establish a web of energy linking the power-pole he had created with every possible point in his territory. Naturally that had required a third mage.

It was possible to do all of that from his own resources, but that would have required exhausting himself completely. That wasn't acceptable at this point. Doing it through others was far less efficient; it took three mages to create what he could have accomplished alone.

The problem with the second method was, of course, that the mages in question would not survive the operation. Which was why the bodies of three of Falconsbane's former servants were littering the floor of his study. If he had more time, he probably would have done it the hard way, through himself. It was difficult finding even ordinary servants; mages were doubly hard to acquire.

He had thought long and hard on the best way to go about claiming the power-locus. He had not been aided by all the distractions taking place in and around his lands. The black riders were everywhere, and although they seldom *did* anything, they rattled his guards and made even his fortress servants nervous. Strange birds had been seen in the forest around his stronghold; and now the woods were reputedly haunted as well, by amorphous, ghostlike shapes and faint, dancing lights.

He had decided at last to set up a power-pole as exactly like the waiting Stone as possible, and anchor *that* within an enormous crystal-cluster he had brought from one of his storage rooms and set up in his study. When he drew the power-locus in near enough, it would snap into the power-pole as it had been intended to do at the Bird-Fools' new Heartstone. Devising the plan had taken much delving into his oldest memories, and he had been a little disturbed at how much he had forgotten. Too many times for comfort, he'd been forced to return to his library and search through his oldest books. In the end, he'd taken scraps of memory, scraps of old knowledge, and a great deal of guessing.

The difference between what he intended to do and what the Tayledras would have done was that when it snapped into the waiting vessel *here*, he would be standing between and would be linked to the crystal. When the power-locus and the power-pole merged into one, *he* would be part of them as well.

It was as inventive in its way as anything that Tayledras Adept had tried; he was quite certain of that. He was thoroughly pleased with his own cleverness. Oh, it was dangerous, surely; the mages who had been sacrificed to give the plan life had advised against it even before they knew they were going to be sucked dry of life and power to fuel it.

"You'll be incinerated by that much power," Atus had protested.

"If you aren't incinerated, you'll go mad. No one can be *part* of a Heartstone!" Renthan had told him.

Preadeth had only shaken his head wordlessly, and cast significant looks at the others.

They thought he was insane even to try it—and at that moment, when he caught them exchanging glances and possibly thoughts, he had known who his sacrificial calves were going to be.

They had doubtless been considering revolt—or at least, escape.

Escape would mean they might even consider going to the Tayledras with what they knew.

It was just as well he had another use for them. It would have been a pity to kill them outright and waste all that potential.

Using his subordinates to supply the power instead of himself was the last element he had needed to make the plan reasonable as well as possible. It meant that at the end of the Working, he was still standing and still capable of acting, instead of unconscious and needing days of rest. Even at that, he was exhausted when he was done.

He sank down on his couch and considered calling in a fourth man and draining him as well, but discarded the idea. It would cause enough trouble that he had killed three of his underlings. There were those who might read it as a desperation measure. It was, on the whole, a bad idea to kill anyone other than a slave or one of the lower servants. It made everyone else unhappy—and inclined to think about defection. Unhappy servants were inefficient servants. They should know the taste of the whip—but also know that it was only there in extreme circumstances, and that they could bring that whip onto their own backs by their own actions. He lay back on the soft black velvet of the couch, and considered his next few moves. First—find a reason for the deaths of his underlings that would disturb the others the least. The mages in particular were a touchy lot; they tended to think of themselves as allies rather than underlings. They were given to occasional minor revolt. It would not do to give them a reason for one of those revolts—not now, when he could ill-afford the energy to subdue them.

Should he claim they had died aiding him in some great work? That was a little too close to the truth, and the next time he called for help in magic-working, he might trigger one of those mass defections. He did not, as a rule, lose even one of his assistants, much less three of them. The mages weren't stupid; they might well guess that "aiding" in a great work meant becoming a sacrifice to it.

The deep-red light flooding in from the window was very soothing to his eyes, and eased the pain at his temples, pain caused by nothing more than overstressing himself. Both temples throbbed, there was a place at the base of his skull that felt as if someone was pressing a dull dagger into it, and sharp stabbing pains over each eye whenever he moved his head too quickly. Hard to think, when one was in pain...

But he must think of a way to explain those bodies. He wished he could simply burn them to ash and pretend that he did not know where they had gone. But *that* might only make the others think their colleagues had run off, and if those three had done so, there might be a good reason for the others to follow their example.

Complications, complications. Everything he did was so complicated. Not like the old days, when he didn't have to justify himself to anyone. When he only had to issue orders and know he would be obeyed.

The cowards. If they hadn't been quite so quick to think of conspiring against him he might not have—

Ah. That was the answer. He would have the bodies dragged from his study and hung from the exterior walls in cages, as traitors were. That would be enough. The rest of his underlings should assume that the three had attempted to overcome him and had fallen in the attempt. A good explanation for why *he* was so weary.

He would not even have to *say* anything himself, just look angry. No one would dare ask him. The rumors would fly, but there was no reason for anyone to guess the truth.

He rang for a servant, and feigning greater strength than he had, contorted his face into a mask of suppressed rage and ordered the bodies taken away and displayed in the cages. Then he called for stimulants, food and drink, as he always did after a battle. Sometimes habits were useful things. When he demanded rare meat, red wine, and *ke-phira*, with a body-slave to be waiting in his bed, the servants all assumed that a fight had aroused his blood and his lust.

The servant left and came back with several more; Falconsbane ignored them as they carried the bodies away, lying back on his couch and staring at the shadow-shrouded ceiling. He often did that after a battle of magic, too. When the servant returned at last with the food and drink he had been sent for, he told the man in a flat, expressionless voice to set it down and take himself out. He did his best to look angry, and not tired. The illusion was what mattered right now.

If I were not so pressed, I would manipulate their minds to reinforce the tale that is spreading, he thought, slowly mustering the strength to reach for a cup of drugged wine. *Perhaps I should do so anyway.*

But at that moment, there came a hesitant tap at the door. He started, and cursed his own jangled nerves, then growled, "Yes? What is it?"

If it's nonsense, I'll kill him. If it's a defection, I'll set the wyrsa *on the fool who ran and see if he can outrun and outlast a pack of forty!*

"Sire," came the timid voice of the servant, muffled by the door, "I beg your pardon for disturbing you, but I'm following your orders. You said to let you know immediately if one of those riders—"

He sat up abruptly, exhaustion and pain completely forgotten. "The riders? Open the damned door, you fool! What about the riders?"

The servant edged the door open, nervously. He peered inside, then slid into the room with one eye on his escape route. There was a small box in his hand.

A small box carved of shining black wood.

Falconsbane's eyes went to it as if drawn there; he stood up and strode over to the man, and stood towering over him, his hands twitching at his sides.

"Sire, one of the riders came right up to the gate just as they were—taking out—" The man gulped, his face pasty white, and Falconsbane repressed the urge to strangle him. He simply tried to ease some of the anger out of his face so that the servant would be able to continue.

"Go on," he said, more gently than he wanted to. He cursed his own weakness; if he had been stronger, he could have seized the man's mind and pulled what he wanted right out of it.

"The rider came up and tossed *this* to the Guard Captain, sire," the servant continued, after visibly trying to calm himself. "Then—he was just gone. The Guard Captain brought this straight to me, like you ordered."

"By 'just gone,' do you mean that he rode away?" Falconsbane asked carefully. *Why didn't they call me? Or was there no time? Can those riders move that fast? Why isn't someone chasing them?*

"No, sire, I mean he was *gone*. Like smoke. There, and then not there." The servant seemed convinced, and there was no real reason for him to lie. "The Guard Captain said so. Said he was gone like he'd been conjured and dispersed."

Falconsbane pondered the box in his hand; this was the first real evidence that the riders were the manifestations of magic. Was his unknown enemy—or friend—showing his hand a little more? They could not have gone through a Gate; he would have sensed that. Therefore they could only have been temporary conjurations, given life and form only so long as the mage needed them, or creatures from another plane. Minor demons, perhaps? Those he might not be able to sense unless he was actually looking for them.

Of the "gifts" that had been sent to him, only one was magical—and it was useless. He cast an eye at the lenticular scrying crystal as the servant waited nervously for his response, and snorted a little.

Scrying crystal, indeed. It was an excellent crystal. The clarity was exceptional, the lenticular form ideal for scrying, the size quite perfect for a detailed image to form. The problem was, no matter how he bent his will upon it, it would show only one thing. The view of some remote mountain peak, and halfway up the side of the mountain, a strange and twisted castle that he did not recognize. A snowstorm swirled about the castle when the crystal was moved.

He dismissed the servant, and reached for the wine, drinking it down in one gulp, before he returned to his couch and contemplated the box. Like the other, it was beautifully carved, and about the same size. There was no sign of magic anywhere about it.

Like the other, this one held something.

Nestled in a nest of black velvet padding was a ring. Not just any ring, either—it held no stone, and was not metal, although it was an intricately carved or molded band. Like a wedding ring, exactly like a wedding ring, it was carved with the symbols of harvest, wheat-ears and grapes—except that this ring was made of a shining, cool black substance. He tried, experimentally, to break it, but it was probably of the same stuff as the horse.

In this part of the world, widows sometimes laid aside their wedding bands to wear a black band like this, made of jet, signifying mourning. Was he being warned? But he had no spouse to mourn, and the very last thing he would weep over was the death of his traitorous daughter.

His predilection for black was apparently well known to these riders—or whoever sent them. There had been the rose, the velvet, the horse, and now the ring. And this would certainly gain his attention far quicker than a simple peasants' gold or silver wedding band.

So, was this an invitation to a "wedding"—an alliance?

Or a funeral?

"I don't like this," Darkwind told Firesong unhappily. "I only told you *my* plan because I hoped you'd have another way of handling this, something that wouldn't put anyone into danger like this. Even if it is my plan, I don't like it."

He had intercepted Firesong as soon as the Adept had anchored the proto-Gate for the night. They had walked back to Firesong's *ekele* together, while Darkwind laid bare his thoughts on Falconsbane and what might be done about him.

To his dismay, Firesong had agreed, completely.

"Nor do I care for your plan," Firesong replied, wearily sagging back against the cushions of his couch. "I dislike sending Nyara into peril of this sort. She is a frail prop for all our hopes—and yet there is a certain symmetry in it, in sending her to avenge her own hurts upon her father."

Darkwind snorted. "Symmetry was not what I had in mind," he said. He would have gone farther than that, but at that same moment, Nyara and Skif arrived, summoned by one of Firesong's ever-present *hertasi*. Skif was unarmed as far as Darkwind could see, but Nyara, as always, had Need; the sword at her side was so much a part of her that he couldn't imagine her without it.

He took a moment to examine her with the dispassionate eyes of a stranger and was a little surprised. He'd thought of Nyara as small and slender, maybe even spidery; well, perhaps she was, compared to himself and to Skif. But she certainly carried her sword with authority—and from what he'd seen, she knew how to use it well. And what skill *she* did not possess, the sword could grant to her, if Elspeth was to be believed.

"Sit," Firesong said, before the other two could say anything. "Please. We have something we need to ask you." He waved to one of the hovering *hertasi*, who converged upon the two Outlanders with food and drink.

They took seats; Nyara a little apprehensively, Skif reluctantly. Darkwind didn't blame them. He'd had the feeling that Nyara knew what he'd had in mind all along, from the nebulous ideas that had formed when he asked her to locate Falconsbane's stronghold, to the crystallized plan that had sent him looking for Firesong. Skif probably didn't know what was in Darkwind's mind, but if it required involving Nyara, he was going to be immediately suspicious.

"I'll come straight to the point," Darkwind said. "Before we take this to a larger forum, we need to know something from you." He waited until they had settled a little, then turned to the Changechild. "Nyara, this afternoon I asked you to help me find your father's stronghold on the map. You thought you located approximately where it is, correct?"

She nodded, slowly, accepting a cup of tea from one of the *hertasi*. It was very hard to read her face; long ago she had probably learned how to control her expressions minutely, and that was a habit that was hard to break.

He hated to ask this of her. He hated to put her back where she might *need* that kind of control. "Well, this is a different question, but related. Could *you* trace your way back to it—and if you found it, get into it?"

Skif yelped and started to rise; she shook her head at him, and placed one hand on his knee to calm him. It didn't calm him a bit, but he subsided, looking sharply at both Firesong and Darkwind.

Hmm. Interesting. I thought he was unarmed, but the way his right hand is tensing—he has a knife hidden somewhere near it. If he had a choice, he probably wouldn't be looking daggers at us, he'd be throwing them.

"Yes to both questions," she replied steadily. "My problem with finding Father's hold upon your map was that I could not see the things I know as landmarks. I have a perfect memory for trails, it seems. I never had occasion to use it before I escaped my father, but it is very difficult for me to become lost. I can easily find the stronghold." She licked her lips, showing the tips of her canine teeth, then took a drink before continuing. "I can find it—and having found it, I know many of the odd ways into it. He does not guard all of them, for many are hidden. Some I was taught, but some I found on my own."

"Yes, but will *he* not know of them as well?" Firesong asked gently. "I would not send you into a trap, dear child. Candidly, that would not serve either of us."

Her lips curved in a faint smile. "I do not think there will be a trap. Since I am only interested in fleeing from him—he thinks—I suspect that the last thing he would look for me to do is return. The ways that I would take inside will be those that only I know, or those that I think he will not bother to trap."

:I can hide her some, if that's your next question,: Need said. *:I can hold a "reflective" illusion on her, the kind that makes her look like part of the landscape to Mage-Sight. More importantly, while I'm doing that, I can hide myself as well. Watch.:*

At that instant, Need ceased to exist, from the point of view of Darkwind's Mage-Sight. She was nothing more sinister to ordinary sight than an ordinary broadsword, and to Mage-Sight, she and Nyara did not exist, and Skif sat alone on the couch.

Then Nyara was "back," all in an instant, and the sword with her.

"Good. Very good," Firesong said, leaning forward a bit, his voice warm with approval. "Well, then, you must know that we have a plan, but the one in greatest danger will be you, Nyara. That is a great burden to be placed upon you, and no one will fault you if you say no."

She shook her head, but not, Darkwind sensed, in denial. "I have been partially to blame for much harm that has come to you," she said. "I feel that I owe some recompense."

:It's not like she's going to do this alone,: Need added dryly. *:I've handled what Falconsbane can throw before. Hmph. Maybe if he throws the right stuff at us this time, I can transmute it and take off a little more of what he did to her.:*

"I will not count upon that," Nyara told her blade, and Darkwind thought he detected a tone of friendly chiding in her voice. "I will not even think of it. It serves little purpose, after all. If you can, I shall be grateful, but do not put yourself into jeopardy by an attempt."

Need couldn't shrug, but Darkwind got the impression she had. *:At any rate, as Nyara and Skif can tell you, I took on this form because there are times when one person can do what an army couldn't. I'm no expert on Falconsbane, but I don't think the odds are any worse now than they were back when I froze myself into this blade.:*

Darkwind looked at Skif, who growled, but shrugged. "She's her own woman," he replied unhappily. "If I tried to make her change her mind, I wouldn't be doing either of us any good. She wants to go through with this—I'll do what I can to help."

Darkwind raised an eyebrow skeptically. Skif grimaced.

"I don't *like* it," he admitted. "I'm scared to death for her, and if I could take her place I would. I won't pretend otherwise. But let's just say I learned how stupid it is to try and stop someone from doing something they have to do. It's even more stupid if you care about them."

Darkwind read the *look* Skif gave both of them, however. If Nyara came to any harm at all, Skif would personally collect the damages due.

"More than good!" Firesong applauded. "Well, then, if Nyara is agreed, I think it is time that we took the idea to the rest. We will discover if anyone can knock holes in this plan—or make it safer in any way."

The gathering in the Council Oak clearing held only part of the usual gathering. Both gryphons, Nyara, Skif, Firesong, Wintermoon, the Companions, Elspeth—and Darkwind himself. No other mages; this would not be a plan that required more mages than they had right here. Starblade and Kethra were back to recovering; Iceshadow and Nightjewel were conserving their strength. And they added no more fighters than Skif and Wintermoon, either. As Need had said, there were times when one—or a handful—could do what an army could not.

Firesong had lost a great deal of his jauntiness in the past few days, and he had put aside his elaborate costumes in favor of simple, flowing clothing like any other mage wore. He could hardly hide the flamboyant bondbird that perched on his shoulder, but other than that, and his incredible beauty, there was nothing that set him apart from the other mages in k'Sheyna.

"Here is the situation as it stands," Firesong began. Using a handful of stones and a bit of string, he began laying out something that looked rather like a very simple spiderweb. "If I had been looking for this earlier, I might have seen it being built—but it has the feeling of something assembled with haste, and we may be able to take advantage of that."

"What is it?" Darkwind was baffled. "I assume Falconsbane has something to do with this, whatever it is."

Firesong flushed, the first time Darkwind had ever seen him truly embarrassed. "Pardon. I forgot that none of you have been working with me upon this. The enemy wants to capture the proto-Gate; to that end he has constructed this web of power-points and interconnecting lines about his stronghold. If you look in the direction of his stronghold with FarSight and Mage-Sight, you will see it."

Treyvan examined the model, and growled. "Thisss isss a new thing, isss it not?"

Firesong shook his head. "Only new to Falconsbane. I have seen this sort of construction before, and it isn't half as effective as those who use it think. It has a vulnerability, a severe one. If the connections were weakened all about the edge so that they might snap beneath a good shock, he likely would not note the weakening. And *if* they snapped, the power would backlash against him in some profound ways."

"What kind of ways?" Wintermoon wanted to know. "Something grievous, I hope."

Firesong smiled faintly. "If he was not prepared with a way to ground it or to escape, he would likely be cast into the void between the Gates— as if he entered a Gate and both the Gate and the terminus were then destroyed. That is because of the way he has set up the tensions among his power-poles and his center. Great concentrations of power warp the world-space as Gates do."

Darkwind shuddered; he had once had a glimpse of that void. He would prefer not to see it again. "That's not a fate I would wish on anyone," he said.

"Not even Falconsbane?" Elspeth asked. "I can think of one or two others I would like to see contemplating their deeds for all eternity!"

Firesong continued, as if they had not interrupted him. "Any shock to him would snap these threads of power once they were weakened— that would be the best way, in fact. A shock at the center will have more effect than one at an edge. But the weakening—that would have to be done quickly, so that he did not have a chance to notice what was being done." He looked up into the gryphons' faces, expectantly.

Treyvan blinked slowly, his eyes distant. "You rrrequirrre ssswiftly trraveling magesss," he said. "And at the sssame time, you rrrequirrre sssomeone to infiltrrrate the beassst'sss home."

Firesong nodded, and waited.

"The ssswift onesss mussst be usss, I think," Treyvan continued. "And the otherrr—Nyarrra."

"If you are willing, yes," Darkwind said awkwardly. "I hate to ask you, but if Falconsbane gains control of the proto-Gate, he'll gain an enormous amount of power. It would be the kind of power that normally goes to establish and maintain an entire Vale; protections, Heartstones, Vale-sculpting, and all."

"He could dessstrroy usss all with a thought," Hydona replied flatly. "He mussst not have that powerrr."

"Bring the little ones here," Darkwind urged. "With the Heartstone gone, there's no longer a danger to them in staying here."

Hydona nodded, but Darkwind sensed that she had something else on her mind. She looked to her mate.

After a moment of wordless exchange, Treyvan sighed. "We wisssh sssomething in return," he said.

"What?" Firesong asked. "If it is in our power—"

"It isss. We requirrre a pricsssse. We want k'Sheyna to not dissolve the Vale when you leave. To give it to usss, Veil, shieldsss, and all." Treyvan tucked his wings closer in to his body. "We had planned to take it oncsssse you left, but—"

"But if you leave it asss it isss, it will be betterrr forr ourrr new *Kla'hessshey'messserin,*" Hydona interrupted. "We might asss well brrring it into clearrr sky, *asshkeyana.*"

Darkwind blinked, trying to identify the two words they had just used. They sounded like Tayledras, but weren't. They weren't Shin'a'in, either.

"Kaled'a'in?" exclaimed Firesong, as he brought his head up, eyes wide with startlement.

Treyvan sighed, as Hydona nodded firmly.

Now that Darkwind knew the tongue, he could translate the words. The second was simply an endearment; "beloved." But the first—it was complicated. The strictest translation would have been "family," or "clan," except that it implied a family made of those who not only were not related by blood—but who might not even be of the same species.

Once again, Firesong beat him to identification. "Pledged-clan?" he exclaimed again. "You're—you can't be Clan k'Leshya!"

Wintermoon quite fell off his seat. "The Lost Ones? The Lost Clan?" he exclaimed, his eyes going so wide with surprise Darkwind was afraid he was going to sprain something. "The Spirit Clan? I thought—but— they were nothing but legend!"

Treyvan's beak gaped in a gryphonic smile. "But we arrre legend, arrre we not? Orrr we werrre, to you."

Elspeth, Skif, and Nyara were looking completely bewildered, as well they might. As Firesong stared and Wintermoon picked himself back up, Darkwind essayed a hasty explanation.

"At the time of the Mage Wars, a group of Kaled'a'in from several clans, a group of outClansmen, and some of the nonhumans all formed a kind of—of—brotherhood, I suppose. They called themselves—"

"*Kena Lessshya'nay,* in the Tongue," Hydona supplied. "It meansss 'clan bound by ssspirit.' Sssssomething like yourrr Heraldsss, but without Companionsss. *Lessshya'nay* could not join, they could only be chosssssen, then agrrreed upon by thrrree morre. Ourrr leaderrrsss werrre two. The great Black Gryphon Ssskandrrranon, and the *kesss-tra'cherrrn,* Amberrdrrrake."

Treyvan chuckled. "Though neitherrr everrr *admitted* to being leaderrr of anything!"

"The Spirit Clan supposedly held many of Urtho's mages, all of the gryphons and *hertasi, kyree, tervardi* and *dyheli,* and a fair number of the Kaled'a'in shamans and Healers," Firesong said to the three Outlanders, leaning forward so that they could hear him. Then he turned to the gryphons, watching them intently. "But during the evacuation of the stronghold, you disappeared."

Treyvan shook his massive head. "No. Herrre isss what happened. We did not ussse the Gatesss the lessser magesss crrreated to evacuate. We had been sssent away—sssupposssedly to find a rrrefuge forrr the rrrest of you and a mysssterriousss weapon. Ssso we werrre not *in* Urrtho'sss landsss when the evacuation came. Insssstead of sssouth or easst, we had gone wesssst, we had with usss a Gate made by Urrtho—hisss verry own Grrreat Gate, anchorrred on a wagon. We ussssed it while you evacuated to brrring the rrrest of *ourr* folk to ourrr rrretrrreat in the wilderrrnessss. But therrre wasss not time to take everrryone thrrrough it—only *Lesssshya'nay.* The ressst of you had to take what Gatesss werrre nearrresssst you."

"And the dessstrrruction of the Ssstrrronghold thrrrew you farrrtherrr than intended. We thought you had perrrisshed," Hydona continued. Then she, too, gaped her beak in a grin. "Imagine ourrr surrrprrrissse to find the legendarrry *Kena Trrrevasho, Kena Sheynarsa,* and the rrresst still in exisssstence. To you, we arrre the Losst Onesss. But to usss, you arrre!"

Firesong shook his head, bemusedly. "Quite amazing. And you still speak the Mother Tongue!"

"Not quite purrrrely, I expect," Treyvan admitted. "But we have not had the prrresssuresss of the Ssstar-Borrrn to sshape our language differrrently. Sssshe doess not meddle ssso much with usss asss with you."

"Thisss all can wait, I think," Hydona interrupted firmly. "What we need to tell you issss thisss. Sssimply—you knew, Darrrkwind, that we werrre forrrerrrunnerrrsss. Of ourrr kind, you thought. Well, morrre of ourrr people arrre coming, and not jussst 'ourrr' kind."

Darkwind shook his head, not quite able to figure out what she meant.

"Not just gryphons, you mean?" Firesong said.

"Gryphonsssss, humanssss, sssome *hertasssi.* And sssoon." Treyvan turned to look at Darkwind. "When k'Sheyna began itsss trrroubleesss, we called them. You rrrecall the booksssshelvesss you helped hang? They werrre not meant forrr us. We knew that thisss place would ssshelterrr usss well, and knew you needed help and would not asssk for it—asss Ssskandranon oft sssaid, 'it isss eassier to beg parrrdon than get perrrmisssion.' Sssince they did not wisssh to ssstir thingsss up by sssetting too many Gatesss, they have been coming acrosss countrrry."

Darkwind had the vague feeling that he should have been outraged by this. He wasn't, but he knew plenty in the Clan who would be. Treyvan, on the other hand, did not look in the least contrite.

"But now, we need magesss, ssswift-trrraveling magesss. Immediately." He turned his attention to Firesong, who nodded, then back to Darkwind. "With yourrr perrrmisssion, I shall ussse the lessser Gate in the rrruinsss and the powerrr of the node to meet *their* Gate, and brrring them herrre in time to help. But for that help, we wisssh the Vale. Intact."

"I can't promise—" Darkwind began helplessly. Firesong interrupted him.

"Is there any reason why k'Sheyna *can't* give them the Vale?" he asked. "Any reason at all?"

The only reason Darkwind could think of was, "because we've never done it before," and that did not seem particularly adequate. Nor did he feel that this would be a true breach of Tayledras territoriality. After all, these people—*beings*—*were* Tayledras. Sort of.

"Not that I can think of," he admitted. He licked his lips thoughtfully. "All we know of the Spirit Clan is out of legend—and by knowing you two," he told the gryphons.

"Leaving a Vale intact—that halves what little power we still possess. And it leaves you with a stronghold. What will we be leaving it to?"

"A Clan like any otherrr," Hydona replied carefully. "A Clan with perrrhapsss only one thing you do not have, and that isss the trrrained *kessstra'cherrrn* crraft. But you have bondbirrrdsss that we do not. We have ourrr lazy folk, ourrr ssstupid folk, ourrr occasssional trrroublemakerrr. I think that no one lazy, at leassst, is likely to make the jourrrney—the ssstupid would likely not surrrvive it—and the trroublemakerrr—" she bobbed her head in a gryphonic shrug. "Therrre will alwaysss be thossse. The humansss, at leassst, *are* Clansssfolk. We will take any oathsss you rrrrequirrre, and willingly, to have the Vale."

"I say that this is aid we dare not reject," Wintermoon said firmly, surprising his brother. "Whatever the cost, ridding us of Falconsbane is worth it."

"Darkwind, I think that anything you, your brother, and I together supported, the Elders would agree to," Firesong told him. "But let's take the advice of the Black Gryphon—that it is easier to beg pardon than gain permission—and go with Treyvan to bring his people through tonight."

Darkwind wavered for a moment, doubtfully. He would be helping to bring an army into the ragged remains of his own people. Would he destroy them? Or would he save them?

He looked into Treyvan's soft-edged raptor eyes, and saw there the friend, the surrogate parent, the ever-present, gentle guide.

The one who had put up with having his feathers pulled by a rambunctious small boy—and his crest snatched by a wayward bondbird.

He smiled, and nodded firmly. "Let's do it."

2 3

The Vale was full of sunlight and gryphons. Elspeth had never seen anything like it, and the sight took her breath away. Everywhere she looked, there was a gryphon—bathing in a pool, lying along a massive branch or the roof of an *ekele*, sunbathing on the cliffs around the Vale.

Gryphons with colors and markings like peregrines or forestgyres, cooperihawks or goshawks. Gryphons in solid colors of gray, gold, rusty-red. Gryphons with accipiter builds, and gryphons as slim as the lightest of falcons. The only markings they all had in common were patently artificial; the final arm's length or so of their first six primaries on each wing were white for four hand-spans, then red for another four hand-spans to the tips. Every time a gryphon moved a wing, the flash of red and white caught the eye like a flash of bright light.

And they had arrived hungry. Fortunately, Treyvan and Hydona had explained to all their fellow flyers just what the bondbirds were and that they were *not* to be eaten. Otherwise there might have been true havoc by now, and a number of damaged Hawkbrothers *and* gryphons. The poor little *hertasi* had worked themselves to exhaustion, finding enough to feed all of them, and probably enjoyed every moment of their work. Hydona had promised that after this, they would hunt their own food.

She thought she had never seen *anything* to match this, not even when the full complement of Heralds and Companions turned out for her mother's wedding. She would much rather look at the gryphons disporting themselves than at the chaos of arguing Clansmen. She would much rather be doing something about Falconsbane or the Heartstone than either...

She shifted impatiently, and tried to concentrate on the meeting below her. The Council Oak clearing was full and overflowing with every Tayledras who could walk, and all of the newcomers—plus Skif and Nyara, up at the front, but she could scarcely see them past the press of bodies. The people who came with the gryphons had been less of a shock than the gryphons themselves; so much like both the Tayledras and the Shin'a'in that she couldn't tell any differences, except in speech and a certain uniformity of dress. They had arrived through the Gate bringing with them curious land-boats; like shallow-draft barges, but with pointed prows and places for rudders. These barges were roofed over and equipped with shutters, fitted up inside for sleeping and storage. Luggage, boxes, and bales of goods were piled upon the roofs and lashed down, and they floated above the ground at about knee-height.

Elspeth had thought her eyes were going to pop out of her head when *those* came through the Veil. She was secretly relieved to find that the Tayledras were equally astonished by the "floating barges;" it made her feel less like a country cousin. Forsaking his place with the Elders, Iceshadow had latched onto one of the mage-pilots of the peculiar constructions, and both of them were whispering to each other even now, ignoring the arguments. She had the feeling that they were planning to spend those waking moments not devoted to moving the proto-Gate to explanations of how the barges were enchanted and worked, and how Heartstones were created and functioned.

The full Clan immediately went into session on demand of a minority of Tayledras who were outraged over this violation of their territory. Wintermoon turned out, surprisingly enough, to be the steadiest voice of reason, reminding the contenders, over and over, that these "Outlanders" *were* Tayledras—or rather, the Hawkbrothers were Kaled'a'in, and that the coming of those of their own blood could hardly be counted as invasion. Elspeth wished that she could have left him to this thankless task, but she was a member of the Clan, and she had to be there, like every other member of the Clan.

There are several other things my time could be spent more profitably on. Wintermoon could probably wear them down into consent within a day or two, with sheer persistence, with or without her help. *I wish they'd simply give up and let the rest of us deal with them later, after things have been settled. Dear gods, this is like having an argument over precedence on the eve of a battle!*

She had been here since sunrise, perched on a shoulder-high tree branch at the back of the mob, and she hadn't heard any variation in the arguments. She stifled a yawn and looked down, catching the amused eyes of Firesong and his new friend, and the shrug of the former.

Firesong was particularly taken by a young man who was supposed to be a *kestra'chern*, whatever that was, and who had offered to teach him some of the craft when there was time. "I think you would have a talent for it," Silverfox had said, with a hint of some kind of innuendo that *she* couldn't read. "You are a Healing Adept, after all—it would be a useful skill to have."

Well, that meant that Firesong was not going to be thinking about Darkwind. Not with the lithe and graceful Silverfox, he of the knowing blue eyes and ankle-length ebony hair, giving silent invitations Firesong seemed to find irresistible. And that was just fine with her.

That left one less thing for both Darkwind and herself to worry about, and they certainly had enough on their hands right now. Even without the contention within the Clan.

A stir of activity near the Elders' seats caught her eye; she was too far away to see what was going on, but there was certainly *something* happening besides the dreary old arguments.

She sent a silent inquiry to Gwena, who was somewhere on the edge of the clearing, but her Companion sent back a wordless negative. Gwena couldn't see anything either.

She narrowed her eyes and peered carefully through the screening of branches and bodies. There was someone coming into the Council Oak clearing from outside—

No, *lots* of someones!

She craned her neck to see, bracing her hands against the branch, and jumped when someone grabbed her wrist. She looked down to find Darkwind tugging her, indicating she should jump down into his arms. "They are calling for us," he said. "The Shin'a'in have arrived."

The Shin'a'in? What did *they* have to do with this mess?

But she obeyed; she jumped and he caught her waist, easing her to the ground with that carefully controlled strength that she never noticed until he did something like this. Together they wound their way through the crowd to the front, where the Elders sat.

As they broke through the final group of Tayledras screening her from the Elders' circle, she stifled a start of surprise. There was old Kra'heera—but with him were six other Shin'a'in—Shin'a'in of a kind she had seen only twice before. Shin'a'in of the kind called "Swordsworn."

They crowded in behind Kra'heera, black-clad, some veiled, some not, leading night-black horses. And the veiled ones seemed to shimmer with power, as if they were not quite of this world.

:So we are not,: said a voice in her head, and she stifled another start. One set of ice-blue eyes over a black veil caught her attention; one of those eyes winked, slowly, and deliberately. *:Be at peace, little sister-in-power, student of my student.:*

"Of course we have known of the coming of the Kaled'a'in," Kra'heera was saying impatiently. The faces of the Elders remained inscrutable, but there was no doubting the surprise and consternation in the expressions of those who had been arguing against permitting the Kaled'a'in to remain. "*She* told us they were coming, and bid us find a place for them on the Plains, if they could not find one here, or chose not to dwell here. We did not expect them to come so soon, or we would have told you long before they arrived." He turned to fix one of the Kaled'a'in spokesmen with an acidic glare. "You were not *supposed* to arrive until midsummer!"

The Kaled'a'in shrugged. "So it goes."

"*She* told you?" one of the most ardent opponents said to Kra'heera, feebly.

"We are here to stand as proof of Her word," one of the veiled ones said, in a strange voice that sounded as if it was coming from the bottom of a well. "Although we are not wont to appear to any save our own. She sent us to prove to you doubters that She approves. Unless you choose to doubt us as well."

The Tayledras in question paled, and shook his head. Kra'heera snorted, and turned back to the Council. "We have been doing what we can, within the limits of Her decree and our own resources, to give you help with your troubles," he told them, sharply. "So, I think it little enough to grant *our brothers* their request, given that they will help us all *deal* with this Great Beast, our enemy! And so, too, does *She* think!"

Skif, who was standing near Starblade with Nyara at his hand, blinked, as if he had suddenly realized something. "Now I know where I saw you!" he said to one of the black-clad Shin'a'in. "Not just at the ruins—you were out in the forest, when we were hunting for Nyara!"

The Shin'a'in shrugged. "Some of us," she said. "Two or three. Keeping an eye on our younger sister, as *She* asked us to, so that we could vouch for her to you as well. The rest—" she chuckled. "The rest of us have been sending the Falconsbane little trinkets, and harassing his borders, to keep his mind puzzling over things with no meaning, and to distract him from *your* doings as much as we could."

:*It is no coincidence that we are black riders upon black horses, little sister,*: said the voice in her head again. :*The Falconsbane knows of your enemy to the north and east—knows that you and yours are white riders. We simply counterfeited something he would expect if that enemy of yours were courting or challenging him; gave him something to think upon, a dangling carrot, as it were, with as many misdirections as we could manage.*:

Elspeth stuffed her hand in her mouth to keep from giggling with a kind of giddy relief. The *Shin'a'in* had been teasing and tormenting Falconsbane. No wonder they'd been able to do as much as they had been! No wonder it seemed as if Falconsbane's attention was divided! She wondered why they'd been doing this, but whys didn't really matter at the moment, only that they had.

She turned her attention back to the Council meeting, but after that, there was very little debate—and a great deal of constructive planning.

* * *

The plan was set; they were about to put it into motion. While most of the gryphons frolicked in the Vale, and barbarically beautiful Kaled'a'in occupied the attentions of most of k'Sheyna, the Council of Elders had already listened to and given consent to what the little "war council" had put together. Surely Selenay would have had a fit if she'd known what her daughter's part in this was to be. Thank all the gods that Gwena had decided to keep discreetly silent on the subject, telling Rolan only that Elspeth's studies "continued."

Well—they did. Sort of.

The gryphons—those dozen or so of the wing of thirty that were full mages, at any rate—were going to solve one problem for them. With seven pairs making the rounds of Falconsbane's web of power, the work of weakening his power-threads should be done between sunset and sunrise, easily. Under the cover of darkness, they were less likely to be spotted from below.

Nyara was going to be the arrow striking for Falconsbane's heart. That was a task Elspeth did not envy her, and she could not imagine how the Changechild managed to be so calm about it. Perhaps it was Need's steadying effect. Perhaps it was because she knew that if *she* betrayed any nervousness, Skif would probably fall to pieces.

Meanwhile, as Nyara crept closer and closer to her father's stronghold, she and Darkwind got to play target to distract him, if they could. The Shin'a'in could no longer play that role; he had started to look for them, and had laid traps for them that would catch them. They had no magic to disarm those traps, not as Darkwind and Elspeth had. The *leshya'e Kal'enedral* would be occupied in another way; helping Kra'heera and Kethra, confusing Falconsbane's FarSight and FarVision spells with their shamanic magic, so that he would not See the newcomers to the Vale, and the special energies of all the new mages there. That was vital to their purposes; if Falconsbane had any idea who and what had arrived to augment the powers of k'Sheyna, he would not hesitate, he would throw everything at them that he had, knowing their massed power could take him. Even with the help of the Kaled'a'in, there was no one in all of the new Council who thought the Vale and the three peoples there would survive that unscathed.

So Darkwind and Elspeth were on their own in supplying a needed distraction. Without distractions, Falconsbane might well notice the gryphons, Nyara, or both. If he noticed them—

She shuddered. Better not to think about it.

With Need's help, she had fashioned a blade that would counterfeit Need at a distance. It had no real power whatsoever—like the sword meant to select the rulers of Rethwellan, *all* it did was burn mage-energy in a spectacular fashion, radiating power to anyone with Mage-Sight. Gwena would supply the energy for that blade. Elspeth would go imperfectly shielded, at least on the surface, looking as ill-trained as possible. Darkwind would simply be himself. That alone should bring Falconsbane down on them.

They would ride north and west, skirting the edge of what was probably Falconsbane's territory, as if they were heading in search of something. Any time they met with one of the enemy's traps, they would destroy it. Any time they found one of his power-sinks, they would drain it. Meanwhile Firesong and the Kaled'a'in mages would be moving the proto-Gate, but with none of the speed they were capable of.

Darkwind hoped that Falconsbane would assume the obvious—that they were trying to distract him from diverting the proto-Gate—and therefore he would not look for something *else* they were distracting him from.

"I really ought to be used to playing target by now," she said, as she tightened Gwena's girth and prepared to ride out into the snow and cold with Darkwind. They looked like a pair of fancy-dress Heralds, the two of them; he wore winter scout gear, which was just as white as any Herald's uniform, and she had *finally* pried her Whites out of the grip of the disapproving *hertasi*. Gwena was champing at her nonexistent bit, ready to go—and Darkwind was going to be riding Firesong's very dear friend, the *dyheli*-mage, Brytha.

What was even more amazing than a *dyheli*-mage, was the fact that Brytha had instantly volunteered for this, before Darkwind could ask any of the other stags to carry him.

:*I am not much of mage,:* Brytha had said, in the stilted thought-forms of his kind. :*I channel power, like Companion. I channel to you; you are less tired, then.:*

No one could deny the truth of that; any power that could be *given* to Darkwind without effort on his part increased his stamina tremendously. But now Elspeth knew why Brytha was white—and why Firesong could accomplish some of the incredible things he'd already done. With that extra reserve of power available, one Healing Adept could act like two, or even three.

That was the edge they had needed to turn this from suicidal to merely horribly dangerous, in Elspeth's opinion. Or at least, to less suicidal.

"I suppose you should be used to being a target, in those 'here I am, please, shoot me,' uniforms you wear," he replied with a grin, carefully tightening Brytha's girth.

"Not you, too," she complained. "Kero calls them the 'oh, shoot me now' uniforms. There are perfectly good reasons why we wear white!"

"I like you better in colors," he said simply and reached out to touch her hand, briefly but gently. "They suit your quiet beauty. White only makes you look remote. An ice-princess. Your spirit is brighter even than my best scarlet."

She flushed and hung her head to cover it. "Thank you," she replied carefully. Slowly, she was learning to accept his compliments without any of the doubt she'd have had if they had come from anyone else. And for a moment, she was back in his *ekele* in memory, surrounded by color and soft silk, warmth and admiration.

Then she shook off the memory. For now, all that was important was the task ahead of them. And for that task, she could not have asked for a better partner than the one she had now. Should they come out of this well enough, they would celebrate in the *ekele* again, in a similar way.

She mounted up; he followed a moment later, and looked into her eyes. She nodded, and he took the lead, riding out through the Veil and into the quiet cold and the snow.

The gauntlet was cast. There was no going back now.

Treyvan launched himself into the wind, his wings spreading wide to catch the updraft, spiraling higher above the Vale with every wingbeat. Behind and below him, Hydona echoed his launch, and once she reached height, the others followed. It was good to see other gryphons taking to the air again; better still to know that they were here to stay. Counting himself and Hydona, there were thirty-two gryphons in the Vale now, a full wing. The little ones would have many teachers, and doubtless there would be playmates for them before too long. The gryphons who had volunteered for this settlement were all paired, and the balmy temperatures of the Vale had sent several of the pairs into pre-courting. It should be very interesting to see the effect on the Tayledras if they had not moved by the time the true courting began...

But that was for later; now there was a job to be done.

They all knew what they were to do. Seven were to go to the south, seven to the north. The web of power gleamed to their inner sight, seen from far above the world; a construction of entirely artificial lines of energy and their anchors, overlaying the natural ley-lines and often conflicting with them. Not exactly a web in shape, only the power-poles were connecting-points. That was what held the whole construction stable—it was *all* that held the whole construction stable.

That would be to their benefit and Falconsbane's detriment. Anything that ran counter to the earth's own ways was subject to extreme stress. Maintaining this web would be much like flying against a headwind. The moment the pressure was released, the entire construction would implode.

The swiftest of the gryphons, two of nearly pure gyrfalcon lineage, would take the farthest points on the web—those two were *not* Treyvan and Hydona, but a much younger pair, Reaycha and Talsheena. Treyvan and Hydona, as senior mages, would take the nearest points, but they would take more of them, making up in work what they were not putting into flight time. All had agreed that this was the fairest way of apportioning the work; since the time of Skandranon, nothing was decreed within a gryphon wing without a majority consenting to it.

The two older gryphons held the middle heights, providing a marker point for the others to use to orient themselves. It was a moonless night, and on such nights, despite mage-enhanced night-sight, distances were often deceptive.

The first pair gained height above Treyvan and his mate, and shot off, barely visible against the swiftly darkening sky, heading southwest and northwest. Then the second pair gained altitude and took to the sky-trail—then the third—

Finally, only he and Hydona were left, gliding in lazy circles on the Vale-generated thermal. The sky was entirely dark now, with wisps of cloud occluding the stars, and a crisp breeze coming up from below. A good night for a flight.

:*Well, my fine-crested lover,*: she said, her mind-voice a warm purring in the back of his mind, :*are you prepared to enchant me with some fancy flying?*:

:*Ever so, my love,*: he replied, and drove his wings in powerful beats that sent him surging upward and outward, as she did the same. He glanced at her, and felt the familiar warmth of love and lust heating him as she showed her strength and beauty, angling against the wind. :*We shall meet at dawn!*:

* * *

Nyara also left at sunset, riding *dyheli*-back. She had not expected that boon, but the *dyheli* themselves had insisted on it. Her partner for this first part of the journey, until the moment that she *must* go on afoot, was a young female, Lareen. Fresh and strong, she promised laughingly that *she* could keep her rider well out of any trouble by strength and speed alone. That suited Nyara perfectly; she had no wish for any kind of a confrontation—it would be far better to reach the borders of Falconsbane's territory without anyone ever getting so much as a glimpse of her.

She had thought that this would be the worst moment of the journey, for Skif had been stiff and silent all during the Council meeting, and she feared he would remain so during the ride. She had not been looking forward to spending what might be their last hours together aching with the weight of his disapproval.

But instead, once the meeting was over, he had taken her aside where no one could overhear them. Except for Need, of course, for the sword had not left her side except for sleep; but the sword had remained silent, and he had ignored the blade entirely.

"Nyara," he had begun, then faltered for a moment, as he looked into her eyes and gripped her shoulders with hands that shook with tension. His usually expressive face had been so full of anxiety that it had become a kind of mask.

She had remained silent, unsure of what to say, only watching him steadfastly. Should she break the silence? Or would that only make things worse?

He had stared at her as if he thought she would vanish or flee with the first word. "Nyara, you know I don't like what they're asking you to do," he said, finally. His voice was hoarse, as if he were forcing the words out over some kind of internal barrier.

She had stared deeply into his eyes, dark with emotions she could not read, and fear (which she could), and nodded slowly, still holding her peace.

"But I also *won't* deny the fact that—that you have a right to do anything you want, and you're *capable* of doing it. And I won't deny you the chance to do what you think is right, what you have to do. You're your own person, and if I tried to stop you, tried to manipulate you by telling you I love you, which I do, absolutely, completely—" He shook his head with a helpless desperation, his eyes never once leaving hers, a frantic plea for understanding in his gaze. "I won't do that to you, I won't manipulate you. Please, understand, I *don't* like this, but I won't stop you, because I know it's something you have to do."

She had reached up to touch his cheek gently, a lump born of mingled emotions briefly stopping her voice. Then she had smiled and said lightly, "But I think you have also learned the futility of trying to stop someone who is set on a course from dealing with Elspeth. Yes?"

Her attempt at lightening the mood had worked. He had growled a little, but a tiny smile crept onto his lips, and a little of the worry eased from his face. "Yes. Minx. You *would* remind me of that, wouldn't you?"

She had sighed as he relaxed his grip on her shoulders and had moved forward so that he could hold her—which is what *she* had wanted him to do, with equal desperation, ever since this morning.

For a long time they simply stood together, holding each other, taking comfort from each other's warmth and nearness. "I think what I hate the most is not what you're doing, but that I can't be with you," he had said, finally, his arms tightening around her. "I feel so damned helpless. I hate feeling helpless."

"We all hate feeling helpless," she had reminded him. Well, so they did, and she was not feeling less helpless than he, though for different reasons.

Her eyes adjusted to the growing darkness as they rode out into the snow, following, for a while, the tracks of Darkwind and Elspeth. The clean, cold air felt very good on her face; in fact, if their situation had not been so tense, she would have enjoyed this. She had discovered out in her tower that she enjoyed the winter, even with all the hardships she had endured once the weather had turned cold. Now she was adequately clothed for winter in Tayledras scout gear; now she was riding upon the back of a creature built for striding through snow, rather than forcing her own way through the drifts. This was winter taken with pure pleasure.

But tension had her stomach in such sour knots that she had not been able to eat much; her back and shoulders were knotted with anxiety, and she was terribly aware of the burden of the sword at her side and what it meant. Need was cloaking her, presumably, as well as itself, but she absolutely required that cloaking, and she would require every bit of her mentor's skill and learning to come through this alive.

The alarms and traps should not react to me, she told herself, once again. *Father has been otherwise occupied. In no way would he ever expect me to return to him of my own will after attacking him and betraying him. Surely he will not have tampered with the defenses since I left him last. He has been beset by the Shin'a'in, launching his own attacks—when has he had time to reset them? Once I leave Skif and Wintermoon at the border, there should be no difficulty in getting within the territory or the stronghold—*

—so why am I as frightened as a rabbit walking into the den of a Changelion?

She shivered, though not with cold, and touched the hilt of the sword unconsciously.

:I'm here, little one,: the sword said calmly. *:I'm screening us both for all I'm worth. You can do this; I trained you, and I know.:*

Some of the sword's calm confidence seeped into her own soul and eased the cramps in muscles and stomach. There was no point in getting so knotted up that she would accomplish nothing, after all. No point in worrying until it was time to worry.

The trail widened at that point, and Skif rode up beside her; she turned to smile at him, but it was so dark that although she could see his face, she doubted that he could see hers.

:We should talk like this, Wintermoon says,: came his mind-voice deep inside her head. Although she had never heard it, she knew it for his and it gave her unexpected comfort, like feeling his hand holding and steadying her. *:I'm not—very good at it, I should warn you. Have to be this close to you.:*

:I will—try,: she replied the same way, stumbling a little despite her practice with Need. Her father had never spoken mind-to-mind with her; he had only used his mind to coerce her, and to hurt her.

:You'd like Valdemar, I think,: he said unexpectedly. *:Especially the hills in the south. They're very beautiful in the winter. You'd probably like the Forest of Sorrows, too; that's way in the north. There are mountains up there so tall that some of them have never been climbed.:*

She Saw the image of the mountains, and the forest at their feet, in his mind; saw it drowsing in the heat of summer, alive with birds in the spring, cloaked in flame in the fall, and sleeping beneath a blanket of snow in winter. *:Why so sad a name?:* she asked.

:Oh—that's because of Vanyel,: he replied, and told her the tale, embellished with images out of his own experiences and imagination. That tale led to another—and another—and soon it was midnight and time to stop for a bit of a rest and a chance to check their bearings against the stars.

Wintermoon oriented himself; she and Skif dismounted and walked a short distance. *:This—being a Herald, I do not understand,:* she told him, as he held her within the warmth of his arms and coat, and they waited for

Wintermoon's two bondbirds to report with their findings.

:Sometimes I don't understand it either,: he admitted. *:I suppose the closest I can come is to say that it's something I have to do—just as what we're doing now is something you have to do. But what I do is not because of hate, or anger, or the feeling that I owe it to anyone.:*

She moved her cheek against his chest and closed her eyes. *:Then why?:* she asked simply, longing, suddenly, to understand.

:Would it sound entirely stupid to say that it was out of love?: he asked. *:That's not the whole of it; that's not even the largest part, but it's the start.:*

She waited, patiently, for the rest of the answer, and it came, in bits and pieces. They were pieces that did not yet fall together to make a whole, but like the pieces of a mirror they reflected bits of *him* that made her see him a little more clearly. When one assembled a broken mirror, one could still discern an image…

Some of his reason was gratitude—the Heralds had literally saved his life and given him something like a real family. That revelation made her feel kinship and a bitter envy; she had known only brief affection and never any sense of real family. She had, now and again, spied upon the lesser creatures of her father's stronghold with wonder and jealousy. She had seen fathers who caressed their children with nothing ever coming of those caresses but care; she had seen children greeting their fathers with joy and not fear. And she had seen that strange and wondrous creature, a mother… a creature that could and would die to save the offspring she had given life to. A creature that gave life and love without asking for anything other than love in return—no matter what the child became, no matter what darkness it turned to.

Skif had not known a mother like that either; in that much, they were kin.

Yet he received that kind of unquestioning love from his Companion.

She suppressed another surge of envy. To have that kind of love—what did he need from her?

Somehow he sensed that doubt, and answered it. Not with words, though; with feeling, feelings that she could not possibly doubt. In her mind, he held her close and warmed her.

Their peaceful reverie was broken by his Companion, who stole up beside them and nudged his shoulder. He turned to her after a moment of silent dialogue.

:Cymry says that Elspeth and Darkwind have managed to attract some attention by springing a trap. She doesn't think Falconsbane is personally involved yet, but

now would be a good time to move on while his guards are occupied with trying to catch them.:

She nodded and sensed Need's agreement as well.

The moment passed, but something of it remained. She examined herself carefully, trying to figure out exactly what it was, and finally gave it up.

The terrain became uneasily familiar, and she felt that cold fear rising up her spine and chilling her throat. Soon now—soon. The first of the border-protections was not that far from here; soon she would have to dismount, shed cloak and coat, and key herself up to the point where she could ignore pain and exhaustion, and run like one of the *dyheli* herself.

By dawn, if all went well, she would be inside the fortress itself. Alone...

:Alone, like bloody hell,: the sword snorted scornfully. *:What am I, an old tin pot?:*

The image that Need sent to her, of Nyara wielding a tin pot against fearful guards, made her smother a giggle, and completely dispelled the fear. Of course she wasn't alone! She had Need beside her, Skif behind her—she would never really be alone again!

:That's the spirit. Just keep thinking that way.:

And somehow, she did, as she and Skif followed Wintermoon deeper into the forest, past the valley where the *dyheli* herd had been caught by one of her father's traps so long ago, closer to the border and the first of the barriers that she must cross.

2 4

Elspeth had been feeling eyes on the back of her neck for the past league and more, ever since they had sprung the trap meant for a bondbird. A particularly nasty thing, Brytha had spotted it and had alerted them to the fact that there were both physical and magical defenses in the trees as well as on the ground. If Vree had encountered such a thing unprepared, it would certainly have caught and hurt him and might well have killed him. But then, Falconsbane was well aware that harming the bondbird meant harming its bondmate.

The night-shrouded forest had held plenty of traps, not all of them Falconsbane's. Rocks and roots lurked beneath the snow, to trip even the wariest. Shadows could hide anything—or nothing. Elspeth's night-sight was not of the best, and she was forced to rely on Gwena's physical senses entirely—although, truthfully, that meant she could devote most of her attention to her mage-senses, spying out trouble.

Trouble there was, right enough, and it increased the closer they got to Falconsbane's lands. Alarms, and more traps, some meant to hold, and some meant to kill. Places where Falconsbane's underlings had simply left things to trip up the unwary, to make them delay. Nothing living, though; Elspeth was not sure if that was a good or bad sign.

Now, with the gray light of dawn creeping over the forest and Vree scouting overhead, she was so tense with anxiety that she felt like a spring too tightly wound—and would have been starting at every little sound, if she had not held herself under careful control. This was the first time she, personally, had played decoy—the Heir to the Throne of Valdemar was far too important to risk as a decoy or bait—and now she knew how Kero and the Skybolts had felt when they were playing this little game.

I can't show I know we're in danger, or we stop being such attractive targets...

If everything was going according to plan, the gryphons would be completing their task if they had not already done so. Nyara would be deep inside her father's stronghold. And very soon *they* would be free to sprint back for the shelter of the Vale and the protections of a Vale full of mages and Adepts.

Nyara was already inside her father's lands, if not his stronghold; Skif had relayed that via Cymry just past midnight. He and Wintermoon had seen her safely past the first line of defenses, and had gone to the rally-point, the place she would reach if she could when this was all over. But there was no way of knowing how far she was at this point.

Please, whatever gods there be—Star-Eyed, Kernos, Astera, whatever you call yourselves—let us all come through this with bodies and minds and hearts intact—

Elspeth was exhausted and getting wearier with every passing moment; this business of springing traps was not as easy as it had sounded. Yes, they could use the power of the ley-lines to augment their own—*when* they could reach them. Some of Falconsbane's own lines overlaid the natural ones, rendering them inaccessible. And some of the lines were protected against meddling by Falconsbane's own power. No, nothing was as simple as it had sounded when they first made this plan, and it had not truly seemed all that simple then!

She caught Darkwind's eye; he smiled at her, but it seemed more than a little strained.

:He's in about the same shape you are,: Gwena said gently. *:And your*

imagination is not acting up. You are *being watched. Imperfectly—the Shin'a'in are doing what they can—but Falconsbane knows you're here and he knows who you are. :*

Well, that was the object of this little excursion, wasn't it? To take the attention off of Nyara and the gryphons? Nevertheless, she felt a chill run up her back as the feeling of *being watched* increased, and the malevolence behind the watching "eyes" made itself felt.

:Vree says the gryphons are done!: Darkwind exulted, suddenly. *:The last line is loose!:*

Distance-Mindspeech was a hazard around Falconsbane—the kind he was watching for, at any rate. But they had something he didn't; the gryphons Mindspoke to Vree, and he in turn to Darkwind—and all at a level it was doubtful Falconsbane was even aware of, much less could eavesdrop upon.

She and Gwena turned, following Darkwind's lead as if they had decided they had come far enough on an ordinary patrol, and were turning back.

Ice crawled up her spine, her stomach was one huge knot of fear and nausea, and she kept looking out of the corners of her eyes for the first signs that Falconsbane was going to attack. *We can't run. If we run, he'll chase us. We can't hold him off if he goes all-out against us. So we have to look as if we're just changing directions, and hope that he doesn't lose interest...*

Huh. Better hope that he doesn't decide he's not going to let us slip away when he realizes we're headed away from him!

At least we know the gryphons succeeded.

If only they had some such bond with Nyara. She licked lips gone dry with a tongue just as dry with fear, and felt her stomach tighten a little more.

Nyara crept along the dusty passages between the walls of her father's stronghold, moving as quietly as only she could. In this, she was her father's superior; he had never mastered the art of moving without noise, without even the sound of a breath. Then again, he had never had need to. He had never had anyone to fear or avoid.

In all his life, he never had to hide from anyone.

Not like a certain small girl, who had huddled for hours in these passageways to avoid him—to avoid what he had in store for her.

She felt fear starting to cramp her stomach, and sternly told it to relax. *Deep breaths. Slowly. Tension brings mistakes; fear is* his *weapon.*

She was glad of the dust, for all that it might have choked her, had she not come prepared for it. She breathed through a silken cloth wrapped closely around nose and mouth; slowly, evenly, taking each step only after testing the surface before her. The dust meant that no one had walked this passage since she had last been here—and that had been years. The last time—certainly it had been two years or more. The last time she had been here was long before she had even dreamed of escape from her father's power. And then it had taken a year of planning before she dared to try.

How bitter it had been to learn that the attempt had been watched and planned by Falconsbane all along...

That thought plays into his hands again. No, Nyara; once you were free of him, you did things he had never anticipated you would. You won *free of him. You turned his own plan against him. Surely it is he who tastes bitterness now.*

She put that old disappointment behind her, throttled her fear again, and concentrated completely on setting each foot down carefully, noiselessly. At the moment, this was the only thing in the universe that was important. What was past could not be changed; the future lay beyond this passageway. *This* was all that she controlled, this moment of *now,* and she must control it completely...

So far, Need had detected no alarms or traps in this passageway itself. Perhaps her father did not feel he needed any. Perhaps he trusted in the narrowness of the passage to keep anything of real danger out of it. Certainly it was much too small to permit the movement of an armed man.

But not too small for one small, slender female, armed with only the sword that she kept out and pointed into the darkness before her.

Thirty steps from here was her goal; her father's study. One of his workrooms; it lay in a suite in the heart of his stronghold, the heart of his power. There was an entrance into this passage from that room; behind a tapestry at the farther end, through the back of a wooden wardrobe that Falconsbane kept some of his special garments in. He knew all about it, of course, for he had built it—but because he knew about it, she did not think he ever thought about it anymore. The passage and the entrance had been there since before she was born, and no one that he knew of had ever used it but him in all that time. If she was very lucky, he might assume that since no one ever had, no one ever would.

Twenty steps more.

:He's ahead up there,: Need cautioned. *:In the suite. No one but him, and he's busy.:*

Ten steps.

She had never prayed before—

:Don't worry about that, kitten. I'm praying enough for both of us. And I'm an expert at it.:

Five…

Elspeth sensed something change, like the sharpness in the air before lightning strikes. Alarm shrilled along her nerves, and every hair on her body stood on end. A bitter, metallic taste filled her throat. Gwena snorted and froze where she stood, sensing it as well—Darkwind and Brytha beside them did the same at the same moment. They were no longer being watched…

They were being targeted!

No use to run now—they couldn't escape what was coming.

:Shields!: Darkwind cried. He stuck out his hand, blindly, as they had planned if it came to this; she linked to Gwena and caught his hand, and with it, his link. *He* was better at shielding; she flung her power to him, taking whatever Gwena could pour into her.

She sensed the blow coming and cringed over Gwena's neck; he met the blow with one of his own—a defense of offense, something she hadn't even thought of.

The two bolts of power met over their heads in a silent explosion of power and a shower of very physical sparks that landed in the snow all around him, sizzling and melting the drifts wherever they landed. He took the moment to weave a hasty shield about them both, but it had none of the layering or complexity he needed.

The next bolt came, splashing and burning against the shield, scorching it half away and blinding her. Physically, as well as in Mage-Sight. A thunderclap of sound deafened her in the next instant. They hadn't had enough time—they hadn't known Falconsbane could strike like this.

Where did he get all that power? Falconsbane should have been wounded, should have been at less power than he'd had before, not *more*.

Unless he was already tapping into the proto-Gate?

Or unless he had ruthlessly sacrificed *many* of his underlings, building a network of death-energies stronger than anything they had. Or unless he'd found an ally somewhere…?

Darkwind couldn't shield all of them; the group was just too big. He reinforced where the shield had burned away, and this time she aided him, weaving light and snow-glare into a dazzle, trying to recreate the kind of shielding they had learned to make in the safety of the Vale.

But Falconsbane was keeping them both off-balance, destroying the rhythm of their dance of power with sheer, brute force. *He* controlled the situation now; it was *his* land they walked on, and the land held energy away from them. She whimpered in sudden pain as a lick of flame burned through and across her hand, the hand that held Darkwind's—but she would not let go, not even if she died in the next moment. Instead, she kneed Gwena closer to Brytha, until their legs were half-crushed between the two mounts to make the physical gap between them smaller. She closed her eyes and sheltered against Darkwind's back, sweat of fear and exertion running down her back under her coat, feeling him tremble with strain.

Falconsbane did not let up, not even for a heartbeat. Blow after blow rained down on them, driving all sense from her, until the last of the shields eroded, and they clung together, waiting for the strike that would take them both.

Together, at least—she thought faintly.

The blow never came; they opened their eyes, fearing something worse.

Then a scream from above made them jump, and look up.

Like two golden streaks of light, the two gryphons plummeted down from above. They crashed through the thin lace of branches, ending their dive barely above the ground, and pulling up with wingbeats that sent the snow spraying in all directions. Both screamed again, an unmistakable note of taunting in their voices, as they plunged upward through the tree canopy.

"Run!" Darkwind found his voice. *"Run! They've made targets out of themselves. If we give him too many to choose from, we may all get away!"*

Brytha broke from his paralysis and hurled himself down their backtrail. Gwena followed a moment later, but not directly behind, making herself and Elspeth into yet another target to track on. Above the interlace of bare branches, Hydona and Treyvan had separated as well, sky dancing as if they were courting—but far enough apart that Falconsbane would have to make a choice of victims. Four targets...

When the two young fools rode along the edge of his territory, at first Falconsbane could not believe the testimony of his own senses. *It must be an illusion,* he thought at first. *It is meant to distract me.* But the closer the pair came, the clearer they were, despite the best attempts of—whatever it was—that was trying to cloud his scrying. Between midnight and dawn, he knew that the pair were something more than they seemed. By false dawn he knew that one of them was the young Outland woman he had wanted so badly to take for his own. By true dawn, he knew that the other was the fool called Darkwind, and that the girl still carried her artifact.

By then, he could not withstand the temptation to attack any longer.

He had not lived this long by neglecting an opportunity when it was given to him. And he would not botch this chance by holding back, or making testing feints.

He gathered all of his power together, prepared his weaponry, and attacked.

Darkwind would die; then the girl and the sword would be his.

There was no point in being prudent or cautious now! Not with *this* prize in his grasp! He rained blow after blow upon them, heedless of the expenditure of power, heedless of anything about him. Elation held him like a powerful drug, making him laugh aloud with every shred of shielding burned away, giving him an elation he had not felt in decades. He held his arms high and power crackled between his hands, power from his network made of the death-energies of his mages. He was draining that network, but it did not matter, for in moments he would have *her,* and the Bird-Fool's power as well, and there would be nothing standing in the way of his revenge and his glory.

And then, just before he was to strike the blow that would take them both—

Gryphons!

The sight of them in his scrying bowl struck like a physical blow, driving the breath from him.

They dove down out of *nowhere,* interposing themselves between him and his quarry; taunting him, flaunting themselves at him, flying as if they thought agility alone would protect them.

Gryphons!

He snarled with overwhelming rage. How *dare* they step between him and his prey?

Anger and hatred filled him, granted him a strength far beyond anything he normally possessed. They thought to confuse him, did they? They thought he could only strike one of them at a time.

They would learn differently—in the few heartbeats it took for *all* of them to die!

He gathered his powers—readied the blast to destroy that entire section of his borderlands—

* * *

Nyara took three deep breaths; focused herself.

There is no future. There is no past. There is only now, and the target. There is no fear. There is only balance. There is only myself and the task.

She slipped through the false wall in the back of the wardrobe and slid soundlessly into the room. Her eyes focused quickly as she swept them from left to right, once, to orient herself.

There. The target. *Yes!*

She took two steps, raising Need high over her head to give additional momentum to her swing—

And brought the mage-blade down squarely on the huge crystal-cluster that Mornelithe Falconsbane had invested and anchored with all of his power—a crystal that cried out to her of death and pain, and even now was glowing with internal fires of red and angry yellow as he drew upon it—

Drew upon it to destroy her friends.

NO!

Sword crashed down upon crystal—and crystal exploded.

Falconsbane brought his hands up, rage a hot taste of blood in his throat.
Then—*What*—

A fractional instant of *something wrong;* no more than that.

—an instant of disorientation—

—searing *pain*—pain, engulfing every nerve, every fiber—

—out of the pain, the void, rushing upon him like the open mouth of a giant to devour him—

—and then, oblivion.

Elspeth picked herself up out of the huge drift of snow she had landed in, slowly. One moment they had been running for their lives, and the next—

Gwena!

She scrambled to her feet, flailing in the deep snow, trying to get herself turned around.

:It's—all right. I'm fine. Mostly.: Elspeth stopped trying to flail her way out of the snow and relaxed.

Thank the gods. Oh, thank the gods. Although Gwena's mind-voice sounded—odd. As if—

:I feel as if I have a hangover.: the Companion replied. *:I—think I may*

be sick.: The overtones of nausea that came with the thoughts almost pushed Elspeth into sickness herself.

She got herself back to her feet and turned around, her head pounding, her stomach heaving along with Gwena's. The Companion was on her knees in another snowdrift, sides heaving as her breath hissed between clenched teeth.

:I will—never again—mock you—when you are—wine-sick,: Gwena managed, closing her eyes as if the sun hurt her.

Elspeth staggered to her side. "Eat some snow," she urged, holding a handful up to Gwena's muzzle. "Do it; I think this might be reaction-sickness, and eating snow will help."

:If you—think so—: Gwena opened her jaws gingerly and accepted a bite of snow, swallowing it quickly. The nausea subsided, and she took another bite. *:That helps. Thank you.:*

"It's not going to help the headache though," Elspeth warned, squinting against the pain in her own head. *We're all alive, I think—*

A shadow loomed beside her; Darkwind, leaning on Brytha. He smiled wanly, and the joy that flooded her almost made her forget her pounding head. She would have jumped up, if she could; as it was, he simply let go of Brytha's shoulder and fell into her arms.

"What happened?" she asked, holding him, being held, and ignoring the chill of the snow penetrating her clothing.

"I think he must have had something ready to hit us with when Nyara destroyed his focus," Darkwind replied unsteadily. "Most of it aborted, but there was enough left to knock us all head-over-hind. I hope Treyvan and Hydona—"

:Were out of range, thank you.: The hearty mind-voice made her wince, and snow blew up in all directions as the gryphon backwinged to a landing. "Arrre you unwell, childrrren?" he continued, folding his wings and cocking his head to one side. Vree landed beside him, imitating his pose in a way that would have been funny if Elspeth's head had not hurt so much.

And not only her head. It felt rather as if someone had been beating her with blunt clubs all over her body.

"I sssee," the gryphon said, although none of them had replied. "Wait a moment."

He walked over to a little sheltered area amid a cluster of bushes. Within a few moments, he had the earth scraped bare and overlaid with pine boughs. "Herrre. I have made you a nessst," he said, turning back to them. "Go and wait therrre, all of you. I ssshall brrring back sssome help. Meanwhile, eat ssssnow."

With that, he launched himself into the air again, vanishing into the bright sky in a few wingbeats.

"Well?" Elspeth said to Darkwind. He shrugged.

"I can't go any further," he replied. "And Brytha's not feeling much better than Gwena. Let's let someone else take charge for a change."

"Good idea," she replied, and the four of them collapsed together into the "nest" that Treyvan had made, to share the heat of their bodies and await *their* rescuers.

Nyara prowled the complex of three rooms, study, library, and workroom, and found only the destruction of a whirlwind in the workroom; Need went quiet for a moment.

:He was here. Kitten, this was mad; he meant to anchor the proto-Gate partially in himself. He's gone now—pulled right into the void, along with half of the stuff in this room.:

"Can he return?" she whispered.

:Don't know. But if he does, he won't be the same.:

She shivered and started back to the hidden passageway. The sound of people murmuring on the other side of the door made her hurry her steps. They might welcome her as savior—but more likely, they'd welcome her with the points of blades. Mornelithe's servants were steeped in suspicion and fear. Time to go. *:You did great, kitten. I was impressed.:*

The Vale had never looked better, and Elspeth felt as if she would like to drink tea and stay in bed for a week. The tea she got, but she wasn't allowed to seek her bed yet. There were a number of people waiting for all of them, chiefest of whom was Firesong.

Firesong actually looked chagrined. Elspeth had never seen that particular expression on his face before and had not ever thought that she would.

"I have some strange news," he said, as she sipped the tea that was slowly dulling her headache to a bearable level. She looked at Darkwind, who only shrugged and accepted another mug from the Healing Adept.

"I'm beginning to think that's the only kind of news we ever have around here," she said dryly, pulling her blanket a little closer.

Firesong sat back on his heels, and shrugged. "This is—news

that will probably not please most of k'Sheyna," he opined. "It is concerning the proto-Gate. It did not settle where I intended. It was pulled away—*very* strongly."

"Not Falconsba—" Elspeth exclaimed, alarmed, when he interrupted her with a shake of his head.

"Nay. But it also did not go to the new k'Sheyna Heartstone." He sighed, and shook his head. "I am at a loss to explain this. It has gone east and north. *Far* east and north." He looked up at her from under long white eyelashes. "To *your* land, to be precise."

She blinked, feeling suddenly very stupid. Was there something here she was missing? "Valdemar?" she replied. "But—why? How?"

"Better to ask, *who*," Firesong replied, standing up again. "There was a force came out of the north, at the moment of backlash. It used the force of backlash to snatch the power-point out of *our* hands, and when all was done, it had settled nicely as a Heartstone in the center of your crown city. Or so I surmise, since I cannot imagine any other place with so many of your Companions in one small area." One corner of his mouth crooked in a slight smile as he nodded at Gwena. "I do suspect that all of them are suffering as much as your—friend—is. The settling of that much power is not an easy thing."

"North?" Elspeth managed, trying not to look too stupid. "North?"

"North?" Darkwind shook his head. "What in the name of the gods is *north* of Valdemar's lands that could do *that?*"

"Nothing—" Elspeth began, then stopped.

"What?" both of them snapped at once.

"The Forest of Sorrows," she said hesitantly. "The Forest—has always had a reputation for strangeness. Since Vanyel died there, anyway."

At the name of "Vanyel," Firesong's eyes narrowed, and he nodded thoughtfully. "You are ready now," he said directly to her. "The rest of your training is largely a matter of practice and learning what will work for you. *I* think you both should go to this Forest."

"Go?" Darkwind said faintly. Elspeth took a glance at him out of the corner of her eye; he was pale, and looked as if someone had just struck him.

"Yes," Firesong repeated forcefully. "Go. And *you* should go with her. It is obvious to a blind man that you wish to—and with all the Kaled'a'in here, there will be nothing that the Clan needs that you alone could provide." He shrugged. "They may even choose to move back here, which *I* think would be an excellent thing. But you should—*must*—go with Elspeth."

"But—I *cannot!*" Darkwind cried out, and winced at the sound of his own cracking voice. "I cannot," he repeated, at a lower volume. "Tayledras never leave their Vales."

"Sheka," Firesong said rudely. "My own foster forefathers did so, to help Herald Vanyel *in Valdemar* when he needed their aid. They have not in centuries, it is true, but this is a time of changes. Or," he finished, his tone heavy with sarcasm, "had that fact escaped you?"

"But the move—" Darkwind said feebly.

"Can be accomplished with the help of the Kaled'a'in. Either bringing them here, or your mages there. Now that the Stone is gone, you could use the node in the ruins to create a new one, or build a Gate to the new Vale." Firesong shrugged, carelessly tossing his hair back over his shoulders. "It matters little to me. My task is done here, and I am returning home."

"Father—" Darkwind began, then shook his head. "Father has Kethra and the Kaled'a'in and Shin'a'in healers. And Wintermoon. I am being foolish. But—" he licked his lips nervously. "This is not easy."

"Fledging rarely is," Firesong said dryly. "I shall leave you to make your decision."

Firesong stood and smiled, and now they saw that he had been toying with a black rose. At Elspeth's curious look, he smiled a little wider and said only, "A gift. Brought to me by a scarlet-crested firebird."

Darkwind's brow creased in concentration. "But—that breed is from the far north."

Firesong closed his eyes and sighed, content as any maiden paid a compliment. "Yes, Darkwind—north of Valdemar."

Elspeth sat quietly as Firesong left them alone in the little clearing below her *ekele*. She wanted to look away from him, but she was afraid that if she did, he would take it as a rejection.

And that was the last thing she wanted.

He stared into his cup for a long, long time, while the tea cooled and both of them were locked inside their own thoughts. Finally, he looked up.

"This will not be easy," he said awkwardly. "I am—I have never been outside our own lands. I know nothing of the Outlands."

"There are good people, bad people, and middling people," she replied as casually as she could. "Just more of them than you're used to,

perhaps. But I would like you to come. I need you; not just the mage—
but yourself, Darkwind."

That last slipped out before she could stop it, but once escaped, she
did not want to take it back.

He let out a breath he had been holding in. "I had hoped you would
say that," he said, and took her hand. "I had hoped, but I had not
expected it."

She felt her heart racing, as she put her own hand over his. "So,"
she said, dizzy with elation, "shall we go see where all these changes are
taking us?"

"Together," he replied. "Yes. I think we should."

Once again, Elspeth made up her full packs, with everything she owned,
and more—all the possessions she had accumulated in the Vale. It was
still the deep of winter, but the expedition that prepared to set out from
Kena Lesheyana Vale was not one that was likely to be daunted by a little
cold and snow. Not only were there three Adepts in the party, Firesong
electing to guide them as far as k'Treva, but there were four gryphons.
Granted that two of them were barely fledged, and would make their
ground-bound way alongside the riders in between their short flights,
but even a *young* gryphon was likely to give predators pause.

That was something Elspeth had *not* expected, but she welcomed
them completely. Treyvan would not say what his ultimate intentions
were, but since he had begun asking for lessons in her tongue, Elspeth
suspected that he and Hydona had been elected as the Kaled'a'in
ambassadors to Valdemar. It made a certain amount of sense—and the
gryphlets would be their wordless assurance to the people of Valdemar
that they intended no ill.

I can't wait to see them in Court. How is the Seneschal going to call their
credentials, I wonder?

Besides, with gryphons to gawk at, Nyara was going to seem almost
commonplace.

Changes indeed.

It would take several weeks to make all the preparations; weeks during
which she and Darkwind could help the Kaled'a'in to build the Gate to
send the mages and scouts of k'Sheyna on to their new Vale. Once that
was complete, there would be nothing more holding Darkwind here—
except dark memories of a kind he would do well to leave behind.

Then—

The unknown—for both of us—

She started to shiver, then a hawk cry made her look up. She wasn't certain *why,* since hawks cried out all the time in a Vale, but something about that cry compelled her to raise her eyes to the sky.

Above her were two vorcel-hawks, skydancing, courting, circling higher and higher into the sun.

AUTHOR'S NOTE

Falcons and horses; bondbirds and Companions. The latter are a *what-if* portrait of the former—but a bondbird is as unlike a real-world hawk or falcon as a zebra is unlike a Companion.

Yet there is always that longing to have something *like* a bondbird or a Companion. Dragons are not possible in this world—but this world does hold hawks and horses. The demand on time, money, and special resources is similar for both the dedicated horseman and the falconer.

First, outfitting the human. Both require specialty items it found in stores. A falconer needs a hawking glove, specially constructed for extra protection where the hawk's talons will be yet flexible enough to handle leash and jesses. They must either make this—expensive in terms of time—or buy it—expensive in terms of money. The horseman requires riding boots if he is going to ride seriously—also expensive.

Next, outfitting the bird or horse. The bird needs a hood—an object very difficult to construct properly, and again expensive either in terms of time or money. She also needs bracelets, jesses, leash, portable perch, transportation box, lining lure—all of which *must* be made to her size by her falconer. The horse requires tack; hackamore, halter, bit, bridle, saddle, saddle-blanket, and grooming materials—all which must be bought.

Housing bird or horse; here is where the horseman has the advantage over the falconer. The bird *must*, by federal regulation, have a house of a certain size and construction, a weathering yard of certain size and construction, and a permanent perch in the weathering yard. All these must be constructed on the falconer's property, for by federal regulations, he must have the bird available for inspection at any reasonable time of the day. There are no boarding stables for birds.

Feeding and veterinary care; expensive propositions for both bird or horse. The bird must have fresh, high-quality food every day—of the kind he would normally eat in the wild. Not hamburger steak, or chicken one can buy in the grocery. Horses eat like—a horse! It is a great deal more difficult to find a vet who will care for a raptor than one who will care for a horse, however, and there is an additional worry. Because hawks and falcons are *protected species*, if a bird becomes ill and dies, the federal government automatically becomes involved to ensure that a death was due to accident and not mistreatment.

Time and training; again, this is something where the falconer has no choice in the matter. He *must* work with his bird on a daily basis, whereas if a horseman has boarded out his horse, he can arrange for other riders to take leave to ride on those days when he may not be able to. In training the birds, there *are* no "bird-breakers." The falconer must do all of his training himself. Unless, of course, he happens to be so wealthy that like the nobility of old, *he* can employ a falconer to man "his" birds—though in that case, they will never be "his," for they will truly answer only to the hand that trained them. By contrast, papers and magazines are full of advertisements for horses in all stages of training. The falconer must have access to land in which to train and exercise, and hunt with his bird. That means that training and hunting with the bird will put many miles on his vehicle. The trained bird requires working every day of the year.

Acquisition; there are captive-bred birds available to both General and Master falconers, but for the Apprentice, obtaining a bird means hours—days—weeks spent attempting to trap a passage redtail or kestrel. The horseman must visit many breeders or dealers and try many horses before he finds one to his liking.

Care; once again, since there are no boarding stables for raptors, the entire burden of care falls to the falconer. And a big bird like a redtail produces an astonishing quantity of leavings. Houses must be scraped and scalded periodically, as must perches; the sand in the house and weathering yard must be raked daily. The bird must be offered his daily bath under conditions that will not leave him open to itching disease. Yards must be inspected and repaired, since many predators—including the large owls—regard a bird on a perch as a meal waiting to be taken.

Outside dangers. Horsemen have to contend with people who honk their car horns at horses being ridden along the side of the road, with dogs who attack horse and rider, and those people who, out of pure maliciousness, will attempt to injure horse, rider, or both. Falconers have to contend with those who are under the mistaken impression that all birds of prey are lawful targets, that birds of prey are taking the game that "belongs to them," and with those who regard birds of prey as "vermin." And with those who, out of pure maliciousness, will attempt to injure or kill the bird.

Both sports require substantial investments of time and money. Neither should be undertaken lightly, or without serious thought. For someone considering becoming a horse owner, there are usually excellent stables offering training care and riding. For someone considering falconry, the best place to consult is the State Fish and Game department; they will have further information on falconers and regulations in your area.

WINDS of FURY

BOOK THREE of
The MAGE WINDS

Dedicated to the teachers of the world.

1

Ancar, King of Hardorn, slumped in the cushioned embrace of his throne and stared out into the empty Great Hall. Empty, because he no longer bothered with holding audiences. He was not here to listen to the complaints of the people of Hardorn. When he wished *them* to learn of his will, there were better ways to inform them than to gather them together like a mass of milling sheep and declaim it to them.

He did not *serve* them, as one petty bureaucrat of his father's reign had whined that he must—just before he had ordered the man given to his mages. They served *him;* his pleasures, his will, his whims. That was what his mother had taught him before she died, and Hulda had simply confirmed those lessons. Now, after all these years, they were finally learning that. He was their ruler by right of arms and strength; he had the power of life and death over them, and all that lay in between.

It had certainly taken them long enough to realize that.

The servants had lit the candles ensconced along the birch-paneled walls, and the dancing flames reflected from the polished gray-granite floor and the varnished maple beams above. Wavering spots of flame twinkled at him from gilt trim and gold fittings, from crystal ornaments and the metal threads of battle flags hanging from the beams. This had been a court of weaklings, once. His few decent enemies had been subdued or annihilated, and their families and lands with them. Now all that remained of them were the flags of their conquered holdings, and a few trophies Ancar kept to remind others of his grasp.

Echoes of his movements came back to him like a whisper. He found a peculiar irony in this empty chamber; a poignancy, yes. He found all of his pensive thoughts poignant. He had run out of challenges. This hall was as empty as his own conquests.

Oh, of course, he had all of Hardorn trembling at his feet—but he could not extend the borders of his Kingdom more than a few shabby leagues in any direction. Even he dared not look Eastward, of course; to the East was the Empire, and the two-hundred-year-old Emperor Charliss. Only a fool would challenge Charliss—or someone who was stronger than Charliss. Ancar knew better than to think that *he* could boast of that.

To the North was Iftel, and he frowned to think of how his single attempt to invade *that* land had ended: with his armies transported bodily back to the capital and deposited there, and not a memory of crossing the border among them—and with his mages vanished utterly, without a trace. There was an invisible wall stretching along the Iftel-Hardorn border, a wall that would allow no one to pass. No, whatever guarded Iftel was as powerful as the Emperor, and there was no point in making It angry.

To the South was Karse. Ruled by priests, at war with Valdemar for hundreds of years—he would have said that Karse was a plum ripe for his picking. Except that he had been unable to gain more than those few leagues; after that, it seemed as if the very land itself rose up against him, and the Sun-priests certainly called up demons against his armies, for scores of men would vanish every night, never to be seen again. And it had become worse since the Priesthood had been taken over by a woman; he had lost even those few leagues he had gained.

But he could have coped with the losses in Karse. It was all hill country, rocky and infertile, of little use. He could have even coped with the humiliation of Iftel. If it hadn't been for Valdemar.

If he lowered his eyes, he would see the map of Hardorn inlaid in the granite of the floor just in front of the throne. The Empire in black terrazzo, Iftel in green marble, Karse in yellow marble, and Valdemar in its everlasting white. Valdemar would be at his left hand; the hand of sorcery, or so the old-wives' tales had it. Valdemar, the unconquered. Valdemar, that should have been first to fall.

Valdemar, the ripe fruit that Hulda had promised him from the beginning.

He felt his lips lifting in a snarl and forced his face back into his mask of calm. And if the truth were to be admitted, he could not have told whether the snarl was meant for Valdemar and her Bitch-Queen, or for Hulda, the Bitch-Adept.

He shifted uncomfortably and the echo whispered back at him, a phantom rustling of fabric. Hulda had promised him Valdemar from the time she began to teach him black sorcery, had promised him the pretty little princess Elspeth, had vowed that he would have both within moments of seizing the throne of Hardorn from his senile old father. He *liked* tender little girls; at sixteen, Elspeth had been a little riper than he preferred but was still young enough to make a good plaything. At a single stroke, he would have doubled the size of his kingdom, and created a platform from which to invade not only Karse but Rethwellan as well. Then, with both these lands firmly in his fist, he could have challenged the old Emperor or simply consolidated his power, making himself Emperor of the West as Charliss was of the East. Hulda had *promised* him that. She had sworn she was the most powerful Adept in seven kingdoms! She had pledged him her help and her teaching; she had certainly not been backward in teaching him the secrets of her body! He had had no reason to doubt her at the time—

Except that it had never happened. *Somehow* the damned Heralds sent to negotiate a marriage with Elspeth got word to their Queen of his plans and the death of his father. *Somehow* one of them even escaped Ancar's prison cell, warned the Queen, and stopped him and his hastily gathered army.

But it got worse with his second attempt. *Somehow* the Queen managed to raise a mercenary army that was capable of defeating his mages as well as his troops. *Somehow* they had cobbled up an alliance with the fanatics of Karse.

Somehow all of this had happened without Hulda, "the most powerful Adept in seven kingdoms," ever becoming aware of what was going on until after the fact. Bitch-Queen Selenay was still firmly on her throne. Another bitch, a mercenary Captain named Kerowyn, now held the border against him, and there didn't seem to be a single trick any of his commanders or mages could work that she hadn't seen before—and countered before. The Herald-Bitch Talia had been made a Sun-priest herself, and vested with the authority of the Arm of Vkandis by yet another bitch, the High Priest Solaris. And Bitch-Princess Elspeth had simply vanished, on some other quest for help, and he had to assume, given the absence of panic, that *she* was succeeding, even though not one of his agents could locate her.

And Bitch-Adept Hulda sat and twiddled her thumbs.

He was beginning to grow very tired of women. He had already grown tired of Hulda.

He was not aware of the fact that he had spoken her name until the echoes sent it back to him. This time he did snarl.

Yes, he was growing very tired of Hulda. He was tired of her whims, her eccentricities, her pretenses. What had been charming and exciting when he was sixteen now bored him—when it didn't disgust him. She was too old to play the coquette, too old for girlish mannerisms. And when she cast them off, she acted as if *she* was the monarch here, and not he.

That galled him almost as much as her consistent failure, and he would have tolerated the former if she had not brought him the latter. But she had the attitude without producing results, and if she weren't an Adept, he'd have had her slow-roasted alive by now.

When he was younger, he had accepted the fact that she virtually ruled him without a thought. But then, he had accepted many things back then without a thought. He was older now.

And wiser.

She treated him exactly as she had when he had taken the throne. She spoke, and expected him to listen attentively; she issued orders, and expected him to fling himself into whatever she ordered him to do.

I could have tolerated all of this if she had only done what she had promised. Out-thinking her was a challenge then...

She had pledged him before he took the throne that he would soon be an Adept to rival her; she swore he would have power beyond his wildest dreams, power enough to level mountains if he chose. She swore that she would teach him everything she knew.

But the power never materialized, and the training she gave him never went beyond the level of Master. She had never taught him how to use all the powers he could Sense, and all the training she had given him until that moment had made it impossible for him to touch them. Or at least he had not been able to touch them during the time that she had been his *only* teacher.

He had encountered this reluctance on Hulda's part to give him any more real teaching two years ago, shortly after he had turned Master. He had been certain at that moment that the powers of an Adept were almost in his grasp, that it would only be a matter of a little more training.

That was when the excuses began. Hulda suspended his regular training sessions, telling him that he was beyond such things. That had made him elated, briefly—until he realized that there was no way other than regular training to achieve his long-sought goal. And when he began to seek her out, asking for more teaching, she was always busy...

And at first, her excuses had seemed plausible. After so many defeats from the west, they were taking no chances. Hulda had mustered a cadre of mages of relatively low power to watch the border for any weaknesses in the force that protected Valdemar from magic. She needed to organize these people, to make certain that the coercion spells upon them were powerful enough to keep them at their work no matter what temptations and opportunities to defect were placed before them. But after weeks of such excuses, they began to wear thin.

After a few months, he took matters into his own hands.

He had been collecting mages since his first, ill-fated attempt to take the Valdemaran throne. Now he began doing more than collecting them and placing them under his coercion spells; now he began finding out, in a systematic sweep through his mage-corps, just what they knew.

He had been collecting and recruiting every kind and type of mage that showed even the faintest traces of power—from hill-shaman to mages of no known school. By aggressively pursuing a course of forced learning, he had picked up every bit of knowledge, however seemingly inconsequential, from any of his "recruits" that had teachings he had not gotten. He had also been collecting every scrap of written information about magic that he could lay his hands on; every grimoire, every mage's personal notebook, every history of ancient times, and *anything* concerning magic to be had from within the Empire. Much of it had been useful. Some of it, he was certain, Hulda herself did not share. But none of it brought him the prize he was trying to reach—

At least, not to his knowledge. As he understood it, only an Adept could use the power of "nodes," those meeting places of the lines of power that he *could* use. Every attempt he had made so far had resulted in failure. He was still not an Adept, and he had no idea how far he was from that goal.

He had been trying to find an Adept to teach him, with no luck. Of course, Adepts could be avoiding Hardorn; everything he had ever heard or read indicated that the kind of Adept willing to teach *him* would also be the kind unwilling to share power, and that was precisely the problem he had with Hulda. Hulda might be warning them off, somehow. It would not surprise him much to discover that she had been working against him, preventing him from locating an Adept so that he would always be her inferior.

But she had underestimated him, and his willingness to tolerate a position as ruler in name only. There could be only one Ruler of Hardorn, and it would not be Hulda.

A servant appeared at the door, waiting silently for him to notice her existence. He admired the woman for a moment—not for her own looks, but for the new livery he had ordered. Scarlet and gold: the scarlet of blood, the gold of the wealth he intended to grasp. The livery matched his new device, now blazoned above his throne, replacing the insipid oak tree of his father. A winged serpent in gold, upon a field of blood-red, poised to strike.

Hulda should have taken note of that new device, and thought about what it meant.

Hulda thought that she had him under control, but she had not counted on the more mundane methods of dealing with an enemy. He had placed spies among her servants, loyal only to him, their loyalty ensured not by spells, but by fear. He had chosen these people carefully, finding those for whom death would be preferable to losing someone—or something. For some, it was a family member or a lover that they would die to protect. For others, it was a secret. And for a few, it was a possession that made life worth living. Such passion meant control—and such control could not be revealed by magical means.

These servants followed Hulda's every move, and let him know when she was so deeply engrossed in some activity that he would be able to act without her guessing what he was up to. She was not infallible—for instance, she did *not* possess a spell that he had read about, one that permitted the caster to see into the past. Whatever he did while she was occupied, she would not know about. She also did not possess the mind-magic that enabled one to read the thoughts of others. Well, neither did he, but that was of little matter at the moment. What was important was that she could not detect his control of her servants from their thoughts. So as long as she did not torture their secrets from them, he would always know where she was and what she was doing.

She might have servants of the same sort watching him; in fact, he had planned on it. His propensity for taking young, barely post-pubescent girls was well known—as was their regrettable tendency to not survive such encounters. He still enjoyed such pleasures, but as often as not, the girl was incidental to something magical he wished to achieve. There was great power in a painful death—something about a life being ended prematurely released incredible power. He did not think Hulda knew that *he* knew this; after all, his preferences had been well established long before he learned of the power these acts released. So he would wait until Hulda was occupied, then select one of the little lambs in his private herd and repair to his own chambers for an enjoyable and profitable candlemark or two.

His hand-picked servants watched Hulda, and guarded his secrets against her.

The woman waiting for him to acknowledge her, for instance, was Hulda's personal maid, and privy to her comings and goings. She was common enough to attract no notice; middle-aged, neither plain nor pretty, neither fat nor thin. And well-trained; she would not have slipped away, she would have waited for Hulda to dismiss her—and yet, at the same time, she would have arranged to be so attentive that Hulda would not dismiss her unless the mage wanted privacy. What a shame she wasn't younger.

He raised his eyes and nodded. The servant crossed the floor silently, her eyes lowered, and prostrated herself at the foot of the throne.

"Speak," he said quietly.

"Hulda has retired to her chamber in the company of the muleteer I told you of, Majesty," the servant replied, in a voice carefully pitched so as not to carry beyond the immediate vicinity. He had not chosen this chamber as a place to sit and brood without thought; it was impossible to be spied upon effectively here, and impossible to be overheard, given the acoustics of the place. It had been built to enable a semi-private audience in the midst of a crowded court. Such clever design gave him true privacy without making it obvious.

He raised his eyebrows in sardonic surprise; the muleteer must be a remarkable man, for this would be the fourth time he had graced Hulda's bed. Then again, Ancar had heard that the man had the strength and stamina of one of his mules... and perhaps shared more with them than Ancar had guessed.

The King had no fear that this muleteer might be an agent of Hulda's own; he knew everything there was to know about the man. Gossip in the kitchens had first alerted him to the muleteer's unusual abilities, although none of his excellence was in the area of intelligence. Hulda's muleteer was as dense as a rock and possessed of very little wit, only one short step above absolute simpleton. And Ancar had, in fact, *arranged* for his erstwhile tutor to hear about the muleteer's physical attributes. It had been no surprise to him when she immediately found an excuse to go down to the secondary stables to see the man for herself. As he had expected, once Hulda had ascertained that there was no hook attached to this very attractive bait, she had taken it.

Yes, well. The "hook" is the man himself, and his ability to keep a woman occupied and heedless of anything else for several candlemarks at a time. Not something Hulda would be looking for.

So, once again, Hulda and her new toy were amusing themselves. He wondered how long this toy would last. She tended to be as hard on her playthings as he was on his.

"Very good," he said in reply. "You may go."

The servant got slowly to her feet and backed out, closing the door behind her. Ancar did not immediately rise from his throne; he would wait, and give Hulda the opportunity to become completely engrossed in her lover before he moved.

No, there could be only one ruler in Hardorn. He was going to find a way to rid himself of Hulda, sooner or later.

That was, in a way, something of a pity. She was the only woman above the age of fifteen that he found desirable; perhaps that was because her sexual experience was so vast, and so unique. She constantly found new ways to amuse him. And it would be *very* pleasurable to somehow reduce her to the level of one of the servants; to strip her of all ability to challenge him, and yet leave her intelligence and her knowledge intact. *That* would be a triumph greater than conquering Valdemar.

No, I don't think that will ever happen. No matter how powerful I became, there would be no way I could strip her mind bare without fearing she would find a way to release herself. She would never accept any kind of role as an underling. It would be a waste of power I could better spend elsewhere. Once I am an Adept, once I have defeated her, that defeat must be followed by her death.

Finally, when he was certain he had given Hulda enough time to put everything except the prowess of her muleteer out of her mind, he rose and took his slow, leisurely way to his own chambers.

And not to his official chambers either.

"Keep watch," he told one of the guards outside the chamber— another of his hand-picked armsmen, but this one controlled directly, as all his personal guards were, by spells controlling his mind. He turned to the other. "Tell my chamberlain I am not to be disturbed unless there is an emergency."

Then he turned just outside of the double doors of the audience chamber and entered one of the corridors of the sort used by the servants. The guard followed him, walking about three paces behind. This was not a heavily trafficked corridor, either; in fact, it was likely that no one walked it except to keep it clean and keep the lights burning along it. It led to a set of dark stairs, which led downward, directly to one of the oldest parts of this castle; one of the round towers that had once anchored this building against siege. Seldom used now, but he found the round shape of the rooms very useful.

He held the only key to the door on this level; he unlocked it, after first making certain the spells and physical devices meant to insure his privacy were still intact. The wooden door had a copper lock; very useful in that copper retained the traces of *any* magic that might be used on it. He let himself into the bottom room of the tower and relocked the door behind him.

This room held his collection of peasant girls, gleaned from the countryside by his troopers, all housed in neat little cells built about the exterior wall of the room. They were carefully chosen by his chamberlain and himself; he looked for deep emotional capacity, and his chamberlain looked for a lack of awkward relatives who might miss them. A spell of silence ensured that they could not speak to one another, nor communicate in any other way. Every day he had food and water delivered to them by a servant; each cell had all the facilities of one of the finer guest rooms in the castle itself, even if the space was a bit cramped. No vermin here, and no dirt either. He was quite fastidious about his person, and what he permitted in close proximity to it. Every girl here was under a minor coercion spell, set by one of his tame mages, that forced her to eat, drink, and keep herself neat and bathed.

The aura of terror in this room was quite astounding, and wonderfully sustaining. The spell of silence only made waiting more frightening to his captives.

Hulda assumed that this was the only purpose of the tower; she had never looked beyond this chamber and the one immediately above. She had no notion of what lay in the windowless third-story room, under the round, peaked roof.

He would not be availing himself of the services of any of the girls today. He had already charged himself with as much power as he could handle yesterday, and the little that had leaked off in the interim was insignificant.

He crossed the chamber to the spiral staircase that rose through the middle, taking it up to the room above. He ignored this room as well; he had no use for the couch, the rack, the chest of instruments. Not today. He permitted the room to remain in darkness, lit only from the chamber below, as he crossed to the staircase that curled up the stone wall and rose to the third and final room.

It, too, lay in near total darkness. He lit a lantern at the head of the stairs—without the use of magic. He would need all the power he had for what lay before him; the manuscript he meant to follow today had made that much quite clear.

Once the lantern gave him some light to see by, he made a circuit of the room, lighting every burnished lantern within it, until it was as bright as possible in a room with no windows.

This wood-floored room was ringed with bookcases, exactly as the ground-floor room was ringed with cells. And here lay the prisoners of his intellectual searches, the captives of his quest for knowledge. Hundreds of books, of book-rolls, of manuscripts; even mere fragments of manuscripts. All of them were handwritten; the kind of knowledge contained in *these* words was not the kind that anyone would ever commit to a printer. He had been collecting these for more than the two years of his disenchantment with his mentor, but it was only within the past two years that he had begun studying them and trying the spells described in them without supervision.

He fully intended to try another of them today.

He did not know what this spell was supposed to do, but he had some hopes that it might be the long-sought way to tap safely into the power of nodes, the spell that would finally make him an Adept. It was in this very manuscript that he first *found* the word "node," and realized from the antique description that these knots of energy at the junction of two or more ley-lines were the same energy nexus-points that he had been, thus far, unable to tap himself.

This was one of the incomplete manuscripts, and it was the many pages missing and paragraphs obliterated that had made him hesitate for so long before trying anything contained in it. The real purpose of this spell was in the pages that were missing, and the pages he possessed were riddled by insects and blurred by time. Still, this was the closest he had come in all the months of searching, and for the past week or so, he had felt ready to attempt this "spell of seeking." For some reason, today *felt* right to try it.

He had managed a week ago to restore some of the manuscript at least; a clear description of the level of Adept that could tap into the "nodes," though *not* the safeguards that would make such tapping less hazardous. This was the first time he had seen such descriptions, or the directions on how to use the node-power once he obtained it.

Hopefully, if he were strong enough, the safeguards would not be necessary. He had never once seen Hulda using any such safeguards when *she* accessed the power of "nodes."

Then again, his more cautious side chided, *she could have established those protections before you were in a position to watch her. She could have been hiding them from you.*

The spell described was not the same one that Hulda used, of that much he was certain. This spell required the construction of some kind of "portal;" he could only assume that it was a portal to the node-power. That made sense; he already *knew* that he, at least, could not touch these things directly.

He settled into a chair he often used for his meditations and suppressed a shiver. He recalled only too well the first and last time he had attempted to touch the nodes directly.

He had been able to see these power nexus-points, as well as the lines leading to them, from the time he reached the level of Journeyman. From the time he was first initiated by Hulda into the world of magic, he had been able to see the power that all things created, all the colors and intensities of it. But until Hulda drew power from those points during an attempt to pierce the sky above one of the Valdemar border towns with magic and let loose a plague of poisonous "insects" there, he had not known they were useful for anything. That was when she had told him—a little *too* proudly, he thought—that he would not be able to copy her example until he was an Adept.

He had tested that himself, when he realized that she was never going to assist him to achieve that status.

The power had been wild and startling; he had known immediately that he did not have the ability to control it at all, much less do so safely. It had felt as if he were suddenly juggling red-hot stones, and he had quickly released his tenuous contact, suddenly grateful that it *was* so tenuous. He had felt "scorched" for days afterward, and he had never again made the attempt.

But this time—perhaps through this "portal"—

The manuscript had been very clear on one point; that the only energy he would be able to use to form this portal was the energy he contained within himself. A pity, but he saw no reason to doubt it; hence the conscientious effort to fully charge himself, as if for a battle. Now he was as ready as he would ever be.

This room was perfect for use as a mage's private workroom; the wooden floor could be inscribed with chalk for diagrams, the peaked roof allowed a great deal of clearance in the center, and the only furniture was the bookcases, two chairs, and one table. There were no windows that needed to be shut or barred, and the stone walls were thick enough that very little sound penetrated. The old tower had been relegated to storage until he took it over, and most of the servants were unaware it was being used for anything else.

The portal required a physical foundation; he used the frame of one of the bookcases, an empty one, since he did not know what would happen to the contents once the portal was complete.

He sat bolt upright in a chair, took a deep, settling breath, and began.

He raised his hands and closed his eyes. He did not need to see the bookcase; what he wanted was not within the level of the visible, anyway. Within the framework of the bookcase he built another framework. Its carefully spun energy intertwined with the grain of the wood. The new framework was composed of energy taken from Ancar's own reserves.

I call upon the Portal—

Those were the words the spell called for; within the structure of those words he built up his frame of power, building it layer upon layer, making it stronger, spinning more and more of himself into it. The words were a mnemonic, a way of keeping track of the anchoring points for the spell; one for each syllable, there, there, and there, seven points. He concentrated on manipulating the energies exactly as the manuscript had described.

Then he reached the place where the manuscript had ended. From this moment on, he would be working blind.

He hoped that at the proper moment the portal would extend to one of the nodes, and enable him to take in the node's wild power without harm. In fact, he thought of that as he built up his portal, hoping that the thought would be echoed in the power, as often happened in higher magery. It was yet another reason why complete control was paramount to an advanced mage; stray thoughts would always affect the final spell.

Steady now; control and command. You rule the power. Shape it to your will, keep it in your hands.

The interior of the bookcase warped away from him and vanished, leaving behind a lightless void. He began to lose strength, as if his life were bleeding away into the void.

No reason to panic. The manuscript said this would happen. I just have to keep it from taking everything.

Then came the unexpected.

The portal's edges pulsed, then extended tendrils in all directions! Lightninglike extrusions of power began spinning out from his carefully wrought framework, waving aimlessly, as if they were searching for something.

Then, as a thread of fear traversed his spine, they reacted as if they felt that fear, and began groping after *him!* And he was paralyzed with weakness, unable to move from his chair!

Gods and demons! No!

He couldn't tell what had gone wrong, or even if this was somehow what was supposed to happen—

No, this couldn't be what was "supposed" to happen; if those tentacles touched him, they would suck the rest of the power from him before he could even blink. He could tell by their color, they *had* to be kept from him. Something had gone wrong—very, very wrong. This was worse than when he had touched the node—for this *thing* he had created was part of him, and he could no more cut himself off from it than he could cut off an arm. What now?

The life-energy tentacles reached blindly for him, threatening to create a power-loop that would devour him. All he could think of was that an Adept would know what to do if this spell was going wrong. At this point, he would gladly have welcomed *any* Adept; Hulda, an Eastern mage, even one of the disgustingly pure White Winds Adepts. *Anyone,* so long as they knew what this thing was and how to save him from it!

At that moment, the groping tendrils stopped reaching for him. They hovered and flickered, then responded to his panicked thoughts and reached instead into the void, growing thinner and thinner...

What—?

Suddenly there was no strength to spare even for a thought; his strength poured from him as from a mortal wound, and he collapsed against the back of his chair. His head spun, his senses began to desert him, and it was all he could do to cling to consciousness and fight the thing he had created.

Then, between one heartbeat and the next, there was a terrible surge of energy back *into* him and through him. Soundless light exploded against his eyelids; he gasped in pain.

That was too much; he blacked out for a moment, all of his senses overloaded, all of his channels struggling to contain the power that had flooded back into him.

Finally, he took a breath. Another. His lungs still worked; he had not been burned to a cinder after all. He blinked, surprised that he could still see.

And as his eyes focused again, he realized that he was no longer alone in his tower room.

There was something—some kind of not-quite-human creature— collapsed at his feet. The portal was gone, and with it, the back and shelves of the empty bookcase.

His first, fleeting thought was that it was a good thing that he had chosen an *empty* bookcase for his experiment. His second, that whatever it was he had created, it had *not* been the means to tap into the nodes that he had thought it would be.

His third—that he had somehow *brought* this creature here. Was that why the manuscript had called the construct a *portal?* Was it a door to somewhere else, not the nodes? If it was, this creature he had somehow summoned through it was from a place stranger than he had ever seen or heard of. It was unconscious, but breathing. He turned it over, carefully, with his foot.

It? No, indisputably "he," not "it."

Whatever he was, this strange creature, he was in very bad condition; in the deep shock only handling too much mage-energy could produce, the shock that Ancar himself had only narrowly escaped just now. He was manlike, but had many attributes of a huge and powerful cat—a golden pelt, manelike hair, the teeth of a carnivore—and the more Ancar examined him, the more certain he became that those "attributes" had been created. This being had somehow been involved in changing his own shape, something that Ancar could not do, and had only seen Hulda do once. This was a more useful ability than a spell of illusion, which could be detected or broken.

Wait a moment, and think. He might have been born this way, and not something changed by magic. Or he could even be a different race than mankind altogether. This could be the creature's natural shape.

That thought was a trifle disappointing, but if it was true, it still meant that the creature was from so far away that Ancar had never even picked up a hint of anything like it before. It had to be involved in magic to have gotten into that void between the Planes. And together, those two facts meant that it must know many things that were not in the magic traditions that Ancar had been using.

And that meant things entirely outside Hulda's scope of knowledge.

Ancar smiled.

He drew upon the energy of his imprisoned girls below, and gained the strength to rise and examine the creature sprawled across the wooden floor of his tower room.

Carefully, warily, Ancar knelt beside him and touched him, extending his own battered probes to the mind and the potentials within that mind.

Whatever shields the creature had once possessed were gone; all of his remaining energies were devoted to simply staying alive. That left him completely naked to Ancar's probes, and what the King found as he explored the creature's potentials startled him into a smothered shout of glee.

The odd half-beast was an Adept! It was clear for anyone of Master rank to read, in the channels, in the strength of his Gift. And a powerful Adept as well... that much was evident from the signs all over him that pointed to constant manipulations of mage-energy on a scale Ancar had only dreamed of.

And with his shields gone, his mind open, he was entirely within Ancar's power. Here it was, exactly what he had been longing for. The power of an Adept was what Ancar wanted; whether it was within himself or in another, it did not matter—as long as it was in his control.

The beast stirred and opened his eyes. Slitted eyes, with rings of gold and green, blinking in a way that could not be counterfeited. The creature was dazed, disoriented, and so weak he could not even manage a coherent thought.

Quickly, before the strange creature could do anything to orient itself, he flung the simplest controlling spell he could think of at it, sending it to sleep. Clumsy with excitement, he lurched to his feet and ran down the two staircases to the room at the base of the tower.

There was no time for finesse, and no time to worry about subtlety. He unlocked the first cell with a touch of his finger, and dragged the shrinking, terrified girl huddled inside out into the light.

She wore a collar and nothing else; a red collar. Good, she was still a virgin.

He snapped a chain onto her collar, and hauled her up the staircase behind him.

* * *

Ancar flung the knife aside, to lie beside the lifeless body of the girl he had brought up from below. He had been a little disappointed in the amount of power he had been able to drain from her before she died. He hoped it would be enough.

He raised his hands and held them palm-down over the creature at his feet. The runes of coercion gleamed wetly on his golden pelt, drawn there in blood while the girl's heart was still beating. This, at least, he had done many times.

He recited the spell under his breath, and chuckled in satisfaction as the runes flared up brightly, then vanished, along with the girl's body. He stepped back a pace or two, then settled himself in his chair again, without once taking his eyes off the body of his new acquisition.

Once he was comfortable, he banished the spell that held the creature unconscious, and watched as the golden eyes flickered open again.

This time there was sense in them; sense, and wariness. But no strength; the creature tried to rise and failed, tasted the strength of the coercive spells binding him, but did not even attempt to test them. Ancar had taken a small risk with one of his spells; he had substituted the glyph for "sound" for the one of "sight" in the only translation spell he knew. He hoped it would enable this strange creature to understand him, and be understood in return.

"Who are you?" he asked carefully.

The creature levered itself into a sitting position, but did not seem able to rise any farther. The man-beast stared at him for a long moment, while Ancar wondered if the spell had worked, or if he should repeat the question.

Then he saw the flicker of sly defiance in the eyes.

...or perhaps a little coercive pressure.

He exerted his will, just a trifle, and had the satisfaction of seeing his captive wince. The sensuous mouth opened.

"Falconsbane." The voice was low, and Ancar had the feeling it could be pleasant, even seductive, if the owner chose. "Mornelithe... Falconsbane."

Oh, how pretentious. At least the creature understood him. "Where do you come from?"

A very pink tongue licked the generous lips; Ancar stared in fascination. This Falconsbane had tremendous powers of recovery! He had gone from comatose to speech in a much shorter time than Ancar had expected, even with the magical assistance of the girl's life-force.

But the question seemed to confuse the creature.

Well, of course it does, fool! If he does not know where he is, how can he know where he is from?

"Never mind that," Ancar amended. "What are you? Is that your natural form?"

"I am... changed," Falconsbane said slowly. "I have changed myself." The words were dragged out of him by the coercion spells, and Ancar clutched the arms of his chair in glee. This had tremendous potential, oh yes, indeed.

Ancar spent as much of the creature's strength as he dared, extracting more information. Some of it he did not understand, although he expected to at some point, when he had time to question Falconsbane in detail. What was a "Hawkbrother," for instance? And what was a "Heartstone?"

But the initial information was enough. Falconsbane was an Adept; he understood the spell that Ancar had botched, although it was fortunate that he *had* botched it, and Ancar had no intention of revealing his inexperience. It was called a "Gate" and Falconsbane had somehow gotten caught in the backlash of a spell that had sent him into the void between Gates. Ancar had hauled him out of there, with his very wish for an Adept to come to his rescue! Falconsbane was not only an Adept, he was probably more powerful and knowledgeable than Ancar had dared to imagine. He had enemies—the "Hawkbrothers" he had mentioned, and "others from his past." He had a vast holding of his own, and Ancar guessed from descriptions that it was to the south and west of Rethwellan, out in the lands purportedly still despoiled by wild magic. He sometimes referred to himself as a "Changechild," and had said things that made Ancar think that what Falconsbane had done with his own body he could do with others. That was an exciting possibility; it meant that Ancar could infiltrate spies anywhere, simply by substituting his own changed men for people in positions of trust.

And Mornelithe Falconsbane was Ancar's entirely.

He was, however, not in very good condition. Even with Ancar's sorcerous support, he had begun to waver during the last few questions. His strength was giving out, and he was still very disoriented. His answers had all come from memory; in order to have an effective servant, he would have to be able to think, and that would require a certain amount of physical recovery.

I am going to have to get this creature back on his feet—and hide him from Hulda.

If I am very, very lucky, she will have attributed the tremors in the fabric of mage-energy to her own passions. If I am not, I shall have to think of something else I could have done that would make the same ripples in the energies.

He had no doubt that if Hulda got wind of Falconsbane's existence—at least up until the Changechild was capable of defending himself—the creature would either vanish or end up in Hulda's control. It was *much* easier to break coercion spells from outside than it was from within them, and Hulda was still stronger than Ancar.

Now, where can I hide this little guest of mine?

He left Falconsbane slumped in the middle of the floor, and hastened down his staircase to summon more of his hand-picked servants. More members of his personal guard; men Hulda never saw, who masqueraded as stable hands and acted as spies among the lowest servants. On his instructions, they brought with them robes and a litter, bundling Falconsbane into it and covering him as if he were sick or injured. Their eyes showed not even a flicker of curiosity at the strange creature. Ancar smiled in satisfaction.

"Take him to the house of Lord Alistair," Ancar told them. "Tell Lord Alistair that he is to take care of this man, and see to it that he receives the best possible care, under constant guard." He pulled off his ring and handed it to the ranking officer. "Give him this; he will understand."

"Lord" Alistair was one of Ancar's own mages, a man he had recruited himself, and on whom he had so many coercions he did not think that Alistair would even be able to use the garderobe without permission.

He's not powerful enough for Hulda to worry about, not attractive enough for Hulda to care about, and I doubt she's going to try to manipulate him. Even if she does, she'll leave her mark on my coercions, and I will have ample time to move my little prize before she learns about him.

The officer accepted the ring and slipped it into his belt-pouch with a bow. He waved to the others to begin the awkward task of taking the litter down the staircase as Ancar stepped back to give them room. But before they had gone more than a step, a voice emerged from the pile of robes on the litter.

"Wait—"

The men stopped, confused. Ancar moved closer to the side of the litter. A pair of feverishly bright eyes looked up at him from under the shadows of a hood.

"Who—are you?"

Ancar grinned, his spirits buoyed up by his new-found feelings of power. This was too great an opportunity to resist.

"King Ancar of Hardorn," he said, softly; then, with steel in his voice that showed he would not be trifled with, added, "But you will call me—'Master.'"

The bright eyes flashed in impotent anger, and Ancar laughed, waving to the litter bearers to be on their way. He had the upper hand here, and he was not going to give Falconsbane a chance to regain it.

2

Herald Elspeth, Heir to the Kingdom of Valdemar, Adept-Mage-In-Training, Wingsister to Tayledras clan k'Sheyna, was in hot water up to her neck—again. She was immersed in a steaming pool, surrounded by Hawkbrother scouts and mages, and members of the legendary Kaled'a'in clan k'Leshya, not all of whom were human...

"This feels marvelous. I say it every day, but I'll say it again: We don't have *anything* like this back in Valdemar. *Yet!*" Elspeth smiled to her counterparts in the hot-spring grotto. "I got word from Gwena there were inventors in Haven working on a water heating system using the fires from forges. If they can make it work, I am definitely going to encourage them to make something like this."

Iceshadow k'Sheyna twisted a few strands of his waist-length, winter-white hair around his finger, and looked thoughtful. It was difficult to tell how old he was, despite the white hair; older than Elspeth, but that was about it. His smooth, sculptured face showed little sign of age, and only a few worry lines creased Iceshadow's brow as a sign of past troubles. He stretched out his arms, popping his joints softly. "You'll be taking many new ways of thinking back to your people. However," he continued, "k'Sheyna will always be a home to you."

"Very true. And while I am proud to be a Wingsister... well, as much as I love the Vales, I would like to see my old familiar surroundings. I like to travel, but I'm not really nomadic. Even people I couldn't stand back at the palace seem pleasant once I've been away from them for a while."

"I feel the same way about our Clan. Those few I disliked in person, I have come to feel affection for when away. Distance and time can do that. But I must admit," he said to Elspeth, "that despite being thrilled at the thought of seeing the rest of k'Sheyna again, this whole Gating business makes me very nervous. Making a Gate, in the heart of this Vale..."

It wasn't Elspeth who answered him. Firesong, who seemingly had not been paying attention to anyone but his black-haired companion Silverfox, grinned back over his shoulder at them. "Ah, there is no unstable Heartstone here, elder cousin. You have no reason to be nervous. Well, not because of Gates, anyway."

When Firesong smiled, it was difficult not to smile back. The supernally handsome Adept from the North could charm just about anyone or anything if he exerted himself, and Iceshadow was no exception to the power of that charm. "Only a node here, and another in the gryphons' ruins. Nothing to fret over. There are more than enough mages here to keep the effects of a Gate Spell balanced, and prevent a spring storm from dropping down upon us."

The older Hawkbrother laughed shakily, returning Firesong's grin. "It is difficult to convince my insides of this, youngling. We lived too long in the shadow of power we dared not trust. It can make anyone wary."

Firesong scowled a little but nodded. He, of all of them, knew best the chill of that shadow, for he had been the one most directly involved in confining it. Elspeth understood Iceshadow's meaning only too easily herself. The little time she had spent in the presence of the rogue, unstable Heartstone of k'Sheyna Vale had been more than enough to convince her that Iceshadow's fears would be hard to lay to rest.

And yet, the real damage that power had done had all been beneath the surface. This Vale had looked to her—and still did—like a little corner of the Havens itself, the realm of the gods. She looked about her, at the luxuriant life of the heart of k'Sheyna, at the incredible beauty of the flowering bushes and vines everywhere, the fluted, sculptured rocks surrounding the hot-spring-fed pool—

Then her senses took in the things that did not fit in a scene from a Valdemaran fantasy or Bardic play.

The huge trees, each supporting as many as a dozen *ekele,* the Tayledras treehouses. The silver-haired mages and mottled-haired scouts taking their ease in the warm waters of the pool, their exotic birds in the branches above them. Hummingbirds drifting by and hovering. The Kaled'a'in, who were clearly some kin to the Tayledras, but of more diverse breeding, some with round faces, some with green or brown eyes instead of silver-blue, and here and there a blond or a redhead. The swirl of silk and the hushed scrape and creak of well-worn leather amidst the calls of immense birds of prey.

And last of all, the gryphons lounging about in the warm sun—

gryphons gray and golden-brown, peregrine-patterned and cooperi-striped, purring or cooing, and talking with Hawkbrothers—

She had a sudden feeling of disorientation, and shook her head. If, a year ago, anyone had told her that she would be soaking in a pool with a half dozen Hawkbrother mages, numbered as a Wingsister to a Hawkbrother Clan, and watching the antics of a score of legendary gryphons, she would have been certain that whoever asserted this had been severely intoxicated.

If they had told her she would be instrumental in the overthrow of a marauding evil Adept, and have a Hawkbrother lover—while her fellow Herald Skif would have an even stranger lover, the half-feline Nyara, daughter of that Adept—and that this same Nyara, and not Elspeth, would be the holder of Elspeth's sword Need—

I would have carefully caught that person off-guard, tied him up, and put in an urgent call to the MindHealers, that's what I would have done.

But MindHealing comes in many forms, and experience is the best of them. Time had passed. She'd experienced all of that and more, and still the future was wide open.

A blazingly white figure appeared at the far side of the pool, just at the edge of the spray from the tiny waterfall that cooled one end.

And right on cue, a beam of sunlight penetrated the clouds and illuminated Elspeth's Companion Gwena, framing her in a rainbow's refracted light, making her look like a horse from the home of the gods, or a Companion-illustration in some book of tales.

Several of the Hawkbrothers gazed appreciatively.

"Good entrance," Firesong laughed, approvingly. "I could not have managed better myself." Silverfox chuckled, and continued to braid the man's waist-length silver hair in an elaborate Kaled'a'in arrangement. Firesong spent most of his time with the Kaled'a'in, and surprisingly, not all of that was with the Kestra'chern Silverfox. Evidently, the Kaled'a'in had explored the usages of magic along much different lines than the Tayledras, and what he was learning from them both excited and fascinated Firesong. Among other things, they had learned how to build Vales without needing a Heartstone; old chronicles spoke of this, but the Tayledras had lost the knack. Elspeth was interested in learning this trick as well, since if it could be managed in Valdemar, it would be possible to create some very comfortable safe-havens in inhospitable territory for, say, Healer's enclaves.

Or Heralds' Resupply Stations… what a lovely thought.

"You look fine today," Firesong continued.

:Thank you for the compliment, my dear,: Gwena replied, winking at the Adept, her calm completely unruffled. *:From you, that is high praise indeed.:*

Elspeth giggled. Gwena was much easier to live with these days, now that she had given up on steering Elspeth to some "destiny," and had resigned herself to the fact that Elspeth was going to make her own way whether or not Gwena liked it. *:So, dearheart, have you finished gossiping with Rolan?:*

Gwena had been giving Rolan—the Queen's Own Companion—daily reports for the past several weeks now, as winter turned to spring, and matters in k'Sheyna Vale were slowly settled. The original plan, made in the euphoria of victory, had been to return to Valdemar immediately, and then, if their enemies gave them a chance, to explore just what, exactly, was going on with the Forest of Sorrows. Several times during their struggle with Mornelithe Falconsbane it seemed as if some power up there was interfering on their behalf. But that plan had to be amended; there were many things she needed to learn from Firesong before he returned to his own Vale, and in the end there seemed to be no real urgency in getting back to Valdemar before winter ended. Ancar had been well confined by the combined armies of Valdemar, Rethwellan, and—miracle of miracles—Karse. His mages seemed to be doing nothing, except waiting and watching. And Elspeth really didn't *want* to go home until the last of winter was over—

—and until memories had faded of the hideous headache that had hit every Herald and Companion in the capital city of Haven, the day that control of the Heartstone's power had been wrested from Mornelithe Falconsbane. The day that same power had come to rest *somewhere* in the Palace/Collegium complex, giving Haven what appeared to be a small, new and, so far, quiescent Heartstone of its own, as if it were to be a new Tayledras Vale.

Elspeth had not known this until after the fact, but as that power snapped into place, every Herald within a few leagues' radius of the capital had been struck down with a blinding, incapacitating headache. So had their Companions. For most, the worst pain had lasted no more than a few hours, but for several others, it had taken days to recover. Elspeth didn't *think* they were going to blame her for it—after all, no one knew the power-locus would go there! It had been intended to go to where most of k'Sheyna Clan waited, to the prepared node and carefully anchored proto-Heartstone they had waiting for it.

K'Sheyna had been very gracious about the theft of their power-source, much more gracious than Elspeth had any right to expect, and quite philosophical about it all.

Still, she didn't think that was going to soothe the ruffled feathers of those Heralds who had found themselves facedown in the snow—or the soup—or otherwise collapsed with indignity and without warning. She absolutely dreaded having to answer to Weaponsmaster Alberich and her own teacher, Herald-Captain Kerowyn. And they were both going to demand answers. They might be contemplating retribution. It would be hard to convince them that *she* had nothing to do with it, and that she had no idea that it was going to happen. It would be even harder to convince them it seemed to be due to some nebulous force living in the Forest of Sorrows. Neither Alberich nor Kerowyn believed in ghosts, not even Herald-Mage ghosts.

Fortunately, Rolan had been mostly immune to what Gwena later said must have been a magical backlash as the great power landed in the middle of the "Web" that connected all Heralds. He had helped calm the panic, had helped Healers and the rescuers find Heralds who had simply dropped, all over Haven. Talia had been one of the first to recover, and she had organized those who bounced back into caring for the rest until the pain passed. And Gwena passed word to Rolan that this was *not* some new and insidious attack from Ancar, that it was—well— an accident.

Since then, Gwena had been in daily contact with Rolan, by order of Elspeth's mother, Queen Selenay. The order had sounded less like an hysterical mother, however, and more as if it had come from Her Majesty the Queen. An hysterical mother was not something Elspeth could handle, but duty to the Queen and Realm was the first order of any Herald's life. Since Falconsbane's banishment into the Void between Gates—and highly probable death—life at k'Sheyna had been *much* less eventful, so it was an easy order to fulfill.

The shaft of sunlight faded; still bright but no longer illuminated like the gods' own Avatar, Gwena surefootedly made her way around the pool to where her Chosen was soaking. Elspeth had been spending a great deal of time with the Kaled'a'in as well, not only to learn magic, but to learn new fighting skills. They had a number of barehanded combat techniques that could allow one who was skilled in them to take on a fighter with a weapon in his hands. Useful techniques for someone who had already faced one assassin.

But occasionally painful to learn…

:It wasn't entirely gossip, dear,: the Companion said, in Mindspeech pitched only for Elspeth to catch. *:Although we've been doing more of that than exchanging any real news lately. Things haven't been all that interesting around Haven or k'Sheyna Vale.:* She chuckled mentally. *:I haven't even had to edit for your mother's consumption once during the last two weeks!:*

Elspeth laughed out loud. "Just remember, heart of mine, that 'may your life be eventful' is the worst curse the Shin'a'in know!"

Iceshadow looked over at her quizzically.

"Oh. I was talking to Gwena. She said things weren't as interesting around here as they used to be."

"Ah. Indeed," Iceshadow agreed. "I will be glad, after all, to see this Gate built to the new Vale, and find myself living in times *much* less interesting!"

He climbed out of the pool; before he had done more than stand, a little lizardlike *hertasi* appeared with a speed that was close to magical. Iceshadow nodded his thanks, and accepted the thick towel the lizard handed him. Again, Elspeth was forced to confront how much she had changed.

Not only in accepting something that looked like an overgrown garden-lizard as an intellectual equal, but in other ways as well. Iceshadow wore nothing more than his long hair; in fact, no one soaking in this pool seemed terribly body-shy. A year ago she would have blushed and averted her eyes. Now she was so much more aware of what each of the Hawkbrothers and Kaled'a'in here *were*, their bodies were simply another garment for the spirit within.

Iceshadow wrapped the towel around himself, and the *hertasi* looked down at Elspeth. The little lizard-folk who had come with the Lost Clan were much bolder than the *hertasi* native to k'Sheyna; she hardly ever saw the latter, while the former bustled about the Vale, undoing the overgrowth of nearly a decade, as oblivious to watchers as a hive of bees. Except, of course, when someone needed something. They seemed to thrive on tending others. Silverfox had said something about that being "part of" them, but hadn't elaborated except to say that it was due to their "recovery" from a long-ago trauma. She wished she knew more; there was such knowledge to learn, and so little time!

"Need towel?" it said to her. "Need drink?" While the *hertasi* seemed to have an instinctive ability to anticipate the needs of the Tayledras and Kaled'a'in, they were at a bit of a loss with her. Gwena and Darkwind had both tried to explain why; she was still at a loss after both explanations. The Lost Clan lizards were perfectly willing to talk to her, sometimes in Mindspeech, and often in audible speech. Even if their speech was a little difficult to understand, if they didn't mind, how could she?

"Thank you, no," she replied. "But when Darkwind gets in, he'll want food and drink, please."

The *hertasi* hissed, "Of course!" and vanished again. Iceshadow gave her a farewell smile, and wandered off to his own *ekele* barefoot. She turned to Firesong, who was leaning back against the stone of the pool's edge and enjoying the massage Silverfox was giving to his long and graceful hands.

It was hard to get her mind on business, but in the next couple of days it *would* be time to leave, and she had better get her mind set about doing so. "Have Treyvan and Hydona made up their minds what they want to do first?" she asked. "I'd be perfectly happy to have them come to Haven as ambassadors, but if there are more Kaled'a'in out there wanting to come back, they *really* ought to go to k'Treva first, as you suggested."

Firesong made a small sigh of utter contentment, and answered without opening his eyes. "I believe that I have talked them into my scheme, cousin," he replied. "K'Treva will not be long in moving on to a new Vale; there have been no troublesome outbreaks of any kind for better than a year now. Indeed, we would have moved on this winter, had it not been for your request for help. And if I may boast—k'Treva Vale is second to none. I think that our Kaled'a'in brethren would be most happy there, taking it after we have gone."

"Is that fulsome description for my benefit, *shaya?*" laughed Silverfox. "I promise you, there are not many who would require convincing. We had not expected to find ourselves offered safe-havens and homes, ready to our hands—yet another miracle of Treyvan and Hydona's doing. And I think that none among you will find fault with our stewardship of what you will leave behind."

The Kestra'chern tossed his dark hair over his shoulder, and moved his graceful fingers along the tendons of Firesong's wrists. Firesong sighed with content.

It was still very hard to think of Firesong as a relative, however distant. She had not even known that Herald-Mage Vanyel had left any offspring—much less that she and a Hawkbrother Healing Adept were descendants of two of them! Really, she had learned more about herself in the time she had been here than she had learned about magic...

"On the whole, I think it's a better idea," Elspeth told him. "I'm glad you talked them into it. My people are going to have enough trouble with Darkwind and a Changechild appearing on their doorstep. I'm not sure I want to subject them to gryphons and gryphlets as well."

"Ah," Silverfox said shrewdly, "but with gryphons and gryphlets, a Changechild and a Hawkbrother Adept might well look less strange. Hmm?"

"The thought had occurred to me," she admitted. "But—well, let's just leave things the way they are. The gryphons can always change their minds when Darkwind and I are ready to Gate out of k'Treva."

"And gryphons are wont to do *just* that," Darkwind said from behind her, where he had already begun undressing.

She turned quickly with a welcoming smile, and he slipped out of the last of his scout gear and into the warm water of the pool. "Gods of my fathers!" he groaned. "That is wonderful! I thought I had become naught but a man of ice! I have never found anything colder than a spring rain."

Elspeth could think of several—such as the snowdrifts that she and Darkwind had collapsed into in the aftermath of Falconsbane's banishment—but then, she hadn't been out on the border all day, either. Temperature seemed to depend on context.

"Just be glad that we're going to k'Treva by Gate, then," she replied. "Skif and I got here the hard way. It's a lot colder outside the Vales up north!"

She tapped his shoulder to get him to turn his back to her so that she could work on his shoulders, and his skin was still cool to the touch. He must have gotten quite thoroughly soaked and chilled while out patrolling the boundaries of k'Sheyna territory for the last few times. Soon, that would be the duty of the Kaled'a'in, and indeed, Kaled'a'in scouts were making the patrols with the Tayledras to learn the lay of the land that would soon be theirs. Darkwind had gone out alone, and come back late; she didn't even have to ask why. She knew that he was gradually saying his farewells to the hills and trees he'd known for so long.

"The gryphons are envious of Treyvan and Hydona," Darkwind continued, with an inquiring glance at Silverfox. "Apparently there's something special about the lake near k'Treva. The one the Valdemarans call Lake Evendim?"

Silverfox nodded. "It is the site of the Black Gryphon's defeat of the Dark Adept Ma'ar. They wish greatly to see this."

Elspeth laughed. "I tried to tell them that they won't *see* anything, that it's all under water, but they didn't care. They are still excited about the whole idea, and every other gryphon is dying for a chance to get up there, too. You'd better be careful about how many of them you let come at once, Firesong, or you'll be up to your eyebrows in gryphons!"

"I shall remember that, cousin. And warn the rest of k'Treva," Firesong replied lazily. "Not that I think such an eventuality would be altogether bad. I find them delightful company, and I'm sure the rest of my Clan will feel the same."

Darkwind snorted. *"You* haven't been responsible for keeping those feathered eating machines fed! Talk to me after you've been hunting for hours, trying to find something larger than a rabbit!"

Silverfox chuckled. "If you think that this is difficult," he pointed out, "think about how it must be in a Vale full of breeding gryphons. The gryphlets eat three times their body weight a day until they are fully fledged!"

Elspeth tried to imagine that, and in the end just shook her head. "No wonder you wanted to move here. How do you keep them from stripping the countryside bare?"

"We have herds," Silverfox replied. "Fear not; we have learned how to manage our own needs and balance them against the needs of the land. We have beasts that are quick to grow, and eat nearly anything. We shall start the herds as soon as you are gone."

As soon as you are gone. Darkwind turned his head to smile into Elspeth's eyes, a glint of anticipation in his, and suddenly she was impatient to get back home. *He* was certainly excited about the prospect of leaving his Clan and kin, and seeing new lands. And there had been so much going on that she had missed out on—the twins getting older, the alliance with Karse, Talia being made a titular Priestess of Vkandis—

Home…

It seemed to beckon her, for all the drawbacks of life there, under a kind of siege.

And now she could hardly wait.

Elspeth folded one of the scarlet silk shirts that Darkwind had designed for her; it rolled up into a surprisingly compact bundle, as did most of her Tayledras clothing. She was certainly going to cut quite a figure when she returned. She had the feeling that a lot of eyebrows were going to go up and stay up.

Things had not been as simple to take care of as they had seemed in the aftermath of the victory over Falconsbane. It had taken most of the winter for the party in search of k'Sheyna to journey overland to the new Vale and return. The very first order of business after everyone had recovered from that last confrontation with Falconsbane had been to *find* the new Vale again. That had taken a great deal of searching by mages who had near relatives or dear friends that had been sent on with the children and artisans. In the end they had found it by sending hummingbirds in the right general direction, keyed to those friends, and waiting for the reply.

Finally, after nerves had been strained to the breaking point, they had found the place, and then with the help of gryphon warriors aloft, two mages, the k'Sheyna Adept Silence and the Kaled'a'in Adept Summerfawn, had gone to find it and return with a mental picture of the place. No Gate could be built without knowing what the destination looked like, which made the things rather limited in practicality, so far as Elspeth was concerned. On the other hand, she was deeply grateful that this *was* the case; she did not even want to think of the Gate Spell in the hands of Ancar, if it made it possible for him to go and come at will to any place he cared.

Silence had returned, thin and travel-worn, but smiling and no longer silent. And now bearing the name "Snowfire," which told everyone that Silence had finally been healed of the emotional trauma that the shattering of the Heartstone and the deaths of so many of k'Sheyna had inflicted, years ago.

With that good omen, it was simply a matter of letting Snowfire rest, and then the Gate between the two Vales, old and new, could be built, and k'Sheyna would be a whole Clan once more. The Kaled'a'in had another trick up their ornamented sleeves as well; not one Adept, but two would build the Gate; Summerfawn from the new Vale and Snowfire from the old. They would build two Gates in parallel, and fuse them into one; halving the fatigue and doubling the strength.

Tomorrow. So many things would begin and end tomorrow—though there would be more endings for Darkwind than for Elspeth.

Now, with the culmination of many weeks of work at hand, Elspeth carefully packed away everything she would not need over the next two or three days. She had been a little dismayed at how much she had accumulated, but now that she had begun, she realized that most of it was clothing, and that packed down into an amazingly small volume. Probably because it was mostly silk, or something like silk…

Darkwind seemed unusually silent, although he was packing just as busily as Elspeth.

I wonder if Gwena made it plain to Mother that I'd been sharing quarters with one of my mage-teachers. Probably not. No point in giving her another thing to get hysterical about. It had seemed rather stupid to keep two *ekeles* when they really only needed one, especially after the arrival of the Kaled'a'in had made things suddenly rather cramped. She had moved in with him, since the *ekele* he had was nearer the entrance to the Vale and had more room than hers.

Perhaps they should have reversed it. Perhaps he would feel the loss less if he had already left his "home."

He tucked a folded garment into the top of a pack and laced the whole thing shut. "I am very glad that I had already left the other *ekele* that I had built before all this happened," he said into the silence. "That was my home—for all that it leaked cold air all winter long. Built by my hands. But it seemed foolish to be living outside the Vale once the Heartstone was shielded, so—" He shrugged. "This place we have shared is dear only because we have shared it. It gives me no great wrench to leave it for another, especially after they have had a long journey."

She stifled a sigh of relief. "I saw how packing up affected Starblade, when he and Kethra had to abandon the place Falconsbane wrecked. It was very emotional for him, and I couldn't help think that leaving your home and your Vale both at once was going to give you some problems."

He made a face and threw a shirt at her; she caught it and began folding it. "Father's emotional condition is a bit less stable than mine, I dare to think."

She nodded agreement. "Well, I for one am truly glad that Kethra is going with your father. I was afraid she might do one of those typically Shin'a'in things and declare she couldn't leave the Plains!"

Darkwind grinned, and this time tossed a pillow at her. She ducked. "You are being silly. How could she do anything like that with one of Hyllarr's feathers, beaded and braided into her hair for all to see? They are mated, silly Herald. She could no more leave him than Hyllarr can."

"Silly Herald, yourself," she retorted. "How am I to know what all these headings and braidings mean? And how in Havens am I to know one feather from another?"

He shook his head sadly. "Barbarian. Barbarian and ignorant. *How* could you not tell that the feather was from Hyllarr? From where else would such a great golden primary have come? There are no other birds the size of a crested hawk-eagle here!"

She cast her eyes up at the ceiling, as if praying for patience. "Just wait," she replied. "Just *wait* until I get you home, and you complain about not being able to tell Companions apart! Revenge will be so-o-o-o sweet!"

He only grinned and went back to his packing, and she to hers and her thoughts. Thinking about the Shin'a'in Healer Kethra made her a great deal happier than worrying about Darkwind. There were going to be problems when she got home that she'd rather not think about right now...

She and Kethra had struck up an odd friendship over the winter, and a bond forged by their love for Darkwind and Darkwind's father Starblade, cemented by the new bondbird that Darkwind and Elspeth had found for the weakened Adept. From the very moment that charming Hyllarr had come into Starblade's life, his recovery from the terrible damage Falconsbane had done to him had been assured. For that alone, Elspeth suspected, Kethra would have been inclined to like her, although Hyllarr's discovery was still sheer good luck in Elspeth's mind. But they were surprisingly alike, and that helped; Kethra had been able to deliver authoritative conversations on caring and partnering that would have been a lecture coming from anyone else, but seemed no more than good advice from Kethra.

It was due to Kethra's suggestions that Darkwind, Skif, and Elspeth, together and separately, had urged Starblade and Wintermoon—Darkwind's half brother—to begin simply *talking* to one another. Wintermoon had long envied Darkwind's favored-son relationship with his father, and had withdrawn from Starblade when quite young. Kethra felt that the time was long past when they should have reversed that withdrawal.

Now—with Kethra, Darkwind, Elspeth, and Skif urging and encouraging, Starblade and Wintermoon had begun building the father-son relationship they had never really enjoyed. Another sign of healing, perhaps, but just as importantly it was a sign that Starblade felt worthy of having relationships at all.

Darkwind had said at one point that he thought in some ways this was the easiest of the relationships for Starblade to establish. There had been so much that had been warped and destroyed of the relationship between Darkwind and his father, that even trying to reestablish it was painful. And so much about loving had been tainted by Falconsbane that simply to permit Kethra into his heart must have been an act of supreme and terrible courage for Starblade.

Yet another thing Falconsbane has to answer for, whatever hell he's in, Elspeth thought angrily. *The beast.*

In many, many ways, it was a good thing that Darkwind and Starblade would be separated for a while. That would give emotional scars a chance to really heal without constant contact irritating them; give Starblade time to find a new way to think of his son—as something other than a little copy of himself that had been his pride.

And it would give Darkwind time to reconcile everything that *he* had endured.

I think emotional damage is harder to heal than physical damage...

Well, tomorrow would put that distance between them. And if it had not been for Clan k'Leshya and the gryphons, instrumental in helping to find the exact physical location of the rest of k'Sheyna, the healing process would have been put off a lot longer. That alone had succeeded in convincing the last diehards of k'Sheyna that the Kaled'a'in *deserved* the stewardship of the old Vale. If they had not generously volunteered their help, it would have taken months to locate the Clan and get an Adept in place who could handle the Gate Spell from the other end.

She looked around for something else to pack, and realized that there was nothing left. Darkwind's collection of feather-masks had been carefully packed up by one of his *hertasi,* and the walls were bare. Books and furniture would be left behind for the next occupant. Small keepsakes and jewelry had been tucked into odd corners of packs; feathers likewise. The few papers and notebooks Darkwind meant to take with him were already in the last pack. That left only the clothing they would need for the next couple of days.

Elspeth was not even taking her old Whites, nor was Skif. The *hertasi,* particularly the Kaled'a'in *hertasi,* had made their disdain of those plain, utilitarian garments very obvious. She had finally given in to their unremitting pressure to let them "make something better." She had only specified that the resulting clothing must follow the same general lines as the old Whites and *must* be completely *white.* Not ecru, not eggshell, not ivory, nor pearl-gray, nor pale pink. *White.* The clothing must be functional; ornamentation must not be any color but white, and it must not catch on things, tear off, or glitter in the sun to give her away—

"As if big white target in green field not give you away," one of the k'Leshya *hertasi* had replied in scorn.

She suspected that in the end the *hertasi,* frustrated, had appealed to Darkwind for help; certainly the new Whites had his touch about them. And it was possible to see the pattern of the originals in the new uniforms. But there the resemblance had ended.

Flowing sleeves caught in long, close cuffs at the wrists, white-on-white embroidery and even beadwork, leathers softer even than deerskin with cut-out patterns as elaborate as lace and long fringe that fell like a waterfall, beautifully tooled and fringed boots and half-boots, and more of the ubiquitous silk so beloved of the Tayledras—the clothing was far more exotic than she could have imagined Whites would be. And, somewhat to her own surprise, she liked them. Even more to her surprise, so did Skif, who asked the *hertasi* to make him something suited to his size and frame—and style.

So the *hertasi* had their hearts' desire, and took apart the old Whites to be used as scrap material and cleaning rags. And the two Heralds would be returning not only splendidly garbed themselves, but with matching gear for their Companions, who gloated that they would be the envy of the Collegium.

"We will do well wherever we go. Home should be in your heart, the Shin'a'in say. Worry not about me," Darkwind said, breaking the silence of Elspeth's thoughts.

"I'll always worry about you. At least a little. I guess we're done," she said, uncertainly. Darkwind laced his pack shut and stood up, smiling.

"Not quite yet, I think," he replied—and before she could react, he caught her up in his arms and tumbled her into their bed.

"We have all evening, and no duties, *kechara*," he said, between kisses. "And *I* at least, had plans—or at least, hopes…"

Given all the unexpected disasters that had followed them, Elspeth more than half expected something to interfere with the opening of the Gate the next morning.

But nothing happened. Those among the gryphons and humans that were relatively low-level mages, or even simply mage-apprentices, contained and smoothed over the power-fluxes caused by diverting the energy-flows at both ends of the Gate. Elspeth had not, in fact, been aware of such work until months ago, after the attempt to move the Heartstone power. Firesong had pointed it out to her with his usual seriousness.

"Never underestimate the importance of even an apprentice," he had told her. "Their work goes on constantly, so that *we* do not so greatly upset all the balances of power and nature that we drive the weather and the ley-lines wild with our actions. If they were not at work, every time an Adept reached out with some major spellcasting, we would be plagued by at least one terrible storm, and perhaps more; the effects tend to be cumulative. Sometimes Adepts forget to thank their so-called 'lesser' cousins, but if it were not for them, we would be greatly handicapped, and everyone for leagues about would curse our names!"

Even so, it was wise to make certain of the weather before attempting a Gate. If there had been any storms in the neighborhood, the attempt would have been delayed.

The appointed day dawned clear and bright, and all of k'Sheyna except Darkwind, Skif, and Elspeth gathered in a pack-burdened crowd before a carved arch, created by the *hertasi* expressly for the purpose of giving the new Gate its physical frame. That it stood on the exact spot where the old Heartstone had been was an irony that was not lost on anyone.

Snowfire stood before the arch, her eyes closed in concentration. A half dozen Hawkbrothers in blue robes cast a carefully prepared, bright-feathered bundle of incense and aromatic leaves into the brazier that honored the Tayledras lost over the years the Vale had been in existence. The entire group bowed their heads in a silent prayer, and the blue smoke from the brazier dwindled down as Snowfire prepared the Gate.

There would be no physical signs of the powers being called into play until the Gate opened, but Elspeth was watching with what Firesong called "the Inner Eye," and the sight was quite impressive.

Snowfire built up the framework of the Gate with power spun from her own resources; she was connected to the Gate by a scintillating cord of energy, multicolored and shining, energy that spun out from her like spidersilk, and came to rest in a continuously shifting pattern laid over the arch. And spinning out from the Gate, reaching off into the void, were more little threads, exactly like the "flying threads" of baby spiders, catching the wind of the void and seeking their anchor.

There was a moment's transition between this Gate-form and the finished Gate. Suddenly, it felt to Elspeth as if the ground dropped out from beneath her for a moment.

Then, instead of the other side of the clearing, there was another side of—something else. Summerfawn k'Leshya stood framed inside the archway, and behind her was a crowd of Tayledras, strangers to Elspeth, who cheered and beckoned.

There might have been sentimental reluctance to leave on the part of some, but at the sight of all those k'Sheyna, a half dozen seized packs and flung themselves through the portal, into the arms of those who awaited them; the rest picked up their belongings and proceeded in a more orderly, but nonetheless eager, fashion. Through it all the two mages holding the Gate stood like rocks, impervious and oblivious.

Starblade came toward Darkwind, with Hyllarr waddling along the ground behind him. The hawk-eagle walked whenever speed was not a factor; his wing never had healed so well that he could fly strongly, and he would have been a terrible burden even for someone like Wintermoon to carry. So he walked. It was not a graceful gait, for no raptor is terribly graceful on the ground, but it served, and it kept Starblade from having to carry him very often. Starblade was the strongest he had been in months, but the weight of a carried raptor seemed to multiply with each passing minute.

Hyllarr leapt to a low branch with only three wing-beats, and regarded the departing Tayledras. Starblade stood on his own before Darkwind, without resting on his walking stick.

"It is time to go, son," the elder Tayledras said quietly, as more of k'Sheyna filed through the arch. "I have not said so until now, but what you are about to do is more important than a single Clan, Darkwind. You carry the bravery of all our ancestors with you, not just k'Sheyna. I am proud of you, and where your mother is, she is proud of you as well."

Darkwind swallowed audibly. Although he had been determined to remain stoic, his throat tightened and his jaw twitched. His father had not spoken to him of his mother with anything besides a tone of self-pity and grief. Now, he spoke of her memory as something factual, not as something that was a knife through his heart. He was healing, and becoming better than he was before. The simple bravery of speaking plainly what was in his heart brought back early childhood memories of how Starblade was invincible and unshakable in Darkwind's eyes.

"I send my prayers with you, my son." Starblade smiled crookedly, and for a moment, many of his years dropped away. The creases of worry and pain changed to become smile-lines, something that hadn't crossed Starblade's face in recent memory. "When you return, you will surely have more tales of life in the Outlands than any scribe will ever be able to pen. And some of them *might* even be true!"

Darkwind laughed, and embraced his father with none of the hesitancy that such embraces had caused before. His own tears touched his father's. "And I expect to hear many tales of your own adventures in dealing with a wild Shin'a'in and a crafty hawkeagle! I think that between them, they will give you no end of excitement!"

:!?: Hyllarr replied, in feigned innocence. :Not I! Am only meek, crippled bird.:

A shadow and rustle of cloth announced Kethra's approach. "I most certainly shall keep his days and nights active," the Shin'a'in Healer said firmly, taking her turn to embrace Elspeth and Darkwind. "Take care of each other, children," she added giving them each a penetrating glance. "Remember, together you are far stronger than you are individually. I think that is something that no enemy will ever be prepared for."

Starblade took Elspeth into his arms, and whispered into her ear, "Watch over my son, dear lady. He is unused to having someone to guard his back, and may not ask for help. Give it anyway, unasked."

"I will," she promised fervently, and kissed him, an act that surprised them both and clearly delighted Starblade.

Starblade lifted his walking stick, and Kethra took the other end onto her shoulder as he did the same. Hyllarr glided down from the branch and alighted between them. His talons closed firmly on the walking stick and he folded his wings, accepting a caress from Starblade. Then it was time, and they took their places as the last in the line.

"Clear skies, Father."

"Wind to thy wings, my son. I love you."

And then they were gone.

Snowfire seemed to wake from her trance; she glanced around the clearing to make certain that there were no stragglers. She saw that Summerfawn already stood on *this* side. Her eyes took in the smoldering embers of the brazier. Then without a single backward look, she strode across the threshold of the Gate.

With a flare of energy, the Gate collapsed.

And for the first time, Darkwind, Elspeth, and Skif were the only k'Sheyna left in the heart of what had been k'Sheyna Vale.

3

The Kaled'a'in clan k'Leshya had been in possession of the Vale for less than a day, and already the place had taken on an entirely new personality.

The Kaled'a'in had waited politely for the former owners to leave before so much as changing a single bush; now they swung into action, taking plans that had been made weeks ago and turning them into reality. The highest *ekeles* were to be converted for use by gryphons after appropriate strengthening, and gryphons and *hertasi* were checking the hillsides around the Vale, and the cliffs at the rear, for suitable lair locations above, and *hertasi* and *kyree* dens below. There were more birds in the air now; not only raptors of bondbird breeding, who had come to the Vale in answer to some unspoken call, but small, colorful creatures in feathered harlequin coats of red, blue, green, and yellow, with raptorial hooked bills and an uncanny ability to mimic human voices. A trio of Kaled'a'in mages began setting up new defenses and Veils to protect the place from the weather as the old Veil faded; rather than receiving power from the nonexistent Heartstone, these defenses would take their energy from a webwork of ley-lines the Kaled'a'in would arrange around the perimeter, lines which would in turn be fed from the node under the ruins where Treyvan and Hydona had nested.

Tervardi and *kyree*, creatures Elspeth had seen only rarely, were part of Clan k'Leshya; considered to be full members and not merely allies. So were the *hertasi*, who bustled about, full of energy, rearranging things to the new Clan's liking now that the old owners had gone.

One thing they were doing was trimming back much of the vegetation. While Elspeth had enjoyed the wildly overgrown Vale with its many shroudings of vine curtains and maskings of flowering bushes, she had to admit that it was a bit difficult to get around in. Every time someone had stormed off in a temper, or had to run somewhere in an emergency, he (or she) had usually wound up with minor scrapes and cuts, leaving behind shredded vegetation. The *hertasi* were taming all that, opening up sunny clearings, making it possible to travel down arched paths without risking strangulation. All the while, those places that needed a certain amount of privacy were left with their surrounding bushes and vines relatively intact. But as Elspeth saw, when she poked her head into the work-in-progress around one of her favorite small hot springs, they were trimming away growth inside the area, so that leaves and dead flowers no longer dropped into the pool to foul it.

Nets were being strung for vines to creep through until they could support themselves and provide more privacy in strategic places. Poles were planted by the *hertasi*, for the greenery to grow against. Dust kicked up by the work filtered through the sunlight as dancing motes of light. Nothing would be quite the same when they were done.

They were scrubbing the stones of the edge, and sifting debris out of the sand at the bottom. Already the water ran clearer. She left the area of the spring much impressed.

The little that Elspeth knew of the Shin'a'in she had learned from

Kethra, but it seemed to her that these people were very different from both the Shin'a'in and the Tayledras. They were less solitary than the Tayledras, though more so than the Shin'a'in. They were certainly noisier than the Tayledras. Every job was accompanied by the murmur of human voices blended with *hertasi* hisses, *tervardi* trills, *kyree* growls, *dyheli* chuckles, and the bass rumblings of gryphons. The Vale as populated by the k'Sheyna had seemed deserted; the Vale as populated by k'Leshya was as full of activity as the Palace/Collegium complex.

Not all of k'Leshya would live inside the Vale. Some would take over the lair begun by Treyvan and Hydona in the ruins overlooking the Dhorisha Plains. They had brought the books that Darkwind had helped build shelves for so long ago.

Others would take the *ekeles* that had been made by the k'Sheyna scouts, surrounding the Vale. Most of the artisans and craftspeople, scholars, and those families with young children would live in the Vale itself—those who were most vulnerable, and most in need of protection. Silverfox had told Elspeth that they hoped to begin a thriving trade with the Shin'a'in, and even with Outsiders. "We use very little magic in everyday things," he had told her. "Mostly for self-defense. But we are fine craftsmen, and trade is how we would prefer to make our Clan prosper."

Even the gryphons? she had wondered. She couldn't see how the gryphons, with those massive talons, could craft anything. Treyvan had needed Darkwind's help just to install a simple set of shelves. But then again, perhaps there were things those talons were good for. Piercing practically anything that needed a hole in it, for one thing…

And gryphons were strong. She'd already seen a gryphon dragging a man-sized log in its beak. Treyvan and Hydona were mages; a little magic went a long way when it came to crafting things. Maybe all the gryphons were mage-craftsmen.

Maybe I just shouldn't worry about it. They hardly need my help or approval!

There seemed to be less activity up near the waterfall, so that was where she went. Everywhere else she got the feeling she was in the way. Perhaps not everything in the Vale would be changed; the k'Leshya had not touched the waterfall and the pool below except to trim back some branches. It was possible to watch several groups hard at work from here without getting underfoot.

She settled down on a sculptured stone, fascinated by the coordinated working party of two gryphons, two humans, a *tervardi,* and three *hertasi* who were opening up an *ekele* for use by gryphons. They were taking out partitions and creating landing platforms on the roof. The gryphons pulled massive coils of twisted cord with their beaks from the corners of the platforms. Steadying themselves with their wings, they increased the tension as a *hertasi* directed them. *Tervardi* scrambled over the construction and reported to the *hertasi,* and holding pins were hammered in by the humans. Elspeth had never taken much notice of construction workers around the Palace, but these workers fascinated her.

Darkwind found her still gazing almost a candlemark later.

He sat down beside her, shaking his head, as his forestgyre Vree winged in and took a perch in a nearby bush. "They confuse me," he said without prompting. "I like them, indeed, but they confuse me deeply. Here—they make so much noise, and yet when we are outside the Vale even the largest gryphon makes no more sound than a leaf falling. They move like they are dancing. And their customs—"

Again he shook his head; Elspeth took his hand and squeezed it. "It's just because they are really *like* your people, but not quite identical," she said comfortingly. "That's all. For you, it's kind of the way I felt when I was learning your tongue. I already knew some Shin'a'in, and it was very confusing when you said something that wasn't *quite* what I knew. It was just similar enough that I felt I ought to know it, and different enough that I couldn't understand."

His puzzled look cleared. "Exactly. That is what I could not put into words. It is very strange to find those who are not human as full Clan members, for instance. I think it a good idea, but I find it strange. They are planning even their homes with that in mind, for instance— rebuilding the stairs to suit not only human feet but *kyree,* and reinforcing the floors and adding landing porches for gryphons. The lower floors even have ramps for *dyheli.* All their thoughts run like that. We built to accommodate our bondbirds, but not to suit anything else other than humans. They consider first how any decision will affect *all* the beings of the Clan."

Elspeth nodded, understanding now what he meant. As considerate as k'Sheyna had been, they would never have considered modifying their homes to suit other creatures. And they would never have taken the needs of the nonhumans into consideration when making any kind of major decision.

Not only the needs, but the abilities—she thought, watching two of the gryphons hovering, holding a thin beam aloft so that it could be set into place and pegged there. Darkwind had seen that they had strengths the humans did not—and his former lover Dawnfire had *used* those often-discounted abilities of the nonhumans. But k'Leshya counted on them; the nonhumans were integral to any plan.

The unfamiliar as an ally.

Darkwind watched the construction work for a moment, and nodded with admiration, his pale blue eyes candid and open. "It is amazing," he said at last. "In a few weeks' time, I shall not know this place." He brushed a strand of silver hair out of his eyes. "In a few years, it will look like nothing that Tayledras built."

"Do you ever want to come back here?" Elspeth asked hesitantly. "I know Firesong is talking about doing so."

But Darkwind shook his head. "I do not think so. I think that no matter what the next few moons bring us, we will be too busy to even consider such a thing. Firesong has good reason to come here, for he is a Healing Adept and k'Leshya has many new magics he wishes to learn. But I am not even well-practiced in our own magics."

"You aren't exactly inept, lover," she smiled.

"Heh. Thank you, bright feather. I would prefer to wait on the learning of new magics until I am more comfortable with the known."

She laughed a little ruefully at that. Over the past several weeks she had found it much easier to admit her own shortcomings since Darkwind had become so open about his. And her shortcomings were many—not the least of which was that she had come so late into her mage-training. She still felt like a stone skipping across ice when she thought about magery in general. "That sounds like something I would say! I had no idea there was so much to learn—nothing I ever read in any of the histories said *anything* about needing lesser mages to take care of the things unbalanced by Adept spells. The histories just said that a great mage did—*thus*—and said nothing about what went on behind the spell-casting."

Darkwind leaned back against the sun-warmed rock. "Not all Adept spells require such a thing," he corrected. "Only those which cannot be performed from within proper shielding—or which *are* not performed from within proper shielding. And then, only those which manipulate great amounts of energy. There are different ways of accomplishing the same result."

She saw the differences, and nodded. "And anything that changes the force-lines, or creates nodes, or whatever, right? Darkwind, just what *is* the difference between a node and a Heartstone?"

He blinked at her, as if he wasn't certain he had heard her correctly, then instead of answering, asked her a question. "Where does the energy go when it flows into a node?"

She was used to that now; if she didn't know the answer, he asked her a question that would make her see the answer for herself, rather than simply telling her. It had been infuriating, at first, but she had to admit that the answers stuck with her much better when she had to deduce them for herself. "It flows right back out on another—oh! Now *why* didn't I see that before?" She shook her head, annoyed. "How could I be so stupid? The difference between a node and a Heartstone is that the energy *doesn't* flow out of a Heartstone. It all stays there. I can't imagine why I didn't see that; it's like a lot of rivers flowing into a sea, and who ever heard of a river flowing *out* of a sea?"

"Well, at least it does not flow out on another ley-line," Darkwind amended. "Power is taken from a Heartstone, of course, or it would build up past the point where it could be contained. It is used to provide the power for all the things in the Vale that require such power. But that is our great secret, the construction of such a thing. Even had Falconsbane succeeded in stealing the proto-Heartstone, I do not think he could have turned it into a real one. He would *have* to have given it an outflowing ley-line, however small, and all he would have had would have been, in the end, no more than an exceptionally strong node. Not that such a node would not have granted him great power! But it would not have been the power of a Heartstone, which has no known equal to my people. It is the fact that a Heartstone has no such way to relieve the pressure of the contained power that makes a Heartstone so very powerful."

"But the one in Haven now is a Heartstone, and not a node, right?" she asked anxiously.

He shrugged. "It appears so, yes, but I cannot be certain until I can view it myself. At the moment it is a guess, an assumption, based on some signs we can See at this great distance. If it is—well, that means that whatever force sent it there knows how to create Heartstones, or cause a waiting one to settle. And what that could portend, I do not know."

"I don't either," she replied. Although that was not strictly true, since the force that had sent the proto-Heartstone to Haven instead of the new k'Sheyna Vale had come from the North of Valdemar, and in the North of Valdemar was the Forest of Sorrows...

"Well, Firesong has cloistered himself away for a day and a night, to rebuild his own energy levels, so we cannot ask him," Darkwind said with a hint of unease in his blue eyes. "I suspect he would only shrug and look mysterious, though."

"Probably," Elspeth chuckled, trying to remove the unease. "You know what a showman he is, he can't even drink a cup of *chava* without making a production out of it. At any rate, in two days we'll have some of our answers, when we get to k'Treva, and we can consult the mages there. The rest can wait until we reach Valdemar. Certainly whatever is under Haven can wait until then." They had all decided that the first step on their journey would be to return to k'Treva with Firesong. Elspeth had hoped that this would make the change from Darkwind's home in the Vale to Valdemar less of a shock. Only Firesong could create the Gate for this journey, but the Gate would not have to be held open for so great a span of time, so only one Adept would be needed. And while the creation of a Gate was no small task, it was one that Firesong had undertaken so many times that with due preparation, he would emerge into his home Vale in fairly good shape, not as drained and exhausted as Darkwind. Besides, once there, he would have his own Heartstone, keyed to the mages of k'Treva, to draw upon to replenish his resources.

Darkwind remained silent after that last comment, and Elspeth wondered now if she should have left all mention of Valdemar out of the conversation. She had been very reluctant to discuss anything past their departure from k'Treva, and she had sensed a corresponding reluctance in Darkwind. He *was* going with her; that much was absolutely certain. But she would no longer be simply Elspeth k'Sheyna k'Valdemar at that point; she would be a princess, the Heir, and on her home ground, with responsibilities to Valdemar that went far beyond personal feelings. For that matter, *she* hadn't thought much about those responsibilities of late.

I should. I need to weigh them all out, and decide what is important and what isn't. And what I am actually able to do. And, a little reluctantly, she decided one other thing. *I need to talk to Gwena. If there's anyone that can discuss where my responsibilities end and stupid customs begin, it's her.* She nibbled her lip uneasily. Gwena had been very agreeable lately; maybe too much so. On the other hand, the Companion had sworn she was not going to attempt to manipulate her Chosen any more.

But did she say she would do so any less? *Hmm…* On the other hand, she admitted she had no real control over her Chosen. And Gwena's disposition lately had been as cheerful as this sunny day. Whether it would continue to be so, if Elspeth did something totally against her

Companion's advice, was a good question.

Well, there was no point in getting worked up over something that was days, weeks, perhaps months away. But it might be a good idea to drag Gwena off for a long heart-to-heart talk now.

She squeezed Darkwind's hand again, and he smiled at her. "I'm going to make a round of the Vale to make sure I haven't forgotten anything we might need," she told him, as an excuse to get Gwena alone for that long talk. "It won't take more than a candlemark or two. Where shall I meet you?"

"Right here?" he offered. His expression lightened considerably, and his eyes crinkled at the corners as he smiled. "It's about the least-busy place in the Vale at the moment; I was half afraid to go to our *ekele* lest I be thrown out by a work crew!"

She laughed, and tossed her hair over her shoulder—now it was long enough to toss, for the first time in years. "I think they'll be polite enough to wait until we're gone, but you ought to take Vree outside the Vale for a hunt. Maybe you and I have been working our tails off, but I think he's been bored."

Nearly invisible in the bush, Vree made a chortling sound. *:Good Elspeth,:* he Mindspoke—more in images than in words. *:Keep this mate, Darkwind. Elspeth bright/clever/wise.:*

Darkwind flushed, but Elspeth only chuckled and made a mock bow to the forestgyre in the branches. "Thank you, Vree, for your unvarnished and candid opinion."

Darkwind rose and offered her his hand to help her up. "I expect I'd better, before he offers any more unvarnished opinions. A good chase followed by a full crop should keep him quiet—so he doesn't lecture me as often as Gwena lectures you!"

Nyara separated her hair with clawed fingertips and began braiding it as she watched Skif from a corner of their shared *ekele*. She had considerably less to pack than anyone else, other than, perhaps, the gryphons. Just herself, two changes of clothing, a set of armor made by the *hertasi*, and a very large and vocal sword...

:I'll thank you not to think of me as baggage, young lady,: Need said dryly, but softened it with a chuckle. *:Baggage can only hinder, after all:*

:Oh, you can hinder, too, my teacher—when you choose to,: Nyara replied saucily, as she bound off the little braid she wore at the side of her head with a thin strip of twine.

"Is Need putting her point in again?" Skif asked, looking up from his own packing. Nyara watched him with a great deal of admiration; she could not for a moment imagine how he was getting so many things into those small packs.

"Why, yes!" she said in surprise. "How can you tell?"

He chuckled and put one gentle finger right between her eyebrows. "Because you get a little crease *here* when you Mindspeak with her, and you only get it then." He raised a bushy eyebrow at the sword, and addressed Need directly. "Well, dear lady, do you think you are prepared for Valdemar?"

:Is Valdemar prepared for me, might be the real question, insolent brat,: Need countered. *:I'm not at all certain that anyone there is.:*

"Well, I'm entirely certain that they're *not*," Skif replied, with a laugh. He ran one hand through his curly dark hair and waggled his eyebrows at both the sword and her bearer. "You're not the same sword that left. I think Kero is going to be quite happy to have you at someone else's side, all things considered. I don't even want to contemplate the clash of personalities that would ensue if you went back to her."

:I'd win,: Need stated arrogantly.

But Skif shook his head. "With all due respect, my lady, I know you both and I think it would be a draw," Skif told her. "Kero is just as stubborn as you are. What's more, that would just be if the confrontation was one-on-one. With Sayvil on her side, you wouldn't stand a chance."

:Hmm.: The sword thought that over for a moment, then turned to a more impartial judge, one who was cropping grass beneath the *ekele* Skif and Nyara shared. *:Cymry? What do you think?:*

Skif's Companion shook her head noisily, and glanced up at the open windows of the *ekele*. Skif had yet to figure out how the sword could talk to both Cymry and Gwena, when Companions were only supposed to be able to Mindspeak their own Heralds.

But then, Need was a law unto herself. How else to characterize a kind of ghost bespelled into a magical blade, an artifact of such age that the places she had known as a woman didn't even exist on maps anymore?

:I think even you would be no match for Kero and Sayvil together,: Cymry said decisively. *:And your magic would give you no edge—pun intended—if Sayvil were to bend her will against yours.:*

If a sword could be said to sigh, Need did so. *:No respect,:* she complained. *:Now silly white horses are punning at me. Ah, well. At least my bearer appreciates me, even if she does think of me as* baggage.*:*

Nyara giggled, and Skif smiled at her. The sound that she made rather surprised her; she had not done much laughing in her short lifetime, and it seemed as if all of it had been occurring in the last year.

Since Skif. The conclusion was as inescapable as her feelings for him. And his feelings for her. When the plans for their departure from the Vale had been discussed, Nyara had entertained no doubts; she would go with Skif, even into a place that had never seen anything like her kind before, and endure whatever came.

Whatever came—it could be some formidable opposition from his own people. She did not look very—human. Her father, Mornelithe Falconsbane, had used her as a kind of experimental model of himself, working the changes he wished to make on his own flesh upon hers first. She had no illusions about herself; she knew there was no disguising her strange, catlike features. What would people who had never seen anything that was not completely human think of her?

What would they think when they learned that Skif, one of their precious Heralds, was her lover?

:Don't lose that smile, Kitten,: Need said, as she tensed unconsciously. *:Remember, you have Cymry favoring you, and you have* me. *These Heralds listen to their horses, and the horses don't give advice so often that they can afford to be ignored. And as Skif pointed out, I'm not the sword that left. I'm better. In fact—:* Need produced another one of her dry mental chuckles, like the creaking of forge bellows. *:—in a sense, you will have them by the proverbial short hairs. They can't afford to offend Skif by treating you poorly; he'll leave. They can't afford the loss of a single Herald right now, not with a war on the horizon. That Ancar character is not going to give up, and we're just lucky he's been so busy stewing his own little pot that he hasn't come roaring up to the Border before this. But besides Skif, they certainly can't afford to do without me! I may not be an Adept by the current standards, but I can do a great many things that an Adept can do, and some that I suspect no one knows how to do anymore. I'm a mage that is utterly unpredictable and unexpected. I can shield my powers and yours; I can look like nothing more than an ordinary sword if I try hard. No one else that I know of can do that. We're too valuable to lose, my dear. Remember, where you go, I go.:*

Nyara considered this seriously; it was an advantage she had not put into her calculations. *:Do you mean you would be willing to coerce all of Valdemar—:*

:Blackmail them to be certain you are happy?: Need finished for her. *:In a moment. Without a second thought. I don't have any stake in their little war, and*

now that I'm awake, I don't send my bearer rushing to the side of whatever female is in trouble. What happens with Ancar is not necessarily my concern. If Selenay wants me fighting on the side of Valdemar, she's going to have to make certain you are treated well.:

Nyara was taken aback, but in a flattered and delighted way. She had not expected such a strong response from her teacher; she hadn't let herself expect any backing at all. Need had taught her to be self-sufficient, at the cost of many hard and bitter lessons. To *depend* on no one but herself—while at the same time learning to give another her trust as a partner.

:Yes, you could *face them alone,:* Need said, answering her unspoken thoughts. *:You have the strength to do so. You are willing to. That's what matters, and if you hadn't been ready, I'd have taken steps to make you ready before you got there, and* then *I would have backed you. You've earned it. Skif will back you; you've more than earned his trust, as well as his—yes, I'll say it—love. And Cymry will back you because she knows you're one of the best partners Skif could have. Kitten, you are a fine person. And we'll give that fine person the support she deserves.:*

Nyara blinked back tears from burning eyes, quickly, before Skif could see them. *:I do not know what to say.:*

:Kitten, don't think this is going to be easy,: the sword cautioned. *:I can't change people's minds or attitudes, nor can Skif or Cymry. People have to change their minds because they want to. You are still going to be the strangest thing they have seen in a long time. But at least I can make certain that you know what a brave child you are. Anything else, you're just going to have to deal with.:*

Nyara nodded, slowly. *:I think I can do that,:* she replied. *:It can be no worse than life in my father's fortress. And I will have Skif, and you, so it will be better, for I will have no chance to be lonely.:*

Again, the dry chuckle. *:I'm glad you remembered to put me in there somewhere!:*

There was not a large gathering at the carved arch the next morning; only a few gryphons, one or two of the Kaled'a'in mages that Firesong had been exchanging techniques with, and of course, Silverfox. That was something of a relief to Elspeth, since she had hoped to slip out of k'Leshya Vale with a minimum of fuss. The less fuss, the better for everyone. She was hoping Darkwind could continue to keep up his eager interest despite leaving everything he had ever known.

She hoped. There was no real way to tell, after all, how he was likely to react.

But he seemed cheerful enough, as the *hertasi* brought the last of their packs to be loaded on the two Companions, Firesong's blazingly white *dyheli* stag, and (temporarily) on the gryphons, who were willing to bear the burdens through the Gate to save strain on Firesong.

And, as usual, the young Adept looked as if he had been groomed to within an inch of his life by an entire troupe of *hertasi*. His long hair flowed down his back in a deceptively simple arrangement. His sculptured face wore an expression of interest and amusement. Although it was warmer, he had donned pristine white robes of exotic style and cut—exotic even by Tayledras standards. His ice-white firebird sat on his shoulder and regarded the company with a resigned silver-blue eye. The snow-white *dhyeli* stag that had brought him to the Vale waited beside him, as still as any marble statue. As usual, he looked magnificent.

"Well, I have had converse with my mother and father," Firesong said, as soon as Skif and Nyara arrived and took their places. "I have warned them that I am about to Gate to k'Treva, as we discussed, and that I will have four of k'Sheyna, Companions, gryphons, and a *most* gallant *kyree* with me."

He bowed gallantly to Rris, who wagged his tail and grinned with his tongue lolling out of his mouth. Rris had agreed to come along both to act as guardian and teacher to the gryphlets, and to chronicle whatever happened as an "impartial" observer. That was Rris' chosen function, after all; the *kyree* had an extensive oral history, and Rris was one of their historians. Although his specialty seemed to be the tales of his "famous cousin Warrl," Elspeth knew that he would rather have had his tail pulled out than miss a chance to see what happened in this new alliance of Tayledras, Kaled'a'in, and Valdemaran.

"So, my ladies and lords, if you are all prepared to depart?" Firesong indicated the arch that would contain the Gate with a nod of his statuesque head, and everyone present made some indication of agreement.

Elspeth had long since gotten over being surprised at how little time it took Firesong to accomplish anything magical. Between one heartbeat and the next, he had established the Gate itself. In the next heartbeat, he had sought out the terminus in k'Treva Vale. In the third, he had anchored it, and the Gate stood open, ready to use, the greenery of k'Treva showing through on the other side, looking disconcertingly like and unlike k'Sheyna Vale.

"After you," Skif said to Elspeth a little nervously, eying the portal which had been empty one moment, then black as pitch, then filled with scenery which was *not* the same as the clearing they stood in. She hid her smile, took Darkwind's hand, and together they stepped through—

She had been told she would feel something like a little jolt; a shock as she passed across the intervening "real" distance. But instead of a shock, she felt a moment of disorientation—

She clutched at Darkwind's hand; there was something pulling and twisting, rippling across the power that held the Gate! He stared at her, his eyes wide—then he and everything else blurred and faded for a moment. Vree spread his wings and mantled in alarm; his beak opened, but nothing emerged.

She might have screamed; it didn't matter, for in that moment that they hung in the Void between Gates, no sound she made would be heard.

Then, just as suddenly, they dropped down with a lurch, safely on the other side. Vree was screaming, still agitated.

They were through. Except—it was not where they were supposed to be.

She looked around wildly, for there was no expanse before a carved archway; no wild and exotic foliage, and no waiting Tayledras. They stood on a dense mat of browned evergreen needles, in a tiny clearing. Behind them was the rough mouth of a cave. Before them was a northern forest, with no one at all in sight. The air was sharp and cool, spicy with pine-scent and mountain-odors. This was upland country; *northern* country—farther north than most of Valdemar.

Darkwind seized her elbow as she stood there aghast, wondering what had gone wrong, and hurried her out of the way. Just in time; first Skif and Nyara emerged, followed by the Companions, then the gryphons and their young, then Rris, the *dyheli*, and Firesong. All of them emerged with the same shocked, puzzled look on their faces.

Firesong was more than shocked, he was startled into speechlessness.

Darkwind seized him, jarring the firebird on his shoulder, which flapped its wings and uttered a high-pitched whistle of distress. "What happened?" he demanded harshly. "This is *not* k'Treva!"

Firesong only shook his head numbly. "I—" he faltered, at a loss for the first time since Elspeth had known him. "I do not know! I might err in just where a Gate opens, any mage might—but it *must* go to some place that I, personally, know! *And I do not know this place.* I have never seen it in my life!"

Skif looked around wildly, as Nyara took a wary grip on Need's hilt. "Where are we, then?" he demanded.

No one had an answer for him.

4

Mornelithe Falconsbane lay quietly in his silk-sheeted bed and feigned sleep. He was still uncertain of many things. His memories were still jumbled, but the bonds upon his powers told him the most important facet of his current condition.

He was a prisoner.

Still, it could be worse. He might be a captive, but at least his captivity featured all the luxurious appointments and appearance of being an honored guest.

But it was captivity nonetheless.

Falconsbane was not the master here; that young upstart puppy called "Ancar" was. That alone rankled, although he endeavored not to show how much.

He spent most of his time in sleep, either real or feigned. He was not at all prosperous at the moment, and he was only too well aware of the fact. Merely to rise and walk across a room cost him more effort than summoning an army of *wyrsa* had when he was at his full powers. And as for working magic—

At the moment, it was simply not possible.

How long had he hovered in that timeless Void? He did not know; it was more than mere days, more like weeks or even months. He had been snatched from that dark and formless space before he had gone quite mad, and he had drained his magical power just to keep his physical body barely alive. Now both were damnably slow to return to him. He had become used to recovering swiftly, taking the lives of his servants to augment his own failed powers. That was not an option open to him at the moment, and his recovery was correspondingly slow.

In fact, even as he lay in his soft, warm cradle, he knew that it was weakness that kept him here rather than his own will. It would be very hard to rise and force his body into some limited form of exercise; very easy to drift from feigned into real sleep. And very attractive as well, for sleep held far more pleasant prospects than reality.

Sleep—where he would forget where he was and the bonds that had been placed upon him, the coercions that now ruled his mind and powers. Where he would forget that it was a mere stripling of a usurping King that he must call "Master."

He had learned his captor had given him his real name quite by accident, during one of those bouts of pretended sleep. The annoying hedge-wizard who played host to him had entered with the servant that had brought him food, and had ordered the frightened man to wake Falconsbane and see that he ate and drank. The servant had objected, clearly thinking Falconsbane some kind of wild beast, half man and half monster, fearing—he little knew how rightly—that Falconsbane might kill him if he ventured too near. The wizard had cuffed his underling, growling that "the King wants him well and what Ancar will do to both of us if he is not is worse than anything this creature ever could do to you!"

At the time, Falconsbane had come very close to betraying his pretense by laughing. Clearly, this foolish magician had *no idea* who and what he was entertaining!

And if he had? Likely he would have fled the country in terror, not trusting to anything but distance to bring him out of Falconsbane's reach. The silly fool; even that would not help him if Mornelithe became *upset* with him.

He still had no real idea why it was that Ancar had placed him under magical coercions—other than the obvious, that the upstart wanted an Adept under his control. Why he wanted and needed an Adept—what purposes he wanted that Adept to serve—that was still a mystery. But at least, after listening covertly to the conversations between the sniveling hedge-wizard and his Master, he now knew *how* Ancar had brought him here.

By accident. Purely and simply, by accident and blundering.

The thought that he, Mornelithe Falconsbane, Adept of power that puny young Ancar could only *dream* of, had been "rescued" entirely by a mistake was enough to make him wild with rage—or hysterical with laughter. It was impossible. It was a thing so absurd that it never should have happened. No mage of any learning would have ever given credit to such a story.

Nevertheless...

It was logical, when analyzed. The backlash of power when his focus had been smashed, his web of power-lines snapped back on him, and the proto-Gate that had been released from his control had sent Falconsbane into the Void. No ordinary Gate could have fetched him back out again, for ordinary Gates were carefully constructed, and the terminus chosen, long before the Gate energy was set in motion. No Gate *could* be set on the Void itself; to attempt such a folly would be to court absolute disaster as the Gate turned back on itself and its creator and devoured both. But Ancar had not created an ordinary Gate; he had not been creating a Gate at all, so far as *he* knew. He had thought then—and *still* thought now—that he had been constructing some safe way for a lesser mage to handle the terrible powers of node-energies, energies only an Adept could safely master. Ancar did not have Adept potential, for all his pretensions; Master was the most the whelp could ever aspire to. But whoever his teacher was, that teacher had evidently chosen not to inform him of this, and he had been searching for a way to make himself an Adept for some time now.

His collections of spellbook fragments must be quite impressive—and the fact that he was willing to risk himself using only fragments proved either that he was very brave, or very stupid.

Or both.

The directions for the Gate had come from one of those fragments, one that had not included the purpose of the spell he had decided to try. As a result of incomplete directions and the utter folly of following them, he had set up a Gate with no terminus. But at the time, at the back of his mind, he had been concentrating on something he wanted very much.

An Adept. If he could not *be* one, then he *wanted* one. Actually, he had probably hoped for both, to become an Adept and to control one, or more than one. A suicidally stupid plan, one that Falconsbane would never have tried. Dark Adepts, the only kind Ancar would be likely to attract, were jealous of their powers, unwilling to share them, and would never stop testing any bonds that were put upon them. And when those bonds broke—

—as eventually, Falconsbane would break his—

—then revenge would be swift and certain.

Falconsbane had known of some of Ancar's activities from his spies; he had been interested in the young King purely because the boy was the enemy of those blasted allies of k'Sheyna, the ones with the white horses. He had briefly toyed with the notion of an alliance himself—with him as the superior, of course. He knew that Ancar had longed for Adepts for some time, and it was logical to assume that he had been concentrating on the need for an Adept at the time the Gate began to fold back in on itself.

Falconsbane knew everything there was to know about Gates, except the few secrets that had disappeared with the Mage of Silence. Oh, *him* again. He could make some deductions now, with the information that he had gleaned from his covert listening, that were probably correct.

The energies making up Gates were remarkably responsive to *wants*, as Falconsbane had every reason to know now. Especially when those wants were triggered by fear as the Gate began to reach for its creator.

Ancar wanted an Adept, and no doubt wanted one very badly when his spell went awry; as it happened, the Void had one. Falconsbane, still caught in nothingness.

And once the Gate had a goal, it "knew" how to reach that goal, given the strength of Ancar's need.

So, taking Ancar's desire as *destination*, the Gate had stopped folding back upon itself, and had reached out to bring Ancar what he wanted.

Falconsbane wondered, as he had wondered before this, what would have happened if the Void had *not* contained what Ancar had wanted. Possibly the Gate would have completed its attempt to double back, and would have destroyed itself and its creator with it. Well, *that* would have been entertaining to watch, but it wouldn't have saved Falconsbane.

Possibly Ancar would have thought of some place he considered safe, and it would have read that as a destination, creating the terminus and thus showing Ancar what it was he had *truly* called into being. It was impossible to say, really, and hard thinking made Mornelithe's head hurt.

Ancar's first Gate had collapsed for lack of further energy. And Ancar still was not aware of what he had created.

Falconsbane had no intention of telling him. He intended to keep as many secrets as he could, given the coercive spells that Ancar had layered on him. He was aided by the fact that Ancar was not aware how much Hardornen Falconsbane knew, or that he had a limited ability to read the unguarded thoughts of the servants to increase his vocabulary. As long as he pretended not to understand, it should be possible to keep quite a bit from Ancar.

He stirred restlessly, clenching his jaw in anger. When he had awakened to himself, he had found himself constrained by so many coercive and controlling spells that he could hardly breathe without permission. And for the first time in a very, very long time, Mornelithe Falconsbane found himself trapped and moving only to another's will.

It was not a situation calculated to make him cooperate with his captor and "rescuer." Not that anything would be, really. Falconsbane was not used to cooperating.

Falconsbane was used to giving orders and having them obeyed. Anything less was infuriating.

In his weakened and currently rather confused state, he often lost track of things. At the moment, he was fairly lucid, but he knew that this condition was only temporary. At any moment, he could slip back into dreams and semiconsciousness.

So while he was in brief control of himself, he laid his own set of coercions on his mind, coercions that would negate the effect of any drugs or momentary weaknesses. He would not answer anything except the most direct of questions, and he would answer those as literally and shortly as possible. If asked if he knew who he was, for instance, he would answer "Yes," and nothing more. If asked if he knew what spell had brought him here, he would also answer "Yes," with no elaboration. If Ancar wanted information, he would have to extract it, bit by painful bit. And Falconsbane would do his best to confuse the issue, by deliberate misunderstandings.

It would be an exercise in patience, to say the least, to learn anything at all of value.

Let Ancar wear himself out. Meanwhile, Falconsbane would be studying him, his spells, and his situation. Let Ancar continue to believe that he was the Master here. Falconsbane would learn to use Ancar even as Ancar thought he was using Falconsbane. He would not remain this fool's captive for long.

Falconsbane had forgotten more about coercion than this piddling puppy King had learned in his lifetime! It would only take time to undo what had been done, or to work his way around what Ancar had hedged him in with. Falconsbane knew above all that any spell created could be broken, circumvented, or twisted.

Even his own, he remembered with some bitterness.

True unconsciousness rose to take him under a blanket of darkness, even as that last sordid thought cut through his mind.

As Falconsbane drifted from pretended slumber into real sleep, An'desha shena Jor'ethan watched from his own starry corner of the Adept's mind.

When Falconsbane's thoughts clouded and drifted into dreams, An'desha opened his shared eyes cautiously, alert to the possibility that such an action might wake Falconsbane again.

But Falconsbane remained asleep, and An'desha reveled in the feeling that his body was his own again—however temporarily that might be. Once Falconsbane woke, he would have to retreat back into the little hidden corner of his mind that Falconsbane did not control, and did not even seem to be aware of. Even his ability to view the world through

Falconsbane's senses was limited to the times when the Adept was very preoccupied, or seriously distracted. Any time there was even the slightest possibility that Falconsbane could sense An'desha's presence, An'desha kept himself hidden in the "dark."

He was not certain why he was still "here." The little he had read in Falconsbane's memories indicated that whenever the Adept took over one of his descendants' bodies, he utterly destroyed the personality, and possibly even the soul, of that descendant. Yet—this time both had remained. An'desha was still "alive," if in a severely limited sense, thanks only to his instincts.

Not that I can do much, he thought with more than a little fear. *And if he ever finds out that I'm still here, he'll squash me like a troublesome insect. He may think he's too weak to do anything, but even now he could destroy me if he wanted to. He'd probably do it just to sharpen his appetite.*

If I'd accepted becoming a shaman... none of this would have happened. There wouldn't even be a Mornelithe Falconsbane, if I hadn't tried to call fire. If only.

If only... easy to say, in retrospect. Half Shin'a'in as he was, would the Plains shaman have even accepted him? There was no telling; the shaman might just as easily have sent him away. Shin'a'in shaman did not practice magic as such—but did they have anything like the fire-calling spell? And if they did, would it have been similar enough to bring Mornelithe out of his limbo? And if it had been—what would have happened then?

If, if, if. Too many "ifs," and none of them of any use.

The past was immutable, the present what it was because of the past. An'desha *had* been gifted with mage-power. He *had* chosen to run away to try to find the Tale'edras and master that magic, rather than become a shaman as the custom of Shin'a'in dictated. He *had* become lost, and he *had* tried to call fire to warm himself the first night he had been on his own. That had been his undoing.

An'desha was a blood-descendant of an Adept called Zendak, who had in turn been the blood-descendant of another and another, tracing their lineage all the way back to the time of the Mage Wars and an Adept called Ma'ar. That Adept had learned a terrible secret; how to defy death by hiding his disembodied self at the moment of his body's death in a pocket of one of the Nether Plains. And Ma'ar had set a trap for every blood-descendant of Adept potential, using the simple fire-spell as the trigger of that trap. A fledgling mage shouldn't know much more than that fire-spell, and so wouldn't be able to effectively defend against the marauder stealing his body.

An'desha, all unknowing and innocent, had called fire. Mornelithe Falconsbane had swarmed up out of his self-imposed limbo to shred An'desha's mind.

But this time, the theft had not taken place completely. An'desha had studied what being a Shin'a'in shaman entailed, and was familiar with some of the ways to control one's own mind. He fled before the Adept's power into a tiny space in his own mind, and had barricaded and camouflaged against the invader. And Falconsbane was completely unaware of that fact.

Sometimes I wish he had gotten rid of me... how can I still be sane? Maybe I'm not...

An'desha had been an unwitting and terrified spectator to far too many of Falconsbane's atrocities—appalled at what was happening, and helpless to do anything about what was being done. And he knew, from stolen glimpses into Falconsbane's thoughts, that the little he had been witness to was only the smallest part of what Falconsbane had done to his victims. His existence had all the qualities of the worst nightmare that anyone could imagine, and more than once he had been tempted to reveal himself, just to end the torment.

But something had always kept him from betraying himself; some hope, however faint, that one day he might, possibly, be able to get his own body back and drive out the interloper. He never gave up on that hope, not even when Falconsbane had changed that body into something An'desha no longer recognized as his.

He had welcomed the embrace of the Void, at least as an end to the madness. He had no more expected release from the Void than Falconsbane had.

He had not been as weakened or as confused as his usurper when that release came, but caution made him very wary of trusting anyone with his secret. He had remained silent and hidden, and that, perhaps, is what had saved him.

The coercions on Falconsbane had not taken hold of *him*, and he had come through the ordeal in far better shape than Falconsbane had. And to his surprise and tentative pleasure, he had discovered that the damage done to Falconsbane had permitted *him* some measure of control again—always provided that he did not try to control something while Falconsbane was using it.

Falconsbane did not seem any more aware of An'desha's presence than he had been before, not even when An'desha, greatly daring, had taken over the body, making it sit up, eat, and even walk, while Falconsbane was "asleep."

What all this meant, An'desha did not dare to speculate.

But there had been other signs to make him hope, signs and even oblique messages, during the time that Falconsbane had waged war on the Tale'edras.

The Black Riders. He had known who and what those mysterious entities were, even though Falconsbane had not. When they had appeared, he had nearly been beside himself with excitement. They were as much a message to him—or so he hoped—as they were a distraction to Falconsbane.

And there had even been an earlier sign, at Falconsbane's battle and subsequent escape from the ruins where the gryphons laired. *He* knew why the Kal'enedral had failed to slay Falconsbane, even if no one else did. They had not missed their mark—nor had they been concerned with sparing the Adept. Their later actions, in the guise of Black Riders, luring Falconsbane into thinking that he was being "courted" by another Adept, only confirmed that.

They—or rather, *She*, the Star-Eyed, the Warrior—knew that An'desha was still "alive." She would; very little was lost to the deity of both the Tale'edras and the Shin'a'in, so long as it occurred either on the Plains or in the Pelagirs. When the Black Riders sent the tiny horse and the ring to Falconsbane, An'desha was certain that they were also sending a message to him. The black horse meant that he had not been forgotten, either by his Goddess or by Her Swordsworn. The ring was to remind him that life is a cycle—and the cycle might bring him a chance to get his body and his life back again.

The question was, now that he was far from the lands that he had known, could *they* act this far from the Plains? The Goddess was not known for being able to do much far from the borders of Her own lands. She had limited Her own power, of Her own will, at the beginning of time—as all the Powers had chosen to do, to keep the world from becoming a battleground of conflicting deities. She would not break Her own rules.

And yet... and yet...

She was clever; She could work around the rules without breaking them. If She chose.

If he proved that he was worthy. That was the other thing to keep in mind; She only helped those who had done *their* part, who had gone to the end of their own abilities, and had no other recourse. If he were to be worthy of Her help, it was up to him to do everything in his power, without waiting for the Star-Eyed to come rescue him.

He would, above all, have to be very, very careful. Just because Falconsbane was damaged now, it did not do to think he would continue to be at a disadvantage. If there was one thing An'desha had learned from watching the Adept, it was this: never underestimate Mornelithe Falconsbane—and always be, not doubly, but *triply* careful whenever doing anything around him.

But—he dared, just for a moment, to send a whisper of prayer into the darkness of the chamber. To Her.

Remember me—and help me, if You will—

Then the sound of footsteps outside the chamber door made him flee back into his hiding place, before Falconsbane was awakened, or woke on his own.

He reached that safety, just as the door opened, and Falconsbane stirred up out of the depths of sleep.

The sound of his door opening and closing roused him from slumber. Falconsbane opened his eyes a mere slit.

It was enough to betray him to his observer.

"I see you are awake." The smooth young voice identified the speaker at once, even before Ancar moved into the faint light cast by a shadowed lantern near the bed. "I hope you are enjoying my hospitality."

Falconsbane refused to allow himself to show any emotion. He simply studied his captor, committing every nuance of expression to memory. Falconsbane knew well the value of every scrap of information, and the more he knew about Ancar of Hardorn, the sooner he would be able to defeat the boy.

He was a handsome young man, showing few signs of the dissipation that Falconsbane suspected. But if he had achieved the position of Master, he surely knew all the tricks by which a mage could delay the onset of aging, strengthen the body, and even make it more comely. Only an Adept could actually *change* the body, as Falconsbane had done with both his own form and that of others. But a Master could hold his own body in youth for a very long time, if he had sufficient energies. Life-energies would serve the best, the life-energies of others. One could steal years, decades, from other lives and add them to one's own. Or one could steal the entire remaining life-span. Easily done; very tempting and a very useful skill to learn. For Mornelithe, in days long ago, it had approached being a hobby.

Ancar of Hardorn was certainly a young man that women would find attractive; his straight black hair was thick and luxuriant, his mustache and beard well-groomed. Neither hid the sensual mouth, a mouth that smiled easily, if falsely. The square face was pleasantly sculptured, the dark eyes neither piggishly small nor bovinely large. But the eyes did give him away, for they were flat, expressionless, and dead. The eyes of someone who sees others only as objects—as things to use, destroy, or ignore. A more experienced man would have learned how even to manipulate the expressions of his eyes, as Falconsbane had. Mornelithe fancied that he could convince anyone of anything, if he chose to. He was certainly convincing this Ancar that his "Master" had him cowed and under control.

Falconsbane considered his answer carefully before making it. How much to reveal? If he seemed *too* submissive, Ancar might suspect something. A mere touch of defiance, perhaps. A faint hint of rebellion. "I cannot say that 'enjoy' is the term I would use."

Ancar laughed, although there was no humor in the sound. "I see you have regained some of your wits at last. Good. I will ask you some questions that have puzzled me."

Since that was not a direct question, Falconsbane made no answering comment. Ancar waited for a moment, then said sharply, "What is your *true* name? And where do you come from?"

The coercions tightened about his mind, forcing answers from him, but he made them as literal as he could. "Mornelithe Falconsbane. I came from the Void, where you found me."

That last was enough to confuse him. Falconsbane preferred that Ancar not learn his true place of origin. Not yet, at least.

Ancar's brow furrowed as he considered this. "Are you an Adept?" he asked at last. "Are you a demon?"

"Yes," Falconsbane replied quickly. "No."

"But you are not human—" Ancar persisted, but since it was not a question, nothing compelled Falconsbane to answer, and Ancar glared at him in frustration. Falconsbane kept his own expression bland and smooth.

"Do you know who I am?" Ancar asked at last—then, finally realizing what game Falconsbane was playing, changed his question to an order, backed by the coercive spells. "Tell me what you know of me!" he demanded.

Mentally cursing, Falconsbane did as he was told. That Ancar was a ruler and a mage, and that his enemies were the Outlanders who rode white horses as a kind of badge. That the king was the one who had cast the spell that had brought Falconsbane out of the Void, and had cast coercive spells to make Falconsbane his captive. Ancar listened to the little that Falconsbane could tell him, then stroked his beard for a moment in thought.

"I am going to give you some information I wish you to think about," he said at last, "because I am certain that once you are aware of who and what you are dealing with, you will be disposed to cooperate. I am Ancar, King of Hardorn, and the most powerful mage in this kingdom. I am, as you surmised, the enemy of those you called 'Outlanders,' the folk of Valdemar who ride those white witch-horses you described. They are known as 'Heralds,' and they possess a certain mastery of mind-magic. I intend to conquer them, and to that end, I require the abilities of an Adept, for their Kingdom has protection against true magic. Not only does it not operate within their border, but mages who attempt to cross that border are driven mad within a short time of trying to exercise their powers. So, you are both useful and necessary to me—but *not* so necessary that I cannot do without you. Keep that in mind."

He smiled, and Falconsbane refrained from snarling. The boy's rhetoric was incredibly heavy-handed. How he had managed to keep himself on his throne, Falconsbane could not imagine. Luck, the help of someone more skilled than he was, or both.

"Now," Ancar continued silkily, "I have every intention of seeing that you are brought to your full health. If you cooperate fully with me, I shall be certain that you are rewarded. If you do not—I shall force your cooperation, and dispose of you when I no longer need you. The situation is just that simple."

He did not wait for an answer this time, but simply turned and left, and Falconsbane felt mage-locks clicking into place behind him.

Slowly, Falconsbane pushed himself into a sitting position, his anger giving him more energy to move than he had thought he possessed. There was food and drink on the table beside the bed; Falconsbane helped himself to both while he still had the strength to do so, and then, when his head began to swim a little, lowered himself back down again.

But although he was prone, his mind continued to work. Ancar had revealed more than he had known, for although he was wearing a mage-constructed shield protecting his thoughts, his expression was perfectly open, and his body had revealed things his words had not.

His hold upon his throne was by no means as secure as he would like Falconsbane to think. There was someone else in the picture—another mage, Falconsbane guessed—who kept the boy in power. That was why Ancar needed Falconsbane. Oh, it was true enough that he also needed an Adept to help defeat these "Heralds" as he had claimed; his body had proclaimed that much also to be true. But his hidden agenda was to rid himself of this other person's influence, if not, indeed, the person.

Now that had a great deal of potential, so far as Falconsbane was concerned. Perhaps when Ancar had first mounted the throne, his people would only have accepted a ruler of the proper lineage. But by now, Falconsbane suspected that Ancar had been foolish enough to mistreat his people very badly indeed. There was only so much mistreatment that a populace would put up with, and after that, they would welcome *any* ruler marginally better than the current despot.

Perhaps this other mage had already calculated precisely that. Perhaps not. It would certainly enter into Falconsbane's calculations.

He would play along with Ancar—perhaps continue to feign weakness, perhaps simply feign complete cooperation. He would work at the coercions until they were no longer a hindrance. Then, when the time was right—Falconsbane would turn the tables on the arrogant brat.

Then this kingdom would be in Falconsbane's hands. That would give him a new base of operations from which to work. He could then discover exactly how far from home he was—and determine if he actually wanted to return home. It might not be worthwhile. After all, one thing he lacked was a decent population base. Such things made real, human armies possible. Add human armies to the armies of his mage-born creatures, and he might well prove to be the most powerful ruler this area had ever seen.

Those Outlanders whose interference had so undone his own plans were almost certainly on their way home. And *now* he knew where that home was. So by furthering Ancar's plans, he would be furthering his own revenge. Then, when *he* was the one in control, he would be able to exact a more complete form of vengeance.

Vengeance again; how it comforted him! It was simple and elegant, however messy or convoluted its execution might be. As it had so many times before, vengeance would pull him through troubles—no, *inconveniences*—like a bright lantern seen through stormy darkness.

Taking their land would be a good start. Finding the girl and the man would complete that particular facet of his revenge.

And from there, with two lands under his control...

Well, it would be much easier to attack the Bird Lovers with a conventional army at his call. They were not prepared for such things. He could take them with little personal effort.

After that—

After that, he might well think about all the blighted ambitions of Leareth and Ma'ar. All the plans he had laid that could actually be brought to fruition. He could become more than a mere "king"—even more than an Emperor. He could have the world calling him Lord and Master.

He closed his eyes, picturing himself as Master of the World, and drifted again into pleasant dreams.

An'desha emerged from hiding as soon as Falconsbane was truly asleep again. This time, although he took care not to move Falconsbane's body, he took a few moments to get some idea of his surroundings.

He was in what seemed to be a very luxurious bedroom. The bed itself was canopied, with heavy curtains that were now pulled back and held against the posts of the bed with straps of fabric. There was a fireplace, although there was no fire burning at the moment. Beside the bed was a table with the remains of Falconsbane's meal still on it. Shadows against the wall hinted at more furniture, but the light from the two heavily shaded lamps beside the bed was not enough for An'desha to make out what kind of furnishings were there.

So much for the physical aspects of the room. As for the nonphysical—

He paused for a moment, then used the Mage-Sight that had become second nature over the years of Mornelithe's dominance.

The door is mage-locked. There are protections on the bed and wards and shields everywhere—baffles and misdirectors. Ancar doesn't want anyone to know that he has a mage in this room.

An'desha hesitated for a moment, trying to decide if he should probe those protections further, or try to investigate the locks on the door.

An odd stirring in the energies surrounding the room alarmed him. Something was coming!

He readied to bolt back into hiding again, when the gentle touch of a thread of Mindspeech touched *his* mind. His—and not Falconsbane's! Was this the madness he had feared? Was his remaining consciousness having fever-dreams of its own now?

:Do not fear, An'desha. We are here to help you.:

He paused in frozen amazement, too shocked at hearing his own name to even think of what to do next. It was the kind of wish fulfillment he had always mistrusted, but it seemed real. Would madness seem so real? Would a madman know?

A sparkling energy coalesced in the room, then formed a rotating center and swirled around it. A column of twisting, glowing mist formed in the center of the room, spreading two wide wings, raising a head—

The image of a ghostly vorcel-hawk, many times life size and made of glowing amber mist, mantled its wings and stared at him for a moment.

A vorcel-hawk—*Her* hawk! This was no trick. Falconsbane knew nothing of Her creatures, nor would the foreigner Ancar have any notion of what a vorcel-hawk meant to a Shin'a'in!

The Hawk gazed at him with star-flecked eyes for three heartbeats. Then it pulled in its wings and became a mist-cloud; the mist swirled again, split into two masses, and began taking shape for a second time.

Not one hawk, but two stared at him, one larger than the other—

Then the hawks folded their wings and the mist clouded; not two hawks, but two people stood there. One, a woman, so faint and tenuous that An'desha could see nothing clearly but her eyes and the vague woman-shape of her. But the other was male.

The other was a man of the Shin'a'in.

He very nearly cried out—but the man motioned him to be silent, and with many years of control and caution behind him, he obeyed instantly. He took a tight rein on his elation and his confusion as well, lest they wake Falconsbane out of slumber. Whoever, whatever these were, they could only be here to help him—but they could not help him if Falconsbane learned of his existence.

:I am Tre'valen shena Tale'sedrin, An'desha,: the spirit-man said in his mind. *:We have been sent to help you as much as we can—but I must warn you, although we come at the order of the Star-Eyed, we are far from our forests and plains. Both we and She are limited in what we can do. She is bound by rules even as we are.:*

There was a little disappointment at learning they would not simply invoke a power and banish Falconsbane, but far more simple relief. He was not alone at least, he had not been forgotten! He nearly wept with the intensity of his emotion.

But like lightning, his relief turned to bewilderment. What, exactly, was this Tre'valen? He didn't *look* anything like one of the Swordsworn... could he be spirit-traveling in some way, and was his real body somewhere nearby? If An'desha had a real, physical ally somewhere, it would be more than he had hoped for. A physical ally *could* free him from Ancar. But on the other hand, wouldn't someone who was *leshy'a* be better suited to free him from Falconsbane?

:What are you?: he asked timidly. *:Are you a spirit?:*

Tre'valen smiled ruefully. *:I am not precisely a spirit—but I am not precisely "alive," either. I was, and am still, a shaman of Tale'sedrin. I do not believe that the term "Avatar" would mean anything to you—:*

An'desha dared not shake his head, but evidently Tre'valen "read" the intention.

:We are "Avatars," for what that is worth. We serve Her a little more directly than the Kal'enedral do. We go where She cannot and where the Kal'enedral are unsuited. As now, when a shaman is needed, and not a warrior. :

A shaman? He couldn't help himself; he had gotten into this mess by trying to *escape* the shaman. He shrank back a little, both afraid of Tre'valen's censure, and ashamed. Surely, since She knew so much, She knew of his foolish attempt to flee, and her—Avatar—knew it, too.

Tre'valen sensed his shame, and Sent him a feeling of reassurance. *:An'desha, you need not fear me because of your past. Would She have sent us to you if She thought you deserved punishment? Would She punish you because you chose to flee instead of being forced into a role you didn't want?:*

A good point. He breathed a little easier.

:And think on it, An'desha. She takes no one who is not willing—Kal'enedral or shaman. She also punishes only those who have betrayed that which they promised. Why should She be angered at you because you were not willing?:

Now he felt twice as stupid. All this could have been avoided if only he had thought before he acted.

Tre'valen shook his head. *:An'desha, I learned to think long before I acted—and when I was young, that broody thoughtfulness became inactivity. I was shocked out of it in my own way, even as you have been shocked. I became what I am now because of a moment when I did not have time to consider hundreds of options. I believe the choice I made was the right one. And perhaps, so was yours.:*

Now he was confused. And what on earth did Tre'valen mean by saying that he was not precisely a spirit, but not precisely alive?

Oh, it didn't matter. What mattered was that he had been forgiven. Tre'valen seemed to be able to follow that thought, for he nodded.

:You were not thinking, An'desha, to run off like that. A better choice would have been to go to another shaman, one of some other Clan, who would have been more objective about you and your life-path. But you were also very young, and being young and stupid is not supposed to open one up to consequences quite as serious as you

suffered. We all learn. That is why we live.: Tre'valen smiled a little and the woman-form behind him took on more substance. And to An'desha's surprise, it was not one of the Kal'enedral as he had suspected it might be, nor was it even another Shin'a'in. Instead, the woman matched all the descriptions of the Tale'edras that he had ever heard! She was very beautiful, and it was clear to An'desha that these two were bound by more than similarity of form and purpose.

:This is Dawnfire,: Tre'valen said, confirming his guess by giving the woman a Hawkbrother name. *:She and I are your friends and your helpers. You know what you want most—:*

:My body!: he cried involuntarily. *:My freedom!:*

:We can free you of your body—permanently, but I suspect that is not your first choice,: Dawnfire replied wryly.

No. For all that he had wished for oblivion and death before, he truly did not want it now.

:In that case, you will have to earn your body and your freedom,: Tre'valen told him. The mist-forms glowed, like dust in a sunbeam, sparkling and dancing. *:And even if you do all that we ask, there is no guarantee that we can grant what you want. We will do our best, but we are very limited in power. There are many other forces at work here.:*

But it was a chance; it was more than he had ever had before. Even a chance was worth fighting for, and especially a chance for freedom.

Both of the spirits nodded encouragingly. *:An'desha, what we want from you is relatively simple. Watch. Listen. Learn. And tell us all that you have learned.:* Tre'valen's mind-voice was earnest. *:This will not be easy, because we will be asking you to do more than simply observe what happens. We will be showing you how to see into Falconsbane's thoughts and memories without him being aware that you are doing so. As you have been, brave one, when Falconsbane is fully aware, you are in limbo. We will show you how to protect yourself so that you are part of everything he thinks and does. Eventually, you will be an unseen witness to what goes on within him and outside of him. Eventually, you will invade his memories and learn the answers to questions we shall ask in the future:*

An'desha writhed with indecision and discomfort for a moment. He had *not* liked the little he had seen; he knew very well that Falconsbane had done horrible things, much more horrible than An'desha had ever been aware of. As Mornelithe had become more intent on his depravities, An'desha had been pushed back into limbo. He had awakened to the aftermath when Mornelithe came down from his twisted pleasure. Could he bear to see and know these things that had been done with *his* body?

:You will not like any of what you find,: Dawnfire warned soberly. *:Falconsbane is a monster in every sense. What you discover for us will bring you pain. But these are things that we must know in order to help you. And—to help others; those Falconsbane would harm.:*

In that case—if they meant to *stop* Falconsbane from hurting anyone else—how could he refuse? How many times had he prayed for a way to stop the madness that he had seen? How many times had he cursed his inability to save even one creature from Falconsbane's evil? The old Shin'a'in proverb of "Beware what you ask for, lest you receive it" seemed particularly apt...

Wordlessly—even though he was full of fear, and already shrinking from what he knew he would find—he gave his assent.

By the time they left him, they had shown him as much as he could encompass in a single lesson. They had coached him through making his little corner of Falconsbane's mind more secure, and even more invisible to the Adept. They had taught him how to gain access to Falconsbane's memory without the Adept being aware that he was doing so. They had shown him how to extend his reach into areas of Falconsbane's waking mind, so that now he would be able to see and hear whatever Falconsbane did, and to read the Adept's waking thoughts at all times, and not just when Falconsbane was extremely preoccupied. And they had gently praised him, something he had not experienced in what felt like eons. He quivered at how it made him feel.

When they took wing into the night, he withdrew again, buttressed up the walls of his defenses, and assimilated everything they had taught him. As Falconsbane continued to sleep, he made his first overt move. He sent the Adept into deeper slumber.

It worked.

Falconsbane descended into a sleep so deep that not even an army marching by would have awakened him. It would not last for long, but it was the first time that An'desha had *dared* do anything directly *against* the Adept.

Encouraged by his success, he thought for a moment.

He did things to my body; I know he did. More things than just changing the way it looks—and I don't even know how far he went with that. I ought to find out.

And the memories of how Falconsbane had done those things were likely to be some of the least noxious.

That would be a good place to start, then.

He settled down, made his own thoughts very quiet, and began his work.

5

Elspeth stared at the enormous conifers surrounding them. Their trunks and branches were not "enormous" by Tayledras standards, but they were huge when compared to the trees around Haven.

If the air had not been so cool, she would have thought they had been transported into a miniature Vale, or part of a larger one. They stood in a pocket-valley, with the cave that had formed the terminus of the Gate behind them, a small, grassy meadow in front of them, and those huge trees climbing up the steep slopes to either side of them. Any place where sunlight might penetrate the canopy, there were bushes and other low-growing plants clustered thickly about the bases of the trees. And yet, the meadow here had nothing taller than a few weeds, and while it was not exactly symmetrical, it still felt artificial—arranged somehow. There were no exotic flowering plants, and no signs of a Veil or other protections. But for all of that, it still reminded her strongly of a Hawkbrother stronghold. There was something about the placement of the trees that gave her the sense that this place had been touched by the hand of man.

Could trees grow that tall without something nurturing them? She didn't think so... but then she was not exactly an expert. Hadn't Darkwind once told her that the trees in the Pelagiris Forest were this tall?

Could they somehow have come out into an *old* Vale, one abandoned long ago? How did they get *here* instead of k'Treva? Certainly Firesong did not seem to recognize this place either. If he had targeted an old Vale by mistake, wouldn't he know it? Wouldn't he *recognize* it, if it was an old k'Treva Vale?

The group moved so their backs faced each other, with the gryphlets in the middle of the circle. Darkwind and Skif had dropped all burdens but their weapons, and Vree was already ranging up onto station to scout. Firesong stood with the most perplexed expression Elspeth had ever seen, one hand to his scalp, pulling his white hair back.

"I have no *clue* how we got here!" he cried, and received a gesture to be quieter from Darkwind, Skif, and Nyara.

A bird called off in the distance somewhere. It sounded like a wood thrush. There weren't any wood thrushes around k' Sheyna, at least not that she had ever heard. She had always thought they were a northern bird... were there other birds that sounded like wood thrushes? Scarlet jays mimicked other birds, so perhaps it was a jay. But would a jay mimic a bird that didn't live in the same region?

"We are definitely far north. I think we can calm down, though—if we were meant to be killed, it would have been done as we exited the Gate. Still," Firesong continued, "this seriously annoys me."

Something about the light shining down into the center of the clearing was unusual. Its color—and the angle at which it fell.

Light in the center of the clearing? But the sun isn't high enough—it's early morning—there can't be a shaft of light in the middle of the clearing!

But there was—only it wasn't a shaft of light coming down through the treetops, but a column of light, taller than a man. Silver-gold light, the kind of light that shines over snow on a winter morning. Everything developed odd double shadows as the light became brighter still.

A ripple in the energies of the place made her redouble her shields quickly, and join them with Darkwind's, in a move that was near-instinctive now. Gods only knew what this thing was, but it surely had something to do with whatever snatched them away from k'Treva.

A vague shape developed, a sculpture of fog—except that it was glowing, and the energies of this place were definitely centered around it. Now that she knew what to look for, the lines of force were as clear as ripples in a pond. This—thing—was a part of the forest—of the energies that lay under the forest.

But it was still changing; it blurred, or perhaps her eyes blurred for a moment. And then, the figure solidified. It was not at all what she had expected.

It was a handsome man, silver-haired, silver-eyed, handsome enough even to cast Firesong into the shade, of no determinate age.

And he was dressed in an antique version of Herald's Whites. He looked like a glowing statue of milky glass, or like—

Oh, gods. Like a ghost, a spirit...

The hair on the back of her neck rose with atavistic fear, and she backed up another pace, holding out one hand as if to ward the thing off.

As if she *could!* This was not the first spirit she had encountered, but how could she know what this spirit could do? How could she hope to hold it off if it chose to attack her?

A crisp, clean breeze rose and fell. It sounded like the forest was sighing.

:Bright Havens!: said a cheerful, gentle voice in her head. *:You all look as if you'd seen a ghost!:*

A quick glance showed her that everyone else had heard that mind-voice as well. Darkwind looked startled; the gryphons were mantling and the little ones hid under their wings. Skif was white—and round-eyed with astonishment, for he was *not* a strong Mindspeaker, and it would take a powerful Mindspeaker indeed to make him Hear. Nyara simply looked frightened and puzzled. The Companions—there was no reading them. They stood as stock still as if they had been carved of snow.

Firesong was as pale as his hair—or the apparition. This was the first time that Elspeth had ever seen the Hawkbrother truly frightened. She'd seen him worried, yes. Anxious and even apprehensive. But never frightened.

Still, it was Firesong who recovered first. He regained a little more color, drew himself erect, and approached the—man.

The apparition simply smiled. For a revenant, this one was remarkably good-natured. Weren't ghosts supposed to rattle chains and moan curses or warnings? But she had never heard of a Herald coming back to haunt anyone before.

"And have we not?" Firesong asked, stopping within touching distance of the spirit and looking challengingly into its "face." "Have we not seen a ghost, Forefather?"

Forefather? "Firesong, what are you talking about?" Elspeth asked in a whisper, as if she really thought the thing wouldn't hear her if she kept her voice down.

Firesong's voice shook, and he was clearly having a hard time keeping it steady. "Don't *you* recognize him, Elspeth?" he asked tremulously. "Have you never seen those features before? Are there no portraits in your home in Valdemar of your ancestor and mine?"

The spirit folded his arms over his chest. It looked, perversely, as if he was enjoying this. It was hard to feel frightened of someone who had that kind of mischievous twinkle in his eyes—or whatever passed for eyes.

"My ancestor?" she repeated, feeling remarkably stupid. "I mean, it looks like he's wearing old Herald's Whites, but I don't—I mean, there isn't anyone in the royal family who looks like—there's no one in the Royal Gallery who—"

Firesong regained a little more color. "Elspeth, have you no eyes in your head?" he asked, in a much steadier—and rather impatient—tone. "Look at him. Look at me! This is *Vanyel.* Your great-great-many-times-great grandfather, and mine. *Herald* Vanyel. The last Herald-Mage, Elspeth. Ally of the Clans."

Her mouth dropped open. The apparition winked broadly. *:Very good, Firesong,:* he said.

:Close your mouth, granddaughter,: said a voice she knew was only in *her* mind this time. *:You look very pretty, but not overly bright that way. There is no Veil to hold insects out; something might fly right down your throat.:*

She snapped her mouth shut and blushed in confusion.

She was not the only one with a reaction to the identification. "If *that* is Vanyel," Skif said, and gulped, "then *this* must be—the Forest of Sorrows!"

She knew even as he said it that Skif was right. But how? How had they gotten here? Skif might well gulp, for she had thought there was a reasonable limit on how far one could Gate—and this was well beyond that limit. As nearly as she could reckon, they were more than the length of Valdemar off-course, and *none* of them had ever been up here before, not even Skif.

This was insane. Or else, *she* had gone insane. Or it was a dream—

:It's not a dream,: Gwena said, lipping her to prove it.

:No, it's not a dream,: the spirit said, still smiling. *:And you haven't all gone mad. This is Sorrows and I am Vanyel Ashkevron. I am still in the service of the Goddess and Valdemar. I brought you here.:*

She could only blink. If this was Vanyel—no, who else could it be? It must be. If her mage-senses weren't supporting his claims, she would have thought he was just someone playing a trick on all of them. "Ah, I'm sorry, but—I've never seen a ghost before—I—" she stammered in confusion.

Firesong continued to stare at the spirit, but there was a certain expression of growing accusation on his face. And well there might be, since this ghostly Vanyel had just run roughshod over their plans with this little excursion.

Elspeth tried to shake her thoughts loose. If this was Vanyel, then *this* was the spirit of one of the most pivotal Heralds of all time. His death had ended the age of Herald-Mages. And if her researches in the Archives were correct, he was also personally responsible for the fact that it was impossible for magic to be performed or even *thought of* inside the borders of Valdemar. She had a million questions in her mind, and was afraid to ask any of them.

But another thought occurred to her suddenly. What if this was still some kind of trick? Just because he was a Herald, *then…*

:It is Vanyel,: Gwena repeated, in reply to the unvoiced suspicion. Elspeth could sense that she was seriously shaken. *:And this is not a trap or, at least, not a trap of an enemy. Trust me in this.:* Then, as if to herself,

she added, *:This was not in the plan....:*

Before Elspeth could react to either statement, the spirit himself replied—his smile fading, and being replaced with a look of stern seriousness. *:There have been many things done that were not in the "plan," sister,:* he said, without apology. *:And for the better. I have many reasons to be less than fond of predestined paths. And it would be wise for you and Rolan to recall that plans seldom survive the first engagement with the enemy. A plan that has been in operation as long as this one of yours should never have lasted as long as it did.:*

Gwena's head came up, and her eyes widened, as if she had not expected to be chided. She staggered back a step.

Vanyel's smile returned, this time for Elspeth. *Personally, I think you have been doing well, especially for someone who had to constantly fight "plans" that had been made without her consent or knowledge.:* He glanced from Elspeth to Darkwind and back. *:I think you will upset a few more plans before you're through. Things should be very interesting for you, at any rate, once you reach Haven. For what it's worth, you have my sympathy.:*

"This is a fine family chat. I'm having a delightful time. May I interrupt and ask how in the silver skies did you bring us here?" Firesong demanded.

:Ah. I'm sorry I had to interfere with your intended destination and your Gate—but this was my only chance to intercept all of you, together. There are forces marshaling now that you need to know about, or Valdemar will be worse off than I can affect. Much worse than what King Valdemar's people fled.:

Elspeth felt a chill run up her back at his words. There were some who had held—sentimentally, she had always thought—that Vanyel somehow protected Valdemar, haunting the Forest of Sorrows. It seemed the sentimentalists were right.

Treyvan's feathers were slowly smoothing down; he clicked his beak twice, and said—with remarkable mildness, Elspeth thought, considering the circumstances—"I did not know you could change the desstination of a Gate." He cocked his head to one side, and continued, making no secret of his surprise, "I know of no one alive who can do ssso—"

Then he stopped short, as he realized that he was not precisely talking to someone who was *alive.*

"Urrr. Apologiesss."

:No need to apologize, Treyvan. I've had a great deal of time to research the subject,: Vanyel replied, actually sounding a bit sheepish.

As he spoke, Elspeth noticed that he faded in and out, as if the amount of power he was using to maintain himself, or his control over it, fluctuated.

:I would imagine you have, youngster,: Need's dry mental voice replied. *:Although Gates are not precisely my specialty, I recall someone in* my *time learning how to kidnap the unwitting by interfering with their Portals.:*

:Ah. So I have not discovered anything new.: Did he sound a little disappointed? *:Well, that means that the rest of you can uncover this "secret" for yourselves, later. Right now, you need to hear some things, and I am the one to tell you. That is why I diverted you.:*

:Kidnapped us, you mean,: Need interrupted. *:There are people in k'Treva Vale who are probably tearing their elaborately braided white hair out with anxiety right now! Never thought of that, did you, boy?:*

Vanyel did not exactly sigh, but Elspeth did get a sense of impatience. *:Then perhaps Firesong ought to send a message telling them you will be all right, shouldn't he?:*

Now it was Firesong's turn to look impatient. "You haven't exactly given me a chance to, Forefather!" he snapped. "If you all don't mind, I shall do exactly that!"

He turned and stalked off into the forest, the white *dyheli* following. His firebird flapped its wings a little to keep its balance as he turned, and favored Vanyel with a contemptuous look and a chitter.

:Oh, dear. I seem to have put my foot in it—and he's as touchy as I used to be,: the spirit said, chagrined. *:I hope he'll accept an apology.:*

"Oh, don't worry too much about it," Darkwind said unexpectedly, giving Vanyel a half grin. "I think he's more upset by the fact that he *isn't* the most powerful Adept around anymore. And it doesn't matter whether you really are what you claim you are, the fact that you played with his Gate proves you're stronger than he is. Besides—you made a better entrance than he did."

Elspeth favored her lover with an odd look. He was certainly taking this apparition rather well—better than she was, in fact. She still wasn't entirely certain that this spirit was who and what he said he was.

No matter what Gwena said. Companions weren't infallible. Could they be fooled?

:Still, I seem to be as bad at handling people's feelings as I was back in my own time...: This time the spirit *did* sigh. *:Shall we take this from the beginning? I need to speak with all of you, but the ones I need to speak with the most are Elspeth and Darkwind—:*

Some of her growing skepticism must have shown, for he stopped and looked only at her.

:You still are not certain that I am genuine, or of my motives. I think you've gotten much more cautious than you once were,: the spirit said at last.

:She's had a good teacher,: Need said gruffly. *:Me. I wouldn't believe the spirit of my own mother if she showed up with as little proof of who she was as you've given us. "Trust me" doesn't fly. If you want her to believe you're what you say you are, you'd better give her some proof she'll recognize.:*

The spirit actually laughed, then turned to Elspeth. *:Will it constitute proof if I answer some questions? Things no one outside of Valdemar could know the answers to except me?:*

She nodded, slowly. It would certainly be a start, anyway.

:The thing that is most on your mind is the "banishment" of magic from Valdemar, and the fact that not only is it impossible for mages to remain, it isn't even possible for magic to be thought of for very long. The two are related, but not from the same cause. The first is my fault, a spell I created. It wasn't supposed to work that way,: he added ruefully. *:I was interrupted by emergencies before I could complete what I'd planned, and I never got back to it. What I did was to set the* vrondi *to watching for mage-energy in use. You know what* vrondi *are, I hope?:*

She did, although she hadn't ever heard the name before she came to k'Sheyna. "The little air-elementals that we call to set the Truth Spell," she replied.

Vanyel nodded vigorously. She noticed then that although his feet touched the ground, the grass stems poked right through them. Hard to counterfeit that effect... *:Exactly. And before you ask, even though it is true magic, since you are Heralds they know not to pester you when you cast the spell that calls them. Heralds casting true magic will never be bothered; I couldn't have them swarming every Herald-Mage in the Kingdom, after all! My aunt would never have let me hear the last of that.:*

Considering what the Herald-Chronicler of the time had to say about Vanyel's formidable aunt, Herald Savil, Elspeth had to chuckle a little at that. She had apparently been a match for Kerowyn.

:So, when the vrondi *saw magic, if it hadn't been cast by a Herald, they were supposed to tell the nearest Herald-Mage, then keep an eye on the person using the mage-energy unless the Herald-Mage told them differently. I was going to change the spell, later—to ask the* vrondi *to "light up" the person who was using the mage-energy the way they do with a Truth Spell, to make the mage rather conspicuous. I thought that was better than having them simply watch the mage, especially since there might not be a Herald-Mage anywhere nearby—:*

"Unfortunately, after you, there weren't *any* Herald-Mages at all," Elspeth said dryly.

:Well, that's true. No active ones, anyway. So now they just watch. The longer the mage sticks around, the more of them come to watch. It's horribly uncomfortable, since mages can sense the vrondi, *and it's rather like being stared at by an increasing crowd all the time.:* The spirit shook his head. *:The borders have changed since I set the spell, and so far as the* vrondi *are concerned, the "border" really ends where the presence of active, on-duty Heralds ends. They don't always notice where Heralds are unless one of them has invoked Truth Spell lately in that area. So the "borders" are changing all the time, and sometimes mages on the Rethwellan or Karsite borders, or the borders on the west, can get fairly far in before they're stopped. I'm afraid that, enthusiastic as they are, well,* vrondi *just aren't too bright themselves.:*

Elspeth nodded; that made sense. The *vrondi* did not seem to be terribly reliable outside of exact instructions, although they were like puppies, and very eager to please. "But what about the way people simply can't *think* about magic?" she persisted. "The *vrondi* couldn't possibly be responsible for that!"

:No, I am. It was something we decided on after Van and I got together again.:

This was a new mind-voice, and after a moment, Elspeth saw the second misty figure beside the first. It was nowhere near as well-defined, but if this was Vanyel—

:Yes, that was Stef's idea,: Vanyel said, confirming Elspeth's guess. *:Tell them why, ashke.:*

:Because we still had a problem with people refusing to give up the notion that Herald-Mages were somehow superior to Heralds with other Gifts,: the new voice sighed. *:It seems to be an inherent weakness of people to think magic cures every ill. The Bards did their best, but there were still those who felt that the young King was hiding the Herald-Mages away somewhere, keeping them for "special purposes" of his own, or reserving their powers for his own personal friends and favorites. So—we decided it would be best for people to simply "forget" that any magic but mind-magic had ever existed in Valdemar, except in old tales and songs.:*

There was a third and larger figure forming behind the other two, and this one was as strong or stronger than Vanyel—and there was no mistake that it was horse-shaped.

Yfandes—Elspeth thought, and as she recognized Vanyel's Companion, the spirit tossed her head in an unmistakable motion of summoning. Without a single word, Gwena and Cymry walked toward her; she led them off into the forest.

:They—ah—need to talk,: Vanyel said delicately. *:Your Gwena, for all that she is Grove-born, is just as fallible as any other mortal.:*

"She's *what?*" Elspeth yelped. Darkwind squinted and scratched his ear to recover from her cry. Grove-born? And no doubt Elspeth had been made to forget *that* as well! This passed everything for sheer, unadulterated gall—

And oddly enough, it was what actually convinced her that Vanyel was Vanyel. No creature born outside Valdemar would know what a Grove-born Companion was. Few inside it would know, for that matter. And no one else would have dared to make such an incredible statement.

:*She's Grove-born,:* Vanyel repeated. :*So, they "forgot" to tell you that, too, hmm? Doubtless "for your own good." It's simple enough, Elspeth; you were going to be the first of the new Herald-Mages, so I suppose they thought you needed something a little more than the ordinary Companion.:* Vanyel's mind-voice dripped irony. :*It never fails to annoy me how little faith people can have in each other, Herald or no. Ah, well. Now that 'Fandes has her away from you, I'll tell you what she may "forget" to tell you about the Grove-born. Be gentle on her, Elspeth; as Companions go—when compared to, say, Sayvil—she is very, very young. No older than you, in fact. She makes all the kinds of mistakes any young thing makes, but because she is Grove-born, she thinks she will always make the right decision.:* He shook his head. :*She forgets that she has no real, human experience to base her decisions on. It is like dictating music when you yourself have never learned to play an instrument.:*

If this was supposed to mollify Elspeth, it didn't work. But on the other hand, she had gotten used to Gwena, and her "habits;" by now she had a fair notion how to figure out what was going on from what Gwena *wouldn't* tell her. Gwena wasn't going to change, so there was really no point in getting upset with her at this late a date. And despite her faults, Gwena had been a good friend for a long time.

:*Actually, it would be a good thing if I could have a word with the two adult gryphons along with Elspeth and Darkwind. Since there are magics to talk of, it would be best to discuss things with all the mages at once.:* Vanyel looked hopefully at Treyvan and Hydona, as the little ones watched the spirit solemnly from behind their parents' wings. :*This valley is quite well shielded and protected; nothing can get in or out unless I permit it. The gryphlets could get some exercise.:*

"While we adultsss ssspeak of thingsss that would bore them into missschief," Hydona laughed. "Well, if Rrisss isss willing to take charge of them—"

The *kyree* nodded his head in a way that made it look like a bow. :*Of course, lovely lady. I can continue hunting lessons if you like.:*

Both gryphlets perked up their ear tufts at that, and suddenly the little round baby faces looked as fierce as the adults'. Elspeth kept forgetting that they were carnivores. They were so baby-fluffy and, well, *cute*. But they were raptorial, like Vree, and like him they enjoyed the hunt and the kill—when they actually succeeded at the latter, which wasn't often.

"Yesss," Hydona replied thoughtfully. "Hunting lessssonsss would be mosssst appreciated."

:Then come along, younglings,: Rris said, trotting off with his tail high, looking surprisingly graceful for a creature the size of a young calf. The gryphlets bounded off after him, with a great deal less grace. Treyvan winced as Lytha crashed into a bush, tumbled head-over-tail, and kept right on going without even a pause. And Jerven was no more coordinated than his sister, blundering through the remains of the bush.

:This is not secret or private,: Vanyel said then, looking at Skif and Nyara, *:But—much will be very technical. You may stay if you wish…:*

"I don't think so—thank you, but I'm not in the least interested. Really. I think I'd be better off not knowing," Skif said hastily. "And I wouldn't have Mage-Gift if you offered it to me. I wouldn't have it if you paid me Cymry's weight in gold to take it!"

He glanced at Nyara, who shrugged. Elspeth hadn't thought she would be interested, and she was not proven wrong. "My abilities are at the level of Journeyman in a school, or so Need tells me. I would be wasting my time with higher magics. The mage who knows how to use simple spells cleverly is just as effective as the Adept with no imagination. I should enjoy simply being with my friends in this lovely place."

And putting off the encounter with more strangers, Elspeth thought. *I can't blame her, either.*

:I'm too old to learn another style of magery without a long time to study it,: Need said. *:To be honest, youngsters, there's things I know you people have forgotten. Simple stuff, but sometimes simple is better. We'll run along, and you'll have your conference without me going "What?" every few moments.:*

Darkwind snickered.

:Van, I can show them the springs,: Stefen offered.

At Vanyel's nod, Skif and Nyara followed the little wisp of mist that was Stefen out of the clearing. Firesong came back a moment later, face impassive and unreadable, but eyes sparkling.

"Mother says that this was quite discourteous and inconsiderate of you, even if you are our forefather," he announced. "She told me to tell you that you are old enough to have better manners, especially by now. The only way she is prepared to forgive you is if you teach me what you did. And how to defend against it, if there is any defense."

The spirit rippled, and Elspeth got the distinct impression Vanyel was either laughing or stifling laughter. *:Very well,:* he said after a moment. *:It is, after all, the least I can do. Now if you could make yourselves comfortable.:*

That was not difficult to do, here. In fact, Elspeth suspected Vanyel *had* taken a leaf or two from the Hawkbrothers' book, and had constructed this place along the lines of a Vale.

The gryphons reclined on the soft grass, and Darkwind and Elspeth used them as backrests. *:The first thing I need to tell you about is what I call the Web,:* Vanyel said. *:I created it because there were too few Herald-Mages left— originally there were four we called Guardians who remained at Haven and kept up a constant watch on the Borders. I changed that; I tied all Heralds and Companions into a net of completely unconscious communication. Now when there is danger in any direction, Heralds with ForeSight who are in a position to alert those who can do something about it have a vision or dream. That's how everyone knows when a Herald dies. And it's one way for the* vrondi *to know where Heralds are.:*

"We have done such things, but only for ssshort periodsss of time," Hydona offered. "Becaussse we did not know how to make it an unconssscious ability."

:The Companions are the key,: Vanyel told her. *:Because they are already linked. I couldn't have managed otherwise.:*

"Hmm." Treyvan nodded thoughtfully.

:I never meant anything but the Web to have to last as long as it has,: Vanyel continued. *:The* vrondi*-spell has eroded near to nothing, and constant attacks on it from Hardorn are taking their toll. I'm going to have to take it down in a controlled manner before someone breaks it and harms the* vrondi *in the process. Whether or not it goes back up again will depend on your choices later.:*

It was a good thing they were well-fed and well-rested, or Elspeth would have asked for a recess to think all this through. This was not precisely what Elspeth had expected to hear—but it was logical enough. Harm to the *vrondi* might mean that they would flee Valdemar altogether, and that would cause more problems than taking down the spell would.

"If you remove the warn-off, then mages will be able to enter Valdemar," Darkwind pointed out, as a light breeze stirred his hair. The breeze was from Vree stooping on Treyvan's head and crest-feathers, then angling up to perch in a tree and preen. "Many mages, in fact, through Valdemar's unfortified borders."

:Precisely.: Vanyel was clearly pleased. *:Now I plan to do several things, besides removing the spell. First, I will need to build a Gate to send you home. This will deplete me seriously for a time, and I do not know how long that will be. I will have to concentrate all my attention on this Border, and I will not be able to even*

offer such paltry distractions as I did against your Falconsbane—along with the Shin'a'in—to make him think that another Adept was courting him for an alliance.:

Darkwind raised an eyebrow at Elspeth. She nodded; she had already known about the Shin'a'in Kal'enedral being involved. Vanyel's help was probably why the ruse had been so effective; Falconsbane would have seen the traces of real magic at work and if the suspicion that the Shin'a'in were running a trick on him had even occurred to him, he would have dismissed it immediately, since the Shin'a'in didn't use magic.

"What about Ancar?" she asked. "He'll know when that spell comes down."

:Ancar, yes. And others. You will have to warn your people through Gwena and Rolan that the barrier is coming down. I will do this just before I send you home. That way they will be prepared for magical incursions—although I do not think that Ancar will be able to react immediately. He is disposed toward grandiose plans, and those take time to prepare.:

"Hmm," Elspeth replied, after a moment of thought. "Even if he's watching for it to break, he likely won't have anyone strong there to do anything. He doesn't trust his powerful mages out of his sight."

:Once the barrier is down and you are home, there is nothing else I can do,: Vanyel said. *:Now, about the new Heartstone in the Palace at Haven…:* Firesong looked up alertly, interest immediately captured. *:I anchored the power in the stone I used to center the Web. You will find it in the old Palace in one of the old mage workrooms, and it is on the middle of a table that seems rooted to the floor. It is not yet activated, and I left it that way, keyed only to Firesong.*

Fortunately for Skif's mental comfort, as they left the clearing, Stefen became gradually less ephemeral and more solid, until at last he seemed almost normal—so long as you ignored the fact that you could see right through him. He seemed a cheerful young man, although his hair couldn't quite seem to make up its mind whether it wanted to be blond or red.

:Here we are—: Stefen announced proudly. *:I thought you'd like this place. It's very romantic.:*

Romantic? Hardly an adequate description for a place where trees overhung a mossy cup of a valley, where delicate flowers bloomed at precisely the right spots, and where a tiny waterfall trickled musically down the back wall of the valley, to fill a perfect, rock-rimmed basin just big enough for two if they cared for a little waterplay. In a candlemark or two the sun would be above the trees, warming this valley and the tiny pool.

Skif had the suspicion that Stefen had a hand in somehow creating this idyllic little hideaway, and was waiting for a reaction.

"This is… this is lovely," he said, finally. "I haven't seen anything prettier even in k'Sheyna Vale."

Stefen looked pleased as Nyara nodded agreement. *:I've been training the trees and the plants,:* he said diffidently. *:Not in the way of a Hawkbrother or anything, but—I'm glad you like it. Van likes it, but he's rather biased on my behalf.:*

"If you don't mind my asking," Skif said hesitantly, "Why have you two—you know, *stuck around* all this time?"

:Gods.: Stefen looked embarrassed. *:Responsibility, I suppose. I mean, we finished off magic in Valdemar, and until people were ready to accept Mage-Gift as just one more Gift,* someone *had to make certain that another wizard-lord like Leareth didn't come down out of the mountains with a mage-army. Van didn't trust his barriers against someone with Adept strength. So—:* he shrugged, *:—here we are.:*

"And I suppose you planned on doing something to educate the next Herald-Mages?" Skif persisted.

:Well, only if there was no other way. We hadn't counted on Gwena getting things mucked up with all her grand plans and predestined paths. If there's anything that Van hates, it's a Glorious Destiny.: Stefen chuckled. *:If he's said it once, he's said it a hundred times: "Glorious Destinies get you Glorious Funerals." Anyway, mostly we're too busy watching for idiot fuzzy barbarians or mages with ambition trying to cross this border to pay too much attention to what's going on down south. Until Elspeth started flinging levin-bolts around, that is.:*

"So you have been aware of that?" Skif asked.

Stefen laughed silently. *:I should say, Van couldn't help but notice, she's in his bloodline, and he put that other spell on all his relatives so he'd know if anyone was trying to turn them into frogs or flatten them or something. That kind of thing persisted a lot longer than he thought it would, too.:*

"Perhaps your Vanyel is a better mage than even he gave himself credit for being," Nyara observed quietly.

Stefen favored her with a sweet smile. *:Once Elspeth started working magic in the Vales, that got his attention and he found out what was going on down there with you folks. He wanted to do something, but he knew his powers were pretty limited that far away. Eventually he started helping the Shin'a'in distract that nasty piece of work, Falconsbane. Sent mage winds to break all his windows, then replaced them with red glass, sent him black roses using a firebird as the carrier—we had a lot of fun with that. And the crystal paperweight with the castle and snow. Even 'Fandes enjoyed that.:*

"I imagine," Skif said dryly. "So now what do you plan for us?"

:Well, Van wanted me to talk to you two, actually. He says I'm better at emotional things, and he's afraid that—well, he knows that you two are not going to have an easy time of it. You know that, but it's still just an intellectual exercise for you. You aren't really prepared for what's going to happen.:

"It would help, Skif, if you tell me who these people are—or were—" Nyara said plaintively, sitting down on a rock and curling her legs underneath her. Skif took a place beside her. "It is obvious that you and Firesong trust them, but—"

Skif hit his forehead with the heel of his palm. "Oh, hellfires. I'm sorry, Nyara—"

:There wasn't time,: Stefen reminded him. *:Why don't you tell her, and I'll fill in what you don't know.:*

:So, there it is. You've seen for yourself that the stories about Van and 'Fandes and me being up here in Sorrows are true,: the spirit said cheerfully. *:It has been fun, actually. Maybe there are people who the Havens just won't have!:*

Skif chuckled. Stefen was making it very easy to simply accept all this, acting quite like an ordinary human and not at all like something out of legends. Perhaps he was making a deliberate effort to do so; to Skif's mind that was a great deal easier than having the two spirits appear, ten feet tall, carrying flaming swords, thundering "Fear not!" There was a vitality and a lightness about the spirit; in fact, there was something about him that kept Skif from feeling worried or anxious when he had every reason to.

For that matter, there was also a feeling of familiarity about Stefen, as if he and the Bard had been old friends of the kind that can say anything to each other, and forgive anything...

"Skif, it seems to me—perhaps I am being forward, but—" Nyara hesitated, then continued as Stefen nodded encouragingly. "What he and Vanyel faced—between them—there is a great deal in common with our situation."

:I think so,: Stefen agreed. *:So does Van. That's part of why I wanted to talk with you.:* He shrugged. *:You'd have thought that once we were a pair, everything would have been lovely, but things kept happening that could have ruined it all. He spent a lot of time away from me. Not everyone accepted it. There were always things coming from outside of us that put strains on us, no matter what we did. Things were never perfect for more than a day at a time. Really—I think you would only harm yourselves if you expected perfection. You'd both just be unhappy when you didn't have*

it.: Stefen's attention was all on Nyara. *:And there is something else Van wanted me to tell you, Nyara. Your father is not sane by anyone's definition. What he did to you wasn't sane. Insane people do things no one can anticipate. Nothing that happened to you is your fault. You didn't "deserve" it, or ask for it, or cause it. And what he did was not right. A parent who does that is a monster, and nothing more.:*

Skif and Need had been trying to tell her the same things, but it was as if a light had suddenly been kindled inside her. And Skif knew why. This was a total stranger, affirming what people she knew cared for her had been saying. And this was a spirit as well, who presumably had a little more insight into things than a still-living mortal...

He shouldn't be jealous, just because it was Stefen who brought that light to her face and not him. And he knew he shouldn't be. But he couldn't help suffering a sharp stab of jealousy anyway.

:This won't be the last time you're jealous, old man,: said Stefen, and he somehow knew Stefen spoke only to him. *:She can't help what she is. There are those who will find her desirable only because she is exotic, and others who will be certain she cannot resist them. She was built for a single purpose, and it still marks her. You have hard times ahead.:*

Skif's jealousy turned to despair; how could he ever hope to hold Nyara once she entered Valdemar and began to meet others? Why should she wish to stay with him? There were people of wealth who had far more to offer than he did. He couldn't even offer her protection from the curious and the unkind. He was a Herald and had duties; he couldn't be with her every moment.

:Don't be a bigger ass than you have to be,: Stefen said sharply. *:She loves you, for one thing. And for another—you will likely be the only creature she ever encounters who sees and desires her for her, herself, and not as an* object *to be possessed. She has had quite enough of that in her life, and believe me, she knows how to recognize it when she sees it.:*

Skif blinked as a bee buzzed near his face. He also would have blushed, if Stefen had not resumed the conversation as casually as if he had not interrupted it to talk to Skif alone. *:There's no great virtue in being lifebonded, you know. It's a lot like having a Predestined Fate; often uncomfortable, frequently inconvenient, usually hazardous.:*

Skif shook his head, and waved the bee away. He had often envied Talia and Dirk—how could Stefen say something like that? Wasn't being lifebonded the ultimate love?

"I thought lifebonding was something to be sought above all else," Nyara replied dubiously.

:That's the poets' and Bards' interpretation,: Stefen said with a grimace. *:It has far more to do with compatibility than with love, and the match is more random than, say—finding two people from different countries with exactly the same eye color. When you're lifebonded, your choices are limited to the things you* both *want, because if your lifebonded is unhappy, so are you. It takes two very strong, well-established personalities to make a lifebonded pair work, because if one is passive, he'll be eaten alive by the other.:*

"That doesn't sound very pleasant," Skif put in. "In fact it doesn't even sound—romantic. It sounds like a disease."

Stefen laughed. *:I don't know about a disease, but it isn't love, that's for certain, even though love usually cements the bond. Van thinks that it's likelier that someone with an extremely powerful Gift of some kind and a tendency to deep depression will be lifebonded than someone who is not so burdened and hag-ridden. That's so the Gifted-and-suicidal half has someone outside of himself to keep him stable and give him an external focus. But all we know is that while it's rare, it isn't something to yearn after.:*

"To think I've envied Talia all this time—" Skif mused. And at Stefen's puzzled look, he added, "That's the current Queen's Own."

:Of course, the one with all the Empathy! 'Fandes almost swatted her once, when she thought the girl was going to lose all control: Before Skif could express his surprise, Stefen went on. *:I liked her, though—so, she lifebonded? You shouldn't be too surprised. I'll bet I can describe her lifemate. Strong, kind, thoughtful, intelligent, tends to keep his feelings to himself, the kind of man everyone knows they can depend on. Little children and animals love him immediately.:*

"That's Dirk!" Skif exclaimed.

:So, that illustrates my point. Love now—a good, solid love is something infinitely rarer and more difficult to maintain, because you don't *know everything your partner is feeling. Love takes work. Love means being able to apologize and mean it when you blunder. Love is worth fighting for!:* Stefen sounded absolutely fierce. *:One of the very things that made what Van and I have a love-match as well as a lifebonding was that we were so different. It is like a marriage—you marry who you* think *your beloved is, and then discover who they really are over the years. It's that discovery that makes a marriage work.:*

:We did have things in common, lots of them, but you would never have assumed that from first seeing us. It made hunting and finding them all the sweeter. And it gave us chances to introduce each other to something new. You two have that same opportunity. Van and I took pride in being different—we enjoyed the diversity to be found among people of all kinds, and we enjoyed the diversity in the two of us.:

Before Skif could react to this, Need spoke up. *:All very pretty, I'm sure,:*

she said scathingly. *:But this is Skif we're talking about. You're assuming the young lout has enough imagination to recognize diversity.:*

"Of course he has imagination!" Nyara exclaimed immediately. "How can you say something so stupid?"

:Oh, he has about as much imagination as he has sensitivity,: Need continued as if she hadn't noticed Nyara's angry exclamation. *:Frankly, I think both of you are giving him more credit than he deserves.:*

Skif wisely kept his mouth shut. He thought he saw what Need was up to. Furthermore, Stefen, after all his impassioned speeches, was keeping quite, quite silent—

And Nyara had taken his hand in a most unmistakably possessive manner. With her other hand, she drew Need from her sheath. Need rasped on. When she insulted Skif's sexual prowess, Nyara pitched the sword away with a hiss.

Skif held Nyara closer. She glared at the discarded sword.

:Well, I've tried to shake you before, but this is going to be the last time,: the sword said, sounding pleased. *:If I can't rattle your faith in each other, no one can.:*

:Exactly so, you crafty woman,: Stefen replied. *:You see, Skif? If her heart doesn't lie with you, then I know nothing of the heart—and as a Bard that has been my special study for a long time. And Nyara—he trusts you enough to allow you to fight your own battle and win, even when he is the target. Love is as much trust as it is devotion.:*

Nyara's face relaxed, then she snorted a tension-breaking laugh and picked up Need. "You fooled me again, you chunk of lead. But—I was not perfectly sure—I—"

Skif smiled. Life was very, very good at the moment.

:Oh, there is no such thing as perfection, or a "perfect" love—Van and I still argue and even become angry with each other,: Stefen countered. *:It annoys the birds and small animals to no end when we do. I doubt there is even perfection in the Havens. Wouldn't perfection be a bore?:*

:Build on what you have, children,: Need said gruffly. *:The foundation is a good one, so now see what kind of a house you can raise. And don't worry if the windows aren't the right size, the door is too tall, or there's dust on the mantelpiece. Just make sure the walls and the ceiling are sound, and make certain your home holds laughter. The dust will take care of itself.:*

"I think we can do that," Skif told Need, feeling much better about the entire relationship than he ever had before. "We'll certainly try." He squeezed Nyara's hand, not noticing the claws. "And we'll succeed. Won't we?" he finished, looking into her eyes.

"Oh, yes," she answered, smiling. "I know we will."

6

Treyvan curled his tail around his haunches and waited beside the cave for his mate. He needed to have a discussion with her that he did not want anyone to overhear. Especially not certain interfering spirits...

It had been two days since their unexpected arrival in the Forest of Sorrows. The gryphlets had taken it all in stride, as they always did, and found excuses to chase things and chew on them at every opportunity. Rris had been as faithful as a *hertasi* and infinitely patient. Firesong had apparently come to grips with his changing status—that is, not being fawned over—and his *dyheli* companion remained nonplussed. And Vree—well, Vree had resumed hunting crest-feathers. Treyvan tolerated that. It was something familiar in an unfamiliar environment.

It had taken that long to make certain everything was ready for the Gate to go up—and for Vanyel's protective spells to come down. When the moment came, it would feel to the gryphons like the magical equivalent of a change in air pressure before a storm, then all would be calm. Valdemar had been alerted, and there would be an escort waiting for Elspeth and her friends at the terminus of the Gate.

That would be at the entrance to the family chapel at Ashkevron Manor. It was the only place still standing intact that Vanyel knew well enough to make into a Gate-terminus. The chapel in Companion's Field was a ruin, and Elspeth could not honestly assure him that the Palace still looked the way it had when he was still alive. Doors had been sealed up, new doors had been cut—trim and decorations had been added and taken away.

But nothing ever changed in the core building of the Ashkevron home. Elspeth had told them all she recalled hearing some of the family actually boasting about just that. There was even a story that if anyone ever did anything besides add to the buildings, the ghost of some long-dead ancestor would rise out of the grave to haunt the one who dared change what he had wrought.

Firesong had been of two minds about going on with Elspeth, until Vanyel had brought out an argument the spirit had held in reserve. It had been on the afternoon of the first day, when the Hawkbrother had said, dubiously, "It is all very well for Darkwind to follow Elspeth into her land, but what ties have I to such a place? Especially when I have duties elsewhere. And while it is true enough that I have experience with a living Heartstone, well, so does Darkwind. He knew enough before he became a scout to be counted among the Adepts."

Vanyel had nodded, acknowledging the truth of that. But then he had countered that argument. *:It is the duty of the Tayledras to heal places where magic has gone wrong,:* he pointed out. *:And that is doubly the duty of a Healing Adept, such as you. True?:*

"True enough," Firesong had replied, warily.

:Well, then, is it not the duty of a Tayledras Healing Adept to prevent the misuse of magic that could poison the earth?:

"I—" Firesong had begun, even more warily. "I suppose so—"

:Then what of the consequences if the Heartstone beneath Haven fell into the hands of Ancar and his mages? What if its power were to be mismanaged through ignorance? Isn't it the duty of a Healing Adept to be as concerned with prevention as with results? Shouldn't, in fact, a Healing Adept be more *concerned with prevention?:* Vanyel had simply looked at Firesong, as a teacher looks at a student who has failed to study.

Treyvan had seen Elspeth suppress a smile. He knew that she wouldn't be able to resist the opportunity to pay Firesong back. "My stepfather has the earth-sense that a lot of the rulers of Rethwellan have," she had put in. "He says that Ancar does horrible things to the earth-magics in Hardorn—that during the last war he rode through a place where the magics had been so misused that the area was dying, and it made him ill just to ride across it."

Vanyel had nodded, as if to say, "There—you see?" and had turned his unwavering gaze back to Firesong.

The young Adept had grumbled something under his breath. "This is blackmail, you know," he had retorted at last. But when Vanyel did not reply, he had shaken his head, and finally given his reluctant agreement to go. "It may be blackmail, but it is also true," he had admitted, and had gone off to tell his Clan of the change in plans. "I shudder to think how fickle my home Vale will regard me after all these changes of plan."

Now it was Treyvan's turn to make a similar decision. Or rather, Treyvan and his mate, together, for he would make no such important decisions without her. They were explorers by choice. They had chosen, together, to be adventurers until the day fortune dashed them on the rocks. Their names would already live on in the stories told by their Clan, Treyvan knew, and perhaps even become legendary after a few more generations. Hadn't they done enough, after all?

Hydona came winging in from above, fanning her wings to break her dive and landing with practiced ease on the grass beside him. "Do not tell me," she said, snatching playfully at his crest-feathers. "I think I can guesss alrready. You wisssh usss to go with young Elssspeth and Darrrkwind."

He felt his eyes going round with surprise, and his beak gaped. "But how did you know?" he exclaimed. "Sssurely I sssaid nothing—"

"No, only you have hung upon everrry worrd of thisss Vanyel, and your earrrtuftssss have twitched each time sssomeone hasss even hinted of the grrryphonsss in the North of Valdemarrr." She shook her head vigorously, and a loose feather flew off and drifted down like a leaf to land in the grass beside her.

He was chagrined, but he had to admit that she was probably right; he *had* been that transparent. But how could he not be? Every Kaled'a'in gryphon knew that of all of the gryphon-wings flying for Mage Urtho, fully half of them had never reached the Gate that had taken the Kaled'a'in safely away before Urtho's stronghold fell. Most of those had been out on the front lines with the army. Of those, some must have died—but surely others had escaped to live elsewhere. There were more than enough mages in Urtho's army to have set up Gates enough to take those fighting to safety as well, before or after the blast that obliterated Urtho's stronghold and Ma'ar's together.

The only way to find out—or at least the only way that would satisfy Treyvan—would be to try to find these gryphons themselves.

"We arrre magesss," Hydona pointed out thoughtfully. "And both the little onesss have Mage-Gift alssso. We will need to trrain them—ssso why not trrain otherrrsss at the sssame time?"

"What, like Herrraldsss?" The idea had already occurred to him, but he was pleased that Hydona had thought of it as well. "It isss trrrue that it would do the little onesss a grrreat deal of good to have sssome competition bessidesss each otherrr. And it could gain usss valuable alliesss."

Her beak gaped in a gentle grin. Oh, how beautiful she was! "My thought prrrecisssely. Thisss issss why I have alrrready told Vanyel that if you wisshed to go, I would not arrrgue with sssuch a change in plansss."

He mock-snapped at her. "Imperrrtinent! Making asssumptionsss—"

"Perrrfectly valid onesss," she pointed out, reaching out to preen his ears. He submitted to her readily, half-closing his eyes in pleasure. "I, of all alive, know you bessst."

"Verrry well, then," he said, with feigned reluctance. "I will misss going to Evendim, but perrrhapsss anotherrr time. If you will have it that way, tell thisss Vanyel that we will be going with Elssspth and our otherrr sssson." He sighed. "I sssuppose it isss jusst asss well. With the way Gating hasss been lately, who knowsss where we might end up otherrrwissse?"

"Mmm," she agreed, mouth full of his feathers.

He closed his eyes completely, and gave himself up to her ministrations.

Ancar started, as a huskily feminine and far-too-familiar voice startled him in the midst of searching through a chest of documents in the war-room.

"Well. What a pleasant surprise. I had *not* expected to find you here."

The silky-smooth tone of Hulda's voice sent a shiver of warning up Ancar's back. She only sounded this sweet when she wanted something— or when she was about to confront him over something, and she knew she had the upper hand.

He straightened, slowly, schooling his face into an impassive mask. He should not fear this woman. He had already subdued a powerful, half-human Adept to his will. She was no greater in power than this "Falconsbane" creature. He had no reason to fear her anger.

But her appearance was not reassuring. She was impeccably gowned and coiffed, looking as near to demure as she ever got. That meant she had found out something that she didn't like, and she was going to have it out with him, here and now.

While he smiled and granted her an ironic little bow, his thoughts raced behind his careful shields. Could she have discovered Falconsbane? But how? He had been so careful. No one came near the creature but those servants he himself controlled.

"Why, my dear teacher, how pleasant to see *you,* after so very long," he replied carefully. "I had thought that your new young friend was occupying all your time—"

"Enough fencing, child," she snapped at him. "We both know you've been up to something, meddling with energies you shouldn't have touched! And so does every mage sensitive to the flows of power! Your fumbling created some unpleasant echoes and ripples that are *still* causing me problems with my own spells, and I wonder how any of your pets are getting anything at all done!"

"My fumblings?" He felt sweat trickling down his back beneath his heavy velvet tunic, and he hoped that he wasn't sweating anywhere that she would notice. "What are you talking about?" Could it be that she actually didn't know what he had done?

"Don't try to toy with me, boy!" she growled. "You were playing with some kind of odd spell or other, and it was either something you made up yourself, or something you got out of one of your damned scraps of half-literate grimoires! Which was it?"

Before he could answer, she cut him off with a gesture. "Never mind," she said. "Don't bother to lie to me. I'll tell you what it was. You were trying to build a Gate, weren't you?"

He stared at her dumbly as she continued, her strange violet eyes flashing with scorn.

"You haven't even the sense to *fear* a Gate Spell, you fool!" she snarled. "Don't you know what the thing would have done if you hadn't broken it first? It would have turned back on you and eaten you alive! Building a Gate without knowing *where* you want it to go, precisely and exactly where, is the kind of mistake that will be your last! You must have used up a lifetime's worth of luck to escape that fate, you blithering idiot."

She went on and on at some length in the same vein; he simply hung his head so that she could not see his eyes and nodded like the foolish child she had named him. He stared at his feet as his sweat cooled, and his flush of fear faded. But beneath his submissive behavior, he was wildly excited and he did not want her to realize what she had just told him.

She had answered his every question about the so-called "portal" he had created! It was not a way to pull in node-energy, but was instead something entirely different, a way to create a doorway that would lead him instantly to any place he chose!

She had given him a weapon of incredible power and versatility, without knowing what she had done. Already he could imagine hundreds of ways to use such doorways.

He could simply step through such a door and into the very heart of a citadel. He could move entire armies without wearying them. He could use these doors to obtain anything or anyone he wanted, without worrying about such pesky complications as guards, locks, or discovery...

As she railed on, pacing back and forth like a restless panther in her black velvet, he also realized from what she did *not* say that she was completely unaware that he had brought anything through his Gate.

She mentioned nothing of the sort, in fact, not even as a horrible possibility. She seemed to be under the impression that he had sensed the Gate turning back on him and, in a panic, had broken the spell, collapsing the Gate upon itself.

He kept his face stiff and expressionless. He answered her, when she demanded answers, in carefully phrased sentences designed to maintain that fiction. The longer he could keep Falconsbane a secret from her, the better.

At least, until the moment that the Adept had recovered enough to bring him openly into the court as a putative ally. That way he would be able to work with Falconsbane without fear of Hulda's reactions.

She has her friends, the ambassador and his entourage from the Emperor... I should introduce Falconsbane as an envoy from the West, beyond Valdemar. She may even try to win him over. He'd appeal to her, I expect. Perhaps I should even let her seduce him—or him, her. I'm not certain which of the two would be the quicker to take the other...

As she used up her anger, wearing it out against the rock of his submission, her voice dropped and her pacing slowed. Finally she stopped and faced him.

"Look at me," she demanded. Slowly, as if he were afraid of her continued wrath, he raised his eyes. "Do not *ever* attempt that spell again," she said, in a tone that brooked no argument. "It is beyond you. It is far more dangerous than you can guess, and it is *well* beyond your current ability and skill. Furthermore, it is obvious that you do not have the whole of the instructions for such a spell. Half-understood spells are more dangerous to the caster than to anyone else. Is that understood?"

He nodded, meekly. "Yes, Hulda," he replied softly. She gave him a sharp look, but evidently did not see anything there to make her suspect his duplicity.

"See that you remember it, then," she said, and turned on her heel and left in a swirl of velvet skirts.

Ancar could hardly contain his excitement. If Hulda knew enough to identify this Gate Spell simply by the effects it had on the mage-energies of the area, how much more could his captive know? He burned to find out.

But he did nothing. Not immediately, anyway. Hulda almost certainly had someone watching him; she might even be watching him herself. If he ran off now, he would lead her to his captive.

So he continued with the task that had brought him here in the first place; unearthing a long-ignored map of the west and south, which included Valdemar and what little was known of the area beyond that land. If Falconsbane came from anywhere about there, he might be able to identify the spot on this map.

The map lay at the very bottom of the document chest, amid the dust and dirt of years of neglect. Ancar unrolled it to be certain that it was still readable, then rolled it back up and inserted it in a map tube for safekeeping.

Even then he did not hurry off to where his captive waited for him. Instead, he tended to several small problems that needed his personal touch, heard the reports of his seneschal and the keeper of his treasury, and looked over the written reports of those mages watching the border of Valdemar. He stuck the map tube in his belt and pretended to forget it was there.

Only then did he leave the central portion of the palace and stroll in the direction of the wing to which he had moved his captive once the creature began to recover properly.

As far as he could tell, there was no one observing his movements at that point, although there had been at least one guard and two servants covertly keeping an eye on him right up until the moment he began looking over the written reports from his mages.

He allowed himself a small smile of victory and put a little more haste into his steps.

The new quarters were an improvement over the old, which had been reasonably luxurious, although not what Falconsbane was used to. This was clearly a suite in Ancar's palace, albeit in a very old section of the palace. Age did not matter; what mattered was that it bore all the signs of having been unused for some time, but it had not been cleaned and refurbished hastily. Some care had been taken to clean and air the place thoroughly, and to ensure that everything was in proper order for the kind of "guest" that the King would consider important.

This somewhat mollified Falconsbane, but only in part. Ancar had not removed or eased the coercions, and his own body continued to betray him with weakness.

He sat now in a supportive chair, padded with cushions. A table within reach bore wine and fruit. Soft light from candles set throughout the room provided ample illumination—making up for the fact that the windows were closely shuttered, and no amount of threat or cajolery on Falconsbane's part would get the servants to open them. Ancar had delivered his orders, it seemed, and they were not to be disobeyed.

The King had arrived for his daily visit, and there seemed to be much on his mind, not all of it satisfactory. He immediately plunged into a flurry of demands for information, demands which had little or no apparent relationship to each other.

"I cannot properly answer your questions," Falconsbane said, with more far more seeming patience than he truly felt, "unless you explain to me what your situation is."

He kept his tone even and calm, pitching it in such a way as to do no more than border on the hypnotic and seductive. He had tried both seduction and fascination a few days ago, in an effort to persuade the upstart to release some of the coercions—and had come up against a surprising wall of resistance. After contemplating the situation, he had come to the conclusion that this resistance to subversion had not come about by accidental *or* true design.

No, there was someone in Ancar's life who had once wielded these very weapons against him to control him, someone he no longer trusted. Thus, the resistance. Falconsbane would have to use a more subtle weapon than body or mind.

He would have to use words.

An exasperating prospect. This sort of thing took time and patience. He did not wish to take the time, and he had little love for exercising patience.

However needful it might be.

However, the fact that Ancar had this core of resistance at all told him one very important fact. There was someone in this benighted place that had once controlled the little fool, and who might still do so.

That someone—given Ancar's biases—was probably female and attractive. That in itself was interesting, because attractive females seldom lost power until they lost their attraction.

He needed to find out more about this woman, whoever, whatever she was. And he needed to discover who had taught the King enough so that the boy was able to command the power of a Gate, however inexpertly and briefly.

Ancar looked away uneasily, as he always did when Falconsbane fixed him with that particular stare. It was as if the youngster found even the appearance of patience unnerving. The soft candlelight touched the boy-King's face; it was a handsome face, with no hint of the excesses fearfully whispered about among the servants.

Had his own servants whispered? Probably. Had their whispers mattered? Only in that rumors made them fear him, and fear made them obey him. Small wonder the child held the reins, given the fear his servants displayed.

"I don't know what you mean," Ancar said. He was lying, but

Falconsbane did not intend him to escape so easily.

"You ask me many questions about magic, in a most haphazard manner, and I can see no pattern behind what you wish to know. Yet there must *be* one. If you will simply tell me what drives these questions, perhaps I can give you better answers."

Ancar contemplated that for a moment, then rubbed his wrist uneasily. "I have enemies," he said, after a long moment.

Falconsbane permitted himself a slight snort of contempt. "You are a King. Every King has enemies," he pointed out. "You must be more specific if I am to help you. Are these enemies within your court, within your land, or outside of both?"

Ancar moved, very slightly.

Falconsbane could read the language of body and expression as easily as a scholar a book in his own language. Ancar had winced when Falconsbane had said, "within your court." So there were forces working against the King from within. Could the woman Falconsbane had postulated be one of those forces?

"Those within it are the ones that most concern me," he finally replied, as Falconsbane continued to fix him with an unwavering gaze.

The Adept nodded shrewdly. "Those who once were friends," he said flatly, making it a statement, and was rewarded once again by that faint wince. And something more. "No," he amended, *"More* than friends." Not relatives; he knew from questioning the servants that Ancar had assassinated his own father. "Lovers?" he hazarded.

Ancar started, but recovered quickly. "A lover," he agreed, the words emerging with some reluctance.

Falconsbane nodded, but lidded his eyes with feigned disinterest. "Such enemies are always the bitterest and most persistent." Dared he make a truly hazardous statement? Well, why not? "And generally, their hate is the greatest. They pursue revenge long past the point when another would have given over."

Slight relaxation told him his shot went wide of the mark. So, this woman was not aware she had lost her powers over the boy!

He made a quick recovery. "But she is foolish not to recognize that you are the one who hates, and not her. So she has lost her power over you, yet thinks she still possesses you." He smiled very slightly as Ancar started again. Good. Now ask a revealing question. "Why do you permit her to live, if you are weary of her?"

His question had caught the King off-guard, enough that the boy actually answered with the truth. "Because she is too powerful for me to be rid of her."

Falconsbane held his own surprise in check. Too powerful? The King could not *possibly* mean that she had secular power; he ruled his land absolutely, and took what he wanted from it. Servants had revealed that much, quite clearly. He could not mean rank, for Ancar had eliminated any other pretender to his throne, and anyone who had force of will or arms to challenge him.

There was only one thing the boy *could* mean, then. The woman was a more powerful mage than Ancar. Too powerful to subvert, too powerful to destroy. Hence, his desire for an equally powerful ally.

Many things fell into place at that moment, and Falconsbane decided to hazard all on a single cast of the dice. "Ah. Your teacher. A foolish thing, to make a lover of a student. It blinds the teacher to the fact that the student develops a will and a series of goals of his own, eventually; goals that may not match with that of the teacher. And it causes the teacher to believe that love or lust are, indeed, enough to make one blind, deaf, and dumb to faults."

Blank astonishment covered Ancar's face for an instant, then once again, he was all smoothness. "I am astonished by your insight," he replied, as if a moment before he had not had every thought frozen with shock. "Is this a power every Adept has?"

"By no means," Falconsbane replied lazily, picking up the goblet of wine on the table beside his chair, and sipping it for a moment. "If your loving teacher had such ability to read people, she would never have lost your affections, and we would not now be having this conversation. You would still be in her control."

Ancar nodded curtly as if he hated having to admit that this unknown woman had *ever* held him under control.

And he did not contradict Falconsbane's implication that his teacher was an Adept. Not surprising, then, the bitterness that crept through his careful mask. This young man was a foolish and proud man, and one who despised the notion that *anyone* could control him, much less a mere woman.

Foolish, indeed. Sex had much to do with power, but little to do with the ability of the wielder to guide it. Falconsbane had seen as many female Adepts in his time as male, and had made a point of eliminating the female rivals as quickly as possible, before they realized that he was a threat. It was easier to predict the thoughts and intentions of one's own sex, and that unpredictability was what made one enemy more dangerous than another.

This changed the complexion of his plans entirely, however. Ancar was not the dangerous one here; this woman was.

"Tell me of this woman," Falconsbane said casually. "All that you know." And as Ancar hesitated, he added, "If I do not know all, I cannot possibly help you adequately."

That apparently decided the boy. Now, at last, the information Falconsbane needed to put together a true picture of the situation here began to flow into his waiting ears and mind.

He felt a certain astonishment and startlement himself, several times, but he fancied he kept his surprise hidden better than Ancar had. This woman—this *Hulda*—was certainly an Adept of great power, and if she had not underestimated her former pupil, he would have granted her the accolade of great cleverness as well.

She was, at the minimum, twice, perhaps three times as old as she looked. This was not necessarily illusion; as Falconsbane knew well, exercise of moderation in one's vices, and access to a ready supply of victims to drain of life-forces, permitted an Adept to reach an astonishing age and still remain in a youthful stasis. One paid for it, eventually, but as Ma'ar had learned, when "eventually" came to pass, all those years might grant one the time needed to find another sort of escape from old age, death, and dissolution.

She had first attempted to subvert the young Heir of Valdemar, that same child he had seen and desired. Had she been aware of the girl's potential? Probably; even as an infant it should have been obvious to an Adept that the girl would be a mage of tremendous strength when she came into her power. Small wonder that "Hulda"—if that was her real name, which Falconsbane privately doubted—had attempted the girl first, before turning to Ancar as a poor second choice.

Ancar was not entirely clear how and why Hulda had been thwarted from her attempt to control the girl. Perhaps he didn't know. There was no reason for Hulda to advertise her defeat, after all, or the reasons for it. Ancar had been given the impression at the time—an impression, or rather illusion, that he still harbored—that Hulda had given up on the girl when she had become aware of *him*.

Falconsbane hid his amusement carefully. There was no point in letting the boy know just how ridiculous a notion that really was. It would gain him nothing, and might lose him yet more freedom if

Ancar tightened his coercions in pique. One *might* choose a handful of wild berries and nuts in preference to a feast of good, red meat, but it would be a stupid choice. So, too, would choosing to subvert Ancar in preference to the young woman.

But apparently she had no options. So, after being routed from Valdemar, Hulda had turned her eyes toward Hardorn and had found fertile ground for her teachings and manipulations in the heir to *that* throne. She had promised, cajoled, and eventually seduced her way into Ancar's life, and had orchestrated everything he did from the moment she climbed into his bed until very recently.

But she had been incredibly stupid, for she had forgotten that all things are subject to change, and had grown complacent of late. She neglected her student for other interests. She promised, but failed to deliver upon those promises. Meanwhile Ancar tasted the exercise of power, and he found it a heady and eye-opening draught. He began to crave more of it, and that was when he realized that Hulda held more of it than he did—or ever would, while she lived.

So, although they had once been allies and even partners, they were now locked in a silent struggle for supremacy that Hulda had only now begun to recognize.

Falconsbane toyed with his goblet, listened, and nodded, saying nothing. Certainly he did not give voice to the contempt that he felt for this petty kinglet and mageling. Under any other circumstances he would have been able to crush Ancar like an overripe grape. He still *could*, if the coercions were eased sufficiently.

He learned also how little Ancar truly knew; how effective Hulda had been in denying him any training that might make him a threat to her power. His obsession with Gates now—if Falconsbane were not certain that the coercions binding him would probably cause the destruction of his mind if Ancar came to harm, he would have encouraged the fool's obsessions and illusions. The boy did not realize that he had no *chance* of ever controlling a real Gate. He simply did not have the strength. He had not figured out that a Gate could only go to places he himself had been, and not, as he fondly imagined, to any place he chose. He didn't really believe, despite the way he had been drained and the warnings in his fragment of manuscript, that Gate-energy came from *him* and not any outside sources of power like a node or energy-reserves.

Continued experiments would be certain to get him killed, and in a particularly nasty and messy fashion. Despite how much fun it would be to watch as his body was drained to a husk, there was the possibility that the royal whelp could tap Falconsbane's energy to save himself. That would be difficult to survive in his present state. So Falconsbane dissuaded Ancar from the idea, gently but firmly, pointing out that Hulda had known that he had been tinkering with the spell, and that she would certainly be on the watch for anything else of the sort. "Patience," he advised, as Ancar frowned. "First, we must rid ourselves of this aged female. *Then* I shall teach you the secrets of Greater Magics."

The power struggle between these two held far more promise of turning the tables on Ancar than anything else Falconsbane had yet observed. He noted how Ancar brightened at his last words, and smiled lazily.

"You can rid me of her?" the boy asked eagerly.

Falconsbane waved his hand languidly. "In time," he said. "I am not yet recovered; I must study the situation—and her. It would assist me greatly if you could manufacture a way to bring me into court, where I could observe her with my own eyes, and see what she is and is not capable of. I may note weaknesses in her armor, and I may know of ways to exploit those weaknesses that you do not."

Ancar nodded, his face now betraying both avidity and anticipation. "I had planned to introduce you as a kind of envoy, an ambassador from a potential Western ally. You must mask your powers from her, of course—"

"Of course," Falconsbane interrupted, with a yawn. "But this must wait until I have recovered all of my strength." He allowed his eyelids to droop. "I am—most fatigued," he murmured. "I become weary so easily…"

He watched from beneath his lids and Ancar was taken in by his appearance of cooperation. Good. Perhaps the boy would become convinced that the coercions were no longer needed. Perhaps he could be persuaded to remove them, on the grounds that they depleted him unnecessarily. Perhaps he would even remove them without any persuasion, secure in his own power and the thought that Falconsbane was his willing ally.

And perhaps Falconsbane would even *be* his willing ally.

For now.

7

An'desha felt sick, smudged with something so foul that he could hardly bear himself. It was a very physical feeling, although, strictly speaking, he no longer had a body to feel any of those things with. The spirits had warned him that he would encounter uncomfortable and unpleasant things in Falconsbane's memories. But neither they nor his own brief glimpses during his years of desperate hiding of what Falconsbane had done with his borrowed body had prepared him for the terrible things he confronted during that first look into Falconsbane's past.

For most of the day after his first foray into the Adept's memory, he had withdrawn quickly into his safe haven and had figuratively curled up there, shaken and nauseated, and unable to think. But his "haven" was really not "safe," and nothing would make the images acid-etched into his own memory go away. Still, he remained knotted about himself, tangled in a benumbed and sickened mental fog, right up until the arrival of some of King Ancar's servants. It seemed that the King had new plans for his captive; they had come to move the Adept to different quarters.

That move shook him out of his shock, although he had not paid a great deal of attention to Ancar before this. It occurred to him that he did not really know much about the Adept's captor. Ancar wanted something of Falconsbane—knowledge, power—but he might simply be ambitious and not evil. That made him think that he might be able to find some kind of ally among these people, someone who could help him to overcome Falconsbane and restore him to control of his much-abused body again.

After all, the spirits had not said he would be unable to find help here, they had simply offered him one possible option. And it was a Shin'a'in belief that the Goddess was most inclined to aid those who first put every effort into helping themselves.

So when Falconsbane was settled into his new, and to Shin'a'in eyes, bewilderingly luxurious suite of rooms, An'desha kept his own "ears" open to the gossip of the servants, hoping to learn something about the young King who had them in his possession. After all, if the King was a strong enough mage to put coercions on Falconsbane and keep them in force, he might be strong enough to overcome the Adept. Mornelithe Falconsbane's contempt of Ancar of Hardorn notwithstanding, the young King might very well have knowledge that would give him an edge even over someone like Mornelithe.

But watching and listening, both to the servants' gossip and to the questions that Ancar put to Falconsbane, dashed An'desha's hopes before they had a chance to grow too far. Ancar was just another sort as Falconsbane—younger, less steeped in depravity, with fewer horrific crimes to his account. But that was all too clearly not for lack of trying.

Ancar cared nothing for others, except to determine if and how they might be used to further his own ends. His only concern was for himself, his powers, and his pleasures. If he learned of An'desha's existence, he would only use that knowledge to get more of an edge over his captive. He might even betray An'desha's presence to the unwitting Adept in the very moment that he learned of it, if he thought it would gain him something. And he would do so without a second thought, destroying a soul as casually as any other man might eat a radish.

He had brief hopes again, when he learned of the existence of the mysterious woman rival in Ancar's life—how could a woman who was Ancar's rival be anything but Ancar's very opposite? But then Ancar's own descriptions destroyed the vision of a woman of integrity opposing the King and his henchmen. Even taking Ancar's words with a great deal of leaven, this *Hulda* was no more to be trusted than Ancar himself.

He learned far more than he cared to about her, nevertheless. Once he had admitted Hulda's existence and their former relationship, Ancar answered all of Falconsbane's questions with casual callousness, describing their relationship in appalling detail, and the things she had taught him, often by example, with a kind of nostalgia. And the woman was just as much a monster as her pupil—perhaps more, for Ancar had no knowledge of anything she might have done before she came into his father's employ. Seducing the young child she had been hired to teach and protect was the least of her excesses...

It was a horrible education for An'desha. His uncle had claimed that the so-called "civilized" people of the other lands were the real barbarians, and at the moment An'desha would vouch for that wholeheartedly. No Shin'a'in would ever sink to the depths that Ancar described, and as for Falconsbane—

No Shin'a'in would ever *believe* anyone would do what the Beast had done.

These people were *all* scum!

He longed, with an intensity that made him sick, for the clean sweep of the Dhorisha Plains and the simpler life of a herd guard. What matter if his kin were sometimes cruel, sometimes taunted him for being a halfbreed? What matter if he had been forced into the life of a shaman? He would *never* have had to experience any of this, never *know* that his body had done *these things*, had performed *those acts*. He would never have been forced to look into the depths of Falconsbane's soul and realize that no matter what he saw now, there was probably something much worse in the Adept's memory that he simply hadn't uncovered yet.

The most evil men in recent Shin'a'in history were those men who had slaughtered Clan Tale'sedrin, down to the last and littlest child— except for the famed Tarma shena Tale'sedrin who had declared blood-feud, been taken as Swordsworn, then tracked them down and eliminated them all. But compared to Mornelithe Falconsbane, all of the crimes of all of those men combined were a single poisonous weed in the poisoned lands of the Pelagir Hills, or a grain of sand in the glass-slagged crater that had in the long-distant past, become the Plains at the Hand of the Star-Eyed.

The young Shin'a'in huddled inside Falconsbane's mind—*no, it is my mind*—as the conversation with Ancar went on and on, trying to hold in his revulsion and mask his presence, and expecting at any moment to be discovered. And An'desha had never in his entire life felt quite so young, petrified with fear, and quite so helpless. Despite the protections the Avatars had taught him, if Falconsbane found him, he would have no way to prevent the Adept from crushing him out of all existence.

But somehow, those protections held. Either Falconsbane was not as all-powerful as he *thought*, or else the Avatars were more powerful than they claimed.

Ancar left at last, as Falconsbane's feigned weariness became real weariness. And when he dozed off in the chair, An'desha crept out of hiding, to stare at a candle flame and try to think out his meager options.

Ancar was repulsive, but an old Shin'a'in proverb held that anything could be used as a weapon in a case of desperation. *You can kill a man who wishes to destroy you with a handful of maggots if you must.* Could An'desha possibly deceive the King long enough to win himself free? *I could reveal myself to Ancar as an ally, and think up some story that makes it look as if I have more power than I really do.* Well, yes. That was a possibility. And if everything worked properly, he *might* get his body back *if* Ancar could overwhelm Falconsbane. But Ancar had no reason to trust An'desha, and every reason to want one more hold over the Adept. What did An'desha have to offer? The knowledge contained in Falconsbane's memory, assuming it was still *there* after Falconsbane was gone—yes, he did have that. But he had no practical experience as a mage; no idea how to handle all these energies. And truth to tell, he was terrified of them. If Ancar asked for proof of his power, what could An'desha offer? Not much. Nothing that would convince Ancar, who was a suspicious man and saw deception everywhere.

Well, what went for Ancar also went for the woman. More so, actually, since Ancar wanted Falconsbane to increase his own power, and the woman would naturally want to eliminate *both* of them once she discovered the conspiracy against her. He would need to offer nothing more than access to Falconsbane—he could turn the tables on both Ancar and Falconsbane, and reveal himself to this "Hulda." But *she* was an Adept as well, and she would be just as likely to use An'desha to destroy Falconsbane, then proceed to finish the job by ridding herself of An'desha. What did *she* need him for, after all? She had power of her own, and no fear of using it. And she was just as depraved as her former pupil. More; after all, she had schooled him in depravity.

There was a last possibility, as disgusting as it was. He could reveal his presence to Falconsbane, and strike a bargain with him. The "coercions" Falconsbane kept thinking about had been put on the Adept, not on An'desha. If Falconsbane cared to remain in a passive mode and simply instruct An'desha, the Shin'a'in might be able to use their powers to free both of them...

Yes, he could try to strike a bargain to that effect. Offer Falconsbane the way out of this gilded trap in return for simple survival; taking no more than he already had, a little corner of the Adept's mind.

Except that such a bargain would make him no better than Falconsbane; to *know* everything the creature had done and turn a blind eye to it in the hope of staying "alive" was as nauseating as anything Falconsbane himself had ever done. It would be a betrayal of all those Falconsbane had destroyed. Further, such a plan assumed Falconsbane would actually keep any bargain he made, and nothing of what An'desha knew of him gave any reassurance the Adept would do any such thing.

He felt tied into a hundred knots by conflicting emotions. Only one thing really seemed clear. None of these folk were worth helping. If any of them had ever done a single decent thing in all their lives, they had certainly taken pains to insure it went undiscovered.

I must listen to the Avatars and remain quiet. That was still not only the best plan, it was the only plan. *I must help the Avatars as they ask; I must hope they can help me. That is the only plan, the only decent course to take.*

:Wise choice, little one.: Tre'valen's voice rang in his mind, so clearly that he glanced around, startled, looking for another physical presence in the room. But there was no one there; Tre'valen and Dawnfire rarely made physical manifestations since their first appearance. He understood why now; such things made a disturbance that could be sensed, if one were looking for it with the inner eye.

:Let the Falconsbane sleep,: the shaman-Avatar continued. *:Meet us upon the Moonpaths, where we cannot be overheard or overlooked.:*

With relief, An'desha abandoned his hold on the body he and Falconsbane shared, and turned his focus in the direction Tre'valen had taught him *within and without.* There was a moment of dizziness, a moment of darkness, and a moment in which he felt he was falling and flying at the same time. Then he found himself standing upon a patch of pristine white sand, in a world made of mist and light, and all that had transpired in the time it took to draw a quick breath.

Tre'valen and Dawnfire were already there, looking quite ordinary, actually, although they glowed with a soft, diffused inner light. It was easier to "see" them here; Tre'valen looked like any of the younger shaman of the Clans, as familiar as his horse or saddle. Lovely Dawnfire on the other hand was garbed in odd clothing that made her look like a slender birch tree wrapped in snow—her hair was long and as white as a snowdrift—and she was as exotic as he had imagined the Hawkbrothers to be when he had first run off to seek them. But her smile and her wink made her still enough like a young scout of the Shin'a'in that he felt comfortable around her.

Except when he looked directly into the eyes of either of them... for they shared the same eyes, eyes without pupil, iris, or white; eyes the same bright-spangled black of a starry night sky. The Eyes of the Warrior... and the single sign that they were truly Her creatures. Those eyes made him shiver with awe and not a little dread, and reminded him that whatever they *had* been, these two Avatars were not human anymore.

So he tried to avoid looking into their eyes at all; not at all difficult, really, since he tended to keep his own glance fixed firmly on his own clasped hands whenever he spoke with them on the Moonpaths. Strange, how his body *here* looked like the one he had worn before he left his Clan and home, and not like the strange half-beast creature that Mornelithe Falconsbane had twisted it into.

"We have a new teaching for you, An'desha," Tre'valen said matter-of-factly. "It should help you seal your control over Falconsbane's body so that when he sleeps you will not awaken him by moving the body about."

Even as he spoke, An'desha felt Dawnfire's mental "hand" brush the surface of his own mind, and he absorbed the lesson effortlessly. And he even managed to smile shyly up into those two pairs of unhuman eyes, in thanks.

He took all the time he needed to study the implanted memory, to examine it and walk its pathway until he was certain he could follow their lesson exactly. And it was a most welcome gift. Such an ability *would* make things easier for him, for if Falconsbane's healing body demanded food while he slept, or made other needs known, such things would eventually wake the Adept so that An'desha must quickly and quietly retreat into watchful hiding. Now he would be able to silence the needs of the body before Falconsbane woke, and that would give him more uninterrupted time in full control. It was only when Falconsbane slept soundly, for instance, that An'desha dared to walk the Moonpaths. He feared, and so had the Avatars warned, that if Falconsbane woke while An'desha was "absent," An'desha would not be able to rejoin his body without the Adept noticing that something was different.

"Be patient, An'desha," Tre'valen said, but in a voice full of sympathy and kindness. "We know how tempting it must be to try to find some other, quicker way to rid yourself of the beast. But truly, our way is the surest, and even it is uncertain. We give you only a *chance*, but it is a chance with honor. There would be much less honor in any of the other paths you have contemplated. None of these people are worth the backing, as you yourself thought, much less worth making even temporary allies of them. Even trying to deceive them would be fraught with both peril and dishonor."

He hung his head in embarrassment and a little shame. Tre'valen was right, of course. And it had been making a choice with no concern for honor that had gotten him here in the first place, a fact that Tre'valen kindly omitted to mention.

"If you are very, very careful," Dawnfire continued in her high, husky voice, "you will even have ample opportunity to undermine *all* of them. *She* knows; She has faith in your good heart. Remember the Black Riders."

He looked up again and nodded. *The Swordsworn seldom miss their marks. The Leshy'a Kal'enedral, never.* That was a Shin'a'in proverb as old as the Swordsworn themselves. And yet, in shooting at Falconsbane, ostensibly to kill, they *had* missed, and had left the body holding both An'desha and Falconsbane alive. Then the Black Riders had appeared, bringing gifts that Falconsbane had thought were for him, but were truly for An'desha—a tiny black horse, the kind given to a child on his birthday, the token that he was ready for his first *real* horse and would be permitted to pick out a foal to train on his own. And the black ring, the ring Tre'valen told him was worn only by those sworn to the service of all *four* faces of the Goddess. An'desha now knew, as Falconsbane did not, that if the Adept had ever held the ring up to strong sunlight, the seemingly opaque black ring would show a fiery heart that contained every color of earth, air, sky and water, a fitting symbol for those sworn to every face of the Shin'a'in Goddess.

And then, after the Black Riders had shown their tokens, Tre'valen and Dawnfire had appeared.

They would not lie. They came to help him; *She* meant to help him save himself, if it could be done. He must not let this fear and uncertainty break him; must not let the filth of Falconsbane destroy his own soul and all his hopes. There was honor in the world, and kindness, and decency.

He must help those who brought those virtues to his aid, even if it meant that he—

He froze for a moment, as the thought ran on to its inescapable conclusion.

Even if it meant giving up his own chance at life and freedom.

There were things worse than death, after delving into Falconsbane's mind he knew that. He would be worse than a rabid animal if he chose his own survival over taking the opportunity to *stop* something like Falconsbane.

And this was a thought that would never have occurred to the "old" An'desha.

Old... He suddenly felt old, a thousand years old, and weary—and very frightened. But quite, quite sure of himself now.

A faintly glowing hand touched his; it was joined by another. He looked up to see the Avatars standing one on either side of him, clasping their hands over the ones he had locked in front of himself. The warmth of their care and concern filled him; their friendship warmed the cold heart of him.

"Thank you, An'desha." That was all that Tre'valen had to say, but An'desha knew that the Avatar had read his internal struggle and his conclusion and approved. He looked down again, but this time it was with a glow of pride. Whatever else came of *this*—*Her* chosen servants had given him their own accolade.

"We did not wish to prompt you into that decision, but now that you have made it, we can be more open with you," Dawnfire told him. She took her hand from his, although the warmth that had filled him remained, and she cupped some of the mist that eddied about them in her hands. "Look here—" she continued, and the handful of mist glowed, and vague figures formed and sharpened within it. He recognized most of them, both from Falconsbane's memories and from stolen glimpses through Falconsbane's eyes.

Two young Hawkbrothers; one ruggedly handsome, though a trifle careworn, and one that he did not recognize, but who was so beautiful that his breath caught. The first was Falconsbane's old enemy, Darkwind k'Sheyna, the son of the Adept he had corrupted. The second—

"He is Firesong k'Treva, a Healing Adept," Dawnfire replied to his unvoiced thought. "He is an ally of yours, although neither of you knew it. It was he that came to the aid of k'Sheyna."

An odd feeling stole over him for a moment, as he stared at that flamboyantly beautiful face. He would like to be more than an ally with *that* one…

He shook his head dismissively as the two figures faded and two more replaced them. One also, he knew. The Outlander from Northern lands, the young woman whose potential Falconsbane desired to devour. Both dressed in white garments, and both with blue-eyed white horses.

"Elspeth and Skif, both what are called 'Heralds' out of Valdemar. The Heralds are Clan-allies to Tale'sedrin," Tre'valen added, in a decisive tone, and An'desha nodded. That was all *he* needed. Anyone who had won acceptance of any of the Clans had won it from all. And if they were Clan-allies, An'desha was honor-bound to assist them.

Honor. There it was again. It became easier to understand when one lived it, rather than looking at it from outside.

A single figure took their place, one that could have been a fragile, feminine version of Falconsbane; a young woman with a feline cast to her features, carrying a sword. And, oh, he knew *this* one from many, many of his worst moments, both within Falconsbane's memories and as unwilling witness to atrocity. "Nyara," he said, biting off the word. His gorge rose at the sight of her, but not because she repulsed him but because what had been done to her by her own father repulsed him.

She is my "daughter" as well, because the body that sired her is mine—but I had nothing to do with it. I did not torture her mind and body. And yet her blood is mine, she is of outClan and Shin'a'in breeding as I am. How much responsibility do I have to her? It was not the first time he had asked himself that question, but it was the first time he had felt there was any chance he could *do* something about the answer.

It was something he would have to think about for a long time. If he had felt old before, he now felt terribly young. His body might be over half a century old, but *he* often felt as if he were still the boy who had run from his Clan and his responsibilities. His "life," such as it was, had been lived in moments and glimpses.

"Yes," Dawnfire replied, "and free of her father. You would find her willing to aid you to the end of her powers. She has a score to settle with Falconsbane."

Lastly, two other creatures crowded the first out of the mist. Gryphons—and Falconsbane harbored a hatred for gryphons that was quite, quite insane, but these two in particular were apt to trigger rages, for they had eluded and defeated him time and time again, and he would likely do *anything* for a chance to destroy them.

"Treyvan and Hydona, and you would find them as apt to your aid as Nyara," said Tre'valen. "They have as much to call Falconsbane to account for as Nyara does. He violated their young, among other things."

Dawnfire opened her hands and the mist flowed away, losing its colors and dispersing into the starlight that surrounded them.

"These are your allies, An'desha," Dawnfire said, her face grave and her night-starred eyes looking somewhere beyond him. In that moment she looked like a beautiful but impassive statue. "They approach this land even now, coming to the land of Ancar's enemies, the land of Valdemar."

An'desha shook his head, puzzled. How could this mean anything to his situation?

"Ancar wars upon Valdemar and plans another attempt to crush them even now. This is what he wishes Falconsbane's powers and teachings for, since he has been unable to defeat their defenses in the past." Tre'valen also looked somewhere beyond An'desha, and he was just as statuelike. "He wishes to become a great emperor, a lord of many kingdoms, but Valdemar stands in his way, by an increasingly lesser margin. These folk we have shown you come to help defend Elspeth's land. We will speak to them, through an intermediary that they trust, letting them know that Falconsbane has come to roost here."

An'desha considered that for a moment, seeing something of what their reaction might be to that unwelcome information. "They will know that Falconsbane is their chiefest enemy. So—what am I to do in all of this? What is it that I can do for them that will help them defeat Ancar and Falconsbane? I can do nothing to prevent him from helping Ancar if he chooses."

"Watch," Dawnfire said immediately. "Delve the depths of Falconsbane's memories. Learn all you can of him and of Ancar and Hulda and *their* plans. We will pass this on as well. You will be the spy that no one can possibly detect; the ideal agent, who is even privy to thoughts. Somewhere, in everything that you learn, there will be a way for your allies to defeat not only Ancar, but Falconsbane as well."

But that did not necessarily mean that they would be able to help him... and he noticed a curious omission. Neither Dawnfire nor Tre'valen had said anything about mentioning *his* existence to these "allies"...

And, feeling a little alarmed, he said so. "You say nothing of me—"

Now Tre'valen looked away, and it was Dawnfire who said, with a peculiar expression of mingled apology and determination, "We cannot tell them of your existence, although we will inform the intermediary, who suspects it already. If we let the others know that you live in Falconsbane's body, they might hesitate to—"

Here she broke off, and An'desha continued, bleakly, with the inescapable. "They might hesitate if it becomes necessary to slay Falconsbane, even if there is no other choice. Is that what you wished to say?"

"The intermediary will know," Tre'valen pointed out, but a little hesitantly. "She can judge best if *they* should know as well... but at the moment, she thinks not."

She thought not, hmm? An'desha pondered that for a moment. How likely was it that these "allies" would come face-to-face with Falconsbane?

But at least three of them were Adepts. When was it necessary for an Adept to come face-to-face with an enemy in order to attack him?

"An'desha, we pledged you that we would do our best to free you and save you. We did *not* mean to 'free you and save you' by slaying you," Dawnfire said, quickly. "You know we cannot lie to you in this. You have already accepted the risk, have you not?"

He sighed. He had. And word once given could not be taken back without becoming an oath-breaker. They were quite right, and besides, what choice did he have? He either faced a lifetime—presumably a long one—of being a prisoner in his own body, forced to watch Falconsbane commit his atrocities and being unable to do anything to prevent them, *or* he could retreat into his "safe haven" in Falconsbane's mind, make himself blind and deaf to all that passed while Falconsbane was awake, and live a kind of prison existence in which he would still *know* what Falconsbane was doing, even if he refused to actually *see* it.

Neither was any kind of a life; a living hell was more like it. He had a *chance* now…

And he certainly did not want Falconsbane making free with his body anymore. The creature must be stopped.

"No matter what happens, we will be with you," Tre'valen said softly.

That decided him. At least his loneliness and isolation were at an end. These two were friends already; it would be no bad thing to come to an ending, if it were in the company of true friends.

"Well, then," he said, steeling himself against the horrid memories he must once again face in order to pass the information on to his protectors. "I must begin my part of the bargain. Here is what I have learned of Ancar…"

It took a surprisingly short time to relate, really. It was astonishing how simply sordid those terrible acts Ancar had recited became, when they were told, not to an avid audience of Mornelithe Falconsbane, but to the impassive witnesses of the two Avatars. They seemed neither disturbed nor impressed; they simply nodded from time to time as if making special note of some point. He added his impressions of what Falconsbane had thought, once he came to the end of that recitation. It had not been flattering, for although Ancar had done his best to shock the Adept, Mornelithe had not been impressed either. He had, in fact, considered Ancar to be little more than a yapping pup, barking his importance to an old, bored dragon.

"Things could be worse," Dawnfire commented, when he came to the end of the recitation. "Falconsbane is still far more interested in regaining control of himself and gaining control of the situation than he is in helping Ancar. He does not know that the Valdemarans are returning to their home, so his thirst for revenge has not yet been awakened against Valdemar. And I suspect he will be investigating this woman Hulda as a possible ally against Ancar, simply because he is not the kind of creature to leave any opportunity without at least looking into it. And meanwhile, Ancar has learned nothing useful from him, which is a good thing, and he intends to withhold real information for as long as possible, which is even better."

An'desha sighed. "Better than you know. The things that Falconsbane has done to gain his powers—"

He shuddered without really intending to. Tre'valen touched his shoulder with sympathy. "I can soften those memories, if you wish," he said quietly. "Make them less—immediate. Give you some detachment."

"Give you the real sense that they are *past*, and there is nothing that you can do to help or hinder now—but that you can learn from them to prevent such things in the future," Dawnfire added, when he looked up in hope. "You must *never* forget that those terrible things were done to other living creatures, An'desha. When those poor victims become only icons, when they lose their power to move you, you will have lost something of your soul."

"I will only see to it that there is that distance," Tre'valen said, with a glance at Dawnfire as if he was amused by her preaching. "Your heart is sound, An'desha, and I have no fear that the plight of others will ever cease to move you. If that is what you want—"

"Please!" he cried, and with a touch, some of the feeling of sickness left him, and some of the feeling of having been rolled in filth until he would never be rid of the taste and smell and feel of it.

It was a blessed, blessed relief. He almost felt clean again, and his nausea subsided completely. Now those memories he had stolen from the Adept were at one remove… as if they were things from very distant childhood, clear, but without the terrible immediacy.

"As if they belonged to someone else, and not to you," Tre'valen said, with a slight smile. "Which they properly do, An'desha. The problem is that they come from your mind, and not Falconsbane's, and that is what made it seem to you as if they were yours."

He sighed, and closed his eyes. "Can you—" he began, and then realized that Tre'valen had already shown him what he needed to do to put any new memories at the same distance.

"You are a good pupil, An'desha," Dawnfire said, a bare hint of teasing in her voice. "You are a credit to your teachers."

He ducked his head shyly, but before he could reply, an internal tug warned him that he must return to the body he and Falconsbane shared before the Adept awakened.

The others understood without a word; they both touched him again, briefly, filling him with that incredible warmth and caring, and then they were gone.

And he closed his eyes, and sought *without, and within—*

And opened the very physical eyes of Mornelithe Falconsbane, who still slept in his heavily cushioned chair. Without even consciously thinking of doing so, he had implemented the new lesson even as he returned to the body. Now *he* was very much in control, although he must make certain that he did nothing abruptly, or made any motion or sound that might wake the Adept.

Still, Falconsbane slept very heavily—and people often walked, talked, and did many other things in their sleep without awakening. An'desha should at least have a limited freedom.

For the first time in years, he had full command of all of his body. He now wore it, rather than being carried by it as a kind of invisible passenger. Senses seemed much sharper now; he became aware of vague aches and pains, of the fact that he was painfully thin, most of the body's resources having been devoured in that terrible time between the Gates. Small wonder Falconsbane ate much, slept much, and tired easily!

The warning that had brought him back was thirst; alive and growing quickly. Moving slowly and carefully, he reached out for the watered wine on the table beside him, poured himself a goblet, and drank it down. He then settled back again with a feeling of triumph. *He* had done that, not Falconsbane—and for the first time, he had done so without feeling Falconsbane would wake while he moved!

An'desha marveled at the feel of the goblet in his hands—*his* hands, at last, *his* arms and body. And now, he had many, many things to think about. He did not feel up to another swim in the cesspool of Falconsbane's memories. Not now.

Later, when Falconsbane truly slept; that would be time enough. But for now—now he had another task in front of him. He had felt very young, a few moments ago. He had *been* very young, a few moments ago.

It was time, finally, to grow up.

By his own will.

8

Elspeth's head felt full-to-bursting, the way it had when she first began learning mage-craft from Need and Darkwind. Or, for that matter, the way it used to feel back when she was still a Herald-trainee, and had been cramming information on laws and customs into her memory as quickly as she could. She had a wealth of information bubbling like a teapot in her mind, and she still hadn't sorted it out yet. But she would; she would. It was all a matter of time.

For now, the best thing was to make as simple a plan as possible and go from there—knowing that even simple plans could go awry. *First we go through the Gate, then Vanyel dispels his protections on Valdemar so that mages can use magic without going mad, then we pelt for Haven as fast as we can. Seems simple enough.* But Elspeth was not inclined to think it would stay simple for very long. There were too many things that could complicate their situation.

Just after the vrondi-*watch is dispelled—that's when Valdemar will be at its most vulnerable. I'd better ask Vanyel if he can make the eastern border protections go down last.*

But risk was part of life. She went through some other things that would be trouble. Communication, for one. She was passing plans on to Gwena, who relayed them to Rolan, who presumably told Talia—a complicated chain in which there were any number of chances for a break in that communication.

They were to return to the Ashkevron estate. Right there, possible problems arose.

Supposedly there were already two Heralds waiting for them at the Ashkevron family manor, who supposedly knew everything that Elspeth had passed on to Gwena and Rolan. They were expecting the Gate, were to have warned the family what was coming.

But just how much were the Heralds really told, how much did they understand, and how much were they able to get the Ashkevrons to believe?

Even if they knew *all* about the Gate, they might not understand what it was. And as for the Ashkevrons believing in magic—that in itself was problematic. Elspeth had on occasion crossed horns with some of the stubborn Ashkevron human oxen, and she knew very well that having been warned and actually doing something about it were two different things.

They were still horse breeders, something that came as no real surprise to Vanyel when she had mentioned it. *:They always have been rather set in tradition,:* was all he had said. He called it "tradition," but she and the Queen had another thing or two to call it, when Ashkevrons showed up at court to protest some edict or other simply because *"We've* never done it that way, and we've never had a problem."

Whether it was sticking younglings with needles dipped in cowpox sores to prevent the Great Pox, or creating a common grazing ground for those folk with single livestock (so that the beasts were not inclined to break free of their tiny yards and roam off to larger and presumably greener pastures), if it was something new and different, the Ashkevrons usually opposed it. Most of them stayed on or near the family property even after marriage, although they were no longer as *prolific* as they had been in Vanyel's day. Most of them were stolid and stubborn, and had to be *shown* why something worked, in detail, and with exhaustive explanations, before they would return home to implement it.

There were no Heralds in this generation of Ashkevrons, although there were two Ashkevron officers in the Guard, one apprentice Bard, and one very ancient Healer. And although the stolid Ashkevrons were always mystified that *anyone* would ever want to leave home, thanks to Vanyel, it was now a *tradition* (and so, unquestioned) that if you didn't feel that you fit in, you left.

Still, Elspeth could just imagine what the two Heralds that had been dragged off their circuits to meet them had gone through, trying to explain to the Ashkevrons just what, exactly, was going to happen. Most likely they themselves didn't even understand it!

The brown-haired, brown-eyed, huskily-built current Lord would blink in puzzlement and say, "You say they're gonna be a-comin' through the chapel door? How in Havens they get in there?" And the Herald in question would have to scratch his head and answer that he really didn't know how, but that they were really going to come through that door—

And then, when the Gate opened—

Gods, it would be a royal mess... she only hoped that everyone would at least keep clear long enough for the Companions to get through. And then the gryphons, both young and old...

Just thinking about what could go wrong gave Elspeth a headache. She closed her eyes and rubbed her temple, then opened them again to meet Darkwind's concerned glance. She smiled slightly, and he squeezed her hand in reassurance.

Ready or not, it was all about to become moot. They gathered once again in the clearing in front of the cave-mouth that had first served as their portal to Vanyel's forest—or his current body, it could be argued. Vanyel's image stood to one side of the Gate he was creating, so thinned and tenuous that he looked like nothing more than a human-shaped wisp of mist. Almost all of his power was going into the building of this Gate—a Gate to a place so far away that Firesong admitted he didn't think *anyone* had the temerity to try such a distance. The only feat that dwarfed it was the one that had brought them here, over an even longer distance. But the energy forming that Gate had come from two Adepts, Vanyel and Firesong; this was coming from Vanyel alone.

Then again, Vanyel had resources no merely human mage could command...

The cave-mouth darkened, blackened—and just as suddenly, gave out on a stone-walled corridor, lit with oil lanterns, filled with strange people gaping in slack-jawed amazement.

"It's up! Go *now!*" Firesong shouted. Gwena and Cymry didn't need any urging. They all knew that the strain of this undertaking, even on a being such as Vanyel, was tremendous; he would only be able to hold the Gate open for a limited time.

The Companions bolted across the portal, hooves kicking up great clods of earth from the soft turf. Elspeth and Skif were right on their heels, followed by Darkwind and Firesong with their bondbirds clinging to their shoulders for dear life. Then came Nyara, Firesong's *dyheli*, and Rris, and bringing up the rear, the four gryphons.

Gwena and Cymry simply kept moving as they passed through, recovering from the disorientation of Gating much more quickly than Elspeth could. Sound did not travel across the barrier of the Gate, and as Elspeth dove through, she saw mouths moving as if people were shouting, although there was nothing to hear.

She passed into blackness, and through that moment of extreme dizziness that made her feel as if she was falling forever and would never touch the ground. There was nothing to concentrate on; no contact even with her own body. She could be screaming and waving her arms around, and she would never know—and if something went wrong with the Gate, wouldn't she be left that way forever?

But her momentum carried her forward, out of the complete silence of the Void and into pandemonium. People shouted, hooves clattered on the stone of the corridor, and all of it echoed so much it made all the sounds into meaningless noise. She glanced around, her eyes still blurred, trying to make sense out of the confusion.

She needn't have bothered. By the time she and Darkwind staggered onto the stone of the Ashkevron corridor and shook their heads clear, the Companions had shoved everyone out of the way and had made enough room even for the gryphons.

Even so, there wasn't a *lot* of room. There was a kind of anteroom in front of the chapel door, and that was what the Companions had cleared. Now there was a horde of people jammed into the corridor itself, beyond the anteroom, all of them jabbering. A strange, faintly unpleasant smell struck Elspeth's nostrils, and she sneezed, wondering what the odd, heavy odor was. Then she remembered; it was fish oil, used for lanterns. She hadn't had fish oil lamps inflicted on her for nearly two years—no wonder the smell made her sneeze!

It appeared that their arrival had been deemed something of a carnival, and the Ashkevrons were always prone to pounce on an excuse to see a marvel. Everyone on the estate had turned out to see just what was supposed to happen.

Or at least, that was the way it seemed to Elspeth. There were three Heralds in the front of the mob, their Whites gleaming in the light from the lanterns, and not the two that she had been told would be here. She didn't recognize any of them, not that she necessarily would; Field Heralds seldom came to Haven, and when they did, they would only be one more stranger in Whites to her. But she had hoped that at least one would be a friend; Jeri or Sherril, even Kero. Her heart sank a little, and she hoped she didn't show her disappointment.

Crowded behind the three Heralds were what appeared to be a hundred other people. All three tried to get past Gwena for what she assumed was a greeting; certainly the relief on their faces spoke volumes for their feelings. Even if her feelings were mixed, theirs certainly were not!

But at that moment, Darkwind and Firesong came stumbling through—then, before anyone could blink, Nyara, the *dyheli* and Rris—

And *then* the gryphons, plunging through the Gate as if they were charging an enemy line, then skidding to a halt just past the threshold.

And the crowd went insane with panic.

A crash of thunder that shook the stones under her drowned out most of the screams, but not all, by any means.

I guess someone forgot to tell them about Treyvan and Hydona—

Thunder faded, but not the shrieks. People stared for a moment, then, like cattle, bolted in the direction of freedom and safety.

That was all she had time to think, before the Ashkevron clan snatched up children, turned tail, and fled the scene, leaving behind three white-faced Heralds to guard their retreating backs.

Crashing thunder covered the sound of their retreat for the most part. All Elspeth could do was stand there, torn between laughter and hysteria.

Meanwhile the three Heralds were apparently convinced they were all about to die at the claws of the strange beasts. All three groped after weapons they weren't wearing, as people shoved and stumbled behind them and thunder crashed again.

Impasse. They were unarmed, but the gryphons weren't moving. And at this point, they must have been wondering why the two Companions didn't do anything! The Heralds stared at the gryphons, paralyzed with indecision, as the Gate vanished behind the winged apparitions, and another blast of thunder deafened them all for a moment.

No one moved.

The gryphons stared back. Elspeth was about to say something to break the deadlock—then stopped herself. Treyvan was an envoy. Let him deal with the situation. If she intervened now, it might look as if he *needed* her intervention. If the Heralds had been armed, it would have been a different story—

In the silence that followed the thunder, Treyvan opened his beak and the three Heralds stepped back a pace as if they expected him to charge them.

"I take it we werrre not exsssspected?" he said, in clear, if heavily accented, Valdemaran.

Eventually, everything was sorted out as the thunderstorm rolled on outside. The Heralds—Cavil, Shion, and Lisha—recovered from their terror very quickly in the face of Treyvan's civilized politeness and sunny charm. As she had expected, he soon had the situation under control, and even had the three Heralds laughing weakly at their own fear.

The antechamber and hallways were too crowded a venue for any kind of discussion, however. As soon as the atmosphere settled for a moment, Elspeth suggested they all move into the chapel.

Like most private chapels, this one was devoid of permanent seats and much in the way of decoration. It was basically a simple stone-walled room, empty at this moment, with a stone altar at one end. More lanterns lit it, but these were candle lamps rather than the fish oil, and the honey scent of beeswax was a great deal easier on Elspeth's nose than the odoriferous oil.

Gwena and Cymry picked their way carefully over the stone floor, leading the way, followed by the *dyheli*. They took places near the altar. The bondbirds flew up to the rafters and began a vigorous preening, oblivious to whatever their bondmates were up to for the moment. And the gryphons herded the young ones into a window alcove that no longer looked out on the outside, as evidenced by the lack of glazing and the view of another fish oil lamp lighting yet another corridor.

At that point, Lord Ashkevron reappeared, armed to the teeth and wearing a hastily donned, antique breastplate. Elspeth would have laughed if she had not been so amazed at his temerity.

She ran quickly to the front of the room, placing herself between him and the gryphons.

"My Lord!" she shouted, pausing for thunder to die down. "My Lord, there is no danger! These are guests of Valdemar. You were supposed to have been warned they were coming!"

His sword point, held in defensive posture, wavered for a moment, then dropped. He raised the visor of his helm.

"The hell you say!" he exclaimed, regarding the gryphons in puzzlement.

She hastened to assure him that there was no danger, and briefly explained the situation.

He in his turn went cautiously to the doorway and peered in.

Treyvan looked up at just that moment. "Hel-lo," he said, in a voice that sounded friendly to Elspeth—although who knew how it sounded to Lord Ashkevron. "May we impossse upon your hossspitality and rrremain herrre, good sirrr? I fearrr we would frrrighten yourrr horrrsesss if we went nearrr yourrr ssstablesss. I would not rrrisssk panic to the horsssesss."

That was enough for Lord Ashkevron; whatever this monster was, it had just demonstrated that it cared not to disturb his precious horseflesh. The gryphons were invited to take over the chapel.

He went off to start collecting the terrified members of his household and explain to them that these were not monsters—or at least, these were monsters that were on the side of Valdemar. Lisha wasted no time in seizing on Elspeth and filling her ears with complaints about how little preparation they'd had.

That was when Elspeth discovered that her worries had been dead on the mark. No one had said anything about the gryphons. In fact, no one had told these three that anyone but Skif and Elspeth were going to arrive—and certainly those assigning them to this task had not been able to explain the manner of Elspeth's arrival in any way the three Heralds were able to understand.

Meanwhile, the storm raged outside, its fury no doubt further frightening everyone who had fled, who must be certain that in the howling wind they heard the hungry cries of man-eating monsters. Finally Elspeth called a halt to further explanations until they helped Lord Ashkevron collect and calm his household.

It took candlemarks to soothe the nerves of the terrified Ashkevrons, who had been certain that they had just witnessed terrible monsters following their Heir—that she and Skif had, in fact, been *fleeing* them when they dashed across the threshold of the Gate. The poor folk had been certain that these monsters came from whatever strange place *she* had been, and were going to eat them all alive as soon as they caught and devoured the Heralds. People had to be hunted out and reassured, one by one; they had fled to every corner of the manor, hiding under beds and behind furniture, in closets and attics, and even cowering in the cellars. Only the storm outside, pouring so hard that it was impossible to see, had kept them from fleeing the building altogether.

Even now, a good half of the inhabitants were still walking softly and fearfully, expecting at any moment that the monsters would show their true nature. Nothing Lord Ashkevron or any of the Heralds could say would convince them otherwise.

Predictably, it was the gryphlets who eventually won over the rest. Lytha and Jerven had begun a game of pounce-and-wrestle as soon as they were settled, including Darkwind in their fun. There was nothing even remotely threatening in their kittenish play, and they soon had Lord Jehan Ashkevron convulsed with laughter. Now those who dared the chapel soon found themselves engaged in cheerful conversation with one or the other of the adults, while the youngsters continued to entertain themselves and anyone else watching them.

With that crisis out of the way, Elspeth and Skif went back to finding out just how things stood—both here, and in the Kingdom as a whole. She could quite cheerfully have shot whoever had made that particular set of omissions. Fortunately, after the gryphons, even the *dyheli* and Nyara didn't seem to cause too much consternation. Rris was simply assumed to be a very large dog, and neither he nor Elspeth saw any reason to enlighten anyone on that score—although his occasionally acidic comments had her choking down laughter she would have been hard put to explain if anyone had noticed.

By the time everyone had been found and calmed, and all misunderstandings sorted out, it was well into night.

Elspeth was tired, hungry, and in no mood to deal with anything other than a meal and a warm bed.

"But like it or not," she said to Darkwind—in Tayledras, so that no one would overhear and be offended—" I'm back at home, which means work, lots of it, starting this very moment. You don't have to sit through this if you don't want to, but I *have* to have a meeting with these Heralds. If *they* didn't get the message about the gryphons, there are probably a hundred equally important messages we haven't gotten."

"I came to help," Darkwind said softly, the lines of worry in his face softened by the light from the candle-lamps. "If you do not object to my presence."

Object? "Not likely," she said with gratitude. "You probably won't understand half of what they say, but you should get the sense of it all if you link with my mind."

Link with my mind—I never thought I would ever say that to anyone, I never thought I would be willing to. She smiled at him, a little shyly. She was so used to linking with him now that it never even caused her a moment of uneasiness; she did it as easily as she opened her thoughts to Gwena.

He smiled, and touched her hand lightly. She gave him a slow wink, then paused for a half breath to settle her thoughts. After speaking only Tayledras for so long, it seemed odd to speak her own tongue again; the words felt strange in her mouth.

Darkwind waited as she attempted to assume an air of authority. At her nod, he followed, as she went right to the corner to interrupt the low-voiced conversation all three Heralds were having with Lord Jehan.

The Heralds started and looked guilty as she cleared her throat. She was struck, at that moment, by how plain and severe their Whites looked, and spared a flicker of thought to wonder if she and Skif looked as outlandish and exotic to them as they looked plain to her.

Although the three Heralds seemed embarrassed—which meant that they had probably been discussing *her*—Sir Jehan, evidently, was just as blunt and forthright as any of his line, and turned to her immediately.

He was a brown and blocky man; brown eyes, hair, and beard, with a square face and a square build, all of it muscle. He looked nothing like Vanyel. She remembered something her mother had said once, though: "The Ashkevron look usually breeds true, and when it doesn't, the poor child generally runs off to Haven!"

"Cavil was just saying that no one told *him* that anyone was coming except you and the other Herald," he said, with a hearty chuckle. "He keeps insisting that I ought to complain to someone. Can't understand why. *I* know how it is. You tell someone, 'I'm coming and bringing an entourage of a hundred,' he tells the next fellow, 'Jehan's bringing an escort,' it keeps getting pared down until your host thinks you're only bringin' a couple of servants, and when you show up with your hundred, there's no place to put 'em all." He shrugged. "It happens. Happens all the time, and no one to blame for it."

She sighed with relief. There was one good thing about dealing with people like Jehan; once they calmed down, they were usually able to take anything in stride, from gryphons in their chapels to Gates in their doorways.

"Thank you for being so understanding," she said. "Could I steal Cavil and the others from you for a little? There's a great deal I have to catch up on."

"Oh, no fear, no fear," Jehan replied affably. "I have to go round up the aunties again and let 'em know they aren't goin' to be eaten in their beds." He grinned hugely, showing very white teeth in a very dark beard, then added, "I never believed 'em when they all said you were dead, Lady. Kept telling 'em they were actin' like a bunch of silly hens, flutterin' around over nothing."

And with that odd comment, he sketched a bow and took his leave.

Elspeth turned to Herald Cavil, who looked profoundly embarrassed. He was an older man, thin and harried-looking, with brown hair going gray at the temples. She had a feeling that after today, there would be a lot more gray there. "Just what in Havens was *that* all about?" she demanded. "About my being dead, I mean."

He flushed; his cheeks turned a brilliant crimson. "Some of what we need to brief you on, my lady," he said, quickly, while the other two Heralds nodded. "There have been rumors over the last several months that you were dead and the Council was trying to conceal that fact. Nothing the Queen or Circle could say or do seemed to calm the alarm. We need to proceed back to Haven at all speed, and as openly as possible—"

"We aren't going to be able to proceed *quietly* with this menagerie!" she pointed out, interrupting him. "But apparently, that's going to be all to the good, from what you're saying. The more people that see me, the better, right?" She shook her head for a moment, and caught Darkwind's eye. He was rather amused by something, although she couldn't imagine what. Perhaps it was the notion of trying to conceal the gryphons.

As what? Statuary?

"Of course, with four gryphons along, I wonder if anyone is going to notice *me!*" she added with a tired smile.

"There is this," Darkwind put in, speaking slowly in his careful, accented Valdemaran. "The notion of you in company with gryphons is so strange that no one would make it up; it is so strange it *must* be believed."

"You don't intend to bring those creatures to Haven!" Cavil exclaimed without thinking.

She started to snap; caught herself, and answered instead, quietly and calmly, "Treyvan and Hydona are not only envoys from the Tayledras and Kaled'a'in, they are mages in their own right. They have offered to teach any Herald with Mage-Gift. Yes, Mage-Gift. They can do that best at Haven, and they are *needed* there. I would be doing everyone a disservice if I insisted they remain here until they were sent for."

The three Heralds exchanged hasty glances, and the one called Shion said, cautiously, "But what of the rest? The other—ah—people?"

A sidelong glance told her that Shion meant Nyara, but she deliberately chose to take her literally.

"Darkwind and Firesong are Tayledras *Adepts*, and they are just as badly needed as the gryphons, if not more so," she replied. "And as for the others, Nyara is Skif's lady, and the *dyheli* and Rris are envoys from their respective peoples. Everyone with me is either a representative of a potential ally, or someone who is practiced in mage-craft and is willing to teach."

At the startled looks she got, she could not repress a chuckle. "It's a strange world out there, my friends," she added. "You can't assume that something that looks like an animal isn't an intelligent person—or that something that looks human is more than a beast. Havens, you should know that from Court duty."

Cavil shook his head, biting his lip in what was obviously a nervous habit. "Lady, this is the single most confusing day of my life," he said at last, with honest bewilderment.

He glanced at the single window in the chapel that still faced the open sky. It was made of thick glass that allowed little view, but enough to show that outside it was black night—except when lightning glared across the sky, turning the window into a patch of white. Obviously the storm had not abated in the least since they had arrived. Here inside thick stone walls, most of the fury of the storm was muffled, but it might very well be the worst storm Elspeth had ever seen.

"It is too late to travel tonight," Cavil said reluctantly. "But in the morning, we must be off. We have taken more time than I like as it is."

That took her a little aback. "In this storm?" she exclaimed without thinking. "The way it's raining, it'll still be going strong in the morning! Can't we wait until it clears, at least?"

Herald Lisha sighed. "It probably won't clear, not for two days at least," she told Elspeth. "Not that I'm a weather-witch or anything, but the weather all over Valdemar has been rotten this year. It got bad around Midwinter, when everyone got hit with that headache, and right before you people popped out of that doorway this storm just blew up out of nowhere. I've never seen anything like it, and I'm not exactly young."

"No one knows what is causing this," Cavil said glumly, "although many people blame Ancar, and a great many more are convinced he has somehow learned to turn the very weather against us. Lisha understates the case, Lady Elspeth. The weather has been simply hellish."

Elspeth noticed that Firesong had been listening intently to this entire conversation, and decided to invite him in on it. "Cavil says the weather has been hellish, that this storm is just one example," she called over to him. He took that as an invitation, and stalked gracefully toward them, his robes flowing about him in a way that made Lisha smile at him appreciatively. "Cavil, Lisha, Shion, this is Firesong k'Treva, another Adept. Firesong, they think Ancar is to blame for the state of the weather. Is this something we need to warn Haven about? Have you any ideas?"

He nodded a greeting to each of the Heralds before replying.

"Of course the weather has been hellish," he said matter-of-factly while Elspeth translated. He understood Valdemaran far better than he could speak it. "There has been a disturbance in the magical currents here, and that *always* makes the weather act up, unless someone is working to balance it. Since you have no weather-wizards and earth-witches working to rebalance the weather, it will continue to be bad."

Lisha's long face was puzzled, Shion's round one thoughtful, but Cavil brightened. "You mean Ancar isn't to blame?"

"In a sense, but it was not deliberate," Firesong explained. He held up a finger. *"First*—that moment when all of you were struck with that blinding headache—that was when a powerful packet of energy was flung up *here* and linked to a physical object in your chief city. That was meant entirely to help you, and indeed you will need it, but it also created great disturbances in the natural order of magic in this land. Weather is influenced by these energy patterns, and so the weather began to turn awry. Now, outside of your land, this Ancar has been mucking about with magic as well, and I suspect without any safeguards at all. That will also stir things up. The forces he has been meddling with are powerful ones, and this has had an effect on the weather over both your lands."

Lisha had the look of a hunter on the track of game. She leaned forward a little. "So what is basically going on is that magic has been like someone rowing across a pond—while the boat is getting from here to there, the rower creates waves and eddies, whether or not he knows it. He maybe stirs up muck from the bottom if he digs his oars in too deep. Yes?"

Firesong's eyes darted from Lisha's face to Elspeth's as she translated, for Lisha had spoken far too quickly for him to understand her. He laughed when Elspeth was done, and nodded vigorously. "Exactly so, and an excellent analogy. Now—we have just opened and closed a Gate in the midst of all this instability, and that has only made things worse. In fact, in this case, it has turned what would have been only a minor storm into a tempest." He shrugged. *"We* do not have these problems, because all Vales have what you call Journeymen and Apprentices balancing the forces while Masters and Adepts work, or doing specific weather-controlling spells to avoid this kind of mess."

He took on a "lecturing" tone, and he might well have gone on in this vein for some time, except that he caught sight of Elspeth's expression. She was directing a rather accusatory glare at him, Darkwind, and Treyvan.

"Why didn't you tell me we'd be doing this to Valdemar?" she demanded, as Firesong broke off, and the three Heralds watched in bewilderment, unable to follow what was going on since she had switched to Tayledras. "Why didn't any of you let me know?"

Firesong shrugged, and crystals braided into his hair reflected flashes of lightning from outside.

"It would have done you no good to know," he pointed out. "What would you have been able to do about it? Nothing. You were a great distance away. Your people have no weather-workers, and until that barrier comes down, you will have none coming in. There was no point in mentioning it."

Shion cleared her throat, her round face telling of her puzzlement and curiosity eloquently. "Please," she said, "What *are* you talking about?"

"The weather," she replied, then took pity on her and gave her a quick translation.

"You mean," she said at last, "it really *is* possible to do something other than complain about the weather?"

She smiled and nodded. "Eventually, we will. But right now, the trouble is that all this wonderful new magic is bringing killer storms down on our own heads."

"Ke'chara, you must think of the other side of this stone," Darkwind put in, speaking again in Valdemaran. "Ancar is getting this weather— ah—in the teeth. And he is getting it as much as we; it must be at least as much of a hindrance. Consider how much magic he works, and completely without safeguards."

He sounded positively cheerful about it. Elspeth couldn't be quite that cheerful, thinking of all the innocent folk who were suffering much more from the wicked weather than Ancar was. But still, it was rather comforting to think that some of Ancar's chickens at least were coming home to roost.

"Oh, quite," Firesong said, just as cheerfully, when Elspeth had finished translating. "In actual fact, I would be much surprised if the effect was not a great deal worse over there in his land. He, after all, is the one who has been working the most magic—and it is he and his mages who also care little for the balances of things."

At Lisha's ironic nod of agreement, Firesong sighed, and shook his head a little. "On reflection, I fear that I will have a great deal of work ahead of me, once the current troubles are settled."

Current troubles—as if the war with Ancar wasn't much more complicated than a brushfire.

"It's going to take a lot to 'settle' Ancar," Lisha replied, with heavy irony. "I don't trust the current stalemate, and neither does anyone else in this Kingdom. You'll have your hands full of more than weather before you're here long."

9

Mornelithe Falconsbane stood in the window of his suite, with the shutters flung open wide and a cold wind whipping his hair about his head. He scowled and watched a night-black storm walking toward his "host's" castle on a thousand legs of lightning. As it neared, the light faded and thunder growled a warning of things to come. The wind picked up and sent the shutters to either side of him crashing against the wall, sending dust and the heavy scent of cold rain into his face. He crossed his arms and watched the storm racing over the empty fields beyond the city walls, lightning licking down and striking the earth for every beat of his heart. This would be a terrible and powerful storm; before it was over, crops would be beaten down in the fields, and many of those fields would lie under water.

He had expected nothing less, given what he already knew.

He waited until the last possible moment before closing windows and shutters against the winds of fury; they howled as if in frustration and lashed at the closed shutters with whips of rain. But the shutters were stoutly built. All the storm could accomplish was to rattle the thick glass of the windows behind them.

Thunder did more than rattle the glass; it shook the palace to the cellars, making all the stones in the walls tremble. Falconsbane felt the vibration under his feet as he turned and walked back to the chair he had abandoned at the first hint of the coming storm.

This was the fourth such storm in the last week. Two of the four had brought little rain, but had sent whirlwinds down out of the clouds and hail to damage roofs and break the glass in windows. Falconsbane had seen one of the whirlwinds firsthand, as it had dropped down out of a black cloud, writhing like a thick snake or the tentacle-arm of a demon. It had withdrawn again without touching ground in the city, but other such whirlwinds had made contact with the ground and wrought great damage out in the countryside. Dead animals had been found high up in the treetops, houses had been destroyed, and crops torn up. There had also been marvels—an unbroken egg driven into the trunk of a tree, straws driven through thick boards.

He had been fascinated by the whirlwinds and the wreckage and bizarre marvels they had left in their wake, but otherwise the storms held no interest for him. In fact, this current outbreak had left him fuming with anger, for he only truly enjoyed storms when *he* had called them and was in control of them. The cold and damp made his wounds ache, and all his joints complained and stiffened, reminding him painfully that this body was not as youthful as it looked.

And reminding him that he had not even overcome Ancar's coercions enough to allow him free reign to recreate that youth and renew the spells that had held age in abeyance. If it had not been for those coercions, he would have been able to choose a victim of his own and Heal himself of his damage. One life would give him the energy to cure himself completely. Two would permit him to reverse some of the ravages of age for a time. More than two would permit him to make any changes to himself that he pleased.

And it would be so pleasant if one of those victims could be Ancar himself...

Failing that, he retreated to his favorite chair, the one nearest the fire, and sat warming himself. Daydreaming of revenge and planning his course to obtain it were his only real amusements at the moment.

He probably should be down among Ancar's courtiers, but this had not been a particularly fruitful day, and he had grown bored rather quickly. He had never had much patience with the witless babble of a court even when it had been his own court. In this current body, he had eliminated holding court altogether. When he wished his underlings to hear something, he gathered them together and told them, then dismissed them. When he wished to hear from *them*—which was rarely— he ordered them before him and stripped their minds.

But Ancar seemed convinced that a "court" was necessary, although he no longer held audiences or even permitted anyone below the rank of noble near him. Perhaps for a ruler like him, it was. Even though it was mostly a sham, and he himself never appeared before his assembled courtiers.

Still, a reasonable amount of information could be obtained if one had the patience to listen to Ancar's brainless toadies, and the wit to read real meaning from what the few foreign ambassadors did and did not say. Today, however, had been hopelessly dull. Even Hulda was off somewhere else, leaving him to mouth meaningless pleasantries at fools who could have served far more useful purposes bleeding their lives away in his hands and granting him the power which they could not use.

The very first person Ancar had introduced him to was Hulda, after warning him far too many times about the woman's perfidy. He had been the consummate gentleman. Hulda amused him. She was quick-witted when she cared to be—much cleverer than she appeared. Complacency was her flaw when it came to Ancar; she obviously still believed she ruled him completely, and if anything would bring her downfall, this complacency would be the cause.

She was much wiser in the ways of magic than her pupil; she knew Falconsbane for a Changechild, for she had made some clever remarks about "changing one's nature" when Ancar had first introduced them. He could certainly see the attraction she must have had for the boy when he was still young and malleable. She was lushly ripe—perhaps a trifle overblown, but some folk liked their fruit well-seasoned and their meat well-aged. With her curving, voluptuous lines, good features, long flow of dark hair, and her startling violet eyes, she cut quite an impressive figure.

Falconsbane had bowed over her hand, but had caressed the palm, unseen, before he let it go. He had noted the flare of interest in her eyes, and had smiled, and nodded knowingly as she lowered her lids to give him a seductive glance from beneath her heavy lashes.

She, too, was older than she looked, he knew that instinctively—but she was not as old as he was, not even in this body. Thus far he had managed to avoid more than speaking to her without ever seeming to avoid her, a fact that must infuriate and frustrate her. He intended to play her a while, before he decided how to handle her over the long run. Let her pursue him; let him be the enigma. It would make her concentrate on his physical presence and not on the threat he might be to her power.

She did not connect his presence with the Gate, and at this moment, he preferred to keep it that way. She recognized him for a mage of some kind, but she did not appear to have any way of judging his true abilities. That was all to the good. If he decided to make a temporary ally of her, he would reveal to her what he chose. And at the moment, he did not know if he cared to make her an ally. It might be amusing, especially since his exotic nature patently attracted her, but it might also be very dangerous. She was playing some deep game, and had secrets that young fool Ancar had not even guessed at. Falconsbane wanted to know just what those secrets were before he even began to consider her as an ally.

And mages were notoriously jealous of their power; if she guessed him to be any kind of a rival, it would not take her long to decide to eliminate him. She would try to do so subtly, but she would not be hampered by coercions. Becoming involved in a covert mage-struggle at this stage could only further delay his plans for freedom.

In the meantime, it suited him to pique her curiosity, and to cast little tidbits of information to her designed to make her think—rightfully— that Ancar was intriguing against her and that he was an unwitting part of that plan. The best thing he could do would be to set these two openly at each others' throats. The more tangled this situation got, the better the outcome for him. The more time they wasted struggling for power, the more time he would have to free himself. The more power they wasted, the weaker they would be when he finally succeeded.

He had been looking forward to tangling the situation a bit more, but Hulda had not even put in an appearance at court this afternoon. Falconsbane had quickly become irritated with the inane chatter and had finally retreated to his suite in boredom and disgust. The joint aches warning of an approaching storm had not sweetened his temper in the least.

He slumped in his chair, stared at the fire, and brooded. He could not recall, in any of his lifetimes, having been so completely cut off from control. It was not possible to forget even for a moment that he was the one being controlled. This was, in many ways, worse than being imprisoned, for he was a prisoner in his own body.

The flames danced wildly in the changing drafts from the chimney, sometimes roaring up the chimney, sometimes flattening against the logs, but he could not hear the crackling of the fire for the howling of the wind and the continual barrage of thunder. Every time the flames flattened for a moment, it simply made his rage smolder a little more.

His several days in the heart of Ancar's court had made it clear that he had been outfoxed by someone he would not even have had in his employ as a menial. *He* knew how disastrous these storms were, not only to the countryside, but to the energy-fields for leagues around. Even if Ancar didn't care what they did to his land, Falconsbane was going to have to put all this back before *he* could work properly. That was what made him the angriest. He had known that the boy was a fool. He had not known the boy was as big a fool as all this.

He did not hear Ancar come in, and was not aware that the young King was in the room until movement at the corner of his vision caught his attention. The noise of the thunder had covered the sounds of the door opening and the boy's footsteps. That irritated him even more. The brat could come and go as he pleased, even in Falconsbane's own rooms, and the Adept was powerless to prevent it!

He looked up, and Ancar's smug expression simply served to ignite his anger.

"What is wrong with you, you little fool?" he snapped furiously. "Why aren't you doing anything about this storm? Or are you simply such an idiot that you don't care what it means?"

Ancar stepped back a pace, doubtless surprised by the venom in his voice, the rage in his eyes. "What it means?" he repeated stupidly. "What do you mean by that? How can a storm mean anything at all? How could I do anything about it even if it did mean something?"

For a moment, Falconsbane stared at him in surprise so great that his anger evaporated. How could anyone who had gotten past Apprentice *not* know weather control, and how magic affected the world about him?

"Hasn't anyone ever taught you weather-magic?" he blurted without thinking. "Don't you realize what you and those idiot mages of yours have been doing?"

Ancar could only blink stupidly at him. "I have no idea what you're talking about," he said. "I don't understand. What have we been doing that makes you so angry?"

Finally, as Ancar continued to stare at him, Falconsbane gathered enough of his temper about him to answer the boy's unspoken questions.

"Evidently, your teacher Hulda has been hiding more from you than you realized," he replied testily. "It is very simple; so simple that you *should* have been able to deduce it from observation alone if you had ever bothered to *observe* anything. Magical energy is created by living things and runs along natural lines, like water. You do know *that* much, I hope?"

Ancar nodded silently.

He snorted, and continued, "Well, then, like water, it can be disturbed, perturbed, and otherwise affected by meddling with it. If you meddle a little, the disturbance is so minor that no one would notice it if they were not looking for it. If you meddle a great deal, as if you had just thrown a mighty boulder into a pond, *everyone* will get splashed and they most certainly will notice. That is how your Hulda knew you were meddling with a Gate. She sensed the ripples in the magical energies, and knew by the pattern they made that you had created a Gate!"

"I know all that—" Ancar began impatiently.

Falconsbane interrupted him, waving him into silence. "Magic also affects the physical elements of the world," he continued, allowing his irritation to show. "You should have noticed this by now. Hadn't you even seen that some kind of weather change always follows a working in the more powerful magics? The more subtle the element, the more it will be affected. Meddle with a Gate, and even the earth will resonate. Meddle enough, you might trigger an earthquake if the earth is unstable at that point. But the most subtle elements are air and water—which make *weather,* you fool. Changes in magical energy change the weather, as the air and water reflect what is happening in the magical fields. You have stirred up the magical fields hereabouts with your little experiments— and now you are reaping the result. Keep this up much more, and you will either be paying a premium price for imported food, or you will have to steal it or starve next year."

Ancar's mouth hung open a little with surprise, his eyes going a little wider. Evidently this was all new to him. And by the growing dismay in his expression, it was not a pleasant revelation.

Falconsbane smiled nastily. "Any mage who is any good at all makes certain that he calms the fields if he can after he is finished. Any mage with the power to command others need only tell *them* to take care of the disturbances, damping them before they cause any great harm. And any mage worthy of his hire could at *least* steer storms over his enemy's territory! By the time I became an Adept, I could do it without even thinking about it when I worked my magics in freedom. I still could, if I had that freedom to work without hindrance." He folded his arms and slumped back down in his chair in a fit of assumed petulance, staring at the flames and ignoring Ancar.

The boy was a fool, but not so great a fool, surely, that he could not understand what Falconsbane had just told him in so many words. Falconsbane could control the weather as he and his own wizards could not—except that Falconsbane was not free to do so. In order to control the weather, Falconsbane must be freed of the coercion spells.

In fact, that was not quite the case. Ancar need only modify the spells in order to give Falconsbane the freedom to work his will on the weather. But Ancar's education was full of some very massive holes, and one of those seemed to be a lack of shading. Things either were, or they were not; there were no indeterminate gradations. So Mornelithe was hoping that his insulting speech would goad Ancar into freeing him, at least a little—

It worked. As Ancar recovered from his surprise, both at the information and at being spoken to as if he were a particularly stupid schoolboy, his face darkened with anger.

"Well," he snarled, just barely audible above the rumble of thunder, "if you can do something, then *do* it, and stop complaining!"

His fingers writhed in a complicated mnemonic gesture, and Falconsbane felt some of the pressure on his powers easing a little. Only a little, but it was a start... a few of the coercions had been dropped. Ancar was not going to release him entirely, but the worst and most confining of the spells were gone.

Without a word, he rose from his chair, and stalked toward the window. Throwing it open with a grandiose gesture, he let the storm come tearing into the room, blowing out all the candles, extinguishing the fire, and plastering his clothing to his body in a breath. He was chilled and soaked in no time, but he ignored the discomforts of both in favor of the impressive show he was creating. Lightning raced across the sky above him, and he flung his arms wide, narrowing his eyes against the pelting rain. A bit of power made his hands glow most convincingly. He didn't need to make his hands glow, of course, but it made Ancar's eyes widen with awe in such a satisfactory manner.

He could have done everything from his comfortable chair, of course, without doing much more than lift a finger or two, but that would not have been dramatic enough. Ancar was stupid enough to be more impressed by dramatics than by results. That was probably why he had ended up with such inferior hirelings in the area of magic. Falconsbane did not need gestures to set his will twisting the forces of magic along the paths he chose. Falconsbane did not even need to close his eyes and drop into trance when the spell he wrought was a simple and familiar one.

Falconsbane sent out his probes, riding the wind until he found the center of the storm, and found the corresponding knot of energy in the ley-lines. He could unknot it, of course, but he didn't want to. Let Ancar's land suffer a little more. Let him see what a weapon controlled weather could be. Seizing the knot of energy, he gave it a powerful shove, sending it farther down the line and taking the storm with it.

Not too far, though. Just far enough from the capital and palace that it would not make his joints ache or interfere with his sleep tonight. He could not actually undo all the things that had *caused* the storm in his present state of coercion, and he did not think that Ancar would be inclined to release him completely just so that he could do so. If the fool asked him why he had not sent the storm into the skies of Valdemar, he would tell the boy that the King's own spells were to blame, interfering with Falconsbane's magic. That might convince him to release a few more of those coercions.

Or perhaps he wouldn't care that his farmers' fields would be flooded, the crops rotting in the sodden earth. It didn't much matter to Falconsbane, except as an example of how short-sighted Ancar was.

The wind and rain died abruptly. As he opened his eyes, he saw with satisfaction that he had not lost his touch. Already the lightning had lessened and the storm was moving off, clouds fleeing into the distance so rapidly that it was obvious something had *made* them change their courses. In a candlemark or two, it would be dry and clear around the palace.

Hopefully, this entire exercise had been showy enough to impress the young idiot. He turned to shrug at his captor. "Well," he said. "There you have it."

Ancar was nodding wisely, his eyes a little wide as he tried unsuccessfully to cover his amazement. "Very good," he said carelessly, still trying to cover his earlier slip. "I can see that you know what you are doing."

Falconsbane simply smiled, then returned to his chair. Now that those particular coercions were off, he relit the candles and the fire with a simple spell. And he noticed, with a twitch of contempt, that Ancar was as impressed by *that* as he had been by how quickly he had sent the storm away.

"I trust that something brought you here other than a wish for my company," he said, carefully keeping any hint of sarcasm from his voice. He gestured at the other chair beside the fire. "Pray, join me."

He was carefully calculating his insolence in being seated in the King's presence to underscore the fact that he *was*, current conditions notwithstanding, the King's equal. And it seemed to be working. Ancar did not say a word about his insulting behavior and, in fact, he took the proffered seat with something as near to humility as Ancar ever came.

"Nothing important," Ancar said airily. It was a lie, of course, and Falconsbane could read his real intentions as easily as if he could read the boy's thoughts. Simple deductions, actually; he knew that Ancar had been reviewing progress—or lack of it—along the border of Valdemar. There had been messengers from that border this very day. Despite Ancar's animosity toward Hulda, in this much he was still of one mind with the sorceress—his hatred of Valdemar. So that particular meeting was probably where Hulda had been this afternoon. It followed that he considered his options to have been exhausted, and now he wanted some help with that particular project from Mornelithe.

"Ah, then since there is nothing in particular you wish to discuss, perhaps you might be willing to satisfy my own curiosity about something," he said, silkily. "This *Valdemar* that troubles you—you can tell me something about the land? How did you choose to quarrel with them in the first place?" He studied his own fingernails intently. "It would seem to me that you have been placing an inordinate amount of effort into attempting to conquer them, when so far as I can see, they are fairly insignificant. They have never attacked you, and they always stop at their own border, even when they are winning. Trying to conquer them seems, at least to an outsider, to be a losing proposition."

He looked up, to see Ancar flushing a little, his eyes showing a hint of anger. But the King did not reply.

He smiled. "And if I understand everything I have heard, now you plan to try for them again. What *is* the point here? Are you so addicted to defeat that you cannot wait to give them another opportunity to deliver it to you?" As Ancar flushed an even deeper shade, he continued, taunting the boy with the litany of his failures, gleaned from questioning servants, courtiers, and some of Ancar's other mages. "First you attack them before you are ready, and you naturally suffer a humiliating defeat. Then you attack them without ever bothering to discover if they had found some military allies and suffer a *worse* defeat. Your people are leaking across the border into their land on a daily basis, and you cannot even manage to insinuate a spy into their midst! Really, Ancar, I should think by now you would know enough to leave these people alone!"

Ancar was nearly purple with anger—and yet he held his peace and his tongue. Ancar did *not* want to talk about it. Now that was a curious combination...

And to Falconsbane's mind, that spelled "obsession."

When one was obsessed with something, logic did not enter into the picture.

When one was obsessed with something, one was often blind to all else. An obsession was a weakness, a place into which a clever man could place the point of his wit, and pry until the shell cracked...

As Ancar sat silently fuming, Falconsbane made some rapid mental calculations, adding up all the information he had been gleaning from courtiers, servants, and underling mages. Ancar was a young male, and any young male hates to be defeated, but that defeat must be doubly bitter coming as it did from the hands of *females.* He had failed to conquer Valdemar, failed to defeat its Queen, failed to get his hands on its Princess. He had failed a military conquest not once, but twice.

But that was by no means all, as Falconsbane's probes had revealed. He had tried, with no success whatsoever, to infiltrate a spy into the ranks of the Heralds. The only agents he had in Valdemar itself were relatively ineffective and powerless ones, placed among the lowest of the merchants and peasantry. Mercenary soldiers under yet another female leader had thwarted every single assassination attempt he had made, even the ones augmented by magic.

In short, the Queen and her nearest and dearest seemed to have some kind of charmed existence. They prevailed against all odds, as if the very gods were on their side. Their success mocked Ancar and all his ambitions, and without a doubt, it all maddened him past bearing.

So Falconsbane thought.

Until Ancar finally spoke, and proved to him that in this one respect, he *had* underestimated the young King.

"I must expand," he said, slowly, his flush cooling. "I am using up the resources of Hardorn at a rapid rate. I need gold to pay my mages, grain to feed my armies, a hundred things that simply must be brought in from outside. I cannot go South—perhaps you will not believe me, but the Karsites are the fiercest fighters you could ever imagine in your wildest nightmares. They are religious, you see. They believe that if they die in the defense of their land, they rise straight to the feet of their God...

and if they take any of the enemies of their God with them, they rise to his right hand."

Falconsbane nodded, a tiny spark of respect kindling for the King. So he understood the power a religion could hold over an enemy? Mornelithe would never have credited him with that much insight. Perhaps there was more to the boy than the Adept had assumed. "Indeed," he said in reply. "There is no more deadly an enemy than a religious fanatic. They are willing to die and desperate to take you with them."

"Precisely," Ancar sighed. "What is more, their priests have a magic that comes from their God that is quite a match for my own. When you add to all that the mountains that border their land—it is an impossible combination. Those mountains are so steep that there is no place to bring a conventional army through without suffering one ambush or trap after another."

"Well, then, what about North?" Falconsbane asked, reasonably. And to his surprise, Ancar whitened.

"Do not even *mention* the North," the King whispered, and glanced hastily from side to side, as if he feared being overheard. "There is something there that dwarfs even the power Karse commands. It is so great—believe me or not, as you will, but I have seen it with my own eyes—that it has created an invisible fence that *no one* can pass. I have found no mage that can breach it, and after the few who attempted it perished, not even Hulda is willing to try."

Falconsbane raised his eyebrows involuntarily. *That* was something new! An invisible wall around a country? Who—or rather, *what*—could ever have produced something like that? What was the name of that land, anyway? Iften? Iftel?

But Ancar had already changed the subject.

"Most of all, I cannot go Eastward," he continued, his voice resuming a normal volume, but taking on an edge of bitterness. "The Eastern Empire is large enough to swallow Hardorn and never notice; the Eastern mages are as good or better than any I can hire, and their armies are vast... and well-paid. And they are watching me. I know it."

That frightened him; Falconsbane had no trouble at all in reading his fear, it was clear in the widening of his eyes, in the tense muscles of his neck and shoulders, in the rigidity of his posture.

"At the moment, they seem to feel that Hardorn is not worth the fight it would take to conquer it. They had a treaty with my father, which they have left in place, but the Emperor has not actually signed a treaty with my regime. Emperor Charliss has not even sent an envoy until very recently. I believe they are watching me, assessing me. But if I fail to take Valdemar, they will assume that I am weak enough to conquer." He grimaced. "My father had treaties of mutual defense with Valdemar and Iftel to protect him. I do not have those. I had not thought I would need them."

"Then do not attempt Valdemar a third time," Falconsbane suggested mildly.

Ancar's jaw clenched. "If I do not, the result will be the same. The Emperor Charliss will assume I am too weak to try. They have sent their ambassador here, and an entourage with him, as if they were planning on signing the treaty soon, but they have not deceived me. These people are not here to make treaties, they are here to spy on me. There are spies all over Hardorn by now. I have found some—"

"I trust you left them in place," Mornelithe said automatically.

He snorted. "Of course I did, I am not that big a fool. The best spy is the one you know! But I am also not so foolish as to think that I have found them all." He rose and began pacing in front of the fire, still talking. "One of the reasons I am sure that I have been unable to attract mages of any great ability is that the Emperor can afford to pay them far more than I can offer. I am fairly certain that the mages *I* have are not creatures of his, but there is no way of telling if he has placed mages as spies in my court and outside of it. So long as they practiced their mage-craft secretly, how would *I* ever know what they were?"

Falconsbane refrained from pointing out that he had just told the boy how he would know, that disturbances in the energy-fields would tell him. Perhaps neither he nor his mages were sensitive to those fields. It was not unheard of, though such mages rarely rose above Master. Perhaps he was sensitive, but only when in trance. If so, that was the fault of his teacher.

Ancar abruptly turned and strode back to the window, standing with his back to Falconsbane and the room, staring at the rapidly clearing clouds.

"This is something I had not seen before," he said, as if to himself. "And I had not known that magic could wreak such inadvertent and accidental havoc. It would be an excellent weapon…"

Falconsbane snorted softly. It had taken the boy long enough to figure that out.

"Men calling themselves 'weather-wizards' have come to me, seeking employment," he continued. "I had thought them little better than herb-witches and charm-makers. They didn't present themselves well enough for me to believe them. I shall have to go about collecting them now."

"That would be wise," Falconsbane said mildly, hiding his contempt.

Ancar turned again and walked back into the room, this time heading for the door, but paused halfway to that portal to gaze back at Falconsbane.

"Is there anything else you need?" he asked.

Falconsbane was quite sure that if he asked for what he *really* wanted—his freedom—he would not get it. Ancar was not yet sure enough of him, or of himself. Rightly so. The moment he had that freedom, Falconsbane would squash the upstart like an insect.

But perhaps—perhaps it was time to ask for something else, something nearly as important.

"Send me someone you wish eliminated," he said. "Permanently eliminated, I mean. Male or female, it does not matter."

He halfway expected more questions—why he wanted such a captive, and what he expected to do with such a sacrificial victim when he had one. But Ancar's eyes narrowed; he smiled, slowly, and there was a dark and sardonic humor about the expression that told Falconsbane that Ancar didn't *care* why he wanted a victim. He nodded, slowly and deliberately. His eyes locked with Falconsbane's, and the Adept once again saw in Ancar's eyes a spirit kindred to his own.

Which made Ancar all the more dangerous. There was no room in the world for two like Falconsbane.

He left without another word, but no more than half a candlemark later, two guards arrived. Between them they held a battered, terrified man, so bound with chains he could scarcely move. When Falconsbane rose, one of them silently handed him the keys to the man's bindings.

The guards backed out, closing the door behind them.

Falconsbane smiled.

And took his time.

10

Chilling rain poured from a leaden sky, a continuous sheet of gray from horizon to horizon. Elspeth silently thanked the far-away *hertasi* for the waterproof coats they had made, and tied her hood a little tighter. They rode right into the teeth of the wind; there was little in the way of lightning and thunder, but the wind and sheeting rain more than made up for that lack. The poor gryphons, shrouded in improvised raincapes made from old tents, would have been soaked to the skin if they had not been able to shield themselves from the worst of it with a bit of magic. The rest of them, however, chose to deal with the elements rather than advertise their presence on the road any further. Admittedly, that was less of a hardship for the Tayledras, Elspeth, Skif, and Nyara, with their coats supplied by the clever fingers of the *hertasi*. She felt very sorry for Cavil, Shion, and Lisha, whose standard-issue raincloaks were nowhere near as waterproof as *hertasi*-made garments.

Still, rain found its way in through every opening, sending unexpected trickles of chill down arms and backs, and exposed legs and faces got the full brunt of the weather. "I may have been more miserable a time or two in my life, but if so, I don't remember it," Skif said to Elspeth.

Nyara grimaced, showing sharp teeth, and nodded agreement. "I do not care to think of spending weeks riding through this," she said. "It must be bad for the hooved ones, yes? And does not cold and wet like this make people ill?"

On the other side of her, Cavil leaned over the neck of his Companion to add his own commentary.

"Now you see what we've been dealing with, off and on, for the past six months or so!" he shouted over the drumming rain, sniffing and rubbing his nose. "The—ah—lady is right; every village is suffering colds or fevers. I *hope* that we manage to ride out of the storm soon, but I am not going to wager on it. You can't predict anything anymore!"

Elspeth glanced back at Firesong, who was huddled in his waterproof cape, his firebird inside his hood, just as Vree was inside Darkwind's. *:Isn't there anything you can do about this?:* she asked him. *:Can't you send the rain away, or something? I thought about doing it, but since I've never done it before, I'm afraid to try.:*

:Rightly,: he replied. *:Weather-work done on mage-disturbance storms after the fact is a touchy business. For that matter, weather-work is always a touchy business. I do not know enough about this land, the countryside hereabouts, to make an informed decision. You do not yet have the skill. We do not know what is safe to do with this storm. Anything either of us do to change the weather-patterns could only mean making a worse disaster than this. Ask your friend if this is going to cause severe enough crop damage to cause shortages later.:*

"Is this bad enough to cause measurable crop damage?" she shouted back to Cavil. He squinted up at the sky for a moment, as if taking its measure, then shook his head. "It won't ruin the grazing, and the hay isn't ripening yet," he replied. "Most people around here are raising beef cattle, milch cows, and sheep, not crops. If this were farther south—" He shook his head. "We've been lucky; storms have been violent, but they haven't caused any major crop damage yet."

Yet. The word hung in the air, as ominous as the lowering clouds.

:Then we do nothing,: Firesong said firmly. *:There is no point in meddling and making a bad situation worse! We can endure some rough weather; the worst we will suffer is a wetting and a chill. When I have an opportunity to meet with those who have records of normal weather patterns, then I will help reestablish those patterns.:* He sighed. *:I fear I was only too prophetic when I said there was a great deal of work ahead of me.:*

Elspeth shrugged and grimaced slightly, but she could certainly see his point. There was only one benefit the foul weather was bestowing. Cavil could not insist on leaving the gryphons or the Tayledras behind on the excuse that they couldn't keep up with the Companions. He'd said something of the sort just before they left the Ashkevron manor, but his own Companion had told him tartly that no one was going to go racing to Haven in a downpour. In weather like this, even the Companions could not make very good time.

Darkwind and Nyara rode on horses borrowed from Lord Ashkevron, at that worthy's insistence. Those horses were what the Lord had referred to as "mudders;" sturdy beasts that could keep up a good pace all day through the worst weather. They were fairly ugly beasts; jug-headed, big-boned, as muscular as oxen, with rough, hairy hides that never could be curried into a shine. But those heavy bones and dense muscles pulled them right through the mire, and their dun-brown coats didn't show mud as badly as Firesong's white *dyheli* or the Companions—all of which were smeared and splattered up to their bellies.

Well, we hardly make a good show, but that's not such a bad thing, she reflected, shoving a strand of wet hair back under the hood of her cloak. *No one even thinks twice about making a State Visit out of us when they see us...*

In fact, the three times they had stopped overnight so far, their hosts had been so concerned by their appearance that they had simply hurried them into warm beds, and had meals sent up to their rooms. They had been able to avoid State nonsense altogether.

Elspeth had just discovered something about herself, something she had learned after a mere twelve candlemarks in Cavil, Shion, and

Lisha's presence. Her tolerance for courtly politics had deteriorated to the point of nonexistence after her stay with k'Sheyna. She just didn't want to hear about it. No gossip, no suppositions, none of it.

At some point during her musing, Skif and Nyara had dropped back as well, leaving her in the lead. Well, that hardly mattered. No one was going to get lost on a perfectly straight road.

Gwena sighed, her sides heaving under Elspeth's legs. *:I will be mortally glad to get to a warm, dry stable,:* she said. *:The Vales spoiled me.:*

The image she sent back included one of both Companions soaking away the cold in one of the hot springs. Elspeth chuckled, a little surprised; she hadn't realized that Gwena and Cymry had made use of the Vale's pools, too.

It made sense, of course, since some things in a Vale had to suit not only humans, but the Hawkbrothers' nonhuman allies. Surely *dyheli* used the hot springs, so why not the Companions?

:They've spoiled me, too, dear,: she replied, feeling her own twinge of longing for those wonderful hot pools. The best she could expect would be a hot bath; not the same thing at all. *:We have got to see about creating something like the springs at Haven. Think about coming in for a soak after a freezing rain—:*

:Like this one? Oh, don't remind me!: Gwena moaned. *:I can't even warm up by all the shoving through the mud!:*

Elspeth patted her shoulder sympathetically. *:It's almost dark,:* she said, with encouragement. *:It's not that far till we stop. I'll make sure you get something warm to eat, a nice hot mash or something like it, and a fire-warmed blanket.:*

Gwena cast a blue eye back at her, an imploring gaze made all the more pathetic by a soaked forelock straggling over the eye. *:Please. And don't forget just because a dozen nobles pounce on you once you're in the door.:*

Any reply she might have made was interrupted by Shion riding up alongside. "Excuse me, Lady," the Herald said, with a sharp and curious glance at Darkwind. "This man you are with? What exactly is his status?"

Shion and Cavil, both born of noble families, had done their level best to get her to talk—or rather, gossip. They were terribly persistent about things Elspeth considered private matters, asking very prying questions whenever Darkwind was out of earshot. Maybe being with the Tayledras had changed her, but she just didn't see why questions like this one were any of Shion's business.

Elspeth narrowed her eyes a bit at that, but kept her tone civil. And she chose to deliberately misunderstand the question. "I suppose that technically he is my equal," she replied evenly. "He is the son of the leader of Clan k'Sheyna, and an ally in his own right—"

She had a suspicion that this was not what Shion meant, and that suspicion was confirmed when the Herald frowned. "Actually, what I meant was—what is he to you? Why is he here, rather than in his own land?"

Elspeth decided to skate right around the question, and continue to give the answers to the questions Shion did have a right to ask. "He is here because he is one of my teachers in magic, and because he has offered to teach however many of our Heralds who have the Mage-Gift as he can. And yes, he *can* tell who has it. He tells me that I am likely not the only Herald to have it." She nodded as Shion bit off an exclamation. "Exactly. Evidently it was never precisely lost, but it was never used for lack of Heralds who could identify it and teach those who had it." She blinked in surprise as she realized something. "For that matter, I can identify people with it, but I'm not qualified to teach."

:*Yet*,: Gwena added.

:*Hush, you'll undermine my credibility*,: she replied.

Shion blinked, and licked her lips. "Do—do I have it?" she asked, as if she hoped to hear she did, and feared it at the same time.

Elspeth Looked for a moment at all three of the Heralds, using that new ability, and shook her head. "Not unless it's latent," she replied honestly. "None of you do, actually. I should tell you it's one of the rarer Gifts anyway. About as common as ForeSight, although that wasn't always the case. People who had it tended to drift out of Valdemar, after Vanyel's time. Most of the time it was identified and trained as if it was FarSight."

She paused for a moment, thinking quickly. "Don't assume I'm something special just because I'm Mage-Gifted. There've been plenty of Heralds who were—and are!—it's just that the Gift wasn't identified as such. Really, the main reason that I'm the first new Herald-Mage is either a matter of accident or divine providence. If a threat like Ancar had come up before, one of the other Heralds with the Gift would have gone outKingdom to get the training. If it hadn't come up now, I would still be sitting in Haven, getting beaten on by Kero and Alberich!"

Shion nodded, looking a little disappointed. Elspeth only chuckled. "Look, I wouldn't worry too much about it if I were you. Any Gift is useful. Any powerful Gift is extremely useful. It's also extremely dangerous to the bearer and those around. Mage-Gift isn't an answer to everything, and sometimes it's less so than mind-magic. What's more, mages don't always think to counter mind-magic. When they do think of it, they don't always succeed."

"That is because they cannot always counter mind-magic," Darkwind said, riding up to join the conversation, as Skif moved obligingly out of the way for him. Elspeth smiled thankfully at him; now maybe Shion would stop prying for a little. Although… perhaps she was being too harsh. She *was* the Heir, and what had happened to her in the Tayledras lands did have some importance for the Kingdom. And it was entirely possible that she was overreacting.

Thank Havens he understands our tongue enough to come rescue me!

Darkwind smiled charmingly at Shion. "There are ways to block some kinds of mind-magic, but they also block all other kinds of magic. A mage-shield powerful enough to block Mindspeaking blocks nearly everything else. So if you wish to keep your enemy from Mindspeaking, you also prevent yourself from working magic upon him."

Shion shook her head. "It's too complicated for me," she replied, and dropped back to ride beside Cavil, leaving Elspeth and Darkwind in the lead.

"Your grasp of my language is improving," she teased. He shrugged. Vree's head peeked out from beneath a fold of the hood for a moment. The bondbird looked at the rain in acute distaste, made a ratcheting sound, and vanished back into Darkwind's voluminous hood. Movement inside the hood showed Vree settling back to wait, probably grumbling to himself.

"My grasp of your language is improving because I am taking most of it from your mind, bright feather," he replied, giving her a glance that warmed her in spite of the freezing rain. "I thought perhaps I ought to save you from that too-curious colleague of yours."

"You noticed that, too, did you?" She grimaced. "All three of them are like that. I suppose it's your exotic nature. It makes them terribly curious."

"I don't know…" He stared off ahead for a moment, then switched to Tayledras. "We have been three days on the road now, and it has not stopped, this questioning. Perhaps it is that we Hawkbrothers are more private, but they seem to see nothing amiss with wishing to know *everything* about me. Not only do they wish to know in detail what I plan to do when we reach Haven, they wish to know things that have *no* bearing on our mission. How I feel about everything, what my personal opinions are on such and such a thing, and most particularly, all the details of what you and I have done together. They seem to think they have a right to this information. It is—rather embarrassing."

She shook her head, puzzled and annoyed. "You may be mistaken," she told him, but with a bit of doubt creeping into her voice. If *he* had gotten the impression that Shion was being a little too personal—

But I am the Heir. Maybe she's under orders from Mother to find out as much as she can about the people with me, and what we might have been—ah—involved in.

"Our cultures are very different, after all," she continued. "What sounds like a question about our personal lives may only be a question about what I was learning with you."

The look he gave her told her that he didn't think that he was mistaken, but he let the matter drop. It wasn't the first time he had complained of the other Heralds' insatiable questioning, but it was the first time he had mentioned their interest in something that could only be fodder for gossip and could serve no other purpose.

"You will probably get the usual greeting when we arrive," he said instead, changing the subject. His eyes twinkled when she grimaced and winced.

"If one more person comes up to me and says 'but I thought you were dead!' I'm going to strangle him," she muttered. "I can't believe people could be so stupid! And what difference would it make if I had been? The twins are perfectly capable, either one of them, of being made Heir. I am *not* indispensable! I'm only another Herald, if it comes right down to that."

"But the rumors made it seem as if you *were* indispensable, *ke'chara*," he pointed out. "The rumors must have implied that your government was in a panic and trying to cover that panic. That makes me think that the rumors must have been more than idle nonsense; they must have been spread persistently and maliciously."

"Persistent and malicious—" Now that had a familiar, nasty ring to it. "Well, that's Ancar all over," Elspeth replied. "I can't think of anyone who deserves that description more. No doubt where it came from. I don't know what in seven hells he hoped to accomplish, though."

"Enough unrest would suit him, I suspect." Darkwind put a hand inside his hood to scratch Vree's breast-feathers. He had warned Elspeth that he was unused to riding, but he seemed to be doing just fine to her. Of course, it helped that their pace was being held to a fast walk. You had to really work to get thrown at that speed. "He wishes, I think, to make as much disturbance and confusion as possible. The Clans have a game like that, from one created by the Shin'a'in. Artful distraction."

She shook her head, and water dribbled into her face. "I just can't believe that disruption would be enough for Ancar."

Darkwind continued to scratch Vree—which looked rather odd, since he seemed to be feeling around inside his hood for something—and his eyes darkened with thought. "What of this, then," he said, after a moment. "You say that your younger siblings would make good Heirs. But their father is not your father, am I correct?" At her nod, he continued. "What if the rumors of your death were only a beginning—that once it was believed that you were dead, Ancar then planned to add rumors that your stepfather had contrived your death, in order to have his own children take the throne?"

She stared at him, mouth dropping open. "That—that's crazy!" she stammered, finally. "No one who knew my stepfather would ever believe that!"

"No one who *knew* him, you say," Darkwind persisted. "But this land of yours is a very large one, larger than I had ever guessed. So how many of these people out here truly know him? How can they? How many have even seen him more than once or twice, and at a distance?"

It made diabolical sense. Especially given that Elspeth's own father—Prince Daren's brother—had tried to murder her mother and take the throne for himself. People would be only too ready to believe in the murderous intentions of another of the Rethwellan royals.

For that matter, they had been perfectly willing to believe that *she* might plot against her mother, as if betrayal were somehow inheritable.

Ancar was even clever enough to spread two conflicting sets of rumors. One set, that Prince Daren had connived at Elspeth's death, and another, that Elspeth was alive and trying to usurp her mother's throne.

"I hate it," she said slowly, "And you are probably right. Especially since my first destination was Rethwellan, *his* land. People would have been only too ready to believe he'd set something up with his brother to get rid of me."

Darkwind nodded. "And what effect would that have upon the rulers of your land?"

"It—at the very best, it would be a distraction and cause a lot of problems at a time when we don't need either." She clenched her jaw. "At the worst, it would undermine confidence in the Queen and everything she stands for. That snake—he is as clever as he is rotten, I swear! He and Falconsbane are two of a kind!"

"Then we must hope he never achieves the kind of power that

Falconsbane had," Darkwind said firmly. "We must work to be rid of him before he does. All the more reason for your friends to be here. We have seen this kind of creature before, and I hope we can second-guess Ancar because of our experience with Falconsbane."

Clouds were too thick for a real sunset, but the light was beginning to fade. Something large and dark, a building of some kind, was looming up in the distance at the side of the road; the rain was falling too thickly for Elspeth to make out what it was, but out here, it was unlikely to be anything other than their next stop, the manor of Lady Kalthea Lyonnes.

Shion looked up and cried, "Look!" in a tone that confirmed Elspeth's guess. They all urged their tired mounts into a little faster pace, and within half a candlemark they were pounding at the gates.

Fortunately, after the trouble at the Ashkevron manor, someone always went on ahead to inform their hosts exactly what was coming. This time Lisha had ridden ahead to warn the Lady and her household about the gryphons; there was a certain amount of trepidation on the part of the servants who came out to meet them, but at least no one fled screaming in fear.

Things were sorted out with commendable haste. The gryphons were conducted off to the chapel—chapels seemed to be the only rooms suitable to their size—the Companions and *dyheli* taken to the stables and a promised hot mash and rubdown. And finally the two-legged members of the party were brought in, still dripping a little, to be presented to their hostess.

"Elspeth!" the Lady cried, clasping Elspeth's hand and kissing it fervently. "Thank the gods! We heard you were dead!"

Darkwind choked, smothering a laugh, and Elspeth only sighed.

But later that night, after all the fuss was over and everyone had been settled into their rooms, Elspeth sagged into a chair beside the fire and stared into the flames. Perhaps this business of staying with the high-born was a mistake...

On the other hand, no inn would ever accept the gryphons. And at least in this way, word was being spread quickly that she *was* alive and she had returned with some real help against Ancar.

But another little conversation with Shion and with a cousin of Shion's who lived here had just proved to her that Darkwind was right. Shion and the others weren't at all concerned with the welfare of Valdemar—or at least that wasn't their motivation in cross-examining her. They were just plain nosy. They wanted gossip-fodder, and what was more, if she didn't give it to them, they were perfectly capable of making things up out of whole cloth!

Shion's cousin had brought Elspeth her supper, using that as an excuse to ask any number of increasingly impertinent questions. Finally she had concluded, shamelessly, with the question of whether it was true that Hawkbrothers only mated in groups, saying as an excuse that she had read about it in "an old story." And it was pretty obvious that the cousin also wanted to know if Elspeth had been a member of one of those groups.

When Elspeth asked her where she had heard such nonsense, the girl had demurred and avoided giving an answer, but Elspeth already had a good idea who had prompted it. After all, until she had gone delving into the old Archives, there hadn't been more than a handful of folk in Valdemar who even knew that the Hawkbrothers existed. So where else would the girl have heard an "old story" about the Tayledras except from Shion?

Elspeth's jaw tightened. The trouble was, no matter what she said or did, it was likely to make the situation worse. If she dressed Shion down for this, Shion would only be more certain that Elspeth was hiding some kind of dreadful secret. If she forbade any more loose talk, that would only make Shion more circumspect in spreading silly gossip. If she ignored it all, Shion would go right on spreading gossip, and making up whatever she didn't know for certain. There was no way Elspeth could win at this.

Heralds were human beings, with all the failings and foibles of any other set of humans. Shion's failing was gossip—harmless enough under most circumstances. Except for this one, where her fantasies could and would cause Elspeth some problems...

A gentle tap at the door made her look up in time to see Darkwind slipping inside. He glanced around the darkened room for a moment, then spotted her at the hearth and came to join her.

"I do not know whether to laugh or snarl, bright feather," he said without preamble. "And if we had not as many notorious gossips in k'Sheyna as anywhere else, I would probably be very annoyed at this moment."

"I take it you met Kalinda," Elspeth said dryly as he took a seat beside the fire.

"Indeed." His mouth twitched. "I was discussing some trifle with Firesong when she brought us our dinners, then, bold as you please, offered to—ah—'join our mating circle.' I confess that I did not know what to say or do."

Elspeth took one look at his face and broke up in a fit of giggling. That set him off, too, and for the next few moments, they leaned against each other, laughing and gasping for breath. Any glance at the other's face only served to set them off again.

"I—dear gods!—you must have done something. How did you get her out of there?" she choked, finally.

He shook his head, and held his side. "I did nothing!" he confessed. "It was Firesong. He just looked at the girl and said, 'the offer is appreciated, but unless you turn male, impossible.' She turned quite scarlet, and stammered something neither of us understood, then left."

That sent Elspeth into convulsions again because she could very easily see Firesong doing exactly that. The wicked creature!

Her gales of laughter started Darkwind giggling again, and the two of them laughed until they simply had no more breath to laugh with anymore. She lay with her head against Darkwind's shoulder while the fire burned a little lower, and only spoke when he moved to throw another branch into the flames.

"I suppose that will take care of Shion for a while," she said, wiping moisture from the corner of one eye. "I wish I'd thought of that as a solution. But you know, now Shion will probably begin telling everyone that you and Firesong are both *shay'a'chern*. The gods only know what *that* will bring out of the corners!"

"I do not care, dearheart," he replied, stroking her hair. "So long as it saves you grief. And I am certain that Firesong will be positively delighted! I tell you, he is as shameless as a cooperihawk!"

She laughed again, for she had seen the cooperihawks in their rounds of spring matings, which were frequent and undiscriminating.

He chuckled with her and caressed her shoulders, then continued. "I have other confessions to make to you, and none so amusing. I had no idea of the size of your land, of the numbers of your people. I had naively supposed your Valdemar must be like a very large Vale. And I had no idea what your status truly was among your people. And—I now realize that all of my assumptions were based on those ideas."

"My status is subject to change, my love," she replied quickly. "As I told you, I am not indispensable."

"But others believe you are." He held her for a long moment in silence, his warm hands clasped across her waist. "You have duties and obligations, and they do not include a—long term relationship with some foreign mage."

She forced herself to remain calm; after all, wasn't this precisely what she had thought, herself, any number of times? She had known since before she left Valdemar that her freedom was severely restricted. Hadn't she rebuffed Skif with that very same argument?

But she no longer accepted that argument, as she had not accepted the "fated" path that the Companions had tried to force her to take.

And even though his tongue was saying that he must let her go, his body was saying quite a different thing. He held her tightly, fiercely, as if to challenge anyone who might try to part them.

She must choose her words very carefully. He had opened his heart to her; she must answer the pain she heard under his words. But he would not respect someone who violated all the vows she had made to her own land and people by willfully deserting them, either. The next few words might be the most important she would ever speak in her life.

"I have duties, true enough," she replied, slowly, turning to stare into his eyes. "I never pretended otherwise. I have to find a way to reconcile those duties with what I want and what you want. I think I can, if you will trust me."

"You know I do. With my very life, *ashke*."

His face looked like a beautiful sculpture by the firelight. Time seemed to slow down. Even Vree was stock-still, watching them both unblinkingly. Darkwind held his breath.

"I think I can be true to Valdemar, Darkwind—and to you. I *know* there has to be a way. I refuse to lose either of you—you or my native land and my duty to it. I refuse to let you go."

The last was said so fiercely that his eyes widened for a moment in surprise. "But how can you possibly reconcile them?" he asked at last. "You are your mother's chosen successor. There is very little freedom for you in that role."

"I have some ideas," she replied. "But they hinge on your not knowing what I'm going to do so you can be just as surprised as everyone else. Otherwise people will think that I'm simply acting like a love-struck wench rather than in the best interests of Valdemar."

He held very still for a moment. "And are you a love-struck wench?"

She reached up, grabbed two handfuls of his hair, and pulled his mouth to hers for a long and passionate kiss.

The touch of his lips made a fire build in the core of her. It made it very difficult to hold to coherent thought. "Of course I am," she replied calmly.

Darkwind smiled and stroked her hair. He closed his eyes and pulled her closer, strong and comforting, protecting her as a great hawk would mantle over its young in a storm. His touch against her cheek was as gentle as a feather's, and his sigh of contentment matched her own.

The scent of his body and the smoky warmth of the room blended. She knew she had said the right thing. She had spoken her heart. She had spoken the truth.

The kiss had made her heart race and drove her thoughts into paths entirely foreign to simple discussion. "But I don't want them to know that. Being love-struck doesn't mean my brains have poured out my ears!"

"I hope not," he murmured, "because I am as much in love with your mind as—"

She did not give him the chance to finish the sentence.

Vree watched the two kiss, then tucked his head to sleep. As far as Vree was concerned, whatever came, whatever they faced, wherever they went, all would now be right with the world.

It was a good bonding. Display done. Mate won. Nesting soon. They would fly high together.

At last, they cleared the area covered by the storm, and the final few days were spent riding under sunnier skies. Sunnier—not sunny; there were no cloudless skies, but at least the roads remained less than mud-pits despite the occasional brief cloudburst. The weather was still odd, though; there were always spectacular sunsets and wild lightning storms at night, although these storms did not necessarily produce rain, and the skies never entirely cleared even when they neared Haven.

The city itself sat under a circle of *blue* sky, rather than clouds; a nearly perfect circle, in fact, and very odd to Elspeth's eyes. When Firesong saw that, he nodded to himself, as if this was something he had anticipated but had not necessarily expected.

At least, when they reached Haven, they were no longer mud-spattered and soggy; they even took a moment to change, when they were within a candlemark or two of the capital. Elspeth had the feeling they were not going to have much of a chance to clean up when they reached the Palace, given the excitement her arrival was generating.

A scant network of signal-towers like the ones in Hardorn had been set up to relay news, although in the foul weather they had been riding through such towers could only be used at night, and often not even then. There were not enough of them to warn their noble hosts that they were coming, but there *were* enough that by now all of Haven knew the approximate candlemark of when they would appear. Once the weather cleared, they had borrowed a cart from one of their hosts, in which the gryphlets and Rris now rode in excited splendor. In every village along the road, even when it was raining, the entire population turned out to see them pass.

Elspeth felt entirely as if she was riding in a circus procession, but she waved and smiled anyway, noting with a great deal of amusement that no one really paid much attention to *her* once they caught sight of the gryphons.

By the time they reached Haven, word had traveled ahead of them by those mirror- and lantern-relays, and as she had expected, the road on both sides was lined with people, four and five deep. It was quite obvious at that point that Elspeth was not the attraction; she was not even a close second. After all, she did not look all that much different than any Herald, and the populace around Haven was quite used to seeing Heralds. The gryphons, gryphlets, and Tayledras were the real attention getters, in that order.

Firesong and Treyvan were in their element, waving genially to the crowd, and occasionally throwing up magical "fireworks" that were insignificant in terms of power, but incredibly showy. They were definitely crowd pleasers. Treyvan would take to the air every few leagues to hover above the procession, while the onlookers ooh-ed and ahh-ed. Hydona simply sighed with patience, and trotted quietly behind the wagon. The gryphlets bounced in the bed of the wagon like a pair of excited kittens, bringing more "ohs" and exclamations of "aren't they *adorable.*" As had happened at the Ashkevron manor, the gryphlets convinced the crowd that these mighty creatures were not monsters at all.

Elspeth might just as well not have been along. People cheered her in a perfunctory sort of way, then riveted their attention on the Hawkbrothers and gryphons. When either Treyvan or Firesong performed, she could have stripped naked and done riding tricks on Gwena's back and no one would have noticed.

She had known this would happen. She had rather expected that she might find herself a little jealous. After all, she was used to being the center of attention—the beloved Heir to the Throne, and all of that.

She had never been forced to share the focus of all eyes, much less been excluded from that focus.

She was rather surprised when all she felt was relief. And in a way, that simply confirmed what she had been thinking since they had arrived back in Valdemar. She was not really happy being the Heir; she was not truly suited to the job. She had been a lot more comfortable back in the Vale, when no one had treated her any differently than anyone else in the Clan. In fact, with the Hawkbrothers, she was judged only by her merits. She had changed a great deal since she had last seen Haven, and nothing showed that change quite so profoundly as this.

When they reached the outskirts of Haven, the crowd had thickened, to the point where there wasn't room for a child between the fronts of the buildings and the street. The noise was deafening; the mass of folk dressed in their best dazzling to the eye. And for someone who had spent so many months out in the wilderness, the crowds were enough to give one a feeling of being crushed.

She spared a thought and a glance for Nyara, who had probably never seen this many people in all of her life put together. The Changechild was clinging to Skif's hand, but seemed to be holding up fairly well.

:*She's all right,*: Need said shortly, in answer to Elspeth's tentative thought. :*I managed to get her used to something like this by feeding her some of my old memories. She doesn't like it much, but then, neither do you.*: A good point. Elspeth tendered her thanks, and turned her attention back toward the crowd, watching for ambushes and traps. This would be a good place to hide an assassin, if Ancar had the time to put one in place. People leaned precariously out of windows to watch them pass, cheering wildly, and still paying very little attention to *her.* It felt like a kind of victory procession. She only hoped the feeling would prove prophetic.

In a way, it was kind of amusing, for the merchants and street vendors had taken advantage of the situation and the advance warning they had of it, to do as much impulse business as they might during a real festival. She noted, chuckling under the roar of the crowd, the number of vendors with merchandise they must have made up specifically for this "processional." There were people hawking gryphon- and Companion-shaped pastries and candies, cheap flags emblazoned with crude gryphons, hawks, and the arms of Valdemar, toy sellers with carved hawks, Companions, and fat little winged cats with beaks that were undoubtably supposed to be gryphons, and one enterprising fellow with stick-horses with white Companion heads *and* feathered gryphon heads. He was doing an especially brisk business.

She was relieved and pleased to see a number of people in Guard blue mingled in with the crowd. Kero's work, no doubt. In fact, she might very well have called in all of the Skybolts to be on assassin-watch. Trust Kero to think of that.

:I'm watching, too, youngling: Need said unexpectedly. *:Keep your eyes sharp, but with all of us working, I think we'll get any assassin before he gets one of us.:*

The crowd continued to be that thick right up to the gates of the Palace/Collegium complex. They passed between the walls and onto the road leading up to the Palace, and there the motley crowd gave way to a crowd of people in discrete knots of Guard Blue, trainee Gray, Healer Green, Bard Red, and Herald White. And it appeared that at least a few of the vendors had penetrated even here—or some enterprising young student had turned vendor himself—for here were the flags they had seen out in the city, being waved just as enthusiastically by usually sober Heralds and Guards. There were, perhaps, a few less gryphons and hawks and a few more of the white horses of Valdemar, but otherwise it looked very much the same. The trainees in particular were loud and enthusiastic, their young voices rising shrilly above those of their elders. It was all but impossible to see much of anything past the crowd. Even the Companions were crowded up behind the humans, tossing their manes, their eyes sparkling with enjoyment.

She caught sight of friends at last among the crowd—some of her year-mates, Keren and Teren, retired Elcarth. The noise was such that she saw their mouths moving, and could only shrug and grin, miming that she would talk to them later.

The procession came to an end at the main entrance to the Palace. It ended there by default, that entrance being the only set of doors large enough to admit the gryphons. There those who were riding dismounted, and an escort of Palace Guards in their dark blue lined up on either side of the group to usher them inside.

Interestingly, Shion, Cavil, and Lisha were neatly cut off from the group and taken aside with the Companions and Firesong's *dyheli*. Elspeth was not particularly sorry to see them leave, she only dreaded the gossip that was sure to follow.

The doors opened—and there was Talia, who ignored gryphons, Hawkbrothers, and protocol, and ran with her arms outstretched to catch Elspeth up in a breathless embrace.

They hugged each other tightly, separating only long enough for searching looks, then embracing again. To Elspeth's surprise, she found herself crying with happiness.

"Oh, *stop* it, you'll make me cry, too," Talia scolded in Elspeth's ear. "Dear gods, you look *wonderful!*"

"You look just as wonderful," Elspeth countered over the cheering.

Talia laughed throatily. "More gray hair, dearheart, I promise you. The children are at the age where someone is always plucking them right out of the arms of trouble, usually by the scruff of the neck. I have to warn you. Your mother has called a full Court, Council and all—"

"So she can prove to everyone at once that I'm still alive. I'd already figured she would." Good. That meant that she would not have to wait to put her plan into motion. "Right now?"

"Right now—" Talia sounded a bit uncertain, and it was Elspeth's turn to laugh and put the Queen's Own at arm's length.

"Look at me," she demanded. Talia cocked her head to one side and did. "I'm a little dusty, but I did take the time to change, so we're all presentable. I've survived fire, flood, and mage-storm, almost daily encounters with the nastiest creatures a perverted Adept could create, and daily border patrols. I'm hardly going to be tired out by a mere ride! Bring on your Council—I'll eat them alive!" And she bared her teeth and growled.

Talia threw her head back and laughed, her chestnut curls trembling, and if there *was* more gray in her hair, Elspeth couldn't see it. "All right, you've convinced me. Now go convince them!"

She stepped back and bowed slightly, gesturing for all of them to precede her into the Palace. Gryphons included. Lytha and Jerven trotted in the shadow of their mother's wings, looking curiously all around with huge, alert eyes.

With Talia and the contingent of the Guard bringing up the rear, Elspeth led the procession through the great double doors—for the first time in her memory, both of them thrown open wide—and down the hall that led to the audience chamber. The gryphons' claws clicked metallically on the marble floor, and the bulk of the Palace muffled the sounds of the crowd outside. Most of the cheering had stopped once they all vanished inside, but there was still some crowd noise. And it was more than likely that Shion, Cavil, and Lisha were being interrogated by all their friends about the ride home and the strange people and creatures that the Heir had brought with her.

The double doors at the end of the hall were thrown open just as they reached them, and a fanfare of trumpets announced them to the expectantly hushed Court.

And it was an announcement of the full complement, as Elspeth had hoped. It included Firesong and Darkwind, as "Ambassadors of the Tayledras;" Nyara as "Lady Nyara k'Sheyna," leaving the assembled courtiers and power brokers to wonder, no doubt, just what a "k'Sheyna" was; and the gryphons as "Lord Treyvan Gryphon and Lady Hydona and children, ambassadors of Kaled'a'in," leaving the courtiers of Valdemar even more baffled. Poor Rris; he was not announced, although he trotted at the heels of the gryphlets. But he did not seem disappointed as Elspeth glanced back. He was simply watching *everything* with that alert expression that told her he was storing it all up, to become yet another tale in the *kyrees'* oral history. The *dyheli* had been taken off with Gwena and Cymry, but he had never shown much interest in being an envoy anyway; he had made it rather clear to Elspeth that he was there mostly to show to Valdemar that there were other intelligent races allied with the Tayledras than just humans and gryphons.

She paused on the threshold, giving the others a chance to compose themselves before striding into the room full of strangers. The room fell silent, and with a whispering rustle of cloth and a creaking of leather, everybody in the room except the four on the dais bent in a bow or curtsy. She paused for another moment, then moved forward, and behind her she heard the same swish of cloth and creaking of leather; the members of Court and Council rising as she passed. Her own eyes were fastened on her mother and stepfather, both in Whites with the royal circlets about their brows, both standing before their thrones, with Heralds flanking them on either hand, and Guards behind the Heralds. One of those Heralds was Kerowyn, who winked broadly as soon as Elspeth was near enough to see her face; the other was Jeri, Alberich's hand-picked successor. The Guards behind both of them were from Kero's Skybolts. Elspeth relaxed at the sight of all these old friends. *They* would understand what she was about to do, even if her mother didn't.

Selenay's gold hair was clearly streaked with silver; Prince Daren showed more worry lines at the corners of his eyes and across his forehead. Both of them widened their eyes and frankly stared for a moment at Elspeth before recovering their "royal masks"—she chuckled under her breath, for she was wearing one of her more elaborate sets of *hertasi*-made working-Whites, and while she was clearly garbed as a Herald, it was not a Herald as Valdemar at large was used to seeing one. She could hardly wait until they got a good look at Firesong, who had chosen to contrast his silver hair and the silver plumage of his firebird with Tayledras mage-robes in a startling shade of blue that could never be mistaken for Guard Blue. In fact, she was not entirely certain *how* the *hertasi* had achieved that eye-blinding color. It certainly was nowhere to be found in nature!

The wood-paneled Throne Room was filled to bursting, with every available light-source fully utilized. If the crowds outside had been dazzling, this crowd was dizzying, each courtier in full dress, with as many jewels as possible within the bounds of taste. And some, predictably, had gone beyond the bounds of taste. The place was ablaze with color and light—

:And all of it pales next to Firesong's self-image,: Gwena commented in the back of her mind. Elspeth stifled a chuckle and kept her face perfectly sober.

She smiled broadly as she neared the throne, but submitted demurely to an "official" greeting, as Selenay announced to the room that her beloved daughter and Heir had returned, and made all the appropriate official motions. Even though she longed to fling her arms around her mother as she had around Talia, that would have to wait until they were in private together.

And by then—

She bowed briefly to her mother, then straightened, and took the steps necessary to place her on the dais in her position as Heir. She turned to face the silent Court, and looked out over the faces of new friends, old, and utter strangers. Firesong winked; so did Treyvan. Nyara managed a tremulous smile. Darkwind simply held her eyes for a long breath.

:Hold onto your feathers, my love,: she Mindsent to Darkwind as she took a deep breath of her own. *:I have a surprise for you.:*

"Thank you, all of you, for your wonderful greetings," she said, carefully pronouncing and projecting each word as she had been taught since she was a child, so that every syllable would reach the back of the room. "I have returned, as I promised, with the help that I went to find—and with more, far more. But with your indulgence, I would like to make an announcement before I introduce our new allies and friends. I, Elspeth, daughter of Queen Selenay and Heir to the throne of Valdemar, hereby renounce my claim to the throne of Valdemar, in favor of my siblings, the Princess Lyra and Prince Kris."

A chorus of whispered comments and oaths came from the courtiers and Guard alike.

"I have been reliably informed by the Companions that both will be Chosen, and thus both are equally suited to the position of Heir to the throne of Valdemar—as I am *not*."

The expressions on the faces nearest her—those not in her own party, that is—were so funny she almost burst out laughing. They were utterly, completely stunned; and she had the feeling that her own mother and stepfather wore identical expressions. It looked almost as if someone had run through the crowd, hitting everyone in the back of the head with a board. They could not have been more startled if she had suddenly sprouted wings and horns.

Quickly, before anyone could interrupt, she enumerated her reasons. "As all well know, my blood-father was a traitor and a would-be assassin, and all my life his crimes have hung over my head, clouding confidence in my trustworthiness and ability to rule. With Lyra and Kris there will be no such doubts. I have heard, before I left and as I returned, the same rumors that many of you had heard both before and during my absence—that I was in reality using that absence to plot against my beloved mother. With Lyra and Kris in the position of Heir, no one need worry when I am absent that I may be thinking of taking the throne before my rightful time. The same rumors have always existed outside this Kingdom as well—and once again, when I no longer hold the position of Heir, the fears that I will attempt to usurp the rule of Valdemar as Ancar of Hardorn usurped his father's throne will be laid to rest. I am not Ancar—and now, no one will ever need to wonder if I could be tempted by the promise of power into following his wretched example."

There, she thought. *Let them think about that, and when they think about it, wonder if those rumors just might have originated with Ancar, since he is so familiar with usurping thrones.*

"But there are additional considerations," she continued quickly, and then surrounded herself in the blink of an eye with a showy glow of magic fires that made everyone gasp and step back a pace. Firesong was grinning and nodding with approval; Darkwind just stared at her, but his mouth was twitching suspiciously. "As you can see," she went on, in ringing, magic-enhanced tones, "I *am* the first of the new Herald-Mages of Valdemar! I am the first and only *trained* Herald-Mage at this moment. There will be others, I promise you, for one of the reasons that I have brought these new allies is to help in the training of new Herald-Mages. And while that is a cause for rejoicing, it is also a cause for concern, for as the sole trained Herald-Mage *and* the Heir, my loyalties and duties are at terrible odds with one another. As Herald-Mage, I must risk myself and my powers in defense of this Kingdom. As Heir, I must *not*, ever, place myself in jeopardy! I have been forced to weigh good against good, duty against duty, and I have concluded that my duty to Valdemar is best served by renouncing the throne and taking my place in the front lines of whatever conflict may come. Valdemar needs my skills and strength far more than it needs me beneath the Heir's coronet."

Now she turned, to see her stepfather beaming with approval, and her mother doing a creditable imitation of a landed fish. Controlling herself carefully, she concluded her speech.

"Therefore, I ask you—you of the Council and Court, and you, Queen and Consort—to accept my abdication and allow me to take my proper place as one Herald among many. I will always be my mother's true daughter, but I no longer wish to be a cause of worry and conflict. And I wish to place my abilities, my life, and my honor fully in the service of my land and people." She looked pleadingly into her mother's eyes. "Will you say me 'aye'?"

Selenay never had a chance to respond, for Prince Daren led the Council and Court in a thundering acceptance of her audacious solution.

It was all over. With weary feet, Elspeth took service corridors rather than the main halls of the Palace. Servants ignored her as just another Herald, although a few stopped to stare at her unique Whites, and one young man paused long enough to whisper, "Herald, that is a *fine* set of Whites!"

She smiled at him and winked. From the look of him, he had a fine sense of fashion himself. Someone had clearly taken a creative hand to his servants' livery. He winked back and hurried on.

But on the whole, Elspeth felt rather as if she had been run through a clothes-wringer in the Palace laundry and hung out to dry. Even after her abdication was a fact, there had still been a hundred things to deal with.

The introduction of the rest of the party, for instance, and the explanations of what, exactly, their positions were, and what they brought to Valdemar's defense. Selenay, still stunned from the abdication, had been taken quite a bit aback by the gryphons, until Hydona had said, quietly, in quite creditable Valdemaran, "I underssstand herrr Majesssty isss the motherrr of twinssss?" and at Selenay's nod had uttered a long-suffering sigh and continued, "Then we have a grrreat deal in common."

And since Lytha had chosen that particular moment to bite Jerven's tail, causing him to squall, and Hydona to reach back absentmindedly and separate them both, Selenay had come out of her stunned trance immediately and graced Hydona with a smile that united them at once in a bond of mother-to-mother. Talia had covered her mouth, hiding a grin. So had Elspeth. No one would ever be able to convince Selenay now that the gryphons were "dangerous animals."

Firesong had quite dazzled the Court; he seemed born to manipulate crowds. And by the time Court had been formally ended, he had collected a little court of his own, both he and his firebird posing and preening quite shamelessly. Darkwind went almost unnoticed, and so did Nyara.

Which had probably been Firesong's intent, or at least one of his intentions.

Then there had been the joyful task of greeting all of her old friends, and explaining to them all that she had thought this through very carefully, and *yes*, it was the best solution to the situation. "Ancar has been focusing on me as a target, one that he knows," she had continued. "He doesn't know anything about the twins, and they're children, much easier to guard day and night because they have no duties. Mother could even send them off into hiding if she had to."

Of all of them, Kero had understood the best, Kero and her stepfather. But eventually all of them accepted it.

She had made a point of not introducing Darkwind specifically. There was no reason to start up rumors yet, not until after she dealt with Selenay.

Then had come the dreaded confrontation with her mother.

Which turned out not to be a confrontation at all.

She still couldn't quite believe it. At some point during her absence, Selenay had come to accept the fact that Elspeth was grown up now, and capable of making her own decisions. "You will always be my darling daughter," she had said, after a long and tear-filled embrace, "but you are also a wise woman, wiser and braver than I am. You *have* seen the best solution to your divided duties. And while I shall *hate* seeing you go into danger, I can't deny you your right to do so."

That had brought out another freshet of tears from both of them, until Selenay was called to a meeting of the Council. Elspeth, no longer Heir and so no longer required to attend, had gone off to her new quarters.

The rooms were the ones assigned to important and high-ranking guests. She had asked to be installed next to Darkwind, in rooms with a connecting door. She hadn't spent all of her childhood running about the Palace without learning the layout of the place. She had made very sure that she knew exactly where each and every member of her group had been housed. The Seneschal had given her a startled look that turned to a knowing one, and nodded once.

And now she no longer had to worry about what people thought. It didn't matter anymore. She was not the Heir; her liaisons were no one's business but her own.

The feeling of freedom was as heady as a draught of strong wine.

She opened the door, and closed it behind her, letting her eyes adjust to the dim light filtering in through the closed curtains. This should be— yes, was—a suite of two rooms, a public room and a bedroom. She pushed away from the door and sought the latter.

There was a basin and pitcher of water on a washstand in her bedroom; once again she had a twinge of nostalgia for the Vale, but this would have to serve until she could get to the shared bathing room. She splashed some water on her face to wash away the marks of tears, brushed out her hair, and then went back into the sitting room and tapped on the door dividing her rooms from Darkwind's.

He opened it, clearly startled that there was anyone seeking entrance, and clearly *not* expecting her. She took advantage of his startlement by flinging herself at him, and within a heartbeat he had recovered quite enough to return her embrace. It was just as heartfelt and passionate as she had hoped, and he left his mind open to her completely, leaving her no doubt whatsoever of how he truly felt. Profound gratitude and relief, a touch of guilt that despite her speech she might have done this only for him, and love and pride.

She was the first to break off the kiss, reluctantly, but he was the first to speak.

"You were magnificent," he said fervently in his own tongue. "Absolutely magnificent. You made me so proud!"

"Good," she replied, taking his hand and pulling him into her room. "Now, let's get to the serious business, before we do or say anything else."

He nodded quickly, following her inside, and closing the connecting door as he did so. "Of course—you are right, we must make war plans, dealing with this Ancar, and how we can identify and train the new mages—"

"No," she told him, laying a finger on his lips to stop the flow of words. "That's serious, but there's something else that needs settling first. You—and me."

He blinked at her a moment, taken quite by surprise. "Ah—I'm not sure—exactly what—" He blinked for a moment more, then let out his breath as if he had been holding it for days. "You and I. Well. Perhaps the first thing we should do is sit down."

She laughed a little. "Good idea."

The rooms that adjoined one another were deliberately designed so that ambassadors could hold informal court. His would be the mirror image of hers, with a fireplace in the wall the two rooms shared, a desk, several chairs, and a small couch where someone who was ailing or infirm (as many senior diplomats were) could recline at his ease. He led the way to the couch, and she sat down beside him. The light from outside was beginning to fade, but no servant would dare venture in here to light candles until they were called for, which was exactly how she had ordered it. They would be undisturbed until she wished otherwise, for the first time in her life.

"I need to know something right now," she said, as he visibly searched for words to begin the conversation. "What are your long-term intentions and plans? As regards us, our relationship, that is."

He swallowed, and took a deep breath. "I'm taking this all very well, am I not?" he replied, with a weak grin. "Actually, you flung a rock into what had been a quiet and ordered pond. I *was* going to keep myself strictly in the background. I had intended to subordinate myself to your needs and wishes, and keep everything so discreet that no one would ever guess what was going on. Firesong and I had even planned on creating the fiction that he and I were *shay'kreth'ashke*, just to throw anyone off the scent. After all, we'd already convinced Shion of that. But now—I suppose I don't need to."

"No, you don't," she replied, then grinned. "In fact, I'd rather like it if you were as blatant as possible. The more *ineligible* I make myself for the throne, the better. Although I know there is going to be at least one person who would prefer the original plan. Poor Firesong is going to be *terribly* disappointed!" She gave him an arch look. "After all, it was your hair that he wanted to braid feathers into!"

He stared at her a moment longer, then broke into laughter that came within a hair of hysteria but never quite crossed the line. She smiled but didn't join him this time. Her neck and stomach were taut with tension, for he still hadn't answered her question. There was something in her pocket that was burning a fiery hole in her heart.

Finally he calmed, and wiped his eyes. "Well," he said at last, "my intentions are honorable, at least. I should like very much, Elspeth k'Sheyna k'Valdemar, if you would accept a feather from my bondbird."

"I hope you have a spare," she replied, with a chuckle born of intense relief and a desire to shout with joy. "I would like very much to accept, but Vree will never forgive me if you run back into your room and pluck him."

But to her surprise, he reached into an inner pocket in the breast of his clothing and brought out a forestgyre primary—one with a shaft covered in beadwork of tiny crystals hardly bigger than grains of sand. It had a hair-tie of a silver clasp with two matching silver chains ending in azure crystals.

"I have held this next to my heart for the past several months," he said solemnly, "never thinking you would be able to wear it openly, and not sure you would even be able to accept it at all."

Her vision blurred as he spoke the traditional words that signified a Hawkbrother marriage. "Elspeth, will you wear my feather, for all the world and skies to see?"

She took it from him, her hands trembling; started to fasten it into her hair, but her hands shook too much to do so and he had to help her. Her heart raced as if she had been running fast, and she could not stop smiling—her skin tingled and burned, and she wanted to laugh, sing, cry—all of them at once.

Instead, she took out her own gift. "I don't have a bondbird," she said. "I don't know how Gwena will feel about this. I can only hope she feels the way I do."

She held out the ring on her open palm, a silver ring with an overlay of crystal. Sandwiched between was an intricately braided band of incandescently white horsehair, hairs carefully pulled from Gwena's tail, one at a time, so that each hair was perfect. She'd had the ring made up by one of the *hertasi* several months ago, never really hoping she would be able to use it, but unable to give up the dream that she might.

He took it and placed it on his ring finger, and she noticed with a certain amount of pleasure that his hands were trembling as much as hers now. "*Hertasi* work, isn't it?" he asked, rather too casually.

She nodded. He looked at the ring closely.

"In fact—I think I know the artisan. Kelee, isn't it?"

Again she nodded. "I've probably had it as long as you've had the feather," she ventured.

He chuckled. "And the *hertasi*, no doubt, have been chortling to themselves for some time. They are inveterate matchmakers, you know."

She thought about the sly way that Kelee had looked at her when he had given her the finished ring, and could only sigh and nod.

"Well," he said at last, after a long silence. "This is a good thing. I think that my parents and Clan would approve."

Elspeth squeezed his hand and said quietly, "It doesn't matter if they do or not. My feelings would be the same."

Darkwind smiled. "Mine as well."

They embraced again. "Perhaps 'Darkwind' is no longer a proper name for me. You have brought too much light into my life for it to apply anymore. I no longer feel like a lowering storm since joining with you, bright feather."

Elspeth nodded and bit her lower lip. "But... there are still storms approaching."

"Yes. We have many plans to make, and many to discard. I think that this is likely to be a very late night..."

I think that this is likely to be a very late night, Talia thought, motioning discreetly to one of the pages near her Council seat. "Go order enough food and wine for all the Councillors, then recruit some of the final-year trainees to serve it and replace the pages," she whispered to him. He was one of the older pages, and nodded with both understanding and relief. He had served the Queen and Council long enough to know how long one of these emergency sessions could last, and while he might have been disappointed at not being able to listen in on the proceedings, the disappointment was countered by the relief that he would not be stuck in the Council chamber until the sun rose.

There was something to be said for having a limited level of responsibility.

As the pages filed out, to be replaced by wide-eyed youngsters in trainee-Grays, Selenay rose to address her Council. The men and women seated around the horseshoe-shaped table fell silent, and lamplight gleamed on jewels and brilliant court-garb. Behind Selenay, the huge crest of Valdemar seemed to glow.

"I am certain that many of you fear that I am going to oppose this abdication," she said, with calm and equanimity. Talia knew better than anyone here that the calm was not feigned, it was real. She and Selenay had spent many nights in Elspeth's absence, trying to find a way to reconcile the conflicts that Elspeth's duties would place her in when she returned, but both of them had assumed that Elspeth would never want to give up her position as Heir. They had both been wrong, and Elspeth's elegant solution to the conflict, while creating several *more* entirely new problems, had solved more than it created.

Selenay locked eyes with each of her Councillors in turn, as Talia assessed their emotional state with her Gift of Empathy. Troubled, most of them, but excited. A bit apprehensive. Afraid that Selenay was going to make difficulties.

"Well," she said, with a wan smile, "Elspeth is wiser than I, and far more expedient. For the moment, although they are not yet Chosen, I am naming Kris and Lyra joint Heir-presumptives. Since they are so very young, being guarded day and night and kept from much public contact is going to do very little harm to them, and given that I am going to assign their safety into the hands of Guardsmen picked by Herald-Captain Kerowyn and Heralds and their Companions picked by my Consort, I think it unlikely that *anyone* will be able to threaten them with such formidable nurses on the watch."

There was overall relief at that, relief so palpable Talia was surprised no one else could feel it, unGifted though they might be.

"It seems to me that the first thing we should do is to ensure that word of Elspeth's abdication spreads as far and as fast as possible," the Queen continued. "This will give her a greater margin of safety, and confuse Ancar completely. And at the same time, we should see to it that the reports of her demonstration of magical powers are as exaggerated as possible." Selenay smiled slyly. "The more Ancar thinks we have, the less he is likely to attempt a sudden attack. Let him believe that Elspeth brought us an army of mages and peculiar creatures, at least until his own spies tell him otherwise. That will give us some breathing space."

Nods and speculative expressions all around the table. Herald-Captain Kerowyn spoke up—and Talia noticed then with some amusement that in the brief time between when Court had been adjourned and the Council had been called, she had managed to change out of her despised "oh-shoot-me-now" Whites. "This is the time to use those night-message relays, Majesty," she said. "Ancar will be sure to read the messages if we make certain that at least one of the towers 'happens' to reflect to the border when they relay on." She grinned. "We can thank him for that much, at least. Companions and Heralds may be invaluable for carrying messages that are supposed to be secret, but the towers are unmatched for relaying anything you *want* your enemy to know."

"See to it," Selenay said with a nod, and Kerowyn frowned with thought for a moment, then scribbled down the message she wanted relayed and handed it to one of the trainees to take outside.

"Now, how can we use this situation to our best advantage?" the Queen continued. "We have the potential to gain a lot of time here, if we use it well." She looked around the table at her Councillors for suggestions. And now the mood had changed, from one of apprehension to one of anticipation and hope.

Talia relaxed further, and surreptitiously gave Selenay the sign that all was well.

For the moment, at any rate. That was all that anyone could count on right now.

1 1

Elspeth knew that Treyvan and Hydona had resigned themselves to some kind of stabling situation when they reached Haven. Instead, somewhat to their astonishment, the gryphons had been housed in the visiting dignitaries' apartments just like the humans. Elspeth was pleased, but not completely surprised. She had recalled a set of two large rooms usually left empty, meant for receptions and the like. When the Seneschal had told her that the gryphons would be treated like any other diplomatic visitor and housed in the Palace, she thought of those two rooms. A question to the pages the next morning confirmed her guess was right. Those rooms were needed often enough that they remained ready and empty at all times; there was no reason why the gryphons couldn't have them. To reach the second room, you had to go through the first, so the arrangement was perfect. The gryphlets could nest in the inner room, and the adults in the outer.

Elspeth, Darkwind, and Firesong went straight to the reception rooms as soon as she confirmed the gryphons were there. The doors— double doors, like the ones in the Throne Room—were standing partially open, as if the gryphons were inviting visitors to come in. The room was completely empty, except for the lanterns on the wall and the adults' nest. She had expected nests of hay and sticks, however, and was greatly surprised to find that instead they had built "nests" of piles of featherbeds, with tough wool blankets over them to save the beds from the punishing effects of sharp talons.

"Featherbeds?" she asked, raising one eyebrow. "My—how luxurious!"

"And why ssshould we make nessstsss of nassty sssticks when we may have sssoft pillowsss?" Treyvan asked genially, lounging at his ease along one side of the "nest."

"I have no idea," she replied with a laugh that made the feather fastened prominently at the side of her head tremble. "I just wasn't aware that featherbeds were part of a gryphon's natural forests. No one ever told me that there were wild featherbed trees."

"And what made you think we werrre wild creaturesss?" Hydona put in, with a sly tilt of the head. "When have we everrr sssaid thisss?"

"She has you there," Darkwind pointed out. Firesong simply shook his head.

"Do not come to me for answers," the Healing Adept said. "What I do not know about gryphons is far more than what I do know! I cannot help you; for all that *I* know, they could nest in crystal spires, live upon pastries, and build those flying barges that we saw Kaled'a'in use—out of spiderwebs."

"We do not build the barrrgesss," was all that Treyvan would say. "And you know well that we do not eat passstrriess! But thisss iss not the point; what isss—we musst find sssomeone who knowsss what has been going on herrre sssince you left, featherrrlesss daughterrrr." He gave her an opaque look. "Desspite that all ssseemsss quiet, it isss a quiet I do not trrrussst."

Somehow it didn't surprise Elspeth to hear Treyvan call her that, as he called Darkwind "featherless son." His sharp eyes had gone straight to the feather braided into her hair the moment she and Darkwind had entered the room. Although he had said nothing, she knew *he* knew what it meant. She felt warmth and pleasure at the gryphons' approval. She had Starblade and Kethra's approval of this liaison, but in many ways the gryphons were a second set of parents to her lover, and winning their approval as well made her spirits rise with a glow of accomplishment. That glow of accomplishment faded quickly, though. Treyvan was right. This was the calm before the storm, and there was no telling how long the calm would last. Days—weeks—or only candlemarks. Too soon, whenever the storm broke.

"If there is anyone in this Kingdom who knows everything important, it's Herald-Captain Kerowyn," she said decisively. Of course Kero knew everything; she was in charge of Selenay's personal spies, and she might have a good guess as to when this calm *would* end.

"Now, we have two choices," she continued. "We can bring her here or we can go to find her. The latter choice is *not* going to be quiet. Treyvan, you and Hydona are the most conspicuous members of this rather conspicuous group; would you rather we brought her to you, or would you rather that as many people saw you as possible?"

"*I* would rather they stayed put," came a clear, feminine voice from the door, "but that's my choice, not theirs. On the other hand, here I am, so you don't have to come looking for me."

Kerowyn pushed the door completely open and gazed on the lounging gryphons with great interest. "We can move elsewhere if you want," she continued, looking into Treyvan's golden gaze, "but there isn't anywhere much more secure than this room, if you're worried about prying eyes and nosy ears, if I may mix my metaphors."

It was Treyvan who answered. "Yesss, warrriorrr. I am trroubled with thosssse who may overrrhearrr. But I alssso wisssh to know why you wisssh usss to rrremain in ourr aerrrie. You do not trrussst usss, perrrhapsss?"

Elspeth didn't know if Kero could read gryphonic body language, but Treyvan was very suspicious. He did not know what Kero's motives were, and he was not taking anything for granted. This set of rooms could easily turn into a prison.

Kero laughed and entered the room, her boots making remarkably little noise on the granite floor. "Simple enough, good sir. You may have convinced the highborn, Heralds, and Companions that you're relatively harmless, but you haven't gotten to all the servants, and you'll never convince some of the beasts. You go strolling about the grounds without giving me the chance to sweep them first, and you'll panic a dozen gardeners, scare the manure out of most of the horses and donkeys, and cause every pampered lapdog that highborn girls are walking in the garden to keel over dead of fright. You don't *really* want angry gardeners and weeping girls coming in here yapping at you, do you?"

Treyvan snapped his beak mischievously. No matter how serious a situation was, he could find something amusing in it. "No," he replied. "I think not." Already he was relaxing; Kero had put him at his ease.

"Excellent." Kero was not in Whites—as usual. She wore riding leathers of a dusty brown, worn and comfortable, her long blonde hair in a single braid down her back. She turned to give Elspeth a long and considered appraisal, lingering over the new Whites. "Well, what is this all about?" she continued. "Trying to set new fashions?"

Elspeth shrugged. "Whatever. I can promise you I can fight in them.

Not that I expect anyone to be able to get close enough to me to have to deal with them hand-to-hand."

"Oh, really?" Kero turned away—then lunged, with no warning at all, not even by the tensing of a single muscle.

But not unexpectedly; Elspeth had been her pupil for too long ever to be taken by surprise, especially after tossing out a challenge like that one. Instead, it was Kero who got the surprise, as Elspeth lashed out with a mage-born whip of power and knocked her feet out from under her. Kero went down onto the marble floor in a controlled tumble, and if Elspeth had not been as well-trained as she was, Kerowyn could have recovered for another try at her. But Elspeth was not going to give her that chance. She kept a "grip" on Kero's ankles to keep her off her feet, then wrapped her up in an invisible binding. Kero did not resist, as most Valdemarans would have. Elspeth knew she had seen magic often enough when she led the Skybolts as a mercenary company in Rethwellan and southward. She simply waited, lying there passively, until Elspeth released her, then got to her feet, dusting off her hands on her breeches.

"You'll do," was all she said, but Elspeth glowed from the compliment, and Darkwind winked at her.

"And you have learned much of magic, lady," Firesong observed. "Enough to know not to fight mage-bonds, which is far more than anyone else in this land would know. And I am curious to know how you came by this knowledge."

Kero gave Firesong a long and penetrating look; in his turn, he graced her with one of his most charming smiles. It would have taken a colder woman than Kero to ignore that smile; it would have taken a more powerful wizard than Firesong for that smile to affect her. But in the end, she decided to answer him.

"Simple enough; I'm not from around here." That was in Shin'a'in, not Valdemaran; Firesong's eyes widened a trifle and he gave her a look full of respect. Kero looked around for somewhere to sit, and finally chose the side of the gryphons' "nest" by default. "I was born and grew up in the south of Rethwellan. I was the granddaughter of a sorceress, trained by a Shin'a'in Swordsworn who was her partner, adopted as a Clan Friend to Tale'sedrin, then took a place in a merc company. Eventually I got the Captain slot, and circumstances brought us up here." She shrugged. "We hired on because I knew Prince Daren, we both trained with the same Shin'a'in, and the Rethwellans owed the Valdemarans a debt that hadn't been discharged. The Skybolts were part-payment on that debt. Never guessed when we came riding over those mountains down south, I'd lose all my mages and pick up a stubborn white talking horse."

:No more stubborn than you.:

Every Mindspeaker in the room looked startled at that, with the sole exception of Kerowyn. She only sighed. "That was my Companion Sayvil," she said, apologetically. "She can Mindspeak with anyone she pleases, and she won't pretend otherwise like the rest of 'em. Next thing is I expect her to start Mindspeaking people without the Gift. She's gotten worse about it lately."

:That's because there's been more need for it lately. And speaking of "Need"—:

"I suppose the damn sword decided you didn't deserve it or something?" Kero asked. "Or did you get fed up with it and drop it down a well like I threatened to do?"

"She's with Skif's lady, Nyara," Elspeth began, hesitantly addressing the air over Kero's head. "That's a long story and—"

:You!: came another, and far more excited voice. From the other room bounded a startled *kyree*, trailed by the gryphlets. *:You had Need! You! You must be the youngling trained by my famous cousin Warrl! Lady Tarma's pupil! The one Lady Kethry gave Need to!:*

He bounded over and prostrated himself at her feet for a moment, in the *kyree* imitation of a courtly bow. *:I have heard so much about you! My famous cousin Warrl said you were destined for greatness! You must tell me all of your life so that I may make it into stories!:*

All the time that Rris was chattering in open Mindspeech, Kero's face had taken on an expression that Elspeth had never, ever expected to see.

Completely blank, and slack-jawed. She was, quite clearly, taken utterly by surprise.

She recovered fairly quickly, however. "I don't believe this," she said under her breath, as Rris finished and waited eagerly for her answer. "I mean—what are the odds? Who ever sees *one kyree* in a lifetime, much less two, and for the two to be *related?* I just don't by-the-gods believe this!"

Rris took on an air of extreme dignity, and fixed Kero with an admonishing gaze. *:My famous cousin Warrl used to say that there is no such thing as coincidence, only mortals who have not fought the winds of fate.:*

"Your famous cousin Warrl stole that particular proverb from the Shin'a'in he ran with," Kero countered. "It happens to be about five hundred years older than your 'famous cousin Warrl.' And believe me, I fought so-called 'fate' plenty. I don't believe in fate." She shook her head again. "All right, *kyree*—what is your name?"

:Rris,: he said proudly. *:Tale-spinner, History-keeper, and Lesson-teacher of the Hyrrrull Pack.:*

"All right, Rris, I'll tell you everything you'd like to know, *but*—" she interjected, holding up a hand to stave off the eager creature, "—*not now.* We have a lot to do, and I have the depressing feeling we have a very short time to do it in. It's only a matter of time before Ancar hits us, and right now we can only pray he follows his old patterns, and makes several feints and tests before he decides to *truly* come after us. Now, unless I miss my guess, what you lot want is intelligence, right?" She looked around at the others. "Not only what dear Ancar has been up to, but all the things that have happened since Elspeth left."

Firesong nodded for all of them. "And let me get the last two of our group," he said. "Skif and his lady, the current bearer of your mage-sword. I think you will be surprised at what has become of the blade. It has changed, warrior, greatly changed. We wish this kept reasonably secret—but not from you. You, I think, need to know what kind of an ally Need has become."

He turned before anyone could stop him and went off at a brisk walk, robes flowing behind him. He returned quickly with Skif and Nyara. Skif also wore the *hertasi*-designed Whites—Whites with a number of surprises built into them—and Nyara wore a *hertasi*-made surcoat and light armor—though it would have been very difficult for anyone who was not aware that it was armor to recognize it as such. As always, Nyara carried Need sheathed at her side, but before anyone could say anything to either of them, the sword spoke up, and Need's mind-voice was sharp with shock.

:I know you!:

Kero jumped this time, she was so startled. She stared at the blade, and then swore, fervently and creatively, using several languages that Elspeth didn't even recognize and describing several acts that Elspeth thought were anatomically impossible.

"—bloody *hell!*" she finished with a wail, throwing up her hands in despair, as if in petition to the unseen gods. "Isn't it bad enough that I get a lover who takes over my dreams, a talking horse, and a uniform like a target? Isn't it enough that I go from being an honest mercenary to some kind of do-gooder? Does *everything* in my life have to come back to haunt me and *talk in my head?*"

* * *

It took all morning to fill Kero in on everything that had happened to Elspeth, Need, and Skif since they left, but the Herald-Captain refused to impart so much as a rumor before she heard Elspeth's story. Occasionally, Kero fixed the sheathed blade with a sharp glance, and Elspeth suspected that Need was gifting her former bearer with choice comments of her own. They were, in many ways, two of a kind. Evidently Kero began to figure that out for herself, for after a while those pointed glances took on a hint of amusement.

Elspeth was just grateful that *she* wasn't "blessed" with the sword's presence anymore. And she had the feeling that Kero felt the same.

Finally, after a break for a noontime meal, Kero made good on her bargain.

Elspeth had pillows brought in so that they could all sit comfortably, while the gryphons lounged with their forequarters draped over the side of their nest. They sat in a ragged circle, with Kero at one end and the gryphons anchoring the other.

"First of all," she said, playing with the end of her braid as she looked at Elspeth, "I want you all to know that not only do I approve of the way Elspeth handled herself yesterday, but the entire Council still approves of the abdication. It's going to confuse Ancar so much he won't know what to make of it. He'll have to wait to see what his spies have to say about it all before he even begins to plan. He's going to be certain that the abdication was a ruse, until he gets reports that Elspeth really *did* give up all of her power. He's going to be hearing all kinds of rumors, and it's going to drive him crazy. He couldn't imagine anyone *ever* giving up a high position."

"I thought as much," Elspeth said with satisfaction.

"Now I've got a little advice for you and your handsome friend," Kero continued, looking directly and only at Elspeth. "I know you're not the Heir anymore, and who you couple with makes no difference. But there are people who are watching you. Don't make any announcements about pairing up for at least a couple of months; that way no one will think to accuse you of being a softheaded female who lets her heart overrule her head, all right?"

Elspeth raised one eyebrow. "Does it matter if people think I'm a softheaded female? As you just said, who I pair with has no real meaning anymore."

Kero gave her *the look*, a scornful expression that had withered sterner hearts than Elspeth's. "It might not to *you*, but you're an example for others, whether or not you realize it. It might seem very romantic to give up throne and duty for the one you love. I'm sure the younger Bards would be thrilled with such a rich topic for balladeering. No one is going to pay any attention to the fact that you're taking on *more* responsibility as the first Herald-Mage in an age. You fell in love, and told your duty to take a long walk, that's how starry-eyed young fluffheads are going to think of it. And while you're at it, think about the hundreds of young people out there who will *use* that as an excuse to abandon responsibilities of their own because they think they are lifebonded! Some chowderheaded young fool who doesn't know the meaning of the word 'duty' is encouraging them to run off to a life of endless love, that's how it would look. Right now, that's the last thing we need."

Elspeth gnawed her lip for a moment, then nodded, slowly. "I can see your point. I'm still someone that people my age look to for an example, and that's not going to change any time soon, if at all. Well, I'm not going to avoid Darkwind, but we can keep from being blatant about things…"

After all, no one knows what the feather and ring mean but the two of us and the folk that came with us. We can make it public knowledge some time later.

"That's all I ask. *Think* before you do something. Always. You may not be the Heir, but you're going to be just as much in the public eye and mind as before, if not more so. You thought being the Heir was bad, I don't think you've thought about how people are going to react to the first Herald-Mage since Vanyel." Kero smirked with satisfaction. "Well, now to the business of catching up. We have agents in Hardorn, Ancar has agents here, but I'm pretty sure I know who most of his are, and I'm equally sure he *hasn't* caught most of ours, so we're able to feed him inaccurate and incomplete information without getting caught in the same trap. His pattern hasn't changed; whenever he thinks he's found a weak spot in our defenses, he generally pokes at it for a while before he actually mounts an attack. He's given up on assassins for a while, or they've given up on him. Hard to hire people who know the last half-dozen wound up very dead." She smiled grimly.

"That's good," Elspeth said fervently. "That's *very* good! What kind of troop strength has he got?"

Kero grimaced. "That's the bad news. It's formidable, and he outnumbers us about three to two. He has a lot of regular troops as well as a lot of mages. You managed to relay that the barrier at the Border was coming down, so we've been acting as if it wasn't there for about a week or so, though he hasn't tried anything yet. I take it that it is down?"

"Probably," Firesong said, tossing his hair back over his shoulder. "Since one of the signs of that barrier was an inability to work unhindered magic, and both Elspeth and I have been able to do so almost from the moment we arrived, I think we can assume Van—the old spells have been banished."

Kero licked her lips thoughtfully. "Right. Well, those mages run test attacks against our Border outposts on a fairly regular basis, so if he doesn't know the barrier is gone now, he will soon. I think we can probably take it as read that he knows *now*. He's learned more caution after getting thrown back twice; he won't rush into an attack right away, I don't think, even after his usual feints and pokes. The abdication and the appearance of Elspeth as a mage, as well as tales that she brought more mages with her, might give him a little more pause. Every day we make him hesitate is one more day *we* have to prepare for his next try at us, and if there's one thing I *know* will happen, it's that he's going to make a try for us."

All of them nodded as Kero finished. "So whatever we can do to confuse him at the moment is going to be of use," Darkwind replied. "Are we waiting for something, ourselves?"

"We are," Kero told him. "When you said you were coming home, I assumed you were going to find some way to get rid of whatever it was that drove Quenten and my other mages off when the Skybolts came north. So I sent some urgent messages asking him to send me as many mages as he could. There are Heralds down in Rethwellan right now, bringing up as many of his White Winds Journeymen and teachers as care to come."

"White Winds is a good, solid school," Firesong spoke up. "It was founded by a *hertasi* mage. We can work with White Winds mages, and I am relieved to learn we will not be the only teachers of Mage-Gifted Heralds."

"Not by a long shot," Kero assured him. "Quenten's White Winds mages will be right up in the front lines, too. They know we're going to have a fight on our hands, and we won't take anyone who isn't willing to work combat-magic. I've got more mages coming, though—and these, I am afraid, are not going to be as easy to work with. Alberich isn't here because he's down south, too. He's bringing back a load of mage-trained Sun-priestesses from Karse."

"He's *what?*" Elspeth gasped. She stared at Kero, wondering for a single wild moment if her teacher had snapped under the strain and had gone quite mad. She had heard about the alliance, of course, but she had assumed all that meant was that Karse was going to present a united front against Hardorn. She had never dreamed that Karse would provide more than that!

"He's bringing back a group of mage-trained Priestesses of Vkandis from Karse," Kero repeated patiently. "I know it sounds crazy, but in case you didn't get all of it from Rolan, this is what happened. There's been a kind of religious upheaval down there, and the Son of the Sun is now a woman, Solaris. Hellfires, that's been going on since before I became the Skybolts' Captain, but it seems that just after you left, this lady organized every priestess and a lot of the Sunsguard, and made her revolt stick. *She* has been watching the situation between us and Hardorn for some time, ever since she was a junior priestess. By my reckoning, that would have been about the time that Ancar usurped the throne. Evidently Solaris decided that Ancar's a snake, old feuds are not worth dying over, and that if the two female rulers of the lands facing his don't drop their differences and decide we're all girls together, Ancar is eventually going to have *both* for lunch." Kero shrugged. "Sounds like the kind of lady I can get along with. So, that's contingent one and two, both on the way. Contingent three is just now getting organized; Daren got in touch with his brother, and the King of Rethwellan is deciding how many of his court mages he can spare, and how many can be trusted to be of real help. He asked us if we wanted him to recruit, but Daren turned that idea down, since there'd be too good a chance a lot of them would be plants from Ancar."

"That's all very good news," Darkwind observed.

But Elspeth frowned. "It is good news, so why are you worried?" she asked Kero.

The Herald-Captain sighed. "Because even with all that help, we're still outnumbered head-to-head, both in mages and in troops, and that's just the troops we know about."

Elspeth thought back to the last conflict, and the mage-controlled troops Valdemar had faced.

"He can take the peasants right out of the fields and throw them into the front lines," she said slowly, her heart sinking.

Kerowyn nodded grimly. "That's right. Ancar doesn't *care* if his country falls to pieces, so he can conscript as many men to fight as he wants to. He doesn't care if they're decent fighters or not; they're fodder, and he can keep throwing them at our lines until they wear us down."

"You are sssaying that he will rissk ssstarrving hissss own people that he may win hisss warrr?" Hydona said, astonished.

All Elspeth and Kero could do was nod.

But Kero wasn't finished with the bad news. "Last of all, he's got some new mage with him; this one just turned up at Ancar's Court fairly recently, and this one worries me." She bit her lip, and looked from the Tayledras to the gryphons and back. "The fellow is so odd that I'm wondering if you lot can't tell me what we can expect out of him. He looks more than half cat, from what my agents tell me, and he keeps pretty much to himself. Only one of them has seen him, and just for a moment. We don't even know his name for certain—just a guess, Falcon's Breath, Falcon's Death, or something like that."

Falcon's—oh, gods. No.

Elspeth felt as if she had taken a blow to the stomach, and Nyara looked stricken. Firesong bit off an exclamation, and Darkwind a curse. The gryphons both jerked bolt upright. Skif looked quite ready to kill something.

Kero looked around at all of them and raised her eyebrows. "I take it you know this person?"

Darkwind was the first to recover. "You could say that," he replied dryly. *"Will we never be rid of the Beast?"*

The last was half-snarled, and Skif's nostrils flared as he nodded in agreement. Firesong shut his gaping mouth with a snap.

"That sincerely annoys me. I can only ask myself what dark demon holds the Beast in high esteem, that he keeps returning," the Healing Adept said after everyone turned to look at him. He bestowed a look full of irony on Kerowyn. "Twice already he has escaped from situations that should have finished him," Firesong continued, "and the next time I shall not believe he is dead until I burn the body, and sow the ashes with salt!"

"I may assume, then, that this is not good news?" Kero asked mildly.

It was Treyvan who answered that question.

"No, warrriorrrr," he growled, crest and hackles up. His voice was so full of venom that Elspeth hardly recognized it. "Thisss isss not good newssss."

By nightfall, they had a basic plan. Firesong would first find the place where the new Heartstone lay and fully activate it. Then he would roam the Palace with Jeri, looking for the old magic workrooms and any artifacts or books that might still be in existence and stored somewhere other than the Archives. Once the rooms were identified and the artifacts found, he would help Jeri get them properly cleaned and restored to their original functions. He did not expect that to take very long. As soon as the workrooms were ready, Firesong would begin training the strongest of the new mages.

The gryphons would identify any Heralds here at the Collegium that had obvious Mage-Gift and begin their basic training if they were not of such potential that they needed Firesong's attention. If there were any doubts whether or not a Herald had Mage-Gift, Darkwind or Elspeth could pass judgment. Need could as well—but the blade opined that it would be better to keep the fact of her existence as an intelligent personality very quiet. A sentient sword would be certain to attract attention, and all of it the wrong kind.

"This group is strange enough without adding a talking sword," Kero agreed. "Good gods, I don't know how I'm going to explain some of you!"

Meanwhile, until the mages from outKingdom arrived, Darkwind and Elspeth would work with Firesong and the new Heartstone, and search the Archives for "lost" books on magic. *She* was certain that there were books they *needed* hidden in there, and that only the prohibition on magic had kept her from finding them in her earlier searches. Now that the prohibition was gone, she should be able to locate them. While books would not replace a real teacher, they could augment what teachers could do. And they might offer spells none of the Tayledras knew, and clues to what Ancar might muster.

Good plans, all of them. Now they would have to see just how long those plans lasted. The worst of their nightmares was now real. Ancar and Mornelithe Falconsbane appeared to be allies. Add in Hulda, and however many mages Ancar had recruited—and Valdemar was racing against time and the most furious of mage winds.

Only Mornelithe and Ancar knew what they were going to do next. Despite what others said about true mages not guarding against mind-magic, Ancar had long ago learned many of the limits of Heraldic abilities. ForeSight or FarSight, neither worked well against him; all they could do was try to outthink him.

:*What have you learned for us?*: Dawnfire asked An'desha, as Falconsbane dozed in his chair beside the fire. :*Is there anything new?*:

She had appeared in the flames of the fireplace itself; if Falconsbane happened to wake, it would be very easy for her to hide herself and her power away. The Avatars often appeared to him in the fireplace now; with Ancar so on edge, he could and did burst into Falconsbane's rooms at any time, waking the Adept, and An'desha did not dare to be away from the body if that happened. An'desha had learned to manipulate Falconsbane's mind and body to make him more aware of his fatigue. The Adept slept most of the time he spent in his rooms, but he was not aware that he was spending a truly inordinate amount of time in slumber. An'desha saw to it that he ate and drank and cared for himself; the rest of that time An'desha spent in rummaging through Falconsbane's memories.

:I have more of Falconsbane's memories,: he replied, and then, with pardonable pride, added, *:and I have been convincing Falconsbane that the defects and faults in his thinking that I cause by accident are truly caused by Ancar, deliberately, to hamper him. It makes him very angry, and less inclined to aid Ancar willingly.:*

Dawnfire was joined by Tre'valen; a pair of graceful forms of gold and blue, with whitely glowing eyes. This time they had both appeared as hawks of flame, rather than in human form. An'desha found their chosen forms oddly comforting, for they were very clearly vorcel-hawks, and they made him think of home every time he saw them.

:Excellent!: Tre'valen applauded, and An'desha flushed with pride. *:Open your thoughts to us, little one, and we shall search through those new memories of yours. Then tell us what else you have learned as we sort them through.:*

That was done quickly; it was a pity there was so little of substance in the memories. This time An'desha had gotten access to the sculpting and training of Falconsbane's daughter Nyara. He could not think of Nyara as *his* daughter; he had not engendered her, and he certainly had nothing to do with her upbringing. He did, however, feel a kinship to her. It seemed to him that they were siblings of a kind; they had both suffered from Falconsbane's whims, and in similar ways. He could empathize and sympathize with her as no one else could.

But the Avatars found more of interest in those pain-filled memories than he had thought they would. *:Oh, this is excellent,:* Tre'valen applauded. *:We shall be able to help Nyara with this. She will never look entirely human again, but there is much that can be undone, now that we know how it was wrought upon her.:*

He hadn't thought of that! The thought that he might be able to help Nyara, even a little, gave him a great deal of pleasure. There was so little he had been able to do for her, and nothing to save her.

:Falconsbane now moves about the court freely,: he reported, as Dawnfire

and Tre'valen sorted through the memories they had taken from him. :*He does little but observes much, and I am able to watch what he thinks.*: For all of his myriad faults, Falconsbane was no fool, and his observations were always worth making note of. :*He has concluded that Ancar is something of a younger, much clumsier, and stupider version of himself. Ancar rules as he did, by fear. Other than those he thinks are valuable, which are mostly great nobles, no one is truly safe from Ancar's mages or his magic.*:

Tre'valen turned his burning white eyes on An'desha. Strange, how he had no trouble telling the two Avatars apart. :*Why is it that Ancar does not molest his great nobles?*: the shaman-Avatar asked sharply.

:*I can only tell you what Falconsbane thinks,*: he said hesitantly. :*The Adept believes that Ancar himself does not know. He thinks in part that Ancar still fears the power those nobles hold, even though he could eliminate them if he chose—it is a fear from the time when he was still the Prince and had little power but that which he stole. And he believes that in part it is because most of them are still his allies, and he knows that if he betrays them, no one will trust him.*: He hesitated again, then added, :*And Falconsbane thinks he is a fool; if he fears the power of these nobles, he should eliminate them quietly, in ways that seem accidental. This is what he would do.*:

Dawnfire's form writhed and distorted. :*Somehow I am not surprised,*: she commented.

An'desha continued. :*He sees that this is how he himself ruled, but he feels that Ancar is being extremely stupid about it. While Falconsbane could have conquered every one of his own underlings, singly or together, if they had chosen to revolt, he would have had sabotage in place already to destroy them and all they held dear. Ancar would not be able to muster a sufficient defense if all of his underlings attacked at once. So he thinks that Ancar is being very foolhardy.*:

Indeed, Falconsbane's thoughts had been far more contemptuous than that. He felt Ancar should eliminate every risk, and saw his failure to do so as a sign of weakness. An'desha had not been so certain. It seemed to him, after watching Ancar among his courtiers, that the young King felt as long as he kept the *threat* of retaliation before his underlings, but only made examples of those few he did not need, he would succeed. People were often like rabbits; frighten them, and their minds ceased to work. And An'desha was by no means as certain as Falconsbane that the Adept *could* have taken all of his underlings if they had chosen to mass against him. Look what one broken Clan, a pair of gryphons, a couple of Outlanders, and his own daughter had managed to do! Twice, it had only been the intervention of the Goddess and her Avatars that had saved him! No, another sign of the damaged state of Falconsbane's mind was this insane overconfidence, this surety that if only Ancar released the coercions, Mornelithe Falconsbane could conquer any obstacle.

Not that he was aware of what the Goddess had done, nor the gaps in his own reasoning, which surely was the cause for his own foolish bravado.

:You have learned much of this Court. What of Ancar's mages?: Tre'valen asked. *:How do they judge their master? Is there any likelihood they will rise up?:*

An'desha considered the question carefully. *:Hulda is the most powerful,:* he said at last. *:She seems to think that Ancar will never escape her influence, and does not realize that he already has done so. The other mages have a hierarchy of their own—the most powerful is a Blood Mountain sorcerer, Pires Nieth. Falconsbane believes that one has ambitions to rule, himself. He comes of a noble family, possibly is of royal blood by bastardy. Falconsbane thinks that if Hulda and Ancar were both to fall, Pires would attempt to seize the throne for himself. But he is only a Master, and not as learned or powerful even as Ancar, and although he rules the other mages, he lives in fear of both Ancar and Hulda.:*

The Avatars communed silently with each other for a moment; the flames danced and hissed about their fire-winged forms. *:Would he intrigue, do you think?:* Dawnfire asked. *:If you revealed yourself to him, could he be counted upon to help you and aid you in getting rid of Falconsbane?:*

An'desha hesitated, then replied, *:I do not know. Falconsbane considered him as a possible ally against Ancar. The Adept would not trust him, so how could we?:*

Tre'valen nodded. *:A good point.:*

:Besides,: An'desha continued, *:He is a blood-path mage. Ancar will have none about him who are not blood-path mages. These men—they are all men, but Hulda—are evil, foul, and the only reason they are not as foul as Falconsbane himself is because they have fewer years, less power, and less imagination. Witting sacrifice is one thing—:*

:You have no argument from me, youngling,: Tre'valen said, hastily. *:You are right; we cannot trust or foster blood-path mages. It would be obscene.:*

An'desha wished he had some way to make notes of what he wished to tell the Avatars; he always had the feeling he was going to forget something important!

:There is only one other thing,: he said finally. *:Falconsbane would never do anything to aid either Hulda or Ancar because he hates them both, so he is fostering the friction between them. I have been trying to make him think this is a good idea. Am I doing rightly?:*

This time Tre'valen chuckled. *:Anything you can do to bring confusion to this nest of* kresh'ta *will be welcome, youngling. You are doing rightly, indeed.:*

The fire popped loudly, and Falconsbane stirred uneasily. He was about to wake.

:Farewell!: Dawnfire said hastily—

—and the Avatars were gone, in the space of an eyeblink.

An'desha withdrew as well, to watch and wait.

Falconsbane stirred as the fire popped again, sending a coal onto the hearth. He opened his eyes, and the coal glared at him from the hearthstone, a baleful fiery eye. He was vaguely aware that there had been something else that had disturbed his sleep but was unable to identify it.

With what had become a habit, he cursed his captor for the clumsy, too-restrictive spells that were making it harder and harder to think or react properly. If that idiot Ancar were only half the mage he thought he was—!

And as if the thought had summoned him, footsteps in the hall heralded Ancar's arrival.

As usual, he burst through the door with no warning and no consideration, as if Falconsbane, like the rooms themselves, was his own personal property. And as usual, he squinted against the perpetual darkness that Falconsbane cloaked himself and his apartment in, a darkness that Falconsbane enhanced with a touch of magery. If the little brat could not learn to announce himself, then Falconsbane would not make it easy for him to fling himself into the suite at will!

"Falconsbane?" Ancar said, peering around the room, and looking, as usual, for a form in one of the hearthside chairs. "Ah—there you are!"

Mornelithe sighed, as Ancar flung himself into the other chair. At least the child didn't have the nerve to order *him* to stand! "I am very fatigued, Majesty," he said, making no effort to mask the boredom in his voice. "What is it that you require of me this time? I fear that no matter what it is, I have little energy to spare for it."

In fact, he was lying; after disposing of a pair of Ancar's political prisoners, he was very nearly at full strength. Granted, he did seem to be sleeping a great deal, but that could be accounted for by the damages he had taken and the coercions he was under. Those things affected the mind and the body, and he did not wish to spare the energy needed to fight the coercions when he might use that same energy to break Ancar.

So far as pure mage-energy, rather than physical energy, was concerned, he felt confident that there was very little he *couldn't* do—if he had not been so hedged about with Ancar's controlling spells.

But he was certainly not going to tell Ancar that.

"I just received word from the border with Valdemar," Ancar blurted, in a state of high excitement. Falconsbane was taken aback by the level of that excitement, the tight anticipation in Ancar's voice. The youngster was as taut as a harpstring! "The barrier against magic is *gone*. I am calling a council of mages; how long until you feel up to joining it?"

Gone? That unbreakable, stubborn barrier was *gone?* Falconsbane's interest stirred, in spite of himself, and his attempt to maintain a pose of indifference and exhaustion. "Not long, a matter of moments—" he began, cautiously, trying to collect his thoughts.

"Good. Come along, then. The walk will wake you up." Ancar sprang to his feet, and Falconsbane fought being pulled out of his chair. Not physically, but via magic, as the young King used his spells to attempt to make Mornelithe rise and follow him. Both the exercise of the coercions and Falconsbane's resistance were automatic. Like the response of a plant to light, or the strike of a snake at prey.

Then he abandoned his struggle, and permitted the King to force his reluctant body to obey. After all, what was the point? He wasted more energy in fighting than he could really afford, and there was no telling when Ancar might send him another prisoner. At the moment Ancar was so wrought up by the news from the border that he wasn't paying a great deal of attention to anything else anyway. Falconsbane wasn't going to make a point of resisting if the King didn't even notice what he was doing.

As they left Mornelithe's rooms, three pairs of guards that had been waiting on either side of the door fell in behind them. The Adept raised a purely mental eyebrow at that. Evidently either Ancar feared attack in his own halls, or else he was not taking any chances on Falconsbane's willingness to come to this "council" of his.

Interesting, in either case. Could it be that he sensed his own coercions weakening, and now was ensuring his captive's compliance with more physical and tangible means?

Ancar led the way out of the guest quarters and down a staircase into a series of dark, stone-faced halls in a direction Falconsbane had never taken. There were no servants about, but several times Falconsbane thought he smelled the scent of cooking food wafting down from above. It must be nearly dinner time, then, and not as late as he had thought.

Finally, Ancar stopped and stood aside while one of his guards opened a perfectly ordinary wooden door, revealing a room that was not ordinary at all.

It was swathed from ceiling to floor in curtains of red satin, and the only furniture in it was a single, large table, with a thronelike chair at one end (currently empty) and several more well-padded chairs on the other three sides. One of those chairs, the one at the throne's right hand, stood empty.

Hulda, looking extremely alert, impeccably and modestly gowned, and without any trace of the sullen sensuality she normally displayed, sat to the throne's immediate left. Her violet eyes fastened on Ancar and Falconsbane, and her lips tightened slightly. More people—all male, mostly the same age as Ancar, and presumably some of his best mages— occupied the other chairs. Most of them Falconsbane recognized; others he had never seen before. All of them wore the same expression of baffled and puzzled excitement, mixed, in varying degrees, with apprehension.

Ancar went straight to the throne and sat down, leaving Falconsbane to make his own way to the sole remaining seat and take it. He did so, taking his time, cloaking his displeasure in immense dignity, wondering if that right-hand seat had been left vacant at Ancar's orders, or not, and what it might mean that it had been left unoccupied. Was it simply that no one else wished to be that close to Ancar, or was Ancar giving a silent but unmistakable sign of Falconsbane's status among the mages by ordering it to stand empty until the Adept arrived?

Ample illumination came from mage-lights hovering above the table; a frivolous display by Falconsbane's reckoning, but there were a few of Ancar's mages who were fairly useless, and could easily be spared to maintain them. It did eliminate the need for servants to come in and tend candles or lanterns, and if this chamber was used for magical purposes, it was best that only a few people ever had access to it. Ancar waited until Falconsbane had taken his seat, and complete silence fell across the table. There was not so much as a whisper.

He did not stand, but he held all eyes. He waited a moment longer, while the silence thickened, and then broke it.

"I have heard from my mages in the West. The barrier that prevents magic from passing the border with Valdemar is down," he said, his voice tense with excitement and anticipation. "It appears to be gone completely. My mages at the border assure me that we can attack at will."

From the stunned looks on the faces of every other mage, including Hulda, Falconsbane concluded that he was the only one besides Ancar to whom this did not come as a revelation. There was a moment more of silence, then all of them tried to speak at once. Hulda was the only one that maintained a semblance of calm; the rest gestured, shouted, even leapt to their feet in an effort to be heard.

The cacophony was deafening, and Falconsbane gave up on trying to understand a single word. Ancar watched all of his mages striving for his attention, each one doing anything short of murder in order to have his say, and the King's face wore a tiny smile of satisfaction. He was enjoying this; enjoying both the fact that the barrier was down and his will would no longer be thwarted, and enjoying being the center of attention.

Then he held up his hand, and the clamor stopped as suddenly as it had started. His smile broadened, and Falconsbane suppressed a flicker of contempt. Pathetic puppy.

He pointed at Hulda, who alone had not contributed to the clamor. She frowned at him, presumably at being designated to speak with such casual disregard for her importance. But that didn't prevent her from speaking up immediately.

"We should be careful," she said, looking cool, intelligent, and businesslike. "We should test the waters first, many, many times, before we even make any plans to attack, much less mount an actual attack. We don't know how or why this happened, but in my opinion, this is very likely to be a trap. Every weakness we have seen in the past has proved to be a trap, and if the pattern holds, this will be as well. The Valdemarans are treacherous and tricky, and this could be just one more trick in a long history of such things. It would be only too easy for them to lure us across their border, then close the jaws of such a trap on us." She shrugged. "They've done so often enough, and they've eaten away at our strength while losing little of their own."

Falconsbane smiled, but only to himself, at the idea of Hulda calling anyone "treacherous and tricky." Then again, it took a traitor to recognize one.

"Precisely!" the mage Pires Nieth cried out before Ancar could designate another to speak. He jumped to his feet, his disheveled hair and beard standing out from his face, making him look like an animal suddenly awakened from a long winter's sleep. "Hulda is right! That was exactly what I wished to say! This requires extreme caution; the Valdemarans have tricked us before by pretending to know nothing of magic, yet turning it on our own troops, and—"

The clamor broke out again, but from what Falconsbane could make out, the consensus was that all of the mages were for caution. Interesting, since from what he had observed, the mages were usually divided on any given subject except when Ancar had previously expressed his own opinion. And from the faint frown on Ancar's face, this did not suit his intentions at all. But there were also signs of hesitation there. Falconsbane guessed that this was an old argument, and that it was one those in favor of caution generally won.

As they babbled on, each one more vehement than the last in urging restraint, Falconsbane analyzed his observations and began to formulate a plan. One thing in particular surprised him, and that was the reaction of Ancar's mages. Apparently, whatever had brought this "barrier" down, it was none of *their* doing. And what truly amazed him was that none of them had the audacity or the brains to claim that it was!

Well, if they would not, Falconsbane would make up for their lack of will and wit. This was another opportunity to impress on Ancar what he could do—and imply he might be able to accomplish far more, if given a free hand. Perhaps this time Ancar might be impressed enough to actually do something.

He let the other mages talk themselves into a standstill, while Ancar's frown deepened, until they began to notice his patent disapproval of their advice. The voices faded, and finally died altogether, leaving an ominous silence. Not even the curtains moved.

Into this silence, Falconsbane dropped his words, cool stones into a waiting pool.

"I am pleased to learn that my tireless efforts upon King Ancar's behalf have not gone unrewarded," he said casually, as if it were of little matter to him. "The cost to me in fatigue has been inconvenient."

There. Now he had a plausible explanation for spending so much time asleep in his rooms, as well as riveting Ancar's attention and gratitude—such as it was—on him. And he had just established himself, not only as Ancar's foreign ally, but as a more potent mage than any in this group. Given the combination of events and the fact that he could now, easily, take on anything covert Hulda would dare to try against him—if she did dare—he felt fairly secure against the woman's machinations.

Ancar's head snapped around, and the King stared into his eyes, dumbfounded. Clearly, this was the very last thing he had expected from his tame Adept.

"*You* broke the barrier?" he blurted. "But—you said nothing of this!"

"You woke me from a sound sleep, Majesty," Falconsbane said smoothly. "I am hardly at my best when half awake. I have labored long and hard in your aid, and I am simply pleased to learn that those labors have borne fruit. It seemed to me that there was no reason to raise your hopes by telling you what I was attempting, when the barrier was at such a great physical distance and I was laboring under so very many handicaps. I never promise what I cannot deliver."

That, in light of the many wonders he had heard Ancar's other mages promise and fail to perform, was a direct slap at most of them. As they gaped at him, he continued, "I dare say that there is no reason to be overly cautious in the light of this development, since it was our doing and not some plot of the Valdemarans. I will be able to do far more for you when I am under less constraint, of course..."

He hoped then that Ancar would say or do something, but his rivals in magic were not about to accept his claims tamely.

Again all the other mages began talking at once, pointing out that there was no way of knowing for certain that it had been Falconsbane who had broken the barrier, each of them eager to discredit him. Mornelithe himself simply ignored their noise, smiling slightly, and steepling his hands in front of his face. It was better not to try to refute them. If he looked as if he did not care, Ancar was more likely to believe he really *had* worked this little miracle.

Or, as one of his long-ago teachers once said, "Tell a big enough lie, and everyone will believe it simply because it is too audacious not to be the truth."

Finally, Ancar brought it all to a halt by raising his hands for quiet.

Silence fell over the table, immediate and absolute. Ancar had his mages firmly under his thumb, that much was certain.

"It does not matter if Mornelithe Falconsbane proves to you that he broke the barrier or not," Ancar said sternly. "It does not even matter to you if I assume that he did. Nothing among the lot of you has changed. The essential fact is that all of *you* have worked in vain to take it down. Now, it is down. And I intend to do something to take advantage of that fact!"

At that, every one of the mages at the table, except for Hulda, looked both chastised and as if he wished he was somewhere else.

And given Ancar's record in the past, perhaps they had reason to wish just that. He had lost more than one of his higher-ranking mages to the Valdemarans during the last two attempts to take their border. Right now, they were probably recalling that and wondering what they could do to keep them from being singled out to "test" whether or not that barrier was really gone. None of them had any wish to risk his precious skin against the Valdemarans. All of them would welcome some idea that would save them from that fate. They licked dry lips and glanced nervously about, and it was fairly obvious that they were unused to really thinking for themselves, or coming up with plans on the spur of the moment.

Once again, it was Falconsbane who broke the thickening and apprehensive silence. This should earn him the gratitude, and at least the temporary support, of every man at this table. Yes, and the woman, too, if she could see a way to profit by it.

"My lord," he said, addressing Ancar directly and ignoring everyone else, "do the lives of common folk in your foot-troops mean anything to you? Are they valuable? Have you any shortage of conscripts? Can you swell your ranks again if they die by the company?"

Ancar stared at him as if he had been speaking Tayledras or Shin'a'in; completely without understanding. Perhaps the concept of valuing the lives of fighters was foreign to him. It would have been foreign to Falconsbane as well, except that he had been in a situation or two where the troops he had were all he would get. At that point, by definition, those lives had value. But finally, Ancar answered.

"Of course not," the King said impatiently, as if only a fool would ask such a question. "I have an endless supply of peasant boys from women who whelp them like puppies. I have mage-controlled troops, and it does not matter if they are real fighters, boys, or graybeards. They will obey and fight as I please, and there are always plenty of peasants from the same source to conscript when they fall."

He did not mention that he had tried armed force before, and failed. Instead, he was giving Falconsbane the compliment of assuming the Adept must have a different plan than the one that had failed.

Falconsbane smiled. "Ah, good," he replied, genially. "That is, on occasion, a concern. If there happens to be a shortage of fighters, or there is no way to make reliable fighters of peasantry, then one must be careful of how the troops are disposed. But in your case—there is your answer. If the lives of troops are meaningless, my lord, then *spend* them."

Ancar shook his head. "Spend them?" he repeated, baffled.

Falconsbane leaned forward over the table, underscoring his intensity with his posture, and the nearest of the mages drew back a little before the avid hunger in his eyes. *"Use* them, my lord. What does it matter if this is a trap? Throw lives at a weak point until you seize it! Their controlling spells will hold past the border now, you have no need to fear that they will no longer obey you once you cross it. So throw them at the border, at one spot, in numbers too great for the Valdemarans to counter." His smile broadened. "I would venture to say that the Valdemarans have a witless concern over the loss of their fighters. That can be used against them, and it is a potent weapon in your arsenal. Throw your troops at the border, march them over the top of their own dead. Take a position, hold it, fortify it, and use it to take another position. Take *land*, my lord, and eat into their side as a canker-worm eats a rosebud. Ignore losses, ignore other targets. Take land, and cut Valdemar in half. If lives do not matter, then use them up to your advantage."

Ancar stared at him, eyes wide, but now it was with an unholy glee, and he drank in the words as a religious zealot would drink in holy writ. Falconsbane mentally congratulated himself. Ancar had known that he was valuable for what he knew. Now the boy knew he was valuable for his intelligence as well.

"Morale is no question when dealing with controlled troops," he added, "but it will be for the Valdemarans. And that is a weapon, as well. Think of how their hearts will quail, when they see the enemy continuing to come, grinding the bodies of their own dead beneath uncaring boots. Think of how they will falter and fail—and finally, flee."

"Yes!" Ancar shouted, crashing his fist down on the table and making his mages jump nervously. "That is precisely what we should do!" He began drawing an invisible diagram on the table with his finger, but only about half his mages bent to follow it. That was the half that Falconsbane needed to keep an eye on, the ones that might, possibly, prove dangerous. "We keep the mages in the rear, where they can be protected by the entire army—and we throw the mage-controlled troops at the border! That is the perfect use of our resources! And when Selenay—"

"No, my lord," Falconsbane interrupted, quickly. The boy was obsessed with the Valdemaran Queen, and now was not the time to permit him to fall into that trap. "Do not make the mistake that has haunted you in the past. Ignore the monarch, ignore your personal enemies. You will have time enough and leisure enough to work your will on them when you have conquered their kingdom. *Land*, my lord. Concentrate only on taking *land*. Capturing and holding large pieces of Valdemar itself. Nothing else."

"This will require a great deal of energy," Hulda interjected. From the expression on her face, thoughtful, and now a little alarmed, Falconsbane judged that she had finally been shaken out of her complacency. She was thinking fast, and did not want to be left out of this, with Falconsbane taking credit not only for breaking the barrier, but for coming up with a battle plan as well. "But it will grant us a great deal *more* energy to replace it!" She turned a brilliant smile on Ancar, but one that was as bloodthirsty as it was broad. "Think of all of the troops, both ours and theirs, dying, and in their deaths, supplying a great crimson stream of blood-magic! Sacrifices, by the hundreds, thousands! We will get back twice the power we expend to control the troops. This is a brilliant plan—"

She smiled brightly at Falconsbane, a smile poisoned with malicious hatred. Falconsbane only raised his eyebrow a trifle.

"—and it is one that, properly managed, will gain us more than we could possibly lose even at the worst case." She settled back in her chair, serene in her confidence that she had at least added her own direction to the flood tide.

But Falconsbane was not yet done.

"In addition, my lord," he continued, seeming to watch only Ancar, but keeping a stealthy eye on Hulda as well, "I would like to add something else for your contemplation. There is another consideration entirely. You have an envoy from the Eastern Emperor here at your court."

Hulda sat bolt upright and fixed him with a hard stare. Ancar nodded cautiously. Obviously he did not see where this was going.

Falconsbane held on to his patience. If this had been a child of his, he'd have had the youngling whipped for stupidity a hundred times over by now.

"You need to give this man information to send his master. You need it to be information of a certain kind. You must show him that you are a powerful ruler. By displaying this kind of—initiative—I think you will give this envoy a great deal to think on. By showing that you know the best way to use your resources, I think you will impress him with your ability to take advantage of any opportunity you are given." He narrowed his eyes a little, and pointed a finger at Ancar. "But most of all, by displaying a ruthless hand toward your own troops, you will prove to him and to his master that you are not to be trifled with."

Ancar smiled broadly, and Hulda's face had become an unreadable mask.

What Falconsbane had suspected, Hulda had just confirmed, although he doubted that Ancar realized this. Hulda was either an ally of the envoy, or a spy of the Emperor. Whether this was an arrangement of long standing or a recent development, it did not matter. The interests of Hulda and that of the Empire were the same, and Ancar was a fool not to have seen it.

This would give him another source of friction between the two of them. Things were looking up.

"You show another side of your powers that I had not expected, Mornelithe Falconsbane," the King replied, unable to keep the glee out of his voice. "And your reasoning is sound. I should have added you to my councillors long ago."

He looked at Hulda. She kept her face as smooth and expressionless as a statue.

"Very sound," Ancar repeated, with emphasis.

He stood up, and looked down at all of them. No one disagreed this time.

"So be it," he said. "We are agreed on a strategy. I will issue the orders immediately. Fedris, Bryon, Willem, you will go with the first contingent of troops to control them. More will follow. Do not risk yourselves, but make certain you drain every bit of blood-magic energy that comes from their deaths."

He looked around the table once again, and his smile did not fade. Nor did Falconsbane's.

"You may leave," King Ancar said, and the smile he wore was the mirror of Falconsbane's.

1 2

"So this is the Heartstone?"

Elspeth sneezed; the dust still in the air even after the room had been cleaned was thick enough to make her eyes water. Even Firesong's bondbird looked dusty—and not at all pleased about it. "Our little gift from V—ah—You Know." She was a little uneasy about mentioning her ancestor. You never knew who might be listening.

"Indeed, and although I assume You Know made it, I truly have *no* idea how this one was made in the first place," Firesong replied ruefully. He appeared to feel the same as she did about saying Vanyel's name out loud. "I seem to be saying that a great deal lately."

The firebird tipped its head sideways, giving him an odd look. He laughed a little, and Elspeth grinned a little, despite the undercurrent of unease she had felt since she got up this morning. "Well, now you have some idea of how much there is that you don't know," she told him, with mockery in her voice. "You can start feeling like the rest of us mortals. Trust me, you'll get used to it."

She turned her attention back to the large globe of crystal on the table in front of her, rubbing her nose to make it stop itching. It didn't work, and she sneezed again.

This Heartstone did not look much like the one she had seen in k'Sheyna Vale. *That* had been a tall, tooth-shaped piece of rough stone set in the center of an open glade, alive with power, but with a cracked and crazed surface and a definite feeling of *wrongness* about it. Not a neatly spherical piece of crystal the size of her head, swirled with hints of color, sitting in the middle of a stone table.

In fact, this room did not look much out of the ordinary at all. It was a direct copy of one on the ground floor of the Palace, one that was probably right above it, if Elspeth had reckoned her distances and angles right. Or maybe—no, probably, this room had to be *much* older—that room was a copy of this one. Why copy it? Perhaps to throw off enemies who were looking for it; this, if she had understood Vanyel correctly, was the physical link to the Web of power that bound all Heralds and all Companions together. Or perhaps the room had been copied because of the magic-prohibition; something like it was needed, but people kept "forgetting" this room existed. Certainly the servants had been surprised to discover a door behind the paintings stacked against it, despite the fact that the door was clearly visible in bright lantern light.

The room itself was not very large; just barely big enough for the round table in the middle and the padded benches around it. The table itself would seat four comfortably, and eight if they were very good friends. A single lantern suspended above the center of that table gave all the light that there was, and that wasn't much; it had been designed to leave the room in a state of twilight, even when the wick was set at its brightest. And in the middle of the table, a globe of pure crystal sat in isolated splendor. Just exactly the same as the room upstairs.

But that was where the similarities with the other room ended. That one was used often for FarSeers, when they needed to exercise their Gift in an atmosphere of undisturbed quiet so that they could concentrate. The crystal globe in the center of the table was used to help them focus that concentration, and it could be picked up and moved, although with difficulty. The globe was very heavy, and the center of the table had a depression carved into it so that the globe could not be moved by accident. That sphere of crystal *was* disturbed often enough that there were a few chips in it, from times when it had rolled off the table and fallen onto the floor. When there were too many chips, someone would take it to one of the jewelers to have it polished smooth again.

The table here was stone, not wood, as were the benches. A lot of the dust had come from cushions that had disintegrated, cushions that Firesong had already replaced. It would take an earthquake that leveled Haven to get *this* globe of crystal to move, and Elspeth was not certain even that would do it. The globe was fused somehow into the stone surface of the table, and the stone pillar supporting the table fused with the stone of the floor.

Firesong assured her that the stone of the floor at that point was fused with the very bedrock the Palace rested on. This arrangement was quite literally a single piece of rock now, and even if the Palace was demolished, that pillar of stone would probably still stand.

No, she decided, it would take more than a mere earthquake or human clumsiness to move *this* crystal stone!

"No one in my knowledge has ever *created* a Heartstone like this one," Firesong told her. "Normally, we simply choose an appropriate outcropping in our Vales—one that goes down to bedrock—and make it into the Heartstone. I don't know of anyone who has ever fused several disparate pieces of stone with the bedrock." The firebird jumped off his shoulder to the table, and stalked over to the crystal globe to examine it with immense dignity from all sides. It even pecked the surface once or twice, but Elspeth did not for a moment assume it was being "birdlike." A bird's eyes saw the world very differently than a human's, and it was entirely possible that Firesong's bondbird was examining the crystal for his bondmate.

The stone itself glowed, very faintly, even to normal sight. The servants had seen that, and commented about it, as they were lighting the lamp. Interestingly, the glow didn't alarm them as Elspeth had assumed it would. There was something very welcoming about this room, very comfortable. One immediately felt at ease, calm, and ready to work.

The visible glow was dim, but to anyone with Mage-Sight, the stone pulsed with power, brightening and dimming with a steady rhythm that Elspeth could only liken to a heartbeat, though one much slower than any human's. Little chasings of sparkles danced across it from time to time.

The other way this room differed was not only in age, but in *feeling*.

Aside from the atmosphere of welcome, there was also an atmosphere of detachment and isolation. Outside sounds were muffled in the room above this one, so that the ringing of the Collegium bells could only be heard faintly. In this chamber, they could not be heard at all. Once the door closed, the Palace seemed to fall away, and as she stood here, the very silence took on a presence, as if every other human being was hundreds of leagues away.

"It is shielded," Firesong said. "The room, I mean. It is shielded as heavily as if it were a mage's workroom, although it appears that you and I and Darkwind have been given the key to those shields. They are powerful, layered, and very old; this room should be able to contain anything. As it must be, if it is to contain a Heartstone and yet be in the center of a populous area. The people of Haven are clearly not prepared to live with the energies of such magics." He raised a snow-white eyebrow at her. "For that matter, I do not know what such magics would do to those who are not Tayledras. There might be problems that one would never encounter in a Vale."

Elspeth licked her lips, and nodded. "I agree with you," she said. Those energies were very real to her; she felt them on her skin, like warm sunlight. They were not unpleasant, not at all, and she had Vanyel's word that she would come to no harm from them, but they were nothing she would want an ordinary person exposed to. These energies might not harm, say, a woman with child—but what if that woman were not a mage? Mages automatically took in energy and incorporated it into themselves, but what if it was not incorporated? All Tayledras were, at least to a tiny extent, mages. It was *born* into them, a gift from their Goddess. What would not harm them might harm someone from outClan.

Mage-energies radiating from the globe made her grateful that Firesong had thought to shield the servants before he allowed them in here to clean. This was like basking in warm summer sunlight! Now she really *knew* why working with this kind of magic bleached the Hawkbrothers' hair and eyes to silver and blue. Firesong had told her that working with node-energy did the same to all Adepts, but living with a Heartstone made it happen more quickly to Tayledras. And for those who actually worked with a Heartstone—well, he claimed his hair was white by the time he was ten. She believed him now. She wondered how long it would take hers to make the change, for when she had looked in the mirror this morning, there had been streaks of silver as wide as her thumb running through her hair, and her eyes were already lighter than they had been. Actually, she had rather liked the effect.

At least when her mother looked at her now, she would never again be haunted by her resemblance to her late and unlamented father.

Actually, maybe it was seeing all the silver hair that made her realize I wasn't her baby anymore... Hmm. Maybe seeing the silver hair was what convinced the Court and Council that I knew what I was doing! People tended to listen more closely to someone their eyes told them was old enough to have attained some wisdom. There could be unexpected benefits to this bleaching business!

"The last of the workrooms is clean," she told the Adept, who had taken a seat on one of the benches and was staring into the Heartstone with a little smile of bemused content. "We moved things that were being stored up into the attics, and the few people who were using them for living places or offices have gotten space elsewhere. They're ready to use, as soon as you have a student you think is dangerous enough to need them."

"Ah, good," he said, proving by his immediate answer that he wasn't as entranced as he looked. "We will be ready for them soon enough. Within a day or two, I think. At the moment you are the only Adept among the Heralds, but that could change at any time. With so many out in the field, one never knows what may ride in."

She nodded. "I think if there really *is* an Adept-potential riding circuit, he or she will be coming in within the next couple of days, Firesong. Remember, the Web holds us all, and the Web 'knows' we need all the strong Mage-Gifts that are out there. Strongly Gifted people are not going to have a choice; *something* will bring them in."

Firesong tilted his head to one side to look at her, and tucked the curtain of his hair behind his ear absently. "Interesting. Very useful." He returned his gaze to the globe of crystal for a moment, as if he might see a vision of those Heralds in its depths. "And have you located all of the books and manuscripts on magic and the histories of Herald-Mages?"

She nodded, as he looked up again. "I think so," she said. "At least, if there are any more, they're hidden in shielded places I can't sense. Thank you for pointing out that books used around magic would pick up some contamination and be visible to Mage-Sight. I never would have found most of them if you hadn't mentioned that."

He simply smiled. "Then let me borrow a single moment of your time. I believe the Stone and I are in full accord now. I know that it is completely active. So there is only one more thing to do, so far as you are concerned—the little triggering I told you of."

Time for him to introduce me—us—to it. Despite Firesong's assurances that the Stone was quite safe, she shivered a little. Her only experience with a Heartstone was with the damaged rogue in k'Sheyna Vale, the "parent," as it were, of this one. It had not been in the least pleasant. On the other hand, if she were going to work as a full Tayledras-trained Adept, she must be able to use not only node-energies, but the powers of her Heartstone. The latter would give her the power to set magics that would outlive her, something few mages ever succeeded in doing. This Heartstone *seemed* "friendly." Yet it had come from a Stone that had tried to kill more than one of the Tayledras she knew, and had succeeded with those she hadn't known.

But she trusted Firesong. He said this Stone was not only safe, but it *must* be keyed to her, even as the shields around this room were keyed to her, so that she, in turn, could key it to other Adepts. Not just her, but Gwena as well—magically speaking, she and Gwena were bonded as closely as a lifebonded couple. So, with some trepidation, she opened herself completely to Gwena, then put her mental "hand" in Firesong's and closed her eyes.

Suddenly, she was enveloped by light and welcome; and a sense of something very, very old, and at the same time, very, very young. The age of stone, the youth of pure power, both were part of this thing that took her into itself.

:Oh, my—: she heard Gwena exclaim, and knew that her Companion had encountered the same feelings. And this was nothing she had expected. There was intelligence, of a sort, but not a "mind." At least, it was nothing she recognized as a mind. Fortunately, it was also utterly unlike the angry, unstable "intelligence" of the k'Sheyna Stone. This intelligence, whatever it was, had a far different view of "time" than she did, and if it had thoughts, they were so alien she could not even begin to grasp them.

But it was alive, there was absolutely no doubt in her mind about that. It recognized the two of them, and it welcomed her and Gwena both and would do so in the future. They "belonged" now. It would give her whatever power she needed, so long as she was in reach. That was what it was supposed to do.

Here was the moment of truth that made her Tayledras; a Heartstone's power was meant for the good of the Clan as a whole—which in her case, was all of Valdemar—and not to be used for an individual's needs. The shielding and the Veils that protected a Vale, the power to sculpt the rocks and create the springs, the force that grew the trees that supported up to a dozen *ekeles* apiece, all this came from the Heartstone. Excess energies were cleansed and stored there, for the use of all.

And for the moment, all that she wanted it to do was to help her create a mage-shield around Haven. For the protection of all. She sensed Firesong's approval as she began.

Not too much protection, for that would block Mindspeech and other Gifts, but about the same as the Vales had when they were not under siege. Firesong understood what she wanted, and lent his own expertise, guiding her, but letting her set her own pace. He had done this before and cheerfully encouraged her as he showed her exactly what needed to be done. But *she* needed to do the actual work; this was her land, her "Vale," her Heartstone.

To her surprise, she discovered that most of what was needed was already in place; either Vanyel's work, or Firesong's, or both. Much of it had a feeling of great age about it. It was possible that there had been mage-shields here before, and they had simply faded with time, leaving behind a framework for her to invest with the new power at her disposal. All she needed to do, really, was to give the shield its proper shape, and define her protections...

When she opened her eyes again, she was sweating with exertion and very tired, but Firesong nodded at her with the satisfaction of a teacher who has just seen his student complete a lesson perfectly. "Good!" he said. "Excellent! Now, since that shield is linked with this Heartstone, and not to *you*, it will hold even after you are gone or dead. That is the advantage of a Heartstone; the magics linked to it are perpetuated long past the death of the caster. Any other spells fade when the caster becomes depleted or dies. Distance can weaken the magic, too. That is why, when an Adept creates a Great Work, he tries to remain with it as much as possible—or else he does it in concert with others of his school and links it to their collective powers. That way the burden can be shared, or even passed on to students. The White Winds and Blue Mountain mages work that way, for instance."

That made sense. She wiped her forehead with a handkerchief and nodded. "I can see that—but there *are* magical devices and artifacts. I distinctly remember Need showing us that she used one to make spell-impregnated swords. Doesn't that imply that some magic *can* be put into things permanently?"

Firesong made a face, and shrugged. "Surely. But *I* do not know how to do so. Perhaps, at some point, that so-stubborn blade may be willing to show us. Until then I must go on as I have."

Well, that made sense, too. She changed the subject. "Should we go see how the gryphons are doing? Treyvan said his batch might be able to start doing something about the wizard-weather today, and I'd like to be there when they start."

"So they have come along that quickly?" Firesong said, with pleasure and surprise. "Wonderful! I should like to see this as well, and select those who might need extra tutoring. We cannot begin teaching them combative magics soon enough. Every hour we gain against the Beast must be used."

Together they left the room, closing the door behind them and blowing out the lantern beside it. Elspeth was surprised at how well the gray wood of the door seemed to fade into the gray stone of the wall in the half-light of the corridor, and Firesong winked at her. "Camouflage of a sort," he told her. "Those who do not need to find this room, probably will not be able to, even though they will no longer 'forget' it existed. This is not a spell, just good building. That was, in part, how it managed to remain overlooked all these years."

They took the steps up to the ground floor, then found one of the corridors leading to a door into the gardens. Treyvan was teaching his "fledgling mages" in an old building in the gardens, a storage shed that had been built in the form of an ornamental tower, complete to being made of stone. It was only three stories tall, but it had a good flat roof and a fine view of the countryside on clear days. It had been placed in a grove of dwarf trees and proportioned to them, so that it appeared to be much taller than it really was. On a clear day, one could see every detail of Elspeth's old pottery shed from its rooftop.

This was not a clear day, however, and the view from the top could be a perilous one in ugly weather. And it had been ugly, ever since the new Heartstone came to rest here. That should change over the course of the next few days; it would take a while to get the local patterns to return. Now the Stone was properly activated, properly shielded, and under supervision. Firesong had done a little about the mage-born storms plaguing the capital, but he had been too busy to learn as much as he needed to about the countryside, so he had erred on the side of caution, refusing to do very much. Another storm had threatened all day without breaking, bringing high winds and moisture-filled clouds in from the east.

The wind whipped their clothes around them; Firesong had dressed for working in the dust of the Heartstone room, wearing relatively subdued grays and greens, but his costume was still that of a Tayledras mage, and as the wind caught his sleeves and hems, it made him look as if he were being attacked by his own clothing. The firebird narrowed its eyes to slits and clung to the padding of his shoulder, hunching down and practically gluing itself to his neck. His hair streamed out behind him, a creature of a hundred wildly whipping tentacles.

:I would not want to have to comb out that hair,: Gwena commented. Elspeth agreed; when the wind got through with it, he'd probably spend hours teasing out all the knots. No wonder the scouts wore theirs short!

:Oh, he'll find someone who's willing to comb it out for him, Gwena,: Elspeth responded cheerfully. *:I've heard rumors of a lovely young Bard!:*

Elspeth smelled rain as another gust hit her face, and winced. The grounds were already sodden, and another drenching would turn the gardens into a swamp. Well, maybe Treyvan would be able to do something about this before it did more than *smell* like rain. The farmlands north of here were parched; if they could just get some of this precipitation up there, the farmers would bless them for the rest of the season.

She and Firesong hurried along one of the gravel-covered paths to the tower. It was easy to see even at a distance a pair of golden-brown wings waving energetically at the top. The rest of the gryphon—and all of his pupils—lay hidden behind the stone coping around the tower's edge.

:Treyvan's in fine fettle,: Gwena said, with an excited laugh. For the moment, even Gwena had put the lowering threat of Ancar out of her mind. *:I'm down below the tower, but I've been able to follow the whole lesson, except while you and I were "talking" to the Heartstone, of course. He's just about ready to have the new mage-trainees try out their weather-working, but I told him you were coming, so he's waiting for you. He wants you and Firesong to see them at work, I think. These are very cooperative students, and they work well together.:*

They rounded a hedge that had been hiding the base of the tower, and there was Gwena, with two other Companions beside her, all of them looking with interest at the tower top. One of those Companions was Rolan; Elspeth recognized him immediately. But she couldn't make out who the other was. Even for a Herald, it was sometimes hard to tell Companions apart.

:I'm Sayvil, dear,: came the dry mind-voice she had heard a time or two before. *:And interested to see how the new teacher was coming. I didn't know gryphons could be mages, although* kyree *can, and you know about* hertasi *and*

dyheli *mages, I presume. He's doing a fine job; I wouldn't change a thing.:*

Oh, so Sayvil was another one of those Companions who knew something of magic? Wasn't *that* interesting…

Was that why she Chose Kero? Or was there some other motivation? It would certainly help to have a Companion who knew about magic in charge of someone who had come riding into your Kingdom wearing a magic sword!

Well, that could wait. There were too many other things that she needed to know. *:I'll let him know you approve, my lady.:* she replied, just as dryly, and got an amused chuckle for her pains.

The bottom stories of the tower were used mostly for storing gardening implements, and the top for storing seeds and bulbs, and wintering dormant plants. The whole building had a pleasant earthy smell about it although it was terribly dark, and she and Firesong had to grope after the ladder. The tiny windows in the sides of the tower were proportioned to make it look as if it were twice the size it actually was, and since the stone walls were a handspan thick, they let in very little light. The "ladders" here were an interesting cross between a ladder and a staircase with alternating steps, made so that they could be climbed by someone with both hands full. Not that Elspeth would want to, but the gardeners scampered up and down them all day without thinking twice about it.

There was more light from the open hatch to the roof, and that made the last of their climb a bit easier. They poked their heads up through the open hatchway cautiously, just as a couple of fat drops fell with identical *splats* onto the wood beside their heads.

"You are in good time, younglingsssss," Treyvan said. "You have ssssaved usss frrrom needing to worrk in the wet." The male gryphon took up half of the roof space; the rest was occupied by two youngsters in trainee Grays, and three adults in Whites. Elspeth didn't recognize any of them. Of the three adults, one could not have been more than twenty at most; the other two were somewhere around thirty. The young one was blond and had the look of a Northerner about him; the other two, male and female, both with brown hair, had the stocky build of the folk on the Rethwellan border. The two trainees were probably in their last year; one was thin and very dark, the other plump and fair.

"I will make introductionsss when we arrre finissshed," the gryphon added hastily, as another set of raindrops joined the first. "Ssstudentsss, you may begin."

Elspeth was a little surprised to see, as they looked at each other and immediately meshed their powers, that he must have directed them to work as a group rather than separately. On the other hand, since the object was not just to train these people, but to actually do something about a bad situation with the weather, his strategy made sense.

The older of the two trainees handled the wind; he began to leech energy away from the weather system that had created this storm in the first place, an odd knot in the sky to the east of Haven. Elspeth couldn't quite see the point of this particular tactic; the wind *did* begin to die down, but that left the storm simply sitting there, right over the capital itself, ready to dump rain on them at any moment. But then the youngster passed the energy he had taken to the oldest of the Heralds, and that lady, rather than trying to change the direction of the existing wind, used the power to start another system north of Haven. Elspeth closed her eyes, and saw what they were Seeing, a "landscape" of weather, exactly like the sculptured terrain in a sandtable. The trainee was taking "sand" from a "hill" in the east and giving it to the woman. She was putting that "sand" in the south, creating another hill there, while the second trainee began to scoop "sand" from the north and pass it along to the woman as well. The air made a kind of thin "liquid" flowing over the sand, too light to move it, but forced to move according to the way it had been sculpted. Where there was a slope, it "flowed" downhill, picking up force. So now there was a new wind that blew in from the south, heading north—

Which, by all reliable reports, could really use the rain that had been dumped uselessly on the capital for the past several weeks. Two more of the Heralds added something else, sculpting the "sand" further, one pulling the air to the north, and one pushing, out of the south. But these two had added something new, to create that push and pull. The one in the north was making things cool and wet, and to the south warm and dry. Elspeth opened her eyes, and saw that the storm really was moving in a new direction; by concentrating, she Saw that "sandtable" as an overlay on the "real" world.

When she had finished making her depression, the second trainee simply held the water in the clouds until they began to move into the north and west and, finally, out of sight.

Firesong smiled; Elspeth "watched" what they were doing using her Mage-Sight and "outer eyes" at once, completely enthralled by the clever way they were accomplishing their goal together. Now she saw why

Firesong didn't want to work any weather-magic without knowing the land around them. It was something that could all too easily go wrong.

On the other hand, this was an application of fairly minor Gifts with major results, and she could well imagine what kind of havoc such weather control could wreak on or before a battle. Bring in a really major storm, and dump a month's worth of rain at once on a battlefield, and you created a quagmire. Force the enemy to come to you across it, and he was exhausted before he reached your lines.

"Well done!" Treyvan said, as the last of the clouds disappeared into the north, leaving behind a warm, cloudless blue sky without even the scent of rain. With a sigh of relief, the five new mages released their hold on the storm, certain now that it was going to behave, and turned to their strange teacher with glowing faces full of the pride of accomplishment. They deserved that glow; even among the Tayledras, Elspeth had never seen mages work together that well. That alone was an accomplishment of major proportions.

"Very well done," Firesong put in. "Fine control, good judgment, and the systems you set up should hold long enough for the rain to travel to where it should have gone in the first place. You are learning quickly. That you work together is a wondrous thing—all of you together can do far more than one of you alone."

One of the Heralds, clearly quite exhausted, sat down on the coping around the edge of the roof. "I'll admit that I was disappointed when my Mage-Gift proved to be just as minor as my FarSight, but now," he shook his head, "I'm not certain I'm ever going to call *any* Gift 'minor' anymore. The idea of actually steering a storm around the sky—in the wrong hands, something like that could be devastating. I don't want to think of someone hitting fields before harvest with hail. You could starve the whole country that way."

:Good man,: Gwena said from below. *:He's thinking, and in combat terms.:*

"You're right, and think about hitting a line of foot-soldiers with hail, while you're at it. FarSight and Mage-Gift are a good pairing," Elspeth told him. "You can use the first to make certain you *don't* dump a storm where it can harm someone, or at least someone on your own side, and just now you saw what you can do with the second."

:Kero would tell you that there is no such thing as a "minor" mage, only a mage who doesn't know how to make the best use of what power he has,: Sayvil observed from below, making all of them start. *:Most of her mages were what they call "earth-witches"—mages of similar power to you. But they knew*

all about holding what you have in reserve until you are in a position where a little application of magic will bring a big result. Think of it as waiting until your enemy is off-balance, then pushing.:

The three Heralds exchanged glances, and nodded; the two trainees just looked very solemn and a little frightened. Elspeth couldn't blame them. They were very young to be thinking of going into battle—only partially trained, and with a new Gift they had no appreciable experience in using—but that was just what they were going to be doing, and soon.

"Listen, we ought to introduce ourselves," the Herald who had spoken said hastily, perhaps hoping to avoid another unsolicited comment from Sayvil. "I'm Herald Rafe—this is Brion and this is Kelsy."

"We're Anda and Chass," said the first trainee shyly. "You're Elspeth, right? Is this the Hawkbrother friend of yours? The one who is a warrior and a mage?"

She nodded. "I'm Elspeth. This is Firesong, not Darkwind. Firesong has never been anything but a mage, but we don't hold that against him!"

Firesong made a face at her, and his firebird gave an audible snort, something that made all five of the students stare and chuckle.

"Darkwind is going through some old books right now, looking for some charts. I'm sure you'll meet him some time soon." She smiled impartially at all five of them. "Actually, my only purpose at the moment, besides watching what you were doing, was to bring Firesong up here to introduce you to him."

Quickly she turned to the Healing Adept and explained in Tayledras what the differences were between a Herald and a Trainee. Then she switched back to speech the others would understand. "So what you have here is a very mixed group of ages and experiences. I'm amazed that they work so well together."

Firesong nodded. "I wish to take these for a day or so, as I think you were hoping. If they can add their powers to work the weather, they can surely add them to shield."

"I have no objection," Treyvan said, cocking his head to one side. "You know more of thisss than I. Gryphonsss are sssolitarrry magesss, mossstly."

"Thanks, both of you." Elspeth turned back to the group. "He'll be another of your mage-teachers, for a couple of specific lessons, probably within the next couple of days."

"In fact, at the moment, we are fairly disorganized," Firesong concluded, granting them all one of his dazzling smiles. "I pledge you, we will do better soon!"

"I sssurely hope sssso," Treyvan hissed wryly. "But Firesssong, if you would ssstay here for a moment, I ssshould like you to begin now, and explain sssomething to thessse ssstudentsss forrr me."

That was clearly a dismissal, and Elspeth ducked back down through the trapdoor. By the time she reached the ground, only Gwena remained of the Companions that had been watching from below.

:One of these days, Sayvil is going to frighten someone right off a roof.: Gwena said, shaking her head and mane vigorously. *:Honestly! Oh, Treyvan's group wasn't the only one doing weather-work today; Hydona had her lot working in the morning, but since they're much stronger, she had them working at a distance. Off to the west a ways, doing something about that horrible Gate-storm we triggered when we came home.:*

Elspeth sighed with relief. "Thank goodness. I was feeling terribly guilty about that mess. Darkwind said that at this point, what with all the new energy-patterns around, there are probably storms over every major node in this Kingdom. Gods, I can't believe the mess we've got."

:I hope he also pointed out we can't take care of them all.: Gwena said with resigned practicality. *:There aren't enough of us, and there isn't enough time. The only reason we can deal with any of it is because it's a way to train our new mages.:*

"He did." Elspeth took a moment to hoist herself up onto Gwena's bare back. "Dearheart, I need a ride. Darkwind said when he finished with the books, he was going to go consult with Kero a bit more and I should meet him at the salle." She stifled a yawn. "There just aren't enough hours in the day. This calm is so deceptive—but under it all, I feel like we can't get everything we need done taken care of fast enough. Ancar is *going* to get us, and only he knows when."

:Right.: Gwena set off at a brisk trot, without a complaint. Elspeth took the brief respite to try to force the knotted muscles of her neck to relax. Before being "introduced" to the Heartstone, she had spent the morning going over the newest set of trainees, testing them for Mage-Gift, then giving them a rush course in the basics of magic. She had an advantage over Darkwind, as a teacher; she *knew* what the mind-magic lessons were like, and she could tell her students exactly how mind-magic and true magic differed. Once they were proficient in those basics, she turned her group over to Hydona.

Then she had gone off to the Archives, and the crates and boxes of books she and Darkwind had discovered late last night, all of them with fading traces of long-ago mage-energies on them. Most of them were handwritten, were either original bound manuscripts, or handmade copies of even older manuscripts. Fortunately, all her delving into the Archives had made her uniquely qualified to sort through them, and determine which were real books teaching magic and which were only contaminated by proximity. Then she had handed the mage-books over to those Heralds that Herald-Chronicler Myste felt could translate them into more modern terms. There had been a few clearly written in Tayledras, which had given Darkwind a bit of a shock, and a couple in no language either could identify. Darkwind was planning to take those to Kerowyn, once he determined if there was anything worth their time in the Tayledras books.

Both of them were running themselves ragged. Her day had started before dawn, and it would last long past midnight. There just weren't enough hours; the peace of the Palace was *so* deceptive. Even with the violent weather plaguing them, it didn't seem as if they were about to be invaded. In fact, things weren't really much different than they had been when she'd left. It was easy to be fooled into thinking there was nothing wrong here, but Ancar was planning something, she knew it...

For that matter, he might well be *doing* something, right this very minute. With all those storms on the borders, the relay-towers were useless except when the weather cleared a bit. At least she had a barrier over Haven now, and Firesong would return to the Heartstone when he was done with Treyvan's students, and use her shield as a model to set other protections in place, as many as he had time and strength for.

And tomorrow, before dawn, it would all begin again.

That was why Gwena was not scolding her for riding the short distance to the salle. Not when riding was quicker than walking, and not as exhausting as running.

She slid off Gwena's back at the door to Kerowyn's domain, and hit the ground at a trot. The salle, a huge, wooden building, with clerestory windows and mirrors on two of the walls, was full of trainees being supervised by Jeri, Kero's assistant, and a Herald who had been hand-picked and personally trained by Alberich, the absent Weaponsmaster. Jeri looked up when she caught Elspeth's reflection in a mirror, nodded at her, and pointed with her chin toward Kero's office, all without missing a command to her line of young, clumsy sword wielders.

Elspeth skirted past the youngsters in their worn practice armor, moving along the wall with the benches between her and them, and avoiding the piles of practice gear strewn in her path. She tapped on Kero's door at the other end of the room, using her own code without thinking twice about it.

It was a good thing she did. The door opened a mere crack, just wide enough for an arm in brown leather to snake out, grab her by the wrist, and pull her inside.

As soon as she cleared the doorway, the reason for Kero's action was obvious. Darkwind was with her, sitting cross-legged in the corner, but so was another man, a stranger, filthy and travel-stained, dressed like a peddler. He had half-risen from his stool at Elspeth's entrance, taking a wary stance and perfectly ready to defend himself.

One of Kero's spies—probably one of her old mercenary company, the Skybolts. That was the only thing he could be. Her heart sank. The man would not be here unless he had some word on Ancar, and from his grim expression, it was probably more trouble.

"I'm glad you're here," Kero said, with a nod to the stranger, and a quick hand-sign Elspeth recognized as being the Skybolts' hand-language for "all clear." He sank back down onto his stool again, and picked up a towel from a pile on the floor next to him. "You and Darkwind know the most about Falcon's Breath, and Ragges here actually managed to see him. He's been describing the man to Darkwind. I want you both to hear what he has to say."

"Bright feather, I fear it really is Falconsbane," Darkwind added. "Ragges has described him perfectly; it could be no other."

Elspeth sat down quickly on another stool, with an explosive sigh. After twice thinking Falconsbane was gone for good, then hearing he had escaped yet again, her reaction to hearing this confirmation that he lived was, oddly enough, simple exhaustion. "Damn. Damn, damn, damn. I didn't really think there was any chance of a mistake. I wish that Beast would just *die*."

"Don't we all," Kero said, leaning up against the door with her ear near enough the crack that she would be able to hear anyone approaching on the other side. "Well, go on, Ragges. Anything you know for a fact could be more important than either of us would guess."

Bleak depression settled over Elspeth as the spy continued his report.

"This Falconsbane is not only advising Ancar, he seems to be very high up in Ancar's mage-ranks," the stranger said, wiping his face vigorously with a towel. As he rubbed, Elspeth realized that what she had taken for dirt and the man's own swarthy complexion was actually makeup or dye. Underneath it he was far paler than he looked. "Rumor had it, literally just as I left, that he is claiming *he* has taken down some kind of protective barrier that keeps magic out of Valdemar. There were so many rumors that war was at hand that I fled the capital, hoping to outrun any army Ancar might mount."

Darkwind looked sardonic. "He would claim anything he thought he could convince folk of," was all the Hawkbrother said, his lips twisted with distaste.

"Well, Hulda is not long for her spot of 'favorite mage' if she can't find a way to counter his influence," Ragges told them, picking off bits of hair and things that counterfeited moles perfectly, which had been glued to his cheeks. "At the moment his star is rising pretty quickly. But there's another player in this little game now, and I have no idea what *he's* about. There's a new envoy at Ancar's court, wearing badges and livery from some lord *I* don't recognize. And mind, most of the allies Ancar picked up in the beginning have pretty well deserted him by now, so whoever sent this lad must be fairly certain there's no way that Ancar can turn on them." He fished a bit of pencil and a scrap of paper out of his pocket and made a quick sketch. "This is the badge, and the man seems to be great friends with Hulda. She does her best not to be seen coming and going, but she spends a great deal of time in his suite. She's so busy watching for spies from her rivals she never noticed me."

Kero gave the sketch a cursory glance, and shrugged. "Nothing I know," she said.

"Let me see that," Darkwind said, suddenly, urgently. She handed it to him, and he frowned over it for a moment.

"I have seen this somewhere—within a day," he said, his brow creased as he stared at it. "No—I saw it today, this very morning. In a book. No, not *in* the book, I remember now!"

He reached down to the pile of books at his feet and looked just inside the covers of each of them in rapid succession. Finally he exclaimed, "Here!" and held up the book for all of them to see.

"That's the device, all right," Ragges said decisively. Kero shrugged again, but Elspeth took the book from Darkwind and leafed through it. It was in Valdemaran so archaic she had taken it for another language entirely until this very moment. But she had not noticed the very first page before, which looked a great deal more modern. She went back to that first page when she simply could not puzzle out any of the script. As she had hoped, in a modern, scholar's hand, she found a history of the book itself. This was a copy, not the original, but the scribes had faithfully reproduced every handwritten marginal note and scribbled diagram.

For this was a copy of a very important tome; one of the books brought to this land before it was a Kingdom, before it was even a nation.

By the Baron Valdemar, who became, by declamation, King Valdemar the First.

"According to this," she said, slowly, puzzling out the words and feeling cold fear growing in the pit of her stomach, "the device inside the cover of this book is that of the former owner—the one that King Valdemar 'borrowed' the book from, when he ran west with his people."

No one would ever have anticipated this; no one could have.

Kero frowned. "I have the sinking feeling I'm not going to like what you're going to tell me."

"It's the personal arms of the ruling family of the Eastern Empire," Elspeth said, her throat closing until her voice was hardly more than a harsh whisper. All her life she had heard tales of the horrors and injustices that the Emperor wrought on his subjects, and always the refrain had been "be glad the Emperor is too far away to notice us." Valdemar had run for *years* with his people before settling here, but the memories of what he had escaped still haunted every scholar's nightmares. There was no name for the Eastern Empire; it didn't need one. It covered the entire Eastern coastline, a monolithic giant from which not even rumors escaped. "The Emperor of the East himself has sent an envoy to Ancar's court—"

"The Emperor's personal envoy is playing footsie with Hulda?" Kero exclaimed, her voice rising sharply. "Old Wizard Charliss? The Emperor of the East? Bloody *hell!*"

Whatever else she might have said was lost as someone pounded urgently on the door. "It's Jeri!" said Kero's assistant, with strain audible in her voice. "There's been a relay-message from the east, and they sent a page out here to get you. They need you people in Council right now! Ancar's troops are attacking our border!"

"Bloody *hell!*" Kero cried again, then snatched open the door and headed out at a dead run, with Elspeth and Darkwind right on her heels.

The ax had fallen, and it was worse than Elspeth had feared. Nightfall brought three more messages as soon as lanterns could be seen from relay-tower to relay-tower, with word that a Herald with more detail was on the way.

But the messages, although they were clear and concise, made absolutely no sense.

Elspeth rubbed her eyes and fought back the urge to sleep; no one in the Council chamber had slept for three days. Right now Selenay was reporting what little the Council knew to her chief courtiers while Prince Daren held her seat. Elspeth was trapped between exhaustion and tension. There was no time for sleep; there was no time for anything, now. A trainee put a mug full of strong, hot tea discreetly by her hand; she took it and emptied it in three swallows.

Ancar's forces had crossed the border shortly after noon on the first day of the attack. As Kero and Elspeth had feared, they seemed to be more of his magically controlled conscript-troops, and they continued to remain under control long past the point when spells had lost their effectiveness in the past. So the barrier was down, just as Vanyel had warned.

What was insane was that they had overrun the first garrison in their path, and had lost at least half their men taking it. Now they were fortifying it and holding it against a counterattack, while more of Ancar's troops came in over the border at their back—and given the rate at which they were losing men, in a day or two they would have to replace the *entire* force that had mounted the attack in the first place!

"This isn't like Ancar," Kero said tiredly, as she and the Lord Marshal shoved counters around on a map in response to every message from the border. "He just doesn't *fight* like this. That garrison is of no value whatsoever; there's no one of any importance there, there's nothing valuable there, it's just one more place on the border. It isn't even *strategically* valuable. He just doesn't go after targets that aren't worth anything—he *certainly* doesn't continue to hold them afterward!"

"I'd say he'd gone mad, except he already was," the Lord Marshal agreed, running his hand through his thinning hair. "I have never seen Ancar strike for anything that did not have a substantial value to it. That was why we didn't bother to fortify that town all that heavily."

"Someone else is dictating his tactics," Darkwind said suddenly, sitting up straight.

All eyes turned toward him. "He's never let anyone dictate his tactics before this," Kero replied skeptically. "That's one reason why we've held him off for so long. He's very predictable, and bad losses have always made him give up. He *always* follows the same pattern; he tests us until he loses his test force, then he falls back. Resist him strongly, and he gives up."

"That was so in the past, but it is not so now," Darkwind replied emphatically. "He has given over his main strategy to someone else, and *we* know who it is that spends the lives of underlings like sand, and leaves a river of the blood of his own people in his wake."

He looked significantly at Elspeth, who nodded. "Mornelithe Falconsbane," she said.

"The *mage?*" was Kero's incredulous reply. "Since when does a mage know anything about tactics?"

"Are these sound *tactical* decisions?" Darkwind countered. "No. But they *will* win the war for Ancar. All he needs do is keep driving his troops in, and they will overwhelm you. He will conquer by sheer numbers. Recall, neither of them care at all for the state either land will be in when the war is over. Falconsbane would as soon both lands were decimated, and he could very well have prodded Ancar until he cares only for revenge."

The rest of the Council stared at him, appalled. Elspeth felt her gut knot with cold fear. This was what she had felt, but had not been able to articulate, probably because she had not wanted to believe it. But now, hearing it spoken aloud, she did believe it.

"No one can win against something like that—" one of the Councillors faltered.

Darkwind only nodded grimly, and Elspeth seconded him.

"Then we are doomed. It is only a matter of time—" The Seneschal did not wail, but he might just as well have. His words, and the fear in them, echoed the feelings of everyone around him.

Black despair descended—eyes widened with incipient hysteria—and the High Council of Valdemar was only a heartbeat away from absolute panic.

"Not if we do something completely unexpected," Elspeth heard herself saying, and she marveled absently at the calm she heard in her own voice. "Something atypical. That was how Darkwind and I defeated him before. We figured out what he thought we would do, and we did something that he couldn't anticipate."

"He'll assume panic," Darkwind put in. "He'll assume that you will mount a rearguard action and attempt to hold a line while the rest of your populace flees, becoming refugees. He will expect you to go north and south, I think; he will try to cut you off from Rethwellan, and count on the mountains to trap you. I would guess that once he panics you, he will come in from a southerly direction to drive you."

Kero studied the map. "That fits," she said at last. "That cuts us off from our allies, although he probably doesn't know about the new alliance with Karse."

"We have an alliance with *Karse?*" squeaked someone to Elspeth's left. Kero ignored whoever it was. "So he's going to be expecting some kind of digging in, a defensive line, you think?"

"Isn't that what logic dictates?" Darkwind replied. "A large defensive attempt. Fortification. So, what is *not* logical? How can we strike at him in a significant way that he will not anticipate?"

Kero stared at him for a very long time, then transferred her gaze to Elspeth. "A dagger strike," she said slowly. "A very small counterattack, inside his own stronghold. We cut off the snake's head. Kill Ancar, Hulda, *and* Falcon's Breath, and the whole thing falls apart."

Darkwind nodded, his mouth set in a thin line, his lips gray with tension and fatigue.

Silence around the Council table, although Elspeth saw her stepfather nodding out of the corner of her eye. Prince Daren knew something of expediency.

"That's murder—" faltered Lady Elibet.

"That's *assassination,*" said the Lord Patriarch sternly. "Cold-blooded, and calculated. A deadly sin by any decent man's moral code."

"Oh, it's a moral dilemma, all right," Kero replied, grimly. "It's murder, it's cold-blooded, it's wrong. If you face an enemy, you should give him a chance to defend himself. Hellfires, killing is wrong. I'm a *mercenary,* my lords and ladies, and I will be the first to tell you that there is no nice way to kill. But what choice do we have? If we try to run, we either abandon *everything* to him—and may I remind you, at least half of our population has no means to escape—or we find ourselves running into a trap he's set for us. So the half that *runs* gets slaughtered, too. If we make a stand, his numbers overrun us and destroy us. And while *we're* dying, so are his own troops. Remember them? They're poor mage-controlled farmers, graybeards, and little boys! In fact, once he starts taking *our* land, he'll start turning our own people against us! *Do we have a choice?*"

Kero looked into the eyes of each Councillor in turn; some returned her stare for stare, and some only dropped their gazes to the table in front of them, but one and all, they only shook their heads.

Elspeth cleared her throat when Kero's gaze reached her. Kero nodded; since she was no longer the Heir, she had no real place in Council, but habit would make them listen to her anyway.

"We can baffle him with strike-and-run tactics," she said. "That will delay him while he tries to take ground. If he is expecting either all-out panic or a defensive line, while the special forces are getting into place, we can puzzle him by not playing either of the games he expects."

Kero nodded cautiously at that. "Is there a plan behind this?" she asked.

"One he wouldn't think of—evacuation," Elspeth replied. "Strike north and lead him up while you evacuate to the south. Then strike from the south and lead him into scorched earth while you evacuate in the west. That way we can get everyone out—and Captain—no one is going to like this—but if people won't leave, pull them out and burn their houses and fields. They won't stay if there's nothing to eat and nowhere to live."

Someone gasped in outrage, but the Lord Marshal nodded, his face a mask of pain. "We have to think of the people first," he said, "And if we deny Ancar any kind of sustenance, he will be forced to march far more slowly than if he can loot as he goes."

"But how can we destroy our own land?" Elibet *did* wail. "How can we simply give him our Kingdom, and lay waste to it ourselves? How can we do this to Valdemar? And how can we explain this to the people?"

Elspeth did not stand, but held herself proud and tall. "Tell them this," she said. "Valdemar is not grainfields, or roads, or cattle; it is not cities, it is not even the land itself. It is people. Grain will grow again— herds can be bred—houses can be rebuilt. It is the lives of our people that are at stake here, and we must preserve them. *That* is what we must fight for, every precious life! There is no book that cannot be rewritten, no temple that cannot be rebuilt, so long as those lives are preserved. So long as the people live—so does Valdemar."

She looked around the table as Kero had, meeting the eyes of every woman and man on the Council.

"There is not a Herald in Valdemar who will not stand between those people and Ancar's forces—even if the only weapons he has are those of his mind and bare hands," she continued. "That includes me—for, my lords and ladies, I will be the first to volunteer for the group that goes into Ancar's land. You know how much he hates me, personally, and what he will do if he takes me. Every Herald will defend our people to his last breath and drop of blood, and lament that he has no more to give. Tell your people that—and remind them that the Heralds have no homes, no belongings, and never have. All that Heralds have comes from the people—and it will all return to their service, first to last, until there is no more to offer."

1 3

Kero sent the trainees out of the Council Chamber—more for their protection than from the need to keep secrets from anyone Chosen. The trainees were as trustworthy as their Companions, but there were a lot of them. It would be difficult to protect all of them from enemy agents if word somehow got out that they knew the contents of a secret plan. Searchingly, she looked at each of the members of the Council in turn. "From here on, nothing leaves this room," she said emphatically. "And I mean *nothing*. If I had a way, I'd put a spell on you people to keep you from even thinking about this when you're outside this room."

Darkwind coughed politely, and Kero's head swiveled like an owl's. Her eyes met his, and he nodded, once. "Don't tell me; you *can* do that," she hazarded. "I should have guessed."

Darkwind shrugged. "It is called a spell of coercion," he offered politely, "And we do not use it except in times of greatest need. We prefer not to use the version that makes one forget something important, unless we think that an enemy may also be a strong Mindspeaker. It can be broken, but the person in question must be in the physical possession of a mage stronger than the one who set it, at least in the areas of mind-magic. It can be worked around, but again, the person must be in the physical possession of a countering mage, and it takes a great deal of time. A Tayledras must also have the consent of the one it is placed upon; others are not so polite about it."

Like Falconsbane, Elspeth thought grimly. She recalled, all too vividly, what Starblade had endured to have his coercions broken.

The other members of the Council, including Heralds Teren, Kyril, and Griffon, stirred uneasily, and there was more than a shadow of fear in some eyes. *Magic;* that was the problem. Mind-magic they knew, but this was different, alien, and fraught with unpleasant implications. About the only times any of them had encountered true magic, it had been in the hands of an enemy.

:Now they know how the unGifted sometimes feel around them,: Gwena commented ironically.

Prince Daren simply looked interested; after all, he had seen magic at work often enough in his days as his brother's Lord Martial. "I'd heard of coercions, but before today I'd never met any mage who could set them," he said. "It was said that the Karsite Priests of Vkandis could set coercions, though, and some things Alberich told me from time to time seemed to confirm that."

Talia, who sat secure in the knowledge her Gift of Empathy gave her, that Darkwind would sooner cut his own arm off than harm *her* or any other Herald, nodded gravely. "I can see where such a precaution would give our force a great deal of protection from slips of the tongue."

"This would be for your protection as well as my team's," Kero said flatly. "What you can't tell, no one can extract from you, even by using drugs. I don't think we need to fear Ancar sending agents in to kidnap any of you, but please remember that illusions work here now. He *could* get someone in to impersonate a servant, drug your food, and get you to babble anything you know, before leaving you to sleep it off. With the right drugs, you'd never even know it had happened."

Talia paled, and rightly. Both she and Elspeth recalled how even when the magic-prohibitions had been in place, Hulda had managed to get in place as an assistant to Elspeth's nurse and drug that nurse so that it was Hulda who issued the orders.

Lady Kester blanched. "You're not serious—" she began, then took a second look at Kero's face. "No. You are. Dear and precious gods. I never thought to see Valdemar in such a pass that Councillors could not be protected in Haven."

"Nor did I," Prince Daren sighed, "But let me be the first to agree to such a spell being set upon me. We are many and the servants here are more numerous still. We have not enough mages to check for the presence of illusions at all times." He raised an eyebrow at Darkwind, who bowed a little in response. "I trust this little spell of yours will be *limited* in scope?"

"If I set it now, and lift it when the discussion is ended, it will be limited to that time period," Darkwind replied. He looked around. "There is this; if any of you feel truly that you cannot bear to have such a spell set upon you, there is always the option to leave and have no part in the decision."

It was an option no one really wanted to take. In the face of Daren's acceptance, and Talia's, which followed immediately upon his, the other Councillors could do nothing else but accept. No one wanted to be left out of the decision, nor did they care for the idea of giving up any of their responsibilities.

Darkwind was exhausted, but he was also an Adept; he was not dependent on his own personal energies to set this spell. Elspeth sensed him fumbling a little in his attempt to find the nearest node; she solved his problem by linking him to it herself. His brief smile was all the thanks she needed.

It was a sad irony that coercive spells were some of the easiest to set. Darkwind was done before half of the Councillors even realized he had begun.

"There," he said, letting his link to the node go and slumping back in his chair. "Now, none of you will be able to speak of this outside the Council chamber, nor with anyone who is not of the Council."

"We won't?" Father Ricard said wonderingly, touching his forehead. "How odd—I don't feel any different—"

"Which is as it should be." For the first time, Firesong, who was sitting behind Elspeth, spoke up. "A coercive spell is an insidious thing. One set well should not be noticed at all. As none of you ever noticed that you could not speak of magic, nor remember its existence, except as an historical anomaly." His lips curved in gentle irony as they started. "Yes, indeed, speakers for k'Valdemar—your land has been under a coercive spell for long and long, and you had never noted it. Such is the usage of magic in skilled and powerful hands. You should be grateful that your last Herald-Mage was a man of deep integrity and great resourcefulness."

:And had a lot of Companions to help him,: Gwena added smugly, confirming Elspeth's suspicion that the Companions had been involved in keeping true magic a "forgotten" resource.

Kero let out a long, deep sigh. "Well, now that we've some assurance we can keep this out of Ancar's hands, we need to put together our team. Ordinarily—I beg your pardons, but ordinarily this is covert work, and none of you would ever hear about it, much less help me agree whom to send. You *might* have heard about the results, if Selenay, Daren, and I agreed that you needed the information. There have been a number of operations you've heard nothing of, and there will be more."

The Lord Patriarch smiled, a little grimly. "We had assumed that, my lady."

Kero coughed. "Well. I had hoped you had. But this time, I *need* that agreement from you, because if we are going to succeed, we must send mages against mages, and we'll be taking those mages away from the direct defense of Valdemar. They're going against Ancar, Hulda, and a mage we *know* is a dangerous Adept, and that means sending in the best we have. So we must accept Elspeth's offer."

"Must we?" Talia asked, but without much hope.

"Speaking as a strategist," the Lord Marshal said unhappily, "I must agree. She has volunteered, and she is a Herald—she knows her duty. And again, it is the last move that Ancar would ever expect."

"The last that Falconsbane would expect, as well," Darkwind put in. "He will be anticipating that every highborn that can will be fleeing to safety in Rethwellan. He cannot conceive of willing self-sacrifice. If he knows that Elspeth is here and not still in k'Sheyna, he will expect her to do the same as he would, to try to escape him and not fly into his reach. After all, she could seek asylum with her kin and be accepted gladly, and she has all the mage-power she needs to escape his minions easily."

"If you send Elspeth, you must send Skif," Lady Kester said firmly. "Whether you will admit it or not, *I* am perfectly aware that he has done this sort of thing before. Send an experienced agent with her, one who has been working with her."

"If I go," Skif replied, from behind Darkwind, "then Nyara comes as well. Cymry backs her to come along. She is clever and skilled, a trained fighter, she has a score of counts to settle with Falconsbane, and she knows him as no one else does."

Kero gave him a long look, transferred it to Nyara, then caught Elpeth's gaze, and did something she seldom resorted to with anyone but her lover, Herald Eldan. She used Mindspeech.

:*Family resemblance, kitten?*: she asked.

Elspeth nodded, very slightly. There was no point in going into excruciating detail at this point. Let Kero simply assume that Nyara was trying to make up for the perfidy of a relative, and perhaps, to extract revenge for something Falconsbane had done to her. That was something Kero could understand.

:*Ah,*: came the reply. :*I'd wondered.*: And she left it at that. Kero was nothing if not expedient. And she trusted Skif's judgment as she trusted her own.

"By the same token, I must go with Elspeth," Darkwind put in. "We have worked together successfully, I am the more experienced mage of the two of us, and as Nyara knows Falconsbane, so she knows Hulda. That will give us four agents to target them, two of them mages and Adepts."

"But you and Elspeth would strike first at Hulda and Ancar," Firesong pointed out. "There is some urgency for *our* people in ridding the world of the Beast, and only an Adept is likely to be able to counter his protective magics. That being the case, I should go with you as well. If you divide, two to target the Hardornens, and two to target the Beast,

Skif and Nyara should have an Adept with them. There is no point in dividing those who have worked together."

Kero nodded. "I have to admit that Falconsbane is not a priority for us—"

Firesong shrugged. "He should be—believe me, even more so than the Hardornens. So, let us plan a two-bladed attack upon *him*. That gives you an Adept that Falconsbane *does not know* to work upon him, and an Adept each for Hulda and Ancar, Adepts who are also well-trained as fighters. I am by no means certain that an Adept can take the Beast; I suspect I will accomplish more by distracting him, making him think I am his only enemy. This means that the physical attack, which he will not anticipate, can come from Skif and Nyara."

:And me,: Need said quietly, for Elspeth's ears alone. *:But the boy will be damned useful. I think I'm going to have to be awfully close to Falconsbane to do any good.:*

Elspeth tried not to look surprised at the Healing Adept's speech, but she had not expected Firesong to volunteer for this. She glanced back at Darkwind, who shrugged.

:He is unique,: Darkwind said wryly. *:With his own will. He does have the mindset of the Healing Adept, and that means he would not care to see Falconsbane working his twisted will on lands that* had *been Cleansed. And I suspect that your mutual ancestor may have impressed some kind of sense of responsibility for your continued health upon him. I certainly would not turn his aid away! But for predictability—I would look upon Firesong as a benevolent trickster.:*

"What are we going to do for mages if you're all leaving?" Lady Kester asked, a little desperately.

"You have the gryphons," Darkwind pointed out. "They are both Masters. You have Heralds and trainees with Mage-Gift, currently being schooled in combative magics."

"Ah…" Kero leaned back in her chair, and hooded her eyes with her lids. "We won't be depending entirely on the gryphons. Since this is all under the rose—I have a surprise for you all. There are more mages coming, and I expect them to start arriving any day now."

As the Councillors turned as one from watching Elspeth and her group to staring at Kero, she revealed to them the news of the three groups of mages currently being brought at top speed toward Haven, riding pillion behind Heralds and trainees released from the Collegium for the duty. She had virtually denuded the Herald's Collegium of all but those Mage-Gifted and first-year students.

"That's why you sent all those so-called 'training groups' off!" exclaimed the Lord Marshal. Kero nodded.

"So, we will have mages. Will they be Adepts?" She shrugged. "I can't tell you. I don't know what they're sending us. What I *can* tell you, since I used mages in my Company, is that a mage is only as good as the tacticians he works with, and his willingness to really use his talents to the fullest. Just because someone is an Adept, that does not mean he is going to be effective."

"I have, in my time, seen a few completely ineffective Adepts," Firesong put in. "I have seen a *Journeyman* defeat one of them in a contest. Kerowyn is correct."

"So there you have it. Are we all agreed on the team?" Kero spread her hands to indicate that she was ready to call a vote on it.

The vote was unanimous, though it was fairly clear that there was some reluctance to place the only Adepts Valdemar had access to, and its former Heir, in such jeopardy.

"Fine." Kero nodded. "Then as far as I am concerned, this meeting can close. We all have things we need to do. I have to find a way to insert these folk into Hardorn. You have things you need to tell your people. Ladies and lords, you will be in charge of the physical defenses and the evacuations. You should consult with the Lord Marshal about that, and how to organize them to coordinate with his strike-and-run raids. I'll join you as soon as we come up with an insertion plan." She raised an eyebrow at Talia, Elspeth, and Prince Daren. "You three have a task I really don't envy. The Queen is not going to like this."

Talia and Elspeth exchanged a knowing glance and a sigh. Daren shook his head.

"Perhaps," he suggested gently, "I should be the one to break the word first to Selenay. I shall remind her of how sad the little ones would be to become half-orphaned; I hope then she will not slay the father of her children out of sheer pique."

Elspeth and Talia waited nervously in the rather austere antechamber to Selenay and Daren's private suite, but it seemed almost no time at all before Daren was back, beckoning to both of them to come with him. They followed him into Selenay's private office, and Elspeth's heart ached to see how drawn and worn her mother's face was. And to add to that burden of grief and worry—

But Selenay only came straight to her, held out her arms, and embraced her tightly but not possessively. Her body shook with tension but not with the tears that Elspeth had feared.

Finally she released her daughter, and held her away at arm's length, searching her face for something, although Elspeth could not tell what it was. Her eyes were narrowed with concentration, and Elspeth saw many fine worry lines around her eyes and creasing her forehead that had not been there when she left.

"Good," she said finally. "This isn't something someone talked you into. You know exactly what you're doing. You thought of this yourself?"

Elspeth nodded. Her mother had pulled her hair back into a no-nonsense braid like Kero's, and like Talia, she was wearing breeches and tunic, her only concession to rank being a bit of gold trim on the tunic hem and her coronet about her brow. Her sword and sword-belt were hanging from the chair beside her desk, and knives lay on top of a pile of papers. Although she had seen her mother in armor and on a battlefield, this was not a Selenay that Elspeth had ever seen before, but she rather expected that anyone who had fought with her mother and grandfather in the Tedrel Wars would find this Queen very familiar. Selenay had pared *everything* from her life that was not relevant to the defense of her land. Valdemar was in peril, and the Queen was ready for personal action.

"I thought about trying to be a commander, but I'm not a tactician, and not even a particularly good fighter. No one knows me to follow me as a charismatic leader," Elspeth said slowly. "In the lines, I would be just one more warrior. Yes, I *could* help with magic defenses—I could even coordinate the mages—but I would be *your* daughter, and the ones from outKingdom would always expect me to favor Herald-Mages and their safety over those from outside. Such suspicion could be fatal. Kero always taught us that you don't stand off and fling sand at a fire from a safe distance; you go in and cut a firebreak right in its path."

"Kero taught you well." Selenay rubbed her eyes with her index finger, and blinked hard against tears. "The Queen agrees with you; the mother—what can I tell you? I hate the idea of sending my child off into this kind of danger, my heart wants to hold you back and keep you safe. But you are a woman grown, Elspeth. You are responsible for your own safety and I can't protect you anymore. Besides, there is no safety anywhere in Valdemar, not now. Elspeth, I am so *proud* of you!"

Elspeth had never expected to hear that last; it caught her by surprise, and her heart swelled and overflowed. She flung herself into her mother's arms again, and this time they both gave way to weeping. Talia, and then Daren, joined them in a fourfold embrace, offering comfort and support. This was sorrow both bitter and sweet, sweet for the accomplishment— bitter for all that accomplishment meant to all of them. Nothing would ever be the same again, even if they all survived this.

When both of them got control over themselves again, they separated, slowly and reluctantly, with tremulous smiles.

"Thank you, Mama," Elspeth managed. "That is the most wonderful thing you have ever said to me. I've always been proud of you, too, but never more than today…"

"When you were such trouble—before Talia came—there were times that I despaired of ever seeing you act like a responsible adult, much less make me so very proud that you are my daughter," Selenay said at last, with a grateful glance at Talia, who only blushed. "No one could ever ask of you what you have just given to Valdemar."

Now it was Elspeth's turn to blush. "I don't know if Papa told you about my rather florid speech in there about saving the people rather than the land," she said. "But being with k'Sheyna and the Hawkbrothers is what showed me that. The way they simply give up their homes and move on when it's time—but mourn the loss of every hawk and owl, *hertasi* and human—that showed me where we should be putting our effort. Let Ancar grab land; the people of Valdemar ran and survived before, and they can now. And if we five can pull this off, they'll have something to return to."

Selenay shook her head in wonder. "You've grown up. And you're wiser than I ever will be—"

Elspeth laughed shakily. "No, just knowledgeable in different things, that's all. Mama, I have to get back to Kero; the sooner we get out of here, the better for all of us."

"If you can spare me for a moment, I'll go with her," Talia added. "I think I have a contact that will give them a way to move across Hardorn quickly."

Selenay nodded. "I will need you in about a candlemark, to help me calm some hysterical highborns when I tell them they are in the path of an invasion we can't stop, but not until then."

Selenay took Elspeth into a quick embrace. "If I don't see you before you leave—remember you take my love with you," she whispered into Elspeth's ear. "And you take my respect and hope as well. I love you, kitten. Come home safe to me. Come home, so I can celebrate your handfasting to that handsome young man who loves you so."

Elspeth returned the embrace fiercely, then fled to resume her duty before Selenay could see that tears threatened to return.

"So. Name everything in this room that can be used as a weapon," Kerowyn grinned at Elspeth.

"Your breath, Firesong's clothes, and that awful tea," Elspeth replied to the old joke. Darkwind and Firesong cracked smiles.

Once again, they all had gathered in Kero's office. Talia was explaining to Kero her link with the secretive and close-knit "clan" of itinerant traveling peddlers. Elspeth had heard it all before, but it was still fascinating, for Talia seemed the last person in the world to keep up an association with the "wagon-families," as they were known. Very often they were regarded as tricksters and only a short step above common thieves. It had been one of the wagon-men who had taken word of her imprisonment out of Hardorn when she had been captured and thrown in a shielded cell by Ancar.

"—so I've kept in constant contact with him, and I've tried to help him get his people out of trouble, when I could," she concluded. "Quite frankly, they can go places we can't, and it occurred to me that it would be very useful to have their cooperation if we needed to get someone into Hardorn, so I've been building up a lot of favors that they owe me."

Kero nodded thoughtfully, tracing little patterns on the table top with her finger. "The gods know I've tried and failed to get an agent in among them. They're very close-mouthed and insular."

Tiredly, Talia ran her fingers through her hair. Elspeth wondered if she would get any sleep at all, or if she'd go on until she collapsed. "Ancar hasn't got any friends among them, I can tell you that. He's taken whole families; I don't care to think what he does with them, but once his men take a wagonload, the people are gone without a trace. Since that started happening, only single men and a few women, all without families, have dared to operate over there—and only in groups, so a single wagon can't just vanish. They've taken to putting together wagon-groups of entertainers and peddlers, and putting on movable fairs. But here's what I think my contact will offer, if I ask him, as the payback for all my favors. I think he'll set our group up with a bigger carnival, give them genuine wagons and things to sell, and basically see that his people protect ours from discovery by outsiders."

Kero made a skeptical face. "Entertainers? Carnival showmen? Gods,

I don't know... I'd thought of something a lot more, well, secretive."

Elspeth snorted. "And how do you propose to hide Nyara or the bondbirds?" she demanded. "The minute anyone gets sight of her *or* the birds, we'd be in trouble, if we were trying to pass ourselves off as simple farmers or something! How many farmers own large exotic birds, or even a hawk? And we'd never pass ourselves off as Hardornen nobles."

"My point exactly," Talia said. "You *can't* hide them, so make them just one more very visible set of entertainers in a sea of flamboyance. After all, where *do* you hide a red fish?"

"In a pond full of other red fish," Kero supplied the tagline of another Shin'a'in proverb. "All right; contact the man. Don't tell him anything until you get his consent to the general idea, and Darkwind can slap one of those coercion things on him."

Talia nodded, and rose from her seat. "I'll have him here by dawn," she said firmly, and left.

Firesong looked highly amused. "Carnival entertainers?" he repeated, "Entertainers, I understand, but what is a carnival?"

After Elspeth explained it to him, he looked even more amused. "You mean—we shall cloak the fact that we are working genuine magic, that we have mage-born creatures, by performing entertainer tricks?"

"*And* selling snake-oil," Kero added, and had to explain the concept of *that* to him as well. By the time she had finished, he was laughing, despite the seriousness of the situation.

"But this is too perfect!" he chuckled. "Oh, please, you *must* let me play a role. The Great Mage Pandemonium! I shall never have another opportunity like this one!"

"I don't know how we could stop you," Skif said dryly. "And your bird is the harder to hide of the two."

Vree cocked his head to one side. *:Tricks, I,:* he offered. Then, to everyone's astonishment, he jumped down onto the table, waddled over to Firesong, and rolled over like a dog, his eyes fixed on the Healing Adept. *:Tricks, I, with Aya. Together.:*

"I think he wants you to have a trick bird act with himself and your firebird," Darkwind said, his eyes still wide with surprise. "I keep thinking he has a limited grasp of abstract concepts, but every once in a while he astonishes me. It would be a *very* good way of explaining the presence of both birds."

"I could assist you, Firesong," Nyara added shyly. "And dance. Falconsbane made me learn to dance, seduction dances, which would be popular, I think. You could say I was your captive."

"And everyone who saw you would be certain *her* looks were due to costume and makeup, and the birds to dye or bleach." Kero nodded. "I like it. You know, I can even show you some things that will make it look as if Nyara's—ah—attributes *are* all makeup and costume. We could shave thin lines of her body-fur to look like seams."

"And I shall dress as flamboyantly and *tastelessly* as Skyseeker k'Treva!" Firesong crowed. "We call him 'Eye-burner' to tease him, for he has *no* taste! A pity I cannot dye Aya a brilliant pink as well—"

The look the firebird gave him, of purest disgust, only sent him into another fit of laughter.

Darkwind shrugged. "For that matter, there's not a reason in the world why we can't bring the *dyheli* along as another one of your 'captives.' There isn't anyone in all of Hardorn except Falconsbane who'd recognize a bondbird, a *dyheli*, or Nyara, and Falconsbane isn't likely to be patronizing a carnival."

"Also an excellent point." Kero pondered a bit more. "But there is the problem that you are all going to have magic associated with you... hmm. Can any of you lot do what Quenten could—layer illusions?"

Elspeth nodded quickly. "All of us can, it's really very simple."

Kero smiled slowly. "Good. Then here's what we'll have. You—" she pointed at Firesong, "—are a very *minor* mage, too minor for Ancar to recruit, but able to cast illusions. You put them on the Companions, the *dyheli*, and possibly yourself. Only you layer the Companions; top is a pair of glossy matched bays, under that is what any other mage will think is the reality, an illusion of a pair of nasty, old, spavined geldings. You layer the *dyheli* the same way; top is the way it really looks, under that is a donkey. You leave Nyara alone—"

:*I can make certain anyone who casts a true-sight on her will see a misshapen girl in cat makeup.:* Need supplied. :*And the assumed presence of an illusion will account for the presence of magic around us.:*

"Right, that was exactly what I was going to suggest." Kero was grinning. "Gods, we are a deceitful bunch! It's a damn good thing we're honest, or no one would be safe!"

Firesong looked supremely content. Elspeth reached for Darkwind's hand under the table, only to find his seeking hers. They exchanged a quick squeeze as Vree, with a very self-satisfied gurgle, returned across the table and leapt back up to Darkwind's shoulder.

"Once you get into Hardorn, you'll have to make it up as you go along," Kero said. "But the way I'll get you across I think can be pretty simple. The bastard can't watch the whole border, but drop a lot of what he thinks are Heralds in one place, and you *bet* he'll watch that spot pretty closely! So I'll turn out a bunch of the Skybolts in fake Whites—send them someplace that looks as if it might be strategic, and you cross wherever else you want. Put what looks like a million Heralds *anywhere*, and Ancar will be certain something is up. Hell, I might just give him something—"

Now *she* began to laugh, wearily, but after a moment, Elspeth realized it was not out of hysteria.

"What is it?" she asked.

"Oh, just something that occurred to me. I'll get one of the Blues to build me some kind of complicated war engine out of broken bits, something that can't possibly work but looks impressive enough to take out a city wall with one blow. I'll have my pseudo-Heralds escort *that* to his fortification, and let him take it. He'll spend forever trying to figure the thing out!" She wiped her eyes with the back of her hand, as the others began to chuckle. "Oh, gods, it is *such* a good thing for the world that we're honest!"

"Speak for yourself!" Firesong replied, with mock-indignation. "I intend to persuade as much coin from the pockets of the unsuspecting as possible!"

The firebird only snorted and resumed its preening.

Falconsbane sipped at a goblet of fine spiced wine and sat back in his chair with a wonderful feeling of pure content. Or, at least, as content as he could be while he was still someone else's captive. Everything was proceeding as it should, and completely in accordance with his plans.

His strategies on the border had succeeded so well that Ancar had sent him several more prisoners to dispose of, by way of reward. He had managed to determine that it was not the coercive spells that were keeping him from access to the local nodes and ley-lines, but a set of complicated keying spells that led back to—surprise!—Hulda. And those spells were keeping Ancar away, too, without a doubt. The only real power that Ancar would be able to touch, other than that derived from the death of underlings, would be through Hulda now. The keying spells would even make it difficult for Falconsbane to access those nodes were he not under coercions.

That made him all the more determined to rid himself of the bitch. He certainly didn't need her, and her overblown and overripe charms had long since lost any attraction for him; her promiscuity was appalling. She *could* have offered him the key; she had not. Therefore, she had no plans to share her power with anyone.

This put Ancar's inability to access power outside himself in another light altogether. If Hulda had locked that power away from him, he might not be altogether incompetent after all.

She was playing some kind of deep game, that one.

Falconsbane was not going to play it, either by her rules or anyone else's.

A slight tap on the door signaled another small triumph. That was Ancar, and Falconsbane had finally convinced him to announce himself before he came barging into Mornelithe's suite. Respect; the boy needed to learn respect, and he might even be worth saving and making into an underling when all this was over.

Meanwhile, the bitch needed to learn a little lesson, too.

"Enter," he said aloud, and Ancar's ever-present escort opened the door silently. Two of the guards entered first, followed by the King, who joined Falconsbane beside his fire. The guards took their positions, one on either side of the door; Falconsbane found their presence rather amusing. Evidently the boy took no chances; he protected himself physically even in the presence of someone he—relatively—trusted. What did he do when he took a wench to his bed? Drug her so that he knew she was harmless? Feh, he was so unappealing, that was probably the only way he would get a bedmate.

Ancar poured himself a cup of wine from the pitcher on the hearth. For all that he took no chances, he was prone to acting very foolishly. Falconsbane was a mage; he could have changed the content of that wine without having any access to poisons. Or didn't Ancar know that was possible?

Falconsbane waited for him to speak first, since it was obvious from the King's manner that nothing urgent had brought him here. But from Ancar's faint frown, something displeased him enough to make him seek Mornelithe's counsel.

Finally, the young King spoke. "I have tried to take power from those lines of energy you spoke about, which seem to be the same thing that Hulda called ley-lines. Something has blocked me from them." His frown deepened. "Although I could never use the nodes you spoke of because they were too powerful for me, I have been able to touch those lines in the past. But now I cannot, and I do not know why."

So, access to the ley-lines had been keyed very recently. Perhaps when Hulda realized that Ancar had attempted a Gate. She knew he was experimenting and had chosen this way to place a limit on what he could do.

"It is none of my doing," he pointed out. "But I had noted this myself; I, too, have been blocked. It is one of the reasons why I can do so little to help you, other than offer advice. I think, however," he added slyly, "that if you would trace the spells that keep you at a distance to their origin, you would find it to be Hulda."

Ancar sat upright. "Oh?" he replied, too casually. "Are you very certain of that?"

Falconsbane only shrugged. "You may see for yourself, Majesty. You certainly have the Mage-Sight to do so. There is nothing preventing you from tracing magic back to its originator."

Ancar sank back into the embrace of the chair, his frown deepening. "She overreaches herself," he muttered to himself. Mornelithe guessed that he had not meant to speak that aloud.

But Falconsbane chose to take the comment as meant for his ears. "Then give her a lesson to put her properly in her place," he said quietly. "Which of you rules here? Will you let her block you from the use of power that is rightfully yours? The coercive spells you have placed upon *me* have certainly worked well enough. Set them on her! Let her cool for a time in your prison cells. Let her see the rewards of thwarting you. Tame the bitch to your hand and muzzle her that she not bite you."

Ancar's jaw clenched and his hands tightened around the goblet. "I do not know that those spells will hold her," he admitted, reluctantly. "She is at her full strength. You were weak when I set them upon you."

Falconsbane laughed aloud, startling him so that his hands jerked, and a few drops of wine splashed out of the goblet. "Majesty, the woman is a bitch in heat when she sees a handsome young man! Lay a trap for her, then bait it with one such, and you will have her at a moment of weakness as great as mine! Only choose your bait wisely, so that he will exhaust her before you spring it."

Ancar brushed absently at the droplets of red on his black velvet tunic, and considered that for a moment. "It might work," he replied thoughtfully. "It might at that."

"If it does not, what have you lost?" Falconsbane countered. "You are something near to a Master mage, and that should suffice that you can set those spells subtly enough that she does not notice them until she tries to act against your interest. Such things are either tough or brittle. If they do not hold, they will break. Few can trace a broken spell if she even notices that the attempt was made to coerce her. If they do hold, then you will have her."

Ancar smiled at him over the edge of the goblet. "You are a good counselor, Mornelithe Falconsbane, and a clever mage. That is *why* I do not lift the spells on you, and do not intend to until I have learned all that you can teach me."

That came as something of a shock to Falconsbane, although he hid his reaction under a smooth expression. He had not given the boy credit for that much cleverness.

He would be more careful in the future.

Ancar left Falconsbane's chambers with a feeling of accomplishment. So, *that* was why he had been denied the power he needed lately! The traces that led back to Hulda were easy enough to see when you looked for them—exactly as Falconsbane claimed. He had not thought she would dare to be so blatant in her attempts to keep a leash on him.

The Adept was right. It was time to teach her a lesson; time to put the leash on *her.*

And he knew exactly the bait for the trap. Hulda was tiring of her mule driver (in no small part because she was using him to exhaustion), but Ancar had anticipated that and had found a replacement a week ago.

This one, a slave—Ancar regretted that his tastes ran to women, and had set his agent to looking for a female counterpart to him—was altogether a remarkable specimen. The agent claimed he had been bred and schooled, like a warhorse, for the private chamber of a lady of wealth from Ceejay. She had met with an accident—quite remarkably, it was a real accident—and the agent had acquired the slave from the innkeeper to whom her lodging-monies were owed. It was then that he had discovered the young man's talents, when he found the boy in bed with his wife...

He was, fortunately for Ancar, a man of phlegmatic temper and a man with his eye on the main chance. He had realized at once that this was an incident of little import. His marriage was one of convenience. The boy was a slave—whom would he tell? And who would believe him if he did speak? The woman would not dare to speak, for she would be the one disgraced if she did. The merchant's reputation was safe enough, provided he rid his household of the boy and sent him far, far away. All he needed to do would be to find a buyer—and he knew he had one in Ancar.

He persuaded his wife that she would not be punished and received such a remarkable tale of the lad's skill, training, and prowess, that he had sent a messenger to the King straight away. Ancar had bought the boy immediately, sight unseen, on the basis of that report, and had set him to work on one of the chambermaids, spying on the two to see if the reports were true.

They were more than true, and Ancar had come very close to envying that fortunate chambermaid. When the lad was through with her, she literally could not move, and she slept for an entire day.

Since then, the boy had been schooled as a page and kept strictly celibate. Reports had him frantic to exercise his craft. He should be quite ready to please Hulda now.

Ancar put the plan in motion, beginning by ordering roughly half of Hulda's staff replaced that very hour, and slipping the boy in with the replacements. The rest would follow, for the slave had been conditioned that *any* female he called "mistress" must be pleased. Hulda would not be able to resist his fresh, innocent fairness, especially in contrast to her swarthy muleteer. She would set out to seduce him, and by the time she realized that the seduction was the other way around, she would be enjoying herself so much she would not think to look any further than the pleasures of the moment.

Ancar waited until his spies told him that Hulda had retired, and not alone. He reckoned that four candlemarks would be enough to give them together, and timed his spells accordingly. Her chamber was guarded against combative magics, but not against this. Then again, she had never dreamed he would be audacious enough to use controlling spells against her.

The spells fell into place, softly as falling snow. Ancar waited a candlemark or two more, then moved in with his escort of guards.

No one tried to stop him; the guards at her doors were all his. But he did not come bursting into her chambers—no, he had the doors opened slowly, carefully, so as not to startle the boy.

After all, he might have use for such a talent some other time.

The boy awakened instantly, and looked up from the wild disarray of the bedclothes, his long blond hair falling charmingly over one sleepy, frightened blue eye. Ancar put his finger to his lips, then motioned to the boy to take himself out of the room.

The slave slipped out of the bed so quietly that he did not even stir the sheets. He did not even stop to gather up his garments; one of the guardsmen, flushing a little, stopped him long enough to hand him a robe before he escaped back to the servants' quarters. Ancar made a mental note to reward the man; a naked page skittering through the halls might cause some awkward comment. Quick thinking deserved a reward.

Ancar motioned to his guards to take up positions around the bed. Then he cleared his throat noisily.

Hulda reacted much faster than he had expected her to. She came up out of the bed like an enraged animal, fully attack-ready, her face a mask of pure anger.

"You!" she spat, seeing Ancar standing at the foot of her bed. "How *dare* you!" And she lashed out at him with her magic, as she would at a disobedient brat that needed a severe correction.

Tried to, that is. Ancar's controlling spells stopped her in mid-strike.

He had expected her to be dumbfounded, perhaps to make another attempt. He had never thought she would go from "correction" into an all-out attempt at attack.

He stepped back a pace as he felt his spells shuddering under the impact of her attempt to break them—break through them, and break *him*. One look at her expression told him that she *knew*—

Knew that her control of him was over. Knew that he now intended to make an obedient servant of her. He was now the enemy, and she would destroy him if she could.

And in that moment, he realized just how tenuous his hold over her was. Suddenly, he was overcome with terror. She could, at any moment, break loose from his control. And when she did—she would go straight for his throat.

He was no match for her.

"Take her!" he shouted at the guards. They did not hesitate—and one of them had been around mages long enough not to give her any chance to turn her spells on *him*. The moment that Ancar snapped out the order, the man seized a rug from the floor and flung it over Hulda's head, following it by flinging himself on her and the rug together. She had a fraction of a breath to be enveloped, realize she was trapped, and start to fight free. By then, he was on the bed, and coolly rapped her on the head with the pommel of his dagger. She collapsed in a heap; he gathered her up, rug and all, bound the entire package with a series of sashes and bedcurtain cords he snatched up from around him. He got to his feet, picked her up, and laid her at Ancar's feet, and then stood back, presenting the "package" as a well-trained hunting dog presented his master with a duck.

Ancar grinned. "Well done!" he applauded, noting that the man was the same one who had given the page a robe. He *would* have to see the man was rewarded well. Perhaps with the page?

Well, that would have to wait. It was not safe to leave Hulda anywhere in the palace proper; the place was rife with her power-objects. But there was one place that would be perfectly safe.

And perfectly ironic.

Long ago, he and she had worked together to make one particular cell completely magic-proof. It had held the Herald Talia for a short time, and Ancar and Hulda both had been determined that once they recaptured the woman, she would become a return visitor to that cell, this time with no means of escape. The cell was so well shielded that not even mind-magic could escape it. The shields were a perfect mirror surface on the inside and would reflect any magic cast right back into the teeth of the caster.

And since Hulda had not been able to follow through on her promise to give him Talia, it was only fitting that she herself should test her handiwork. The irony was that although she herself had set the shields, from the inside she would not be able to take them down. Delightful.

He signed to the guard who had captured Hulda to pick her up again, and noted with approval that the man took the precaution of administering another carefully calculated rap to Hulda's skull before picking her up. He was taking no chances—and Hulda would have a terrible headache when she woke.

The page was standing just inside the door to the pages' quarters as they passed, still wrapped in Hulda's fine silk robe, but with his long blond hair now neatly tied back, and his fair young face flushed. The guard carrying Hulda looked at him briefly and flushed, but it was not a blush of embarrassment. Ancar suppressed a smile of amusement.

Yes, he would certainly reward the man with the page. One night with the boy, and the guard would probably die for his lord out of purest gratitude.

With one guard leading, and the man with the Hulda-bundle following, he led the way down into the dungeons.

On the way, he ordered some servants' livery to be brought along.

He would leave nothing to chance, allow nothing from her chambers to enter the cell. If she wished to remain naked rather than clothe herself as his servant, that was her choice. If she chose to clothe herself—well, perhaps the lesson would be taken. If he could only *control* her, she could still be a useful tool…

Almost as useful as Mornelithe Falconsbane.

Falconsbane did not move from the chair when Ancar left. He was fairly certain the boy was going to take his advice. He was also fairly certain the boy would succeed.

Temporarily.

Hulda was a powerful Adept. The boy had never actually fought any mage head-to-head, much less an Adept, before this moment. When she recovered her strength, she would be perfectly capable of breaking anything that held her and quite ready to kill the one that had ordered her humiliation.

It might take a great deal of time—but she would do so, eventually, and she would devote every waking moment to the task. Hadn't Falconsbane? And Hulda would not be hindered by physical weakness or unfamiliar surroundings.

The only question in Falconsbane's mind was whether or not Ancar would succeed in killing her before she broke free of his control entirely.

The situation was perfect. He sipped his wine, and smiled.

One way or another, whether Ancar won or lost—*he* would be free, and both Hulda and Ancar would die. If Hulda killed Ancar, the coercions would go with him, and Hulda would be weak enough to destroy.

Falconsbane did not intend to leave an angry Adept on his backtrail when he left. The woman might make the mistake of trying to take him for herself.

If Ancar killed Hulda, he would have to devote everything he had to the attempt, and Falconsbane could break free as soon as the last bit of Ancar's strength and attention went to the struggle. He might even help Ancar, a little and unobtrusively.

Then when Ancar lay completely exhausted, Falconsbane would kill *him*. Sadly, it would be so swift he would not gain much blood-magic power from it, but not all things in the world were ideal.

And then—he would have to flee. Either westward or southward; things should be chaotic enough with both obvious leaders gone that he could get back into territory he knew without recapture. If he had to cross Valdemar—well, he could simply cloak himself in the illusion of a simple human peasant, fleeing the war. He could feign being simple-minded to cover his lack of the language.

He toyed briefly with the notion of staying here and attempting to take the kingdom over—but no. Firstly, Ancar had laid waste to it in his foolish warring. At the moment, it was not worth having. There would be two hostile forces inclined to move in, at least, and perhaps more. He did not know this land, and all it would take would be one lucky fool at a moment of his own weakness to kill *him*. No one native to this place would ever suffer his rule willingly.

No, he must return home, pick up the pieces, build his power back to what it had been, and see what had happened to the Hawkfools in his absence. There were still the artifacts under the Dhorisha Plains to acquire—the permanent Gate beneath the ruins near k'Sheyna to explore—and revenge to be taken. His daughter was still loose, somewhere. And that most desirable mage-sword.

And gryphons…

Gryphons…

1 4

Falconsbane drifted off into sleep, dreaming of gryphons in torment. Some were faded memories, some were fancies of his, a few cruelties he hadn't yet tried. The dreams were as tortured as the man was twisted, and An'desha could hardly wait for them to fade into the formlessness of deep sleep. When Falconsbane slept, An'desha relaxed and waited for the Avatars to appear. If he'd had a stomach, it would have been twisted with nerves; if he'd had a body, he would have paced. That was one of the problems—there was a body, but it was no longer his.

The last time the Avatars came to him, they promised him that they had found his outside allies on the way, and that he would be able to Mindspeak with one in particular directly—and very soon. They warned him that this would only be possible while Falconsbane was deeply asleep and An'desha could walk the Moonpaths, but the prospect of actually having someone who could speak to him and help him in a real and physical way was so wonderful that it had not mattered. One person, at least, would know his secret and would work to free him.

As Falconsbane's breathing slowed, the fire on the hearth flared for a moment, and a pair of glowing eyes in a tiny human face winked into existence. It was Tre'valen; he spread his arms there in the flames for the briefest of moments. The halo of transparent hawk wings shone around them.

:Come,: he said, and beckoned. An'desha did not need a second invitation; nervous energy catapulted him from this world into the next. As Tre'valen passed from the fire to the other worlds that held the Moonpaths, An'desha followed in his now-familiar wake.

He flung himself after Tre'valen with heart and will, going *in* and then *out*—

And, as he had so many times before, found himself standing beside the Avatar, on a pathway made of pearlescent light, surrounded by luminescent gray mist. Once again, he walked the Moonpaths with the Avatar of the Star-Eyed. But next to the Avatar was not Dawnfire, but someone entirely new.

The newcomer was an old woman, but strong and built like a fighter, with knotted muscles and face and arms burned brown by the sun and toughened with work in all weathers. She wore strange garments made of dark leather, simple breeches and an odd cape-shirt that seemed to have been made of an entire brain-tanned deerhide. Her hair was cut off at chin length and was as gray as iron and straight as grass. She stood beside Tre'valen with her hands on her hips, and although her face was seamed with wrinkles that indicated a certain stern character, he caught a kindly twinkle in her black eyes.

He liked her instinctively; if *this* had been his Clan shaman, he might never have tried to run away.

"So this is the boy," she said, and reached out to seize his chin so she could peer into his eyes. He had the distinct impression that she was weighing and measuring everything he was and had ever been. "Huh. You need some shaping, some tempering, and that's for certain. You're not pot-metal, but you're not battle-steel either, not yet."

He traded her look for look, sensing that shyness and diffidence would win nothing from her but contempt. "I haven't exactly had an opportunity for tempering, Wise One," he replied. "My experiences have been limited by circumstance."

Tre'valen laughed silently, his star-filled eyes somehow seeming more human than usual, and the old woman's lips twitched as if she were trying not to laugh herself. "And why is that, boy?"

"Because—" he faltered for a moment, losing his courage as he was forced to actually *say* what he was. Or rather, was not, anymore. "—because my body belongs to Falconsbane, and any moments that I live I must steal from him."

She raised an eyebrow, as if she did not find this to be so terrible. "Oh, so? And I suppose you feel very sorry for yourself, eh? You feel the fates have mistreated you?"

He shook his head. "Yes. No. I mean—"

"Ha. You don't even know your own mind." She lifted her lip in a faint sneer and narrowed her gaze. "Well, this fellow here has told me all about you, and I'll tell you what *I* think. I *could* feel sorry for you, but I won't. I've known too many people with hard lives or harder deaths to feel sorry for you. And what's more, if you indulge yourself in self-pity, I'm gone! I don't waste my time on people who spend all their time pitying themselves and not doing anything. You want out of this situation, boy, you help make it happen!"

The words stung, but not with the crack of a whip, or as salt in a wound, but rather as a brisk tap to awaken him. He lifted his chin and straightened his back. For all the harshness of her words, there was a kindliness in her tone that made him think she really *did* feel sorry for him, and would help him the best way she knew how.

And she was right; was Nyara's lot not much harder than his own? And any of Falconsbane's victims that had perished in pain surely exceeded anything that had happened to him! "Yes, Wise One," he said, forthrightly. "Tre'valen has already explained all this to me. If I am to take my body and my life back, I must earn the aid to do so. I was a coward, Wise One, but not a fool. Or rather, I was a fool before, but I am no longer one, I hope."

She snorted, but the smile was back and the sneer was gone. "Piff. A brave man is simply someone who doesn't let his cowardice and fear stop him. Hellfires, boy, we're *all* cowards at some time or another. Me, I was afraid of deep water. Never did learn to swim."

He had to smile at that. Oh, this was a crusty old woman, but she had a good heart, and a keen mind that must make her a kind of shaman among her own people. And she *did* want to help him, he knew it now as well as he knew his own predicament. Somehow her will to help him made him more confident than the Avatars' promises. They were otherworldly and uncanny, but she was as earthy and real as a good loaf of bread. As the Shin'a'in proverb went, "It is easier to believe in grain than spirits."

"I should rather think that the water would fear *you*, Wise One, and part to let you pass," he said, greatly daring but feeling she would like the attempt at a joke.

She did; she laughed, throwing her head back and braying like a donkey. "All right, Tre'valen, you were right, he'll do. He'll do."

:I said so, did I not?: Tre'valen countered, amused.

She turned serious, all in a moment. "Now listen, boy. You remember those people Falconsbane wanted to get his claws into so much? The daughter, the girl in white, the Hawkbrother boy? The ones Tre'valen told you were going to be coming this way to do something about Ancar and Falconsbane?"

He nodded. Nyara he knew too well. The girl of the white spirit-steed was one that Falconsbane had coveted, and had never even touched. The Hawkbrother—*Darkwind*, he remembered—was the son of Starblade, the Hawkbrother mage Falconsbane had gleefully corrupted.

He winced away from the memories that name called up, and not just because they were unpleasant, but because there had been moments of pleasure there, too. Falconsbane was an Adept at combining pleasure and pain, as well as an Adept mage. And he had taken pleasure *in* the pain, and used the pleasure to *cause* pain. That was what made An'desha so uncomfortable with those memories… that was what felt so… unclean. Falconsbane knew so much—and to use what he knew in the way he did—that made him all the worse, for he could have used it to such good ends had he wished. The Avatars did, and this woman had power. And the others—

"Well, those three are coming. To Hardorn, here. They are on the way right this very moment. They intend to get Ancar and Hulda—and Falconsbane; eliminate them completely, before Ancar can destroy Valdemar. What we—you, me, and the Avatars—want to do is see if they can't get Falconsbane without getting *you*. Do you understand what I'm saying?" She cocked her head to one side and regarded him carefully.

"Somehow we have to find a way to kill Falconsbane without killing my body, so I can have it back." He shook his head, feeling a sudden sinking of spirits. Put baldly, he could not see how they could manage this. "I am no mage, Wise One, but that seems an impossible task," he faltered.

She snorted. "Hellfires, boy, I've seen less likely than that come to pass in my time. Improbable, maybe. What's impossible is how he has managed to flit from body to body, down all these years," she countered.

"We don't know how he's done it. If you can find that out for me, we have a chance."

His spirits soared again. She had a point! Falconsbane *had* to have a way for his spirit to remain intact down all the centuries. And she was clearly a mage, so perhaps once she knew how the Adept had done this, perhaps she could see a way to force him out again.

He nodded with excitement, and she smiled. "Right," she said. "Now, there are actually five people coming in on this, and three of 'em are Adepts, so among all of us, I think we have a pretty good chance of coming up with an answer for you. Say—" she added as an afterthought. "You want to see what they look like right now? I tell you, it's worth seeing, you will not believe what they're doing."

"Oh—yes, please," he replied, eagerly. Tre'valen had shown him these people once, but he was starved for another sight of them. One, in particular...

A circular section of the mist between her and Tre'valen brightened— and then suddenly it was as if he were staring out a round window onto a road.

There were three riders framed in that "window," riding side-by-side. First was that incredibly handsome young man, this time with his long hair bound in a single braid down the back of his neck, and dressed in a motley of robes that would have been, separately, breathtaking and striking, but worn together presented a vision of the most appalling bad taste that An'desha had ever seen in his life. Around his neck, the young man bore a jangling tangle of cheap and tawdry jewelry, and surmounting his head was a—

Well, An'desha could not call this "creation" a hat. It was turbanlike, but so huge that it made his head look as if he were the stem of a mushroom, with a huge, scarlet cap. It, too, was covered with tinsel and jewelry, and rising in moth-eaten splendor in the front was a cluster of the saddest plumes ever to have sprung from some unfortunate bird.

His mount was a *dyheli*, but one with gilded horns, ribbons woven in his tail, and mismatched bells jangling all over some kind of harness as bright and tasteless as the rider's robes. The *dyheli* seemed to find this as amusing as the rider did.

And perched on his shoulder, in a state of resigned disgust, was a white firebird, wing-primaries and tail-feathers dyed in rainbow colors, with a huge ribbon-cluster tied onto its head, and ribbon-jesses trailing from bracelets on its legs. It was most definitely *not* amused.

An'desha smothered a giggle.

"Makes quite a sight, doesn't he, our young Firesong," the old woman said, grinning. "Now, looking at *that*, would you ever guess him to be a Tayledras Healing Adept?"

"Never," An'desha said firmly. "Nor would I take him to be other than a charlatan."

"Most wouldn't take him at all," she said dryly, "for fear his clothes might stick to them."

It was hard to turn his attention away from Firesong—for even done up in all that laughable "finery" he made An'desha ache with odd longings. He did look away, though, for the other two riders would be just as important to him as the handsome young Hawkbrother.

They rode a pair of glossy, matched bays, but were otherwise completely unremarkable. They were just another pair of shifty-eyed toughs. Under the slouches and the skin-dye, the oily hair, the sneers and the scuffed leather armor, he *could* see that the two were that Elspeth and Skif he had also seen before, in Tre'valen's vision. But it would have taken the eye of someone who knew them to see a pair of fine young Heralds in these two ne'er-do-wells. He guessed, from their postures, that when they walked, Skif would swagger, and Elspeth would slink. He would not have trusted either of them with a clipped coin, and he rather fancied that when they entered a place, women rushed to hide their children.

The vision shifted, and it was clear that the three were riding in front of a wagon, drawn by mules. And there was Nyara, beside the driver, wearing practically nothing at all, with a collar and chain holding her to a huge iron ring beside the wagon seat. She did not seem in any distress, however; in fact, she had draped herself across the seat in a languorous and seductive—and very animalistic—pose. Beside her, wearing a less flamboyant version of Firesong's motley, was Darkwind. He slouched over the reins, his posture suggesting that he was both submissive and bored. His hawk sat on his shoulder, looking around alertly, with ribbon-jesses like the firebird's, but without the ribbon-hat.

But the collar and leash on Nyara bothered him, and made him worried for her. What would she do if some toady of Ancar's attempted some kind of attack? "The collar snaps right off," the old woman assured him, evidently reading his mind as easily as the Avatars did. "She can be rid of it any time she likes. They're playing at being entertainers, with a traveling Faire. Firesong's a magician with a trick-bird act, Darkwind is his assistant, Nyara is his 'captive cat-woman.' She does a dance where she takes off most of her clothes, too; I tell you *that* makes the hair on these villagers curl. The other two are selling a bogus cure-all that Firesong supposedly makes. It's spiced brandy with some good herbs in it, which is more than I can say for most quack cure-alls, and they price it about the same as a bottle of brandy, so people are willing to buy."

An'desha stared at Nyara, not because he found her seductive, but because an idea was slowly beginning to form in his mind. "Wise One," he offered, hesitantly, "You do know that if Falconsbane should hear rumors of a cat-woman, he would be eager to know more. He might even try to see her for himself. He does not know it was Nyara who smashed his crystal and flung him into the Void."

"He doesn't?" the old woman replied, her eyes brightening with interest.

"No," An'desha said firmly. "I know his mind, and I know that he never knew that. At the moment, he believes that she fled into the East. He could readily believe she came far enough to be caught by these folk. And *he* does not know *how* far to the East he truly is from his home."

"Really?" The old woman's eyes narrowed in sudden concentration. "Now isn't that a bit of interesting thought! I'll pass that on, and we'll see if we can't build on it, eh?"

He smiled shyly back at her, and was about to ask her where she was in this caravan—and then felt the laggings that meant Falconsbane was about to awaken.

"I must go!" he said—and plunged away.

The sparse crowd on either side of the road was quiet. In Valdemar they'd have been cheering.

But this wasn't Valdemar, and these people had little energy for cheers.

:You don't deserve me,: Cymry said to Skif, with a chuckle in her mind-voice.

:So long as it's mutual,: Skif replied. From anyone besides Cymry, he'd have taken offense, but such jabs between close friends were amusing, in a situation where little else was. He was worried about Nyara, wondering if she had overestimated her ability to cope with her role of sexual object. The stares of the men made her tenser than she admitted, and the strain of the dancing-show left her trembling with fear after every performance.

He scowled at the townsfolk, who stood outside their doors and stared at the passing wagons, a bit of interest coming into their otherwise sad and bleak-eyed faces. He didn't really want to scowl, and it made him sorry to see the fear in their eyes when he gave them that unfriendly look, but the scowl fit the persona he wore. Hardorn had gotten worse since the last time he had been through it, and things hadn't been all that good then. Most of the people had lost all hope, and it showed, in the untended streets, in the threadbare clothing, in the ill-kept houses.

:I know I don't deserve you, but what brought that on?: he asked her.

:There's a young man over there with a bad leg—see him?: she replied, pointing with her nose to the road just ahead. *:He was in the cavalry, got hurt, and got kicked out, and he thinks you stole me—and he knows you don't deserve me. He's got some rudimentary Mindspeech, so I can hear him.:*

And from the frown on the young man's face, he was resentful enough to make his thoughts heard to anyone unshielded. It was fairly easy to see why he'd gotten the boot from the cavalry; he'd broken his leg and no one had bothered to set it properly, so it had healed all wrong. He could use it, but not well and he needed a cane; the leg jutted at a crooked angle that must have made walking an agony. Skif grimaced; that sort of thing would never have happened in Valdemar. It would never even have happened in Kero's Skybolts, or any other good merc company.

It appeared that the rotten weather was plaguing Hardorn just as badly as Valdemar, and Ancar had not even bothered to try to do anything about it. The town was between storms at the moment, but the streets were deeply rutted, as muddy as a river, and the skies were overcast.

But Firesong would make certain the bad weather held off so that the troupe could hold its entertainments as soon as they set up. *They* traveled under cloudy but rainless skies, thanks to him, Darkwind, and Elspeth.

The traveling Faire needed that break in the local weather, if they were going to make any money; that had been part of the bargain Kero and Talia had made for the protection of the wagon-folk. Wherever the carnival went, the weather would be as close to clear as they could manage, so the tents would go up without hindrance, and the performers' shows could go on without a downpour. And, as usual, Nyara would be one of the most popular acts in the carnival.

He thrust down his surge of jealousy and anxiety at that thought, his hands tightening on Cymry's reins. And he vowed, once again, that he would not take that jealousy out on her. She was doing her part—she didn't like what she was doing any better than he did. She had told him it made her feel greasy, as if the men watching her had been running their hands on her and leaving oily marks behind. It frightened her although she would never admit it to anyone but him. And he was afraid it called up old, bad memories as well.

That didn't make the jealousy go away, but it made it a little easier to live with and control. Perhaps simply thinking about it was giving him more control over it. He hoped so, because Nyara's exotic beauty was likely to bring the attraction of men wherever she went, even if she wore the robes of a cloistered sister.

There had been some muttering about Nyara's popularity as an act among the rest of the troupe after their first stop and her first performances. That muttering had ended when he and Nyara distributed the "take" among the rest of the entertainers. That had been Nyara's idea, and he was glad she had suggested it, for it had turned what might have become an ugly situation into a pleasant one. Now everyone watched cheerfully as their tent filled for Nyara's show, for the bigger the audience, the more there would be for all to share. Their cover story, of searching for lost relatives with a view to extracting them from Hardorn, was holding water, given more credence by the fact that among the troupers, they were making no attempt to conceal the fact that they had no interest in making a profit.

As Talia had warned, there were no families with this troupe; only single men and very few women. Most of those women were actually as hardened and tough as Elspeth looked to be. Only people willing to risk everything for a fast profit would make such a journey. There were no real Faires in Hardorn anymore, and no single peddlers providing the country folk with goods. This might be the only entertainment these people would see for the next year—and it would certainly be the only chance they'd have to spend a coin or two on something besides day-to-day necessities. Ancar might be grinding his people into poverty, but there were still youngsters falling in love and wanting love-tokens; still pretty girls wishing for something bright to attract someone's eye; still loving husbands wanting a special little gift for a new mother. Ordinary life went on, even while war raged over the border, and Ancar despoiled his own land...

The houses ended, and the road came out on the village common— high ground, thank goodness, and not as sodden as the last place they'd played. Ahead of him, the other members of the troupe had begun to form the rows of wagons that became the carnival. Every wagon had its particular place; closest to the village, the food sellers and the trained beasts. Next, the folk with fairings and other goods to sell. Farthest away, entertainment tents. There were reasons for the placement, based on how people spent their money; Skif didn't pretend to understand any of it, but he followed the wagon-master's waved direction, and led the way for Darkwind to bring the wagon up beside the one with the contortionist and jugglers. They were, as always, the last in the row, since Nyara was the most popular of acts. Anyone who wanted to see her had to make his way past the temptation of every other peddler, vendor, and entertainer in the carnival.

Firesong didn't even pretend to be an "act" anymore; his show was strictly to attract people to the tent between Nyara's shows, so that Skif and Darkwind could try and sell them bottles of cure-all. He was having the time of his life. He combined sleight-of-hand with genuine illusions, ending with bird tricks, which Aya suffered through and Vree positively bounced through. There was one trick, however, that all of them enjoyed—

—the one where Aya would sail out into the audience, and pick out particularly impoverished-looking children, bringing one back to his bondmate. Then Firesong would pluck gilded "coins" from the child's ears, hair, pockets—any place he could think of—until the child's hands were overflowing with the bounty of what appeared to be gold-painted mock-coins. Then he would send the little one back out to his or her parents, who were always indulgently pleased with the little one's "treasure," assuming it to be as tawdry as Firesong's jewelry.

Of course, the next day, when the illusion wore off and the coins proved to be real copper and silver, their reaction would probably be something else entirely. Every member of the assassination team wished they could see that moment. There was something redeeming about doing small acts of kindness while they faced their necessary task with varying measures of reluctance.

The wagon slowed and was parked. Elspeth and Skif left their Companions to join Darkwind in readying their show.

Elspeth unhitched the mules and picketed them. Skif went to the back of the wagon and jumped up onto the little porch there, reached up to release a latch at the top, just under the roof, while Darkwind did the same at the front.

Skif watched Darkwind, reflexively analyzing his weak points and noting his handyness. Skif had been going over parts of his past during this trip, and remembered the knife-edges of resentment he had suppressed while Elspeth and Darkwind grew closer. He remembered analyzing Darkwind for the quickest elimination many times, in case he became a threat to Valdemar or Elspeth. Now, though, there was no animosity toward him—it was simply habit.

Darkwind stepped back and signaled. Carefully, they brought what had appeared to be the side of the wagon down on its hinges; this was the stage. This would be where Firesong would work his magic; behind the stage-platform was the real side of the wagon, and there were racks of "Magic Pandemonium Cure-All" in scarlet bottles, built into the recess the stage had covered. The stage itself was hinged its entire length, and he and Darkwind dropped it down onto four stout legs they pulled from under the wagon to support its weight.

While he and Darkwind set up the stage, Elspeth and Nyara crawled under the wagon to take the tent and tent poles from the rack beneath. By the time the stage was set up, they had the tent spread out on the other side, ready to erect. He and Darkwind pounded stakes into the soft earth at each corner, ready to take the guy ropes.

Another stage dropped down from this side of the wagon, but this one had a curtain behind it and was the actual wagon wall. Nyara would appear and retreat into the wagon itself, which doubled as their living-quarters. The wagon formed the back wall of the tent, with the canvas forming the other three walls and roof. It only held about ten people crowded in together, but the stage was high enough that no one could reach Nyara without encountering either him or Elspeth. Lanterns on either side of the curtain gave enough light to see most of Nyara's performance.

Ten was as many people as they wanted to have to handle, just in case anyone decided to try to get more out of Nyara than a dance. Darkwind provided the "music" she danced to—a drum—and Skif and Elspeth stood guard over the stage while Firesong guarded the outside. If the men ever got to the point where swords weren't deterrent enough, Darkwind or Elspeth would hit them with true magic to get rid of them.

The canvas was heavy and unwieldy; he and Firesong—who had shed the hat and most of the robes to help with the work—took one side, while Darkwind and Elspeth wrestled with the other, and Nyara crawled inside to set up the tent poles. He sneaked a look at her receding—anatomy.

The first few times they'd done this, it had taken so long that the other wagon-folk had given them a hand so that the carnival could open before dark. Now they were only a little slower than the rest, which was fine, since they were at the end of the line anyway. They would be set up by the time people actually got here.

He sniffed; there was hot oil and spice from the food-vendors, who sold grease-fried bits of salty dough and other things, cups of sweetened water with vegetable dyes in them, and very cheap beer. He knew better than to eat anything from the vendors; one of the reasons that "Pandemonium Cure-All" made money was that it had stomach-soothers in it, and the Great Mage Pandemonium could usually effect a cure or two right on the spot. The vendors shrugged and said philosophically that Faire-food was always pretty awful; if you wanted a good meal, you ate at home. But given the hungry stares some of the people of Hardorn had, Skif had to wonder if this *was* good food now, to them. Gods, that was a frightening thought.

The center of the tent rose to a peak; Nyara had gotten the middle pole up. She always had a knack for that. A moment later, the two corner poles went in. Skif and Darkwind pulled the corner ropes as tight as they could, then tied them to the stakes they'd pounded into the ground. The canvas by the wagon bobbed as Nyara tied it to the top of the wagon from inside. He dusted off his muddy hands on his breeches and went around to the front to join the others.

Darkwind and Elspeth were already at the edge of the outer stage, and a moment later, Firesong emerged from the back of the wagon, his dubious finery back in place and a grin on his face. His firebird stretched its wings by flying to the front of the carnival and back, causing cries of excitement from the gathering townsfolk as it flew overhead, streaming ribbons. Vree did the same, indulging in some aerobatics to make up in showmanship what he lacked in appearance.

"We've got everything well in hand," Darkwind said, as he looked around for something to do. "Why don't you go into the wagon and spend a little time with Nyara before the first show? You two have little enough time with each other."

It was a suggestion Darkwind didn't have to make twice. Skif ran up the set of stairs at the tail of the wagon and joined Nyara.

She was putting on little bits of makeup and rabbit fur to make her look as if she was wearing a costume. They included a preposterous pair of artificial ears that she could have used as sails, if they'd had a boat.

She was holding them with an expression of distaste. "I do not like these," she sighed. "They do not fit well, and they are very itchy!"

He chuckled and took one for her, carefully fitting it over her own, delicately pointed ear. "If you wouldn't be so impatient, and wait for me to come and help you, they wouldn't itch as badly," he told her, carefully gluing it in place along her cheek.

She smiled wryly, and handed him the other one to put on for her, then began to add cat-stripes to her forehead and cheekbones. "I wish we did not have to do this," she said pensively. But behind the pensive expression, he sensed real strain and fear. Was there more strain there tonight than last night?

"I do, too," he told her, his voice husky with the effort of holding back emotions. She turned, then, and quickly laid the palm of her hand against his cheek, staring up into his eyes.

"If you dislike it so greatly that it hurts you—I will stop—" she faltered, searching his face for his true feelings. "We could—I could be displayed in a cage, perhaps—"

But that notion clearly made her more afraid than the dancing did. He shook his head, his stomach in turmoil, and captured her hand in his own. "No," he told her. "No, this is the best and fastest way to get Him to hear about you. We need that. But—I worry about you," he continued, his throat feeling choked and thick. "I know that this could be hurting you, all these men, staring at you, and thinking the way your father did. I worry if you think *I'm* thinking that, too, if you wonder if that's the only way I see you, as something to use—to own—"

She licked her lips and swallowed. "Yes," she admitted after a long moment. "Yes, sometimes I do wonder that. And sometimes I wonder if that is the only real worth I have—"

He started to blurt something, but she laid her finger against his lips, and smiled, a thin, sad smile but a real one. "But then," she continued, "you say something like you just did—or Need tells me to stop being a stupid little kitten and get *on* with my job, and I know it is not true."

She took her finger away, pulled him close, and locked him in another of her impossible, indescribable embraces.

When she released him again, she said only, "I love you, Herald-man."

He kissed her gently, but with no less passion. "I love you, too, cat-lady."

She laughed at the grease-makeup that smeared his face and delicately touched a clawed finger to the tip of his nose.

And then Darkwind began to beat the drum for Firesong's first turn, and there was no time...

Treyvan narrowed his eyes, and regarded a scarlet-clad Sun-priestess with what he hoped was a predatory expression. "I agrrree with you that Rassshi isss a young idiot," he said carefully, "and he isss likely mosssst difficult to worrrk with. He isss ssscatterrrbrrrained."

The priestess nodded, her mouth forming a tight, angry line.

"But," he continued, "you will worrrk with him. He knowsss the ssspellsss that you do not, and you need to know them. Morrre, you need to learrrn how to worrrk with thossse you do not carrre forrr."

The priestess tossed her head; he had been warned about her. She was formerly from a noble Karsite family, and she was very conscious of her birth-rank. She had made trouble before this, during her training as a priestess. Rashi, besides being scatterbrained, was the son of a pigkeeper. But he was kindhearted as well, and he knew a series of protective spells that no one else here had mastered—and whether she liked it or not, Treyvan was determined that Gisell *would* learn them, and would learn to work with him.

Treyvan rose to his full height, and towered over her. "You will worrrk with him," he repeated. "A mage who will not cooperrrate isss a dangerrr to all of usss. And I am *not* of Valdemarrr, Karrrse, orrr Rrrethwellan. I do not *carrre* about you orrr yourrrr alliancesss. I will be gone when thisss warrr isss overrr. I do thisss asss a perrrsssonal favorrr to Darrrkwind. And I will sssnap the sssspine of anyone who makesss thisss tasssk morrrre difficult!"

Her face went blank, as she picked his words out of the tangle of trills and hisses, and then she paled. He snapped his beak once, loudly, by way of emphasis, a sound like two dry skulls crunching against each other.

"I have younglingssss to feed," Hydona added suggestively, looking over Treyvan's shoulder. "Meat-eaterrrsss. They *do* ssso love meat of good brrreeding."

The priestess swallowed once, audibly, then tried to smile. "Perhaps Rashi simply needs some patience?" she suggested meekly.

"Patiencssse isss a good thing," Treyvan agreed, lying back down again. "Patiencssse isss a jewel in the crrrown of any prrriesssstesss."

The priestess bowed with newly born meekness, then turned to go back to poor young Rashi, her assigned partner, who probably had no idea the young woman had come storming up to Treyvan to demand someone else. The trouble was, there *was* no one else. The priestess had alienated every Herald and most of the Rethwellan mages except dim but good-natured Rashi.

Gisell was only half-trained, but would certainly be Master rank when she finally completed her schooling. Rashi was only a bottom-rank Journeyman, a plain and simple earth-wizard, and never would be any more powerful than that—but his training had been the best. His instincts were sharp, and his skills were sound.

This was the essence of all the pairs, triads, and quartets that Treyvan and Hydona were setting up. Powerful but half-trained mages were partnered with educated but less powerful mages, with the former working *through* the latter, as Elspeth had worked in partnership with Need. To the knowledge of any of the fully schooled mages, no one had ever tried this before. All the better. What had never been tried, Ancar could not anticipate.

Some of these teams were already out with the Guard or the Skybolts—and there had been not one, but *two* Adept-class potential Heralds among the two dozen or so that had come riding in, responding to the urgent need sent out on the Web. Both of them had been paired immediately, one with the single White Winds teacher young enough to endure the physical hardships of this war, and one with the Son of the Sun's right-hand wizard, a surprisingly young man with a head full of good sense and a dry sense of humor that struck chords with Treyvan's own. They were doing a very fine job of holding Ancar's progress to a crawl, simply by forcing Ancar's mages to layer protections on the coercive spells controlling his fighters. Ancar had, in fact, been forced to send in the Elite Guard, putting them immediately behind the coerced troops to supply a different kind of motivation to advance.

Treyvan and Hydona were in complete charge of Valdemar's few mages and mage-allies, simply because they *were* the most foreign. Their ongoing story, at least so far as anyone other than Selenay and her Council were concerned, was just what Treyvan had told that young priestess. They were doing this as a favor to Darkwind; they were completely indifferent to Valdemaran politics, external or internal. Add to that their size and formidable appearance... thus far, no one had cared to challenge any of their edicts. When they needed to coordinate with Valdemar's forces, they went through subcommanders Selenay had assigned.

Treyvan turned his attention back to the trio he had been working with before Gisell interrupted. "Yourr parrrdon," he said, thinking as he did so that at any other time and place, these three would have been at such odds that there would probably have been bloodshed. Not that they weren't getting along; they were cooperating surprisingly well. But a south-border Herald, a red-robed Priest of Vkandis, and a mage who had once fought Karse under Kerowyn... it could have been trouble.

The priest shrugged, the Herald chuckled, and the merc mage shook his head. "Gisell always difficult has been," the priest said, in his stilted Valdemaran. "Young, she is."

"Just wait until she gets out on the lines, she'll settle down," the Herald advised. The mage, an older man, bent and wizened, nodded.

"They gen'rally do," he said comfortably. "Either that, or they don' last past their first fight." He glanced at the other two. "You, now—I kin work with the both of ye."

"Query, one only, had I," the priest said, looking at Treyvan, but with a half-smile for the old man. Treyvan waited, but the priest, oddly, hesitated. Treyvan wished he could read human faces better; this man's expression was an odd one. It looked like his face-skin was imploding.

"Red-robe, I am not, truly," he said after a moment. "Black-robe am I. Or was I."

He looked from the Herald to the other mage, who shrugged without comprehension, and sighed.

"Black-robe, the Son has said, no more to be. Black-robes, demon-runners are." And he watched, warily, for a reaction.

He got one. The old mage hissed and stepped back a pace; the Herald's eyes widened. It was the Herald who spoke first, not to Treyvan, but to the priest.

"I'd heard rumors some of you could control demons," he said, his eyes betraying his unease, "but I never believed it—I never saw anything to make me believe it."

"Control?" The priest shrugged. "Little control. As—control great rockfall. Take demon—send demon—capture demon. The Son likes demons not; the Son has said: 'Demons be of the dark, Vkandis is all of the light.' Therefore, no more demon-runners."

"So she demoted you?" the mage demanded. "Uh—took your rank."

But the priest shook his head. "No. Rank stays, robe goes, and no more demon-runners." He turned back to Treyvan. "Question: demons terrible be and all of the dark. Yet them do we use now, here?"

Treyvan lidded his eyes, thinking quickly. How he wished this man's superior was here! "Jussst what doesss he mean by 'demonsss'?" he asked the Herald, who seemed to have some inkling of what the priest was talking about.

"There've always been stories that some of the Vkandis priests could control supernatural night-creatures," the Herald replied. The priest followed the words closely, nodding vigorously from time to time when the Herald hit precisely on the facts. "They're supposed to be unstoppable—they keep whole villages indoors at night for fear of them, and they are said to be able to take individuals right out of their beds in locked homes, with no one the wiser. What these things are, I don't know—though from what you and Jonaton there have taught me so far, my guess is they're from the Abyssal Plane, which would mean they aren't real bright. Basically, you haul them out, give them a target or an area to patrol, turn them loose—and try to stay out of their way."

The priest was nodding so hard now that Treyvan was afraid his head would come off. "Yes, yes," he said. "Yes, and terrible, terrible."

Treyvan's own magic was of the direct sort; he had little experience in using or summoning creatures of any of the Planes. The closest he had ever come was in calling an elemental or two, like a *vrondi*. This sort of thing was usually undertaken by a mage with little mind-magic and a fairly weak Mage-Gift, but with a great deal of trained will. A focused and trained will could accomplish a great deal, even when the sorcerer's own powers were slight, provided the sorcerer had a known source of energy. Unfortunately, when a mage's own abilities were poor, the most certain source of energy was that of pain and death. Which was why most of the mages summoning other-Planar creatures were blood-path mages.

This priest seemed to be the exception to that rule; he was somewhere on the border between Journeyman and Master, and he certainly didn't *need* demons to help him. He seemed very sincere, and very anxious that they know both that he *could* call demons, and that they were pretty dreadful creatures.

"Terrible, terrible," the priest repeated. "But Ancar terrible is. Yes?"

Ah, so what he was saying was that the demons were a dreadful weapon, but they were a weapon Ancar might deserve to get in his teeth.

Now here was a dilemma, if ever there was one. A terrifying weapon, an evil enemy. Did the one deserve the other?

Treyvan ground his beak, frustrated. He had flown out to the front lines once, and it was a damned mess. It had Falconsbane written all over it; there was that kind of callous disregard for life. The carnage could not have been described. Ancar was driving his troops over ground so thick with the bodies of the dead that there wasn't a handspan of dirt or grass visible anywhere. If a soldier lost a limb, he could bend over and pick up a new one.

To use the weapon, or not?

"Could Ancarrr take yourrr demonsss, once you loosssed them?" he asked the priest urgently. "Could *he* ussse them?"

The man looked very startled, as if he had not considered that question. Then, after a moment of thought, he nodded slowly.

Treyvan let out a growling breath he did not realize he had been holding in. So much for the moral question. You do not fling a weapon at your enemy that he may then pick up and use.

Or, as the Shin'a'in said, "Never *throw* your best knife at your foe."

"No demonsss," he said firmly. "We do not give Ancarrr demonsss he can ssssend back." The priest looked relieved. The Herald and old Jonaton definitely looked relieved.

"Now," he continued, "let usss once again trrry thisss messshing of sssshieldsss…"

The gryphlets and the two royal twins were playing a game of tag. Of all of them, Hydona reflected, it was the children who were affected the least. For as long as Lyra and Kris had been alive, there had been war with Ancar and danger in Valdemar. For as long as Lytha and Jerven had been alive, they had nested in a perilous world. For both sets of twins, the danger was only a matter of degree. And the tension their parents were under was offset by the joy of having a new set of playmates.

For the two human children, having the fascinating Rris as a new teacher and nurse only made things better. And as for the gryphlets, they now had a brand new playground, and an entire new set of toys and lessons. For the four of them, life was very good.

The youngsters all lived together during the day in the salle. Lessons at the Collegium had been canceled for the duration, and the trainees set to running errands—or, if they were about to graduate, were thrown into Whites and put under the direct tutelage of an experienced Herald. The salle had only one entrance, and that could be easily guarded— and was, not only by armed Guardsmen but by every unpartnered Companion at the Collegium, in teams of four pairs. Inside, ropes could be strung from the ceiling for young gryphlets to climb, practice dummies set up for them to wrestle, and a marvelous maze of things to climb on, slide down, and crawl about in could be constructed for both species. All of these things were done. They caused twice the noise of a war themselves when they were in full swing.

When the children tired, there was always Rris or the two human nurses—a pair of retired Heralds—who were ready to tell stories or teach reading and writing—well, reading, anyway. The gryphlets' talons were not made for holding human-sized pens. The nurses also instructed the youngsters in the rudiments of any of the four languages now being spoken on the Palace grounds.

Already it was a race to see if the human children picked up more Kaled'a'in, or the gryphlets more Valdemaran, just from playing with each other.

Hydona sighed, thinking wistfully how much she wished she could join the little ones, if only for an hour. But at least she had them when the day was done... and Rris was the best teacher anyone could ever have asked for. It was a truism that those who provided support were greater heroes than the ones who fought the wars, so Rris was as much a hero as his "Famous Cousin Warrl."

She knew that Selenay felt the same, but Selenay spent far more time away from her little ones than Hydona did, for Selenay's day did not end when she and a set of pupils were exhausted. The Queen and Kerowyn coordinated everything from the War Room in the Palace.

And it could not be done, save for the Mindspeaker among the Heralds.

Valdemar's greatest advantage remained its communications. Tactics could be put hand in hand with strategy from the Palace, thanks to Mindspoken dispatches, read in condensed battle-code, from field scoutings. Valdemar's second advantage was knowledge of the land; Heralds on circuit for so many generations had kept precise maps. Whether the land was high or low, wet or dry, resources could be moved rapidly with a minimum of waste.

Ancar had taken a bite from the side of Valdemar; Selenay and Kerowyn were ensuring that he did not find it an easy bite to digest. Treyvan's mages harried his mages, concentrating all their power on simply disrupting whatever spells had been set, by targeting the mages for specific, personalized nuisance attacks as well as attempting to break the spells themselves. This, evidently, was a strategy no one had used here. Ancar had not anticipated that FarSeers could identify his mages at a distance, and pass that information to mages who could then tailor their spells to suit. It did seem to be helping. And the Guard and Skybolts ran constant hit-then-run-away attacks against his lines, never letting Ancar's troops rest quietly, and doing their best to disrupt the supply lines.

The good news was that the civilian evacuation was working. There were a minimum of civilian casualties, those mostly too stupid or stubborn to leave when they were told to. This was something Hydona could not understand. How could humans be so attached to *things* and *property* that they would lose their lives simply to stay with those things? Nesting for the deranged.

She watched the youngsters a moment more, her heart aching with the need to cuddle them, human and gryphlet alike. But they had not noticed her, and she would not disturb their moment of joy for the world. Too often, the appearance of a parent meant the bad news that the parent would be away for a while. And while the younglings were amazingly resilient and seemed able to play no matter what, there were dark fears lurking beneath their carefree exteriors. When Mummy or Daddy came to say they would be "away," there was always that fear that "away" would mean far away, like Teren and Jeri, and Darkwind and Elspeth—and they might not come back again...

Hydona slipped out again, with a nod of thanks to the Guard and a feather touch for three of the Companions. Her pupils were ready for the front lines; soon all of the mages would be with the troops, and it *would* be time for that dreaded "going away." Treyvan and Hydona would have to leave the little ones, to take personal command of the mage-troops.

But as she neared the Palace, she saw a horse being led to the stables, and took a second, sharper look at it.

Rough gray coat; dense muscles; huge, ugly head—

It was! It was a Shin'a'in battle mare!

She spread her wings and bounded a few steps, taking to the air to fly the rest of the distance to the Palace. As she neared, she saw someone— one of the gray-clad trainees—waving frantically to her.

She backwinged to a landing, trying not to knock the poor child off her feet, as the girl braced herself against the wash from her wings.

"There's some 'un t' see ye, Lady," the girl said. "What I mean is, she's seen th' Queen, now she wants t' see one o' ye gryphons."

"Do I go to herrr, orrr doesss ssshe come to me?" Hydona asked logically.

"I come to you, Lady," replied the black-clad Shin'a'in Swordsworn, who emerged from the door behind the trainee. To Hydona's amazement she used Kaled'a'in, not Shin'a'in or Valdemaran.

This plethora of tongues could get to be very confusing, she thought fleetingly as the Shin'a'in sketched a salute.

"It would, of course, be far too difficult for you to enter this door," the woman continued. "I bring greetings Lady, from your kin—"

Then before Hydona could say or do anything, the woman closed her eyes in concentration and began to rattle off a long series of personal messages, messages that were, unmistakably, from Hydona's kin and friends still in the Kaled'a'in Vale. There were something like twenty of them, and the poor trainee simply stood there in bafflement while the Swordsworn recited.

Hydona simply absorbed it all, lost in admiration. "Rrremarkable. How did you do that?" she asked when the Shin'a'in was done.

The woman smiled. "I was shaman-trained before the Star-Eyed called me to this," she said simply. Hydona nodded. Since half of the shamanic training required memorization of verbal histories, twenty messages would be no great burden.

Then Hydona noticed something else. The woman was not black-clad, as she had thought, but was garbed in very deep blue.

Well, at least she is not here on blood-feud! That would have been a complication no one needed right now.

"I am here," the woman said, answering Hydona's unspoken question, "for the same reason that you are here. I am the emissary from my people to k'Valdemar, and in token of that, I brought the Queen a true alliance gift. And I see no reason why you should not know it, since shortly all will." She smiled widely. "It is good news, I think, in a time of bad. Tayledras, Kaled'a'in, and Shin'a'in have united, and are holding open safe exit routes upon the Valdemar border to the west and south. Those places will stay in safe hands. Should all fail, the people of k'Valdemar can do as they did in their past—retreat, and find safe-havens. We, our warriors and yours, shall stay and survive, and work to set all aright."

Hydona felt limp with relief. That had been her unvoiced, worst fear—that somehow Falconsbane would raise the western border against Valdemar, and trap everyone between an army of his creatures and Ancar's forces.

And—k'Valdemar? So, the Kingdom of Valdemar was being counted as one great Clan. And by all the Clans…?

Shin'a'in, Tayledras, and Kaled'a'in… Hydona could guess at only one thing that could have pried the Shin'a'in out of their Plains, or the Tayledras from their forests—

She sent a glance of inquiry at the woman, who nodded significantly and cast her eyes briefly upward.

So. *She* had sent forth an edict, had She? Interesting. Very interesting. It made sense, as much as anything did these days—and after all,

Treyvan and Hydona had been part of bringing it all about. Of course, it was also entirely possible that the Star-Eyed was being opportunistic.

She could be claiming responsibility for events that simply *happened,* as if it were part of a great Cosmic Plan. Most of this uniting of the Clans and People could have been dumb luck. Still, for whatever reason it happened, there it was, and it was a relief indeed.

This Shin'a'in must have ridden day and night to get here as fast as she did, even with Tayledras Gating to get her to the Vale nearest the Valdemar border!

"Yourrr parrrdon," Hydona said, as she read the signs of bone-deep, profound fatigue that the woman's control had hidden with fair success. "I am keeping you frrrom a rrressst that isss sssurely well-earrrned."

"And I will accept your pardon and take that rest," the woman said, with a quick smile of gratitude. "And when you meet me later—I am called Querna, of Tale'sedrin." Then she turned to the poor, baffled trainee, who could not have been much older than twelve or thirteen, and spoke in careful Valdemaran. "My thanks, child. I have discharged the last of my immediate duties, and I will now gladly take your guidance to the room you spoke of."

"Thank you, warrriorrr! Rrressst well!" Hydona called after her. How many languages did these people know? Hydona felt a moment of embarrassment at her growling accent. Ah, but accents were unimportant as long as words were understood. And those words! Treyvan would be so pleased!

She hurried to find her mate, to give him the good news, with a lightness of step she hadn't felt in a long time.

Now, if their tactics of mistake and harassment would hold, if the innocents could escape, if they could only hold Hardorn's forces long enough for their real weapon to find its mark, *then* they could celebrate. All the People and their friends together, and the children...

1 5

Firesong rode in front of Skif and Elspeth, telling himself that there was no reason to give in to depression. Things were no different now than they had been when this journey began, but giving himself encouraging lectures did not really help. For the past several days he had hidden his growing and profound unhappiness, feigning a careless enjoyment of his role. There was no point in inflicting any further strain on the others, who had their own worries and stresses.

But this land was appalling. The farther into it they came, the worse it got, as if the closer they went to Ancar's "lair," the worse his depredations on his land and people.

Firesong had grown up around the gray and brown of lightbark and willow, sighing-leaf, loversroot and sweet-briar, but the overcast and mud of Hardorn were different, even if the colors were the same as those Vale plants and trees. The grays and browns of Hardorn were those of life departed, not the colors of the life itself. The colors of his robes that had seemed so outrageously bright in Valdemar were sullen and sad. It felt like life had seeped away into the ever-present mud, and he had faded like the colors.

Intellectually, he knew that he had not been prepared for the experience of so many people living together in their cities and towns, and for the problems that caused. Tayledras simply did not live like that, giving each person in a Vale a reasonable amount of space and privacy—and outside their Vales, the land was always wild and untamed in every sense. However, he fancied he had come to grips with the way folk lived here, and certainly he had even come to appreciate some of the advantages.

But that had been in Valdemar, not Hardorn. This was *not* just his reaction to seeing folk crowding themselves like sheep in a pen, and not only his reaction to the joyless and uncreative lives most of them led. That, in itself, was quite bad enough. For most of these folk, their days were an unending round of repetitive labor, from sunup to sundown, tasks that varied only with the season, and not much even then. A dreadful amount of time was spent simply in obtaining enough food for themselves and their families. The "wizard-weather," as folks called it here, had been hard on Valdemar, but it was only a small part of what was destroying Hardorn.

There were better ways, ways to make an ordinary man's life more fulfilling—he had seen that much in Valdemar—but Skif told him that the ruler of this land wanted things this way. A hungry man is concerned with the filling of his belly and not with attempts to free himself from a vile overlord. Being forced to toil to exhaustion each day left no one any time to think of aught but how the next day's toil could be endured.

In Valdemar, at least, while the poorest folk did labor mightily to feed themselves, they also had some leisure, some time to devote to things outside that round of work. Time to make things purely for the sake of ornament, time to talk, time to sing and dance.

But here... here there was no escape from grueling labor, for before one could even work to gain one's bread, one must labor in the service of the King. Only after much work was put in—tilling the King's fields, mending the King's roads, minding the King's herds—could one return to one's own tiny holding and work for one's own self. And this went on, every day, week in, week out, with never a holiday and never a day of rest.

And meanwhile, the very land itself suffered. Firesong had never seen anything like this, and had only heard of it from his own teachers. Few mages, even those following dark and blood-stained paths, ever did this to the lands they claimed, for they planned to use those lands and took thought not to use them up.

All things living produced tiny amounts of mage-energy which gathered like dew and flowed down into the ley-lines and thence to the nodes. There was some energy available at the sources, weak, but easy to tame, and accessible to a Journeyman. There was more to be had from the lines, though it was stronger, and took a Master's hand. And the magic of nodes, of course, was something only an Adept could ever hope to control. All this power flowed naturally, in good time, and as both King and mage, Ancar should have husbanded those resources. But Ancar was not content with that. His magics forced the energy from the land, taking the life with it. Small wonder that folks felt drained and without hope! Ancar was stealing their life-force away from them, from their children, from their crops and their animals!

Ancar was a study in malicious negligence, who had risen to power by gradual theft overshadowed by visible force.

The only bright side to all of this was that what Ancar was doing was relatively easy to cure. Even the cure itself was the essence of simplicity.

Dispatch the monster. Get rid of him, and he would no longer be a leech on the side of this land. His lingering spells would decay, ley-lines would drift back to normal, and things would, in time, return to normal.

Even Ancar's wizard-weather was not as violent as it could have been. He had not been creating any great pools of power to disturb weather patterns as had happened purely by accident in Valdemar, as the Haven Heartstone in turn woke other long-dormant places. Those wells of power had collected without the kind of control and supervision there would have been if there had been a Vale of Tayledras in charge. The weather over Valdemar was steadying now, and centuries' worth of aged power, steeped into the rocks and trees, was unfolding like a fresh flower-bloom.

Once Ancar was dead, the weather in *his* land would also return to normal.

But this place made him itch to have the job done and be gone. The despair here spread like a slow poison into his own veins, and made his muscles tight. The sooner they were all gone from here, the sooner he would be able to get back to Valdemar and begin Healing the damage there. He could nudge the land into some kind of magical order, so that Elspeth and her Heralds could work their magics properly. Despite the arrogant poses he kept, mainly for his own amusement, Firesong knew he could only influence the natural order, not control it. Healers, hunters, artists, and farmers knew that.

They passed a knot of farmers in their fields, filthy and mired, stooping over a plot of tubers, half of which were already rotting in the ground. Their threadbare, shabby clothes were nearly the same color as the mud they labored in. Their faces were blank and bleak, with no strength wasted on expression. He shuddered and turned away.

This place was cancerous. Its slow death was palpable, and came from the capital, enforced by marauding soldiers, steel-handed police, and insidious magics. Falconsbane was not much better, but he had never drunk up the life of his land the way these fools were.

The mood of the place had infected Firesong enough that things that had been amusing in the beginning of this trek no longer seemed clever. He had ceased to ask Aya to wear his ribbons, although when the firebird made his flights to attract the customers, he carried his trailing ribbons in his claws rather than wearing them. And he himself no longer donned that silly turban or bright robes until just before they came to a village. There was nothing to distinguish him from Darkwind, save length of hair.

Soon, he told himself. *It will be over soon.*

All that really gave him pleasure was to brighten the hearts of the children with his magic tricks, and to know that they were going home with enough money to buy their families a few days of decent meals.

If there were any food to buy.

That might be enough to hold them in hope until help really came, for the carnival was within a few days of the city where Ancar held abode.

Soon. Soon.

He fretted about Nyara, about her ability to handle what was surely the most onerous position in this little band, and about her mental stability, given her background. He would have fretted more, if not for Need. The sword spoke to him often, as often as he wished; they had spoken together of this more than once. He believed Need when she assured him that she could hold Nyara if the strain became too much to bear and she snapped beneath it. She had more than once proved herself equal to the task of controlling an adult mage; he had no doubt she could control Nyara if she had to, at least physically. Firesong, as one familiar with Healer-skills, recommended that Nyara's body could be influenced to calm or comfort her. Need understood.

He had confidence that between them, Skif and the blade could bring Nyara back to her senses if something went horribly wrong. But none of that would be good for Nyara, or help her own sense of self-worth in any way, and he prayed that it would never come to a testing.

There was one source of personal irritation that he could do nothing about. He had not had a lover since they left Valdemar—and for Firesong, who had not slept alone for any length of time since he was old enough to send feathers to suitors, this was an irritation indeed. There had been that charming young Bard in Haven… but that had been all. Nothing in Vanyel's Forest, of course. Nor on the road between the Gate and Haven. And from Haven to this moment, nothing again. No one in the carnival had even approached him.

He would not, even for a moment, consider Darkwind. Not that Darkwind wasn't devastatingly attractive. It simply would not be fair. Elspeth did not understand all the nuances of Tayledras courting-play or customs, and she might well be hurt and unhappy if Firesong—

Besides, Darkwind had not reacted in any way as if he was interested in Firesong, which was irritating in itself, though Darkwind could hardly be faulted for personal tastes. Still. There it was. Even if Elspeth could be persuaded it was all completely harmless, Darkwind was simply not going to play.

There was Skif, however… Skif had not shown any interest either, but that could be for lack of opportunity.

He considered that for a bit longer. Nyara had such a warped childhood that there was *nothing* she took for granted. If he made it clear to her that there was nothing in this but a kind of exchange between friends—

She would still feel badly. I would damage her self-esteem. She would be certain that she is worthless to Skif if he "must" go elsewhere for a partner. I cannot do that to a friend. And to do that to someone already under as much as she is—would be as if I plunged a blade into her back.

Nothing came without a price. There was no hope for it. Unless someone else in this carnival approached the outsiders, he would just have to remain chaste.

Horrid thought.

But there it was.

The bonds between Skif and Nyara, as those between Darkwind and Elspeth, were simply too new and too fragile to disturb. Those love-bonds were like blood-feathers; if he touched them, they might break, and if they broke, the birds would bleed—if not to death, certainly to sickness. Their relationships were too important to jeopardize, and their friendships too valuable. He would survive his longing. But even once...

No, and no, and no.

He sighed, and Skif looked at him curiously. He indicated the farmers with a jerk of his head, and Skif grimaced. Evidently the young Herald also felt some of the sickness affecting this land, even if he had no mage-senses.

And amidst all the more serious troubles in this unhappy land, amidst all the dangers and uncertainties of this mission, his lack of partners was hardly more than trivial.

But as Skif turned away, he caught himself admiring the young man's profile. Not his usual type, but variety was the essence of life, and—

Oh, Firesong, he scolded himself. *Do grow up. Try to treat this as a serious situation! Your needs are certainly not the only ones in this world!*

Odd, how one never noticed a need, though, until it was no longer being filled.

Or until it was being discovered.

Darkwind listened to Nyara stirring about restlessly for a moment, before she settled on a bunk. She had chosen to hide herself away; now they needed to keep her appearances as secretive as possible, so that only rumors of her existence would reach Falconsbane. He might dismiss them, but if he didn't, she could be the bait in a trap designed to bring the Beast to them, to their choice of ground. It would depend on what his spies told him; whether they were convinced that her appearance was all sham, or whether they thought, given that they knew Falconsbane was real, that this might be another of his kind. It was just one plan of several, but it was the plan that had the greatest potential.

There was another reason to keep her out of sight, a very ugly reason. The nearer they got to the capital, the more of Ancar's Elite

Guards there were, prowling about and helping themselves to whatever they wanted from the cowed populace.

So far there had not been more than two or three at once, either riding patrol along the road, or apparently stationed at the villages. They had taken note of Darkwind, Skif, and Elspeth, measured them with their eyes, and evidently concluded that the cat-girl was not worth a fight with skilled mercenaries.

Better to keep Nyara out of their sight as much as possible, however, and keep the trouble to a minimum. It was like the mercy of hooding a skittish hunting-hawk in a strange environment, too—she would not have enjoyed being outside to see the land anyway.

It was relatively easy to deal with the men when they were in the tent audience; the one time there had been four willing to start some trouble, he and Elspeth had used a spell they had devised between them to take the troublemakers under control and make them forget what they wanted. They did this in such a way that seemed, later on, to have been nothing more than intoxication. It was a combination of mind-magic and true magic, and it took two to work it; once again, he and Elspeth were proving themselves as a partnership. Nyara had never even known there had been potential trouble; that was how skillfully Elspeth had worked with him. He would not have her know, either. These days, Nyara was a fragile thing; he would not allow anything to crush her.

That meshing with Elspeth though—so effortless, and so seamless, despite the danger—had matched anything they had done together outside of the bedchamber for sheer intoxicating pleasure. Magic had been like that before, when he was younger. Thanks to Elspeth, it was now that way again. It made for a tiny bright spot in the gloom of tensions that surrounded them all.

He knew that Skif was worried, for they had hurried this plan through, and it was not as well-thought-out as Skif liked. Skif fretted about the other members of the carnival, and how much they could be trusted. He had a point, too—there were too many pressures that could be brought to bear on one of these folk if Ancar's men got wind of something wrong and decided to haul someone away for questioning. And now that they were within a few days of the capital, he knew that Skif and Elspeth both had another overwhelming fear. They had been gone for a long time—long enough for a war to be won or lost. Although news of a real, stunning victory would surely have reached even their carnival, there was no way of telling what was truly happening on the front if the victories were small ones. The word in Hardorn would be the same for small victories, small defeats, or stalemate—the same bombastic assurance that the war was going well, and victory was assured. What was going on back home? What was Ancar doing to their beloved land? Were the tactics they had sketched out working? Could Treyvan and Hydona handle all those varied mages? How much of Valdemar had been lost already?

The Companions refused to contact others of their kind any more than absolutely necessary, and then only briefly, for fear of detection. Elspeth told Darkwind with unhappy certainty that her mother would misinform the team about how the war was going if it was necessary. It did nothing to ease his worries.

In fact, all of them were acting as if they were preoccupied and fretting about something, with nerves on edge and tempers short. It didn't take any great wizard to understand why. They *all* wanted this done, for good or ill, and over with. They were taking action, pursuing the best solution they could come up with, using what resources and fortunes they had. As always, they had hope—and each other.

Some of the members of their troupe were already expressing misgivings about forming this carnival, and not because the Valdemarans were with them either. Everyone rode with weapons near to hand, for Ancar's Elite Guard had already made trouble at the last two stops. At the first, they had tried to force one of the women-contortionists to give them pleasure; that time he and Elspeth had worked their magics and sent them all into a deep sleep, implanting memories of a great deal of ale and a bet on who could drink the most. At the second, a group had overwhelmed one of the peddlers who had been alone for a moment, taken all his money, and scattered his goods into the mud. Darkwind was not looking forward to tonight's performance.

He checked back with Nyara, and found she had fallen asleep. He envied her that escape. No doubt, Need had a great deal to do with it. In this situation, the blade was not above imposing her will on the girl.

This must be purest hell for poor Skif, who had less trust in Need—and the rest of the world—than Darkwind had.

Thanks to the gods for a partner who is strong enough to bear as much as I. The sheer relief of knowing that Elspeth could and would take not only an equal share of the load, but would take up the slack if he faltered, was something Skif could not enjoy. It was another tiny source of pleasure in this perilous situation.

The task—the danger—the tension—

It was hard to concentrate on performing with everything else that was going on in his mind and heart, and he knew the others felt the same pressures. And yet, if they did not perform well, they would stand out among the others. Being drab among the other peacocks could be fatal.

For that matter, giving a bad performance could easily bring another kind of attention; that of Ancar's men, who could decide to take out their disappointment on the performers.

:Darkwind.:

The gravellike mind-voice could only be Need, and despite his worries he smiled. He was beginning to like the old creature. She had a good sense of humor, and what was more, she was just as ready to tell a joke at her own expense as at anyone else's. With Need along, he did not fear for Nyara's physical safety; however, he worried for her mental safety. If Need had not been with them, it would have been a different story entirely.

She had waited until Nyara slept to speak with him.

:Yes, Lady?: he responded immediately.

:I have some news that may cheer you up.:

:Please, Lady, tell.:

:I have an informant inside Ancar's Court.:

He could not have been more stunned if Nyara had risen from her bed and clubbed him with a frying pan.

Need had an informant? In *Ancar's Court?* How in the name of—well, all the gods at once, had she managed that? The blade sounded very smug, and well she should be!

His spirits rose immediately—just, no doubt, as she had assumed they would. But if he had not been Mindspeaking, he surely would have stuttered his reply, he was that flabbergasted. *:Lady, that is excellent, incredible news indeed! How does this happen?:*

:Let's just say I have my means.: She chuckled. *:And my methods. This is a good source, trustworthy, and most unlikely to be uncovered; he's got mind-magic, and he's close enough to the Beast that he can, if he's very careful, not only find out what is going on with Falconsbane, but influence him as well:*

His elation to turned to alarm. An informant was one thing—and he had to assume that this person had Mindspeech—but to use that mind-magic on Falconsbane? That was more peril than he himself would have cared to undertake! *:Lady, do either of you know how dangerous that is?:* He could think of any number of things that could go wrong, *particularly* with an outsider trying to influence Falconsbane's thoughts. The Beast had very little Mindspeech, if any at all, and much less in the way of tolerance. There was always the chance that he would detect anyone who touched his thoughts. He had not gotten as far as he had by being stupid—and what was more, Darkwind *knew* that Mornelithe was skilled at shielding against mind-magic. How could even an expert hope to touch his mind undetected?

:Steady on. We're not dealing with the Falconsbane you knew,: she said, so calmly that it made his spinning thoughts slow down and calm. *:Hear me out before you panic.:*

As he kept a fraction of his attention on the road, she detailed what had happened to Mornelithe Falconsbane from the time after he was lost in the Void and up to this very day.

In some ways, he was forced into a reluctant admiration, simply for the Beast's ability to survive. But all that punishment had taken a toll on Falconsbane. And she was right; from all she described, he was a very depleted, mentally damaged individual, and one who did not even realize the extent of his handicaps.

:So, you see,: she concluded, *:he's damaged goods, so to speak. But he's not aware of the fact. Between the coercions that Ancar has him under, and the fragmenting of his own personality, he's just not up to noticing anything subtle. For that matter, he often doesn't notice something blatant, so long as it doesn't make him act against his own best interest.:*

Darkwind ground his teeth a little. It sounded too good to be true. Was it? Or was there a great deal that Need had eliminated in the name of an expedient explanation? She had known what they were going to do from the very moment they had begun planning it. She had even taken part in the discussions. But that did not prevent her from running her own schemes to augment theirs. *:Let me contemplate this for a moment before I answer you,:* he hedged.

The sword sounded amused. *:Contemplate all you like. We've got the time, as long as you don't take a week. I know this is sudden, but I didn't want to break it to you until it was a reality. I'm the last person to tell you to rush into anything. I'm awake now.:*

The mules flicked their ears at him as his hands tightened on the reins. If it had been anyone else telling him all this, he would never consider it seriously. Everything hinged on being able to trust someone they didn't know, had never seen, would not be able to contact directly. Someone they had never even dreamed existed.

But it was not just anyone claiming all this. It was Need. She was caution personified. She never trusted anything or anyone entirely— even less than Skif. If his instincts said to check something twice, hers would move her to check it a dozen times. She simply did not rush into anything; she left that to her bearers.

It followed, then, that she had already done far more about this "informant" than she had told him. Perhaps that was why it had taken her so long to report it. She had said that she had not wanted to tell him of this before it was a reality—and she had plenty of time and opportunity, if distance was no great deterrent to this contact. When it came right down to it, he had no idea what her abilities really were. So.

He weighed everything he knew about Need and her ways and decided to ask two questions.

:How long have you been cultivating this contact?: he asked. *:Is there more about him you can't tell me yet?:*

She chuckled, as if she had expected those very questions. *:That's what I like about you, Darkwind. You're a suspicious one. To answer your questions, there's quite a bit I can't tell you about him yet, and I've been in one form of contact or another with him for some time. My indirect contacts started even before we crossed the border. I can't tell you how it all came about, but I can promise you that those who put me in contact with him are trustworthy entities.:*

Entities? An interesting choice of words. One could describe the Companions as "entities." Were the Companions behind this?

:Not exactly, but something very like the Companions. Someone you would trust if I could tell you:

Something—oh—like the Swordsworn, then? The Kal'enedral had certainly been helpful in the past with regard to Falconsbane.

Need laughed. *:Persistent, aren't you? And a good guesser, too.:*

He nodded, and his hands relaxed. In that case—it must be *leshy'a Kal'enedral;* that would explain a great deal. What the spirit-Kal'enedral were doing in Hardorn he had no idea, but poor Tre'valen had said that She had told him the interests of the Shin'a'in were now carrying beyond the Plains. Perhaps this was one of the things She had meant.

:Do I take it that you are bringing this through me and not through Nyara to spare her distress?: He could well imagine what unhappiness receiving any information about her father at this moment would cause. She didn't enjoy being used as bait for him, but it was the one useful thing she could think to contribute. He suspected that a burning desire for revenge held her steady in the day-to-day strain of being "staked out" like a stalking-

horse. And as for actually seeing Mornelithe face-to-face again—he was certain that Nyara tried not to think of that. She probably tried not to think of him at all. This would not help her precarious peace of mind.

:Precisely.: Need seemed very satisfied with his sensitivity. *:Ah—have you noticed that on the whole she is looking and acting more—human? One of the things my time with her has accomplished is that I am able to find the memories of what the Beast did to her. Knowing that, I can do some things to reverse his changes.:* Need sounded smug again. He did not in the least blame her.

:I'm no god or Avatar, but there are a few things I can still do.:

:I had noticed. My plaudits, Lady. You may not call yourself Adept, but you cannot be far from one.: He smiled at her raspy chuckle.

:So, can I count on you to break this to the others? If you want to make it sound as if you've been in on this from the beginning, that's fine, if it makes the rest more inclined to trust the information.: Need apparently felt that she required his support on this; very well, she would have it. He assented readily. This was too great an opportunity to allow anything to spoil it.

:There is one small blessing in Nyara's lack of confidence in herself, Lady,: he pointed out. *:Poor little thing, she has been so used to thinking of herself as useless that it will not even occur to her that you might have brought this word to her, and not me.:*

He sensed something like a sigh from her. *:Sad, but true. Well, Skif and I are working on that. And if all of this falls out as best as possible, she'll have a boost in that direction.:*

The next village was coming up; he saw the huddle of buildings through a curtain of trees just beyond the first wagon. He could deal with all of this later. Right now there was a persona to keep up, a show to stage, and hopefully there would be no trouble from Ancar's men to complicate matters.

However, on that last, the odds weren't with them, and he knew it only too well.

The carnival-wagons drew nearer the cluster of buildings, then entered the edge of the town. He and Elspeth both sensed the tension as they drove through the village. The townspeople did not even gather to watch them as they passed through; instead, they watched furtively from their windows and doorways, trying to be as unobtrusive as possible. Their faces were even more haggard than was usual in Hardorn.

As the procession reached the common, the reason for the tension became clear.

More of Ancar's Elite, some in armor and some only in uniform, were gathered outside a large building on the edge of the common to watch them pull in. It looked as if there were about twenty or thirty of them. He had no idea what so many of the Elite were doing here in this tiny town; it seemed that they were garrisoned here on a permanent basis, but there didn't seem to be a reason for a garrison. No one in the last town had bothered to warn them about this—and it was something new since the last time any of the wagon-folk had been here.

Whatever it was that caused the Elite to be here—well, the carnival was running a risk in setting up tonight. The Elite always had money and few enough places to spend it. But one of the reasons that they always had money was that they were in the habit of taking whatever they wanted. They seldom needed to actually buy anything, and when they did—well, there were always plenty of people to steal more money from under the guise of "donations for the troops."

Still, it was difficult to force a good performance out of an artist. A frightened musician forgot words and music; a terrified dancer would move like a wooden doll. A juggler under duress dropped things. And no one could give any kind of a performance with a sword at his throat, or a knife pointed at a loved one. The effect of terror on a performer would only be funny for a limited number of times before the amusement began to pall. If luck was with them, some of these men had figured that out by now.

The routine was the same as always, but the tension had spread to everyone else in the troupe by the time all the tents and wagons were set up. Darkwind's stomach was in an uproar and his shoulders a mass of knots before they even set up the tent. And before the customers began to trickle in, word was passing among the wagon-folk; sensible word, by Darkwind's way of thinking.

Ancar's men were to be *given* anything they expressed an interest in. Free food, free entertainment, free drink. Smile at the nice soldiers, and tell them fervently how much you support them. *Encourage them to toss coin in a hat if you must have it, but do not charge them,* ran the advice. *If we get out of here whole, that will be enough.* He passed on the advice to the others, who agreed fervently. There was no point in antagonizing these men, and if they were in a good mood and remained so, they might even avoid more trouble later.

"Hoo, I'll *give* them bottles of Cure-All if they'll take it!" Firesong said fervently. "In fact… hmm… that's not a bad idea. They'll be stuffing themselves from the Mystery Meat sellers. All that grease would give a goat a bellyache. I'll prescribe Cure-All to the ones that look bilious. It's a lot stronger than anything they're used to gulping down, and given all the soothing herbs in it, it might make them *pleasant* drunks. If nothing else, it will knock them out much more quickly than the ale."

That was a notion that had a lot of merit. "Mention it has a base of brandy-wine in your selling speech, Firesong," Darkwind advised. "That will surely catch their interest. Something like—ah—'made of the finest brandy-wine, triply distilled, of vintage grapes trodden out by virgin girls in the full of the moon, and laden with the sacred herbs of the forest gods guaranteed to put heat in an old man and fire in a young one, to make weeping women smile and young maidens dance—' How does that sound?"

"You know, you are good at that." Firesong gave him a strained, ironic half-smile.

"Perhaps I should consider making an honest living," Darkwind replied with heavy irony.

"Sounds good enough to make me drink it, and I made the last batch," Skif observed, coming around the corner of the tent. "And I've got an idea. Nyara *doesn't* dance. It's too dangerous; maybe we can hold four or five armed men off her, but we can't take on thirty. And if ten of them are in the tent, that's twenty somewhere outside where you can't see them. Tonight, the performance in the tent is you, the birds, and Darkwind. Nyara stays hidden. They don't know she's here, so let's not stretch our luck by letting them see her."

"I wish this," Nyara said from the dark of the wagon, her voice trembling in a way that made Darkwind ache with pity for her. How many times had her father made her perform in just such a way for his men? "I greatly wish this. What need have we of showing my face here and now? And there will be no one expecting shared monies tonight, yes?"

"Quite true," Elspeth said firmly. "After all, the last thing that anyone in this carnival wants is to give these men any cause at all to make trouble, and one look at Nyara will *make* trouble. In fact, I'm going over to the contortionists' tent to advise all their women stay out of sight, too."

It seemed to be a consensus.

While they readied the tent for the shows, Darkwind related everything Need had told him. The news was enough to make everyone a little more cheerful, so when the Elite did show up, Firesong was able to give them a good performance.

At first, only one of the Elite would accept a bottle of the Cure-

All. From the grimace on his face, he had eaten far too much of what Firesong called "Mystery Meat," and far too many greasy fried pies. He took the Cure-All dubiously, with much jibing from his friends—

Until he downed the first swallow, and came up sputtering. His face was a study in astonishment.

"That bad, eh, Kaven?" one of them laughed.

"Hellfires *no*," the man exclaimed, wiping his face on the back of his arm and going back for another pull. "That *good!* This here's prime drink!" With one bottle at his lips, he was already reaching toward Firesong, who divined his intention and quickly gave him a second flask. He polished off the first bottle, and got halfway through the second, with his mates watching with great interest, when the alcohol caught up with him. He took the bottle from his mouth, corked it carefully, and stowed it in the front of his tunic. Then, with a beatific smile on his face, he passed out cold, falling over backward like a stunned ox.

Firesong ran out of Cure-All immediately, but he made certain that every man of the Elite got at least one bottle. After that, they could fight it out among themselves.

Some of them did, in fact; brawling in the "streets" between the wagons in a display of undiscipline that should have shamed them, but which seemed, from the lack of intervention by the officers, to be standard behavior.

Thereafter, they wandered the carnival, bottles in one hand and whatever had taken their fancy in the other, moving from one entertainer to the next. While they were sober, Firesong and Darkwind took pains to make certain that they never repeated a trick from one show to the next—and in desperation, they were using small feats of real magic instead of sleight-of-hand. But once the men were drunk, it made no difference, for they could not remember what they had just seen, much less what they had seen in the show before. The small size of the tent was a definite advantage now, for only ten of them could crowd in at a time, which meant they never had the same audience twice in a row. But the alcohol fumes were enough to dizzy the birds, and the stench of unwashed bodies was enough to choke a sheep.

As darkness fell, the aisles between the wagons were both too crowded and too empty. The Elite filled it with their swaggering presence. There were *no* townsfolk brave enough to dare the carnival; the Elite held it all to themselves. By now all of the Faire-folk were knotted with fear and starting at any odd sound. This was horribly like being under siege. Darkwind wondered grimly why they had not helped themselves to the women of the town, as they seemed to help themselves to everything else, but Skif had an answer for that when he murmured the question out loud.

"Any attractive women that have relatives out of town have probably gone to those relatives," Skif told them. "Those that are left are being very careful never to be where one of the Elite can grab them without a lot of fuss. These men aren't totally undisciplined, and even if Ancar doesn't care what they do, their local commander knows that if they take their excesses beyond a little bullying and petty pilfering, the whole town will revolt. He doesn't want that; he has a quota of goods or food he has to meet, and he can't do that without the local labor. But we're outsiders, so we're fair prey. No one here will care if anything happens to us."

A good reason for the women of the carnival to stay out of sight…

At that moment, shouts and pain-filled cries rang out above the noise of the peddlers and entertainers—exactly what Darkwind had been dreading, yet expecting.

Thirty-one bodies lay unconscious in the middle of the carnival, laid out in neat rows; two of the peddlers were bringing in the thirty-second and last. Virtually all of the rest of the wagon-folk were getting their animals from the picket lines and hitching up.

These two men, a pair of burly drivers, hauled him by wrists and ankles. They let him drag on the ground, taking no care to be gentle, and flung him down beside the rest.

Every one of these men had collapsed where he stood, within moments of the first cry. Most of them had been within a few feet of the victim.

Firesong knelt at the end of one of the rows, his face gray with exhaustion. He was responsible for the mass collapse, and it had taken everything he had; an ordinary and simple spell of sleep had been made far more complicated by the need to target *only* the Elite, and to strike all of them at once. This was more complicated than either Darkwind or Elspeth could handle, and he had acted while they were still trying to organize themselves. Firesong's spell had taken long enough to set up that some of the damage had already been done.

The victim of the attack was one of the peddlers; not a particularly feminine-looking lad, but beardless and, most importantly, alone at the moment when four of the Elite came upon him, completely alone, in between two sets of deserted stalls. At this point, the Elite had all realized that there were no females anywhere in the carnival; that there would be no sexual favors here. His stock-in-trade, ribbons, were something none of the men wanted, but they *did* serve as a reminder that there were none of the easy—or at least, accessible—women they had anticipated getting their hands on.

As Darkwind understood it, the only warning the young man had was when the first four soldiers began an argument with him, claiming they had been cheated. Since he hadn't given away a ribbon all night, much less sold any, he hadn't the faintest notion what they meant and had tried to back his way out of the situation.

Then they had surrounded him, informed him that what they had been cheated of was *women*, and told him he'd just have to make it up to them.

By then, there were ten, not four, and he hadn't a chance. By the time the first four had pushed him to the ground, there were even more.

One man, at least, had beaten the lad before Firesong's spell took effect.

This had all been an incredible shock to Firesong, who had spent all of his life in the Vales. Darkwind was not foolish enough to think that molestation was unknown among his people—but it was *very* uncommon, given that most women *and* men could very well defend themselves against an attacker. As a scout, he had seen the worst possible behavior on the part of Falconsbane's men and creatures and had some armoring against what had come. Firesong had no such protection; Firesong was a rare and precious commodity, a Healing Adept, and as such he had been protected more than the ordinary Hawkbrother.

He had never seen anyone victimized like the boy. Others, who had MindHealing skills, would have dealt with such cases, which would probably have involved an enemy from outside the Vale. It was the attack itself that had him in shock, far more than the drain on his resources.

Darkwind had never thought to feel pity for the handsome Adept— but he did now, and he longed to be able to give Firesong some comfort in the name of clean and uncomplicated friendship. But there was too much to do, and no time for such niceties.

Darkwind laid a hand gently on Elspeth's shoulder. "Are you ready?" he asked. "It's our turn now."

She nodded, her mouth in a tight, grim line.

"I don't like this, you know," she said conversationally, although he sensed the anger under the casual tone. "If it were up to me, these bastards would all wake up eunuchs—if I let them wake up at all. I'd rather get rid of them altogether. Permanently. Let their gods sort them out."

"If it were my judgment, I would agree with you." He shook his head and sighed. If this were home, he could do as she preferred without a second thought. But it was not; they were not alone, they could not fade into the scenery and vanish. More importantly, however, neither could the people of the carnival and town.

If these men were maimed or killed, retribution would fall, and swiftly, on both the wagon-folk and the village. The only people who had even a chance to escape that punishment would be the Valdemarans, who had magic that would help them get away. Assuming that Ancar's mages did not try to track them. To put the villagers and Faire-folk into such danger would be an act of unforgivable arrogance.

No, there was no real choice in the matter; he and Elspeth would simply follow the plan they always used. These men would sleepwalk themselves back to their barracks. They would wake up tomorrow with no memory of the molestation, and no memory of being struck down as they either participated, watched and cheered, or waited their turn. They would only remember that they had a good time at the carnival, that they drank more than they should of that drink of dubious origin, and that they had crawled back to their quarters and passed out.

"At least let me give them the worst hangovers they've ever had in their lives," Elspeth begged fiercely. "And make them impotent while the hangovers last!"

He sighed, not because he didn't agree with her but because it seemed far too petty a punishment, but it was all they dared mete out.

"I wish we could do worse to them," he said. "I wish we could fix everything. Our best chance at that is to do what we came here to do. Get rid of Ancar, Falconsbane, and Hulda."

She nodded grimly but softened as she meshed her mind and talents with his. In a few moments, it was done, and the men began to rise woodenly, stumbling to their feet and bumbling in the direction of their barracks. Their faces were blank, their eyes glazed, and they looked altogether like walking corpses.

"I'd like to give them plague," Elspeth muttered, staring after them. "I would, if I didn't think the townsfolk would catch it. Maybe some lice or social disease. Genital leprosy?"

As the last of them rose and bumbled off, Firesong stood up, slowly, looking a little better, but still drained and sickly. The last of the wagon-folk were gone, too, and from the sounds all over the encampment, they were getting ready to leave. There were two torches stuck into the ground that gave fitful, sputtering light. "It is hard on a mage to cast magics when there has been no time to prepare for them," he murmured, his expression open and vulnerable and showing much of the pain he must be feeling. And also some guilt. "Had to push it through with personal power, and damp it all down, so we wouldn't be discovered." Firesong rubbed his eyes. "Still. I feel I could have prevented this if I had only acted sooner."

"You need not feel guilty," Darkwind said quietly as Elspeth nodded, trying to put some force into his words so that Firesong would believe him. "You were faster than we were. And you did the best you could."

Firesong looked down at his hands. "But it was not enough," he said unhappily, the strain in his voice betraying how deeply he ached over this. "Where is the poor lad? Liam was his name? I do not like to think of him being alone—"

"Gerdo has him," Elspeth said. "He carried him off to their wagon."

Firesong looked astonished at that; Darkwind was a little surprised himself. Gerdo was one of the contortionists, and if he'd spoken a dozen words to Liam in all the time they'd been in Hardorn, Darkwind, at least, didn't know about it. They were, at best, casual acquaintances.

"He said Sara would understand," Elspeth continued, "since she was attacked herself. And he said something else, that he knew how Liam felt, sort of, because the same thing happened to him when he was a boy. He said they could at least tell Liam that it wasn't his fault. Maybe if they tell him often enough, he'll start to believe it."

"I feel I must go apologize," Firesong said after a moment.

Darkwind nodded, and sensed Elspeth's agreement and Gwena's gentle urging. "Do you mind if we join you?" he said simply.

There was no rest for them that night; the entire carnival packed up and moved in the dark. They did not stop until the next village that did *not* have a garrison of Ancar's men. Darkwind, Elspeth, Nyara, and Skif took turns driving the wagon and sleeping in it. The poor Companions and the *dyheli* had no such luxury; they had to make their way on their own four hooves. Firesong spent most of that day and night with Gerdo, helping with Liam. Darkwind was not surprised at that; Firesong was a Healing Adept, after all, even though he was not a body-Healer *per se.* He had the ability to do Liam a great deal of good—and Liam's plight could do Firesong an equal amount of good.

Firesong was talented, Gifted, beautiful, and arrogant. In many ways, he had seen himself as above everyone else in this mission, even his fellow Tayledras. Nothing had really touched him except the damage done to the land; he had, for the most part, ignored the damage done to the people. Up until this moment, the pain of these people had been mostly an abstraction to the Adept—something to be deplored and kept at a distance, but nothing that really affected him. *Now* it had hit home. He had seen willful, cruel violence close at hand. Firesong had opened himself to pain and could not avoid it any more.

Firesong returned to his fellows late in the afternoon, uncharacteristically sober and silent, but with a certain amount of weary satisfaction on his face. When Liam finally appeared as the wagons were setting up for the shows, Darkwind understood the expression.

Liam appeared to have found a kind of peace and support. He was ready to get to work, and could look his fellows in the face. The young man had come through the immediate crisis well; while he would bear scars, they would not be as devastating as they might have been.

And Firesong seemed to have learned a great deal, too. When he looked about him, his beautiful face radiated empathy and compassion for those people who felt pain.

He no longer wore a mask of any kind, frivolous or haughty. "Saving the defenseless" appeared no longer to be a meaningless phrase spoken as any other platitude, but rather a goal to be understood as a way of life. Real pain had been touched and understood; Healing was no longer simply a mental exercise for Firesong.

That night, Need finally conveyed to them what she had learned from her "contact."

Darkwind wished devoutly that he could go to bed early, but he had done with less sleep in his life, and this was more important. They wanted things to look as normal as possible, though, and "normal" meant that the wagon should at least *look* as if they were all asleep. So the five of them sat on two of the beds, heads together, whispering into the darkness of the wagon.

:*Firstly*—*we've all had some ideas about who was the real power in Hardorn, the one who's responsible for the way things have gone to pot around here,*: Need said. :*We all thought it was Ancar, but it wasn't. He isn't more than a Master, if that. It was Hulda.*:

Elspeth choked. "Hulda?" she whispered urgently.

:That's right. She *is an Adept.:*

"But—the protections that were on Valdemar when she was there—how could she have been an Adept?" Elspeth sputtered.

:Apparently she never used any magic while she was there, child, so she never invoked the interest of the vrondi. *She knew what she was doing, and understood the nature of the protections. Anyway. She set up this draining effect that's been pulling life-force out of this land; Ancar's been getting all the loot, all the gold and the pretties, baubles to keep the baby happy, but she's been hoarding the power for herself. What she's done with it, though—I don't know, and neither does Mornelithe. Falconsbane thinks she was courting the Emperor's envoy; they use magic over there, so maybe she was sending them the power. If she was, it's the first time I've ever heard of people being able to do that sort of thing.:*

Darkwind shook his head, feeling nauseous. That had to be one of the strangest and most perverted things he'd ever heard. "So Hulda has been deliberately wrecking this land?"

:Pretty much. Encouraging Ancar to do what he wants, without ever giving him any real power or training past a certain point. Huh. Maybe I do know what she was doing with all that power. Those magical attacks, coercive spells on the troops—all of that is far too powerful for the mages Ancar has in his employ to be able to successfully invoke—unless someone was feeding them the energy to do it. Interesting idea.:

"That makes a great deal of sense," Firesong agreed, his voice flat with exhaustion. "More sense than that she would be making courting-gifts of mage-power. So Ancar has been the puppet, and she the manipulator?"

:Until lately. She's been sloppy, and he's been chafing at the constraints she put on him. She made the mistake of promising him more training and not delivering. So he started experimenting on his own; that's how he got Falconsbane. Put up half a Gate without knowing what he was doing or what it was for, wished desperately *for an Adept to get him out of it before he got eaten alive, the Gate took the wish for the destination, and delivered Falconsbane with a bow on him.:*

Firesong bit off an exclamation. Darkwind could only sit and shake his head with weary astonishment. "Either he is the stupidest lucky man in the world, or the luckiest stupid one," Darkwind said at last. "I would not have given him the chance of a dewdrop in an inferno of surviving such a blunder."

"And Mornelithe has the luck of a god, I swear it," Firesong snorted with a little more energy.

:He put Falconsbane under coercion while still magically naked and helpless—for once in his life, the Beast couldn't fight or break what was put on him. So; now Ancar has an Adept, he starts to feel as if he can do without Hulda. Falconsbane has been

encouraging this, figuring on setting both of them against each other and running out while they get rid of each other. Except that Ancar managed to catch Hulda in a moment of weakness, and right now he has her inside a mage-mirrored prison cell she helped create. So she's out of the way, for the moment.:

"So, what we have is the three powers at the top, who should be working together, who we've assumed have been working together, actually fighting each other?" That was Skif, and he sounded incredulous despite his own weariness. "We might yet be able to pull this off!"

:Before you get too confident, let me give you the details,: Need said dryly.

The details were many, and often baffling. Only by assuming that Need's assessment of Falconsbane was accurate could Darkwind even begin to understand how the Beast had made so many fundamental blunders. It was incredible, impossible, insane. But, he realized, that described Falconsbane perfectly.

Still, it was terrifying to think what would happen if Falconsbane should happen to change his mind about cooperating with Ancar. The damage that had been wrought without that cooperation was terrible. And the number of successes the army of Hardorn had against Valdemar without Falconsbane's real help was even worse. But *with* it—

And Falconsbane was capricious. He could change his mind at any time. *Their* only chance was to strike for him while he was still Ancar's captive, for if he became Ancar's comrade before they reached the capital—the odds in their favor were not good.

The odds for Valdemar would be even worse.

1 6

An'desha waited on the Moonpaths; alone this time, for Dawnfire had appeared only long enough to summon him and then had left him. That might mean the old woman wished to speak with him, then. That was good, for An'desha had been keeping Falconsbane annoyed with Ancar, as she had asked him to do, and at the moment it would be more likely for a pig to stoop on a hawk than that Falconsbane should become Ancar's willing helper.

Still, the Adept was a slippery and unpredictable creature. An'desha had been forced to play fast and loose with Mornelithe's mind to stave off the thought that it *might* not be such a bad thing to cooperate with the King. He'd had to remind Falconsbane of the coercions, and the King's own word that he had no intention of taking them off.

The trouble was that Hulda was still incarcerated. The protections she herself had put on the cell were better than Falconsbane had given her credit for. There was no sign that she was going to come bursting out of there and finish Ancar off any time soon, and the Adept was growing impatient.

He heard footsteps—real footsteps, on the Moonpath to his right. He turned to peer into the glittery fog. It had to be the old woman, for the Avatars had never made the sound of footsteps, and she was just contrary enough to create a sound in a place where such things were superfluous.

The old woman emerged out of the fog; from the set of her jaw, she had much to tell him.

"Well, boy," she said, stopping within a few paces of him, and looking him up and down as if to take his measure, "I hope you're as ready for this as your friends think because this is where we gamble everything."

"Friends?"

"The Avatars."

A chill of anticipation mingled with fear threaded his veins, for all that his "veins" were as illusory as the old woman's footsteps. "I can only try," he said carefully. "I have kept Falconsbane at odds with Ancar. He was beginning to think it might be good to ally with King Ancar after all."

She nodded brusquely. "That's good. You've done very well, boy. But this is going to take a surer, more delicate touch, and constant work. I mean that. We've come to the real turning point, and there's no way back now. You won't be able to leave him alone for a heartbeat, and you'll have to be absolutely certain he doesn't know you're playing with him. My people aren't more than a day away."

An'desha felt very much as if he had been suddenly immersed in ice water, but his voice remained steady. "So, whatever we do, it must be done soon. You have a plan, and its success depends upon my performance. If I fail, we all will lose."

"Exactly." She gave him another of those measuring looks. "This is where we see if you can really come up to what we're going to ask of you. You're going to have to create memories for Falconsbane from whole cloth, boy—memories of one of the servants telling him about the carnival, and that there's a captive cat-woman dancing in one of the tent-shows there. We want him to hear about Nyara, we want him to come after her. We intend for him to walk into ambush. Can you do that?"

Create whole memories... he had been making fragments, adding to things Ancar truly had said so that they could be read as being insulting, for instance. Falconsbane had no idea his memories had been tampered with. An'desha had plenty of memories to use to make this one, memories that featured the servants talking. Was there any reason why he couldn't do this?

"I believe I can, Lady," he replied, trying to sound confident.

She smiled for the first time in this meeting. "Good. Then I'll leave you. You're going to need a lot of time to do this right, and I'm only wasting it."

And with that, she turned and walked off into the mist, and was gone.

Part of the plan, however, was not going to work. Having a servant tell Falconsbane about the carnival was simply not believable, no matter what the old woman thought. *No*, he thought, as he examined Falconsbane's sleeping mind and all the memories of servants in it. *No, I cannot have a memory of a servant* telling *him something. They do not speak to him unless they need to, for they fear him. But a memory of him overhearing them—yes, that I can do. There are plenty of those, and they will be less obtrusive, for he listens to the servants speak when they do not think he can hear them.*

The memory, he decided after some thought, should be just a little vague. Perhaps if Falconsbane had been sleeping?

He selected something that had happened in the recent past, a recollection of a pair of servants coming into Falconsbane's room to tend the fire, and waking him. That time they had been gossiping about Ancar and Hulda and had not known he was awake. It was a good choice for something like this; Mornelithe had been half-asleep, and had only opened his eyes long enough to see which of the servants were whispering together. It was another measure of how damaged he was that he didn't think of the servants as any kind of threat. The old Falconsbane would never have been less than fully alert with even a single, well-known person in the same room with him, however apparently helpless or harmless that person was.

He took the memory, laid it down, then began to create his dialogue. It wasn't easy. He had to steal snippets of conversation from other memories, then blend them all in a harsh whisper, since Hardornen was neither his native tongue nor Falconsbane's. He did not *think* in this language, so he had to fabricate what he needed, making his dialogue from patchwork, like a quilt.

He kept Falconsbane sleeping deeply as he labored through the night. If he had been able to sweat, he would have; this was hard labor, as hard as horse-taming or riding night-guard. It was so much like weaving a tapestry—like he imagined the legendary history-tapestries were. But at last it was done, and he watched it himself, to examine it as a whole with a weary mental "eye." He was so weary that even his fear was a dull and distant thing, secondary to simply finishing what had been asked of him.

The two servants entered the room; the memory of this was only the sound of the door opening and closing. They were whispering, but too softly to make out more than a word or two—"show," and "faire," and some chuckling. Then—a bit of vision as if Falconsbane had opened his eyes and shut them again quickly. A glimpse of two menservants, one with logs and the other with a poker, silhouetted against the fire.

"...what could be worth going back there?" asked one, over the sound of the fire being stirred with the poker.

"There's a dancer. They call her Lady Cat, and she looks half cat. I tell you, when she's done dancing, you wish she'd come sit on your lap! When she moves, you can't think of anything but sex. She's supposed to be a slave; she's got a collar and a chain, but she doesn't act much like a slave, more like she owns the whole show."

Another laugh, this one knowing. "I'll bet she does! I'll bet she does things besides dance when the show closes, too!"

"Well, that's what I mean to find out—"

Sounds of logs being put on the fire, then of the servants leaving the room and closing the door behind them.

It looked good, what vision there was behind it. It sounded good, solid and real. *Well, now to wake Falconsbane up, and make him think the little conversation has just now occurred.*

He woke the Adept with the sound of the door closing, and a little jolt, then left the memory out in Falconsbane's mind where it was the very first thing he would "see."

And it worked! The Adept thought he had actually witnessed the entire conversation!

He watched as Falconsbane mulled it over, wondering if this so-called "Cat Lady" was a carnival fake, created because of his own growing notoriety, or was real—

Oh, no—oh, no. She can't be a fake—he can't even think she might be a fake. Quickly An'desha shunted that thought away, guiding Falconsbane's sleep-fogged mind in the direction *he* wanted.

No, of course the cat-woman wasn't a fake. No one would dare counterfeit a Changechild, much less counterfeit Falconsbane; his own reputation would frighten anyone who dared to try it! No, it had to be real, and if it was real, there was only one creature it could be.

Nyara, An'desha whispered, keeping his own terror of being caught under tight control.

Nyara. Falconsbane's claws tightened on the bedclothes, piercing holes in the cloth. She had run eastward, after all! Probably she had started running when he had escaped death at the hands of the cursed Shin'a'in, and had not stopped until she had been captured. Now was his chance to catch her and make her pay for her treachery!

But I must hide her existence from Ancar, An'desha prompted.

But of course he would have to hide her very existence from Ancar. He would have to slip out of the palace, go alone and unobserved, and take her himself. If Ancar learned about her, he would want to see her, and the moment he saw her he would know she was Falconsbane's handiwork. Ancar was not the fool Falconsbane had thought—although a fool he certainly was—and he would certainly use Nyara as an additional hold over his captive Adept. Falconsbane had invested a great deal of power in making Nyara what she was, and any mage higher than Journeyman would know that using her he could control the creator. The old law of contamination. Any mage left some of himself along with his power, even an Apprentice knew that. There was the likelihood that even Hulda's old toy knew it as well.

Going to this carnival alone and unobserved, though—that would take some creativity. There were always guards at his door, and more guards throughout the palace. He would have to find a way to avoid them, and a time when Ancar was occupied elsewhere. This would take a great deal of advance preparation, and no small amount of power to come and go without detection.

Why else have I been storing up mage-energy? An'desha asked.

But then, why else had he been storing up mage-energy? Even with the coercions, he could still work spells that would make him ignored by anyone who set eyes on him. He could even work a true spell of invisibility for a short period of time. He could stun the guards for as long as he needed, and he had certainly picked up enough information from the servants' gossip to know the easiest clandestine ways in and out of the palace. If he picked a time when Ancar was busy with the war plans, he could be down to the carnival and back with no one being the wiser.

And as for Nyara—once he had her, even though her death would of necessity be rushed, he could make it seem an eternity to her. Perhaps—perhaps he could enhance all her senses, and stretch her time perception, so that every tiny cut seemed to take a year.

Such a sweet reunion it would be...

Falconsbane began to plan what he would do to his daughter when he finally had his hands on her. An'desha shuddered but did not pull back into the familiar corner of his mind.

Skif couldn't help but notice the air of relaxation all through the carnival this afternoon. Wagon-folk all over the carnival had breathed a sigh of relief as they set up just outside the walls of the capital, at the gate nearest the palace itself. Ancar might permit his men to do as they willed anywhere else, but here they were as restrained as good, disciplined troops in any other land. Pairs of Elite Guards with special armbands patrolled the streets, and today while running his errands, Skif had seen one man hauled off for public drunkenness, and another for robbing a street peddler.

Skif only wished that he and the others could share in the general feeling of relief. For the Valdemarans and their allies, the dangers had just increased exponentially.

The general consensus among the wagon-folk was that it would be well worth staying a week or so here, and safe enough to let the women come out of hiding. There were good pickings to be had in this city. Many of them had constructed clever hiding places in their wagons for a small hoard of coins in anticipation of a good run.

No one among the wagon-folk knew what the Valdemarans were really up to; their story—which still seemed to be holding under the pressure of passing time—was that they were going into the city; that they had found out that their missing relatives had last been heard of here, and they were going to get them out, if they were still alive. Missing relatives was a common enough tale in Hardorn these days, and if the wagon-folk wondered about the odd group, they had so far kept their speculations to themselves.

Skif had gone out into the city to get the lay of the land; now he returned to the carnival with the provisions he had been "sent" for, and a great deal of information. Last night Nyara had danced in three shows; and his every muscle had been tight with strain at each one, wondering if she would be able to continue the charade. This morning there were at least a few people in the marketplace talking about her. If

Falconsbane would just hear about her and come looking...

Already townsfolk threaded the aisles of the carnival, looking, fingering, and sometimes buying. He pushed his way through them until he came to "Great Mage Pandemonium's" stand. At the moment it was closed; the five of them had decided it would be better only to perform after nightfall, and to keep the use of magic to a minimum. Nyara was only a draw to the adult crowd, anyway, and the day-goers seemed to be families and older children.

The rest should be in the tent, relaxing; the wagon was too cramped for anything except sleeping. And *just* sleeping; he was far too shy to do anything with Nyara in company, and Elspeth and Darkwind felt the same. They'd been making it a habit to eat, lounge, and carry on the things that had to be tended to, day-to-day, in the larger area of the show-tent.

He had expected the atmosphere to be tense when he entered the tent, but he had not expected the set of peculiar expressions on the faces of his friends as they turned toward him. They were seated on makeshift stools of whatever equipment boxes happened to be handy. Even in the dim light beneath the heavy canvas, they looked as if they were suffering from sunstroke. Stunned, and quite at a loss.

"Our sharp friend has handed us a complication," Darkwind said, his own expression swiftly changing from irritation to apprehension and back again as he glanced at the sword at Nyara's side.

"It seems that Falconsbane isn't really Falconsbane."

What? "An imposter?" Skif blurted, that being the only thing he could think of. "We've been chasing an—"

"No, no, no," Elspeth interrupted. "No, that's not it at all! But—the Beast is not exactly *alone.*"

Now Skif was even more bewildered, and he shook his head violently, as if by shaking it, the words would make some sense. "What in Havens are you talking about?"

:Damn it, you're all missing the point,: Need said with irritation. *:Except Firesong, but I've been talking to him all morning. Here, let me show you.:*

Then, without even a "by your leave," Skif found himself inside the thoughts of some *other* person entirely, just as Need had once flung him inside her own memories when she had first awakened, to explain what she was by showing him. But this was not Need's memory; this person was young, male, and seemed to be Shin'a'in—

:Halfbreed,: Need interrupted. *:Trust me, it made a difference in how things came out.:*

He watched, a silent observer, as the boy discovered his mage-powers, determined to run away to the Hawkbrothers, got lost in the Pelagiris Forest, tried to light a fire—

—and the entity that called itself Mornelithe Falconsbane—in *this* lifetime—came flooding in to take his mind and body and make them his own.

Abruptly, Need flung Skif out of those memories, and he found himself back in the carnival tent, blinking, the others shaking their heads as they, too, recovered from the experience. "I wish you wouldn't do that without warning a man," Skif complained, hitting the side of his head lightly with the heel of his hand. "It—"

:It saves time,: Need replied testily. *:Well, now you know.* That's *who my informant has been.:*

"The boy?" Skif chewed his lip a little. "And presumably he still lives within Falconsbane's body. Forgive me, but I don't see how that changes anything."

:He lives inside his body. Falconsbane has stolen it. What changes everything is that the boy found out how *Falconsbane's been doing this. An'desha's body is far from the first he's stolen. Unless we stop Falconsbane in a way that keeps him from taking his spirit off to hide again, it won't be the last. People, this has been happening since the time your folk call the 'Mage Wars.' All he needs is a body out of his bloodline, with Mage-Gift. And trust me on this; he spent a lot of time back then making certain he'd have a lot of descendants. Usually he does the same any time he's had a body for a while.:*

After a moment the sense of that penetrated, and Skif cursed softly. "You mean if we take him the way we had planned and kill him, we might be facing him *again* in a couple of years?"

:If he finds somebody else with his bloodline, yes. Or takes over Nyara's children. You see, he had another motive for trying out all his Changes on her first. Mage-Gift will always breed true in her children now, and if and when she decides to have them, despite the lies her father told her, she'll be very—ah—prolific. Catlike in more than looks, it seems.:

Skif froze in place, his body and mind chilled, as his eyes sought Nyara's. She nodded unhappily. "I could not fight him, Skif. Need could help me, but she cannot be everywhere, at all times, and what are we to do? Insist that our grown children stay with us all their lives?"

:Even if you don't have children, there are always more where An'desha came from. His father was out spending his seed all over the south. Sooner or later, Falconsbane will be back.:

"We can't capture him—we can't kill him—what in the nine hells *can* we do with him?" Skif demanded, his voice rising. He threw his hands up in the air, exasperated. "What are we here for? Why don't we just give up? Why are we even trying?"

Firesong gave him a look that shut him up abruptly. "We can kill him, Skif," the Healing Adept said calmly, his face an inhuman mask of serenity. "Need and I have been discussing this since you left. We can be rid of him, forever, *and* in a way that will allow An'desha to reclaim his body. But it will take four of us working together; you, Nyara, Need, and myself. Possibly even your Companion. It will take superb timing and equally superb cooperation. And it will not be silent."

"By silent, you mean that it is going to take some very obvious magic?" Skif hazarded. This time it was Darkwind who nodded.

"That's why Elspeth, Vree, Gwena, and I will not be here. *We* will have to strike after Ancar takes the backlash of this magic or detects it in other ways, but before he has a chance to act on that knowledge. Since Falconsbane bears a great many of his coercion spells, slaying the Beast should snap them, and they will recoil on him like snapped bowstrings." Darkwind rubbed one temple, then moved his hand up higher to scratch Vree. "More timing, you see. There will be a moment when he is very stunned, and that is when *we* must strike. Firesong will give us a signal when Falconsbane is gone. First we will take out Ancar. Then we will deal with Hulda."

After all the time it had taken to get to this point, things seemed to be cascading much too fast, one plan running into the next like an avalanche. But so far as Skif was concerned there was still one question to be asked.

"If you can kill Falconsbane without killing the other fellow, wouldn't it be easier to kill him straight off and not worry about this boy?" There, it was out. He didn't like it, but how could seeing her father's body walking around do Nyara any good? And why complicate matters? It was very nice that this An'desha fellow had helped them, but sometimes you had to accept innocent casualties…

The realist and the Herald warred within him, and the realist looked to be winning, but it was not making him feel anything other than soiled, old, and terribly cynical.

"We could, and it would be simpler," Firesong admitted reluctantly. "But it is something I do not care for. On the other hand, one less complication might increase our chances for surviving this." It looked to Skif as if he were facing his own internal struggle, and didn't care for the realities of the situation either.

Skif nodded; Elspeth looked uncomfortable and distressed, but nodded also, for she had learned long ago to accept that the expedient way might be the best way. But to Skif's surprise, it was Nyara who spoke up against the idea.

"Need has given me a sense of what An'desha has dwelt within, all these years," she said slowly. "What Falconsbane did to me is nothing to what he has done to this boy. He has helped us at risk of real death—and he has done so knowing we might decide not to help him. *I* say it would reflect ill upon us all our days if we were to pretend he did not exist. I say we should save him if we can, and I put my life up for trying."

She looked at Skif as if she were afraid he would think her to be crazed. He did—but it was the kind of "crazed" that he could admire. He crossed the tent and took her in his arms for a moment, then turned to the others.

"Nyara's right. It's stupid, it's suicidal, but Nyara's right and I was wrong." He gulped, shaking all over, but feeling an odd relief as well. "We have to help this boy, if we can."

:And that is why you were Chosen,: Cymry said softly, into his mind.

"All right, Great Mage Pandemonium," he said. "Then let's do this all or nothing. After all—" he grinned tautly as he remembered his old motto, the one he had told Talia so very long ago, "—if you're going to traverse thin ice, you might as well dance your way across!"

Night fell, and Falconsbane's preparations were all in place. They were in for another bout of wizard-weather, this time an unseasonable cold, and as far as he was concerned, that was all to the good. Bad weather would make it easier for him to disguise himself.

There was a very convincing simulacrum of himself in the bed, apparently sleeping, in case anyone came in while he was gone.

Ancar was in his war-room, a large chamber with a balcony overlooking the courtyard of the palace. Hulda, of course, was still in her cell, and showing no signs of breaking free. The other mages were all with Ancar, but the King did not trust Falconsbane enough to allow him access to the actual battle plans unless things had unraveled to the point that there was no choice.

The servants were mostly elsewhere. Rumors of what Falconsbane had done to the prisoners Ancar had given him insured that, except when he was known to be sleeping. There were two guards at his door, however...

Falconsbane moved soundlessly to the doorway, and placed his hands at head-height on either side of the doorframe. This would be very tricky; he had very little mind-magic, so this would all be true spellcasting. Difficult, when one could not see one's target...

He gathered his powers; closed his eyes, concentrating, building up the forces. And then, at the moment of greatest tension, let them fly, arrows of power from each hand that pierced the wall without a sound.

He opened his eyes. There was no noise, no hint of disturbance, on the other side of the door.

He reached for the voluminous cloak he'd had one of the servants bring him this morning and swirled it over his shoulders. It fell gracefully to his feet in heavy folds; he pulled the hood up over his head, using it to cover his face, so that nothing showed but his eyes. As cold as it was tonight, no one would think anything wrong, seeing a man muffled to the nose in a cloak. Likely, everyone else on the street would be doing the same thing and hoping that it would not rain.

He opened the door. The two guards still stood there, at rigid attention. Perhaps—a trifle too rigid?

Mornelithe chuckled and waved his hand in front of their glazed eyes. "Hello?" he said, softly, knowing there would be no response.

Nor was there. Ancar had not thought to armor the guards he had on Falconsbane against spell-casting, trusting in the coercions to keep Falconsbane from doing anything to them. But Mornelithe was not doing anything against Ancar's interests, no indeed...

"Just going for a little walk, men," Mornelithe whispered to the unresponsive guards in a moment of perverse whimsy. "I'll be back before you miss me, I promise!"

He closed the door carefully and set off down the hallway in a swirl of dark fabric. He was not worried about the servants seeing him; if they caught sight of him, they would never imagine the stranger was Falconsbane, and Mornelithe's authoritative stride was enough to make most of them think twice about challenging his presence in these halls. Ancar had a great many visitors who did not wish to be seen or challenged, and people who were foolhardy enough to do so often disappeared. In a few moments, the two men he had bespelled would wake from their daze, quite unaware that anything had happened to them. He would bespell them again on his return.

It was Ancar's other guards and soldiers Mornelithe wished to avoid.

He hoped there would be none of them to challenge him, but the best chance of avoiding them lay in getting outside quickly.

He could bespell more guards if he had to, but then he would have to find a way to dispose of them. They might be missed. That would be awkward, and not as much fun as he'd prefer.

He continued down the hall without meeting any more men in Ancar's uniform, but as he rounded a corner and drew within a few feet of his goal he heard the distinctive slap of military boots on the wooden floor. Four sets, at least.

He gambled; made a dash for the door leading to the staircase and wrenched it open. He slipped inside just before the guards came into view, and ran right into a young servingman, just as he closed the door and turned on the landing.

The boy opened his mouth. Falconsbane seized him by the throat before he even managed to squeak. There was no time for finesse; he simply choked the boy so that he could not make a sound. He then wrapped them both in silence, drained the servingboy of life-force, and left him on the landing.

Let whoever found him figure out how he had died.

The staircase led directly to the public corridors of the palace. Here he was even less likely to be challenged, and he opened the door at the bottom with confidence, striding out into the corridor and taking a certain enjoyment in the way people avoided looking at him directly. Anyone who walked in such a confident, unhurried manner in *Ancar's* palace must be powerful and dangerous... both attributes belonged to people that the folk here would rather avoid. Especially if the strangers took pains to hide their faces.

Unhindered, he passed out into the chill and darkness and paused for a moment on the landing above the courtyard. The guards at the doors did not even look at him; after all, they were there to keep people out, not in. He trotted quickly down the steps to the courtyard, casting a covert glance as he did so to the room behind the balcony immediately above the main doors. Lights were still burning brightly, and shadows were moving about inside. The war-council was still going strong.

Good. Let the children play.

There were more guards at the various gates he had to pass to get to the city itself, but once again, they were there to keep people out, not in, and they ignored him. On his return journey, he would come in through another way, via the gardens, and an ingenious series of gates with locks that could be picked with a pin or latches that could be lifted with a twig, holes under walls, and trees with overhanging limbs. This was the route that the servants used to slip in after a clandestine night in the town. Pity it only worked to get *in* by, but overhanging limbs that permitted a drop *down* were not very useful when the reverse was needed. He was a mage, not an acrobat.

He passed the last gate and a squad of very bored, very hardened soldiers who looked as if they would have welcomed an intruder just so that they could alleviate their boredom by killing him. Then he was out in streets of the city, and free.

For one brief moment, he was tempted to just keep walking. Forget a cat-woman who might or might not be Nyara; forget that he might be hundreds of leagues from his own territory. He was free—he could take that freedom and just walk away from here.

But as he thought that, he suddenly felt the jerk of the coercions on him, a chain jerking a dog back to its kennel. The force was sufficient to make him stagger. And he snarled inside the shadow of his hood.

No, this breath of freedom was an illusion after all. And he could not simply walk away. Ancar's coercive spells were set too well, and the King had evidently planned against this very possibility. He had the freedom of the city—but that was all.

At least, until Ancar was dead.

Very well. Let him see if this Lady Cat was indeed Nyara. And if she was, he would use her death to fuel his own powers, taking back into himself all that he had used to make her.

Then he would return to Ancar's palace… and lay some new plans.

An'desha was very glad that his link with his physical body was so tenuous that as long as Falconsbane was awake it might just as well have not existed. If he—or rather, his body—had broken into a sweat of nervous fear, Falconsbane would *certainly* have noticed something was going on!

That moment when Falconsbane had thought to simply walk off—An'desha had taken a gamble and given the Adept a jolt he *hoped* Falconsbane would interpret as Ancar's coercions. The gamble had worked, but the old woman had been only too correct when she had warned that this was going to take every bit of cleverness and concentration he had. The Adept had come within a heartbeat of bringing down all their plans.

The die was cast. Whatever happened would follow from this, win or lose.

Falconsbane moved swiftly through the darkened, noisome streets to the city gate. His nose wrinkled in distaste at the odor of offal in the gutters, an odor even the bitter cold could not suppress. And this was supposed to be one of the better parts of this city! An'desha could not for a moment fathom why anyone would want to live in one of these hives. He felt a pang of longing as sharp as any blade for his long-lost Plains, or even the Pelagir territory Falconsbane had taken for his own. *Wilderness,* he thought achingly, as a vision of the endless sea of grass that was the Plains in late spring danced before his mind's eye. *Shall I ever see it again?*

On the other side of the gate in the city wall, the Faire spread out on the long slope of a meadow, inclining away from the city. Lighted stalls, wagons, and tents showed that the carnival was in full swing, and streams of people going to and from the Faire proved that folk still craved entertainment. Perhaps they craved it even more, under Ancar's repressions.

Falconsbane made his way through the crowds; most folk ignored him or avoided him, but he hardly noticed. His eyes searched out and dismissed every occupant of every stage. He passed a wealth of jugglers, musicians, conjurers, salesmen of every sort of strange brew and device—

And finally, where the crowd was thickest, he found what he sought.

He could not get too near the wagon-stage in question, for the people were piled ten and twenty deep around it. The performance he had heard so much about was just ending, but Falconsbane saw more than enough to make his heart race.

Dancing provocatively to the throbbing of a drum, posing and twisting in positions that rivaled the contortionists on the next stage, was Nyara.

Even with the foolish and patently false ears and tail she wore, and the peculiar makeup that added stripes to her face, it was clearly Nyara, dressed in a few veils and a singlet—And a collar and chain-leash.

She posed once more, dropped a veil, and whisked around the corner of the wagon, to what was obviously a performance tent—where, presumably, she would remove more than a single veil.

A fellow in an impossibly gaudy costume began chanting something to that effect, inviting the crowd to see "more of her," in just a half candlemark. Then he followed after Nyara, presumably to ready the stage inside the tent.

And after the initial shock and elation, Falconsbane could only think of one thing.

This is a trap.

An'desha panicked. To have come so far, and to have Falconsbane flee on the threshold—no, it could not happen! There had to be something that would push him past this, to the place where caution didn't exist! To the point of madness, of obsession—

Yes! There was!

Quickly, even as Falconsbane completed that thought, An'desha added another, praying to the Star-Eyed that he would not notice An'desha's "voice" in his head.

She was with the gryphons; they must have the gryphons with them!

Falconsbane's field of vision narrowed and tinged red with a rush of rage that sent a flood of blood to his head, and burned along his veins.

:Good boy! I'll warn the girl,: came a harsh whisper to An'desha, as the mere mention of gryphons triggered Falconsbane's powerful, ancient obsession. Now it did not matter to Falconsbane that this might be a trap. Nothing mattered—except that there might—no, *must*—be gryphons, the two gryphons who had twice escaped his wrath. Maybe the little ones, too!

An'desha felt a new fear now as he realized that his thoughts and Mornelithe's were intertwining the more he manipulated the Adept's thoughts. He was inserting thoughts and ideas so much quicker than before—what if Mornelithe left this body and took *An'desha's* consciousness with him, instead of abandoning the body to its rightful owner?

Then that is the price I must pay, An'desha thought, with smothered despair, and spurred Mornelithe forward. *Either way, may the Goddess ensure Mornelithe is done for.*

Quickly, Falconsbane shoved his way through the crowd, ignoring protests and return shoves, working his way to the end of the row where he could get to the back of the tents. There, if anywhere, would be the gryphons. They were too big to hide anywhere else.

He shoved his way into clear space and darkness, out of the reach of the torches illuminating the public areas of the carnival. He had squeezed his way between two of the wagons, and was now in an area of the carnival meant only for the Faire-folk. There were at least a dozen large tents here, all in a neat row, most glowing softly from within. Beside one, a horse was grazing quietly. It screamed to his mage-senses of illusion; he looked below the illusion—to see a poor old broken-down nag where the glossy bay was standing.

Amusing. Typical trickster's chicanery.

And even as he got his bearings, he saw the shadow of a gryphon, briefly, against the side of one of the tents.

Falconsbane took in that shadow, those waving wings, and went quite mad—a madness like a deadly storm, built over the course of centuries.

Falconsbane's hands blazed with power, ready to strike. He rushed at the tent, screaming at the top of his lungs in anger, burning the canvas away as he neared, and came to a halt—

And saw Nyara; she held a sword as if she actually knew how to use it! Behind her, a young, curly-haired man was using a lantern to make clever shadow-shapes with his fingers against the canvas.

It *was* a trap! But he would trap *them!* This had become absurdly funny. He—

Something dark loomed up behind him and struck like a lightning bolt before he could twist to evade it. He fell forward with a shock onto—

The point of the sword.

Held by Nyara.

But—there were no gryphons—

Falconsbane felt his rage ebbing, along with his power, and a great surge of bitter disappointment, just as the first wave of pain hit him.

No—

Firesong waited in the shadows of the back of the tent—

—when suddenly Nyara cried out desperately, "A gryphon! Somebody make a gryphon, one he can see! He's about to get away!"

Taken by surprise, with no illusion ready, he could only fumble after a bit of power to obey her.

Oh, please, don't let everything fall apart now—

Skif thrust his hands up in front of the lantern, as if he were doing a shadow-puppet play, and writhed his clever fingers into something that cast an amazingly lifelike shadow of a nodding gryphon on the back wall of the tent. The lower mandible opened and closed in a remarkable imitation of a gryphon talking, and his fingers made wingtips.

But would it be enough to fool Falconsbane?

He got his answer a breath later, as something—someone—shrieked with towering rage, then terrible power burned through the canvas and Falconsbane stood there—hands blazing, eyes afire with madness, teeth bared in an animalistic growl as if he would rend them apart like a beast of the forest or one of his own monsters.

He faced Nyara, his hands aglow with raw power; she brought Need up into a guard position. From the way her stance changed, Skif knew she had given control of her body over to the old woman.

But magic does not need a blade to strike, and can kill from afar. Only Need had the ability to destroy the Adept. But if Falconsbane did not find a target other than his daughter, she might not survive to close with him.

Fear acted on him like a drug, sharpening his own reflexes, and making it seem as if everyone else moved at a crawl while he ran. Firesong was only now bringing up his hands to strike at the Adept, and he would be too late to stop the first attack on Nyara unless Skif redirected it.

He reached for his own blade, knowing he stood no chance against Falconsbane—but at least he could defend Nyara. Even if he died doing so—

:No, Chosen!: There was an equine scream and a flurry of hoofbeats. Cymry loomed up out of the darkness and rushed into Falconsbane. Mornelithe stumbled forward, face gone blank with surprise.

To meet Nyara, standing with Need braced, ready for him.

They had expected a combat, with Firesong taking on Falconsbane's magic, and Nyara striking at a moment of distraction.

Cymry evidently had other ideas.

She continued her rush right into the tent, and shoved the Adept right up onto the blade, impaling him on its full length.

Somehow, Nyara held steady, under the double impact of his body and the surprise that their clever foe had been so incredibly *stupid.*

Mornelithe gathered his power, instinctively grasping after the one thing he still controlled.

The witch-horse danced backward, neighing with triumph.

Nyara braced herself against him, but even so, she staggered back. He was half again her weight, after all. The force of the shove had carried him halfway up the blade; he stared stupidly at her, face-to-face. Pain took him as a triumphant conqueror, and death beckoned. His eyes flitted to the blade as his power ran away along with his own life-force and his red, red blood, flowing into the ground before him.

His magics failed, aborted by the trauma to his body.

His power was draining away, and so was his life. This body was dying, very quickly.

He could use what was left to have revenge on them—or he could escape and get his revenge another time.

He chose as he had always chosen, laughing in spite of the terrible pain that wracked this latest body he had stolen.

An'desha felt Falconsbane gather the last of his energies, and leap—

—and now, completely in control, he stared down with his own eyes. Pain seized him as a dog would seize a rag doll, and shook him, and he screamed as his vision failed and darkness came down around him— darkness, and despair—

But as the darkness descended, he saw light—

The Moonpaths! It was the old woman, standing on the Moonpaths, with a black abyss between him and her. She held out a hand to him.

"Here!" she said. "To me!"

He hesitated.

"Do you trust your Goddess?" she said. "Jump to me!"

A thousand thoughts flitted through his mind, but uppermost was that *this* must also be an Avatar of the Goddess, one that had cloaked Herself in the seeming of an old woman—yes, that made sense, for how else could he have spoken with Her? No human woman could have touched his mind on the Moonpaths!

—yes, and wasn't the last face of the Goddess that of the Crone? She who gave life and death?

Wasn't She the Goddess?

He *must* trust Her!

He leapt; She caught and held him—

And She clung to him, and held him out of the abyss even as it opened up under his feet.

Skif caught the crumpling body, lowering it to the ground *far* more gently than he would have if he hadn't seen the ghost of a frightened child looking out of the eyes just before the body fell. Nyara's eyes were closed, her face a wooden mask of concentration.

:Hold onto him, son. I'll be leeching a lot of your energy for this. Keep him steady. Nyara is going to have to pull me out a hair at a time.:

He stared at the wound; at the ashen face of what had been

Falconsbane. Surely, Need could not save anything this time!

:Hush, fool. I have to Heal it all in my wake, but I can do it. I've Healed worse, once, and I wasn't even awake at the time. 'Course, I did have help.

He had to close his eyes; a wave of dizziness came over him and did not pass, but only got worse. It felt like that moment, years ago, when he and Cymry had gotten washed over that cliff, and fell, and fell—

He was going to die like this, falling forever!

Panic—

:Chosen—touch me—:

It was Cymry; he caught her presence and held her, even as he was holding Falconsbane—

:An'desha, Chosen. Never Falconsbane again. Don't worry, I can hold you forever, if I must. My strength is yours. Take whatever is there for your own. With you always.:

The dizziness steadied, ebbed, faded. He opened his eyes.

Nyara stood beside him, leaning on the blade, panting as if she had just run for miles. There was no sign of the wound except the dark slit in An'desha's shirt, and the blood soaking into the ground. The chest rose and fell with full, even breaths, and under his hand the pulse was strong and steady. And even as he stared down at the miracle in his arms, the eyes opened, and looked up into his.

Innocent. Vulnerable. Terrified.

And no more Falconsbane's eyes than Nyara's were.

An'desha looked up into the face of the stranger, the one who had been making shadow-gryphons with his fingers, and who now held him carefully, with no sign of the hatred he must feel toward Falconsbane. He looked over at Nyara, who leaned heavily and wearily on a sword but took a moment to smile encouragingly.

They *did* know who and what he was!

And he looked at the sword. Which, he now realized, *was* the old woman.

:You lied to me!: he wailed, as he started to shake, still held in the terror of near-death.

:I never told you I was your Goddess,: came the tart reply. *:I only asked if you trusted Her.:*

Firesong was hot on Falconsbane's trail, flying through the spirit-realms, a silver falcon. The traces faded with preternatural speed, and Firesong poured even more of his own life into tracing Falconsbane back to the little pocket of the Nether Planes where he had made his hiding place, his place of refuge, where death and time could not touch him. Through the swirling colors and chaos of the paths of power, he followed the spark that was Falconsbane, until he watched it dive into a pocket of blackness, an opening into a greater darkness. Small wonder he had not gone mad when trapped in the Gate's greater Void! He had practice, after all, in coping with such things.

Falconsbane reached the shelter of his refuge, fled inside, and sealed it up from within. If you had not seen the rabbit dive into its warren, you would never have noticed it. Clever, clever Falconsbane, to have seen that the Void held all in stasis, and to realize that in the shifting swirls of the paths of power, no one would ever notice a little flaw, a seam, where none should be.

But Firesong *did* know. And what was more, he knew how to get into it.

Death was about to keep a long-overdue appointment with Mornelithe Falconsbane.

He paused for a moment, then allowed himself a grim smile. He *had* told Elspeth and Darkwind that there would be a sign when it was time to attack Ancar. And here was all that energy, so much, in such a tiny and compressed package. Granted, it was blood and death energy, and too tainted for a Healing Adept to actually use. But it would be a shame to get rid of Falconsbane and allow it all to go to waste, drifting back into the currents of energy and fading away…

And fire purified. Wasn't that why his use-name was "Firesong?"

So it was, and it was time to sing. He seized the shelter in fiery hands—talons—of energy.

As he tore open the walls Falconsbane had built, he sensed an instant of surprise, followed by pure panic.

But that was all he allowed time for.

In passion, he took on the aspect of his firebird, and used every last bit of his powers to sink talonlike fingers and sharp, silvery-white beak into Falconsbane, shelter and all, tearing them into motes and ribbons and sparks, flinging them across the sky of Hardorn in a burst of fireworks that would be seen for leagues—

Every mote, every ribbon, every spark, he personally and completely purified with his own soul's fire while he sang in triumphant ecstasy. He wiped it all clean of every sickening memory, every jot of personality, and scattered it far and wide into the bitter night air.

If he ever comes back again, it will be as a cloud of gnats!

Firesong burned away the last little bit of the shelter within the Void, released the magical "ash" of it into the flow of the Void, and then sank back into his own body.

He opened his eyes to find himself on the ground, with Nyara propping him up, and Skif and Fal—no, *An'desha*—staring at him intently. It *was* An'desha; Falconsbane would never, ever have had traces of tears on his cheeks. Falconsbane would never have had Nyara's hand resting on his shoulder in a gesture of protective comfort.

It was An'desha who broke the waiting silence, as outside, people still exclaimed over the fading fireworks.

"Is he gone?" An'desha asked tremulously.

Firesong nodded wearily but with immense satisfaction.

An'desha stared at him for a moment, and then, unexpectedly, began weeping again; hoarse, racking sobs of long-pent and terrible grief.

Sobs that sounded uncannily like the ones Liam had made…

Firesong hesitated for a moment. Was there anything he could offer this poor boy? Would he believe comfort coming from another Adept such as his tormenter had been? Yet—oh, how he *wanted* to offer comfort and have it taken!

:You're a Healing Adept, boy,: Need reminded him, gruffly. *:But you don't need magic to Heal. Just words. And kindness, and care.:*

Firesong shakily levered himself up off the ground, knelt beside An'desha, and offered his arms tentatively.

An'desha folded into them as into a haven of safety. Firesong cradled the boy carefully, murmuring into his ear.

"It's all right, An'desha. It's all right now. He can never hurt anyone again. You beat him. You are safe now, and we will always be here to help you. *I* will always be here to help you…"

1 7

The sky overhead erupted into a garden of fiery flowers. Darkwind jerked up his head like a startled horse, and he stared at the odd-colored flashes, showers of sparks, and soundless lightning playing across the sky and lighting up the clouds.

"Damned showman," he muttered under his breath. "That 'Pandemonium' persona is rubbing off on him!"

:Time to move, ashke,: he sent to Elspeth, who nodded.

Darkwind was on a horse he'd stolen from the stable of an inn; the horse, if not the current rider, belonged to Ancar's Elite. Elspeth was on Gwena, still cloaked in her illusion. Both of them were in stolen uniforms, with Elspeth's hair tucked up under her uniform hat, and her breasts bound flat, so that she looked like a very slender man. The uniforms hadn't been very difficult to get; there were plenty of troopers getting drunk in the city taverns, and if two of them woke up in the morning to find themselves stark naked, bound and gagged—well, it probably wasn't the first time something like that had happened. And by then, he and Elspeth would either be long gone, or no longer in a position to worry about the consequences of being identified.

He had cobbled together something that looked enough like a messenger pouch to pass at a distance, supposedly containing dispatches from the front lines. That had gotten them as far as the courtyard; they were about to dismount, when the fires in the sky began, and the currents of power around them bucked and heaved like a herd of startled *dyheli.*

To anyone with a scrap of mage-sense, it was distressing. He had never felt quite so violent a disturbance in the energy-currents before.

:Ancar can't possibly miss this!: Elspeth cried, as they both tried to look as if everything was normal—except for the fireworks, of course; she shouted and pointed upward as all the ordinary people on the walls and in the courtyard were doing. *:And I can feel a mage-storm building very fast. People are probably getting nosebleeds all over the city—:* Even now, a huge anvil-shaped cloud was boiling up over the city seemingly from nowhere.

And now every man guarding the walls and the gates, every servant that heard the cries of surprise, and every stableboy came running out to gape at the skies like a parcel of fools. Their cries brought others.

And, unbelievably, *Ancar!*

He could hardly have missed the upheavals in the magic-currents, and given how many spells he had tied into Falconsbane, he must have been knocked metaphorically head-over-arse when they snapped back on him at the Beast's death. But they had never, in all their wildest hopes, imagined he would come running out onto the landing in front of the main doors of his palace like any other fool, just to look up at the sky!

And no one, *no one,* was paying any attention to Elspeth and Darkwind in the middle of the courtyard.

They didn't even pause to think; as one, they drew strung bows and a pair of arrows from the cases on their saddles. As one, they nocked and fired and followed the first arrows with a second, then snatched for a third while the first two were still in the air.

Ancar was a mage; he was likely to be shielded against a magical attack, but not necessarily a physical one...

So they hoped, anyway. It was the best chance for a physical attack that they were likely to get. Darkwind watched the arrows arc toward the oblivious King and held his breath, not even daring to mutter a prayer for success, his whole being straining after the streaking shafts.

All four arrows hit the edge of a mage-shield set against physical attacks, and disintegrated in a shower of sparks.

Well, that certainly got his attention, he thought fleetingly as Ancar spotted them.

Ancar's eyes slid right over Darkwind and fixed on Elspeth. And even from halfway across the courtyard, there was no doubt in Darkwind's mind that he *recognized* Elspeth. There was an instant of frozen shock, and his lips moved as his eyes widened. *He knew.* Somehow, through disguise and illusion, he knew *who* it was who came to kill him wearing the cold mask of diamond-pure Vengeance. Elspeth was an arrow of justice sped from the hand of the Queen and the bow of Valdemar.

Ancar seemed to go mad then, his eyes blazing with anger. His hands flared up in an instant with blood-red mage-energy. Rather than stunning him, the shock of recognition seemed to galvanize him into sudden action. Darkwind and Elspeth both dropped their useless bows; Darkwind ducked over his horse's neck and kicked free of his stirrups, just as Ancar let fly a mage-bolt that passed through the space where he had been and shattered the pavestones, making Darkwind's stolen horse buck and jump sideways. The Hawkbrother rolled out of the way, shoulder against the hard stone.

Elspeth tumbled in a more controlled manner off Gwena's back. Darkwind reached out an ephemeral "hand" to her; the two of them meshed powers with the ease of long practice, joining shields, just as a second mage-bolt crashed into their united defenses.

They were not given a chance to breathe—bolt after bolt of raw power crashed into them, burning away outer shields and forcing them to devote all of their attention to defenses...

Nor was that all; the death of Falconsbane, the battle, all these had tipped the precarious balance over Hardorn's capital. For too long Ancar and his mages had worked their magics without regard for the world around them, throwing it further and further out of balance.

Now something had thrown it too far, as Firesong had warned might happen. Nature went as berserk as the King.

As Ancar cast his deadly bolts of power, another equally deadly bolt lanced down out of the clouds overhead and struck somewhere in the back of the palace. It hung, shattering the night as it lanced from the skies and lingered, momentarily deafening and blinding them, signaling the worst lightning-storm Darkwind had ever seen. It easily surpassed the storm they had triggered over Ashkevron Manor with their Gate for sheer fury.

Twice, as they bowed beneath the battering of Ancar's mage-bolts, lightning hit the palace itself, setting fires on the roof. Ancar seemed oblivious to it all, intent only on pounding the two of them into red dust on the cobbles of the courtyard.

Then a third bolt struck the doors behind the King. The bolt's thinnest tendrils—enough to split huge trees—licked Ancar's shields, then the charred, exploding doors knocked Ancar to the courtyard itself. It left his clothes singed, but it didn't seem to affect his concentration; he came to his feet immediately and resumed his attack, even as Darkwind was still trying to clear his vision from the flash. Vree and Gwena were nowhere to be seen.

He *could not* imagine where Ancar was getting all this power! The man couldn't be more than a Master—how was he holding off two Adepts?

"He's mad!" Elspeth cried out, as another bolt of lightning struck and exploded the wall above the metal gates, scattering bricks and bodies down onto the pavement below. Another bolt followed it, and by its light, Darkwind caught a good look at Ancar's face.

He realized that she was, literally, right. Ancar had bitten through his own lip and hadn't even noticed. He *was* mad; mad enough to burn himself out, crazed enough not to care, using himself up in a prolonged version of a mage's final strike. What was more, the King was insane enough to *use* the lightning-power. Darkwind felt his skin prickle, his only warning of a bolt coming in the next instant. He leapt to catch Elspeth's wrist, and jerked her aside only to see a bolt of lightning sear the stones where they had just been.

And Ancar laughed, a high-pitched cackle that held nothing of sanity in it, his eyes so wide that the white showed all around, reflecting hellish-red from the blazing mage-energy of his hands. He pointed his finger at them; this time it was Elspeth who shoved Darkwind, and once again they evaded a lightning-strike by no more than a few arms' lengths.

Ancar pointed again—in the flash of a secondary strike behind him,

Darkwind saw all of Ancar's hair standing on end as he absorbed the chaotic power of the storm. His aim was improving with every strike, and this time they were both flat on the ground. They would never get out of the way in time!

Two ghostly shapes moved on the scene. One fell from the sky, pale compared to the lightning, but almost as swift.

Vree!

Gwena reared up out of the shadows of the staircase where she had been hidden. Vree dove at Ancar and struck, clawing the King's face to distract him, tearing huge furrows in his scalp and forehead to keep him from seeing the Companion.

Ancar shrieked with pain and his blazing hands rose to engulf the bird.

Gwena came down on Ancar with all the force of her powerful body behind her forehooves and knocked him to the ground. The bones of his shoulders shattered audibly even above the thunder.

Ancar screamed again, first in pain and anger, then in sheer terror, as he saw the hooves coming down on him where he lay.

A single blow of those silver hooves to his head would have killed him instantly, and with a malicious intent Darkwind would never have credited if he had not seen it himself, she deliberately avoided such a blow. No—perhaps it was to avoid striking Vree, who struggled from where he'd bound to Ancar's scalp and flapped away, wing-wrenched and upset, but alive. In a frenzy of rage nearly as mad as Ancar's, Gwena trampled him, dancing on him with all four hooves until the screaming stopped, and he was nothing more than red pulp seeping into flagstones.

:That!: Her mind-voice was a scream, and she was still pounding the inert meat with her wet, red hooves. *:That! That's for Talia! That's for Kris! That's for—:*

"Laugh now, horse!" came a shout from the palace, and a mage-bolt took Gwena in the side, lifting her right off the ground with the force. Gwena hit the ground, hooves slipping beneath her, and landed on her side with a *thud.*

Darkwind's gaze snapped up, to the balcony above the doors.

Hulda!

That was the only person it could be, even though the woman was dressed in servants' livery, and was as wild-eyed as Ancar had been.

"Go ahead and laugh at *this*—" the woman cried, raising her hands for another blow. Darkwind erected hasty shields over Gwena, who moved her legs feebly and flailed her head as she tried to rise.

Behind Hulda, a man grabbed her arm, distracting her for a moment. "Don't be a fool!" he shouted in oddly accented Hardornen over the roar of the thunder. "We have to get out of here! Leave these idiots!"

She pulled away from him and started to build power for another attack—but once again he pulled her away, this time succeeding in drawing her back inside.

Darkwind was *not* going to let her escape—and there was no sign that anyone was going to interfere at this point. The mage-storms and lightning had driven everyone out of the courtyard and off the walls.

He scrambled to his feet and ran up to the sundered stairs, then hooked his fingers around stonework, climbing to reach the balcony. :*Go!*: he shouted at Elspeth, :*Get inside and cut them off from below!*:

This kind of climb was nothing to a Tayledras. As Elspeth dashed into the doors below him, his hand reached the balcony itself, and he pulled himself up and over the railing.

And just as he burst into the ravaged room, he felt the unmistakable shivering in the power-currents of someone building a Gate nearby...

They had all studied the plans of Ancar's palace until they could have walked the place blindfolded. Elspeth remembered a stair going right up into the hallway above, just inside the main doors. The place was deserted; everyone had either gone off to fight the fires or fled in terror when the mage-battle began. She ran up the stairs two at a time, and as she reached the top and the corridor that it led to, she heard the sound of a fight on the other side of the second door along the corridor.

She didn't stop to think; she just gathered power and blasted, disintegrating the door and running through the hole while the dust was still raining down.

And she stumbled to a halt as she hit something that felt like a web, a net that closed around her in a heartbeat and held her immobile.

But her eyes still worked, and the very first thing she saw, by the white light of pure power, was the man that had pulled Hulda inside.

The man who bore a distinctive device on his tunic—

Dear gods—the Emperor's envoy!—

—was building a *Gate!* He already had the framework up. He wasn't even using a real door as his anchor, he was simply building the thing in midair!

How much of what's happened has been his *doing?*

Darkwind knelt on the floor, beside the shattered doors to the balcony, cringing beneath his shields as Hulda rained blow after fiery blow down on him. So far, Hulda hadn't even noticed *her*. The hinged splinters of the balcony doors slammed against the wall, as the rainless mage-storm raged outside, whitening the room in flashes from the lightning. Thunder roared, drowning out any other sounds, and smoke crept in the window from the fires outside.

Elspeth fought the bonds that held her, frantically seeking a weak spot.

Suddenly, the darkness in the Gate brightened—and became a hole in the air, a hole leading to a brightly lit room somewhere, filled with furnishings in a sinuous style Elspeth had never seen before.

The man turned toward Hulda. "Are you coming?" he snarled. "Or are you enjoying yourself too much to leave?"

Elspeth realized his lips had not moved with his words. He had projected them in open Mindspeech so strong that anyone, Gifted or not, would have Heard him. As his attention wavered for a moment, split between the Gate and Hulda, so did the bonds holding her. She freed one hand, and shook a knife from her sleeve down into it—her old, reliable, predictable, *material* knives. *No pottery to hurl this time...*

As Hulda turned to answer him, Elspeth cast the knife, knowing that if the envoy went down, the Gate would go with him.

He was not expecting a physical attack; the knife caught him in the throat. It buried itself to the hilt. Blood spurted from a severed artery, a fountain of ebony-red in the hellish white light. The envoy's face convulsed; both hands clutched at his throat. He staggered backward, across the threshold, and through the Gate itself.

The Gate collapsed as he fell through it.

The bonds holding her faded away. And *now* Hulda saw her.

There was no recognition in Hulda's eyes, but there was plenty of pure rage.

Elspeth readied a mage-bolt of her own, but Hulda was faster. And Hulda was trapped, with nowhere to escape to; Darkwind was between her and the balcony, Elspeth was between her and the hallway. So she fought with all the desperate strength of any cornered creature, and with the stores of energy she had drained from the land of Hardorn for all these past years...

She was an Adept, easily the equivalent of Falconsbane—and she was not handicapped by having an agent in her own mind, or by a disintegrating personality.

Within moments, Elspeth knew with rising panic that stole her breath that she was in trouble, trying to hold eroded shields against a barrage of mage winds, each of them geared to a specific energy, that began to eat their way down through her protections. They circled her in a whirlwind that caught up papers, bits of wood, shattered glass, and other debris, pelting her with physical as well as magical weapons.

But panic made her mind clearer, and a sudden memory matched the whirlwind. *Firesong—the lesson—*

She spun her shields until they mated with the whirlwinds; then reached through them, and began to absorb the energies of the attack into her own. But the instant Hulda realized that she had found a counter, the woman set the winds on Darkwind, and attacked Elspeth with—

Demons!

Creatures of shadow and teeth boiled up from the floor, and a hundred taloned hands reached for her. Fear sent arcs of cold down her limbs. Elspeth backpedaled and came up against the wall; for a moment, she was lost in panic. She had no counter to *this—*

Panicked, until in the next heartbeat, she remembered that these might be illusions. Illusions vanished if challenged! She pulled her sword, forgotten until now, and swung.

The "demons" vanished without a sound. Hulda then flung a wall of fire at her. Her confidence increased. *This* she could handle! Perhaps Hulda was not so formidable after all!

She countered it by absorbing it—took another step toward the woman—

And then Hulda recognized her. "You! The Brat!"

"The *Adept*," Elspeth screamed back defiantly. "Your better, bitch!"

Hulda's reply was drowned out by another thunderclap; there was a trace of real fear in her eyes, and her face was like a stone mask. Elspeth laughed hysterically. Hulda was *afraid!* Afraid of *her!* They could take the bitch, they could!

But Hulda evidently decided that if *she* was doomed, she would take her enemies with her.

Hulda reached out with her powers in a thrust that knocked Elspeth back into the wall again, and with great shudders of power that shook her body as they shook the walls, she began to tear the building down around them.

The walls and ceiling screamed with the shrieks of tortured stone and wood. Elspeth dodged a falling chandelier that brought a quarter of the ceiling down with it—

—just in time to see Darkwind falling beneath the outer wall, going down under a cascade of stone and burning wall-maps that buried him completely in an instant.

"No!" she screamed, reaching for him with mind, heart, and powers, forgetting her own peril—

Only to receive, not an answer, but a flood of energy. Energy that felt—final, as if it was all he had.

Her heart convulsed, but her body acted.

She shook her arm and felt her other knife fall into her hand. She screamed again, a wordless howl of rage and anguish; invested every last bit of power in the second knife—and threw it.

The knife cut through the air and ripped through Hulda's shields.

Hulda collapsed in a boneless heap, her howling winds collapsing at the same instant, leaving behind an echoing silence filled only by thunder, and the crunch of an occasional brick falling. A glittering knife-hilt shone from her left eye socket.

She was dead, but she had taken Darkwind with her.

Elspeth turned and stared at the heap of broken stones, her throat choked with grief so all-consuming that she could not think, could not even weep. She stumbled a step or two toward the pile—

And Vree came winging in out of the darkness, through the gaping, broken wall. He landed beside the stones, and hopped over to them—to the only part of Darkwind that she could see, his hand. He nibbled the fingers, as if to try to coax life into them, and Elspeth's grief overflowed into scalding tears that blurred her vision. Her throat closed, and she sobbed, then moaned with pain.

He was gone. She was alone. Hulda had won, after all. His loss was an ache that would never be healed.

:Damn... bird.: A whisper in her mind.

What?

:Elspeth... ashke:

Grief turned to hysterical joy, all in a heartbeat. He was alive!

She shook her head, frantically wiping at her eyes to clear them, then ran to the pile of stones and began to pull them off of him. Vree hopped excitedly beside her, making odd creaking sounds, as she managed to clear his head and shoulders of debris.

He looked terrible, bruised and bleeding from a dozen small cuts, and she trembled to think how many bones might be broken. But he was alive!

:Gods.: He opened his eyes for a moment, then closed them. *:I feel... awful. Like... a wall... just fell on me.:*

Her heart overflowing, she resumed pulling stones from his body, ignoring splitting nails and sharp edges that cut her hands, thankful that the winds had snuffed out the earlier fires. Finally she came to a thick slab of wood—a strategic map, showing invasion plans. A map of Valdemar.

It had protected Darkwind from the heaviest of the stones, prevented his lungs and ribs from being crushed. Paint flaked from the board as she twisted it free of him, and troop-counters fell like rain from the "Losses" box she found propping up one end of it. She kept having to shake her head to clear her eyes of tears as she pulled debris away from him, trying to figure out how badly he *had* been hurt.

:Wait. Check Gwena...: he began, his thoughts coming to her from a haze of generalized pain.

:No need,: Gwena said weakly. *:I'm going to live. And there's no one down here to bother me while I decide if I still* want *to. No bones broken, I don't think—some burns, and bruises that go to the bone. Keep him from fading, I'll call Cymry. And you send Vree for him, in case I can't reach him!:*

Although that was somewhat confused, Elspeth had no trouble figuring out which "he" Gwena meant. *:Vree,:* she said intently, turning to the falcon, concentrating on trying to impress him with her urgency. *:Vree, we need Skif. Find Skif. Bring him here quickly!:*

Vree bobbed his head once, then nibbled Darkwind's finger, spread his wings, and flapped heavily off into the darkness again.

:He's... a horrible night flyer, ashke. *Hope he doesn't hit anything.:*

"Just stay with me," she said aloud, fiercely, starting with that hand to check for broken bones, since it was the piece of him least likely to cause problems if she accidentally moved it. Or held it. "Don't pass out on me."

:I'll try.:

"Stop that!" she snapped, still rubbing away tears. "Stay awake, stop fading! Or—or I'll tell you Hawkbrother jokes! How many Hawkbrothers does it take for a mating circle?"

:No... not that... anything but that.:

"Only one, but he has to be flexible!"

:I'm doomed.:

* * *

When Skif arrived, he brought Nyara and Need with him, and his expression betrayed his relief at finding the situation nowhere near as desperate as he had feared from Gwena's weak Mindcall. He told Elspeth that he'd seen worse injuries than Darkwind's out in the field, when miners or builders had been trapped under collapsing walls. Darkwind would not only live, he would do so with all organs and limbs intact…

That gave her some measure of comfort and calmed her shattered nerves a little. And although at some point she would be mad with impatience to hear his side of the story, and the confrontation with Falconsbane, at the moment there was enough on her plate to worry about. They still had to get out of here.

They laid Need down beside Darkwind with his hand on the hilt—her complaining the whole time that she had done enough Healing for one day—and carefully lifted the last of the stones from Darkwind's back and legs. By the time they finished, people were drifting back into the palace, and coming to stare curiously at the wreckage in the room.

But Elspeth and Darkwind still wore their purloined uniforms, and when Elspeth turned and barked "Out!" at the onlookers, they quickly found something else to do.

They limped their way out of the building without being stopped, carrying Darkwind on the map that had saved him, using it as a stretcher. Skif did pause long enough to look down at Hulda and make a *tsk*ing sound.

"A knife," he sighed. "How—predictable."

She thought about hitting him, but she was just too weary—mentally, emotionally, and physically.

He reached down for the offending object, cleaning it on his none-too-clean sleeve and handed it back to her. "Where's the other one?" he asked, as she slipped it into her arm sheath and pulled her sleeve back down over it.

"In the throat of the Eastern Envoy—who is, I suppose, back in his Master's domain," she replied. "He was building a Gate, I got him with the knife, and he fell through it."

Another curious onlooker peeked in the door but vanished before she could even snarl at him.

"Falling dead, with a knife bearing the crest of Valdemar on the pommel-nut," he said dryly. "Very subtle, Elspeth. Couldn't you have sent a more direct message to the Emperor? Like, perhaps, 'Your father won the Horse Faire. Your mother tracks rabbits by scent. Love and kisses, Elspeth of Valdemar.'"

A bit of the ceiling dropped, breaking the silence, followed by the sound of someone picking his way across the floor upstairs. She growled at him, at the end of her patience. "I didn't exactly have much choice," she pointed out. "And if we're going to get out of here before someone names us the assassins of the King, we'd better move now!"

"A good point," he acknowledged, and picked up his end of the board holding Darkwind. "Need—Gwena's rather handicapped at the moment. I don't suppose—"

:Gods. Can't you people do anything for yourselves?:

"We are not Healers," Nyara pointed out sweetly. "You are."

:Right. Bring logic into this.: Elspeth could have sworn that the sword sighed. *:All right. Bring on the horses.:*

:I am not—: Gwena snapped, *:a horse!:*

Skif helped Darkwind up into Cymry's saddle. Gwena's worst injuries were mostly to muscle, and easily within Need's purview; Darkwind's to bone, which took several days to Heal, and the best Need could do was set them and hold them in place. With Gwena Healed enough to carry her own weight, Elspeth elected to put Darkwind on Cymry's back and walk, with her on one side, steadying him, and Nyara on the other.

"I'll catch up with you," Skif told them. "You get back to the carnival and warn everyone that—let's see—" He thought quickly. "Falconsbane and Hulda tried to kill Ancar; he got both of them, but not before they called up a demon that mashed him to a pulp. Anyway, tell them all that, and tell them it's going to be hell around here when everyone realizes all three top people are gone. They may want to get out."

"They may want to stay and loot," Elspeth pointed out, tilting her head at the number of people trickling out of the palace carrying things—and the growing stream going in, unhindered by threat of fire, lightning, or remaining guards.

He shrugged. "Doesn't bother me; they'll just be getting back some of what Ancar's been taking, indirectly. There's just a few things of Ancar's I want to make sure don't survive."

Elspeth looked at him curiously, one hand on Darkwind's leg, supporting him. "What, documents? How could you know where—" Then she shook her head. "Never mind. I don't want to know how you know. We'll get ourselves ready for fast travel and meet you at the camp."

Cymry started forward, through what was left of the main gates. Gwena limped along behind.

Skif took himself into the palace.

By the time he slipped back out of the doors, there were people looting already—running through the hall, grabbing whatever they could carry, and dashing back out again. Most of those people wore the uniforms of Ancar's Elite Guard, which didn't surprise him in the least. None of them offered any kind of hindrance to him, once they saw *he* wasn't carrying any choice bits of loot. And every once in a while, he saw one of the political prisoners or kidnapped girls he'd just freed from the dungeons making for the city, some bauble or valuable in hand.

Behind him, one room and all its contents were burning merrily. One more small fire among the other three or four started by the lightning, anyone would assume. It was likely that looters would add to those fires before the night was over.

He stopped long enough at the royal stables to steal a pair of strong, fast horses, and a small carriage; they'd need both for An'desha and Darkwind. Some of the stable hands seemed to have had the same idea, for the really fine horseflesh and the royal carriages were all gone. As an afterthought, he stopped long enough in the courtyard to pitch a kind of souvenir into the back of the wagon he'd appropriated—the map that had saved Darkwind. He thought Elspeth would like to have it.

And as he passed through the gates, he was already making plans for the fastest route out, one that passed through the fewest number of towns that might hold garrisons. Getting to the border was going to be tricky.

Getting across was going to be even more fun…

Maybe we ought to see if old Firesong has one more trick in him. Or maybe Elspeth? A Gate into Valdemar would be damned useful about now…

Pires Nieth settled himself gingerly into Ancar's throne. To say that he was exhausted was understating the case, but he dared not allow that to show. He had only taken control of the chaotic situation by the thinnest of margins, and only because the commanders of the Elite were more afraid of mages than they were greedy. His illusions of demons alone had been enough to convince them that he held all the power of his late master; if he'd had to produce more than illusions, he'd have been in desperate trouble.

Fortunately, the commanders had taken the illusion for the real thing, and had brought *their* men back under control. Now the palace was completely cleared of looters, the city was rapidly being pacified, and *he* was the man who was going to inherit Ancar's rather damaged crown. Once anyone thought to contest him for it, well, it would be too late.

Hardorn was not what it had been—but it was more than he had ever owned before.

The throne was mostly intact, a few semiprecious stones missing. The throne-room itself was smoke-stained and bore the muddy footprints of looters. But it was still a throne and an audience chamber, and there were plenty of servants to repair both.

Oh, you've done very well by yourself, Pires, he congratulated himself as his cowed and frightened sheep—ah, *courtiers and mages*—gathered to pay him their homage officially. *You have done very well by yourself, and all by being clever, watching everything, knowing when to play your hand—*

A commotion at the end of the room made him frown. The courtiers swirled like little fish disturbed by the passing of a larger, hungry fish. What now?

A battered and disheveled messenger came pushing through the crowd, his eyes wild, his face sweat- and dirt-streaked. "The border!" he panted, frantically. "An attack on the border!"

Damn—the Valdemarans—well, I have no quarrel with them, I can simply make a truce— "What are the Valdemarans doing?" he asked. "Who's the commander in charge? How quickly can he retreat from—"

"Not the *western* border!" the man wailed. "The *eastern* border! The towers just relayed a message from the eastern border! There's an army there, a *huge* army, it outnumbers us by a hundred to one, and it's rolling over *everything!*"

It was at this time that Pires Nieth realized his throne might not be valuable for very much longer. And he tried to think of who he could go to that would trade Ancar's flattened crown for a fast horse.

Treyvan mantled his wings over the youngsters, cradling gryphlet and human alike. The salle was warm and bright, but the little ones took no notice of the sunlight, nor of the toys piled all around them. All four were distressed, for all four knew that their parents were going away, and where they were going, people got hurt.

He was making soothing little sounds, when suddenly his feathers all stood on end, and he felt the unique trembling in the forces of magic that signaled a Gate forming in this very room.

His first thought was that Falconsbane had found a way to build a

Gate here, to attack the children. He shoved them all behind him, turning with foreclaws outstretched, building his shields and his powers to strike at anything that struck at him. His action took the two Heralds on guard entirely by surprise, but they reacted with the speed of superbly trained fighters, drawing their weapons and facing the direction he faced.

A haze of power shimmered in the doorway to the salle. Then—the door vanished, to be replaced by a meadow of sad, yellowed grasses—

A meadow?

And Firesong and Elspeth came stumbling through, followed by Nyara and Skif, the *dyheli,* the birds, and the two Companions, one of whom carried Darkwind on her back, and dragged a slab of wood. The other Companion carried someone else, wrapped up in so much cloth as to be unidentifiable.

The Gate came down immediately. So did Firesong, collapsing where he stood. Darkwind looked none too good either.

"Get a Healerrrr!" Treyvan snapped; one of the Heralds sheathed her blade and took off at a dead run before he even finished the sentence. The other joined him at Firesong's side.

"What happened?" the young man demanded. "Is—"

"We got Falconsbane, Ancar, and Hulda, in that order, yesterday," Elspeth replied, helping Darkwind down off Gwena's back. "All hell broke loose over there. We'll probably see the effects of it on the border, in a day or a week, depending on if anyone thinks to use the relay-towers to get word to the front lines. There was rioting in the city as we left, and we traveled just long enough for Firesong to get back the strength to Gate us home. The unrest was spreading faster than we could move."

"What isss the wood?"

Darkwind chuckled weakly, still clearly in some pain. "A trophy. A lifesaver of a trophy."

Just then, the first Herald returned with not one, but three Healers, and right behind them were Selenay and Prince Daren and their bodyguards, followed by a runner from one of the Valdemaran relay-towers. It looked as if the man had been bringing an urgent message, had seen the Queen and her consort running like *dyheli* for the salle, and had followed them instead of going to the Palace.

He nearly got skewered by the bodyguards until he flung up both hands, showing himself weaponless, and panted out, "Message from the border!"

"Ten to one it's starting—" Treyvan heard Skif mutter to Nyara, who nodded wisely, as she aided the unknown down from the second

Companion's saddle. He, she, or it also simply slumped down to the floor, but not until Firesong had gotten to his (her?) side with one of the Healers.

Skif was right. The message from the border was of chaos.

Some of Ancar's army—the Elite—continued to attack. Most were fleeing. Even Ancar's mages were no longer a factor, for they were actually fighting among *themselves*.

"We need to get out there," Selenay said, immediately. "All of us. Companion-back it shouldn't take that long."

Elspeth shook her head. "I'm still in good shape, Mother. I can build a Gate for you. The only reason Firesong brought us here was because of the distance; it isn't even half that far to Landon Castle, and that should be right near the front." She grinned wanly. "I certainly saw enough of *that* place the last time Ancar hit us to put a Gate in the chapel door."

"Done," Selenay said instantly, and turned to Treyvan. He waved a claw at her. "Fearrr not, Lady. We shall be rrrready. Hydona and I can deal with sssuch magesssss asss may get thisss farrr."

"Be here in a candlemark with whoever and whatever you want to take with you," Elspeth said, and looked at Darkwind. "I should go, too."

Selenay shook her head. "No, love, not really. Daren and I will go because there will be decisions on what must be done with Hardorn, but now—this is hardly more than a matter of cleaning up."

Darkwind nodded agreement. "The danger will not be to you. The dangers are all in a disorderly retreat, to keep the forces from hurting each other. Your people know you; you are the one in charge. And they no longer need an Adept out there."

"My thoughtsss exactly." Treyvan nodded. Selenay was not going to waste time or words; she and Daren hurried back out, trailed by guards, messengers, and Heralds.

Selenay and Daren returned with their Companions, all armed and provisioned, and a guard of six Heralds and six Royal Guardsmen. They were ready, Elspeth was ready—Treyvan was very proud of his young human pupil, who was showing her true mettle. He gently reminded her of how the Gate Spell worked, and stood ready to guide her "hands."

Elspeth took *her* place before the salle doors to create her very first Gate.

Treyvan watched her with the critical eye of a teacher but could find nothing to criticize. She had not needed his aid at all; she had done her work flawlessly. The portal filled with the image of a dark, ill-lit, stone-walled room. "That old miser never will buy enough candles to light that great barn properly," Selenay muttered, covering her amazement with the rather flippant remark. Treyvan thought it rather brave of her, when she did not ask, "Is it safe?" but rather, "Is everything ready?"

A chorus of "ayes" answered her, and the Queen herself, with her Companion, was the first one through the Gate. Two by two, the entourage went through.

Elspeth dissolved the Gate—and sat down herself, abruptly. Treyvan was expecting it, however, and helped her to sit, waving away the Healer who had been tending Firesong. "It isss wearrrinesss, only," he assured the woman. "Gate-enerrrgy."

He bent over Elspeth. *:Silly child,:* he chided, mind-to-mind. *:You have all of the Heartstone to regain your energies! Use it! Firesong assuredly is!:*

:Oh,: she replied sheepishly. *:I—ah—forgot:* And only then did the Healer tending the unknown persuade her (him?) to remove the cloak swathing his face and body.

Treyvan flashed into "kill" stance, shoving the youngsters behind him with his outstretched wings. *:Falconsbane!:*

Then, before anyone could do or say anything, he looked deeply into the creature's eyes and saw there, not the ages-old tyrant, but a young and vulnerable boy.

He relaxed, flattening his feathers, and tucking his wings in with a flip. "Ssso," he said, "and who isss thiss, that wearrrsss the body of ourrr old foe?"

It was Firesong who answered, with one hand protectively on the boy's shoulder. "This is An'desha, old friend. And—"

:And he has earned more than the reward he sought.: The mental voice boomed through his head, resonating in his bones. Every feather on Treyvan's body stood on end, as he felt the stirrings of energies deeper and stranger than the local mage-currents. Light filled the room, a warm and sourceless light as bright as sunlight on a summer day. A faint scent of sun-warmed grasses wafted across the salle—

The light collected behind An'desha; more light formed into an identical column behind a very startled Nyara. The columns of light spread huge, fiery wings over the two; Treyvan's skin tingled and Darkwind and Firesong gasped.

:These twain have given selflessly. It is the will of the Warrior that what was stolen from them be returned.:

A female voice this time—and Darkwind reached toward the pillar of light behind Nyara as if he recognized it, and soundlessly mouthed a name. Treyvan realized that, no, these were not winged columns of golden light, but a pair of huge golden birds, shining so brightly that Treyvan squinted and the humans' eyes watered. But the birds had human eyes—eyes as black as night, but spangled with stars.

:So let the balance be restored.: Both voices called, in glorious harmony, a peal of trumpets, the cry of hawks—

The light flared, and Treyvan cried out involuntarily, blinded, deafened, able to see only the light and hear only the joined and wordless song of those two voices, which went on, and on—

And was, as suddenly, gone.

He blinked, his beak still agape. The light was gone, and with it the two huge hawks of light—

Then his beak gaped even farther as he looked down at what had been An'desha/Mornelithe.

A young, bewildered, and clearly *human* man sat there now; as he looked up in shock and wonder at Treyvan, his golden skin betrayed his Shin'a'in blood, although his golden-brown hair spoke of an outClan parent somewhere. His eyes were still green-gold and slitted like a cat's, and there was still a feline cast to his features; his build was still powerful and his fingernails still talonlike—but no one would ever look askance at him in a crowd now.

Treyvan looked quickly to Nyara, who was staring at An'desha, and saw that similar changes had been made to her. She looked down at her hands, at skin that no longer bore a coat of sleek, short fur—and burst into tears.

It took a while for Skif and Treyvan to understand her distress, and longer for Skif to persuade Nyara that he still *would* love her now that she was no longer so exotic. Treyvan advised the blade Need to stay out of it; wisely, she did.

An'desha was simply overjoyed. He had never expected to look human again—he had only wanted *a* body back, not necessarily the original body Mornelithe had taken. It was from him that they learned what the two fiery birds were—"Avatars of the Shin'a'in Warrior"—and *who*—"A shaman of my people, Tre'valen, and his lady, Dawnfire."

Darkwind nodded as if he had expected something of the sort; he and Elspeth shared a warm and secret smile of pleasure. Firesong looked as if he had gotten a revelation from the gods. The gryphlets and children, who had been quiet witnesses to all of this, simply watched with wide, delighted eyes.

* * *

Finally, they packed themselves back up to the palace, silent, awestruck youngsters and all. Treyvan was simply afire by then with impatience. "I *mussst* know!" he exclaimed as they settled into the gryphons' rooms, and another small army of Healers and servants descended on them. "I ssssee that thisss An'desssha isss not Falconsssbane, but how, *how*, did he become Falconsssbane? Orrrr did Falconsssbane become him?"

Firesong had his arm about the young man's shoulders, in a gesture both protective and proprietary. "Falconsbane became him, old bird," the Adept replied. "And how he got there is a very, very, long story."

:A long story? A long story?: Rris came bounding up at last, dashing in from the hallway, ears and tail high. *:Knowledge is good! History is better! Tell me! Tell me all!:*

Treyvan grinned to himself. Once the *kyree* discovered what he had missed witnessing, they were never going to hear the last of it!

Firesong laughed tiredly; An'desha stared at the *kyree* in utter fascination, and Treyvan only shook his head and sighed at Rris' unbounded enthusiasm.

"We will have time enough to tell you all you wish, Rris," Firesong said. "An'desha and Darkwind and I are the most weary of this company, and I think—"

"If you think that we're going to order the lot of you to stay here and recover, you're right!" snapped one of the Healers. "You're in no shape to go haring around on a battlefield." He turned back to An'desha, muttering something about "Heralds."

"Well, Rris," Elspeth said with a smile, getting up off the floor to go sit with Darkwind. She leaned gingerly into his shoulder, "It looks as if you're going to have all of us at your disposal for some time."

:Yes!: Rris replied, bounding in place. *:Yes! I will make histories of all of it!:* And he abruptly settled, fixed Darkwind with his direct and intelligent gaze, and demanded, *:Now. You, Darkwind. Begin at the beginning, and leave nothing out.:*

Darkwind slowly picked up the battered map of Valdemar and threatened Rris with it.

Elspeth burst into laughter, laughing until tears came to her eyes. "Don't kill him, *ashke;* he's a Bard and has immunity here."

"Impudence, you mean," Darkwind muttered. Then smiled, and gently put the map back down.

"It all began," he said, as if he were a master storyteller, "on the day we left home."

Rris cocked his head to one side, curiously. *:K'Sheyna?:* he asked, puzzled.

"No," Darkwind replied, his eyes on Elspeth and not the *kyree*. "Home. Valdemar."

Treyvan thought that the blinding light of the Avatars could never be matched. But it was challenged and eclipsed then, by the light in Elspeth's eyes.

AUTHOR'S NOTE

No one works in a vacuum; a creation can only reach people with the help of more than merely the creator. In the case of a book, the reader seldom sees all those people, often never knows that they exist.

At DAW Books, it all began with tireless First Reader, Peter Stampfel, a fine musician in his own right (catch him and his group, the Bottle Caps, when you're in New York). He is the man who reads hundreds, if not thousands, of manuscripts every year and picks out those he thinks the editors would like to see. One of the ones he picked out was *Arrows of the Queen*, for which I owe him eternal gratitude.

Then comes Editor in Chief, Elizabeth Wollheim, whose critique has made what had been good books into much, much better books, and who also has taken the courageous steps of publishing a trilogy with a *shaych* hero and of putting illustrations back into books. No one could ever want a better editor; no one could ever have an editor who was easier to work with. Without her, Valdemar would never have been what it has become. Without her, I would not be the writer I am today. A good writer never stops learning, and I could have no better teacher than Elizabeth Wollheim.

Also entering the fray, in the times when Betsy was juggling too many red-hot pokers to manage another, is Sheila Gilbert. This is the lady who has been bringing you the fine work of Tanya Huff as well.

Of course I can't fail to mention Elsie Wollheim and her late husband Don, without whom there would not be a DAW Books, and very likely would not be a Heralds of Valdemar series. Elsie and Don discovered far too many science fiction talents to ever list here, and with their unfailing honesty and determination to "do right" by their writers, have won the admiration and love of so many of us.

The stalwart centurion of the copy-editing line, Paula Greenberg, makes certain that all my capitalizations and spellings match and imparts as much consistency as anyone can to someone as chaotic as I am.

The patient Joe Schaumburger ensures that none of us forget anything, keeping track of it all, occasionally proofreading, reminding us that we haven't sent our proof corrections, and a million other things, all at once. I can only conclude he has a monumental memory, as well as a charming personality, and it is always a pleasure to hear from him.

Out in the "field" are all the booksellers—the independents, who start so many careers, and the chains, who nourish careers. We have the American Booksellers Association to thank for the fact that there is scarcely a town in the United States that does not have a bookstore, which was *not* the case when I was a youngster. We have the ABA to thank for crusading tirelessly against those who would have books taken off the shelves, censored, and banned.

And we have the American Library Association, who make certain that those who can't afford to buy *all* the books they want can still read them!

On the home front, I have my personal set of High Flight folks to thank, and very first and foremost is Larry Dixon. A talented artist and writer, he also is my "first editor;" everything he has touched has always been immeasurably better for it. He is the best partner anyone could want; he has also become my husband which makes it even better! Interestingly, we began with a working relationship, he as artist, I as writer. It was a collaboration begun the first weekend we met, called "Ties Never Binding." It evolved into the "Winds" trilogy.

Another co-writer, Mark Shepherd, is our secretary in addition to being my protégé. He is the one who keeps track of fan mail, release forms for fan-fiction, insurance papers, correspondence, schedules, and all the rest. Without his help, we would be in a far greater mess than we are!

And riding tail-guard at the Aerie is Victor Wren, Larry's assistant and computer guru extraordinaire. It is Victor's expertise that makes it possible for us to bring you the images you have seen in this book; Larry's pencil drawings are scanned into their computer imaging system, Larry and Victor retouch them there, add special effects, then print them out as camera-ready halftones.

We have had the help of fellow wildlife rehabbers, fellow members of NAFA (North American Falconry Association), and others who devote themselves to preserving the wild for future generations.

There are our friends in the field—Andre Norton, Marion Zimmer

Bradley, Anne McCaffrey, Ellen Guon, Holly Lisle, Josepha Sherman, Martin Greenberg, Mike Resnick, Judith Tarr, Esther Friesner, Lisa Waters, Ru Emerson, Tanya Huff, Elizabeth Moon, C.J. Cherryh, Terri Lee, Nancy Asire, and many others.

Last, and surely the best, are the fans. "Herald House-Mother," Judith Louvis, who runs the fan club "Queen's Own," all of the editors and contributors of the fanzines, the folk in "Queen's Own Online— Modems of the Queen" on GEnie, and all of you who have enjoyed these stories and keep asking for more. This is a heartfelt acknowledgment and sincere thanks to all of you. We will be writing of Heralds and Companions, Shin'a'in, Tayledras, and Kaled'a'in, the past and future of Valdemar—oh yes, and the Eastern Empire—for as long as you care to read the stories.

Zhai'helleva!
Mercedes Lackey

ABOUT THE AUTHOR

Mercedes Lackey is a full-time writer and has published numerous novels and works of short fiction, including the bestselling *Heralds of Valdemar* series. She is also a professional lyricist and licensed wild bird rehabilitator. She lives in Oklahoma with her husband and collaborator, artist Larry Dixon, and their flock of parrots.

www.**mercedeslackey**.com

THE COLLEGIUM CHRONICLES
Mercedes Lackey

Follow Magpie, Bear, Lena and friends as they face their demons and find their true strength on the road to becoming full Heralds, Bards and Healers of Valdemar.

Book One: Foundation
Book Two: Intrigues
Book Three: Changes
Book Four: Redoubt
Book Five: Bastion

"Lackey makes a real page-turner out of Mags' and the collegia's development… this book's outstanding characters, especially Mags, will greatly please Valdemar fans." *Booklist*

"The tone, characterization, and rampant angst recall Lackey's earliest Valdemar books… this is a worthy entry in the overall saga." *Publishers Weekly*

"Lackey's Valdemar series is already a fantasy classic, and these newest adventures will generate even more acclaim for this fantasy superstar." *Romantic Times*